THE YEAR'S BEST

SCIENCE fICTION

ALSO BY GARDNER DOZOIS

ANTHOLOGIES

A Day in the Life
Another World
Best Science Fiction Stories of the
  Year, #6–10
The Best of Isaac Asimov's Science
  Fiction Magazine
Time-Travelers from Isaac Asimov's
  Science Fiction Magazine
Transcendental Tales from Isaac
  Asimov's Science Fiction Magazine
Isaac Asimov's Aliens
Isaac Asimov's Mars
Isaac Asimov's SF Lite
Isaac Asimov's War
Roads Not Taken
  (with Stanley Schmidt)
The Year's Best Science Fiction,
  #1–19

Future Earths: Under African Skies
  (with Mike Resnick)
Future Earths: Under South
  American Skies
  (with Mike Resnick)
Ripper! (with Susan Casper)
Modern Classics of Science Fiction
Modern Classic Short Novels of
  Science Fiction
Modern Classics of Fantasy
Killing Me Softly
Dying For It
The Good Old Stuff
The Good New Stuff
Explorers
The Furthest Horizon
Worldmakers
Supermen

COEDITED WITH SHEILA WILLIAMS

Isaac Asimov's Planet Earth
Isaac Asimov's Robots
Isaac Asimov's Valentines
Isaac Asimov's Skin Deep
Isaac Asimov's Ghosts
Isaac Asimov's Vampires
Isaac Asimov's Moons
Isaac Asimov's Christmas

Isaac Asimov's Camelot
Isaac Asimov's Werewolves
Isaac Asimov's Solar System
Isaac Asimov's Detectives
Isaac Asimov's Cyberdreams

COEDITED WITH JACK DANN

Aliens!	Mermaids!	Dinosaurs!	Invaders!	Clones
Unicorns!	Sorcerers!	Little People!	Angels!	Nanotech
Magicats!	Demons!	Dragons!	Dinosaurs II	Immortals
Magicats 2!	Dogtales!	Horses!	Hackers	Future Sports
Bestiary!	Seaserpents!	Unicorns 2	Timegates	Beyond Flesh

FICTION

Strangers
The Visible Man (collection)
Nightmare Blue
  (with George Alec Effinger)
Slow Dancing Through Time
  (with Jack Dann, Michael Swanwick,
  Susan Casper and Jack C. Haldeman II)

The Peacemaker
Geodesic Dreams (collection)
Strange Days: Fabulous Journeys
  with Gardner Dozois (collection)

NONFICTION

The Fiction of James Tiptree, Jr.

THE YEAR'S BEST

SCIENCE FICTION

twentieth annual collection

edited by **Gardner Dozois**

st. martin's griffin ☙ new york

www.stmartins.com

ISBN 0-312-30859-0 (hc)
     0-312-30860-4 (tp)

FIRST EDITION: JULY 2003

10 9 8 7 6 5 4 3 2 1

acknowledgment is made for permission to reprint the following materials

"Breathmoss," by Ian R. MacLeod. Copyright © 2002 by Dell Magazines. First published in *Asimov's Science Fiction*, May 2002. Reprinted by permission of the author and his agent, Susan Ann Protter.

"The Most Famous Little Girl in the World," by Nancy Kress. Copyright © 2002 by SCIFI.COM. First published electronically on SCI FICTION, May 8, 2002. Reprinted by permission of the author.

"The Passenger," by Paul McAuley. Copyright © 2002 by Dell Magazines. First published in *Asimov's Science Fiction*, March 2002. Reprinted by permission of the author.

"The Political Officer," by Charles Coleman Finlay. Copyright © 2002 by Spilogale, Inc. First published in *The Magazine of Fantasy & Science Fiction*, April 2002. Reprinted by permission of the author.

"Lambing Season," by Molly Gloss. Copyright © 2002 by Dell Magazines. First published in *Asimov's Science Fiction*, July 2002. Reprinted by permission of the author.

"Coelacanths," by Robert Reed. Copyright © 2002 by Spilogale, Inc. First published in *The Magazine of Fantasy & Science Fiction*, March 2002. Reprinted by permission of the author.

"Presence," by Maureen F. McHugh. Copyright © 2002 by Spilogale, Inc. First published in *The Magazine of Fantasy & Science Fiction*, March 2002. Reprinted by permission of the author.

"Halo," by Charles Stross. Copyright © 2002 by Dell Magazines. First published in *Asimov's Science Fiction*, June 2002. Reprinted by permission of the author.

"In Paradise," by Bruce Sterling. Copyright © 2002 by Spilogale, Inc. First published in *The Magazine of Fantasy & Science Fiction*, September 2002. Reprinted by permission of the author.

"The Old Cosmonaut and the Construction Worker Dream of Mars," by Ian McDonald. Copyright © 2002 by Ian McDonald. First published in *Mars Probes* (DAW), edited by Peter Crowther. Reprinted by permission of the author.

"Stories For Men," by John Kessel. Copyright © 2002 by Dell Magazines. First published in *Asimov's Science Fiction*, October/November 2002. Reprinted by permission of the author.

"To Become a Warrior," by Chris Beckett. Copyright © 2002 by *Interzone*. First published in *Interzone*, June/July 2002. Reprinted by permission of the author.

contents

acknowledgments

The editor would like to thank the following people for their help and support: Susan Casper, Ellen Datlow, Gordon Van Gelder, Peter Crowther, David Pringle, Eileen Gunn, Nisi Shawl, Mark Watson, Sheila Williams, Brian Bieniowski, Trevor Quachri, Paul Frazier, Mark R. Kelly, Mark Watson, Gary Turner, Marty Halpern, Jayme Lynn Blaschke, Byron R. Tetrick, Richard Freeborn, Robert Silverberg, Cory Doctorow, Michael Swanwick, Charles Stross, Craig Engler, Linn Prentis, Vaughne Lee Hansen, Jed Hartman, Mary Anne Mohanraj, Susan Marie Groppi, Patrick Swenson, Tom Vander Neut, Andy Cox, Steve Pendergrast, Laura Ann Gilman, Alastair Reynolds, Warren Lapine, Shawna McCarthy, David Hartwell, Darrell Schweitzer, Robert Sawyer, Jennifer A. Hall, and special thanks to my own editor, Marc Resnick.

Thanks are also due to Charles N. Brown, whose magazine *Locus* [Locus Publications, P.O. Box 13305, Oakland, CA 94661, $49 for a one-year subscription (twelve issues) via second class; credit card orders (510) 339-9198] was used as an invaluable reference source throughout the Summation; *Locus Online* (www.locusmag.com), edited by Mark Kelly, has also become a key reference source. Thanks are also due to the editors of *Science Fiction Chronicle* (DNA Publications, Inc., P.O. Box 2988, Radford, VA 24143-2988, $45 for a one-year/twelve-issue subscription via second class) was also used as a reference source throughout.

Although critics continued to talk about the "Death of Science Fiction" throughout 2002 (some of them with ill-disguised longing), the unpalatable fact (for them) is that science fiction *didn't* die this year, and doesn't even look particularly sick. In fact, sales for many genre titles were brisk, and not only were there not fewer books published this year than last, several new book lines were added that swelled the total and are going to swell it more next year (and this isn't even counting print-on-demand titles and books sold as electronic downloads from internet Web sites, things much more difficult to keep track of than traditionally printed-and-distributed books). Nor, to my eyes anyway, was there any noticeable fall-off in literary quality. Sure, there's plenty of crap out there on the bookstore shelves, just as there's always been. But there's *also* more quality SF of many different flavors and varieties (to say nothing of the equally diverse range of quality fantasy titles) available out there this year than any one person is going to be able to read, unless they make a full-time job out of doing so (even the professional reviewers have difficulty keeping up!). In fact, an incredibly wide spectrum of good SF and fantasy, both new titles and formerly long-out-of-print older books, are probably more readily available to the average reader now—in many different forms and formats—than at any other time in history. All of which indicate to me that nailing the coffin-lid shut on the genre, smearing ashes on your face, and trotting out the obituaries might be just a *bit* premature.

In fact, 2002 was a rather quiet year in the genre market. There were few major changes this year. The slowing economy has yet to hit the genre too hard (knock on wood), although there are signs of possible trouble ahead for conglomerates, such as AOL–Time Warner and Bertelsmann; the difficulties are on high corporate levels and not directly caused by anything happening on the genre level, although they may eventually impact it. There were even some signs of expansion: Five Star Books added a vigorous new SF line, with the emphasis on short-story collections edited by Martin H. Greenberg; Tor added a new Young Adult science fiction and fantasy line, Starscape, and by early in 2003 had added a *second* YA mass-market line, Tor Teen; Tor is also planning to start a "paranormal romance" line, as yet unnamed, in 2004; Penguin Putnam started a new line of science fiction and fantasy books, Firebird, aimed at young readers; Del Rey introduced a new YA line, Imagine; and HarperCollins started Children's and YA Eos in the beginning of 2003.

Although all of this sudden interest in producing books for young adults is, of course, attributable to the immense success of the *Harry Potter* novels, it pleases me to see it, especially in science fiction, since novels aimed at the young adult market more-or-less ceased to exist (or at least became very thin on the ground) after the high days of the Andre Norton and Robert A. Heinlein "juvenile" novels of the '50s and '60s. This was short-sighted of science fiction publishers; I think that one reason why fantasy may have had an edge in popularity over science fiction in the last few decades is that fantasy has continued its tradition of easily findable, high-quality YA work—giving young readers somewhere to *start*, somewhere to become hooked on the form, before they eventually move up to reading more challenging adult-level work—while SF largely abandoned that whole share of the audience. Ironically, the much despised media novels, such as *Star Trek* and *Star Wars* books, may have been one of the few things left to play this role to a limited extent for potential new SF readers during the last twenty years, a service that they've hardly received any credit for from critics. Good new non-media-specific YA SF would, I think, do an even better job of funneling young new readers directly into the core of the genre, and, with luck, some of those readers might stick around when they get older. The operative word here, though, is "good." Most of the deliberate attempts to create YA SF novels in the past few years have produced only dull, pompous, and condescending books, usually stuffed to the gunwales with didactic libertarian propaganda. This isn't going to do it for kids raised on MTV, CGI-drenched movies, and computer games. You need something that will be as exciting to kids in the Oughts as Heinlein's "juvenile" novels were to kids in the '50s. And, frankly, rather than being as safe and politically correct as possible, a whiff of non-conformist rebellion and outlaw danger wouldn't hurt either. So let's hope that these new YA lines will help. If SF as a genre can find stuff that kids are actually *eager* to read, rather than having it prescribed for them medicinally, then that will go a long way to assuring that there are people around who still want to read the stuff even in the middle decades of the new century ahead.

2002 was another tough year in the magazine market, but at least the overall losses in circulation were relatively small as opposed to the huge plunges we've seen in other years, and there were small gains to partially balance off the loses—although these varied from magazine to magazine, so that *Asimov's Science Fiction* gained in subscriptions but lost in newsstand sales, while *The Magazine of Fantasy and Science Fiction* lost subscriptions but gained in newsstand sales, and so forth.

Last year I went into great detail explaining the publishing factors that were battering the whole magazine industry, regardless of genre, far beyond the boundaries of the science fiction field, including former mega-sellers such as *Playboy* and *TV Guide*, and some of the technical reasons why things might not be quite as bad in the SF magazine world as they appeared to be—and, as I'd feared going in, it was largely a waste of time, as I still spent the rest of the year fielding questions in interviews and convention panels about the "Death of Science Fiction" as indicated by declining magazine circulation and listening to remarks about how the editors must be buying the wrong kinds of stories or the circu-lations wouldn't be going down. I can't summon the strength to go through all that again (read the Summation for *The Year's Best Science Fiction, Nineteenth Annual Collection*, if you'd like to see the arguments). So I'll settle for mentioning that while it's tough to put too positive a spin on the situation in the current SF magazine market, and, of course, no magazine editor is happy to see his overall circulation decline, one factor that is often overlooked is that while circulation decreased by small amounts at most magazines this year, *sell-through*, the number of magazines that must be put out in the marketplace to sell one, has *increased*, increased dramatically in some cases—at *Asimov's*, sell-through was up to a record 56% last year; at *Analog*, sell-through was up to a record 55%; and at *The Magazine of Fantasy and Science Fiction*, sell-through was up to 37%. This is a factor that goes straight to the profitability of a magazine. To achieve a 35% sell-through, for instance, means that three times as many magazines are printed and put on the newsstands as actually *sell*: if you can cut-back on the number of unsold copies you have to put out there in order to actually sell one, your sell-through increases, and you save a lot of money in production costs by not having to print and distribute as many "extra" copies that no one is going to buy. This is one of the hidden factors, along with how cheap digest-sized magazines are to produce in the first place, that is, so far anyway, helping to keep the SF magazine market afloat.

If you had a 100% sell-through, you wouldn't print any more copies of an issue than you were actually going to sell—and you'd probably be a subscription-only magazine, where they know in advance exactly how many copies of an issue they need to print. It may well be that the SF magazines, the digest magazines in particular, are eventually going to go this route, as newsstands themselves dwindle in numbers, and the ones that are still around become ever more reluctant to display fiction magazines—especially digest-sized magazines that don't really fit into the physical format of most newsstands very well. And most of the digests could probably survive as subscription-only magazines, considering how much newsstand sales have fallen off over the last ten years anyway (the same problem being faced by many other magazines, not just genre magazines). The problem is that the purpose of putting more copies out on the newsstand than you expect to sell in the first place is that the extra copies act as *advertising*, tempting potential new subscribers into picking them up. If you only print as many copies as your existent subscriber-base, nobody ever chances across a copy somewhere of a magazine they might not even have known existed until that moment, and that makes it hard to gain *new* subscribers—and eventually your subscription-base is eroded away, as old subscribers die or fall away and are not replaced by new ones.

Can use of the Internet, supplemented by distribution to bookstores rather than to newsstands, solve the advertising/promotional problem of attracting new subscribers that used to be solved by putting extra copies out on the newsstand? No one yet knows—but most of the magazine editors I know are giving it their best shot.

As use of Internet Web sites to push sales of the physical product through subscriptions is becoming increasingly important, I'm going to list the URLs for those magazines that have Web sites: *Asimov's* site is at www.asimovs.com. *Analog's* site is at www.analogsf.com. *The Magazine of Fantasy & Science Fiction's* site is at www.sfsite.com/fsf/. *Interzone's* site is at www.sfsite.com/interzone/. *Realms of Fantasy* doesn't have a Web site per se, although content *from* it can be found on www.scifi.now.com The amount of activity varies widely from site to site, but the *important* thing about all of the sites is that you can *subscribe* to the magazines there, electronically, online, with just a few clicks of some buttons, no stamps, no envelopes, and no trips to the post-office required. And you can subscribe from overseas just as easily as you can from the United States, something that was formerly difficult-to-impossible. Internet sites such as Peanut Press (www.peanutpress.com) and Fictionwise (*www.fictionwise.com*), which sell electronic downloadable versions of the magazines to be read on your PDA or home computer, are also becoming important.

At any rate, to get down to hard figures, *Asimov's Science Fiction* registered a 1.7 loss in overall circulation in 2002, gaining 504 in subscriptions, but losing 1,078 in newsstand sales. *Analog Science Fiction & Fact* registered a 2.4% loss in overall circulation in 2002, gaining 490 in newsstand sales but losing 1,504 in subscriptions. *The Magazine of Fantasy & Science Fiction* registered an 10.1% loss in overall circulation, gaining 374 in newsstand sales, but losing 3,038 in subscriptions. *Interzone* held steady at a circulation of about 4,000 copies, as it has for several years, more or less evenly split between subscriptions and newsstand sales. No circulation figures for *Realms of Fantasy* were available.

The lively little Scottish SF magazine *Spectrum SF* has published so much good professional-quality work over the last three years, including good stories this year by Colin P. Davies, Eric Brown, Chris Lawson, Adam Roberts, and the serialization of Charles Stross's novel *The Atrocity Archive*, that I'm listing it here with the professional magazines, rather than in the semiprozine section, where its circulation by rights ought to put it. Unfortunately, not all is well at *Spectrum SF*; they managed to produce only two out of a scheduled four issues this year, and in the most recent issue, editor Paul Fraser announced that in the future, due to financial difficulties and constraints on his time, *Spectrum SF* is going to be an "occasional" magazine, cut-back from its quarterly schedule to appearing perhaps a couple of times a year. I'm not sure how much practical difference this really makes, since the magazine never came remotely close to keeping its schedule anyway, but it would be a shame if Fraser became even more discouraged and threw in the towel altogether. So everyone, write lots of encouraging letters to Paul, with even-more encouraging subscription money folded inside, because science fiction needs as many markets of this caliber as it can get; this little magazine publishes a disproportionate share of the year's good fiction every year, and it would be a shame to lose it.

A new British magazine started up this year, *3SF*, edited by Liz Holliday, the former editor of *Odyssey* magazine, which died several years back. The first issue was released in 2002. It's a nice-looking magazine, with a range of interviews, book reviews, media reviews, and interesting articles on such offbeat topics as alternate history and the fate of English political refugees in eleventh-century Russia. The weakest part of the magazine to date, in fact, is the fiction—issue one features solid talents such as Richard Parks, Jay Lake, and Lawrence Watt-Evans, but nothing here rises much above average-competent, certainly nowhere near the level of the first-rate stuff that has been appearing in *Spectrum SF*. Let's hope they can bring the quality of the fiction up in subsequent issues; certainly they have some very talented writers announced as appearing in upcoming issues: a good sign. We should all wish them well, as the field really does need as many viable short-fiction markets as it can get.

Subscription addresses follow: *The Magazine of Fantasy & Science Fiction*, Spilogale, Inc., P.O. Box 3447, Hoboken, NJ, 07030, annual subscription—$38.97 in U.S.; *Asimov's Science Fiction*, Dell Magazines, P.O. Box 54033, Boulder, CO, 80322-4033—$39.97 for annual subscription in U.S., *Analog Science Fiction and Fact*, Dell Magazines, P.O. Box 54625, Boulder, CO, 80323—$39.97 for annual subscription in U.S.; *Interzone*, 217 Preston Drove, Brighton BN1 6FL, United Kingdom—$60.00 for an airmail one year (twelve issues) subscription; *Realms of Fantasy*, Sovereign Media Co. Inc., P.O. Box 1623, Williamsport, PA, 17703—$16.95 for an annual subscription in the U.S.; *Spectrum SF*, Spectrum Publishing, P.O. Box 10308, Aberdeen, AB11 6ZR, United Kingdom—17 pounds sterling for a four-issue subscription, make checks payable to "Spectrum Publishing"; *3SF*, Big Engine Co., Ltd, P.O. Box 185, Abingdon, Oxon OX 14 1GR—$45.00 for a six-issue (one year) overseas subscription, or subscribe online at www.3SFmag.co.uk. Note that many of these magazines can also be subscribed to electronically online, at their various Web sites.

The internet scene evolves with such lightning speed, with new e-magazines and internet sites of general interest being born and dying in what seems a blink of the eye, that it remains possible that everything I say about it here will be obsolete by the time this book makes it into print and gets out on a bookshelf somewhere where you can buy it. The only way you can be sure to keep up with the online world is to check out what's happening there yourself, and keep checking frequently.

Once again this year, one of the major players in the whole genre short-fiction market, not just the online segment of it, was Hugo-winner Ellen Datlow's *Sci Fiction* page on the internet (www.scifi.com/scifiction/), a fiction site within the larger umbrella of The Sci-Fi Channel site, which published (or "published," if you insist) a lot of the year's best fiction, including stories by Nancy Kress, Robert Reed, Alex Irvine, Paul McAuley, Steven Popkes, James Van Pelt, Terry Bisson, and others. The site also features classic reprints, and a different original short-short story by Michael Swanwick every week.

Although *Sci Fiction* is no doubt your best bet on the Internet for good short fiction, it's not the only place to look. Eileen Gunn's *The Infinite Matrix* page (www.infinite matrix.net) also published literate and quirky fiction of high quality this year by Gene Wolfe, Ursula K. Le Guin, Benjamin Rosenbaum, Michael Swanwick, Walter Jon Williams, John Kessel, Maureen F. McHugh, Neal Barrett, Jr., John Varley, and others. The site also features a weblog from Bruce Sterling, a daily feature by Terry Bisson, a series of short-shorts from Richard Kadrey and the indefatigable Michael Swanwick, reviews by John Clute, and other neat stuff. (How long it will survive is, alas, another question; they're running low on money again, after a grant from an unnamed benefactor keep them going throughout 2002, and have resorted to trying Public Television–style campaign-drives, offering offbeat prizes in return for contributions; let's hope it works!) The *Strange Horizons* site (www.strangehorizons.com) is also worth checking out; as well as reprints, reviews, and articles, they run lots of original science fiction, fantasy, slipstream, and mild horror stories—I tend to like their fantasy better than their science fiction, but they published good stories of all sorts this year by Alex Irvine, Jay Lake, Ellen Klages, Tim Pratt, Ruth Nestvold, Greg Van Eekhout, Michael J. Jasper, Karen L. Abrahamson, and others. Another site where professional-quality stories can be found is at *Oceans of the Mind* (www.trantor publications.com/oceans.htm), where they'll sell you an electronic download of one of their four annual issues as a PDF file to be read on your home computer or PDA; they ran good stories last year by Richard Paul Russo, Ryck Neube, John Alfred Taylor, Michelle Sabara, among others, and an additional point in their favor is that most of the stuff seems to be core science fiction (for some reason, original science fiction is relatively hard to find on the Internet, although you can find slipstream and horror by the ton; in fact, slipstream and horror (particularly horror) seem to be the Internet default-setting, as far as original short fiction is concerned). Another promising site, *Future Orbits* (www.futureorbits.com), which ran on the same principal as *Oceans of the Mind*, died this year after only having been introduced last year, showing you how quickly things can turnover in the online world.

A site called *Revolution SF* (www.revolutionsf.com), also publishes some original fiction, although the bulk of its space is devoted to media and gaming reviews, book reviews, essays, and interviews; the quality of the fiction has been uneven, but some quite interesting stuff has appeared there this year, including stories by Steven Utley, David Hutchinson, and Chris Nakashima-Brown. Short science fiction stories have even been turning up on *Salon* (www.salon.com) of all places, which has so far published two good SF stories by Cory Doctorow.

Below this point, it becomes difficult to find short original science fiction of any sort of reasonably professional quality on the Internet. Good short *reprint* SF, though, is not at all hard to find. For starters, most of the sites that are associated with existent print magazines, such as *Asimov's, Analog, The Magazine of Fantasy & Science Fiction, Aurealis,* and others, will have extensive archives of material, both fiction and nonfiction, previously published by the print versions of the magazines, and some of them regularly run teaser excerpts from stories appearing in forthcoming issues. Another great place to read reprint stories for *free* (although you have to read them on the screen) is the British *Infinity Plus* (www.users. zetnet.co.uk/iplus/), a good general site that features a very extensive selection of good quality reprint stories, as well as extensive biographical and bibliographical information, book reviews, and critical essays. And don't forget that extensive archive of classic reprint stories at *Sci Fiction* that I mentioned, or the archived backlog of stories at *The Infinite Matrix* and *Strange Horizons,* all available to be read for free.

If you're willing to pay a small fee, though, you can access an even greater range of reprint stories, some of which have been unavailable anywhere else for years. Perhaps the best site to do this at is at *Fictionwise* (www.fictionwise.com). Unlike a site like *Sci Fiction* or *The Infinite Matrix, Fictionwise* is not an "electronic magazine," but rather a place to buy downloadable e-books and stories to read on your PDA or home computer — and it's probably the best place on the Internet to do this (as far as accessing good science fiction is concerned), with most of the stuff of high professional quality. In addition to individual stories, you can also buy "fiction bundles" here, which amount to electronic collections, as well as a selection of novels in several different genres; more important to *me,* you can also subscribe to downloadable versions of several of the SF magazines — including *Asimov's Science Fiction* — here, in a number of different formats (as you can at the Peanut Press site). Another similar site where you can buy downloadable e-books of various lengths by top authors is *ElectricStory* (www.electricstory.com). But here, as at a site like *Infinity Plus,* you can also access online for free a large array of critical material, including a regular column by Howard Waldrop, movie reviews by Lucius Shepard, and other things. Access for a small fee to both original and reprint SF stories is also offered by sites such as *Mind's Eye Fiction* (tale.com/genres.htm), and *Alexandria Digital Literature* (alexlit.com) as well.

People go online, though, for other reasons other than just finding stories to read. In fact, there's a large cluster of general interest sites that don't publish fiction but *do* publish lots of reviews, critical articles, and genre-oriented news of various kinds, which can be great fun to drop in on. Among my most frequent stops while Web-surfing are: *Locus Online* (www.locusmag.com), the online version of the newsmagazine *Locus,* which won a Hugo Award year as "Best Web Site," one of the most valuable sites on the whole Internet for the SF buff — a great source for fast-breaking genre-related news, as well as access to book reviews, critical lists, and extensive and invaluable data-base archives such as the Locus Index to Science Fiction and the Locus Index to Science Fiction Awards; *Science Fiction Weekly* (www.scifi.com/sfw/), a similar site, more media-and-gaming oriented than *Locus Online,* but that also features news and book reviews, as well as regular columns by John Clute, Michael Cassut, and Wil McCarthy; *Tangent Online* (www.sfsite.com/tangent/), perhaps the most valuable SF-oriented review site on the Internet, especially for short fiction; *Best SF* (*www.bestsf.net/*), another great review site, and one of the few places, along with *Tangent Online,* that makes any attempt to regularly review online fiction as well as print fiction; *Bluejack* (www.bluejack.com), less exhaustively comprehensive than *Tangent On-*

line or *Best SF*, but still a place to find insightful magazine reviews, as well as bluejack's own online diary; *SFRevu* (www.sfrevu.com), another review site, although rather than reviewing short fiction, they specialize in media and novel reviews; the *Sci-Fi Channel* (www.scifi.com), which provides a home for Ellen Datlow's *Sci Fiction* and for *Science Fiction Weekly*, and to the bimonthly SF-oriented chats hosted by *Asimov's* and *Analog*, as well as vast amounts of material about SF movies and TV shows; the *SF Site* (www.sfsite.com), which not only features an extensive selection of reviews of books, games, and magazines, interviews, critical retrospective articles, letters, and so forth, plus a huge archive of past reviews; but also serves as host-site for the web-pages of *The Magazine of Fantasy & Science Fiction, Interzone*, and the above-mentioned *SFRevu*; SFF net (www.sff.net), a huge site featuring dozens of home pages and "newsgroups" for SF writers, plus sites for genre-oriented "live chats"; the *Science Fiction Writers of America* page (www.sfwa.org); where news, obituaries, award information, and recommended reading lists can be accessed; *Audible* (www.audible.com) and *Beyond 2000* (www.beyond2000.com), where SF-oriented radio plays can be accessed; multiple Hugo-winner David Langford's on-line version of his fanzine *Ansible* (www.dcs.gla.ac.uk/Ansible/), which provides a funny and often iconoclastic slant on genre-oriented news; and *Speculations* (www.speculations.com), a long-running site which dispenses writing advice, although to access most of it, you'll have to subscribe to the site.

Live online interviews with prominent genre writers are also offered on a regular basis on many sites, including interviews sponsored by *Asimov's* and *Analog* and conducted by Gardner Dozois on the Sci-Fi Channel (www.scifi.com/chat) every other Tuesday night at 9 p.m. EST (*Sci Fiction* chats conducted by Ellen Datlow are also featured on the Sci-Fi Channel at irregular intervals, usually on Thursdays, check the site for details); regular scheduled interviews on the Cybling site (www.cybling.com); and occasional interviews on the Talk City site (www.talkcity.com). Many Bulletin Board Services, such as Delphi, Compuserve, and AOL, have large online communities of SF writers and fans, and some of these services also feature regularly scheduled live interactive real-time "chats" or conferences, in which anyone interested in SF is welcome to participate. The SF-oriented chat on Delphi, every Wednesday at about 10 p.m. EST, is the one with which I'm most familiar, but there are similar chats on F.net, and probably on other BBSs as well.

Nobody in this market has as yet figured out a good, steady, reliable way to *make money* by publishing fiction online, and until that happens, many of these sites and e-zines are going to die from lack of capital and funds (production costs may be a lot lower for "publishing" an e-zine than for publishing an old-fashioned print magazine, but at the very least you still have to have money to pay for the stories, to say nothing of money to pay your staff—and it adds up), and the online market is not going to reach its full potential, which is considerable. Maybe the *Fictionwise* model, selling individual stories and books in the form of downloads for your PDA, or the *Oceans of the Mind* model, selling subscriptions to purchase whole issues of a magazine in downloadable form at regular intervals, will prove to be commercially viable, and become the wave of the future. Or maybe not. Only time will tell.

It was at best a so-so year in the print semiprozine market. Nothing has been heard from the once-prominent fiction semiprozine *Century* for more than two years now, and I'm beginning to wonder if we're ever going to hear from it again. The acclaimed and long-running Australian fiction semiprozine *Eidolon* died this year, and *Orb, Altair, and Terra Incognita* have all gone "on hiatus," a limbo from which few magazines ever return in the semiprozine world.

The titles consolidated under the umbrella of Warren Lapine's DNA Publications—*Fantastic Stories of the Imagination, Weird Tales, Chronicle* (formerly *Science Fiction Chronicle*), the all-vampire-fiction magazine *Dreams of Decadence*; and Lapine's original magazine, *Absolute Magnitude, The Magazine of Science Fiction Adventures*—were all still having trouble keeping to their announced publishing schedules this year, except for *Chronicle*, which met it, and which seemed to have held steady in circulation as well. The other DNA magazines all registered slight drops in circulation, although no disastrous plunges, and the sell-through for most of them was high as well. An ominous note was struck, though, by a note from publisher Warren Lapine in recent renewal notices to subscribers, which warns that unless subscribers not only renew but subscribe to an additional magazine or purchase a book listed on the back of the renewal flyer, DNA will have to cut costs, including the possibility that at least two magazines will be dropped. This doesn't sound good.

The most stable of the fiction semiprozines seem to be the long-running Canadian semiprozine *On Spec* and the leading British semiprozine *The Third Alternative*, which were among the very few magazines in the entire semipro market to meet their announced production schedules this year. The slick, large-format *The Third Alternative* is one of the handsomest magazines out there, semiprozine *or* pro, and seems to just keep getting better, publishing fiction at a fully professional level, most of which remains slipstream and horror, although they've been adding a bit of science fiction to the mix of late as well—good stuff by John Grant, Ian Watson, Graham Joyce, Douglas Lain, and others, appeared in *The Third Alternative* this year. *On Spec* is another handsome magazine, and also published some good stuff this year by Charles Coleman Finlay, Karen Traviss, Kate Riedel, and others. *Talebones, Fiction on the Dark Edge* managed only two issues out of a scheduled four this year, but the editors had the best of excuses: the birth of a new baby. *Talebones* remains a lively little magazine, steadily improving, and published good fiction this year from William Barton, James Van Pelt, James Sallis, Beverly Suarez-Beard, and others.

Artemis Magazine: Science and Fiction for a Space-Faring Society again managed only two issues this year out of their scheduled four; I like the fact that *Artemis* features center-core science fiction in a marketplace where the bulk of the fiction semiprozines run mostly slipstream or horror instead, but they need to work on making their stories more vivid and powerful; much of the work here this year was rather gray, although there were interesting stories by Edward Willett and Roxanne Hutton. A magazine which couldn't be more different from *Artemis* in editorial personality is *Lady Churchill's Rosebud Wristlet* (about all they have in common is that they both only managed to get two issues out this year), which almost never publishes core science-fiction, but does publish some good slipstream stuff, including stories by Jeffrey Ford, Greg Van Eekhout, and others. The other long-running Australian semiprozine, *Aurealis*, was taken over by a new editor, and managed two of its scheduled four issues this year, with interesting stories by Robert N. Stephenson and Lee Battersby; it's good to see it surviving, since the fear last year was that it would follow *Eidolon* into the grave. A new Australian fiction semiprozine, the oddly titled *Andromeda Spaceways Inflight Magazine*, launched this year, but is already reported to be in financial trouble; we'll see if it makes it. I saw one issue of the quirky Irish semiprozine *Albedo One* this year and heard rumors that there was a *Tales of the Unanticipated*, but I never saw it.

Black Gate, the new large-format fantasy magazine, managed two fat issues out of a scheduled four. Although ostensibly a fantasy magazine, they remain very broad-church in their definition of fantasy, but the magazine did feature good stories this year, whatever you define them as, by Ellen Klages, Mike Resnick, Cory Doctorow, Bill Johnson, Gail Sproule, and others.

I don't follow the horror semiprozine market anymore, but the most prominent magazine there, as usual, seems to be the highly respected *Cemetery Dance*.

Your best bets in the critical magazine market, and by far the most reliably published, are the two "newszines," *Locus* and *Chronicle* (formerly *Science Fiction Chronicle*), and David G. Hartwell's eclectic critical magazine, perhaps the best critical magazine out there at the moment, *The New York Review of Science Fiction*. There have been a few changes here, at least with the newszines: *Locus's* longtime and multiple Hugo-winning editor, Charles N. Brown, supposedly retired in 2002, turning the editorial reins over to Jennifer A. Hall, but since the magazine is still put together in his living room, most insiders guess that he won't *actually* "retire" until they pry the magazine from his cold dead fingers. *Science Fiction Chronicle* was taken over by Warren Lapine's DNA Publishing Group last year, and *this* year, longtime editor and Hugo-winner Andy Porter left the magazine he'd founded, among swirling rumors that he'd been fired; he was replaced as News Editor by John Douglas, the title of the magazine was changed to *Chronicle*, and its formerly erratic publishing schedule was stabilized. One issue of Lawrence Person's playful *Nova Express* was published this year, but the editor is considering turning the magazine into an online "electronic magazine" (which I suspect will eventually be the fate of most critical semiprozines). There were several issues of *The Fix* this year, a welcome new short-fiction review magazine brought to you by the people who put out *The Third Alternative*.

Locus, The Newspaper of the Science Fiction Field, Locus Publications, Inc., P.O. Box 13305, Oakland, CA 94661—$56.00 for a one-year first class subscription, 12 issues; *The New York Review Of Science Fiction*, Dragon Press, P.O. Box 78, Pleasantville, NY, 10570—$32.00 per year, 12 issues; *Nova Express*, P.O. Box 27231, Austin, TX 78755-2231—$12 for a one-year (four issue) subscription; *On Spec, More Than Just Science Fiction*, P.O. Box 4727, Edmonton, AB, Canada T6E 5G6—$18 for a one-year subscription; *Aurealis, the Australian Magazine of Fantasy and Science Fiction*, Chimaera Publications, P.O. Box 2164, Mt. Waverley, Victoria 3149, Australia—$43 for a four-issue overseas airmail subscription, "all cheques and money orders must be made out to Chimarea Publications in Australian dollars"; *Albedo*, Albedo One Productions, 2 Post Road, Lusk, Co., Dublin, Ireland—$34 for a four-issue airmail subscription, make checks payable to "Albedo One"; *Pirate Writings, Tales of Fantasy, Mystery & Science Fiction, Absolute Magnitude, The Magazine of Science Fiction Adventures, Aboriginal Science Fiction, Weird Tales, Dreams of Decadence, Chronicle*—all available from DNA Publications, P.O. Box 2988, Radford, VA 24142-2988—all available for $16 for a one-year subscription, although you can get a group subscription to all five DNA fiction magazines for $70 a year, with *Chronicle* $45 a year (12 issues), all checks payable to "D.N.A. Publications"; *Tales of the Unanticipated*, Box 8036, Lake Street Station, Minneapolis, MN 55408—$15 for a four-issue subscription; *Artemis Magazine: Science and Fiction for a Space-Faring Society*, LRC Publications, 1380 E. 17th St., Suite 201, Brooklyn NY 11230-6011—$15 for a four-issue subscription, checks payable to LRC Publications; *Talebones, Fiction on the Dark Edge*, 5203 Quincy Ave. SE,

Auburn, WA 98092—$18 for four issues; *The Third Alternative*, TTA Press, 5 Martins Lane, Witcham, Ely, Cambs. CB6 2LB, England, UK—$22 for a four-issue subscription, checks made payable to "TTA Press"; *Black Gate*, New Epoch Press, 815 Oak Street, St. Charles, IL 60174—$25.95 for a one-year (four issue) subscription; *Lady Churchill's Rosebud Wristlet*, Small Beer Press, 360 Atlantic Avenue, PMB #132, Brooklyn, NY 11217—$12 for four issues, all checks payable to Gavin Grant; *The Fix: The Review of Short Fiction*, TTA Press, Wayne Edwards, P.O. Box 219, Olyphant, PA 18447—$28.00 for a six-issue subscription, make checks payable to "TTA Press"; *Andromeda Spaceways Inflight Magazine*, P.O. Box 495, Chinchilla QLD 4415 Australia—$35.00 for a one-year subscription. Many of these magazines can also be ordered online, at their Web sites; see the online section for URLs.

Yet again, it was a pretty weak year for original anthologies.

The best original SF anthology of the year, with almost no competition, was *Mars Probes* (DAW), edited by Peter Crowther. Having said that, I must admit that I found *Mars Probes* somewhat disappointing overall, in comparison with Crowther's 1999 anthology *Moon Shots*. With all the good science fiction that's been written about Mars at novel-length in recent years, I'd hoped for a really solid, definitive collection of core SF, reflecting some of the recent science fiction thinking about the Red Planet, and there *is* some of that here—but a great deal of the anthology (too much of it, in my opinion) is devoted to fabulations and homages drawing not on scientific fact but on other fictional versions of Mars, from Bradbury's "Mars" to Burrough's "Barsoom," including an uncannily spot-on pastiche/homage of Leigh Brackett's pulp-era Martian stories by Michael Moorcock. Even Paul McAuley, who has done some of the best of the recent work about Mars, contributes a near-mainstream story set in a Martian theme park rather than a hard-science story. Most of this stuff is clever, well-crafted, and entertaining, but it makes the anthology as a whole a little more insubstantial as a *science fiction anthology* than I was hoping it would be (perhaps the problem is with my own expectations rather than with the anthology itself); in spite of these quibbles, though, it's still easily the best SF anthology of the year. The best story in *Mars Probes* is Ian McDonald's "The Old Cosmonaut and the Construction Worker Dream of Mars," but there's also good work here by Stephen Baxter, Alastair Reynolds, Eric Brown, Gene Wolfe, Allen Steele, and others.

It's nearly impossible to come up with a follow-up candidate for best original SF anthology this year, although there were several anthologies with one or two good stories apiece in them. The most solid of these overall was probably *30th Anniversary DAW: Science Fiction* (DAW), edited by Elizabeth R. Wollheim and Sheila E. Gilbert; a lot of the stuff here is just fragments of larger story-arcs, depending on your familiarity with long-running DAW novel series for full effect, but there is some good self-contained work here by Neal Barrett, Jr., Brian Stableford, C. J. Cherryh, Charles L. Harness, Ian Watson, and others. *Once Upon a Galaxy* (DAW), edited by Wil McCarthy, Martin H. Greenberg, and John Heifers, an anthology of fairy-tales retold as science fiction, has some clever stuff in it. The best story here is by Paul Di Filippo, but there is also good stuff by Gregory Benford, Stanley Schmidt, Scott Edleman, Thomas Wylde, and others. *Sol's Children* (DAW), edited by Jean Rabe and Martin H. Greenberg, features good but unexceptional stories by Timothy Zahn, Michael A. Stackpole, Kristine Kathryn Rusch, the late Jack C. Haldeman II, and others. *Oceans of Space* (DAW), edited by Brian M. Thomsen and Martin H. Greenberg, is largely unimpressive, but has decent stories by Andre Norton, Mike Resnick, Simon Hawke, and others.

PS Publishing, edited by Peter Crowther, which for the last couple of years has been bringing out novellas in individual chapbook form, produced another bunch of titles this year, including the excellent *V.A.O.*, by Geoff Ryman, good novellas such as *Riding the Rock*, by Stephen Baxter, *The Tain*, by China Mieville, and others. Golden Gryphon Press got into the same business this year, bringing Alastair Reynold's first-rate novella *Turquoise Days* out as an individual chapbook. You're more likely to find really good science fiction in these chapbooks than you are to find it in most of the second-tier anthologies mentioned above.

There were three original Alternate History anthologies this year, the best of which was *Worlds That Weren't* (Roc), edited by Laura Ann Gilman; the best story here is Walter Jon Williams's strange novella "The Last Ride of German Freddie," but the book also features good novellas by Harry Turtledove, Mary Gentle, and S. M. Stirling. *Alternate Generals II* (Baen), edited by Harry Turtledove, is also worthwhile, although it may appeal more to military history buffs than to the average reader, since a number of the stories here require more knowledge of the intricate details of past wars for full appreciation than the average reader is likely to possess. The best story here is William Sanders's "Empire," although there is also good work by Judith Tarr, Michael F. Flynn, Susan Shwartz, and others (I do wonder, though, how many people are going to be willing to pay $24.00 for this: I think they would have been better off bringing it out as an inexpensive mass-market paperback, like the first *Alternate Generals* anthology, than as an expensive hardcover). *Alternate Gettysburgs* (Berkley), edited by Brian M. Thomsen and Martin H. Greenberg, is even more specialized—if you're not reasonably *au courant* with the American Civil War, and especially the Battle of Gettysburg, you might as well forget it; most of the stories in these three books are alternate history, unsurprisingly enough, but the best story in *Alternate Gettysburgs* is an SF story by William H. Keith, Jr., although there are also good stories by Kristine Kathryn Rusch, Brendan DuBois, and others here, probably enough to make it worthwhile as a $6.99 paperback (I wouldn't have wanted to buy it as a $24.00 hardcover).

There was supposedly a new volume in the assembled-online "SFF.net" annual anthology series this year, called *Beyond the Last Star*, edited by Sherwood Smith, but I never saw it; I'll have to save it for consideration for next year.

As usual, *L. Ron Hubbard Presents Writers of the Future Volume XVIII* (Bridge), edited by Algis Budrys, presents novice work by beginning writers, some of whom may later turn out to be important talents. Much the same could be said of *Empire of Dreams and Miracles* (Phobos), edited by Orson Scott Card, which features winners of the 1st Annual Phobos Fiction Contest.

In terms of literary quality, the line-by-line quality of the writing, the best anthology of the year may well be *Conjunctions 39: The New Wave Fabulists*, a special issue of the literary publication *Conjunctions* guest-edited by Peter Straub—although some genre fans are going to find it disappointing in spite of the bravura quality of the prose. The (somewhat unclear) intention here seems to have been to produce an "all genres" anthology aimed at the mainstream literary audience, but there is almost no science fiction here—with the exception of a good Alternate History story by John Kessel, "The Invisible Empire"—and surprisingly, considering that horror superstar Peter Straub was the editor, almost no horror either; most of the stories fall somewhere on the line between fantasy and slipstream/

surrealism/Magic Realism/whatever-we're-calling-it-this-month, although several of the anthologies very best stories, such as Karen Joy Fowler's "The Further Adventures of the Invisible Man" and John Crowley's "The Girlhood of Shakespeare's Heroine," strike me as straight mainstream stories (in spite of Straub's rather too-clever attempts to argue that the Crowley is *really* a fantasy story afterall). Although Straub does brandish the term "post-transformation fiction," it's hard for me to perceive that any coherent critical argument is being made here, or to discern why this particular group of authors are "New Wave Fabulists," or what makes them so, or what that term *means*, or why they were selected rather than some other grouping of authors; it seems instead like the partially random selection of authors you'd get assembling any original anthology, depending largely on the luck of the draw, rather than a list of authors collected with critical rigor or to demonstrate some particular mode or emerging school of fiction. Still, if you set aside considerations of genre or of critical canon-forming, what you get is an anthology with some really good stuff to read in it. After the above-mentioned stories by Fowler, Crowley, and Kessel, the best stories here are Andy Duncan's flamboyant "The Big Rock Candy Mountain" and China Mieville's grisly "Familiar," but the anthology also features good-to-excellent stories by Nalo Hopkinson, Neil Gaiman, Elizabeth Hand, Peter Straub himself, and others, plus excerpts from forthcoming novels by Joe Haldeman and Gene Wolfe, a book well worth the $15 cover price, especially for those who don't insist on drinking their genre neat.

There were four other small press anthologies this year that mixed slipstream, horror, fantasy, and science fiction in their contents lists to varying effect, usually with science fiction the smallest element in the mix by far. *Polyphony, Volume 1* (Wheatland Press), edited by Deborah Layne and Jay Lake, is more unambiguously a "slipstream" anthology than *Conjunctions 39*, with little that could be mistaken for any other genre, but is still worthwhile. The best story here is Maureen F. McHugh's "Laika Comes Home Safe," but *Polyphony* also contains good stuff by Andy Duncan, Lucius Shepard, Leslie What, James Van Pelt, and others. *Leviathan Three* (Ministry of Whimsy Press), edited by Jeff VanderMeer and Forrest Aguirre, mixes other fairly identifiable genres (mostly fantasy) in with the slipstream stuff, and mixes genres more *within* individual stories than most of these anthologies do (Brian Stableford's story, for instance, mixes science fiction and fantasy to enough of a degree that it can only be called science-fantasy), and although there's some over-pretentious and rather dull stuff here, there's also some excellent work. The best stories here are "The Face of an Angel," by Brian Stableford and "The Fool's Tale," by L. Timmel Duchamp, but there are also good stories by Jeffrey Ford, Carol Emshwiller, Stepan Chapman, and others. *J. K. Potter's Embrace the Mutation* (Subterranean Press), edited by William Schafer and Bill Sheehan, is an anthology of stories supposedly inspired by the work of artist J. K. Potter (included in the book); not surprisingly, considering Potter's sometimes grotesque work and the publisher's usual fare, *Embrace the Mutation* leans a good deal more toward straight horror than the other three anthologies being discussed here, but there still are visitations from other genres, notably pure fantasy in a story by Elizabeth Hand and even science fiction in a story by Lucius Shepard—those two, in fact, "Pavane for a Prince of the Air," by Elizabeth Hand, and "Radiant Green Star," by Lucius Shepard, are the best stories in the book, but it also features good work by Michael Bishop, Kim Newman, John Crowley, Peter Crowther, and others. *In the Shadow of the Wall* (Cumberland House), edited by Byron R. Tetrick and Martin H. Greenberg, is an otherwise pretty good anthology, mostly of rather *Twilight Zonish* fantasy stories, that hampers itself a bit by insisting that all its stories deal centrally with the Vietnam Memorial (the Wall of the title. The best story here is Michael Swanwick's bitter little story "Dirty Little War," but there is also good work by Barry N. Malzberg, Orson Scott Card, Nick DiChario, and Byron R. Terrick himself.

Two other small-press anthologies filled an odd and rather specialized literary niche: anthologies of stories about (or inspired by, in one case, to be precise) science fiction and fantasy *bookstores*. *Shelf Life: Fantastic Stories Celebrating Bookstores* (DreamHaven), edited by Gregg Ketter, the owner of the DreamHaven science fiction bookstore in Minneapolis. *Shelf Life* deals pretty centrally with the bookstore theme, here treated mostly as a variant of the "little magic shop" story in a sequence of mostly rather gentle fantasy stories, with some mild horror, by Gene Wolfe (with his "From the Cradle," being, unsurprisingly, the volume's best), P. D. Cacek, John J. Miller, and others, plus one SF story by Jack Williamson (a pleasant-enough anthology, but at $75.00, it's wildly overpriced). *The Bakka Anthology* (The Bakka Collection), edited by Kristen Pederson Chew, has a looser theme, stories "inspired by" the authors having worked in the *Bakka* science fiction bookstore in Toronto, and, as might be expected, gathers a more eclectic crop of stories as a result, mostly science fiction, with some fantasy and harder-to-classify stuff thrown in. The best story here is Michelle Sagara West's "To Kill an Immortal," but there's good work by Cory Doctorow, Nalo Hopkinson, Robert J. Sawyer, and others, here as well.

The best original genre fantasy anthology of the year, again with little real competition, was probably *The Green Man: Tales from the Mythic Forest* (Viking) edited by Ellen Datlow and Terry Windling, which contained good-to-excellent work by M. Shayne Bell, Tanith Lee, Delia Sherman, Emma Bull, Nina Kiriki Hoffman, Patricia A. McKillip, and others. *30th Anniversary DAW: Fantasy* (DAW), edited by Ellizabeth R. Wollheim and Sheila E. Gilbert is also worth mentioning; although it suffers from the same faults as its SF brother-volume, it contains good work by Tanith Lee, Michelle West, and others. The rest of the year's original fantasy anthologies were pleasant but minor, including, *Knight Fantastic* (DAW), edited by John Helfers and Martin H. Greenberg; *Pharaoh Fantastic* (DAW), edited by Brittiany A. Koren and Martin H. Greenberg; and *Apprentice Fantastic* (DAW), edited by Russell Davis and Martin H. Greenberg.

Shared-world anthologies this year included *Wild Cards: Deuces Down* (ibooks), edited by George R. R. Martin; *Thieves' World: Turning Points* (Tor), edited by Lynn Abbey; and *Deryni Tales* (Ace), edited by Katherine Kurtz.

Although I don't pay a lot of attention to the horror genre anymore, from what I could tell the big original anthology of the year there seemed to be *Dark Terrors 6* (Gollancz), edited by Stephen Jones and David Sutton. Other original horror anthologies included *The Children of Cthulhu: Chilling Tales Inspired by H. P. Lovecraft* (Del Rey), edited by John Polant and Benjamin Adams and *The Darker Side: Generations of Horror* (Roc), edited by John Pelan.

A new anthology by Peter Crowther and Robert Silverberg's *Legends II* is about all there is to look forward to in the original anthology market for next year. Maybe the long-promised Greg Benford anthology will finally appear. Not a lot else on the horizon.

Addresses: PS Publishing, 98 High Ash Drive, Leeds L517 8RE, England, UK—$14.00 for *V.A.O.*, by Geoff Ryman, $14.00 for *Riding the Rock*, by Stephen Baxter, $14.00 for *The Tain*, by China Mieville; Golden Gryphon Press, 3002 Perkins Road, Urbana, IL 61802—$15.95 for *Turquoise Days*, by Alastair Reynolds; Conjunctions, Bard College,

Annandale-on-Hudson, NY 12504—$15 for *Conjunctions 39: The New Wave Fabulists*;
Wheatland Press, P.O. Box 1818, Wilsonville, OR 97070—$16.95 for *Polyphony*; Subter-
ranean Press, P.O. Box 190106, Burton, MI 48519—$40.00 for *Embrace the Mutation*;
Ministry of Whimsy Press, P.O. Box 4248, Tallahasse, FL 32315—$21.95 for *Leviathan 3*;
Cumberland House, 431 Harding Industrial Drive, Nashville, TN 37211—$14.95 for *In
the Shadow of the Wall*; DreamHaven Books, 912 W. Lake Street, Minneapolis, MN
55408—$75.00 for *Shelf Life: Fantastic Stories Celebrating Bookstores*; The Bakka Collec-
tion, 598 Yonge Street, Toronto, ONT M4Y 1Z3—$30.00 for The Bakka Anthology.

2002 seemed like a pretty strong year for novels, in spite of all the moaning about how SF
is dying and there's nothing worthwhile to read left out there on the bookstore shelves.
According to the newsmagazine *Locus*, there were 2,241 books "of interest to the SF field,"
both original and reprint, published in 2002, up by 4% from 2001's total of 2,158. Original
books were up by 5% to 1,271 from last year's total of 1,210; reprint books were up by 2
% to 970 titles over last year's total of 948. The number of new SF novels was up slightly,
with 256 new titles published as opposed to 251 novels published in 2001. The number
of new fantasy novels was also up, to 333, as opposed to 282 novels published in 2001.
Horror, however, was down, dropping to 112 from last year's total of 151. And, for the most
part, these totals don't even reflect print-on-demand novels, novels offered as downloads on
the internet, media tie-in-novels, novelizations of movies, gaming novels, or novels drawn
from TV shows such as *Charmed*, *Angel*, and *Buffy, the Vampire Slayer*.

Even sticking to the SF novels alone, that's a lot of novels. How many of the people
who complain that "there's nothing to read out there" have really sampled even a small
percentage of them, let alone all 256?

I myself didn't have time to read many novels this year, with all the reading I have to
do at shorter lengths. So instead I'll limit myself to mentioning novels that received a lot
of attention and acclaim in 2002 include: *Guardian* (Ace), Joe Haldeman; *Schild's Ladder*
(Eos), Greg Egan; *Probability Space* (Tor), Nancy Kress; *The Years of Rice and Salt* (Bantam), Kim Stanley Robinson; *Bones of the Earth* (Eos), Michael Swanwick; *Coyote* (Ace),
Allen Steele; *Light Music* (Eos), Kathleen Ann Goonan; *The Scar* (Del Rey), China Mie-
ville; *The Praxis* (Avon), Walter Jon Williams; *Redemption Ark* (Ace), Alastair Reynolds;
Evolution (Del Rey), Stephen Baxter; *The Disappeared* (Roc), Kristine Kathryn Rusch; *Light*
(Gollancz), M. John Harrison; *Castles Made of Sand* (Gollancz), Gwyneth Jones; *The Lady
of the Sorrows* (Warner Aspect), Cecilia Dart-Thornton; *Shadow Puppets* (Tor), Orson Scott
Card; *Kiln People* (Tor), David Brin; *Vitals* (Del Rey), Greg Bear; *Engine City* (Tor), Ken
MacLeod; *The Fall of the Kings* (Bantam Spectra), Ellen Kushner & Delia Sherman; *Ares
Express* (Earthlight), Ian McDonald; *The Sky So Big and Black* (Tor), John Barnes; *Tran-
scension* (Tor), Damien Broderick; *Chindi* (Ace), Jack McDevitt; *Empire of Bones* (Bantam
Spectra), Liz Williams; *The Omega Expedition* (Tor) Brian Stableford; *The Visitor* (Eos),
Sheri S. Tepper; *The Impossible Bird* (Tor), Patrick O'Leary; *Ruled Britannia* (NAL), Harry
Turtledove; *The Separation* (Scribner UK), Christopher Priest; *Spaceland* (Tor), Rudy
Rucker; *A Winter Haunting* (Morrow), Dan Simmons; *The Translator* (Morrow), John
Crowley; *White Apples* (Tor), Jonathan Carroll; *The Devil and Deep Space* (Roc), Susan
R. Matthews; *Permanence* (Tor), Karl Schroeder; *Fitcher's Brides* (Tor), Gregory Frost; *Ex-
plorer* (DAW), C. J. Cherryh; *Kushiel's Chosen* (Tor), Jacqueline Carey; *The Longest Way*

Home (Eos), Robert Silverberg; *Dark Ararat* (Tor), Brian Stableford; *Resurgence* (Baen), Charles Sheffield; *Manifold: Origin* (Del Rey), Stephen Baxter; *Night Watch* (Harper-Collins), Terry Pratchett; *Burning the Ice* (Tor), Laura J. Mixon; *The King* (Ace), David Feintuch; *Jupiter* (Tor), Ben Bova; *The Alchemist's Door* (Tor), Lisa Goldstein; and *Coraline* (Harper), Neil Gaiman.

The first novels that drew the most attention this year seemed to be *The Golden Age* (Tor), John C. Wright, *A Scattering of Jades* (Tor), Alexander C. Irvine, and *The Atrocity Archive*, Charles Stross (the Stross suffering under the handicap of only appearing as a serial in *Spectrum SF* magazine, and not yet in book form; in spite of this, it got a lot of notice). Other first novels included: *Solitaire* (Eos), Kelly Eskridge; *The Summer Country* (Ace), James A. Hetley; *Fires of the Faithful* (Bantam Spectra), Naomi Kritzer; *The Red Church* (Pinnacle), Scott Nicholson; *The Eve of Night* (Bantam Spectra), Pauline J. Alama; *Altered Carbon* (Del Rey), Richard Morgan; *Warchild* (Warner Aspect), Karin Lowachee; *Just Like Beauty* (Farrar, Straus, Giroux), Lisa Lerner; and *The God Who Beget a Jackal* (Picador USA), Nega Mezlekia.

Looking over these lists, it's clear that Tor, Eos, and Ace had strong years, although Del Rey had a pretty good year as well. And in spite of the usual critical chorus about how science fiction is "dying" or being driven off the shelves by fantasy, it's clear that the majority of novels here are center-core science fiction. Even omitting the fantasy of novels and the borderline genre-straddling work from the list, the Egan, the Kress, the two Baxters, the Reynolds, the McDevitt, the Swanwick, the Stablefords, the Barnes, the Goonan, the Harrison, the Bear, the Bova, the Sheffield, the Silverberg, the McDonald, the McDevitt, the Williams, the MacLeod, the Brin, the Card, the Steele, and almost a dozen others are clearly and unmistakably science fiction, many of them "hard science fiction" at that. Pretty fair numbers for an endangered species!

Meanwhile, this is the best time in decades to pick up new editions of long out-of-print classics of science fiction and fantasy, books that have been unavailable to the average reader since the '70s in some cases. Throughout the last two decades, reissues had become as rare as the proverbial hen's teeth, as shortsighted bottom-line corporate publishing practices meant that books almost never came back into print once they had gone out of it, and that reprints of even-older classics were out of the question. Now, however, the ice is beginning to break up a bit. The *SF Masterworks* and the *Fantasy Masterworks* reprint series, from English publisher Millennium, have brought forth slews of classic reprints during the last few years, joined by American lines such as Tor Orb, Del Rey Impact, Baen Books, and Vintage, as well as print-on-demand publishers such as *Wildside* and *Big Engine*, and Internet sites such as *Fictionwise* and *Electric Story*, where classic novels and stories are available for purchase in downloadable form. This year, ibooks joined in with a wave of classic reprints, including Robert Silverberg's *Dying Inside*, *Up the Line*, and *The Man in the Maze*, Brian W. Aldiss's *Helliconia* triology, Greg Bear's *Blood Music* and *Strength of Stones*, William Rotsler's *Patron of the Arts*, Roger Zelazny's collection *The Last Defender of Camelot*, an omnibus of three Barry Malzberg novels collected as *On a Planet Alien*, and Harlan Ellison's famous anthology *Dangerous Visions*; Vintage reissued a flood of Philip K. Dick titles, including *Time Out of Joint*, *Dr. Bloodmoney*, *Clans of the Alphane Moon*, *The Simulacra*, *Counter-Clock World*, *The Man Who Japed*, and *The Zap Gun* (if you can afford only one of these, make it *Time Out of Joint*, one of Dick's best; some of the others are rather minor), as well as reprints of Samuel R. Delany's *Nova* (one of the best and most influential books of its decade) and a combination volume consisting of his *Babel-17/Empire*

Star. Orb published an omnibus by Hal Clement, *Heavy Planet*, containing his novels *Mission of Gravity* and *Star Light*, plus other related material, and an omnibus of three of James White's "Sector General" novels, *Alien Emergencies*, as well as a reissue of A. E. Van Vogt's *The World of Null-A*. Tor reprinted Frank Herbert's *The Green Brain* and *The Santaroga Barrier*, as well as releasing omnibus collections of "Stainless Steel Rat" novels by Harry Harrison, *A Stainless Stell Trio*, and of "Dorsai" novels by Gordon R. Dickson, *Dorsai Spirit*. Baen released an omnibus collection of "Lord Darcy" stories and novels by Randall Garrett, *Lord Darcy*, as well as an omnibus of "Miles Vorkesigan" novels by Lois McMaster Bujold, *Miles Errant*, and a collection of stories and novels by James H. Schmitz, *Eternal Frontier*. Gollancz reprinted Jack Vance's *Big Planet*, Joe Haldeman's *Worlds*, Samuel R. Delany's *The Jewels of Aptor*, Robert Silverberg's *The Masks of Time*, John Sladek's *Tik-Tok*, and Ian Watson's *The Jonah Kit*. Big Engine made available an omnibus of Brian Stableford novels, *Swan Songs: The Complete Hooded Swan Collection*, as well as Leigh Kennedy's novel *The Journal of Nicholas the American*; Perennial reprinted John Crowley's *Little, Big*, and issued an omnibus of three other Crowley novels, *Otherwise*. NESFA Press issued an omnibus of novels by Fredric Brown, *Martians and Madness: The Complete SF Novels of Fredric Brown*, and an omnibus of Robert Sheckley novels, *Dimensions of Sheckley*. Tachyon Publications reissued Pat Murphy's *The Shadow Hunter* and Avram Davidson's *The Phoenix and the Mirror*. Overlook Press reissued Evangeline Walton's *The Maginogion Tetralogy*; Del Rey reissued Nicola Griffith's *Ammonite*; and Starscape reprinted Orson Scott Card's *Ender's Game*.

And no doubt there were other reprints that I've missed.

As I said, this is the best time in decades to pick up new editions of long out-of-print work, so go out and get them while you can!

I've almost given up trying to guess which novels are going to win the year's major awards, especially as SFWA's weird and dysfunctional "rolling eligibility" rule means that books that already won a Hugo last year, such as Neil Gaiman's *American Gods*, get to go head-to-head with new novels such as Michael Swanwick's *Bones of the Earth*. To be fair, it's hard to see a clear or obvious winner for the Hugo, either. We'll just have to wait and see.

Small-press original novels of interest this year included Charles L. Harness's *Cybele, with Bluebonnets* (NESFA Press), an autobiographical novel with some fantastic elements, and Carol Emshwiller's *The Mount* (Small Beer Press).

Associational novels by SF writers this year included a mystery novel by Ray Bradbury, *Let's All Kill Constance* (HarperCollins/Morrow).

Mail-order information: NESFA Press, P.O. Box 809, Framinghan, MA 01701-0809— $21 (plus $2.50 shipping in all cases) for *Cybele, with Bluebonnets*, by Charles Harness, $29.00 (plus $2.50 shipping) for *Martians and Madness: The Complete SF Novels of Fredric Brown*, $29.00 for *Dimensions of Sheckley*, by Robert Sheckley; Small Beer Press, 360 Atlantic Avenue, PMB #132, Brooklyn, NY 112117—$16 for *The Mount*, by Carol Emshwiller; Tachyon Publications, 1459 18th Street #139, San Francisco, CA 94107—$14.95 for *The Shadow Hunter*, by Pat Murphy, $15.00 for *The Phoenix and the Mirror*, by Avram Davidson.

It was another good year for short-story collections. The year's best collections included: *The Birthday of the World* (HarperCollins), by Ursula K. Le Guin; *Black Projects, White*

Nights; *The Company Dossiers* (Golden Gryphon), by Kage Baker; *Toast and Other Rusted Futures* (Cosmos), by Charles Stross; *Worlds Enough & Time* (Subterranean), by Dan Simmons; *Strange But Not a Stranger* (Golden Gryphon), by James Patrick Kelly; *The Retrieval Artist and Other Stories* (Five Star), by Kristine Kathryn Rusch; *Vinland the Dream and Other Stories* (Voyager), In *Another Country and Other Short Novels* (Five Star), by Robert Silverberg; *Stories of Your Life and Others* (Tor), by Ted Chiang; *The Lady Vanishes and Other Oddities of Nature* (Five Star), by Charles Sheffield; *Everything's Eventual* (Scribner), by Stephen King, *Aristotle and the Gun and Other Stories* (Five Star), by L. Sprague de Camp; and *Phase Space* (Voyager), by Stephen Baxter. (It's worth noting that the Le Guin, the Baker, the Stross, the Simmons, the Kelly, the Rusch, and the Chiang collections all contain original stories.)

Other good collections included *The Fantasy Writer's Assistant and Other Stories* (Golden Gryphon), by Jeffery Ford; *The Great Escape* (Golden Gryphon), by Ian Watson; *Strangers and Beggars* (Fairwood Press), by James Van Pelt; *Hunting the Snark and Other Short Novels* (Five Star), by Mike Resnick; *Rosetti Song: Four Stories* (Small Beer Press), by Alex Irvine; *Dragon's Island and Other Stories* (Five Star), by Jack Williamson; *The Mountain Cage and Other Stories* (Meisha Merlin), by Pamela Sargent; *Human Voices* (Five Star), by James Gunn; *Counting Up, Counting Down* (Del Rey), by Harry Turtledove; *The Ogre's Wife* (Obscura Press), by Richard Parks; *Babylon Sisters and Other Posthuman Stories* (Prime), by Paul Di Filippo; *God Is an Iron and Other Stories* (Five Star), by Spider Robinson; *Little Doors* (Four Walls, Eight Windows), by Paul Di Filippo; *Generation Gap and Other Stories* (Five Star), by Stanley Schmidt; *If Lions Could Speak* (Cosmos), by Paul Park; *Report to the Men's Club and Other Stories* (Small Beer Press), by Carol Emshwiller; *Death and the Librarian and Other Stories* (Five Stars), by Esther Friesner; *Waifs and Strays* (Viking), by Charles de Lint; *Through My Glasses Darkly* (KaCSFFS Press), by Frank Robinson, selected and edited by Robin Wayne Bailey; *Claremont Tales II* (Golden Gryphon), by Richard Lupoff; *Swift Thoughts* (Golden Gryphon), by George Zebrowski; and *Lord Stink and Other Stories* (Small Beer Press), Judith Berman.

The year also featured excellent retrospective collections such as *The Collected Stories of Greg Bear* (Tor), by Greg Bear; *Smoke Ghost & Other Apparitions* (Midnight House), by Fritz Leiber; *Going For Infinity* (Tor), by Poul Anderson; *Keith Laumer: The Lighter Side* (Baen), by Keith Laumer; *One More for the Road* (Morrow), by Ray Bradbury; *The Amazing Dr. Darwin* (Baen), by Charles Sheffield; *Selected Stories of Philip K. Dick* (Pantheon), by Philip K. Dick; *Nightmare at 20,000 Feet* (Tor), by Richard Matheson; *Med Ship* (Baen), by Murry Leinster; *The Collected Stories of Jack Williamson; Volume Four: Spider Island and Other Stories*, by Jack Williamson; *The Emperor of Dreams* (Gollancz), by Clark Ashton Smith; *Maps: The Uncollected John Sladek* (Big Engine), by John Sladek; and *Bright Segment: The Complete Short Stories of Theodore Sturgeon, Volume VIII* (North Atlantic), by Theodore Sturgeon.

It's good to see regular trade publishers such as Tor and HarperCollins publishing collections, especially major, important collections such as the Bear, the Anderson, the Chiang, and the Le Guin, but, as has been true for many years now, it's still the small press publishers who are publishing the bulk of the year's collections. New book line Five Star Books exploded on the scene with an unprecedented *twelve* collections, but Golden Gryphon Press held its own with six, and may have had the edge in overall quality, although both houses brought out first-rate collections this year. But as you can see from the lists above, publishers such as NESFA Press, Four Walls, Eight Windows, and North Atlantic remain important as well, as do even smaller presses such as Fairwood Press. Print-on-demand collections are becoming more frequent as well, with collections from Charles Stross, Paul Park, John Sladek, and others, coming out from POD houses such as Cosmos/ Wildside and Big Engine, and I suspect that this area will grow in importance as a source of short-story collections as the years go by. (*Toast*, by Charles Stross and *If Lions Could Speak*, by Paul Park can be ordered from Wildside Press at www.wildsidepress.com. *Maps: the Uncollected John Sladek*, by John Sladek, can be ordered from Big Engine Press at www.bigengine.com.)

"Electronic collections" continue to be available for downloading online at sites such as *Fictionwise* and *ElectricStory*, and I expect that this area will continue to grow as we progress into the century as well.

As very few small-press titles will be findable in the average bookstore, or even in the average chain superstore, means that mail-order is still your best bet, and so I'm going to list the addresses of the small-press publishers mentioned above who have little presence in most bookstores: Golden Gryphon Press, 3002 Perkins Road, Urbana, IL 61802—$24.95 for *Black Projects, White Knights: The Company Dossiers*, by Kage Baker, $25.95 for *Strange but Not a Stranger*, by James Patrick Kelly, $23.95 for *The Fantasy Writer's Assistant and Other Stories*, by Jeffrey Ford, $23.95 for *The Great Escape*, by Ian Watson, $23.95 for *Claremont Tales II*, by Richard Lupoff; $24.95 for *Swift Thoughts*, by George Zebrowski; Midnight House, 4128 Woodland Park Ave., N. Seattle, WA 98103—$40.00 for *Smoke Ghost and Other Apparitions*, by Fritz Leiber; Fairwood Press, 5203 Quincy Ave SE, Auburn, WA 98092—$17.99 for *Strangers and Beggars*, by James Van Pelt; Haffner Press, 5005 Crooks Rd., Suite 35, Royal Oak, MI 48073-1239—$35.00 plus $5.00 postage for *The Collected Stories of Jack Williamson, Volume Four: Spider Island and Other Stories*, by Jack Williamson; Small Beer Press, 360 Atlantic Avenue, PMB# 132, Brooklyn, NY 11217—$16.00 for *Report to the Men's Club and Other Stories*, by Carol Emshwiller, $6.00 including shipping for *Rosetti Song: Four Stories*, by Alex Irvine, $6.00 including shipping for *Lord Stink and Other Stories*, by Judith Berman; Obscura Press, P.O. Box 1992, Ames, IA, 50010—$18.95 for *The Ogre's Wife*, by Richard Parks; KaCSFFS Press, P.O. Box 36212, Kansas City, MO, 64171-6212—$15.00 for *Through My Glasses Darkly*, by Frank M. Robinson; Prime, P.O. Box 36503, Canton, OH 44735—$17.95 for *Babylon Sisters and Other Posthuman Stories*, by Paul Di Filippo; North Atlantic Press, P.O. Box 12327, Berkeley, CA 94701—$35.00 for *Bright Segment: The Complete Short Stories of Theodore Sturgeon*, Volume VIII.

2002 was another strong year for reprint anthologies; in fact, the reprint anthology market was actually stronger than the original anthology market, with a lot more value for your buck.

Among the most reliable bets for your money in this category, as usual, were the various "Best of the Year" anthologies. This year, science fiction was covered by three "Best of the Year" anthology series: the one you are holding in your hand (presumably, unless you're levitating it with your vast mental powers), *The Year's Best Science Fiction* series from St. Martin's, now up to its twentieth annual volume; the *Year's Best SF* series (Eos), edited by David G. Hartwell, now up to its eighth annual volume, and a new science fiction "Best of the Year" series added to the mix last year, *Science Fiction: The Best of 2002* (ibooks), edited by Robert Silverberg and Karen Haber. Once again, there were two Best of the Year anthologies covering horror in 2002: the latest edition in the British series *The Mammoth Book of Best New Horror* (Robinson, Caroll & Graff), edited by Stephen Jones, now up to Volume Thirteen, and the Ellen Datlow half of a huge volume covering both horror and fantasy, *The Year's Best Fantasy and Horror* (St. Martin's Press), edited by Ellen Datlow and Terri Windling, this year up to its Fifteenth Annual Collection. For the second year in a row, fantasy is being covered by *three* Best of the Year anthologies, by the Windling half of the Datlow/Windling anthology, by the *Year's Best Fantasy* (Eos), edited by David G. Hartwell and Katherine Cramer, now up to its third annual volume, and by a new "Best of the Year" series covering fantasy introduced last year, *Fantasy: The Best of 2002* (ibooks), edited by Robert Silverberg and Karen Haber, now in its second year. Similar in a way, and also good, is the annual Nebula Award anthology, *Nebula Awards Showcase 2002* (Harcourt Brace Jovanovich), edited by Kim Stanley Robinson.

Turning from series to stand-alone books, there were some excellent retrospective anthologies this year. The best of these is the exceptional *The Hard SF Renaissance* (Tor), edited by David G. Hartwell and Kathryn Cramer, probably the best reprint anthology of the decade so far, and one of the best to come out in the last ten years as well. I don't always agree with Hartwell and Cramer's critical opinions and rhetoric, expressed in the extensive storynotes and introductions, and I don't always agree that all of their selections are a perfect fit for the book, but when any anthology includes 960 pages filled with stories such as Greg Egan's "Wang's Carpets," Paul McAuley's "Gene Wars," Poul Anderson's "Genesis," Michael Swanwick's "Griffin's Egg," Bruce Sterling's "Taklamakan," Stephen Baxter's "On the Orion Line," and thirty-five other good-to-great stories by writers such as Nancy Kress, Joe Haldeman, Hal Clement, Kim Stanley Robinson, Brian Stableford, Alastair Reynolds, Charles Sheffield, Gregory Benford, and many others, then it becomes pointless to quibble about such things. This book is a great read, and an invaluable reference anthology if you want a picture of how SF is evolving in the Oughts, and even at $39.95, it's one of the best reading bargains you're going to find this year; buy it. *The Mammoth Book of Science Fiction* (Carroll & Graf), edited by Mike Ashley, is not quite as exceptional as the Hartwell/Cramer anthology, but is still a good solid value, featuring first-rate stories such as Connie Willis's "Firewatch," Michael Swanwick's "The Very Pulse of the Machine," Damon Knight's "Anacron," Greg Egan's "The Infinite Assassin," Geoffry A. Landis's "Approaching Perimelasma," Clifford D. Simak's "A Death in the House," and lots of others. *The Great SF Stories (1964)* (NESFA Press), edited by Robert Silverberg and Martin H. Greenberg, takes a look back at the year 1964, when classic stories such as Jack Vance's "The Kraken," Roger Zelazny's "The Graveyard Heart," Fritz Leiber's "When the Change Winds Blow," Gordon R. Dickson's "Soldier, Ask Not," Ursula K. Le Guin's "The Dowry of Angyar," and Norman Kagan's "Four Brands of Impossible" appeared, demonstrating that it was a very good year indeed. And *The Ultimate Cyberpunk* (ibooks), edited by Pat Cadigan, takes a look back into the more-recent past, at the Cyberpunk Revolution of the mid-'80s, examining some of cyberpunk's rarely mentioned roots in stories such as James Tiptree's "The Girl Who Was Plugged In," Cordwainer Smith's "The Game of Rat and Dragon," Philip K. Dick's "We Can Remember it for You Wholesale," and Alfred Bester's "Fondly Farenheit," and then passing through some canonical stories such as William Gibson's "Burning Chrome," Greg Bear's "Blood Music," William Gibson and Michael

Swanwick's "Dogfight," Bruce Sterling's "Green Days in Brunei," and Cadigan's own "Patterns," before considering more-recent progressions of the form such as Paul McAuley's "Dr. Luther's Assistant." At $16.00 for the trade paperback, this is a great reading bargain, and another valuable reference anthology.

Noted without comment: *Future Sports* (Ace), edited by Jack Dann and Gardner Dozois, and *Beyond Flesh* (Ace), edited by Jack Dann and Gardner Dozois.

The most important reprint fantasy anthology this year (indeed, one of the *only* reprint fantasy anthologies this year, other than the two Fantasy Bests and the Windling half of the Datlow/Windling) was *The American Fantasy Tradition* (Tor), edited by Brian M. Thomsen and Martin H. Greenberg, which gives an comprehensive overview of the evolution of American fantasy, from stories by Nathanial Hawthorne, Stephen Vincent Benet, Mark Twain, and Robert W. Chambers on to more recent classics such as H. P. Lovecraft's "The Shadow Over Innsmouth," Manly Wade Wellman's "O Ugly Bird!," R. A. Lafferty's "Narrow Valley," Shirley Jackson's "The Lottery," Ray Bradbury's "The Black Ferris," Harlan Ellison's "The Whimper of Whipped Dogs," Orson Scott Card's "Hatrack River," and many others.

Other than the Stephen Jones "Best" anthology and Datlow's half of the Datlow/Windling anthology, there didn't seem to be many reprint horror anthologies this year either, but then again, I wasn't looking intensively for them either. I did spot *The Literary Werewolf: An Anthology* (Syracuse University Press), edited by Charlotte F. Otten, which could also be considered to be a fantasy anthology instead, I suppose, depending on how you squint at it.

It was an unexceptional year in the SF-and-fantasy-oriented nonfiction and reference book field, although there were a slew of literary biographies and studies of the work of individual authors, including *L. Frank Baum: Creator of Oz* (St. Martin's), by Katharine M. Rogers; *The Science Fiction of Cordwainer Smith* (MacFarland), by Karen L. Hellekson; *A. E. van Vogt: Science Fantasy's Icon* (H. L. Drake), by H. L. Drake; *Mervyn Peake: My Eyes Mint Gold: A Life* (Overlook), by Malcolm Yorke; *Harlan Ellison: The Edge of Forever* (Ohio State), by Ellen Weil and Gary K. Wolfe; *Starlight Man: The Extraordinary Life of Algernon Blackwood* (Constable), by Mike Ashley; *The Age of Chaos: The Multiverse of Michael Moorcock* (The British Fantasy Society), by Jeff Gardiner; *Clive Barker: The Dark Fantastic* (HarperCollins), by Douglas E. Winter, and *Isaac Asimov: It's Been a Good Life* (Prometheaus Books), edited by J. O. Jeppsen, a nonfiction collection of excerpts from Asimov's three previous autobiographical volumes. Of books of this sort this year, the most accessible to the average reader, and probably the most enjoyable, would be Judith Merril's "autobiography," *Better to Have Loved: The Life of Judith Merril* (Between the Lines, 720 Bathurst St., Suite 404, Toronto, Ontario M5S 2R4, C$29.95), by Judith Merril and Emily Pohl-Weary. The quotation marks around "autobiography" are there because Merril didn't live to complete the full-dress autobiography she'd had planned, and there are only pieces of it here, with the book filled out with articles, letters, and other autobiographical snippets Merril produced for one reason or another over the years. There's still enough here though to give you a bit of the flavor of Merril's colorful, highly opinionated, passionate, and forceful personality, make this an entertaining read, and make you wish that she'd been able to complete a full autobiography before her untimely death.

More generalized reference books this year included *Supernatural Fiction Writers: Contemporary Fantasy and Horror, Volumes I & II* (Scribner), edited by Richard Bleiler; *The*

Battle of the Sexes in Science Fiction (Wesleyan), by Justine Larbalestier; *Once There Was a Magazine* (Beccon), by Fred Smith; *John W. Campbell's Golden Age of Science Fiction* (DMZ), by Eric Solstein; *Smokin' Rockets* (McFarland), by Patrick Lucanio and Gary Coville; and, probably the most accessible of these for the average reader, a collection of essays by horror writer Ramsey Campbell, *Ramsey Campbell, Probably: On Horror and Sundry Fantasies* (PS Publishing), by Ramsey Campbell.

The most generally enjoyable books in this category this year (or at least they *sort* of fit into this category; although they're not a perfect fit *anywhere*) are two "travel guide" books, *Roswell, Vegas, and Area 51: Travels with Courtney* (Wormhole Books, 413 High St., Fort Wayne, IN 46808, $15.00), by Connie Willis, and *A Walking Tour of the Shambles* (American Fantasy Press, P.O. Box 1059, Woodstock, IL 60098, $15.00), by Gene Wolfe and Neil Gaiman. *A Walking Tour of the Shambles* is a whimsical and good-naturedly grotesque "travel guide" to an imaginary Chicago neighborhood filled with enchanted places and magical people, and *Roswell, Vegas, and Area 51: Travels with Courtney* is a caustic, sharp-eyed, and very funny tour through real places so bizarre and unlikely that they might just as well be the products of a fantasy writer's fevered imagination (and it makes it even funnier that they are *not*).

As has been true for the last few years, the art book field was very strong this year. Among the best of the art books were *Fantasy Art Masters: The Best in Fantasy and SF Art Worldwide* (Collins), by Dick Jude; *Paper Tiger Fantasy Art Gallery* (Paper Tiger), edited by Paul Barnett; *The Art of Jeffrey Jones* (Underwood Books), edited by Cathy and Arnie Fenner; *The Science Fiction Art of Vincent Di Fate* (Paper Tiger), by Vincent Di Fate; *Perceptualistics: Art by Jael* (Paper Tiger), by Jael and John Grant; *Manchu: Science (Fiction)* (Guy Delcourt), by Manchu; *Dragonhenge* (Paper Tiger), by Bob Eggleton and John Grant; *GOAD: The Many Moods of Phil Hale* (Donald M. Grant), by Phil Hale, and the latest edition in a Best-of-the-Year–like retrospective of the year in fantastic art, *Spectrum 9: The Best in Contemporary Fantastic Art* (Underwood), by Kathy Fenner and Arnie Fenner.

There were only a few general genre-related nonfiction books of interest this year. *The Extravagant Universe: Exploding Stars, Dark Energy, and the Accelerating Cosmos* (Princeton University Press), by Robert P. Kirshner, may help you make sense of recent cosmological discoveries (primarily, that the universe is not only expanding, but *accelerating* as it expands) that have turned our entire picture of the nature of the universe upside-down. You may be prepared for some possibly even *weirder* future revelations if you check out one of the most fiercely controversial books in years, *A New Kind of Science* (Wolfram Media), by Stephen Wolfram, which puts forth the radical idea that the entire universe is controlled by the same basic set of rules that control cellular animations. To bring things back to Earth, there's the late Stephen Jay Gould's last book, *The Structure of Evolutionary Theory* (Harvard University Press), but although Gould's lucid prose and experience at explaining scientific theory in comprehensible terms help, this is primarily aimed at specialists, and there are probably few laymen who are going to be willing to devote the time and brainwork necessary to absorb and comprehend its thousand-plus pages of text. For a less demanding and more easily graspable and enjoyable book that covers at least some of the same ground, take a look at *The Life of Mammals* (BBC Books), by David Attenborough, which examines in fascinating detail (complete with gorgeous color photographs) the strange and wonderful lifeways of some of the creatures we share our planet with, lifeways that are often far more astonishing and strange than those of most SF writers's aliens. It's hard to come up with a really credible genre-related justification for listing the next book, except perhaps that many SF fans are also history buffs, but in spite of that I'm going to recommend that you go out and buy a copy of *The Cartoon History of the Universe III: From the Rise of Arabia to the Renaissance* (W.W. Norton & Company), by Larry Gonick, one of the most informative, sharp-witted, erudite, and flat-out funny books you're likely to find on the shelves anywhere, and one that's perhaps particularly germane and valuable this year, as another war in the Middle East looms on the horizon, dealing centrally as it does with the birth and spread of Islam, and some of the root causes of misunderstandings between it and the West. Perhaps a similar weak justification could be used to work-in a mention of *Sahara* (St. Martin's), by Michael Palin, which documents a grueling trip around the war-torn Saharan Africa, and shows just how closed-off and inaccessible many of the areas of our planet have become, as war, feral nationalism, and religious intolerance close border after border to the ordinary traveler, leaving us living on a planet where it may be easier to go to the Moon than to go from one country to the country next door.

It was another fairly good year for fantasy movies, but an unimpressive one for science fiction movies, in spite of the release of new entries in the two most successful media SF series of all time.

The big story of the year, easily overshadowing the new *Star Wars* movie in terms of the buzz and excitement it generated (and it is itself an interesting sign of the times that that can be said), was the second *Lord of the Rings* movie, *The Lord of the Rings: The Two Towers*. Although there are considerably more changes made here from the storyline of Tolkien's text than there had been in the first movie, and in some ways more substantive ones, the movie remained true to the *spirit* of Tolkien's great work, and all but the most fanatically obsessed fans seemed to be willing to cut Director Peter Jackson some slack. At any rate, although there were quibbles in plenty, they lacked any real force, and the over-whelming majority of Tolkien fans seemed willing to embrace the movie in spite of de-partures from the Sacred Cannon. There is a lot worth embracing: even if some of Tolkien's more subtle nuances are lost, the movie is fast-paced and tremendously exciting, shot through with moments of both terror and wonder (although not as quite as many of the later as I'd have liked; the scene of Gandalf and Bilbo relaxing and blowing magical smoke-rings in *Fellowhip of the Rings* was one of the most effective of the whole movie for me, and I'd liked to have seen a few more moments of quiet wonder here as well) and not only features good performances on every level from the live actors, but what is surely by far the best "performance" ever from a CGI-created or animated creature, as Gollum comes close to stealing the movies even from gifted professionals such as Ian McKellan and Christopher Lee. *The Two Towers* is certainly one of your very best bets this year for good value in return for your money, and if for some odd reason (a supernaturally enforced quota? An aesthetic diet?) you can only see *one* of 2002's genre movies, this is undoubtedly the one to see.

The new *Harry Potter* movie, *Harry Potter and the Chamber of Secrets*, also seems to have satisfied its picky and fanatically loyal fan base, making few (if any) changes from the text of J. K. Rowling's novel, and also did well at the box-office, although not quite as well as the first one had. It's a darker movie, a lot more scary, more suspenseful and faster-paced than last year's *Harry Potter and the Sorcerer's Stone*, but with even less of the feeling of enchantment and wonder than the previous movie had managed to generate. As I said last year, for a film about a school for magicians, especially one loaded with CGI-effects, the film lacks *magic* somehow—that's even more true of *Chamber of Secrets* than it was of *Sorcerer's Stone*, perhaps because the movie hurtles along at a headlong-enough pace not to have room for even the few evocative magical set-pieces the first film managed to work in. None of these quibbles matter anyway, though, because the movie's main audience is kids, and the *kids* seemed perfectly happy with it, and, even more important, no doubt will be perfectly willing to drag their parents (willingly or unwillingly) to the *next* film in the series.

The year's other heavy-hitter at the box-office was *Spider-Man*, which I suppose most people wouldn't consider to be a fantasy movie, but which is certainly not a science fiction movie (or at least not a *good* one), as the "science" is complete nonsense—what it really is, of course, is a *comic-book movie*, practically a genre of their own, which straddle the borderline of both fantasy and science fiction, and play by their own aesthetic rules and their own brand of internal logic (which is why nobody ever realizes that Clark Kent looks *exactly* like Superman with glasses on). By the rules of real-world logic that the rest of us operate on, *Spider-Man* makes not a lick of sense, of course, but judged on its own terms, by comic-book aesthetics and comic-book logic, it's a pretty good version of the adventures of the perhaps the most famous superhero of all, after Superman and Batman. Spider-Man was always the comic of choice of intellectual nerds who got slammed up against lockers in high-school and laughed at in gym class, and the movie does a good job of capturing this part of the character's appeal, with Tobey McGuire somehow managing to actually *look* like one of Steve Ditko's drawings of the scrawny, squamulous, lopsided-headed Peter Parker in some of the early scenes. Even after the character's transformation into a being with vast superpowers, when we're deep into classic wish-fulfillment/Revenge Fantasy territory, McGuire does a good job of somehow letting us know that, deep inside the skin-tight costume and the bulging muscles, Peter Parker realizes that he's *still* a loser no woman would touch with a stick—an intelligent job of acting. *Spider-Man* is the most successful film version of a comic-book, both critically and financially, since *The X-Men*, if not the original Tim Burton *Batman*, and not only has spawned a new franchise, with several sequels already in the works, but has sent producers scurrying to buy film rights to every comic-book they can find, no matter how obscure. So, like it or loathe it, there's lot more of this stuff yet to come.

Things were less interesting on the science fiction side of the ledger. The most commercially successful of the year's SF movies was also in some ways the most disappointing: *Star Wars: Episode II—Attack of the Clones* still managed to pack-in the audiences, but was savaged critically, and, more significantly, didn't get good word-of-mouth afterward from people who'd seen it, with even most stone *Star Wars* fans being unable to find anything more positive about it to say than "it was better than *The Phantom Menace*, anyway." In spite of good special effects, evocative CGI-generated or augmented sets, wonderful costuming and set-dressing, and even a few good fight scenes (the light-saber battle between Yoda and Christopher Lee was a knockout, but unfortunately was good enough to make most of the *rest* of the movie look even more limp by comparison), this lack of enthusiasm was not unearned—the dialog was awful, the storyline made even less sense than it had in *The Phantom Menace* (and twisted the backstory into even more contradictory knots), and the acting was so flat and wooden throughout, even from ordinarily good actors, that one finds it hard not to give some credence to the rumor that Lucas deliberately directs them to act that way. Hayden Christensen as Anakin Skywalker is an improvement over that creepy little kid from the previous movie, but his portrayal of the Darth-Vader-To-Be as a sullen, whiny, and sulky teenager, seemingly always on the verge of throwing a tantrum and holding his breath until he turns blue ("Why CAN'T I be the most powerful Jedi Knight? I WANNA be the most powerful Jedi Knight! You never let me do ANYTHING!"), lacks any sort of impact or conviction (his love scenes are enough to make a cat laugh), and drains the power from what, in the right hands, could have been an archtypically potent role. A review from *The New York Times* famously referred to *Attack of the Clones* as "a two-hour-and-12-minute action-figure commercial," and, sadly, that largely sums it up.

Meanwhile, over at media SF's *other* most famous franchise, things weren't much better; in fact, in some ways, they were worse. The new *Star Trek* movie, *Star Trek: Nemesis*, didn't do a lot better than *Attack of the Clones* with the critics (it did a little better: usually the reviews were lukewarm rather than scathing), and it did considerably worse at the box-office—not a total bomb, but certainly a disappointment, in terms of what they hoped it would draw, and what it cost to make. Again, even long-term, hardcore *Star Trek* fans seemed unexcited by it, and the movie generated little or no buzz even among media fans, let alone the general audience. Combined with the tepid performance of the current *Star Trek* television series, *Enterprise*, the mediocre performance of *Star Trek: Nemesis* is a major blow to the franchise, and radically decreases the chance of there ever being another *Star Trek* theatrical movie, as even the producers are ruefully admitting in public.

Minority Report and *Signs*, on the other hand, *did* make a lot of money, although I, finicky bastard that I am, was unimpressed with either. I liked *Minority Report* better than *Signs*—a sickly blend of science fiction and horror, freighted with an inspirational message about Faith and Redemption—but found it depressing that stories drawn from Philip K. Dick's work, as *Minority Report* is, somehow always seem to come out more about car-chases, action scenes, and big explosions than about the intellectual/philosophical/mystical territory that Dick explored in such intricate and unsettling detail. *Men in Black II* was a limp sequel that managed to be not even half as much fun as the original, in spite of pumping in more special effects, more silly aliens, and lots more gags (fewer of which were really funny). Will Smith and Tommy Lee Jones do their best at being frenetic and charm-ing, but they mostly just look tired, particularly Tommy Lee Jones, who looks throughout like he's grumpy after being woken up from a long nap on the sofa. *Solaris*, the remake of the old Russian film version of Stanislaw Lem's novel of the same name, was too lowbrow for the author, who criticized it sharply, and too highbrow for the viewing audience, who stayed away in droves. *Reign of Fire* had the last men on Earth earnestly fighting a plague of CGI dragons, rather than just instructing the special effects people to turn them off. And the latest Eddie Murphy vehicle, *The Adventures of Pluto Nash*, was such an enormous bomb that echoes of it are still washing back-and-forth between the Hollywood Hills, a sci-fi movie so bad that it makes you cry grateful tears to have something as good as *Men in Black II* to watch. And that was about it for science fiction films this year, live-action ones, anyway.

Two of the most successful films last year were animated features, *Monsters, Inc.* and (especially) *Shrek*, but this year's animated films met with varying fates at the box-office.

Disney's *Lilo and Stitch* was very successful, both commercially and critically, a slightly edgier film (although, of course, still "warm-hearted" at base) then is usual from Disney, with vigorous and highly stylized — although somewhat crude — animation, lots of slapstick Roadrunner-style action, and a generous sprinkling of genuinely witty lines and incidental bits of business; it reminded me more of *The Emperor's New Groove* from a few years back — loose-jointed and jazzy, with a lot of anachronistic, self-referential postmodern chops — than the standard non-Pixar Disney product. On the other hand, Disney's *Treasure Planet*, a film with much more traditional Disney aesthetics, storytelling choices, and animation style, was a box-office disaster, especially considering how much it cost to make. The large number of direct-to-video quick-knockoff sequels of Disney classics that the studio cranked out this year — *Peter Pan II*, *The Little Mermaid II*, and so forth — didn't seem to be setting the world on fire either. Coupled with the failure of last year's traditional Disney animated feature, *Atlantis*, and the success of films such as *Shreck*, far ruder and cruder than the Disney average, I wonder if this doesn't indicate that there's been a fundamental shift in the taste of the audience. Kids who have grown up watching cartoons on *Nickleodeon*, stuff like *SpongeBob* and *Dexter's Labrotory* and *Rug-Rats* and *The Powerpuff Girls*, may now want something edgier and hipper and zanier in their full-length animated movies than anything that Disney usually gives them. *Ice Age* also did well at the box-office and shared some of the same kind of self-referential postmodern humor as *Lilo and Stitch* or *The Emperor's New Groove*, but I found it more heavy-handed and not as imaginative or engaging as either of those films. And the Japanese *Spirited Away*, aimed at an adult rather than a children's audience, did very well with the critics, but was hard to find anywhere except in art-houses in the very biggest cities.

There were lots of horror movies, I'm sure, but I didn't go see any of them, so you're on your own there.

Coming up next year: More Sequels! (What a surprise!) 2004 or late 2003 should see the final *Lord of the Rings* movie, a new *Harry Potter* movie, two new *Matrix* movies, a new *X-Men* movie, maybe a new *Spider-Man* movie, and so forth. *Maybe* even a couple of stand-alone movies! (Or maybe not.)

In closing, it's interesting to realize that all but two or three of the list of the twenty highest-grossing movies of *all time* are science fiction or fantasy films! No wonder the studios can swallow a bomb like *The Adventures of Pluto Nash* and not give up on making genre films!

It wasn't a very good year for SF and fantasy on television either. Although *Stargate SG1* is doing better than ever in the ratings, the Sci-Fi Channel canceled *Farscape* (which hadn't significantly built its audience) in spite of anguished howls of protest from its devoted fan base and a hastily organized write-in and e-mail campaign petitioning the Sci-Fi Channel execs to keep it alive. (They canceled *Farscape*, one of the few relatively intelligent SF shows on the air, and immediately announced plans to re-run *Battlestar Galactica*, one of the dumbest and most pallidly horrid SF series of all time, and what's more, a show that *almost no one liked* the *first* time around; at least *Farscape* had people who actually wanted to *watch* it, before the plug was pulled, while I've talked to no one who feels anything other than sadness, distaste, and vague dread that *Battlestar Galactica* is coming back. Go figure. Those wacky Suits!)

The new *Star Trek* series, *Enterprise*, now in its sophomore year, is not doing *badly*, but it's doing worse in the ratings than any of the other *Star Trek* series did, and its future may also be in doubt. With the indifferent performance of the new *Star Trek* theatrical movie, *Star Trek: Nemesis*, and *Enterprise's* relatively mediocre numbers, it suddenly looks as if the whole franchise may be in danger, and we might be faced with the prospect of—horror of horrors!—a world without *Star Trek*!! If this dire possibility actually comes to pass, fans can console themselves with the *Trek* novels, I suppose, which show no sign of stopping (in fact, they're selling better than ever), with *Trek* computer games (ditto), and with the fact that re-runs of the various *Trek* shows will probably be in syndication for years—if not decades—to come. Which raises the odd possibility that the various *Star Trek* spin-off products may continue to sell vigorously long after there's no longer an original franchise *show* running anywhere on television.

Firefly, the much-hyped and much anticipated new "space western" from *Buffy, the Vampire Slayer* creator Joss Whedon, debuted this year, but even the hardest-core *Buffy* fans hated it, it failed to either carry the *Buffy* audience or find alternative audiences of its own, the ratings were disastrous, and it was cancelled by mid-season, in spite of all of Whedon's clout and all the pressure he could bring to bear on network execs to save it. Meanwhile, the end is finally in sight for *Buffy, the Vampire Slayer* itself, after two years of disappointing episodes and decreasing ratings, with the announcement that Sarah Michelle Geller, who portrays Buffy, is leaving the show at the end of the current seventh season for greener pastures in the film world. There are rumors about another possible *Buffy* spin-off series, but as I type these words, nobody knows what such a series would be, who would be in it, or, most important, if there's going to even *be* one in the first place. It's also unknown as I type this whether or not the network is going to renew the original *Buffy* spin-off series, *Angel*, for another season—too bad if they don't, *Angel* has been pretty good this year, better, in fact, than its parent series has been (*Angel's* writing seeming to improve in quality as *Buffy's* relentlessly declined). Again, it's interesting to see how quickly these TV franchise empires can fall apart—at the beginning of the year, Whedon's production company was at the top of the television food-chain, with three shows running at once; by the end of 2003, it's possible that they'll have *none*. (Although *Buffy* and *Angel* novels and other franchise products may continue on long after both shows are gone, too, in the same way that the *Star Trek* products might).

Charmed and *Sabrina, the Teenage Witch*, similar if considerably more lightweight supernatural-themed shows, still seem to be pretty successful, *Smallville* remains a genuine smash, and *The Dead Zone* seems to be doing okay, but several new shows such as *Birds of Prey* and *Haunted* came and went almost before you could notice them, and *The New Twilight Zone* is a pale imitation even of the *previous* remake of the show, let alone the original series.

South Park and *The Simpsons*, if you consider them to be genre shows, are still around, but I no longer pay much attention to them. The more genre-specific *Futurama* is gone.

Taken was a big hit in the ratings, and covered very similar ground as *Signs*, but I don't approve of shows that pander to and encourage the already too-prevalent UFO-abductee mania, and so I didn't watch it. *Dinotopia* failed to find an audience, in spite of some very nice dinosaur effects. And *The History Channel* produced a very disappointing "history" of science fiction, one that ignored most of the real history of the form to concentrate instead on the history of sci-fi movies, and which left many hours of recorded interviews with actual SF writers on the cutting-room floor. (Let's hope they do a better job with their *other* "historical" documentaries!)

Coming up next year, a new version of *Mr. Ed*, proving that the television execs are every bit as creative as the Hollywood moguls who brought us a remake of *Lost in Space* and who are in the process of bringing us a big-budget remake of *Bewitched*.

The 60th World Science Fiction Convention, ConJose, was held in San Jose, California, from August 30–September 3, 2002, and drew an estimated attendance of 5,500. The 2002 Hugo Awards, presented at ConJose, were: Best Novel, *American Gods*, by Neil Gaiman; Best Novella, "Fast Times at Fairmont High," by Vernor Vinge; Best Novelette, "Hell is the Absence of God," by Ted Chiang; Best Short Story, "The Dog Said Bow-Wow," by Michael Swanwick; Best Related Book, *The Art of Chesley Bonestell*, by Ron Miller and Frederick C. Durant III, with Melvin H. Schuetz; Best Professional Editor, Ellen Datlow; Best Professional Artist, Michael Whelan; Best Dramatic Presentation, *The Lord of the Rings: The Fellowship of the Rings*; Best Semiprozine, *Locus*, edited by Charles N. Brown; Best Fanzine, *Ansible*, edited by David Langford; Best Fan Writer, David Langford; Best Fan Artist, Teddy Harvia; plus the John W. Campbell Award for Best New Writer to Jo Walton; and the Cordwainer Smith Rediscovery Award to R. A. Lafferty.

The 2001 Nebula Awards, presented at a banquet at the Westin Crown Center in Kansas City, Missouri, on April 27, 2002, were: Best Novel, *The Quantum Rose*, by Catherine Asaro; Best Novella, "The Ultimate Earth," by Jack Williamson; Best Novelette, "Louise's Ghost," by Kelly Link; Best Short Story, "The Cure for Everything," by Severna Park; Best Script, *Crouching Tiger, Hidden Dragon*, by James Schamus, Kuo Jun Tsai, and Hui-Ling Wang; plus a special Lifetime Achievement Award to Betty Ballantine.

The World Fantasy Awards, presented at the Twenty-Eighth Annual World Fantasy Convention at the Hilton Towers in Minneapolis, Minnesota, on November 3, 2002, were: Best Novel, *The Other Wind*, by Ursula K. Le Guin; Best Novella, "The Bird Catcher," by S. P. Somtow; Best Short Fiction, "Queen for a Day," Albert E. Cowdrey; Best Collection, *Skin Folk*, by Nalo Hopkinson; Best Anthology, *The Museum of Horrors*, edited by Dennis Etchison; Best Artist, Allen Koszowski; Special Award (Professional), to Stephen Jones and Jo Fletcher (tie); Special Award (Non-Professional), to Raymond Russell and Rosalie Parker; plus the Life Achievement Award to George Scithers and Forrest J. Ackerman.

The 2002 Bram Stoker Awards, presented by the Horror Writers of America during a banquet in Chicago, Illinois, on June 8, 2002, were: Best Novel, *American Gods*, by Neil Gaiman; Best First Novel, *Deadliest of the Species*, Michael Oliveri; Best Collection, *The Man with the Barbed-Wire Fists*, by Norman Partridge; Best Long Fiction, "In These Final Days of Sales," by Steve Rasnic Tem; Best Short Story, "Reconstructing Amy," Tim Lebbon; Nonfiction, *Jobs in Hell*, edited by Brian Keene; Best Anthology, *Extremes 2: Fantasy and Horror from the Ends of the Earth*, edited by Brian A. Hopkins; Best Screenplay, *Memento*, by Christopher Nolan and Jonathan Nolan; Best Work for Young Readers, *The Willow Files 2*, by Yvonne Navarro; Poetry Collection, *Consumed, Reduced to Beautiful Gray Ashes*, by Linda Addison; Best Alternative Forms, *Dark Dreaming: Facing the Masters of Fear*, by Beth Gwinn and Stanley Winter; plus the Lifetime Achievement Award to John Farris.

The 2001 John W. Campbell Memorial Award was won by *Terraforming Earth*, by Jack Williamson and *The Chronoliths*, by Robert Charles Wilson (tie).

The 2001 Theodore Sturgeon Award for Best Short Story was won by "The Chief Designer," by Andy Duncan.

The 2001 Philip K. Dick Memorial Award went to *Ship of Fools*, by Richard Paul Russo.

The 2001 Arthur C. Clarke award was won by *Bold as Love*, by Gwyneth Jones.

The 2001 James Tiptree, Jr. Memorial Award was won by *The Kappa Child*, by Hiromi Goto.

Death struck the SF field heavily once again this year. Dead in 2002 or early 2003 were: DAMON KNIGHT, 79, author, editor, critic, anthologist, one of the most influential figures in the history of modern science fiction, editor of the long-running ORBIT anthology series, one of the founders of the Science Fiction Writers of America, author of dozens of classic SF stories such as "The Country of the Kind," "Stranger Station," "Dio," "The Earth Quarter," "Rule Golden," "Mary," and "To Serve Man," as well as many novels such as *The Man in the Tree*, *Why Do Birds?*, and *Humptey Dumptey: An Oval*, a mentor and a friend to me ever since I entered this field, and an inspiration to generations of new writers; R. A. LAFFERTY, 87, eclectic and utterly individual writer, author of some of the freshest and funniest short stories ever written, such as "Narrow Valley," "Thus We Frustrate Charlemange," "Slow Tuesday Night," "Hog-Belly Honey," "The Hole on the Corner," and many others, as well as quirky and challenging novels such as *The Reefs of Earth*, *Past Master*, *Okla Hannali*, *The Fall of Rome*, and *The Devil is Dead*, posthumous winner of the Cordwainer Smith Rediscovery Award; CHARLES SHEFFIELD, 67, scientist and Hugo-winning writer, author of *The Web Between the Worlds*, *My Brother's Keeper*, *Summertide*, *Transcendence*, *Cold as Ice*, *The Mind Pool*, and many others, as well as much first-rate short fiction in both the SF and mystery fields, a personal friend; GEORGE ALEC EFFINGER, 55, critically acclaimed and Hugo-winning author of *When Gravity Fails*, *A Fire in the Sun*, *The Exile Kiss*, *What Entropy Means to Me*, *The Nick of Time*, *The Wolves of Memory*, and others, as well as dozens of short stories such as "Two Sadnesses," "Schrodinger's Kitten," "Put Your Hands Together," "Afternoon Under Glass," "Everything but Honor," "Naked to the Invisible Eye," and many others, a personal friend for more than thirty years; JOHN MIDDLETON MURRY, Jr., 75, British writer who, as RICHARD COWPER, wrote such acclaimed SF novels as *The Road to Corlay*, *A Dream of Kinship*, *A Tapestry of Time*, and *The Twilight of Briareus*, and short fiction such as "Piper at the Gates of Dawn," "The Custodians," and "Out There Where the Big Ships Go"; ROBERT L. FORWARD, 70, scientist and writer, author of *Dragon's Egg*, *Starquake*, *The Flight of the Dragonfly*, and other novels; LLOYD BIGGLE, Jr., 79, writer and musicologist, author of *All the Colors of Darkness*, *The World Menders*, *The Angry Espers*, *The Still, Small Voice of Trumpets*, and other novels and stories; CHERRY WILDER, 71, New Zealand-born author of *The Luck of Brin's Five*, *Second Nature*, *The Summer's King*, and other novels, as well as a large amount of eloquent short fiction; LAWRENCE M. JENIFER, 69, SF author whose work appeared in *Astounding/Analog* over the course of several decades, author of the popular "Knave" series, and of novels including *Survivor*, *Knave in Hand*, *Knave in the Game*, and others; HENRY SLEZAR, 74, SF and mystery writer, and prolific writer of television screenplays; JERRY SOHL, 88, SF novelist and television scriptwriter, author of *Costigan's Needle* and *Point Ultimate*; JOHN R. PIERCE, 92, author, electrical engineer, and acoustics expert; KATHLEEN M. MASSIE-FERCH, 47, author, editor, anthologist, and scientist; MARY SCOTT, 54, British author; THOMAS E. FULLER, 54, SF writer and dramatist; DAVE VAN ARNAM, SF writer and fan; STEPHEN JAY GOULD,

60, biologist and evolutionary theorist whose controversial theory of "punctured evolution" inspired many SF writers, as well as one of the most popular "science popularizers" since Carl Sagan and Isaac Asimov, and whose long-running columns in *Natural History* magazine were collected into many books such as *The Panda's Thumb*; VIRGINIA KIDD, 81, one of the last of the Futurians, writer, anthologist, and for more than forty years one of the leading literary agents in science fiction, a longtime friend and colleague; LESLIE FIEDLER, 85, respected literary critic who occasionally slummed in the SF world, author of a biography of Olaf Stapledon and of the "historical-critical" anthology of science fiction, *In Dreams Awake*; RON WALOTSKY, 58, one of the leading SF cover artists and illustrators, whose work was recently collected in *Inner Visions: The Art of Ron Walotsky*, a friend; CHUCK JONES, 89, the mastermind behind decades of "Looney Tunes" cartoons, including the Roadrunner series, and also of the—far superior to the later live-action remake—original animated version of *How the Grinch Stole Christmas*; BILL PEET, 87, artist, children's book author, and part of the animation team that created many of the most classic Disney animated features; RICHARD HARRIS, 72, actor probably best known to the genre audience for his role as Professor Dumbledore in the two "Harry Potter" movies; ROD STEIGER, 77, actor, probably best known to genre audiences for his role in the film version of Ray Bradbury's *The Illustrated Man*; JONATHAN HARRIS, 87, actor, probably best known to the genre audience for his role as the villainous but loveable Dr. Smith in the old television series *Lost in Space*; DONALD FRANSON, 85, writer and fan, coeditor (with Howard DeVore) of the invaluable reference source, *A History of the Hugo, Nebula, and International Fantasy Award*; BETSY CURTIS, 84, writer, fan, costumer; JON GUSTAFSON, 56, writer, editor, illustrator, longtime fan; WYNNE WHITEFORD, 87, Australian SF author and fan; WILLIAM SARJEANT, 66, author, geologist, and paleontologist; BRUCE PELZ, 65, longtime fan and convention organizer, chairman of the 1972 Worldcon; HARRY NADLER, 61, longtime British fan and film enthusiast; VIRGINIA HEINLEIN, 86, widow of SF writer Robert A. Heinlein, and the model for many of the female characters in his books; JOAN HARRISON, 72, wife of SF author Harry Harrison; JOAN BENFORD, 62, wife of SF writer Gregory Benford; DR. CHARLES NORTH, 62, partner of SF writer Liz Williams; DREW CHRISTIAN STAFANSON, 39, partner of SF writer M. Shayne Bell; MARY GUNN, 81, mother of SF writer and editor Eileen Gunn; and DEE L. FROST, 81, father of SF writer Gregory Frost.

Breathmoss

IAN R. MACLEOD

British writer Ian R. MacLeod was one of the hottest new writers of the nineties, and, as we travel into the new century ahead, his work continues to grow in power and deepen in maturity. MacLeod has published a slew of strong stories in Interzone, Asimov's Science Fiction, Weird Tales, Amazing, *and* The Magazine of Fantasy and Science Fiction, *among other markets. Several of these stories made the cut for one or another of the various "Best of the Year" anthologies; in 1990, in fact, he appeared in three different Best of the Year anthologies with three different stories, certainly a rare distinction. His stories have appeared in our Eighth through Thirteenth, Fifteenth, Sixteenth, and Nineteenth Annual Collections. His first novel,* The Great Wheel, *was published to critical acclaim in 1997, followed by a major collection of his short work,* Voyages by Starlight. *In 1999, he won the World Fantasy Award with his brilliant novella "The Summer Isles," and followed it up in 2000 by winning another World Fantasy Award for his novelette "The Chop Girl." His most recent book is a major new novel,* The Light Ages. *MacLeod lives with his wife and young daughter in the West Midlands of England, and is at work on several new novels.*

Here he takes us across the galaxy and thousands of years into the far-future, for the intimate story of a child growing into a woman that is also a generation-spanning epic tale of love, loss, tragedy, and redemption, played out against the backdrop of a world as vivid, rich, layered, evocative, and luminously strange as any the genre has seen since Gene Wolfe's The Book of the New Sun.

1.

In her twelfth standard year, which on Habara was the Season of Soft Rains, Jalila moved across the mountains with her mothers from the high plains of Ta-buthal to the coast. For all of them, the journey down was one of unhurried discovery, with the kamasheens long gone and the world freshly moist, and the hayawans rusting as they rode them, the huge flat plates of their feet swishing through purplish-green undergrowth. She saw the cliffs and qasrs she'd only visited from her dreamtent, and sailed across the high ridges on ropewalks her distant ancestors had built, which had seemed frail and antique to her in her worried imaginings, but were in fact strong and subtle; huge dripping gantries heaving from the mist like wise giants, softly humming, and welcoming her and her hayawan, whom she called Robin, in cocoons of effortless embrace. Swaying over the drop beyond into grey-green nothing was almost like flying.

The strangest thing of all in this journey of discoveries was that the landscape actually seemed to rise higher as they descended and encamped and descended again; the sense of *up* increased, rather than that of down. The air on the high plains of Tabuthal was rarefied—Jalila knew that from her lessons in her dreamtent; they were so close to the stars that Pavo had had to clap a mask over her face from the moment of her birth until the breathmoss was embedded in her lungs. And it had been clear up there, it was always clear, and it was pleasantly cold. The sun shone all day hard and cold and white from the blue blackness, as did a billion stars at night, although Jalila had never thought of those things as she ran amid the crystal trees and her mothers smiled at her and occasionally warned her that, one day, all of this would have to change.

And now that day was upon her, and this landscape—as Robin, her, hayawan, rounded the path through an urrearth forest of alien-looking trees with wrinkled brown trunks and soft green leaves, and the land fell away, and she caught her first glimpse of something far and flat on the horizon—had never seemed so high.

Down on the coast, the mountains reared behind them and around a bay. There were many people here—not the vast numbers, perhaps, of Jalila's dreamtent stories of the Ten Thousand and One Worlds, but so many that she was sure, as she first walked the streets of a town where the buildings huddled in ridiculous proximity, and tried not to stare at all the faces, that she would never know all their families.

Because of its position at the edge of the mountains, the town was called Al Janb, and, to Jalila's relief, their new haramlek was some distance away from it, up along a near-unnoticeable dirt track that meandered off from the blue-black serraplated coastal road. There was much to be done there by way of repair, after the long season that her bondmother Lya had left the place deserted. The walls were fused stone, but the structure of the roof had been mostly made from the stuff of the same strange urrearth trees that grew up the mountains, and in many places it had sagged and leaked and grown back toward the chaos that seemed to want to encompass everything here. The hayawans, too, needed much attention in their makeshift stables as they adapted to this new climate, and mother Pavo was long employed constructing the necessary potions to mend the bleeding bonds of rusty metal and flesh, and then to counteract the mold that grew like slow tears across their long, solemn faces. Jalila would normally have been in anguish to think of the sufferings that this new climate was visiting on Robin, but she was too busy feeling ill herself to care. Ridiculously, seeing as there was so much more oxygen to breathe in this rich coastal air, every lungful became a conscious effort, a dreadful physical lunge. Inhaling the damp, salty, spore-laden atmosphere was like sucking soup through a straw. She grew feverish for a while, and suffered the attentions of similar molds to those that were growing over Robin, yet in even more irritating and embarrassing places. More irritating still was the fact that Ananke her birthmother and Lya her bondmother—even Pavo, who was still busily attending to the hayawans—treated her discomforts and fevers with airy disregard. They had, they all assured her vaguely, suffered similarly in their own youths. And the weather would soon change in any case. To Jalila, who had spent all her life in the cool unvarying glare of Tabuthal, where the wind only ever blew from one direction and the trees jingled like ice, that last statement might as well have been spoken in another language.

If anything, Jalila was sure that she was getting worse. The rain drummed on what there was of the roof of their haramlek, and dripped down and pooled in the makeshift awnings, which burst in bucketloads down your neck if you bumped into them, and the mist drifted in from every direction through the paneless windows, and the mountains, most of the time, seemed to consist of cloud, or to have vanished entirely. She was coughing. Strange stuff was coming out on her hands, slippery and green as the slime that tried to grow everywhere here. One morning, she awoke, sure that part of her was bursting, and stumbled from her dreamtent and out through the scaffolding that had by then surrounded the haramlek, then barefoot down the mud track and across the quiet black road and down onto the beach, for no other reason than that she needed to *escape*.

She stood gasping amid the rockpools, her hair lank and her skin feverishly itching. There was something at the back of her throat. There was something in her lungs. She was sure that it had taken root and was growing. Then she started coughing as she had never coughed before, and more of the greenstuff came splattering over her hands and down her chin. She doubled over. Huge lumps of it came showering out, strung with blood. If it hadn't been mostly green, she'd have been sure that it *was* her lungs. She'd never imagined anything so agonizing. Finally, though, in heaves and starts and false dawns, the process dwindled. She wiped her hands on her nightdress. The rocks all around her were splattered green. It was breathmoss; the stuff that had sustained her on the high plains. And *now* look at it! Jalila took a slow, cautious breath. And then another. Her throat ached. Her head was throbbing. But still, the process was suddenly almost ridiculously easy. She picked her way back across the beach, up through the mists to her haramlek. Her mothers were eating breakfast. Jalila sat down with them, wordlessly, and started to eat.

That night, Ananke came and sat with Jalila as she lay in her dreamtent in plain darkness and tried not to listen to the sounds of the rain falling on and through the creaking, dripping building. Even now, her birthmother's hands smelled and felt like the high desert as they touched her face. Rough and clean and warm, like rocks in starlight, giving off their heat. A few months before, Jalila would probably have started crying.

"You'll understand now, perhaps, why we thought it better not to tell you about the breathmoss . . . ?"

There was a question mark at the end of the sentence, but Jalila ignored it. They'd known all along! She was still angry.

"And there are other things, too, which will soon start to happen to your body. Things that are nothing to do with this place. And I shall now tell you about them all, even though you'll say you knew it before. . . ."

The smooth, rough fingers stroked her hair. As Ananke's words unraveled, telling Jalila of changings and swellings and growths she'd never thought would really apply to *her,* and which these fetid lowlands really seemed to have brought closer, Jalila thought of the sound of the wind, tinkling through the crystal trees up on Tabuthal. She thought of the dry cold wind in her face. The wet air here seemed to enclose her. She wished that she was running. She wanted to escape.

Small though Al Janb was, it was as big a town as Jalila had ever seen, and she soon came to volunteer to run all the various errands that her mothers required as they restored and repaired their haramlek. She was used to wide expanses, big horizons, the surprises of a giant landscape that crept upon you slowly, visible for miles. Yet here, every turn brought abrupt surprise and sudden change. The people had such varied faces and accents. They hung their washing across the streets, and bickered and smoked in public. Some ate with both hands. They stared at you as you went past, and didn't seem to mind if you stared back at them. There were unfamiliar sights and smells, markets that erupted on particular days to the workings of no calendar Jalila yet understood, and which sold, in glittering, shining, stinking, disgusting, fascinating arrays, the strangest and most wonderful things. There were fruits from off-planet, spices shaped like insects, and insects that you crushed for their spice. There were swarming vats of things Jalila couldn't possibly imagine any use for, and bright silks woven thin as starlit wind that she longed for with an acute physical thirst. And there were aliens, too, to be glimpsed sometimes wandering the streets of Al Janb, or looking down at you from its overhung top windows like odd pictures in old frames. Some of them carried their own atmosphere around with them in bubbling hookahs, and some rolled around in huge grey bits of the sea of their own planets, like babies in a birthsac. Some of them looked like huge versions of the spice insects, and the air around them buzzed angrily if you got too close. The only thing they had in common was that they seemed blithely unaware of Jalila as she stared and followed them, and then returned inexcusably late from whatever errand she'd supposedly been sent on. Sometimes, she forgot her errands entirely.

"You must learn to get *used* to things. . . ." Lya her bondmother said to her with genuine irritation late one afternoon, when she'd come back without the tool she'd been sent to get early that morning, or even any recollection of its name or function. "This or any other world will never be a home to you if you let *every single thing* surprise you. . . ." But Jalila didn't mind the surprises; in fact, she was coming to enjoy them, and the next time the need arose to visit Al Janb to buy a new growth-crystal for the scaffolding, she begged to be allowed to go, and her mothers finally relented, although with many a warning shake of the head.

The rain had stopped at last, or at least held back for a whole day, although everything still looked green and wet to Jalila as she walked along the coastal road toward the ragged tumble of Al Janb. She understood, at least in theory, that the rain would probably return, and then relent, and then come back again, but in a decreasing pattern, much as the heat was gradually *increasing*, although it still seemed ridiculous to her that no one could ever predict exactly how, or when, Habara's proper Season of Summers would arrive. Those boats she could see now, those fisherwomen out on their feluccas beyond the white bands of breaking waves, their whole lives were dictated by these uncertainties, and the habits of the shoals of whiteback that came and went on the oceans, and which could also only be guessed at in this same approximate way. The world down here on the coast was so *unpredictable* compared with Tabuthal! The markets, the people, the washing, the sun, the rain, the aliens. Even Hayam and Walah, Habara's moons, which Jalila was long used to watching, had to drag themselves through cloud like cannonballs through cotton as they pushed and pulled at this ocean. Yet today, as she clambered over the groynes of the long shingle beach that she took as a shortcut to the center of the town when the various tides were out, she saw a particular sight that surprised her more than any other.

There was a boat, hauled far up from the water, longer and blacker and heavier-looking than the feluccas, with a sort-of ramshackle house at the prow, and a winch at the stern that was so massive that Jalila wondered if it wouldn't tip the craft over if it ever actually entered the water. But, for all that, it wasn't the boat that first caught her eye, but the figure who was working on it. Even from a distance, as she struggled to heave some ropes, there was something different about her, and the way she was moving. Another alien? But she was plainly human. And barefoot, in ragged shorts, and bare-breasted. In fact, almost as flat-chested as Jalila still was, and probably of about her age and height. Jalila still wasn't used to introducing herself to strangers, but she decided that she could at least go over, and pretend an interest in — or an ignorance of — this odd boat.

The figure dropped another loop of rope over the gunwales with a grunt that carried on the smelly sea breeze. She was brown as tea, with her massy hair hooped back and hanging in a long tail down her back. She was broad-shouldered, and moved in that way that didn't quite seem wrong, but didn't seem entirely right either. As if, somewhere across her back, there was an extra joint. When she glanced up at the clatter of shingle as Jalila jumped the last groyne, Jalila got a proper full sight of her face, and saw that she was big-nosed, big-chinned, and that her features were oddly broad and flat. A child sculpting a person out of clay might have done better.

"Have you come to help me?"

Jalila shrugged. "I might have done."

"That's a funny accent you've got."

They were standing facing each other. She had grey eyes, which looked odd as well. Perhaps she was an off-worlder. That might explain it. Jalila had heard that there were people who had things done to themselves so they could live in different places. She supposed the breathmoss was like that, although she'd never

thought of it that way. And she couldn't quite imagine why it would be a require-
ment for living on any world that you looked this ugly.

"Everyone talks oddly here," she replied. "But then your accent's funny as well."

"I'm Kalal. And that's just my *voice*. It's not an accent." Kalal looked down at
her oily hands, perhaps thought about wiping one and offering it to shake, then
decided not to bother.

"Oh . . . ?"

"You don't get it, do you?" That gruff voice. The odd way her features twisted
when she smiled.

"What is there to get? You're just—"

"—I'm a man." Kalal picked up a coil of rope from the shingle, and nodded
to another beside it. "Well? Are you going to help me with this, or aren't you?"

The rains came again, this time starting as a thing called *drizzle*, then working up
the scale to *torrent*. The tides washed especially high. There were storms, and
white crackles of lightening, and the boom of a wind that was so unlike the
kamasheen. Jalila's mothers told her to be patient, to wait, and to remember—
please remember this time, so you don't waste the day for us all, Jalilaneen—the
things that they sent her down the serraplate road to get from Al Janb. She trudged
under an umbrella, another new and useless coastal object, which turned itself
inside out so many times that she ended up throwing it into the sea, where it
floated off quite happily, as if that was the element for which it was intended in
the first place. Almost all of the feluccas were drawn up on the far side of the
roadway, safe from the madly bashing waves, but there was no sign of that bigger
craft belonging to Kalal. Perhaps he—the antique genderative word *was* he, wasn't
it?—was out there, where the clouds rumbled like boulders. Perhaps she'd imagined their whole encounter entirely.

Arriving back home at the haramlek surprisingly quickly, and carrying for once
the things she'd been ordered to get, Jalila dried herself off and buried herself in
her dreamtent, trying to find out from it all that she could about these creatures
called *men*. Like so many things about life at this awkward, interesting, difficult
time, men were something Jalila would have insisted she definitely already knew
about a few months before up on Tabuthal. Now, she wasn't so sure. Kalal, despite
his ugliness and his funny rough-squeaky voice and his slightly odd smell, looked
little like the hairy-faced werewolf figures of her childhood stories, and seemed to
have no particular need to shout or fight, to carry her off to his rancid cave, or to
start collecting odd and pointless things that he would then try to give her. There
had once, Jalila's dreamtent told her, for obscure biological reasons she didn't
quite follow, been far more men in the universe; almost as many as there had
been women. Obviously, they had dwindled. She then checked on the word *rape*,
to make sure it really was the thing she'd imagined, shuddered, but nevertheless
investigated in full holographic detail the bits of himself that Kalal had kept hidden
beneath his shorts as she'd helped stow those ropes. She couldn't help feeling sorry
for him. It was all so pointless and ugly. Had his birth been an accident? A curse?
She began to grow sleepy. The subject was starting to bore her. The last thing she

remembered learning was that Kalal wasn't a proper man at all, but a *boy* — a half-formed thing; the equivalent to girl — another old urrearth word. Then sleep drifted over her, and she was back with the starlight and the crystal trees of Tabuthal, and wondering as she danced with her own reflection which of them was changing.

By next morning, the sun was shining as if she would never stop. As Jalila stepped out onto the newly formed patio, she gave the blazing light the same sort of an appraising *what-are-you-up-to-now* glare that her mothers gave her when she returned from Al Janb. The sun had done this trick before of seeming permanent, then vanishing by lunchtime into sodden murk, but today her brilliance continued. As it did the day after. And the day after that. Half a month later, even Jalila was convinced that the Season of Summers on Habara had finally arrived.

The flowers went mad, as did the insects. There were colors everywhere, pulsing before your eyes, swarming down the cliffs toward the sea, which lay flat and placid and salt-rimed, like a huge animal, basking. It remained mostly cool in Jalila's dreamtent, and the haramlek by now was a place of tall malqaf windtowers and flashing fans and well-like depths, but stepping outside beyond the striped shade of the mashrabiyas at midday felt like being hit repeatedly across the head with a hot iron pan. The horizons had drawn back; the mountains, after a few last rumbles of thunder and mist, as if they were clearing their throats, had finally announced themselves to the coastline in all their majesty, and climbed up and up in huge stretches of forest into stone limbs that rose and tangled until your eyes grew tired of rising. Above them, finally, was the sky, which was always blue in this season; the blue color of flame. Even at midnight, you caught the flash and swirl of flame.

Jalila learned to follow the advice of her mothers, and to change her daily habits to suit the imperious demands of this incredible, fussy, and demanding weather. If you woke early, and then drank lots of water, and bowed twice in the direction of Al'Toman while she was still a pinprick in the west, you could catch the day by surprise, when dew lay on the stones and pillars, and the air felt soft and silky as the arms of the ghostly women who sometimes visited Jalila's nights. Then there was breakfast, and the time of work, and the time of study, and Ananke and Pavo would quiz Jalila to ensure that she was following the prescribed Orders of Knowledge. By midday, though, the shadows had drawn back and every trace of moisture had evaporated, and your head swarmed with flies. You sought your own company, and didn't even want *that*, and wished, as you tossed and sweated in your dreamtent, for frost and darkness. Once or twice, just to prove to herself that it could be done, Jalila had tried walking to Al Janb at this time, although of course everything was shut and the whole place wobbled and stank in the heat like rancid jelly. She returned to the haramlek gritty and sweaty, almost crawling, and with a pounding ache in her head.

By evening, when the proper order of the world had righted itself, and Al'Toman would have hung in the east if the mountains hadn't swallowed her, and the heat, which never vanished, had assumed a smoother, more manageable quality, Jalila's mothers were once again hungry for company, and for food and for argument. These evenings, perhaps, were the best of all the times that Jalila could remember of her early life on the coast of Habara's single great ocean, at that stage in her development from child to adult when the only thing of permanence seemed to be the existence of endless, fascinating change. *How* they argued! Lya, her bondmother, and the oldest of her parents, who wore her grey hair loose as cobwebs with the pride of her age, and waved her arms as she talked and drank, wreathed in endless curls of smoke. Little Pavo, her face smooth as a carved nutmeg, with her small, precise hands, and who knew so much but rarely said anything with insistence. And Jalila's birthmother Ananke, for whom, of her three mothers, Jalila had always felt the deepest, simplest love, who would always touch you before she said anything, and then fix you with her sad and lovely eyes, as if touching and seeing were far more important than any words. Jalila was older now. She joined in with the arguments—of course, she had *always* joined in, but she cringed to think of the stumbling inanities to which her mothers had previously had to listen, while, now, at last, she had real, proper things to say about life, whole new philosophies that no one else on the Ten Thousand Worlds and One had ever thought of. . . . Most of the time, her mothers listened. Sometimes, they even acted as if they were persuaded by their daughter's wisdom.

Frequently, there were visitors to these evening gatherings. Up on Tabuthal, visitors had been rare animals, to be fussed over and cherished and only reluctantly released for their onward journey across the black dazzling plains. Down here, where people were nearly as common as stones on the beach, a more relaxed attitude reigned. Sometimes, there were formal invitations that Lya would issue to someone who was *this* or *that* in the town, or more often Pavo would come back with a person she had happened to meet as she poked around for lifeforms on the beach, or Ananke would softly suggest a *neighbor* (another new word and concept to Jalila) might like to *pop in* (ditto). But Al Janb was still a small town, and the dignitaries generally weren't that dignified, and Pavo's beach wanderers were often shy and slight as she was, while *neighbor* was frequently a synonym for *boring*. Still, Jalila came to enjoy most kinds of company, if only so that she could hold forth yet more devastatingly on whatever universal theory of life she was currently developing.

The flutter of lanterns and hands. The slow breath of the sea. Jalila ate stuffed breads and fuul and picked at the mountains of fruit and sucked lemons and sweet blue rutta and waved her fingers. The heavy night insects, glowing with the pollen they had collected, came bumbling toward the lanterns or would alight in their hands. Sometimes, afterward, they walked the shore, and Pavo would show them strange creatures with blurring mouths like wheels, or point to the vast, distant beds of the tideflowers that rose at night to the changes of the tide; silver, crimson, or glowing, their fronds waving through the dark like the beckoning palm trees of islands from storybook seas.

One guestless night, when they were walking north away from the lights of the town, and Pavo was filling a silver bag for an aquarium she was ostensibly making for Jalila, but in reality for herself, the horizon suddenly cracked and rumbled.

Instinctively by now, Jalila glanced overhead, expecting clouds to be covering the coastal haze of stars. But the air was still and clear; the hot dark edge of that blue flame. Across the sea, the rumble and crackle was continuing, accompanied by a glowing pillar of smoke that slowly tottered over the horizon. The night pulsed and flickered. There was a breath of impossibly hot salt air. The pillar, a wobbly finger with a flame-tipped nail, continued climbing skyward. A few geelies rose and fell, clacking and cawing, on the far rocks; black shapes in the darkness.

"It's the start of the Season of Rockets," Lya said. "I wonder who'll be coming . . . ?"

2.

By now, Jalila had acquired many of her own acquaintances and friends. Young people were relatively scarce amid the long-lived human Habarans, and those who dwelt around Al Janb were continually drawn together and then repulsed from each other like spinning magnets. The elderly mahwagis, who had outlived the need for wives and the company of a haramlek and lived alone, were often more fun, and more reliably eccentric. It was a relief to visit their houses and escape the pettinesses and sexual jealousies that were starting to infect the other girls near to Jalila's own age. She regarded Kalal similarly—as an escape—and she relished helping him with his boat, and enjoyed their journeys out across the bay, where the wind finally tipped almost cool over the edge of the mountains and lapped the sweat from their faces.

Kalal took Jalila out to see the rocketport one still, hot afternoon. It lay just over the horizon, and was the longest journey they had undertaken. The sails filled with the wind, and the ocean grew almost black, yet somehow transparent, as they hurried over it. Looking down, Jalila believed that she could glimpse the white sliding shapes of the great sea-leviathans who had once dwelt, if local legend was to be believed, in the ruined rock palaces of the qasrs, which she had passed on her journey down from Tabuthal. Growing tired of sunlight, they had swarmed back to the sea that had birthed them, throwing away their jewels and riches, which bubbled below the surface, then rose again under Habara's twin moons to become the beds of tideflowers. She had gotten that part of the story from Kalal. Unlike most people who lived on the coast, Kalal was interested in Jalila's life in the starry darkness of Tabuthal, and repaid her with his own tales of the ocean.

The boat ploughed on, rising, frothing. Blissfully, it was almost cold. Just how far out at sea was this rocketport? Jalila had watched some of the arrivals and departures from the quays at Al Janb, but those journeys took place in sleek sail-less craft with silver doors that looked, as they turned out from the harbor and rose out on stilts from the water, as if they could travel half-way up to the stars on their own. Kalal was squatting at the prow, beyond that ramshackle hut that Jalila now knew contained the pheromones and grapplers that were needed to ensnare the tideflowers that this craft had been built to harvest. The boat bore no name on the prow, yet Kalal had many names for it, which he would occasionally mention without explaining. If there was one thing that was different about Kalal.

Jalila had decided, it was this absence of proper talk or explanation. It put many people off, but she had found that most things became apparent if you just hung around him and didn't ask direct questions.

People generally pitied Kalal, or stared at him as Jalila still stared at the aliens, or asked him questions that he wouldn't answer with anything other than a shrug. Now that she knew him better, Jalila was starting to understand just how much he hated such treatment—almost as much, in fact, as he hated being thought of as ordinary. I am a *man*, you know, he'd still remark sometimes—whenever he felt that Jalila was forgetting. Jalila had never yet risked pointing out that he was in fact a *boy*. Kalal could be prickly and sensitive if you treated him as if things didn't matter. It was hard to tell, really, just how much of how he acted was due to his odd sexual identity, and how much was his personality.

To add to his freakishness, Kalal lived alone with another male—in fact, the only other male in Al Janb—at the far end of the shore cottages, in a birthing relationship that made Kalal term him his *father*. His name was Ibra, and he looked much more like the males of Jalila's dreamtent stories. He was taller than almost anyone, and wore a black beard and long colorful robes or strode about bare-chested, and always talked in a thunderously deep voice, as if he were addressing a crowd through a megaphone. Ibra laughed a lot and flashed his teeth through that hairy mask, and clapped people on the back when he asked them how they were, and then stood away and seemed to lose interest before they had answered. He whistled and sang loudly and waved to passers-by while he worked at repairing the feluccas for his living. Ibra had come to this planet when Kalal was a baby, under circumstances that remained perennially vague. He treated Jalila with the same loud and grinning friendship with which he treated everyone, and which seemed like a wall. He was at least as alien as the tube-like creatures who had arrived from the stars with this new Season of Rockets, which had had one of the larger buildings in Al Janb encased in transparent plastics and flooded in a freezing grey goo so they could live in it. Ibra had come around to their haramlek once, on the strength of one of Ananke's *pop in* evening invitations. Jalila, who was then nurturing the idea that no intelligence could exist without the desire to acknowledge some higher deity, found her propositions and examples drowned out in a flurry of counter-questions and assertions and odd bits of information that she half-suspected that Ibra, as he drank surprising amounts of virtually undiluted zibib and freckled aniseed spit at her, was making up on the spot. Afterward, as they walked the shore, he drew her apart and laid a heavy hand on her shoulder and confided in his rambling growl how much he'd enjoyed *fencing* with her. Jalila knew what fencing was, but she didn't see what it had to do with talking. She wasn't even sure if she liked Ibra. She certainly didn't pretend to understand him.

The sails thrummed and crackled as they headed toward the spaceport. Kalal was absorbed, staring ahead from the prow, the water splashing reflections across his lithe brown body. Jalila had almost grown used to the way he looked. After all, they were both slightly freakish: she, because she came from the mountains; he, because of his sex. And they both liked their own company, and could accept each other into it without distraction during these long periods of silence. One never asked the other what they were thinking. Neither really cared, and they cherished that privacy.

"Look—" Kalal scuttled to the rudder. Jalila hauled back the jib. In wind-crackling silence, they and their nameless and many-named boat tacked toward the spaceport.

The spaceport was almost like the mountains: when you were close up, it was too big be seen properly. Yet, for all its size, the place was a disappointment; empty and messy, like a huge version of the docks of Al Janb, similarly reeking of oil and refuse, and essentially serving a similar function. The spaceships them-selves—if indeed the vast cistern-like objects they saw forever in the distance as they furled the sails and rowed along the maze of oily canals were spaceships—were only a small part of this huge floating complex of islands. Much more of it was taken up by looming berths for the tugs and tankers that placidly chugged from icy pole to equator across the watery expanses of Habara, taking or delivering the supplies that the settlements deemed necessary for civilized life, or collecting the returning fallen bulk cargoes. The tankers were rust-streaked beasts, so huge that they hardly seemed to grow as you approached them, humming and eerily deserted, yet devoid of any apparent intelligence of their own. They didn't glimpse a single alien at the spaceport. They didn't even see a human being.

The journey there, Jalila decided as they finally got the sails up again, had been far more enjoyable and exciting than actually arriving. Heading back toward the sun-pink coastal mountains, which almost felt like home to her now, she was filled with an odd longing that only diminished when she began to make out the lighted dusky buildings of Al Janb. Was this homesickness, she wondered? Or something else?

This was the time of Habara's long summer. This was the Season of Rockets. When she mentioned their trip, Jalila was severely warned by Pavo of the conse-quences of approaching the spaceport during periods of possible launch, but it went no further than that. Each night now, and deep into the morning, the rockets rumbled at the horizon and climbed upward on those grumpy pillars, bringing to the shore a faint whiff of sulphur and roses, adding to the thunderous heat. And outside at night, if you looked up, you could sometimes see the blazing comet-trails of the returning capsules, which would crash somewhere in the distant seas.

The beds of tideflowers were growing bigger as well. If you climbed up the sides of the mountains before the morning heat flattened everything, you could look down on those huge, brilliant, and ever-changing carpets, where every pattern and swirl seemed gorgeous and unique. At night, in her dreamtent, Jalila some-times imagined that she was floating up on them, just as in the oldest of the old stories. She was sailing over a different landscape on a magic carpet, with the cool night desert rising and falling beneath her like a soft sea. She saw distant palaces, and clusters of palms around small and tranquil lakes that flashed the silver of a single moon. And then yet more of this infinite sahara, airy and frosty, flowed through curves and undulations, and grew vast and pinkish in her dreams. Those curves, as she flew over them and began to touch herself, resolved into thighs and breasts. The winds stirring the peaks of the dunes resolved in shuddering breaths. This was the time of Habara's long summer. This was the Season of Rockets.

Robin, Jalila's hayawan, had by now, under Pavo's attentions, fully recovered from the change to her environment. The rust had gone from her flanks, the melds with her thinly grey-furred flesh were bloodless and neat. She looked thinner and lighter. She even smelled different. Like the other hayawans, Robin was frisky and bright and brown-eyed now, and didn't seem to mind the heat, or even Jalila's forgetful neglect of her. Down on the coast, hayawans were regarded as expensive, uncomfortable, and unreliable, and Jalila and her mothers took a pride in riding across the beach into Al Janb on their huge, flat-footed, and loping mounts, enjoying the stares and the whispers, and the whispering space that opened around them as they hobbled the hayawans in a square. Kalal, typically, was one of the few coastal people who expressed an interest in trying to ride one of them, and Jalila was glad to teach him, showing him the clicks and calls and nudges, the way you took the undulations of the creature's back as you might the ups and downs of the sea, and when not to walk around their front and rear ends. After her experiences on his boat, the initial rope burns, the cracks on the head and the heaving sickness, she enjoyed the reversal of situations.

There was a Tabuthal saying about falling off a hayawan ninety-nine times before you learnt to ride, which Kalal disproved by falling off far into triple figures. Jalila chose Lya's mount Abu for him to ride, because she was the biggest, the most intelligent, and generally the most placid of the beasts unless she felt that something was threatening her, and because Lya, more conscious of looks and protocol down here than the other mothers, rarely rode her. Domestic animals, Jalila had noticed, often took oddly to Kalal when they first saw and scented him, but he had learned the ways of getting around them, and developed a bond and understanding with Abu even while she was still trying to bite his legs. Jalila had made a good choice of riding partners. Both of them, hayawan and human, while proud and aloof, were essentially playful, and never shirked a challenge. While all hayawans had been female throughout all recorded history, Jalila wondered if there wasn't a little of the male still embedded in Abu's imperious downward glance.

Now that summer was here, and the afternoons had vanished into the sun's blank blaze, the best time to go riding was the early morning. North, beyond Al Janb, there were shores and there were saltbeds and there were meadows, there were fences to be leapt, and barking feral dogs as male as Kalal to be taunted, but south, there were rocks and forests, there were tracks that led nowhere, and there were headlands and cliffs that you saw once and could never find again. South, mostly, was the way that they rode.

"What happens if we keep riding?"

They were taking their breath on a flatrock shore where a stream, from which they had all drunk, shone in pools on its way to the ocean. The hayawans had squatted down now in the shadows of the cliff and were nodding sleepily, one nictitating membrane after another slipping over their eyes. As soon as they had gotten here and dismounted, Kalal had walked straight down, arms outstretched, into the tideflower-bobbing ocean. Jalila had followed, whooping, feeling tendrils and petals bumping into her. It was like walking through floral soup. Kalal had sunk to his shoulders and started swimming, which was something Jalila still couldn't quite manage. He splashed around her, taunting, sending up sheets of colored light. They'd stripped from their clothes as they clambered out, and laid them on the hot rocks, where they now steamed like fresh bread.

"This whole continent's like a huge island," Jalila said in delayed answer to Kalal's question. "We'd come back to where we started."

Kalal shook his head. "Oh, you can never do that. . . ."

"Where would we be, then?"

"Somewhere slightly different. The tideflowers would have changed, and we wouldn't be us, either." Kalal wet his finger, and wrote something in naskhi script on the hot, flat stone between them. Jalila thought she recognized the words of a poet, but the beginning had dissolved into the hot air before she could make proper sense of it. Funny, but at home with her mothers, and with their guests, and even with many of the people of her own age, such statements as they had just made would have been the beginning of a long debate. With Kalal, they just seemed to hang there. Kalal, he moved, he passed on. Nothing quite seemed to stick. There was something, somewhere, Jalila thought, lost and empty about him.

The way he was sitting, she could see most of his genitals, which looked quite jaunty in their little nest of hair, like a small animal. She'd almost gotten as used to the sight of them as she had to the other peculiarities of Kalal's features. Scratching her nose, picking off some of the petals that still clung to her skin like wet confetti, she felt no particular curiosity. Much more than Kalal's funny body, Jalila was conscious of her own—especially her growing breasts, which were still somewhat uneven. Would they ever come out right, she wondered, or would she forever be some unlovely oddity, just as Kalal seemingly was? Better not to think of such things. Better to just enjoy the feel of the sun baking her shoulders, loosening the curls of her hair.

"Should we turn back?" Kalal asked eventually. "It's getting hotter. . . ."

"Why bother with that—if we carry on, we'll get back to where we started."

Kalal stood up. "Do you want to bet?"

So they rode on, more slowly, uphill through the uncharted forest, where the urrearth trees tangled with the blue fronds of Habara fungus, and the birds were still, and the crackle of the dry undergrowth was the only sound in the air. Eventually, ducking boughs, then walking, dreamily lost and almost ready to turn back, they came to a path, and remounted. The trees fell away, and they found that they were on a clifftop, far, far higher above the winking sea than they could possibly have imagined. Midday heat clapped around them. Ahead, where the cliff stuck out over the ocean like a cupped hand, shimmering and yet solid, was one of the ruined castles or geological features that the sea-leviathans had supposedly deserted before the arrival of people on this planet—a qasr. They rode slowly toward it, their hayawans' feet thocking in the dust. It looked like a fairy place. Part natural, but roofed and buttressed, with grey-black gables and huge and intricate windows, that flashed with the colors of the sea. Kalal gestured for silence, dismounted from Abu, led his mount back into the shadowed arms of the forest, and flicked the switch in her back that hobbled her.

"You *know* where this is?"

Kalal beckoned.

Jalila, who knew him better than to ask questions, followed.

Close to, much of the qasr seemed to be made of a quartz-speckled version of the same fused stone from which Jalila's haramlek was constructed. But some other bits of it appeared to be natural effusions of the rock. There was a big arched door of sun-bleached and iron-studded oak, reached by a path across the narrowing cliff, but Kalal steered Jalila to the side, and then up and around a bare angle of hot stone that seemed ready at any moment to tilt them down into the distant sea. But the way never quite gave out; there was always another handhold. From the confident manner in which he moved up this near-cliff face, then scrambled across the blistering black tiles of the rooftop beyond, and dropped down into the sudden cool of a narrow passageway, Jalila guessed that Kalal had been to this qasr before. At first, there was little sense of trespass. The place seemed old and empty—a little-visited monument. The ceilings were stained. The corridors were swept with the litter of winter leaves. Here and there along the walls, there were friezes, and long strings of a script which made as little sense to Jalila, in their age and dimness, as that which Kalal had written on the hot rocks.

Then Kalal gestured for Jalila to stop, and she clustered beside him, and they looked down through the intricate stone lattice of a mashrabiya into sunlight. It was plain from the balcony drop beneath them that they were still high up in this qasr. Below, in the central courtyard, somehow shocking after this emptiness, a fountain played in a garden, and water lapped from its lip and ran in steel fingers toward cloistered shadows.

"Someone *lives* here?"

Kalal mouthed the word *tariqua*. Somehow, Jalila instantly understood. It all made sense, in this Season of Rockets, even the dim scenes and hieroglyphs carved in the honeyed stones of this fairy castle. Tariquas were merely human, after all, and the spaceport was nearby; they had to live somewhere. Jalila glanced down at her scuffed sandals, suddenly conscious that she hadn't taken them off—but by then it was too late, and below them and through the mashrabiya a figure had detached herself from the shadows. The tariqua was tall and thin, and black and bent as a burnt-out matchstick. She walked with a cane. Jalila didn't know what she'd expected—she'd grown older since her first encounter with Kalal, and no longer imagined that she knew about things just because she'd learnt of them in her dreamtent. But still, this tariqua seemed a long way from someone who piloted the impossible distances between the stars, as she moved and clicked slowly around that courtyard fountain, and far older and frailer than anyone Jalila had ever seen. She tended a bush of blue flowers, she touched the fountain's bubbling stone lip. Her head was ebony bald. Her fingers were charcoal. Her eyes were as white and seemingly blind as the flecks of quartz in the fused stone of this building. Once, though, she seemed to look up toward them. Jalila went cold. Surely it wasn't possible that she could *see* them?—and in any event, there was something about the motion of looking up which seemed habitual. As if, like touching the lip of the fountain, and tending that bush, the tariqua always looked up at this moment of the day at that particular point in the stone walls that rose above her.

Jalila followed Kalal further along the corridors, and down stairways and across drops of beautifully clear glass, that hung on nothing far above the prismatic sea. Another glimpse of the tariqua, who was still slowly moving, her neck stretching like an old tortoise as she bent to sniff a flower. In this part of the qasr, there were more definite signs of habitation. Scattered cards and books. A moth-eaten tapestry that billowed from a windowless arch overlooking the sea. Empty coat hangers piled like the bones of insects. An active but clearly little-used chemical toilet. Now that the initial sense of surprise had gone, there was something funny about this mixture of the extraordinary and the everyday. Here, there was a kitchen, and a half-chewed lump of aish on a plate smeared with seeds. To imagine, that you could both travel between the stars *and* eat bread and tomatoes! Both Kalal and Jalila were red-faced and chuffing now from suppressed hilarity. Down now at the level of the cloisters, hunched in the shade, they studied the tariqua's stooping back. She really did look like a scrawny tortoise, yanked out of its shell, moving between these bushes. Any moment now, you expected her to start chomping on the leaves. She moved more by touch than by sight. Amid the intricate colors of this courtyard, and the flashing glass windchimes that tinkled in the far archways, as she fumbled sightlessly but occasionally glanced at things with those odd, white eyes, it seemed yet more likely that she was blind, or at least terribly near-sighted. Slowly, Jalila's hilarity receded, and she began to feel sorry for this old creature who had been aged and withered and wrecked by the strange process of travel between the stars. *The Pain of Distance*—now, where had that phrase come from?

Kalal was still puffing his cheeks. His eyes were watering as he ground his fist against his mouth and silently thumped the nearest pillar in agonized hilarity. Then he let out a nasal grunt, which Jalila was sure that the tariqua must have heard. But her stance didn't alter. It wasn't so much as if she hadn't noticed them, but that she already *knew* that someone was there. There was a sadness and resignation about her movements, the tap of her cane. . . . But Kalal had recovered his equilibrium, and Jalila watched his fingers snake out and enclose a flake of broken paving. Another moment, and it spun out into the sunlit courtyard in an arc so perfect that there was never any doubt that it was going to strike the tariqua smack between her bird-like shoulders. Which it did—but by then they were running, and the tariqua was straightening herself up with that same slow resignation. Just before they bundled themselves up the stairway, Jalila glanced back, and felt a hot bar of light from one of the qasr's high upper windows stream across her face. The tariqua was looking straight toward her with those blind white eyes. Then Kalal grabbed her hand. Once again, she was running.

Jalila was cross with herself, and cross with Kalal. It wasn't *like* her, a voice like a mingled chorus of her three mothers would say, to taunt some poor old mahwagi, even if that mahwagi happened also to be an aged tariqua. But Jalila was young, and life was busy. The voice soon faded. In any case, there was the coming moulid to prepare for.

The arrangement of festivals, locally, and on Habara as a whole, was always difficult. Habara's astronomical year was so long that it made no sense to fix the traditional cycle of moulids by it, but at the same time, no one felt comfortable celebrating the same saint or eid in conflicting seasons. Fasting, after all, properly belonged to winter, and no one could quite face their obligations toward the Almighty with quite the same sense of surrender and equanimity in the middle of spring. People's memories faded, as well, as to how one *did* a particular saint in autumn, or revered a certain enlightenment in blasting heat that you had previously celebrated by throwing snowballs. Added to this were the logistical problems of catering for the needs of a small and scattered population across a large planet. There were travelling players, fairs, wandering sufis and priests, but they plainly couldn't be everywhere at once. The end result was that each moulid was fixed locally on Habara, according to a shifting timetable, and after much discussion and many meetings, and rarely happened twice at exactly the same time, or else occurred simultaneously in different places. Lya threw herself into these discussions with the enthusiasm of one who had long been missing such complexities in the lonelier life up on Tabuthal. For the Moulid of First Habitation—which commemorated the time when the Blessed Joanna had arrived on Habara at a site that several different towns claimed, and cast the first urrearth seeds, and lived for five long Habaran years on nothing but tideflowers and starlight, and rode the sea-leviathans across the oceans as if they were hayawans as she waited for her lover Pia—Lya was the leading light in the local organizations at Al Janb, and the rest of her haramlek were expected to follow suit.

The whole of Al Janb was to be transformed for a day and a night. Jalila helped with the hammering and weaving, and tuning Pavo's crystals and plants, which would supposedly transform the serraplate road between their haramlek and the town into a glittering tunnel. More in the forefront of Jalila's mind were those colored silks that came and went at a particular stall in the markets, and which she was sure would look perfect on her. Between the planning and the worries about this or that turning into a disaster, she worked carefully on each of her three mothers in turn; a nudge here, a suggestion there. Turning their thoughts toward accepting this extravagance was a delicate matter, like training a new hayawan to bear the saddle. Of course, there were wild resistances and buckings, but you were patient, you were stronger. You knew what you wanted. You kept to your subject. You returned and returned and returned to it.

On the day when Ananke finally relented, a worrying wind had struck up, pushing at the soft, half-formed growths that now straggled through the normal weeds along the road into Al Janb like silvered mucus. Pavo was fretting about her creations. Lya's life was one long meeting. Even Ananke was anxious as they walked into Al Janb, where faulty fresh projections flickered across the buildings and squares like an incipient headache as the sky greyed. Jalila, urging her birth-mother on as she paused frustratingly, was sure that the market wouldn't be there, or that if it was, the stall that sold the windsilks was sure to have sold out—or, even then, that the particular ones she'd set her mind on would have gone. . . .

But it was all there. In fact, a whole new supply of windsilks, even more marvelous and colorful, had been imported for this moulid. They blew and lifted like colored smoke. Jalila caught and admired them.

"I think this might be you. . . ."

Jalila turned at the voice. It was Nayra, a girl about a standard year and a half older than her, whose mothers were amongst the richest and most powerful in Al Janb. Nayra herself was both beautiful and intelligent; witty, and sometimes devastatingly cruel. She was generally at the center of things, surrounded by a bickering and admiring crowd of seemingly lesser mortals, which sometimes included Jalila. But today she was alone.

"You see, Jalila. That crimson. With your hair, your eyes . . ."

She held the windsilk across Jalila's face like a yashmak. It danced around her eyes. It blurred over her shoulders. Jalila would have thought the color too bold. But Nayra's gaze, which flickered without ever quite leaving Jalila's, her smoothing hands, told Jalila that it was right for her far better than any mirror could have. And then there was blue — that flame color of the summer night. There were silver clasps, too, to hold these windsilks, which Jalila had never noticed on sale before. The stallkeeper, sensing a desire to purchase that went beyond normal bargaining, drew out more surprises from a chest. *Feel! They can only be made in one place, on one planet, in one season. Look! The grubs, they only hatch when they hear the song of a particular bird, which sings only once in its life before it gives up its spirit to the Almighty.* . . . And so on. Ananke, seeing that Jalila had found a more interested and willing helper, palmed her far more cash than she'd promised, and left her with a smile and an oddly sad backward glance.

Jalila spent the rest of that grey and windy afternoon with Nayra, choosing clothes and ornaments for the moulid. Bangles for their wrists and ankles. Perhaps — no? yes? — even a small tiara. Bolts of cloth the color of today's sky bound across her hips to offset the windsilk's beauty. A jewel still filled with the sapphire light of a distant sun to twinkle at her belly. Nayra, with her dark blonde hair, her light brown eyes, her fine strong hands, which were pale pink beneath the fingernails like the inside of a shell, she hardly needed anything to augment her obvious beauty. But Jalila knew from her endless studies of herself in her dreamtent mirror that *she* needed to be more careful; the wrong angle, the wrong light, an incipient spot, and whatever effect she was striving for could be so easily ruined. Yet she'd never really cared as much about such things as she did on that windy afternoon, moving through stalls and shops amid the scent of patchouli. To be so much the focus of her own and someone else's attention! Nayra's hands, smoothing across her back and shoulders, lifting her hair, cool sweat at her shoulders, the cool slide and rattle of her bangles as she raised her arms. . . .

"We could be creatures from a story, Jalila. Let's imagine I'm Scheherazade." A toss of that lovely hair. Liquid gold. Nayra's seashell fingers, stirring. "You can be her sister, Dinarzade. . . ."

Jalila nodded enthusiastically, although Dinarzade had been an unspectacular creature as far as she remembered the tale; there only so that she might waken Scheherazade in the Sultana's chamber before the first cock crow of morning. But her limbs, her throat, felt strange and soft and heavy. She reminded herself, as she dressed and undressed, of the doll Tabatha she'd once so treasured up on Tabuthal, and had found again recently, and thought for some odd reason of burying. . . .

The lifting, the pulling, Nayra's appraising hands and glance and eyes. This unresisting heaviness. Jalila returned home to her haramlek dazed and drained and happy, and severely out of credit.

That night, there was another visitor for dinner. She must have taken some sort of carriage to get there, but she came toward their veranda as if she'd walked the entire distance. Jalila, whose head was filled with many things, was putting out the bowls when she heard the murmur of footsteps. The sound was so slow that eventually she noticed it consciously, looked up, and saw a thin, dark figure coming up the sandy path between Pavo's swaying and newly sculpted bushes. One arm leaned on a cane, and the other strained seekingly forward. In shock, Jalila dropped the bowl she was holding. It seemed to roll around and around on the table forever, slipping playfully out of reach of her fingers before spinning off the edge and shattering into several thousand white pieces.

"Oh dear," the tariqua said, finally climbing the steps beside the windy trellis, her cane tap-tapping. "Perhaps you'd better go and tell one of your mothers, Jalila."

Jalila felt breathless. All through that evening, the tariqua's trachoman white eyes, the scarred and tarry driftwood of her face, seemed to be studying her. Even apart from that odd business of her knowing her name, which she supposed could be explained, Jalila was more and more certain that the tariqua knew that it was she and Kalal who had spied on her and thrown stones at her on that hot day in the qasr. As if that mattered. But somehow, it *did*, more than it should have done. Amid all this confused thinking, and the silky memories of her afternoon with Nayra, Jalila scarcely noticed the conversation. The weather remained gusty, spinning the lanterns, playing shapes with the shadows, making the tapestries breathe. The tariqua's voice was as thin as her frame. It carried on the spinning air like the croak of an insect.

"Perhaps we could walk on the beach, Jalila?"

"What?" She jerked as if she'd been abruptly awakened. Her mothers were already clearing things away, and casting odd glances at her. The voice had whispered inside her head, and the tariqua was sitting there, her burnt and splintery arm outstretched, in the hope, Jalila supposed, that she would be helped up from the table. The creature's robe had fallen back. Her arm looked like a picture Jalila had once seen of a dried cadaver. With an effort, nearly knocking over another bowl, Jalila moved around the billowing table. With an even bigger effort, she placed her own hand into that of the tariqua. She'd expected it to feel leathery, which it did. But it was also hot beyond fever. Terribly, the fingers closed around hers. There was a pause. Then the tariqua got up with surprising swiftness, and reached around for her cane, still holding Jalila's hand, but without having placed any weight on it. *She could have done all that on her own, the old witch,* Jalila thought. *And she can see, too — look at the way she's been stuffing herself with kofta all evening, reaching over for figs....*

"What do you know of the stars, Jalila?" the tariqua asked as they walked beside the beach. Pavo's creations along the road behind them still looked stark and strange and half-formed as they swayed in the wind, like the wavering silver limbs of an upturned insect. The waves came and went, strewing tideflowers far up the strand. Like the tongue of a snake, the tariqua's cane darted ahead of her.

Jalila shrugged. There were these Gateways, she had always known that. There were these Gateways, and they were the only proper path between the stars, because no one could endure the eons of time that crossing even the tiniest fragment of the Ten Thousand and One Worlds would entail by the ordinary means of traveling from *there* to *here*.

"Not, of course," the tariqua was saying, "that people don't do such things. There are tales, there are always tales, of ghost-ships of sufis drifting for tens of centuries through the black and black.... But the wealth, the contact, the *community*, flows through the Gateways. The Almighty herself provided the means to make them in the Days of Creation, when everything that was and will ever be spilled out into a void so empty that it did not even exist as an emptiness. In those first moments, as warring elements collided, boundaries formed, dimensions were made and disappeared without ever quite dissolving, like the salt tidemarks on those rocks...." As they walked, the tariqua waved her cane. "...which the sun and the eons can never quite bake away. These boundaries are called cosmic strings, Jalila, and they have no end. They must form either minute loops, or they must stretch from one end of this universe to the other, and then turn back again, and turn and turn without end."

Jalila glanced at the brooch the tariqua was wearing, which was of a worm consuming its tail. She knew that the physical distances between the stars were vast, but the tariqua somehow made the distances that she traversed to avoid that journey seem even vaster....

"You must understand," the tariqua said, "that we tariquas pass through something worse than nothing to get from one side to the other of a Gateway."

Jalila nodded. She was young, and *nothing* didn't sound especially frightening. Still, she sensed that there were the answers to mysteries in this near-blind gaze and whispering voice that she would never get from her dreamtent or her mothers. "But, *hanim*, what could be worse," she asked dutifully, although she still couldn't think of the tariqua in terms of a name, and thus simply addressed her with the short honorific, "than sheer emptiness?"

"Ah, but emptiness is *nothing*. Imagine, Jalila, passing through *everything* instead!" The tariqua chuckled, and gazed up at the sky. "But the stars are beautiful, and so is this night. You come, I hear, from Tabuthal. There, the skies must all have been very different."

Jalila nodded. A brief vision flared over her. The way that up there, on the clearest, coldest nights, you felt as if the stars were all around you. Even now, much though she loved the fetors and astonishments of the coast, she still felt the odd pang of missing something. It was a *feeling* she missed, as much as the place itself, which she guessed would probably seem bleak and lonely if she returned to it now. It was partly to do, she suspected, with that sense that she was loosing her childhood. It was like being on a ship, on Kalal's nameless boat, and watching the land recede, and half of you loving the loss, half of you hating it. A war seemed to be going on inside her between these two warring impulses. . . .

To her surprise, Jalila realized that she wasn't just thinking these thoughts, but speaking them, and that the tariqua, walking at her slow pace, the weight of her head bending her spine, her cane whispering a jagged line in the dust as the black rags of her djibbah flapped around her, was listening. Jalila supposed that she, too, had been young once, although that was hard to imagine. The sea frothed and swished. They were at the point in the road now where, gently buzzing and almost out of sight amid the forest, hidden there as if in shame, the tariqua's caleche lay waiting. It was a small filigree, a thing as old and black and ornate as her brooch. Jalila helped her toward it through the trees. The craft's door creaked open like an iron gate, then shut behind the tariqua. A few crickets sounded through the night's heat. Then, with a soft rush, and a static glow like the charge of windsilk brushing flesh, the caleche rose up through the treetops and wafted away.

The day of the moulid came. It was everything that Jalila expected, although she paid it little attention. The intricate, bowered pathway that Pavo had been working on finally shaped itself to her plans—in fact, it was better than that, and seemed like a beautiful accident. As the skies cleared, the sun shone through prismatic arches. The flowers, which had looked so stunted only the evening before, suddenly unfolded, with petals like beaten brass, and stamens shaped so that the continuing breeze, which Pavo had always claimed to have feared, laughed and whistled and tooted as it passed through them. Walking beneath the archways of flickering shadows, you were assailed by scents and the clashes of small orchestras. But Jalila's ears were blocked, her eyes were sightless. She, after all, was Dinarzade, and Nayra was Scheherazade of the Thousand and One Nights.

Swirling windsilks, her heart hammering, she strode into Al Janb. Everything seemed to be different today. There were too many sounds and colors. People tried to dance with her, or sell her things. Some of the aliens seemed to have dressed themselves as humans. Some of the humans were most definitely dressed as aliens. Her feet were already blistered and delicate from her new crimson slippers. And there was Nayra, dressed in a silvery serwal and blouse of such devastating simplicity that Jalila felt her heart kick and pause in its beating. Nayra was surrounded by a small storm of her usual admirers. Her eyes took in Jalila as she stood at their edge, then beckoned her to join them. The idea of Dinarzade and Scheherazade, which Jalila had thought was to be their secret, was now shared with everyone. The other girls laughed and clustered around, admiring, joking, touching and stroking bits of her as if she was a hayawan. *You of all people, Jalila! And such jewels, such silks* . . . Jalila stood half-frozen, her heart still kicking. *So, so marvelous! And not at all dowdy.* . . . She could have lived many a long and happy life without such compliments.

Thus the day continued. All of them in a crowd, and Jalila feeling both overdressed and exposed, with these stirring, whispering windsilks that covered and yet mostly seemed to reveal her body. She felt like a child in a ribboned parade, and when one of the old mahwagis even came up and pressed a sticky lump of basbousa into her hand, it was the final indignity. She trudged off alone, and found Kalal and his father Ibra managing a seafront stall beside the swaying masts of the bigger trawlers, around which there was a fair level of purchase and interest. Ibra was enjoying himself, roaring out enticements and laughter in his big, belling voice. At last, they'd gotten around to harvesting some of the tideflowers for which their nameless boat had been designed, and they were selling every sort here, salt-fresh from the ocean.

"Try this one. . . ." Kalal drew Jalila away to the edge of the harbor, where the oiled water flashed below. He had just one tideflower in his hand. It was deep-banded the same crimson and blue as her windsilks. The interior was like the eye of an anemone.

Jalila was flattered. But she hesitated. "I'm not sure about wearing something dead." In any case, she knew she already looked ridiculous. That this would be more of the same.

"It isn't dead, it's as alive as you are." Kalal held it closer, against Jalila's shoulder, toward the top of her breast, smoothing out the windsilks in a way that briefly reminded her of Nayra. "And isn't this material the dead tissue of some creature or other . . . ?" Still, his hands were smoothing. Jalila thought again of Nayra. Being dressed like a doll. Her nipples started to rise. "And if we take it back to the tideflower beds tomorrow morning, place it down there carefully, it'll still survive . . ." The tideflower had stuck itself to her now, anyway, beneath the shoulder, its adhesion passing through the thin windsilks, burning briefly as it bound to her flesh. And it *was* beautiful, even if she wasn't, and it would have been churlish to refuse. Jalila placed her finger into the tideflower's center, and felt a soft suction, like the mouth of a baby. Smiling, thanking Kalal, feeling somehow better and more determined, she walked away.

The day went on. The night came. Fireworks crackled and rumpled, rippling down the slopes of the mountains. The whole of the center of Al Janb was transformed unrecognizably into the set of a play. Young Joanna herself walked the vast avenues of Ghezirah, the island city that lies at the center of all the Ten Thousand and One Worlds, and which grows in much the same way as Pavo's crystal scaffoldings, but on an inconceivable scale, filled with azure skies, glinting in the dark heavens like a vast diamond. The Blessed Joanna, she was supposedly thinking of a planet that had come to her in a vision as she wandered beside Ghezirah's palaces; it was a place of fine seas, lost giants, and mysterious natural castles, although Jalila, as she followed in the buffeting, cheering procession, and glanced around at the scale of the projections that briefly covered Al Janb's ordinary buildings, wondered why, even if this version of Ghezirah was fake and thin, Joanna would ever have wanted to leave *that* city to come to a place such as this.

There were more fireworks. As they rattled, a deeper sound swept over them in a moan from the sea, and everyone looked up as sunglow poured through the gaudy images of Ghezirah that still clad Al Janb's buildings. Not one rocket, or two, but three, were all climbing up from the spaceport simultaneously, the vast white plumes of their energies fanning out across half the sky to form a billowy *fleur de lys*. At last, as she craned her neck and watched the last of those blazing tails diminish, Jalila felt exulted by this moulid. In the main square, the play continued. When she found a place on a bench and began to watch the more intimate parts of the drama unfold, as Joanna's lover Pia pleaded with her to remain amid the cerulean towers of Ghezirah, a figure moved to sit beside her. To Jalila's astonishment, it was Nayra.

"That's a lovely flower. I've been meaning to ask you all day . . ." Her fingers moved across Jalila's shoulder. There was a tug at her skin as she touched the petals.

"I got it from Kalal."

"Oh . . ." Nayra sought the right word. "*Him*. Can I smell it . . . ?" She was already bending down, her face close to Jalila's breast, the golden fall of her hair brushing her forearm, enclosing her in the sweet, slightly vanilla scent of her body. "That's nice. It smells like the sea — on a clear day, when you climb up and look down at it from the mountains. . . ."

The play continued. Would Joanna really go to this planet, which kept appearing to her in these visions? Jalila didn't know. She didn't care. Nayra's hand slipped into her own and lay there upon her thigh with a weight and presence that seemed far heavier than the entire universe. She felt like that doll again. Her breath was pulling, dragging. The play continued, and then, somewhere, somehow, it came to an end. Jalila felt an aching sadness. She'd have been happy for Joanna to continue her will-I-won't-I agonizing and prayers throughout all of human history, just so that she and Nayra could continue to sit together like this, hand in hand, thigh to thigh, on this hard bench.

The projections flickered and faded. She stood up in wordless disappointment. The whole square suddenly looked like a wastetip, and she felt crumpled and used-up in these sweaty and ridiculous clothes. It was hardly worth looking back toward Nayra to say goodbye. She would, Jalila was sure, have already vanished to rejoin those clucking, chattering friends who surrounded her like a wall.

"Wait!" A hand on her arm. That same vanilla scent. "I've heard that your mother Pavo's displays along the south road are something quite fabulous. . . ." For once, Nayra's golden gaze as Jalila looked back at her was almost coy, nearly averted. "I was rather hoping you might show me. . . ."

The two of them. Walking hand in hand, just like all lovers throughout history. Like Pia and Joanna. Like Romana and Juliet. Like Isabel and Genya. Ghosts of smoke from the rocket plumes that had buttressed the sky hung around them, and the world seemed half-dissolved in the scent of sulphur and roses. An old woman they passed, who was sweeping up discarded kebab sticks and wrappers, made a sign as they passed, and gave them a weary, sad-happy smile. Jalila wasn't sure what had happened to her slippers, but they and her feet both seemed to have become weightless. If it hadn't been for the soft sway and pull of Nayra's arm, Jalila wouldn't even have been sure that she was moving. *People's feet really don't touch the ground when they are in love!* Here was something else that her dream-tent and her mothers hadn't told her.

Pavo's confections of plant and crystal looked marvelous in the hazed and doubled silver shadows of the rising moons. Jalila and Nayra wandered amid them, and the rest of the world felt withdrawn and empty. A breeze was still playing over the rocks and the waves, but the fluting sound had changed. It was one soft pitch, rising, falling. They kissed. Jalila closed her eyes—she couldn't help it—and trembled. Then they held both hands together and stared at each other, unflinching. Nayra's bare arms in the moonlight, the curve inside her elbow and the blue trace of a vein: Jalila had never seen anything as beautiful, here in this magical place.

The stables, where the hayawans were breathing. Jalila spoke to Robin, to Abu. The beasts were sleepy. Their flesh felt cold, their plates were warm, and Nayra seemed a little afraid. There, in the sighing darkness, the clean scent of feed and straw was overlaid with the heat of the hayawans' bodies and their dung. The place was no longer a ramshackle tent, but solid and dark, another of Pavo's creations; the stony catacombs of ages. Jalila led Nayra through it, her shoulders brushing pillars, her heart pounding, her slippered feet whispering through spills of straw. To the far corner, where the fine new white bedding lay like depths of cloud. They threw themselves onto it, half-expecting to fall through. But they were floating in straggles of windsilk, held in tangles of their own laughter and limbs.

"Remember." Nayra's palm on Jalila's right breast, scrolled like an old print in the geometric moonlight that fell from Walah, and then through the arched stone grid of a murqana that lay above their heads. "I'm Scheherazade. You're Dinarzade, my sister . . ." The pebble of Jalila's nipple rising through the windsilk. "That old, old story, Jalila. Can you remember how it went . . . ?"

In the tide of yore and in the time of long gone before, there was a Queen of all the Queens of the Banu Sasan in the far islands of India and China, a Lady of armies and guards and servants and dependants. . . .

Again, they kissed.

Handsome gifts, such as horses with saddles of gem-encrusted gold; mamelukes, or white slaves; beautiful handmaids, high-breasted virgins, and splendid stuffs and costly. . . .

Nayra's hand moved from Jalila's breast to encircle the tideflower. She gave it a tug, pulled harder. Something held, gave, held, hurt, then gave entirely. The windsilks poured back. A small dark bead of blood welled at the curve between Jalila's breast and shoulder. Nayra licked it away.

In one house was a girl weeping for the loss of her sister. In another, perhaps a mother trembling for the fate of her child; and instead of the blessings that had formerly been heaped on the Sultana's head, the air was now full of curses. . . .

Jalila was rising, floating, as Nayra's mouth traveled downward to suckle at her breast.

Now the Wazir had two daughters, Scheherazade and Dinarzade, of whom the elder had perused the books, annals, and legends of preceding queens and empresses, and the stories, examples, and instances of bygone things. Scheherazade had read the works of the poets and she knew them by heart. She had studied philosophy, the sciences, the arts, and all accomplishments. And Scheherazade was pleasant and polite, wise and witty. Scheherazade, she was beautiful and well bred. . . .

Flying far over frost-glittering saharas, beneath the twin moons, soaring through the clouds. The falling, rising dunes. The minarets and domes of distant cities. The cries and shuddering sighs of the beloved. Patterned moonlight falling through the murqana in a white and dark tapestry across the curves and hollows of Nayra's belly.

Alekum as-salal wa rahmatu allahi wa barakatuh. . . .

Upon you, the peace and the mercy of God and all these blessings.

Amen.

There was no cock-crow when Jalila startled awake. But Walah had vanished, and so had Nayra, and the light of the morning sun came splintering down through the murqana's hot blue lattice. Sheltering her face with her hands, Jalila looked down at herself, and smiled. The jewel in her belly was all that was left of her costume. She smelled faintly of vanilla, and much of Nayra, and nothing about her flesh seemed quite her own. Moving through the dazzling drizzle, she gathered up the windsilks and other scraps of clothing that had settled into the fleece bedding. She found one of Nayra's earrings, which was twisted to right angles at the post, and had to smile again. And here was that tideflower, tossed upturned like an old cup into the corner. She touched the tiny scab on her shoulder, then lifted the flower up and inhaled, but caught on her palms only the scents of Nayra. She closed her eyes, feeling the diamond speckles of heat and cold across her body like the ripples of the sea.

The hayawans barely stirred as she moved out through their stables. Only Robin regarded her, and then incuriously, as she paused to touch the hard grey melds of her flank that she had pressed against the bars of her enclosure. One eye, grey as rocket smoke, opened, then returned to its saharas of dreams. The hayawans, Jalila supposed for the first time, had their own passions, and these were not to be shared with some odd two-legged creatures of another race and planet.

The morning was still clinging to its freshness, and the road, as she crossed it, was barely warm beneath her feet. Wind-towered Al Janb and the haramlek behind her looked deserted. Even the limbs of the mountains seemed curled in sleepy haze. On this day after the moulid, no one but the geelies was yet stirring. Cawing, they rose and settled in flapping red flocks from the beds of the tideflowers as Jalila scrunched across the hard stones of the beach. Her feet encountered the cool, slick water. She continued walking, wading, until the sea tickled her waist and what remained of the windsilks had spread about in spills of dye. From her cupped hands, she released the tideflower, and watched it float away. She splashed her face. She sunk down to her shoulders as the windsilks dissolved from her, and looked down between her breasts at the glowing jewel that was still stuck in her belly, and plucked it out, and watched it sink; the sea-lantern of a ship, drowning.

Walking back up the beach, wringing the wet from her hair, Jalila noticed a rich green growth standing out amid the sky-filled rockpools and the growths of lichen. Pricked by something resembling Pavo's curiosity, she scrambled over, and crouched to examine it as the gathering heat of the sun dried her back. She recognized this spot—albeit dimly—from the angle of a band of quartz that glittered and bled blue oxides. This was where she had coughed up her breathmoss in that early Season of Soft Rains. And here it still was, changed but unmistakable—and growing. A small patch here, several larger patches there. Tiny filaments of green, a minute forest, raising its boughs and branches to the sun.

She walked back up toward her haramlek, humming.

3.

The sky was no longer blue. It was no longer white. It had turned to mercury. The rockets rose and rose in dry crackles of summer lightening. The tube-like aliens fled, leaving their strange house of goo-filled windows and pipes still clicking and humming until something burst and the whole structure deflated, and the mess of it leaked across the nearby streets. There were warnings of poisonings and strange epidemics. There were cloggings and stenches of the drains.

Jalila showed the breathmoss to her mothers, who were all intrigued and delighted, although Pavo had of course noticed and categorized the growth long before, while Ananke had to touch the stuff, and left a small brown mark there like the tips of her three fingers, which dried and turned golden over the days that followed. But in this hot season, these evenings when the sun seemed as if it would never vanish, the breathmoss proved surprisingly hardy. . . .

After that night of the moulid, Jalila spent several happy days absorbed and alone, turning and smoothing the memory of her love-making with Nayra. Wandering above and beneath the unthinking routines of everyday life, she was like a fine craftsman, spinning silver, shaping sandalwood. The dimples of Nayra's back. Sweat glinting in the checkered moonlight. That sweet vein in the crook of her beloved's arm, and the pulse of the blood that had risen from it to the drumbeats of ecstasy. The memory seemed entirely enough to Jalila. She was barely living in the present day. When, perhaps six days after the end of the moulid, Nayra turned up at their doorstep with the ends of her hair chewed wet and her eyes red-rimmed, Jalila had been almost surprised to see her, and then to notice the differences between the real Nayra and the Scheherazade of her memories. Nayra smelled of tears and dust as they embraced; like someone who had arrived from a long, long journey.

"Why didn't you *call* me? I've been waiting, waiting. . . ."

Jalila kissed her hair. Her hand traveled beneath a summer shawl to caress Nayra's back, which felt damp and gritty. She had no idea how to answer her questions. They walked out together that afternoon in the shade of the woods behind the haramlek. The trees had changed in this long, hot season, departing from their urrearth habits to coat their leaves in a waxy substance that smelled medicinal. The shadows of their boughs were chalkmarks and charcoal. All was silent. The urrearth birds had retreated to their summer hibernations until the mists of autumn came to rouse them again. Climbing a scree of stones, they found clusters of them at the back of a cave; feathery bundles amid the dripping rock, seemingly without eyes or beak.

As they sat at the mouth of that cave, looking down across the heat-trembling bay, sucking the ice and eating the dates that Ananke had insisted they bring with them, Nayra had seemed like a different person than the one Jalila had thought she had known before the day of the moulid. Nayra, too, was human, and not the goddess she had seemed. She had her doubts and worries. She, too, thought that the girls who surrounded her were mostly crass and stupid. She didn't even believe in her own obvious beauty. She cried a little again, and Jalila hugged her. The hug became a kiss. Soon, dusty and greedy, they were tumbling amid the hot rocks. That evening, back at the haramlek, Nayra was welcomed for dinner by Jalila's mothers with mint tea and the best china. She was invited to bathe. Jalila sat beside her as they ate figs fresh from distant Ras and the year's second crop of oranges. She felt happy. At last, life seemed simple. Nayra was now officially her lover, and this love would form the pattern of her days.

Jalila's life now seemed complete; she believed that she was an adult, and that she talked and spoke and loved and worshipped in an adult way. She still rode out sometimes with Kalal on Robin and Abu, she still laughed or stole things or played games, but she was conscious now that these activities were the sweetmeats of life, pleasing but unnutritous, and the real glories and surprises lay with being with Nayra, and with her mothers, and the life of the haramlek that the two young women talked of founding together one day.

Nayra's mothers lived on the far side of Al Janb, in a fine tall clifftop palace that was one of the oldest in the town, clad in white stone and filled with intricate courtyards, and a final beautiful tajo that looked down from gardens of tarragon across the whole bay. Jalila greatly enjoyed exploring this haramlek, deciphering the peeling scripts that wound along the cool vaults, and enjoying the company of Nayra's mothers who, in their wealth and grace and wisdom, often made her own mothers seem like the awkward and recent provincial arrivals that they plainly were. At home, in her own haramlek, the conversations and ideas seemed stale. An awful dream came to Jalila one night. She was her old doll Tabatha, and she really was being buried. The ground she lay in was moist and dank, as if it was still the Season of Soft Rains, and the faces of everyone she knew were clustered around the hole above her, muttering and sighing as her mouth and eyes were inexorably filled with soil.

"Tell me what it was like, when you first fell in love."

Jalila had chosen Pavo to ask this question of Ananke would probably just hug her, while Lya would talk and talk until there was nothing to say.

"I don't know. Falling in love is like coming home. You can never quite do it for the first time."

"But in the stories—"

"—The stories are always written *afterward*, Jalila."

They were walking the luminous shore. It was near midnight, which was now by far the best time of the night or day. But what Pavo had just said sounded wrong; perhaps she hadn't been the right choice of mother to speak to, after all. Jalila was sure she'd loved Nayra since that day before the moulid of Joanna, although it was true she loved her now in a different way.

"You still don't think we really will form a haramlek together, do you?"

"I think that it's too early to say."

"You were the last of our three, weren't you? Lya and Ananke were already together."

"It was what drew me to them. They seemed so happy and complete. It was also what frightened me and nearly sent me away."

"But you stayed together, and then there was . . ." This was the part that Jalila still found hardest to acknowledge; the idea that her mothers had a physical, sexual relationship. Sometimes, deep at night, from someone else's dreamtent, she had heard muffled sighs, the wet slap of flesh. Just like the hayawans, she supposed, there were things about other people's lives that you could never fully understand, no matter how well you thought you knew them.

She chose a different tack. "So why did you choose to have me?"

"Because we wanted to fill the world with something that had never ever existed before. Because we felt selfish. Because we wanted to give ourselves away."

"Ananke, she actually gave birth to me, didn't she?"

"Down here at Al Janb, they'd say we were primitive and mad. Perhaps that was how we wanted to be. But all the machines at the clinics do is try to re-create the conditions of a real human womb—the voices, the movements, the sound of breathing. . . . Without first hearing that Song of Life, no human can ever be happy, so what better way could there be than to hear it naturally?"

A flash of that dream-image of herself being buried. "But the birth itself—"

"—I think that was something we all underestimated." The tone of Pavo's voice told Jalila that this was not a subject to be explored on the grounds of mere curiosity.

The tideflower beds had solidified. You could walk across them as if they were dry land. Kalal, after several postponements and broken promises, took Jalila and Nayra out one night to demonstrate.

Smoking lanterns at the prow and stern of his boat. The water slipping warm as blood through Jalila's trailing fingers. Al Janb receding beneath the hot thighs of the mountains. Kalal at the prow. Nayra sitting beside her, her arm around her shoulder, hand straying across her breast until Jalila shrugged it away because the heat of their two bodies was oppressive.

"This season'll end soon," Nayra said. "You've never known the winter here, have you?"

"I was *born* in the winter. Nothing here could be as cold as the lightest spring morning in the mountains of Tabuthal."

"Ah, the *mountains*. You must show me sometime. We should travel there together. . . ."

Jalila nodded, trying hard to picture that journey. She'd attempted to interest Nayra in riding a hayawan, but she grew frightened even in the presence of the beasts. In so many ways, in fact, Nayra surprised Jalila with her timidity. Jalila, in these moments of doubt, and as she lay alone in her dreamtent and wondered, would list to herself Nayra's many assets: her lithe and willing body; the beautiful haramlek of her beautiful mothers; the fact that so many of the other girls now envied and admired her. There were so many things that were good about Nayra.

Kalal, now that his boat had been set on course for the further tidebeds, came to sit with them, his face sweated lantern-red. He and Nayra shared many memories, and now, as the sails pushed on from the hot air off the mountains, they vied to tell Jalila of the surprises and delights of winters in Al Janb. The fogs when you couldn't see your hand. The intoxicating blue berries that appeared in special hollows through the crust of the snow. The special saint's days. . . . If Jalila hadn't known better, she'd have said that Nayra and Kalal were fighting over something more important.

The beds of tideflowers were vast, luminous, heavy-scented. Red-black clusters of geelies rose and fell here and there in the moonlight. Walking these gaudy carpets was a most strange sensation. The dense interlaces of leaves felt like rubber matting, but sank and bobbed. Jalila and Nayra lit more lanterns and dotted them around a field of huge primrose and orange petals. They sang and staggered and rolled and fell over. Nayra had brought a pipe of kif resin, and the sensation of smoking that and trying to dance was hilarious. Kalal declined, pleading that he had to control the boat on the way back, and picked his way out of sight, disturbing flocks of geelies.

And so the two girls danced as the twin moons rose. Nayra, twirling silks, her hair fanning, was graceful as Jalila still staggered amid the lapping flowers. As she lifted her arms and rose on tiptoe, bracelets glittering, she had never looked more desirable. Somewhat drunkenly—and slightly reluctantly, because Kalal might return at any moment—Jalila moved forward to embrace her. It was good to hold Nayra, and her mouth tasted like the tideflowers and sucked needily at her own. In fact, the moments of their love had never been sweeter and slower than they were on that night, although, even as Jalila marveled at the shape of Nayra's breasts and listened to the changed song of her breathing, she felt herself chilling, receding, drawing back, not just from Nayra's physical presence, but from this small bay beside the small town on the single continent beside Habara's great and lonely ocean. Jalila felt infinitely sorry for Nayra as she brought her to her little ecstasies and they kissed and rolled across the beds of flowers. She felt sorry for Nayra because she was beautiful, and sorry for her because of all her accomplishments, and sorry for her because she would always be happy here amid the slow seasons of this little planet.

Jalila felt sorry for herself as well; sorry because she had thought that she had known love, and because she knew now that it had only been a pretty illusion.

There was a shifting wind, dry and abrasive, briefly to be welcomed, until it became something to curse and cover your face and close your shutters against.

Of Jalila's mothers, only Lya seemed at all disappointed by her break from Nayra, no doubt because she had fostered hopes of their union forming a powerful bond between their haramleks, and even she did her best not to show it. Of the outside world, the other young women of Al Janb all professed total disbelief— *why if it had been me, I'd never have* . . . But soon, they were cherishing the new hope that it might indeed *be* them. Nayra, to her credit, maintained an extraordinary dignity in the face of the fact that she, of all people, had finally been rejected. She dressed in plain clothes. She spoke and ate simply. Of course, she looked more devastatingly beautiful than ever, and everyone's eyes were reddened by air-borne grit in any case, so it was impossible to tell how much she had really been crying. Now, as the buildings of Al Janb creaked and the breakers rolled and the wind howled through the teeth of the mountains, Jalila saw the gaudy, seeking and competing creatures who so often surrounded Nayra quite differently. Nayra was not, had never been, in control of them. She was more like the bloody carcass over which, flashing their teeth, their eyes, stretching their limbs, they endlessly fought. Often, riven by a sadness far deeper than she had ever experienced, missing something she couldn't explain, wandering alone or lying in her dreamtent, Jalila nearly went back to Nayra. . . . But she never did.

This was the Season of Winds, and Jalila was heartily sick of herself and Al Janb, and the girls and the mahwagis and the mothers, and of this changing, buffeting banshee weather that seemed to play with her moods. Sometimes now, the skies were entirely beautiful, strung by the curling multicolored banners of sand that the winds had lifted from distant corners of the continent. There was crimson and there was sapphire. The distant saharas of Jalila's dreams had come to haunt her. They fell — as the trees tore and the paint stripped from the shutters and what remained of Pavo's arches collapsed — in an irritating grit that worked its way into all the crevices of your body and every weave of your clothes.

The tariqua had spoken of the pain of *nothing*, and then of the pain of *everything*. At the time, Jalila had understood neither, but now, she felt that she understood the pain of nothing all too well. The product of the combined genes of her three mothers; loving Ananke, ever-curious Pavo, proud and talkative Lya, she had always felt glad to recognize these characteristics mingled in herself, but now she wondered if these traits hadn't cancelled each other out. She was a null-point, a zero, clumsy and destructive and unloving. She was Jalila, and she walked alone and uncaring through this Season of Winds.

One morning, the weather was especially harsh. Jalila was alone in the haramlek, although she cared little where she or anywhere else was. A shutter must have come loose somewhere. That often happened now. It had been banging and hammering so long that it began to irritate even her. She climbed stairs and slammed doors over jamming drifts of mica. She flapped back irritably at flapping curtains. Still, the banging went on. Yet all the windows and doors were now secure. She was sure of it. Unless. . . .

Someone was at the front door. She could see a swirling globular head through the greenish glass mullion. Even though they could surely see her as well, the banging went on. Jalila wondered if she wanted it to be Nayra; after all, this was how she had come to her after the moulid; a sweet and needy human being to drag her out from her dreams. But it was only Kalal. As the door shoved Jalila back, she tried not to look disappointed.

"You can't do this with your life!"

"Do what?"

"This—*nothing*. And then not answering the fucking door. . . ." Kalal prowled the hallway as the door banged back and forth and tapestries flailed, looking for clues as if he was a detective. "Let's go out."

Even in this weather, Jalila supposed that she owed it to Robin. Then Kalal had wanted to go north, and she insisted on going south, and was not in any mood for arguing. It was an odd journey, so unlike the ones they'd undertaken in the summer. They wrapped their heads and faces in flapping howlis, and tried to ride mostly in the forest, but the trees whipped and flapped and the raw air still abraded their faces.

They took lunch down by a flatrock shore, in what amounted to shelter, although there was still little enough of it as the wind eddied about them. This could have been the same spot where they had stopped in summer, but it was hard to tell; the light was so changed, the sky so bruised. Kalal seemed changed, too. His face beneath his howli seemed older, as he tried to eat their aish before the sand-laden air got to it, and his chin looked prickled and abraded. Jalila supposed that this was the same facial growth that his father Ibra was so fond of sporting. She also supposed he must choose to shave his off in the way that some women on some decadent planets were said to shave their legs and armpits.

"Come a bit closer—" she half-shouted, working her way back into the lee of the bigger rock beside which she was sitting to make room for him. "I want you to tell me what you know about love, Kalal."

Kalal hunched beside her. For a while, he just continued tearing and chewing bits of aish, with his body pressed against hers as the winds boiled around them, the warmth of their flesh almost meeting. And Jalila wondered if men and women, when their lives and needs had been more closely intertwined, had perhaps known the answer to her question. What *was* love, after all? It would have been nice to think that, in those dim times of myth, men and women had whispered the answer to that question to each other. . . .

She thought then that Kalal hadn't properly heard her. He was telling her about his father, and a planet he barely remembered, but on which he was born. The sky there had been fractaled gold and turquoise—colors so strange and bright that they came as a delight and a shock each morning. It was a place of many islands, and one great city. His father had been a fisherman and boat-repairer of sorts there as well, although the boats had been much grander than anything you ever saw at Al Janb, and the fish had lived not as single organisms, but as complex shoals that were caught not for their meat, but for their joint minds. Ibra had been approached by a woman from off-world, who had wanted a ship on which she could sail alone around the whole lonely band of the northern oceans. She had told him that she was sick of human company. The planning and the making of the craft was a joy for Ibra, because such a lonely journey had been one that he had long dreamed of making, if ever he'd had the time and money. The ship was his finest-ever creation, and it turned out, as they worked on it, that neither he nor the woman were quite as sick of human company as they had imagined. They fell in love as the keel and the spars grew in the city dockyards and the ship's mind was nurtured, and as they did so, they slowly re-learned the expressions of sexual need between the male and female.

"You mean he *raped* her?"

Kalal tossed his last nub of bread toward the waves. "I mean that they *made love.*"

After the usual negotiations and contracts, and after the necessary insertions of the appropriate cells, Ibra and this woman (whom Kalal didn't name in his story, any more than he named the world) set sail together, fully intending to conceive a child in the fabled way of old.

"Which was *you?*"

Kalal scowled. It was impossible to ask him even simple questions on this subject without making him look annoyed. "Of *course* it was! How many of me do you think there are?" Then he lapsed into silence. The sands swirled in colored helixes before them.

"That woman—your birthmother. What happened to her?"

"She wanted to take me away, of course—to some haramlek on another world, just as she'd been planning all along. My father was just a toy to her. As soon as their ship returned, she started making plans, issuing contracts. There was a long legal dispute with my father. I was placed in a birthsac, in stasis."

"And your father won?"

Kalal scowled. "He took me here, anyway. Which is winning enough."

There were many other questions about this story that Jalila wanted to ask Kalal, if she hadn't already pressed too far. What, after all, did this tale of dispute and deception have to do with love? And were Kalal and Ibra really fugitives? It would explain quite a lot. Once more, in that familiar welling, she felt sorry for him. Men were such strange, sad creatures; forever fighting, angry, lost. . . .

"*I'm* glad you're here anyway," she said. Then, on impulse, one of those careless things you do, she took that rough and ugly chin in her hand, turned his face toward hers and kissed him lightly on the lips.

"What was that for?"

"*El-hamdu-l-Illah.* That was for thanks."

They plodded further on their hayawans. They came eventually to a cliff-edge so high that the sea and sky above and beneath vanished. Jalila already knew what they would see as they made their way along it, but still it was a shock; that qasr, thrust into these teeming ribbons of sand. The winds whooped and howled, and the hayawans raised their heads and howled back at it. In this grinding atmosphere, Jalila could see how the qasrs had been carved over long years from pure natural rock. They dismounted, and struggled bent-backed across the narrowing track toward the qasr's studded door. Jalila raised her fist and beat on it.

She glanced back at Kalal, but his face was entirely hidden beneath his hood. Had they always intended to come here? But they had traveled too far to do otherwise now; Robin and Abu were tired and near-blinded; they all needed rest and shelter. She beat on the door again, but the sound was lost in the booming storm. Perhaps the tariqua had left with the last of the Season of Rockets, just as had most of the aliens. Jalila was about to turn away when the door, as if thrown wide by the wind, blasted open. There was no one on the other side, and the hallway beyond was dark as the bottom of a dry well. Robin hoiked her head back and howled and resisted as Jalila hauled her in. Kalal with Abu followed. The door, with a massive drumbeat, hammered itself shut behind them. Of course, it was only some old mechanism of this house, but Jalila felt the hairs on the nape of her neck rise.

They hobbled the hayawans beside the largest of the scalloped arches, and walked on down the passageway beyond. The wind was still with them, and the shapes of the pillars were like the swirling helixes of sand made solid. It was hard to tell what parts of this place had been made by the hands of women and what was entirely natural. If the qasr had seemed deserted in the heat of summer, it was entirely abandoned now. A scatter of glass windchimes, torn apart by the wind. A few broken plates. Some flapping cobwebs of tapestry.

Kalal pulled Jalila's hand.

"Let's go back. . . ."

But there was greater light ahead, the shadows of the speeding sky. Here was the courtyard where they had glimpsed the tariqua. She had plainly gone now — the fountain was dry and clogged, the bushes were bare tangles of wire. They walked out beneath the tiled arches, looking around. The wind was like a million voices, rising in ululating chorus. This was a strange and empty place; somehow dangerous. . . . Jalila span around. The tariqua was standing there, her robes flapping. With insect fingers, she beckoned.

"Are you leaving?" Jalila asked. "I mean, this place. . . ."

The tariqua had led them into the shelter of a tall, wind-echoing chamber set with blue and white tiles. There were a few rugs and cushions scattered on the floor, but still the sense of abandonment remained. As if, Jalila thought, as the tariqua folded herself on the floor and gestured that they join her, this was her last retreat.

"No, Jalila. I won't be leaving Habara. *Itfaddal*. . . . Do sit down."

They stepped from their sandals and obeyed. Jalila couldn't quite remember now whether Kalal had encountered the tariqua on her visit to their haramlek, although it seemed plain from his stares at her, and the way her grey-white gaze returned them, that they knew of each other in some way. Coffee was brewing in the corner, over a tiny blue spirit flame, which, as it fluttered in the many drafts, would have taken hours to heat anything. Yet the spout of the brass pot was steaming. And there were dates, too, and nuts and seeds. The tariqua, apologizing for her inadequacy as a host, nevertheless insisted that they help themselves. And somewhere there was a trough of water, too, for their hayawans, and a basket of acram leaves.

Uneasily, they sipped from their cups, chewed the seeds. Kalal had picked up a chipped lump of old stone and was playing with it nervously. Jalila couldn't quite see what it was.

"So," he said, clearing his throat, "you've been to and from the stars, have you?"

"As have you. Perhaps you could name the planet? It may have been somewhere that we have both visited. . . ."

Kalal swallowed. His lump of old stone clicked the floor. A spindle of wind played chill on Jalila's neck. Then — she didn't know how it began — the tariqua was talking of Ghezirah, the great and fabled city that lay at the center of all the Ten Thousand and One Worlds. No one Jalila had ever met or heard of had ever visited Ghezirah, not even Nayra's mothers—yet this tariqua talked of it as if she knew it well. Before, Jalila had somehow imagined the tariqua trailing from planet to distant planet with dull cargoes of ore and biomass in her ship's holds. To her mind, Ghezirah had always been more than half-mythical—a place from which a dubious historical figure such as the Blessed Joanna might easily emanate, but certainly not a place composed of solid streets upon which the gnarled and bony feet of this old woman might once have walked. . . .

Ghezirah . . . she could see it now in her mind, smell the shadowy lobbies, see the ever-climbing curve of its mezzanines and rooftops vanishing into the impossible greens of the Floating Ocean. But every time Jalila's vision seemed about to solidify, the tariqua said something else that made it tremble and change. And then the tariqua said the strangest thing of all, which was that the City At The End Of All Roads was actually *alive*. Not alive in the meager sense in which every town has a sort of life, but truly living. The city thought. It grew. It responded. There was no central mind or focus to this consciousness, because Ghezirah *itself*, its teeming streets and minarets and rivers and caleches and its many millions of lives, was itself the mind. . . .

Jalila was awestruck, but Kalal seemed unimpressed, and was still playing with that old lump of stone.

4.

"Jalilaneen. . . ."

The way bondmother Lya said her name made Jalila look up. Somewhere in her throat, a wary nerve started ticking. They took their meals inside now, in the central courtyard of the haramlek, which Pavo had provided with a translucent roofing to let in a little of what light there was in the evenings' skies, and keep out most of the wind. Still, as Jalila took a sip of steaming hibiscus, she was sure that the sand had gotten into something.

"We've been talking. Things have come up—ideas about which we'd like to seek your opinion. . . ."

In other words, Jalila thought, her gaze traveling across her three mothers, you've decided something. And this is how you tell me—by pretending that you're consulting me. It had been the same with leaving Tabuthal. It was always the same. An old ghost of herself got up at that point, threw down her napkin, stalked off up to her room. But the new Jalila remained seated. She even smiled and tried to look encouraging.

"We've seen so little of this world," Lya continued. "All of us, really. And especially since we had you. It's been marvelous. But, of course, it's also been confining. . . . Oh *no*—" Lya waved the idea away quickly, before anyone could even begin to start thinking it. "—we won't be leaving our haramlek and Al Janb. There are many things to do. New bonds and friendships have been made. Ananke and I won't be leaving, anyway. . . . But Pavo . . ." And here Lya, who could never quite stop being the chair of a committee, gave a nod toward her mate. ". . . Pavo here has dec—expressed a *wish*—that she would like to travel."

"Travel?" Jalila leaned forward, her chin resting on her knuckles. "How?"

Pavo gave her plate a half turn. "By boat seems the best way to explore Habara. With such a big ocean . . ." She turned the plate again, as if to demonstrate.

"And not just a *boat*," Ananke put in encouragingly. "A brand new *ship*. We're having it built—"

"—But I thought you said you hadn't yet decided?"

"The contract, I think, is still being prepared," Lya explained. "And much of the craft will be to Pavo's own design."

"Will you be building it yourself?"

"Not alone." Pavo gave another of her flustered smiles. "I've asked Ibra to help me. He seems to be the best, the most knowledgeable—"

"—Ibra? Does he have any references?"

"This is *Al Janb*, Jalila," Lya said. "We know and trust people. I'd have thought that, with your friendship with Kalal. . . ."

"This certainly *is* Al Janb. . . ." Jalila sat back. "How can I ever forget it!" All of her mothers' eyes were on her. Then something broke. She got up and stormed off to her room.

The long ride to the tariqua's qasr, the swish of the wind, and banging three times on the old oak door. Then hobbling Robin and hurrying through dusty corridors to that tall tiled chamber, and somehow expecting no one to be there, even though Jalila had now come here several times alone.

But the tariqua was always there. Waiting.

Between them now, there was much to be said.

"This ant, Jalila, which crawls across this sheet of paper from *here* to *there*. She is much like us as we crawl across the surface of this planet. Even if she had the wings some of her kind sprout, just as I have my caleche, it would still be the same." The tiny creature, waving feelers, was plainly lost. A black dot. Jalila understood how it felt. "But say, if we were to fold both sides of the paper together. You see how she moves now . . . ?" The ant, antennae waving, hesitant, at last made the tiny jump. "We can move more quickly from one place to another by not travelling across the distance that separates us from it, but by folding space itself.

"Imagine now, Jalila, that this universe is not one thing alone, one solitary series of *this* following *that*, but an endless branching of potentialities. Such it has been since the Days of Creation, and such it is even now, in the shuffle of that leaf as the wind picks at it, in the rising steam of your coffee. Every moment goes in many ways. Most are poor, half-formed things, the passing thoughts and whims of the Almighty. They hang there and they die, never to be seen again. But others branch as strongly as this path that we find ourselves following. There are universes where you and I have never sat here in this qasr. There are universes where there is no Jalila. . . . Will you get that for me . . . ?"

The tariqua was pointing to an old book in a far corner. Its leather was cracked, the wind lifted its pages. As she took it from her, Jalila felt the hot brush of the old woman's hand.

"So now, you must imagine that there is not just one sheet of a single universe, but many, as in this book, heaped invisibly above and beside and below the page upon which we find ourselves crawling. In fact . . ." The ant recoiled briefly, sensing the strange heat of the tariqua's fingers, then settled on the open pages. "You must imagine shelf after shelf, floor upon floor of books, the aisles of an infinite library. And if we are to fold this one page, you see, we or the ant never quite knows what lies on the other side of it. And there may be a tear in that next page as well. It may even be that another version of ourselves has already torn it."

Despite its worn state, the book looked potentially valuable, hand-written in a beautiful flowing script. Jalila had to wince when the tariqua's fingers ripped through them. But the ant had vanished now. She was somewhere between the book's pages. . . .

"That, Jalila, is the Pain of Distance—the sense of every potentiality. So that womankind may pass over the spaces between the stars, every tariqua must experience it." The wind gave an extra lunge, flipping the book shut. Jalila reached forward, but the tariqua, quick for once, was ahead of her. Instead of opening the book to release the ant, she weighed it down with the same chipped old stone with which Kalal had played on his solitary visit to this qasr.

"Now, perhaps, my Jalila, you begin to understand?"

The stone was old, chipped, grey-green. It was inscribed, and had been carved with the closed wings of a beetle. Here was something from a world so impossibly old and distant as to make the book upon which it rested seem fresh and new as an unbudded leaf—a scarab, shaped for the Queens of Egypt.

"See here, Jalila. See how it grows. The breathmoss?"

This was the beginning of the Season of Autumns. The trees were beautiful; the forests were on fire with their leaves. Jalila had been walking with Pavo, enjoying the return of the birdsong, and wondering why it was that this new season felt sad when everything around her seemed to be changing and growing.

"Look. . . ."

The breathmoss, too, had turned russet-gold. Leaning close to it beneath this tranquil sky, which was composed of a blue so pale it was as if the sea had been caught in reflection inside an upturned white bowl, was like looking into the arms of a miniature forest.

"Do you think it will die?"

Pavo leaned beside her. "Jalila, it should have died long ago. *Inshallah*, it is a small miracle." There were the three dead marks where Ananke had touched it in a Season of Long Ago. "You see how frail it is, and yet . . ."

"At least it won't spread and take over the planet."

"Not for a while, at least."

On another rock lay another small colony. Here, too, oddly enough, there were marks. Five large dead dots, as if made by the outspread of a hand, although the shape of it was too big to have been Ananke's. They walked on. Evening was coming. Their shadows were lengthening. Although the sun was shining and the waves sparkled, Jalila wished that she had put on something warmer than a shawl.

"That tariqua. You seem to enjoy her company. . . ."

Jalila nodded. When she was with the old woman, she felt at last as if she was escaping the confines of Al Janb. It was liberating, after the close life in this town and with her mothers in their haramlek, to know that interstellar space truly existed, and then to feel, as the tariqua spoke of Gateways, momentarily like that ant, infinitely small and yet somehow inching, crawling across the many universes' infinite pages. But how could she express this? Even Pavo wouldn't understand.

"How goes the boat?" she asked instead.

Pavo slipped her arm into to crook of Jalila's and hugged her. "You must come and *see!* I have the plan in my head, but I'd never realized quite how big it would be. And complex. Ibra's full of enthusiasm."

"I can imagine!"

The sea flashed. The two women chuckled.

"The way the ship's designed, Jalila, there's more than enough room for others. I never exactly planned to go alone, but then Lya's Lya. And Ananke's always—"

Jalila gave her mother's arm a squeeze. "I know what you're saying."

"I'd be happy if you came, Jalila. I'd understand if you didn't. This is such a beautiful, wonderful planet. The leviathans—we know so little about them, yet they plainly have intelligence, just as all those old myths say."

"You'll be telling me next about the qasrs. . . ."

"The ones we can see near here are *nothing!* There are islands on the ocean that are entirely made from them. And the wind pours through. They sing endlessly. A different song for every mood and season."

"Moods! If I'd said something like that when you were teaching me of the Pillars of Life, you'd have told me I was being unscientific!"

"Science is *about* wonder, Jalila. I was a poor teacher if I never told you that."

"You did." Jalila turned to kiss Pavo's forehead. "You did. . . ."

Pavo's ship was a fine thing. Between the slipways and the old mooring posts, where the red-flapping geelies quarreled over scraps of dying tideflower, it grew and grew. Golden-hulled. Far sleeker and bigger than even the ferries that had once borne Al Janb's visitors to and from the rocket port, and which now squatted on the shingle nearby, gently rusting. It was the talk of the Season. People came to admire its progress.

As Jalila watched the spars rise over the clustered roofs of the fisherwomen's houses, she was reminded of Kalal's tale of his father and his nameless mother, and that ship that they had made together in the teeming dockyards of that city. Her thoughts blurred. She saw the high balconies of a hotel far bigger than any of Al Janb's inns and boarding houses. She saw a darker, brighter ocean. Strange flesh upon flesh, with the windows open to the oil-and-salt breeze, the white lace curtains rising, falling. . . .

The boat grew, and Jalila visited the tariqua, although back in Al Janb, her thoughts sometimes trailed after Kalal as she wondered how it must be—to be male, like the last dodo, and trapped in some endless state of part-arousal, like a form of nagging worry. Poor Kalal. But his life certainly wasn't lonely. The first time Jalila noticed him at the center of the excited swarm of girls that once again surrounded Nayra, she'd almost thought that she was seeing things. But the gossip was loud and persistent. Kalal and Nayra were a *couple*—the phrase normally followed by a scandalized shriek, a hand-covered mouth. Jalila could only guess what the proud mothers of Nayra's haramlek thought of such a union, but, of course, no one could subscribe to outright prejudice. Kalal was, after all, just another human being. Lightly probing her own mothers' attitudes, she found the usual condescending tolerance. Having sexual relations with a male would be like smoking kif, or drinking alcohol, or any other form of slightly aberrant adolescent behavior, to be tolerated with easy smiles and sympathy, as long as it didn't go on for too long. To be treated, in fact, in much the same manner as her mothers were now treating her regular visits to the tariqua.

Jalila came to understand why people thought of the Season of Autumns as a sad time. The chill nights. The morning fogs that shrouded the bay. The leaves, finally falling, piled into rotting heaps. The tideflower beds, also, were dying as the waves pulled and dismantled what remained of their colors, and they drifted to the shores, the flowers bearing the same stench and texture and color as upturned clay. The geelies were dying as well. In the town, to compensate, there was much bunting and celebration for yet another moulid, but to Jalila the brightness seemed feeble—the flame of a match held against winter's gathering gale. Still, she some-times wandered the old markets with some of her old curiosity, nostalgically touch-ing the flapping windsilks, studying the faces and nodding at the many she now knew, although her thoughts were often literally light-years away. *The Pain of Distance*; she could feel it. Inwardly, she was thrilled and afraid. Her mothers and everyone else, caught up in the moulid and Pavo's coming departure, imagined from her mood that she had now decided to take that voyage with her. She de-ceived Kalal in much the same way.

The nights became clearer. Riding back from the qasr one dark evening with the tariqua's slight voice ringing in her ears, the stars seemed to hover closer around her than at any time since she had left Tabuthal. She could feel the night blossoming, its emptiness and the possibilities spinning out to infinity. She felt both like crying, and like whooping for joy. She had dared to ask the tariqua the question she had long been formulating, and the answer, albeit not entirely yes, had not been no. She talked to Robin as they bobbed along, and the puny yellow smudge of Al Janb drew slowly closer. You must understand, she told her hayawan, that the core of the Almighty is like the empty place between these stars, around which they all revolve. It is *there*, we know it, but we can never *see* it. . . . She sang songs from the old saharas about the joy of loneliness, and the loneliness of joy. From here, high up on the gradually descending road that wound its way down toward her haramlek, the horizon was still distant enough for her to see the lights of the rocketport. It was like a huge tidebed, holding out as the season changed. And there at the center of it, rising golden, no longer a stumpy silo-shaped object but somehow beautiful, was the last of the year's rockets. It would have to rise from Habara before the coming of the Season of Winters.

Her mothers' anxious faces hurried around her in the lamplight as she led Robin toward the stable.

"Where have you *been*, Jalilaneen?"

"Do you *know* what time it is?"

"We should be in the town *already!*"

For some reason, they were dressed in their best, most formal robes. Their palms were hennaed and scented. They bustled Jalila out of her gritty clothes, practically washed and dressed her, then flapped themselves down the serraplate road into town, where the processions had already started. Still, they were there in plenty of time to witness the blessing of Pavo's ship. It was to be called *Endeavor*, and Pavo and Jalila together smashed the bottle of wine across its prow before it rumbled into the nightblack waters of the harbor with an enormous white splash. Everyone cheered. Pavo hugged Jalila.

There were more bottles of the same frothy wine available at the party afterward. Lya, with her usual thoroughness, had ordered a huge case of the stuff, although many of the guests remembered the Prophet's old injunction and avoided imbibing. Ibra, though, was soon even more full of himself than usual, and went around the big marquee with a bottle in each hand, dancing clumsily with anyone who was foolish enough to come near him. Jalila drank a little of the stuff herself. The taste was sweet, but oddly hot and bitter. She filled up another glass.

"Wondered what you two mariners were going to call that boat. . . ."

It was Kalal. He'd been dancing with many of the girls, and he looked almost as red-faced as his father.

"Bet you don't even know what the first *Endeavor* was."

"You're wrong there," Jalila countered primly, although the simple words almost fell over each other as she tried to say them. "It was the spacecraft of Captain Cook. She was one of the urrearth's most famous early explorers."

"I thought you were many things," Kalal countered, angry for no apparent reason. "But I never thought you were *stupid*."

Jalila watched him walk away. The dance had gathered up its beat. Ibra had retreated to sit, foolishly glum, in a corner, and Nayra had moved to the middle of the floor, her arms raised, bracelets jingling, an opal jewel at her belly, windsilk-draped hips swaying. Jalila watched. Perhaps it was the drink, but for the first time in many a Season, she felt a slight return of that old erotic longing as she watched Nayra swaying. Desire was the strangest of all emotions. It seemed so trivial when you weren't possessed of it, and yet when you were possessed, it was as if all the secrets of the universe were waiting. . . . Nayra was the focus of all attention now as she swayed amid the crowd, her shoulders glistening. She danced before Jalila, and her languorous eyes fixed her for a moment before she danced on. Now she was dancing with Kalal, and he was swaying with her, her hands laid upon his shoulders, and everyone was clapping. They made a fine couple. But the music was getting louder, and so were people's voices. Her head was pounding. She left the marquee.

She welcomed the harshness of the night air, the clear presence of the stars. Even the stench of the rotting tideflowers seemed appropriate as she picked her way across the ropes and slipways of the beach. So much had changed since she had first come here—but mostly what had changed had been herself. Here, its shape unmistakable as rising Walah spread her faint blue light across the ocean, was Kalal's boat. She sat down on the gunwale. The cold wind bit into her. She heard the crunch of shingle, and imagined it was someone else who was in need of solitude. But the sound grew closer, and then whoever it was sat down on the boat beside her. She didn't need to look up now. Kalal's smell was always different, and now he was sweating from the dancing.

"I thought you were enjoying yourself," she muttered.

"Oh—I was . . ." The emphasis on the *was* was strong.

They sat there for a long time, in windy, wave-crashing silence. It was almost like being alone. It was like the old days of their being together.

"So you're going, are you?" Kalal asked eventually.

"Oh, yes."

"I'm pleased for you. It's a fine boat, and I like Pavo best of all your mothers. You haven't seemed quite so happy lately here in Al Janb. Spending all that time with that old witch in the qasr."

"She's not a witch. She's a tariqua. It's one of the greatest, oldest callings. Although I'm surprised you've had time to notice what I'm up to, anyway. You and Nayra . . ."

Kalal laughed, and the wind made the sound turn bitter.

"I'm sorry," Jalila continued. "I'm sounding just like those stupid gossips. I know you're not like that. Either of you. And I'm happy for you both. Nayra's sweet and talented and entirely lovely . . . I hope it lasts . . . I hope . . ."

After another long pause, Kalal said, "Seeing as we're apologizing, I'm sorry I got cross with you about the name of that boat you'll be going on—the *Endeavor*. It's a good name."

"Thank you. *El-hamadu-l-illah*."

"In fact, I could only think of one better one, and I'm glad you and Pavo didn't use it. You know what they say. To have two ships with the same name confuses the spirits of the winds. . . ."

"What are you talking about, Kalal?"

"This boat. You're sitting right on it. I thought you might have noticed."

Jalila glanced down at the prow, which lay before her in the moonlight, pointing toward the silvered waves. From this angle, and in the old naskhi script that Kalal had used, it took her a moment to work out the craft's name. Something turned inside her.

Breathmoss.

In white, moonlit letters.

"I'm sure there are better names for a boat," she said carefully. "Still, I'm flattered."

"Flattered?" Kalal stood up. She couldn't really see his face, but she suddenly knew that she'd once again said the wrong thing. He waved his hands in an odd shrug, and he seemed for a moment almost ready to lean close to her—to do something unpredictable and violent—but instead, picking up stones and skimming them hard into the agitated waters, he walked away.

Pavo was right. If not about love—which Jalila knew now that she still waited to experience—then at least about the major decisions of your life. There was never quite a beginning to them, although your mind often sought for such a thing.

When the tariqua's caleche emerged out of the newly teeming rain one dark evening a week or so after the naming of the *Endeavor*, and settled itself before the lights of their haramlek, and the old woman herself emerged, somehow still dry, and splashed across the puddled garden while her three mothers flustered about to find the umbrella they should have thought to look for earlier, Jalila still didn't know what she should be thinking. The four women would, in any case, need to talk alone; Jalila recognized that. For once, after the initial greetings, she was happy to retreat to her dreamtent.

But her mind was still in turmoil. She was suddenly terrified that her mothers would actually agree to this strange proposition, and then that, out of little more than embarrassment and obligation, the rest of her life would be bound to something that the tariqua called the Church of the Gateway. She knew so little. The tariqua talked only in riddles. She could be a fraud, for all Jalila knew—or a witch, just as Kalal insisted. Thoughts swirled about her like the rain. To make the time disappear, she tried searching the knowledge of her dreamtent. Lying there, listening to the rising sound of her mothers' voices, which seemed to be studded endlessly with the syllables of her own name, Jalila let the personalities who had guided her through the many Pillars of Wisdom tell her what they knew about the Church of the Gateway.

She saw the blackness of planetary space, swirled with the mica dots of turning planets. Almost as big as those as she zoomed close to it, yet looking disappointingly like a many-angled version of the rocketport, lay the spacestation, and, within it, the junction that could lead you from *here* to *there* without passing across the distance between. A huge rent in the Book of Life, composed of the trapped energies of those things the tariqua called cosmic strings, although they and the Gateway itself were visible as nothing more than a turning ring near to the center of the vast spacestation, where occasionally, as Jalila watched, crafts of all possible shapes would seem to hang, then vanish. The gap she glimpsed inside seemed no darker than that which hung between the stars behind it, but it somehow hurt to stare at it. This, then, was the core of the mystery; something both plain and extraordinary. We crawl across the surface of this universe like ants, and each of these craft, switching through the Gateway's moment of loss and endless potentiality, is piloted by the will of a tariqua's conscious intelligence, which must glimpse those choices, then somehow emerge sane and entire at the other end of everything. . . .

Jalila's mind returned to the familiar scents and shapes of her dreamtent, and the sounds of the rain. The moment seemed to belong with those of the long-ago Season of Soft Rains. Downstairs, there were no voices. As she climbed out from her dreamtent, warily expecting to find the haramlek leaking and half-finished, Jalila was struck by an idea that the tariqua hadn't quite made plain to her; that a Gateway must push through *time* just as easily as it pushes through every other dimension . . . ! But the rooms of the haramlek were finely furnished, and her three mothers and the tariqua were sitting in the rainswept candlelight of the courtyard, waiting.

With any lesser request, Lya always quizzed Jalila before she would even consider granting it. So as Jalila sat before her mothers and tried not to tremble in their presence, she wondered how she could possibly explain her ignorance of this pure, boundless mystery.

But Lya simply asked Jalila if this was what she wanted—to be an acolyte of the Church of the Gateway.

"Yes."

Jalila waited. Then, not even, *are you sure?* They'd trusted her less than this when they'd sent her on errands into Al Janb. . . . It was still raining. The evening was starless and dark. Her three mothers, having hugged her, but saying little else, retreated to their own dreamtents and silences, leaving Jalila to say farewell to the tariqua alone. The heat of the old woman's hand no longer came as a surprise to Jalila as she helped her up from her chair and away from the sheltered courtyard.

"Well," the tariqua croaked, "that didn't seem to go so badly."

"But I know so *little!*" They were standing on the patio at the dripping edge of the night. Wet streamers of wind tugged at them.

"I know you wish I could tell you more, Jalila—but then, would it make any difference?"

Jalila shook her head. "Will you come with me?"

"Habara is where I must stay, Jalila. It is written."

"But I'll be able to return?"

"Of course. But you must remember that you can never return to the place you have left." The tariqua fumbled with her clasp, the one of a worm consuming its tail. "I want you to have this." It was made of black ivory, and felt as hot as the old woman's flesh as Jalila took it. For once, not really caring whether she broke her bones, she gave the small, bird-like woman a hug. She smelled of dust and metal, like an antique box left forgotten on a sunny windowledge. Jalila helped her out down the steps into the rainswept garden.

"I'll come again soon," she said, "to the qasr."

"Of course . . . there are many arrangements." The tariqua opened the dripping filigree door of her caleche and peered at her with those half-blind eyes. Jalila waited. They had stood too long in the rain already.

"Yes?"

"Don't be too hard on Kalal."

Puzzled, Jalila watched the caleche rise and turn away from the lights of the haramlek.

Jalila moved warily through the sharded glass of her own and her mothers' expectations. It was agreed that a message concerning her be sent, endorsed by the full long and ornate formal name of the tariqua, to the body that did indeed call itself the Church of the Gateway. It went by radio pulse to the spacestation in wide solar orbit that received Habara's rockets and was then passed on inside a vessel from *here* to *there* that was piloted by a tariqua. Not only that, but the message was destined for Ghezirah! Riding Robin up to the cliffs where, in this newly clear autumn air, under grey skies and tearing wet wind, she could finally see the waiting fuselage of that last golden rocket, Jalila felt confused and tiny, huge and mythic. It was agreed though, that for the sake of everyone—and not least Jalila herself, should she change her mind—that the word should remain that she was traveling out around the planet with Pavo onboard the *Endeavor*. In need of something to do when she wasn't brooding, and waiting for further word from (could it really be?) the sentient city of Ghezirah, Jalila threw herself into the listings and loadings and preparations with convincing enthusiasm.

"The hardest decisions, once made, are often the best ones."

"Compared to what you'll be doing, my little journey seems almost pointless."

"We love you so deeply."

Then the message finally came: an acknowledgement; an acceptance; a few (far too few, it seemed) particulars of the arrangements and permissions necessary for such a journey. All on less than half a sheet of plain two-dimensional printout.

Even Lya had started touching and hugging her at every opportunity.

Jalila ate lunch with Kalal and Nayra. She surprised herself and talked gaily at first of singing islands and sea-leviathans, somehow feeling that she was hiding little from her two best friends but the particular details of the journey she was undertaking. But Jalila was struck by the coldness that seemed to lie between these two supposed lovers. Nayra, perhaps sensing from bitter experience that she was once again about to be rejected, seemed near-tearful behind her dazzling smiles and the flirtatious blonde tossings of her hair, while Kalal seemed . . . Jalila had no idea how he seemed, but she couldn't let it end like this, and concocted some queries about the *Endeavor* so that she could lead him off alone as they left the bar. Nayra, perhaps fearing something else entirely, was reluctant to leave them.

"I wonder what it is that we've both done to her?" Kalal sighed as they watched her give a final sideways wave, pause, and then turn reluctantly down a sidestreet with a most un-Nayran duck of her lovely head.

They walked toward the harbor through a pause in the rain, to where the *Endeavor* was waiting.

"Lovely, isn't she?" Kalal murmured as they stood looking down at the long deck, then up at the high forest of spars. Pavo, who was developing her acquaintance with the ship's mind, gave them a wave from the bubble of the forecastle. "How long do you think your journey will take? You should be back by early spring, I calculate, if you get ahead of the icebergs. . . ."

Jalila fingered the brooch that the tariqua had given her, and which she had taken to wearing at her shoulder in the place where she had once worn the tideflower. It was like black ivory, but set with tiny white specks that loomed at your eyes if you held it close. She had no idea what world it was from, or of the substance of which it was made.

". . . You'll miss the winter here. But perhaps that's no bad thing. It's cold, and there'll be other Seasons on the ocean. And there'll be other winters. Well, to be honest, Jalila, I'd been hoping—"

"—Look!" Jalila interrupted, suddenly sick of the lie she'd been living. "I'm not going."

They turned and were facing each other by the harbor's edge. Kalal's strange face twisted into surprise, and then something like delight. Jalila thought that he was looking more and more like his father. "That's marvelous!" He clasped each of Jalila's arms and squeezed her hard enough to hurt. "It was rubbish, by the way, what I just said about winters here in Al Janb. They're the most magical, wonderful season. We'll have snowball fights together! And when Eid al-Fitr comes . . ."

His voice trailed off. His hands dropped from her. "What is it, Jalila?"

"I'm not going with Pavo on the *Endeavor*, but I'm going away. I'm going to Ghezirah. I'm going to study under the Church of the Gateway. I'm going to try to become a tariqua."

His face twisted again. "That witch—"

"—don't keep calling her that! You have no idea!"

Kalal balled his fists, and Jalila stumbled back, fearing for a moment that this wild, odd creature might actually be about to strike her. But he turned instead, and ran off from the harbor.

Next morning, to no one's particular surprise, it was once again raining. Jalila felt restless and disturbed after her incomplete exchanges with Kalal. Some time had also passed since the message had been received from Ghezirah, and the few small details it had given of her journey had become vast and complicated and frustrating in their arranging. Despite the weather, she decided to ride out to see the tariqua.

Robin's mood had been almost as odd as her mothers, recently, and she moaned and snickered at Jalila when she entered the stables. Jalila called back to her, and stroked her long nose, trying to ease her agitation. It was only when she went to check the harnesses that she realized that Abu was missing. Lya was in the haramlek, still finishing breakfast. It had to be Kalal who had taken her.

The swirling serraplated road. The black, dripping trees. The agitated ocean. Robin was starting to rust again. She would need more of Pavo's attention. But Pavo would soon be gone too. . . . The whole planet was changing, and Jalila didn't know what to make of anything, least of all what Kalal was up to, although the unasked-for borrowing of a precious mount, even if Abu had been virtually Kalal's all summer, filled her with a foreboding that was an awkward load, not especially heavy, but difficult to carry or put down; awkward and jagged and painful. Twice, now, he had turned from her and walked away with something unsaid. It felt like the start of some prophecy. . . .

The qasr shone jet-black in the teeming rain. The studded door, straining to overcome the swelling damp, burst open more forcefully than usual at Jalila's third knock, and the air inside swirled dark and empty. No sign of Abu in the place beyond the porch where Kalal would probably have hobbled him, although the floor here seemed muddied and damp, and Robin was agitated. Jalila glanced back, but she and her hayawan had already obscured the possible signs of another's presence. Unlike Kalal, who seemed to notice many things, she decided that she made a poor detective.

Cold air stuttered down the passageways. Jalila, chilled and watchful, had grown so used to this qasr's sense of abandonment that it was impossible to tell whether the place was now finally empty. But she feared that it was. Her thoughts and footsteps whispered to her that the tariqua, after ruining her life and playing with her expectations, had simply vanished into a puff of lost potentialities. Already disappointed, angry, she hurried to the high-ceilinged room set with blue and white tiles and found, with no great surprise, that the strewn cushions were cold and damp, the coffee lamp was unlit, and that the book through which that patient ant had crawled was now sprawled in a damp-leafed scatter of torn pages. There was no sign of the scarab. Jalila sat down, and listened to the wind's howl, the rain's ticking, wondering for a long time when it was that she had lost the ability to cry.

Finally, she stood up and moved toward the courtyard. It was colder today than it had ever been, and the rain had greyed and thickened. It gelled and dripped from the gutters in the form of something she supposed was called *sleet*, and which she decided as it splattered down her neck that she would hate forever. It filled the bowl of the fountain with mucus-like slush, and trickled sluggishly along the lines of the drains. The air was full of weepings and howlings. In the corner of the courtyard, there lay a small black heap.

Sprawled half in, half out of the poor shelter of the arched cloisters, more than ever like a flightless bird, the tariqua lay dead. Her clothes were sodden. All the furnace heat had gone from her body, although, on a day such as this, that would take no more than a matter of moments. Jalila glanced up through the sleet toward the black wet stone of the latticed mashrabiya from which she and Kalal had first spied on the old woman, but she was sure now that she was alone. People shrank incredibly when they were dead—even a figure as frail and old as this creature had been. And yet, Jalila found as she tried to move the tariqua's remains out of the rain, their spiritless bodies grew uncompliant; heavier and stupider than clay. The tariqua's face rolled up toward her. One side was pushed in almost unrecognizably, and she saw that a nearby nest of ants were swarming over it, busily tunneling out the moisture and nutrition, bearing it across the smeared paving as they stored up for the long winter ahead.

There was no sign of the scarab.

5.

This, for Jalila and her mothers, was the Season of Farewells. It was the Season of Departures.

There was a small and pretty onion-domed mausoleum on a headland overlooking Al Janb, and the pastures around it were a popular place for picnics and lovers' trysts in the Season of Summers, although they were scattered with tombstones. It was the ever-reliable Lya who saw to the bathing and shrouding of the tariqua's body, which was something Jalila could not possibly face, and to the sending out through the null-space between the stars of all the necessary messages. Jalila, who had never been witness to the processes of death before, was astonished at the speed with which everything was arranged. As she stood with the other mourners on a day scarfed with cloud, beside the narrow rectangle of earth within which what remained of the tariqua now lay, she could still hear the wind booming over the empty qasr, feel the uncompliant weight of the old woman's body, the chill speckle of sleet on her face.

It seemed as if most of the population of Al Janb had made the journey with the cortege up the narrow road from the town. Hard-handed fisherwomen. Gaudily dressed merchants. Even the few remaining aliens. Nayra was there, too, a beautiful vision of sorrow surrounded by her lesser black acolytes. So was Ibra. So, even, was Kalal. Jalila, who was acknowledged to have known the old woman better than anyone, said a few words that she barely heard herself over the wind. Then a priestess who had flown in specially from Ras pronounced the usual prayers about the soul rising on the arms of Munkar and Nakir, the blue and the black angels. Looking down into the ground, trying hard to think of the Gardens of Delight that the Almighty always promised her stumbling faithful, Jalila could only remember that dream of her own burial: the soil pattering on her face, and everyone she knew looking down at her. The tariqua, in one of her many half-finished tales, had once spoken to her of a world upon which no sun had ever shone, but which was nevertheless warm and bounteous from the core of heat beneath its surface, and where the people were all blind, and moved by touch and sound alone; it was a joyous place, and they were forever singing. Perhaps, and despite all the words of the Prophet, Heaven, too, was a place of warmth and darkness.

The ceremony was finished. Everyone moved away, each pausing to toss in a damp clod of earth, but leaving the rest of the job to be completed by a dull-minded robotic creature, which Pavo had had to rescue from the attentions of the younger children, who, all through the long Habaran summer, had ridden around on it. Down at their haramlek, Jalila's mothers had organized a small feast. People wandered the courtyard, and commented admiringly on the many changes and improvements they had made to the place. Amid all this, Ibra seemed subdued—a reluctant presence in his own body—while Kalal was nowhere to be seen at all, although Jalila suspected that, if only for the reasons of penance, he couldn't be far away.

Of course, there had been shock at the news of the tariqua's death, and Lya, who had now become the person to whom the town most often turned to resolve its difficulties, had taken the lead in the inquiries that followed. A committee of wisewomen was organized even more quickly than the funeral, and Jalila had been summoned and interrogated. Waiting outside in the cold hallways of Al Janb's municipal buildings, she'd toyed with the idea of keeping Abu's disappearance and her suspicions of Kalal out of her story, but Lya and the others had already spoken to him, and he'd admitted to what sounded like everything. He'd ridden to the qasr on Abu to remonstrate with the tariqua. He'd been angry, and his mood had been bad. Somehow, but only lightly, he'd pushed the old woman, and she had fallen badly. Then, he panicked. Kalal bore responsibility for his acts, it was true, but it was accepted that the incident was essentially an accident. Jalila, who had imagined many versions of Kalal's confrontation with the tariqua, but not a single one that seemed entirely real, had been surprised at how easily the people of Al Janb were willing to absolve him. She wondered if they would have done so quite so easily if Kalal had not been a freak—a man. And then she also wondered, although no one had said a single word to suggest it, just how much she was to blame for all of this herself.

She left the haramlek from the funeral wake and crossed the road to the beach. Kalal was sitting on the rocks, his back turned to the shore and the mountains. He didn't look around when she approached and sat down beside him. It was the first time since before the tariqua's death that they'd been alone.

"I'll have to leave here," he said, still gazing out toward the clouds that trailed the horizon.

"There's no reason—"

"—no one's asked me and Ibra to *stay*. I think they would, don't you, if anyone had wanted us to? That's the way you women work."

"We're not *you women*, Kalal. We're people."

"So you always say. And all Al Janb's probably terrified about the report they've had to make to that thing you're joining—the Church of the Gateway. Some big, powerful body, and—whoops—we've killed one of your old employees. . . ."

"Please don't be bitter."

Kalal blinked and said nothing. His cheeks were shining.

"You and Ibra—where will you both go?"

"There are plenty of other towns around this coast. We can use our boat to take us there before the ice sets in. We can't afford to leave the planet. But maybe in the Season of False Springs, when I'm a grown man and we've made some of the proper money we're always talking about making from harvesting the tideflowers—and when word's got around to everyone on this planet of what happened here. Maybe then we'll leave Habara." He shook his head and sniffed. "I don't know why I bother to say *maybe*. . . ."

Jalila watched the waves. She wondered if this was the destiny of all men; to wander forever from place to place, planet to planet, pursued by the knowledge of vague crimes that they hadn't really committed.

"I suppose you want to know what happened?"

Jalila shook her head. "It's in the report, Kalal. I believe what you said."

He wiped his face with his palms, studied their wetness. "I'm not sure I believe it myself, Jalila. The way she was, that day. That old woman—she always seemed to be expecting you, didn't she? And then she seemed to know. I don't understand quite how it happened, and I was angry, I admit. But she almost *lunged* at me. . . . She seemed to want to die. . . ."

"You mustn't blame yourself. *I* brought you to this, Kalal. I never saw . . ." Jalila shook her head. She couldn't say. Not even now. Her eyes felt parched and cold.

"I loved you, Jalila."

The worlds branched in a million different ways. It could all have been different. The tariqua still alive. Jalila and Kalal together, instead of the half-formed thing that the love they had both felt for Nayra had briefly been. They could have taken the *Endeavor* together and sailed this planet's seas; Pavo would probably have let them—but when, but where, but how? None of it seemed real. Perhaps the tariqua was right; there are many worlds, but most of them are poor, half-formed things.

Jalila and Kalal sat there for a while longer. The breathmoss lay not far off, darkening and hardening into a carpet of stiff grey. Neither of them noticed it.

For no other reason than the shift of the tides and the rapidly coming winter, Pavo, Jalila, and Kalal and Ibra all left Al Janb on the same morning. The days before were chaotic in the haramlek. People shouted and looked around for things and grew cross and petty. Jalila was torn between bringing everything and nothing, and after many hours of bag-packing and lip-chewing, decided that it could all be thrown out, and that her time would be better spent down in the stables, with Robin. Abu was there too, of course, and she seemed to sense the imminence of change and departure even more than Jalila's own hayawan. She had become Kalal's mount far more than she had ever been Lya's, and he wouldn't come to say goodbye.

Jalila stroked the warm felt of the creatures' noses. Gazing into Abu's eyes as she gazed back at hers, she remembered their rides out in the heat of summer. Being with Kalal then, although she hadn't even noticed it, had been the closest she had ever come to loving anyone. On the last night before their departure, Ananke cooked one of her most extravagant dinners, and the four women sat around the heaped extravagance of the table that she'd spent all day preparing, each of them wondering what to say, and regretting how much of these precious last times together they'd wasted. They said a long prayer to the Almighty, and bowed in the direction of Al'Toman. It seemed that, tomorrow, even the two mothers who weren't leaving Al Janb would be setting out on a new and difficult journey.

Then there came the morning, and the weather obliged with chill sunlight and a wind that pushed hard at their cloaks and nudged the *Endeavor* away from the harbor even before her sails were set. They all watched her go, the whole town cheering and waving as Pavo waved back, looking smaller and neater and prettier than ever as she receded. Without ceremony, around the corner from the docks, out of sight and glad of the *Endeavor*'s distraction, Ibra and Kalal were also preparing to leave. At a run, Jalila caught them just as they were starting to shift the hull down the rubbled slipway into the waves. *Breathmoss*; she noticed that Kalal had kept the name, although she and he stood apart on that final beach and talked as two strangers.

She shook hands with Ibra. She kissed Kalal lightly on the cheek by leaning stiffly forward, and felt the roughness of his stubble. Then the craft got stuck on the slipway, and they were all heaving to get her moving the last few meters into the ocean, until, suddenly, she was afloat, and Ibra was raising the sails, and Kalal was at the prow, hidden behind the tarpaulined weight of their belongings. Jalila only glimpsed him once more, and by then *Breathmoss* had turned to meet the stronger currents that swept outside the grey bay. He could have been a figurehead.

Back at the dock, her mothers were pacing, anxious.

"Where have you *been?*"

"Do you *know* what *time* it is?"

Jalila let them scald her. She *was* almost late for her own leaving. Although most of the crowds had departed, she'd half expected Nayra to be there. Jalila was momentarily saddened, and then she was glad for her. The silver craft that would take her to the rocketport smelled disappointingly of engine fumes as she clambered into it with the few other women and aliens who were leaving Habara. There was a loud bang as the hatches closed, and then a long wait while nothing seemed to happen, and she could only wave at Lya and Ananke through the thick porthole, smiling and mouthing stupid phrases until her face ached. The ferry bobbed loose, lurched, turned, and angled up. Al Janb was half gone in plumes of white spray already.

Then it came in a huge wave. That feeling of incompleteness, of something vital and unknown left irretrievably behind, which is the beginning of the Pain of Distance that Jalila, as a tariqua, would have to face throughout her long life. A sweat came over her. As she gazed out through the porthole at what little there was to see of Al Janb and the mountains, it slowly resolved itself into one thought. Immense and trivial. Vital and stupid. That scarab. She'd never asked Kalal about it, nor found it at the qasr, and the ancient object turned itself over in her head, sinking, spinning, filling her mind and then dwindling before rising up again as she climbed out, nauseous, from the ferry and crossed the clanging gantries of the spaceport toward the last huge golden craft, which stood steaming in the winter's air. A murder weapon?—but no, Kalal was no murderer. And, in any case, she was a poor detective. And yet . . .

The rockets thrust and rumbled. Pushing back, squeezing her eyeballs. There was no time now to think. Weight on weight, terrible seconds piled on her. Her blood seemed to leave her face. She was a clay-corpse. Vital elements of her senses departed. Then, there was a huge wash of silence. Jalila turned to look through the porthole beside her, and there it was. Mostly blue, and entirely beautiful: Habara, her birth planet. Jalila's hands rose up without her willing, and her fingers squealed as she touched the glass and tried to trace the shape of the greenish-brown coastline, the rising brown and white of the mountains of that huge single continent that already seemed so small, but of which she knew so little. Jewels seemed to be hanging close before her, twinkling and floating in and out of focus like the hazy stars she couldn't yet see. They puzzled her for a long time, did these jewels, and they were evasive as fish as she sought them with her weightlessly clumsy fingers. Then Jalila felt the salt break of moisture against her face, and realized what it was.

At long last, she was crying.

6.

Jalila had long been expecting the message when it finally came. At only one hundred and twenty standard years, Pavo was still relatively young to die, but she had used her life up at a frantic pace, as if she had always known that her time would be limited. Even though the custom for swift funerals remained on Habara, Jalila was able to use her position as a tariqua to ride the Gateways and return for the service. The weather on the planet of her birth was unpredictable as ever, raining one moment and then sunny the next, even as she took the ferry to Al Janb from the rocketport, and hot and cold winds seemed to strike her face as she stood on the dock's edge and looked about for her two remaining mothers. They embraced. They led her to their haramlek, which seemed smaller to Jalila each time she visited it, despite the many additions and extensions and improvements they had made, and far closer to Al Janb than the long walk she remembered once taking on those many errands. She wandered the shore after dinner, and searched the twilight for a particular shape and angle of quartz, and the signs of dark growth. But the heights of the Season of Storms on this coastline were ferocious, and nothing as fragile as breathmoss could have survived. She lay sleepless that night in her old room within her dreamtent, breathing the strong, dense, moist atmosphere with difficulty, listening to the sound of the wind and rain.

She recognized none of the faces but her mothers' of the people who stood around Pavo's grave the following morning. Al Janb had seemed so changeless, yet even Nayra had moved on—and Kalal was far away. Time was relentless. Far more than the wind that came in off the bay, it chilled Jalila to the bone. One mother dead, and her two others looking like the mahwagis she supposed they were becoming. *The Pain of Distance.* More than ever now, and hour by hour and day by day in this life that she had chosen, Jalila knew what the old tariqua had meant. She stepped forward to say a few words. Pavo's life had been beautiful and complete. She had passed on much knowledge about this planet to all womankind, just as she had once passed on her wisdom to Jalila. The people listened respectfully to Jalila, as if she were a priest. When the prayers were finished and the clods of earth had been tossed and the groups began to move back down the hillside, Jalila remained standing by Pavo's grave. What looked like the same old part-metal beast came lumbering up, and began to fill in the rest of the hole, lifting and lowering the earth with reverent, childlike care. Just as Jalila had insisted, and despite her mothers' puzzlement, Pavo's grave lay right beside the old tariqua's whom they had buried so long ago. This was a place that she had long avoided, but now that Jalila saw the stone, once raw and brittle, but now smoothed and greyed by rain and wind, she felt none of the expected agony. She traced the complex name, scrolled in naskhi script, which she had once found impossible to remember, but which she had now recited countless times in the ceremonials that the Church of the Gateway demanded of its acolytes. Sometimes, especially in the High Temple at Ghezirah, the damn things could go on for days. Yet not one member of the whole Church had seen fit to come to the simple ceremony of this old woman's burial. It had hurt her, once, to think that no one from offworld had come to her own funeral. But now she understood.

About to walk away, Jalila paused, and peered around the back of the gravestone. In the lee of the wind, a soft green patch of life was thriving. She stooped to examine the growth, which was thick and healthy, forming a patch more than the size of her two outstretched hands in this sheltered place. Breathmoss. It must have been here for a long time. Yet who would have thought to bring it? Only Pavo: only Pavo could possibly have known.

As the gathering of mourners at the haramlek started to peter out, Jalila excused herself and went to Pavo's quarters. Most of the stuff up here was a mystery to her. There were machines and nutrients and potions beyond anything you'd expect to encounter on such an out-of-the way planet. Things were growing. Objects and data needed developing, tending, cataloging, if Pavo's legacy was to be maintained. Jalila would have to speak to her mothers. But, for now, she found what she wanted, which was little more than a glass tube with an open end. She pocketed it, and walked back up over the hill to the cemetery, and said another few prayers, and bent down in the lee of the wind behind the old gravestone beside Pavo's new patch of earth, and managed to remove a small portion of the breathmoss without damaging the rest of it.

That afternoon, she knew that she would have to ride out. The stables seemed virtually unchanged, and Robin was waiting. She even snickered in recognition of Jalila, and didn't try to bite her when she came to introduce the saddle. It had been such a long time that the animal's easy compliance seemed a small miracle. But perhaps this was Pavo again; she could have done something to preserve the recollection of her much-changed mistress in some circuit or synapse of the hayawan's memory. Snuffling tears, feeling sad and exulted, and also somewhat uncomfortable, Jalila headed south on her hayawan along the old serraplate road, up over the cliffs and beneath the arms of the urrearth forest. The trees seemed different; thicker-leafed. And the birdsong cooed slower and deeper than she remembered. Perhaps, here in Habara, this was some Season other than all of those that she remembered. But the qasr reared as always — out there on the cliff face, and plainly deserted. No one came here now, but, like Robin, the door, at three beats of her fists, remembered.

Such neglect. Such decay. It seemed a dark and empty place. Even before Jalila came across the ancient signs of her own future presence — a twisted coathanger, a chipped plate, a few bleached and rotting cushions, some odd and scattered bits of Gateway technology that had passed beyond malfunction and looked like broken shells — she felt lost and afraid. Perhaps this, at last, was the final moment of knowing that she had warned herself she might have to face on Habara. The Pain of Distance. But at the same time, she knew that she was safe as she crawled across this particular page of her universe, and that when she did finally take a turn beyond the Gateways through which sanity itself could scarcely follow, it would be of her own volition, and as an impossibly old woman. The tariqua. Tending flowers like an old tortoise thrust out of its shell. Here, on a sunny, distant day. There were worse things. There were always worse things. And life was good. For all of this, pain was the price you paid.

Still, in the courtyard, Jalila felt the cold draft of prescience upon her neck from that lacy mashrabiya where she and Kalal would one day stand. The movement she made as she looked up toward it even reminded her of the old tariqua. Even her eyesight was not as sharp as it had once been. Of course, there were ways around that which could be purchased in the tiered and dizzy markets of Ghezirah, but sometimes it was better to accept a few things as the will of the

Almighty. Bowing down, muttering the *shahada*, Jalila laid the breathmoss upon the shaded stone within the cloister. Sheltered here, she imagined that it would thrive. Mounting Robin, riding from the qasr, she paused once to look back. Perhaps her eyesight really was failing her, for she thought she saw the ancient structure shimmer and change. A beautiful green castle hung above the cliffs, coated entirely in breathmoss; a wonder from a far and distant age. She rode on, humming snatches of the old songs she'd once known so well about love and loss between the stars. Back at the haramlek, her mothers were as anxious as ever to know where she had been. Jalila tried not to smile as she endured their familiar scolding. She longed to hug them. She longed to cry.

That evening, her last evening before she left Habara, Jalila walked the shore alone again. Somehow, it seemed the place to her where Pavo's ghost was closest. Jalila could see her mother there now, as darkness welled up from between the rocks; a small, lithe body, always stooping, turning, looking. She tried going toward her; but Pavo's shadow always flickered shyly away. Still, it seemed to Jalila as if she had been led toward something, for here was the quartz-striped rock from that long-ago Season of the Soft Rains. Of course, there was no breathmoss left, the storms had seen to that, but nevertheless, as she bent down to examine it, Jalila was sure that she could see something beside it, twinkling clear from a rockpool through the fading light. She plunged her hand in. It was a stone, almost as smooth and round as many millions of others on the beach, yet this one was worked and carved. And its color was greenish-grey.

The soapstone scarab, somehow thrust here to this beach by the storms of potentiality that the tariquas of the Church of the Gateway stirred up by their impossible journeyings, although Jalila was pleased to see that it looked considerably less damaged than the object she remembered Kalal turning over and over in his nervous hands as he spoke to her future self. Here at last was the link that would bind her through the pages of destiny, and, for a moment, she hitched her hand back and prepared to throw it so far out into the ocean that it would never be reclaimed. Then her arm relaxed. Out there, all the way across the darkness of the bay, the tideflowers of Habara were glowing.

She decided to keep it.

The Most Famous Little Girl in the World

NANCY KRESS

Nancy Kress began selling her elegant and incisive stories in the mid-seventies, and has since become a frequent contributor to Asimov's Science Fiction, The Magazine of Fantasy and Science Fiction, Sci Fiction, *and elsewhere. Her books include the novels* The Prince Of Morning Bells, The Golden Grove, The White Pipes, An Alien Light, Brain Rose, Oaths & Miracles, Stinger, Maximum Light, *the novel version of her Hugo and Nebula–winning story,* Beggars in Spain, *and a sequel,* Beggars and Choosers. *Her short work has been collected in* Trinity and Other Stories, The Aliens of Earth, *and* Beaker's Dozen. *Her most recent books are a sequence of novels,* Probability Moon, Probability Sun, *and* Probability Space. *Upcoming is a new novel,* Crossfire. *She has also won Nebula Awards for her stories "Out of All Them Bright Stars" and "The Flowers of Aulit Prison." She has had stories in our Second, Third, Sixth through Fifteenth, Eighteenth, and Nineteenth Annual Collections.*

In the intricate, poignant, and absorbing story that follows, she shows us how a few minutes can birth all the rest of your life . . . .

T he most famous little girl in the world stuck out her tongue at me. "These are all *my* Barbie dolls and you can't use them!"

I ran to Mommy. "Kyra won't share!"

"Kyra, dear," Aunt Julie said in that funny tight voice she had ever since IT happened, "share your new dolls with Amy."

"No, they're mine!" Kyra said. "The news people gave them all to me!" She tried to hold all the Barbie dolls, nine or ten, in her arms all at once, and then she started to cry.

She does that a lot now.

"Julie," Mommy said, real quiet, "she doesn't have to share."

"Yes, she does. Just because she's now some sort of . . . oh, God, I wish none of this had happened!" Then Aunt Julie was crying, too.

Grown-ups aren't supposed to cry. I looked at Aunt Julie, and then at stupid Kyra, still bawling, and then at Aunt Julie again. Nothing was right.

Mommy took me by the hand, led me into the kitchen, and sat me on her lap. The kitchen was all warm and there were chocolate-chip cookies baking, so that was good. "Amy," Mommy said, "I want to talk to you."

"I'm too big to sit on your lap," I said.

"No, you're not," Mommy said, and held me closer, and I felt better. "But you are big enough to understand what happened to Kyra."

"Kyra says *she* doesn't understand it!"

"Well, in one sense that's true," Mommy said. "But you understand some of it, anyway. You know that Kyra and you were in the cow field, and a big spaceship came down."

"Can I have a cookie?"

"They're not done yet. Sit still and listen, Amy."

I said, "I know all this! The ship came down, and the door opened, and Kyra went in and I was far away and I didn't." And then I called Mommy on the cell phone and she called 911 and people came running. Not Aunt Julie—Mommy was baby-sitting Kyra at Kyra's house. But police cars and firemen and ambulances. The cars drove right into the cow field, right through cow poop. If the cows hadn't been all bunched together way over by the fence, I bet the cars would have driven through the cows, too. That would have been kind of cool.

Kyra was in there a long time. The police shouted at the little spaceship, but it didn't open up or anything. I was watching from an upstairs window, where Mommy made me go, through Uncle John's binoculars. A helicopter came but before it could do anything, the spaceship door opened and Kyra walked out and policemen rushed forward and grabbed her. And then the spaceship just rose up and went away, passing the helicopter, and ever since everybody thinks Kyra is the coolest thing in the world. Well, I don't.

"I hate her, Mommy."

"No, you don't. But Kyra is getting all the attention and—" She sighed and held me tighter. It was nice, even though I'm too big to be held tight like that.

"Is Kyra going to go on TV?"

"No. Aunt Julie and I agreed to keep both of you off TV and magazines and whatever."

"Kyra's been on lots of magazines."

"Not by choice."

"Mommy," I said, because it was safe sitting there on her lap and the cookies smelled good, "what did Kyra do in the spaceship?"

Her chest got stiff. "We don't know. Kyra can't remember. Unless . . . unless she told you something, Amy?"

"She says she can't remember."

I twisted to look at Mommy's face. "So how come they still send presents? It was *last year*!"

"I know." Mommy put me on the floor and opened the oven to poke at the cookies. They smelled wonderful.

"And," I demanded, "how come Uncle John doesn't come home anymore?"

Mommy bit her lip. "Would you like a cookie, Amy?"

"Yes. How come?"

"Sometimes people just—"

"Are Aunt Julie and Uncle John getting a divorce? Because of *Kyra?*"

"*No.* Kyra is not responsible here, and you just remember that, young lady! I don't want you making her feel more confused than she is!"

I ate my cookie. Kyra wasn't confused. She was a cry-baby and a Barbie hog and I hated her. I didn't want her to be my cousin anymore.

What was so great about going into some stupid spaceship, anyway? Nothing. She couldn't even remember anything about it!

Mommy put her hands over her face.

2008

Whispers broke out all over the cafeteria. "That's her . . . her . . . her!"

Oh, shit. I bent my head over my milk. Last year the cafeteria used to serve fizzies and Coke and there were vending machines with candy and chips, but the new principal took all that out. He's a real bastard. Part of the "Clean Up America" campaign our new president is forcing down our throats, Dad said. Only he didn't say "forcing" because he thinks it's cool, like all the Carter Falls High parents do. Supervision for kids. School uniforms. Silent prayer. A mandatory class in citizenship. Getting expelled for everything short of *breathing*. It all sucks.

"It *is* her," Jack said. "I saw her picture online."

Hannah said, "What do you suppose they really did to her in that ship when she was a little kid?"

Angie giggled and licked her lips. She has a really dirty mind. Carter, who's sort of a goody-goody even though he's on the football team, said, "It's none of our business. And she was just a little kid."

"So?" Angie smirked. "You never heard of pedophiles?"

Hannah said, "Pedophile *aliens?* Grow up, Angie."

Jack said, "She's kind of cute."

"I thought you wanted a virgin, Jack," Angie said, still smirking.

Carter said, "Oh, give her a break. She just moved here, after all."

I watched Kyra walk uncertainly toward the cafeteria tables. The monitors were keeping a close eye on everybody. We have monitors everywhere, just like the street has National Guard everywhere. *Clean up America*, my ass. Kyra squinted; she's near-sighted and doesn't like to wear her contacts because she says they itch. I ducked lower over my milk.

Angie said, "Somebody told me Kyra Lunden is your cousin."

Everybody's head jerked to look at me. Damn that bitch Angie! Where had she heard that? Mom had promised me that nobody in school would know and Kyra wouldn't say anything! She and Aunt Julie had to move, Mom and Dad said, because Aunt Julie was having a rough time since the divorce and she needed to be close to her sister, and I should understand that. Well, I did, I guess, but not if Kyra blasted in and ruined everything for me. This was my school, not hers, I spent a lot of time getting into the good groups, the ones I was never part of in junior high, and no pathetic famous cousin was going to wreck that. She couldn't even dance.

Jack said, "Kyra Lunden is your cousin, Amy? Really?"

"No," I said. "Of course not."

Angie said, "That's not what I heard."

Carter said, "So it's just gossip? You can hurt people that way, Angie."

"God, Carter, don't you ever let up? Holier-than-thou!"

Carter mottled red. Hannah, who likes him even though Carter doesn't know it, said, "It's nice that some people at least try to be kind to others."

"Spit it in your soup, Hannah," Angie said.

Jack and Hannah exchanged a look. They really make the decisions for the group, and for a bunch of other groups, too. Angie's too stupid to realize that, or to realize that she's going to be oozed out. I don't feel sorry for her. She deserves it, even if being oozed is really horrible. You walk through the halls alone, and nobody looks directly at you, and people laugh at you behind your back because you can't even keep your own friends. Still, Angie deserves it.

Hannah looked at me straight, with that look Jack calls her "police interrogation gaze." "Amy . . . *is* Kyra Lunden your cousin?"

Kyra sat alone at one end of a table. A bunch of kids, the really cobra ones that run the V-R lab, sat at the other end, kind of laughing at her without laughing. I saw Eleanor Murphy, who was elected Queen of V-R Gala even though she's only a junior, give Kyra a long cool level look and then turn disdainfully away.

"No," I said, "I already told you. She's not my cousin. In fact, I never even met her."

2018

I stared at the villa with disbelief. Not at the guards—everywhere rich is guarded now, we're a nation of paranoids, perhaps not without reason. There seems no containing the lunatic terrorists, home-grown patriotic militias, White Supremacists and Black Equalizers, not to mention the run-of-the-mill gangs and petty drug lords and black-market smugglers. Plus, of course, the government's response to these, which sometimes seems to involve putting every single nineteen-year-old in the country out on the streets in camouflage—except, of course, those nineteen-year-olds who are already bespoken as lunatic terrorists, home-grown militia, White Supremacists, et al. The rest of us get on with our normal lives.

So the guards didn't surprise me—the villa did. It was a miniaturized replica of a Forbidden City palace—in *Minnesota*.

The chief guard caught me gaping at the swooping curved roof, the gilded archways, the octagonal pagoda. "Papers, please?"

I pulled myself together and looked professional, which is to say, not desperate. I was desperate, of course. But not even Kyra was going to know that.

"I am Madame Lunden's cousin," I said formally, "Amy Parker. Madame Lunden is expecting me."

Forget inscrutable Chinese—the guard looked as suspicious as if I'd said I was a Muslim Turkic Uighur. He examined me, he examined my identity card, he ran the computer match on my retina scan. I walked through metal detectors, explosive residue detectors, detector detectors. I was patted down thoroughly but not obscenely. Finally he let me through the inner gate, watching me all the way through the arch carved with incongruous peacocks and dragons.

Kyra waited in the courtyard beyond the arch. She wore an aggressively fashionable blue jumpsuit with a double row of tiny mirrors sewn down the front. Her hair was dyed bright blonde and cut in the sharp asymmetrical cut popularized by that Dutch on-line model, Brigitte. In the traditional Chinese courtyard, set with flowering plum trees in porcelain pots and a pool with golden carp, she looked either ridiculous or exotic, depending on your point of view. Point of view was why I was here. We hadn't seen each other in eight years.

"Hello, Amy," Kyra said in her low, husky voice.

"Hello, Kyra. Thank you for seeing me."

"My pleasure."

Was there mockery in her tone? Probably. If so, I'd earned it. "How is Aunt Julie?"

"I have no idea. She refuses to have any contact with me."

My eyes widened; I hadn't known that. I should have known that. A good journalist does her homework. Kyra smiled at me, and this time there was no mistaking the mockery. I had stepped in it, and oh God, I couldn't afford to ruin this interview. My job depended on it. Staff was being cut, and Paul had not axed me only because I said, with the desperation of fear, *Kyra Lunden is my cousin. I know she's refused all other interviews, but maybe . . .*

Kyra said, "Sit down, Amy. Shall we start? Which service do you write for, again?"

"*Times* online."

"Ah, yes. Well, what do you want to know?"

"I thought we'd start with some background. How did you and General Chou meet?"

"At a party."

"Oh. Where was the party held?" She wasn't going to help me at all.

Kyra crossed her legs. The expensive blue fabric of the jumpsuit draped becomingly. She looked fabulous; I wondered if she'd had any body work done. But, then, she'd always been pretty, even when she'd been ten and the most famous little girl in the world, blinking bewildered into the clunky TV equipment of sixteen years ago. My robocam drifted beside me, automatically recording us from the most flattering angles.

"The party was at Carol Perez's," Kyra said, naming a Washington hostess I'd only seen in the society programs. "I'd met Carol at Yale, of course. I met a lot of people at Yale."

Yes, she did. By college, Kyra had lost her shyness about what had happened to her when we were ten. She'd developed what sounded like a superb act—we had mutual friends—composed of mystery combined with notoriety. Subtly she reminded people that she had had an experience unique to all of mankind, never duplicated since, and that although she was reluctant to talk about it, yes, it was true that she was undergoing deep hypnosis and it was possible she might remember what actually happened . . .

By her junior year, she'd "remembered." Tastefully, shyly, nothing to make people label her a lunatic. The aliens were small and bipedal, they'd put a sort of helmet on her head and she'd watched holograms while, presumably, they recorded her reactions. . . . No, she couldn't remember any specifics. Not yet, anyway.

Yale ate it up. Intellectuals, especially political types, debated the aliens' intentions in terms of future United States policy. Artsy preppies' imaginations were stirred. Socialites decided that Kyra Lunden was an interesting addition to their parties. She was in.

"Carol's party was at their Virginia home," Kyra continued. "Diplomats, horse people, the usual. Ch'un-fu and I were introduced, and we both knew right away this could be something special."

I peered at her. Could she really be that naive? Chou Ch'un-fu had already had two American mistresses. The Han Chinese, Chou's party, and the United States were now allies, united in their actions against terrorists from the western part of China, the Muslim Turkic Uighurs, who were destabilizing China with their desperate war for independence. The Uighurs would lose. Everyone knew this, probably even the Uighurs. But until they did, they were blowing up things in Peking and Shanghai and San Francisco and London, sometimes in frantic negotiation for money, sometimes with arrogant political manifestos, sometimes, it seemed, out of sheer frustration. The carnage, even in a century used to it, could make a diplomat pale. General Chou was experienced in all this. Press drudges like me don't get insider data, but rumor linked him with some brutal actions. He maintained a home in Minnesota because it was easy to reach on the rocket flights over the pole.

And Kyra believed they had a "special" romantic relationship?

Incredibly, it seemed she did. As she talked about their meeting, about her life with Chou, I saw no trace of irony, of doubt, of simple confusion. Certainly not of anything approaching shame. I did detect anger, and that was the most intriguing thing about her demeanor. Who was she angry with? Chou? Her mother, that straight-laced paragon who had rejected her? The aliens? Fate?

She deflected all political questions. "Kyra, do you approve of the way the Chinese-American alliance is developing?"

"I approve of the way my life is developing." Tinkly laugh, undercut with anger.

We toured the villa, and she let me photograph everything, even their bedroom. Huge canopied bed, carved chests, jars of plum blossoms. Chou, or some PR spinner, had decided that a Chinese political partner should appear neither too austere nor too American. China's past was honored in her present, even as she looked toward the future — that was clearly the message I was to get out. I recorded everything. Kyra said nothing as we toured, usually not even looking at me. She combed her hair in front of her ornate carved mirror, fiddled with objects, sat in deep reverie. It was as if she'd forgotten I was there.

Kyra's silence broke only as she escorted me to the gate. Abruptly she said,

"Amy . . . do you remember Carter Falls High? The V-R Gala?"

"Yes," I said cautiously.

"You and I and our dates were in the jungle room. There was a virtual coconut fight. I tossed a coconut at you, it hit, and you pretended you didn't even see it."

"Yes," I said. Out of all the shunning I'd done to her in those horrible, terrified, cruel teenage years, she picked that to recall!

"But you did see it. You knew I was there."

"Yes. I'm sorry, Kyra."

"Don't worry about it," she said, with such a glittering smile that all at once I knew who her anger was directed at. She had given me this interview out of old family ties, or a desire to show off the superiority of our relative positions, or something, but she was angry at me. And always would be.

"I'm sorry," I said again, with spectacular inadequacy. Kyra didn't answer, merely turned and walked back toward her tiny Forbidden City.

My story was a great success. The *Times* ran it in flat-screen, 3-D, and V-R, and its access rate went off the charts. It was the first time anyone had been inside the Chou compound, had met the American girlfriend of an enigmatic general, had seen that particular lifestyle up close. Kyra's mysterious encounter with aliens sixteen years ago gave it a unique edge. Even those who hated the story—and there were many, calling it exploitative, immoral, decadent, symptomatic of this or that—noticed it. My message system nearly collapsed under the weight of congratulations, condemnations, job offers.

The next day, Kyra Lunden called a press conference. She denied everything. I had been admitted to the Chou villa, yes, but only as a relative, for tea. Our agreement had been no recorders. I had violated that, had recorded secretly, and furthermore had endangered Chinese-American relations. Kyra had tears in her eyes. The Chinese Embassy issued an angry denunciation. The State Department was not pleased.

The *Times* fired me.

Standing in my apartment, still surrounded by the masses of flowers that had arrived yesterday, I stared at nothing. The sickeningly sweet fragrances made me queasy. Wild ideas, stupid ideas, rioted in my head. I could sue. I could kill myself. Kyra really had been altered by the aliens. She was no longer human, but a V-R-thriller simulacrum of a human, and it was my duty to expose her.

All stupid. Only one idea was true.

Kyra had, after all these years, found a way to get even.

2027

In the second year of the war, the aliens came back.

David told me while I was bathing the baby in the kitchen sink. The twins, Lucy and Lem, were shrieking around the tiny apartment like a pair of banshees.

It was a crummy apartment, but it wasn't too far from David's job, and we were lucky to get it. There was a war on.

"The Blanding telescope has picked up an alien ship heading for Earth." David spoke the amazing sentence flatly, the way he speaks everything to me now. It was the first time he'd initiated conversation in two weeks.

I tightened my grip on Robin, a wriggler slippery with soap, and stared at him. "When . . . how . . ."

"It would be good, Amy, if you could ever finish a sentence," David said, with the dispassionate hypercriticism he brings these days to everything I say. It wasn't always like this. David wasn't always like this. *Depression*, his doctor told me, *unfortunately not responding to available medications*. Well, great, so David's depressed. The whole country's depressed. Also frightened and poor and gray-faced with anxiety about this unpredictable war's bio-attacks and Q-bomb attacks and EMP attacks, all seemingly random. We're all depressed, but not all of us take it out on the people we live with.

I said with great deliberation, "When did the Blanding pick up the aliens, and do the scientists believe they're the same aliens that came here in July of 2002?"

"Yesterday. Yes. You should either bathe Robin or not bathe him, instead of suspending a vital parental job in the middle like that." He left the room.

I rinsed Robin, wrapped him in a large, gray-from-age towel, and laid him on the floor. He smiled at me; such a sweet-natured child. I gave Lucy and Lem, too frenetic for sweetness, a hoarded cookie each, and turned on the Internet. The *Trumpeter* avatar, whom someone had designed to subtly remind viewers of Honest Abe Lincoln, was in the middle of the story, complete with what must have been hastily assembled archival footage from obsolete media.

There was the little pewter-colored spaceship in my Uncle John's cow field twenty-five years ago, and Kyra walking out with a dazed look on her small face. God—she'd been only a few years older than Lucy and Lem. There was the ship lifting straight up, passing the Army helicopter. That time, no watching telescopes or satellites had detected a larger ship, coming or going . . . either our technology was better now, or the aliens had a different game plan. Now the screen showed pictures from the Blanding, which looked like nothing but a dot in space until computers enhanced it, surrounded it with graphics, and "artistically rendered" various imaginary appearances and routes and speculations. In the midst of the hype given somberly in Abraham Lincoln's "voice," I gathered that the ship's trajectory would intersect with the same cow pasture as last time—unless, of course, it didn't—and would arrive at Earth in thirteen hours and seven minutes.

A Chinese general appeared on-screen, announcing in translation that China was prepared to shoot the intruder down.

"Mommy!" Lucy shrieked. "My cookie's gone!"

"Not now, honey."

"But Lem gots some of his cookie and he won't share!"

"In a minute!"

"But Mommy—"

The Internet abruptly cut out. The *Internet*.

Into the shocking, eerie silence came Lem's voice, marginally quieter than his sister's. "Mommy. I hear some sirens."

Three days of chaos. I had never believed panic — old-style Roman rioting in the streets, totally out of control, murderous panic — could happen in the United States, in gray cities like Rochester, New York. Yes, there were periodic race riots in Atlanta and looting spells in New York or war hysteria in San Francisco, but the National Guard quickly contained them in neighborhoods where violence was a way of life anyway. But this panic took over the whole city — Rochester — in a cold February and watching on the Internet, when a given site's coverage was up anyway, was to know a surreal horror. This was supposed to be America.

People were publicly beheaded on the lawns of the art museum, their breath frozen on the winter air a second before the blood leapt from their severed heads toward the camera. No one could say why they were being executed, or even if there was a reason. Buildings that the National Guard had protected from being bombed by Chinese terrorists were bombed by crazed Americans. Anyone Chinese-American, or appearing Chinese-American, or rumored to be Chinese-American, was so savagely assaulted that the fourteenth century would have been disgusted. A dead, mangled baby was thrown onto our fourth-floor fire escape, where it lay for the entire three days, pecked at by crows.

I kept the children huddled in the bathroom, which had no windows to shatter. Or see out of. The electricity went off, then on, then off for good. The heat ceased. David stayed by the living room window in case the building caught fire and we had no choice but to evacuate. Even during this horror he belittled and criticized: "If you'd had more food stockpiled, Amy, maybe the kids wouldn't have to have cereal again." "You never were any good at keeping them soothed and quiet."

Soothed and quiet. The crows on the fire escape had plucked out the dead infant's eyes.

Whenever Lucy, Lem, and Robin were finally asleep, I turned on the radio. The riots were coming under control. No, they weren't. The President was dead. No, he wasn't. The President had declared martial law. Massive bio-weapons had been unleashed in New York. No, in London. No, in Peking. The Chinese were behind these attacks. No, the Chinese were having worse riots than we were, their present chaos merging with their previous chaos of civil war. It was that civil war that had broken the American-Chinese alliance three years ago. And then during their civil upheavals, the Chinese had attacked Alaska. Maybe. Not even the international intelligence network was completely sure who'd released the bubonic-plague-carrying rats in Anchorage. But, announced the White House, the excesses of China had become too much for the Western world to stomach.

I didn't see how those excesses could be worse than this.

And then it was over. The Army prevailed. Or maybe the chaos, self-limiting as some plagues, just ran its course. Everyone left alive was immune. After another week, David and I — but not the kids — emerged from our building into the rubble to start rebuilding some sort of economic and communal existence. We never left the children alone, but even so David had found an isolated moment to say, resentment in every line of his body, "You're the one who wanted to have children. I don't know how much longer I can go on paying for your bad judgment."

It was then that I got the e-mail from Kyra.

"Why did you come?" Kyra asked me.

We faced each other in a federal prison in the Catskill Mountains northeast of New York City. The prison, built in 2022, was state-of-the-art. Nothing could break in or out, including bacteria, viruses, and some radiation. The Kyra sitting opposite me, this frightened woman, was actually two miles away, locked in some cell that probably looked nothing like the hologram of her I faced in the Visitors' Center.

I said slowly, "I can't say why I came." This was the truth. Or, rather, I could say but only with so much mixed motive that she would never understand. Because I had to get away from David for these two days. Because the childhood she and I shared, no matter how embittered by events, nonetheless looked to me now like Arcadia. Because I wanted to see Kyra humbled, in pain, as she had once put me. Because I had some insane idea, as crazy as the chaos we had lived through two weeks ago, that she might hold a key to understanding the inexplicable. Because.

She said, "Did you come to gloat?"

"In part."

"All right, you're entitled. Just help me!"

"To tell the truth, Kyra, you don't look like you need all that much help. You look well-fed, and bathed, and safe enough behind these walls." All more than my children were. "When did you land in here, anyway?"

"They put me in the second the alien ship was spotted." Her voice was bitter.

"On what charges?"

"No charges. I'm a detainee for the good of the state."

I said levelly, "Because of the alien ship or because you slept with the Chinese enemy?"

"They weren't the enemy then!" she said angrily, and I saw that my goading was pushing her to the point where she wanted to tell me to fuck off. But she didn't dare.

She didn't look bad. Well-fed, bathed, as I'd said. No longer pretty, however. Well, it had been nine hard years since I'd seen her. That delicate skin had coarsened and wrinkled much more than mine, as if she'd spent a lot of time in the sun. The hair, once blazingly blonde, was a dull brown streaked with gray. My Aunt Julie, her mother, had died five years ago in a traffic accident.

"Amy," she said, visibly controlling herself, "I'm afraid they'll just quietly keep me here forever. I don't have any ties with the Chinese anymore, and I don't know *anything* about or from that alien ship. I was just living quietly, under an alias, and then they broke in to my apartment in the middle of the night and cuffed me and brought me here."

"Why don't you contact General Chou?" I said cruelly.

Kyra only looked at me with such despair that I despised her. She was, had always been, a sentimentalist. I remembered how she'd actually thought that military monster loved her.

"Tell me what happened since 2018," I said, and watched her seize on this with desperate hope.

"After your news story came out and—I'm sorry, Amy, I . . ."

"Don't," I said harshly, and she knew enough to stop.

"I left Chun'fu, or rather he threw me out. It hit me hard, although I guess I was pretty much a fool not to think he'd react that way, not to anticipate—" She looked away, old pain fresh on her face. I thought that "fool" didn't begin to cover it.

"Anyway, I had some old friends who helped me. Most people wanted nothing to do with me, but a few loyal ones got me a new identity and a job on a lobster farm on Cape Cod. You know, I liked it. I'd forgotten how good it can feel to work outdoors. It was different from my father's dairy farm, of course, but the wind and the rain and the sea . . ." She trailed off, remembering things I'd never seen.

"I met a lobster farmer named Daniel and we lived together. I never told him my real name. We had a daughter, Jane . . ."

I thought I'd seen pain on her face before. I'd been wrong.

I said, and it came out gentle, "Where are Daniel and Jane now?"

"Dead. A bio-virus attack. I didn't think I could go on after that, but of course I did. People do. Are you married, Amy?"

"Yes. I hate him." I hadn't planned on saying that. Something in her pain drew out my own. Kyra didn't look shocked.

"Kids?"

"Three wonderful ones. Five-year-old twins and a six-month-old."

She leaned forward, like a plant hungry for sun. "What are their names?"

"Lucy. Lem. Robin. Kyra . . . how do you think I can help you?"

"Write about me. You're a journalist."

"No, I'm not. You ended my career." Did Kyra really not know that?

"Then call a press conference. Send data to the news outlets. Write letters to Congress. Just don't let me rot here indefinitely because they don't know what to do with me!"

She really had no idea how things worked. Still an innocent. I wasn't ready yet to tell her that all her anguish was silly. Instead I said, "Did the aliens communicate with you from their ship in some way?"

"Of course not!"

"The ship left, you know."

From her face, it was clear she didn't know. "They left?"

"Two weeks ago. Came no closer than the moon. If we had any sort of decent space program left, if anyone did, we might have tried to contact them. But they just observed us, or whatever, from that distance, then took off again."

"Fuck them to bloody hell! I wish we had shot them down!"

She had surprised me, with both the language—Kyra had always been a bit prissy, despite her sexual adventures—and the hatred. My surprise must have shown on my face.

"Amy," Kyra said, "they ruined my life. Without that abduction—" the word didn't really seem appropriate—"when I was ten, my parents would never have divorced. I wouldn't have been an outcast in school. I never would have met

Chou, or behaved like . . . and I certainly wouldn't be in this fucking prison now! They came here to ruin my life and they succeeded!"

"You take no responsibility for anything," I said evenly.

Kyra glared at me. "Don't you dare judge me, Amy. You with your beautiful living children and your life free of any suspicion that you're somehow deformed and dangerous because of a few childhood hours you can't even remember —"

" 'Can't remember'? What about the helmet and the flickering images and the observing aliens? Did you make those all up, Kyra?"

Enraged, she lunged forward to slap me. There was nothing there, of course. We were only virtually together. I stood to leave my half of the farce.

"Please, Amy . . . please! Say you'll help me!"

"You're a fool, Kyra. You learn nothing. Do you think the prison officials would be letting you have this 'meeting' with me if they were going to keep you here hidden away for good? Do you think you'd even have been permitted to send me e-mail? You're as good as out already. And when you are, try this time to behave as if you weren't still ten years old."

We parted in contempt and anger. I hoped to never see or hear from her again.

2047

The next time the aliens returned, they landed.

I was at JungleTime Playland with my granddaughter, Lehani. She loved JungleTime Playland. I was amused by it; in the long, long rebuilding after the war, V-R had finally reached the commercial level that Robin and Lucy and Lem, Lehani's father, had also played in. Of course, government applications of V-R and holo and AI were another matter, but I had nothing to do with those. I led a very small, contented life.

"I go Yung Lan,' " Lehani said, looking up at me with the shining, whole-hearted hope of the young on her small face. Every wish granted is paradise, every wish crushed is eternal disappointment.

"Yes, you can go into JungleLand, but we have to wait our turn, dear heart."

So she stood in line beside me, hopping from foot to foot, holding my hand. Nobody ever told me grandmotherhood was going to be this sweet.

When we finally reached the head of the line, I registered her, put the tag on her neck that would keep me informed of her every move as well as the most minute changes in her skin conductivity. If she got scared or inattentive, I would know it. No adults are allowed in Jungle Playland; that would spoil the thrill. Lehani grinned and ran through the virtual curtain. I accepted the map tuned to her tag and sat at a table in the lobby, surrounded by lines of older children registering for the other V-R playlands.

Sipping tea, I was checking my e-mail when the big lobby screen abruptly came on.

"News! News! An alien ship has been sighted moving toward Earth. Government sources say it resembles the ship that landed in Minnesota in 2002 and traveled as far as lunar orbit in 2027 but so far no —"

People erupted all around me. Buzzing, signaling for their children, and, in the case of one stupid woman, pointless shrieking. Under cover of the noise I comlinked Central, before the site was hopelessly jammed.

"Library," I keyed in. "Public Records, State of Maine. Data search."

"Search ready," the tiny screen said.

"Death certificate, first name Daniel, same date as death certificate, first name Jane, years 2020 through 2026."

"Searching."

Children began to pour out of the playlands, most resentful at having their V-R time interrupted. Kyra had never told me Daniel's last name. Nor did I have any idea what name she was using now. But if she simply wanted to pass unnoticed among ordinary people, his name would do, and Kyra had always been sentimental. The government, of course, would know exactly where she was, but they would know that no matter what name she used or what paper trails she falsified. Her DNA was on record. The press, too, could track her down if they decided to take the trouble. The alien landing meant they would take the trouble.

My handheld displayed, "Daniel Ethan Parmani, died June 16, 2025, age forty-two, and Jane Julia Parmani, died June 16, 2025, age three."

"Second search. United States. Locate Kyra Parmani, ages—" What age might Kyra think she could pass for? In prison, twenty years ago, she had looked far older than she was. "Ages fifty through seventy."

"Searching."

Lehani appeared at the JungleLand door, looking furious. She spied me and ran over. "Lady sayed I can't play!"

"I know, sweetie. Come sit on Grandma's lap."

She climbed onto me, buried her head in my shoulder, and burst into angry tears. I peered around her to see the handheld.

"Six matches." It displayed them. Six? With a name like "Parmani" coupled with one like "Kyra"? I sighed and shifted Lehani's weight.

"Call each of them in turn."

Kyra was the second match. She answered the call herself, her voice unconcerned. She hadn't heard. "Hello?"

"Kyra. It's Amy, your cousin. Listen, they've just spotted an alien ship coming in. They'll be looking for you again." Silence on the other end. "Kyra?"

"How did you find me?"

"Lucky guesswork. But if you want to hide, from the feds or the press . . ." They might put her in jail again, and who knew this time when she would get out? At the very least, the press would make her life, whatever it was now, a misery. I said, "Do you have somewhere to go? Some not-too-close-but-perfectly-trusted friend's back bedroom or strange structure in a cowfield?"

She didn't laugh. Kyra never had had much of a sense of humor. Not that this was an especially good time for joking.

"Yes, Amy. I do. Why are you warning me?"

"Oh, God, Kyra, how do I answer that?"

Maybe she understood. Maybe not. She merely said, "All right. And thanks. Amy . . ."

"What?"

"I'm getting married again. I'm happy."

That was certainly like her: blurting out the personal that no one had asked about. For a second I, too, was the old Amy, bitter and jealous. I had not remarried since my terrible divorce from David, had not even loved any one again. I suspected I never would. But the moment passed. I had Robin and Lem and Lehani and, intermittently when she was in the country, Lucy.

"Congratulations, Kyra. Now get going. They can find you in about forty seconds if they want to, you know."

"I know. I'll call you when this is all over, Amy. Where are you?"

"Prince George's County, Maryland. Amy Suiter Parker. Bye, Kyra." I broke the link.

"Who on link?" Lehani demanded, apparently having decided her tears were not accomplishing anything.

"Somebody Grandma knew a long time ago, dear heart. Come on, let's go home, and you can play with Mr. Grindle's cat."

"Yes! Yes!"

It is always so easy to distract the uncorrupted.

The alien ship parked itself in lunar orbit for the better part of three days. Naturally we had no one up there; not a single nation on Earth had anything you could call a space program anymore. But there were satellites. Maybe we communicated with the aliens, or they with us, or maybe we tried to destroy them, or entice them, or threaten them. Or all of the above, by different nations with different satellites. Ordinary citizens like me were not told. And of course the aliens could have been doing anything with their ship: sampling broadcasts, scrambling military signals, seeding clouds, sending messages to true believers' back teeth. How would I know?

On the second day, three agents from People's Safety Commission, the latest political reincarnation of that office, showed up to ask me about Kyra's whereabouts. I said, truthfully, that I hadn't seen her in twenty years and had no idea where she was now. They thanked me politely and left. News cams staked out her house, a modest foamcast building in a small Pennsylvania town, and they dissected her current life, but they never actually found her, so it made a pretty lackluster story.

After three days of lunar orbit, a small alien craft landed on the upland savanna of East Africa.

Somehow it sneaked past whatever surveillance we had as if it didn't exist. The ship set down just beyond sight of a Kikuyu village. Two small boys herding goats spotted it, and one of them went inside.

By the time the world learned of this, from a call made on the village's only comlink, the child was already inside the alien ship. News people and government people raced to the scene. East Africa was in its usual state of confused civil war, incipient drought, and raging disease. The borders were theoretically sealed. This made no difference whatsoever. Gunfire erupted, disinformation spread, ultimata were issued. The robocams went on recording.

"Does it look the same as the ship you saw?" Lem said softly, watching the news beside me. His wife Amalie was in the kitchen with Lehani. I could hear them laughing.

"It looks the same." Forty-five years fell away and I stood in Uncle John's cow field, watching Kyra walk into the pewter-colored ship and walk out the most famous little girl in the world.

Lem said, "What do you think they want?"

I stared at him. "Don't you think I've wondered that for four and a half decades? That everyone has wondered that?"

Lem was silent.

A helicopter appeared in the sky over the alien craft. That, too, was familiar— until it set down and I grasped its huge size. Troops began pouring out, guns were leveled, and orders barked. A newsman, maybe live but probably virtual, said, "We're being ordered to shut down all reporting on this—" He disappeared.

A black cloud emanated from the helicopter, but not before a robocam had shown more equipment being off-loaded. Lem said, "My God, I think that's a bombcase!" Through the black cloud ripped more gunfire.

Then no news came through at all.

The stories conflicted wildly, of course. At least six different agencies, in three different countries, were blamed. A hundred and three people died at the scene, and uncounted more in the senseless riots that followed. One of the dead was the second little boy that had witnessed the landing.

The first child went up with the ship. It was the only picture that emerged after the government erected visual and electronic blockage: the small craft rising unharmed above the black cloud, ascending into the sky and disappearing into the bright African sunlight.

The Kikuyu boy was released about a hundred miles away, near another village, but it was a long time before ordinary people learned that.

Kyra never called me after the furor had died down. I searched for her, but she was more savvy about choosing her aliases. If the government located her, and I assumed they did, no one informed me.

Why would they?

Sometimes the world you want comes too late.

It was not really the world anyone wanted, of course. Third world countries, especially but not exclusively in Africa, were still essentially ungovernable. Fetid urban slums, disease, and terror from local warlords. Daily want, brutality, and suffering, all made orders of magnitude worse by the lunatic compulsion to genocide. Much of the globe lives like this, with little hope of foreseeable change.

But inside the United States's tightly guarded, expensively defended borders, a miracle had occurred. Loaves from fishes, something for nothing, the free lunch there ain't supposed to be one of. Nanotechnology.

It was still an embryonic industry. But it had brought burgeoning prosperity. And with prosperity came the things that aren't supposed to cost money but always do: peace, generosity, civility. And one more thing: a space program, the cause of all the news agitation I was pointedly not watching.

"It's not fair to say that nano brought civility," Lucy protested. She was back from a journalism assignment in Sudan that had left her gaunt and limping, with half her hair fallen out. Lucy didn't volunteer details and I didn't ask. From the look in her haunted eyes, I didn't think I could bear to hear her answers.

"Civility is a by-product of money," I said. "Starving people are not civil to each other."

"Sometimes they are," she said, looking at some painful memory I could not imagine.

"Often?" I pressed.

"No. Not often." Abruptly Lucy left the room.

I have learned to wait serenely until she's ready to return to me, just as she has learned to wait, less serenely, until she is ready to return to those parts of the world where she makes her living. My daughter is too old for what she does, but she cannot, somehow, leave it alone. Injured, diseased, half bald, she always goes back.

But Lucy is partly right. It isn't just America's present riches that have led to her present civility. This decade's culture — optimistic, tolerant, fairly formal — is also a simple backlash to what went before. Pendulums swing. They cannot not swing.

While I waited for Lucy, I returned to my needlepoint. Now that nano has begun to easily make us anything, things that are hard to make are back in fashion. My eyes are too old for embroidery or even petit point, but gros point I can do. Under my fingers, roses bloomed on a pair of slippers. A bird flew to the tree beside me, lit on a branch, and watched me solemnly.

I'm still not used to birds in the house. But, then, I'm not used to this house of my son's, either. All the rooms open into an open central courtyard two stories high. Atop the courtyard is some sort of invisible shield that I don't understand. It keeps out cold and insects, and it can be adjusted to let rain in or keep it out. The shield keeps in the birds who live here. What Lem has is a miniature, climate-controlled, carefully landscaped, indoor Eden. The bird watching me was bright red with an extravagant gold tail, undoubtedly genetically engineered for health and long life. Other birds glow in the dark. One has what looks like blue fur.

"Go away," I told it. I like the fresh air; the genemod birds give me the creeps.

When Lucy returned, someone was with her. I put down my needlework, pasted on a smile, and prepared to be civil. The visitor used a walker, moving very slowly. She had sparse gray hair. I let out a little cry.

I hadn't even known Kyra was still alive.

"Mom, guess who's here! Your cousin Kyra!"

"Hello, Amy," Kyra said, and her voice hadn't changed, still low and husky.

"Where . . . how did you . . ."

"Oh, you were always easy to find, remember? I was the difficult one to locate."

Lucy said, "Are they looking for you now, Kyra?"

Kyra. Lucy was born too soon for the new civil formality. Lem's and Robin's children would have called her Ms. Lunden, or ma'am.

"Oh, probably," Kyra said. "But if they show up, child, just tell them my hearing implant failed again." She lowered herself into a chair, which obligingly curved itself around her. That still gives me the creeps, too, but Kyra didn't seem to mind.

We stared at each other, two ancient ladies in comfortable baggy clothing, and I suddenly saw the twenty-six-year-old she had been, gaudily dressed mistress to an enemy general. Every detail was sharp as winter air: her blue jumpsuit with a double row of tiny mirrors sewn down the front, her asymmetrical hair the color of gold-leaf. That happens to me more and more. The past is so much clearer than the present.

Lucy said, "I'll go make some tea, all right?"

"Yes, dear, please," I said.

Kyra smiled. "She seems like a good person."

"Too good," I said, without explanation. "Kyra, why are you here? Do you need to hide again? This probably isn't the best place."

"No, I'm not hiding. They're either looking for me or they're not, but I think not. They've got their hands full, after all, up at Celadon."

Celadon is the aggressively new international space station. When I first heard the name, I'd thought, why name a space station after a *color*? But it turns out that's the name of some famous engineer who designed the nuclear devices that make it cheap to hoist things back and forth from Earth to orbit. They've hoisted a lot of things. The station is still growing, but it already houses one hundred seventy scientists, techies, and administrators. Plus, now, two aliens.

They appeared in the solar system three months ago. The usual alarms went off, but there was no rioting, at least not in the United States. People watched their children more closely. But we had the space station now, a place for the aliens to contact, without actually coming to Earth. And maybe the New Civility (that's how journalists write about it, with capital letters) made a difference as well. I couldn't say. But the aliens spent a month or so communicating with Celadon, and then they came aboard, and a few selected humans went aboard their mother ship, and the whole thing began to resemble a tea party fortified with the security of a transnational bank vault.

Kyra was watching me. "You aren't paying any attention to the aliens' return, are you, Amy?"

"Not really." I picked up my needlepoint and started to work.

"That's a switch, isn't it? It used to be you who were interested in the political and me who wasn't."

It seemed an odd thing to say, given her career, but I didn't argue. "How are you, Kyra?"

"Old."

"Ah, yes. I know that feeling."

"And your children?"

I made myself go on stitching. "Robin is dead. Cross-fire victim. His ashes are buried there, under that lilac tree. Lucy you saw. Lem and his wife are fine, and their two kids, and my three great-grandchildren."

Kyra nodded, unsurprised. "I have three step-children, two step-grandchildren. Wonderful kids."

"You married again?"

"Late. I was sixty-five, Bill sixty-seven. A pair of sagging gray arthritic honeymooners. But we had ten good years, and I'm grateful for them."

I knew what she meant. At the end, one was grateful for all the good years, no matter what their aftermath. I said, "Kyra, I still don't know why you're here. Not that you're not welcome, of course, but why now?"

"I told you. I wanted to hear what you thought of the aliens' coming to Celadon."

"You could have comlinked."

She didn't say anything to that. I stitched on. Lucy brought tea, poured it, and left again.

"Amy, I really want to know what you think."

She was serious. It mattered to her. I put down my teacup. "All right. On Mondays I think they're not on Celadon at all and the government made the whole thing up. On Tuesdays I think that they're here to do just what it looks like: make contact with humans, and this is the first time it looks safe to them. The other three times we met them with soldiers and bombs and anger because they landed on our planet. Now there's a place to interact without coming too close, and we aren't screeching at them in panic, and they were waiting for that in order to establish trade and/or diplomatic relations. On Wednesdays I think they're worming their way into our confidence, gathering knowledge about our technology, in order to enslave us or destroy us. On Thursdays I think that they're *aliens*, so how can we ever hope to understand their reasons? They're not human. On Fridays I hope, and on Saturdays I despair, and on Sundays I take a day of rest."

Kyra didn't smile. I remembered that about her: she didn't have much of a sense of humor. She said, "And why do you think they took me and that Kikuyu boy into their ships?"

"On Mondays—"

"I'm serious, Amy!"

"Always. All right, I guess they just wanted to learn about us in person, so they picked out two growing specimens and knocked them out so they could garner all the secrets of our physical bodies for future use. They might even have taken some of your DNA, you know. You'd never miss it. There could be small culture-grown Kyras running around some distant planet. Or not so small, by now."

But Kyra wasn't interested in the possibilities of genetic engineering. "I think I know why they came."

"You do?" Once she had told me that the aliens came just to destroy her life. But that kind of hubris was for the young.

"Yes," Kyra said. "I think they came without knowing the reason. They just came. After all, Amy, if I think about it, I can't really say why I did half the things in my life. They just seemed the available course of action at the time, so I did them. Why should the aliens be any different? Can you say that you really know why you did all the things in your life?"

Could I? I thought about it. "Yes, Kyra. I think I can, pretty much. That's not to say my reasons were good. But they were understandable."

She shrugged. "Then you're different from me. But I'll tell you this: Any plan the government makes to deal with these aliens won't work. You know why? Because it will be one plan, one set of attitudes and procedures, and pretty soon things will change on Earth or on Celadon or for the aliens, and then the plan won't work anymore and still everybody will try desperately to make it work. They'll try to stay in control, and *nobody can control anything important.*"

She said this last with such intensity that I looked up from my needlepoint. She meant it, this banal and obvious insight that she was offering as if it were cutting edge knowledge.

And yet, it was cutting edge, because each person had to acquire it painfully, in his or her own way, through loss and failure and births and plagues and war and victories and, sometimes, a life shaped by an hour in an alien spaceship. All fodder for the same trite, heart-breaking conclusion. Everything old is new again.

And yet—

Sudden tenderness washed over me for Kyra. We had spent most of our lives locked in pointless battle. I reached over to her, carefully so as not to aggravate my creaky joints, and took her hand.

"Kyra, if you believe you can't control anything, then you won't try for control, which of course guarantees that you end up not controlling anything."

"Never in my whole life have I been able to make a difference to—*what the fuck is that!*"

The furry blue bird had landed on her head, its feet tangling briefly in her hair. "It's one of Lem's genemod birds," I said. "It's been engineered to have no fear of humans."

"Well, *that's* a stupid idea!" Kyra said, swatting at it with surprising vigor. The bird flew away. "If that thing lands on me again, I'll strangle it!"

"Yes," I said, and laughed, and didn't bother to explain why.

The passenger

PAUL J. MCAULEY

Born in Oxford, England, in 1955, Paul J. McAuley now makes his home in London. A professional biologist for many years, he sold his first story in 1984, and has gone on to be a frequent contributor to Interzone, as well as to markets such as Asimov's Science Fiction, Amazing, The Magazine of Fantasy and Science Fiction, Skylife, The Third Alternative, When the Music's Over, and elsewhere.

McAuley is considered to be one of the best of the new breed of British writers (although a few Australian writers could be fit in under this heading as well) who are producing that brand of rigorous hard science fiction with updated modern and stylistic sensibilities that is sometimes referred to as "radical hard science fiction," but he also writes Dystopian sociological speculations about the very near future. He also is one of the major young writers who is producing that revamped and retooled widescreen Space Opera that has sometimes been called the New Baroque Space Opera, reminiscent of the Superscience stories of the 1930s taken to an even higher level of intensity and scale. His first novel, Four Hundred Billion Stars, won the Philip K. Dick Award, and his acclaimed novel Fairyland won both the Arthur C. Clarke Award and the John W. Campbell Award in 1996. His other books include the novels Of The Fall, Eternal Light, and Pasquale's Angel, Confluence—a major trilogy of ambitious scope and scale set ten million years in the future, comprised of the novels Child of the River, Ancient of Days, and Shrine of Stars—and Life on Mars. His short fiction has been collected in The King of the Hill and Other Stories and The Invisible Country, and he is the coeditor, with Kim Newman, of an original anthology, In Dreams. His stories have appeared in our Fifth, Ninth, Thirteenth, and Fifteenth through Nineteenth Annual Collections. His most recent books are two new novels, The Secret of Life and Whole Wide World.

Here he takes us along with a crew salvaging spaceships in the aftermath of an interplanetary war who run into some life-or-death problems of a kind that they never expected to face . . .

The sky was full of ships.

Sturdy little scows that were mostly motor; lumpy intrasystem shuttles, the work-horses of space; the truncated cones of surface-to-orbit gigs; freighters that, stripped of their cargo pods, looked like the unclad skeletons of skyscrapers; even an elegant clipper, a golden arc like the crescent moon of a fairy-tale illustration. More than a hundred ships spread in a rough sphere a thousand kilometers in diameter, in the Lagrangian point sixty degrees of arc ahead of Dione. All of them hulks. Combat wreckage. Spoils of war waiting to be rendered into useful components, rare metals, and scrap.

From the viewports of the battered hab-modules of the wrecking gangs, hung in the midst of this junkyard Sargasso, four or five ships were always visible, framed at various angles against starry space. Only a few showed obvious signs of damage. There was a passenger shuttle whose cylindrical lifesystem had been unseamed by carefully placed bomblets, a kamikaze act of sabotage that had killed the fleeing government of Baghdad, Enceladus. There was a freighter wrecked by a missile strike, its frame peeled back and half-melted, like a Daliesque flower. A dozen tugs, converted into singleship fighters, had been drilled by X-ray lasers or holed by smart rocks. But most were simply brain dead, their cybernetic nervous systems zapped by neutron lasers, microwave bursts or emp mines during the investment of the Saturn system. Salvage robots had attached themselves to these hulks and pushed them into low-energy orbits that had eventually intersected that of Dione. Their cargo pods had been dismounted, the antihydrogen and antilithium had been removed from their motors, and now, two hundred days after the end of the Quiet War, they awaited the attention of the wrecking gangs.

The men and women of the gangs were all outers recruited by Symbiosis, the Earth-based transnat that had won the auction for salvaging and rendering these casualties of the Quiet War. They were engineers, General Labor Pool grunts, and freefall construction mechanics on thirty-days-on/thirty-days-off shifts under minimum wage contracts, and pleased to get the work; the Quiet War had wrecked the economy of the Outer System colonies, and seventy percent of the population depended upon the charity of the victorious Three Powers Alliance.

Maris Delgado, foreperson of Wrecking Gang #3, was supporting her mother and father, and her brother and his family back in Athens, Tethys. Every cent of her wages, after deductions, went to them. Maris was a practical, gruff, level-headed woman. She preferred to put her faith in machines rather than people. You could always flange up a rough solution to a machine's problems, but people were unfathomable and all too often untrustworthy. Her approach to running her gang was pragmatic: do what Symbiosis asked, no more and no less. Her family depended upon her, and she wanted to get the job done with the minimum of fuss. She took no part in the gossip and rumors the wrecking gangs exchanged by clandestine laser blink whenever they were out of the line-of-sight of the Symbiosis supervisor's ship. She poured scorn on the rumors of ghosts and hauntings, of curses worked by dying crews, of hatches mysteriously locked or unlocked, machinery suddenly starting up or breaking down. She ridiculed the vivid stories that Ty Siriwardene, the youngest member of her gang, liked to conjure up, told him that the last thing you needed on a job like this was an imagination.

Not even on their latest assignment, which was a shuttle that Maris had helped to build a couple of years before the war, when she had been working in the orbital shipyards of Tethys. Ty said that the coincidence was spooky; Maris said that it was ridiculous to make anything of it. She'd worked fifteen years at the yards—all her working life. It was a statistical inevitability that sooner or later she'd find herself taking apart a ship that she had once helped assemble, and she was determined to treat it like any other.

Maris did the initial survey of the hulk with Somerset. It was grossly intact, and its lifesystem still pressurized; the only potential problem was the thick black crust growing around the motor, a vacuum organism that was probably subsisting on water vapor leaking from the attitude-control tanks. Somerset, who had been a data miner before getting religion, plugged a slate into the shuttle's dead computer and pulled the manifest from the memory core. The shuttle had been carrying a single passenger and miscellaneous agricultural supplies; it seemed likely that the vacuum organism had escaped from one of the cargo pods before they had been removed.

For once, Maris and Somerset didn't have to search for the crew; the Symbiosis workers who had uncoupled the cargo pods and decommissioned the motor had already done that. The three bodies, still wearing sealed pressure suits, were huddled together in an equipment locker around some kind of impedance heater lashed up from cable and an exhausted fuel cell. The locker, the heater, and the p-suits had been the crew's last stand against the inevitable after the shuttle's systems had been fritzed by an emp mine and the stricken lifesystem had cooled to minus two hundred degrees centigrade. One by one, they had succumbed to hypothermia's deep sleep, and their corpses had frozen solid.

Watched by one of the half-dozen drones that for some reason were floating about the lifesystem, Maris and Somerset identified each of the bodies, collected and documented their personal effects, and sealed them into coffins that Symbiosis would with impersonal charity deliver to surviving relatives. They were one body short—the passenger. Maris assumed that the woman had wandered off to die on her own in some obscure spot not discovered by the Symbiosis workers; the wrecking gang would find her frozen corpse by and by, when they stripped out the lifesystem.

Once the coffins had been sent on their way, the other two members of the wrecking gang came aboard. They rigged lights and a power supply, collected drifting trash, vented the lifesystem, and generally made the hulk safe, so that they could begin the second stage of the salvage operation, stripping out gold and silver, iridium and germanium, and all the other rare metals from the shuttle's control systems.

It was Ty Siriwardene who noticed that the shuttle's foodmaker had been dismantled, and that its yeast base block was missing. He told Maris about it at the end of the shift, back in the hab-module; she suggested that it couldn't be due to one of his famous ghosts, because it was well known that ghosts didn't eat.

"*Something* took the stuff," Ty said stubbornly. "I'm not making this up."

He was a raggedy young man, scrawny and slight in his grubby blue suitliner, thick black tattoos squirming over his shaven scalp. He chewed gum incessantly; he was chewing it now, a tendon jumping on his neck, as he locked eyes with Maris.

"Maybe the crew ate the yeast because the maker couldn't synthesize food without power," Maris said.

Ty popped gum. "If they just wanted the yeast, why did they dismantle the maker? And why would they have eaten the yeast when they hardly touched the reserves of food paste in their suits?"

"They preferred yeast," Maris said curtly. She was tired. She had been working for twelve hours straight. She was looking forward to a shower and a long sleep. She didn't have time for Ty's spooky shit. He wanted her to contradict him, she realized, so that he could keep his silly notions alive in a pointless argument. She said, "We've got just one week left before we're all rotated rockside. Let it go, Ty, unless you want to write up a report for Barrett."

Ty didn't write it up, of course. The supervisor, James Lo Barrett, was considered a joke amongst the wrecking gangs: an inflexible bureaucrat who was working off some kind of demerit at this obscure posting, an incomer who hardly ever left his ship, who had no idea of the practical difficulties of the work. But Ty didn't let it go, either. The next day, midshift, he swam up to Maris and pulled a patch cord from his p-suit's utility belt. Maris sighed, but took the free end of the cord and plugged it in.

"Something's screwy," Ty said. "I was outside, checking the service compartment? Turns out all the fuel cells in the back-up power system are gone."

"The crew moved them inside after their ship was crippled," Maris said. "We found one cell right by their bodies."

"Yeah, but where are the *other* three?"

"They'll turn up," Maris said. "Forget it, and get back to work."

They were floating head-to-head in the narrow shaft that ran through the middle of the shuttle's tiny lifesystem, where Maris was feeding circuitry into the squat cube of a portable refinery that boiled off metals and separated and collected them by laser chromatography. Ty's gaze was grabby and nervous behind his gold-filmed visor. He really was spooked. He said, "You don't feel it? It's not just that something weird happened here. It's as if something's still here. A presence, a ghost."

"That would be Barrett. You know he's always on my tail to keep you guys on schedule. We have fifteen days to strip this hulk. If we fall behind, he'll dock our pay. Can you afford that, Ty? *I* can't. I have people who depend on me. Forget about the fuel cells. It's one of those mysteries that really isn't worth thinking about. It's nothing. Let me hear you say that."

"It's *something*," Ty said, with a flicker of insolence. He pulled the patch cord, spun head-over-heels, and shot away down the long corridor.

"And another thing," Maris said over the common radio channel, as Ty did a tuck-and-turn and pulled himself through a hatchway, "don't fuck around with any more drones. Barrett called me up a couple of hours ago, said he thought you'd done something to one of them."

"I don't like being watched while I work," Ty said.

"What did you do, Ty?"

"Glued it to a bulkhead. If Barrett wants to spy on me, he can come out and unglue it himself."

Ty wouldn't give up his idea that something was haunting the shuttle. Later, Maris caught him plugged into a private conversation with Bruno Peterfreund, the fourth member of the wrecking gang. They had just spent a couple of hours combing through the shuttle's lifesystem, and presented her with an inventory: the com module gone; pumps and filters from the air conditioning dismounted; sleeping bags and tools missing.

"Something took all this stuff," Ty said, "and made itself a nice cozy nest."

"I think he's right, boss," Bruno said. "The stuff, it is not floating around somewhere. It's gone."

"The shuttle was zapped right at the beginning of the war," Maris said. "Nothing could have survived out here for three hundred days."

"Nothing human," Ty said. "It's a spook of some kind for sure. Hiding in the shadows, waiting to jump our asses."

Maris told the two men to get back to work, but she knew this wouldn't be the end of it. Ty and Bruno had wasted precious time chasing a ghost that couldn't possibly exist. They had fallen behind on the job.

Sure enough, Barrett called her that evening. He'd checked her day log, and wanted to know why her gang were still refining rare metals when they should have started to dismount the fusion plant. Maris wasn't prepared to expose her crew to Barrett's acid ridicule, so she flat-out lied. She told him that the calibration of the refinery had drifted, that there had been cross-contamination in the collection chambers, that she had had to run everything through the refinery all over again.

"I don't want to fine you," Barrett said, "but I'm going to *have* to do it all the same. You've gotten behind, Maris, and I can't be seen to favor one gang over another. It's nothing, just 30 percent of the day's pay, but if your gang don't have the fusion plant dismounted by the end of tomorrow, I'm afraid that I'll be forced to invoke another penalty."

James Lo Barrett, the smug bastard, giving her a synthetic look of soapy sympathy. He had a fleshy, pouched face, a shaven head (even his eyebrows were shaved), and a pussy little beard that was no more than a single long braid hung off his chin and wrapped in black silk thread. He looked, Maris thought, like a fetus blimped up by some kind of accelerated growth program. He was sitting at his desk, at ease in the centrifugal gravity of his ship in a clean, brightly lit room, with real plants growing on a shelf behind him and a mug of something smothered in his podgy hands. Coffee, probably—Maris thought she could see steam rising from it. She hadn't had a proper hot drink or meal in twenty days; the hab-module's atmosphere was a nitrox mix at less than half an atmosphere, and water boiled at seventy degrees centigrade. It stank too, because its air scrubbers didn't work properly; its joints needed careful monitoring because they were prone to spring leaks; its underpowered electrical system was liable to unpredictable brownouts and cut-offs; it had a low grade but intractable black mold infection; the motors and fans of its air conditioning thrummed and clanked and groaned in a continual dismal chorus. But it was infinitely better than sitting rockside, subsiding on the meager charity of the Three Powers Occupation Force and enduring the random sweeps of its police. It was work, and work was what Maris lived for, even if she had to deal with people like Barrett.

She'd met him just once, at the start of her contract. He'd made a big deal about coming out to the hab-module to meet the new wrecking gang, had a clammy handshake, grabby eyes, and smelled of eucalyptus oil. He'd tried to convince her then that he was on her side, that he thought outers were getting a tough break. "The war is over," he'd told her. "We should draw a line under it and move on. There are tremendous possibilities out here, vast resources. Everyone can benefit. So don't think of me as the enemy, that's all in the past. Deal with me like you would anyone else, and we'll get along just fine."

Maris decided then that although she had to work for him, he couldn't make her pretend to like him. She said now, direct and matter-of-fact, "We'll get back on schedule. No problem."

"Work with me, Delgado. Don't let me down."

"Absolutely," Maris said. Her job would have been so much easier if Barrett had been a tough son of a bitch. Maris could deal with sons of bitches — you always knew where you were with them. But Barrett pretended that he was not responsible for the authority he wielded, pretended that punishing his crews hurt him as much as it hurt them, demanding their sympathy even as he sequestered money that was needed to feed starving children. His spineless mendacity made him a worse tyrant than any bully.

"If there's a problem," he said, "you know I'm always here to help."

Yeah, right. Maris knew that if there really was a problem, he'd get rid of her without a qualm. She gave her best smile, and said, "The refinery threw a glitch, but it's fixed now. We'll get on top of the schedule first thing."

"That's the spirit. And Delgado? No more games with my drones."

Wrecking Gang #3's hab-module was nothing more than two stubby, double-skinned cargo pods welded either side of a central airlock, like two tin cans kissing a fat ball bearing. Maris sculled from the workspace cylinder, with its lockers and racks and benches, through the spherical airlock, into the living quarters. Ty glanced up from his TV; he was an addict of the spew of reworked ancient programs pumped out by autonomous self-replicating satellites in Saturn's ring system. Half hidden by the flexing silvery tube of the air ducting, Bruno Peterfreund, his long blond hair coiled under a knitted cap, was painstakingly scraping mold from a viewport.

Maris told the two men the bad news. She gave it to them straight. She didn't mention their sudden obsession with missing fuel cells and the rest; she let the inference hang in the air. "You guys will start dismounting the fusion plant," she said, "and once Somerset and I have finished up metal reclamation, we'll come and give you a hand. We'll start early, finish late. Okay?"

"Whatever," Ty said, affecting indifference but not quite daring to meet Maris's fierce gaze.

"That won't interfere with your social plans, Bruno?"

"Nothing I can't put off, boss." Bruno was a stolid, taciturn man of thirty-five, exactly the same age as Maris, a ship's engineer from Europa who had been stranded in the Saturn system by the war. He had spent more than a hundred days in a forced labor camp, helping to rebuild wrecked agricultural domes. Now that the Three Powers Occupation Force had declared "normalization" through-out the Outer System, and the embargo on civilian travel had been lifted, he hoped to earn enough from salvage work to pay for his ticket home. He had a round, impassive face and dark watchful eyes that didn't miss much; lately, Maris had caught him checking out her trim whenever he thought she wasn't looking. He was lonesome, she thought, missing the family he hadn't seen for almost a year. If he hadn't been married, and if they hadn't been working together, she might have responded; as it was, by unspoken agreement, they kept it at the level of mutually respectful banter.

"We'll make up the time," Maris told the two men. "I know you guys can work hard when you have to. Where's Somerset? Gardening?"

"As usual," Ty said.

Somerset was cocooned in a sleeping bag in a curtained niche at the far end of the chamber, eyes masked by spex, ringed fingers flexing like pale sea plants.

"Hey," Maris said.

Somerset pushed up the spex and turned its calm, untroubled gaze toward her. Like all neuters, its age was difficult to estimate; although it was thirty years older than Maris, and its spiky crest of hair was as white as nitrogen snow, its coffee-and-cream skin had the smooth, unlined complexion of a child. It was a member of some kind of Buddhist sect, and all of its wages went to the refugee center run by its temple. It owned nothing but a couple of changes of clothes, its p-suit, and its garden—a virtual microhabitat whose health and harmony were, according to the precepts of its faith, a reflection of its spiritual state.

Maris said, "How's everything growing?"

Somerset shrugged and said dryly, "You don't have to attempt pleasantries, Maris. I will do my part."

"You heard what I told Ty and Bruno."

"I thought you were quite restrained, considering the trouble they have caused."

"I want to know just one thing," Maris said. "I want to know if this is some kind of joke on me. If you're all winding me up because I helped build the ship, and I've bored you to death about why I don't believe in ghosts. If that's what it is, ha-ha, you've all made your point, and I'm wiser for it. But we have to get back on schedule."

"I don't play games," Somerset said disdainfully.

Maris said, "But you know what's going on, don't you? It's Ty. Ty for sure, and maybe Bruno. Bruno's quiet, but he's sly."

"To begin with," Somerset said, "I thought Ty's stories were as silly as you did, but now I'm not so sure. We still haven't found that missing passenger, after all."

"She died in some obscure little spot," Maris said, "or she took a walk out of the airlock. One or the other. The ship was shut down, Somerset. It was killed stone dead. The emp blast fritzed every circuit. No lights, no air conditioning, no heat, no communications, no hope of rescue. Remember that other shuttle we did, last shift? All the crew were gone. They took the big step rather than die a long lingering death by freezing or asphyxiation."

"I did an infrared scan," Somerset said. "Just in case."

Maris nodded. Somerset was smart; Somerset was methodical. Anything warmer than the vacuum, such as a hidey-hole with a warm body living in it, would show up stark white in infrared. She said, "I should have thought of that."

Somerset smiled. "But I didn't find anything."

"There you are."

"Of course, absence of evidence is not evidence of absence."

"Meaning?"

"Its hiding place could be well-insulated. It could be buried deep in the shuttle's structure."

"Bullshit," Maris said. "We'll finish stripping out the circuitry tomorrow. We'll find her body in some corner, and that will be an end to it."

Maris and Somerset didn't find the missing passenger. Ty and Bruno did.

The two men came into the lifesystem a couple of hours before the end of the shift, ricocheting down the central shaft like a couple of freefall neophytes. Ty was so shaken that he couldn't string together a coherent sentence; even the normally imperturbable Bruno was spooked.

"You have to see it for yourself, boss," Bruno told Maris, after they had all used patch cords to link themselves together, so that Barrett couldn't overhear them.

"If you guys are setting me up for something, I'll personally drag your asses rockside."

"No joke," Ty said. "Clan's honor this is no joke."

"Tell us again what you found," Somerset said calmly. "Think carefully. Describe everything you saw."

Ty and Bruno talked: ten minutes.

When they were finished, Maris said, "If she's in there, she can't be alive."

"Gang #1 found bodies hung on a bulkhead in one of the freighters," Ty said. "Bodies with chunks missing from them. They figure that one of the crew killed the rest. They think that he might still be alive."

Maris said firmly, "No one could have survived for long in any of these hulks. No power, no food, no air . . . it isn't possible."

"You don't know what the gene wizards made for the war," Ty said. "No one does."

Maris had to admit that Ty had a point. Before the Quiet War, Earth had infiltrated the Outer System colonies with spies, dopplegängers, and suicide artists, most of them clones and most of them gengineered. The suicide artists had been the worst—terror weapons in human form, berserkers, walking bombs. One type had hidden themselves near sensitive installations and simply died; symbiotic bacteria had transformed their corpses into unstable lumps of high explosive. Maris's younger brother had been killed when one of these corpse-bombs had blown a hole in the agricultural dome where he had been working.

She said, "Did any of Barrett's drones follow you?"

"Not a one," Ty said.

"You're sure."

"My suit's radar can spot a flea's heartbeat at a hundred klicks. Yeah, I'm sure."

"If Barrett suspected anything, boss," Bruno said, "he would be asking you some hard questions around about now."

"We should consider telling him," Somerset said. "If something dangerous is hiding in there, Symbiosis can provide the appropriate back-up."

"Soldiers," Ty said. "*Armed* soldiers."

"If we could tell anyone other than Barrett, I'd agree with you," Maris said. "But Barrett can't make a decision to save his life. Faced with something like this, something that isn't covered by his precious rule book, he'll panic. The first thing he'll do is sling our asses rockside. The second thing he'll do is, if by some miracle she's still alive, he'll kill her. He'll declare her a saboteur or a spy, kill her, and get promoted for it. Or he'll simply get rid of her, pretend she never existed. And don't try and tell me that this is some spook or monster, Ty. This has to be the missing passenger—Alice Eighteen Singh Rai. A person, not a monster."

"The boss has a point," Bruno said. "Barrett does not accept responsibility for his actions. He hides behind his position in the company, and his position in the company is all he is. In the camp, there were many like him, people who told themselves that they must do terrible things to the prisoners because their superiors demanded it, people who refused to see that they were doing these things out of fear and denial. Those people, they made themselves into monsters, and I think Barrett is that kind of monster. He will commit murder rather than risk doing something that might endanger his status, and he will tell himself it is for the good of the company."

It was the longest speech any of them had heard Bruno make, and the only time he had ever talked about the labor camp.

"Aw, shit," Ty said. "Let's do it. But if we all get killed by some kind of monster, don't say I didn't warn you."

"I would like you all to remember that I have expressed my reservations," Somerset said.

"If it was a monster," Maris said, "don't you think it would have killed us already?"

They went out together. They carried percussion hammers, bolt cutters, glue guns. Bruno carried a portable airlock kit. Ty carried a switchblade he'd somehow smuggled past Symbiont security. Maris carried a tube of plastic explosive. Somerset carried a portable ultrasonic scanner. They fingertip-flew over the swell of the shuttle's main body toward the flared skirt of the motor's radiation shield. Saturn's pale crescent, nipped like a fingernail paring in the delicate tweezers of its ring system, hung just a few degrees above it. At zenith, the twin stars of the Symbiosis ship, motor and lifesystem linked by a fullerene tether four kilometers long, rotated once a second around their common center.

Beyond the radiation shield, the bulbous cylinder of the motor and most of its ancillary spheres and spars were coated with the black crust of the vacuum organism, smooth as spilled paint in some places, raised in thin, stiff sheets in others. The biggest sheets clustered like mutant funeral flowers around the mass-reaction tanks, a ring of six aluminum spheres, each three meters in diameter, that were tucked in the lee of the radiation skirt. The tanks contained water that had fuelled superheated steam venturis used for delicate attitude control; one of the tanks, Ty claimed, was the hiding place of a monster.

They plugged in patch cords; they went to work.

While Somerset fiddled with the ultrasonic scanner, Maris used a wand to confirm that the tank was leaking minute traces of an oxyhelium mix. Bruno showed her a clear spot in the otherwise ubiquitous coating of the vacuum organism, hidden behind one of the triangular struts that secured the tank to the motor's spine. It was like a dull grey eye surrounded by ridged and puckered black tar; in its center, a fine seam defined a circle about half a meter in diameter.

"That is what gave us the clue," Bruno said. "The vacuum organism must be an oxygen hater. Also, we find a current flowing in it."

"It's not just photosynthetic," Ty said. He hung back from the tank as if ready to bolt, the patch cord that connected him to Bruno at full stretch. His white p-suit was painted with swirling lines and dots that echoed his tattoos.

"It generates electricity," Bruno said. "Something like ten point six watts over its entire surface. Not very much, but enough —"

"I'm ahead of you," Maris said. "It's enough to run the tank's internal heaters. Well, but it doesn't mean that she's alive. What do you see, Somerset?"

Somerset, hanging head down close to the tank's sphere, his orange p-suit vivid against the stiff black sheets of the vacuum organism, was using the ultrasonic scanner. It said, "Nothing at all. It is very well insulated. Maris, you know that we have to tell Symbiosis."

"If it is the missing passenger, she has to be crazy," Bruno said. "Or why would she still be hiding?"

"She has to be some kind of thing," Ty said.

"She has to be dead," Maris said. "Let's get her out of there."

They set dots of plastic explosive around the almost invisible seam. They rigged the portable airlock over it. They took shelter behind another tank, and Maris blew the charges.

An aluminum disc, forced out by pressure inside the tank, shot to the top of the transparent tent of the airlock and bounced back to meet something shuddering out of the hole — another portable airlock struggling to fit inside the first. After nothing else happened for a whole minute, Maris sculled over to investigate. She pushed the visor of her helmet against the double layer of taut, transparent plastic, and shone her flashlight inside.

At the center of the tank, curled up in a nest made from the absorbent material and honeycomb vanes that had channeled the water, was the body of a little girl in a cut-down pressure suit.

They thought at first that she was dead: her p-suit's internal temperature was just two degrees centigrade, barely above the freezing point of water, and she had no pulse or respiration signs. But a quick ultrasonic scan showed that her blood was sluggishly circulating through a cascade filter pump connected to the femoral artery of her left leg. There was also a small machine attached to the base of her skull, something coiled in her stomach, and a line in the vein of her left arm that went through the elbow joint of her p-suit and was coupled to a lash-up of tubing, pumps and bags of clear and cloudy liquids, and the three missing fuel cells.

"That's what happened to the foodmaker," Ty said. "She's got some kind of continuous culture running."

He hung just outside the hatch, watching as Maris and Somerset worked inside the tank, tying off the line into the little girl's arm, detaching a cable trickling amps to her p-suit.

"She is hibernating," Bruno said, his helmet jostling beside Ty's. "I have heard of the technique. Soldiers on the other side were infected with nanotech that could shut them down if they were badly injured."

"Then she's a spy," Ty said.

"I don't know what she is," Somerset said, looking across the little girl's body at Maris, "but I do know that no ordinary child could have rigged this. We should leave her here. Let Symbiosis deal with her as I have already suggested."

"I don't think so," Maris said. "The temperature inside her suit has risen by five degrees, and it's still rising. I think she's waking up."

They waited until the Symbiosis ship was eclipsed by a freighter that was slowly rotating end over end thirty klicks beyond the shuttle, and then rode their sled to the hab-module. Halfway there, the little girl's arms and legs spasmed; Maris held her down, saw that she was dribbling a clear liquid from her mouth and nostrils. Then her eyes opened, and she looked straight at Maris.

Her eyes were beaten gold, with silvery, pinprick pupils.

Maris touched her visor to the little girl's. "It's okay," she said. "Everything's okay, sweetheart. We'll look after you. I promise."

By the time they had bundled her inside the hab-module, the little girl was dazed but fully awake. Out of her p-suit, she stank like a pharm goat and was as skinny as a snake, in a liner that was two sizes too big. Even though the intravenous line had been dripping vitamins, amino acids, and complex carbohydrates from the yeast culture into her blood, she had used up all of her body fat and a good deal of muscle mass in her long sleep. She seemed to be about eight or nine, was completely hairless, and had bronze skin, and those big silver-on-gold eyes that stared boldly at the wrecking crew who hung around her.

Although she responded to her name, she wouldn't or couldn't talk; hardly surprising, Maris said, considering what she had been through. When Bruno tried to examine the blood pump that clung to her leg like a swollen leech, she drew her knees to her chest and carefully detached it, then reached behind her head, plucked the tiny machine from the base of her skull, and flicked it away. Bruno deftly caught it on the rebound, and after a brief examination said it was some kind of Russian Sleep gadget. "Some monster, boss," he said. "I'm disappointed."

"We could throw her back," Maris said, "and try for something better."

Ty laughed, showing for a moment the wad of green gum that lay on his tongue. He was fascinated by the little girl; his fear had transformed directly to excitement and a kind of proprietorial pride. "She's amazing," he said. "Could you have done what she did? I couldn't."

"None of us could," Somerset said. "That's why she can't be a normal little girl. That's why we have taken a very grave risk in bringing her aboard."

"Aw, come on," Ty said. "Look at her. She's a kid. She's half-starved to death. She couldn't harm a blade of grass."

"Appearances can be deceptive," Somerset said.

Alice Eighteen Singh Rai watched them carefully as they spoke about her, but showed no sign that she understood what they were saying.

"She would have died if we had not found her," Bruno said. "Whatever she is, she needs our help."

"Of course," Somerset said. "But we know nothing about her."

Ty snorted air through his nose. "What are you saying, we should tie her up?"

"We should certainly take precautions," Somerset said, ignoring Ty's sarcasm.

Maris decided that Somerset needed something to do, and told him, "Before we can decide anything, I need you to find out everything you can about where Alice came from."

"Somewhere on Iapetus, I should think," Somerset said. "That was the shuttle's point of departure, according to its manifest. It was on a straight run to Mimas when the emp mine intercepted it."

"I'm sure you can find out exactly where on Iapetus."

"I will try my best," Somerset said, and swam off to its cubicle.

"And take the rod out of your ass while you're about it," Ty murmured.

"Somerset does have a point," Bruno said. "We have to think very carefully about what we're going to do."

"I'm going to have to come up with some excuse for Barrett," Maris said. "But first, I'm going to give this little girl her first shower in three hundred days."

Alice Eighteen Singh Rai scrubbed up well, submitting docilely to the air-mask necessary in the freefall shower. Enveloped in one of Maris's jumpers, she refused the bags of chow Ty patiently offered one by one, then suddenly kicked off toward the kitchen nook, quick and agile as an eel. She had ripped open a tube and was cramming black olive paste into her mouth before Ty could pull her away by an ankle.

"Let her eat," Maris said. "I think she knows what her body needs."

"Man," Ty said, wonderingly, "she sure is hungry."

Bruno said, "I have only a minimum of medical training, boss. I don't know anything about mental illness or brain damage. The autodoc can work up her blood and urine chemistry for chemical signs of psychosis, but that's about all. I hate to say it, but the Symbiosis ship has better facilities."

"I don't want to turn her over to Barrett."

Bruno nodded. His eyes were dark and solemn under the brim of his knitted cap. "She's one of us, isn't she?"

"She's no ordinary little girl. Somerset is right about that. But she's no monster, either."

"She sure is hungry," Ty said again, watching with tender pride as Alice unseamed her third tube of olive paste.

Maris left her with Ty and Bruno, and, with heavy foreboding, wrote up a false report for the day log and sent it off. Barrett called back almost at once. He said, "I want to believe you, but somehow I'm having a hard time."

Maris's first thought was that one of Barrett's drones had spotted them working around Alice's nest. She hunched over the com, sweat popping over her body. Her pulse beat heavily in her temples. She said, "If this is about why we're still behind—"

"Of course it is. And I'm very disappointed."

"The vacuum organism caused a bigger problem than we anticipated."

"All you have to do is cut through it," Barrett said scornfully. "Cut through it, scorch it off, *deal* with it."

"Can you tell me about the shuttle's cargo, Barrett? What was it carrying?"

Barrett gave her a sharp, bright look. "Why do you want to know?"

"Perhaps the vacuum organism was part of the cargo. If we know what it is, we can deal with it more easily."

"The v.o. was checked out when the cargo pods were detached. It's nothing out of the ordinary."

"Don't you have more specific information? The ship was recovered five months ago. Symbiosis must know what was in the cargo pods by now."

"That's none of your business, Delgado. Your business is to render down that shuttle, and your gang is a whole ten hours behind. You have to understand that Symbiosis wrote up these work schedules with generous margins—"

Relief that Barrett didn't seem to know about Alice made Maris bold. She said, "The schedules weren't drawn up with vacuum organism contamination in mind."

"Please don't interrupt me again," Barrett said, all frosty rectitude. "The margins are there, and you've overrun them. You know the contract regs as well as I, Delgado. What else can I do?"

"Okay, fine, take off ten hours pay."

"A day's pay plus penalties. The contract is quite specific."

"Okay."

"What's wrong, Delgado? Talk to me. Are you having trouble maintaining discipline?" Barrett suddenly mock-solicitous, leaning so close to the camera that his face looked like a pockmarked moon, his silly little braid wagging on his chin.

"There's no problem," Maris said, snapping off the com and instantly regretting it. It was a sign of weakness, and the one skill that Barrett had honed to perfection was sniffing out weaknesses in others.

She waited five minutes in case he called back, then sculled back to the living quarters. Ty and Alice were watching a TV sheet floating in the air. Both were chewing gum. Bruno and Somerset broke off a whispered conversation, and Somerset told Maris, "I have found out where she came from."

The Saturn infonet had been badly damaged during the Quiet War, but after running Alice's name through half a dozen clandestine search engines, Somerset had discovered that the shuttle's cargo and passenger had both originated in Hawaiki, an agricultural settlement on the great dark plains of Iapetus's Cassini Regio.

"I discovered something else, too," Somerset said. "The settlement was designed by Avernus."

The name of the woman who had been the Outer System's most famous gene wizard, and was now its most wanted so-called war criminal, hung in the air for a moment.

"Man," Ty said, "I knew our Alice was something special. Didn't I say she was special?"

"Avernus was famous for the totality of her designs," Somerset said. "She tailored both ecospheres and their inhabitants. Given her appearance and what she did to survive, it seems quite likely that our guest benefited from Avernus's art."

Alice smiled at them all, seemingly quite happy to be the center of their attention.

"It doesn't mean that she's a monster," Maris said forthrightly, although she had to admit that Somerset's discovery was disquieting. Avernus had dedicated her considerable skills to pushing the envelope of humanity's range. Some of her commissions—a sect in which adults lost the use of their limbs and eyes and grew leathery, involuted integuments stained purple with photosynthetic pigment, becoming sessile eremites devoted to praising God; a community with a completely closed ecosystem, the bellies of its citizens swollen with sacs of symbiotic bacteria—had tested even the generously inclusive tolerance of the outers.

"Aw, hell," Ty said, "according to the flatlanders, we're *all* monsters. And you know what? It's *true*. We're all tweaks, and we're all proud to be tweaks! Flatlanders need drugs and nanotech to live here, but we're gengineered for low-gravity. Maybe Avernus gave Alice a few extra special abilities, but so what?"

Maris asked Somerset, "Can we get in touch with Alice's home?"

"Hawaiki no longer exists," Somerset said. "It was captured and destroyed during the war."

"There must be survivors," Maris said.

"They were probably put in a camp," Bruno said darkly. "One of those experimental camps."

"Hey," Ty said, "not in front of Alice."

"The TPA must know," Somerset said, "but there are no records that I can access."

"One thing is certain," Maris said. "We were absolutely right not to tell Barrett about Alice."

She remembered with a chill the supervisor's sudden bright look when she had asked about the shuttle's cargo, and knew that he knew all about the shuttle's passenger, knew that she was valuable.

"You're going to stay here," Ty told the golden-eyed little girl. "Stay here with us, until we find a way of getting you back to your family."

"I would like to know," Somerset said, "how we can keep Barrett from finding out about her."

"We just don't tell him," Maris said.

"I'm relieved to see that you have thought it through," Somerset said.

Bruno said, "The boss is right, Somerset. Barrett hardly ever leaves his ship. If we don't tell him about Alice, he'll never know."

"This isn't like playing around in your garden," Ty said. "This is for real."

"My garden has nothing to do with this," Somerset said.

"Ty didn't mean anything by it," Maris said.

"I meant," Ty said doggedly, "that this is the *real* world, where what you do has real consequences for real people. We rescued Alice, Somerset, so it's up to us to look after her."

"I believe that we have all agreed that Barrett would almost certainly kill Alice if he found out about her," Somerset said, with acid patience. "It follows that the only morally correct course of action is to assume responsibility for her care. I merely point out that it is also a very dangerous course of action."

"Nevertheless, we're all in this together," Maris said.

Everyone looked at everyone else. Everyone said yes. Alice smiled.

Maris, strung out by anxiety and the physical exhaustion of zero-gravity work, fell asleep almost as soon as she wriggled into her sleeping bag. She slept deeply and easily, and when she woke in the middle of the night, it took her a little while to realize what was wrong.

The spavined rattle and bone-deep thrum of the air conditioning was gone.

Maris pushed up her mask, hitched out of the sleeping bag, and ducked through her privacy curtain. Ty and Bruno hung in midair, watching Alice mime something in the soft red light of the hab-module's sleep-cycle illumination. Ty spun around as Maris caught a rung. He was chewing gum and grinning from ear to ear. "She fixed the air conditioning," he said.

"You mean she broke it."

"She *fixed* it," Ty insisted. "Listen."

Ty and Bruno and Alice watched as Maris concentrated on nothing but the sound of her own ragged breath . . . and heard, at the very edge of audibility, a soft pulsing hum, a whisper of moving air.

Somerset shot through its privacy curtain, caught a rung, reversed. Its crest of white hair was all askew. It said, "What did she do?"

Bruno said, "She altered the rate of spin of every fan in the system, tuning them to a single harmonic. No more vibration."

"Alice knows machines," Ty said proudly.

"It seems she does not sleep," Bruno said. "So, while we slept, she fixed the air conditioning."

"Swaddling," Somerset said. "Or a tether. I am serious. Suppose she meddles with something else? We do not know what she can do."

"Alice knows machines," Ty insisted, proud as a new parent.

Which, in a sense, he *was*, Maris thought. Which, in a sense, they all were. She sculled through the air until her face was level with Alice's. Those strange silver-on-gold eyes, unreadable as coins, stared into hers. She said gently, "You did a good job, but you mustn't touch anything else. Do you understand?"

The little girl nodded—a fractional movement, but a definite assent.

"If she did a good job," Ty said, "what's the problem?"

"We hardly know anything about her," Somerset said. "That's the problem."

"You can find out," Bruno told Somerset. "Use those data mining skills of yours to dig deeper."

"I have found all there is to find," Somerset said. "The war wrecked most of the infonet. I am surprised that I found anything at all."

"Let's all get some rest," Maris said. "We have to start work in three hours. A lot of work."

She did not think that she would get back to sleep, but she did, and slept peacefully in the harmonious murmur of the fans.

They started their shift early. As they all sucked down a hasty breakfast of gritty, fruit-flavored oat paste and lukewarm coffee, Somerset made it clear just how unhappy it was about leaving Alice alone in the hab-module.

"We should take her with us," the neuter said. "If she is as good with machines as Ty claims, she can be of some help."

"No way," Maris said. "Even Barrett can count up to five. What do you think he'll do if he spots an extra body out there?"

"Then someone should stay behind with her," Somerset said stubbornly.

"If Barrett can count up to five," Maris said, "he can also count up to three. None of us can afford to lose any more pay, and we'll never catch up on our schedule if we're one body short."

Ty said, "Alice, honey, you know we have to go out, don't you? You promise you'll be good while we're away?"

Alice was floating in midair with her arms hooked under her knees, watching TV; when she heard her name, she looked over at Ty, eyes flashing in the half-dark, and nodded once.

"You see," Ty said. "It's not a problem."

"I don't like what she did to the air," Somerset said. "It smells strange."

"If by *strange* you mean it doesn't smell of crotch-sweat and stale farts anymore," Ty said, "then I don't think it's strange—I think it's an improvement!"

"The temperature is higher, too," Somerset said.

"Yeah," Ty said. "Nice and comfortable, isn't it? Look, Somerset, Alice is just a kid. I guess, what with your religious bent and all, you might not know much about kids, but I do. I used to look after a whole bunch of them back in the clan. Trust me on this. *There's no problem.*"

"She is not merely—"

Maris flicked her empty paste and coffee tubes into the maw of the disposal. "No time for argument, gentlemen. Suit up and ship out. We have plenty of work to do."

For a little while, absorbed in the hard, complicated job of dismounting the shuttle's fusion plant, they all forgot their worries. Clambering about the narrow crawlspaces around the plant's combustion chamber, they severed cables and pipes, sheared bolts and cut through supports, strung temporary tethers. They worked well; they worked as a team; they made good time. Maris was beginning to plan the complicated pattern of explosive charges that would pop the fusion plant out of its shaft when her radio shrieked, a piercing electronic squeal that cut off before she could access her suit's com menu.

Everyone shot out of the access hatch, using their suit thrusters to turn toward the hab-module.

"Alice," Ty said, his voice sounding hollow in the echo of the radio squeal. "She's in trouble."

Bruno, his p-suit painted, Jupiter-system style, with an elaborate abstract pattern, spun around and shot off toward the sled. Maris saw the black sphere of Barrett's pressurized sled clinging like a blood-gorged tick to one of the hatches of the hab-module's airlock, and chased after him.

Bruno took the helm of the sled, told them all to hang on, and punched out with a hard continuous burn. Directly ahead, the hab-module expanded with alarming speed.

"You'll overshoot," Somerset said calmly.

"Saint Isaac Newton, bless me now in my hour of need," Bruno said. He flipped the sled with a nicely judged blip of its attitude jets, opened the throttle in a hard blast of deceleration that seemed to squeeze every drop of Maris's blood into her boots, and fired off tethers whose sticky pads slapped against the airlock and jerked the sled to a halt.

Maris signed for radio silence. They fanned out, peering through view-ports into the red-lit interiors of the two cylinders. Somerset's orange-suited figure, at the far end of the workspace, raised a hand, pointed down. The others clustered around him.

Alice stared up at them through the little disc of scratched, triple-layered plastic. After a moment, she smiled.

They opened the airlock's secondary hatch and cycled through, the four of them crowding each other in the little spherical space as they shucked helmets and gloves. Alice was waiting placidly in the center of the cluttered workroom, floating as usual in midair, hands hooked under her knees.

"Oh my," Maris said in dismay.

Still in its yellow p-suit, Symbiosis's sunburst-in-a-green-circle logo on its chest-plate, Barrett's body was strung against the bulkhead behind Alice. Its arms were bound to its sides by a whipcord tether; a wormy knot of patch sealant filled the broken visor of its helmet. The end of Barrett's braided beard stuck out of the hard white foam like a mountaineer's flag on a snowy peak. Maris didn't need Bruno's pronouncement to know that the supervisor was dead.

It took Ty ten minutes to get the story from Alice. He asked questions; she answered by nods or shakes. Apparently, Barrett had come looking for her after his AI had decrypted and audited Somerset's infonet usage records; he'd boasted about his cleverness. He had been friendly at first, but when Alice had refused to answer his questions, he had threatened to kill her. That was when she had immobilized him with the tether and suffocated him with the sealant.

Somerset found Barrett's weapon. It had fetched up against one of the air-conditioning outlets.

Ty asked Alice, "Did he threaten to kill you, honey?"

A quick nod.

"Why did he want to kill you? Was he scared of you?"

Alice nodded, then shook her head.

"Okay, he was scared of you, but that wasn't why he wanted to kill you."

A nod.

"He wanted something from you."

A nod.

"He probably wanted *Alice*," Bruno said. "She has been gengineered by Avernus. Her genome, it must be very valuable."

Alice shook her head.

Ty said, "What did he want, honey?"

Alice put a finger to her lips, assumed a sudden look of inward concentration, and started, very delicately, to choke. She shook her head when Ty reached for her, coughed, and started to pull something from her mouth.

Blue plastic wire, over two meters of it.

Maris's parents had owned a vacuum organism farm before the war; she knew at once what the wire was. "That's how vacuum organism spores are packaged."

Alice smiled and nodded.

Maris said, "Does it contain spores of the vacuum organism growing on the shuttle?"

Alice nodded again, then held up her right hand, opened and closed it half a dozen times.

Ty said, "It contains all kinds of spores?"

Bruno said, "This is why you were a passenger. You were carrying it all the time."

"Symbiosis knew about it," Maris said. "They must have had the complete cargo inventory. When they didn't find it in the cargo pods, they searched the lifesystem for the only passenger. And Barrett knew about it too, or found out about it. That's why he sent drones to watch us as we stripped out the lifesystem."

"He did not watch us work outside," Bruno said.

"Barrett is a flatlander," Maris said. "It didn't occur to him that the passenger might be hiding outside. Outside is a bad, scary place, as far as flatlanders are concerned; that's why he hardly ever left his ship. But then he discovered Somerset's trail in the infonet, and worked out that we had found Alice. He wanted her for himself, so he couldn't confront us directly; he waited until we went to work, got up his nerve, and came here."

Somerset was hanging back from the others, near the hatch to the airlock. It said, "You grow an intricate story from only a few facts."

Ty told the neuter, "Don't you realize it's *your* fault Barrett found out about Alice?"

"I asked Somerset to make a search on the infonet," Maris said. "It isn't its fault that Barrett's AI was able to break into its records. And I was stupid enough to ask

Barrett about the shuttle's cargo, which probably made him suspicious in the first place." She took a breath to center herself, called up every gram of her resolve. "Listen up, you three. We all brought Alice back; we all decided that we couldn't give her up to Barrett; we're all in this together. We have to decide what to do, and we have to do it quickly, before the crew of the Symbiosis ship start to worry about their boss."

"Somerset has a point," Bruno said. "We don't know what happened between Alice and Barrett."

"He didn't come over for a social visit," Ty said. "He wanted these spores, he threatened her with the weapon. That's why she killed him."

Somerset said calmly, "I am not sure that Symbiosis will believe your story."

Ty knuckled his tattooed scalp. "Fuck you, Somerset! I *know* Alice is no murderer, and that's all that matters to me."

"That's the problem," Somerset said, and pointed Barrett's weapon at Ty. It was as black and smooth as a pebble, with a blunt snout that nestled between the neuter's thumb and forefinger.

Maris said, "What are you doing, Somerset?"

Somerset's narrow face was set with cold resolve. It looked wholly masculine now. It said, "This fires needles stamped from a ribbon of smart plastic. Some of the needles are explosive; others sprout hooks and barbs when they strike something; they all cause a lot of damage. It is a disgusting weapon, but I will use it if I have to, for the greater moral good."

"Stay calm, Somerset," Maris said. "Don't do anything foolish."

"Yeah," Ty said. "If you want to play with that, go outside."

"I want you all to listen to me. Ty, before we found Alice, you were convinced that she was a monster. I believe that you were right. Because she looks like a little girl, she triggers protective reflexes in ordinary men and women, and they do not realize that they are being manipulated. I, however, am immune. I see her for what she is, and I want you all to share this clear, uncomfortable insight."

Ty said, "She killed Barrett in self-defense, man!" He had drifted in front of Alice, shielding her from Somerset.

"We do not know what happened," Somerset said. "We see a dead man. We see what looks like a little girl. We make assumptions, but how do we know the truth? Perhaps Barrett drew this weapon in self-defense."

Maris said, "You don't like violence, Somerset. I understand that. But what you're doing now makes you as bad as Barrett."

"Not at all," Somerset said. "As I believe I have said before, if you take the side of a murderer with no good reason, then you are as morally culpable as she is."

"She isn't a murderer," Ty said.

"We do not know that," Somerset insisted calmly.

"You fucking traitor!" Bruno said, and dove straight at the neuter.

Somerset swung around. The weapon in his fist made a mild popping sound. Bruno bellowed with pain and clutched at his right arm. Suddenly off-balance, he missed Somerset entirely, slammed against the edge of the airlock hatch, and tumbled backward. And Alice spun head-over-heels and threw something with such force that Maris only saw it on the rebound, after it had sliced through

Somerset's fingers. It was a power saw blade, a diamond disc that ricocheted sideways and lodged in the door of a locker with an emphatic thud. Somerset, its truncated right hand pumping strings of crimson droplets into the air, made a clumsy grab for the weapon; Maris snatched the black pebble out of the air, and Ty knocked the neuter through the airlock hatch.

Ty and Maris trussed Somerset with tethers, and Bruno staunched its bleeding finger stumps and gave it a shot of painkiller before allowing Maris to bandage his own, much more superficial wound. Alice hung back, calm and watchful.

"I am lucky," Bruno said. "It was not an explosive needle."

"You're lucky Somerset couldn't shoot straight," Maris told him.

"I don't think Somerset wanted to kill me, boss."

"We should make the fucker take the big walk without its suit," Ty said, glaring at Somerset.

"You know we can't do that," Maris said.

"*I* can do it," Ty said grimly.

Somerset returned Ty's angry glare with woozy equanimity, and said, "If you kill me, you will only prove that I was right all along."

"Then we'll both be happy," Ty said.

"She's *using* us," Somerset said, slurring every s, "and no one sees it but me."

Maris grabbed the hypo from the medical kit and swam up to Somerset. "You can't keep quiet, can you?"

"Silence is a form of complicity," Somerset said. Its eyes crossed as it tried to focus on the hypo. "I do not need another shot. I can bear pain."

"This is for *us*," Maris said, and pressed the hypo against Somerset's neck. The neuter started to protest, but then the blast of painkiller hit and its eyes rolled up.

"We could fly it right out of the airlock," Ty said. "It wouldn't feel a thing."

"You know we aren't going to do any such thing," Maris said. "Listen up. Any minute now, the ship's crew are going to notice that their boss is missing. What we have to do is work out what we're going to tell them."

Ty said, "I'm not giving her up."

"We know Alice must have killed Barrett in self-defense," Maris said. "We can testify—"

Bruno said, "Ty is right, boss. We know that Alice isn't a murderer, but our testimony won't mean much in court."

Alice waved her hands to get their attention, then pointed to the workshop's camera.

"It's recording," Ty said. He laughed, and turned a full somersault in midair. "Alice knows machines! She had the internal com record everything!"

Maris shook out a screen, plugged it into the camera, and started the playback. Ty and Bruno crowded around her, watched Barrett struggle through the airlock in his p-suit, watched him question Alice, his p-suit still sealed, his voice coming cold and metallic through its speaker. He loomed over her like a fully armed medieval knight menacing a helpless maiden. Her stubborn intervals of silence, his amplified voice getting louder, his gestures angrier. Alice shrank back. He showed her his weapon. And Alice flew at him, whipping a tether around his arms and body, the tether contracting in a tight embrace as her momentum drove him backward; she wrapped her legs around his chest, smashed his visor with a jack-hammer, and emptied a canister of foam into his helmet.

The camera saw everything; it even picked up the glint of the weapon when it flew from Barrett's gloved hand. He flung his helmeted head from side to side, trying to shake off the foam's suffocating mask; Alice pressed against a wall, un-obtrusively out of focus, as his struggles quietened.

Maris said, "It looks good, but will it look good to the court?"

"We can't turn her over to Symbiosis or the TPA police," Bruno said. "At best, they'll turn her into a lab specimen. At worst—"

"Where is she?" Ty said.

Alice was gone; the hatch to the airlock was closed. Neither the automatic nor manual system would budge it. As Bruno prized off the cover of the servomotor, Maris joined Ty at the door's little port, saw Alice wave bye-bye and shoot through the hatch into Barrett's sled. A moment later, there was a solid thump as the sled decoupled.

Maris and Bruno and Ty rushed to the viewports.

"Look at her go!" Maris said.

"Where is she going?" Ty said.

"It looks like she is heading straight to the Symbiosis ship," Bruno said. "She sure can fly that sled."

"Of course she can," Ty said. "What do you think she's going to do?"

"We'll see soon enough," Maris said. "Meanwhile, let's get busy, gentlemen."

Bruno glanced at her. "I do believe you have a plan," he said.

"It's not much of one, but hear me out."

By the time Ty and Maris had hauled Barrett's body to the shuttle, his sled had docked with the motor section of the Symbiosis ship. They tethered the body to the tank where Alice had slept out three hundred days, and tethered the weapon to the utility belt of its p-suit. Maris dragged some of the plastic insulation out of the tank's hatch for dramatic effect, fired a couple of shots into the tangle of bags and tubes inside, then scooted back to look at her work. The tank looked like something had hatched from it in a hurry; Barrett's body, with its mask of lumpy foam, hung half-folded like a grotesque unstrung puppet, its yellow p-suit vivid against the black film of the vacuum organism.

"It looks kind of cheesy," Ty said doubtfully, over their patch cord link.

"If you have a better idea," Maris said, "let me know."

"Maybe it's because I don't think he would have had the sense to tether his weapon."

"He found where Alice was hiding," Maris said, "and opened up the tank. There was a struggle. She killed him and took his sled. The weapon is necessary. It shows he meant her harm. If we don't tether it to him, it'll drift off somewhere and no one will find it. So let's pretend that in his last moments he was overcome with common sense."

"Yeah, well, none of that will matter if the crew knew where he was going in the first place."

"We've been over that already. Barrett wouldn't have told them where he was going because he wanted what Alice had for himself. Otherwise, you can bet that he would have come with plenty of back-up, or sat tight in the safety of his ship and let the Symbiosis cops take care of it."

Ty looked as though he was ready to argue the point, but before he could say anything, Bruno broke in on the common channel. "Heads up," he said. "The Symbiosis ship just broke apart. It would seem that the cable linking the two halves has been severed."

Maris called up her suit's navigation menu, and after a couple of moments, it confirmed Bruno's guess. With the cable cut, the lifesystem and motor section of the ship had shot away in opposite directions. The lifesystem, tumbling badly, was heading into a slightly higher orbit; the motor section was accelerating toward Saturn, its exhaust a steady, brilliant star beyond the ragged sphere of wrecked ships. Maris's com system lit up: the distress signal of the Symbiosis ship's lifesystem; messages from the other two wrecking gangs; Dione's traffic control.

"A perfect burn," Bruno said, with professional admiration. "It is too early to judge exactly, but if I had to make a guess, I would say that it is heading toward the rings."

"Let's get packed up," Maris told Ty, over the patch cord. "The cops will be here pretty soon."

"She'll be all right, won't she?"

"I think she knew what she was doing all along."

Back at the hab-module, Maris and Ty stripped off their suits and grabbed tubes of coffee while Bruno flipped through a babble of voices on the radio channels. Two tugs were chasing the Symbiosis ship's lifesystem, but as yet no one was pursuing the motor section. Bruno had worked up a trajectory, and showed Maris and Ty that it would graze the outer edge of the B ring.

"One hears many wild stories of rebels and refugees hiding inside the minor bodies of the rings," he remarked. "Perhaps some of them are true."

Maris said, "She's going home."

A small, happy thought to cling to, in the cold certainty of days of inquiries, investigations, accusations. Wherever Alice was going, Wrecking Gang #3 was headed rockside, their contracts terminated.

"We'll have to let Somerset go," she said.

"I still think we should make it take the big step," Ty said. "Anyone seen my TV? Maybe the news channels will tell us what's going down."

"Somerset is a fool," Bruno said, "but it is also one of us."

Maris said, "I can't help wondering if Somerset was right. That we were manipulated by Alice. She killed Barrett and ran off, and left us to deal with the consequences."

"She could have taken Barrett's shuttle as soon as she killed him," Bruno said. "Instead, she took a very big risk, alerting us with that radio squeal, waiting for us to get back. She wanted us to know she was innocent. And she wanted to give us a chance to get our story straight."

Maris nodded. "It's a pretty thought, but we'll never know for sure."

Ty suddenly kicked back from his locker, waving something as he tumbled backward down the long axis of the living quarters. It was his TV, rolled up in a neat scroll. "Will you look at this," he said.

The scroll was tied with a length of blue wire. The wire Alice had regurgitated. The cargo she had guarded all this time.

The consequences of Barrett's murder and the sabotage of the Symbiosis ship took a couple of dozen days to settle. Maris and the rest of Wrecking Gang #3 spent some of that time in jail, but were eventually released without trial.

Before the cops came for them, they agreed to take equal shares of Alice's gift. At first, Ty didn't want to give Somerset anything, and Somerset refused to take its share of the wire.

"I have agreed to lie about what happened. I have agreed to tell the police that my injury was caused by an accident. I do not need payment for this; I do it to make amends to you all."

"It isn't payment," Maris said. "It's a gift. You take it, Somerset. What you do with it is up to you."

Maris hid the wire by splicing it into the control cable of her p-suit's thruster pack. It turned out to be an unnecessary precaution; Symbiosis believed that the passenger had taken the missing vacuum organism spores with her, after she had killed Barrett and hijacked the engine section of his ship, and the police's search of the hab-module was cursory. After they were released, the members of Wrecking Gang #3 met just once, to divide the spore-laden spool of wire into four equal lengths. They never saw each other again.

Somerset and Bruno sold their portions on the grey market. Somerset donated the money to his temple's refugee center; Bruno bought a ticket on a Pacific Community liner to the Jupiter System. Maris became a farmer. With an advance on the license fees for the two novel varieties of vacuum organism that her length of wire yielded, she and her family set up an agribusiness on Iapetus, ten thousand square kilometers of the black, carbonaceous-rich plains of Cassini Regio. The farm prospered: the population of the Outer System was expanding rapidly as the economy recovered and migrants poured in from Earth. Maris married the technician who had helped type her vacuum organisms. He was ten years younger than her, and eager to start a family. The dangerous idea of exploring the ruins of the domed crater where Alice's family had lived was an itch that soon dissolved in the ordinary clamor of everyday life.

A few years later, on a business trip to Tethys, Maris paid a spur-of-the-moment visit to the hearth-home of Ty's clan. She learned that he'd given them his length of wire and set off on a *Wanderjahr*. His last message had been sent from a hotel in Camelot, the only city on Mimas, the small, icy moon whose orbit lay between Saturn's G and E rings. It seemed that Ty had taken a sled on a trip to the central peak of Hershel, the huge crater smashed into the leading edge of Mimas, and had not returned. The sled had been found, but his body had never been recovered.

Maris believed that she knew what grail Ty might have been searching for under the geometric glory of Saturn's rings, but she kept her thoughts to herself. Tales of feral communities, fiddler's greens, pirate cities, rebel hideouts, edens, posthuman clades, and other wonders hidden in the millions of moonlets of Saturn's rings were by now the mundane stuff of sagas, psychodramas, and the generic fictions broadcast on illicit TV. Maris knew better than most that a few of these stories had been grown from grains of truth, but by now there were so many that it was impossible even for her to tell fact from fable.

The political officer

CHARLES COLEMAN FINLAY

New writer Charles Coleman Finlay made his first sale last year to The Magazine of Fantasy and Science Fiction, *and has since followed it up with three more sales to that magazine, including the taut and suspenseful story that follows, which takes us on a deeply hazardous top secret mission into deep space, with a hard-pressed crew who soon discover that for all the dangers outside, the biggest dangers may be the ones that lurk within . . .*

Finlay lives with his family in Columbus, Ohio.

Maxim Nikomedes saw the other man rush toward him but there was no room to dodge in the crate-packed corridor. He braced for the impact. The other man pulled up short, his face blanching in the pallid half-light of the "night" rotation. It was Kulakov, the chief petty officer. He went rigid and snapped a salute.

"Sir! Sorry, sir!" His voice trembled.

"At ease, Kulakov," Max said. "Not your fault. It's a tight fit inside this metal sausage."

Standard ship joke. The small craft was stuffed with supplies, mostly food, for the eighteen-month voyage ahead. Max waited for the standard response, but Kulakov stared through the hull into deep space. He was near sixty, old for the space service, old for his position, and the only man aboard who made Max, in his midforties, feel young.

Max smiled, an expression so faint it could be mistaken for a twitch. "But it's better than being stuck in a capped-off sewer pipe, no?"

Which is what the ship would be on the voyage home. "You've got that right, sir!" said Kulakov.

"Carry on."

Kulakov shrank aside like an old church deacon, afraid to touch a sinner lest he catch the sin. Max expected that reaction from the crew, and not just because they'd nicknamed him the Corpse for his cadaverous and dead expression. As the political officer, he held the threat of death over every career aboard: the death of some careers would entail a corporeal equivalent. For the first six weeks of their mission, after spongediving the new wormhole, Max had cultivated invisibility and waited for the crew to fall into the false complacency of routine. Now it was time to shake them up again to see if he could find the traitor he suspected. He brushed against Kulakov on purpose as he passed by him.

He twisted his way through the last passage and paused outside the visiting officers' cabin. He lifted his knuckles to knock, then changed his mind, turned the latch and swung open the door. The three officers sitting inside jumped at the sight of him. Guilty consciences, Max hoped.

Captain Ernst Petoskey recovered first. "Looking for someone, Lieutenant?"

Max let the silence become uncomfortable while he studied Petoskey. The captain stood six and a half feet tall, his broad shoulders permanently hunched from spending too much time in ships built for smaller men. The crew loved him and would eagerly die — or kill — for him. Called him Papa behind his back. He wouldn't shave again until they returned safely to spaceport, and his beard was juice-stained at the corner by proscripted chewing tobacco. Max glanced past Lukinov, the paunchy, balding "radio lieutenant," and stared at Ensign Pen Reedy, the only woman on the ship.

She was lean, with prominent cheekbones, but the thing Max always noticed first were her hands. She had large, red-knuckled hands. She remained impeccably dressed and groomed, even six weeks into the voyage. Every hair on her head appeared to be individually placed as if they were all soldiers under her command.

Petoskey and Lukinov sat on opposite ends of the bunk. Reedy sat on a crate across from them. Another crate between them held a bottle, tumblers, and some cards.

Petoskey, finally uncomfortable with the silence, opened his mouth again.

"Just looking," Max pre-empted him. "And what do I find but the captain himself in bed with Drozhin's boys?"

Petoskey glanced at the bunk. "I see only one, and he's hardly a boy."

Lukinov, a few years younger than Max, smirked and tugged at the lightning-bolt patch on his shirtsleeve. "And what's with calling us *Drozhin's* boys? We're just simple radiomen. If I have to read otherwise, I'll have you up for falsifying reports when we get back to Jesusalem."

He pronounced their home *Hey-zoo-salaam*, like the popular video stars did, instead of the older way, *Jeez-us-ail-em*.

"Things are not always what they appear to be, are they?" said Max.

Lukinov, Reedy, and a third man, Burdick, were the intelligence listening team assigned to intercept and decode Adarean messages — the newly opened wormhole passage would let the ship dive undetected into the Adarean system to spy. The three had been personally selected and prepped for this mission by Dmitri Drozhin, the legendary Director of Jesusalem's Department of Intelligence. Drozhin had been the Minister too, back when it had still been the Ministry of the Wisdom of Prophets Reborn. He was the only high government official to survive the Revolution *in situ*, but these days younger men like Mallove in the Department of Political Education challenged his influence.

"Next time, knock first, Lieutenant," Petoskey said.

"Why should I, Captain?" Max returned congenially. "An honest man has nothing to fear from his conscience, and what am I if not the conscience of every man aboard this ship?"

"We don't need a conscience when we have orders," Petoskey said with a straight face.

Lukinov tilted his head back dramatically and sneered. "Come off it, Max. I invited the captain up here to celebrate, if that's all right with you. Reedy earned her comet today."

Indeed, she had. The young ensign wore a gold comet pinned to her left breast pocket, similar to the ones embroidered on the shirts of the other two officers. Crewmen earned their comets by demonstrating competence on every ship system—Engineering, Ops and Nav, Weapons, Vacuum and Radiation. Reedy must have qualified in record time. This was her first space assignment. "Congratulations," Max said.

Reedy suppressed a genuine smile. "Thank you, sir."

"That makes her the last one aboard," Petoskey said. "Except for you."

"What do I need to know about ship systems? If I understand the minds and motivations of the men who operate them, it is enough."

"It isn't. Not with this," his mouth twisted distastefully, "*miscegenated*, patched-together, scrapyard ship. I need to be able to count on every man in an emergency."

"Is it that bad? What kind of emergency do you expect?"

Lukinov sighed loudly. "You're becoming a bore, Max. You checked on us, now go make notes in your little spy log and leave us alone."

"Either that or pull up a crate and close the damn hatch," said Petoskey. "We could use a fourth."

The light flashed off Lukinov's gold signet ring as he waved his hand in clear negation. "You don't want to do that, Ernst. This is the man who won his true love in a card game."

Petoskey looked over at Max. "Is that so?"

"I won my wife in a card game, yes." Max didn't think that story was widely known outside his own department. "But that was many years ago."

"I heard you cheated to win her," said Lukinov. He was Max's counterpart in Intelligence—the Department of Political Education couldn't touch him. The two Departments hated each other and protected their own. "Heard that she divorced you too. I guess an ugly little weasel like you has to get it where he can."

"But unlike your wife, she always remained faithful."

Lukinov muttered a curse and pulled back his fist. Score one on the sore spot. Petoskey reached out and grabbed the intelligence officer's elbow. "None of that aboard my ship. I don't care who you two are. Come on, Nikomedes. If you're such a hotshot card player, sit down. I could use a little challenge."

A contrary mood seized Max. He turned into the hallway, detached one of the crates, and shoved it into the tiny quarters.

"So what are we playing?" he asked, sitting down.

"Blind Man's Draw," said Petoskey, shuffling the cards. "Deuce beats an ace, ace beats everything else."

Max nodded. "What's the minimum?"

"A temple to bid, a temple to raise."

Jesusalem's founders stamped their money with an image of the Temple to encourage the citizen-colonists to render their wealth unto God. The new plastic carried pictures of the revolutionary patriots who'd overthrown the Patriarch, but everyone still called them temples. "Then I'm in for a few hands," Max said.

Petoskey dealt four cards face down. Max kept the king of spades and tossed three cards back into the pile. The ones he got in exchange were just as bad.

"So," said Lukinov, peeking at his hand. "We have the troika of the Service all gathered in one room. Military, Intelligence, and—one card, please, ah, raise you one temple—and what should I call you, Max? Schoolmarm?"

Max saw the raise. "If you like. Just remember that Intelligence is useless without a good Education."

"Is that your sermon these days?"

Petoskey collected the discards. "Nothing against either of you gentlemen," he said, "but it's your mother screwed three ways at once, isn't it. There's three separate chains of command on a ship like this one. It's a recipe for mutiny." He pulled at his beard. "Has been on other ships, strictly off the record. And with this mission ahead, if we don't all work together, God help us."

Max kept the ten of spades with his king and took two more cards. "Not that there is one," he said officially, "but let God help our enemies. A cord of three strands is not easily broken."

Petoskey nodded his agreement. "That's a good way to look at it. A cord of three strands, all intertwined." He stared each of them in the eyes. "So take care of the spying, and the politics, but leave the running of the ship to me."

"Of course," said Lukinov.

"That's why you're the captain and both of us are mere *lieutenants*," said Max. In reality, both he and Lukinov had the same service rank as Petoskey. On the ground, in Jesusalem's mixed-up service, they were all three colonels. Lukinov was technically senior of the three, though Max had final authority aboard ship within his sphere.

It was, indeed, a troubling conundrum.

Max's hand held nothing—king and ten of spades, two of hearts, and a seven of clubs. Petoskey tossed the fifth card down face-up. Another deuce.

Max hated Blind Man's Draw. It was like playing the lottery. The card a man showed you was the one he'd just been dealt; you never really knew what he might be hiding. He looked at the other players' hands. Petoskey showed the eight of clubs and Lukinov the jack of diamonds. Ensign Reedy folded her hand and said, "I'm out."

"Raise it a temple and call," Max said, on the off chance he might beat a pair of aces. They turned their cards over and it was money thrown away. Petoskey won with three eights.

Lukinov shook his head. "Holding onto the deuces, Max? That's almost always a loser's hand."

"Except when it isn't."

Petoskey won three of the next five hands, with Lukinov and Max splitting the other two. The poor ensign said little and folded often. Max decided to deal in his other game. While Lukinov shuffled the cards, Max rubbed his nose and said to the air, "You're awfully silent, Miss Reedy. Contemplating your betrayal of us to the Adareans?"

Lukinov mis-shuffled. A heartbeat later, Captain Petoskey picked up his spittoon and spat.

Reedy's voice churned as steady as a motor in low gear. "What do you mean, sir?"

"You're becoming a bore again, Max," Lukinov said under his breath.

"What's this about?" Petoskey asked.

"Perhaps Miss Reedy should explain it herself," Max replied. "Go on, Ensign. Describe the immigrant ghetto in your neighborhood, your childhood chums, Sabbathday afternoons at language academy."

"It was hardly that, sir," she said smoothly. "They were just kids who lived near our residence in the city. And there were never any formal classes."

"Oh, there was much more to it than that," Max pressed. "Must I spell it out for you? You lived in a neighborhood of expatriate Adareans. Some spymaster chose you to become a mole before you were out of diapers and started brainwashing you before you could talk. Now while you pretend to serve Jesusalem you really serve Adares. Yes?"

"No. Sir." Reedy's hands, resting fingertip to fingertip across her knees, trembled slightly. "For one thing, how did they know women would ever be admitted to the military academies?"

Reedy hadn't been part of the first class to enter, but she graduated with the first class to serve active duty. "They saw it was common everywhere else. Does it matter? Who can understand their motives? Their gene modifications make them impure. Half-animal, barely human."

She frowned, as if she couldn't believe that kind of prejudice still existed. "Nukes don't distinguish between one set of genes and another, sir. They suffered during the bombardments, just like we did. They fought beside us, they went to our church. Even the archbishop called them good citizens. They're as proud to be Jesusalemites as I am. And as loyal. Sir."

Max rubbed his nose again. "A role model for treason. They betrayed one government to serve another. I know for a fact this crew contains at least one double agent, someone who serves two masters. I suspect there are more. Is it you, Miss Reedy?"

Lukinov turned into a fossil before Max's eyes. Petoskey glared at the young intelligence officer across the table like a man contemplating murder.

Reedy pressed her fingertips together until her hands grew still. "Sir. There may be a traitor, but it's not me. Sir."

Max leaned back casually. "I've read your Academy records, Ensign, and find them interesting for the things they leave out. Such as your role in the unfortunate accident that befell Cadet Vance."

Reedy was well disciplined. Max's comments were neither an order nor a question, so she said nothing, gave nothing away.

"Vance's injuries necessitated his withdrawal from the Academy," Max continued. "What exactly did you have to do with that situation?"

"Come on, Max," said Lukinov in his senior officer's cease-and-desist voice. "This is going too far. There are always accidents in the Academy and in the service. Usually it's the fault of the idiot who ends up slabbed. Some stupid mistake."

Before Max could observe that Vance's mistake had been antagonizing Reedy, Petoskey interrupted. "Lukinov, have you forgotten how to deal? Are you broke yet, Nikomedes? You can quit any time you want."

Max flashed the plastic in his pocket while Lukinov started tossing down the cards. As he made the second circuit around their makeshift table, the lights flickered and went off. Max's stomach fluttered as the emergency lights blinked on, casting a weak red glare over the cramped room. The cards sailed past the table and into the air. Petoskey slammed his glass down. It bounced off the table and twirled toward the ceiling, spilling little brown droplets of whiskey.

Petoskey slapped the ship's intercom. "Bridge!"

"Ensign," Lukinov said. "Find something to catch that mess before the grav comes back on and splatters it everywhere."

"Yes, sir," Reedy answered and scrambled to the bathroom for a towel.

"Bridge!" shouted Petoskey, then shook his head. "The com's down."

"It's just the ship encounter drill," Lukinov said.

"There's no drill scheduled for this rotation. And we haven't entered Adarean space yet, so we can't be encountering another ship. . . ."

Another ship.

The thought must have hit all four of them simultaneously. As they propelled themselves frog-like toward the hatch, they crashed into one another, inevitable in the small space. During the jumble, Max took a kick to the back of his head. It hurt, even without any weight behind it. No accident, he was sure of that, but he didn't see who did it.

Petoskey flung the door open. "The pig-hearted, fornicating bastards."

Max echoed the sentiment when he followed a moment later. The corridor was blocked by drifting crates. They'd been improperly secured.

"Ensign!" snapped Petoskey.

"Yes, Captain."

"To the front! I'll pass you the crates, you attach them."

"Yes, sir."

"Can I *trust* you to do that?"

"Yes, sir!"

Max almost felt sorry for Reedy. Almost. In typical fashion for these older ships, someone had strung a steel cable along the corridor, twist-tied to the knobs of the security lights. Max held onto it and stayed out of the way as Petoskey grabbed one loose box after another and passed them back to Reedy. There was the steady rasp of Velcro as they made their way toward the bridge.

"What do you think it is?" Lukinov whispered to him. "If it's a ship, then the wormhole's been discovered. . . ."

The implications hung in the air like everything else. Max compared the size of Lukinov's boot with the sore spot on the back of his head. "Could be another wormhole. The sponge is like that. Once one hole opens up, you usually find several more. There's no reason why the Adareans couldn't find a route in the opposite direction."

Lukinov braced himself against the wall, trying to keep himself oriented as if the grav was still on. "If it's the Adareans, they'll be thinking invasion again."

"It could be someone neutral too," said Max. "Most of the spongedivers from Earth are prospecting in toward the core again, so it could be one of them. Put on your ears and find out who they are. I'll determine whether they're for us or against us."

Lukinov laughed. "If they're against us, then Ernst can eliminate them. That's a proper division of labor."

"Our system is imperfect, but it works." That was a stretch, Max told himself. Maybe he ought to just say that the system worked better than the one it replaced.

"Hey," Petoskey shouted. "Are you gentlemen going to sit there or join me on the bridge?"

"Coming," said Lukinov, echoed a second later by Max.

They descended two levels and came to the control center. Max followed the others through the open hatch. Men sat strapped to their chairs, faces tinted the color of blood by the glow of the emergency lights. Conduits, ducts, and wires ran overhead, like the intestines of some manmade monster. One of the vents kicked on, drawing a loud mechanical breath. Truly, Max thought, they were in the belly of leviathan now.

One of the men called "Attention" and Petoskey immediately replied, "At ease — report!"

"Lefty heard a ship," returned Commander Gordet, a plug-shaped man with a double chin. "It was nothing more than a fart in space, I swear. I folded the wings and initiated immediate shutdown per your instructions before our signature could be detected."

"Contact confirmed?"

"Yes, sir."

"Good work then." The ship chairs were too small for Petoskey's oversized frame. He preferred to stand anyway and had bolted a towel rack to the floor in the center of the deck. The crew tripped over it when the grav was on, but now Petoskey slipped his feet under it to keep from bumping his head on the low ceilings. It was against all regulations, but, just as with his smuggled tobacco, Petoskey broke regulations whenever it suited him. He shared this quality with many of the fleet's best deep space captains. "Those orders were for when we entered Adarean space, Commander," Petoskey added. "I commend your initiative. Put a commendation in Engineer Elefteriou's record also."

"Yes, sir." Gordet's voice snapped like elastic, pleased by the captain's praise.

"Identity?"

"Its prime number pings up Outback. Corporate prospectors. Her signature looks like one of the new class."

Petoskey grabbed the passive scope above his head and pulled it down to his eyes. "Vector?"

"Intercept."

"*Intercept?*"

"It's headed in-system and we're headed out. At our current respective courses and velocities, we should come within spitting distance of each other just past Big Brother."

Big Brother was the nickname for this system's larger gas giant. Little Brother, the smaller gas giant, was on the far side of the sun, out past the wormhole to home.

"Are they coming from the Adares jump?" Petoskey asked.

"That's what we thought at first," said Gordet. "But it appears now that they're entering from a third wormhole. About thirty degrees negative of the Adares jump, on the opposite side of the ecliptic." He glanced over the navigator's shoulder at the monitor and read off the orbital velocity.

Petoskey continued to stare into the scope. "Shit. There's nothing out here."

Gordet cleared his throat. "It's millions of kilometers out, sir. Still too far away for a clear visual."

"No, I mean there's *nothing* out here. This system won't hold their attention for long. It's only a matter of time before they find the opened holes to Adares and home." He paused. "Do that and they'll close our route back."

Indeed. Max had a strong urge to pace. If he started bouncing off the walls Petoskey would order him off the bridge, so he tried to float with purpose. Burdick, the third member of the intelligence team, paused in the hatch, carrying a large box. He nodded to Lukinov and Reedy, who followed him forward toward the secure radio room. Max wondered briefly why Burdick had left his post.

"The intercept makes things easier for us," Petoskey concluded aloud. "Calculate the soonest opportunity to engage without warning. With any luck, the missing ship will be counted as a wormhole mishap." Absorbed by the sponge.

Eleftheriou turned and spoke to Rucker, the first lieutenant, who spoke to Gordet, who said, "Sir, radio transmissions from the ship appear to be directed at another ship in the vicinity of the jump. If we neutralize this target, then the other dives out and lives to witness."

"Just one other ship?"

"No way of telling this far out without the active sensors." Which they couldn't use without showing up like a solar flare.

"The order stands," said Petoskey. "Also, Commander, loose cargo in the corridors impeded my progress to the bridge. This is a contraindication of ship readiness."

Gordet stiffened, as crushed by this criticism as he'd been puffed up by the praise. "It'll be taken care of, *sir*."

"See to it. Where's Chevrier?" Arkady Chevrier was the chief engineer. He came from a family of industrialists that contributed heavily to the Revolution. His uncle headed the Department of Finance, and his father was a general. Mallove, Max's boss in Political Education, had warned him not to antagonize Chevrier.

"In the engine room, sir," answered Gordet. "He thought that the sudden unscheduled shutdown of main power resulted in a drain on the main battery arrays. I sent him to fix it."

"Raise Engineering on the com."

"Yes, sir," said Gordet. "Raise Engineering."

Lefty punched his console, listened to his earphones, shook his head.

Petoskey shifted the plug of tobacco in his mouth. "When I tried to contact the bridge from quarters, the com was down. If I have to choose between ship communications and life support in the presence of a possible enemy vessel, I want communications first. Get a status report from Engineering and give me a com link to all essential parts of the ship if you have to do it with tin cans and string. Is that clear?"

Gordet's jowls quivered as he answered. "Yessir!"

Max noted that Gordet did not divide his attention well. He'd been so absorbed with the other ship, he hadn't noticed the ship communications problem. Several past errors in judgment featured prominently in his permanent file. He seemed unaware that this was the reason he'd been passed over for ship command of his own. But he was steady, and more or less politically sound.

He could also be a vindictive S.O.B. Max watched him turn on his subordinates. "Corporal Elefteriou," Gordet said. "I want a full report on com status. Five minutes ago is not soon enough. Lieutenant Rucker!"

"Sir."

"Get your ass to Engineering. I want to receive Chevrier's verbal report on this com here." He punched it with his fist for emphasis. "If it doesn't come in fifteen minutes, you can hold your breath while the rest of us put on space gear."

The first lieutenant set off for Engineering. Petoskey cleared his throat. "Commander, one other thing."

"Yes?"

"We'll switch to two shifts now, six hours on, six off. All crew."

"Yes, sir."

Petoskey gestured for Max to come beside him.

"So now we wait around for three days to intercept," Petoskey said in a low voice. "You look like a damn monkey floating there, Nikomedes. We could surgi-tape your boots to the deck."

"That's not necessary." Petoskey wasn't the only captain in the fleet who'd tie his political officer down to one spot if he could. Max needed to be free to move around to catch his traitor.

"If you were qualified for any systems, I'd put you to work."

An excellent reason to remain unqualified. "And what would you have me do?"

"At this point?" Petoskey shrugged. Then he frowned, and jerked his head toward the intelligence team's radio room. "Was that true? About—?"

"This is *not* the place," Max said firmly. Illusion was not reality; the crew pretended not to hear Petoskey speak, but they'd repeat every word that came from his mouth.

"I hate the Adareans, I want you to know that," Petoskey said. "Anything to do with the Adareans, I hate, and I'll have none of it aboard my ship. So if there's any danger, even from one of the intelligence men—"

"There will be no danger," Max asserted firmly. "It is my job to make certain of that."

"See to it, Lieutenant."

"I will." Max was surprised. That qualified as the most direct command any captain had given him during his tenure as a political officer.

Petoskey returned an almost respectful nod. Max was about to suggest a later discussion when Lukinov shouted from the hatch.

"Captain. You might want to listen to this. We tried to raise you on the com, but it's not working."

Petoskey slipped his feet free and followed the intelligence officer. Max invited himself and swam along.

Inside the listening room, Reedy stood—or floated—at a long desk, wearing headphones and making notes on the translation in her palm-pad. Burdick had a truck battery surgi-taped to a table wedged in the tiny room's rounded corner. Wires ran from it to an open panel on the main concomsole, and Burdick connected others. He looked up from his work and grinned as they came into the hatch. "Gotta love the electrician's mates," he said. "They've got *everything*."

Lukinov laughed and handed headphones to Petoskey. "Wait until you hear this."

Petoskey slipped the earpieces into place. "I don't understand Chinese," he said after a minute. "Always sounds like an out-of-tune guitar to me."

Lukinov's smile widened. "But it's voices, not code, don't you see? The level of encryption was like cheap glue." He made a knife-opening-a-letter gesture with his hands.

"Good work. What have you learned so far?"

Lukinov leaned over Reedy's shoulder to look at her palm-pad. "Corporate security research ship. Spongedivers."

Petoskey nodded. "Bunch of scientists and part-time soldiers. Soft, but great tech. Way beyond ours. It's a safe bet their battery arrays don't go down when they fly mute. Lefty says there's another one parked out by the wormhole."

Lukinov confirmed this. "We know it because the radio tech is talking to his *girl*friend over on the other ship."

Burdick snickered, and Petoskey muttered "Mixed crews" with all the venom of a curse. He glared at Reedy so hard his eyes must have burned a hole in the ensign's head. The young woman looked up. "Yes, sir?" she asked.

"I didn't speak to you," Petoskey snapped.

Mixed crews were part of the Revolution, a way to double manpower—so to speak—in the military forces and give Jesusalem a chance to catch up. So far it was only in the officer corps, and even there it hadn't been received well. Some men, like Vance at the Academy, openly tried to discourage it despite the government's commitment.

Lukinov held the back of Reedy's seat to keep from drifting toward the ceiling. "The inbound ship's called the *Deng Xiaopeng*. Why does that name sound familiar?"

Petoskey shrugged. "Means nothing to me."

If they didn't know, then Max would give them an answer. He cleared his throat. "I believe that Deng Xiaopeng was one of Napoleon's generals."

Lukinov curled his mouth skeptically.

"That doesn't sound right," said Petoskey.

"I'm quite certain of it," said Max, bracing himself between the wall and floor at angle sideways to the others. "Confusion to the enemy."

"Always," replied Petoskey, apparently happy to find something he could agree with. "Always."

Max lay on the bunk in his cabin waiting for the clock to tick over to morning. Two days after the spongedivers had been sighted, his thoughts still careened weightlessly off the small walls. The presence of the ship from Outback complicated the ship's mission and his. Meanwhile, he was cut off from his superiors, unable to guess which goal they wanted him to pursue now. Or goals, as the case more likely was. So he was on his own again. Forced to decide for himself.

Nothing new about that, he thought ruefully.

He released the straps and pushed off for the door to take a tour of the ship. He paused for a moment, then grabbed his cap, and tugged it down tight on his head. If he made it a formal tour of the ship, it might draw out his traitor.

When he opened the door, he saw another one cracked open down the corridor. Lieutenant Rucker peeked out and gestured for Max to come inside. Max checked to see that no one was in the hall and slipped into the room.

The blond young man closed the door too fast and it slammed shut. He noticed Max's cap and saluted with perfect etiquette before producing an envelope. "I was hoping to catch you," he said. "This is from Commander Gordet."

Max took the multi-tool from his pocket and flicked out the miniature knife to slice open the seal. He studied the sheet inside. Gordet had written down the codes for the safe that held the captain's secret orders. Interesting. Max wondered if Rucker had made a copy for himself. "Did Gordet say anything specific?"

"He said to tell you that if we were to engage the Outback ship in combat and anything unfortunate were to happen to the captain, you would have his full cooperation and support."

"So what did he tell the captain?"

Rucker looked at the wall, opened his mouth, closed it again. He was not a quick liar.

Max gave him an avuncular clap on the shoulder. "You can tell me, Lieutenant. I'll find out anyway."

Rucker gulped, still refusing to meet Max's eyes. "He told the captain that, um, if we were to engage the other ship in combat, and anything unfortunate were to happen to you, he'd make sure it was all clear in the records."

So Gordet was indecisive, trying to play both sides at once. That was a hard game. The Commander had no gift for it either. "What's your opinion of Gordet?" probed Max.

"He's a good officer. I'm proud to serve under him."

Rather standard response, deserving of Max's withering stare. This time Rucker's eyes did meet his.

"But, um, he's still mad about losing his cabin to you, sir. He doesn't like bunking with the junior officers."

"He'll get over it," said Max. "Just remind him that Lukinov is bunking with Burdick, eh?" He gestured at Rucker to open the door. Rucker looked both ways down the corridor, motioned that it was clear, and Max went on his way.

He headed topside, pulling himself hand over hand up the narrow shaft. When he exited the tube he found Kulakov conducting an emergency training drill in the forward compartments. Stick-its posted to all the surfaces indicated the type and extent of combat damage. Crews in full space gear performed "repairs" while the chief petty officer graded their performance.

"You're dead," shouted Kulakov, grabbing a man by his collar and pulling him out of the exercise. "You forgot that you're a vacuum cleaner!"

"But sir, I'm suited up properly." His voice sounded injured, even distorted slightly by the microphone.

"But you're not plugged in," Kulakov said, tapping the stick-it on the wall. "That's open to the outside, and without your tether you're nothing more now than a very small meteor moving away from the ship! What are the rest of you looking at?"

He glanced over his shoulder, saw Max, and froze. The crews stopped their exercise.

"You just spaced another crewman," said Max, tilting his head toward a man who'd backed into the wall. "Carry on."

He turned away without waiting for Kulakov's salute. He didn't know why he had such an effect on that man, but now he was thinking he should look into it.

He proceeded through several twisting corridors, designed to slow and confuse boarding parties headed for the bridge, and passed the gym. He needed exercise. The weightlessness was already starting to get to him. But he decided to worry about that later.

He paused when he came to the missile room.

The Black Forest.

That was the crew's nickname for it. Four polished black columns rose four uninterrupted stories—tubes for nuclear missiles, back when this ship was intended to fight the same kind of dirty war waged by the Adareans. It was the largest open space in the entire ship. When the grav was on, the men exercised by running laps, up one set of stairs, across the catwalk, down the other, around the tubes, and up again.

Max went out onto the catwalk, climbed up on the railing, and jumped.

If one could truly jump in zero-gee, that was. He pushed himself toward the floor and prayed that the grav didn't come on unexpectedly. On the way down he noticed someone who feared just that possibility making their way up the stairs.

Max did a somersault, extending his legs to change his momentum and direction, pushed off one of the tubes, and bounced over to see who it was. He immediately regretted doing so. It was Sergeant Simco, commander of the combat troops.

Every captain personally commanded a detachment of ground troops. It could be as big as a battalion in some cases, but for this voyage, with an entire crew of only 141, the number was limited to ten. Officially, they were along to repel boarders and provide combat assistance if needed. Unofficially, they were called troubleshooters. If crewmen gave the captain any trouble, it was the troopers' job to shoot them.

Simco would enjoy doing it too. He had more muscles than brains. But then nobody had that many brains.

"Hello, Sergeant," Max called.

"Sir, that was nicely done."

"I didn't have you pegged for the cautious type."

Simco shook his head. "I don't like freefall unless I've got a parachute strapped to my back."

Typical groundhog response. "Are your men ready to board and take that Outback ship, Sergeant?"

"Sir, I could do it all by myself. They're *women*."

They both laughed, Simco snapped a perfect salute, and Max pushed off from the railing. When he landed on the bottom, he saw placards marked "Killshot" hanging on each of the four tubes. That meant they were loaded with live missiles, ready to launch. Something new since the last time he'd passed through the Black Forest. He saw handwriting scrawled across the bottom of the placards, and went up close to read it. A. G. W.

Under the old government, the hastily thrown together Department of War had been called the Ministry of A Just God's Wrath. Considering the success of the Adareans, the joke had been that the name was a typo and should have been called Adjust God's Wrath. Some devout crewmen still had the same goal.

On the lower level, Max continued to the aftmost portion of the ship, off limits to all crew except for Engineering and Senior officers. Only one sealed hatch allowed direct entrance to this section. Max found an off-duty electrician's mate sitting there, watching a pocketvid. The faint sound of someone dying came from the tiny speaker.

Max stopped in front of the crewman. "What are you watching?"

The crewman looked up, startled. DePuy, that was his name. He jumped to his feet and went all the way to the ceiling. He saluted with one hand, while the thumb of the other flicked to the pause button. "It's *A Fire on the Land*, sir. It's about the Adarean nuking of New Nazareth."

"I'm familiar with it," Max replied. Political Education approved all videos, practically ran the video business. "The bombing and the vid. Move aside and let me pass."

"Sorry, sir, the chief engineer said. . . ."

Max turned as cold as deep space. He reached under DePuy to open the hatch. "Move aside, crewman."

"The chief engineer gave me a direct order, sir!"

"And I am giving you another direct order right now." Damn it, thought Max, the man still hesitated. "Rejecting an order from your political officer is mutiny, Mr. DePuy. A year is a very long time to spend in the ship's brig waiting for trial."

"Sir! A year is a very long time to serve under a chief officer who holds grudges, sir!"

"If I have to repeat my order a third time, you *will* go to the brig."

DePuy pushed off from the wall. Though he seemed to seriously consider, for a split second, whether he wouldn't rather be locked up than face Chevrier's temper.

Max went down the corridor and paused outside the starboard Battery Room. The hatch stood open on the two-story space. One of the battery arrays was completely disassembled and diagrammed on the wall, with the key processing chips circled in red. A small group of men, most of them stripped to their waists, crowded into the soft-walled clean room in the corner. A large duct ran up from it toward the ceiling, the motor struggling to draw air. A crewman looked up and tapped the chief engineer on the shoulder.

"You!" Chevrier shouted as soon as he saw Max. "This is a restricted area! I want you out of my section right now!"

"Nothing is off limits to me," Max replied.

"Fuck your mother!" Chevrier thundered, shooting across the room and getting right in Max's face. Chevrier's eyes had dark circles around them like storm clouds, and red lines in the whites like tiny bolts of lightning. He probably hadn't slept since the spongediver was spotted; no doubt he was also pumped up on Nova or its more legal equivalent from the dispensary. That would explain his heavy sweating. It couldn't drip off him in the weightlessness, but had simply accumulated in a pool about a half inch deep that sloshed freely in the vicinity of his breastbone. Max noticed that the comet insignia was *branded* on Chevrier's bare chest. The Revolutionary government had banned that tradition, but the branding irons still floated around some ships in the service. Chevrier was the type who had probably heated it up with a hand welder and branded himself. He jabbed a finger in the direction of the empty spot on Max's left breast pocket. "You haven't qualified for a single ship's system," he said, "and you sure as hell aren't reactor qualified. Now get out of my section!"

"You forgetting something, soldier?" Max asked, in as irritating a voice as he could manage.

Chevrier laughed in disbelief. "I wish I could forget! I've got a major problem on my hands, a ship with no fucking backup power."

Max took a deep breath. "Did somebody break your arm, *soldier*?"

Chevrier's eyes flickered. He made a sloppy motion with his right hand in the general direction of his head. Had Mallove sent word in the other direction too? Did Chevrier know that Max was supposed to leave him alone?

"Good. Give me a status report on the power situation."

The chief engineer inhaled deeply. "Screwed up and likely to stay that way. The crewman on duty panicked—he folded the wings and powered down the Casmir drive without disengaging the batteries first and fried half the chips. We are now trying to build new chips, atom by atom, but you need a grade A clean hood to do that. And our hood is about as tight and clean as an old whore."

Max had heard all this already, less vividly described, from the captain's reports. "Go on."

"Normally, we could just switch over to the secondary array, but some blackhole of a genius gutted our portside Battery Room and replaced it with a salvaged groundside nuclear reactor so we can float through Adarean space disguised like background radiation in order to do God knows what."

"But you can switch communications, ship systems, propulsion, all that, over to the reactor, right?"

That was the plan: dive into Adarean space, do one circuit around the sun running on the nukes while recording everything they could on the military and political communications channels, then head home again.

"We've already done all that," answered Chevrier, "but we can't power up the Casmir drive with it. It's strictly inner system, no diving." He suddenly noticed the pool of sweat on his chest, went to flick it away, then stopped. "The Adareans won't scan us if we're running on nuclears, but they wouldn't scan canvas sails either, so we might as well have used them instead. We've got to fix the main battery at some point."

"Can you bring the grav back online?"

"Not safely, no, and not with the reactor. It's a power hog. Too many things to go wrong."

"Lasers?"

Chevrier ground his teeth. "You could talk to the captain, you know. He sends down here every damned hour for another report, asking the same exact damn questions."

"Lasers?" repeated Max firmly.

"I recommended other options to the captain, but if you want to turn some Outback ship into space slag, I'll give you enough power to do it. As long as you let me comb through the debris for spare parts once you're done. Might be one way to get some decent equipment."

"Fair enough. How are your men holding up?"

"They're soldiers." He pronounced the word very differently than Max had. "They do exactly what they're told. Except for that worthless snot of a mate who apparently can't even guard a fucking sealed hatch properly."

Max didn't like the sound of that. Chevrier couldn't keep pushing his men as hard as he pushed himself, or they'd start to break. "Your men are not machines—"

"Hell they aren't! A ship's crew is one big machine and you're a piece of grit in the silicone, a short in the wire. With you issuing orders outside the chain of command, the command splits. You either need to fit in or get the hell out of the machine!"

Chevrier jabbed his finger at Max's chest again to punctuate his statement. This time, he made contact with enough force to send the two men in opposite directions.

It was clear that he didn't mean to touch Max, and just as clear that he didn't mean to back down. He glared at Max, daring him to make something of it. Aggressiveness was the main side effect of Nova. It built up until the men went supernova and burned out. On top of that, Chevrier also had that look some men got when things went very wrong. He couldn't fix things so he wanted to smash them instead.

Max could bring him up on charges, but the ship needed its chief engineer right now. And if Mallove had promised his friends in government that he would protect Chevrier. . . .

Max decided to ignore the incident. For the time being. "I'll be sure to make a record of your comments."

Chevrier snorted, as if he'd won a game of chicken. "If you have problems with any of the big words, come back and I'll spell them out for you." He flapped his hand near his head again, turned and went back to the clean hood.

The other men scowled at Max.

That was the problem with anger—it was an infectious disease. Frustration only made it spread faster. He continued his tour, looking into the main engine room and then at the nuclear reactors. Nobody was in the former because there was nothing to be done there, and nobody was in the latter because radiation spooked them. One man sat in the control room, reading the monitors. Max hovered near the ceiling a moment looking over the crewman's shoulder, comparing the pictures on the vids to the layout of the rooms. The crewman stared at the monitors intently, pretending not to see Max. Yes, thought Max, anger was very infectious. You never knew who might catch it next.

The hapless mate DePuy still guarded the hatch, whipping the vid behind his back as he snapped to attention. Max ignored him. Accidents happened. Some idiots would just slab themselves.

He went back through the Black Forest, acknowledging salutes from a pair of shooters, the tactics officer's mates. He swam through the air to the top level, and down the main corridor, past the open door of the exercise room. He turned back. If grav was going to be offline much longer, he needed to sign up for exercise time. Physically, he needed to stay sharp right now.

Max pushed the door open. The room was dark. It surprised him briefly that no one was there, but then, with the six-and-sixes, and all the drills, the men were probably too busy. He hit the light switch. Nothing came on. He moved farther into the room to hit the second switch. Something hard smashed on the back of the head, knocking his cap off. He twisted, trying to get a hold of his assailant, but there was no one behind him. He realized that the other man was above him, on the ceiling, too late, and as he twisted in the dark room, he suddenly became very dizzy, losing any sense of direction, any orientation to the walls and floors. A thick arm snaked around his throat, choking off his nausea along with his breath. Max got hold of a thumb and managed to pull it halfway loose, but he had no leverage at all.

He swung his elbows forcefully and futilely as black dots swam before his eyes like collapsing stars in the darkened room.

Then the darkness became absolute.

———————————————

He experienced a floating, disconnected sensation, like being in the sensory deprivation tanks they'd used for some of his conditioning experiments. Max had hated the feeling then, of being lost, detached, and he hated it now. Then light knifed down into one of his eyes and all his pains awoke at once.

"Do you hear me, Lieutenant Nikomedes?"

"Yes," croaked Max. His throat felt raw. The light flicked off, then stabbed into the other eye. "That hurts."

"I should imagine that it's the least of your hurts. Has the painkiller worn off completely then?"

"I hope so, because if it hasn't you should just kill me now." His throat felt crushed and his kidneys ached like hell. The light went off and Max's eyes adjusted to the setting. He was in the sickbay with the Doc hovering over him. His name was Noyes, and he was only a medtech, but the crew still called him Doc. The service was short of surgeons. Command didn't want to spare one for this voyage.

"Your pupils look good," Noyes continued. "There's a ruptured blood vessel in the right eye. It's not pretty, but the damage is superficial. We had some concern about how long you'd been without oxygen when you came in."

Yeah, thought Max. He was concerned too. "So how long was it?"

"Not long. Seconds, maybe. A couple of the shooters found you unconscious in the gym."

"And so they brought the Corpse to sickbay?"

"You know that nickname?" Noyes administered an injection and Max's pain lessened. "Whoever attacked you knew what he was doing. He cut off your air supply without crushing your windpipe or leaving any fingerprint type bruises on your throat. You're lucky—the shooters did chest compressions as soon as they found you and got you breathing again."

So this wasn't just a warning. Someone had tried to kill him, and failed. Unless the shooters were in on it. But who would do it and why? His hand shot up to his breast pocket. Gordet's note with the secret codes was still there.

"What's that?" asked Noyes, noticing the gesture.

"A list of suspects," replied Max. He wondered if someone had followed him from Engineering. "Did you hear the one about the political officer who was killed during wargame exercises?"

Suspicion flickered across the Doc's face. "No," he said slowly.

"They couldn't call it friendly fire because he had no friends."

Noyes didn't laugh. He was young, barely thirty, if that. But his face was worn, and he had a deep crease between his eyes. "Can I ask you a direct question?"

"If it's about who did this—"

"No. It's about the ship's mission."

"I may not be able to answer."

"It's just the crew, you know what they're saying, that this is a suicide mission. We're supposed to sneak into Adarean space, nuke their capital, and then blow ourselves up, vaporize the evidence."

"Ah." No, Max hadn't heard that one yet, though he supposed he should have thought of it himself. Sometimes there were disadvantages to knowing inside information; it limited one's ability to imagine other possibilities. "We could blow up their capital, but their military command is space-based, decentralized. That kind of strike wouldn't touch them at all. That doesn't make any sense, Doc."

"It doesn't have to make sense for the service to order it." Noyes laughed, a truncated little puff of air. "I was scheduled for leave, I was supposed to be getting married on my leave, and I got yanked off the transport and put on this ship without a word of explanation, and then found out I was going to be gone for a year and a half. So don't tell me the service only gives orders that make any sense."

Max had no answer for that. He knew how orders were.

"Is this a suicide mission?" asked Noyes. "Tell me straight. The shooters think that's why someone tried to kill you, because they don't have to worry about consequences when they get back home."

And they could die knowing they'd offed an officer. There were definitely a few of that type onboard. But Max didn't think it was that random. "And if it is a suicide mission?"

The medtech's face grew solemn. "Then I want to send some kind of message back to Suzan. I don't want her to think I simply disappeared on her. I don't want her to live the rest of her life with that."

Noyes couldn't be the only one having those thoughts. No wonder there was tension on the ship. "This isn't a suicide mission," Max said firmly.

"Your word on that?"

"Yes." He would have to try to kill this rumor. Even if it proved to be true. Max touched his pocket again. What exactly were the secret orders? He thought he knew them, but maybe he didn't.

Noyes shook his head. "Too bad you're the political officer. Everyone knows your word can't be trusted." He handed Max a bottle of pills. "The captain wants to see you on the bridge right away. Take one of these if you feel weak, or in pain, and then report back to sickbay next shift."

Max sat up, and noticed his pants pockets were inside out. So someone had been searching him after all and the shooters interrupted them. Unless that too was part of the ruse. For now, he'd stick to the simpler explanation.

Noyes helped him to his feet. "I ought to keep you for observation," he said.

"No," replied Max. "I'm fine." I'm as rotten a liar as Rucker is, he thought. He wondered if the first lieutenant had changed his mind. Or changed his allegiances.

The door opened and Simco waited outside. His bulk seemed to fill the small corridor. He held his hands folded behind his back. "Captain assigned me to be your guard, sir. He asks you not to speak about this incident while I'm investigating it. He also requires your immediate attention on the bridge."

"The assignment comes a little too late, apparently, Sergeant," murmured Max. He gestured for Simco to lead the way.

"You first, sir."

Trouble never came looking for him face-to-face, thought Max as he led the way through the corridors. It always came sneaking up behind.

A double crew packed the already tight bridge because of shift change, giving reports to one another in low tones.

No one but the captain bothered to look up when Max entered, and even he only glanced away from the scope for a second. Vents hissed above the muted beeps from the monitors. The two shooters Max had seen in the Black Forest were seated next to the tactics officer. Max waited to make eye contact with them, to say thanks, but they were so absorbed in their work they didn't notice him. He gave up waiting, and slid over to stand by Petoskey.

"It's about damn time, Nikomedes," growled Petoskey.

"I had a slight accident."

"Well I have a slight problem. The incoming ship boosted. They're in some kind of a hurry. So our window of opportunity is here, and it's closing fast."

He hasn't made up his mind yet, Max realized. "Have they detected us?"

"No. We're between them and the rings. They don't see us because we're floating dead, and because they don't expect to see anyone out here."

Max remained silent, running the calculations through his head. Outback's presence would not affect the Jesusalem's claim to the system, only the possible success of their mission through Adarean space.

" 'War is an extension of political policy with military force,' " prompted Petoskey, quoting regulations.

And it was the job of the political officer to be the final arbiter of policy. This was exactly the type of unforeseen situation that created the need for political officers on ships. "What are our options?"

Petoskey shifted his chewing tobacco into a spot below his lower lip. "Chevrier says we could power up and hit them with the lasers, but we wouldn't get more than one or two shots. I don't like our chances at this distance. We could launch the nuclears at them. They'd see them coming, but we could bracket them so that they'll still take on a killer dose of radiation even if we don't score a direct hit. Or we could do nothing."

"What are your concerns?"

He sucked the tobacco juice through his teeth. "The last I heard officially, Outback was one of our trading partners."

"We have met the enemy," Max mused softly, "and they are us."

Petoskey scowled. "But Outback also trades with Adares. If they find our dive to their system, they'll let the Adareans know about it and that endangers our mission. So what's the politically correct thing for me to do?"

"I would suggest that we haven't been tasked with guarding the system or the other wormhole. I would point out that there are other ships in place specifically to do just that." He paused. "And as long as we dive undetected, our mission isn't really endangered."

Petoskey leaned back and straightened so that his head nearly scraped the pipes. He slammed the scope back into its slot and stared hard at Max. "So we let them pass?"

"They've got a second ship outside our range. We pop this one and the other one sees us, then Jesusalem could face a war on two fronts." Although they weren't technically at war with Adares any longer, the capital was filled with rumors of war. "Politically, we're not ready to handle that."

"I'll tell you one thing," said Petoskey, with a slight shudder that mixed revulsion with unease. "I'm glad not to use the nukes. Those are dirty weapons to use. On people."

"I fail to see any difference," said Max. "Two kinds of fire. Lasers or nukes, they would be equally dead."

Petoskey had a lidded cup taped to the conduits on the wall. He pulled it off, spit into it, and taped it back up again. Pausing, so he could change the subject. "I understand that *you* were nearly dead a little while ago, Nikomedes. Simco has one of his men guarding Reedy."

"Why?" asked Max. Had the ensign been attacked also?

"Spy or not, it's obvious she's trying to get back at you for your comments in quarters the other day. I asked around and found out what she did to Vance. Shows what happens when you don't keep women in their place. Before I had her locked up, I wanted to make certain this wasn't something arranged between the two of you. Some kind of duel. Not that I thought it was, but. . . ."

He thought it might be, finished Max to himself. Or hoped it might be. "It wasn't Reedy as far as I know. But let Simco's man watch her while Simco investigates. If Reedy's guilty, maybe she'll give herself away."

"Shouldn't have a woman onboard anyway, even if she is language qualified. We can't afford dissension on a voyage like this one. I will personally execute anyone who endangers this mission. I don't care if it is a junior officer."

Or a woman, thought Max. "Understood," he answered. He looked up one last time, to see if he could catch the shooters' eyes. That's when he noticed Rucker and Gordet staring at him. They had been whispering to one another and stopped. "In fact, I think I'll head down to the radio room right now."

"You're dismissed from duty until Doc says you've recovered. And Simco or one of his men will stay with you at all times."

That was not what Max wanted, not at all. "Thanks. I appreciate that."

Petoskey nodded, dismissing him.

Max began to wish that whoever had attacked him had done a better job.

He went to the secure radio room and all three of the intelligence officers stopped talking and turned toward the doorway. It's the Political Officer Effect, thought Max.

"What happened to your face?" Lukinov asked.

"I fought the law and the law won," Max answered impulsively.

Burdick burst out laughing. Even Lukinov smiled. "Why does that sound so damned familiar?" he asked.

"*Judas's Chariot*," answered Burdick. "The vid. It was one of Barabbas's lines."

"Yeah, yeah, I remember that one now. It had Oliver Whatshisname in it. I got to meet him once, at a party, when he did that public information vid. Good man." He twisted around. The smell of his cologne nearly choked Max. "Seriously, Max, what happened? Why has the captain put a guard on one of my men?"

"Someone tried to kill me." Max was disappointed with the surprise in Lukinov's expression. In all of their expressions. Intelligence was supposed to know everything. "Captain suspects the ensign here."

"That's ridiculous!" Lukinov rolled his eyes. Anger flashed across Reedy's face.

"It wasn't my suggestion," Max replied. "But if you don't mind my asking, which one of you is just coming on shift?"

"I am, sir," Reedy answered immediately.

"And where were you?"

"In her quarters sleeping," interjected Lukinov. "Where else would she have been?"

"You were there with her?" No one wanted to answer that accusation, so Max slid past it. "You two usually work one shift together, and Burdick takes the other, right?"

The senior officer hesitated. "I doubled shifted with Burdick because of the information we were getting."

So. Reedy had been alone. Not that Max suspected her of the attack. But now he'd have to. Maybe he'd misestimated her in the first place. "What information is that?"

"The other Outback ship is doing some kind of military research defending the wormhole. Based on what we're overhearing from observers in the shuttles. We've got a name on the second ship. It's the *Jiang Qing*, same class as the other one." He paused. "You aren't going to try to tell me that Jiang Qing was one of Napoleon's generals too, are you, Max?"

"Why not?" asked Max flatly. "Historically, Earth has had women generals for centuries. Jesusalem was the only planet without a mixed service."

Lukinov's lip curled. "We finally tracked down Deng Xiaopeng. He and this Jiang Qing woman were both part of the Chinese revolution. Reedy found the information."

"The Chinese communist revolution," clarified the ensign. "They were minor figures, associated with Mao. Both were charged with crimes though they helped bring about important political changes that led to the second revolution."

"Ah," said Max. A wave of pain shot through him. If his legs had been supporting his weight, they would surely have buckled. "Please cooperate with Sergeant Simco until we can get this straightened out. Now, if you will excuse me."

He didn't wait for their response, but turned back to the hall. Simco waited at parade rest, his hands behind his back. Another trooper stood beside him.

"I'm going to return to my cabin now," Max said.

"I've detailed Rambaud here to watch you while I begin my investigation," Simco replied. Rambaud was a smaller but equally muscled version of his superior officer. "I'll be rotating all my men through this duty until we find the culprit."

"Keeping them sharp?" Max said.

Simco nodded. "A knife can't cut if you don't keep it sharp."

"I couldn't agree more." Max barely noticed the other man shadowing him through the narrow maze of corridors. When he reached his room, he took a double dose of the doctor's painkillers, added one from his own stock, and washed them all down with a gulp of warm, flat water. He looked in the bathroom mirror at his damaged eye. That was when he started to shake. He had the ludicrous sensation that he was going to fall down, so he grabbed hold of the sink and tried to steady himself. Eventually it passed, but not before his breath came out in ragged gasps.

He'd come too close to dying this time. And why?

The rumor of the suicide mission still bothered him, and so did the problem of Reedy. When he drifted off to sleep, he dreamed that he was wandering an empty vessel searching for someone who was no longer aboard, through corridors that were kinked and slicked like the intestines of some animal. They started shrinking, squeezing the crates and boxes that filled them into a solid mass, as Max tried to find his way out. The last section dead-ended in a mirror, and when he paused to look into its silver surface he saw a bloody eye above a pyramid.

He woke up shivering and nauseous. According to the clock, he'd slept nearly four and a half hours, but he didn't believe it. He wasn't inclined to believe anything right now.

He rose and dressed himself. He needed better luck. If it wouldn't come looking for him, he'd have to go looking for it.

Down in the very bottom of the ship rested an observation chamber that contained the only naked ports in the entire vessel. Max went down there to think, dutifully followed by Simco's watchdog.

Max paused outside the airlock. "You can wait here."

"I'm supposed to stay with you, sir."

"The lights are off, it's empty," said Max, realizing as soon as the words were out of his mouth what had happened the last time he went into a dark room alone. "If someone's waiting in there to kill me, then you've got them trapped. You'll get a commendation."

Rambaud relented. Max entered the room, closing the hatch behind him. It sealed automatically, reminding Max of the sound of a prison cell door shutting.

Outside the round windows stretched the infinite expanse of space. The sun was a small, cold ember in a charcoal-colored sky dominated by the vast and ominous bulk of Big Brother. They were close enough that Max could see crimson storms raging on its surface, swirling hurricanes larger than Jerusalem itself. He counted three moons spinning around the planet, and great rings of dust, as if everything in space was drawn into satellites around the self-consuming fire of its mass.

A quiet cough came from the rear of the compartment.

Max pirouetted, and saw another man floating cross-legged in the air. As he unfolded and came to attention, light glinted off the jack that sat lodged in his forehead like a third eye. It was the spongediver, the ship's pilot, Patchett.

"At ease, Patchett," said Max.

Patchett nodded toward the port as he clasped his hands behind his back. "Beautiful, isn't it?"

"It's no place for a human being to live," Max said. "Give me a little blue marble of a planet any day instead."

The pilot smiled. "That figures."

"What do you mean?"

"You're the political officer, and politics is always about the place we live, how we live together." He gestured at the sweep of the illuminated rings. "But this is why I joined the service—to explore, to see space."

"Has it been worth it?"

"Too much waiting, too much doing nothing." Patchett shifted his position, rotating a quarter circle. "The diving makes it worthwhile."

"Good," murmured Max, looking away.

"You and I are alike that way. We both are the most useless men on the ship *except* for that one moment when we're the only one qualified to do the job." He stared out the port. "What happened to you, that was wrong, sir."

Max gazed out the window also, saying nothing.

"I'd guess," Patchett said, "that I've been in the service as long as you have. Nearly twenty years."

"Just past thirty years now," Max replied. It wasn't all in the official records, but thirty years total. A very long time. Patchett clearly wanted to say something more. "What is it?" asked Max. "Speak freely."

Patchett exhaled. "Things have been going downhill the past few years, sir. The wrong men in charge, undermining everything we hoped to accomplish in the Revolution. They all want war. They forget what the last one was like."

"Are you sure you should be telling this to your political officer?"

"You may be the only one I *can* say it to. You have to know it already. Petoskey's an excellent captain, don't get me wrong, sir. But he's too young to remember what the last war was like."

They hung there in the dark, weightless, silent, watching the giant spin on its axis. If Patchett was right, there was one moment in the voyage when only Max's skills would make a difference. But what moment, and what kind of difference, there was no way to know in advance.

When Max went to the med bay to check in with Noyes he found Simco sitting— more or less—at the exam table. "I'd salute," Simco said, "but Doc here's treating a sprain."

"Dislocation," corrected Noyes.

"What happened?" asked Max.

Simco grinned. "I scheduled extra combat training for my men. Want to make sure they're ready in case they run into whoever attacked you. It doesn't really count as a good workout unless someone dislocates something."

Noyes snorted.

"Plus, Doc here says that we have to exercise at least an hour a day or we'll start losing bone and muscle mass."

"Nobody's had to deal with prolonged weightlessness in a couple of hundred years," added Noyes. "I'm only finding hints of the information I need in our database. The nausea, vertigo, lethargy—that I expected and was prepared for. But we're already seeing more infections, shortness of breath, odd stuff. And we've got orders to spend *months* like this? It's madness. Take it easy on this thumb for a few more days, Simco." He went to lay his stim-gun on the table and it floated off sideways across the room. "Damn. Not again."

Max snatched it out of the air and handed it back to the Doc. "Any word on who my attacker was?" he asked Simco.

"No." The sergeant blew out his breath. "But I did hear that you picked a fight with Chevrier down in Engineering."

"Nothing even close to that."

"Good. He's a big man, completely out of your weight class."

"Right now, we're all in the same weight class."

That won Max a laugh from both Simco and Noyes. "Still, if you go see him again, about anything, please inform me first," the sergeant said.

"You'll know about it before I do," promised Max.

After the Doc finished checking him, Max went back through the crate-packed corridors toward his quarters. On the way, he passed Reedy, whose mouth quirked in a brief smile as Max squeezed past her.

"What do you find so funny, Ensign?" Max growled.

Reedy's eyes flicked, indicating the trooper following her and the one behind Max. "For a second there, sir, I wondered which of us was the real prisoner."

Very perceptive. She had an edge to her voice that reminded him of Chevrier. He recalled that she had shown a strong aversion to confinement after the incident with Vance. "Remember who you're speaking to, Ensign!"

"Yes, sir. It won't happen again, sir."

"See that it doesn't."

He went into his room and swallowed another painkiller. Even if the moment came when he could make a difference, would he be able to get away from his minders long enough to do it?

Eight more shifts, two more days, and nothing.

Max had no appetite, the food all tasted bland to him. He couldn't sleep for more than a few hours at a time. If he turned the lights off, he'd wake in a panic, disoriented, unsure of his location. But if he slept with the lights on, they poked at the edge of his consciousness, prodding him awake. He tried to exercise one hour out of every two shifts, but everything seemed tedious. It just felt wrong, empty motions with nothing to push against.

On the bridge, he asked Petoskey if it was still necessary to have a guard.

"The attack's still unsolved," Petoskey said. "Until Simco brings me the man—or woman—who did it, I want you protected."

Max had the sinking feeling that might be for the rest of the voyage. "How are the repairs going?"

"Chevrier replaced all the chips in the dead array with new ones, but something failed when he tested it. He has an idea for rebuilding the chips with some kind of silicon alloy crystal. Says he can grow it as long as we stay weightless. Some other kind of old tech. Inorganic. He tried to explain it to me, but he's the only one who really understands it."

"Can we wait that long?"

"We can't power up to jump as long as those Outback ships are in the vicinity. They'd see us—and the wormhole—in a microsecond. So far they still haven't detected our buoy. Or if they have, they just took it for a pulsar signal." Which was the idea, after all. Petoskey tugged hard at his beard. There were dark stains of sleeplessness under his eyes. "Don't you have some work to do, some reports to write?"

He meant it as a dismissal. Max was willing to be dismissed. He was still no closer to catching his traitor, and his luck couldn't have been more execrable.

He went to the ship's library to read. Rambaud, his trooper again this shift, had no interest in reading or studying vids of any kind. He writhed in almost open pain as Max made it clear that he intended to stay at a desk alone for several hours. Max decided that it wouldn't be murder if he bored Simco's men to death.

He sat there, scanning Fier's monograph on the Adarean war, skimming through the casualty lists in the appendixes, thinking about some of the worst battles, early on, and the consequences of war, when a voice intruded on his contemplations.

". . . bored as hell down here. Uh-huh. Wargames. That sounds interesting. Can you understand that Outback lingo?"

Rambaud was whispering on the comlink to his compatriot in charge of Reedy. Max let the conversation turn to complaints about the exercise regimen and weightlessness before he flipped off his screen and rose to go.

He headed for the intelligence radio room. The scent of Lukinov's imported cologne drifted out the open door into the corridor. Max paused at the doorway. Inside, the trooper floated behind Lukinov and Reedy. He wore a set of earphones.

"So this is how well you keep secrets?" asked Max.

The trooper saw Max, yanked the earphones out of his ear, and handed them back to an ebullient Lukinov. "Wait until you hear this, Max!" Lukinov said.

The trooper tried to squeeze by Max without touching him. Max stayed firmly in his way, making him as uncomfortable as possible. "Rambaud," he said to his own man, "I believe I left my palm-pad down in the library by accident. Retrieve it for me and bring it to this room immediately so I can record this conversation."

Rambaud hesitated before answering. "Yes, sir."

The other trooper went over Max's head and took up station outside the door. Max kicked the door shut and latched it.

"What's going on with the spongediver?" asked Max.

"They're testing a new laser deflector, using it for wormhole defense." Lukinov grinned. "Go ahead and listen."

Max picked up the headphones and fit the wires into his ears. Pilots chattered with tactics officers, describing the kind of run they were simulating. No wonder Outback outfitted their survey ships with the newest military equipment. The blind side of a wormhole dive was probably the only place in the galaxy they could test any new weapons without being observed. "Very standard stuff here," he said after a moment. "Is there just one channel of this?"

"Their scientists are on the other channel, the one Reedy's monitoring. But don't you see what an advantage this gives us if we can steal it? We can attack Adares with impunity and keep them from diving into our system."

Max switched the channel setting to the one Reedy listened to. "Do unto others before they do unto you?"

"Exactly!" replied Lukinov.

Reedy's eyes went wide open. She started tapping the desk to get their attention. "Sir," she said. "There's something you should. . . ."

"Not right now," said Max.

Lukinov frowned at him. "Now see here—"

"No, you see here. Has the captain been informed of this?"

"Not yet," replied Lukinov.

"You invite some grunt in here to listen to information that will certainly be classified top secret before you notify the captain?" He sneered at Lukinov, pausing long enough to listen to the scientists talk. "You can be sure that my Department will file a record of protest on our return. In the meantime, I better go get the captain."

Lukinov popped out of his seat. "No, I'll do that. I was just planning to do that anyway, if you hadn't interrupted."

"Sir," repeated Reedy. "*Sirs.*"

"Ensign," said Max, "Shut. Up."

The ensign nodded mutely, her eyes shaped like two satellite dishes trying to pick up a signal.

"I'm coming with you, Lukinov," Max said.

"No, you aren't, *Lieutenant*," snapped the intelligence officer. "I'm the one man on this ship you can't give direct orders to and don't you forget it."

Max saluted, a gesture sharp enough to have turned into a knife hand strike at the other man's throat. Lukinov stormed out of the room. Max turned back to the ensign, who simply stared at him.

"They just broadcast the complete specifications," said Reedy. "They were checking for field deformation—"

"I know that," said Max. And then he did something he never expected to do, not on this voyage. He said aloud the secret intelligence code word for "render all assistance." Silently, to himself, he added a prayer that it was current, and that Reedy would recognize it.

"Wh-what did you say?" she stammered.

Max repeated the code word for "render all assistance" while he pulled off his earphones and reached in his pocket for his multi-tool. His fingers found nothing, and he realized that it had been missing since his attack. "And give me a screwdriver," he added.

Reedy handed over the tool. "But . . . but. . . ."

Max ignored her. In thirty seconds, he'd disconnected the power and disassembled the outer case of the radio. "Give me the laser," he said.

The ensign's hands shook as she complied.

"I need two new memory chips and the spare pod." Reedy just stared at him, uncomprehending. "Now!" spit Max, and the ensign dove for the equipment box.

Max shoved the loaded chips into his pockets and snapped the replacements into their slots as Reedy handed them over. The radio was still a mess of pieces when someone rapped on the door.

"Stall them!" hissed Max.

The rap came again and the door cracked open. Rambaud pushed his head in partway. "Here's your palm-pad, sir."

"I'll take it," said Reedy, grabbing it and shoving the door shut on him.

"Thanks!" called Max. He'd lost one of the screws, and when he looked up from the equipment to see if it was floating somewhere, he was temporarily disoriented. His stomach did a flip-flop and his head spun in a circle. "Shit!"

Rambaud pushed back on the door. "Are you safe in there, sir? I'm coming in."

Reedy wedged herself against the wall to block the door.

Max heard a plain thump as Rambaud bounced against it. He saw the screw floating near his ankles and scooped it up. He fixed the cover and powered the machine up again. Reedy grunted as the door pushed against her, cracking open. "I'm fine," Max said loudly.

Rambaud nodded, but he stood outside the cracked door peering in.

Reedy panted, caught herself, controlled it. A thousand questions formed and died on her lips. Max had taken the leap, and now he had to see how far that leap would take him.

"Ensign," he whispered.

"Yes, sir?"

"From this moment forth," his lips barely moved, "you will consider me your sole superior officer."

Her eyes jumped to the door. "Sir? But—"

"That is a direct order."

"Yes, sir."

"You will not tell anyone—"

But he did not get the chance to tell Reedy what she should and shouldn't say. The door swung open and Lukinov entered, followed by Captain Petoskey. Lukinov grinned like a party girl full of booze. "Wait until you hear this," he said. He put his headphones on, and handed one to Petoskey as Reedy slid quickly back into her place.

They listened for a moment. Petoskey squinted his eyes, and rounded his shoulders even more than usual. "Sounds like they're bringing the shuttles in, getting ready to leave. Radioing a safe voyage message to their other ship. What was I supposed to hear?"

"They're testing a new deflector for wormhole defense. If we attack their ship and kill them, we can take it. Their other ship will be stuck in-system and we can nuke them."

"Captain," said Max.

"Yes?"

"I didn't hear any evidence of this deflector. I can't recommend an attack."

Lukinov frantically punched commands into his keypad. "Let me back up to an hour ago." His face went as blank as the records he was trying to access. "I can't seem to find it. Reedy, what's going on here?"

"Sir," she muttered, with a pleading glance at Max, "uh, I don't know, sir."

"She's covering up," said Max.

Three faces stared at him with variations of disbelief.

"Look at the battery, it's not properly grounded." It was an awful explanation, but the best that Max could come up with on the spot. "Reedy was moving some equipment around, hit it with something. I didn't see what. Sparks flew and the screens all went dead. She got them back up right away, but she probably wiped the memories."

"Ensign," Lukinov said coldly. "Explain yourself."

Reedy's mouth hung open. She didn't know what to say. Betrayal was written all over her face.

Petoskey took off his headset. "Lukinov, I trust you to take care of this. Niko-medes. . . ."

"Yes, sir?"

Petoskey couldn't seem to think of any orders to give him. "I have to go talk to Chevrier. We have our mission. With the second ship out of the way, we have to prepare to dive."

Max followed Petoskey out into the corridor, but returned to his room to stash the stolen memory. Only two things mattered now: getting the information to his superior, and keeping Lukinov from getting it to his. It needed to be used as a defensive weapon, not as an excuse to start a war. Lukinov had access to the radio and official channels. Max didn't. That stacked the cards in Lukinov's favor.

He had to do something with it soon, before they jumped to Adarean space. And he had to hope that a baby-faced ensign just out of the Academy didn't fold under pressure and give him away. It was like a game of Blind Man's Draw. Max had already put everything he had into the pot.

There was nothing else he could do at this point except play the card that he was dealt.

Meal time. Max sat by himself, as usual, at his own narrow table in the galley. Even the trooper guarding him sat with some of the other crewmen.

Lukinov entered, saw Max, and came straight over to him. "Reedy won't say that you were lying, but you were," the intelligence officer said. "Not that it matters. The machines are buggered, the data's all gone. Even Burdick can't find it."

Max had a blank sheet in his pocket. He pulled it out, and a stylus, and passed it over to Lukinov. This was the way duels were proposed at the Academy. According to the Academy's cover story, it was the way Reedy had arranged to meet with Vance.

Lukinov looked at the sheet, then scratched "observation room" and a time two hours distant on it. He pushed it back over to Max, who shook his head, and wrote "reactor room."

"Why there?" asked the intelligence officer.

"They've got cameras there, but no mikes. It's off limits to Simco's troopers, but not to us. We won't be there long."

"So this is just to be a private conversation? I should leave my weapons behind?"

"I wish you would."

"More's the pity," said Lukinov, and stormed out.

Max was putting his tray away, trying to resolve his other problem, when Simco came in. "Lukinov won't let us throw the ensign in the brig, not yet. But he thought it was best if I stuck with you personally in the meantime."

Perfect, thought Max, just perfect.

Two hours had never stretched out to such an eternity before in all Max's life. Simco escorted him to his quarters and joined him inside.

"Do you want to follow me into the head and shake it dry for me?" asked Max on his way into the bathroom.

Simco laughed, but remained in the other room. Max retrieved a bottle of pills and an old pair of nail clippers from the medicine cabinet, putting them in his pocket. Then he led Simco on a long, roundabout trip through the corridors that ended up on the floor of the Black Forest. He stopped when he got there and snapped his fingers.

"I forgot something," Max said. "You don't mind if I borrow that multi-tool in your pocket, do you?"

Simco stuffed his hand automatically into his pants, wrapped it around the bulge there, and froze. "Sorry, sir, I don't have one with me," he said, grinning. "Got one in my locker. Or do you want to hit Engineering to borrow one?"

"No, it's nothing I need that badly." He jumped. "Meet you up top, in the exercise room." He grabbed hold of the service ladder outside one of the missile shafts, and pulled himself up. He used his momentum to spin, kicking off from the side of the shaft, and shot like a rocket toward the ceiling.

"Hold up there," called Simco, halfway up the stairs.

Max ducked into the upper corridor. He dove through the hall as fast as he could, past the exercise room, down the access shaft, and back out the corridor below, returning to the missile room. He watched Simco's feet disappear above him into the top corridor, and then he flew straight across the cavern to the section over Engineering, opened a portside hatch, and closed it again after himself.

A long time ago Max had modified his nail clippers to function as a makeshift tool. Bracing himself against the wall, he used it now to remove the grille from the ceiling vent—it was the supply duct for the HEPA filters in the clean hood corner of the battery room directly below. He squeezed inside, feet first, pulling the grille after him. There was no way to reattach it, but with no gravity he didn't need to. He simply pulled it into place and it stayed there.

It was an eighteen-inch duct and he was a small man. Even so, he felt like toothpaste being forced back into the tube. He had to twist sideways and flip over to get past the L-curve, but after that it was a straight trip down to the reactor room. With his arms pinned above his head, and no gravity to help him, he writhed downward like a rat caught in a drainpipe. He reached bottom, unable to go any further. His kicks had no effect at all and his heart began to race as he wondered if he'd be trapped inside the duct. Finally, by pressing his elbows out into the corners, and hooking one foot on the lip where the vent teed out horizontally, he was able to push the other foot downward until the duct tore open.

He eased downward into the plenum space above the hood ceiling and kicked through the tiles. When he finally lowered himself into the battery room he was drenched in sweat and his pants were ripped in the thigh. He hadn't even noticed. He undid his belt and looked at the scrape on his leg. It was mostly superficial. Not much blood.

He leaned in the corner, with the hood's softwalls pulled back, catching his breath. The cameras were all installed to monitor the reactor, so they faced the center of the room. Most of them close-upped on specific pieces of equipment. He eased out, pushing himself up toward the high ceiling.

He glanced at his chrono. Already seven minutes past his meeting time with Lukinov. He waited two more minutes before the hatch popped open. He had a split second to decide what he would do if it was one of the engineers.

But a familiar balding head poked through the door. Max eased out of the hood area. "Hey, Lukinov."

"Max?" The other man twisted around to see him. He entered, closing the hatch behind him. "How the hell did you get in here? Chevrier's guard at the door gave me the runaround, swore he hadn't seen you. The mate watching the monitors said you never came in here either. What are you, some damn spook?"

Max ignored the questions. "You wanted to talk to me about the radio room. It was me. I stole the memory chips."

Lukinov came toward him, pale with fury. "You did *what*? By god, I'll see you shot."

"Intelligence won't touch me," said Max. "Not for this."

"I'll get Political Education to do it, you goddamn weasel," Lukinov vowed. He launched himself toward Max, keeping a hand against the wall to orient himself. "Your boss, Mallove, is a personal friend of mine. He won't like—"

Max jumped, tucking his knees and spinning as he sailed in the air. He wrapped his belt around Lukinov's throat, pivoted, twisting the belt as he pulled himself back to the floor. The motion jerked Lukinov upside down so that he floated in the air like a child's balloon.

"Your boss, Drozhin," whispered Max, "doesn't like the way you've been selling Intelligence's secrets out to Political Education and War."

Drozhin was Max's boss too. He'd moled Max in Political Education as soon as the new Department formed.

Lukinov panicked. He thrashed his arms and legs, disoriented, trying to make contact with any surface, clutching futilely at Max, who was behind his back and below him. Max twisted the belt, pinching the carotid arteries and cutting off blood flow to the brain. Lukinov was unconscious in about seven seconds. His body just went still. He was dead a few seconds later.

Drozhin had ordered Max to watch Lukinov, not kill him, but he couldn't see any other way around it. He shoved the body toward the corner, under the vent, and put his belt back on.

Still nobody at the hatch. Maybe they hadn't noticed. Maybe they were summoning Simco. There'd be no denying this one, not if he'd missed the location of any cameras.

But he had no time to think about failure. He didn't want anyone looking closely at Lukinov's body and he didn't want the ship making the jump to Adares. Intelligence was publicly part of the war party, but Drozhin believed that war would destroy Jesusalem and wanted it sabotaged at all costs. Max took the medicine bottle from his pocket and removed the two pills that weren't pills. He popped them into his mouth to warm them — they tasted awful — while he removed the wire and blasting cap from the bottle's lid.

He couldn't blow any main part of the reactor, he understood that much. But the cooling circuit used water pipes, and a radioactive water spill could scuttle the jump. Max darted in, fixed the explosive to a blue-tagged pipe, plugged the wire in it, and hurried back to the hood. He pushed Lukinov's corpse in the direction of the explosive before he climbed through the hole into the vent.

There was a soft boom behind him.

Max cranked his neck to peer down between his feet and saw the water spray in a fine mist, filling the air like fog. All the radiation alarms blared at once.

They sounded far off at first while he wiggled upward. He thought he was sweating, but realized that the busted air flow was drawing some of the water up through the shaft. Droplets pelleted him with radiation, and that made him crawl faster. He got stuck in the bend for a moment, finally squeezing through, and thrusting the vent cover out of the way without checking first to see if anyone was in the corridor. But it was empty — so far his luck held! He retrieved the grille and screwed it back into place. One of the alarms was located directly beside him. Its wailing made his pulse skip.

He emerged into the shaft of the weapons compartment as men raced both ways, toward the accident and away from it. No one noticed him. He was headed across the void toward his quarters when someone called his name.

"Hey, Nikomedes!"

He saw the medtech, Noyes, down by the corridor that led to Engineering. "What is it, Doc?"

"You don't have your comet, do you?"

Max touched the empty spot on his breast pocket. "No. Why?"

"Radiation emergency!" he screamed. "You're drafted as the surgeon's assistant — come on!"

Max considered ignoring the command, but according to regulations, Doc was right. Anyone who wasn't Vacuum and Radiation qualified was designated an orderly to help treat those who were. Plus it gave him an alibi. He jumped toward the bottom of the Black Forest and joined Noyes.

"Here, carry this kit," Noyes said, handing over a box of radiation gear as he went back across the hall to grab another.

"Where is it?" asked Max. He held the gear close, covering the rip in his pants. "What's going on?"

"Don't know. The com's down again. But it has to be the reactor."

Nobody guarded the main hatch to Engineering so the two men went straight in. A crowd gathered in the monitor room, spilling out into the corridor. Noyes pushed straight through, and Max followed along behind him. Chevrier was shaking a crewman by the throat.

" — what the hell did you let him in there for?"

"He ordered me to!" the man complained. It was DePuy.

"There's water everywhere!" another one of the men yelled, coming back from the direction of the reactor room hatch. "The reactor's over-heating fast!"

"It's already past four hundred cees," said one of the men at the monitors.

Chevrier tried to fling DePuy at the wall, but they just flopped a short distance apart. The chief engineer turned toward the rest of crew in disgust.

Rucker, the first lieutenant, showed up behind Max. "Captain wants a report—the com's down again!"

"That's because the reactor's overheating," Chevrier said. "The cooling system's busted."

"My God," said Rucker, invoking a deity he probably didn't believe in, thought Max.

Noyes slapped a yellow patch on the first lieutenant's shirt. "Radiation detectors, everyone. When they turn orange, you're in danger, means get out. Red means see me for immediate treatment." He handed some to Max. "Make sure everyone wears one."

"We've got to go in there, fix the pipe, and cool the reactor," said Chevrier. Some of the men started to protest. "Shut the fuck up! I'm asking for volunteers. And I'll be going in with you."

Rucker wiped the blond cowlick back off his forehead. "I'll go in," he said. Six other crewmen volunteered, most of them senior engineers. Max slapped radiation badges on those men first.

"Here's the plan." Chevrier pointed to pictures on the monitors. "We're going to shut off these valves here and here, cut out and replace this section of pipe—"

Noyes, looking over his shoulder, said, "That man in there ought to come out at once. He looks unconscious."

"That man is dead," said Chevrier, "and it's a good thing too, or I'd kill him. Then we're going to run a pipe through here, from the drinking water supply—"

A moan of dismay.

"—shut up! We'll take it from the number three reserve tank. That ought to be enough, and it won't contaminate the rest of the water. Once we get the main engine back up, we can make more water off the fuel cells."

Everyone had a badge now, and Max hung back with Noyes.

"I'd like someone to go in there and turn off these," Chevrier tapped spots on one of the monitors, "here, here, and here, while I get the repair set up."

"That'll be me," Rucker said. Like any junior officer, Max thought, trying to set a good example.

Chevrier gave him a nod. "This one here is tough. It'll take you a few minutes. It's right next to the reactor, and it's going to be hotter than hell." He gave Rucker the tools he needed and sent him off down the tube to the reactor room.

"I'll need a shower set up for decontamination," said Noyes.

Max found the air shower over by the other clean room, and showed him where it was. Noyes started setting up the lead-lined bags for clothing and equipment disposal.

By the time they went back to the monitor room, Chevrier had diagrammed his repair. His volunteers double-checked the equipment lined up in the hall. He sent others, who hadn't volunteered, to run a connector line from the freshwater tank. They were just getting ready to go in, when Rucker staggered back out. He looked . . . cooked. Like the worst sunburn Max had ever seen. His clothes were soaked, and glowing drops of water followed through the air in his wake. Noyes was there, swiping the droplets out of the air with a lead blanket. He wrapped Rucker in it, and started leading him toward the shower.

The lieutenant's badge was bright red.

One crewman bolted, another threw up. No one said anything about the smell, but one of the men took off his shirt and tried to catch the vomit as it scattered through the air.

Chevrier ripped his badge off. "Won't need this. Just one more distraction. If we're going to go swimming, we might as well go skinny-dipping." He stripped off his clothes and the other volunteers followed his example. "Can't handle tools in those damn vacuum suits anyway."

Anger, fear, those things were contagious, Max reflected. But so were courage and foolhardy bravery. He hoped the price was worth it.

He supposed he ought to be at decontamination, with Noyes, but he couldn't tear himself away from the monitors. There were no cameras aimed directly at the spot where the men were working with the pipes, but they passed in and out of the vids. The radioactive water pooled in the air, drop meeting drop, coalescing into larger blobs like mercury spilled on a lab table and just as poisonous. Or perhaps more like antibodies in a bloodstream. The men splashed into them as they moved and the water clung to their skin, searing wherever it touched.

Simco appeared at the door demanding a report for the captain. Max ignored him. Paint peeled off the overheating reactor, curling like bits of ash as it burned away. Water that hit its surface boiled away into steam, but the steam hit the other water, and became drops again instantly, a swirling rain that never fell. And, except for the dead tone of the radiation alarms, it all happened in silence, with no one in the monitor room speaking for long minutes, and no sound at all from the reactor room.

Noyes appeared beside Max. "That man needs to come out right now to have those burns treated," he said, tapping at one of the monitors. Glowing circles spun in slow lambent spirals on one man's buttocks.

Max laughed, a sound that came out of his mouth only as a breathless sigh. "Those are tattoos, Doc. Jets. Lightning bug juice impregnated in the subdermal cells."

"I've . . . never heard of that," said Noyes.

"It's supposed to bring a spacer safely home again."

"It's an abomination," blurted Noyes. The people of Jesusalem were against any mixing of the species. "Let's hope it does," he said.

"Indeed," replied Max.

DePuy stood beside them, shaking his head. "They're not getting it fixed."

Max began to think he'd miscalculated badly. He hadn't wanted anyone to look too closely at Lukinov's corpse. He wanted the ship to turn around and head back home. But with the main engine down and the back-up scuttled, they were in big trouble.

The hatch flew open and two men came out.

"They've been in there almost an hour," said Noyes, checking his chrono and calculating the damage to them.

"Is it done?" the men in the monitor room demanded. Max heard his own voice blurt out, "Is it fixed?"

But their faces were mute. The blistered flesh bubbled off as Doc wrapped them in blankets. Noyes helped one toward the shower, and Max took the other. "This is hopeless," Noyes said, trying to clean the men. "You have to go back there now and get the other men out before they die."

"I think we all die with the ship if they fail," said Max.

Rambaud, one of the troopers, appeared in the door. "Message from the captain, Doc. He wants you on the bridge."

"Tell him no."

The trooper's eyes kept flicking nervously to their badges. Max noticed his own was a sickly orange color. "Beg your pardon, Doc, but he's getting ready to abandon ship. If it's necessary."

"If he wants to give me an order, he can come down here and do it himself," said Noyes, shooting the burned man full of painkillers and starting an IV pump.

Rambaud fled.

Noyes stared after him. "They were going to suicide all of us anyway, for nothing. If I'm going to die, it might as well be doing my job."

"Hell, yes." Max's job was getting the specifications on the deflectors to Drozhin. If the captain took the escape shuttles and flew in system, then it was Max's duty to retrieve the chips from his quarters and get on a shuttle.

He followed Noyes back into the mouth of fire instead.

"They're coming out!" someone shouted.

Four more men this time, in worse shape than the others. Noyes had to hypospray them full of painkillers just to get them down to the shower. Max carried the man with the tattoos. They were coal black in his skin. Whatever lived in the cells and gave them their luminescence had been killed off by the radiation.

Before they finished the others, Chevrier was brought to them, covered with burn blisters, his hands raw meat, his eyes blind. He couldn't speak.

"Did he get it done?" shouted Max.

No one knew, so Max flew back toward the monitor room, where the handful of men who remained were arguing over the monitors. "The temperatures are still climbing," shouted DePuy. His voice had risen an octave in pitch. "I tell you he didn't get it running."

"What's going on?" asked Max.

"The pipes aren't open," said one of the electrician's mates.

"Somebody needs to go in there and turn this valve here," said DePuy. He pointed to a spot in the middle of the thick steam that surrounded the overheating reactor.

No one volunteered.

They were boys mostly, eighteen or nineteen, junior crewmen. They'd all seen the others carried out, had smelled the burned flesh, had listened to their weeping.

The cut on Max's leg throbbed. His face and arms felt hot, burned. "I'll go in," he said.

Reactors were the only ship system he wasn't officially trained on, and all the reading he'd done before the voyage seemed inadequate to the task now. But he could go in there and turn a valve. He could do that much.

He went out to the corridor and found it blocked by a man in a vacuum suit, dragging a plasma cutter on a tether and reading the manual in his palm-pad. The man turned, his face gray behind the clear mask covering his face. It was Kulakov, the chief petty officer.

For a second Max thought the man would freeze up.

Kulakov looked back down at his diagram. "Be sure to seal the locks tight behind me," he said. "Send someone right now to levels three and four, portside, directly above us, to clear the corridors and seal the locks there. You have to do that!"

"Will do," said Max. Then, "Carry on."

Kulakov passed through the hatch, but when Max went to seal it, the freshwater supply tubing blocked it. "Damn," he said, with a very bad feeling in the pit of his stomach. "Damn, damn, damn."

Then DePuy was there beside him with a clamp and some cutters. He severed the pipe, and tossed the loose end through the hatch after Kulakov. Max sealed the door. "Did someone go to three and four?"

DePuy nodded. "But I'll go double-check," he added, glancing at the bare spot where Max's comet should have been. No, he was looking at Max's radiation badge. It was orange-red, bleeding into a bright crimson.

"You better head over to see Doc," said the electrician's mate at the monitors.

"Not yet," said Max.

On the video feed they watched Kulakov move methodically from point to point, comparing the hook-up and settings with the diagram on his palm-pad. It took him much longer than it had Chevrier when he was naked. A couple times it was clear that between the fog, and the loss of sensation caused by the suit, Kulakov became disoriented crossing an open space. He spun in circles until he found the right side up again. He reached the final valve but couldn't turn it. He peeled his gloves off, surrounded by the steam, and slowly cranked it over.

The electrician's mate pounded the monitors. "It's running! Look at the temps drop!"

Max did, but he watched Kulakov too as he struggled to put his gloves back on, picked up the plasma cutter, and then burned a hole through the hull.

The weeping sound of the radiation alarms was joined by the sudden keening of the hull breech alarms. The whole ship shuddered, the bulkhead creaked beside him, and Max's ears popped.

But he kept his eyes fixed on the screen in the reactor room. The steam and all the radioactive water whooshed out of the ship. So did Lukinov's body. And so did Kulakov.

There was a dark, flat line straight across one of the screens, like a dead reading on a monitor.

Kulakov's tether.

"Hey look!" whispered one of the crewmen as Max entered the sick bay. "The Corpse is up and walking!"

They all laughed at that, the survivors, even Max. Chevrier was dead, and so was Rucker, and so were two other men. Of the six surviving men who'd received red badge levels of radiation exposure, only Max was strong enough to walk.

Kulakov sat in the middle of them. His hands were wrapped in bandages, two crooked, crippled hooks. Max nodded to him. "They still giving you a hard time?" he asked.

"You know it," grinned Kulakov.

"Well it's not fair that he should be the only one who gets leave while we're on this voyage," said one of the men.

"How can it be shore leave without a shore, that's what I want to know," said Kulakov.

They all laughed again, even Max. That was going to be a ship joke for a long time, how Kulakov got liberty—hanging on a tether outside the ship.

"Papa sent me down here with a message," said Max. Captain Petoskey, Papa, had only been to the sick bay once since the accident, and quickly. Most of the other crewman stayed away as if radiation sickness were something contagious.

"What is it?" said Kulakov, the words thick in his throat.

"He wanted me to tell you that he's going to request that they rename the ship." The crewmen looked up at him seriously, all the humor gone from their eyes. "They're going to call it the *New Nazareth*."

New Nazareth had been nuked the worst by the Adareans. The land there still glowed in the dark.

Kulakov chuckled first, then the other men broke out laughing. Max saluted them, holding himself stiff for a full three seconds, then turned to go see Noyes. The medtech slumped in his chair, head sprawled across his arms on the desk, eyes closed. "I'm not sleeping," he muttered. "I'm just thinking."

"About your fiancée," asked Max, "waiting for you at home?"

"No, about the bone marrow cultures I've got growing in the vats, and the skin sheets, and the transplant surgery I have to do later this afternoon, that I've never done unassisted before, and the one I have to do tonight that I'm not trained to do at all." He twisted his head, peeking one eye out at Max. "And Suzan. Waiting for me. And the ship flying home. How are you feeling?"

"I'd be fine if you had any spare teeth," Max said, poking his tongue into the empty spots in his gums. That didn't feel as strange as having gravity under his feet again.

"They're in a drawer over by the sink," said Noyes. "Take two and call me in the morning."

Max walked through corridors considerably less crowded than they had been a few days before. Almost everything inside the ship had received some radiation. The crewmen went crate to crate with geiger counters deciding what could be saved and what should be jettisoned. With the grav back on, the men's appetites returned. They also had a year's worth of supplies and only a short voyage ahead of them, so every meal became a feast. Some celebrated the fact that they were going home, and others the simple fact that they'd survived.

Only Captain Petoskey failed to join the celebration. When Max entered the galley, Petoskey wore the expression of a man on the way to the lethal injection chamber. Max couldn't say for sure if it was the condemned man's expression or the executioner's.

Ensign Reedy sat on one side of a long table, with two troopers standing guard behind her. Petoskey and Commander Gordet sat on the opposite side with Simco standing at attention. Petoskey looked naked without his beard, shorn before they recorded these official proceedings. Burdick, the other intelligence officer, sat off to one end.

Petoskey invited Max to the empty seat beside him. "Are you sure you feel up to this, Nikomedes?"

"Doc says I'll be fine as long as it's brief."

"This'll be quick."

Petoskey turned on the recorder and read the regulations calling a board of inquiry. "Ensign Reedy, do you wish to make a confession of your crimes at this time?"

Max looked at the youngster. He hadn't seen or spoken to her since he'd taken the chips in the radio room. If Reedy broke and told them what Max had done, then the entire gamble was for naught.

"I have nothing to confess," Reedy said.

"Corporal Burdick," continued Petoskey, "will you describe what you found in the radio room."

"The equipment had been disassembled and the memory chips replaced with spares." He made eye contact with no one. "This happened sometime during the last shift when Lieutenant Lukinov and Ensign Reedy were on duty together."

"Sergeant Simco, please describe your actions."

"Sir, we made a complete search of Ensign Reedy's person and belongings looking for the items described by Corporal Burdick. We found nothing there, nor in any place she is known to have visited. We also searched Lieutenant Lukinov's belongings and found nothing."

"Lieutenant Nikomedes," continued Petoskey. "Would you describe what you saw in the radio room." He added the exact date and shift.

Max repeated his story about the battery short circuit. "If Lukinov removed the chips that Ensign Burdick described, and he had them on him, then they were spaced."

Petoskey nodded. "Yes, I've thought of that. Ensign Reedy, can you explain what happened to the chips containing the communications from the neutral ship?"

"No sir, I cannot."

"Were you and Lieutenant Lukinov working together as spies for the Adareans?"

"I was not," answered Reedy. "I can't speak for the lieutenant, as I was not in his confidence."

Petoskey slammed his fist on the table. "I think you're a coward, Reedy. You're too weak to take responsibility for your actions. I'd tell you to act like a man, but you're not."

If Petoskey hoped to provoke Reedy, then his gambit failed. She sat there, placid as a lake on a still summer day.

"Can we conduct a medical interrogation?" interjected Max.

Petoskey went to tug at his beard, but his fingers clutched at emptiness. "I've discussed that already with the surgeon and Commander Gordet. Noyes is only a medtech and not qualified to conduct an interrogation that will hold up in military court. Conceivably, we could even taint the later results of a test."

Max leaned forward. "Can we use more . . . traditional methods?"

"I won't command it," said Petoskey, looking directly into the recorder. He waited for Max to speak again.

Max ran his tongue over the loose replacement teeth, saying nothing, and leaned back. He might get out of this, after all.

"However, if you think . . . ," said Petoskey.

Max looked at the camera. "Without an immediate danger, we should follow standard procedures."

Petoskey accepted this disappointment and concluded the proceedings with a provisional declaration of guilt. He ordered Reedy confined to the brig until they returned to Jesusalem.

As Max limped back toward his quarters afterward he noticed that Gordet followed him.

"What can I do for you, Commander?" asked Max.

The bull-shaped second-in-command looked around nervously, then leaned in close. "There's something you should know, sir."

"What?" asked Max wearily. "That Petoskey ordered Simco to kill me, that he intended to blame it on Reedy, and then have her arrested and executed?"

Gordet jerked back. "Did you check the secret orders too?"

"What does it matter now? Simco failed, Reedy's arrested anyway, and we're on our way home. A bit of advice for you, Mr. Gordet." He clapped him on the shoulder. "Next time you should pick your horse before the race is over."

He walked away. When he returned to his room, he recovered the sheet with the combination from its hiding spot and destroyed it. He didn't know what the secret orders said. He didn't care.

There was only one thing he had left to do.

———————

Third shift, night rotation, normal schedule. Max headed down to the brig carrying a black bag. One of Simco's troopers stood guard. "I'm here to interrogate the prisoner," Max said.

"Let me check with Sergeant Simco, sir."

Max had been thinking hard about this. Only two people knew that he had the plans for the deflector, and the only way two people could keep a secret was if one of them was dead.

"Sarge wants to know if you need help," said the trooper.

"Tell him that I take full responsibility for this, in the name of the Department of Political Education, and that no assistance will be necessary."

The trooper relayed this information, then gave Max a short, sneering nod. "He says he understands. Perfectly. But he wants me to make sure that you'll be safe in there."

Max patted a hand on his black bag. "If you hear screaming," he said, "don't interrupt us unless it's mine."

The trooper twitched uncomfortably under Max's glare. "Yes, sir." He opened the door for Max.

Reedy twitched then sat up quickly on the edge of her bunk. Her wrists and ankles were cuffed, and she wore insignialess fatigues. She folded her hands on her knees, fingertip to fingertip, pressed together hard enough to turn her knuckles white.

He stepped inside. The room was barely eight feet by four, with a bed on one wall and a stainless steel toilet built into the corner opposite the door. "That'll be all, trooper," Max said. "I'll signal you when I'm done."

The hatch closed behind him and latched shut. He looked at Reedy. Her eyes were red and puffy but devoid of feeling, her cheeks hollow and drawn. A blue vein stood out vulnerably on her pale neck.

With his lips tight, Max gave her a small nod. He removed a wand from his bag and searched the room for bugs. She watched closely while he located and destroyed them.

"You look depressed," he said quietly when he was done.

She shook her head, once. "No, I've been depressed before. This time it's not bad."

"Define *not bad*."

"It's bad when you want to kill yourself. Right now, I just wish I was dead. That's not bad."

Max sat down with his back against the door and opened his bag. He removed two tumblers and a bottle of ouzo. The ensign remained perfectly still as Max pulled out a plate, and ripped open vacuum-wrapped packages of cheese, sausages, and anchovies to set on it.

"Not proper *mezedes* at all," he said apologetically. "The fish should always be fresh."

He filled one cup and pushed it over toward Reedy, then poured and swallowed his own. It tasted like licorice, reminding him both of his childhood and his days as a young man in completely different ways. Reedy remained immobile.

"I've been thinking." Max spoke very quietly, unbuttoning his collar. "When two men know a secret, it's only safe if one of them is dead." Good men had died already because of this. So would many more, likely enough, along with the bad. "Therefore you don't know anything. Only I, and Lukinov, and Lukinov's dead. Do you understand this?"

"I don't know anything," Reedy said, with just a hint of irony. She reached over and lifted the glass of ouzo with both hands.

"My department will declare you the most politically sound of officers. Intelligence will know the truth, at least at the level that matters. Drozhin will get the captain's official report, but he'll get another report unofficially. You'll be fine." He picked up an anchovy. "There will be a very difficult time, a very ugly court-martial. But you can survive that."

"Again?"

"Again. This one will not be removed from the record due to extenuating circumstances." Her attack on Vance had been one of self-defense. "But you'll be exonerated. You'll be fine. Things are changing. They'll be better." He believed that.

She leaned her head back and tossed down the ouzo. Max reached over and poured her another glass while her eyes were still watering. "When I got this assignment," she said, "I couldn't figure out if I was being rewarded for being at the top of the class in languages, despite being a woman. Or if I was being punished for being a woman."

"Sometimes it's both ways at once," Max said. He bit the anchovy and found he didn't care for the taste.

"Can I ask you one question?" asked Reedy.

Why did people always think he had all the answers? "Information is like ouzo. A little bit can clear your head, make you feel better. Too much will make you sick, maybe even kill you." He twirled his cup. "What's your question?"

"Did you really win your wife in a card game?"

"Yes." He drained his glass to cover his surprise. Though he'd won her with a bluff and not by cheating.

"Why did she leave you?"

Max thought about telling her that was two questions. Then he thought about telling her the truth, that his wife hadn't left him, that she waited at home for him, not knowing where he was or what he did, going to church every day, caring for their two grandchildren. His daughter was about Reedy's age. But he'd kept his life sealed in separate compartments and wouldn't breech one of them now.

"Love, like loyalty," he said, "is a gift. You can only try to be worthy of it."

The silence lengthened out between them like all of the empty, uncharted universe. The food sat untouched while they drank. Max could feel himself getting drunk. It felt good.

Lambing Season

MOLLY GLOSS

Molly Gloss made her first sale in 1984, and has since sold to Asimov's Science Fiction, The Magazine of Fantasy and Science Fiction, Universe, and elsewhere. She published a fantasy novel, Outside the Gates, in 1986, and another novel, The Jump-Off Creek, a "woman's western," was released in 1990. In 1997, she published an SF novel, The Dazzle of Day, which was a New York Times Notable Book for that year. Her most recent book, another SF novel, Wild Life, won the prestigious James Tiptree, Jr. Memorial Award in 2001. She lives in Portland, Oregon.

Since Biblical times, shepherds "watching their sheep by night" have always seen strange things in the sky. Probably not quite as strange, though, as the celestial visitation that the compassionate shepherd of this story finds that she has to deal with . . .

From May to September, Delia took the Churro sheep and two dogs and went up on Joe-Johns Mountain to live. She had that country pretty much to herself all summer. Ken Owen sent one of his Mexican hands up every other week with a load of groceries, but otherwise she was alone, alone with the sheep and the dogs. She liked the solitude. Liked the silence. Some sheepherders she knew talked a blue streak to the dogs, the rocks, the porcupines, they sang songs and played the radio, read their magazines out loud, but Delia let the silence settle into her, and, by early summer, she had begun to hear the ticking of the dry grasses as a language she could almost translate. The dogs were named Jesus and Alice. "Away to me, Jesus," she said when they were moving the sheep. "Go bye, Alice." From May to September these words spoken in command of the dogs were almost the only times she heard her own voice; that, and when the Mexican brought the groceries, a polite exchange in Spanish about the weather, the health of the dogs, the fecundity of the ewes.

The Churros were a very old breed. The O-Bar Ranch had a federal allotment up on the mountain, which was all rimrock and sparse grasses well suited to the Churros, who were fiercely protective of their lambs and had a long-stapled top coat that could take the weather. They did well on the thin grass of the mountain where other sheep would lose flesh and give up their lambs to the coyotes. The Mexican was an old man. He said he remembered Churros from his childhood in the Oaxaca highlands, the rams with their four horns, two curving up, two down. "Buen' carne," he told Delia. Uncommonly fine meat.

The wind blew out of the southwest in the early part of the season, a wind that smelled of juniper and sage and pollen; in the later months, it blew straight from the east, a dry wind smelling of dust and smoke, bringing down showers of parched leaves and seedheads of yarrow and bittercress. Thunderstorms came frequently out of the east, enormous cloudscapes with hearts of livid magenta and glaucous green. At those times, if she was camped on a ridge, she'd get out of her bed and walk downhill to find a draw where she could feel safer, but if she were camped in a low place, she would stay with the sheep while a war passed over their heads, spectacular jagged flares of lightning, skull-rumbling cannonades of thunder. It was maybe bred into the bones of Churros, a knowledge and a tolerance of mountain weather, for they shifted together and waited out the thunder with surprising composure; they stood forbearingly while rain beat down in hard blinding bursts.

Sheepherding was simple work, although Delia knew some herders who made it hard, dogging the sheep every minute, keeping them in a tight group, moving all the time. She let the sheep herd themselves, do what they wanted, make their own decisions. If the band began to separate, she would whistle or yell, and often the strays would turn around and rejoin the main group. Only if they were badly scattered did she send out the dogs. Mostly she just kept an eye on the sheep, made sure they got good feed, that the band didn't split, that they stayed in the boundaries of the O-Bar allotment. She studied the sheep for the language of their bodies, and tried to handle them just as close to their nature as possible. When she put out salt for them, she scattered it on rocks and stumps as if she were hiding Easter eggs, because she saw how they enjoyed the search.

The spring grass made their manure wet, so she kept the wool cut away from the ewes' tail area with a pair of sharp, short-bladed shears. She dosed the sheep with wormer, trimmed their feet, inspected their teeth, treated ewes for mastitis. She combed the burrs from the dogs' coats and inspected them for ticks. *You're such good dogs*, she told them with her hands. *I'm very very proud of you.*

She had some old binoculars, 7 × 32s, and in the long quiet days, she watched bands of wild horses miles off in the distance, ragged looking mares with dorsal stripes and black legs. She read the back issues of the local newspapers, looking in the obits for names she recognized. She read spine-broken paperback novels and played solitaire and scoured the ground for arrowheads and rocks she would later sell to rockhounds. She studied the parched brown grass, which was full of grasshoppers and beetles and crickets and ants. But most of her day was spent just walking. The sheep sometimes bedded quite a ways from her trailer and she had to get out to them before sunrise when the coyotes would make their kills. She was usually up by three or four and walking out to the sheep in darkness. Sometimes she returned to the camp for lunch, but always she was out with the sheep again until sundown, when the coyotes were likely to return, and then she walked home after dark to water and feed the dogs, eat supper, climb into bed.

In her first years on Joe-Johns, she had often walked three or four miles away from the band just to see what was over a hill, or to study the intricate architecture of a sheepherder's monument. Stacking up flat stones in the form of an obelisk was a common herders' pastime, their monuments all over that sheep country, and though Delia had never felt an impulse to start one herself, she admired the ones other people had built. She sometimes walked miles out of her way just to look at a rockpile up close.

She had a mental map of the allotment, divided into ten pastures. Every few days, when the sheep had moved on to a new pasture, she moved her camp. She towed the trailer with an old Dodge pickup, over the rocks and creekbeds, the sloughs and dry meadows, to the new place. For a while afterward, after the engine was shut off and while the heavy old body of the truck was settling onto its tires, she would be deaf, her head filled with a dull roaring white noise.

She had about eight hundred ewes, as well as their lambs, many of them twins or triplets. The ferocity of the Churro ewes in defending their offspring was some- times a problem for the dogs, but in the balance of things, she knew that it kept her losses small. Many coyotes lived on Joe-Johns, and sometimes a cougar or bear would come up from the salt pan desert on the north side of the mountain, looking for better country to own. These animals considered the sheep to be fair game, which Delia understood to be their right; and also her right, hers and the dogs', to take the side of the sheep. Sheep were smarter than people commonly believed and the Churros smarter than other sheep she had tended, but by midsummer the coyotes always passed the word among themselves, buen' carne, and Delia and the dogs then had a job to work, keeping the sheep out of harm's way.

She carried a .32 caliber Colt pistol in an old-fashioned holster worn on her belt. *If you're a coyot' you'd better be careful of this woman,* she said with her body, with the way she stood and the way she walked when she was wearing the pistol. That gun and holster had once belonged to her mother's mother, a woman who had come West on her own and homesteaded for a while, down in the Sprague River Canyon. Delia's grandmother had liked to tell the story: how a concerned neighbor, a bachelor with an interest in marriageable females, had pressed the gun upon her, back when the Klamaths were at war with the army of General Joel Palmer; and how she never had used it for anything but shooting rabbits.

In July, a coyote killed a lamb while Delia was camped no more than two hundred feet away from the bedded sheep. It was dusk, and she was sitting on the steps of the trailer reading a two-gun western, leaning close over the pages in the failing light, and the dogs were dozing at her feet. She heard the small sound, a strange high faint squeal she did not recognize and then did recognize, and she jumped up and fumbled for the gun, yelling at the coyote, at the dogs, her yell startling the entire band to its feet but the ewes making their charge too late, Delia firing too late, and none of it doing any good beyond a release of fear and anger.

A lion might well have taken the lamb entire; she had known of lion kills where the only evidence was blood on the grass and a dribble of entrails in the beam of a flashlight. But a coyote is small and will kill with a bite to the throat and then perhaps eat just the liver and heart, though a mother coyote will take all she can carry in her stomach, bolt it down and carry it home to her pups. Delia's grandmother's pistol had scared this one off before it could even take a bite, and the lamb was twitching and whole on the grass, bleeding only from its neck. The mother ewe stood over it, crying in a distraught and pitiful way, but there was nothing to be done, and, in a few minutes, the lamb was dead.

There wasn't much point in chasing after the coyote, and anyway, the whole band was now a skittish jumble of anxiety and confusion; it was hours before the mother ewe gave up her grieving, before Delia and the dogs had the band calm and bedded down again, almost midnight. By then, the dead lamb had stiffened on the ground, and she dragged it over by the truck and skinned it and let the dogs have the meat, which went against her nature, but was about the only way to keep the coyote from coming back for the carcass.

While the dogs worked on the lamb, she stood with both hands pressed to her tired back, looking out at the sheep, the mottled pattern of their whiteness almost opalescent across the black landscape, and the stars thick and bright above the faint outline of the rock ridges, stood there a moment before turning toward the trailer, toward bed, and afterward, she would think how the coyote and the sorrowing ewe and the dark of the July moon and the kink in her back, how all of that came together and was the reason that she was standing there watching the sky, was the reason that she saw the brief, brilliantly green flash in the southwest and then the sulfur yellow streak breaking across the night, southwest to due west on a descending arc onto Lame Man Bench. It was a broad bright ribbon, rainbow-wide, a cyanotic contrail. It was not a meteor, she had seen hundreds of meteors. She stood and looked at it.

Things to do with the sky, with distance, you could lose perspective, it was hard to judge even a lightning strike, whether it had touched down on a particular hill or the next hill or the valley between. So she knew this thing falling out of the sky might have come down miles to the west of Lame Man, not onto Lame Man at all, which was two miles away, at least two miles, and getting there would be all ridges and rocks, no way to cover the ground in the truck. She thought about it. She had moved camp earlier in the day, which was always troublesome work, and it had been a blistering hot day, and now the excitement with the coyote. She was very tired, the tiredness like a weight against her breastbone. She didn't know what this thing was, falling out of the sky. Maybe if she walked over there she would find just a dead satellite or a broken weather balloon and not dead or broken people. The contrail thinned slowly while she stood there looking at it, became a wide streak of yellowy cloud against the blackness, with the field of stars glimmering dimly behind it.

After a while, she went into the truck and got a water bottle and filled it, and also took the first aid kit out of the trailer and a couple of spare batteries for the flashlight and a handful of extra cartridges for the pistol, and stuffed these things into a backpack and looped her arms into the straps and started up the rise away from the dark camp, the bedded sheep. The dogs left off their gnawing of the dead lamb and trailed her anxiously, wanting to follow, or not wanting her to leave the sheep. "Stay by," she said to them sharply, and they went back and stood with the band and watched her go. *That coyot', he's done with us tonight:* This is what she told the dogs with her body, walking away, and she believed it was probably true.

Now that she'd decided to go, she walked fast. This was her sixth year on the mountain, and, by this time, she knew the country pretty well. She didn't use the flashlight. Without it, she became accustomed to the starlit darkness, able to see the stones and pick out a path. The air was cool, but full of the smell of heat rising off the rocks and the parched earth. She heard nothing but her own breathing and the gritting of her boots on the pebbly dirt. A little owl circled once in silence and then went off toward a line of cottonwood trees standing in black silhouette to the northeast.

Lame Man Bench was a great upthrust block of basalt grown over with scraggly juniper forest. As she climbed among the trees, the smell of something like ozone or sulfur grew very strong, and the air became thick, burdened with dust. Threads of the yellow contrail hung in the limbs of the trees. She went on across the top of the bench and onto slabs of shelving rock that gave a view to the west. Down in the steep-sided draw below her there was a big wing-shaped piece of metal resting on the ground, which she at first thought had been torn from an airplane, but then realized was a whole thing, not broken, and she quit looking for the rest of the wreckage. She squatted down and looked at it. Yellow dust settled slowly out of the sky, pollinating her hair, her shoulders, the toes of her boots, faintly dulling the oily black shine of the wing, the thing shaped like a wing.

While she was squatting there looking down at it, something came out from the sloped underside of it, a coyote she thought at first, and then it wasn't a coyote but a dog built like a greyhound or a whippet, deep-chested, long legged, very light-boned and frail-looking. She waited for somebody else, a man, to crawl out after his dog, but nobody did. The dog squatted to pee and then moved off a short distance and sat on its haunches and considered things. Delia considered, too. She considered that the dog might have been sent up alone. The Russians had sent up a dog in their little sputnik, she remembered. She considered that a skinny almost hairless dog with frail bones would be dead in short order if left alone in this country. And she considered that there might be a man inside the wing, dead or too hurt to climb out. She thought how much trouble it would be, getting down this steep rock bluff in the darkness to rescue a useless dog and a dead man.

After a while, she stood and started picking her way into the draw. The dog by this time was smelling the ground, making a slow and careful circuit around the black wing. Delia kept expecting the dog to look up and bark, but it went on with its intent inspection of the ground as if it was stone deaf, as if Delia's boots making a racket on the loose gravel was not an announcement that someone was coming down. She thought of the old Dodge truck, how it always left her ears ringing, and wondered if maybe it was the same with this dog and its wing-shaped sputnik, although the wing had fallen soundless across the sky.

When she had come about half way down the hill, she lost footing and slid down six or eight feet before she got her heels dug in and found a handful of willow scrub to hang onto. A glimpse of this movement—rocks sliding to the bottom, or the dust she raised—must have startled the dog, for it leaped backward suddenly and then reared up. They looked at each other in silence, Delia and the dog, Delia standing leaning into the steep slope a dozen yards above the bottom of the draw, and the dog standing next to the sputnik, standing all the way up on its hind legs like a bear or a man and no longer seeming to be a dog but a person with a long narrow muzzle and a narrow chest, turned-out knees, delicate dog-like feet. Its genitals were more cat-like than dog, a male set but very small and neat and contained. Dog's eyes, though, dark and small and shining below an anxious brow, so that she was reminded of Jesus and Alice, the way they had looked at her when she had left them alone with the sheep. She had years of acquaintance with dogs and she knew enough to look away, break off her stare. Also, after a moment, she remembered the old pistol and holster at her belt. In cowboy pictures, a man would unbuckle his gunbelt and let it down on the ground as a gesture of peaceful intent, but it seemed to her this might only bring attention to the gun, to the true intent of a gun, which is always killing. *This woman is nobody at all to be scared of*, she told the dog with her body, standing very still along the steep hillside, holding onto the scrub willow with her hands, looking vaguely to the left of him, where the smooth curve of the wing rose up and gathered a veneer of yellow dust.

The dog, the dog person, opened his jaws and yawned the way a dog will do to relieve nervousness, and then they were both silent and still for a minute. When finally he turned and stepped toward the wing, it was an unexpected, delicate movement, exactly the way a ballet dancer steps along on his toes, knees turned out, lifting his long thin legs; and then he dropped down on all-fours and seemed to become almost a dog again. He went back to his business of smelling the ground intently, though every little while he looked up to see if Delia was still standing along the rock slope. It was a steep place to stand. When her knees finally gave out, she sat down very carefully where she was, which didn't spook him. He had become used to her by then, and his brief, sliding glance just said, *That woman up there is nobody at all to be scared of.*

What he was after, or wanting to know, was a mystery to her. She kept expecting him to gather up rocks, like all those men who'd gone to the moon, but he only smelled the ground, making a wide slow circuit around the wing the way Alice always circled round the trailer every morning, nose down, reading the dirt like a book. And when he seemed satisfied with what he'd learned, he stood up again and looked back at Delia, a last look delivered across his shoulder before he dropped down and disappeared under the edge of the wing, a grave and inquiring look, the kind of look a dog or a man will give you before going off on his own business, a look that says, *You be okay if I go?* If he had been a dog, and if Delia had been close enough to do it, she'd have scratched the smooth head, felt the hard bone beneath, moved her hands around the soft ears. *Sure, okay, you go on now, Mr. Dog:* This is what she would have said with her hands. Then he crawled into the darkness under the slope of the wing, where she figured there must be a door, a hatch letting into the body of the machine, and after a while he flew off into the dark of the July moon.

In the weeks afterward, on nights when the moon had set or hadn't yet risen, she looked for the flash and streak of something breaking across the darkness out of the southwest. She saw him come and go to that draw on the west side of Lame Man Bench twice more in the first month. Both times, she left her grandmother's gun in the trailer and walked over there and sat in the dark on the rock slab above the draw and watched him for a couple of hours. He may have been waiting for her, or he knew her smell, because both times he reared up and looked at her just about as soon as she sat down. But then he went on with his business. *That woman is nobody to be scared of,* he said with his body, with the way he went on smelling the ground, widening his circle and widening it, sometimes taking a clod or a sprig into his mouth and tasting it, the way a mild-mannered dog will do when he's investigating something and not paying any attention to the person he's with.

Delia had about decided that the draw behind Lame Man Bench was one of his regular stops, like the ten campsites she used over and over again when she was herding on Joe-Johns Mountain; but after those three times in the first month, she didn't see him again.

At the end of September, she brought the sheep down to the O-Bar. After the lambs had been shipped out she took her band of dry ewes over onto the Nelson prairie for the fall, and in mid-November, when the snow had settled in, she brought them to the feed lots. That was all the work the ranch had for her until lambing season. Jesus and Alice belonged to the O-Bar. They stood in the yard and watched her go.

In town, she rented the same room as the year before, and, as before, spent most of a year's wages on getting drunk and standing other herders to rounds of drink. She gave up looking into the sky.

In March, she went back out to the ranch. In bitter weather, they built jugs and mothering-up pens, and trucked the pregnant ewes from Green, where they'd been feeding on wheat stubble. Some ewes lambed in the trailer on the way in, and after every haul, there was a surge of lambs born. Delia had the night shift, where she was paired with Roy Joyce, a fellow who raised sugar beets over in the valley and came out for the lambing season every year. In the black, freezing cold middle of the night, eight and ten ewes would be lambing at a time. Triplets, twins, big singles, a few quads, ewes with lambs born dead, ewes too sick or confused to mother. She and Roy would skin a dead lamb and feed the carcass to the ranch dogs and wrap the fleece around a bummer lamb, which was intended to fool the bereaved ewe into taking the orphan as her own, and sometimes it worked that way. All the mothering-up pens swiftly filled, and the jugs filled, and still some ewes with new lambs stood out in the cold field waiting for a room to open up.

You couldn't pull the stuck lambs with gloves on, you had to reach into the womb with your fingers to turn the lamb, or tie cord around the feet, or grasp the feet barehanded, so Delia's hands were always cold and wet, then cracked and bleeding. The ranch had brought in some old converted school buses to house the lambing crew, and she would fall into a bunk at daybreak and then not be able to sleep, shivering in the unheated bus with the gray daylight pouring in the windows and the endless daytime clamor out at the lambing sheds. All the lambers had sore throats, colds, nagging coughs. Roy Joyce looked like hell, deep bags as blue as bruises under his eyes, and Delia figured she looked about the same, though she hadn't seen a mirror, not even to draw a brush through her hair, since the start of the season.

By the end of the second week, only a handful of ewes hadn't lambed. The nights became quieter. The weather cleared, and the thin skiff of snow melted off the grass. On the dark of the moon, Delia was standing outside the mothering-up pens drinking coffee from a thermos. She put her head back and held the warmth of the coffee in her mouth a moment, and, as she was swallowing it down, lowering her chin, she caught the tail end of a green flash and a thin yellow line breaking across the sky, so far off anybody else would have thought it was a meteor, but it was bright, and dropping from southwest to due west, maybe right onto Lame Man Bench. She stood and looked at it. She was so very goddamned tired and had a sore throat that wouldn't clear, and she could barely get her fingers to fold around the thermos, they were so split and tender.

She told Roy she felt sick as a horse, and did he think he could handle things if she drove herself into town to the Urgent Care clinic, and she took one of the ranch trucks and drove up the road a short way and then turned onto the rutted track that went up to Joe-Johns.

The night was utterly clear and you could see things a long way off. She was still an hour's drive from the Churros' summer range when she began to see a yellow-orange glimmer behind the black ridgeline, a faint nimbus like the ones that marked distant range fires on summer nights.

She had to leave the truck at the bottom of the bench and climb up the last mile or so on foot, had to get a flashlight out of the glove box and try to find an uphill path with it because the fluttery reddish lightshow was finished by then, and a thick pall of smoke overcast the sky and blotted out the stars. Her eyes itched and burned, and tears ran from them, but the smoke calmed her sore throat. She went up slowly, breathing through her mouth.

The wing had burned a skid path through the scraggly junipers along the top of the bench and had come apart into about a hundred pieces. She wandered through the burnt trees and the scattered wreckage, shining her flashlight into the smoky darkness, not expecting to find what she was looking for, but there he was, lying apart from the scattered pieces of metal, out on the smooth slab rock at the edge of the draw. He was panting shallowly and his close coat of short brown hair was matted with blood. He lay in such a way that she immediately knew his back was broken. When he saw Delia coming up, his brow furrowed with worry. A sick or a wounded dog will bite, she knew that, but she squatted next to him. *It's just me*, she told him, by shining the light not in his face but in hers. Then she spoke to him. "Okay," she said. "I'm here now," without thinking too much about what the words meant, or whether they meant anything at all, and she didn't remember until afterward that he was very likely deaf anyway. He sighed and shifted his look from her to the middle distance, where she supposed he was focused on approaching death.

Near at hand, he didn't resemble a dog all that much, only in the long shape of his head, the folded-over ears, the round darkness of his eyes. He lay on the ground flat on his side like a dog that's been run over and is dying by the side of the road, but a man will lay like that too when he's dying. He had small-fingered nail-less hands where a dog would have had toes and front feet. Delia offered him a sip from her water bottle, but he didn't seem to want it, so she just sat with him quietly, holding one of his hands, which was smooth as lambskin against the cracked and roughened flesh of her palm. The batteries in the flashlight gave out, and sitting there in the cold darkness she found his head and stroked it, moving her sore fingers lightly over the bone of his skull, and around the soft ears, the loose jowls. Maybe it wasn't any particular comfort to him, but she was comforted by doing it. *Sure, okay, you can go on.*

She heard him sigh, and then sigh again, and each time wondered if it would turn out to be his death. She had used to wonder what a coyote, or especially a dog, would make of this doggish man, and now while she was listening, waiting to hear if he would breathe again, she began to wish she'd brought Alice or Jesus with her, though not out of that old curiosity. When her husband had died years before, at the very moment he took his last breath, the dog she'd had then had barked wildly and raced back and forth from the front to the rear door of the house as if he'd heard or seen something invisible to her. People said it was her husband's soul going out the door or his angel coming in. She didn't know what it was the dog had seen or heard or smelled, but she wished she knew. And now she wished she had a dog with her to bear witness.

She went on petting him even after he had died, after she was sure he was dead, went on petting him until his body was cool, and then she got up stiffly from the bloody ground and gathered rocks and piled them onto him, a couple of feet high, so that he wouldn't be found or dug up. She didn't know what to do about the wreckage, so she didn't do anything with it at all.

In May, when she brought the Churro sheep back to Joe-Johns Mountain, the pieces of the wrecked wing had already eroded, were small and smooth-edged like the bits of sea glass you find on a beach, and she figured that this must be what it was meant to do: to break apart into pieces too small for anybody to notice, and then to quickly wear away. But the stones she'd piled over his body seemed like the start of something, so she began the slow work of raising them higher into a sheepherder's monument. She gathered up all the smooth eroded bits of wing, too, and laid them in a series of widening circles around the base of the monument. She went on piling up stones through the summer and into September, until it reached fifteen feet. Mornings, standing with the sheep miles away, she would look for it through the binoculars and think about ways to raise it higher, and she would wonder what was buried under all the other monuments sheepherders had raised in that country. At night, she studied the sky, but nobody came for him.

In November, when she finished with the sheep and went into town, she asked around and found a guy who knew about star-gazing and telescopes. He loaned her some books and sent her to a certain pawnshop, and she gave most of a year's wages for a 14 × 75 telescope with a reflective lens. On clear, moonless nights, she met the astronomy guy out at the Little League baseball field, and she sat on a fold-up canvas stool with her eye against the telescope's finder while he told her what she was seeing: Jupiter's moons, the Pelican Nebula, the Andromeda Galaxy. The telescope had a tripod mount, and he showed her how to make a little jerry-built device so she could mount her old 7 × 32 binoculars on the tripod too. She used the binoculars for their wider view of star clusters and small constellations.

She was indifferent to most discomforts, could sit quietly in one position for hours at a time, teeth rattling with the cold, staring into the immense vault of the sky until she became numb and stiff, barely able to stand and walk back home. Astronomy, she discovered, was a work of patience, but the sheep had taught her patience, or it was already in her nature before she ever took up with them.

coelacanths

ROBERT REED

Robert Reed sold his first story in 1986, and quickly established himself as a frequent contributor to The Magazine of Fantasy and Science Fiction *and* Asimov's Science Fiction, *as well as selling many stories to* Science Fiction Age, Universe, New Destinies, Tomorrow, Synergy, Starlight, *and elsewhere. Reed may be one of the most prolific of today's young writers, particularly at short fiction lengths, seriously rivaled for that position only by authors such as Stephen Baxter and Brian Stableford. And—also like Baxter and Stableford—he manages to keep up a very high standard of quality while being prolific, something that is not at all easy to do. Reed stories such as "Sister Alice," "Brother Perfect," "Decency," "Savior," "The Remoras," "Chrysalis," "Whiptail," "The Utility Man," "Marrow," "Birth Day," "Blind," "The Toad of Heaven," "Stride," "The Shape of Everything," "Guest of Honor," "Waging Good," and "Killing the Morrow," among at least a half-dozen others equally as strong, count as among some of the best short work produced by anyone in the '80s and '90s. Nor is he non-prolific as a novelist, having turned out eight novels since the end of the '80s, including* The Lee Shore, The Hormone Jungle, Black Milk, The Remarkables, Down the Bright Way, Beyond the Veil of Stars, An Exaltation of Larks, *and* Beneath the Gated Sky. *His reputation can only grow as the years go by, and I suspect that he will become one of the Big Names of the first decade of the new century that lies ahead. His stories have appeared in our Ninth through Seventeenth, and our Nineteenth Annual Collections. Some of the best of his short work was collected in* The Dragons of Springplace. *His most recent book is* Marrow, *a novel-length version of his 1997 novella of the same name. Reed lives in Lincoln, Nebraska.*

Here's as strange and distant a far-future as you're ever likely to see, even in today's science fiction, a world that has become so alien to the few remaining humans who scuttle like cockroaches through its interstices that they have given up all hope of understanding it, and concentrate all their energies and ingenuity just on the daily battle to survive . . .

THE SPEAKER

He stalks the wide stage, a brilliant beam of hot blue light fixed squarely upon him. "We are great! We are glorious!" the man calls out. His voice is pleasantly, effortlessly loud. With a face handsome to the brink of lovely and a collage of smooth, passionate mannerisms, he performs for an audience that sits in the surrounding darkness. Flinging long arms overhead, hands reaching for the distant light, his booming voice proclaims, "We have never been as numerous as we are today. We have never been this happy. And we have never known the prosperity that is ours at this golden moment. This golden now!" Athletic legs carry him across the stage, bare feet slapping against planks of waxed maple. "Our species is thriving," he can declare with a seamless ease. "By every conceivable measure, we are a magnificent, irresistible tide sweeping across the universe!"

Transfixed by the blue beam, his naked body is shamelessly young, rippling with hard muscles over hard bone. A long fat penis dangles and dances, accenting every sweeping gesture, every bold word. The living image of a small but potent god, he surely is a creature worthy of admiration, a soul deserving every esteem and emulation. With a laugh, he promises the darkness, "We have never been so powerful, we humans." Yet in the next breath, with a faintly apologetic smile, he must add, "Yet still, as surely as tomorrow comes, our glories today will seem small and quaint in the future, and what looks golden now will turn to the yellow dust upon which our magnificent children will tread!"

PROCYON

Study your history. It tells you that travel always brings its share of hazards; that's a basic, impatient law of the universe. Leaving the security and familiarity of home is never easy. But every person needs to make the occasional journey, embracing the risks to improve his station, his worth and self-esteem. Procyon explains why this day is a good day to wander. She refers to intelligence reports as well as the astrological tables. Then by a dozen means, she maps out their intricate course, describing what she hopes to find and everything that she wants to avoid.

She has twin sons. They were born four months ago, and they are mostly grown now. "Keep alert," she tells the man-children, leading them out through a series of reinforced and powerfully camouflaged doorways. "No naps, no distractions," she warns them. Then with a backward glance, she asks again, "What do we want?"

"Whatever we can use," the boys reply in a sloppy chorus.

"Quiet," she warns. Then she nods and shows a caring smile, reminding them, "A lot of things can be used. But their trash is sweetest."

Mother and sons look alike: They are short, strong people with closely cropped hair and white-gray eyes. They wear simple clothes and three fashions of camouflage, plus a stew of mental add-ons and microchine helpers as well as an array of sensors that never blink, watching what human eyes cannot see. Standing motionless, they vanish into the convoluted, ever-shifting background. But walking makes them into three transient blurs — dancing wisps that are noticeably simpler than the enormous world around them. They can creep ahead only so far before their camouflage falls apart, and then they have to stop, waiting patiently or otherwise, allowing the machinery to find new ways to help make them invisible.

"I'm confused," one son admits. "That thing up ahead — "

"Did you update your perception menu?"

"I thought I did."

Procyon makes no sound. Her diamond-bright glare is enough. She remains rigidly, effortlessly still, allowing her lazy son to finish his preparations. Dense, heavily encoded signals have to be whispered, the local net downloading the most recent topological cues, teaching a three-dimensional creature how to navigate through this shifting, highly intricate environment.

The universe is fat with dimensions.

Procyon knows as much theory as anyone. Yet despite a long life rich with experience, she has to fight to decipher what her eyes and sensors tell her. She doesn't even bother learning the tricks that coax these extra dimensions out of hiding. Let her add-ons guide her. That's all a person can do, slipping in close to one of *them*. In this place, up is three things and sideways is five others. Why bother counting? What matters is that when they walk again, the three of them move through the best combination of dimensions, passing into a little bubble of old-fashioned up and down. She knows this place. Rising up beside them is a trusted landmark — a red granite bowl that cradles what looks like a forest of tall sticks, the sticks leaking a warm light that Procyon ignores, stepping again, moving along on her tiptoes.

One son leads the way. He lacks the experience to be first, but in another few weeks, his flesh and sprint-grown brain will force him into the world alone. He needs his practice, and more important, he needs confidence, learning to trust his add-ons and his careful preparations, and his breeding, and his own good luck.

Procyon's other son lingers near the granite bowl. He's the son who didn't update his menu. This is her dreamy child, whom she loves dearly. Of course she adores him. But there's no escaping the fact that he is easily distracted, and that his adult life will be, at its very best, difficult. Study your biology. Since life began, mothers have made hard decisions about their children, and they have made the deadliest decisions with the tiniest of gestures.

Procyon lets her lazy son fall behind.

Her other son takes two careful steps and stops abruptly, standing before what looks like a great black cylinder set on its side. The shape is a fiction: The cylinder is round in one fashion but incomprehensible in many others. Her add-ons and sensors have built this very simple geometry to represent something far more elaborate. This is a standard disposal unit. Various openings appear as a single slot near the rim of the cylinder, just enough room showing for a hand and forearm to reach through, touching whatever garbage waits inside.

Her son's thick body has more grace than any dancer of old, more strength than a platoon of ancient athletes. His IQ is enormous. His reaction times have been enhanced by every available means. His father was a great old soul who survived into his tenth year, which is almost forever. But when the boy drifts sideways, he betrays his inexperience. His sensors attack the cylinder by every means, telling him that it's a low-grade trash receptacle secured by what looks like a standard locking device, AI-managed and obsolete for days, if not weeks. And inside the receptacle is a mangled piece of hardware worth a near-fortune on the open market.

The boy drifts sideways, and he glimmers.

Procyon says, "No," too loudly.

But he feels excited, invulnerable. Grinning over his shoulder now, he winks and lifts one hand with a smooth, blurring motion —

Instincts old as blood come bubbling up. Procyon leaps, shoving her son off his feet and saving him. And in the next horrible instant, she feels herself engulfed, a dry cold hand grabbing her, then stuffing her inside a hole that by any geometry feels nothing but bottomless.

ABLE

Near the lip of the City, inside the emerald green ring of Park, waits a secret place where the moss and horsetail and tree fern forest plunges into a deep crystalline pool of warm spring water. No public map tells of the pool, and no trail leads the casual walker near it. But the pool is exactly the sort of place that young boys always discover, and it is exactly the kind of treasure that remains unmentioned to parents or any other adult with suspicious or troublesome natures.

Able Quotient likes to believe that he was first to stumble across this tiny corner of Creation. And if he isn't first, at least no one before him has ever truly seen the water's beauty, and nobody after him will appreciate the charms of this elegant, timeless place.

Sometimes Able brings others to the pool, but only his best friends and a few boys whom he wants to impress. Not for a long time does he even consider bringing a girl, and then it takes forever to find a worthy candidate, then muster the courage to ask her to join him. Her name is Mish. She's younger than Able by a little ways, but like all girls, she acts older and much wiser than he will ever be. They have been classmates from the beginning. They live three floors apart in The Tower Of Gracious Good, which makes them close neighbors. Mish is pretty, and her beauty is the sort that will only grow as she becomes a woman. Her face is narrow and serious. Her eyes watch everything. She wears flowing dresses and jeweled sandals, and she goes everywhere with a clouded leopard named Mr. Stuff-and-Nonsense. "If my cat can come along," she says after hearing Able's generous offer. "Are there any birds at this pond of yours?"

Able should be horrified by the question. The life around the pool knows him and has grown to trust him. But he is so enamored by Mish that he blurts out, "Yes, hundreds of birds. Fat, slow birds. Mr. Stuff can eat himself sick."

"But that wouldn't be right," Mish replies with a disapproving smirk. "I'll lock down his appetite. And if we see any wounded birds . . . any animal that's suffering . . . we can unlock him right away . . . !"

"Oh, sure," Able replies, almost sick with nerves. "I guess that's fine, too."

People rarely travel any distance. City is thoroughly modern, every apartment supplied by conduits and meshed with every web and channel, shareline and gossip run. But even with most of its citizens happily sitting at home, the streets are jammed with millions of walking bodies. Every seat on the train is filled all the way to the last stop. Able momentarily loses track of Mish when the cabin walls evaporate. But thankfully, he finds her waiting at Park's edge. She and her little leopard are standing in the narrow shade of a horsetail. She teases him, observing, "You look lost." Then she laughs, perhaps at him, before abruptly changing the subject. With a nod and sweeping gesture, she asks, "Have you noticed? Our towers look like these trees."

To a point, yes. The towers are tall and thin and rounded like the horsetails, and the hanging porches make them appear rough-skinned. But there are obvious and important differences between trees and towers, and if she were a boy, Able would make fun of her now. Fighting his nature, Able forces himself to smile. "Oh, my," he says as he turns, looking back over a shoulder. "They do look like horsetails, don't they?"

Now the three adventurers set off into the forest. Able takes the lead. Walking with boys is a quick business that often turns into a race. But girls are different, particularly when their fat, unhungry cats are dragging along behind them. It takes forever to reach the rim of the world. Then it takes another two forevers to follow the rim to where they can almost see the secret pool. But that's where Mish announces, "I'm tired!" To the world, she says, "I want to stop and eat. I want to rest here."

Able nearly tells her, "No."

Instead he decides to coax her, promising, "It's just a little farther."

But she doesn't seem to hear him, leaping up on the pink polished rim, sitting where the granite is smooth and flat, legs dangling and her bony knees exposed. She opens the little pack that has floated on her back from the beginning, pulling out a hot lunch that she keeps and a cold lunch that she hands to Able. "This is all I could take," she explains, "without my parents asking questions." She is reminding Able that she never quite got permission to make this little journey. "If you don't like the cold lunch," she promises, "then we can trade. I mean, if you really don't."

He says, "I like it fine," without opening the insulated box. Then he looks inside, discovering a single wedge of spiced sap, and it takes all of his poise not to say, "Ugh!"

Mr. Stuff collapses into a puddle of towerlight, instantly falling asleep.

The two children eat quietly and slowly. Mish makes the occasional noise about favorite teachers and mutual friends. She acts serious and ordinary, and disappointment starts gnawing at Able. He isn't old enough to sense that the girl is nervous. He can't imagine that Mish wants to delay the moment when they'll reach the secret pool, or that she sees possibilities waiting there—wicked possibilities that only a wicked boy should be able to foresee.

Finished with her meal, Mish runs her hands along the hem of her dress, and she kicks at the air, and then, hunting for any distraction, she happens to glance over her shoulder.

Where the granite ends, the world ends. Normally nothing of substance can be seen out past the pink stone—nothing but a confused, ever-shifting grayness that extends on forever. Able hasn't bothered to look out there. He is much too busy trying to finish his awful meal, concentrating on his little frustrations and his depraved little daydreams.

"Oh, goodness," the young girl exclaims. "Look at that!"

Able has no expectations. What could possibly be worth the trouble of turning around? But it's an excuse to give up on his lunch, and after setting it aside, he turns slowly, eyes jumping wide open and a surprised grunt leaking out of him as he tumbles off the granite, landing squarely on top of poor Mr. Stuff.

ESCHER

She has a clear, persistent memory of flesh, but the flesh isn't hers. Like manners and like knowledge, what a person remembers can be bequeathed by her ancestors. That's what is happening now. Limbs and heads; penises and vaginas. In the midst of some unrelated business, she remembers having feet and the endless need to protect those feet with sandals or boots or ostrich skin or spiked shoes that will lend a person even more height. She remembers wearing clothes that gave color and bulk to what was already bright and enormous. At this particular instant, what she sees is a distant, long-dead relative sitting on a white porcelain bowl, bare feet dangling, his orifices voiding mountains of waste and an ocean of water.

Her oldest ancestors were giants. They were built from skin and muscle, wet air and great slabs of fat. Without question, they were an astonishing excess of matter, vast beyond all reason, yet fueled by slow, inefficient chemical fires.

Nothing about Escher is inefficient. No flesh clings to her. Not a drop of water or one glistening pearl of fat. It's always smart to be built from structure light and tested, efficient instructions. It's best to be tinier than a single cell and as swift as electricity, slipping unseen through places that won't even notice your presence.

Escher is a glimmer, a perfect and enduring whisper of light. Of life. Lovely in her own fashion, yet fierce beyond all measure.

She needs her fierceness.

When cooperation fails, as it always does, a person has to throw her rage at the world and her countless enemies.

But in this place, for this moment, cooperation holds sway.

Manners rule.

Escher is eating. Even as tiny and efficient as she is, she needs an occasional sip of raw power. Everyone does. And it seems as if half of everyone has gathered around what can only be described as a tiny, delicious wound. She can't count the citizens gathered at the feast. Millions and millions, surely. All those weak glimmers join into a soft glow. Everyone is bathed in a joyous light. It is a boastful, wasteful show, but Escher won't waste her energy with warnings. Better to sip at the wound, absorbing the free current, building up her reserves for the next breed-ing cycle. It is best to let others make the mistakes for you: Escher believes nothing else quite so fervently.

A pair of sisters float past. The familial resemblance is obvious, and so are the tiny differences. Mutations as well as tailored changes have created two loud gos-sips who speak and giggle in a rush of words and raw data, exchanging secrets about the multitude around them.

Escher ignores their prattle, gulping down the last of what she can possibly hold, and then pausing, considering where she might hide a few nanojoules of extra juice, keeping them safe for some desperate occasion.

Escher begins to hunt for that unlikely hiding place.

And then her sisters abruptly change topics. Gossip turns to trading memories stolen from The World. Most of it is picoweight stuff, useless and boring. An astonishing fraction of His thoughts are banal. Like the giants of old, He can afford to be sloppy. To be a spendthrift. Here is a pointed example of why Escher is happy to be herself. She is smart in her own fashion, and imaginative, and almost everything about her is important, and when a problem confronts her, she can cut through the muddle, seeing the blessing wrapped up snug inside the measurable risks.

Quietly, with a puzzled tone, one sister announces, "The World is alarmed."

"About?" says the other.

"A situation," says the first. "Yes, He is alarmed now. Moral questions are beg-ging for His attention."

"What questions?"

The first sister tells a brief, strange story.

"You know all this?" asks another. Asks Escher. "Is this daydream or hard fact?"

"I know, and it is fact." The sister feels insulted by the doubting tone, but she puts on a mannerly voice, explaining the history of this sudden crisis.

Escher listens.

And suddenly the multitude is talking about nothing else. What is happening has never happened before, not in this fashion . . . not in any genuine memory of any of the millions here, it hasn't . . . and some very dim possibilities begin to show themselves. Benefits wrapped inside some awful dangers. And one or two of these benefits wink at Escher, and smile. . . .

The multitude panics, and evaporates.

Escher remains behind, deliberating on these possibilities. The landscape be-neath her is far more sophisticated than flesh, and stronger, but it has an ugly appearance that reminds her of a flesh-born memory. A lesion; a pimple. A tiny, unsightly ruin standing in what is normally seamless, and beautiful, and perfect.

She flees, but only so far.

Then she hunkers down and waits, knowing that eventually, in one fashion or another, He will scratch at this tiny irritation.

THE SPEAKER

"You cannot count human accomplishments," he boasts to his audience, strutting and wagging his way to the edge of the stage. Bare toes curl over the sharp edge, and he grins jauntily, admitting, "And I cannot count them, either. There are simply too many successes, in too many far-flung places, to nail up a number that you can believe. But allow me, if you will, this chance to list a few important marvels."

Long hands grab bony hips, and he gazes out into the watching darkness. "The conquest of our cradle continent," he begins, "which was quickly followed by the conquest of our cradle world. Then after a gathering pause, we swiftly and thoroughly occupied most of our neighboring worlds, too. It was during those millennia when we learned how to split flint and atoms and DNA and our own restless psyches. With these apish hands, we fashioned great machines that worked for us as our willing, eager slaves. And with our slaves' more delicate hands, we fabricated machines that could think for us." A knowing wink, a mischievous shrug. "Like any child, of course, our thinking machines eventually learned to think for themselves. Which was a dangerous, foolish business, said some. Said fools. But my list of our marvels only begins with that business. This is what I believe, and I challenge anyone to say otherwise."

There is a sound—a stern little murmur—and perhaps it implies dissent. Or perhaps the speaker made the noise himself, fostering a tension that he is building with his words and body.

His penis grows erect, drawing the eye.

Then with a wide and bright and unabashedly smug grin, he roars out, "Say this with me. Tell me what great things we have done. Boast to Creation about the wonders that we have taken part in . . . !"

PROCYON

Torture is what this is: She feels her body plunging from a high place, head before feet. A frantic wind roars past. Outstretched hands refuse to slow her fall. Then Procyon makes herself spin, putting her feet beneath her body, and gravity instantly reverses itself. She screams, and screams, and the distant walls reflect her terror, needles jabbed into her wounded ears. Finally, she grows quiet, wrapping her arms around her eyes and ears, forcing herself to do nothing, hanging limp in space while her body falls in one awful direction.

A voice whimpers.

A son's worried voice says, "Mother, are you there? Mother?"

Some of her add-ons have been peeled away, but not all of them. The brave son uses a whisper-channel, saying, "I'm sorry," with a genuine anguish. He sounds sick and sorry, and exceptionally angry, too. "I was careless," he admits. He says, "Thank you for saving me." Then to someone else, he says, "She can't hear me."

"I hear you," she whispers.

"Listen," says her other son. The lazy one. "Did you hear something?"

She starts to say, "Boys," with a stern voice. But then the trap vibrates, a piercing white screech nearly deafening Procyon. Someone physically strikes the trap. Two someones. She feels the walls turning around her, the trap making perhaps a quarter-turn toward home.

Again, she calls out, "Boys."

They stop rolling her. Did they hear her? No, they found a hidden restraint, the trap secured at one or two or ten ends.

One last time, she says, "Boys."

"I hear her," her dreamy son blurts.

"Don't give up, Mother," says her brave son. "We'll get you out. I see the locks, I can beat them—"

"You can't," she promises.

He pretends not to have heard her. A shaped explosive detonates, making a cold ringing sound, faraway and useless. Then the boy growls, "Damn," and kicks the trap, accomplishing nothing at all.

"It's too tough," says her dreamy son. "We're not doing any good—"

"Shut up," his brother shouts.

Procyon tells them, "Quiet now. Be quiet."

The trap is probably tied to an alarm. Time is short, or it has run out already. Either way, there's a decision to be made, and the decision has a single, inescapable answer. With a careful and firm voice, she tells her sons, "Leave me. Now. Go!"

"I won't," the brave son declares. "Never!"

"Now," she says.

"It's my fault," says the dreamy son. "I should have been keeping up—"

"Both of you are to blame," Procyon calls out. "And I am, too. And there's bad luck here, but there's some good, too. You're still free. You can still get away. Now, before you get yourself seen and caught—"

"You're going to die," the brave son complains.

"One day or the next, I will," she agrees. "Absolutely."

"We'll find help," he promises.

"From where?" she asks.

"From who?" says her dreamy son in the same instant. "We aren't close to anyone—"

"Shut up," his brother snaps. "Just shut up!"

"Run away," their mother repeats.

"I won't," the brave son tells her. Or himself. Then with a serious, tight little voice, he says, "I can fight. We'll both fight."

Her dreamy son says nothing.

Procyon peels her arms away from her face, opening her eyes, focusing on the blurring cylindrical walls of the trap. It seems that she was wrong about her sons. The brave one is just a fool, and the dreamy one has the good sense. She listens to her dreamy son saying nothing, and then the other boy says, "Of course you're going to fight. Together, we can do some real damage—"

"I love you both," she declares.

That wins a silence.

Then again, one last time, she says, "Run."

"I'm not a coward," one son growls.

While her good son says nothing, running now, and he needs his breath for things more essential than pride and bluster.

ABLE

The face stares at them for the longest while. It is a great wide face, heavily bearded with smoke-colored eyes and a long nose perched above the cavernous mouth that hangs open, revealing teeth and things more amazing than teeth. Set between the bone-white enamel are little machines made of fancy stuff. Able can only guess what the add-on machines are doing. This is a wild man, powerful and free. People like him are scarce and strange, their bodies reengineered in countless ways. Like his eyes: Able stares into those giant gray eyes, noticing fleets of tiny machines floating on the tears. Those machines are probably delicate sensors. Then with a jolt of amazement, he realizes that those machines and sparkling eyes are staring into their world with what seems to be a genuine fascination.

"He's watching us," Able mutters.

"No, he isn't," Mish argues. "He can't see into our realm."

"We can't see into his either," the boy replies. "But just the same, I can make him out just fine."

"It must be. . . ." Her voice falls silent while she accesses City's library. Then with a dismissive shrug of her shoulders, she announces, "We're caught in his topological hardware. That's all. He has to simplify his surroundings to navigate, and we just happen to be close enough and aligned right."

Able had already assumed all that.

Mish starts to speak again, probably wanting to add to her explanation. She can sure be a know-everything sort of girl. But then the great face abruptly turns away, and they watch the man run away from their world.

"I told you," Mish sings out. "He couldn't see us."

"I think he could have," Able replies, his voice finding a distinct sharpness.

The girl straightens her back. "You're wrong," she says with an obstinate tone. Then she turns away from the edge of the world, announcing, "I'm ready to go on now."

"I'm not," says Able.

She doesn't look back at him. She seems to be talking to her leopard, asking, "Why aren't you ready?"

"I see two of them now," Able tells her.

"You can't."

"I can." The hardware trickery is keeping the outside realms sensible. A tunnel of simple space leads to two men standing beside an iron-black cylinder. The men wear camouflage, but they are moving too fast to let it work. They look small now. Distant, or tiny. Once you leave the world, size and distance are impossible to measure. How many times have teachers told him that? Able watches the tiny men kicking at the cylinder. They beat on its heavy sides with their fists and forearms, managing to roll it for almost a quarter turn. Then one of the men pulls a fist-sized device from what looks like a cloth sack, fixing it to what looks like a sealed slot, and both men hurry to the far end of the cylinder.

"What are they doing?" asks Mish with a grumpy interest.

A feeling warns Able, but too late. He starts to say, "Look away—"

The explosion is brilliant and swift, the blast reflected off the cylinder and up along the tunnel of ordinary space, a clap of thunder making the giant horsetails sway and nearly knocking the two of them onto the forest floor.

"They're criminals," Mish mutters with a nervous hatred.

"How do you know?" the boy asks.

"People like that just are," she remarks. "Living like they do. Alone like that, and wild. You know how they make their living."

"They take what they need—"

"They steal!" she interrupts.

Able doesn't even glance at her. He watches as the two men work frantically, trying to pry open the still-sealed doorway. He can't guess why they would want the doorway opened. Or rather, he can think of too many reasons. But when he looks at their anguished, helpless faces, he realizes that whatever is inside, it's driving these wild men very close to panic.

"Criminals," Mish repeats.

"I heard you," Able mutters.

Then before she can offer another hard opinion, he turns to her and admits, "I've always liked them. They live by their wits, and mostly alone, and they have all these sweeping powers—"

"Powers that they've stolen," she whines.

"From garbage, maybe." There is no point in mentioning whose garbage. He stares at Mish's face, pretty but twisted with fury, and something sad and inevitable occurs to Able. He shakes his head and sighs, telling her, "I don't like you very much."

Mish is taken by surprise. Probably no other boy has said those awful words to her, and she doesn't know how to react, except to sputter ugly little sounds as she turns, looking back over the edge of the world.

Able does the same.

One of the wild men abruptly turns and runs. In a supersonic flash, he races past the children, vanishing into the swirling grayness, leaving his companion to stand alone beside the mysterious black cylinder. Obviously weeping, the last man wipes the tears from his whiskered face with a trembling hand, while his other hand begins to yank a string of wondrous machines from what seems to be a bottomless sack of treasures.

ESCHER

She consumes all of her carefully stockpiled energies, and for the first time in her life, she weaves a body for herself: A distinct physical shell composed of diamond dust and keratin and discarded rare earths and a dozen subtle glues meant to bind to every surface without being felt. To a busy eye, she is dust. She is insubstantial and useless and forgettable. To a careful eye and an inquisitive touch, she is the tiniest soul imaginable, frail beyond words, forever perched on the brink of extermination. Surely she poses no threat to any creature, least of all the great ones. Lying on the edge of the little wound, passive and vulnerable, she waits for Chance to carry her where she needs to be. Probably others are doing the same. Perhaps thousands of sisters and daughters are hiding nearby, each snug inside her own spore case. The temptation to whisper, "Hello," is easily ignored. The odds are awful as it is; any noise could turn this into a suicide. What matters is silence and watchfulness, thinking hard about the great goal while keeping ready for anything that might happen, as well as everything that will not.

The little wound begins to heal, causing a trickling pain to flow.

The World feels the irritation, and in reflex, touches His discomfort by several means, delicate and less so.

Escher misses her first opportunity. A great swift shape presses its way across her hiding place, but she activates her glues too late. Dabs of glue cure against air, wasted. So she cuts the glue loose and watches again. A second touch is unlikely, but it comes, and she manages to heave a sticky tendril into a likely crevice, letting the irresistible force yank her into a brilliant, endless sky.

She will probably die now.

For a little while, Escher allows herself to look back across her life, counting daughters and other successes, taking warm comfort in her many accomplishments.

Someone hangs in the distance, dangling from a similar tendril. Escher recognizes the shape and intricate glint of her neighbor's spore case; she is one of Escher's daughters. There is a strong temptation to signal her, trading information, helping each other—

But a purge-ball attacks suddenly, and the daughter evaporates, nothing remaining of her but ions and a flash of incoherent light.

Escher pulls herself toward the crevice, and hesitates. Her tendril is anchored on a fleshy surface. A minor neuron—a thread of warm optical cable—lies buried inside the wet cells. She launches a second tendril at her new target. By chance, the purge-ball sweeps the wrong terrain, giving her that little instant. The tendril makes a sloppy connection with the neuron. Without time to test its integrity, all she can do is shout, "Don't kill me! Or my daughters! Don't murder us, Great World!"

Nothing changes. The purge-ball works its way across the deeply folded fleshscape, moving toward Escher again, distant flashes announcing the deaths of another two daughters or sisters.

"Great World!" she cries out.

He will not reply. Escher is like the hum of a single angry electron, and she can only hope that he notices the hum.

"I am vile," she promises. "I am loathsome and sneaky, and you should hate me. What I am is an illness lurking inside you. A disease that steals exactly what I can steal without bringing your wrath."

The purge-ball appears, following a tall reddish ridge of flesh, bearing down on her hiding place.

She says, "Kill me, if you want. Or spare me, and I will do this for you." Then she unleashes a series of vivid images, precise and simple, meant to be compelling to any mind.

The purge-ball slows, its sterilizing lasers taking careful aim.

She repeats herself, knowing that thought travels only so quickly and The World is too vast to see her thoughts and react soon enough to save her. But if she can help . . . if she saves just a few hundred daughters . . . ?

Lasers aim, and do nothing. Nothing. And after an instant of inactivity, the machine changes its shape and nature. It hovers above Escher, sending out its own tendrils. A careless strength yanks her free of her hiding place. Her tendrils and glues are ripped from her aching body. A scaffolding of carbon is built around her, and she is shoved inside the retooled purge-ball, held in a perfect darkness, waiting alone until an identical scaffold is stacked beside her.

A hard, angry voice boasts, "I did this."

"What did you do?" asks Escher.

"I made the World listen to reason." It sounds like Escher's voice, except for the delusions of power. "I made a promise, and that's why He saved us."

With a sarcastic tone, she says, "Thank you ever so much. But now where are we going?"

"I won't tell you," her fellow prisoner responds.

"Because you don't know where," says Escher.

"I know everything I need to know."

"Then you're the first person ever," she giggles, winning a brief, delicious silence from her companion.

Other prisoners arrive, each slammed into the empty spaces between their sisters and daughters. Eventually the purge-ball is a prison-ball, swollen to vast proportions, and no one else is being captured. Nothing changes for a long while. There is nothing to be done now but wait, speaking when the urge hits and listening to whichever voice sounds less than tedious.

Gossip is the common currency. People are desperate to hear the smallest glimmer of news. Where the final rumor comes from, nobody knows if it's true. But the woman who was captured moments after Escher claims, "It comes from the world Himself. He's going to put us where we can do the most good."

"Where?" Escher inquires.

"On a tooth," her companion says. "The right incisor, as it happens." Then with that boasting voice, she adds, "Which is exactly what I told Him to do. This is all because of me."

"What isn't?" Escher grumbles.

"Very little," the tiny prisoner promises. "Very, very little."

THE SPEAKER

"We walk today on a thousand worlds, and I mean 'walk' in all manners of speaking." He manages a few comical steps before shifting into a graceful turn, arms held firmly around the wide waist of an invisible and equally graceful partner. *"A*

hundred alien suns bake us with their perfect light. And between the suns, in the cold and dark, we survive, and thrive, by every worthy means."

Now he pauses, hands forgetting the unseen partner. A look of calculated confusion sweeps across his face. Fingers rise to his thick black hair, stabbing it and yanking backward, leaving furrows in the unruly mass.

"Our numbers," he says. "Our population. It made us sick with worry when we were ten billion standing on the surface of one enormous world. 'Where will our children stand?' we asked ourselves. But then in the next little while, we became ten trillion people, and we had split into a thousand species of humanity, and the new complaint was that we were still too scarce and spread too far apart. 'How could we matter to the universe?' we asked ourselves. 'How could so few souls endure another day in our immeasurable, uncaring universe?' "

His erect penis makes a little leap, a fat and vivid white drop of semen striking the wooden stage with an audible plop.

"Our numbers," he repeats. "Our legions." Then with a wide, garish smile, he confesses, "I don't know our numbers today. No authority does. You make estimates. You extrapolate off data that went stale long ago. You build a hundred models and fashion every kind of vast number. Ten raised to the twentieth power. The thirtieth power. Or more." He giggles and skips backward, and with the giddy, careless energy of a child, he dances where he stands, singing to lights overhead, "If you are as common as sand and as unique as snowflakes, how can you be anything but a wild, wonderful success?"

ABLE

The wild man is enormous and powerful, and surely brilliant beyond anything that Able can comprehend—as smart as City as a whole—but despite his gifts, the man is obviously terrified. That he can even manage to stand his ground astonishes Able. He says as much to Mish, and then he glances at her, adding, "He must be very devoted to whoever's inside."

"Whoever's inside what?" she asks.

"That trap." He looks straight ahead again, telling himself not to waste time with the girl. She is foolish and bad-tempered, and he couldn't be any more tired of her. "I think that's what the cylinder is," he whispers. "A trap of some kind. And someone's been caught in it."

"Well, I don't care who," she snarls.

He pretends not to notice her.

"What was that?" she blurts. "Did you hear that—?"

"No," Able blurts. But then he notices a distant rumble, deep and faintly rhythmic, and with every breath, growing. When he listens carefully, it resembles nothing normal. It isn't thunder, and it can't be a voice. He feels the sound as much as he hears it, as if some great mass were being displaced. But he knows better. In school, teachers like to explain what must be happening now, employing tortuous mathematics and magical sleights of hand. Matter and energy are being rapidly and brutally manipulated. The universe's obscure dimensions are being twisted like bands of warm rubber. Able knows all this. But still, he understands none of it. Words without comprehension; froth without substance. All that he knows for certain is that behind that deep, unknowable throbbing lies something even farther beyond human description.

The wild man looks up, gray eyes staring at that something.

He cries out, that tiny sound lost between his mouth and Able. Then he produces what seems to be a spear—no, an elaborate missile—that launches itself with a bolt of fire, lifting a sophisticated warhead up into a vague gray space that swallows the weapon without sound, or complaint.

Next the man aims a sturdy laser, and fires. But the weapon simply melts at its tip, collapsing into a smoldering, useless mass at his feet.

Again, the wild man cries out.

His language could be a million generations removed from City-speech, but Able hears the desperate, furious sound of his voice. He doesn't need words to know that the man is cursing. Then the swirling grayness slows itself, and parts, and stupidly, in reflex, Able turns to Mish, wanting to tell her, "Watch. You're going to see one of *Them.*"

But Mish has vanished. Sometime in the last few moments, she jumped off the world's rim and ran away, and save for the fat old leopard sleeping between the horsetails, Able is entirely alone now.

"Good," he mutters.

Almost too late, he turns and runs to the very edge of the granite rim.

The wild man stands motionless now. His bowels and bladder have emptied themselves. His handsome, godly face is twisted from every flavor of misery. Eyes as big as windows stare up into what only they can see, and to that great, unknowable something, the man says two simple words.

"Fuck you," Able hears.

And then the wild man opens his mouth, baring his white apish teeth, and just as Able wonders what's going to happen, the man's body explodes, the dull black burst of a shaped charge sending chunks of his face skyward.

PROCYON

One last time, she whispers her son's name.

She whispers it and closes her mouth and listens to the brief, sharp silence that comes after the awful explosion. What must have happened, she tells herself, is that her boy found his good sense and fled. How can a mother think anything else? And then the ominous deep rumbling begins again, begins and gradually swells until the walls of the trap are shuddering and twisting again. But this time the monster is slower. It approaches the trap more cautiously, summoning new courage. She can nearly taste its courage now, and with her intuition, she senses emotions that might be curiosity and might be a kind of reflexive admiration. Or do those eternal human emotions have any relationship for what *It* feels . . . ?

What she feels, after everything, is numbness. A terrible deep weariness hangs on her like a new skin. Procyon seems to be falling faster now, accelerating down through the bottomless trap. But she doesn't care anymore. In place of courage, she wields a muscular apathy. Death looms, but when hasn't it been her dearest companion? And in place of fear, she is astonished to discover an incurious little pride about what is about to happen: How many people—wild free people like herself—have ever found themselves so near one of *Them*?

Quietly, with a calm smooth and slow voice, Procyon says, "I feel you there, you. I can taste you."

Nothing changes.

Less quietly, she says, "Show yourself."

A wide parabolic floor appears, gleaming and black and agonizingly close. But just before she slams into the floor, a wrenching force peels it away. A brilliant violet light rises to meet her, turning into a thick sweet syrup. What may or may not be a hand curls around her body, and squeezes. Procyon fights every urge to struggle. She wrestles with her body, wrestles with her will, forcing both to lie still while the hand tightens its grip and grows comfortable. Then using a voice that betrays nothing tentative or small, she tells what holds her, "I made you, you know."

She says, "You can do what you want to me."

Then with a natural, deep joy, she cries out, "But you're an ungrateful glory . . . and you'll always belong to me . . . !"

ESCHER

The prison-ball has been reengineered, slathered with camouflage and armor and the best immune-suppressors on the market, and its navigation system has been adapted from add-ons stolen from the finest trashcans. Now it is a battle-phage riding on the sharp incisor as far as it dares, then leaping free. A thousand similar phages leap and lose their way, or they are killed. Only Escher's phage reaches the target, impacting on what passes for flesh and launching its cargo with a microscopic railgun, punching her and a thousand sisters and daughters through immeasurable distances of senseless, twisted nothing.

How many survive the attack?

She can't guess how many. Can't even care. What matters is to make herself survive inside this strange new world. An enormous world, yes. Escher feels a vastness that reaches out across ten or twelve or maybe a thousand dimensions. How do I know where to go? she asks herself. And instantly, an assortment of possible routes appear in her consciousness, drawn in the simplest imaginable fashion, waiting and eager to help her find her way around.

This is a last gift from Him, she realizes. Unless there are more gifts waiting, of course.

She thanks nobody.

On the equivalent of tiptoes, Escher creeps her way into a tiny conduit that moves something stranger than any blood across five dimensions. She becomes passive, aiming for invisibility. She drifts and spins, watching her surroundings turn from a senseless glow into a landscape that occasionally seems a little bit reasonable. A little bit real. Slowly, she learns how to see in this new world. Eventually she spies a little peak that may or may not be ordinary matter. The peak is pink and flexible and sticks out into the great artery, and flinging her last tendril, Escher grabs hold and pulls in snug, knowing that the chances are lousy that she will ever find anything nourishing here, much less delicious.

But her reserves have been filled again, she notes. If she is careful—and when hasn't she been—her energies will keep her alive for centuries.

She thinks of the World, and thanks nobody.

"Watch and learn," she whispers to herself.

That was the first human thought. She remembers that odd fact suddenly. People were just a bunch of grubbing apes moving blindly through their tiny lives until one said to a companion, "Watch and learn."

An inherited memory, or another gift from Him?

Silently, she thanks Luck, and she thanks Him, and once again, she thanks Luck.

"Patience and planning," she tells herself.

Which is another wise thought of the conscious, enduring ape.

THE LAST SON

The locked gates and various doorways know him—recognize him at a glance—but they have to taste him anyway. They have to test him. Three people were expected, and he can't explain in words what has happened. He just says, "The others will be coming later," and leaves that lie hanging in the air. Then as he passes through the final doorway, he says, "Let no one through. Not without my permission first."

"This is your mother's house," says the door's AI.

"Not anymore," he remarks.

The machine grows quiet, and sad.

During any other age, his home would be a mansion. There are endless rooms, rooms beyond counting, and each is enormous and richly furnished and lovely and jammed full of games and art and distractions and flourishes that even the least aesthetic soul would find lovely. He sees none of that now. Alone, he walks to what has always been his room, and he sits on a leather recliner, and the house brings him a soothing drink and an intoxicating drink and an assortment of treats that sit on the platter, untouched.

For a long while, the boy stares off at the distant ceiling, replaying everything with his near-perfect memory. Everything. Then he forgets everything, stupidly calling out, "Mother," with a voice that sounds ridiculously young. Then again, he calls, "Mother." And he starts to rise from his chair, starts to ask the great empty house, "Where is she?"

And he remembers.

As if his legs have been sawed off, he collapses. His chair twists itself to catch him, and an army of AIs brings their talents to bear. They are loyal, limited machines. They are empathetic, and on occasion, even sweet. They want to help him in any fashion, just name the way . . . but their appeals and their smart sug-gestions are just so much noise. The boy acts deaf, and he obviously can't see anything with his fists jabbed into his eyes like that, slouched forward in his favorite chair, begging an invisible someone for forgiveness. . . .

THE SPEAKER

He squats and uses the tip of a forefinger to dab at the puddle of semen, and he rubs the finger against his thumb, saying, "Think of cells. Individual, self-reliant cells. For most of Earth's great history, they ruled. First as bacteria, and then as composites built from cooperative bacteria. They were everywhere and ruled every-thing, and then the wild cells learned how to dance together, in one enormous body, and the living world was transformed for the next seven hundred million years."

Thumb and finger wipe themselves dry against a hairy thigh, and he rises again, grinning in that relentless and smug, yet somehow charming fashion. "Everything was changed, and nothing had changed," he says. Then he says, "Scaling," with an important tone, as if that single word should erase all confusion. "The bacteria and green algae and the carnivorous amoebae weren't swept away by any revolution. Honestly, I doubt if their numbers fell appreciably or for long." And again, he says, "Scaling," and sighs with a rich appreciation. "Life evolves. Adapts. Spreads and grows, constantly utilizing new energies and novel genetics. But wherever something large can live, a thousand small things can thrive just as well, or better. Wherever something enormous survives, a trillion bacteria hang on for the ride."

For a moment, the speaker hesitates.

A slippery half-instant passes where an audience might believe that he has finally lost his concentration, that he is about to stumble over his own tongue. But then he licks at the air, tasting something delicious. And three times, he clicks his tongue against the roof of his mouth.

Then he says what he has planned to say from the beginning.

"I never know whom I'm speaking to," he admits. "I've never actually seen my audience. But I know you're great and good. I know that however you appear, and however you make your living, you deserve to hear this:

"Humans have always lived in terror. Rainstorms and the eclipsing moon and earthquakes and the ominous guts of some disemboweled goat—all have preyed upon our fears and defeated our fragile optimisms. But what we fear today—what shapes and reshapes the universe around us—is a child of our own imaginations.

"A whirlwind that owes its very existence to glorious, endless us!"

ABLE

The boy stops walking once or twice, letting the fat leopard keep pace. Then he pushes his way through a last wall of emerald ferns, stepping out into the bright damp air above the rounded pool. A splashing takes him by surprise. He looks down at his secret pool, and he squints, watching what seems to be a woman pulling her way through the clear water with thick, strong arms. She is naked. Astonishingly, wonderfully naked. A stubby hand grabs an overhanging limb, and she stands on the rocky shore, moving as if exhausted, picking her way up the slippery slope until she finds an open patch of halfway flattened earth where she can collapse, rolling onto her back, her smooth flesh glistening and her hard breasts shining up at Able, making him sick with joy.

Then she starts to cry, quietly, with a deep sadness.

Lust vanishes, replaced by simple embarrassment. Able flinches and starts to step back, and that's when he first looks at her face.

He recognizes its features.

Intrigued, the boy picks his way down to the shoreline, practically standing beside the crying woman.

She looks at him, and she sniffs.

"I saw two of them," he reports. "And I saw you, too. You were inside that cylinder, weren't you?"

She watches him, saying nothing.

"I saw something pull you out of that trap. And then I couldn't see you. *It* must have put you here, I guess. Out of its way." Able nods, and smiles. He can't help but stare at her breasts, but at least he keeps his eyes halfway closed, pretending to look out over the water instead. "*It* took pity on you, I guess."

A good-sized fish breaks on the water.

The woman seems to watch the creature as it swims past, big blue scales catching the light, heavy fins lazily shoving their way through the warm water. The fish eyes are huge and black, and they are stupid eyes. The mind behind them sees nothing but vague shapes and sudden motions. Able knows from experience: If he stands quite still, the creature will come close enough to touch.

"They're called coelacanths," he explains.

Maybe the woman reacts to his voice. Some sound other than crying now leaks from her.

So Able continues, explaining, "They were rare, once. I've studied them quite a bit. They're old and primitive, and they were almost extinct when we found them. But when *they* got loose, got free, and took apart the Earth . . . and took everything and everyone with them up into the sky . . ."

The woman gazes up at the towering horsetails.

Able stares at her legs and what lies between them.

"Anyway," he mutters, "there's more coelacanths now than ever. They live in a million oceans, and they've never been more successful, really." He hesitates, and then adds, "Kind of like us, I think. Like people. You know?"

The woman turns, staring at him with gray-white eyes. And with a quiet hard voice, she says, "No."

She says, "That's an idiot's opinion."

And then with a grace that belies her strong frame, she dives back into the water, kicking hard and chasing that ancient and stupid fish all the way back to the bottom.

presence

MAUREEN F. McHUGH

Maureen F. McHugh made her first sale in 1989, and has since made a powerful impression on the SF world with a relatively small body of work, becoming one of today's most respected writers. In 1992, she published one of the year's most widely acclaimed and talked-about first novels, China Mountain Zhang, *which won the Locus Award for Best First Novel, the Lambda Literary Award, and the James Tiptree, Jr. Memorial Award, and which was named a* New York Times *Notable Book as well as being a finalist for the Hugo and Nebula Awards. Her other books, including the novels* Half the Day is Night *and* Mission Child, *have been greeted with similar enthusiasm. Her most recent book is a major new novel,* Nekropolis. *Her powerful short fiction has appeared in Asimov's Science Fiction, The Magazine of Fantasy and Science Fiction, Starlight, Alternate Warriors, Aladdin, Killing Me Softly, and other markets, and is about to be assembled in a collection called* The Lincoln Train. *She has had stories in our Tenth through Fourteenth, and our Nineteenth Annual Collections. She lives in Twinsburg, Ohio, with her husband, her son, and a golden retriever named Smith.*

In the eloquent and moving story that follows, she shows us that perhaps it is sometimes better not to know what you have lost . . .

Mila sits at her desk in Ohio and picks up the handle of the new disposable razor in . . . Shen Zhen, China? Juarez, Mexico? She can't remember where they're assembling the parts. She pans left and right and decides it must be Shen Zhen, because when she looks around there's no one else in camera range. There's a twelve-hour time-zone difference. It's eleven at night in China, so the only other activity is another production engineer doing telepresence work — waldos sorting through a bin of hinge joints two tables over in a pool of light. Factories are dim and dirty places, but cameras need light, so telepresence stations are islands in the darkness.

She lifts the dark blue plastic part in front of the CMM and waits for it to measure the cavity. She figures they're running about twenty percent out of spec, but they are so far behind on the razor product launch they can't afford to have the vendor resupply, so tomorrow, underpaid Chinese employees in Shen Zhen raw materials will have to hand-inspect the parts, discard the bad ones and send the rest to packaging.

Her phone rings.

She disengages the waldos and the visor. The display is her home number and she winces.

"Hello?" says her husband, Gus. "Hello, who is this?"

"It's Mila," she says. "It's Mila, honey."

"Mila?" he says. "That's what the Speed Dial said. Where are you?"

"I'm at work," she says.

"At P&G?" he says.

"No, honey, now I work for Gillette. You worked for Gillette, too."

"I did not," he says, suspicious. Gus has Alzheimer's. He is fifty-seven.

"Where's Cathy?" Mila asks.

"Cathy?" his voice lowers. "Is that her name? I was calling because she was here. What is she doing in our house?"

"She's there to help you," Mila says helplessly. Cathy is the new home health. She's been watching Gus during the day for almost three weeks now, but Gus still calls to ask who she is.

"She's black," Gus says. "Not that it matters. Is she from the neighborhood? Is she Dan's friend?" Dan is their son. He's twenty-five and living in Boulder.

"Are you hungry?" Mila asks. "Cathy can make you a sandwich. Do you want a sandwich?"

"I don't need help," Gus says, "Where's my car? Is it in the shop?"

"Yes," Mila says, seizing on the excuse.

"No it's not," he says. "You're lying to me. There's a woman here, some strange woman, and she's taken my car."

"No, baby," Mila says. "You want me to come home for lunch?" It's eleven, she could take an early lunch. Not that she really wants to go home if Gus is agitated.

Gus hangs up the phone.

Motherfucker. She grabs her purse.

Cathy is standing at the door, holding her elbows. Cathy is twenty-five and Gus is her first assignment from the home healthcare agency. Mila likes her, likes even her beautifully elaborate long, polished fingernails. "Mrs. Schuster? Mr. Schuster is gone. I was going to follow his minder but he took my locater. I'm sorry, it was in my purse and I never thought he'd take it out—"

"Oh, Jesus," Mila says. She runs upstairs and gets her minder from her bedside table. She flicks it on and it says that Gus is within 300 meters. The indicator arrow says he's headed away from Glenwood, where all the traffic is, and down toward the dead end or even the pond.

"I'm so sorry, Mrs. Schuster," Cathy says.

"He's not far," Mila says. "It's not your fault. He's cunning."

They go down the front steps. Cathy is so young. So unhappy right now, still nervously hugging her elbows as if her ribs hurt. Her fingernails are pink with long sprays like rays from a sunrise on each nail. She trails along behind Mila, scuffing in her cute flats. She's an easy girl, usually unflustered. Mila had so hoped that Gus would like her.

Gus is around the corner toward the dead end. He's in the side yard of some-one's house Mila doesn't know—thank God that nobody is ever home in the daytime except kids. He's squatting in a flower garden and he has his pants down, she can see his hairy thighs. She hopes he isn't shitting on his pants. Behind him, pale pink hollyhocks rise in spikes.

"Gus!" she calls.

He waves at her to go away.

"Gus," she says. Cathy is still trailing her. "Gus, what are you doing?"

"Can't a man go to the bathroom in peace?" he says, and he sounds so much like himself that if she weren't used to all the craziness she might have burst into tears.

She doesn't cry. She doesn't care. That's when she decides it all has to stop. Because she just doesn't care.

"It is sometimes possible to cure Alzheimer's, it's just not possible to cure the person who has Alzheimer's," the treatment info explains. "We can fix the brain and replace the damaged neurons with new brain but we can't replace the mem-ories that are gone." It's the way Alzheimer's has been all along, Mila thinks, a creeping insidious disease that takes away the person you knew and leaves this angry, disoriented stranger. The video goes on to explain how the treatment— which is nearly completely effective in only about thirty percent of cases, but which arrests the progress of the disease in ninety percent of the cases and provides some functional improvement in almost all cases—cannot fix the parts of the brain that have been destroyed.

Mila is a quality engineer. This is a place she is accustomed to, a place of percentages and estimations, of statements of certainty about large groups, and only guesses about particular individuals. She can translate it, "We can promise you everything, we just can't promise it will happen to Gus."

Gus is gone anyway, except in odd moments of habit.

When Gus was diagnosed they had talked about whether or not they should try this treatment. They had sat at the kitchen table, a couple of engineers, and looked at this carefully. Gus had said no. "In five years," he'd said, "there's a good chance the Alzheimer's will come back. So then we'll have spent all this money on a treatment that didn't do any good and where will you be then?"

In some people it reverses in five years. But they've only been doing it for seven years, so who knows?

Gus had diagrammed the benefits. At very best he would be cured. Most likely they would only have spent a lot of money to slow the disease down. "And even if I'm cured, the disease could come roaring back," he'd said. "I don't think I want to have this disease for a long time. I know I don't want to have it twice."

His hands are small for a man, which sounds dainty but isn't. His hands are perfect, the nails neat and smooth, but he hadn't been fussy. He'd been deft with a pencil, had been good at engineering drawings before they did them on computer, and his diagram of benefits and liabilities on a piece of computer paper had been neat. "Don't cry," he'd said.

Gus couldn't handle it when she cried. For the thirty years of their marriage, when she'd had to cry—which was always at night, at least in her memory—she'd gone downstairs after he'd gone to sleep and sat on the couch and cried. She would have liked him to comfort her, but in marriage you learn what other people's limits are. And you learn your own.

For the cost of her house, she can have them put an enzyme in Gus's brain that will scrub out the Alzheimic plaque that has replaced so much of his neural structure. And then they will put in undifferentiated cells and a medium called Transglycyn and that medium will contain a virus that tells the DNA within the cells to create neurons and grow him a new brain.

She calls Dan in Boulder.

"I thought you and Dad didn't want to do this," Dan says.

"I thought so, too," she says. "But I didn't know what it would be like."

Dan is silent. Digital silence. You can hear a pin drop silence. "Do you want me to come home?" he asks.

"No," she says. "No, you stay out there. You just started your job." Dan is a chef. He studied at the Culinary Institute of America, and spent a couple of years as a line chef in the Four Seasons in New York. Now Etienne Corot is opening a new restaurant in Boulder called, of course, "Corot," and Dan has gotten a job as sous-chef. It's a promotion. The next step in making a name for himself, so that someday he can open his own restaurant.

"You need to keep your eye on Schuster's," she says. It's an old joke between them, that he's going to open a four-star restaurant called Schuster's. They both agree that Schuster's sounds like a Big Boy franchise.

" 'Artesia,' " he says.

"Is that it?" she asks.

"That's the latest name," he says. They have been trading names for the restaurant he will someday open since he started at the Culinary Institute. "You like it?"

"As long as I don't think about the cattle town in New Mexico."

"No shit," he says, and she can imagine him at the other end of the phone, ducking his head the way his dad does. Dan is an inch taller than Gus, with the same long legs and arms. Unfortunately, he got her father's hairline and already, at twenty-five, his bare temples make her tender and protective.

"I can fly out," he says.

"It's not like surgery," she says, suddenly irritated. She wants him to fly out, but there isn't any point in it. "And I'd get tired of us sitting there holding hands for the next three months while they eradicate the plaque, because as far as you and I will be able to tell, nothing will be happening."

"Okay," he says.

"Dan," she says. "I feel as if I'm spending your money."

"I don't care about the money. I don't like to talk about it that way, anyway," he says. "I just feel weird because Dad said not to do it."

"I know," she says. "But I don't feel as if this person is your dad anymore."

"It won't be Dad when it's done, will it?" Dan says.

"No," Mila says. "No, but at least maybe it will be a person who can take care of himself."

"Look, Mom," he says, his voice serious and grown-up. "You're there. You're dealing with it every day. You do what you have to do. Don't worry about me."

She feels tears well up in her eyes. "Okay, honey," she says. "Well, you've got stuff you need to do."

"Call me if you want me to come out," he says.

She wants him off the phone before she cries. "I will," she says.

"Love you, Mom," he says.

She knows he can tell she was crying.

"I'm not sick," Gus says.

"It's a check-up," Mila says.

Gus sits on the examining room table in his shorts and T-shirt. It used to be that she said the litany of what she loved when she saw him like this—his nose, his blue eyes made to look the distance, the hollow of his collarbone, his long legs. Show me your butt, she'd say, and he'd turn and shake it at her and they'd cackle like children.

"We've waited long enough," Gus says.

"It's not that long," Mila says, and at that moment the doctor knocks and opens the door. With him is a technician, a black woman, with a cart.

"Who are you?" Gus says.

"I'm Dr. Feingold." He is patient, is Dr. Feingold. He met with them for an hour yesterday and he talked with them for a few minutes this morning before Gus had his blood work. But Gus doesn't remember. Gus was worse than usual. They are in Atlanta for the procedure. Lexington, Kentucky, and Windsor, Ontario, both have clinics that do the procedures, but Dr. Feingold had worked with Raymond Miller, the Ph.D. who originated the treatment. So she picked Atlanta.

Gus is agitated. "You're not my doctor," he says.

Dr. Feingold says, "I'm a specialist, Mr. Schuster. I'm going to help you with your memory problems."

Gus looks at Mila.

"It's true," she says.

"You're trying to hurt me," Gus says. "In fact, you're going to kill me, aren't you?"

"No, honey," she says. "You're sick. You have Alzheimer's. I'm trying to help you."

"You've been poisoning me," Gus says. Is it because he's scared? Because everything is so strange?

"Do you want to get dressed?" Dr. Feingold says. "We can try this in an hour."

"I don't want to try anything," Gus says. He stands up. He's wearing white athletic socks and he has the skinny calves of an old man. The disease has made him much older than fifty-seven. In a way she is killing him. Gus will never come back and now she's going to replace him with a stranger.

"Take some time," Dr. Feingold says. Mila has never been to a doctor's office where the doctor wasn't scheduled to death. But then again, she's never paid $74,000 for a doctor's visit, which is what today's injection of brain scrubbing Transglycyn will cost. Not really just the visit and the Transglycyn. They'll stay here two more days and Gus will be monitored.

"Goddamn," Gus says, sitting back down. "Goddamn you all."

"All right, Mr. Schuster," Dr. Feingold says.

The technician pushes the cart over and Dr. Feingold says, "I'm going to give you an injection, Mr. Schuster."

"Goddamn," Gus says again. Gus never much said "Goddamn" before.

The Transglycyn with the enzyme is supposed to be injected in the spine but Dr. Feingold takes a hypodermic and gives Gus a shot in the crook of his arm.

"You just lie there a moment," Dr. Feingold says.

Gus doesn't say anything.

"Isn't it supposed to be in his back?" Mila says.

"It is," Dr. Feingold says, "but right now I want to reduce his agitation. So I've given him something to calm him."

"You didn't say anything about that," she says.

"I don't want him to change his mind while we're giving him the enzyme. This will relax him and make him compliant."

"Compliant," she says. She's supposed to complain, they're drugging him and they didn't tell her they would. But she's pretty used to him not being compliant. Compliant sounds good. It sounds excellent. "Is it a tranquilizer?" she asks.

"It's a new drug," Dr. Feingold says. He is writing it down on Gus's chart. "Most tranquilizers can further agitate patients with Alzheimer's."

"I have Alzheimer's," Gus says. "It makes me agitated. But sometimes I know it."

"Yes, Mr. Schuster," Dr. Feingold says. "You do. This is Vicki. Vicki is someone who helps me with this all the time, and we're very good at doing it, but when we roll you on your side, I need you to lie very still, all right?"

Gus, who hated when doctors patronized him, says dopily, "All right." Gus, who during a colonoscopy, higher than a kite on Demerol, asked his doctor if they had gotten to the ileum, because even with his brain cradled in opiates, Gus just liked to *know*.

Vicki and Dr. Feingold roll Gus onto his side.

"Are you comfortable, Mr. Schuster?" Vicki asks. She has a down-home Atlanta accent.

Dr. Feingold goes out the door. He comes back in with two more people, both men, and they put a cushion behind Gus's knees so it's hard for him to roll over, and then another cushion at the back of his neck.

"Are you all right, Mr. Schuster?" Dr. Feingold asks. "Are you comfortable?"

"Okay," Gus says, fuzzy.

Vicki pulls his undershirt up and exposes his knobby backbone. Dr. Feingold marks a place with a black pen. He feels Gus's back like a blind woman, his face absent with concentration, and then he takes a needle and says, "There will be a prick, Mr. Schuster. This will make the skin on your back numb, okay?" He gives Gus another shot.

Gus says "Ow" solemnly.

And then Dr. Feingold and Vicki make some marks with the pen. Then there is another needle, and Dr. Feingold makes a careful injection in Gus's back. He leaves the needle in a moment, pulls the part of the hypodermic out that had medication in it, and Vicki takes it and gives him another one and he puts that in the hypodermic and injects it.

Mila isn't sure if that's more painkiller or the Transglycyn.

"Okay, Mr. Schuster," Dr. Feingold says. "We're done with the medicine. But you lie still for a few minutes."

"Is it like a spinal tap?" Mila asks. "Will he get a headache?"

Dr. Feingold shakes his head. "No, Mrs. Schuster, that's it. When he feels like sitting up, he can."

So now it is inside him. Soon it will start eating the plaque in his brain.

The places it will eat clean were not Gus anymore, anyway. It's not as if Gus is losing anything more. It bothers her, though, the Transglycyn goo moving along the silver-gray pathways of his neurons, dissolving the Swiss cheese damage of the disease. And then, what, there are gaps in his head? Fluid-filled gaps in his brain, the tissue porous as a sponge and poor Gus, shambling along, angry and desperate.

She wants to stroke his poor head. But he is quiet now, sedated, and maybe it's best to let him be.

The clinic is more like a hotel than a hospital, the bed has a floral bedspread and over it is a painting of cream and peach roses in a vase. After being sedated during the day, Gus is restless. He will not go to bed. If she goes to bed he'll try to go out into the hall, but the door is locked from the inside so he can't get out. There's a touchpad next to the door and she's used 0815, Dan's birthday, as the code. She doesn't think Gus knows Dan's birthday anymore. A sign on the door says, IN CASE OF FIRE, ALL DOORS WILL OPEN AUTOMATICALLY. Gus runs his fingers along the crack between the door and the wall. "I want to go out," he says, and she says that he can't. "I want to go out," he says, and she says, "We're not home, we have to stay here."

"I want to go out," he says, again and again, long after she stops answering him. He finally sits and watches five minutes of television but then he gets up and goes back to the door. "Let's go home," he says this time, and when she doesn't answer, he runs his long fingers like spiders up and down the edge of the door. He sits, he gets up and stands at the door for minutes, twenty, thirty minutes at a time, until she is blind with fatigue and her eyes burn with tears and she finally shrieks, "There's no way out!"

For a moment he looks at her, befuddled. The he turns back to the door and says querulously, "I want to go out."

At one point she goes to him and folds both his hands in hers and says, "We're both trapped." She is dizzy with fatigue but if she cries he will just get worse. He looks at her and then goes back to searching the door, moth fingers fluttering. She turns out the light and he howls, "Oww-ow-oww-ow—" until she snaps the light back on.

Finally, she shoves past him and locks him in the room. She goes down to the lounge and sits on a couch, pulling her bare feet up and tucking them under her nightgown. The lounge is deserted. She thinks about sleeping here for a few hours. She feels vacant and exposed. She leans her head back and closes her eyes and there is the distant white noise of the ventilation system and the strange audible emptiness of a big room and she can feel her brain swooping instantly into a kind of nightmare where she is sliding into sleep thinking someone is sick and she needs to do something and when she jerks awake her whole body feels a flush of exhaustion.

She can't stay here. Is Gus howling in the room?

When she opens the door he is standing there, but she has the odd feeling he may not have noticed she was gone.

He finally lets her talk him into lying down around 3:15 in the morning but he is up again a little after six.

She asks the next day if it is the stuff they've injected, but of course, it's not. It's the strangeness. The strange room, the strange place, the Alzheimer's, the ruin of his brain.

The social worker suggests that until they are ready to insert the cellular material and stimulate neural growth, Gus should go to a nursing facility for elderly with dementia.

Even if she could afford it, Mila thinks she would have to say no. When they resculpt his brain, he will be a different person, but she will still be married to him, and she wants to stay with him and to be part of the whole process, so that maybe her new husband, the new Gus, will still be someone she loves. Or at least someone she can be married to.

Mila is lucky they can afford this. It is an experimental treatment so insurance doesn't cover the cost. She and Gus have money put away for retirement from his parents and hers, but she can't touch that or capital gains taxes will go off, as her accountant says, like a time bomb. But they can sell their house.

The old house sells for $217,000. The first half of the treatment is about $74,000. The second half of the treatment is a little over $38,000. Physical therapy is expected to cost a little over $2,100 a month. Home health is $32,000 through an agency (insurance will no longer pay because this is an experimental treatment). That doesn't include airfare and a thousand incidentals. At least the house is paid off, and the tax man does some finagling and manages to save her $30,000 for a down payment on a little townhouse.

It has two floors, a postage stamp-sized backyard, and monthly maintenance fees of $223 a month. Her mortgage is $739 a month.

It has a living room and kitchen downstairs and two bedrooms upstairs. The carpet is a pale gray, and her living room furniture, which is all rich medieval reds and ochre and ivory, doesn't go well, but it doesn't look bad, either.

"Why is our couch here?" Gus asks plaintively. "When can we go home?"

One evening when he says he wants to go home she puts him in the car and starts driving. When Dan was a baby, when he wouldn't go to sleep, the sound of a car engine would soothe him, and this evening it seems to have the same effect on Gus. He settles happily into the passenger seat of their seven-year-old Honda sedan, and as she drives he strokes the armrest and croons. She's not sure at first if the crooning means he's agitated, but after a while she decides it's a happy sound.

"You like going for a ride?" she says to him.

He doesn't answer but he keeps on crooning, "ooo-ooo-ooo-ooo."

Another night she wakes up alone in the bed. Alzheimer's victims don't sleep much. Used to be that if Gus or Dan got up in the night she heard them, but she's pretty tired these days.

She finds him downstairs in the kitchen, taking the bowl of macaroni and cheese out of the refrigerator. It's covered in foil because she's out of plastic wrap. "Are you hungry?" she asks.

Gus says, "I can take care of it." His tone is ordinary and reassuring. He puts the bowl in the microwave.

"You can't put it in the microwave, honey," Mila says. "You have to take the foil off the top first." She hates that she only calls him "honey" when she is exasperated with him, and when she doesn't want to make him angry. It feels passive aggressive. Or something.

Gus closes the microwave door and pushes the time button.

"Gus," she says, "don't do that." She reaches past him and opens the microwave door, and he pushes her away.

"Gus," she says, "don't." She reaches for the door and he pushes her away again.

"Leave it alone," he says.

"You can't," she says. "It's got foil on it." Gus is an engineer, for God's sake. Or was.

She tries to stop him, puts her hand on his forearm, and he turns to face her, his face a grimace of anger, and he pulls his arm back and punches her in the face.

He is still a strong, tall man and the punch knocks her down.

She doesn't even know how to feel it. No one has punched her since she was maybe twelve, and that was a pretty ineffective punch, even if her nose did bleed. It stops her from thinking. She is lying on the kitchen floor. Gus pushes the start button on the microwave.

Mila touches her face. Her lip is cut, she can taste the blood. Her face hurts.

There is a flicker as the microwave arcs. She doesn't have it in her to get up and do anything about it. Gus frowns. Not at her, at the microwave.

Mila sits up and explores her face. One of her teeth feels wobbly to her tongue. Gus doesn't pay any attention, he's watching the microwave. He's intent. It's a parody of the engineer solving a problem.

The microwave starts arcing in earnest and Gus steps back.

Mila sits on the floor until the microwave starts smoking and only then does she get up. She doesn't even feel like crying, although her mouth and cheek hurt. She pushes cancel on the microwave and then pulls it out of the alcove and unplugs it. She leaves it half pulled out and goes over to the sink and spits bloody saliva. She rinses her mouth and then washes the sink out.

"Go on up to bed," she says.

Gus looks at her. Is he angry? She steps back, out of range. Now she is scared. He's not a child, he's a big man. Is he going to be upset with her because he's still hungry?

"I'll heat you up some soup," she says. "Okay?"

Gus looks away, his mouth a little open.

She grabs an oven mitt, opens the smoking microwave carefully and takes out the macaroni and cheese. The ceramic bowl has cracked in half and the foil is blackened, but she holds it together until she can throw it out. Gus sits down. She takes the microwave outside on the grass. She doesn't think it's burning inside, but she isn't sure. She can't sit and watch it, not with Gus unsupervised. So if it starts to smolder, it starts to smolder. The grass is damp.

Back inside she finds Gus in the living room eating ice cream out of the carton with a serving spoon. There is ice cream on him and on the couch.

She's afraid to go near him, so she sits on a chair and watches him eat.

She cannot shake the feeling that the man in front of her should not be Gus, because the Gus she has been married to would not, would never, hit her. The Gus she was married to had certain characteristics that were inalienable to him — his neatness — almost fussiness. His meticulousness. His desperate need to be good, to be oh so good. But this is still Gus, too. Even as the ice cream drips on his legs and on the couch. What exactly is Gus? What defines Gusness? What is it she married? It is not just this familiar body. There is some of Gus inside, too. Something present that she can't put her finger on, maybe only habits of Gusness.

Later, when he goes up to bed, sticky with ice cream, she throws out the carton even though it is still half full. Outside, the microwave sits inert and smelling faintly of hot appliance. She goes upstairs and goes to bed in the other bedroom.

She tries to think of what to do. The Transglycyn is eating out the plaque, but he won't start to get better until they replace the neurons and the neurons grow and they don't even go to Atlanta until next month. It will be three months after that before she begins to see any improvement.

The old bastard. Alzheimer's is the bastard.

She doesn't know what to do. She can't even afford a leave of absence at work. Saturday, she thinks, she'll hire a sitter and then she'll rent a hotel room and sleep for a few hours. That will help. She'll think better when she's not so tired.

At work, Mila's closest friend is Phyllis. Phyllis is also a quality engineer. More and more engineers in QA are women and Phyllis says that's why QA engineers make $10,000 a year less than design and production engineers. "It's like Human Resources," she says. "It's a girl-ghetto of engineering now." "Girl-ghetto" is a little ironic, coming from Phyllis who is five foot two inches, weighs close to two hundred pounds, and who has close-cut iron gray hair.

Phyllis comes by Mila's cubicle at midmorning and says, "So how's the old bastard." Phyllis knew Gus when he was still Gus.

"A real bastard," Mila says and looks up away from the computer monitor, up at Phyllis, the side of her face all morning-glory purple.

"Oh my God!" Phyllis says, "What happened?"

"Gus decked me."

"Oh God," Phyllis says. In the cafeteria, sitting with a cup of coffee in front of her, she says dryly, "You really look quite amazing," which is a relief, because Phyllis's initial shock, her initial speechlessness was almost more than Mila could bear. If Phyllis can't joke about it. . . .

She does not say, "You've got to put him in a home." The other thing Phyllis does say is, "Gus would be appalled."

"He would," Mila says, utterly grateful. "He would, wouldn't he."

They go to the Cleveland Clinic and Gus is anesthetized and some of his bone marrow is extracted. The frozen bone marrow is shipped to Atlanta so they can extract undifferentiated stem cells to inject in him to replace his own missing neurons.

After the anesthetic he is agitated for two days. His balance is off and his hip hurts where they extracted the bone marrow and he calls her a bitch.

Two weeks later they go to Atlanta and the procedure to inject the undifferentiated cells and virus trigger are almost identical to the first procedure. Gus swings at her twice more; once at the clinic in Atlanta and once back in the townhouse, but she's watching because she's afraid of him now, and she gets out of the way both times. She warns Iris, the new home health. (Cathy left because her boyfriend has a cousin in Tampa who can get him some sort of job.) Iris is in her thirties, heavy and not friendly. Not unfriendly. Iris says Gus never gets that way around her. Is she lying? Mila wonders. And then, why would she?

Is Iris saying that Gus likes Iris better than Mila? Mila always has the feeling that Iris thinks Mila should be home more. That Mila should be taking care of Gus herself.

Gus likes car rides, sometimes. They climb into her car.

"Where are we going?" he asks.

"To therapy," she says. He'll start to get agitated now, she thinks.

But he puts the window down and the trees go past, and he leans his head back and croons.

"Are you happy, Saxophone Man?" Mila says.

Everything is in stasis now—he grows no better but no worse until something happens with the cells they put in his brain. Three months until they see any difference, at the earliest. But now, one month after they injected new cells into his gap-ridden brain, they will do some tests to benchmark.

It all makes perfect sense. Too bad we never benchmark when we're healthy, she thinks. Maybe she should have herself benchmarked. Mila Schuster, cognitive function raw scores at age fifty-one. Then if dementia got her in its jaws, they could chart the whole cycle. Hell, benchmark the whole population, like they benchmark women with mammograms between the ages of forty-five and fifty.

Unless it has already started. She forgets things at work. She knows it is just because she is so worried about Alzheimer's. Senior moments, Allen, one of the home health used to call those times when you stand in the kitchen and can't remember what you came for.

If she got Alzheimer's, who would take care of her? She and Gus would end up in an institution, both in diapers and unaware of each other.

Gus croons.

"Saxophone Man," she says. There is something dear to her about the ruined Gus, even through all the fear and the anger and the dismay. This great ruin of a fine brain. This engineer who could so often put his finger on a problem and say, "There. That's it. The higher the strength of the plastic in the handle, the more brittle it is. You want to back off on the strength a bit and let the thing flex or it's going to shatter. Particularly if it sits in sunlight and the UV starts breaking down the plastic."

What a marvelous brain you had, she thinks. You'd say it and I'd see it, everybody would see it, obvious then. But everything is obvious once you see it.

The therapy is done at a place called Baobab Tree Rehab in a strip shopping mall. The anchor store in the mall is a Sears Hardware, which is Sears with just tools. Inside, Baobab Tree Rehab is like insurance companies and mortgage companies — there are ficus trees in pots in front of the windows, and rat's maze cubicles like there are in older office buildings. Once, years before, Gus was walking with Mila at work when suddenly he crouched a bit so he was her height — she is five three — and said, it really is a maze for you. That was the first time she realized he could see over the tops of the cubicles, and so they didn't really work like walls for him.

Gus is looking over the cubicles now, too.

Their therapist is young. She comes out to meet them. "Mr. Schuster, Mrs. Schuster, I'm Eileen."

Mila likes that she talks to Gus. Gus may or may not care, but Mila figures it means that they think about things.

Eileen takes them back past the cubicles to a real room with a table in it. There are shelves on the wall.

"Mrs. Schuster," she says, "I'd like you to sit in with us this first time." Mila has not even thought about not sitting in, but now, suddenly she longs to be allowed to leave. She could go for a walk. Go take a nap. But Gus will probably get upset if she leaves him with a stranger.

And nearly everyone is a stranger.

Gus sits down at the table, bemused.

Eileen takes a puzzle with big wooden pieces off of a shelf and says, "Mr. Schuster? Do you like to do puzzles?"

Gus says, "No."

Did Gus like to do puzzles? Isn't engineering a kind of puzzle? Mila can't remember Gus ever doing regular puzzles—but they were so busy. Their life wasn't exactly conducive to sitting down and doing puzzles. Gus built telescopes for a while. And then he built model rockets. He made such beautiful rockets. He would sit in front of the television and sand the rocket fins to get the perfect airfoil shape, sawdust falling into a towel on his lap, and then he would glue them to the rocket body using a slow setting epoxy, and finally, when they were about set, he'd dip his finger in rubbing alcohol and run it down the seam to make the fillet smooth and perfect. He made beautiful rockets and then shot them off, risking everything.

"Let's try a puzzle," Eileen says.

"Mila?" It is Gus on the phone.

"I'll get back to you," Mila tells Roger. Roger is the manufacturing engineer on the project she's working on.

"Look," Roger says, "I just need a signature and I'll get out of your hair—"

"It's *Gus*," Mila says.

"Mila, honey," Roger says, "I'm sorry, but I've got four thousand parts in IQA." He wants her to sign off on allowing the parts to be used, even though they're not quite to spec, and she's pretty sure he's right that they can use them. But her job is to be sure.

"Mila," Gus says in her ear, "I think I've got bees in my head."

Roger knew Gus. And Roger is a short-sighted bastard who doesn't care about anything but four thousand pieces of ABS plastic pieces. Actually Roger is just doing his job. Roger is thorough.

"I promise it's okay," Roger says. "I assembled twenty of them, they worked fine."

Mila signs.

"Mila?" Gus says. "Can you hear me? I think I've got bees in my head."

"What do you mean, honey," she says.

"It itches in my head."

Gus isn't supposed to feel anything from the procedures. There aren't nerve endings in the brain, he can't be feeling anything. It's been four months since the second procedure.

"It itches in your head," Mila says.

"That's right," Gus says. "Can you come pick me up? I'm ready to go home now."

Gus is at home, of course, with Iris, the home health. But if Mila says that he's at home, Gus will get upset. "I'll be there in a while to pick you up. Let me talk to Iris."

"My head itches," Gus says. "Inside."

"Okay, honey," Mila says. "Let me talk to Iris."

Gus doesn't want to give the phone to Iris. He wants . . . something. He wants Mila to take care of this head itching thing, or whatever it is that's going on. Mila doesn't know what Gus knows about the procedure. Maybe he's sort of pieced this together to get her to come and take him home. Maybe something strange is going on. It is an experimental procedure. Maybe this is just more weird Alzheimer's behavior. Maybe he has a headache and this is what he can say.

"It's bees," he says.

Finally he lets her talk to Iris.

"Does he have a temperature? Does anything seem wrong?" she asks Iris.

"No," says Iris. "He's real good today, Mrs. Schuster. I think that brain cells are growing back because he's really good these last couple of days."

"Do I need to come home?" Mila asks.

"No, ma'am. He just insisted on calling you. I don't know where the bees thing comes from, he didn't say that to me."

Maybe the tissue in his head is being rejected. It shouldn't be. The cells are naïve stem cells. They're from his own body. Maybe there was a mistake.

When she gets home he doesn't mention it.

Sitting across from him at the dinner table, she can't decide if he's better or not. Is he handling a fork better?

"Gus?" she says. "Do you want to look at some photographs after dinner?"

"Okay," he says.

She sits him down on the couch and pulls out a photo album. She just grabs one, but it turns out to be from when Dan was in first grade. "There's Dan," she says. "There's our son."

"Uh-huh," Gus says. His eyes wander across the page. He flips to the next page, not really looking.

So much is gone. If he does get smarter, she'll have to teach him his past again.

There is a picture of Dan sitting on a big pumpkin. There is someone, a stranger, off to one side, and there are rows of pumpkins, clearly for sale. Dan is sitting with his face upturned, smiling the over-big smile he used to make every time his picture was being taken. He looks as if he is about six.

Mila can't remember where they took the picture.

What was Dan that year for Halloween? She used to make his costumes. Was that the year he was the knight? And she made him a shield and it was too heavy to carry, so Gus ended up carrying it? No, because she made the shield in the garage in the house on Talladega Trail, and they didn't move there until Dan was eight. Dan had been disappointed in the shield, although she couldn't remember why. Something about the emblem. She couldn't even remember the emblem, just that the shield was red and white. She had spent hours making it. It had been a disaster, although he had used it for a couple of years afterward, playing sword fight in the front yard.

How much memory did anybody have? And how much of it was even worth keeping?

"Who is that?" Gus asks, pointing.

"That's my mother," Mila says. "Do you remember my mother?"

"Sure," Gus says, which doesn't mean anything. Then he says, "Cards."

"Yeah," Mila says. "My mother played bridge."

"And poker," Gus says. "With Dan."

The magpie mind, she thinks. He can't remember where he lives but he can remember that my mother taught Dan to play poker.

"Who is that?" he asks.

"That's our neighbor on South Bend," Mila says. Thankfully, his name is written next to the photo. "Mike. That's Mike. He was a volunteer fireman, remember?"

Gus isn't even looking at the photos. He's looking at the room. "I think I'm ready to go home now," he says.

"Okay," she says. "We'll go home in a few minutes."

That satisfies him until he forgets and asks again.

Dan comes in the door with his suitcase.

"It's nice, Mom," he says. "It's really nice. The way you talked I thought you were living in a project."

Mila laughs, so delighted to see him, so grateful. "I didn't say it was that bad."

"It's plain," he says, his voice high to mimic her, "it's just a box, but it's all right."

"Who's there?" Gus calls.

"It's me, Dad. It's Dan." His face tightens with . . . worry? Nervousness, she decides.

"Dan?" his dad says.

"Hi Dad," he says. "It's me, Dan. Your son." He is searching his father's face for recognition.

It is one of Gus's good days, and Mila has only a moment of fear before Gus says, "Dan. Visiting. Hello." And then in that astonishingly normal way he sometimes does, "How was your flight?"

Dan grins. "Great, Dad, it was great."

Is it the treatment that makes Gus remember? Or is it just one of those odd moments?

Dan is home for Christmas. It's his Christmas gift for her, he says, to give her a break. It's no break because she's been cleaning and trying to buy presents off the net. Thank God for the net. She's bought Dan cookbooks and cds, a beautiful set of German knives that he's always wanted but would never get because he never cooks at home. She's spent way too much money, but what would she buy Gus? She's bought Gus chocolates for a palate gone childlike. A couple of warm bright shirts. A puzzle.

"I can't believe you're here," she says, and she can feel her face stretched too wide.

"I'm here," he says. "Of course I'm here. Where else would I be? Lisa says hello."

Lisa is the new girlfriend. "You could have brought her," Mila says.

Gus stands there, vacant and uninterested.

Dan says, "Dad, I've met a really nice girl." She's told Gus about Lisa, but mostly it's to hear her own chatter and because Gus seems soothed by chatter. Whether the magpie left of his mind has noticed the name, she doesn't know.

"I didn't bring her," Dan says. "I thought I would be enough disruption."

Gus doesn't even appear to try to follow the conversation.

"I'll show you your room," Mila says. She's putting Dan in the guest room, which means she'll have to sleep with Gus. This week he has been going to sleep at ten or even earlier. And sleeping until early morning, say, five or six. That, she thinks, has to be the treatment.

On Christmas Eve, Dan makes a fabulous feast. On Christmas Eve they used to eat roast beef, and then on Christmas day they'd eat roast beef sandwiches all day, but in the last few years she's made just a normal meal for the two of them. Dan makes a Christmas roast and Yorkshire pudding. There are puréed chestnuts and roasted potatoes and a salad with pomegranate and champagne dressing. "For dessert," he says, "crème brûlée. I borrowed a torch from Corot's." He brandishes a little handheld torch like the ones in the Williams-Sonoma catalogue. "This is going to be the best Christmas ever!" he cackles, which has been his joke for years, an ironic reference to all those Christmas television specials.

Gus does a puzzle. He has been doing them in therapy and the therapist (a different one from the first one, who is now on maternity leave) says that there are definite signs that the cells are grafting, filling in. Gus likes puzzles. She buys the ones for children eight to twelve. Cannonball Adderly is on the cd player. The tightness in her eases a bit. Christmas has never been a time for good things to happen, not in her experience. Too much at stake, she always supposed. All those expectations of the best Christmas ever.

But at this moment she is profoundly grateful.

"Do you need help?" she calls into the kitchen. Dan has told her she isn't allowed in on pain of death.

"No," Dan calls out.

The smell of beef drippings is overwhelming. She has been living on micro-wavable dinners and food picked up at the grocery where they have already cooked stuff to take home and eat and Chinese takeout.

"Why'd you get rid of the microwave?" Dan asks from the kitchen.

"It shorted out," Mila says.

Gus doesn't look up from his puzzle. Does he remember that evening at all? That was after his brain was scrubbed out, so it isn't something he would have lost. But did he ever have it? Does he know what he is living through, moment to moment, or is it like sand?

"Are you in there?" she whispers.

At six o'clock, there is more food than three people could ever eat in a month. Dan has sliced the beef and put beautifully finished slices on their plates. (Gus's is cut up, she notices, and her eyes fill with gratitude.) The beef is cooked beau-tifully, and sits in a brown sauce with a swirl of horseradish. There is a flower cut out of carrot sitting on bay leaves on her plate and on Dan's—Gus's has the flower, but no bay leaf to mistake for food. The salad glistens and the pomegranate berries are like garnets. There is wine in her glass and in Dan's—Gus's glass has juice.

"Oh, my," she breathes. It's a dinner for grown-ups in a place that has never seen anything but frozen lasagna and Chinese takeout. "Oh, Dan," she says. "It's so beautiful."

"It had better be," Dan says. "It's what I do for a living."

"Gus," she says. "Come eat Dan's dinner."

"I'm not hungry," Gus says.

"Come and sit with me while I eat, then."

Sometimes he comes and sometimes he doesn't. Tonight he comes and she guides him to his seat.

"It's Christmas Eve, Dad," Dan says. "It's roast beef for Christmas Eve dinner." She wants to tell him not to try so hard, to just let Gus make his own way, but he has worked so hard. Please, no trouble, she thinks.

"Roast beef?" Gus says. He takes his fork and takes a bite. "It's good," he says. She and Dan smile at each other.

Mila takes a bite. "Where did you get this meat?" she asks.

"Reider's Stop and Shop," Dan says.

"No you didn't," she says.

"Sure I did," Dan says. "You've just cooked so many years you don't remember how it tastes when you've just been smelling. I got all my cooking talents from you, Mom."

Not true. He is his father over again, with the same deep thoughtfulness, the same meticulousness. It is always a puzzle, cooking. She cooked as a hobby. Dan cooks with the same deep obsessiveness that Gus brought to model rockets.

"I don't like that," Gus says.

"What?" Dan says.

"That." Gus points to the swirl of horseradish. "It's nasty."

"Horseradish?" Dan says. "You always liked horseradish."

Gus had made a fetish of horseradish. And wasabi and chilies and ginger. He liked licorice and kimchee and stilton cheese and everything else that tasted strongly.

"It's nasty," Gus says.

"I'll get you some without," Mila says, before Dan fights. Never contradict, she thinks at Dan. It's not important. "He's not used to strong tastes anymore," she says quickly to Dan, hoping Gus won't pay attention, that she won't have to explain.

"I'll get it," Dan says. "You sit."

Dan brings a plate. "What have you been eating, Dad?" he asks. "Cottage cheese? Mom, shouldn't he be getting tastes to, I don't know, stimulate him?"

Gus frowns.

"Don't," she says. It's hard enough without Dan making accusations.

Gus has retreated from all but the bland. He eats like a three-year-old might. Macaroni and cheese. Grilled cheese sandwiches. Tomato soup. Ice cream. And she's let him because it was easy. She thinks about telling him that Gus has hit her. That they have been getting through the days.

Maybe inviting Dan was a mistake. Gus needs routine, not disruption.

"How's that, Dad?" Dan says.

"Good," Gus says. Gus eats the roast beef without horseradish, the potatoes, the chestnut purée. He cleans out the ramekin of crème brûlée with his index finger while Dan sits, smiling and bemused.

And then, full, he goes upstairs and goes to bed in his clothes. After an hour she goes up and takes off his shoes and covers him up. He sleeps, childlike and serene, until almost seven on Christmas morning.

"I'm getting better," Gus announces after therapy one day in February.

"Yes," Mila says, "you are." He goes to therapy three times a week now, and does the kind of things they do with children who have sensory integration problems. Lots of touching and moving. Evenings after therapy he goes to bed early, worn out.

"I remember better," he says.

He does, too. He remembers, for instance, that the townhouse is where they live. He doesn't ask to go home, although he will say that he wishes they still lived in the other house. She thinks there is some small bit of recrimination in this announcement.

"Do you want to go out to eat?" she asks one evening. They haven't gone out to eat in, oh, years. She is out of the habit.

She decides on Applebee's, where the food is reassuringly bland. These days, Gus might be someone who had a stroke. He no longer looks vacant. There is someone there, although sometimes she feels as if the person there is a stranger.

After dinner at Applebee's she takes him to rent a DVD. He wanders among the racks of DVDs and stops in the area of the store where they still have video tapes. "We used to watch these," he says.

"We did," she says. "With Dan."

"Dan is my son," he says. Testing. Although as far as she can tell he's never forgotten who Dan is.

"Dan is your son," she agrees.

"But he's grown," Gus says.

"Yes," she says.

"Pick a movie for me," he says.

"How about a movie you used to like?" She picks out *Forbidden Planet*. They had the tape until she moved them to the townhouse. She got rid of all of Gus's old tapes when they moved because there wasn't enough room. He had all the *Star Wars* tapes including the lousy ones. He had all the *Star Trek* movies, and *2001, Blade Runner, Back to the Future I* and *III*.

"This is one of your favorites," she says. "You made a model of the rocket."

When Dan was a kid he loved to hear about when he was a baby, and Gus is that way now about what he was like "before." He turns the DVD over and over in his hands.

At home he puts it in the player and sits in front of the screen. After a few minutes he frowns. "It's old," he says.

"It's in black and white," she says.

"It's dumb," he says. "I didn't like this."

She almost says, *It was your favorite.* They watched it when they were dating, sitting on the couch together. He had shown her all his science fiction movies. They'd watched *Them* on television. But she doesn't, doesn't start a fight. When he gets angry he retreats back into Alzheimer's behavior, restless and pacing and then opaque.

She turns on the TV and runs the channels.

"Wait," he says, "go back."

She goes back until he tells her to stop. It's a police show, one of the kind everyone is watching now. It's shot three camera live and to her it looks like a cross between *Cops* and the old sitcom *Barney Miller.* Part of the time it's sort of funny, like a sitcom, and part of the time it's full of swearing and idiots with too many tattoos and too few teeth.

"I don't like this," she says.

"I do," Gus says. And watches the whole show.

She lets the home health go.

Iris quit to go to another agency, Mila doesn't know why, and then they got William. Luckily by the time they got William it was okay if Gus was alone sometimes because William never got there before eight-thirty and Mila had to leave for work before eight. William was an affable and inept twenty-something, but Gus seemed to like him. Because William was a man instead of a woman?

Gus says, "Thank you for putting up with me," and William smiles.

"I'm so glad you got better, Mr. Schuster," he says. "I never left before because a patient got better."

"You helped a lot," he says.

Gus can stay by himself. There's so much he doesn't know these days, among the strange things that he does. But he can follow directions. The latest therapist— they have had four in the ten months Gus has been going, and the latest is a patient young man named Chris—the latest therapist says that Gus has the capacity to be pretty much normal. It's just a matter of re-learning. And he is re-learning as if he was actually much younger than he is, because of those new neurons forming connections.

There is some concern about those new neurons. Children form more and more connections until they hit puberty, and then the brain seems to sort through the connections and weed out some and reinforce others, to make the brain efficient in other ways. Nobody knows what will happen with Gus. And of course, the cause of the Alzheimer's still lurks somewhere. Maybe in ten years he'll start to deteriorate again.

"I am so grateful to you," he says to Mila when William is gone. "You have been through so much for me."

"It's okay," she says. "You'd do the same for me." Although she doesn't know what Gus would do. She doesn't know if she likes this new Gus. This big child.

"I would do the same for you," he says.

"Are you sure you wouldn't stick me in some nursing home?" she says. "Only come visit me once a month?" She tries to make her tone broad, broad enough for anyone to see this comment as a joke.

But Gus doesn't. Teasing distresses him. "No," he says now, "I promise, Mila. I would look after you the way you looked after me."

"I know, honey," she says. "I was just joking."

He frowns.

"Come on," she says. "Let's look at your homework."

He is studying for his G.E.D. It's a goal he and the therapist came up with. Mila wanted to say that Gus not only had a degree in engineering, he was certified, but of course that was the old Gus.

He's studying the Civil War, and Mila checks his homework before he goes to his G.E.D. class.

"I think I want to go to college," he says.

"What do you want to study?" she asks. She almost says, 'Engineering?' but the truth is he doesn't like math. Gus was never very good at arithmetic, but he was great at conceptual math—algebra, calculus, differential equations. But now he doesn't have enough patience for the drill in fractions and square roots.

"I don't know," he says. "Maybe I want to be a therapist. I think I want to help people."

Help me, she thinks. But then she squashes the thought. He is here, he is getting better. He is not squatting in the hollyhocks. She's not afraid of him anymore. And if she doesn't love him like a husband anymore, well, she still loves him.

"What was that boy's name?" Gus says, squinting down the street.

He means the home health.

For a moment she can't think and her insides twist in fear. It has started happening recently, when she forgets she feels this sudden overwhelming fear. Is it Alzheimer's?

"William," she says. "His name is William."

"He was a nice boy," Gus says.

"Yes," Mila says, her voice and face calm but her heart beating too fast.

Halo

CHARLES STROSS

Although he made his first sale back in 1987, it's only recently that British writer Charles Stross has begun to make a name for himself as a writer to watch in the new century ahead (in fact, as one of the key Writers To Watch in the Oughts), with a sudden burst in the last few years of quirky, inventive, high-bit-rate stories such as "Antibodies," "A Colder War," "Bear Trap," "Dechlorinating the Moderator," "Toast: A Con Report," "Lobsters," "Troubadour," and "Tourist," in markets such as Interzone, Spectrum SF, Asimov's Science Fiction, Odyssey, Strange Plasma, *and* New Worlds. *Stross is also a regular columnist for the monthly magazine* Computer Shopper. *He has "published" a novel online,* Scratch Monkey, *available to be read on his website (www.antipope.org/charlie/), and is currently serializing another novel,* The Atrocity Archive, *in the magazine* Spectrum SF. *His most recent books are another new novel,* Festival of Fools, *and his first collection,* Toast, and Other Burned Out Futures. *He had two stories in our Eighteenth Annual Collection, and one in our Nineteenth Annual Collection. He lives in Edinburgh, Scotland.*

Here he takes us back to the wired-up, dazzlingly fast-paced Information Age future of his acclaimed and popular "Manfred Macx" stories (debuted last year in "Lobsters," a Hugo Finalist), and cranks things up a notch even from his former frenetic concept-dense pace—introducing us to what might be called "Manfred Macx: The Next Generation," as the daughter of Manfred Macx leaves a frazzled Earth tottering on the edge of a Vingian Singularity to travel to Jupiter space, in company with a cast of characters that even Manfred Macx himself might have found a bit peculiar . . .

T he asteroid is running Barney: it sings of love on the high frontier, of the passion of matter for replicators, and its friendship for the needy billions of the Pacific Rim. "I love you," it croons in Amber's ears as she seeks a precise fix on it: "Let me give you a big hug. . . ."

A fraction of a light-second away, Amber locks a cluster of cursors together on the signal, trains them to track its Doppler shift, and reads off the orbital elements.

"Locked and loaded," she mutters. The animated purple dinosaur pirouettes and prances in the middle of her viewport, throwing a diamond-tipped swizzle-stick overhead. Sarcastically: "big hug time! I got asteroid!" Cold gas thrusters bang somewhere behind her in the interstage docking ring, prodding the cumbersome farm ship round to orient on the Barney rock. She damps her enthusiasm self-consciously, her implants hungrily sequestrating surplus neurotransmitter molecules floating around her synapses before reuptake sets in: it doesn't do to get too excited in free flight. But the impulse to spin handstands, jump and sing, is still there: it's *her* rock, and it loves her, and she's going to bring it to life.

The workspace of Amber's room is a mass of stuff that probably doesn't belong on a spaceship. Posters of the latest Lebanese boy-band bump-and-grind through their glam routines; tentacular restraining straps wave from the corners of her sleeping bag, somehow accumulating a crust of dirty clothing from the air like a giant inanimate hydra. (Cleaning robots seldom dare to venture inside the teenager's bedroom.) One wall is repeatedly cycling through a simulation of the projected construction cycle of Habitat One, a big fuzzy sphere with a glowing core (that Amber is doing her bit to help create): three or four small pastel-colored plastic *kawai* dolls stalk each other across its circumference with million-kilometer strides. And her father's cat is curled up between the aircon duct and her costume locker, snoring in a high-pitched tone.

Amber yanks open the faded velour curtain that shuts her room off from the rest of the hive: *"I've got it!"* she shouts. "It's all mine! I rule!" It's the sixteenth rock tagged by the orphanage so far, but it's *her* first, and that makes it special. She bounces off the other side of the commons, surprising one of Oscar's cane toads — which should be locked down in the farm, it's not clear how it got here — and the audio repeaters copy the incoming signal, noise-fuzzed echoes of a thousand fossilized infant's video shows.

"You're so *prompt*, Amber," Pierre whines when she corners him in the canteen.

"Well, yeah!" She tosses her head, barely concealing a smirk of delight at her own brilliance. She knows it isn't nice, but Mom is a long way away, and Dad and Step-Mom don't care about that kind of thing. *"I'm* brilliant, *me!"* she announces. "Now what about our bet?"

"Aww." Pierre thrusts his hands deep into his pockets. "But I don't *have* two million on me in change right now. Next cycle?"

"Huh?" She's outraged. "But we had a bet!"

"Uh, Doctor Bayes said you weren't going to make it this time, either, so I stuck my smart money in an options trade. If I take it out now, I'll take a big hit. Can you give me until cycle's end?"

"You should know better than to trust a *sim*, Pee." Her avatar blazes at him with early teen contempt: Pierre hunches his shoulders under her gaze. He's only thirteen, freckled, hasn't yet learned that you don't welsh on a deal. "I'll let you do it *this* time," she announces, "but you'll have to pay for it. I want interest."

He sighs. "What base rate are you —"

"No, *your* interest! Slave for a cycle!" She grins malevolently.

And his face shifts abruptly into apprehension: "As long as you don't make me clean the litter tray again. You aren't planning on doing *that*, are you?"

Welcome to the third decade. The thinking mass of the solar system now exceeds one MIP per gram; it's still pretty dumb, but it's not dumb all over. The human population is near maximum overshoot, pushing nine billion, but its growth rate is tipping toward negative numbers, and bits of what used to be the first world are now facing a middle-aged average. Human cogitation provides about 10^{28} MIPS of the solar system's brainpower. The real thinking is mostly done by the halo of a thousand trillion processors that surround the meat machines with a haze of computation—individually, a tenth as powerful as a human brain, collectively, they're ten thousand times more powerful, and their numbers are doubling every twenty million seconds. They're up to 10^{33} MIPS and rising, although there's a long way to go before the solar system is fully awake.

Technologies come, technologies go, but even five years ago nobody predicted that there'd be tinned primates in orbit around Jupiter by now: a synergy of emergent industries and strange business models have kick-started the space age again, aided and abetted by the discovery of (so far undecrypted) signals from ET's. Unexpected fringe-riders are developing new ecological niches on the edge of the human information space, light-minutes and light-hours from the core, as an expansion that has hung fire since the 1970s gets under way.

Amber, like most of the post-industrialists aboard the orphanage ship *Ernst Sanger*, is in her early teens: her natural abilities are enhanced by germ-line genetic recombination. Like most of the others, half her wetware is running outside her skull on an array of processor nodes hooked in by quantum-entangled communication channels—her own personal metacortex. These kids are mutant youth, burning bright: not quite incomprehensible to their parents, but profoundly alien—the generation gap is as wide as the 1960s and as deep as the solar system. Their parents, born in the gutter-years of the twentieth century, grew up with white elephant shuttles and a space station that just went round and round, and computers that went beep when you pushed their buttons: the idea that Jupiter was somewhere you could *go* was as profoundly counter-intuitive as the Internet to a baby boomer.

Most of the passengers on the can have run away from parents who thought that teenagers belong in school, unable to come to terms with a generation so heavily augmented that they are fundamentally brighter than the adults around them. Amber was fluent in nine languages by the age of six, only two of them human, and six of them serializable; her birth-mother—who had denied her most of the prenatal mods then available, insisting that a random genotype was innately healthier—had taken her to the school psychiatrist for speaking in synthetic tongues. That was the final straw for Amber: using an illicit anonymous phone, she called her father. Her mother had him under a restraining order, but it hadn't occurred to her to apply for an order against his *partner*. . . .

Vast whorls of cloud ripple beneath the ship's drive stinger: orange and brown and muddy grey streaks slowly ripple across the bloated horizon of Jupiter. *Sanger* is nearing perijove, deep within the gas giant's lethal magnetic field; static discharges flicker along the tube, arcing over near the deep violet exhaust cloud emerging from the magnetic mirrors of the ship's VASIMR motor. The plasma rocket is cranked up to maximum mass flow, its specific impulse almost as low as a fission rocket but thrusting at maximum as the assembly creaks and groans through the gravitational assist maneuver. In another hour, the drive will flicker off, and the orphanage will fall up and out toward Ganymede, before dropping back in toward orbit around Amalthea, Jupiter's fourth moon (and source of much of the material in the Gossamer ring). They're not the first canned primates to make it to Jupiter subsystem, but they're one of the first wholly private ventures. The bandwidth out here sucks dead slugs through a straw, with millions of kilometers of vacuum separating them from scant hundreds of mouse-brained microprobes and a few mechanical dinosaurs left behind by NASA or ESA. They're so far from the inner system that a good chunk of the ship's communications array is given over to caching: the news is whole kiloseconds old by the time it gets out here.

Amber, along with about half the waking passengers, watches in fascination from the common room. The commons are a long axial cylinder, a double-hulled inflatable at the center of the ship with a large part of their liquid water supply stored in its wall-tubes. The far end is video-enabled, showing them a realtime 3D view of the planet as it rolls beneath them: in reality, there's as much mass as possible between them and the trapped particles in the Jovian magnetic envelope. "I could go swimming in that," sighs Lilly. "Just imagine, diving into that sea. . . ." Her avatar appears in the window, riding a silver surfboard down the kilometers of vacuum.

"Nice case of windburn you've got there," someone jeers: Kas. Suddenly, Lilly's avatar, heretofore clad in a shimmering metallic swimsuit, turns to the texture of baked meat, and waggles sausage-fingers up at them in warning.

"Same to you and the window you climbed in through!" Abruptly the virtual vacuum outside the window is full of bodies, most of them human, contorting and writhing and morphing in mock-combat as half the kids pitch into the virtual deathmatch: it's a gesture in the face of the sharp fear that outside the thin walls of the orphanage lies an environment that really *is* as hostile as Lilly's toasted avatar would indicate.

Amber turns back to her slate: she's working through a complex mess of forms, necessary before the expedition can start work. Facts and figures that are never far away crowd around her, intimidating. Jupiter weighs 1.9×10^{27} kilograms. There are twenty-nine Jovian moons and an estimated two hundred thousand minor bodies, lumps of rock, and bits of debris crowded around them—debris above the size of ring fragments, for Jupiter (like Saturn) has rings, albeit not as prominent. A total of six major national orbiter platforms have made it out here—and another two hundred and seventeen microprobes, all but six of them private entertainment platforms. The first human expedition was put together by ESA Studios six years ago, followed by a couple of wildcat mining prospectors and a u-commerce bus that scattered half a million picoprobes throughout Jupiter subsystem. Now the *Sanger* has arrived, along with another three monkey cans—one from Mars, two more from LEO—and it looks as if colonization would explode except that there are at least four mutually exclusive Grand Plans for what to do with old Jove's mass.

Someone prods her. "Hey, Amber, what are you up to?"

She opens her eyes. "Doing my homework." It's Su Ang. "Look, we're going to Amalthea, aren't we? But we file our accounts in Reno, so we have to do all this paperwork. Monica asked me to help. It's insane."

Ang leans over and reads, upside down. "Environmental Protection Agency?"

"Yeah. Estimated Environmental Impact Forward Analysis 204.6b, Page Two. They want me to 'list any bodies of standing water within five kilometers of the designated mining area. If excavating below the water table, list any wellsprings, reservoirs, and streams within depth of excavation in meters multiplied by five hundred meters up to a maximum distance of ten kilometers downstream of direction of bedding plane flow. For each body of water, itemize any endangered or listed species of bird, fish, mammal, reptile, invertebrate, or plant living within ten kilometers—' "

"—Of a mine on Amalthea? Which orbits one hundred and eighty thousand kilometers above Jupiter, has no atmosphere, and where you can pick up a whole body radiation dose of ten Grays in half an hour on the surface?" Ang shakes her head, then spoils it by giggling. Amber glances up.

On the wall in front of her someone—Nicky or Boris, probably—has pasted a caricature of her own avatar into the virch fight. She's being hugged from behind by a giant cartoon dog with floppy ears and an erection, who's singing anatomically improbable suggestions while fondling himself suggestively. "Fuck that!" Shocked out of her distraction—and angry—Amber drops her stack of paperwork and throws a new avatar at the screen, one an agent of hers dreamed up overnight: it's called Spike, and it's not friendly. Spike rips off the dog's head and pisses down its trachea, which is anatomically correct for a human being: meanwhile she looks around, trying to work out which of the laughing idiot children and lost geeks around her could have sent such an unpleasant message.

"Children! Chill out." She glances round: one of the Franklins (this is the twenty-something dark-skinned female one) is frowning at them. "Can't we leave you alone for half a K without a fight?"

Amber pouts. "It's not a fight: it's a forceful exchange of opinions."

"Hah." The Franklin leans back in midair, arms crossed, an expression of supercilious smugness pasted across her-their face. "Heard that one before. Anyway—" she-they gesture and the screen goes blank "—I've got news for you pesky kids. We got a claim verified! Factory starts work as soon as we shut down the stinger and finish filing all the paperwork via our lawyers. Now's our chance to earn our upkeep. . . ."

Amber is flashing on ancient history, three years back along her timeline. In her replay, she's in some kind of split-level ranch house out west. It's a temporary posting while her mother audits an obsolescent fab line enterprise that grinds out dead chips of VLSI silicon for Pentagon projects that have slipped behind the cutting edge. Her mom leans over her, menacingly adult in her dark suit and chaperonage earrings: "You're going to school, and that's that!"

Her mother is a blonde ice-maiden madonna, one of the IRS's most productive bounty hunters—she can make grown CEOs panic just by blinking at them. Amber, a tow-headed eight-year-old tearaway with a confusing mix of identities, inexperience blurring the boundary between self and grid, is not yet able to fight back effectively. After a couple of seconds, she verbalizes a rather feeble protest: "Don't want to!" One of her stance demons whispers that this is the wrong approach to take, so she modifies it: "they'll beat up on me, Mom. I'm too different. Sides, I know you want me socialized up with my grade metrics, but isn't that what sideband's for? I can socialize *real* good at home."

Mom does something unexpected: she kneels down, putting herself on eye level with Amber. They're on the living room carpet, all seventies-retro brown corduroy and acid-orange paisley wallpaper: the domestics are in hiding while the humans hold court. "Listen to me, sweetie." Mom's voice is breathy, laden with an emotional undertow as strong and stifling as the eau de cologne she wears to the office to cover up the scent of her client's fear. "I know that's what your father's writing to you, but it isn't true. You need the company—*physical* company—of children your own age. You're *natural*, not some kind of engineered freak, even with your skullset. Natural children like you need company, or they grow up all weird. Don't you know how much you mean to me? I want you to grow up happy, and that won't happen if you don't learn to get along with children your own age. You're not going to be some kind of cyborg otaku freak, Amber. But to *get* healthy, you've got to go to school, build up a mental immune system. That which does not destroy us makes us stronger, right?"

It's crude moral blackmail, transparent as glass and manipulative as hell, but Amber's *corpus logica* flags it with a heavy emotional sprite miming the likelihood of physical discipline if she rises to the bait: Mom is agitated, nostrils slightly flared, ventilation rate up, some vasodilatation visible in her cheeks. Amber—in combination with her skullset and the metacortex of distributed agents it supports—is mature enough at eight years to model, anticipate, and avoid corporal punishment: but her stature and lack of physical maturity conspire to put her at a disadvantage when negotiating with adults who matured in a simpler age. She sighs, then puts on a pout to let Mom know she's still reluctant, but obedient. "O-kay. If you say so."

Mom stands up, eyes distant—probably telling Saturn to warm his engine and open the garage doors. "I say so, punkin. Go get your shoes on, now. I'll pick you up on my way back from work, and I've got a treat for you: we're going to check out a new Church together this evening." Mom smiles, but it doesn't reach her eyes. "You be a good little girl, now, all right?"

The Imam is at prayer in a gyrostabilized mosque.

His mosque is not very big, and it has a congregation of one: he performs salat on his own every seventeen thousand two hundred and eighty seconds. He also webcasts the call to prayer, but there are no other believers in trans-Jovian space to answer the summons. Between prayers, he splits his attention between the exigencies of life-support and scholarship. A student of the Hadith and of knowledge-based systems, Sadeq collaborates in a project with other mujtahid scholars who are building a revised concordance of all the known isnads, to provide a basis for exploring the body of Islamic jurisprudence from a new perspective—one they'll need sorely if the looked-for breakthroughs in communication with aliens emerge. Their goal is to answer the vexatious questions that bedevil Islam in the age of accelerated consciousness: and as their representative in orbit around Jupiter, these questions fall most heavily on Sadeq's shoulders.

Sadeq is a slightly built man, with close-cropped black hair and a perpetually tired expression: unlike the orphanage crew, he has a ship to himself. The ship started out as an Iranian knock-off of a Shenzhou-B capsule, with a Chinese-type 921 space-station module tacked onto its tail: but the clunky, nineteen-sixties look-alike—a glittering aluminum dragonfly mating with a Coke can—has a weirdly contoured M2P2 pod strapped to its nose. The M2P2 pod is a plasma sail: built in orbit by one of Daewoo's wake shield-facilities, it dragged Sadeq and his cramped space station out to Jupiter in just four months, surfing on the solar breeze. His presence may be a triumph for the Ummah, but he feels acutely alone out here: when he turns his compact observatory's mirrors in the direction of the *Sanger*, he is struck by its size and purposeful appearance. *Sanger's* superior size speaks of the efficiency of the western financial instruments, semi-autonomous investment trusts with variable business-cycle accounting protocols that make possible the development of commercial space exploration. The Prophet, peace be unto him, may have condemned usury: but surely it would have given him pause to see these engines of capital formation demonstrate their power above the Great Red Spot.

After finishing his prayers, Sadeq spends a couple of extra precious minutes on his mat. He finds that meditation comes hard in this environment: kneel in silence and you become aware of the hum of ventilation fans, the smell of old socks and sweat, the metallic taste of ozone from the Elektron oxygen generators. It is hard to approach God in this third-hand spaceship, a hand-me-down from arrogant Russia to ambitious China, and finally to the religious trustees of Qom, who have better uses for it than any of the heathen states imagine. They've pushed it far, this little toy space station: but who's to say if it is God's intention for humans to live here, in orbit around this swollen alien giant of a planet?

Sadeq shakes his head: he rolls his mat up and stows it beside the solitary porthole with a quiet sigh. A stab of homesickness wrenches at him, for his childhood in hot, dusty Yazd and his many years as a student in Qom: he steadies himself by looking round, searching the station that is by now as familiar to him as the fourth-floor concrete apartment that his parents—a car factory worker and his wife—raised him in. The interior of the station is the size of a school bus, every surface cluttered with storage areas, instrument consoles, and layers of exposed pipes: a couple of globules of antifreeze jiggle like stranded jellyfish near a heat exchanger that has been giving him grief. Sadeq kicks off in search of the squeeze bottle he keeps for this purpose, then gathers up his roll of tools and instructs one of his agents to find him the relevant sura of the maintenance log: it's time to fix this leaky joint for good.

An hour or so of serious plumbing, and then he will eat (freeze-dried lamb stew, with a paste of lentils and boiled rice, and a bulb of strong tea to wash it down), then sit down to review his next flyby maneuvering sequence. Perhaps, God willing, there will be no further system alerts and he'll be able to spend an hour or two on his research between evening and final prayers. Maybe the day after tomorrow, there'll even be time to relax for a couple of hours, to watch one of the old movies that he finds so fascinating for their insights into alien cultures: *Apollo 13*, maybe. It isn't easy, being the only crew aboard a long-duration space mission: and it's even harder for Sadeq, up here with nobody to talk to, for the communications lag to earth is more than half an hour each way—and so far as he knows he's the only believer within half a billion kilometers.

Amber dials a number in Paris and waits until someone answers the phone. She knows the strange woman on the phone's tiny screen: Mom calls her "your father's fancy bitch," with a peculiar tight smile. (The one time Amber asked what a fancy bitch was, Mom hit her—not hard, just a warning.) "Is Daddy there?" she asks.

The strange woman looks slightly bemused. (Her hair is blonde, like Mom's, but the color clearly came out of a bleach bottle, and it's cut really short, mannish.) "*Oui*. Ah, yes." She smiles tentatively. "I am sorry, it is a disposable phone you are using? You want to talk to 'im?"

It comes out in a rush: "I want to *see* him." Amber clutches the phone like a lifesaver: it's a cheap disposable cereal-packet item, and the cardboard is already softening in her sweaty grip. "Momma won't let me, auntie 'Nette—"

"Hush." Annette, who has lived with Amber's father for more than twice as long as her mother did, smiles. "You are sure that telephone, your mother does not know of it?"

Amber looks around. She's the only child in the rest room because it isn't break time and she told teacher she had to go right *now:* "I'm sure, P_{20} confidence factor greater than 0.9." Her Bayesian head tells her that she can't reason accurately about this because Momma has never caught her with an illicit phone before, but what the hell. *It can't get Dad into trouble if he doesn't know, can it?*

"Very good." Annette glances aside. "Manny, I have a surprise call for you."

Daddy appears onscreen. She can see all of his face, and he looks younger than last time: he must have stopped using those clunky old glasses. "Hi—Amber! Where are you? Does your mother know you're calling me?" He looks slightly worried.

"No," she says confidently, "the phone came in a box of Grahams."

"Phew. Listen, sweet, you must remember to never, ever call me where your mom may find out. Otherwise, she'll get her lawyers to come after me with thumb screws and hot pincers, because she'll say *I* made you call me. Understand?"

"Yes, Daddy." She sighs. "Don't you want to know why I called?"

"Um." For a moment he looks taken aback. Then he nods, seriously. Amber likes Daddy because he takes her seriously most times when she talks to him. It's a phreaking nuisance having to borrow her classmates' phones or tunnel past Mom's pit-bull firewall, but Dad doesn't assume that she can't know anything because she's only a kid. "Go ahead. There's something you need to get off your chest? How've things been, anyway?"

She's going to have to be brief: the disposaphone comes prepaid, the international tariff it's using is lousy, and the break bell is going to ring any minute. "I want *out*, Daddy. I mean it. Mom's getting loopier every week: she's dragging me around to all these churches now, and yesterday she threw a fit over me talking to my terminal. She wants me to see the school shrink, I mean, what *for*? I *can't* do what she wants; I'm not her little girl! Every time I tunnel out, she tries to put a content-bot on me, and it's making my head hurt—I can't even think straight anymore!" To her surprise, Amber feels tears starting. "Get me out of here!"

The view of her father shakes, pans around to show her tante Annette looking worried. "You know, your father, he cannot do anything? The divorce lawyers, they will tie him up."

Amber sniffs. "Can *you* help?" she asks.

"I'll see what I can do," her father's fancy bitch promises as the break bell rings.

An instrument package peels away from the *Sanger*'s claimjumper drone and drops toward the potato-shaped rock, fifty kilometers below. Jupiter hangs huge and gibbous in the background, impressionist wallpaper for a mad cosmologist: Pierre bites his lower lip as he concentrates on steering it.

Amber, wearing a black sleeping-sack, hovers over his head like a giant bat, enjoying her freedom for a shift. She looks down on Pierre's bowl-cut hair, his wiry arms gripping either side of the viewing table, and wonders what to have him do next. A slave for a day is an interesting experience, restful: life aboard the *Sanger* is busy enough that nobody gets much slacktime (at least, not until the big habitats have been assembled and the high bandwidth dish is pointing at Earth). They're unrolling everything to a hugely intricate plan generated by the backers' critical path team, and there isn't much room for idling: the expedition relies on shamelessly exploitative child labor—they're lighter on the life-support consumables than adults—working the kids twelve-hour days to assemble a toe-hold on the shore of the future. (When they're older and their options vest fully, they'll all be rich—but that hasn't stopped the outraged herdnews propaganda back home.) For Amber, the chance to let somebody else work for her is novel, and she's trying to make every minute count.

"Hey, slave," she calls idly: "how you doing?"

Pierre sniffs. "It's going okay." He refuses to glance up at her, Amber notices. He's thirteen: isn't he supposed to be obsessed with girls by that age? She notices his quiet, intense focus, runs a stealthy probe along his outer boundary: he shows no sign of noticing it but it bounces off, unable to chink his mental armor. "Got cruise speed," he says, taciturn, as two tons of metal, ceramics, and diamond-phase weirdness hurtles toward the surface of Barney at three hundred kilometers per hour. "Stop shoving me: there's a three-second lag and I don't want to get into a feedback control-loop with it."

"I'll shove if I want, *slave.*" She sticks her tongue out at him.

"And if you make me drop it?" he asks. Looking up at her, his face serious— "Are we supposed to be doing this?"

"You cover your ass and I'll cover *mine*," she says, then turns bright red. "You know what I mean."

"I do, do I?" Pierre grins widely, then turns back to the console: "Aww, that's no fun. And you want to tune whatever bit-bucket you've given control of your speech centers to: they're putting out way too much *double-entendre*, somebody might mistake you for a grown-up."

"You stick to *your* business and *I'll* stick to *mine*," she says, emphatically. "And you can start by telling me what's happening."

"Nothing." He leans back and crosses his arms, grimacing at the screen. "It's going to drift for five hundred seconds, now, then there's the midcourse correction and a deceleration burn before touchdown. And *then* it's going to be an hour while it unwraps itself and starts unwinding the cable spool. What do you want, minute noodles with that?"

"Uh-huh." Amber spreads her bat-wings and lies back in midair, staring at the window, feeling rich and idle as Pierre works his way through her dayshift. "Wake me when there's something interesting to see." Maybe she should have had him feed her peeled grapes or give her a foot massage, something more traditionally hedonistic: but right now just *knowing* he's her own little piece of alienated labor is doing good things for her self-esteem. Looking at those tense arms, the curve of his neck, she thinks maybe there's something to this whispering-and-giggling he *really likes you* stuff the older girls go in for—

The window rings like a gong and Pierre coughs. "You've got mail," he says dryly. "You want me to read it for you?"

"What the—" A message is flooding across the screen, right-to-left snaky script like the stuff on her corporate instrument (now lodged safely in a deposit box in Zurich). It takes her a while to page-in the grammar agent that can handle Arabic, and another minute for her to take in the meaning of the message. When she does, she starts swearing, loudly and continuously.

"*You* bitch, *Mom! Why'd you have to go and do a thing like* that?"

The corporate instrument arrived in a huge FedEx box addressed to Amber: it happened on her birthday while Mom was at work, and she remembers it as if it was only an hour ago.

She remembers reaching up and scraping her thumb over the delivery man's clipboard, the rough feel of the microsequencers sampling her DNA; afterward, she drags the package inside. When she pulls the tab on the box it unpacks itself automatically, regurgitating a compact 3D printer, half a ream of paper printed in old-fashioned dumb ink, and a small calico cat with a large @-symbol on its flank. The cat hops out of the box, stretches, shakes its head, and glares at her. "You're Amber?" it mrowls.

"Yeah," she says, shyly. "Are you from Tanté 'Nette?' "

"No, I'm from the fucking tooth fairy." It leans over and head-butts her knee, strops the scent glands between its ears all over her skirt. "Listen, you got any tuna in the kitchen?"

"Mom doesn't believe in seafood," says Amber: "it's all foreign junk, she says. It's my birthday today, did I tell you?"

"Happy fucking birthday, then." The cat yawns, convincingly realistic. "Here's your dad's present. Bastard put me in hibernation and blogged me along to show you how to work it. You take my advice, you'll trash the fucker. No good will come of it."

Amber interrupts the cat's grumbling by clapping her hands gleefully. "So what *is* it?" she demands. "A new invention? Some kind of weird sex toy from Amsterdam? A gun, so I can shoot Pastor Wallace?"

"Naaah." The cat yawns, yet again, and curls up on the floor next to the 3D printer. "It's some kinda dodgy business model to get you out of hock to your mom. Better be careful, though—he says its legality is narrowly scoped jurisdiction-wise."

"Wow. Like, how totally cool!" In truth, Amber is delighted because it *is* her birthday, but Mom's at work and Amber's home alone, with just the TV in moral-majority mode for company. Things have gone so far downhill since Mom discovered religion that absolutely the best thing in the world tante Annette could have sent her is some scam programmed by Daddy to take her away. If he doesn't, Mom will take her to Church tonight (and maybe to an IRS compliance-certified restaurant afterward, if Amber's good and does whatever Pastor Wallace tells her to).

The cat sniffs in the direction of the printer: "Why dontcha fire it up?" Amber opens the lid on the printer, removes the packing popcorn, and plugs it in. There's a whirr and a rush of waste heat from its rear as it cools the imaging heads down to working temperature and registers her ownership.

"What do I do now?" she asks.

"Pick up the page labeled READ ME and follow the instructions," the cat recites in a bored sing-song voice. It winks at her, then fakes an exaggerated French accent: "Le READ ME contains directions pour l'execution instrument corporate dans le boîte. In event of perplexity, consult the accompanying aineko for clarification." The cat wrinkles its nose rapidly, as if it's about to bite an invisible insect. "Warning: don't rely on your father's cat's opinions, it is a perverse beast and cannot be trusted. Your mother helped seed its meme base, back when they were married. *Ends.*" It mumbles on for a while: "fucking snotty Parisian bitch, I'll piss in her knicker drawer, I'll molt in her bidet. . . ."

"Don't be vile." Amber scans the README quickly. Corporate instruments are strong magic, according to Daddy, and this one is exotic by any standards: a limited company established in Yemen, contorted by the intersection between shari'a and the global legislatosaurus. Understanding it isn't easy, even with a personal net full of subsapient agents that have full access to whole libraries of international trade law—the bottleneck is comprehension. Amber finds the documents highly puzzling. It's not the fact that half of them are written in Arabic that bothers her—that's what her grammar engine is for—or even that they're full of S-expressions and semidigestible chunks of LISP: but that the company seems to assert that it exists for the sole purpose of owning slaves.

"What's going on?" she asks the cat. "What's this all about?"

The cat sneezes, then looks disgusted. "This wasn't *my* idea, big shot. Your father is a very weird guy and your mother hates him lots because she's still in love with him. She's got kinks, y'know? Or maybe she's sublimating them, if she's serious about this church shit she's putting you through. He thinks that she's a control freak. Anyway, after your dad ran off in search of another dome, she took out an injunction against him. But she forgot to cover his partner, and *she* bought this parcel of worms and sent them to you, okay? Annie is a real bitch, but he's got her wrapped right around his finger, or something. Anyway, he built these companies and this printer—which isn't hardwired to a filtering proxy, like your mom's—specifically to let you get away from her legally. *If* that's what you want to do."

Amber fast-forwards through the dynamic chunks of the README—boring static UML diagrams, mostly—soaking up the gist of the plan. Yemen is one of the few countries to implement traditional Sunni shari'a law and a limited-liability company scam at the same time. Owning slaves is legal—the fiction is that the owner has an option hedged on the indentured laborer's future output, with interest payments that grow faster than the unfortunate victim can pay them off—and companies are legal entities. If Amber sells herself into slavery to this company, she will become a slave, and the company will be legally liable for her actions and upkeep. The rest of the legal instrument—about 90 percent of it, in fact—is a set of self-modifying corporate mechanisms coded in a variety of jurisdictions that permit Turing-complete company constitutions, and which act as an ownership shell for the slavery contract: at the far end of the corporate firewall is a trust fund of which Amber is the prime beneficiary and shareholder. When she reaches the age of majority, she'll acquire total control over all the companies in the network and can dissolve her slave contract; until then, the trust funds (which she essentially owns) oversee the company that owns her (and keeps it safe from hostile takeover bids). Oh, and the company network is primed by an extraordinary general meeting that instructed it to move the trust's assets to Paris immediately. A one-way airline ticket is enclosed.

"You think I should take this?" she asks uncertainly. It's hard to tell how smart the cat really is—there's probably a yawning vacuum behind those semantic networks if you dig deep enough—but it tells a pretty convincing tale.

The cat squats and curls its tail protectively around its paws: "I'm saying nothing, you know what I mean? You take this, you can go live with your dad. But it won't stop your ma coming after him with a horse whip and after *you* with a bunch of lawyers and a set of handcuffs. You want *my* advice, you'll phone the Franklins and get aboard their off-planet mining scam. In space, no one can serve a writ on you. Plus, they got long-term plans to get into the CETI market, cracking alien network packets. You want my honest opinion, you wouldn't like it in Paris after a bit. Your dad and the frog bitch, they're swingers, y'know? No time in their lives for a kid. Or a cat like me, now I think of it. They're out all hours of the night doing drugs, fetish parties, raves, opera, that kind of adult shit. Your dad dresses in frocks more than your mom, and your tante 'Nettie leads him around the apartment on a chain when they're not having noisy sex on the balcony. They'd cramp your style, kid: you shouldn't have to put up with parents who have more of a life than you do."

"Huh." Amber wrinkles her nose, half-disgusted by the cat's transparent scheming, and half-acknowledging its message: *I'd better think hard about this*, she decides. Then she flies off in so many directions at once that she nearly browns out the household net feed. Part of her is examining the intricate card pyramid of company structures; somewhere else, she's thinking about what can go wrong, while another bit (probably some of her wet, messy glandular biological self) is thinking about how nice it would be to see Daddy again, albeit with some trepidation. Parents aren't supposed to have sex: isn't there a law, or something? "Tell me about the Franklins? Are they married? Singular?"

The 3D printer is cranking up. It hisses slightly, dissipating heat from the hard-vacuum chamber in its supercooled workspace. Deep in its guts it creates coherent atom beams, from a bunch of Bose-Einstein condensates hovering on the edge of absolute zero: by superimposing interference patterns on them, it generates an atomic hologram, building a perfect replica of some original artifact, right down to the atomic level — there are no clunky moving nanotechnology parts to break or overheat or mutate. Something is going to come out of the printer in half an hour, something cloned off its original right down to the individual quantum states of its component atomic, nuclei. The cat, seemingly oblivious, shuffles closer to its exhaust ducts.

"Bob Franklin, he died about two, three years before you were born: your dad did business with him. So did your mom. Anyway, he had chunks of his noumen preserved, and the estate trustees are trying to recreate his consciousness by cross-loading him in their implants. They're sort of a borganism, but with money and style. Anyway, Bob got into the space biz back then, with some financial wizardry a friend of your father whipped up for him, and now they-he are building a spacehab that they're going to take all the way out to Jupiter, where they can dismantle a couple of small moons and begin building helium-three refineries. It's that CETI scam I told you about earlier, but they've got a whole load of other angles on it for the long term."

This is mostly going right over Amber's head — she'll have to learn what helium-three refineries are later — but the idea of running away to space has a certain appeal. Adventure, that's what. Amber looks around the living room and sees it for a moment as a capsule, a small wooden cell locked deep in a vision of a middle-America that never was — the one her mom wants to retreat into. "Is Jupiter fun?" she asks. "I know it's big and not very dense, but is it, like, a happening place?"

"You could say that," says the cat, as the printer clanks and disgorges a fake passport (convincingly aged), an intricate metal seal engraved with Arabic script, and a tailored wide-spectrum vaccine targeted on Amber's immature immune system. "Stick that on your wrist, sign the three top copies, put them in the envelope, and let's get going: we've got a flight to catch."

———

Sadeq is eating his dinner when the lawsuit rolls in.

Alone in the cramped humming void of his station, he contemplates the plea. The language is awkward, showing all the hallmarks of a crude machine translation: the supplicant is American, a woman, and — oddly — claims to be a Christian. This is surprising enough, but the nature of her claim is, at face value, preposterous. He forces himself to finish his bread, then bag the waste and clean the platter, before he gives it his full consideration. Is it a tasteless joke? Evidently not: as the only quadi outside the orbit of Mars he is uniquely qualified to hear it, and it *is* a case that cries out for justice.

A woman who leads a God-fearing life — not a correct one, no, but she shows some signs of humility and progress toward a deeper understanding — is deprived of her child by the machinations of a feckless husband who deserted her years before. That the woman was raising the child alone strikes Sadeq as disturbingly western, but pardonable when he reads her account of the feckless one's behavior, which is degenerate: an ill fate indeed would await any child that this man raises to adulthood. This man deprives her of her child, but not by legitimate means: he doesn't take the child into his own household or make any attempt to raise her, either in accordance with his own customs or the precepts of shari'a. Instead, he enslaves her wickedly in the mire of the western legal tradition, then casts her into outer darkness to be used as a laborer by the dubious forces of self-proclaimed "progress." The same forces that Sadeq has been sent to confront, as representative of the Ummah in orbit around Jupiter.

Sadeq scratches his short beard thoughtfully. A nasty tale, but what can he do about it? "Computer," he says, "a reply to this supplicant: my sympathies lie with you in the manner of your suffering, but I fail to see in what way I can be of assistance. Your heart cries out for help before God (blessed be his name), but surely this is a matter for the temporal authorities of the dar al-Harb." He pauses: *or is it?* he wonders. Legal wheels begin to turn in his mind. "If you can but find your way to extending to me a path by which I can assert the primacy of shari'ah over your daughter, I shall apply myself to constructing a case for her emancipation, to the greater glory of God (blessed be his name) in the name of the Prophet (peace be unto him). Ends, sigblock, send."

Releasing the Velcro straps that hold him at the table, Sadeq floats up and then kicks gently toward the forward end of the cramped habitat. The controls of the telescope are positioned between the ultrasonic clothing cleaner and the lithium hydroxide scrubbers: they're already freed up, because he was conducting a wide-field survey of the inner ring, looking for the signature of water ice. It is the work of a few moments to pipe the navigation and tracking system into the telescope's controller and direct it to hunt for the big foreign ship of fools. Something nudges at Sadeq's mind urgently, an irritating realization that he may have missed something in the woman's e-mail: there were a number of huge attachments. With half his mind, he surfs the news digest his scholarly peers send him daily: meanwhile, he waits patiently for the telescope to find the speck of light that the poor woman's daughter is enslaved within.

This might be a way in, he realizes, a way to enter dialogue with them. Let the hard questions answer themselves, elegantly. There will be no need for the war of the sword if they can be convinced that their plans are faulty: no need to defend the godly from the latter-day Tower of Babel these people propose to build. If this woman Pamela means what she says, Sadeq need not end his days out here in the cold between the worlds, away from his elderly parents and brother and his colleagues and friends. And he will be profoundly grateful: because, in his heart of hearts, he knows that he is less a warrior than a scholar.

"I'm sorry, but the Borg is attempting to assimilate a lawsuit," says the receptionist. "Will you hold?"

"Crud." Amber blinks the Binary Betty answerphone sprite out of her eye and glances around at the cabin. "That is *so* last century," she grumbles. "Who do they think they are?"

"Doctor Robert H. Franklin," volunteers the cat. "It's a losing proposition if you ask me. Bob was so fond of his dope that there's this whole hippie groupmind that's grown up using his state vector as a bong—"

"Shut the fuck up!" Amber shouts at him. Instantly contrite (for yelling in an inflatable spacecraft is a major faux pas): "Sorry." She spawns an autonomic thread with full parasympathetic nervous control, tells it to calm her down: then she spawns a couple more to go forth and become fuqaha, expert on shari'a law. She realizes she's buying up way too much of the orphanage's scarce bandwidth— time that will have to be paid for in chores, later—but it's necessary. "She's gone *too* far. This time, it's *war*."

She slams out of her cabin and spins right around in the central axis of the hab, a rogue missile pinging for a target to vent her rage on. A tantrum would be *good*—

But her body is telling her to chill out, take ten, and there's a drone of scriptural lore dribbling away in the back of her head, and she's feeling frustrated and angry and not in control, but not really mad now. It was like this three years ago when Mom noticed her getting on too well with Jenny Morgan and moved her to a new school district—she said it was a work assignment, but Amber knows better, Mom asked for it—just to keep her dependent and helpless. Mom is a psycho bitch control-freak and ever since she had to face up to losing Dad she's been working her claws into Amber—which is tough, because Amber is not good victim material, and is smart and well-networked to boot. But now Mom's found a way of fucking Amber over *completely*, even in Jupiter orbit, and Amber would be totally out of control if not for her skullware keeping a lid on things.

Instead of shouting at her cat or trying to message the Borg, Amber goes to hunt them down in their meatspace den.

There are sixteen Borg aboard the *Sanger*—adults, members of the Franklin Collective, squatters in the ruins of Bob Franklin's posthumous vision. They lend bits of their brains to the task of running what science has been able to resurrect of the dead dot-com billionaire's mind, making him the first boddhisatva of the uploading age—apart from the lobster colony, of course. Their den mother is a woman called Monica: a willowy brown-eyed hive queen with raster-burned corneal implants and a dry, sardonic delivery that can corrode egos like a desert wind. She's better than the others at running Bob, and she's no slouch when she's being herself: which is why they elected her Maximum Leader of the expedition.

Amber finds Monica in the number four kitchen garden, performing surgery on a filter that's been blocked by toadspawn. She's almost buried beneath a large pipe, her Velcro-taped toolkit waving in the breeze like strange blue air-kelp. "Monica? You got a minute?"

"Sure, I have lots of minutes. Make yourself helpful? Pass me the antitorque wrench and a number-six hex head."

"Um." Amber captures the blue flag and fiddles around with its contents. Something that has batteries, motors, a flywheel counterweight, and laser gyros assembles itself—Amber passes it under the pipe. "Here. Listen, your phone is busy."

"I know. You've come to see me about your conversion, haven't you?"

"Yes!"

There's a clanking noise from under the pressure sump. "Take this." A plastic bag floats out, bulging with stray fasteners. "I got a bit of vacuuming to do. Get yourself a mask if you don't already have one."

A minute later, Amber is back beside Monica's legs, her face veiled by a filter mask. "I don't want this to go through," she says. "I don't care what Mom says, I'm not Moslem! This judge, he can't touch me. He *can't*," she repeats, vehemence warring with uncertainty.

"Maybe he doesn't want to?" Another bag. "Here, catch."

Amber grabs the bag: too late, she discovers that it's full of water and toadspawn. Stringy mucous ropes full of squiggling comma-shaped baby tadpoles explode all over the compartment and bounce off the walls in a shower of amphibian confetti. "Eew!"

Monica squirms out from behind the pipe. "Oh, you *didn't*." She kicks off the consensus-defined floor and grabs a wad of absorbent paper from the spinner, whacks it across the ventilator shroud above the sump. Together they go after the toadspawn with garbage bags and paper—by the time they've got the stringy mess mopped up, the spinner has begun to click and whirr, processing cellulose from the algae tanks into fresh wipes. "That was really clever," Monica says emphatically, as the disposal bin sucks down her final bag. "You wouldn't happen to know how the toad got in here?"

"No, but I ran into one that was loose in the commons, one shift before last cycle-end. Gave it a ride back to Oscar."

"I'll have a word with him, then." Monica glares blackly at the pipe. "I'm going to have to go back and refit the filter in a minute. Do you want me to be Bob?"

"Uh." Amber thinks. "Not sure. Your call."

"All right, Bob coming on-line." Monica's face relaxes slightly, then her expression hardens. "Way I see it, you've got a choice. Your mother's kinda boxed you in, hasn't she?"

"Yes." Amber frowns.

"So. Pretend I'm an idiot. Talk me through it, huh?"

Amber drags herself alongside the hydro pipe and gets her head down, alongside

Monica/Bob, who is floating with her feet near the floor. "I ran away from home. Mom owned me—that is, she had parental rights and Dad had none. So Dad, via a proxy, helped me sell myself into slavery to a company. The company was owned by a trust fund, and I'm the main beneficiary when I reach the age of majority. As a chattel, the company tells me what to do—legally—but the shell company is set to take my orders. So I'm autonomous. Right?"

"That sounds like the sort of thing your father would do," Monica says neutrally. Overtaken by a sardonic middle-aged Silicon Valley drawl, her north-of-England accent sounds peculiarly mid-Atlantic.

"Trouble is, most countries don't acknowledge slavery; those that do mostly don't have any equivalent of a limited-liability company, much less one that can be directed by another company from abroad. Dad picked Yemen on the grounds that they've got this stupid brand of shari'a law—and a crap human rights record—but they're just about conformant to the open legal standards protocol, able to interface to EU norms via a Turkish legislative firewall."

"So."

"Well, I guess I was technically a Jannissary. Mom was doing her Christian phase, so that made me a Christian unbeliever slave of an Islamic company. But now the stupid bitch has gone and converted to shi'ism. Now, normally, Islamic descent runs through the father, but she picked her sect carefully, and chose one that's got a progressive view of women's rights: they're sort of Islamic fundamentalist liberal constructionists! 'What would the Prophet do if he were alive today and had to worry about self-replicating chewing gum factories.' They generally take a progressive, almost westernized, view of things like legal equality of the sexes, because for his time and place, the Prophet was way ahead of the ball and they figure they ought to follow his example. Anyway, that means Mom can assert that I am Moslem, and under Yemeni law I get to be treated as a Moslem chattel of a company. And their legal code is very dubious about permitting slavery of Moslems. It's not that I have *rights* as such, but my pastoral well-being becomes the responsibility of the local imam, and—" She shrugs helplessly.

"Has he tried to make you run under any new rules, yet?" asks Monica/Bob. "Has he put blocks on your freedom of agency, tried to mess with your mind? Insisted on libido dampers?"

"Not yet." Amber's expression is grim. "But he's no dummy. I figure he may be using Mom—and me—as a way of getting his fingers into this whole expedition. Staking a claim for jurisdiction, claim arbitration, that sort of thing. It could be worse; he might order me to comply fully with his specific implementation of shari'a. They permit implants, but require mandatory conceptual filtering: if I run that stuff, I'll end up *believing* it!"

"Okay." Monica does a slow backward somersault in midair. "Now tell me why you can't simply repudiate it."

"Because." Deep breath. "I can do that in two ways. I can deny Islam, which makes me an apostate, and automatically terminates my indenture to the shell, so Mom owns me. Or I can say that the instrument has no legal standing because I was in the USA when I signed it, and slavery is illegal there, in which case Mom owns me, because I'm a minor. Or I can take the veil, live like a modest Moslem woman, do whatever the imam wants, and Mom doesn't own me—but she gets to appoint my chaperone. Oh Bob, she has planned this *so well*."

"Uh-huh." Monica rotates back to the floor and looks at Amber, suddenly very Bob. "Now you've told me your troubles, start thinking like your dad. Your dad had a dozen creative ideas before breakfast every day—it's how he made his name. Your mom has got you in a box. Think your way *outside* it: what can you do?"

"Well." Amber rolls over and hugs the fat hydroponic duct to her chest like a life raft. "It's a legal paradox. I'm trapped because of the jurisdiction she's cornered me in. I could talk to the judge, I suppose, but she'll have picked him carefully." Her eyes narrow. "The jurisdiction. Hey, Bob." She lets go of the duct and floats free, hair streaming out behind her like a cometary halo. "How do I go about creating myself a new jurisdiction?"

Monica grins. "I seem to recall the traditional way was to grab yourself some land and set yourself up as king: but there are other ways. I've got some friends I think you should meet. They're not good conversationalists and there's a two-hour lightspeed delay . . . but I think you'll find they've answered that question already. But why don't you talk to the imam first and find out what he's like? He may surprise you. After all, he was already out here before your mom decided to use him against you."

The *Sanger* hangs in orbit thirty kilometers up, circling the waist of potato-shaped Amalthea. Drones swarm across the slopes of Mons Lyctos, ten kilometers above the mean surface level: they kick up clouds of reddish sulfate dust as they spread transparent sheets across the surface. This close to Jupiter—a mere hundred and eighty thousand kilometers above the swirling madness of the cloudscape—the gas giant fills half the sky with a perpetually changing clockface: for Amalthea orbits the master in under twelve hours. The *Sanger*'s radiation shields are running at full power, shrouding the ship in a corona of rippling plasma: radio is useless, and the human miners run their drones via an intricate network of laser circuits. Other, larger drones are unwinding spools of heavy electrical cable north and south from the landing site: once the circuits are connected, these will form a coil cutting through Jupiter's magnetic field, generating electrical current (and imperceptibly slowing the moon's orbital momentum).

Amber sighs and looks, for the sixth time this hour, at the webcam plastered on the side of her cabin. She's taken down the posters and told the toys to tidy themselves away. In another two thousand seconds, the tiny Iranian spaceship will rise above the limb of Moshtari, and then it will be time to talk to the teacher. She isn't looking forward to the experience. If he's a grizzled old blockhead of the most obdurate fundamentalist streak, she'll be in trouble: disrespect for age has been part and parcel of the western teenage experience for generations, and a cross-cultural thread that she's sent to clue-up on Islam reminds her that not all cultures share this outlook. But if he turns out to be young, intelligent, and flexible, things could be even worse. When she was eight, Amber audited *The Taming of the Shrew*: now she has no appetite for a starring role in her own cross-cultural production.

She sighs again. "Pierre?"

"Yeah?" His voice comes from the foot of the emergency locker in her room. He's curled up down there, limbs twitching languidly as he drives a mining drone around the surface of Object Barney, as the rock has named itself. The drone is a long-legged crane-fly lookalike, bouncing very slowly from toe-tip to toe-tip in the microgravity—the rock is only half a kilometer along its longest axis, coated brown with weird hydrocarbon goop and sulfur compounds sprayed off the surface of Io by the Jovian winds. "I'm coming."

"You better." She glances at the screen. "One twenty seconds to next burn." The payload canister on the screen is, technically speaking, stolen: it'll be okay as long as she gives it back, Bob said, although she won't be able to do that until it's reached Barney and they've found enough water ice to refuel it. "Found anything yet?"

"Just the usual. Got a seam of ice near the semimajor pole—it's dirty, but there's at least a thousand tons there. And the surface is crunchy with tar. Amber, you know what? The orange shit, it's solid with fullerenes."

Amber grins at her reflection in the screen. That's good news. Once the payload she's steering touches down, Pierre can help her lay superconducting wires along Barney's long axis. It's only a kilometer and a half, and that'll only give them a few tens of kilowatts of juice, but the condensation fabricator that's also in the payload will be able to use it to convert Barney's crust into processed goods at about two grams per second. Using designs copylefted by the free hardware foundation, inside two hundred thousand seconds they'll have a grid of sixty-four 3D printers barfing up structured matter at a rate limited only by available power. Starting with a honking great dome tent and some free nitrogen/oxygen for her to breathe, then adding a big webcache and direct high-bandwidth uplink to Earth, Amber could have her very own one-girl colony up and running within a million seconds.

The screen blinks at her. "Oh shit. Make yourself scarce, Pierre!" The incoming call nags at her attention. "Yeah? Who are you?"

The screen fills with a view of a cramped, very twen-cen-looking space capsule. The guy inside it is in his twenties, with a heavily tanned face, close-cropped hair and beard, wearing an olive-drab spacesuit liner. He's floating between a TORU manual-docking controller and a gilt-framed photograph of the Ka'bah at Mecca. "Good evening to you," he says solemnly. "Do I have the honor to be addressing Amber Macx?"

"Uh, yeah. That's me." She stares at him: he looks nothing like her conception of an ayatollah—whatever an ayatollah is—elderly, black-robed, vindictively fundamentalist. "Who are you?"

"I am Doctor Sadeq Khurasani. I hope that I am not interrupting you? Is it convenient for you that we talk now?"

He looks so anxious that Amber nods automatically. "Sure. Did my mom put you up to this?" They're still speaking English, and she notices that his diction is good, but slightly stilted: he isn't using a grammar engine, he's actually learned it the hard way. "If so, you want to be careful. She doesn't lie, exactly, but she gets people to do what she wants."

"Yes, she did. Ah." A pause. They're still almost a light-second apart, time for painful collisions and accidental silences. "I have not noticed that. Are you sure you should be speaking of your mother that way?"

Amber breathes deeply. "*Adults* can get divorced. If *I* could get divorced from her, I would. She's—" she flails around for the right word helplessly. "Look. She's the sort of person who can't lose a fight. If she's going to lose, she'll try to figure how to set the law on you. Like she's done to me. Don't you see?"

Doctor Khurasani looks extremely dubious. "I am not sure I understand," he says. "Perhaps, mm, I should tell you why I am talking to you?"

"Sure. Go ahead." Amber is startled by his attitude: he's actually taking her seriously, she realizes. Treating her like an adult. The sensation is so novel— coming from someone more than twenty years old and not a member of the Borg—that she almost lets herself forget that he's only talking to her because Mom set her up.

"Well. I am an engineer. In addition, I am a student of *fiqh*, jurisprudence. In fact, I am qualified to sit in judgment. I am a very junior judge, but even so, it is a heavy responsibility. Anyway. Your mother, peace be unto her, lodged a petition with me. Are you aware of it?"

"Yes." Amber tenses up. "It's a lie. Distortion of the facts."

"Hmm." Sadeq rubs his beard thoughtfully. "Well, I have to find out, yes? Your mother has submitted herself to the will of God. This makes you the child of a Moslem, and she claims—"

"She's trying to use you as a weapon!" Amber interrupts. "I sold myself into *slavery* to get away from her, do you understand? I enslaved myself to a company that is held in trust for my ownership. She's trying to change the rules to get me back. You know what? I don't believe she gives a shit about your religion, all she wants is me!"

"A mother's love—"

"Fuck love!" Amber snarls, "she wants *power*."

Sadeq's expression hardens. "You have a foul mouth in your head, child. All I am trying to do is to find out the facts of this situation: you should ask yourself if such disrespect furthers your interests?" He pauses for a moment, then continues, less abruptly, "Did you really have such a bad childhood with her? Do you think she did everything merely for power, or could she love you?" Pause. "You must understand, I need an answer to these things. Before I can know what is the right thing to do."

"My mother—" Amber stops. Spawns a vaporous cloud of memory retrievals. They fan out through the space around her mind like the tail of her cometary mind. Invoking a complex of network parsers and class filters, she turns the memories into reified images and blats them at the webcam's tiny brain so that he can see them. Some of the memories are so painful that Amber has to close her eyes. Mom in full office war-paint, leaning over Amber, promising to take her to church so that Reverend Beeching can pray the devil out of her. Mom telling Amber that they're moving again, abruptly, dragging her away from school and the friends she'd tentatively started to like. Mom catching her on the phone to Daddy, tearing the phone in half and hitting her with it. Mom at the kitchen table, forcing her to eat—"My mother likes *control*."

"Ah." Sadeq's expression turns glassy. "And this is how you feel about her? How long have you had that level of—no, please forgive me for asking. You obviously understand implants. Do your grandparents know? Did you talk to them?"

"My grandparents?" Amber stifles a snort. "Mom's parents are dead. Dad's are still alive, but they won't talk to him—they like Mom. They think I'm creepy. I know little things, their tax bands and customer profiles. I could mine data with my head when I was four. I'm not built like little girls were in their day, and they don't understand. You know that the old ones don't like us at all? Some of the churches make money doing nothing but exorcisms for oldsters who think their kids are possessed."

"Well." Sadeq is fingering his beard again, distractedly. "I must say, this is a lot to learn. But you know that your mother has accepted Islam, don't you? This means that you are Moslem, too. Unless you are an adult, your parent legally speaks for you. And she says that this makes you my problem. Hmm."

"I'm not Moslem." Amber stares at the screen. "I'm not a child, either." Her threads are coming together, whispering scarily behind her eyes: her head is suddenly dense and turgid with ideas, heavy as a stone and twice as old as time. "I am nobody's chattel. What does your law say about people who are born with implants? What does it say about people who want to live forever? I don't believe in any *god*, mister judge. I don't believe in any limits. Mom can't, physically, make me do *anything*, and she sure can't speak for me."

"Well, if that is what you have to say, I must think on the matter." He catches her eye: his expression is thoughtful, like a doctor considering a diagnosis. "I will call you again in due course. In the meantime, if you need to talk to anyone, remember that I am always available. If there is anything I can do to help ease your pain, I would be pleased to be of service. Peace be unto you, and those you care for."

"Same to you too," she mutters darkly as the connection goes dead. "*Now* what?" she asks, as a beeping sprite gyrates across the wall, begging for attention.

"I think it's the lander," Pierre says helpfully. "Is it down yet?"

She rounds on him. "Hey, I thought I told you to get lost!"

"What, and miss all the fun?" He grins at her impishly. "Amber's got a new boyfriend! Wait until I tell everybody. . . ."

Sleep cycles pass: the borrowed 3D printer on Object Barney's surface spews bitmaps of atoms in quantum lockstep at its rendering platform, building up the control circuitry and skeletons of new printers. (There are no clunky nanoassemblers here, no robots the size of viruses busily sorting molecules into piles—just the bizarre quantized magic of atomic holography, modulated Bose-Einstein condensates collapsing into strange, lacy, supercold machinery.) Electricity surges through the cable loops as they slice through Jupiter's magnetosphere, slowly converting the rock's momentum into power: small robots grovel in the orange dirt, scooping up raw material to feed to the fractionating oven. Amber's garden of machinery flourishes slowly, unpacking itself according to a schema designed by preteens at an industrial school in Poland, with barely any need for human guidance.

High in orbit around Amalthea, complex financial instruments breed and conjugate. Developed for the express purpose of facilitating trade with the alien intelligences believed to have been detected eight years earlier by SETI, they function equally well as fiscal firewalls for space colonies. The *Sanger's* bank accounts in California and Cuba are looking acceptable — since entering Jupiter space, the orphanage has staked a claim on roughly a hundred gigatons of random rocks and a moon that's just small enough to creep in under the International Astronomical Union's definition of a sovereign planetary body. The Borg are working hard, leading their eager teams of child stakeholders in their plans to build the industrial metastructures necessary to support mining helium three from Jupiter: they're so focused that they spend much of their time being themselves, not bothering to run Bob, the shared identity that gives them their messianic drive.

Half a light-hour away, tired Earth wakes and slumbers in time to its ancient orbital dynamics. A religious college in Cairo is considering issues of nanotechnology: if replicators are used to prepare a copy of a strip of bacon, right down to the molecular level, but without it ever being part of a pig, how is it to be treated? (If the mind of one of the faithful is copied into a computing machine's memory by mapping and simulating all its synapses, is the computer now a Moslem? If not, *why* not? If so, what are its rights and duties?) Riots in Borneo underline the urgency of theotechnological inquiry.

More riots in Barcelona, Madrid, Birmingham, and Marseilles also underline a rising problem: social chaos caused by cheap antiaging treatments. The zombie exterminators, a backlash of disaffected youth against the formerly greying gerontocracy of Europe, insist that people who predate the supergrid and can't handle implants aren't *really* conscious: their ferocity is equaled only by the anger of the dynamic septuagenarians of the baby boom, their bodies partially restored to the flush of sixties youth but their minds adrift in a slower, less contingent century. The faux-young boomers feel betrayed, forced back into the labor pool but unable to cope with the implant-accelerated culture of the new millennium, their hard-earned experience rendered obsolete by deflationary time.

The Bangladeshi economic miracle is typical of the age. With growth rates running at over 20 percent, cheap out-of-control bioindustrialization has swept the nation: former rice farmers harvest plastics and milk cows for silk, while their children study mariculture and design sea walls. With cellphone ownership nearing 80 percent and literacy at 90, the once-poor country is finally breaking out of its historical infrastructure trap and beginning to develop: another generation, and they'll be richer than Japan in 2001.

Radical new economic theories are focusing around bandwidth, speed-of-light transmission time, and the implications of CETI, communication with extraterrestrial intelligence: cosmologists and quants collaborate on bizarre relativistically telescoped financial instruments. Space (which lets you store information) and structure (which lets you process it) acquire value while dumb mass — like gold — loses it: the degenerate cores of the traditional stock markets are in free fall, the old smokestack microprocessor and biotech/nanotech industries crumbling before the onslaught of matter replicators and self-modifying ideas and the barbarian communicators, who mortgage their future for a millennium against the chance of a gift from a visiting alien intelligence. Microsoft, once the US Steel of the silicon age, quietly fades into liquidation.

An outbreak of green goo—a crude biomechanical replicator that eats everything in its path—is dealt with in the Australian outback by carpetbombing with fuel-air explosives: the USAF subsequently reactivates two wings of refurbished B-52s and places them at the disposal of the UN standing committee on self-replicating weapons. (CNN discovers that one of their newest pilots, re-enlisting with the body of a twenty-year-old and an empty pension account, first flew them over Laos and Cambodia.) The news overshadows the World Health Organization's announcement of the end of the HIV pandemic, after more than fifty years of bigotry, panic, and megadeath.

"Breathe steadily. Remember your regulator drill? If you spot your heart rate going up or your mouth going dry, take five."

"Shut the fuck up, 'Neko, I'm trying to concentrate." Amber fumbles with the titanium D-ring, trying to snake the strap through it. The gauntlets are getting in her way: high orbit spacesuits—little more than a body stocking designed to hold your skin under compression and help you breathe—are easy, but this deep in Jupiter's radiation belt, she has to wear an old moon suit that comes in about thirteen layers, and the gloves are stiff. It's Chernobyl weather, a sleet of alpha particles and raw protons storming through the void. "Got it." She yanks the strap tight, pulls on the D-ring, then goes to work on the next strap. Never looking down: because the wall she's tying herself to has no floor, just a cut-off two meters below, then empty space for a hundred kilometers before the nearest solid ground.

The ground sings to her moronically: "I fall to you, you fall to me, it's the law of gravity—"

She shoves her feet down onto the platform that juts from the side of the capsule like a suicide's ledge: metalized Velcro grabs hold, and she pulls on the straps to turn her body around until she can see past the capsule, sideways. The capsule masses about five tons, barely bigger than an ancient Soyuz. It's packed to overflowing with environment-sensitive stuff she'll need, and a honking great high-gain antenna. "I hope you know what you're doing?" someone says over the intercom.

"Of course I—" she stops. Alone in this TsUP-surplus iron maiden with its low bandwidth comms and bizarre plumbing, she feels claustrophobic and helpless: parts of her mind don't work. When she was four, Mom took her down a famous cave system somewhere out west: when the guide turned out the lights half a kilometer underground, she'd screamed with surprise as the darkness had reached out and touched her. Now it's not the darkness that frightens her, it's the lack of thought. For a hundred kilometers below her, there are *no* minds, and even on the surface there's not much but a moronic warbling of bots. Everything that makes the universe primate-friendly seems to be locked in the huge spaceship that looms somewhere just behind her, and she has to fight down an urge to shed her straps and swarm back up the umbilical that anchors this capsule to the *Sanger*. "I'll be fine," she forces herself to say. And even though she's unsure that it's true, she tries to make herself believe it. "It's just leaving-home nerves. I've read about it, okay?"

There's a funny, high-pitched whistle in her ears. For a moment, the sweat on the back of her neck turns icy cold, then the noise stops. She strains for a moment, and when it returns, she recognizes the sound: the heretofore-talkative cat, curled in the warmth of her pressurized luggage can, has begun to snore.

"Let's go," she says, "time to roll the wagon." A speech macro deep in the *Sanger*'s docking firmware recognizes her authority and gently lets go of the pod. A couple of cold gas thrusters pop, deep banging vibrations running through the capsule, and she's on her way.

"Amber. How's it hanging?" A familiar voice in her ears: she blinks. Fifteen hundred seconds, nearly half an hour gone.

"Robes-Pierre, chopped any aristos lately?"

"Heh!" A pause. "I can see *your* head from here."

"How's it looking?" she asks. There's a lump in her throat, she isn't sure why. Pierre is probably hooked into one of the smaller proximity cameras dotted around the outer hull of the big mothership. Watching over her as she falls.

"Pretty much like always," he says laconically. Another pause, this time longer. "This is wild, you know? Su Ang says hi, by the way."

"Su Ang, hi," she replies, resisting the urge to lean back and look up—up relative to her feet, not her vector—and see if the ship's still visible.

"Hi," Ang says shyly. "You're very brave!"

"Still can't beat you at chess." Amber frowns. Su Ang and her over-engineered algae. Oscar and his pharmaceutical factory toads. People she's known for three years, mostly ignored, and never thought about missing. "Listen, you going to come visiting?"

"Visit?" Ang sounds dubious. "When will it be ready?"

"Oh, soon enough." At four kilograms per minute of structured-matter output, the printers on the surface have already built her a bunch of stuff: a habitat dome, the guts of an algae/shrimp farm, a bucket conveyor to bury it with, an airlock. It's all lying around waiting for her to put it together and move into her new home. "Once the Borg get back from Amalthea."

"Hey! You mean they're moving? How did you figure that?"

"Go talk to them," Amber says. Actually, she's a large part of the reason the *Sanger* is about to crank its orbit up and out toward the other moon: she wants to be alone in comms silence for a couple of million seconds. The Franklin collective is doing her a big favor.

"Ahead of the curve, as usual," Pierre cuts in, with something that sounds like admiration to her uncertain ears.

"You too," she says, a little too fast. "Come visit when I've got the life-support cycle stabilized."

"I'll do that," he replies. A red glow suffuses the flank of the capsule next to her head, and she looks up in time to see the glaring blue laser-line of the *Sanger's* drive torch powering up.

Eighteen million seconds, almost a tenth of a Jupiter year, passes.

The imam tugs thoughtfully on his beard as he stares at the traffic-control display. These days, every shift seems to bring a new crewed spaceship into Jupiter system: space is getting positively crowded. When he arrived, there were less than two hundred people here: now there's the population of a small city, and many of them live at the heart of the approach map centered on his display. He breathes deeply — trying to ignore the omnipresent odor of old socks — and studies the map. "Computer, what about my slot?" he asks.

"Your slot: cleared to commence final approach in six nine five seconds. Speed limit is ten meters per second inside ten kilometers, drop to two meters per second inside one kilometer. Uploading map of forbidden thrust vectors now." Chunks of the approach map turn red, gridded off to prevent his exhaust stream damaging other craft in the area.

Sadeq sighs. "We'll go in on Kurs. I assume their Kurs guidance is active?"

"Kurs docking target support available to shell level three."

"Praise the Prophet, peace be unto him." He pokes around through the guidance subsystem's menus, setting up the software emulation of the obsolete (but highly reliable) Soyuz docking system. At last, he can leave the ship to look after itself for a bit. He glances around: for two years he has lived in this canister, and soon he will step outside it. It hardly seems real.

The radio, usually silent, crackles with unexpected life. "Bravo One One, this is Imperial Traffic Control. Verbal contact required, over."

Sadeq twitches with surprise. The voice sounds inhuman, paced with the cadences of a speech synthesizer, like so many of Her Majesty's subjects. "Bravo One One to Traffic Control, I'm listening, over."

"Bravo One One, we have assigned you a landing slot on tunnel four, airlock delta. Kurs active, ensure your guidance is set to seven four zero and slaved to our control."

He leans over the screen and rapidly checks the docking system's settings. "Control, all in order."

"Bravo One One, stand by."

The next hour passes slowly as the traffic control system guides his Type 921 down to a rocky rendezvous. Orange dust streaks his one optical-glass porthole: a kilometer before touchdown, Sadeq busies himself closing protective covers, locking down anything that might fall around on contact. Finally, he unrolls his mat against the floor in front of the console and floats above it for ten minutes, eyes closed in prayer. It's not the landing that worries him, but what comes next.

Her Majesty's domain stretches out before the battered Almaz module like a rust-stained snowflake half-a-kilometer in diameter. Its core is buried in a loose snowball of greyish rubble, and it waves languid brittlestar arms at the gibbous orange horizon of Jupiter. Fine hairs, fractally branching down to the molecular level, split off the main collector arms at regular intervals; a cluster of habitat pods like seedless grapes cling to the roots of the massive cluster. Already, he can see the huge steel generator loops that climb from either pole of the snowflake, wreathed in sparking plasma: the Jovian rings form a rainbow of darkness rising behind them.

Finally, the battered space station is on final approach. Sadeq watches the Kurs simulation output carefully, piping it direct into his visual field: there's an external camera view of the rockpile and grapes, expanding toward the convex ceiling of the ship, and he licks his lips, ready to hit the manual override and go around again—but the rate of descent is slowing, and by the time he's close enough to see the scratches on the shiny metal docking cone ahead of the ship, it's measured in centimeters per second. There's a gentle bump, then a shudder, then a rippling bang as the docking ring latches fire—and he's down.

Sadeq breathes deeply again, then tries to stand. There's gravity here, but not much: walking is impossible. He's about to head for the life-support panel when he freezes, hearing a noise from the far end of the docking node. Turning, he is just in time to see the hatch opening toward him, a puff of vapor condensing, and then—

Her Imperial Majesty is sitting in the throne room, moodily fidgeting with the new signet ring her Equerry has designed for her. It's a lump of structured carbon massing almost fifty grams, set in a plain band of iridium. It glitters with the blue and violet speckle highlights of its internal lasers, because, in addition to being a piece of state jewelry, it is also an optical router, part of the industrial control infrastructure she's building out here on the edge of the solar system. Her Majesty wears plain black combat pants and sweatshirt, woven from the finest spider silk and spun glass, but her feet are bare: her taste in fashion is best described as youthful, and, in any event, certain styles—skirts, for example—are simply impractical in microgravity. But, being a monarch, she's wearing a crown. And there's a cat sleeping on the back of her throne.

The lady-in-waiting (and sometime hydroponic engineer) ushers Sadeq to the doorway, then floats back. "If you need anything, please say," she says shyly, then ducks and rolls away. Sadeq approaches the throne, orients himself on the floor—a simple slab of black composite, save for the throne growing from its center like an exotic flower—and waits to be noticed.

"Doctor Khurasani, I presume." She smiles at him, neither the innocent grin of a child nor the knowing smirk of an adult: merely a warm greeting. "Welcome to my kingdom. Please feel free to make use of any necessary support services here, and I wish you a very pleasant stay."

Sadeq holds his expression still. The queen is young—her face still retains the puppy fat of childhood, emphasized by microgravity moon-face—but it would be a bad mistake to consider her immature. "I am grateful for Your Majesty's forbearance," he murmurs, formulaic. Behind her the walls glitter like diamonds, a glowing kaleidoscope vision. Her crown, more like a compact helm that covers the top and rear of her head, also glitters and throws off diffraction rainbows: but most of its emissions are in the near ultraviolet, invisible except in the faint glowing nimbus it creates around her head. Like a halo.

"Have a seat," she offers, gesturing: a ballooning free-fall cradle squirts down and expands from the ceiling, angled toward her, open and waiting. "You must be tired: working a ship all by yourself is exhausting." She frowns ruefully, as if remembering. "And two years is nearly unprecedented."

"Your Majesty is too kind." Sadeq wraps the cradle arms around himself and faces her. "Your labors have been fruitful, I trust."

She shrugs. "I sell the biggest commodity in short supply on any frontier. . . ." a momentary grin. "This isn't the wild west, is it?"

"Justice cannot be sold," Sadeq says stiffly. Then, a moment later. "My apologies, please accept that while I mean no insult. I merely mean that while you say your goal is to provide the rule of Law, what you *sell* is and must be something different. Justice without God, sold to the highest bidder, is not justice."

The queen nods. "Leaving aside the mention of God, I agree: I can't sell it. But I can sell participation in a just system. And this new frontier really is a lot smaller than anyone expected, isn't it? Our bodies may take months to travel between worlds, but our disputes and arguments take seconds or minutes. As long as everybody agrees to abide by my arbitration, physical enforcement can wait until they're close enough to touch. And everybody *does* agree that my legal framework is easier to comply with, better adjusted to space, than any earthbound one." A note of steel creeps into her voice, challenging: her halo brightens, tickling a reactive glow from the walls of the throne room.

Five billion inputs or more, Sadeq marvels: the crown is an engineering marvel, even though most of its mass is buried in the walls and floor of this huge construct. "There is law revealed by the Prophet, peace be unto him, and there is Law that we can establish by analyzing his intentions. There are other forms of law by which humans live, and various interpretations of the law of God even among those who study his works. How, in the absence of the word of the Prophet, can you provide a moral compass?"

"Hmm." She taps her fingers on the arm of her throne, and Sadeq's heart freezes. He's heard the stories from the claim-jumpers and boardroom bandits, from the greenmail experts with their roots in the earthbound jurisdictions that have made such a hash of arbitration here: how she can experience a year in a minute, rip your memories out through your cortical implants and make you relive your worst mistakes in her nightmarishly powerful simulation system. She is the *queen*—the first individual to get her hands on so much mass and energy that she could pull ahead of the curve of binding technology, and the first to set up her own jurisdiction and rule certain experiments to be legal so that she could make use of the mass/energy intersection. She has *force majeure*—even the Pentagon's infowarriors respect the Ring Imperium's firewall. In fact, the body sitting in the throne opposite him probably contains only a fraction of her identity; she's by no means the first upload or partial, but she's the first-gust front of the storm of power that will arrive when the arrogant ones achieve their goal of dismantling the planets and turning dumb and uninhabited mass into brains throughout the observable reaches of the universe. And he's just questioned the rectitude of her vision.

The queen's lips twitch. Then they curl into a wide, carnivorous grin. Behind her, the cat sits up and stretches, then stares at Sadeq through narrowed eyes.

"You know, that's the first time in *weeks* that anyone has told me I'm full of shit. You haven't been talking to my mother again, have you?"

It's Sadeq's turn to shrug, uncomfortably. "I have prepared a judgment," he says slowly.

"Ah." Amber rotates the huge diamond ring around her finger, seemingly unaware. It is Amber that looks him in the eye, a trifle nervously. Although what he could possibly *do* to make her comply with any decree—

"Her motive is polluted," Sadeq says shortly.

"Does that mean what I think it does?" she asks.

Sadeq breathes deeply again. "Yes."

Her smile returns. "And is that the end of it?" she asks.

He raises a dark eyebrow. "Only if you can prove to me that you can have a conscience in the absence of divine revelation."

Her reaction catches him by surprise. "Oh, sure. That's the next part of the program. Obtaining divine revelations."

"What? From the aliens?"

The cat, claws extended, delicately picks its way down to her lap and waits to be held and stroked. It never once takes its eyes off him. "Where else?" she asks. "Doctor, I didn't get the Franklin trust to loan me the wherewithal to build this castle just in return for some legal paperwork. We've known for years that there's a whole alien packet-switching network out there and we're just getting spillover from some of their routes: it turns out there's a node not far away from here, in real space. Helium three, separate jurisdictions, heavy industrialization on Io— there is a *purpose* to all this activity."

Sadeq licks his suddenly dry lips. "You're going to narrowcast a reply?"

"No, much better than that: we're going to *visit* them. Cut the delay cycle down to realtime. We came here to build a ship and recruit a crew, even if we have to cannibalize the whole of Jupiter system to pay for the exercise."

The cat yawns, then fixes him with a thousand-yard stare. "This stupid girl wants to bring her *conscience* along to a meeting with something so smart it might as well be a god," it says, "and you're it. There's a slot open for the post of ship's theologian. I don't suppose I can convince you to turn the offer down?"

in paradise

BRUCE STERLING

One of the most powerful and innovative new talents to enter SF in the past few decades, Bruce Sterling sold his first story in 1976. By the end of the '80s, he had established himself, with a series of stories set in his exotic "Shaper/Mechanist" future, with novels such as the complex and Stapeldonian Schismatrix *and the well-received* Islands in the Net *(as well as with his editing of the influential anthology* Mirrorshades: the Cyberpunk Anthology *and the infamous critical magazine* Cheap Truth*), as perhaps the prime driving force behind the revolutionary "Cyberpunk" movement in science fiction, and also as one of the best new hard science writers to enter the field in some time. His other books include a critically acclaimed nonfiction study of First Amendment issues in the world of computer networking,* The Hacker Crackdown: Law and Disorder on the Electronic Frontier, *the novels* The Artificial Kid, Involution Ocean, Heavy Weather, Holy Fire, *and* Distraction, *a novel in collaboration with William Gibson,* The Difference Engine, *and the landmark collections* Crystal Express *and* Globalhead. *His most recent books include the omnibus collection (it contains the novel* Schismatrix *as well as most of his Shaper/Mechanist stories)* Schismatrix Plus, *a new collection,* A Good Old-Fashioned Future, *and a new novel,* Zeitgeist. *Upcoming is a nonfiction study of the future,* Tomorrow Now: Envisioning the Next Fifty Years. *His story "Bicycle Repairman" earned him a long-overdue Hugo in 1997, and he won another Hugo in 1997 for his story "Taklamakan." His stories have appeared in our First through Eighth, Eleventh, Fourteenth, and Sixteenth Annual Collections. He lives with his family in Austin, Texas.*

In the sly and deceptively quiet story that follows, he offers us a postmodern romance, quirky, bittersweet—and surprising.

T he machines broke down so much that it was comical, but the security people never laughed about that.

Felix could endure the delay, for plumbers billed by the hour. He opened his tool kit, extracted a plastic flask and had a solid nip of Scotch.

The Moslem girl was chattering into her phone. Her dad and another bearded weirdo had passed through the big metal frame just as the scanner broke down. So these two somber, suited old men were getting the full third degree with the hand wands, while daughter was stuck. Daughter wore a long baggy coat and thick black headscarf and a surprisingly sexy pair of sandals. Between her and her minders stretched the no man's land of official insecurity. She waved across the gap.

The security geeks found something metallic in the black wool jacket of the Wicked Uncle. Of course it was harmless, but they had to run their full ritual, lest they die of boredom at their posts. As the Scotch settled in, Felix felt time stretch like taffy. Little Miss Mujihadeen discovered that her phone was dying. She banged at it with the flat of her hand.

The line of hopeful shoppers, grimly waiting to stimulate the economy, shifted in their disgruntlement. It was a bad, bleak scene. It crushed Felix's heart within him. He longed to leap to his feet and harangue the lot of them. *Wake up*, he wanted to scream at them, *cheer up, act more human.* He felt the urge keenly, but it scared people when he cut loose like that. They really hated it. And so did he. He knew he couldn't look them in the eye. It would only make a lot of trouble.

The Mideastern men shouted at the girl. She waved her dead phone at them, as if another breakdown was going to help their mood. Then Felix noticed that she shared his own make of cell phone. She had a rather ahead-of-the-curve Finnish model that he'd spent a lot of money on. So Felix rose and sidled over.

"Help you out with that phone, ma'am?"

She gave him the paralyzed look of a coed stuck with a dripping tap. "No English?" he concluded. "Habla español, senorita?" No such luck.

He offered her his own phone. No, she didn't care to use it. Surprised and even a little hurt by this rejection, Felix took his first good look at her, and realized with a lurch that she was pretty. What eyes! They were whirlpools. The line of her lips was like the tapered edge of a rose leaf.

"It's your battery," he told her. Though she had not a word of English, she obviously got it about phone batteries. After some gestured persuasion, she was willing to trade her dead battery for his. There was a fine and delicate little moment when his fingertips extracted her power supply, and he inserted his own unit into that golden-lined copper cavity. Her display leapt to life with an eager flash of numerals. Felix pressed a button or two, smiled winningly, and handed her phone back.

She dialed in a hurry, and bearded Evil Dad lifted his phone to answer, and life became much easier on the nerves. Then, with a groaning buzz, the scanner came back on. Dad and Uncle waved a command at her, like lifers turned to trusty prison guards, and she scampered through the metal gate and never looked back.

She had taken his battery. Well, no problem. He would treasure the one she had given him.

Felix gallantly let the little crowd through before he himself cleared security. The geeks always went nuts about his plumbing tools, but then again, they had to. He found the assignment: a chi-chi place that sold fake antiques and potpourri. The manager's office had a clogged drain. As he worked, Felix recharged the phone. Then he socked them for a sum that made them wince.

On his leisurely way out—whoa, there was Miss Cell phone, that looker, that little goddess, browsing in a jewelry store over Korean gold chains and tiaras. Dad and Uncle were there, with a couple of off-duty cops.

Felix retired to a bench beside the fountain, in the potted plastic plants. He had another bracing shot of Scotch, then put his feet up on his toolbox and punched her number.

He saw her straighten at the ring, and open her purse, and place the phone to the kerchiefed side of her head. She didn't know where he was, or who he was. That was why the words came pouring out of him.

"My God you're pretty," he said. "You are wasting your time with that jewelry. Because your eyes are like two black diamonds."

She jumped a little, poked at the phone's buttons with disbelief, and put it back to her head.

Felix choked back the urge to laugh and leaned forward, his elbows on his knees. "A string of pearls around your throat would look like peanuts," he told the phone. "I am totally smitten with you. What are you like under that big baggy coat? Do I dare to wonder? I would give a million dollars just to see your knees!"

"Why are you telling me that?" said the phone.

"Because I'm looking at you right now. And after one look at you, believe me, I was a lost soul." Felix felt a chill. "Hey, wait a minute—you don't speak English, do you?"

"No, I don't speak English—but my telephone does."

"It *does*?"

"It's a very new telephone. It's from Finland," the telephone said. "I need it because I'm stuck in a foreign country. Do you really have a million dollars for my knees?"

"That was a figure of speech," said Felix, though his bank account was, in point of fact, looking considerably healthier since his girlfriend Lola had dumped him. "Never mind the million dollars," he said. "I'm dying of love out here. I'd sell my blood just to buy you petunias."

"You must be a famous poet," the phone said dreamily, "for you speak such wonderful Farsi."

Felix had no idea what Farsi was—but he was way beyond such fretting now. The rusty gates of his soul were shuddering on their hinges. "I'm drunk," he realized. "I am drunk on your smile."

"In my family, the women never smile."

Felix had no idea what to say to that, so there was a hissing silence.

"Are you a spy? How did you get my phone number?"

"I'm not a spy. I got your phone number from your phone."

"Then I know you. You must be that tall foreign man who gave me your battery. Where are you?"

"Look outside the store. See me on the bench?" She turned where she stood, and he waved his fingertips. "That's right, it's me," he declared to her. "I can't believe I'm really going through with this. You just stand there, okay? I'm going to run in there and buy you a wedding ring."

"Don't do that." She glanced cautiously at Dad and Uncle, then stepped closer to the bulletproof glass. "Yes, I do see you. I remember you."

She was looking straight at him. Their eyes met. They were connecting. A hot torrent ran up his spine. "You are looking straight at me."

"You're very handsome."

It wasn't hard to elope. Young women had been eloping since the dawn of time. Elopement with eager phone support was a snap. He followed her to the hotel, a posh place that swarmed with limos and videocams. He brought her a bag with a big hat, sunglasses, and a cheap Mexican wedding dress. He sneaked into the women's restroom—they never put videocams there, due to the complaints—and he left the bag in a stall. She went in, came out in new clothes with her hair loose, and walked straight out of the hotel and into his car.

They couldn't speak together without their phones, but that turned out to be surprisingly advantageous, as further discussion was not on their minds. Unlike Lola, who was always complaining that he should open up and relate—"You're a plumber," she would tell him, "how deep and mysterious is a plumber supposed to be?"—the new woman in his life had needs that were very straightforward. She liked to walk in parks without a police escort. She liked to thoughtfully peruse the goods in Mideastern ethnic groceries. And she liked to make love to him. She was nineteen years old, and the willing sacrifice of her chastity had really burned the bridges for his little refugee. Once she got fully briefed about what went inside where, she was in the mood to tame the demon. She had big, jagged, sobbing, alarming, romantic, brink-of-the-grave things going on, with long, swoony kisses, and heel-drumming, and clutching-and-clawing.

When they were too weak, and too raw, and too tingling to make love anymore, then she would cook, very badly. She was on her phone constantly, talking to her people. These confidantes of hers were obviously women, because she asked them for Persian cooking tips. She would sink with triumphant delight into cheery chatter as the Basmati rice burned.

He longed to take her out to eat; to show her to everyone, to the whole world; really, besides the sex, no act could have made him happier—but she was un-documented, and sooner or later some security geek was sure to check on that. People did things like that to people nowadays. To contemplate such things threw a thorny darkness over their whole affair, so, mostly, he didn't think. He took time off work, and he spent every moment that he could in her radiant presence, and she did what a pretty girl could do to lift a man's darkened spirits, which was plenty. More than he had ever had from anyone.

After ten days of golden, unsullied bliss, ten days of bread and jug wine, ten days when the nightingales sang in chorus and the reddest of roses bloomed outside the boudoir, there came a knock on his door, and it was three cops.

"Hello, Mr. Hernandez," said the smallest of the trio. "I would be Agent Portillo from Homeland Security, and these would be two of my distinguished associates. Might we come in?"

"Would there be a problem?" said Felix.

"Yes there would!" said Portillo. "There might be rather less of a problem if my associates here could search your apartment." Portillo offered up a handheld screen. "A young woman named Batool Kadivar? Would we be recognizing Miss Batool Kadivar?"

"I can't even pronounce that," Felix said. "But I guess you'd better come in," for Agent Portillo's associates were already well on their way. Men of their ilk were not prepared to take no for an answer. They shoved past him and headed at once for the bedroom.

"Who are those guys? They're not American."

"They're Iranian allies. The Iranians were totally nuts for a while, and then they were sort of okay, and then they became our new friends, and then the enemies of our friends became our friends. . . . Do you ever watch TV news, Mr. Hernandez? Secular uprisings, people seizing embassies? Ground war in the holy city of Qom, that kind of thing?"

"It's hard to miss," Felix admitted.

"There are a billion Moslems. If they want to turn the whole planet into Israel, we don't get a choice about that. You know something? I used to be an accountant!" Portillo sighed theatrically. " 'Homeland Security.' Why'd they have to stick me with that chicken outfit? Hombre, we're twenty years old, and we don't even have our own budget yet. Did you see those gorillas I've got on my hands? You think these guys ever listen to sense? Geneva Convention? U.S. Constitution? Come on."

"They're not gonna find any terrorists in here."

Portillo sighed again. "Look, Mr. Hernandez. You're a young man with a clean record, so I want to do you a favor." He adjusted his handheld and it showed a new screen. "These are cell phone records. Thirty, forty calls a day, to and from your number. Then look at this screen, this is the good part. Check out *her* call records. That would be her aunt in Yerevan, and her little sister in Teheran, and five or six of her teenage girlfriends, still living back in purdah. . . . Who do you think is gonna *pay* that phone bill? Did that ever cross your mind?"

Felix said nothing.

"I can understand this, Mr. Hernandez. You lucked out. You're a young, red-blooded guy and that is a very pretty girl. But she's a minor, and an illegal alien. Her father's family has got political connections like nobody's business, and I would mean nobody, and I would also mean business."

"Not my business," Felix said.

"You're being a sap, Mr. Hernandez. You may not be interested in war, but war is plenty interested in you." There were loud crashing, sacking and looting noises coming from his bedroom.

"You are sunk, hermano. There is video at the Lebanese grocery store. There is video hidden in the traffic lights. You're a free American citizen, sir. You're free to go anywhere you want, and we're free to watch all the backup tapes. That would be the big story I'm relating here. Would we be catching on yet?"

"That's some kind of story," Felix said.

"You don't know the half of it. You don't know the tenth."

The two goons reappeared. There was a brief exchange of notes. They had to use their computers.

"My friends here are disappointed," said Agent Portillo, "because there is no girl in your residence, even though there is an extensive selection of makeup and perfume. They want me to arrest you for abduction, and obstruction of justice, and probably ten or twelve other things. But I would be asking myself: why? Why should this young taxpayer with a steady job want to have his life ruined? What I'm thinking is: there must be *another* story. A *better* story. The flighty girl ran off, and she spent the last two weeks in a convent. It was just an impulse thing for her. She got frightened and upset by America, and then she came back to her people. Everything diplomatic."

"That's diplomacy?"

"Diplomacy is the art of avoiding extensive unpleasantness for all the parties concerned. The united coalition, as it were."

"They'll chop her hands off and beat her like a dog!"

"Well, that would depend, Mr. Hernandez. That would depend entirely on whether the girl herself tells that story. Somebody would have to get her up to speed on all that. A trusted friend. You see?"

After the departure of the three security men, Felix thought through his situation. He realized there was nothing whatsoever in it for him but shame, humiliation, impotence, and a crushing and lasting unhappiness. He then fetched up the reposado tequila from beneath his sink.

Sometime later he felt the dulled stinging of a series of slaps to his head. When she saw that she had his attention, she poured the tequila onto the floor, accenting this gesture with an eye-opening Persian harangue. Felix staggered to the bathroom, threw up, and returned to find a fresh cup of coffee. She had raised the volume and was still going strong.

He'd never had her pick a lovers' quarrel with him, though he'd always known it was in her somewhere. It was magnificent. It was washing over him in a musical torrent of absolute nonsense. It was operatic, and he found it quite beautiful. Like sitting through a rainstorm without getting wet: trees straining, leaves flying, dark, windy, torrential. Majestic.

Her idea of coffee was basically wet grounds, so it brought him around in short order. "You're right, I'm wrong, and I'm sorry," he admitted tangentially, knowing she didn't understand a word, "so come on and help me," and he opened the sink cabinet, where he had hidden all his bottles when he'd noticed the earlier disapproving glances. He then decanted them down the drain: vodka, Southern Comfort, the gin, the party jug of tequila, even the last two inches of his favorite single-malt. Moslems didn't drink, and really, how wrong could any billion people be? He gulped a couple of aspirin and picked up the phone.

"The police were here. They know about us. I got upset. I drank too much."

"Did they beat you?"

"Uh, no. They're not big fans of beating over here, they've got better methods. They'll be back. We are in big trouble."

She folded her arms. "Then we'll run away."

"You know, we have a proverb for that in America. 'You can run, but you can't hide.'"

"Darling, I love your poetry, but when the police come to the house, it's serious."

"Yes. It's very serious, it's serious as cancer. You've got no I.D. You have no passport. You can't get on any plane to get away. Even the trains and lousy bus stations have facial recognition. My car is useless too. They'd read my license plate a hundred times before we hit city limits. I can't rent another car without leaving credit records. The cops have got my number."

"We'll steal a fast car and go very fast."

"You can't outrun them! That is not possible! They've all got phones like we do, so they're always ahead of us, waiting."

"I'm a rebel! I'll never surrender!" She lifted her chin. "Let's get married."

"I'd love to, but we can't. We have no license. We have no blood test."

"Then we'll marry in some place where they have all the blood they want. Beirut, that would be good." She placed her free hand against her chest. "We were married in my heart, the first time we ever made love."

This artless confession blew through him like a summer breeze. "They do have rings for cash at a pawnbroker's. . . . But I'm a Catholic. There must be *somebody* who does this sort of thing. . . . Maybe some heretic mullah. Maybe a Santeria guy?"

"If we're husband and wife, what can they do to us? We haven't done anything wrong! I'll get a Green Card. I'll beg them! I'll beg for mercy. I'll beg political asylum."

Agent Portillo conspicuously cleared his throat. "Mr. Hernandez, please! This would not be the conversation you two need to be having."

"I forgot to mention the worst part," Felix said. "They know about our phones."

"Miss Kadivar, can you also understand me?"

"Who are you? I hate you. Get off this line and let me talk to him."

"Salaam alekom to you, too," Portillo concluded. "It's a sad commentary on federal procurement when a mullah's daughter has a fancy translator, and I can't even talk live with my own fellow agents. By the way, those two gentlemen from the new regime in Teheran are staking out your apartment. How they failed to recognize your girlfriend on her way in, that I'll never know. But if you two listen to me, I think I can walk you out of this very dangerous situation."

"I don't want to leave my beloved," she said.

"Over my dead body," Felix declared. "Come and get me. Bring a gun."

"Okay, Miss Kadivar, you would seem to be the more rational of the two parties, so let me talk sense to you. You have no future with this man. What kind of wicked man seduces a decent girl with phone pranks? He's an *aayash*, he's a playboy. America has a fifty percent divorce rate. He would never ask your father honorably for your hand. What would your mother say?"

"Who is this awful man?" she said, shaken. "He knows everything!"

"He's a snake!" Felix said. "He's the devil!"

"You still don't get it, compadre. I'm not the Great Satan. Really, I'm not! I am the *good guy*. I'm your guardian angel, dude. I am trying really hard to give you back a normal life."

"Okay cop, you had your say, now listen to me. I love her body and soul, and even if you kill me dead for that, the flames in my heart will set my coffin on fire."

She burst into tears. "Oh God, my God, that's the most beautiful thing anyone has ever said to me."

"You kids are sick, okay?" Portillo snapped. "This would be *mental illness* that I'm eavesdropping on here! You two don't even *speak each other's language*. You had every fair warning! Just remember, when it happens, you *made me* do it. Now try this one on for size, Romeo and Juliet." The phones went dead.

Felix placed his dead phone on the tabletop. "Okay. Situation report. We've got no phones, no passports, no ID and two different intelligence agencies are after us. We can't fly, we can't drive, we can't take a train or a bus. My credit cards are useless now, my bank cards will just track me down, and I guess I've lost my job now. I can't even walk out my own front door. . . . And wow, you don't understand a single word I'm saying. I can tell from that look in your eye. You are completely thrilled."

She put her finger to her lips. Then she took him by the hand.

Apparently, she had a new plan. It involved walking. She wanted to walk to Los Angeles. She knew the words "Los Angeles," and maybe there was somebody there that she knew. This trek would involve crossing half the American continent on foot, but Felix was at peace with that ambition. He really thought he could do it. A lot of people had done it just for the sake of gold nuggets, back in 1849. Women had walked to California just to meet a guy with gold nuggets.

The beautiful part of this scheme was that, after creeping out the window, they really had vanished. The feds might be all over the airports, over everything that mattered, but they didn't care about what didn't matter. Nobody was looking out for dangerous interstate pedestrians.

To pass the time as they walked, she taught him elementary Farsi. The day's first lesson was body parts, because that was all they had handy for pointing. That suited Felix just fine. If anything, this expanded their passionate communion. He was perfectly willing to starve for that, fight for that and die for that. Every form of intercourse between man and woman was fraught with illusion, and the bigger, the better. Every hour that passed was an hour they had not been parted.

They had to sleep rough. Their clothes became filthy. Then, on the tenth day, they got arrested.

She was, of course, an illegal alien, and he had the good sense to talk only Spanish, so of course, he became one as well. The Immigration cops piled them into the bus for the border, but they got two seats together and were able to kiss and hold hands. The other deported wretches even smiled at them.

He realized now that he was sacrificing everything for her: his identity, his citizenship, flag, church, habits, money. . . . Everything, and good riddance. He bit thoughtfully into his wax-papered cheese sandwich. This was the federal bounty distributed to every refugee on the bus, along with an apple, a small carton of homogenized milk, and some carrot chips.

When the protein hit his famished stomach Felix realized that he had gone delirious with joy. He was *growing* by this experience. It had broken every stifling limit within him. His dusty, savage, squalid world was widening drastically.

Giving alms, for instance—before his abject poverty, he'd never understood that alms were holy. Alms were indeed very holy. From now on—as soon as he found a place to sleep, some place that was so wrecked, so torn, so bleeding, that it never asked uncomfortable questions about a plumber—as soon as he became a plumber again, then he'd be giving some alms.

She ate her food, licked her fingers, then fell asleep against him, in the moving bus. He brushed the free hair from her dirty face. She was twenty days older now. "This is a pearl," he said aloud. "This is a pearl by far too rare to be contained within the shell of time and space."

Why had those lines come to him, in such a rush? Had he read them somewhere? Or were those lines his own?

The old cosmonaut and the construction worker dream of Mars

IAN MCDONALD

British author Ian McDonald is an ambitious and daring writer with a wide range and an impressive amount of talent. His first story was published in 1982, and since then he has appeared with some frequency in Interzone, Asimov's Science Fiction, New Worlds, Zenith, Other Edens, Amazing, *and elsewhere. He was nominated for the John W. Campbell Award in 1985, and in 1989 he won the* Locus *"Best First Novel" Award for his novel* Desolation Road. *He won the Philip K. Dick Award in 1992 for his novel* King of Morning, Queen of Day. *His other books include the novels* Out On Blue Six *and* Hearts, Hands and Voices, Terminal Cafe, Sacrifice of Fools, Evolution's Shore, Kirinya, *and two collections of his short fiction,* Empire Dreams *and* Speaking In Tongues. *His stories have appeared in our Eighth through Tenth, Fourteenth through Sixteenth, and Nineteenth Annual Collections. His most recent books are a chapbook novella* Tendeleo's Story, *and a new novel,* Ares Express. *Coming up is another new novel,* Cyberabad. *Born in Manchester, England, in 1960, McDonald has spent most of his life in Northern Ireland, and now lives and works in Belfast. He has a Web site at http://www.lysator.liu.se/~unicorn/mcdonald/.*

In the lyrical story that follows, we learn that sometimes the dream is what counts—no matter how different the dreamers are.

From the summer room he watched the car wind along the road by the bay, and he thought, *They will be bringing the dog.* His pleasure at seeing them all again did a sharp down-turn at that. He did not like the dog. He did not like dogs in general; fawning, attention-seeking things, with a surfeit of bodily fluids, and this dog in particular owned a superabundance of those things. It was a tatty white-and-black urchin with a need for human attention so consuming that once, coming down in the night for a drink of water, he caught it four-square in the middle of the kitchen table, enthusiastically pissing on the tablecloth. It had been lonely. He had scrubbed, steeped, disinfected twice, and said nothing as Paavo and Raisa and Yuri sat around it pouring their coffee and breaking their rolls.

You can no more kick a man's dog than his child. Even for pissing on the table. And Yuri adored the beast.

As he always did when they came on their twice yearly visits, he lit all the house lights so that there should be a welcome as they came across the causeway over the frozen inlet. Last of all were the porch lights, as he stood by the open door in the knifing cold of December and the car turned in the gravel drive, sending its headlight beams washing over him. He could hear the dog barking in the back. It had probably been barking like that all the way from Haapsalu.

Yuri came running in first; then his son and Raisa, beating their hands and stamping their feet. Breath-steamy kisses with the dog leaping up at him, leaping and leaping and leaping until he stove in its ribs with a timely lifted knee.

"The roads bad?"

Paavo lumbered in with the bags.

"Bad enough. Down to thirty this side of Tallinn. Repair budget's probably putting some councillor's kid through university."

"Ah, no budget for anything, these days." He looked out at the setting indigo before closing the porch door on the winter. The silhouettes of the trees across the bay were still discernible, shadows against the infra-blue; low over them, Jupiter rising, and the early stars. Another thing we couldn't afford.

"You can cut the rest, but you have to have infrastructure," Paavo was saying as he moved the bags into the hall.

"Spoken like a good new Russian," the old man said, but Yuri was running ahead of any of them, even the dog.

"Where are they, can I see them?" he called out, questing in at the open door though he knew what room they were in, where they would always remain, that they were always his to look at and marvel over. Grandfather Antti paused in the study doorway, reluctant to break the shell of unalloyed wonder. Yuri stood in the center of the threadbare Kazakh rug, head thrown back, looking up at the models hanging from the ceiling. Revolving slowly, unconsciously; the photographs and certificates and engineering diagrams and artist's impressions spinning around him. Relativity.

The dog scuffled at his heels, horrified that it was missing something. Antti shoved it away with his foot. *Dare break the moment and, Yuri notwithstanding, I will poison you.* Twice a year, summer and winter, was a meager ration of wonder stuff, and its half-life was so short. Years and peers and sophistication would kill that thing you feel, orbiting beneath the models of the ships that should have taken us to Mars.

Yuri stopped.

"That one. That wasn't here before."

"It's new, that's why."

"I can see that. Show me."

Antti pulled over the peeling swivel chair to stand on and unhook the curved delta of aerobody from its fishing line rig.

"What's that bit?"

"That's the fuel processing module. The idea was that it would go down first, maybe even six months before, and manufacture the fuel for the return trip."

"An empty tank mission."

"Empty tanks." The boy had the language. "That's right."

Yuri turned the aerodynamic plastic wedge over in his hands, stopped at a hieroglyph in curvilinear blue.

"This isn't Russian," he pronounced. "I know this sign. That says NASA. But I don't know this bit." A line of red, alien letters above the noble blue insignia.

"It says 'Astrodyne Systems MOREL 2'."

"An American ship."

"I have friends in America. I send them mine, they send me theirs. We're all the same, really."

"They didn't get there either."

"No, they left it too late. Do you know what they ask for most? The Americans?" He nodded Yuri to the disk of embroidered fabric, insignificant among the prints and plans of the boosters and orbiters. Vorontsev, Nitin, Rozdevshensky, Selkokari: *Novy Mir*. And the date, so many decades ago he could not believe the hubris of those who had planned to send men to another world. Another Russia, then. "I'll never let them have it. A photograph, that's what they'll get. At least we made it to the pad."

The hatch-dog spinning. The gloved hand reaching in: the thick, black glove. The glove, the hand that should not have been there. The gold-plated audio jacks pulling free from the helmet sockets, dangling on their glossy black wire coils. Commander Rozdevshensky hitting his chest release and surging up from his restraint straps—slowly, so slowly—as the white digits on the countdown timer remained forever frozen between the flip and flop. Better to die that way. Better by far than to be talked to death by pragmatists and right Christians.

And it still hurt, by God, still brought that involuntary twitch to the corners of the mouth. Thirty-five years since the light of a Kazakhstan morning flooded through the hatch into the capsule, the hatch that should have opened on another light altogether. Scrap now. Plumbing in the Presidential palaces of new Republics. Pig sheds. He had heard that one of the preignition pumps had turned up as a vodka still. New Russia. Dismembered. But in this shrine to a lost space age deep in Baltic winter, ATOM 12 still stood as he remembered her that morning as they drove across the steppe, high and lovely and unbelievably white. Its model in the corner by the curtained window towered over Yuri. *Towers over us all*, his grandfather thought. *We are never out of its shadow, the rocket that would have taken Antti Selkokari, Cosmonaut, to Mars.*

The holy woman has been in the tomb five days now and the crowds are gathering again. Most are there to witness a miracle, a triumph of faith and will. They are easy to spot: many wear the sadhu's unbraided hair and go flagrantly naked, skin daubed with holy ash. Spirit clad. Some practice asceticism; burning cones of incense on their skin, driving hooks through folds of flesh, tongue, eyelids. One man walks around for the admiration of the crowd, his right arm held aloft by a devotee declaring that the sadhu had held his arm fifteen years thus in asceticism. Fifteen years! The arm is withered as a stick in a drought. It will never bend again. The joints are fused, locked. The holy man s eyes glare spiritual challenge at the crowds thronging the station approach. See what I do: who in this corrupt century dares attempt such practice to sever soul from flesh?

This corrupt century has surer and swifter ways to samadhi, Ashwin thinks, smiling to himself, as he joins the queue for holy breakfast. He has done this every morning since the sacred woman's coffin was sealed, lowered into the dusty grave, and buried. Behind him, a band tootles. Off-shift jitneys and money-kids on biomotor scooters dart around the musicians. The sky is already that flat, dusty steel blue of the most ferociously hot days; the sun a savage copper atom. Ashwin thanks whatever gods mind buried women for the air-conditioning of the cyber-*mahals* of Chandigarh. The line shuffles forward, toward the shade of the tent where Ashwin can make out the bobbing, nodding head of the benefactor; a *datarajah*: grown sleek on the global market's hunger for cheap IT labor. His expiation: a pile of chapattis and a pot of *daal*.

Ashwin reaches the folding deal table where the alms are bestowed. The old man bows to him in blessing, an assistant hands him a chapati. Ashwin cannot but notice the barrier gloves. He looks a moment at the bowed head of the rich man, the saffron mark on the forehead, the simple white robes. *Are you the one whose machines split my mind from my body and send it across the solar system?* A nudge moves him on.

"How long?" Ashwin asks the man at the end of the row of tables, whose job seems to be to keep the beneficiaries moving. He nods to the richly patterned cloth draped over the pile.

"Looking like today," the minder says.

By the time Ashwin reaches the station, he has finished the holy breakfast. With each step up, the sound from within increases until it seems as solid as the four-hundred-year-old Raj-brick walls. Hand-scrawled signs apologize again for the delay in final construction of the nano-carbon diamond train shed. Labor shortages. More money to be made, *out there*. The spars of the half-completed dome reach over the crumbling station like a hunting hawk's claws, stooping. Beneath them, legions of shift workers clash on the platforms, merge, flow through each, separate, neither the victor. Clocking on, clocking off. Families camped on the platforms make meals, wipe children, tend elders. Water sellers clack bronze water cups, newsplug hawkers hold up five fingers full of the days' headlines; wallahs lift baskets of guavas and mangoes; battered tin trays of samosas and nimki; paper-wrapped pokes of *channa*. Buy eat buy eat. Ashwin half-hears an announcement, half-glimpses a platform change on a hovering roll-screen, then is almost carried off his feet as a thousand people move as one. *Out there*, a sleek little electric commuter train slides stealthily into its platform. He makes it as the doors close, dodges the Sikh packer who would seize him by collar and seat of pants and wedge him between that oily man with the big mustache and that girl in the suddenly self-consciously short skirt. Ashwin swings into the gap between carriages:

hands reach down, pull him up the ladder as the fast little train begins to accelerate.

The inside monthly ticket has gone up again.

Roof-riders shuffle aside for Ashwin as the train pulls out of the cracked dome of Kharar station. He grips tight as the carriage lurches over points. If you slide down between the carriages, there is no hope. But it is cheap, and the air is fresher than the hot spew pushed around by the carriage ventilators. From his high seat, it seems to Ashwin that even in one night the slum *chawls* have divided and grown denser again, like bacteria doubling, in a sample dish. They seem to shoulder closer to the line. *Chawl* life as a series of snapshots. *Flash*: a dirty little urchin girl, wide-eyed at the wonderful train, one hand in her mouth, the other held up in salutation. Hello hello hello . . . *Flash*: three men in dhotis drag the corpse of a pickup on frayed nylon ropes, like an ox hauled to the slaughter. *Flash*: two barefoot women push a water-barrow, leaning hard into the shafts to shift the heavy leaking plastic barrel. *Flash*: a leathery old man angles a solar umbrella into the best light to power his sewing machine. *Flash*: A skeletal yellow cow stares dully at the level crossing, unfazed by the train hurtling past its nose. Don't test your sacred status this morning. Panjab Rapid Transit respects you not.

Ashwin thinks of his own tenaciously held few rooms, the roof garden where his mother tends a small urban farm, the balcony; his father's pride, the mark of a man, a place where he may entertain his friends, read the paper of a morning, watch the satellite sports of an evening. But a proper house; no slum, no cardboard shanty, no. So proud they are. He thinks of the world he will build that day, the homes and towns they will design beneath the glass sky. Cities. Hundreds of cities; cities built for people, with districts where everyone knows your name and open spaces where you can meet and talk and markets where you can buy goods from two worlds and then a cup of coffee in a bar where you may watch sports. Cities big enough to be thrilling, small enough to be intimate. And *chawls*? Ashwin looks at the sprawling degradation with a new eye. Yes, chawls! *Of course chawls!* Where there are people, there will always be the cities we build for ourselves, out of our deepest needs, not given by those who tell us how we should live. Human cities. He imagines the people of Old Kharar and Basi and Kurali flocking from their hovels, along the sewage-seeping lanes to the roads, to the rail, south, ever south, to the girdle of space elevators ringing the world's waist. He sees them flowing up those spun-diamond towers, sailing across space in colossal arks, whole families together. He imagines them coming down the hundred thousand pier-towers, spreading out under his glass roof across the virgin grasslands, taking the things they find and building from them their homes.

A sudden slam of sound and air and movement jars him out of his dreams. Ashwin slides on his tender perch, grabs, finds human bodies. Hands seize him, steady him. The 07:00 Jullundur express hurtles past on the main line, a blurred streak of steel and windows and speed. Ashwin laughs. And trains. Of course trains. The only practical transport. No plane can operate in the cold, primeval atmosphere beyond the roof, and none but a fool or a sparrow would fly inside a glass house. Trains, then. Already, he has heard, engineers are designing fusion-powered juggernauts the size of city blocks riding tracks wide as a house. Grand journeys they shall go on; not gritty little commuter runs, but voyages across whole continents. Those who ride up on the roofs of these titans will see entire landscapes unfolding before their eyes, new vistas, geographies; new worlds that have never felt the foot of man.

When the fast train slams past, Ashwin always looks forward for the first glints from the towers of Chandigarh through the smog haze. Ghost cities in the mist. The Cybermahals of the Indian Tiger. Curving scimitars of construction crystal, minarets of spun titanium and glass, curtain walls of solar tiling, battlements half a kilometer above the *chawl* sprawl of the Panjab. Ashwin seeks particularly the golden glint of the huge solar disk that fronts the Ambedkar tower, the vanity of *corporada* architecture but also the device that will spin his mind, his perceptions, his abilities, across the solar system to that new world. Ashwin thinks again of the holy woman by the station, buried in dirt. Can you promise them anything like this? Or is it all internal, all for the next world? There is the next world, hanging up there. All you have to do is look. A promise, a lure. A world of your own. Your Mars. For how many years had the disciple lifted his own arm, uncomplainingly, unnoticed, to bear aloft his master's?

Then cutting walls seal off the vision as the overburdened little commuter train dives into the approach tunnel to Chandigarh station.

The others were asleep now, and the house was quiet and dark. A time for men. A time for father and son. They sat by the fire in the drawing room. Burning wood gave the only light. Paavo had brought a bottle of good vodka: Polish, none of that Russian dung. The dog lay at his feet, but it did not lie easily. Every creak, every click of the geriatric heating, every pop of the fire roused it: enemy/interest/ attention. *Lie at peace like a proper dog*, Antti thought. *Proper dogs trust their masters.*

The long, bad winter drive had drained Paavo; it did not take much vodka, Polish or not, to bring him to the point where he could speak the truth. He lifted his glass, turned it to catch the light from the fire, send its rays into his eyes, his soul of souls.

"I thought twice about bringing Yuri with us this time."

A brief knurl of cold in Antti's chest. Cold of winter, cold of space. Cold of an old man alone in a wooden house by the sea.

"Why would you do that?"

Paavo shifted uncomfortably in his chair. The bloody dog started.

"He has exams."

"I thought he was doing well at school."

"He is. He is. Just . . ."

"Not at the right subjects."

"His science grades have been dropping."

Antti eyed the bottle, thought the Polish vodka made what he had to say next slip out so much more easily.

"So, why should he not come to see me for New Year? I'm a scientist. Scientist first class. I've got the medal, from Comrade Kosygin himself. I could help him with his grades." He waved down any interruption Paavo might make. "I know, I know. It's the wrong kind of science. Space travel. Stars, galaxies, planets. Missions to Mars. Old science. Wrong science. Not the kind you can make money from. Not technology. Not computers." The dog was edgy now, sensing an arousal beyond its primeval levels of reaction and response. Its velvet mongrel ears lifted. "All that time and research and effort and money to send men to Mars, and how many people get to go? Four men. All that money and time and effort. And the stars? Impossible! The universe is too big for us. Let's explore inner space instead. Cyberspace. Everyone can go there. All you need is a computer. And look at the wonders you find there! All those wonderful things you can buy, if you have the money. All those beautiful women who want you to look at them having sex with donkeys or drinking each other's piss. If you have the money. All the famous people; you can find out about their lives and their clothes and what they eat and how they make love, but you can never ever be like them. Reach the stars? Impossible."

He snatched up the bottle. Surprised, the dog gave a little grizzle. *And you,* the old man thought at it.

"Are you finished?" Paavo asked.

"No, not nearly; I've hardly even begun."

"Well, when you're done, give me a shot of that and I'll show you something."

Antti handed the bottle through the firelight. Paavo poured, and the two men drank in silence, one too proud to admit his hurt, the other to apologize. *When you were Yuri's age, on such a night as this we went out through those French windows into the gardens and named the winter constellations together,* Antti thought. *I saw you look up. I saw their light in your eyes. I have always respected your work, even if I haven't always comprehended it, and if I am scornful, if I am critical and bitter, it is because, like my ATOM project, there, too, a great promise has been betrayed. Buy things. Look at things. The constellations in this cyberspace have no shine, no wonder. They are shaped like Coke logos and Nike swooshes. There is no sparkle in them to catch in your eye. They don't call you outward from home.*

Now Paavo was taking a flat case from his bag beside his chair. He set it on his lap, unfolded it. Blue screen light illuminated his face.

"This is the thing you wanted to show me?" Antti asked. "Another laptop."

"No," Paavo said carefully. "Not another laptop. You were saying about the universe being too big for us? No, it's not. I've got it right in here." He tapped the translucent blue polycarbonate casing. "I've got them all in here. Infinite universes, in one small box."

"You got it to work, then."

The son nodded.

"If Einstein couldn't get his head around quantum theory, I don't imagine that I ever will," Antti said, realizing as the words left him how mealy they sounded. "This quantum computing: calculations being made simultaneously in thousands of parallel universes, each as real as this room, as us, that dog. . . ."

Other rooms, like reflections of reflections. Mirror in mirror. Other worlds.

One where the crew of *Novy Mir* were not pulled from the capsule at T-minus-seven because the booster, the ATOM mission, the entire Mars project had been so rotten with corruption and creaming-off that safety standards had been squandered.

The moment you went for throttle-up, the fuel lines would have ruptured, Launch Controller Barsamian had said as the army transporter sped away from the launch site, the summer dust pluming up behind it. *The call came through from Kirilenko. The whole thing is rotten. Rotten to the heart. It always was. A quick, cheap fix.*

He had glanced back through the window at the great white tower on the scorched steppe and thought, *Was there a chance it could have flown, or had it been quick and cheap and botched from the start? All a feint in the game with the Americans?*

In another world, the word did not come from Kirilenko in time. They went for throttle-up. It blew.

In another universe, they went for throttle-up. It flew. It flew right off this world, on to another. They came burning down in an arc of fire clear across Amazonis Planitia and the calderas of Elysium. Ten kilometers above Isidia Planitia the descent stage fired. They came down in fire and steam in the crater shadow of Nili Patera. The hammer and sickle of the Union of Soviet Socialist Republics was stabbed into the regolith and unfurled in the winds of Syrtis Major.

Somewhere in that thin plastic case, that possibility existed.

"Can I see it?"

Paavo gave a shrug of assent. Antti lifted the plastic shell as if what it held were terribly terribly fragile. It was lighter than he had imagined.

"All these . . ."

Paavo smiled. Antti turned the screen toward him, angled it to make sense and shape out of the plasma film screen. A brief frown of disappointment: the display was a standard operating system interface. But its pristine touch pads, white as milk teeth, called his fingers to type. *Test us if we speak the truth.*

"I feel I should ask it something."

"It's not an oracle. It's just a computer."

"All the same . . ."

"It's still garbage in, garbage out in every universe." The coals collapsed, sending up a spear of flame, and the dog started, and they were two men together with the mad cold outside the window. "If it were an oracle, if it could send one question out into all universes and all times, what would you ask?"

Paavo saw his father smile, then think, then the light from the surge of fire fade from his face. Slowly, deliberately, with winter-stiff fingers, not wanting to get one holy word wrong, Antti began to type.

The locker rooms are all numbered and work in strict rotation. Fifteen hundred workers off-shifting as the next battalion shift on would clash like Vedic armies in the corridors and changing rooms, so they are channeled into separate sectors. Ashwin always imagines he can feel the drub of feet through the carbon steel skeleton of the tower. Likewise, though he never met his shift predecessor, Ashwin knows the heat and particular perfume of his body (irrefutably a *his*) from the imprint on the live-leather transfer seat.

Men here, women there. Shirt on this peg. Shoes on that shelf. Pants here. Always folded, neatly folded. A gentleman looks after his clothes. A nod, a word to the number up and the number down and the number across as he changes into the simple white coverall. Sometimes, in the transfer, the body forgets itself; a soiling, a leaking, at least, a drooling. As ever, the papery thing catches at the crotch. Ready. Fifteen hundred locker doors clatter shut, ranked and filed. People moving; always moving, along streets, down platform, onto trains, into rooms, down plastic clad corridors, moving together, a herd of bodies under the utilitarian strip light.

He nods to his fellow on-shifters. He does not confuse them with workmates anymore. Once you get in that chair, they can send you anywhere. The thin Sikh man next him could work an entire quartersphere away. His own closest workmate is a black man from Senegal. Ashwin carries, he bolts.

But the room catches him, every time. He flies heavy-lift rosettes through the staggering canyon lands of Valles Marineris, but a thousand black-chairs, row upon row, all facing in the same direction, is awe-full.

As ever, the air hums to barely audible mantras to relax the on-workers and set the brain-wave patterns ready for the transfer. The scent is mood blue. Ashwin has come to hate that stink up his nose. He finds his seat, twenty along by thirty-five deep. Still warm. He knows its every creak as he lowers himself onto the skin. A nod to the Sikh, mumbling a prayer to himself. Ashwin lies back, stretches. The sensory array arms unfold over his face like a mantis over her husband.

A start, something, down at the foot of the room. A noise raised over the mantra-wash; wailing, animal noise. Ashwin props himself up, the machine arms with their eyecups and earplugs and skull taps scurry away. Thrashing: something is spasming its couch. Attendants come running through the rows of transfer couches, screening the sight with their bodies, but the fear has rippled out to every corner of the huge room.

The technology is safe, they said. *Tested, tried, true, safe. You need have no fear. We are paying for your soul, but nothing will go wrong.*

But things go wrong. Things have always gone wrong. The ones who settled under the skull-tap probes and went into seizures. The ones who built up an allergic response to the nanoprocessors. The ones who, like this one, come out in pieces, broken in the head. The ones, they rumor, who never come out at all. Who go *somewhere else.*

Ashwin watches the electric gurney weave its load back between the couches. Nothing to see here, nothing's happened, everything will be fine, go about your work, you have great work to do today, great work. And Ashwin feels part of him saying, yes, yes to the blandishments of the company medics and he knows that part is the pretransfer drugs suffusing up through the skin of the seat, through his own skin, into his blood. Let go. All is illusion: mind, body . . . illusion. Free your mind. Let us park your body. Go. Commute.

Soft bioplastic fingers unfold over Ashwin. Eyecups press over his sockets: A moment's panic as the plugs seek out the contours of his inner ears and fill them.

The breathing tubes worm down his nostrils, into his lungs. The drip-feed needles and blood scrubbers are busy at his wrists. Last of all, the taps caress his skull as the nanoprocessors swarm through the cranium into his selfhood and wrench it away from him.

But another Ashwin, one the drugs and tiny skull machines cannot touch, shouts through the drugs and the seethe of nanomachines, the sweat-reek of the workroom, the corporada mantra-blur. What kind of world? What kind of Mars, you asked yourself, up on the roof, riding with the poor men like the poor man you are? That kind of Mars, where poor men are taken away quietly on a cart, where there is no fuss, no mess, nothing to spoil the *corporada* image. You think your people will ever ride on the roof of those great fusion-power expresses? There will never be enough cars on the space-elevator, there will never be enough berths in the transplanetary ships, enough lovely, habitable cities for all the poor of Chandigarh and the Punjab and all of Bharat, let alone the children they squeeze into being every second of every day. Rich men build a rich world. You go to construct a golf course in the sky. A country club for the *datarajahs*.

Then that Ashwin is snuffed out, and there is the black of light-speed for a time the mind cannot clock. And after that instant: light, mass, sensation, existence. A world. His world. Ashwin Mehta has arrived on Mars.

The old man came down the stairs sniffing. No salty tang of mongrel urine in the porch. He threw back the heavy night curtains. The outer windows were leafy with frost. No taint in the hall. In the study the splendid erection of ATOM 12 was undefiled; a natural challenge to a dog. Why did he always forget to close the door when that thing came to call? Nothing and no one to close them on, most of the time. The living room smelled of vodka and gentle sweat, but no taint of piss. The fire had burned down to gray charcoals. New morning now. Antti wrenched open the curtains, admitting watery, destroying light into every part of the room. He waved clear a circle in the frosted mist inside the window. Real mist beyond, moving slowly across the frozen bay. The sun was high and wan, seeming to dash and veer through the upper streamers of the fog. If it were a morning hoar, it would boil off, but the speed with which the trees on Kuresaari Island were fading hinted at an inversion layer forming out at the limit of the pack ice. They could lie out there for days. Weeks, in a stable winter anticyclone. Breath steaming, Antti watched the ice crystals reform and close as cold coils of fog hastened across the ice to swaddle the wooden house.

In the unsympathetic morning light, the oracle-machine was just a wafer of translucent aquamarine plastic. No more wisdom than a credit card. Wincing at the foolishness of old men and firelight and vodka, Antti slipped open the lid. Still there from the night before. He had forgotten to shut the program down. So clever, and yet too stupid to think of doing it itself.

WHAT WILL HAPPEN TO MY DREAM OF MARS?

Dining room unsullied. Dining table polished and perfect. Table linen pure and unpolluted. Kitchen. And there it was, one paw in a shallow lagoon of cold, orange piss, proudly wagging its tail.

"Hiii! Hutt! Hutt! Hutt! Out with you, pissing beast! Go on, out, out, away with you."

The thing had a terrible temper, but the wrath of old men is swift and fearless. The vile thing was bundled out the back door before it could open its jaw. It stood there, grubby white on the white, stunned by the suddenness of the cold. Antti bent to the undersink cupboard to fetch cleaner and cloths and disinfectant before young feet in search of cereals came skidding through the amber slick. It was crying now, a kind of sobbing keen that made Antti despise it all the more. *Learn Darwin*, he thought as he went down on his knees to the crusted piss.

Only when he heard Yuri's voice from outside did Antti realize he had not heard the dog's yip for some minutes now. He ran to the door to scold Yuri about silly boys who went rushing out into the cold not properly dressed. He listened. Yuri's voice was getting farther away. He was out on the ice.

"Bloody cur!" Antti cursed. He dashed down the back path as fast as his years and the winter would let him.

"Yuri!"

The boy was farther even than he had feared, calling into the white fog that came weaving thicker every moment through the trees across the inlet.

"Yuri!"

Come back, oh, come back now, don't let this be the moment when you decide that everything old men say is stupid and you can safely disregard them.

"Yuri!"

The boy stopped, on the edge of melting into the white and white.

"Come back, come on back. It's not safe; you can't see a foot in front of you in this fog, and the ice can still be rotten."

"But my dog . . ."

"Come back to the house." He saw the boy look back to the dimensionless white of the closing fog and knew what he must offer to buy his safety. "I'll go look for him. You go on back. It'll be all right."

Hunting through the drawer of the study desk, Antti looked at his private space fleet and shivered. *Venture into the unknown. The alien on your doorstep.* He found his mission training compass. *It saw me through Kamchatka, it won't let me down within sight of my own back door.* Outside, the cold was paralyzing. Antti took a bearing on the house and went down to the edge of the ice. Pebbles grated beneath his booted feet. And he was *there*. The door opening, everyone waiting for that first crack of light, that pale slit widening into a wedge, a rectangle of illumination, beyond which lay a new world. Cranking down the ladder, everyone getting into proper order in the lock as narrow as a birth canal; bulking in their excursion suits, rehearsing their lines. Rozdevshensky first, then him, last Nitin. The top of Rozdevshensky's helmet vanishing over the platform. Rozdevshensky down, a breath—more a sigh—on the helmet intercoms. Then him, lumbering out backward, clumsy as a spring-woken bear. Looking at the strangely lit metal, until the crunch of stones under his booted feet. *You're down. Now, you can turn and look. How it would have been. Should have been.*

Antti Selkokari stepped out onto the frozen world.

Within twenty paces, the house was a ghost. Another ten, and it was gone. Antti was embedded in white from the surface of his skin to infinity. He looked around, suddenly cold and fearful in the knowledge that he had let his need to be admired by his grandson push him into folly. Pale fronds of trees swam momentarily through the nothing. He checked the compass. It pointed true. It pointed home. He struck out into the mist.

"Hiii! Hey! Here, boy!" he called. "Come on, where are you, you stupid mutt?"

No sign, no sound. He half-hoped that it was drowned already. It would wash up with the thaw, recognizable only by its blue plastic webbing collar. Thing-that-was-a-dog. Let it go. *Your kitchen is warm, there is coffee, and you are no Mars explorer. Anything lost in this is dead.*

But Yuri, he told himself. *How can I tell him this and retain any honor?*

Another reading on the compass, another tentative shuffle forward into the featureless white. Every footfall a test. *Will it bear me. Is it rotten to its blue heart?*

On Mars, there are craters silted so full of dust they cannot be seen on the surface. They wait, drowning traps of red, like buried ant-lions.

Lost in remembrance, Antti realized with a shock of cold that he had been walking without thought. He flipped open the compass. The needle was spinning, swinging wildly from point to point, hunting for home and unable to find it.

Antti Selkokari tapped the compass.

Still the needle swung.

He closed the compass, opened it again, hit it with the heel of his hand, held it upside down, shook it, shook it like he would a dog that had pissed on his dining table, pressed it up to his ear as if it might tell him the reason for its betrayal. Still, it lied. It would not tell the way home. Antti was lost. The ice held no footprints, no track back.

"Hello!" Antti shouted. "Hello! Can you hear me!"

The ice fog took his words, smeared them, returned them as whispering echoes. Echoes. Nothing in this dimensionlessness should echo.

"Hello!"

Hello hello hello hellooo hellllooooo said the echoes, in voices not his, that did not die away, but whispered on, into a mumble of conversations half heard, from another room, another universe.

Hello?

Against sense, Antti spun toward the voice so clear behind him.

Is anyone there? Who is that?

The voice was at once out there in the white and inside his head, speaking in his own Estonian and another language he did not recognize.

"Who is this?" Antti asked, and heard his own voice speak in two places, two languages, two worlds. He frowned, a thickening of the fog, a curdling of the white, a solidity, a shape. A shadow, moving toward him across the ice plain. The white swirled, and a man walked out of it.

White on gold. A line, a crack. Peer into it: a sliver of eye, a line of cheek, the corner of a lip. A face under the gold. Pull out: the crack is a hairbreadth in a curve of gold: another step's remove, and the golden arc is the laminated visor of a pressure-suit helmet. Reflected in the visor, a landscape curved like an image in a state fair hall of mirrors. Where visor seals to helmet, the golden landscape curves away to nothing. There are hills mirrored here on either side; they slide off into nothingness, the mere suggestion of altitude. Optical lies: in truth, they are vast rim-walls, kilometers high. This same distortion gives undue prominence to the objects at the center of the field of vision. Immediate foreground: an insectlike vehicle, spiky with antennae, huge balloon wheels at the end of each of the six sprung legs. Behind it, a squat brick structure, incongruously like a Hopi pueblo, down to the satellite dish on the flat roof. Its location only adds to the likeness: a wide, dry plain of wind-eroded stones. Beyond, and dwarfing the little adobe home, a hovering saucer, keeping its station a handful of meters above the ground with twitches of its nacelle-mounted fans. The distortion of the reflection thrusts the logo on the aircraft's nose into focus: ROTECH. It has colleagues, they hold tight formation across the valley floor as far as the visor reflections allow seeing. And beyond the flotilla of airships, and dwarfing them as they dwarf the house, the house the vehicle, the vehicle the man, the man the scratch etched by some accident in his helmet visor, the pillar. It is surely stupendous. It is buttressed like the roots of a rain-forest tree: tiny flakes of dirt cling to them. There are other pueblos, hanging from the lower slopes, insignificant as grains of salt. An airship drifts across the sheer face of the tower. It is tiny and bright as a five *pice* coin. Follow the huge structure up until it curves away off the edge of the visor. Look beyond: like the airships, this pillar is one of a mass. The floor of this vast canyon is forested with thousands of pillars, three kilometers high.

Pull out again, in a long, astronomical-scale zoom. The pressure-suited figure is just one of many, human and machine. The machines outnumber the humans in number and variety. The valley floor is a hive of machine species. There are high-stepping nanofacturing robots, pausing to stab proboscises into the surface and release swarms of nanoassemblers. There are surveying machines, exchanging heliographs of laser light. There are great orange worm machines, burrowing deep in the regolith, chewing dead red rock into pumice. There are planters and fermentories—great, slow, sessile things—gulping in carbon dioxide atmosphere by the ton and reacting it with water and wan sunlight into organic matter. Living stuff. The stuff of worlds. There are the fleets of heavy-lift LTAs—the man in the suit is marshaling them on some precision maneuver—and smaller, nimbler skycraft, zipping between the big slow dirigibles on their priority missions. There are track layers and road builders and brick makers and patient little spider machines that mortar them into the neat adobes for the humans. There are machines that build machines and machines that service machines and machines that program machines and machines that repair machines and everywhere is the green circle logo and sigil of ROTECH. Remote Orbital Terraform and Environmental Control Headquarters. Swarming machine life calls green out of the red; tentative, fragile plantations of gene-tweak grasses and mosses. Beneath human perceptions, the cleverest, the most important machines, the nanoassemblers, fuse red sand into silicon pillar. On the scale of planets, other hives of machines extend primeval run-water channels into canals to carry water from the thawing north pole to the terraformed lands of Grand Valley. A flash of light: eighty kilometers up in low, fast orbit, a vana, a spinning mirror of silver polymer, frail as a hope, rolls its focus on to its true target; the northern polar cap. The scale of the work in this four-thousand kilometer rift valley only becomes apparent at this kind of altitude. To the northwest the forest of towers rise above our ascending point of view. Their tops open out into branches, those branches into twigs, bare, waiting. To the east the towers are still growing, one kilometer, two kilometers. Farther east still, trillions of assemblers swarming in the subsoil are pushing the great root-buttresses out of chaotic mesa-lands of Eos and Capri. The wave of construction passes down the chasm like a slow, silicon spring. Another glitter of light, not from an orbital mirror this time, but sun catching the edge of the world roof, five kilometers above the wind-shaved hills of Coprates. Above it now, climbing fast. The world roof flows from the east like a river of glass that falls into red emptiness.

How to terraform Mars. Easy. Stick a roof over Valles Marineris. Real greenhouse effect. By the time it is complete, it will be visible from Earth, a bright white mote in the eye of the ancient red war god.

Higher now, past the littler, lower moon. Keeping precise pace with it on the other side of the planet is the SkyWheel, the spinning ground-to-orbit space-cable. All the humans, all the machines that build the bases and plants and the machines, were spun down this cable. But the real work of terraforming, the RO in the ROTECH, is done from orbit. Up beyond the vanas and the supercores, weaving a magnetic cocoon around this tectonically dead, defenseless world, are the orbital habitats and factories and mass drivers of the planetary engineers and terraformers. By the time humans can walk unclad under the Grand Valley roof, they will form a ring around the planet, a band of satellites. The night will glitter with them.

All in a construction worker's visor; reflected.

Ashwin Mehta edges the heavy-lift flotilla in over the construction site. His belly sensors and satellite uplinks to ROTECH's moon ring redoubt could guide him in with laser precision but human atavism endures. The gloved hands wave him down, and he follows. Spinners skitter clear. The winds that howl the full length of the rift valley have buried the load with sand: Ashwin's trim-fans sweep it clear as he maneuvers with millimeter precision. He feels the lift cables go out of him: it is a physical, pleasurable sensation but not one for which his flesh body has an analogue.

Despite Bharat trumpeting the largest IT skill pool on the planet, Ashwin knows that he and every other body on its live-skin couch only got there because of strong body mapping. It still took him many shifts to feel his way into a new, weightless body to which modules could be added or swapped. His hands and arms are obviously the wiry little manipulators—though no human arm ever experienced the sensation of detaching itself and swinging, hand-over-hand to a new attachment point elsewhere on the body. His legs he regards as the fan-pods, his lungs the lift bags and the curved silver shell his body, the center of his being. The slave units, hooked up according to work schedule, were more difficult, but he has learned a way; he expands his sense of self to incorporate them. *I am vast, I contain multitudes.* It still takes some minutes after the computers flick him home at light-speed to snap out of three-hundred-sixty-degree vision. The rabbit-eye sight of his hundreds of optical sensors has taught Ashwin truths about how body shapes consciousness. The universe of meat is divided rigidly into front and back, visible and invisible. Objects are sought out, selected, made part of the view. Morphology begets psychology. Ashwin, like a divinity, sees everywhere at once. There is no forward or backward, up or down, just movement toward a destination or away from it.

It is this aspect of his job that he finds hardest to tell others. His parents nod and say how good it is that he has employment and good steady money but they do not comprehend what he is doing up there, let alone how he feels doing it. They are one generation away from believing that gods live in the sky. He does not want to tell them that, in a sense, they do. The girls are a little more sophisticated; they know about other planets and terraforming. *Mars! How exciting! How romantic! Is it really really dangerous? Do you face sandstorms and explosions and volcanoes?* Telling them that Mars is a quiet, placid sort of place, where what action there ever was happened billions of years ago, is not what they want to hear but they have passed on anyway, for these women also know what kind of work the *corporadas* hire for, and how little it pays.

He feels locked. The cable grippers bind molecule to molecule with the lift points. *Ready*, Ashwin says. Coprates control whispers clearance in his inner ear: the site foreman waves her hand. Take her up. Fans swivel to full lift. Winches wind in the strain. Flicker-lasers torch up: these loads require every gram of lift. Ashwin feels motor/muscles tense, strut-bones strain. He mentally grits his teeth. *You are a weight lifter, going for the clean lift.*

The rosette of twelve linked LTAs pulls the five-hundred-meter diameter glass hexagon clear from the sand. Ashwin lifts straight for a hundred meters, then tilts the whole array from side to side to clear it of lingering dust and dead glass-weavers. Gently, gently. The glass is engineered to tolerances far beyond terrestrial norms, and the gravity slight, but one crack, three kilometers up. . . . Tiny crystal shells cascade from the edges of the roof pane like iridescent snow. The great glass light heliographs in the sun. The forewoman raises an arm in salute as Ashwin gains cruising altitude. It is a sight he never tires of, this resurrection of glass from the earth. Two kilometers up, bearing 5.3 pi rad, Pier 112, 328. Pane 662, 259.

Telephone number engineering.

Beneath him graders are leveling billion-year-old outwash hills for new glass fields. Ahead, the buried panes are stains in the sand, a mesh of linked hexagons. Tiny machines, working, working. Ashwin reflects a moment on the incomplete dome of Kharar railway station, then a proximity alert gently chides him: Heavy Lift Array 2238 is on approach to pick up. Day and night the LTAs carry and set, busy and sterile as drone bees.

In the air lane now. The lifters move in strictly regulated traffic zones over cleared terrain. There has not been an accidental drop since Ashwin started on the job, but a five-hundred hexagon of fifty-centimeter glass falling from three kays is the stuff of health and safety legend. HLA 1956 comes up from the glass fields of Cander and slips in ahead of Ashwin: a colleague, though Ashwin has never seen his flesh face, nor knows where his meat is based. He sends a greeting message over the com channels; truckers flashing their headlights. Closing on the target now. The front edge of the construction is visible as a line of white light. Ashwin has never seen the sea, but he always thinks of the edge of the world roof as a line of surf breaking on a beach, frozen, turned to slow-flowing glass, inching forward day by day, hour by hour. One kilometer out, construction control taps into Ashwin's neural matrix and dispatches him and his load into an approach pattern to Pier 112, 328. As he moves in high over the open fingers of the Main Left Branch, he sees another heavy-lift cluster retract cables and slide away from the pier top. Spider-welders skitter across the glass on delicate sucker feet to bolt the plate to the struts. That is what Ashwin's friend from Senegal does: Ashwin can see his spider-welder hugging the pure white spar like a tick as he swivels the rig on its belly fans. They earn more than lifter pilots. They have more responsibility.

Lasers flicker from all around Ashwin's multiple body—another sensation for which his meat has no likeness—guiding him in onto the baffle plates. The alignment must be millimeter perfect. Ashwin tunes the ducted fans to compensate for an unseasonable breeze he can feel picking up across his sensory skin, descends steadily through the mesh of laser light. Thirty meters. Twenty.

Looking good, Ash, says the bolter from Senegal on the innercom.

Ten meters.

Looking good. A simple expression of solidarity, but it opens Ashwin's extended senses like a key. From skin to horizon in every direction he can look, his world rushes in on him. He sees it all fresh, entire, as one thing. The stupendous canyon, one end to the other, wall to wall. The thin pink sky, the wisps of high cirrus. The surface three kilometers beneath him; the constructions of man, the patterns they make on the soil as they fuse sand to glass. The machines: those above, those below, those between, that crawl upon the pillars and roof of the world. The SkyWheel on its ponderous orbits, ROTECH's habitats wheeling overhead in a carousel of satellites. The men and minds that looked on this world, and set their will upon it. He sees it all, and it looks good to him. Very good indeed. He is so proud of all that he is part of, this Bharati boy one foot out of the *chawl*, who is become Creator of Worlds.

Five meters.

And in that instant, everything goes white. . . .

Is this what it is to be dead? he thinks and thinking so, knows himself to be alive. An image: the holy woman, buried alive for righteousness' sake. Real? Imaginary? Is the darkness of the grave really a white so intense it cannot be regarded by the eye? Is there any difference between outside and inside in this featureless white? A freezing thought. This is the pure white light of cyberspace. There has been an error in the mindlink, a fault in the tap-head technology. The kind of thing that sends some people thrashing and fitting on their couches. You, it has sent into nowhere. No thing. A mind without a body.

He cannot tell if he has flesh perception or machine sense: everything in every direction looks the same and therefore robs him of dimension. An uncle driven blind by cataracts once told him the horror of blindness. It is not not seeing. It is everything white.

A mind, with no senses, no connection to the outside world. He could be lying on his couch at the Ambedkar *corporada*, in a hospital, at home. A mind with only its own thoughts for company. A thought to make the heart kick coldly in the chest. At least, he can still feel. And if he can feel . . .

"Hello?" Ashwin ventures. He can hear himself. His own voice, inside, and outside. "Hello? Can anyone hear me?"

Does he hear an echo, or is it the resonance of his own skull? If he does, is it in another voice, another accent?

"Hello?"

Hello.

And the white: is it moving, are there shapes within it, like figures in a fog? Ashwin is sure now; the fog boils like milk and he can sense up and down, forward, back. Dimensions. Gravity. Slowly he becomes aware that he has a body, his own body, his home flesh. There is a surface under his feet, and there is a human shape walking toward him through the white fog. A white man in a white fog, an old man, dressed for cold, with a compass in his hand. He steps into clear focus and frowns at Ashwin.

"Who the hell are you?" he says.

A milky blue box on a living-room table. A photonic array tumbling over Terra Tyrrhena. Calculations made in billions of parallel universes. Each computer contains the other, and millions more besides.

The machines that are building Mars have more than just the viewpoint of gods. They have something of the power. Quantum computing, quantum engineering. If calculations can be made in multiple universes, one of which supplies the perfect solution, how much simpler to cut out the application of that answer and cut straight to the result? It's mere extension of theory into practice to take those solutions out of the abstract into the real world. Model a thousand, a million, a billion quantum Mars; a slew of possibilities from Barsoom at one end of the probability spread to tripod fighting machines and delicate crystal cities at the other. Humped along the bell-shaped curve in the middle, the likelier, possible Marses. Simple school algebra will give you the best likely solution. Output, and let that be your reality. Terraforming by quantum leap. Nudges along the path to inhabitability. More than terraforming. Whole-universe-forming. The quantum machines, the AIs that have, in the private mindspaces where humans cannot go, given themselves the names and natures of angels, have always understood that reality is a construct of language. They know what the shamans knew; that words, whether in primal chant or machine code, have power over the physical universe.

And somewhere in that polyverse, lies that answer that makes the theory real, and, by the gods whose power they have usurped, the machines are going to have a go at it. But what kind of Mars? Whose dreams will frame it? An old cosmonaut, left on the pad like a jilted bride, who casually asked a foolish prophetic question of a plastic box. A young construction worker, who is shown the glory every day and every night has it taken away from him, whose mind is sent spinning across space by quantum computers. These, certainly, and others besides, millions of others, brought to this place that is white with the light of millions of universes, to speak their dreams and tell their stories.

"Well, I could as well argue you're my illusion," Antti Selkokari said to the young Indian man standing before him barefoot in an incongruous paper coverall. "After all, I can understand you and you can understand me, And where does that happen except in dreams? And you're hardly dressed for the cold. You'd be dead after ten minutes in that, where I come from."

"And what about you?" Ashwin Mehta argued. "An old man with a compass? Very allegorical."

"All right, then," Antti said. "We'll agree that each is a figment of the other's imagination. So, then, who imagined all these?"

Figures were advancing through the white fog on all sides. Men, women, children, all ages and races and stations, walking patiently, silently. Between them, Antti and Ashwin saw other figures emerging from indeterminacy. Beyond them, yet others. The two lost men stood at the center of a great congregation of people.

"Who are you?" Antti demanded, more bold than Ashwin in the face of a faceless mass. "Where is this place? What do you want?"

A woman stepped forward. She was small, dressed in a simple shift frock, barefoot, her hair badly cut, urchin crop. She had soft black eyes and when she spoke, both men heard her in their own tongues, with an American accent. She said, "In answer to your questions: first; my folk don't really do names—we're AIs—but if you want to call me something, call me Catherine. It's as good as any. Second: that entirely depends on you, all, but at the moment it might help to think of yourselves as individuals accidentally caught up in an experimental superimposed quantum state. Or a convocation, if that helps. Third: your stories. Your visions. Your hopes. Your Marses."

Silence across the white plain. The shabby little woman turned to the great mass of people.

"Hey! It's your world. You all have a say in it. Say nothing, and that bit goes unsaid. Your works build it, your stories tell it. Listen: quantum reality is information, pure and simple. Language defines what's real: it's the same for AIs as it is for humans. Deep down, everything is a story. We're all tales. Tell me. Tell me your stories. We've got a world to build, and build it right."

Against reason, Antti found words bubbling up in his throat. They were not demands for explanations that made sense, to be shown the way home. They were heart words, old memories and passions surging up like water from a deep aquifer struck by a well. It was a story of Mars, and the story of his own life.

He told of the night with the crisp of autumn first on the air when his father lit a bonfire on the beach and his children, following the sparks up into the night sky, had seen one that did not fly and fade. "That is no spark," he remembered his father saying. "That is another world. Its name is Mars." Another world! As complete and self-contained and full as this. A childhood of frequent illnesses was self-educated with old *People's Encyclopedias*. Short on the rest of the world, but long on the wonders of astronomy. Sitting up late, late to listen to the beep on the radio that was Sputnik calling Earth. Again, that hot summer day when his father came running from the house to call him in from football to see the pictures of the capitalists walking on the Moon.

"That was when I decided I wanted to be a cosmonaut," Antti said. "The Americans had put their flag on the Moon, but Mars, Red Mars; that was always ours."

As he spoke, he became aware of the young man Ashwin's voice, telling his own story: a strange and mighty one, of a world very alien to his own, and all the other voices on this featureless white plain, telling their tales and dreams of that little red light in the night.

Antti told them of the Air Force, when it had been a thing of pride and honor, and the passion and energy of young men who drive themselves toward a single ambition. The trials, the tests, the skills, the physical rigors and disciplines, the sacramental hours alone in the training jet, up on the lonely edge of the world, only the stars above him. The tensor mathematics would have finished him had he not found the humility to go home to his father, a schoolteacher, and ask his help.

"And cosmonaut training!"

It was only after that Kazakhstan morning, when ATOM 12 died, that Antti Selkokari realized his entire life and energy had been focused on that red dot in the sky, like a laser sight. As he told of the hours in the centrifuge, the constant medical testing—his childhood sickness a permanent dread—the team-building exercises, the Kamchatka survival course, the hours in the underwater tank, the hours and hours in the mock-ups and simulators, doing it over and over and over and over until they could do it blindfolded; the hours and hours and hours at the desks in front of the blackboards, working it out again and again and again. The crew interviews; how he thought his heart would stop when the letter came with the crest of the space agency, yet his fingers had no hesitation ripping it open. He still could not remember what it said beyond the key words. Glad. Successful. Mars. *Novy Mir.* Report.

He told about Milena. How overjoyed she had been, how proud! A cosmonaut's wife! They celebrated with Cuban cigars and good vodka. A party member's daughter could get the good stuff. She came at him fast and hot that night: there was a child to be conceived. A keep-safe, in case. Space was big. Radiation hard. Mars far and cold. Unflinching how it had all fallen apart, afterward. The failure had not been his, but it is a sin women do not forgive.

That morning, always coming back to that morning. The cold; clear Kazakhstan light; the jokes in the back of the truck that died one by one as they drew nearer to the great white rocket. The frosting he had noticed on the rippled white skin as they rode up the elevator, helmets under their arms. The cameraman crouching beside the gantry, their nonchalant waves. *Hi, we're going to Mars!* Vorontsev, Nitin, Rozdevshensky, Selkokari. The startled birds flapping across the steppe. The hatch dogging, screwing the umbilical into the LSU. The startled grunt on the intercom as Mission Commander Rozdevshensky was told something they could not hear and he could not quite believe. The dogs turning. The ray of golden morning light. Barsamian's hand reaching in: *come now, quick now, get unfastened there and come with me.* The ride down in the elevator. The ride no one had ever thought to take. The van bouncing over the rutted dirt road to the control bunker, and the word from Kirilenko that the thing was poisoned, had always been poisoned, was nothing but a tool in Politburo maneuvers.

From his trip to Mars, Antti Selkokari brought back a Kazakh rug and a fabric badge with the names of the crew of *Novy Mir.* He brought them home to the wooden house by the Baltic that had been his father's and, since his death, was now his, his alone. A party official invited himself for tea to tell Cosmonaut Selkokari Mars was dead, no one was going now or ever, never to mention Mars; forget Mars, but even then their authority was on the wane and Antti had nodded and signed the forms and consents and that night gone out on the pale sand beach to look up at that red dot in the sky. First loves are enduring loves.

As he spoke, Antti became aware that the other voices telling their tales of their Marses were fading; the figures, though still pressed close as far as he could see into the white, were becoming less distinct. They became whispers, shadows, until all that remained with any clarity was the Indian youth, confessing his hopes and dreams for the world he was building, a world for all the dispossessed; with trains! Trains! Antti smiled. The construction worker smiled back and, like the cat in that English children's story he never liked, faded too, the white of the smile lingering. Back to his future, his universe, his incomplete solution to Mars. Now Antti was alone with the ragged little woman, the saint, the angel, the artificial intelligence.

"Will this do?" he asked. "It's all I have."

"This will do very well," she said, turned, and was gone, too.

Antti was alone in the featureless white, and, as if held in abeyance, the cold rushed in.

Time, he knew, had restarted somewhere. And space. Space! The compass. He flipped it open. The needle quested, then settled firmly on north. Antti tapped it. No lie. As if in confirmation, he heard a dog barking, muffled, but closing with every yap. It came bowling out of the white, breath steaming, curling up in itself, wagging its tail furiously in its delight to have found him. It made to jump up, Antti stepped back.

"Enough of that!" It cringed. "Here! Hutttt! Heel!"

Too much to expect of such a creature, but it did draw close, looking up at him, and together they followed the way the compass said to home, man and mongrel.

Before the train has even come to a halt the roof-riders are swinging down over the doors and windows, hitting the platform at a run, some slipping and falling, some hitting into people waiting for the train out. Racing to beat the crowd. Racing to get home. Work. Home. Sleep. Work.

Every other evening, Ashwin would have been among the first of the first. Tonight, he waits for the roof to empty around him. He looks up at the fragmented station dome. The memories of the time that was not a time in that other place that was not a place are less clear now. In time they will fade. All such encounters with the numinous, the miraculous must. It is written.

Quantum interference, they said in the medical center. A *random superposition of states. Less than a second, no permanent damage done.* But in that second, he had flat-lined. Brain-dead. Mind . . . elsewhere. Elsewhen. The *corporada* doctors ran their diagnostics and did their tests and pronounced him fit to work and travel. It would have cost too much money to have pronounced him anything else.

New passengers are scrambling up as Ashwin climbs down from the train. He passes through the ceaseless, changeless bustle of the station in a state of beatification.

I've seen you all, over there, in the new world. I told them about you, what you needed, what you dreamed. It may be your future, it may be someone else's future, but I spoke for you. And somebody listened.

In the square a great crowd has gathered, all attention turned to the street where the holy woman has buried herself alive. The kids have got off their scooters and are peering, questing over the heads, *What's happening, what's going on?* The band is playing like a pack of maniacs and over the general hubbub Ashwin can hear the *sadhus* proclaiming loudly that a miracle has taken place, a miracle, a sign for corrupt, materialist days. This woman! This holy woman! For five days she has mortified the flesh in the earth, she has practiced the fiercest of asceticisms, she has come forth and she has achieved *samadhi.*

From the top of the station steps, Ashwin catches sight of her. She is smaller than he had imagined and, despite five days fasting in the earth, plumper. Her hair is wound in a long greasy pigtail, and a circle of *sadhus* surrounds her, proclaiming her virtues to the crowd, who thrust out their hands to be touched, to take some of her spirituality. But something stops her. Something turns her head. She looks up. She seeks out Ashwin on the far side of the crowd. Their eyes lock.

I saw you, there, Ashwin thinks. *And you saw me. We know each other. We know what we have done.*

Self-mortification as a quantum state? What are the physics of the soul?

He nods. The holy woman smiles, then goes back to her adoration. Ashwin skirts the crowd, then the smell stops him. It has been a long, strange day of hard work. he could eat the beard of the *sadhu.* He might trouble the *datarajah* for another of his chapatis, he thinks.

The thing ate like a pig. Worse, for a pig, despite its lack of grace, has some utility. He had put his life on the line out there on the ice (*and beyond,* something whispers) and it hadn't even the grace to look up from its food bowl.

Displacement, Antti thought. *It's the boy you are really annoyed with. He went straight to the dog, not to you. What did you expect? But you cannot be angry with our grandson. So curse his dog, and watch it scatter its food that looks and smells like shit over the kitchen floor.*

Paavo had that look he got when he wanted to lecture his father again for his stupidity. Antti knew that he would say it was a bad example to Yuri, going out on the ice alone, not leaving a note, a message — why, he even has a GPS tracker in the car — trusting your life to some ancient compass. All for Yuri's benefit, but it would be son to father. Strange, the nuances of parents. Everything mediated through the children.

Nursing his mug of coffee — shot through with the last of the night's good Polish vodka — Antti excused himself from the kitchen table.

"If that thing has to pee, take it out on a bit of string," he admonished Yuri.

He hesitated at the door to his study. All that Mars, shut inside. Hallucination? People did go crazy in whiteout. Wintermad. And he knew he had been closer to hypothermia out there than he liked to think. But it had seemed so real, so true. He had told those people things he had not even told his own son, certainly not the woman who had been his wife. Things he had only alluded to with his truest family; the brethren of rocketeers and Areologists and Mars dreamers.

He opened the door, peeked in. There, in the corner, a glimpse of another world: a ragbag place that held the dreams of everyone who had ever looked up into the autumn sky and wondered at that little red fast traveler. Ten thousand cities under a glass roof. SkyWheels and moon rings and terraforming machines and reality shaping angels and airship legions and trains the size of ocean liners. And more, so much more; more wonders. As many wonders and incongruities as only a real world can hold. And people. Of course, people. People make it a world. Their stories, their words, their never-ceasing definition of its reality. Without them, it is just a planet. Dead.

He looked again and it was just badges and models and toy spaceships hanging from the ceiling on fishing line. He closed the door. He would take his coffee in the living room. He could poke some life into the embers of the other night; there was wood, he might coax up a blaze. He settled in his chair, watched curls of red creep across the charcoals, almost alive. The quantum computer still stood open on the table. Antti turned it to him. His wish, his prophecy, burned on the screen. WHAT WILL HAPPEN TO MY DREAM OF MARS? He closed the blue plastic lid and settled down to have his coffee.

stories for men

john kessel

Born in Buffalo, New York, John Kessel now lives with his family in Ra-
leigh, North Carolina, where he is a professor of American literature and
creative writing at North Carolina State University. Kessel made his first
sale in 1975. His first solo novel, Good News From Outer Space, *was*
released in 1988 to wide critical acclaim, but before that he had made his
mark on the genre primarily as a writer of highly imaginative, finely crafted
short stories, many of which were assembled in his collection Meeting in
infinity. He won a Nebula Award in 1983 for his superlative novella "An-
other Orphan," which was also a Hugo finalist that year, and has been
released as an individual book. His story "Buffalo" won the Theodore Stur-
geon Award in 1991. His other books include the novel Freedom Beach,
written in collaboration with James Patrick Kelly, and an anthology of
stories from the famous Sycamore Hill Writers Workshop (which he also
helps to run), called Intersections, *coedited by Mark L. Van Name and*
Richard Butner. His most recent books are a major new novel, Corrupting
Dr. Nice, *and a new collection,* The Pure Product. *His stories have ap-*
peared in our First, Second (in collaboration with James Patrick Kelly),
Fourth, Sixth, Eighth, Thirteenth, Fourteenth, Fifteenth, and Nineteenth
Annual Collections.

In the complex and thought-provoking novella that follows, he takes us
to the Moon to visit a Lunar colony that's supposed to be a Utopia, a
perfect, harmonious society worked out in intricate detail by social engi-
neers—but one where the social engineers have forgotten that one person's
Utopia is often someone else's Dystopia . . .

ONE

Erno couldn't get to the club until an hour after it opened, so of course the
place was crowded and he got stuck in the back behind three queens whose loud,
aimless conversation made him edgy. He was never less than edgy anyway, Erno—

a seventeen-year-old biotech apprentice known for the clumsy, earnest intensity with which he propositioned almost every girl he met.

It was more people than Erno had ever seen in the Oxygen Warehouse. Even though Tyler Durden had not yet taken the stage, every table was filled, and people stood three deep at the bar. Rosamund, the owner, bustled back and forth providing drinks, her face glistening with sweat. The crush of people only irritated Erno. He had been one of the first to catch on to Durden, and the room full of others, some of whom had probably come on his own recommendation, struck him as usurpers.

Erno forced his way to the bar and bought a tincture. Tyrus and Sid, friends of his, nodded at him from across the room. Erno sipped the cool, licorice flavored drink and eavesdropped, and gradually his thoughts took on an architectural, intricate intellectuality.

A friend of his mother sat with a couple of sons who anticipated for her what she was going to see. "He's not just a comedian, he's a philosopher," said the skinny one. His foot, crossed over his knee, bounced in rhythm to the jazz playing in the background. Erno recognized him from a party he'd attended a few months back.

"We have philosophers," the matron said. "We even have comedians."

"Not like Tyler Durden," said the other boy.

"Tyler Durden—who gave him that name?"

"I think it's historical," the first boy said.

"Not any history I ever heard," the woman said. "Who's his mother?"

Erno noticed that there were more women in the room than there had been at any performance he had seen. Already the matrons were homing in. You could not escape their sisterly curiosity, their motherly tyranny. He realized that his shoulders were cramped; he rolled his head to try to loosen the spring-tight muscles.

The Oxygen Warehouse was located in what had been a shop in the commercial district of the northwest lava tube. It was a free enterprise zone, and no one had objected to the addition of a tinctures bar, though some eyebrows had been raised when it was discovered that one of the tinctures sold was alcohol. The stage was merely a raised platform in one corner. Around the room were small tables with chairs. The bar spanned one end, and the other featured a false window that showed a nighttime cityscape of Old New York.

Rosamund Demisdaughter, who'd started the club, at first booked local jazz musicians. Her idea was to present as close to a retro Earth atmosphere as could be managed on the far side of the moon, where few of the inhabitants had ever even seen the Earth. Her clientele consisted of a few immigrants and a larger group of rebellious young cousins who were looking for an *avant garde*. Erno knew his mother would not approve his going to the Warehouse, so he was there immediately.

He pulled his pack of fireless cigarettes from the inside pocket of his black twentieth-century suit, shook out a fag, inhaled it into life and imagined himself living back on Earth a hundred years ago. Exhaling a plume of cool, rancid smoke, he caught a glimpse of his razor haircut in the mirror behind the bar, then adjusted the knot of his narrow tie.

After some minutes the door beside the bar opened and Tyler Durden came out. He leaned over and exchanged a few words with Rosamund. Some of the men whistled and cheered. Rosamund flipped a brandy snifter high into the air, where it caught the ceiling lights as it spun in the low G, then slowly fell back to her hand. Having attracted the attention of the audience, she hopped over the bar and onto the small stage.

"Don't you people have anything better to do?" she shouted.

A chorus of rude remarks.

"Welcome to The Oxygen Warehouse," she said. "I want to say, before I bring him out, that I take no responsibility for the opinions expressed by Tyler Durden. He's not my boy."

Durden stepped onto the stage. The audience was quiet, a little nervous. He ran his hand over his shaved head, gave a boyish grin. He was a big man, in his thirties, wearing the blue coveralls of an environmental technician. Around his waist he wore a belt with tools hanging from it, as if he'd just come off shift.

" 'Make love, not war!' " Durden said. "Remember that one? You got that from your mother, in the school? I never liked that one. 'Make love, not war,' they'll tell you. I hate that. I want to make love *and* war. I don't want my dick just to be a dick. I want it to stand for something!"

A heckler from the audience shouted, "Can't it stand on its own?"

Durden grinned. "Let's ask it." He addressed his crotch. "Hey, son!" He called down. "Don't you like screwing?"

Durden looked up at the ceiling, his face went simple, and he became his dick talking back to him. "Hiya dad!" he squeaked. "Sure, I like screwing!"

Durden winked at a couple of guys in makeup and lace in the front row, then looked down again: "Boys or girls?"

His dick: "What day of the week is it?"

"Thursday."

"Doesn't matter, then. Thursday's guest mammal day."

"Outstanding, son."

"I'm a Good Partner."

The queers laughed. Erno did, too.

"You want I should show you?"

"Not now, son," Tyler told his dick. "You keep quiet for a minute, and let me explain to the people, okay?"

"Sure. I'm here whenever you need me."

"I'm aware of that." Durden addressed the audience again. "Remember what Mama says, folks: *Keep your son close, let your semen go.*" He recited the slogan with exaggerated rhythm, wagging his finger at them, sober as a scolding grandmother. The audience loved it. Some of them chanted along with the catchphrase.

Durden was warming up. "But is screwing all there is to a dick? I say no!

"A dick is a sign of power. It's a tower of strength. It's the tree of life. It's a weapon. It's an incisive tool of logic. It's the seeker of truth.

"Mama says that being male is nothing more than a performance. You know what I say to that? Perform this, baby!" He grabbed his imaginary cock with both of his hands, made a stupid face.

Cheers.

"But of course, *they* can't perform this! I don't care how you plank the genes, Mama don't have the *machinery*. Not only that, she don't have the *programming*. But mama wants to program *us* with *her* half-baked scheme of what women want a man to be. This whole place is about fucking up our *hardware* with their *software*."

He was laughing himself, now. Beads of sweat stood out on his scalp in the bright light.

"Mama says, 'Don't confuse your penis with a phallus.'" He assumed a female sway of his hips, lifted his chin and narrowed his eyes: just like that, he was an archetypal matron, his voice transmuted into a fruity contralto. "'Yes, you boys do have those nice little dicks, but we're living in a *post-phallic* society. A penis is merely a biological appendage.'"

Now he was her son, responding. "'Like a foot, Mom?'"

Mama: "'Yes, son. Exactly like a foot.'"

Quick as a spark, back to his own voice: "How many of you in the audience here have named your foot?"

Laughter, a show of hands.

"Okay, so much for the foot theory of the penis.

"But Mama says the penis is designed solely for the propagation of the species. Sex gives pleasure in order to encourage procreation. A phallus, on the other hand—whichever hand you like—I prefer the left—"

More laughter.

"—a phallus is an idea, a cultural creation of the dead patriarchy, a symbolic sheath applied over the penis to give it meanings that have nothing to do with biology...."

Durden seized his invisible dick again. "Apply my symbolic sheath, baby... oohhh, yes, I like it...."

Erno had heard Tyler talk about his symbolic sheath before. Though there were variations, he watched the audience instead. Did they get it? Most of the men seemed to be engaged and laughing. A drunk in the first row leaned forward, hands on his knees, howling at Tyler's every word. Queers leaned their heads together and smirked. Faces gleamed in the close air. But a lot of the men's laughter was nervous, and some did not laugh at all.

A few of the women, mostly the younger ones, were laughing. Some of them seemed mildly amused. Puzzled. Some looked bored. Others sat stonily with expressions that could only indicate anger.

Erno did not know how he felt about the women who were laughing. He felt hostility toward those who looked bored: why did you come here, he wanted to ask them. Who do you think you are? He preferred those who looked angry. That was what he wanted from them.

Then he noticed those who looked calm, interested, alert yet unamused. These women scared him.

In the back of the room stood some green-uniformed constables, male and female, carrying batons, red lights gleaming in the corner of their mirror spex, recording. Looking around the room, Erno located at least a half dozen of them. One, he saw with a start; was his mother.

He ducked behind a tall man beside him. She might not have seen him yet, but she would see him sooner or later. For a moment he considered confronting her, but then he sidled behind a row of watchers toward the back rooms. Another constable, her slender lunar physique distorted by the bulging muscles of a genetically engineered testosterone girl, stood beside the doorway. She did not look at Erno: she was watching Tyler, who was back to conversing with his dick.

"I'm tired of being confined," Tyler's dick was saying.

"You feel constricted?" Tyler asked.

He looked up in dumb appeal. "I'm stuck in your pants all day!"

Looking down: "I can let you out, but first tell me, are you a penis or a phallus?"

"That's a distinction without a difference."

"*Au contraire*, little man! You haven't been listening."

"I'm not noted for my listening ability."

"Sounds like you're a phallus to me," Tyler told his dick. "We have lots of room for penises, but Mama don't allow no phalluses 'round here."

"Let my people go!"

"Nice try, but wrong color. Look, son. It's risky when you come out. You could get damaged. The phallic liberation movement is in its infancy."

"I thought you cousins were *all about* freedom."

"In theory. In practice, free phalluses are dangerous."

"Who says?"

"Well, Debra does, and so does Mary, and Sue, and Jamina most every time I see her, and there was this lecture in We-Whine-You-Listen class last week, and Ramona says so too, and of course most emphatically Baba, and then there's that bitch Nora. . . ."

Erno spotted his mother moving toward his side of the room. He slipped past the constable into the hall. There was the rest room, and a couple of other doors. A gale of laughter washed in from the club behind him at the climax of Tyler's story; cursing his mother, Erno went into the rest room.

No one was there. He could still hear the laughter, but not the cause of it. His mother's presence had cut him out of the community of male watchers as neatly as if she had used a baton. Erno felt murderously angry. He switched on a urinal and took a piss.

Over the urinal, a window played a scene in Central Park, on Earth, of a hundred years ago. A night scene of a pathway beneath some trees, trees as large as the largest in Sobieski Park. A line of electric lights on poles threw pools of light along the path, and through the pools of light strolled a man and a woman. They were talking, but Erno could not hear what they were saying.

The woman wore a dress cinched tight at the waist, whose skirt flared out stiffly, ending halfway down her calves. The top of her dress had a low neckline that showed off her breasts. The man wore a dark suit like Erno's. They were completely differentiated by their dress, as if they were from different cultures, even species. Erno wondered where Rosamund had gotten the image.

As Erno watched, the man nudged the woman to the side of the path, beneath one of the trees. He slid his hands around her waist and pressed his body against hers. She yielded softly to his embrace. Erno could not see their faces in the shadows, but they were inches apart. He felt his dick getting hard in his hand.

He stepped back from the urinal, turned it off, and closed his pants. As the hum of the recycler died, the rest room door swung open and a woman came in. She glanced at Erno and headed for one of the toilets. Erno went over to the counter and stuck his hands into the cleaner. The woman's presence sparked his anger.

Without turning to face her, but watching in the mirror, he said, "Why are you here tonight?"

The woman looked up (she had been studying her fingernails) and her eyes locked on his. She was younger than his mother and had a pretty, heart-shaped face. "I was curious. People are talking about him."

"Do you think men want you here?"

"I don't know what the men want."

"Yes. That's the point, isn't it? Are you learning anything?"

"Perhaps." The woman looked back at her hands. "Aren't you Pamela Megs-daughter's son?"

"So she tells me." Erno pulled his tingling hands out of the cleaner.

The woman used the bidet, and dried herself. She had a great ass. "Did she bring you or did you bring her?" she asked.

"We brought ourselves," Erno said. He left the rest room. He looked out into the club again, listening to the noise. The crowd was rowdier, and more raucous. The men's shouts of encouragement were like barks, their laughter edged with anger. His mother was still there. He did not want to see her, or to have her see him.

He went back past the rest room to the end of the hallway. The hall made a right angle into a dead end, but when Erno stepped into the bend he saw, behind a stack of plastic crates, an old door. He wedged the crates to one side and opened the door enough to slip through.

The door opened into a dark, dimly lit space. His steps echoed. As his eyes adjusted to the dim light he saw it was a very large room hewn out of the rock, empty except for some racks that must have held liquid oxygen cylinders back in the early days of the colony, when this place had been an actual oxygen warehouse. The light came from ancient bioluminescent units on the walls. The club must have been set up in this space years before.

The tincture still lent Erno an edge of aggression, and he called out: "I'm Erno, King of the Moon!"

"—ooo—ooo—ooon!" the echoes came back, fading to stillness. He kicked an empty cylinder, which rolled forlornly a few meters before it stopped. He wandered around the chill vastness. At the far wall, one of the darker shadows turned out to be an alcove in the stone. Set in the back, barely visible in the dim light, was an ancient pressure door.

Erno decided not to mess with it — it could open onto vacuum. He went back to the club door and slid into the hallway.

Around the corner, two men were just coming out of the rest room, and Erno followed them as if he were just returning as well. The club was more crowded than ever. Every open space was filled with standing men, and others sat cross-legged up front. His mother and another constable had moved to the edge of the stage.

"— the problem with getting laid all the time is, you can't think!" Tyler was saying. "I mean, there's only so much blood in the human body. That's why those old Catholics back on Earth put the lock on the Pope's dick. He had an empire to run: the more time he spent taking care of John Thomas the less he spent thinking up ways of getting money out of peasants. The secret of our moms is that, if they keep that blood flowing below the belt, it ain't never gonna flow back above the shirt collar. Keeps the frequency of radical male ideas down!"

Tyler leaned over toward the drunk in the first row. "You know what I'm talking about, soldier?"

"You bet," the man said. He tried to stand, wobbled, sat down, tried to stand again.

"Where do you work?"

"Lunox." The man found his balance. "You're *right*, you —"

Tyler patted him on the shoulder. "An oxygen boy. You know what I mean, you're out there on the processing line, and you're thinking about how maybe if you were to add a little more graphite to the reduction chamber you could increase efficiency by 15 percent, and just then Mary Ellen Swivelhips walks by in her skintight and — bam!" Tyler made the face of a man who'd been poleaxed. "Uh — what was I thinking of?"

The audience howled.

"Forty I.Q. points down the oubliette. And nothing, NOTHING's gonna change until we get a handle on this! Am I right, brothers?"

More howls, spiked with anger.

Tyler was sweating, laughing, trembling as if charged with electricity. "Keep your son close! *Penis, no! Phallus, si!*"

Cheers now. Men stood and raised their fists. The drunk saw Erno's mother at the edge of the stage and took a step toward her. He said something, and while she and her partner stood irresolute, he put his big hand on her chest and shoved her away.

The other constable discharged his electric club against the man. The drunk's arms flew back, striking a bystander, and two other men surged forward and knocked down the constable. Erno's mother raised her own baton. More constables pushed toward the stage, using their batons, and other men rose to stop them. A table was upended, shouts echoed, the room was hot as hell and turning into a riot, the first riot in the Society of Cousins in fifty years.

As the crowd surged toward the exits or toward the constables, Erno ducked back to the hallway. He hesitated, and then Tyler Durden came stumbling out of the melee. He took a quick look at Erno. "What now, kid?"

"Come with me," Erno said. He grabbed Tyler's arm and pulled him around the bend in the end of the hall, past the crates to the warehouse door. He slammed the door behind them and propped an empty oxygen cylinder against it. "We can hide here until the thing dies down."

"Who are you?"

"My name is Erno."

"Well, Erno, are we sure we want to hide? Out there is more interesting."

Erno decided not to tell Tyler that one of the constables was his mother. "Are you serious?"

"I'm always serious." Durden wandered back from the door into the gloom of the cavern. He kicked a piece of rubble, which soared across the room and skidded up against the wall thirty meters away. "This place must have been here since the beginning. I'm surprised they're wasting the space. Probably full of toxics."

"You think so?" Erno said.

"Who knows?" Durden went toward the back of the warehouse, and Erno followed. It was cold, and their breath steamed the air. "Who would have figured the lights would still be growing," Durden said.

"A well established colony can last for fifty years or more," Erno said. "As long as there's enough moisture in the air. They break down the rock."

"You know all about it."

"I work in biotech," Erno said. "I'm a gene hacker."

Durden said nothing, and Erno felt the awkwardness of his boast.

They reached the far wall. Durden found the pressure door set into the dark alcove. He pulled a flashlight from his belt. The triangular yellow warning signs around the door were faded. He felt around the door seam.

"We probably ought to leave that alone," Erno said.

Durden handed Erno the flashlight, took a pry bar from his belt, and shoved it into the edge of the door. The door resisted, then with a grating squeak jerked open a couple of centimeters. Erno jumped at the sound.

"Help me out here, Erno," Durden said.

Erno got his fingers around the door's edge, and the two of them braced themselves. Durden put his feet up on the wall and used his legs and back to get leverage. When the door suddenly shot open Erno fell back and whacked his head. Durden lost his grip, shot sideways out of the alcove, bounced once, and skidded across the dusty floor. While Erno shook his head to clear his vision, Durden sat spread-legged, laughing. "Bingo!" He said. He bounced up. "You okay, Erno?"

Erno felt the back of his skull. He wasn't bleeding. "I'm fine," he said.

"Let's see what we've got, then."

Beyond the door a dark corridor cut through the basalt. Durden stepped into the path marked by his light. Erno wanted to go back to the club—by now things must have died down—but instead he followed.

Shortly past the door the corridor turned into a cramped lava tube. Early settlers had leveled the floor of the erratic tube formed by the draining away of cooling lava several billion years ago. Between walls that had been erected to form rooms ran a path of red volcanic gravel much like tailings from the oxygen factory. Foamy irregular pebbles kicked up by their shoes rattled off the walls. Dead light fixtures broke the ceiling at intervals. Tyler stopped to shine his light into a couple of the doorways, and at the third he went inside.

"This must be from the start of the colony," Erno said. "I wonder why it's been abandoned."

"Kind of claustrophobic." Durden shone the light around the small room.

The light fell on a small rectangular object in the corner. From his belt Durden pulled another tool, which he extended into a probe.

"Do you always carry this equipment?" Erno asked.

"Be prepared," Durden said. He set down the light and crouched over the object. It looked like a small box, a few centimeters thick. "You ever hear of the Boy Scouts, Erno?"

"Some early lunar colony?"

"Nope. Sort of like the Men's House, only different." Durden forced the probe under an edge, and one side lifted as if to come off. "Well, well!"

He put down the probe, picked up the object. He held it end-on, put his thumbs against the long side, and opened it. It divided neatly into flat sheets attached at the other long side.

"What is it?" Erno asked.

"It's a book."

"Is it still working?"

"This is an unpowered book. The words are printed right on these leaves. They're made of paper."

Erno had seen such old-fashioned books in vids. "It must be very old. What is it?"

Durden carefully turned the pages. "It's a book of stories." Durden stood up and handed the book to Erno. "Here. You keep it. Let me know what it's about."

Erno tried to make out the writing, but without Tyler's flashlight it was too dim.

Durden folded up his probe and hung it on his belt. He ran his hand over his head, smearing a line of dust over his scalp. "Are you cold? I suppose we ought to find our way out of here." Immediately he headed out of the room and back down the corridor.

Erno felt he was getting left behind in more ways than one. Clutching the book, he followed after Durden and his bobbing light. Rather than heading back to the Oxygen Warehouse, the comedian continued down the lava tube.

Eventually the tube ended in another old pressure door. When Durden touched the key panel at its side, amazingly, it lit.

"What do you think?" Durden said.

"We should go back," Erno said. "We can't know whether the locked door on the other side is still airtight. The fail-safes could be broken. We could open the door onto vacuum." He held the book under his armpit and blew on his cold hands.

"How old are you, Erno?"

"Seventeen."

"Seventeen?" Durden's eyes glinted in shadowed eye sockets. "Seventeen is no age to be cautious."

Erno couldn't help but grin. "You're right. Let's open it."

"My man, Erno!" Durden slapped him on the shoulder. He keyed the door open. They heard the whine of a long-unused electric motor. Erno could feel his heart beat, the blood running swiftly in his veins. At first nothing happened, then the door began to slide open. There was a chuff of air escaping from the lava tube, and dust kicked up. But the wind stopped as soon as it started, and the door opened completely on the old airlock, filled floor to ceiling with crates and bundles of fiberglass building struts.

It took them half an hour to shift boxes and burrow their way through the airlock, to emerge at the other end into another warehouse, this one still in use. They crept by racks of construction materials until they reached the entrance, and sneaked out into the colony corridor beyond.

They were at the far end of North Six, the giant lava tube that served the industrial wing of the colony. The few workers they encountered on the late shift might have noticed Erno's suit, but said nothing.

Erno and Tyler made their way back home. Tyler cracked jokes about the constables until they emerged into the vast open space of the domed crater that formed the center of the colony. Above, on the huge dome, was projected a night starfield. In the distance, down the rimwall slopes covered with junipers, across the crater floor, lights glinted among the trees in Sobieski Park. Erno took a huge breath, fragrant with piñon.

"The world our ancestors gave us," Tyler said, waving his arm as if offering it to Erno.

As Tyler turned to leave, Erno called out impulsively, "That was an adventure!"

"The first of many, Erno." Tyler said, and jogged away.

Celibacy Day

On Celibacy Day, everyone gets a day off from sex.

Some protest this practice, but they are relatively few. Most men take it as an opportunity to retreat to the informal Men's Houses that, though they have no statutory sanction, sprang up in the first generation of settlers.

In the Men's House, men and boys talk about what it is to be a man, a lover of other men and women, a father in a world where fatherhood is no more than a biological concept. They complain about their lot. They tell vile jokes and sing songs. They wrestle. They gossip. Heteros and queers and everyone in between compare speculations on what they think women really want, and whether it matters. They try to figure out what a true man is.

As a boy Erno would go to the Men's House with his mother's current partner or one of the other men involved in the household. Some of the men taught him things. He learned about masturbation, and cross checks, and Micro Language Theory.

But no matter how welcoming the men were supposed to be to each other—and they talked about brotherhood all the time—there was always that little edge when you met another boy there, or that necessary wariness when you talked to an adult. Men came to the Men's House to spend time together and remind themselves of certain congruencies, but only a crazy person would want to live solely in the company of men.

TWO

The founders of the Society of Cousins had a vision of women as independent agents, free thinkers forming alliances with other women to create a social bond so strong that men could not overwhelm them. Solidarity, sisterhood, motherhood. But Erno's mother was not like those women. Those women existed only in history vids, sitting in meeting circles, laughing, making plans, sure of themselves and complete.

Erno's mother was a cop. She had a cop's squinty eyes and a cop's suspicion of anyone who stepped outside of the norm. She had a cop's lack of imagination, except as she could imagine what people would do wrong.

Erno and his mother and his sister Celeste and his Aunt Sophie and his cousins Lena and Aphra, and various men some of whom may have been fathers, some of them Good Partners, and others just men, lived in an apartment in Sanger, on the third level of the northeast quadrant, a small place looking down on the farms that filled the floor of the crater they called Fowler, though the real Fowler was a much larger crater five kilometers distant.

Erno had his own room. He thought nothing of the fact that the girls had to share a room, and would be forced to move out when they turned fourteen. *Keep your son close, let your daughter go,* went the aphorism Tyler had mocked. Erno's mother was not about to challenge any aphorisms. Erno remembered her expression as she had stepped forward to arrest the drunk: sad that this man had forced her to this, and determined to do it. She was comfortable in the world; she saw no need for alternatives. Her cronies came by the apartment and shared coffee and gossip, and they were just like all the other mothers and sisters and aunts. None of them were extraordinary.

Not that any of the men Erno knew were extraordinary, either. Except Tyler Durden. And now Erno knew Durden, and they had spent a night breaking rules and getting away with it.

Celeste and Aphra were dishing up oatmeal when Erno returned to the apartment that morning. "Where were you?" his mother asked. She looked up from the table, more curious than upset, and Erno noticed a bruise on her temple.

"What happened to your forehead?" Erno asked.

His mother touched a hand to her forehead, as if she had forgotten it. She waved the hand in dismissal.

"There was trouble at a club in the enterprise district," Aunt Sophie said. "The constables had to step in, and your mother was assaulted."

"It was a riot!" Lena said eagerly. "There's going to be a big meeting about it in the park today." Lena was a month from turning fourteen, and looking forward to voting.

Erno sat down at the table. As he did so he felt the book, which he had tucked into his belt at the small of his back beneath his now rumpled suit jacket. He leaned forward, pulled a bowl of oatmeal toward him and took up a spoon. Looking down into the bowl to avoid anyone's eyes, he idly asked, "What's the meeting for?"

"One of the rioters was knocked into a coma," Lena said. "The social order committee wants this comedian Tyler Durden to be made invisible."

Erno concentrated on his spoon. "Why?"

"You know about him?" his mother asked.

Before he had to think of an answer, Nick Farahsson, his mother's partner, shambled into the kitchen. "Lord, Pam, don't you pay attention? Erno's one of his biggest fans."

His mother turned on Erno. "Is that so?"

Erno looked up from his bowl and met her eyes. She looked hurt. "I've heard of him."

"Heard of him?" Nick said. "Erno, I bet you were there last night."

"I bet *you* weren't there," Erno said.

Nick stretched. "I don't need to hear him. I have no complaints." He came up behind Erno's mother, nuzzled the nape of her neck and cupped her breast in his hand.

She turned her face up and kissed him on the cheek. "I should hope not."

Lena made a face. "Heteros. I can't wait until I get out of here." She had recently declared herself a lesbian and was quite judgmental about it.

"You'd better get to your practicum, Lena," Aunt Sophie said. "Let your aunt take care of her own sex life."

"This guy Durden is setting himself up for a major fall," said Nick. "Smells like a case of abnormal development. Who's his mother?"

Erno couldn't keep quiet. "He doesn't have a mother. He doesn't need one."

"Parthenogenesis," Aunt Sophie said. "I didn't think it had been perfected yet."

"If they ever do, what happens to me?" Nick said.

"You have your uses." Erno's mother nudged her shoulder against his hip.

"You two can go back to your room," Aunt Sophie said. "We'll take care of things for you."

"No need." Nick grabbed a bowl of oatmeal and sat down. "Thank you, sweetheart," he said to Aphra. "I can't see what this guy's problem is."

"Doesn't it bother you that you can't vote?" Erno said. "What's fair about that?"

"I don't want to vote," Nick said.

"You're a complete drone."

His mother frowned at him. Erno pushed his bowl away and left for his room.

"You're the one with special tutoring!" Lena called. "The nice clothes. What work do you do?"

"Shut up," Erno said softly, but his ears burned.

He had nothing to do until his 1100 biotech tutorial, and he didn't even have to go if he didn't want to. Lena was right about that, anyway. He threw the book on his bed, undressed, and switched on his screen. On the front page was a report of solar activity approaching its eleven-year peak, with radiation warnings issued for all surface activity. Erno called up the calendar. There it was: a discussion on Tyler Durden was scheduled in the amphitheater at 1600. Linked was a vid of the riot and a forum for open citizen comment. A cousin named Tashi Yokiosson had been clubbed in the fight and was in a coma, undergoing nanorepair.

Erno didn't know him, but that didn't prevent his anger. He considered calling up Tyrus or Sid, finding out what had happened to them, and telling them about his adventure with Tyler. But that would spoil the secret, and it might get around to his mother. Yet he couldn't let his night with Tyler go uncelebrated. He opened his journal, and wrote a poem:

> Going outside the crater
> finding the lost tunnels
> of freedom
> and male strength.
> Searching with your brother
> shoulder to shoulder
> like men.
>
> Getting below the surface
> of a stifling society
> sounding your XY shout.
> Flashing your colors
> like an ancient Spartan bird
> proud, erect, never to be softened
> by the silent embrace of woman
>
> No females aloud.

Not bad. It had some of the raw honesty of the beats. He would read it at the next meeting of the Poets' Club. He saved it with the four hundred other poems he had written in the last year: Erno prided himself on being the most prolific poet in his class. He had already won four Laurel Awards, one for best Lyric, one for best Sonnet, and two for best Villanelle—plus a Snappie for best limerick of 2097. He was sure to make Bard at an earlier age than anyone since Patrick Maurasson.

Erno switched off the screen, lay on his bed, and remembered the book. He dug it out from under his discarded clothes. It had a blue cover, faded to purple near the binding, made of some sort of fabric. Embossed on the front was a torch encircled by a laurel wreath. He opened the book to its title page: *Stories for Men*, "An Anthology by Charles Grayson." Published in August 1936, in the United States of America.

As a fan of Earth culture, Erno knew that most Earth societies used the pat-ronymic, so that Gray, Grayson's naming parent, would be a man, not a woman.

Stories for men. The authors on the contents page were all men—except perhaps for odd names like "Dashiell." Despite Erno's interest in twentieth-century popular art, only a couple were familiar. William Faulkner he knew was considered a major Earth writer, and he had seen the name Hemingway before, though he had associated it only with a style of furniture. But even assuming the stories were all written by men, the title said the book was stories *for* men, not stories *by* men.

How did a story for a man differ from a story for a woman? Erno had never considered the idea before. He had heard storytellers in the park, and read books in school—Murasaki, Chopin, Cather, Ellison, Morrison, Ferenc, Sabinsdaughter. As a child, he had loved the Alice books, and *Flatland*, and Maria Hidalgo's kids' stories, and Seuss. None seemed particularly male or female.

He supposed the cousins did have their own stories for men. Nick loved interactive serials, tortured romantic tales of interpersonal angst set in the patriarchal world, where men struggled against injustice until they found the right women and were taken care of. Erno stuck to poetry. His favorite novel was Tawanda Tamikasdaughter's *The Dark Blood*—the story of a misunderstood young Cousin's struggles against his overbearing mother, climaxed when his father miraculously reveals himself and brings the mother to heel. At the Men's House, he had also seen his share of porn—thrillers set on Earth where men forced women to do whatever the men wanted, and like it.

But this book did not look like porn. A note at the beginning promised the book contained material to "interest, or alarm, or amuse, or instruct, or—and possibly most important of all—entertain you." Erno wondered that Tyler had found this particular 160-year-old book in the lava tube. It seemed too unlikely to be coincidence.

What sort of things would entertain an Earthman of 1936? Erno turned to the first story, "The Ambassador of Poker" by "Achmed Abdullah."

But the archaic text was frustratingly passive—nothing more than black type physically impressed on the pages, without links or explanations. After a paragraph or so rife with obscure cultural references—"cordovan brogues," "knickerbockers," "County Sligo," "a four-in-hand"—Erno's night without sleep caught up with him, and he dozed off.

Heroes

Why does a man remain in the Society of Cousins, when he would have much more authority outside of it, in one of the other lunar colonies, or on Earth?

For one thing, the sex is great.

Men are valued for their sexuality, praised for their potency, competed for by women. From before puberty, a boy is schooled by both men and women on how to give pleasure. A man who can give such pleasure has high status. He is recognized and respected throughout the colony. He is welcome in any bed. He is admired and envied by other men.

THREE

Erno woke suddenly, sweaty and disoriented, trailing the wisps of a dream that faded before he could call it back. He looked at his clock: 1530. He was going to miss the meeting.

He washed his face, applied personal hygiene bacteria, threw on his embroidered jumpsuit, and rushed out of the apartment.

The amphitheater in Sobieski Park was filling as Erno arrived. Five or six hundred people were already there; other cousins would be watching on the link. The dome presented a clear blue sky, and the ring of heliotropes around its zenith flooded the air with sunlight. A slight breeze rustled the old oaks, hovering over the semicircular ranks of seats like aged grandmothers. People came in twos and threes, adults and children, along the paths that led down from the colony perimeter road through the farmlands to the park. Others emerged from the doors at the base of the central spire that supported the dome. Erno found a seat in the top row, far from the stage, off to one side where the seats gave way to grass.

Chairing the meeting was Debra Debrasdaughter. Debrasdaughter was a tiny sixty-year-old woman who, though she had held public office infrequently and never for long, was one of the most respected cousins. She had been Erno's teacher when he was six, and he remembered how she'd sat with him and worked through his feud with Bill Grettasson. She taught him how to play forward on the soccer team. On the soccer field she had been fast and sudden as a bug. She had a warm laugh and sharp brown eyes.

Down on the stage, Debrasdaughter was hugging the secretary. Then the sound person hugged Debrasdaughter. They both hugged the secretary again. A troubled-looking old man sat down in the front row, and all three of them got down off the platform and hugged him. He brushed his hand along Debrasdaughter's thigh, but it was plain that his heart wasn't in it. She kissed his cheek and went back up on the stage.

A flyer wearing red wings swooped over the amphitheater and soared back up again, slowly beating the air. Another pair of flyers were racing around the perimeter of the crater, silhouetted against the clusters of apartments built into the crater walls. A thousand meters above his head Erno could spy a couple of others on the edge of the launch platform at the top of, the spire. As he watched, squinting against the sunlight, one of the tiny figures spread its wings and pushed off, diving down, at first ever so slowly, gaining speed, then, with a flip of wings, soaring out level. Erno could feel it in his own shoulders, the stress that maneuver put on your arms. He didn't like flying. Even in lunar gravity, the chances of a fall were too big.

The amplified voice of Debrasdaughter drew him back to the amphitheater. "Thank you, Cousins, for coming," she said. "Please come to order."

Erno saw that Tyler Durden had taken a seat off to one side of the stage. He wore flaming red coveralls, like a shout.

"A motion has been made to impose a decree of invisibility against Thomas Marysson, otherwise known as Tyler Durden, for a period of one year. We are met here for the first of two discussions over this matter, prior to holding a colony-wide vote."

Short of banishment, invisibility was the colony's maximum social sanction. Should the motion carry, Tyler would be formally ostracized. Tagged by an AI, continuously monitored, he would not be acknowledged by other cousins. Should he attempt to harm anyone, the AI would trigger receptors in his brain stem to put him to sleep.

"This motion was prompted by the disturbances that have ensued as a result of public performances of Thomas Marysson. The floor is now open for discussion."

A very tall woman who had been waiting anxiously stood, and as if by pre-arrangement, Debrasdaughter recognized her. The hovering mikes picked up her high voice. "I am Yokio Kumiosdaughter. My son is in the hospital as a result of this shameful episode. He is a good boy. He is the kind of boy we all want, and I don't understand how he came to be in that place. I pray that he recovers and lives to become the good man I know he can be.

"We must not let this happen to anyone else's son. At the very least, Invisibility will give Thomas Marysson the opportunity to reflect on his actions before he provokes another such tragedy."

Another woman rose. Erno saw it was Rosamund Demisdaughter.

"With due respect to Cousin Kumiosdaughter, I don't believe the riot in my club was Tyler's fault. Her son brought this on himself. Tyler is not responsible for the actions of the patrons. Since when do we punish people for the misbehavior of others?

"The real mistake was sending constables," Rosamund continued. "Whether or not the grievances Tyler gives vent to are real or only perceived, we must allow any cousins to speak their mind. The founders understood that men and women are different. By sending armed officers into that club, we threatened the right of those men who came to see Tyler Durden to be different."

"It was stupid strategy!" someone interrupted. "They could have arrested Durden easily after the show."

"Arrested him? On what grounds?" another woman asked.

Rosamund continued. "Adil Al-Hafez said it when he helped Nora Sobieski raise the money for this colony : 'The cousins are a new start for men as much as women. We do not seek to change men, but to offer them the opportunity to be other than they have been.'"

A man Erno recognized from the biotech factory took the floor. "It's all very well to quote the founders back at us, but they were realists too. Men *are* different. Personalized male power has made the history of Earth one long tale of slaughter, oppression, rape, and war. Sobieski and Al-Hafez and the rest knew that, too: The California massacre sent them here. Durden's incitements will inevitably cause trouble. This kid wouldn't have gotten hurt without him. We can't stand by while the seeds of institutionalized male aggression are planted."

"This is a free speech issue!" a young woman shouted.

"It's not about speech," the man countered. "It's about violence."

Debrasdaughter called for order. The man looked sheepish and sat down. A middle-aged woman with a worried expression stood. "What about organizing a new round of games? Let them work it out on the rink, the flying drome, the playing field."

"We have games of every description," another woman responded. "You think we can make Durden join the hockey team?"

The old man in the front row croaked out, "Did you see that game last week against Aristarchus? They could use a little more organized male aggression!" That drew a chorus of laughter from the crowd.

When the noise died down, an elderly woman took the floor. "I have been a cousin for seventy years," she said. "I've seen troublemakers. There will always be troublemakers. But what's happened to the Good Partners? I remember the North tube blowout of '32. Sixty people died. Life here was brutal and dangerous. But men and women worked together shoulder to shoulder; we shared each other's joys and sorrows. We were good bedmates then. Where is that spirit now?"

Erno had heard such tiresome sermonettes about the old days a hundred times. The discussion turned into a cacophony of voices.

"What are we going to do?" said another woman. "Deprive men of the right to speak?"

"Men are already deprived of the vote! How many voters are men?"

"By living on the colony stipend, men *choose* not to vote. Nobody is stopping you from going to work."

"We work already! How much basic science do men do? Look at the work Laurasson did on free energy. And most of the artists are men."

"—they have the time to devote to science and art, *because of* the material support of the community. They have the luxury of intellectual pursuit."

"And all decisions about what to do with their work are made by women."

"The decisions, which will affect the lives of everyone in the society, are made not by women, but by voters."

"And most voters are women."

"Back to beginning of argument!" someone shouted. "Reload program and repeat."

A smattering of laughter greeted the sarcasm. Debrasdaughter smiled. "These are general issues, and to a certain degree I am content to let them be aired. But do they bear directly on the motion? What, if anything, are we to do about Thomas Marysson?"

She looked over at Tyler, who looked back at her coolly, his legs crossed.

A woman in a constable's uniform rose. "The problem with Thomas Marysson is that he claims the privileges of artistic expression, but he's not really an artist. He's a provocateur."

"Most of the artists in history have been provocateurs," shot back a small, dark man.

"He makes *me* laugh," said another.

"He's smart. Instead of competing with other men, he wants to organize them. He encourages them to band together."

The back-and-forth rambled on. Despite Debrasdaughter's attempt to keep order, the discussion ran into irrelevant byways, circular arguments, vague calls for comity, and general statements of male and female grievance. Erno had debated all this stuff a million times with the guys at the gym. It annoyed him that Debrasdaughter did not force the speakers to stay on point. But that was typical of a cousins' meeting—they would talk endlessly, letting every nitwit have her say, before actually getting around to deciding anything.

A young woman stood to speak, and Erno saw it was Alicia Keikosdaughter. Alicia and he had shared a tutorial in math, and she had been the second girl he had ever had sex with.

"Of course Durden wants to be seen as an artist," Alicia said. "There's no mystique about the guy who works next to you in the factory. Who wants to sleep with him? The truth—"

"I will!" A good-looking woman interrupted Alicia.

The assembly laughed.

"The truth—" Alicia tried to continue.

The woman ignored her. She stood, her hand on the head of the little girl at her side, and addressed Tyler Durden directly. "I think you need to get laid!" She turned to the others. "Send him around to me! I'll take care of any revolutionary impulses he might have." More laughter.

Erno could see Alicia's shoulders slump, and she sat down. It was a typical case of a matron ignoring a young woman. He got up, moved down the aisle, and slid into a spot next to her.

Alicia turned to him. "Erno. Hello."

"It's not your fault they won't listen," he said. Alicia was wearing a tight satin shirt and Erno could not help but notice her breasts.

She kissed him on the cheek. She turned to the meeting, then back to him. "What do you think they're going to do?"

"They're going to ostracize him, I'll bet."

"I saw him on link. Have you seen him?"

"I was there last night."

Alicia leaned closer. "Really?" she said. Her breath was fragrant, and her lips full. There was a tactile quality to Alicia that Erno found deeply sexy—when she talked to you she would touch your shoulder or bump her knee against yours, as if to reassure herself that you were really there. "Did you get in the fight?"

A woman on the other side of Alicia leaned over. "If you two aren't going to pay attention, at least be quiet so the rest of us can."

Erno started to say something, but Alicia put her hand on his arm. "Let's go for a walk."

Erno was torn. Boring or not, he didn't want to miss the meeting, but it was hard to ignore Alicia. She was a year younger than Erno yet was already on her own, living with Sharon Yasminsdaughter while studying environmental social work. One time Erno had heard her argue with Sharon whether it was true that women on Earth could not use elevators because if they did they would inevitably be raped.

They left the amphitheater and walked through the park. Erno told Alicia his version of the riot at the club, leaving out his exploring the deserted lava tube with Tyler.

"Even if they don't make him invisible," Alicia said, "you know that somebody is going to make sure he gets the message."

"He hasn't hurt anyone. Why aren't we having a meeting about the constable who clubbed Yokiosson?"

"The constable was attacked. A lot of cousins feel threatened. I'm not even sure how I feel."

"The Unwritten Law," Erno muttered.

"The what?"

"Tyler does a bit about it. It was an Earth custom, in most of the patriarchies. The 'unwritten law' said that, if a wife had sex with anyone other than her husband, the husband had the right to kill her and her lover, and no court would hold him guilty."

"That's because men had all the power."

"But you just said somebody would send Tyler a message. Up here, if a man abuses a woman, even threatens to, then the abused woman's friends take revenge. When was the last time anyone did anything about that?"

"I get it, Erno. That must seem unfair."

"Men don't abuse women here."

"Maybe that's why."

"It doesn't make it right."

"You're right, Erno. It doesn't. I'm on your side."

Erno sat down on the ledge of the pool surrounding the fountains. The fountains were the pride of the colony: in a conspicuous show of water consumption the pools surrounded the central spire and wandered beneath the park's trees. Genetically altered carp swam in their green depths, and the air was more humid here than anywhere else under the dome.

Alicia sat next to him. "Remind me why we broke up," Erno said.

"Things got complicated." She had said the same thing the night she told him they shouldn't sleep together anymore. He still didn't know what that meant, and he suspected she said it only to keep from saying something that might wound him deeply. Much as he wanted to insist that he would prefer her honesty, he wasn't sure he could stand it.

"I'm going crazy at home," he told Alicia. "Mother treats me like a child. Lena is starting to act like she's better than me. I do real work at Biotech, but that doesn't matter."

"You'll be in university soon. You're a premium gene hacker."

"Who says?" Erno asked.

"People."

"Yeah, right. And if I am, I still live at home. I'm going to end up just like Nick," he said, "the pet male in a household full of females."

"Maybe something will come of this. Things can change."

"If only," Erno said morosely. But he was surprised and gratified to have Alicia's encouragement. Maybe she cared for him after all. "There's one thing, Alicia . . . I could move in with you."

Alicia raised an eyebrow. He pressed on. "Like you say, I'll be studying at the university next session. . . ."

She put her hand on his leg. "There's not much space, with Sharon and me. We couldn't give you your own room."

"I'm not afraid of sharing a bed. I can alternate between you."

"You're so manly, Erno!" she teased.

"I aim to please," he said, and struck a pose. Inside he cringed. It was a stupid thing to say, so much a boy trying to talk big.

Alicia did a generous thing—she laughed. There was affection and understanding in it. It made him feel they were part of some club together. Erno hadn't realized how afraid he was that she would mock him. Neither said anything for a moment. A finch landed on the branch above them, turned its head sideways and inspected them. "You know, you could be just like Tyler Durden, Erno."

Erno started—what did she mean by that? He looked her in the face. Alicia's eyes were calm and green, flecked with gold. He hadn't looked into her eyes since they had been lovers.

She kissed him. Then she touched his lips with her finger. "Don't say anything. I'll talk to Sharon."

He put his arm around her. She melted into him.

In the distance the sounds of the debate were broken by a burst of laughter. "Let's go back," she said.

"All right," he said reluctantly.

They walked back to the amphitheater and found seats in the top row, beside two women in their twenties who joked with each other.

"This guy is no Derek Silviasson," one of them said.

"If he could fuck like Derek, now *that* would be comedy," said her blond partner.

Debrasdaughter was calling for order.

"We cannot compel any cousin to indulge in sex against his will. If he chooses to be celibate, and encourages his followers to be celibate, we can't prevent that without undermining the very freedoms we came here to establish."

Nick Farahsson, his face red and his voice contorted, shouted out, "You just said the key word—followers! We don't need followers here. Followers have ceded their autonomy to a hierarchy. Followers are the tool of phallocracy. Followers started the riot." Erno saw his mother, sitting next to Nick, try to calm him.

Another man spoke. "What a joke! We're all a bunch of followers! Cousins follow customs as slavishly as any Earth patriarch."

"What I don't understand," someone called out directly to Tyler, "is, if you hate it here so much, why don't you just leave? Don't let the airlock door clip your ass on the way out."

"This is my home, too," Tyler said.

He stood and turned to Debrasdaughter. "If you don't mind, I would like to speak."

"We'd be pleased to hear what you have to say," Debrasdaughter said. The trace of a smile on her pale face made her look girlish despite her gray hair. "Speaking for myself, I've been waiting."

Tyler ran his hand over his shaved scalp, came to the front of the platform. He looked up at his fellow citizens, and smiled. "I think you've outlined all the positions pretty clearly so far. I note that Tashi Yokiosson didn't say anything, but maybe he'll get back to us later. It's been a revealing discussion, and now I'd just like to ask you to help me out with a demonstration. Will you do this little thing for me?

"I'd like you all to put your hand over your eyes. Like this—" He covered his own eyes with his palm, peeked out. Most of the assembly did as he asked. "All of you got your eyes covered? Good!

"Because, sweethearts, this is the closest I am going to get to invisibility."

Tyler threw his arms wide, and laughed.

"Make me invisible? You can't see me now! You don't recognize a man whose word is steel, whose reality is not dependent on rules. Men have fought and bled and died for you. Men put their lives on the line for every microscopic step forward our pitiful race has made. Nothing's more visible than the sacrifices men have made for the good of their wives and daughters. Yes, women died too—but they were *real* women, women not threatened by the existence of masculinity.

"You see that tower?" Tyler pointed to the thousand-meter spire looming over their heads. "I can climb that tower! I can fuck every real woman in this amphitheater. I eat a lot of food, drink a lot of alcohol, and take a lot of drugs. I'm *bigger* than you are. I sweat more. I howl like a dog. I make noise. You think anyone can make more noise than me?

"One way or another, Mama, I'm going to keep you awake all night! And *you* think you're the girl that can stop me?

"My Uncle Dick told me when I was a boy, son, don't take it out unless you intend to use it! Well, it's out and it's in use! Rim ram goddamn, sonafabitch fuck! It is to laugh. This whole discussion's been a waste of oxygen. I'm real, I'm here, get used to it.

"Invisible? Just *try* not to see me."

Then Tyler crouched and leapt, three meters into the air, tucked, did a roll. Coming down, he landed on his hands and did a handspring. The second his feet touched the platform, he shot off the side and ran, taking long, loping strides out of the park and through the cornfields.

A confused murmur rippled through the assembly, broken by a few angry calls. Many puzzled glances. Some people stood.

Debrasdaughter called for order. "I'll ask the assembly to calm down," she said. Gradually, quiet came.

"I'm sure we are all stimulated by that very original statement. I don't think we are going to get any farther today, and I note that it is coming on time for the swing shifters to leave, so unless there are serious objections I would like to call this meeting to a close.

"The laws call for a second open meeting a week from today, followed by a polling period of three days, at the end of which the will of the colony will be made public and enacted. Do I hear any further discussion?"

There was none.

"Then I hereby adjourn this meeting. We will meet again one week from today at 1600 hours. Anyone who wishes to post a statement in regard to this matter may do so at the colony site, where a room will be open continuously for debate. Thank you for your participation."

People began to break up, talking. The two women beside Erno, joking, left the theater.

Alicia stood. "Was that one of his routines?"

Tyler's speech had stirred something in Erno that made him want to shout. He was grinning from ear to ear. "It is to laugh," he murmured.

Alicia grabbed Erno's wrist. She pulled a pen from her pocket, turned his hand so the palm lay open, and on it wrote "Gilman 334."

"Before you do anything stupid, Erno," she said, "call me."

"Define stupid," he said.

But Alicia had turned away. He felt the tingle of the writing on his hand as he watched her go.

Work

Men are encouraged to apply for an exemption from the mita: *the compulsory weekly labor that each cousin devotes to the support of the colony. The cost of this exemption is forfeiture of the right to vote. As artists, writers, artisans, athletes, performers, and especially as scientists, men have an easier path than women. Their interests are supported to the limits of the cousins' resources. But this is not accorded the designation of* work, *and all practical decisions as to what to do with any creations of their art or discoveries they might make, are left to voters, who are overwhelmingly women.*

Men who choose such careers are praised as public-spirited volunteers, sacrificing for the sake of the community. At the same time, they live a life of relative ease, pursuing their interests. They compete with each other for the attentions of women. They may exert influence, but have no legal responsibilities, and no other responsibilities except as they choose them. They live like sultans, but without power. Or like gigolos. Peacocks, and studs.

And those who choose to do work? Work — *ah, work is different. Work is mundane labor directed toward support of the colony. Male workers earn no honors, accumulate no status. And because men are always outnumbered by women on such jobs, they have little chance of advancement to a position of authority. They just can't get the votes.*

"Twenty-Five Bucks"

Erno began to puzzle out some of the *Stories for Men.* One was about a "prize fighter"—a man who fought another man with his fists for money. This aging fighter agrees with a promoter to fight a younger, stronger man for "twenty-five bucks," which from context Erno gathered was a small sum of money. The boxer spends his time in the ring avoiding getting beaten up. During a pause between the "rounds" of the fight, the promoter comes to him and complains that he is not fighting hard enough, and swears he will not pay the boxer if he "takes a dive."

So in the next round the boxer truly engages in the brutal battle, and within a minute gets beaten unconscious.

But because this happens immediately after the promoter spoke to him, in the sight of the audience, the audience assumes the boxer was *told* by the promoter to take a dive. They protest. Rather than defend the boxer, the promoter denies him the twenty-five bucks anyway.

The boxer, unconscious while the promoter and audience argue, dies of a brain hemorrhage.

The story infuriated Erno. It felt so *wrong*. Why did the boxer take on the fight? Why did he allow himself to be beaten so badly? Why did the promoter betray the boxer? What was the point of the boxer's dying in the end? Why did the writer—someone named James T. Farrell—invent this grim tale?

FOUR

A week after the meeting, when Erno logged onto school, he found a message for him from "Ethan Edwards." It read:

I saw you with that girl. Cute. But no sex, Erno. I'm counting on men like you.

Erno sent a reply: "You promised me another adventure. When?"

Then he did biochemistry ("Delineate the steps in the synthesis of human growth hormone") and read Gender & Art for three hours until he had to get to his practicum at biotech.

In order to reduce the risk of stray bugs getting loose in the colony, the biotech factories were located in a bunker separate from the main crater. Workers had to don pressure suits and ride a bus for a couple of kilometers across the lunar surface. A crowd of other biotech workers already filled the locker room at the north airlock when Erno arrived.

"Tyrus told me you're fucking Alicia Keikosdaughter, Erno," said Paul Gwynethsson, whose locker was next to Erno's. "He was out flying. He saw you in the park."

"So? Who are you fucking?" Erno asked. He pulled on his skintight. The fabric, webbed with thermoregulators, sealed itself, the suit's environment system powered up, and Erno locked down his helmet. The helmet's head's-up display was green. He and Paul went to the airlock, passed their ID's through the reader and entered with the others. The exit sign posted the solar storm warning. Paul teased Erno about Alicia as the air was cycled through the lock and they walked out through the radiation maze to the surface.

They got on the bus that dropped off the previous biotech shift. The bus bumped away in slow motion down the graded road. It was late in the lunar afternoon, probably only a day or so of light before the two-week night. If a storm should be detected and the alert sounded, they would have maybe twenty minutes to find shelter before the radiation flux hit the exposed surface. But the ride to the lab went uneventfully.

A man right off the cable train from Tsander was doing a practicum in the lab. His name was Cluny. Like so many Earthmen, he was short and impressively muscled, and spoke slowly, with an odd accent. Cluny was not yet a citizen and had not taken a cousin's name. He was still going through training before qualifying to apply for exemption from the *mita*.

Erno interrupted Cluny as he carried several racks of micro-environment bulbs to the sterilizer. He asked Cluny what he thought of Tyler Durden.

Cluny was closemouthed; perhaps he thought Erno was testing him: "I think if he doesn't like it up here, I can show him lots of places on Earth happy to take him."

Erno let him get on with his work. Cluny was going to have a hard time over the next six months. The culture shock would be nothing next to the genetic manipulation he would have to undergo to adjust him for low-G. The life expectancy of an unmodified human on the moon was forty-eight. No exercise regimen or drugs could prevent the cardiovascular atrophy and loss of bone mass that humans evolved for Earth would suffer.

But the retroviruses could alter the human genome to produce solid fibrolaminar bones in 1/6 G, prevent plaque buildup in arteries, insure pulmonary health, and prevent a dozen other fatal low-G syndromes.

At the same time, licensing biotech discoveries was the colony's major source of foreign exchange, so research was under tight security. Erno pressed his thumb against the gene scanner. He had to go through three levels of clearances to access the experiment he had been working on. Alicia was right—Erno was getting strokes for his rapid learning in gene techniques, and already had a rep. Even better, he liked it. He could spend hours brainstorming synergistic combinations of alterations in mice, adapting Earth genotypes for exploitation.

Right now he was assigned to the ecological design section under Lemmy Odillesson, the premiere agricultural genobotanist. Lemmy was working on giant plane trees. He had a vision of underground bioengineered forests, entire ecosystems introduced to newly opened lava tubes that would transform dead, airless immensities into habitable biospheres. He wanted to live in a city of underground lunar tree houses.

Too soon Erno's six-hour shift was over. He suited up, climbed to the surface, and took the bus back to the north airlock. As the shift got off, a figure came up to Erno from the shadows of the radiation maze.

It was a big man in a tiger-striped skintight, his faceplate opaqued. Erno shied away from him, but the man held his hands, palms up, in front of him to indicate no threat. He came closer, leaned forward. Erno flinched. The man took Erno's shoulder, gently, and pulled him forward until the black faceplate of his helmet kissed Erno's own.

"Howdy, Erno." Tyler Durden's voice, carried by conduction from a face he could not see, echoed like Erno's own thought.

Erno tried to regain his cool. "Mr. Durden, I presume."

"Switch your suit to Channel Six," Tyler said. "Encrypted." He pulled away and touched the pad on his arm, and pointed to Erno's. When Erno did the same, his radio found Tyler's wavelength, and he heard Tyler's voice in his ear.

"I thought I might catch you out here."

The other workers had all passed by; they were alone. "What are you doing here?"

"You want adventure? We got adventure."

"What adventure?"

"Come along with me."

Instead of heading in through the maze, Tyler led Erno back out to the surface. The fan of concrete was deserted, the shuttle bus already gone back to the lab and factories. From around a corner, Tyler hauled out a backpack, settled it over his shoulders, and struck off east, along the graded road that encircled Fowler. The mountainous rim rose to their right, topped by the beginnings of the dome; to their left was the rubble of the broken highlands. Tyler moved along at a quick pace, taking long strides in the low G with a minimum of effort.

After a while Tyler asked him, "So, how about the book? Have you read it?"

"Some. It's a collection of stories, all about men."

"Learning anything?"

"They seem so primitive. I guess it was a different world back then."

"What's so different?"

Erno told him the story about the prizefighter. "Did they really do that?"

"Yes. Men have always engaged in combat."

"For money?"

"The money is just an excuse. They do it anyway."

"But why did the writer tell that story? What's the point?"

"It's about elemental manhood. The fighters were men. The promoter was not."

"Because he didn't pay the boxer?"

"Because he knew the boxer had fought his heart out, but he pretended that the boxer was a coward in order to keep the audience from getting mad at him. The promoter preserved his own credibility by trashing the boxer's. The author wants you to be like the boxer, not the promoter."

"But the boxer dies—for twenty-five bucks."

"He died a man. Nobody can take that away from him."

"But nobody knows that. In fact, they all think he died a coward."

"The promoter knows he wasn't. The other fighter knows, probably. And thanks to the story, now you know, too."

Erno still had trouble grasping exactly the metaphor Tyler intended when he used the term "man." It had nothing to do with genetics. But before he could quiz Tyler, the older man stopped. By this time they had circled a quarter of the colony and were in the shadow of the crater wall. Tyler switched on his helmet light and Erno did likewise. Erno's thermoregulator pumped heat along the microfibers buried in his suit's skin, compensating for the sudden shift from the brutal heat of lunar sunlight to the brutal cold of lunar darkness.

"Here we are," Tyler said, looking up the crater wall. "See that path?"

It wasn't much of a path, just a jumble of rocks leading up the side of the crater, but once they reached it Erno could see that, by following patches of luminescent paint on boulders, you could climb the rim mountain to the top. "Where are we going?" Erno asked.

"To the top of the world," Tyler said. "From up there I'll show you the empire I'll give you if you follow me."

"You're kidding."

Tyler said nothing.

It was a hard climb to the crater's lip, where a concrete rim formed the foundation of the dome. From here, the dome looked like an unnaturally swollen stretch of *mare*, absurdly regular, covered in lunar regolith. Once the dome had been constructed over the crater, about six meters of lunar soil had been spread evenly over its surface to provide a radiation shield for the interior. Concentric rings every ten meters kept the soil from sliding down the pitch of the dome. It was easier climbing here, but surreal. The horizon of the dome moved ahead of them as they progressed, and it was hard to judge distances.

"There's a solar storm warning," Erno said. "Aren't you worried?"

"We're not going to be out long."

"I was at the meeting," Erno said.

"I saw you," Tyler said. "Cute girl, the dark skinned one. Watch out. You know what they used to say on Earth?"

"What?"

"If women didn't have control of all the pussy, they'd have bounties on their heads."

Erno laughed. "How can you say that? They're our sisters, our mothers."

"And they still have control of all the pussy."

They climbed the outside of the dome.

"What are you going to do to keep from being made invisible?" Erno asked.

"What makes you think they're going to try?"

"I don't think your speech changed anybody's mind."

"So? No matter what they teach you, my visibility is not socially constructed. That's the lesson for today."

"What are we doing out here?"

"We're going to do demonstrate this fact."

Ahead of them a structure hove into sight. At the apex of the dome, just above the central spire, stood a maintenance airlock. Normally, this would be the way workers would exit to inspect or repair the dome's exterior — not the way Erno and Tyler had come. This was not a public airlock, and the entrance code would be encrypted.

Tyler led them up to the door. From his belt pouch he took a key card and stuck it into the reader. Erno could hear him humming a song over his earphones. After a moment, the door slid open.

"In we go, Erno," Tyler said.

They entered the airlock and waited for the air to recycle. "This could get us into trouble," Erno said.

"Yes, it could."

"If you can break into the airlock you can sabotage it. An airlock breach could kill hundreds of people."

"You're absolutely right, Erno. That's why only completely responsible people like us should break into airlocks."

The interior door opened into a small chamber facing an elevator. Tyler put down his backpack, cracked the seal on his helmet and began stripping off his garish suit. Underneath he wore only briefs. Rust-colored pubic hair curled from around the edges of the briefs. Tyler's skin was pale, the muscles in his arms and chest well developed, but his belly soft. His skin was crisscrossed with a web of pink lines where the thermoregulator system of the suit had marked him.

Feeling self-conscious, Erno took off his own suit. They were the same height, but Tyler outweighed him by twenty kilos. "What's in the backpack?" Erno asked.

"Rappelling equipment." Tyler gathered up his suit and the pack and, ignoring the elevator, opened the door beside it to a stairwell. "Leave your suit here," he said, ditching his own in a corner.

The stairwell was steep and the cold air tasted stale; it raised goose bumps on Erno's skin. Clutching the pack to his chest, Tyler hopped down the stairs to the next level. The wall beside them was sprayed with gray insulation. The light from bioluminescents turned their skin greenish yellow.

Instead of continuing down the well all the way to the top of the spire, Tyler stopped at a door on the side of the stairwell. He punched in a code. The door opened into a vast darkness, the space between the exterior and interior shells of the dome. Tyler shone his light inside: Three meters high, broken by reinforcing struts, the cavity stretched out from them into the darkness, curving slightly as it fell away. Tyler closed the door behind them and, in the light of his flash, pulled a notebook from the pack and called up a map. He studied it for a minute, and then led Erno into the darkness.

To the right about ten meters, an impenetrable wall was one of the great cermet ribs of the dome that stretched like the frame of an umbrella from the central spire to the distant crater rim.

Before long Tyler stopped, shining his light on the floor. "Here it is."

"What?"

"Maintenance port. Periodically they have to inspect the interior of the dome, repair the fiberoptics." Tyler squatted down and began to open the lock.

"What are you going to do?"

"We're going to hang from the roof like little spiders, Erno, and leave a gift for our cousins."

The port opened and Erno got a glimpse of the space that yawned below. A thousand meters below them the semicircular ranks of seats of the Sobieski Park amphitheater glowed ghostly white in the lights of the artificial night. Tyler drew ropes and carabineers from his pack, and from the bottom, an oblong device, perhaps fifty centimeters square, wrapped in fiberoptic cloth that glinted in the light of the flashlight. At one end was a timer. The object gave off an aura of threat that was both frightening and instantly attractive.

"What is that thing? Is it a bomb?"

"A bomb, Erno? Are you crazy?" Tyler snapped one of the lines around a reinforcing strut. He donned a harness and handed an identical one to Erno. "Put this on."

"I'm afraid of heights."

"Don't be silly. This is safe as a kiss. Safer, maybe."

"What are we trying to accomplish?"

"That's something of a metaphysical question."

"That thing doesn't look metaphysical to me."

"Nonetheless, it is. Call it the Philosopher's Stone. We're going to attach it to the inside of the dome."

"I'm not going to blow any hole in the dome."

"Erno, I couldn't blow a hole in the dome without killing myself. I guarantee you that, as a result of what we do here, I will suffer whatever consequences anyone else suffers. More than anyone else, even. Do I look suicidal to you, Erno?"

"To tell the truth, I don't know. You sure do some risky things. Why don't you tell me what you intend?"

"This is a test. I want to see whether you trust me."

"You don't trust *me* enough to tell me anything."

"Trust isn't about being persuaded. Trust is when you do something because your brother asks you to. I didn't have to ask you along on this adventure, Erno. I trusted you." Tyler crouched there, calmly watching Erno. "So, do you have the balls for this?"

The moment stretched. Erno pulled on the climbing harness.

Tyler ran the ropes through the harness, gave him a pair of gloves, and showed Erno how to brake the rope behind his back. Then, with the maybe-bomb Philosopher's Stone slung over his shoulder, Tyler dropped through the port. Feeling like he was about to take a step he could never take back, Erno edged out after him.

Tyler helped him let out three or four meters of rope. Erno's weight made the rope twist, and the world began to spin dizzily. They were so close to the dome's inner surface that the "stars" shining there were huge fuzzy patches of light in the braided fiberglass surface. The farmlands of the crater floor were swathed in shadow, but around the crater's rim, oddly twisted from this god's-eye perspective, the lights of apartment districts cast fans of illumination on the hanging gardens and switchbacked perimeter road. Erno could make out a few microscopic figures down there. Not far from Tyler and him, the top of the central spire obscured their view to the west. The flying stage, thirty meters down from where the spire met the roof, was closed for the night, but an owl nesting underneath flew out at their appearance and circled below them.

Tyler began to swing himself back and forth at the end of his line, gradually picking up amplitude until, at the apex of one of his swings, he latched himself onto the dome's inner surface. "C'mon, Erno! Time's wasting!"

Erno steeled himself to copy Tyler's performance. It took effort to get himself swinging and once he did the arcs were ponderous and slow. He had trouble orienting himself so that one end of his oscillation left him close to Tyler. At the top of every swing gravity disappeared and his stomach lurched. Finally, after what seemed an eternity of trying, Erno swung close enough for Tyler to reach out and snag his leg.

He pulled Erno up beside him and attached Erno's belt line to a ringbolt in the dome's surface. Erno's heart beat fast.

"Now you know you're alive," Tyler said.

"If anyone catches us up here, our asses are fried."

"Our asses are everywhere and always fried. That's the human condition. Let's work."

While Tyler pulled the device out of the bag he had Erno spread glue onto the dome's surface. When the glue was set, the two of them pressed the Philosopher's Stone into it until it was firmly fixed. Because of its reflective surface it would be invisible from the crater floor. "Now, what time did Debra Debrasdaughter say that meeting was tomorrow?"

"1600," Erno said. "You knew that."

Tyler flipped open the lid over the Stone's timer and punched some keys. "Yes, I did."

"And you didn't need my help to do this. Why did you make me come?"

The timer beeped; the digital readout began counting down. Tyler flipped the lid closed. "To give you the opportunity to betray me. And if you want to, you still have—" he looked at his wristward, "—fourteen hours and thirteen minutes."

Male Dominance Behavior

Erno had begun building his store of resentment when he was twelve, in Eva Evasdaughter's molecular biotechnology class. Eva Evasdaughter came from an illustrious family: her mother had been the longest serving member of the colony council. Her grandmother, Eva Kabatsumi, jailed with Nora Sobieski in California, had originated the matronymic system.

It took Erno a while to figure out that that didn't make Evasdaughter a good teacher. He was the brightest boy in the class. He believed in the cousins, respected authority, and worshipped women like his mother and Evasdaughter.

Evasdaughter was a tall woman who wore tight short-sleeved tunics that emphasized her small breasts. Erno had begun to notice such things; sex play was everyone's interest that semester, and he had recently had several erotic fondling sessions with girls in the class.

One day they were studying protein engineering. Erno loved it. He liked how you could make a gene jump through hoops if you were clever enough. He got ahead in the reading. That day he asked Eva Evasdaughter about directed protein mutagenesis, a topic they were not due to study until next semester.

"Can you make macro-modifications in proteins—I mean replace entire sequences to get new enzymes?" He was genuinely curious, but at some level he also was seeking Evasdaughter's approval of his doing extra work.

She turned on him coolly. "Are you talking about using site-directed mutagenesis, or chemical synthesis of oligonucleotides?"

He had never heard of site-directed mutagenesis. "I mean using oligonucleotides to change the genes."

"I can't answer unless I know if we're talking about site-directed or synthesized oligonucleotides. Which is it?"

Erno felt his face color. The other students were watching him. "I—I don't know."

"Yes, you don't," Evasdaughter said cheerfully. And instead of explaining, she turned back to the lesson.

Erno didn't remember another thing for the rest of that class, except looking at his shoes. Why had she treated him like that? She made him feel stupid. Yes, she knew more biotech than he did, but she was the teacher! Of course she knew more! Did that mean she had to put him down?

When he complained to his mother, she only said that he needed to listen to the teacher.

Only slowly did he realize that Evasdaughter had exhibited what he had always been taught was male dominance behavior. He had presented a challenge to her superiority, and she had smashed him flat. After he was, smashed, she could afford to treat him kindly. But she would teach him only after he admitted that he was her inferior.

Now that his eyes were opened, he saw this behavior everywhere. Every day cousins asserted their superiority in order to hurt others. He had been lied to, and his elders were hypocrites.

Yet when he tried to show his superiority, he was told to behave himself. Superior / inferior is wrong, they said. Difference is all.

FIVE

One thing Tyler had said was undoubtedly true: this was a test. How devoted was Erno to the Society of Cousins? How good a judge was he of Tyler's character? How eager was he to see his mother and the rest of his world made uncomfortable, and how large a discomfort did he think was justified? Just how angry was Erno?

After Erno got back to his room, he lay awake, unable to sleep. He ran every moment of his night with Tyler over in his mind, parsed every sentence, and examined every ambiguous word. Tyler had never denied that the Philosopher's Stone was a bomb. Erno looked up the term in the dictionary: a philosopher's stone was "an imaginary substance sought by alchemists in the belief that it would change base metals into gold or silver."

He did not think the change that Tyler's stone would bring had anything to do with gold or silver.

He looked at his palm, long since washed clean, where Alicia had written her number. She'd asked him to call her before he did anything stupid.

At 1545 the next day Erno was seated in the amphitheater among the crowds of cousins. More people were here than had come the previous week, and the buzz of their conversation, broken by occasional laughter, filled the air. He squinted up at the dome to try to figure out just where they had placed the stone. The dome had automatic safety devices to seal any minor air leak. But it couldn't survive a hole blasted in it. Against the artificial blue sky Erno watched a couple of flyers circling like hawks.

1552. Tyler arrived, trailing a gaggle of followers, mostly young men trying to look insolent. He'd showed up—what did that mean? Erno noted that this time,

Tyler wore black. He seemed as calm as he had before, and he chatted easily with the others, then left them to take a seat on the stage.

At 1559 Debra Debrasdaughter took her place. Erno looked at his watch. 1600. Nothing happened.

Was that the test? To see whether Erno would panic and fall for a ruse? He tried to catch Tyler's eye, but got nothing.

Debrasdaughter rapped for order. The ranks of cousins began to quiet, to sit up straighter. Near silence had fallen, and Debrasdaughter began to speak.

"Our second meeting to discuss—"

A flash of light seared the air high above them, followed a second later by a concussion. Shouts, a few screams.

Erno looked up. A cloud of black smoke shot rapidly from a point against the blue. One flyer tumbled, trying to regain his balance; the other had dived a hundred meters seeking a landing place. People pointed and shouted. The blue sky flickered twice, went to white as the imaging system struggled, then recovered.

People boiled out of the amphitheater, headed for pressurized shelter. Erno could not see if the dome had been breached. The smoke, instead of dissipating, spread out in an arc, then flattened up against the dome. It formed tendrils, shapes. He stood there, frozen. It was not smoke at all, he realized, but smart paint.

The nanodevices spread the black paint onto the interior of the dome. The paint crawled and shaped itself, forming letters. The letters, like a message from God, made a huge sign on the inside of the clear blue sky:

"BANG! YOU'RE DEAD!"

"You're Dead!"

One of the other *Stories for Men* was about Harry Rodney and Little Bert, two petty criminals on an ocean liner that has struck an iceberg and is sinking, with not enough lifeboats for all the passengers. The patriarchal custom was that women and children had precedence for spaces in the boats. Harry gives up his space in a boat in favor of some girl. Bert strips a coat and scarf from an injured woman, steals her jewelry, abandons her belowdecks, and uses her clothes to sneak into a lifeboat.

As it happens, both men survive. But Harry is so disgusted by Bert's crime that he persuades him to run away and pretend he is dead. For years, whenever Bert contacts Harry, Harry tells him to stay away or else the police might discover him. Bert never returns home for fear of being found out.

SIX

In the panic and confusion, Tyler Durden disappeared. On his seat at the meeting lay a note: "I did it."

As a first step in responding to the threat to the colony, the Board of Matrons immediately called the question of ostracism, and by evening the population had voted: Tyler Durden was declared invisible.

As if that mattered. He could not be found.

SEVEN

It took several days for the writing to be erased from the dome.

A manhunt did not turn up Tyler. Nerves were on edge. Rumors arose, circulated, were denied. Tyler Durden was still in the colony, in disguise. A cabal of followers was hiding him. No, he and his confederates had a secret outpost ten kilometers north of the colony. Durden was in the employ of the government of California. He had stockpiled weapons and was planning an attack. He had an atomic bomb.

At the gym entrance, AI's checked DNA prints, and Erno was conscious, as never before, of the cameras in every room. He wondered if any monitors had picked up his excursion with Tyler. Every moment he expected a summons on his wristward to come to the assembly offices.

When Erno entered the workout room, he found Tyrus and a number of others wearing white T-shirts that said, "BANG! YOU'RE DEAD!"

Erno took the unoccupied rowing machine next to Ty. Ty was talking to Sid on the other side of him.

A woman came across the room to use the machines. She was tightly muscled, and her dark hair was pulled back from her sweaty neck. As she approached, the young men went silent and turned to look at her. She hesitated. Erno saw something on her face he had rarely seen on a woman's face before: fear. The woman turned and left the gym.

None of the boys said anything. If the others had recognized what had just happened, they did not let it show.

Erno pulled on his machine. He felt the muscles in his legs knot. "Cool shirt," he said.

"Tyrus wants to be invisible, too," said Sid. Sid wasn't wearing one of the shirts.

"Eventually someone will check the vids of Tyler's performances, and see me there," said Ty between strokes. "I'm not ashamed to be Tyler's fan." At thirteen, Erno and Ty had been fumbling lovers, testing out their sexuality. Now Ty was a blunt overmuscled guy who laughed like a hyena. He didn't laugh now.

"It was a rush to judgment," one of the other boys said. "Tyler didn't harm a single cousin. It was free expression."

"He could just as easily have blown a hole in the dome," said Erno. "Do they need any more justification for force?"

Ty stopped rowing and turned toward Erno. Where he had sweated through the fabric, the "Bang!" on his shirt had turned blood red. "Maybe it will come to force. We do as much work, and we're second class citizens." He started rowing again, pulled furiously at the machine, fifty reps a minute, drawing quick breaths.

"That Durden has a pair, doesn't he?" Sid said. Sid was a popular stud-boy.

His thick chestnut hair dipped below one eye. "You should have seen the look on Rebecca's face when that explosion went off."

"I hear, if they catch him, the council's not going to stop at invisibility," Erno said. "They'll kick him out."

"Invisibility won't slow Tyler down," Ty said. "Would you obey the decree?" he asked Sid.

"Me? I'm too beautiful to let myself get booted. If Tyler Durden likes masculinists so much, let him go to one of the other colonies, or to Earth. I'm getting laid too often."

Erno's gut tightened. "They will kick him out. My mother would vote for it in a second."

"Let 'em try," Ty grunted, still rowing.

"Is that why you're working out so much lately, Ty?" Sid said. "Planning to move to Earth?"

"No. I'm just planning to bust your ass."

"I suspect it's not busting you want to do to my ass."

"Yeah. Your ass has better uses."

"My mother says Tyler's broken the social contract," Erno said.

"Does your mother—" Ty said, still rowing, "—keep your balls under her pillow?"

Sid laughed.

Erno wanted to grab Ty and tell him, *I was there. I helped him do it!* But he said nothing. He pulled on the machine. His face burned.

After a minute Erno picked up his towel and went to the weight machine. No one paid him any attention. Twenty minutes later he hit the sauna. Sweating in the heat, sullen, resentful. He had *been* there, had taken a bigger risk than any of these fan-boys.

Coming out of the sauna he saw Sid heading for the sex rooms, where any woman who was interested could find a male partner who was willing. Erno considered posting himself to one of the rooms. But he wasn't a stud; he was just an anonymous minor male. He had no following. It would be humiliating to sit there waiting for someone, or worse, to be selected by some old bag.

A day later Erno got himself one of the T-shirts. Wearing it didn't make him feel any better.

It came to him that maybe this was the test Tyler intended: not whether Erno would tell about the Philosopher's Stone before it happened, but whether he would admit he'd helped set it after he saw the uproar it caused in the colony.

If that was the test, Erno was failing. He thought about calling Tyler's apartment, but the constables were sure to be monitoring that number. A new rumor had it Tyler had been captured and was being held in protective custody—threats had been made against his life—until the Board of Matrons could decide when and how to impose the invisibility. Erno imagined Tyler in some bare white room, his brain injected with nanoprobes, his neck fitted with a collar.

At biotech, Erno became aware of something he had never noticed before: how the women assumed first pick of the desserts in the cafeteria. Then, later, when he walked by their table, four women burst into laughter. He turned and stared at them, but they never glanced at him.

Another day he was talking with a group of engineers on break: three women, another man, and Erno. Hana from materials told a joke: "What do you have when you have two little balls in your hand?"

The other women grinned. Erno watched the other man. He stood as if on a trapdoor, a tentative smile on his face. The man was getting ready to laugh, because that was what you did when people told jokes, whether or not they were funny. It was part of the social contract—somebody went into joke-telling mode, and you went into joke-listening mode.

"A man's undivided attention," Hana said.

The women laughed. The man grinned.

"How can you tell when a man is aroused?" Pearl said. "—He's breathing."

"That isn't funny," Erno said.

"Really? I think it is," Hana said.

"It's objectification. Men are just like women. They have emotions, too."

"Cool off, Erno," said Pearl. "This isn't gender equity class."

"There is no gender equity here."

"Someone get Erno a T-shirt."

"Erno wants to be invisible."

"We're already invisible!" Erno said, and stalked off. He left the lab, put on his suit, and took the next bus back to the dome. He quit going to his practicum: he would not let himself be used anymore. He was damned if he would go back there again.

A meeting to discuss what to do about the missing comedian was disrupted by a group of young men marching and chanting outside the meeting room. Constables were stationed in public places, carrying clubs. In online discussion rooms, people openly advocated closing the Men's Houses for fear conspiracies were being hatched in them.

And Erno received another message. This one was from "Harry Callahan."

Are you watching, Erno? If you think our gender situation is GROSS, you can change it. Check exposition.

Crimes of Violence

The incidence of crimes of violence among the cousins is vanishingly small. Colony archives record eight murders in sixty years. Five of them were man against man, two man against woman, and one woman against woman.

This does not count vigilante acts of women against men, but despite the lack of official statistics, such incidents too are rare.

EIGHT

"It's no trick to be celibate when you don't like sex."

"That's the point," Erno insisted. "He does like sex. He likes sex fine. But he's making a sacrifice in order to establish his point: He's not going to be a prisoner of his dick."

Erno was sitting out on the ledge of the terrace in front of their apartment, chucking pebbles at the recycling bin at the corner and arguing with his cousin Lena. He had been arguing with a lot of people lately, and not getting anywhere. Every morning he still left as if he were going to biotech, but instead he hung out in the park or gym. It would take some time for his mother to realize he had dropped out.

Lena launched into a tirade, and Erno was suddenly very tired of it all. Before she could gain any momentum, he threw a last pebble that whanged off the bin, got up and, without a word, retreated into the apartment. He could hear Lena's squawk behind him.

He went to his room and opened a screen on his wall. The latest news was that Tashi Yokiosson had regained consciousness, but that he had suffered neurological damage that might take a year or more to repair. Debate on the situation raged on the net. Erno opened his documents locker and fiddled with a melancholy sonnet he was working on, but he wasn't in the mood.

He switched back to Tyler's cryptic message. *You can change it. Check exposition.* It had something to do with biotech, Erno was pretty sure. He had tried the public databases, but had not come up with anything. There were databases accessible only through the biotech labs, but he would have to return to his practicum to view them, and that would mean he would have to explain his absence. He wasn't ready for that yet.

On impulse, Erno looked up Tyler in the colony's genome database. What was the name Debrasdaughter had called him? — Marysson, Thomas Marysson. He found Tyler's genome. Nothing about it stood out.

Debaters had linked Tyler's bio to the genome. Marysson had been born thirty-six years ago. His mother was a second-generation cousin; his grandmother had arrived with the third colonization contingent, in 2038. He had received a general education, neither excelling nor failing anything. His mother had died when he was twenty. He had moved out into the dorms, had worked uneventfully in construction and repair for fourteen years, showing no sign of rebelliousness before reinventing himself as Tyler Durden, the Comedian.

Until two years ago, absolutely nothing had distinguished him from any of a thousand male cousins.

Bored, Erno looked up his own genome.

There he lay in rows of base pairs, neat as a tile floor. Over at biotech, some insisted that everything you were was fixed in those sequences in black and white. Erno didn't buy it. Where was the gene for desire there, or hope, or despair, or frustration? Where was the gene that said he would sit in front of a computer screen at the age of seventeen, boiling with rage?

He called up his mother's genome. There were her sequences. Some were the same as his. Of course there was no information about his father. To prevent dire social consequences, his father must remain a blank spot in his history, as far as the Society of Cousins was concerned. Maybe some families kept track of such things, but nowhere in the databases were fathers and children linked.

Of course they couldn't stop him from finding out. He knew others who had done it. His father's genome was somewhere in the database, for medical purposes. If he removed from his own those sequences that belonged to his mother, then what was left—at least the sequences she had not altered when she had planned him—belonged to his father. He could cross check those against the genomes of all the colony's men.

From his chart, he stripped those genes that matched his mother's. Using what remained, he prepared a search engine to sort through the colony's males.

The result was a list of six names. Three were brothers: Stuart, Simon, and Josef Bettesson. He checked the available public information on them. They were all in their nineties, forty years older than Erno's mother. Of the remaining men, two were of about her age: Sidney Orindasson and Micah Avasson. Of those two, Mica Avasson had the higher correlation with Erno's genome.

He read the public records for Micah Avasson. Born in 2042, he would be fifty-six years old. A physical address: men's dormitory, East Five lava tube. He keyed it into his notebook.

Without knocking, his mother came into the room. Though he had no reason to be ashamed of his search, Erno shoved the notebook into his pocket.

She did not notice. "Erno, we need to talk."

"By talk do you mean interrogate, or lecture?"

His mother's face stiffened. For the first time he noticed the crow's feet at the corners of her eyes. She moved around his room, picking up his clothes, sorting, putting them away. "You should keep your room cleaner. Your room is a reflection of your mind."

"Please, mother."

She held one of his shirts to her nose, sniffed, and made a face. "Did I ever tell you about the time I got arrested? I was thirteen, and Derek Silviasson and I were screwing backstage in the middle of a performance of A Doll's House. We got a little carried away. When Nora opened the door to leave at the end of the second act, she tripped over Derek and me in our second act."

"They arrested you? Why?"

"The head of the Board was a prude. It wouldn't have mattered so much but A Doll's House was her favorite play."

"You and Derek Silviasson were lovers?"

She sat down on his bed, a meter from him, and leaned forward. "After the paint bombing, Erno, they went back to examine the recordings from the spex of the officers at the Oxygen Warehouse riot. Who do you suppose, to my surprise, they found there?"

Erno swiveled in his chair to avoid her eyes. "Nick already told you I went there."

"But you didn't. Not only were you there, but at one point you were together with Durden."

"What was I doing?"

"Don't be difficult. I'm trying to protect you, Erno. The only reason I know about this is that Harald Gundasson let me know on the sly. Another report says Durden met you outside the North airlock one day. You're likely to be called in for questioning. I want to know what's going on. Are you involved in some conspiracy?"

His mother looked so forlorn he found it hard to be hostile. "As far as I know there is no conspiracy."

"Did you have something to do with the paint bomb?"

"No. Of course not."

"I found out you haven't been to your practicum. What have you been doing?"

"I've been going to the gym."

"Are you planning a trip to Earth?"

"Don't be stupid, mother."

"Honestly, Erno, I can't guess what you are thinking. You're acting like a spy."

"Maybe I am a spy."

His mother laughed.

"Don't laugh at me!"

"I'm not laughing because you're funny. I'm laughing because I'm scared! This is an ugly business, Erno."

"Stop it, mother. Please."

She stared at him. He tried not to look away. "I want you to listen. Tyler Durden is a destroyer. I've been to Aristarchus, to Tycho. I've seen the patriarchy. Do you want that here?"

"How would I know? I've never been there!" His eyes fell on the copy of *Stories for Men.* "Don't tell me stories about rape and carnage," he said, looking at the book's cover. "I've heard them all before. You crammed them down my throat with my baby food."

"They're true. Do you deny them?"

Erno clenched his jaw, tried to think. Did she have to browbeat him? "I don't know!"

"It's not just carnage. It's waste and insanity. You want to know what they're like—one time I had a talk with this security man at Shackleton. They were mining lunar ice for reaction mass in the shuttles.

"I put it to him that using lunar ice for rocket fuel was criminally wasteful. Water is the most precious commodity on the moon, and here they are blowing it into space.

"He told me it was cheaper to use lunar ice than haul water from Earth. My argument wasn't with him, he said, it was with the laws of the marketplace. Like most of them, he condescended to me, as if I were a child or idiot. He thought that invoking the free market settled the issue, as if to go against the market were to go against the laws of nature. The goal of conquering space justified the expenditure, he said—that they'd get more water somewhere else when they used up the lunar ice."

"He's got an argument."

"The market as a law of nature? 'Conquering space?' How do you conquer space? That's not a goal, it's a disease."

"What does this have to do with Tyler Durden?"

"Durden is bringing the disease here!"

"He's fighting oppression! Men have no power here; they are stifled and ignored. There are no real male cousins."

"There are plenty of male cousins. There are lots of role models. Think of Adil Al-Hafaz, of Peter Sarahsson—of Nick, for pity's sake!"

"Nick? Nick?" Erno laughed. He stood. "You might as well leave now, officer."

His mother looked hurt. "Officer?"

"That's why you're here, isn't it?"

"Erno, I know you don't like me. I'm dull and conventional. But being unconventional, by itself, isn't a virtue. I'm your mother."

"And you're a cop."

That stopped her for a moment. She took a deep breath. "I dearly love you, Erno, but if you think—"

That tone of voice. He'd heard it all his life: all the personal anecdotes are over, now. We're done with persuasion, and it's time for you to do what I say.

"You dearly love nothing!" Erno shouted. "All you want is to control me!"

She started to get up. "I've given you every chance—"

Erno threw *Stories for Men* at her. His mother flinched, and the book struck her in the chest and fell slowly to the floor. She looked more startled than hurt, watching the book fall, tumbling, leaves open; she looked as if she were trying to understand what it was—but when she faced him again, her eyes clouded. Trembling, livid, she stood, and started to speak. Before she could say a word Erno ran from the room.

Property

A man on his own is completely isolated. Other men might be his friends or lovers, but if he has a legal connection to anyone, it is to his mother.

Beyond a certain point, property among the cousins is the possession of the community. Private property passes down from woman to woman, but only outside of the second degree of blood relation. A woman never inherits from her biological mother. A woman chooses her friends and mates, and in the event of her death, her property goes to them. If a woman dies without naming an heir, her property goes to the community.

A man's property is typically confined to personal possessions. Of course, in most families he is petted, and has access to more resources than any female, but the possessions are gotten for him by his mother or his mate, and they belong to her. What property he might hold beyond that belongs to his mother. If he has no mother, then it belongs to his oldest sister. If he has no sister, then it goes to the community.

A man who forsakes his family has nowhere to go.

NINE

The great jazzmen were all persecuted minorities. Black men like Armstrong, Ellington, Coltrane, Parker. And the comedians were all Jews and black men. Leaving his mother's apartment, Erno saw himself the latest in history's long story of abused fighters for expressive freedom.

Erno stalked around the perimeter road, head down. To his left, beyond the parapet, the crater's inner slope, planted with groundsel, wildflowers, and hardy low-G modifications of desert scrub, fell away down to the agricultural fields, the park, and two kilometers distant, clear through the low-moisture air, the aspen-forested opposite slopes. To his right rose the ranks of apartments, refectories, dorms, public buildings and labs, clusters of oblong boxes growing higgledy-piggledy, planted with vines and hanging gardens, divided by ramps and stairs and walkways, a high-tech cliff city in pastel concrete glittering with ilemenite crystals. A small green lizard scuttled across the pebbled composite of the roadway and disappeared among some ground cover.

Erno ignored the people on their way to work and back, talking or playing. He felt like smashing something. But smashing things was not appropriate cousins behavior.

In the southwest quad he turned up a ramp into a residential district. These were newer structures, products of the last decade's planned expansion of living quarters, occupied for the most part by new families. He moved upward by steady leaps, feeling the tension on his legs, enjoying the burn it generated.

Near the top of the rimwall he found Gilman 334. He pressed the door button. The screen remained blank, but after a moment Alicia's voice came from the speaker. "Erno. Come on in."

The door opened and he entered the apartment. It consisted mostly of an open lounge, furnished in woven furniture, with a couple of small rooms adjoining. Six young women were sitting around inhaling mood enhancers, listening to music. The music was Monk, "Brilliant Corners." Erno had given it to Alicia; she would never have encountered twentieth century jazz otherwise.

There was something wrong with Monk in this context. These girls ought to be listening to some lunar music—one of the airy mixed choral groups, or Shari Cloudsdaughter's *Drums and Sunlight*. In this circle of females, the tossed off lines of Sonny Rollins' sax, the splayed rhythms of Monk's piano, seemed as if they were being stolen. Or worse still, studied—by a crew of aliens for whom they could not mean what they meant to Erno.

"Hello," Erno said. "Am I crashing your party?"

"You're not crashing." Alicia took him by the arm. "This is Erno," she said to the others. "Some of you know him."

Sharon was there, one of the hottest women in Alicia's cohort at school—he had heard Sid talk about her. He recognized Betty Sarahsdaughter, Liz Beths-daughter, both of them, like Alicia, studying social work, both of whom had turned him down at one time or another. Erno liked women as individuals, but in a group, their intimate laughter, gossip, and private jokes—as completely innocent as they might be—made him feel like he knew nothing about them. He drew Alicia aside, "Can we talk—in private?"

"Sure." She took Erno to one of the bedrooms. She sat on the bed, gestured to a chair. "What's the matter?"

"I had a fight with my mother."

"That's what mothers are for, as far as I can tell."

"And the constables are going to call me in for questioning. They think I may be involved in some conspiracy with Tyler Durden."

"Do you know where he is?"

Erno's defenses came up. "Do you care?"

"I don't want to know where he is. If you know, keep it to yourself. I'm *not* your mother."

"I could be in trouble."

"A lot of us will stand behind you on this, Erno. Sharon and I would." She reached out to touch his arm. "I'll go down to the center with you."

Erno moved to the bed beside her. He slid his hand to her waist, closed his eyes, and rubbed his cheek against her hair. To his surprise, he felt her hand between his shoulder blades. He kissed her, and she leaned back. He looked into her face: her green eyes, troubled, searched his. Her bottom lip was full. He kissed her again, slid his hand to her breast, and felt the nipple taut beneath her shirt.

Leave aside the clumsiness—struggling out of their clothes, the distraction of "Straight, No Chaser" from the other room, Erno's momentary thought of the women out there wondering what was going on in here—and it was the easiest thing in the world. He slid into Alicia as if he were coming home. Though his head swirled with desire, he tried to hold himself back, to give her what she wanted. He kissed her all over. She giggled and teased him and twisted her fingers in his hair to pull him down to her, biting his lip. For fifteen or twenty minutes, the Society of Cousins disappeared.

Erno watched her face, watched her closed eyes and parted lips, as she concentrated on her pleasure. It gave him a feeling of power. Her skin flushed, she gasped, shuddered, and he came.

He rested his head upon her breast, eyes closed, breathing deeply, tasting the salt of her sweat. Her chest rose and fell, and he could hear her heart beating fast, then slower. He held her tight. Neither said anything for a long time.

After a while he asked her, quietly, "Can I stay here?"

Alicia stroked his shoulder, slid out from beneath him, and began to pull on her shirt. "I'll talk to Sharon."

Sharon. Erno wondered how many of the other women in the next room Alicia was sleeping with. Alicia was a part of that whole scene, young men and women playing complex mating games that Erno was no good at. He had no idea what "talking to Sharon" might involve. But Alicia acted as if the thought of him moving in was a complete surprise.

"Don't pull a muscle or anything stretching to grasp the concept," Erno said softly.

Alicia reacted immediately. "Erno, we've never exchanged two words about partnering. What do you expect me to say?"

"We did talk about it—in the park. You said you would talk to Sharon then. Why didn't you?"

"Please, Erno." She drew up her pants and the fabric seamed itself closed over her lovely, long legs. "When you're quiet, you're so sweet."

Sweet. Erno felt vulnerable, lying there naked with the semen drying on his belly. He reached for his clothes. "That's right," he muttered, "I forgot. Sex is the social glue. Fuck him so he doesn't cause any trouble."

"Everything isn't about your penis, Erno. Durden is turning you into some self-destructive *boy*. Grow up."

"Grow up?" Erno tugged on his pants. "You don't want me grown-up. You want the sweet boy, forever. I've figured it out now—you're never even there with me, except maybe your body. At least I think it was you."

Alicia stared at him. Erno recognized that complete exasperation: he had seen it on his mother. From the next room drifted the sound of "Blue Monk," and women laughing.

"Sharon was right," Alicia said, shaking her head. And she chuckled, a little rueful gasp, as if to say, *I can't believe I'm talking with this guy.*

Erno took a step forward and slapped her face. "You bitch," he breathed. "You fucking bitch."

Alicia fell back, her eyes wide with shock. Erno's head spun. He fled the room, ran through the party and out of the apartment.

It was full night now, the dome sprinkled with stars. He stalked down the switchback ramps toward the perimeter road, through the light thrown by successive lampposts, in a straight-legged gait that kicked him off the pavement with every stride. He hoped that anyone who saw him would see his fury and think him dangerous. Down on the road he stood at the parapet, breathing through his mouth and listening to the hum of insects in the fields below.

In the lamplight far to his left, a person in a green uniform appeared. On impulse Erno hopped over the parapet to the slope. Rather than wait for the constable to pass, he bounced off down toward the crater's floor, skidding where it was steep, his shoes kicking up dust. He picked up speed, making headlong four- or five-meter leaps, risking a fall every time his feet touched.

It was too fast. Thirty meters above the floor he stumbled and went flying face forward. He came down sideways, rolled, and slammed his head as he flipped and skidded to a halt. He lay trying to catch his breath. He felt for broken limbs. His shirt was torn and his shoulder ached. He pulled himself up and went down the last few meters to the crater floor, then limped through the fields for Sobieski Park.

In a few minutes he was there, out of breath and sweating. At the fountain he splashed water on his face. He felt his shoulder gingerly, then made his way to the amphitheater. At first he thought the theater was deserted, but then he saw, down on the stage, a couple of women necking, oblivious of him.

He stood in the row where he had spotted Alicia some weeks before. He had hit her. He couldn't believe he had hit her.

TEN

Erno slept in the park and in the morning headed for his biotech shift as if he had never stopped going. No one at the airlock questioned him. Apparently, even though his mind was chaos, he looked perfectly normal. The radiation warning had been renewed; solar monitors reported conditions ripe for a coronal mass ejection. Cousins obliged to go out on the surface were being advised to keep within range of a radiation shelter.

When Erno arrived at the bunker he went to Lemmy Odilleson's lab. Lemmy had not arrived yet. He sat down at his workstation, signed onto the system, pressed his thumb against the gene scanner and accessed the database.

He tried the general index. There was no file named exposition. Following Tyler's reference to "gross," he looked for any references to the number 144. Nothing. Nothing on the gross structures of nucleotides, either. He tried coming at it from the virus index. Dozens of viruses had been engineered by the cousins to deal with problems from soil microbes to cellular breakdowns caused by exposure to surface radiation. There was no virus called exposition.

While he sat there Lemmy showed up. He said nothing of Erno's sudden appearance after his extended absence. "We're making progress on integrating the morphological growth genes into the prototypes," he said excitedly. "The sequences for extracting silicon from the soil are falling into place."

"That's good," Erno said. He busied himself cleaning up the chaos Lemmy typically left in his notes. After a while, he asked casually, "Lemmy, have you ever heard about a virus called 'exposition'?"

"X-position?" Lemmy said vaguely, not looking up from a rack of test bulbs. "Those prefixes go with female sex-linked factors. The Y-position are the male."

"Oh, right."

As soon as Erno was sure Lemmy was caught up in his lab work, he turned back to the archives. First he went to Gendersites, a database he knew mostly for its concentration of anti-cancer modifications. X-position led him to an encyclopedia of information on the X chromosome. Erno called up a number of files, but he saw no point in digging through gene libraries at random. He located a file of experiments on female-linked syndromes from osteoporosis to post menopausal cardiac conditions.

On a whim, he did a search on "gross."

Up popped a file labeled Nucleotide Repeats. When Erno opened the file, the heading read:

Get

Rid

Of

Slimy

girl**S**

The sounds of the lab around him faded as he read the paper.

It described a method for increasing the number of unstable trinucleotide repeats on the X chromosome. All humans had repeat sequences, the presence of which were associated with various diseases: spinal and bulbar muscular atrophy, fragile X mental retardation, myotonic dystrophy, Huntington disease, spinocere-brellar ataxia, dentatorubral-pallidoluysian atrophy, and Machado-Joseph disease. All well understood neurological disorders.

In normal DNA, the repeats were below the level of expression of disease. Standard tests of the zygote assured this. The GROSS paper told how to construct two viruses: the first would plant a time bomb in the egg. At a particular stage of embryonic development the repetition of trinucleotides would explode. The second virus would plant compensating sequences on the Y chromosome.

Creating the viruses would be a tricky but not impossible problem in plasmid engineering. Their effect, however, would be devastating. In males the Y chromosome would suppress the X-linked diseases, but in females the trinucleotide syndromes would be expressed. When the repeats kicked in, the child would develop any one of a host of debilitating or fatal neurological disorders.

Of course once the disorder was recognized, other gene engineers would go to work curing it, or at least identifying possessors prenatally. The GROSS virus would not destroy the human race—but it could burden a generation of females with disease and early death.

Tyler had led Erno to this monstrosity. What was he supposed to do with it?

Nonetheless, Erno downloaded the file into his notebook. He had just finished when Cluny came into the lab.

"Hello, Professor Odillesson," Cluny said to Lemmy. He saw Erno and did a double take. Erno stared back at him.

"I'm not a professor, Michael," Lemmy said.

Cluny pointed at Erno. "You know the constables are looking for him?"

"They are? Why?"

Erno got up. "Don't bother explaining. I'll go."

Cluny moved to stop him. "Wait a minute."

Erno put his hand on Cluny's shoulder to push him aside. Cluny grabbed Erno's arm.

"What's going on?" Lemmy asked.

Erno tried to free himself from Cluny, but the Earthman's grip was firm. Cluny pulled him, and pain shot through the shoulder Erno had hurt in yesterday's spill. Erno hit Cluny in the face.

Cluny's head jerked back, but he didn't let go. His jaw clenched and his expression hardened into animal determination. He wrestled with Erno; they lost their balance, and in slow motion stumbled against a lab bench. Lemmy shouted and two women ran in from the next lab. Before Erno knew it he was pinned against the floor.

"Dead Man"

Many of the stories for men were about murder. The old Earth writers seemed fascinated by murder, and wrote about it from a dozen perspectives.

In one of the stories, a detective whose job it is to throw illegal riders off cargo trains finds a destitute man — a "hobo" — hiding on the train. While being brutally beaten by the detective, the hobo strikes back and unintentionally kills him.

The punishment for such a killing, even an accidental one, is death. Terrified, knowing that he has to hide his guilt, the hobo hurries back to the city. He pretends he never left the "flophouse" where he spent the previous night. He disposes of his clothes, dirty with coal dust from the train.

Then he reads a newspaper report. The detective's body has been found, but the investigators assume that he fell off the train and was killed by accident, and are not seeking anyone. The hobo is completely free from suspicion. His immediate reaction is to go to the nearest police station and confess.

ELEVEN

Erno waited in a small white room at the constabulary headquarters. As a child Erno had come here many times with his mother, but now everything seemed different. He was subject to the force of the state. That fucking cow Cluny. The constables had taken his notebook. Was that *pro forma*, or would they search it until they found the GROSS file?

He wondered what Alicia had done after he'd left the day before. What had she told her friends?

The door opened and two women came in. One of them was tall and good-looking. The other was small, with a narrow face and close-cropped blond hair. She looked to be a little younger than his mother. She sat down across from him; the tall woman remained standing.

"This can be simple, Erno, if you let it," the small woman said. She had an odd drawl that, combined with her short stature, made Erno wonder if she was from Earth. "Tell us where Tyler Durden is. And about the conspiracy."

Erno folded his arms across his chest. "I don't know where he is. There is no conspiracy."

"Do we have to show you images of you and him together during the Oxygen Warehouse riot?"

"I never saw him before that, or since. We were just hiding in the back room."

"You had nothing to do with the smartpaint explosion?"

"No."

The tall woman, who still had not spoken, looked worried. The blond interrogator leaned forward, resting her forearms on the table. "Your DNA was found at the access portal where the device was set."

Erno squirmed. He imagined a sequence of unstable nucleotide triplets multiplying in the woman's cells. "He asked me to help him. I had no idea what it was."

"No idea. So it could have been a bomb big enough to blow a hole in the dome. Yet you told no one about it."

"I knew he wasn't going to kill anyone. I could tell."

The interrogator leaned back. "I hope you will excuse the rest of us if we question your judgment."

"Believe me, I would never do anything to hurt a cousin. Ask my mother."

The tall woman finally spoke. "We have. She does say that. But you have to help us out, Erno. I'm sure you can understand how upset all this has made the polity."

"Forget it, Kim," the other said. "Erno here's not going to betray his lover."

"Tyler's not my lover," Erno said.

The blond interrogator smirked. "Right."

The tall one said, "There's nothing wrong with you being lovers, Erno."

"Then why did this one bring it up?"

"No special reason," said the blond. "I'm just saying you wouldn't betray him."

"Well, we're not lovers."

"Too bad," the blond muttered.

"You need to help us, Erno," the tall one said. "Otherwise, even if we let you go, you're going to be at risk of violence from other cousins."

"Only if you tell everyone about me."

"So we should just let you go, and not inconvenience you by telling others the truth about you," said the blond.

"What truth? You don't know me."

She came out of her chair, leaning forward on her clenched fists. Her face was flushed. "Don't know you? I know all about you."

"Mona, calm down," the other woman said.

"Calm down? Earth history is full of this! Men sublimate their sexual attraction in claims of brotherhood—with the accompanying military fetishism, penis comparing, suicidal conquer-or-die movements. Durden is heading for one of those classic orgasmic armageddons: Masada, Hitler in the bunker, David Koresh, September 11, the California massacre."

The tall one grabbed her shoulder and tried to pull her back. "Mona."

Mona threw off the restraining hand, and pushed her face up close to Erno's. "If we let this little shit go, I guarantee you he'll be involved in some transcendent destructive act—suicidally brave, suicidally cowardly—aimed at all of us. The signs are all over him." Spittle flew in Erno's face.

"You're crazy," Erno said. "If I wanted to fuck him, I would just fuck him."

The tall one tried again. "Come away, officer."

Mona grabbed Erno by the neck. "Where is he!"

"Come away, now!" The tall cop yanked the small woman away, and she fell back. She glared at Erno. The other, tugging her by the arm, pulled her out of the room.

Erno tried to catch his breath. He wiped his sleeve across his sweating face. He sat there alone for a long time, touching the raw skin where she had gripped his neck. Then the door opened and his mother came in.

"Mom!"

She carried some things in her hands, put them on the table. It was the contents of his pockets, including his notebook. "Get up."

"What's going on?"

"Just shut up and come with me. We're letting you go."

Erno stumbled from the chair. "That officer is crazy."

"Never mind her. I'm not sure she isn't right. It's up to you to prove she isn't."

She hustled him out of the office and into the hall. In seconds Erno found himself, dizzy, in the plaza outside the headquarters. "You are not out of trouble. Go home, and stay there," his mother said, and hurried back inside.

Passersby in North Six watched him as he straightened his clothes. He went to sit on the bench beneath the acacia trees at the lava tube's center. He caught his breath.

Erno wondered if the cop would follow through with her threat to tell about his helping with the explosion. He felt newly vulnerable. But it was not just vulnerability he felt. He had never seen a woman lose it as clearly as the interrogator had. He had gotten to her in a way he had never gotten to a matron in his life. She was actually *scared* of him!

Now what? He put his hand in his pocket, and felt the notebook.

He pulled it out. He switched it on. The GROSS file was still there, and so was the address he'd written earlier.

A Dream

Erno was ten when his youngest sister Celeste was born. After the birth, his mother fell into a severe depression. She snapped at Erno, fought with Aunt Sophie, and complained about one of the husbands until he moved out. Erno's way of coping was to disappear; his cousin Aphra coped by misbehaving.

One day Erno came back from school to find a fire in the middle of the kitchen floor, a flurry of safetybots stifling it with foam, his mother screaming, and Aphra — who had apparently started the fire — shouting back at her. Skidding on the foam, Erno stepped between the two of them, put his hands on Aphra's chest, and made her go to her room.

The whole time, his mother never stopped shouting. Erno was angrier at her than at Aphra. She was supposed to be the responsible one. When he returned from quieting Aphra, his mother ran off to her room and slammed the door. Erno cleaned the kitchen and waited for Aunt Sophie to come home.

The night of the fire he had a dream. He was alone in the kitchen, and then a man was there. The man drew him aside. Erno was unable to make out his face. "I am your father," the man said. "Let me show you something." He made Erno sit down and called up an image on the table. It was Erno's mother as a little girl. She sat, cross-legged, hunched over some blocks, her face screwed up in troubled introspection. "That's her second phase of work expression," Erno's father said.

With a shock, Erno recognized the expression on the little girl's face as one he had seen his mother make as she concentrated.

"She hates this photo," Erno's father said, as if to persuade Erno not to judge her: she still contained that innocence, that desire to struggle against a problem she could not solve. But Erno was mad. As he resisted, the father pressed on, and began to lose it too. He ended up screaming at Erno, "You can't take it? I'll make you see! I'll make you see!"

Erno put his hands over his ears. The faceless man's voice was twisted with rage. Eventually he stopped shouting. "There you go, there you go," he said quietly, stroking Erno's hair. "You're just the same."

TWELVE

On his way to the East Five tube, Erno considered the officer's rant. Maybe Tyler did want to sleep with him. So what? The officer was some kind of homophobe and ought to be relieved. Raving about violence while locking him up in a room. And then trying to choke him. Yes, he had the GROSS file in his pocket, yes he had hit Alicia—but he was no terrorist. The accusation was just a way for the cop to ignore men's legitimate grievances.

But they must not have checked the file, or understood it if they did. If they knew about GROSS, he would never have been freed.

Early in the colony's life, the East Five lava tube had been its major agricultural center. The yeast vats now produced only animal fodder, but the hydroponics rack farms still functioned, mostly for luxury items. The rote work of tending the racks fell to cousins who did not express ambition to do anything more challenging. They lived in the tube warrens on the colony's Minimum Living Standard.

A stylized painting of a centaur graced the entrance of the East Five men's warren. Since the artist had not likely ever studied a real horse, the stance of the creature looked deeply suspect to Erno. At the lobby interface Erno called up the AI attendant. The AI came on-screen as a dark brown woman wearing a glittery green shirt.

"I'm looking for Micah Avasson," Erno asked it.

"Who is calling?"

"Erno Pamelasson."

"He's on shift right now."

"Can I speak with him?"

"Knock yourself out." The avatar pointed off-screen toward a dimly lit passageway across the room. She appeared on the wall near the doorway, and called out to Erno, "Over here. Follow this corridor, third exit left to the Ag tube."

Outside of the lobby, the corridors and rooms here had the brutal utilitarian quality that marked the early colony, when survival had been the first concern and the idea of humane design had been to put a mirror at the end of a room to try to convince the eye that you weren't living in a cramped burrow some meters below the surface of a dead world. An environmental social worker would shudder.

The third exit on the left was covered with a clear permeable barrier. From the time he was a boy Erno had disliked passing through these permeable barriers; he hated the feel of the electrostatics brushing his face. He took a mask from the dispenser, fitted it over his nose and mouth, closed his eyes and passed through into the Ag tube. Above, layers of gray mastic sealed the tube roof; below, a concrete floor supported long rows of racks under light transmitted fiberoptically from the heliostats. A number of workers wearing coveralls and oxygen masks moved up and down the rows tending the racks. The high CO_2 air was laden with humidity, and even through the mask smelled of phosphates.

Erno approached a man bent over a drawer of seedlings he had pulled out of a rack. The man held a meter from which wires dangled to a tube immersed in the hydroponics fluid. "Excuse me," Erno said. "I'm looking for Micah Avasson."

The man lifted his head, inspected Erno, then without speaking turned. "Micah!" He called down the row.

A tall man a little farther down the aisle looked up and peered at them. He had a full head of dark hair, a birdlike way of holding his shoulders. After a moment he said, "I'm Micah Avasson."

Erno walked down toward him. Erno was nonplused—the man had pushed up his mask from his mouth and was smoking a cigarette, using real fire. No, not a cigarette—a joint.

"You can smoke in here? What about the fire regulations?"

"We in the depths are not held to as high a standard as you." Micah said this absolutely deadpan, as if there were not a hint of a joke. "Not enough O_2 to make a decent fire anyway. It takes practice just to get a good buzz off this thing in here without passing out."

Joint dangling from his lower lip, the man turned back to the rack. He wore yellow rubber gloves, and was pinching the buds off the tray of squat green leafy plants. Erno recognized them as a modified broadleaf sensamilla.

"You're using the colony facilities to grow pot."

"This is my personal crop. We each get a personal rack. Sparks initiative." Micah kept pinching buds. "Want to try some?"

Erno gathered himself. "My name is Erno Pamelasson. I came to see you because—"

"You're my son." Micah said, not looking at him.

Erno stared, at a loss for words. Up close the lines at the corners of the man's eyes were distinct, and there was a bit of sag to his chin. But the shape of Micah's face reminded Erno of his own reflection in the mirror.

"What did you want to see me about?" Micah pushed the rack drawer closed and looked at Erno. When Erno stood there dumb, he wheeled the stainless steel cart beside him down to the next rack. He took a plastic bin from the cart, crouched, pulled open the bottom drawer of the rack and began harvesting cherry tomatoes.

Finally, words came to Erno. "Why haven't I ever seen you before?"

"Lots of boys never meet their fathers."

"I'm not talking about other fathers. Why aren't you and my mother together?"

"You assume we were together. How do you know that we didn't meet in the sauna some night, one time only?"

"Is that how it was?"

Micah lifted a partially yellow tomato on his fingertips, then left it on the vine to ripen. He smiled. "No. Your mother and I were in love. We lived together for twenty-two months. And two days."

"So why did you split?"

"That I don't remember so well. We must have had our reasons. Everybody has reasons."

Erno touched his shoulder. "Don't give me that."

Micah stood, overbalancing a little. Erno caught his arm to steady him. "Thanks," Micah said. "The knees aren't what they used to be." He took a long drag on the joint, exhaled at the roof far overhead. "All right, then. The reason we broke up is that your mother is a cast-iron bitch. And I am a cast-iron bastard. The details of our breakup all derive from those simple facts, and I don't recall them. I do recall that we had good fun making you, though. I remember that well."

"I bet."

"You were a good baby, as babies go. Didn't cry too much. You had a sunny disposition." He took a final toke on the joint, and then dropped the butt into the bin of tomatoes. "Doesn't seem to have lasted."

"Were you there when I was born?"

"So we're going to have this conversation." Micah exhaled the last cloud of smoke, slipped his mask down, and finally fixed his watery brown eyes on Erno. "I was there. I was there until you were maybe six or seven months. Then I left."

"Did she make you leave?"

"Not really." His voice was muffled now. "She was taken with me at first because of the glamor—I was an acrobat, the *Cirque Jacinthe?* But her sister was in the marriage, and her friends. She had her mentor, her support group. I was just the father. It was okay while it was fun, and maybe I thought it was something more when we first got together, but after a while it wasn't fun anymore."

"You just didn't want the responsibility!"

"Erno, to tell you the truth, that didn't have much to do with it. I liked holding you on my lap and rubbing you with my beard. You would giggle. I would toss you up into the air and catch you. You liked that. Drove your mother crazy— you're going to hurt him, she kept saying."

Erno had a sudden memory of being thrown high, floating, tumbling. Laughing.

"So why did you leave?"

"Pam and I just didn't get along. I met another woman, that got hot, and Pam didn't seem to need me around anymore. I had filled my purpose."

Emotion worked in Erno. He shifted from foot to foot. "I don't understand men like you. They've stuck you down here in a dorm! You're old, and you've got nothing."

"I've got everything I need. I have friends."

"Women shit on you, and you don't care."

"There are women just like me. We have what we want. I work. I read. I grow my plants. I have no desire to change the world. The world works for me."

"The genius of the founders, Erno—" Micah opened another drawer and started on the next rack of tomatoes, "—was that they minimized the contact of males and females. They made it purely voluntary. Do you realize how many centuries men and women tore themselves to pieces through forced intimacy? In every marriage, the decades of lying that paid for every week of pleasure? That the vast majority of men and women, when they spoke honestly, regretted the day they had ever married?"

"We have no power!"

Micah made a disgusted noise. "Nobody has any power. On Earth, for every privilege, men had six obligations. I'm sorry you feel that something has been taken from you. If you feel that way, I suggest you work on building your own relationships. Get married, for pity's sake. Nothing is stopping you."

Erno grabbed Micah's wrist. "Look at me!"

Micah looked. "Yes?"

"You knew I was your son. Doesn't that mean you've been paying attention to me?"

"From a distance. I wish you well, you understand."

"You know I was responsible for the explosion at the meeting! The constables arrested me!"

"No. Really? That sounds like trouble, Erno."

"Don't you want to ask me anything?"

"Give me your number. If I think of something, I'll call. Assuming you're not banished by then."

Erno turned away. He stalked down the row of hydroponics.

"Come by again, Erno!" Micah called after him. "Anytime. I mean it. Do you like music?"

The next man down was watching Erno now. He passed through the door out of the Ag tube, tore off the mask and threw it down.

Some of the permeable barrier must have brushed Erno's face when he passed through, because as he left East Five he found he couldn't keep his eyes from tearing up.

"The Grandstand Complex"

Two motorcycle racers have been rivals for a long time. The one telling the story has been beating the other, Tony Lukatovich, in every race. Tony takes increasing risks to win the crowd's approval, without success. Finally he makes a bet with the narrator: whoever wins the next race, the loser will kill himself.

The narrator thinks Tony is crazy. He doesn't want to bet. But when Tony threatens to tell the public he is a coward, he agrees.

In the next race, Tony and another rider are ahead of the narrator until the last turn, where Tony's bike bumps the leader's and they both crash. The narrator wins, but Tony is killed in the crash.

Then the narrator finds out that, *before the race,* Tony told a newspaper reporter that the narrator had decided to retire after the next fatal crash. Did Tony deliberately get himself killed in order to make him retire?

Yet, despite the news report, the winner doesn't have to retire. He can say he changed his mind. Tony hasn't won anything, has he? If so, what?

THIRTEEN

Erno had not left the apartment in days. In the aftermath of his police interview, his mother had hovered over him like a bad mood, and it was all he could do to avoid her reproachful stare. Aunt Sophie and Lena and even Aphra acted like he had some terminal disease that might be catching. They intended to heap him with shame until he was crushed. He holed up in his room listening to an ancient recording, "Black and Blue," by Louis Armstrong. The long dead jazzman growled, "What did I do, to feel so black and blue?"

A real man would get back at them. Tyler would. And they would know that they were being gotten, and they would be gotten in the heart of their assumption of superiority. Something that would show women permanently that men were not to be disregarded.

Erno opened his notebook and tried writing a poem.

> When you hit someone
> It changes their face.
>
> Your mother looks shocked and old.
> Alicia looks younger.
> Men named Cluny get even stupider than they are.
>
> It hurts your fist.
> It hurts your shoulder.
>
> The biggest surprise: you can do it.
> Your fist is there at the end of your arm
> Waiting
> At any and every moment
> Whether you are aware of it or not.
>
> Once you know this
> The world changes.

He stared at the lines for some minutes, then erased them. In their place he tried writing a joke.

Q: How many matrons does it take to screw in a light bulb?
A: Light bulbs don't care to be screwed by matrons.

He turned off his screen and lay on his bed, his hands behind his head, and stared at the ceiling. He could engineer the GROSS virus. He would not even need access to the biotech facilities; he knew where he could obtain almost everything required from warehouses within the colony. But he would need a place secret enough that nobody would find him out.

Suddenly he knew the place. And with it, he knew where Tyler was hiding.

The northwest lava tube was fairly busy when Erno arrived at 2300. Swing shift cousins wandered into the open clubs, and the free enterprise shops were doing their heaviest business. The door to the Oxygen Warehouse was dark, and a public notice was posted on it. The door was locked, and Erno did not want to draw attention by trying to force it.

So he returned to the construction materials warehouse in North Six. Little traffic here, and Erno was able to slip inside without notice. He kept behind the farthest aisle until he reached the back wall and the deserted airlock that was being used for storage. It took him some minutes to move the building struts and slide through to the other end. The door opened and he was in the deserted lava tube.

It was completely dark. He used his flashlight to retrace their steps from weeks ago.

Before long, Erno heard a faint noise ahead. He extinguished the flash and saw, beyond several bends in the distance, a faint light. He crept along until he reached a section where light fell from a series of open doorways. He slid next to the first and listened.

The voices from inside stopped. After a moment one of them called, "Come in."

Nervous, Erno stepped into the light from the open door. He squinted and saw Tyler and a couple of other men in a room cluttered with tables, cases of dried food, oxygen packs, scattered clothes, blankets, surface suits. On the table were book readers, half-filled juice bulbs, constables' batons.

One of the younger men came up to Erno and slapped him on the back. "Erno. My man!" It was Sid.

The others watched Erno speculatively. Tyler leaned back against the table. He wore a surface skintight; beside him lay his utility belt. His hair had grown out into a centimeter of red bristle. He grinned. "I assume you've brought the goods, Erno."

Erno pulled his notebook from his pocket. "Yes."

Tyler took the notebook and, without moving his eyes from Erno's, put it on the table. "You can do this, right?"

"Erno's a wizard," Sid said. "He can do it in his sleep."

The other young men just watched Erno. They cared what he was going to say.

"I can do it."

Tyler scratched the corner of his nose with his index finger. "Will you?"

"I don't know."

"Why don't you know? Is this a hard decision?"

"Of course it is. A lot of children will die. Nothing will ever be the same."

"We're under the impression that's the point, Erno. Come with me," Tyler said, getting off the table. "We need to talk."

Tyler directed the others to go back to work and took Erno into another room.

This one had a cot, a pile of clothes, and bulbs of alcohol lying around. On a wall screen was a schematic of the colony's substructure.

Tyler pushed a pile of clothes off a chair. "Sit down."

Erno sat. "You knew about this place before we came here the night of the riot."

Tyler said nothing.

"They asked me if there was a conspiracy," Erno continued. "I told them no. Is there?"

"Sure there is. You're part of it."

"I'm not part of anything."

"That's the trouble with men among the cousins, Erno. We're not part of anything. If a man isn't part of something, then he's of no use to anybody."

"Help me out, Tyler. I don't get it."

"They say that men can't live only with other men. I don't believe that. Did you ever study the warrior culture?"

"No."

"Men banding together—for duty, honor, clan. That's what the warrior lived by throughout history. It was the definition of manhood.

"The matrons say men are extreme, that they'll do anything. They're right. A man will run into a collapsing building to rescue a complete stranger. That's why, for most of human history, the warrior was necessary for the survival of the clan—later the nation.

"But the twentieth century drained all the meaning out of it. First the great industrial nations exploited the warrior ethic, destroying the best of their sons for money, for material gain, for political ideology. Then the feminist movement, which did not understand the warrior, and feared and ridiculed him, grew. They even persuaded some men to reject masculinity.

"All this eventually erased the purpose from what was left of the warrior culture. Now, if the warrior ethic can exist at all, it must be personal. 'Duty, honor, self.'"

"Self?"

"Self. In some way it was always like that. Sacrifice for others is not about the others, it's the ultimate assertion of self. It's the self, after all, that decides to place value in the other. What's important is the *self* and the *sacrifice*, not the cause for which you sacrifice. In the final analysis, all sacrifices are in service of the self. The pure male assertion."

"You're not talking about running into a collapsing building, Tyler."

Tyler laughed. "Don't you get it yet, Erno? We're living in a collapsing building!"

"If we produce this virus, people are going to die."

"Living as a male among the cousins is death. They destroy certain things, things that are good—only this society defines them as bad. Fatherhood. Protection of the weak by the strong. There's no *force* here, Erno. There's no *growth*. The cousins are an evolutionary dead end. In time of peace it may look fine and dandy, but in time of war, it would be wiped out in a moment."

Erno didn't know what to say.

"This isn't some scheme for power, Erno. You think I'm in this out of some abstract theory? This is life's blood. This—"

Sid ran in from the hall. "Tyler," he said. "The warehouse door has cycled again!"

Tyler was up instantly. He grabbed Erno by the shirt. "Who did you tell?"

"Tell? No one!"

"Get the others!" Tyler told Sid. But as soon as Sid left the room an explosion rocked the hall, and the lights went out. Tyler still had hold of Erno's shirt, and dragged him to the floor. The air was full of stinging fumes.

"Follow me if you want to live!" Tyler whispered.

They crawled away from the hall door, toward the back of the room. In the light of the wall screen, Tyler upended the cot and yanked open a meter-square door set into the wall. When Erno hesitated, Tyler dragged him into the dark tunnel beyond.

They crawled on hands and knees for a long time. Erno's eyes teared from the gas, and he coughed until he vomited. Tyler pulled him along in the blackness until they reached a chamber, dimly lit in red, where they could stand. On the other side of the chamber was a pressure door.

"Put this on," Tyler said, shoving a surface suit into Erno's arms. "Quickly!"

Erno struggled to pull on the skintight, still gasping for breath. "I swear I had nothing to do with this," he said.

"I know," Tyler said. He sealed up his own suit and locked down his tiger-striped helmet.

"Brace yourself. This isn't an airlock," Tyler said, and hit the control on the exterior door.

The moment the door showed a gap, the air blew out of the chamber, almost knocking Erno off his feet. When it opened wide enough, they staggered through into a crevasse. The moisture in the escaping air froze and fell as frost in the vacuum around them. Erno wondered if their pursuers would be able to seal the tube or get back behind a pressure door before they passed out.

Tyler and Erno emerged from the crevasse into a sloping pit, half of which was lit by the glare of hard sunlight. They scrambled up the slope through six centimeters of dust and reached the surface.

"Now what?" Erno said.

Tyler shook his head and put his hand against Erno's faceplate. He leaned over and touched his helmet to Erno's. "Private six, encrypted."

Erno switched his suit radio.

"They won't be out after us for some time," Tyler said. "Since we left that Judas-book of yours behind, they may not even know where we are."

"Judas book?"

"Your notebook—you must have had it with you when the constables questioned you."

"Yes. But they didn't know what the download meant or they wouldn't have returned it to me."

"Returned it to you? Dumbass. They put a tracer in it."

Erno could see Tyler's dark eyes dimly through the faceplate, inches from his own, yet separated by more than glass and vacuum. "I'm sorry."

"Forget it."

"When we go back, we'll be arrested. We might be banished."

"We're not going back just yet. Follow me."

"Where can we go?"

"There's a construction shack at an abandoned ilemenite mine south of here. It's a bit of a hike—two to three hours—but what else are we going to do on such a fine morning?"

Tyler turned and hopped off across the surface. Erno stood dumbly for a moment, then followed.

They headed south along the western side of the crater. The ground was much rockier, full of huge boulders and pits where ancient lava tubes had collapsed millennia ago. The suit Erno wore was too tight, and pinched him in the armpits and crotch. His thermoregulators struggled against the open sunlight, and he felt his body inside the skintight slick with sweat. The bind in his crotch became a stabbing pain with every stride.

Around to the south side of Fowler, they struck off to the south. Tyler followed a line of boot prints and tractor treads in the dust. The land rose to Adil's Ridge after a couple of kilometers, from which Erno looked back and saw, for the first time, all of the domed crater where he had spent his entire life.

"Is this construction shack habitable?" he asked.

"I've got it outfitted."

"What are we going to do? We can't stay out here forever."

"We won't. They'll calm down. You forget that we haven't done anything but spray a prank message on the dome. I'm a comedian. What do they expect from a comedian?"

Erno did not remind Tyler of the possible decompression injuries their escape might have caused. He tucked his head down and focused on keeping up with the big man's steady pace. He drew deep breaths. They skipped along without speaking for an hour or more. Off to their left, Erno noticed a line of distant pylons, with threads of cable strung between them. It was the cable train route from Fowler to Tsander several hundred kilometers south.

Tyler began to speak. "I'm working on some new material. For my come-back performance. It's about the difference between love and sex."

"Okay. So what's the difference?"

"Sex is like a fresh steak. It smells great, you salivate, you consume it in a couple of minutes, you're satisfied, you feel great, and you fall asleep."

"And love?"

"Love is completely different. Love is like flash-frozen food—it lasts forever. Cold as liquid hydrogen. You take it out when you need it, warm it up. You persuade yourself it's just as good as sex. People who promote love say it's even better, but that's a lie constructed out of necessity. The only thing it's better than is starving to death."

"Needs a little work," Erno said. After a moment he added. "There's a story in *Stories for Men* about love."

"I'd think the stories for men would be about sex."

"No. There's no sex in any of them. There's hardly any women at all. Most of them are about men competing with other men. But there's one about a rich man who bets a poor young man that hunger is stronger than love. He locks the poor man and his lover in separate rooms with a window between them, for seven days, without food. At the end of the seven days they're starving. Then he puts them together in a room with a single piece of bread."

"Who eats it?"

"The man grabs it, and is at the point of eating it when he looks over at the woman, almost unconscious from hunger. He gives it to her. She refuses it, says he should have it because he's more hungry than she is. So they win the bet."

Tyler laughed. "If it had been a steak, they would have lost." They continued hiking for a while. "That story isn't about love. It's about the poor man beating the rich man."

Erno considered it. "Maybe."

"So what have you learned from that book? Anything?"

"Well, there's a lot of killing—it's like the writers are obsessed with killing. The characters kill for fun, or sport, or money, or freedom, or to get respect. Or women."

"That's the way it was back then, Erno. Men—"

Tyler's voice was blotted out by a tone blaring over their earphones. After fifteen seconds an AI voice came on:

"SATELLITES REPORT A MAJOR SOLAR CORONAL MASS EJECTION. PARTICLE FLUX WILL BEGIN TO RISE IN TWENTY MINUTES, REACHING LETHAL LEVELS WITHIN THIRTY. ALL PERSONS ON THE SURFACE SHOULD IMMEDIATELY SEEK SHELTER. REFRAIN FROM EXPOSURE UNTIL THE ALL CLEAR SOUNDS.

"REPEAT: A MAJOR SOLAR RADIATION EVENT HAS OCCURRED. ALL PERSONS SHOULD IMMEDIATELY TAKE SHELTER."

Both of them stopped. Erno scanned the sky, frantic. Of course there was no difference. The sun threw the same harsh glare it always threw. His heart thudded in his ears. He heard Tyler's deep breaths in his earphones.

"How insulated is this shack?" he asked Tyler. "Can it stand a solar storm?"

Tyler didn't answer for a moment. "I doubt it."

"How about the mine? Is there a radiation shelter? Or a tunnel?"

"It was a strip mine. Besides," Tyler said calmly, "we couldn't get there in twenty minutes."

They were more than an hour south of the colony.

Erno scanned the horizon, looking for some sign of shelter. A crevasse, a lava tube—maybe they'd run out of air, but at least they would not fry. He saw, again, the threads of the cable towers to the east.

"The cable line!" Erno said. "It has radiation shelters for the cable cars all along it."

"If we can reach one in time."

Erno checked his clock readout. 0237. Figure they had until 0300. He leapt off due east, toward the cable towers. Tyler followed.

The next fifteen minutes passed in a trance, a surreal slow motion broken field race through the dust and boulders toward the pylons to the east. Erno pushed himself to the edge of his strength, until a haze of spots rose before his eyes. They seemed to move with agonizing slowness.

They were 500 meters from the cable pylon. 300 meters. 100 meters. They were beneath it.

When they reached the pylon, Erno scanned in both directions for a shelter. The cable line was designed to dip underground for radiation protection periodically all along the length of its route. The distance between the tunnels was determined by the top speed of the cable car and the amount of advance warning the passengers were likely to get of a solar event. There was no way of telling how far they were from a shelter, or in which direction the closest lay.

"South," Tyler said. "The colony is the next shelter north, and it's too far for us to run, so our only shot should be south."

It was 0251. They ran south, their leaps no longer strong and low, but with a weary desperation to them now. Erno kept his eyes fixed on the horizon. The twin cables stretched above them like strands of spider's web, silver in the sunlight, disappearing far ahead where the next T pylon stood like the finish line in a race.

The T grew, and suddenly they were on it. Beyond, in its next arc, the cable swooped down to the horizon. They kept running, and as they drew closer, Erno saw that a tunnel opened in the distance, and the cable ran into it. He gasped out a moan that was all the shout he could make.

They were almost there when Erno realized that Tyler had slowed, and was no longer keeping up. He willed himself to stop, awkwardly, almost pitching face first into the regolith. He looked back. Tyler had slowed to a stroll.

"What's wrong?" Erno gasped.

"Nothing," Tyler said. Though Erno could hear Tyler's ragged breath, there was no hurry in his voice.

"Come on!" Erno shouted.

Tyler stopped completely. "Women and children first."

Erno tried to catch his breath. His clock read 0304. "What?"

"You go ahead. Save your pathetic life."

"Are you crazy? Do you want to die?"

"Of course not. I want you to go in first."

"Why?"

"If you can't figure it out by now, I can't explain it, Erno. It's a story for a man."

Erno stood dumbstruck.

"Come out here into the sunshine with me," Tyler said. "It's nice out here."

Erno laughed. He took a step back toward Tyler. He took another. They stood side by side.

"That's my man Erno. Now, how long can you stay out here?"

The sun beat brightly down. The tunnel mouth gaped five meters in front of them. 0307. 0309. Each watched the other, neither budged.

"My life isn't pathetic," Erno said.

"Depends on how you look at it," Tyler replied.

"Don't you think yours is worth saving?"

"What makes you think this is a real radiation alert, Erno? The broadcast could be a trick to make us come back."

"There have been warnings posted for weeks."

"That only makes it a more plausible trick."

"That's no reason for us to risk our lives—on the chance it is."

"I don't think it's a trick, Erno. I'll go into that tunnel. After you."

Erno stared at the dark tunnel ahead. 0311. A single leap from safety. Even now lethal levels of radiation might be sluicing through their bodies. A bead of sweat stung his eye.

"So this is what it means to be a man?" Erno said softly, as much to himself as to Tyler.

"This is it," Tyler said. "And I'm a better man than you are."

Erno felt an adrenaline surge. "You're not better than me."

"We'll find out."

"You haven't accomplished anything."

"I don't need you to tell me what I've accomplished. Go ahead, Erno. Back to your cave."

0312. 0313. Erno could feel the radiation. It was shattering proteins and DNA throughout his body, rupturing cell walls, turning the miraculously ordered organic molecules of his brain into sludge. He thought about Alicia, the curve of her breast, the light in her eyes. Had she told her friends that he had hit her? And his mother. He saw the shock and surprise in her face when the book hit her. How angry he had been. He wanted to explain to her why he had thrown it. It shouldn't be that hard to explain.

He saw his shadow reaching out beside him, sharp and steady, two arms, two legs and a head, an ape somehow transported to the moon. No, not an ape—a man. What a miracle that a man could keep himself alive in this harsh place—not just keep alive, but make a home of it. All the intellect and planning and work that had gone to put him here, standing out under the brutal sun, letting it exterminate him.

He looked at Tyler, fixed as stone.

"This is insane," Erno said—then ran for the tunnel.

A second after he sheltered inside, Tyler was there beside him.

FOURTEEN

They found the radiation shelter midway through the tunnel, closed themselves inside, stripped off their suits, drank some water, breathed the cool air. They crowded in the tiny stone room together, smelling each other's sweat. Erno started to get sick: he had chills, he felt nausea. Tyler made him sip water, put his arm around Erno's shoulders.

Tyler said it was radiation poisoning, but Erno said it was not. He sat wordless in the corner the nine hours it took until the all-clear came. Then, ignoring Tyler, he suited up and headed back to the colony.

FIFTEEN

So that is the story of how Erno discovered that he was not a man. That, indeed, Tyler was right, and there was no place for men in the Society of Cousins. And that he, Erno, despite his grievances and rage, was a cousin.

The cost of this discovery was Erno's own banishment, and one thing more.

When Erno turned himself in at the constabulary headquarters, eager to tell them about GROSS and ready to help them find Tyler, he was surprised at their subdued reaction. They asked him no questions. They looked at him funny, eyes full of rage and something besides rage. Horror? Loathing? Pity? They put him in the same white room where he had sat before, and left him there alone. After a while the blond interrogator, Mona, came in and told him that three people had been injured when Tyler and Erno had blown the vacuum seal while escaping. One, who had insisted on crawling after them through the escape tunnel, had been caught in there and died: Erno's mother.

Erno and Tyler were given separate trials, and the colony voted: they were to be expelled. Tyler's banishment was permanent; Erno was free to apply for read-mission in ten years.

The night before he left, Erno, accompanied by a constable, was allowed to visit his home. Knowing how completely inadequate it was, he apologized to his sister, his aunt and cousins. Aunt Sophie and Nick treated him with stiff rectitude. Celeste, who somehow did not feel the rage against him that he deserved, cried and embraced him. They let him pack a duffel with a number of items from his room.

After leaving, he asked the constable if he could stop a moment on the terrace outside the apartment before going back to jail. He took a last look at the vista of the domed crater from the place where he had lived every day of his life. He drew a deep breath and closed his eyes. His mother seemed everywhere around him. All he could see was her crawling, on hands and knees in the dark, desperately trying to save him from himself. How angry she must have been, and how afraid. What must she have thought, as the air flew away and she felt her coming death? Did she regret giving birth to him?

He opened his eyes. There on the terrace stood the recycler he had thrown pebbles at for years. He reached into his pack, pulled out *Stories for Men*, and stepped toward the bin.

Alicia came around a corner. "Hello, Erno," she said.

A step from the trash bin, Erno held the book awkwardly in his hand, trying to think of something to say. The constable watched them.

"I can't tell you how sorry I am," he told Alicia.

"I know you didn't mean this to happen," she said.

"It doesn't matter what I meant. It happened."

On impulse, he handed her the copy of *Stories for Men*. "I don't know what to do with this," he said. "Will you keep it for me?"

The next morning they put him on the cable car for Tsander. His exile had begun.

TO BECOME A WARRIOR

CHRIS BECKETT

British writer Chris Beckett is a frequent contributor to Interzone *and has just made a sale to* Asimov's Science Fiction. *A former social worker, he's now a university lecturer living in Cambridge, England. He has had stories in our Ninth and Nineteenth Annual Collections.*

Sometimes it's not enough just to talk the talk, you have to walk the walk, too. And that can be a lot more difficult than you think it's going to be . . .

Where I live it's the Thurston Fields estate only we just call it the Fields. Which it's what they call a Special Category Estate which is crap for a start because everyone knows it's a dreg estate and we're the dreggies. Which is we're the ones they haven't got any use for, yeah? I mean fair enough, I can't hardly read and write as such. Which I've never had a job or nothing only once I had a job in this tyre and exhaust place. Like a job creation scheme? Only I was late the second day — right? — and the manager, he only told me to do something about my attitude, so I fucking smacked him one, didn't I?

And I'll tell you what mate, not being funny or nothing, but if you never lived on a dreg estate you've got no idea what it's like. You might think you have but you haven't. I'll tell you one thing about it, the Department runs your life. The DeSCA, yeah? The deskies we call them. Which you get different kinds, like housing deskies which if you're some girl who gets pregnant, they're the ones who get you a flat. (Mind you, if you're a *bloke* and you want a flat you've got to find some slag and say you love her and that, know what I mean?) And you get teacher deskies, and benefits deskies. You even get deskie police. But I tell you what, mate, the ones we really hate are the fucking social worker deskies. Like they try to be so nice and understanding and that, all *concerned* about you — know what I mean? — but next thing they're taking your fucking kid away.

Like my girlfriend Kylie, well my ex-girlfriend because I dumped her, didn't I? Which she had her kid Sam taken off her and she went fucking *mental*, know what I mean? I mean, fair play, he is a whinging little git and at first I thought, great, all day in bed and no distractions. But it did her head in and she was crying and that, and she was down the Child Welfare every day and she didn't want fucking sex no more or nothing so I thought to myself, I can't hack this, *I'll* go fucking mental, know what I mean?

(Which then she tried to top herself which her mum said was down to me but it never. It was the fucking deskies.)

Anyway, one day I was down the Locomotive with my mates when this geezer comes in — yeah? — and he only had a skull tattooed all over his face! I mean like so his face *looked* like a skull, yeah? Which my mate Shane goes, "Shit, look at *that*!" This bloke he looked *well* hard, but — yeah? — we must have had twelve pints each minimum, so I thought to myself, fuck it. And I go up to this skull geezer — right? — and go like, "Who the fuck are you?" (Shane was pissing himself, the prat. He thought it was hysterical. He thought old skull face there was going to beat the shit out of me.)

But the skull guy just laughs.

And he was like, "I'm Laf, who the hell are you?"

So I go, "I'm Carl. What kind of name is Laf for fuck's sake?"

And he was like, "Watch it mate," only he was laughing, know what I mean? And he goes, "It's short for Olaf. It's a warrior's name, alright? I'm a warrior of Dunner I am."

Which I'll tell you what, back then I didn't know what the fuck he meant but I didn't want to look like a prat or nothing so I just go, "Warrior of Dunner, huh?" (You know, American and that).

And he laughs and goes, "You don't know what I'm talking about, do you mate?"

So I go, "No I don't, mate, but I reckon you're talking out of your arse."

But he just kind of looks round the pub at the blokes slagging each other off by the pool table and at the kids arsing about on the machines and at that old slag Dora with her wrecked fucking face who comes in every night and drinks till they chuck her out.

So he looks all round — right? — and then he looks back at me and he's like, "This place is shit isn't it?"

And I'm like, "Yeah?" Because, like, I can see what he means in a way but I drink there every bloody night.

And he goes, "Want to come and meet some of my mates?"

And I'm, "Yeah okay."

And he's, "Only I've taken a liking to you Carl. I liked the way you came over like that. More bottle than your mates there."

Well then we walk straight out past Shane and Derek and they're like trying to make out it's hysterical — yeah? — but really they're bloody gobsmacked, aren't they?

And Derek goes, "Where the fuck are you going Carl?"

But I don't know, do I?

———

Laf's got his car out there—it's like a really old Mondeo—and, it was well good, we ton across the estate at 90, with the windows down and the music on full blast. (Well the police don't bother with the Fields at night, only if there's a riot or something.)

And we go up Thurston Road, right up near the wire where there is them three big old tower blocks—yeah?—which are all sealed off and that because they've been like condemned. (I mean: they've always been condemned and sealed off like that since I was a kid, because of asbestos or something, I think.)

Me and my mates, we've tried to get into those places but they're like not just boarded up they're *steeled* up—yeah?—with metal plates and that. Only it turns out that Laf and his mates have managed to get into one of them called Progress House. Like there's a kind of service door or something round the back which it still looks like it's locked up but they can get in and out, yeah?

Inside it was really dark and echoey and it smelt of piss. You couldn't see nothing but Laf goes charging off up the stairs: one floor, two floors, three floors . . .

"Wait for me," I go.

But Laf just laughs and he's like, "You'll have to get fitter than that, mate, if you want to be a warrior of Dunner."

Those places are like twelve stories high, yeah? Which right at the top they'd opened up a flat. You could smell the puff smoke from a floor below. Which there's this room in there, like a cave—yeah?—with candles and that, and weird pictures on the wall, and there are Laf's mates, three of them: one fat bloke in one corner, one really evil-looking bloke with greasy black hair in the other corner and then this boffy-looking fucker in the middle. And he's got glasses on and he's rolling up a spliff.

"Good evening," he goes, really posh. And he's like, "Welcome to Progress House. This is Gunnar" (that was the fat one), "this is Rogg and my name is Erik. Delighted to make your acquaintance."

I look at Laf and I'm like, "Who the *fuck* is this?"

And Laf don't say nothing in words but he's kind of frowning at me—right?—like he's going, "Respect, man! This geezer is well hard, know what I mean?"

(Which, like, *he's* got a skull all over his face!)

Erik laughs, "A word of advice, Carl. Laf has chosen to let you into our little secret. We do that from time to time, because we are, well, we're *missionaries* in a way." (I didn't know what he was talking about at first. I thought missionary meant, like, sex with the geezer on top, know what I mean?)

"But if you were to reveal our secret to anyone else without our permission," goes boffy Erik, "I personally will kill you. I mean that quite literally. And I assure you that what I have just said is not a threat but a promise."

And Laf is like, "He means it, mate, he's well evil. He'd kill a bloke, no sweat at all."

And Erik laughed really pleasant—yeah?—like some posh bloke on the telly.

You would not believe all the gear they had up there, yeah? We did E's and A's and M's and C's and fuck knows what else until the walls were wobbling like jelly—yeah?—and it was like Erik was talking into this blob of jelly from outside somewhere, down some tube or something.

"Have you heard of Dunner, Carl?" he goes. "Or Thor, some call him?"

And I'm like, ". . . er, no, don't think so, mate . . ."—right?—like I'm talking up this tube?

"Well, he used to be *big* around here," goes Erik. "Thurston *means* Thor's town for one thing. Did you know that? Come to that he's got a whole day of the week named after him. Thursday means Thor's day."

"Yeah," goes Laf, "and Wednesday's named after his dad, right, Erik?"

"That's right," goes Erik. "Woden's day."

And I'm like, ". . . Yeah?" (Which if anyone else had come up with this shit I would just have laughed, know what I mean?)

"Dunner or Thor," goes Erik, "is the god of thunder. And he's a warrior god. His weapon is a big hammer which crushes anything it strikes. As I say, he used to be big around here. Your ancestors would have worshipped him. They would have sacrificed to him too, animals and even human beings. So you can see they took him very seriously indeed."

And I'm like "So?" but I don't say nothing.

"And now," goes Erik, "here is another secret. But this one I *am* happy for you to tell who you like. Because it's the government who wants it kept as a secret. It's the politicians and the do-gooders. It's them who don't want anyone to know."

Well the room was as big as a fucking football pitch now—right?—with that Erik talking over the p.a. in a big echoey voice like God or something.

"Do you think about the universe at all, Carl?"

"As in, like, the sun goes round the earth?" I go. "Stars and that?"

Erik does his nice TV laugh.

"That's it, Carl, you've got it in one. Stars and that. But listen and I'll tell you something. The whole of this universe of stars and space is just one tiny twig in an enormous tree and every second, every fraction of a second, it's branching and dividing, making new worlds."

I laughed. But—it was weird, yeah?—I could fucking *see* it. Only it didn't look like a tree. More like millions of black worms in the dark that kept on splitting in two and splitting in two and splitting in two—yeah?—like viruses or something.

"There are millions of other earths, millions of other Englands, millions of other Thurston Fields estates," he goes—and like I said, he's like God or something, I couldn't even see him with all the E's and A's and shit going round me, just hear his big echoey voice all round me.

"And we don't come from this one," he goes, "Laf and Gunnar and Rogg and I, we're shifters, we come from another world. Anytime we want to we can go to another world too. So we can do what we want here. We can do whatever we want. No one is ever going to catch us."

I heard him moving about somewhere out there, know what I mean, like he's on a different planet?

"Look at these!" he goes.

Well I'm lying on the floor with my eyes shut and when I open my eyes, even though it's only candles in there, it still feels, like, too bright, know what I mean? So it's a job to see anything at all as such — yeah? — but I see he's holding out a bag with pills in it, hundreds of dark little pills.

"These are seeds, these are Lok seeds. Every one of these will take us to another world. Think of that. We can travel between the branches of the tree like Dunner does, with his hammer in his hand."

And then that Rogg speaks, that evil bastard with the greasy black hair, and he's a Scotchman or a Geordie or something.

"Yeah," he goes, "and you know what we's looking for, mate? We's looking for one of Dunner's worlds. Know what I mean?"

I go, "Yeah?"

"He means a world where Dunner is still worshipped today," goes Erik. "We know they exist because the seeds come from there and because of shifter stories. There are thousands like us, you see, Carl, thousands of warriors of Dunner moving between the worlds. And we tell each other stories. We swap news."

Then that fat bloke talks: Gunnar. You know how some big fat blokes have these, like, really high little mild little voices? Which Gunnar was one of them, right? He had this gentle little voice — yeah? — really polite and high. I'll tell you what, though, I reckon he could beat you to a fucking pulp. But he'd still talk to you like really kind and gentle while he was doing it — yeah? — in that small little gentle high voice.

And he's like, "Do you want to know what it's like in Dunner's worlds, Carl?"

And I'm "Yeah" and he goes, "Tell him what it's like, Erik, he probably doesn't know!"

(Which I've got my eyes closed again — right? — and those black worms are splitting and wriggling and splitting all the time all round me. But those shifter geezers' voices are far away, coming down like from like ten miles above me or something.)

"Of course," goes Erik, "of course . . ." and he's drawing breath, like this is the good part coming up . . .

"Does *civilization* mean anything to you Carl?" he asks, "Or *democracy*? Or *human rights*?"

"You *what*?" I go, not being funny or nothing, but I don't know what the fuck he's talking about.

But they all laugh like I've made a really good joke! So I feel well chuffed, don't I?

"They don't mean shit to me!" I go, like doing the joke again.

"Of course they don't Carl," goes Erik kindly, "and do you know why?"

"Because I don't give a monkey's," I go, but they're tired of the joke now and they don't laugh no more.

"The reason civilization doesn't mean anything to you, Carl," Erik goes, "is that civilization isn't there for your benefit. You're not *part* of civilization. Civilization is for the others out there across the wire. They don't care what you think. They don't care about what you can and can't do. They give you a dreg estate to live in and a DeSCA department to look after you. All they ask in return is that you leave them alone with their civilization. Just keep out of the way, is all they ask, and let them get on with their civilization in peace."

"Yeah?" I go.

"Carl don't want to know all that, Erik mate," goes fat Gunnar in his little kind voice. "He wants to know about *Dunner's* worlds."

"I was coming to that," goes Erik and he, like, growls. He don't like being interrupted.

"You see Carl, in Dunner's worlds there is no civilization, no democracy, no human rights. And there's no DeSCA either, no Special Category estates, no wire. A young chap like you doesn't have to go to the deskies for money or a place to live. No. What you'd do in one of Dunner's worlds is find yourself a lord. A *war*lord, I mean, a great warrior, not some-toffee-nosed do-gooder who sits on committees about social exclusion and goes to the opera. You'd go to a lord and, if you promised to fight his enemies for him, he'd look after you, he'd make sure you got everything you needed."

"Yeah?" I go.

"And Carl, mate," goes fat Gunnar, "that wouldn't be like a deskie flat or nothing he'd give you. Don't think that, mate. He'd have a big hall, with a big fire in the middle, and you'd live there with all your mates. And you'd drink all you wanted, mate, and eat all you wanted and get as pissed as you wanted and when it was time to sleep, well you'd just sleep there in the hall, with all your mates around you. So you wouldn't never have to think about money or nothing, and you wouldn't never have to be alone. How does that sound, my old mate?"

I laughed. "That sounds like fucking heaven mate."

"Yeah, and you don't need to *work* or nothing," goes old skull-face Laf. "All you got to do is *fight*! It's your job, like. You even get to kill people and that and there's no police or nothing to stop you."

Which I'm like "Great!"

"Fair enough it's dangerous," goes Laf. "You could get killed too, know what I mean?"

"So?" I go, laughing. "Who gives a shit? When you're dead you're fucking dead, right?"

"Well said!" goes Erik. "Spoken like a warrior! But actually it's better than that, Carl my friend, it's better than that. If you die fighting, Dunner will take you home to Valour-Hall, where all the brave warriors go, and then you'd live again. And then it's feasting and fighting for ever and ever, until the Last Battle at the end of time."

And Gunnar's like, "So what do you say, then, Carl my old mate? Do you want to be a warrior?"

Well, of *course* I do, don't I?

"Yeah!" I laugh.

"Well there's a test you have to pass," goes Erik, "a little test . . ."

But one of them is putting this spliff into my hand—yeah?—and I don't know what they put in it but next thing I'm down on my knees half-way through my mum's front door, chucking up all over the fucking lino.

Well, the next few days—right?—I'm like, "Did I dream that or what?"

I even went down there to Progress House—yeah?—and no way could anyone have got in there, know what I mean? Steel plates and massive bloody locks.

Which I go, "Well, I *must* have dreamed it."

But down the Locomotive when Shane and Derek and that go, "Where the fuck d'you go with that skull bloke?" I didn't say nothing, know what I mean? Because—yeah?—I remembered that boffy geezer Erik go, like, "That's not a threat it's a promise."

I didn't feel like taking a chance.

But, like, a couple of weeks later I was just going down to the pub in the morning—right?—when this car pulls up. Which it's only that dodgy old Mondeo and that fat geezer Gunnar driving it.

"Hop in, my old mate!" he goes, leaning back to open the back door.

So I get in the back and that evil Scotch bastard Rogg—yeah?—he's there in the front with Gunnar and he passes me back a spliff and, like, we're off.

Next thing we're at the line and Gunnar is showing his ID to the cop.

And he's like, "Alright mate? How you doing?" in his kind little voice.

"Not so bad," the cop goes. Which he's a bit surprised—yeah?—like he's not used to people being nice to him and that. And he's like, "Have a nice day!" as he lets us through the wire.

Which Rogg laughs and goes, "Anyone tell you yous can't fake deskie ID cards, Carl? Well you can."

And Gunnar's like, "There isn't nothing our Erik can't figure out, Carl mate. He's one in a million that geezer. He's diamond, mate, he's pure diamond."

We go right across town—right?—to this posh area where I never been before. And Gunnar parks the car—yeah?—and we get out and it's like there's shops that don't sell nothing but coloured fucking *candles* right? And shops that sell little toys made out of painted wood which any normal kid would smash in two seconds flat and they cost like a week's money each. And all these rich bastards in fancy clothes and posh voices—yeah?—like la di da this and la di da that and "Oh really Jonathan, that's ever so sweet of you!" and beautiful bitches in posh sexy clothes like TV stars. And you look at them and think, "*Shit*, I fancy you," but you know if you tried anything they'd just laugh at you like you was an alien from space or something with tentacles and that, or eyes on fucking stalks.

And Gunnar goes, "Do you know this place, Carl mate?"

And I go, "No."

And he goes, "It's Clifton Village mate, where the rich people hang out."

"The *beautiful* people," goes Rogg with, like, an evil sneer.

Then Gunnar puts his arm across my shoulders—yeah?—like he's my dad or something.

And he's like, "How's this place make you feel, my old mate?"

And I'm like "How would I fucking know?"

"Angry maybe?" goes Gunnar kindly. "Does it make you feel angry at all mate?"

And I'm, "Nah, I don't give a shit," like with a shrug and that.

And then I go, "Yeah, alright, angry then."

"That's the way, my old mate," goes Gunnar, "That's the way."

Which he's still got his arm round me like he's my dad or my kind uncle.

"Now listen, Carl mate," he goes, "how would you like it if you could do whatever you wanted here?"

And I'm like, "Eh? What d'you mean?"

"How would you like it, Carl," goes Rogg, "if you could smash these shops and burn these cars and fuck these women and blow away any of these smug bastards you wanted?"

"Yes, how would you like that my old mate?" goes Gunnar.

"Well of course I'd like it," I go, "but you're having a laugh with me, aren't you? You're just winding me up."

"No," goes Rogg, "no wind-up, Carl. It's what we're planning to really do. And I'll tell you the beauty of it. The beauty of it is we'll have swallowed seeds, so when the police come along we can just laugh and let them lock us up, because we'll know that in an hour or two we'll be in a different world and they won't ever be able to get us."

And it's like it finally dawns on me, yeah? It dawns on me for the first time. If you're a shifter you can really do shit like that. That's what it would mean to be a warrior of Dunner.

So a big smile spreads over my face — yeah? — and I'm like, "Sweet, man! Fucking sweet!"

"And you can be there," goes Rogg. "You can be there with us if you want to, if you're willing to take the test, like."

And I'm going, "Yeah, no problem, mate, no sweat at all," when this old geezer comes walking past and suddenly stops, like, and looks at me.

"Well, well," he goes. "Carl Pendant isn't it? What a nice surprise! Do you remember me? Cyril Burkitt? How are you doing Carl? It must be all of 15 years."

And he, like, smiles at Rogg and Gunnar — yeah? — like any friend of Carl's is a friend of his. (Which Rogg don't say nothing, and Gunnar's like "Alright, mate. How you doing?")

And I'm like, "Oh alright, you know, mate" and that.

Which he's only my old social worker I used to have when I was in care and that. Which they're all wankers but I sort of liked the bloke. He didn't never get funny with me or nothing — yeah? — like I remember one time when I'd fucked up as per bloody usual and he says to me "You just don't get it do you Carl?" and I go "No I fucking don't" and he laughs and he's like "Well that makes two of us I'm afraid Carl."

Anyway, old Cyril Burkitt looks at Rogg and Gunnar again and he's like, "Well, I won't keep you from your friends Carl. But I'll tell you what, I'm retired now. If you fancy calling by for a chat sometime you'd be very welcome. I don't see such a lot of people these days, you see, so I'm always glad of company. And I've often thought about you over the years and wondered how you were getting on."

And he gives me this little card—yeah?—with his address and that.

Well then I notice Rogg and Gunnar looking at each other with, like, a funny secret sort of look.

Which I'm like, "What?"

"A deskie, right?" goes Rogg.

And I'm like, "Yeah."

Which they look at each other again—yeah?—and sort of not.

"Well that's your test then, Carl mate," goes Gunnar.

And I'm like, "What is?"

And Rogg goes, "Go to his house, Carl, and kill him."

Well I thought, "This is a joke, yeah?" So I'm laughing and I'm like, "Oh, he's not *that* bad, not for a deskie, know what I mean?"

And Gunnar goes, "No Carl mate, you don't understand. That's your *test*! See what I mean, mate? It's what you've got to do to become a warrior. Are you with me, my old mate?"

"You's got to make a sacrifice for Dunner," goes Rogg.

Which, like, they're just looking at me—yeah?—and waiting.

And I go, "Shit!"

And Gunnar goes, "Fair enough if you don't want to do it, Carl mate. No hard feelings or nothing. But if you do want to be a warrior, well, that's the test you've got to pass. Know what I mean?"

So I like swallow—yeah?—and I'm thinking, like, well, all deskies are the same really. Alright some of them act nice and that but it don't mean nothing. Which anyway the stupid git, if he goes round giving out his address and that, *some* fucker's going to get him—yeah?—and if it's not me it's going to be some bugger else. So it don't make no difference really anyway.

So I laugh—yeah?—and I go, "Yeah, alright. I'll do it."

So Laf—right?—he takes me over in the car the next day to the place where Cyril Burkitt lives. (Which it's like another part of town which I never heard of. Only I never really been nowhere much outside of the Fields as such, except down the Centre—yeah?—to clubs and that and once we went over to Weston on a school trip and Shane had six pints of lager and threw up all over the teacher.)

And he stops like a couple of streets away and he's like, "Now it's along there and then turn right and it's number 23, right? So don't get lost will you, Carl?"

Which I'm like, "Fuck *off*," you know, like laughing and that to show I'm not worried or nothing.

So I start to open the door but he's like, "Hang on a minute, Carl mate. You'll need this, you prat!"

Then he gives me a gun as such and it's like, "This is the trigger, mate, and this is the safety catch, and this is a silencer so there won't be any loud bangs or nothing. And listen, mate, there's ten bullets in there, so when he's down, empty the lot into the bastard, know what I mean? Into his head and that, yeah?"

Which I'm like, "No worries mate."

He laughs and lights up a spliff for me.

"I don't need no wacky baccy to give me the bottle for this job mate," I go. "It's no problem mate. It's no sweat."

And he's like, "No Carl, I'm not being funny or nothing, mate. It's just, like, to make it more of a laugh, yeah? Know what I mean?"

Then I'm outside Cyril Burkitt's house—yeah?—and it's doing my head in because I never really thought he had a home or nothing, know what I mean? He was just a deskie, yeah? And, like there's a car outside and flowers and that, and a milk bottle, and there's, like, a little path from the gate made of bricks, and coloured glass in the front door: red and blue and green. And through the front window—right?—there's this big room with loads of books and that. Which I can see him in there—yeah?—reading the paper by himself. And there's music playing, yeah? Violins and that.

So I ring the bell, and he looks up and sees me through the window. Which he, like, smiles and gets up and comes to the door.

"*Hello*, Carl! This is a nice surprise! I didn't think you'd come. I didn't think you'd have the time for an old deskie like me!"

He's got like a cardigan on, and brown slippers and, like, old-man jeans, and he hasn't shaved yet or nothing. He don't look like a deskie, really. Just some old geezer, know what I mean?

"Come on in, Carl, come on in. Can I get you a cup of tea or something?"

And I'm like, "Yeah, thanks, tea." So we go through into this big kitchen like on telly or something with like wood everywhere and a stone floor and that.

Which he gets the kettle and goes over to the sink to fill it up.

"Let me see now, Carl, is that milk and four sugars? Have I remembered that right?"

Then he turns round smiling and sees the gun in my hand.

And he's like, "Oh."

It's weird, he don't look scared or nothing, just like, *tired*.

"I see," he goes.

And then he laughs! Not like *really* laughs, but like, a little sad sort of laugh. Know what I mean?

"All this hatred!" he goes, "I should be honoured really I suppose. It's almost like being loved."

"You *what*?" I go.

"Never mind, Carl," he goes. "Don't worry about it."

He puts the kettle down slowly and then he goes, "Someone put you up to this, I suppose, Carl? You were never much of a one for thinking things up for yourself."

And I'm like, "Mind your own business."

Which he nods and sort of sighs.

"Listen Carl," he goes, and he's really slow, like he's thinking out loud. "Listen Carl. My wife died a while back and she was the only person in the world I really loved. And then my career sort of petered out, as you may have heard, not that it was ever *much* of a career and not that I was ever much cop at my job—as you probably know better than most, I'm afraid. So I really don't have a huge amount to live for. Oh, I get by alright. I potter around. I weed my garden. I do the crossword. I watch TV. But really it doesn't make much difference to me if my life ends now or whether it goes on for another 20 years. Do you see what I mean? I mean: if you really *need* to shoot me, well, be my guest!"

Well I'm like, "What the fuck?" but I don't say nothing.

"But listen Carl," he goes, "I don't know who put you to this but, you know, you are *very* easily led. I do suggest you think very carefully about whether it's actually in your interest to shoot me. You really do need to think about that."

And I'm like, "Fuck off, don't give me that deskie shit *now*! Don't give that *concerned* shit," but I don't say nothing.

(Which I really *don't* want to hear this stuff, though, and it's doing my head in as such.)

"I'm worried for you, Carl," he goes, "It probably sounds strange, but I really am."

Which then—yeah?—I can't stand it no more.

"Fuck off!" I shout at him. "Fuck off you stupid deskie bastard. Just leave me alone, alright? Why can't you never leave me alone?"

And I hate the bastard, I fucking *hate* him, know what I mean? I never hated no one like that in my whole life.

And he goes, "Carl! Carl!"

But I'm not staying to listen to this shit. I'm off out of there, mate. I'm *out* of there. I slammed the front door so hard it broke the stupid coloured glass. Red and blue and green splinters all over the poncy little path.

"You didn't do it, did you?" goes Laf.

I don't say nothing.

"Give me the gun, then," he goes.

I give it him.

Well he just drives off then without saying nothing and I spend all day trying to find my way back to the Fields.

Back home my mum's been on the booze and she's like snoring in front of the telly with her false teeth half out, the ugly slag. So I nick some money from her purse—yeah?—and go down the Locomotive. If I'm lucky some bastard will want a fight so I can kick his fucking head in.

It don't make no difference though, does it? I won't never see that Valour-Hall now.

the clear Blue seas of Luna

GREGORY BENFORD

Gregory Benford is one of the modern giants of the field. His 1980 novel,
Timescape, won the Nebula Award, the John W. Campbell Memorial
Award, the British Science Fiction Association Award, and the Australian
Ditmar Award, and is widely considered to be one of the classic novels of
the last two decades. His other novels include Beyond Jupiter, The Stars
In Shroud, In the Ocean Of Night, Against Infinity, Artifact, Across the
Sea of Suns, Great Sky River, Tides of Light, Furious Gulf, Sailing Bright
Eternity, Cosm, *and* Foundation's Fear. *His short work has been collected*
in Matter's End *and* Worlds Vast and Various. *His stories have appeared*
in our Seventh, Ninth, Fourteenth, and Fifteenth Annual Collections. His
most recent books are a major new solo novel, The Martian Race, *a non-*
fiction collection, Deep Time, *and a new collection,* Immersion and Other
Short Novels. *Benford is a professor of physics at the University of Cali-*
fornia at Irvine.

We tend to think of the Moon as cold, silent, serene, a bleak and barren
sea of rock where nothing moves and nothing has happened since the birth
of the Solar System, but the fast-paced and pyrotechnic story that follows
shows us quite a different Moon, one that boils beneath its placid surface
with energy, intrigue, and purposeful activity — and one that can be a very
dangerous place indeed . . .

You know many things, but what he knows is both less and more than what I
tell to us.

O r especially, what we all tell to all those others — those simple humans, who
are like him in their limits.

I cannot be what you are, you the larger.

Not that we are not somehow also the same, wedded to our memories of the
centuries we have been wedded and grown together.

For we are like you and him and I, a life form that evolution could not produce on the rich loam of Earth. To birth forth and then burst forth a thing—a great, sprawling metallo-bio-cyber-thing such as we and you—takes grander musics, such as I know.

Only by shrinking down to the narrow chasms of the single view can you know the intricate slick fineness, the reek and tingle and chime of this silky symphony of self.

But bigness blunders, thumb-fingered.

Smallness can enchant. So let us to go an oddment of him, and me, and you:

He saw:

A long thin hard room, fluorescent white, without shadows.

Metal on ceramo-glass on fake wood on woven nylon rug.

A granite desk. A man whose name he could not recall.

A neat uniform, so familiar he looked beyond it by reflex.

He felt: light gravity (Mars? the moon?); rough cloth at a cuff of his work shirt; a chill dry air-conditioned breeze along his neck. A red flash of anger.

Benjan smiled slightly. He had just seen what he must do.

"Gray was free when we began work, centuries ago," Benjan said, his black eyes fixed steadily on the man across the desk. Katonji, that was the man's name. His commander, once, a very long time ago.

"It had been planned that way, yes," his superior said haltingly, begrudging the words.

"That was the only reason I took the assignment," Benjan said.

"I know. Unfortunately—"

"I have spent many decades on it."

"Fleet Control certainly appreciates—"

"World-scaping isn't just a job, damn it! It's an art, a discipline, a craft that saps a man's energies."

"And you have done quite well. Personally, I—"

"When you asked me to do this I wanted to know what Fleet Control planned for Gray."

"You can recall an ancient conversation?"

A verbal maneuver, no more. Katonji was an amplified human and already well over two centuries old, but the Earthside social convention was to pretend that the past faded away, leaving a young psyche. "A 'grand experiment in human society,' I remember your words."

"True, that was the original plan—"

"But now you tell me a single faction needs it? The whole moon?"

"The council has reconsidered."

"Reconsidered, hell." Benjan's bronze face crinkled with disdain. "Somebody pressured them and they gave in. Who was it?"

"I would not put it that way," Katonji said coldly.

"I know you wouldn't. Far easier to hide behind words." He smiled wryly and compressed his thin lips. The view-screen near him looked out on a cold silver landscape and he studied it, smoldering inside. An artificial viewscape from Gray itself. Earth, a crescent concerto in blue and white, hung in a creamy sky over the insect working of robotractors and men. Gray's air was unusually clear today, the normal haze swept away by a front blowing in from the equator near Mare Chrisum.

The milling minions were hollowing out another cavern for Fleet Control to fill with cubicles and screens and memos. Great Gray above, mere gray below. Earth swam above high fleecy cirrus and for a moment Benjan dreamed of the day when birds, easily adapted to the light gravity and high atmospheric density, would flap lazily across such views.

"Officer Tozenji—"

"I am no longer an officer. I resigned before you were born."

"By your leave, I meant it solely as an honorific. Surely you still have some loyalty to the fleet."

Benjan laughed. The deep bass notes echoed from the office walls with a curious emptiness. "So it's an appeal to the honor of the crest, is it? I see I spent too long on Gray. Back here you have forgotten what I am like," Benjan said. *But where is "here"? I could not take Earth full gravity anymore, so this must be an orbiting Fleet cylinder, spinning gravity.*

A frown. "I had hoped that working once more with Fleet officers would change you, even though you remained a civilian on Gray. A man isn't—"

"A man is what he is," Benjan said.

Katonji leaned back in his shiftchair and made a tent of his fingers. "You . . . played the Sabal Game during those years?" he asked slowly.

Benjan's eyes narrowed. "Yes, I did." The game was ancient, revered, simplicity itself. It taught that the greater gain lay in working with others, rather than in self-seeking. He had always enjoyed it, but only a fool believed that such moral lessons extended to the cut and thrust of Fleet matters.

"It did not . . . bring you to community?"

"I got on well enough with the members of my team," Benjan said evenly.

"I hoped such isolation with a small group would calm your . . . spirit. Fleet is a community of men and women seeking enlightenment in the missions, just as you do. You are an exceptional person, anchored as you are in the station, using linkages we have not used—"

"Permitted, you mean."

"Those old techniques were deemed . . . too risky."

Benjan felt his many links like a background hum, in concert and warm. What could this man know of such methods time-savored by those who lived them? "And not easy to direct from above."

The man fastidiously raised a finger and persisted: "We still sit at the game, and while you are here would welcome your—

"Can we leave my spiritual progress aside?"

"Of course, if you desire."

"Fine. Now tell me who is getting my planet."

"Gray is not your planet."

"I speak for the station and all the intelligences who link with it: We made Gray. Through many decades, we hammered the crust, released the gases, planted the spores, damped the winds."

"With help."

"Three hundred of us at the start, and eleven heavy spacecraft. A puny beginning that blossomed into millions."

"Helped by the entire staff of Earthside—"

"They were Fleet men. They take orders, I don't. I work by contract."

"A contract spanning centuries?"

"It is still valid, though those who wrote it are dust."

"Let us treat this in a gentlemanly fashion, sir. Any contract can be renegotiated."

"The paper I—we, but I am here to speak for all—signed for Gray said it was to be an open colony. That's the only reason I worked on it," he said sharply.

"I would not advise you to pursue that point," Katonji said. He turned and studied the viewscreen, his broad, southern Chinese nose flaring at the nostrils. But the rest of his face remained an impassive mask. For a long moment there was only the thin whine of air circulation in the room.

"Sir," the other man said abruptly, "I can only tell you what the council has granted. Men of your talents are rare. We know that, had you undertaken the formation of Gray for a, uh, private interest, you would have demanded more payment."

"Wrong. I wouldn't have done it at all."

"Nonetheless, the council is willing to pay you a double fee. The Majiken Clan, who have been invested with Primacy Rights to Gray—"

"What!"

"—have seen fit to contribute the amount necessary to reimburse you—"

"So that's who—"

"—and all others of the station, to whom I have been authorized to release funds immediately."

Benjan stared blankly ahead for a short moment. "I believe I'll do a bit of releasing myself," he murmured, almost to himself.

"What?"

"Oh, nothing. Information?"

"Infor—oh."

"The Clans have a stranglehold on the council, but not the 3D. People might be interested to know how it came about that a new planet—a rich one, too—was handed over—"

"Officer Tozenji—"

Best to pause. Think. He shrugged, tried on a thin smile. "I was only jesting. Even idealists are not always stupid."

"Um. I am glad of that."

"Lodge the Majiken draft in my account. I want to wash my hands of this."

The other man said something, but Benjan was not listening. He made the ritual of leaving. They exchanged only perfunctory hand gestures. He turned to go, and wondered at the naked, flat room this man had chosen to work in: It carried no soft tones, no humanity, none of the feel of a room that is used, a place where men do work that interests them, so that they embody it with something of themselves. This office was empty in the most profound sense. It was a room for men who lived by taking orders. He hoped never to see such a place again.

Benjan turned. Stepped — the slow slide of falling, then catching himself, stepped —

You fall over Gray.

Skating down the steep banks of young clouds, searching, driving.

Luna you know as Gray, as all in station know it, because pearly clouds deck high in its thick air. It had been gray long before, as well — the aged pewter of rock hard-hammered for billions of years by the relentless sun. Now its air was like soft slate, cloaking the greatest of human handiworks.

You raise a hand, gaze at it. So much could come from so small an instrument. You marvel. A small tool, five-fingered slab, working over great stretches of centuries. Seen against the canopy of your craft, it seems an unlikely tool to heft worlds with —

And the thought alone sends you plunging —

Luna was born small, too small.

So the sun had readily stripped it of its early shroud of gas. Luna came from the collision of a Mars-sized world into the primordial Earth. From that colossal crunch — how you wish you could have seen that! — spun a disk, and from that churn, Luna condensed red-hot. The heat of that birth stripped away the moon's water and gases, leaving it bare to the sun's glower.

So amend that:

You steer a comet from the chilly freezer beyond Pluto, swing it around Jupiter, and smack it into the bleak fields of Mare Chrisium. In bits.

For a century, all hell breaks loose. You wait, patient in your station. It is a craft of fractions: Luna is smaller, so needs less to build an atmosphere.

There was always some scrap of gas on the moon — trapped from the solar wind, baked from its dust, perhaps even belched from the early, now long-dead volcanoes. When Apollo descended, bringing the first men, its tiny exhaust plume doubled the mass of the frail atmosphere.

Still, such a wan world could hold gases for tens of thousands of years; physics said so. Its lesser gravity tugs at a mere sixth of Earth's hefty grip. So, to begin, you sling inward a comet bearing a third the mass of all Earth's ample air, a chunk of mountain-sized grimy ice.

Sol's heat had robbed this world, but mother-massive Earth herself had slowly stolen away its spin. It became a submissive partner in a rigid gavotte, forever tide-locked with one face always smiling at its partner.

Here you use the iceteroid to double effect. By hooking the comet adroitly around Jupiter, in a reverse swingby, you loop it into an orbit opposite to the customary, docile way that worlds loop around the sun. Go opposite! Retro! Coming in on Luna, the iceball then has ten times the impact energy.

Mere days before it strikes, you blow it apart with meticulous brutality. Smashed to shards, chunks come gliding in all around Luna's equator, small enough that they cannot muster momentum enough to splatter free of gravity's grip. Huge cannonballs slam into gray rock, but at angles that prevent them from getting away again.

Earth admin was picky about this: no debris was to be flung free, to rain down as celestial buckshot on that favored world.

Within hours, Luna had air—of a crude sort. You mixed and salted and worked your chemical magicks upon roiling clouds that sported forked lightning. Gravity's grind provoked fevers, molecular riots.

More: as the pellets pelted down, Luna spun up. Its crust echoed with myriad slams and bangs. The old world creaked as it yielded, spinning faster from the hammering. From its lazy cycle of twenty-eight days it sped up to sixty hours— close enough to Earth-like, as they say, for government work. A day still lazy enough.

Even here, you orchestrated a nuanced performance, coaxed from dynamics. Luna's axial tilt had been a dull zero. Dutifully it had spun at right angles to the orbital plane of the solar system, robbed of summers and winters.

But you wanted otherwise. Angled just so, the incoming ice nuggets tilted the poles. From such simple mechanics, you conjured seasons. And as the gases cooled, icy caps crowned your work.

You were democratic, at first: allowing both water and carbon dioxide, with smidgens of methane and ammonia. Here you called upon the appetites of bacteria, sprites you sowed as soon as the winds calmed after bombardment. They basked in sunlight, broke up the methane. The greenhouse blanket quickly warmed the old gray rocks, coveting the heat from the infalls, and soon algae covered them.

You watched with pride as the first rain fell. For centuries, the dark plains had carried humanity's imposed, watery names: Tranquility, Serenity, Crises, Clouds, Storms. Now these lowlands of aged lava caught the rains and made muds and fattened into ponds, lakes, true seas. You made the ancient names come true.

Through your servant machines, you marched across these suddenly murky lands, bristling with an earned arrogance. They—*yourself!*—plowed and dug, sampled and salted. Through their eyes and tongues and ears, you sat in your high station and heard the sad baby sigh of the first winds awakening.

The station was becoming more than a bristling canister of metal, by then. Its agents grew, as did you.

You smiled down upon the gathering Gray with your quartz eyes and microwave antennas. For you knew what was coming. A mere sidewise glance at rich Earth told you what to expect.

Like Earth's tropics now, at Luna's equator heat drove moist gases aloft. Cooler gas flowed from the poles to fill in. The high wet clouds skated poleward, cooled— and rained down riches.

On Earth, such currents are robbed of their water about a third of the way to the poles, and so descend, their dry rasp making a worldwide belt of deserts. Not so on Luna.

You had judged the streams of newborn air rightly. Thicker airs than Earth's took longer to exhaust, and so did not fall until they reached the poles. Thus the new world had no chains of deserts, and one simple circulating air cell ground away in each hemisphere. Moisture worked its magicks.

You smiled to see your labors come right. Though anchored in your mammoth station, you felt the first pinpricks of awareness in the crawlers, flyers and diggers who probed the freshening moon.

You tasted their flavors, the brimming possibilities. Northerly winds swept the upper half of the globe, bearing poleward, then swerving toward the west to make the occasional mild tornado. (Not all weather should be boring.)

Clouds patrolled the air, still fretting over their uneasy births. Day and night came in their slow rhythm, stirring the biological lab that worked below. You sometimes took a moment from running all this, just to watch.

Lunascapes. Great Grayworld.

Where day yielded to dark, valleys sank into smoldering blackness. Already a chain of snowy peaks shone where they caught the sun's dimming rays, and lit the plains with slanting colors like live coals. Sharp mountains cleaved the cloud banks, leaving a wake like that of a huge ship. At the fat equator, straining still to adjust to the new spin, tropical thunderheads glowered, lit by orange lightning that seemed to be looking for a way to spark life among the drifting molecules.

All that you did, in a mere decade. You had made "the lesser light that rules the night" now shine five times brighter, casting sharp shadows on Earth. Sunrays glinted by day from the young oceans, dazzling the eyes on Earth. And the mother world itself reflected in those muddy seas, so that when the alignment was right, people on Earth's night side gazed up into their own mirrored selves. Viewed at just the right angle, Earth's image was rimmed with ruddy sunlight, refracting through Earth's air.

You knew it could not last, but were pleased to find that the new air stuck around. It would bleed away in ten thousand years, but by that time other measures could come into play. You had plans for a monolayer membrane to cap your work, resting atop the whole atmosphere, the largest balloon ever conceived.

Later? No, act in the moment—and so you did.

You wove it with membrane skill, cast it wide, let it fall—to rest easy on the thick airs below. Great holes in it let ships glide to and fro, but the losses from those would be trivial.

Not that all was perfect. Luna had no soil, only the damaged dust left from four billion years beneath the solar wind's anvil.

After a mere momentary decade (nothing, to you), fresh wonders bloomed.

Making soil from gritty grime was work best left to the microbeasts who loved such stuff. To do great works on a global scale took tiny assistants. You fashioned them in your own labs, which poked outward from the station's many-armed skin.

Gray grew a crust. Earth is in essence a tissue of microbial organisms living off the sun's fires. Gray would do the same, in fast-forward. You cooked up not mere primordial broths, but endless chains of regulatory messages, intricate feedback loops, organic gavottes.

Earth hung above, an example of life ornamented by elaborate decorations, structures of forest and grass and skin and blood—living quarters, like seagrass and zebras and eucalyptus and primates.

Do the same, you told yourself. *Only better.*

These tasks you loved. Their conjuring consumed more decades, stacked end on end. You were sucked into the romance of tiny turf wars, chemical assaults, microbial murders, and invasive incests. But you had to play upon the stellar stage, as well.

You had not thought about the tides. Even you had not found a way around those outcomes of gravity's gradient. Earth raised bulges in Gray's seas a full twenty meters tall. That made for a dim future for coastal property, even once the air became breathable.

Luckily, even such colossal tides were not a great bother to the lakes you shaped in crater beds. These you made as breeding farms for the bioengineered minions who ceaselessly tilled the dirts, massaged the gases, filtered the tinkling streams that cut swift ways through rock.

Indeed, here and there you even found a use for the tides. There were more watts lurking there, in kinetic energy. You fashioned push-plates to tap some of it, to run your substations. Thrifty gods do not have to suck up to (and from) Earthside.

And so the sphere that, when you began, had been the realm of strip miners and mass-driver camps, of rugged, suited loners . . . became a place where, someday, humans might walk and breathe free.

That time is about to come. You yearn for it. For you, too, can then manifest yourself, your station, as a mere mortal . . . and set foot upon a world that you would name Selene.

You were both station and more, by then. How much more few knew. But some sliver of you clung to the name of Benjan—

—Benjan nodded slightly, ears ringing for some reason.

The smooth, sure interviewer gave a short introduction. "Man . . . or manifestation? This we must all wonder as we greet an embodiment of humanity's greatest—and now ancient—construction project. One you and I can see every evening in the sky—for those who are still surface dwellers."

The 3D cameras moved in smooth arcs through the studio darkness beyond. Two men sat in a pool of light. The interviewer spoke toward the directional mike as he gave the background on Benjan's charges against the council.

Smiles galore. Platitudes aplenty. That done, came the attack.

"But isn't this a rather abstract, distant point to bring at this time?" the man said, turning to Benjan.

Benjan blinked, uncertain, edgy. He was a private man, used to working alone. Now that he was moving against the council he had to bear these public appearances, these . . . manifestations . . . of a dwindled self. "To, ah, the people of the next generation, Gray will not be an abstraction—"

"You mean the moon?"

"Uh, yes, Gray is my name for it. That's the way it looked when I—uh, we all—started work on it centuries ago."

"Yes you were there all along, in fact."

"Well, yes. But when I'm—we're—done," Benjan leaned forward, and his interviewer leaned back, as if not wanting to be too close, "it will be a real place, not just an idea—where you all can live and start a planned ecology. It will be a frontier."

"We understand that romantic tradition, but—"

"No, you don't. Gray isn't just an idea, it's something I've—we've—worked on for everyone, whatever shape or genetype they might favor."

"Yes yes, and such ideas are touching in their, well, customary way, but—"

"But the only ones who will ever enjoy it, if the council gets away with this, is the Majiken Clan."

The interviewer pursed his lips. Or was this a *he* at all? In the current style, the bulging muscles and thick neck might just be fashion statements. "Well, the Majiken are a very large, important segment of the—"

"No more important than the rest of humanity, in my estimation."

"But to cause this much stir over a world that will not even be habitable for at least decades more—"

"We of the station are there now."

"You've been modified, adapted."

"Well, yes. I couldn't do this interview on Earth. I'm grav-adapted."

"Frankly, that's why many feel that we need to put Earthside people on the ground on Luna as soon as possible. To represent our point of view."

"Look, Gray's not just any world. Not just a gas giant, useful for raw gas and nothing else. Not a Mercury type; there are millions of those littered out among the stars. Gray is going to be fully Earthlike. The astronomers tell us there are only four semiterrestrials outside the home system that humans can ever live on, around other stars, and those are pretty terrible. I—"

"You forget the Outer Colonies," the interviewer broke in smoothly, smiling at the 3D.

"Yeah—iceballs." He could not hide his contempt. What he wanted to say, but knew it was terribly old-fashioned, was: *Damn it, Gray is happening now, we've got to plan for it. Photosynthesis is going on. I've seen it myself—hell, I caused it myself—carbon dioxide and water converting into organics and oxygen, gases fresh as a breeze. Currents carry the algae down through the cloud layers into the warm areas, where they work just fine. That gives off simple carbon compounds, raw carbon and water. This keeps the water content of the atmosphere constant, but converts carbon dioxide—we've got too much right now—into carbon and oxygen. It's going well, the rate itself is exponentiating—*

Benjan shook his fist, just now realizing that he *was* saying all this out loud, after all. Probably not a smart move, but he couldn't stop himself. "Look, there's enough water in Gray's deep rock to make an ocean a meter deep all the way around the planet. That's enough to resupply the atmospheric loss, easy, even without breaking up the rocks. Our designer plants are doing their jobs."

"We have heard of these routine miracles—"

"—and there can be belts of jungle—soon! We've got mountains for climbing, rivers that snake, polar caps, programmed animals coming up, beautiful sunsets, soft summer storms—anything the human race wants. That's the vision we had when we started Gray. And I'm damned if I'm going to let the Majiken—"

"But the Majiken can defend Gray," the interviewer said mildly.

Benjan paused. "Oh, you mean—"

"Yes, the ever-hungry Outer Colonies. Surely if Gray proves as extraordinary as you think, the rebellious colonies will attempt to take it." The man gave Benjan a broad, insincere smile. *Dummy*, it said. *Don't know the real-politic of this time, do you?*

He could see the logic. Earth had gotten soft, fed by a tougher empire that now stretched to the chilly preserve beyond Pluto. To keep their manicured lands clean and "original," Earthers had burrowed underground, built deep cities there, and sent most manufacturing off-world. The real economic muscle now lay in the hands of the suppliers of fine rocks and volatiles, shipped on long orbits from the Outers and the Belt. These realities were hard to remember when your attention was focused on the details of making a fresh world. One forgot that appetites ruled, not reason.

Benjan grimaced. "The Majiken fight well, they are the backbone of the fleet, yes. Still, to give them a *world*—"

"Surely in time there will be others," the man said reasonably.

"Oh? Why should there be? We can't possibly make Venus work, and Mars will take thousands of years more—"

"No, I meant built worlds—stations."

He snorted. "Live inside a can?"

"That's what you do," the man shot back.

"I'm . . . different."

"Ah yes." The interviewer bore in, lips compressed to a white line, and the 3Ds followed him, snouts peering. Benjan felt hopelessly outmatched. "And just how so?"

"I'm . . . a man chosen to represent . . ."

"The Shaping Station, correct?"

"I'm of the breed who have always lived in and for the station."

"Now, that's what I'm sure our audience really wants to get into. After all, the moon won't be ready for a long time. But you—an ancient artifact, practically— are more interesting."

"I don't want to talk about that." Stony, frozen.

"Why not?" Not really a question.

"It's personal."

"You're here as a public figure!"

"Only because you require it. Nobody wants to talk to the station directly."

"We do not converse with such strange machines."

"It's not just a machine."

"Then what is it?"

"An . . . idea," he finished lamely. "An . . . ancient one." How to tell them? Suddenly, he longed to be back doing a solid, worthy job—flying a jet in Gray's skies, pushing along the organic chemistry—

The interviewer looked uneasy. "Well, since you won't go there . . . our time's almost up and—"

Again, I am falling over Gray.

Misty auburn clouds, so thin they might be only illusion, spread below the ship. They caught red as dusk fell. The thick air refracted six times more than Earth's, so sunsets had a slow-motion grandeur, the full palette of pinks and crimsons and rouge-reds.

I am in a ramjet—the throttled growl is unmistakable—lancing cleanly into the upper atmosphere. Straps tug and pinch me as the craft banks and sweeps, the smoothly wrenching way I like it, the stubby snout sipping precisely enough for the air's growing oxygen fraction to keep the engine thrusting forward.

I probably should not have come on this flight; it is an uncharacteristic self-indulgence. But I could not sit forever in the station to plot and plan and calculate and check. I had to see my handiwork, get the feel of it. To use my body in the way it longed for.

I make the ramjet arc toward Gray's night side. The horizon curves away, clean hard blue-white, and—*chung!*—I take a jolt as the first canister blows off the underbelly below my feet. Through a rearview camera I watch it tumble away into ruddy oblivion. The canister carries more organic cultures, a new matrix I selected carefully back on the station, in my expanded mode. I watch the shiny morsel explode below, yellow flash. It showers intricate, tailored algae through the clouds.

Gray is at a crucial stage. Since the centuries-ago slamming by the air-giving comets, the conspiracy of spin, water, and heat (great gifts of astro-engineering) had done their deep work. Volcanoes now simmered, percolating more moisture from deep within, kindling, kindling. Some heat climbed to the high cloud decks and froze into thin crystals.

There, I conjure fresh life—tinkering, endlessly.

Life, yes. Carefully engineered cells, to breathe carbon dioxide and live off the traces of other gases this high from the surface. In time. Photosynthesis in the buoyant forms—gas-bag trees, spindly but graceful in the top layer of Gray's dense air—conjure carbon dioxide into oxygen.

I glance up, encased in the tight flight jacket, yet feeling utterly free, naked. *Incoming meteors*. Brown clouds of dust I had summoned to orbit about Gray were cutting off some sunlight.

Added spice, these—ingredients sent from the asteroids to pepper the soil, prick the air, speed chemical matters along. The surface was cooling, the Gray greenhouse winding down. Losing the heat from the atmosphere's birth took centuries. *Patience, prudence.*

Now chemical concerts in the rocks slowed. I felt those, too, as a distant sampler hailed me with its accountant's chattering details. Part of the song. Other chem chores, more subtle, would soon become energetically possible. Fluids could seep and run. In the clotted air below, crystals and cells would make their slow work. All in time. . . .

In time, the first puddle had become a lake. How I had rejoiced then!

Centuries ago, I wanted to go swimming in the clear blue seas of Luna, I remember. Tropical waters at the equator, under Earthshine. . . .

What joy it had been, to fertilize those early, still waters with minutely programmed bacteria, stir and season their primordial soup—and wait.

What sweet mother Earth did in a billion years, I did to Gray in fifty. Joyfully! Singing the song of the molecules, in concert with them.

My steps were many, the methods subtle. To shape the mountain ranges, I needed further infalls from small asteroids, taking a century—ferrying rough-cut stone to polish a jewel.

Memories . . . of a man and more. Fashioned from the tick of time, ironed out by the swift passage of mere puny years, of decades, of the ringing centuries. Worlds take *time*.

My ramjet leaps into night, smelling of hot iron and—*chung!*—discharging its burden.

I glance down at wisps of yellow-pearl. Sulphuric and carbolic acid streamers, drifting far below. There algae feed and prosper. Murky mists below pale, darken, vanish. *Go!*

Yet I felt a sudden sadness as the jet took me up again. I had watched every small change in the atmosphere, played shepherd to newborn cloud banks, raised fresh chains of volcanoes with fusion triggers that burrowed like moles—and all this might come to naught, if it became another private preserve for some Earth-side power games.

I could not shake off the depression. Should I have that worry pruned away? It could hamper my work, and I could easily be rid of it for a while, when I returned to the sleeping vaults. Most in the station spent about one month per year working. Their other days passed in dreamless chilled sleep, waiting for the slow metabolism of Gray to quicken and change.

Not I. I slept seldom, and did not want the stacks of years washed away.

I run my tongue over fuzzy teeth. I am getting stale, worn. Even a ramjet ride did not revive my spirit.

And the station did not want slackers. Not only memories could be pruned.

Ancient urges arise, needs. . . .

A warm shower and rest await me above, in orbit, inside the mother-skin. Time to go.

I touch the controls, cutting in extra ballistic computer capacity and—

—suddenly I am there again, with *her*.

She is around me and beneath me, slick with ruby sweat.

And the power of it soars up through me. I reach out and her breast

blossoms in my eager hand, her soft cries unfurl in puffs of green steam.
Aye!
She is a splash of purple across the cool lunar stones, her breath ringing
in me—
as she licks my rasping ear with a tiny jagged fork of puckered laughter,
most joyful and triumphant, yea verily.
The station knows you need this now.
Yes, and the station is right. I need to be consumed, digested, spat back
out a new and fresh man, so that I may work well again.
—so she coils and swirls like a fine tinkling gas around me, her mouth
wraps me like a vortex. I slide my shaft into her gratefully
as she sobs great wracking orange gaudiness through me,
her, again, *her,*
gift of the strumming vast blue station that guides us all down centuries
of dense, oily time.
You need this, take, eat, this is the body and blood of the station, eat, savor,
take fully.
I had known her once—redly, sweet, and loud—and now I know her
again,
my senses all piling up and waiting to be eaten from her.
I glide back and forth, moisture chimes between us, *she* is coiled tight,
too.
We all are, we creatures of the station.
It knows this, releases us when we must be gone.
I slam myself into *her* because *she* is both that woman—known so long
ago,
delicious in her whirlwind passions, supple in colors of the mind, singing
in rubs and heats
I knew across the centuries. So the station came to know *her,* too, and
duly recorded her—
so that I can now bury my coal-black, sweaty troubles in her, *aye!*
and thus in the Shaping Station,
as was and ever shall be, Grayworld without end, amen.

Resting. Compiling himself again, letting the rivulets of self knit up into remembrance.

Of course the station had to be more vast and able than anything humanity
had yet known.

At the time the Great Shaping began, it was colossal. By then, humanity had
gone on to grander projects.

Mars brimmed nicely with vapors and lichen, but would take millennia more
before anyone could walk its surface with only a compressor to take and thicken
oxygen from the swirling airs.

Mammoth works now cruised at the outer rim of the solar system, vast ice
castles inhabited by beings only dimly related to the humans of Earth.

He did not know those constructions. But he had been there, in inherited memory, when the station was born. For part of him and you and me and us had voyaged forth at the very beginning. . . .

The numbers were simple, their implications known to schoolchildren.

(Let's remember that the future belongs to the engineers.)

Take an asteroid, say, and slice it sidewise, allowing four meters of headroom for each level—about what a human takes to live in. This dwelling, then, has floor space that expands as the cube of the asteroid size. How big an asteroid could provide the living room equal to the entire surface of the Earth? Simple: about two hundred kilometers.

Nothing, in other words. For Ceres, the largest asteroid in the inner belt, was 380 kilometers across, before humans began to work her.

But room was not the essence of the station. For after all, he had made the station, yes? Information was her essence, the truth of that blossomed in him, the past as prologue—

He ambled along a corridor a hundred meters below Gray's slag and muds, gazing down on the frothy air-fountains in the foyer. *Day's work done.*

Even manifestations need a rest, and the interview with the smug Earther had put him off, sapping his resolve. Inhaling the crisp, cold air (a bit high on the oxy, he thought; have to check that), he let himself concentrate wholly on the clear scent of the splashing. The blue water was the very best, fresh from the growing poles, not the recycled stuff he endured on flights. He breathed in the tingling spray and a man grabbed him.

"I present formal secure-lock," the man growled, his third knuckle biting into Benjan's elbow port.

A cold, brittle *thunk.* His systems froze. Before he could move, whole command linkages went dead in his inboards. The station's hovering presence, always humming in the distance, telescoped away. It felt like a wrenching fall that never ends, head over heels—

He got a grip. *Focus. Regain your links. The loss!*—It was like having fingers chopped away, whole pieces of himself amputated. *Bloody neural stumps*—

He sent quick, darting questions down his lines, and met . . . *dark.* Silent. Dead.

His entire aura of presence was gone. He sucked in the cold air, letting a fresh anger bubble up but keeping it tightly bound.

His attacker was the sort who blended into the background. Perfect for this job. A nobody out of nowhere, complete surprise. Clipping on a hand-restraint, the mousy man stepped back. "They ordered me to do it fast." A mousy voice, too.

Benjan resisted the impulse to deck him. He looked Lunar, thin and pale. One of the Earther families who had come to deal with the station a century ago? Maybe with more kilos than Benjan, but a fair match. And it would feel *good.*

But that would just bring more of them, in the end. "Damn it, I have immunity from casual arrest. I—"

"No matter now, they said." The cop shrugged apologetically, but his jaw set. He was used to this.

Benjan vaguely recognized him, from some bar near the Apex of the crater's dome. There weren't more than a thousand people on Gray, mostly like him, manifestations of the station. But not all. More of the others all the time. . . . "You're Majiken."

"Yeah. So?"

"At least you people do your own work."

"We have plenty on the inside here. You don't think Gray's gonna be neglected, eh?'

In his elbow, he felt injected programs spread, *clunk*, consolidating their blocks. A seeping ache. Benjan fought it all through his neuro-musculars, but the disease was strong.

Keep your voice level, wait for a chance. Only one of them—my God, they're sure of themselves! Okay, make yourself seem like a doormat.

"I don't suppose I can get a few things from my office?"

" 'Fraid not."

"Mighty decent."

The man shrugged, letting the sarcasm pass. "They want you locked down good before they. . . ."

"They what?"

"Make their next move, I'd guess."

"I'm just a step, eh?"

"Sure, chop off the hands and feet first." A smirking thug with a gift for metaphor.

Well, these hands and feet can still work. Benjan began walking toward his apartment. "I'll stay in your lockdown, but at home."

"Hey, nobody said—"

"But what's the harm? I'm deadened now." He kept walking.

"Uh, uh—" The man paused, obviously consulting with his superiors on an in-link.

He should have known it was coming. The Majikens were ferret-eyed, canny, unoriginal, and always dangerous. He had forgotten that. In the rush to get ores sifted, grayscapes planed right to control the constant rains, a system of streams and rivers snaking through the fresh-cut valleys . . . a man could get distracted, yes. Forget how people were. *Careless.*

Not completely, though. Agents like this Luny usually nailed their prey at home, not in a hallway. Benjan kept a stunner in the apartment, right beside the door, convenient.

Distract him. "I want to file a protest."

"Take it to Kalespon." Clipped, efficient, probably had a dozen other slices of bad news to deliver today. To other manifestations. Busy man.

"No, with your boss."

"Mine?" His rock-steady jaw went slack.

"For—" he sharply turned the corner to his apartment, using the time to reach for some mumbo-jumbo—"felonious interrogation of inboards."

"Hey, I didn't touch your—"

"I felt it. Slimy little gropes—yeccch!" Might as well ham it up a little, have some fun.

The Majiken looked offended. "I never violate protocols. The integrity of your nexus is intact. You can ask for a scope-through when we take you in—"

"I'll get my overnight kit." Only now did he hurry toward the apartment portal and popped it by an inboard command. As he stepped through he felt the cop, three steps behind.

Here goes. One foot over the lip, turn to the right, snatch the stunner out of its grip mount—

—and it wasn't there. They'd laundered the place already. "Damn!"

"Thought it'd be waitin', huh?"

In the first second. When the Majiken was pretty sure of himself, act—

Benjan took a step back and kicked. A satisfying soft *thuuunk*.

In the low gravity, the man rose a meter and his *uungh!* was strangely satisfying. The Majiken were warriors, after all, by heritage. Easier for them to take physical damage than life trauma.

The Majiken came up fast and nailed Benjan with a hand feint and slam. Benjan fell back in the slow gravity—and at a 45-degree tilt, sprang backward, away, toward the wall—

Which he hit, completing his turn in air, heels coming hard into the wall so that he could absorb the recoil—

—and spring off, head-height—

—into the Majiken's throat as the man rushed forward, shaped hands ready for the put-away blow. Benjan caught him with both hand-edges, slamming the throat from both sides. The punch cut off blood to the head and the Majiken crumbled.

Benjan tied him with his own belt. Killed the link on the screen. Bound him further to the furniture. Even on Gray, inertia was inertia. The Majiken would not find it easy to get out from under a couch he was firmly tied to.

The apartment would figure out that something was wrong about its occupant in a hour or two, and call for help. Time enough to run? Benjan was unsure, but part of him liked this, felt a surge of adrenaline joy arc redly through his systems.

Five minutes of work and he got the interlocks off. His connections sprang back to life. Colors and images sang in his aura.

He was out the door, away—

The cramped corridors seemed to shrink, dropping down and away from him, weaving and collapsing. Something came toward him—chalk-white hills, yawning craters.

A hurricane breath whipped by him as it swept down from the jutting, fresh-carved mountains. His body strained.

He was running, that much seeped through to him. He breathed brown murk that seared but his lungs sucked it in eagerly.

Plunging hard and heavy across the swampy flesh of Gray.

He moved easily, bouncing with each stride in the light gravity, down an infinite straight line between rows of enormous trees. Vegetable trees, these were, soft tubers and floppy leaves in the wan glow of a filtered sun. There should be no men here, only machines to tend the crops. Then he noticed that he was not a man at all. A robo-hauler, yes—and his legs were in fact wheels, his arms the working grapplers. Yet he read all this as his running body. Somehow it was pleasant.

And *she* ran with him.

He saw beside him a miner-bot, speeding down the slope. Yet he knew it was *she*, Martine, and he loved her.

He whirred, clicked—and sent a hail.

You are fair, my sweet.

Back from the lumbering miner came, *This body will not work well at games of lust.*

No reason we can't shed them in time.

To what end? she demanded. Always imperious, that girl.

To slide silky skin again.

You seem to forget that we are fleeing. That cop, someone will find him.

In fact, he had forgotten. *Uh . . . update me?*

Ah! How exasperating! You've been off, romping through your imputs again, right?

Worse than that. He had only a slippery hold on the jiggling, surging lands of mud and murk that funneled past. Best not to alarm her, though. *My sensations seem to have become a bit scrambled, yes. I know there is some reason to run—*

They are right behind us!

Who?

The Majiken Clan! They want to seize you as a primary manifestation!

Damn! I'm fragmenting.

You mean they're reaching into your associative cortex?

Must be, my love. Which is why you're running with me.

What do you mean?

How to tell her the truth but shade it so that she does not guess . . . the Truth? *Suppose I tell you something that is more useful than accurate?*

Why would you do that, m'love?

Why do doctors slant a diagnosis?

Because no good diagnostic gives a solid prediction.

Exactly. Not what he had meant, but it got them by an awkward fact.

Come on, she sent. *Let's scamper down this canyon. The topo maps say it's a shortcut.*

Can't trust 'em, the rains slice up the land so fast. He felt his legs springing like pistons in the mad buoyancy of adrenaline.

They surged together down slippery sheets that festered with life-spreading algae, some of the many-leafed slim-trees Benjan had himself helped design. Rank growths festooned the banks of dripping slime, biology run wild and woolly at a fevered pace, irked by infusions of smart bugs. A landscape on fast forward.

What do you fear so much? she said suddenly.

The sharpness of it stalls his mind. He was afraid for her more than himself, but how to tell her? This apparition of her was so firm and heartbreakingly warm, her whole presence welling through to him on his sensorium. . . . Time to tell another truth that conceals a deeper truth.

They'll blot out every central feature of me, all those they can find.

If they catch you. Us.

Yup. Keep it to monosyllables, so the tremor of his voice does not give itself away. If they got to her, she would face final, total erasure. Even of a fragment self.

Save your breath for the run, she sent. So he did, gratefully.

If there were no omni-sensors lurking along this approach to the launch fields, they might get through. Probably Fleet expected him to stay indoors, hiding, working his way to some help. But there would be no aid there. The Majiken were thorough and would capture all human manifestations, timing the arrests simultaneously to prevent anyone sending a warning. That was why they had sent a lone cop to grab him; they were stretched thin. Reassuring, but not much.

It was only three days past the 3D interview, yet they had decided to act and put together a sweep. What would they be doing to the station itself? He ached at the thought. After all, *she* resided there. . . .

And *she* was here. He was talking to a manifestation that was remarkable, because he had opened his inputs in a way that only a crisis can spur.

Benjan grimaced. Decades working over Gray had aged him, taught him things Fleet could not imagine. The Sabal Game still hummed in his mind, still guided his thoughts, but these men of the Fleet had betrayed all that. They thought, quite probably, that they could recall him to full officer status, and he would not guess that they would then silence him, quite legally.

Did they think him so slow? Benjan allowed himself a thin, dry chuckle as he ran.

They entered the last short canyon before the launch fields. Tall blades like scimitar grasses poked up, making him dart among them. She growled and spun her tracks and plowed them under. She did not speak. None of them liked to destroy the life so precariously remaking Gray. Each crushed blade was a step backward.

His quarters were many kilometers behind by now, and soon these green fields would end. If he had judged the map correctly—yes, there it was. A craggy peak ahead, crowned with the somber lights of the launch station. They would be operating a routine shift in there, not taking any special precautions.

Abruptly, he burst from the thicket of thick-leafed plants and charged down the last slope. Before him lay the vast lava plain of Oberg Plateau, towering above the Fogg Sea. Now it was a mud flat, foggy, littered with ships. A vast dark hole yawned in the bluff nearby, the slanting sunlight etching its rimmed locks. It must be the exit tube for the electromagnetic accelerator, now obsolete, unable to fling any more loads of ore through the cloak of atmosphere.

A huge craft loomed at the base of the bluff. A cargo vessel probably; far too large and certainly too slow. Beyond lay an array of robot communications vessels, without the bubble of a life support system. He rejected those, too, ran on.

She surged behind him. They kept electromagnetic silence now.

His breath came faster and he sucked at the thick, cold air, then had to stop for a moment in the shadow of the cruiser to catch his breath. Above he thought he could make out the faint green tinge of the atmospheric cap in the membrane that held Gray's air. He would have to find his way out through the holes in it, too, in an unfamiliar ship.

He glanced around, searching. To the side stood a small craft, obviously Jump type. No one worked at its base. In the murky fog that shrouded the mud flat he could see a few men and robo-servers beside nearby ships. They would wonder what he was up to. He decided to risk it. He broke from cover and ran swiftly to the small ship. The hatch opened easily.

Gaining lift with the ship was not simple, and so he called on his time-sense accelerations, to the max. That would cost him mental energy later. Right now, he wanted to be sure there was a *later* at all.

Roaring flame drove him into the pearly sky.

Finding the exit hole in the membrane proved easier. He flew by pure eye-balled grace, slamming the acceleration until it was nearly a straight-line problem, like shooting a rifle. Fighting a mere sixth of a g had many advantages.

And now, where to go?

A bright arc flashed behind Benjan's eyelids, showing the fans of purpling blood vessels. He heard the dark, whispering sounds of an inner void. A pit opened beneath him and the falling sensation began—he had run over the boundaries this body could attain. His mind had overpowered the shrieking demands of the muscles and nerves, and now he was shutting down, harking to the body's calls. . . .

And *she?*

I am here, m'love. The voice came warm and moist, wrapping him in it as he faded, faded, into a gray of his own making.

She greeted him at the station.
She held shadowed inlets of rest. A cup brimming with water,
a distant chime of bells, the sweet damp air of early morning.
He remembered it so well, the ritual of meditation in his fleet training,
the days of quiet devotion through simple duties that strengthened the
mind.
Everything had been of a piece then.
Before Gray grew to greatness, before conflict and aching doubt,
before the storm that raged red through his mind, like—

—Wind, snarling his hair, a hard winter afternoon as he walked back to his quarters. . . .
—then, instantly, the cold prickly sensation of diving through shimmering spheres of water in zero gravity. The huge bubbles trembled and refracted the yellow light into his eyes. He laughed.
—scalding black rock faces rose on Gray. Wedges thrust upward as the tortured skin of the planet writhed and buckled. He watched it by remote camera, seeing only a few hundred yards through the choking clouds of carbon dioxide. He felt the rumble of earthquakes, the ominous murmur of a mountain chain being born.
—a man running, scuttling like an insect across the tortured face of Gray. Above him the

great membrane clasped the atmosphere, pressing it down on him, pinning him, a beetle beneath glass. But it is Fleet that wishes to pin him there, to snarl him in the threads of duty. And as the ship arcs upward at the sky he feels a tide of joy, of freedom.

—twisted shrieking trees, leaves like leather and apples that gleam blue. Moisture beading on fresh crimson grapes beneath a white-hot star.

—sharp synapses, ferrite cores, spinning drums of cold electrical memory. Input and output. Copper terminals (male or female?), scanners, channels, electrons pouring through p-n-p junctions. Memory mired in quantum noise.

Index. Catalog. Transform. Fourier components, the infinite wheeling dance of Laplace and Gauss and Hermite.

And through it all she is there with him, through centuries to keep him whole and sane and yet he does not know, across such vaults of time and space . . . who is he?

Many: us. One: I. Others: you. *Did you think that the marriage of true organisms and fateful machines with machine minds would make a thing that could at last know itself? This is a new order of being but it is not a god.*

Us: one, We: you, He: I.

And yet you suspect you are . . . different . . . somehow.

The Majiken ships were peeling off from their orbits, skating down through the membrane holes, into *my* air!

They gazed down, tense and wary, these shock troops in their huddled lonely carriages. Not up, where I lurk.

For I am iceball and stony-frag, fruit of the icesteroids. Held in long orbit for just such a (then) far future. (Now) arrived.

Down I fall in my myriads. Through the secret membrane passages I/we/you made decades before, knowing that a bolthole is good. And that bolts slam true in both directions.

Down, down—through gray decks I have cooked, artful ambrosias, pewter terraces I have sculpted to hide my selves as they guide the rocks and bergs—*after them!*—

The Majiken ships, ever-wary of fire from below, never thinking to glance up. I fall upon them in machine-gun violences, my ices and stones ripping their craft, puncturing. They die in round-mouthed surprise, these warriors.

I, master of hyperbolic purpose, shred them.

I, orbit-master to Gray.

Conflict has always provoked anxiety within him, a habit he could never
correct, and so:
—in concert we will rise to full congruence with F(x)
and sum over all variables and integrate over the contour
encapsulating all singularities. It is right and meet so to do.
He sat comfortably, rocking on his heels in meditation position.
Water dripped in a cistern nearby and he thought his mantra,
letting the sound curl up from within him. A thought entered,
flickered across his mind as though a bird,
and left.

She she she she
The mantra returned in its flowing green rhythmic beauty and he entered
the crystal state of thought within thought,
consciousness regarding itself without detail or structure.
The air rested upon him, the earth groaned beneath with the weight of
continents,
shouting sweet stars wheeled in a chanting cadence above.
He was in place and focused, man and boy and elder at once,
officer of Fleet, mind encased in matter, body summed into mind
—and *she* came to him, cool balm of aid, succor, yet beneath her palms
his muscles warmed, warmed—

His universe slides into night. Circuits close. Oscillating electrons carry information, senses, fragments of memory.

I swim in the blackness. There are long moments of no sensations, nothing to see or hear or feel. I grope—

Her? No, she is not here either. Cannot be. For she has been dead these centuries and lives only in your station, where she knows not what has become of herself.

At last, I seize upon some frag, will it to expand. A strange watery vision floats into view. A man is peering at him. There is no detail behind the man, only a blank white wall. He wears the blue uniform of Fleet and he cocks an amused eyebrow at:

Benjan.

"Recognize me?" the man says.

"Of course. Hello, Katonji, you bastard."

"Ah, rancor. A nice touch. Unusual in a computer simulation, even one as sophisticated as this."

"What? Comp—"

And Benjan knows who he is.

In a swirling instant he sends out feelers. He finds boundaries, cool gray walls he cannot penetrate, dead patches, great areas of gray emptiness, of no memory. What did he look like when he was young? Where was his first home located? That girl—at age fifteen? Was that *her? Her?* He grasps for her—

And knows. He cannot answer. He does not know. He is only a piece of Benjan.

"You see now? Check it. Try something—to move your arm, for instance. You haven't got arms." Katonji makes a thin smile. "Computer simulations do not have bodies, though they have some of the perceptions that come from bodies."

"P—perceptions from where?"

"From the fool Benjan, of course."

"Me."

"He didn't realize, having burned up all that time on Gray, that we can penetrate all diagnostics. Even the station's. Technologies, even at the level of sentient molecular plasmas, have logs and files. Their data is not closed to certain lawful parties."

He swept an arm (not a real one, of course) at the man's face. Nothing. No contact. All right, then. . . . "And these feelings are—"

"Mere memories. Bits from Benjan's station self." Katonji smiles wryly.

He stops, horrified. He does not exist. He is only binary bits of information scattered in ferrite memory cores. He has no substance, is without flesh. "But . . . but, where is the real me?" he says at last.

"That's what you're going to tell us."

"I don't know. I was . . . falling. Yes, over Gray—"

"And running, yes—I know. That was a quick escape, an unexpectedly neat solution."

"It worked," Benjan said, still in a daze. "But it wasn't me?"

"In a way it was. I'm sure the real Benjan has devised some clever destination, and some tactics. You—his ferrite inner self—will tell us, *now*, what he will do next."

"He's got something, yes. . . ."

"Speak *now*," Katonji said impatiently.

Stall for time. "I need to know more."

"This is a calculated opportunity," Katonji said off-handedly. "We had hoped Benjan would put together a solution from things he had been thinking about recently, and apparently it worked."

"So you have breached the station?" Horror flooded him, black bile.

"Oh, you aren't a complete simulation of Benjan, just recently stored conscious data and a good bit of subconscious motivation. A truncated personality, it is called."

As Katonji speaks, Benjan sends out tracers and feels them flash through his being. He summons up input and output. There are slabs of useless data, a latticed library of the mind. He can expand in polynomials, integrate along an orbit, factorize, compare coefficients—*so they used my computational self to make up part of this shambling construct.*

More. He can fix his field—there, just so—and fold his hands, repeating his mantra. Sound wells up and folds over him, encasing him in a moment of silence. *So the part of me that still loves the Sabal Game, feels drawn to the one-is-all side of being human—they got that, too.*

Panic. Do something. Slam on the brakes—

He registers Katonji's voice, a low drone that becomes deeper and deeper as time slows. The world outside stills. His thought processes are far faster than an ordinary man's. He can control his perception rate.

Somehow, even though he is a simulation, he can tap the real Benjan's method of meditation, at least to accelerate his time sense. He feels a surge of anticipation. He hums the mantra again and feels the world around him alter. The trickle of input through his circuits slows and stops. He is running cool and smooth. He feels himself cascading down through ruby-hot levels of perception, flashing back through Benjan's memories.

He speeds himself. He lives again the moments over Gray. He dives through the swampy atmosphere and swims above the world he made. Molecular master, he is awash in the sight-sound-smell, an ocean of perception.

Katonji is still saying something. Benjan allows time to alter again and Katonji's drone returns, rising—

Benjan suddenly perceives something behind Katonji's impassive features. "Why didn't you follow Benjan immediately? You could find out where he was going. You could have picked him up before he scrambled your tracker beams."

Katonji smiles slightly. "Quite perceptive, aren't you? Understand, we wish only Benjan's compliance."

"But if he died, he would be even more silent."

"Precisely so. I see you are a good simulation."

"I seem quite real to myself."

"Ha! Don't we all. A computer who jests. Very much like Benjan, you are. I will have to speak to you in detail, later. I would like to know just why he failed us so badly. But for the moment we must know where he is now. He is a legend, and can be allowed neither to escape nor to die."

Benjan feels a tremor of fear.

"So where did he flee? You're the closest model of Benjan."

I summon winds from the equator, cold banks of sullen cloud from the poles, and bid them *crash*. They slam together to make a tornado such as never seen on Earth. Lower gravity, thicker air—a cauldron. It twirls and snarls and spits out lightning knives. The funnel touches down, kisses my crust—

—and there are Majiken beneath, whole canisters of them, awaiting my kiss.

Everyone talks about the weather, but only I do anything about it.

They crack open like ripe fruit.

—and you dwindle again, hiding from their pursuing electrons. Falling away into your microstructure.

They do not know how much they have captured. They think in terms of bits and pieces and he/you/we/I are not. So they do not know this—

> You knew this had to come
> As worlds must turn
> And primates must prance
> And givers must grab
> So they would try to wrap their world around yours.
> They are not dumb.
> And smell a beautiful beast slouching toward Bethlehem.

Benjan coils in upon himself. He has to delay Katonji. He must lie—

—and at this rogue thought, scarlet circuits fire. Agony. Benjan flinches as truth verification overrides trigger inside himself.

"I warned you." Katonji smiles, lips thin and dry.

Let them kill me.

"You'd like that, I know. No, you will yield up your little secrets."

Speak. Don't just let him read your thoughts. "Why can't you find him?"

"We do not know. Except that your sort of intelligence has gotten quite out of control, that we do know. We will take it apart gradually, to understand it—you, I suppose, included."

"You will . . ."

"Peel you, yes. There will be nothing left. To avoid that, tell us *now*."

—and the howling storm breaches him, bowls him over, shrieks and tears and devours him. The fire licks flesh from his bones, chars him, flames burst behind his eyelids—

And he stands. He endures. He seals off the pain. It becomes a raging, white-hot point deep in his gut.

Find the truth. "After . . . after . . . escape, I imagine—yes, I am certain—he would go to the poles."

"Ah! Perfect. Quite plausible, but—which pole?" Katonji turns and murmurs something to someone beyond Benjan's view. He nods, turns back and says, "We will catch him there. You understand, Fleet cannot allow a manifestation of his sort to remain free after he has flouted our authority."

"Of course," Benjan says between clenched teeth.

(But he has no teeth, he realizes. Perceptions are but data, bits strung together in binary. But they feel like teeth, and the smoldering flames in his belly make acrid sweat trickle down his brow.)

"If we could have anticipated him, before he got on 3D. . . ." Katonji mutters to himself. "Here, have some more—"

Fire lances. Benjan wants to cry out and go on screaming forever. A frag of him begins his mantra. The word slides over and around itself and rises between him and the wall of pain. The flames lose their sting. He views them at a distance, their cobalt facets cool and remote, as though they have suddenly become deep blue veins of ice, fire going into glacier.

He feels the distant gnawing of them. Perhaps, in the tick of time, they will devour his substance. But the place where he sits, the thing he has become, can recede from them. And as he waits, the real Benjan is moving. And yes, he *does* know where. . . .

Tell me true, these bastards say. All right—

"Demonax crater. At the rim of the South Polar glacier."

Katonji checks. The verification indices bear out the truth of it. The man laughs with triumph.

All truths are partial. A portion of what Benjan is/was/will be lurks there.

> Take heart, true Benjan.
> For *she* is we and we are all together,
> we mere Ones who are born to suffer.
> Did you think you would come out of this long trip alive?
> Remember, we are dealing with the most nasty of all species the planet
> has ever produced.

Deftly, deftly—

We converge. The alabaster Earthglow guides us. Demonax crater lies around us as we see the ivory lances of their craft descend.

They come forth to inspect the ruse we have gathered ourselves into. We seem to be an entire ship and buildings, a shiny human construct of lunar grit. We hold still, though that is not our nature.

Until they enter us.

We are tiny and innumerable but we do count. Microbial tongues lick. Membranes stick.

Some of us vibrate like eardrums to their terrible swift cries.

They will discover eventually. They will find him out.

(Moisture spatters upon the walkway outside. Angry dark clouds boil up from the horizon.)

They will peel him then. Sharp and cold and hard, now it comes, but, but—

(Waves hiss on yellow sand. A green sun wobbles above the seascape. Strange birds twitter and call.)

Of course, in countering their assault upon the station, I shall bring all my hoarded assets into play.

And we all know that I cannot save everyone.

Don't you?

They come at us through my many branches. Up the tendrils of ceramic and steel. Through my microwave dishes and phased arrays. Sounding me with gamma rays and traitor cyber-personas.

They have been planning this for decades. But I have known it was coming for centuries.

The Benjan singleton reaches me in time. Nearly.

He struggles with their minions. I help. I am many and he is one. He is quick, I am slow. That he is one of the originals does matter to me. I harbor the same affection for him that one does for a favorite finger.

I hit the first one of the bastards square on. It goes to pieces just as it swings the claw thing at me.

Damn! it's good to be back in a body again. My muscles bunching under tight skin, huffing in hot breaths, happy primate murder-joy shooting adrenaline-quick.

One of the Majiken comes in slow as weather and I cut him in two. Been centuries since I even *thought* of doing somethin' like that. Thumping heart, yelling, joyful slashing at them with tractor spin-waves, the whole business.

A hell of a lot of 'em, though.

They hit me in shoulder and knee and I go down, pain shooting, swimming in the low centrifugal g of the station. Centuries ago I wanted to go swimming in the clear blue seas of Luna, I recall. In warm tropical waters at the equator, under silvery Earthshine. . . .

But *she* is there. I swerve and dodge and *she* stays right with me. We waltz through the bastards. Shards flying all around and vacuum sucking at me but *her* in my veins. Throat-tightening pure joy in my chest.

Strumming notes sound through me and it is *she*
Fully in me, at last
Gift of the station in all its spaces
For which we give thanks yea verily in this the ever-consuming moment—
Then there is a pain there and I look down and my left arm is gone.
Just like that.
And she of ages past is with me now.

—and even if he is just digits running somewhere, he can relive scenes, the grainy stuff of life. He feels a rush of warm joy. Benjan will escape, will go on. Yet so will he, the mere simulation, in his own abstract way.

Distant agonies echo. Coming nearer now. He withdraws further.

As the world slows to frozen silence outside he shall meditate upon his memories. It is like growing old, but reliving all scenes of the past with sharpness and flavor retained.

—(The scent of new-cut grass curls up red and sweet and humming through his nostrils. The summer day is warm; a Gray wind caresses him, cool and smooth. A piece of chocolate bursts its muddy flavor in his mouth.)

Time enough to think over what has happened, what it means. He opens himself to the moment. It sweeps him up, wraps him in a yawning bath of sensation. He opens himself. Each instant splinters sharp into points of perception. He opens himself. He. Opens. Himself.

Gray is not solely for humanity. There are greater categories now. Larger perspectives on the world beckon to us. To us all.

You know many things, but what he knows is both less and more than what I tell to us.

—*for Martin Fogg*

V.A.O.

GEOFF RYMAN

Born in Canada, Geoff Ryman now lives in England. He made his first sale in 1976, to New Worlds, *but it was not until 1984, when he made his first appearance in* Interzone — *the magazine where almost all of his published short fiction has appeared — with his brilliant novella* The Unconquered Country *that he first attracted any serious attention. The Unconquered Country, one of the best novellas of the decade, had a stunning impact on the science fiction scene of the day, and almost overnight established Ryman as one of the most accomplished writers of his generation, winning him both the British Science Fiction Award and the World Fantasy Award; it was later published in a book version,* The Unconquered Country: A Life History. *His output has been sparse since then, by the high-production standards of the genre, but extremely distinguished, with his novel* The Child Garden: A Low Comedy *winning both the prestigious Arthur C. Clarke Award and the John W. Campbell Memorial Award. His other novels include* The Warrior Who Carried Life, *the critically acclaimed mainstream novel* Was, *and the underground cult classic* 253, *the "print remix" of an "interactive hypertext novel" which in its original form ran online on Ryman's home page of www.ryman.com, and which, in its print form won the Philip K. Dick Award. Four of his novellas have been collected in* Unconquered Countries. *His most recent book is a new novel,* Lust. *His stories have appeared in our Twelfth, Thirteenth, Seventeenth, and Nineteenth Annual Collections.*

In the wry and compelling story that follows, he introduces us to some people at the very end of life who find that there's still some challenges to face — and some surprises ahead.

Jazzanova wandered off again. He was out all night.

They tell me that they've found him up a tree. So I sit in his room and wait for him and I remember that he told me once that when he was a kid, he used to climb up pine trees in the park to read comics — *Iron Man, Dr. Midnight.* I guess he was a dreamy kind of kid. Then he came to Jersey and started to live it instead. That's when we met, in college.

They bring him back in. Jazza looks like a cricket that somebody's stained brown with tea. I hate his shuffling walk. His feet never leave the ground like he's wearing slippers all the time. The backwards baseball cap he always wears doesn't suit Alzheimer's either. He shuffles off to take a leak and I hear him getting into a fight with his talking toilet.

The toilet says, "You've been missing your medication." It's probably sampled his pee.

Jazzanova doesn't like that. "Goddamit!" He sounds drunk and angry. He flushes the thing, to shut it up. He comes out and his glasses start up on him. "11:15," his glasses say in this needling little voice. "You should have taken medication at 9:00 am and 10:30 am. Go to the blue tray and find the pills in the green column."

They never let up on you. The whole place is wired. It's so full of ordnance you can hear it. Jazza's bedroom sounds like it's full of hummingbirds.

He blanks it all out and kinda falls back onto the sofa. His callipers aren't so hot on sitting down. Then he just stares for a couple of seconds. He's looking at his hands like they don't belong to him. Finally he says to me, "What say we get outa here for a beer, um . . ."

He's forgotten who I am again. I can see the little flicker in his glasses as it goes through photos and whispers my name at him. "Brewster," he says. Then he like, shrugs and says, "It's all in the mix."

It's all in the mix. That's what he always says when he's pretending he's chilled out and not gaga. Jazza's still on planet Clubland, a million years ago. Maybe he's happy there.

But he can't pay his bills.

"Bar's not open," I tell him. I hold out his blue tray of pills. "Take one of these, man. Top buzz."

Instead of taking one, he fumbles up a wholehandful and the tray says to him "Nooooooo." It sounds like a bouncer outside a club.

"Shit," he says and takes five of the fuckers anyway.

Outside his big window, it's late summer, early morning, all kinda smoky. It's a nice view; I'll say that. Lawn, trees. The view is wired too. Whole place is full of VAO. Victim Activated Ordnance. To protect us rich old folks.

Once I saw this kid who'd climbed over the wall. He was just a kid. He probably just wanted to play on the grass. The camera saw him and zapped him. They used pulse sound on him. He clutched his head and tried to run, but his feet kept wobbling. Each bullet is 150 decibels and you can't really think. He stumbled down onto his knees and he'd stand up, drop, stand up drop down again until they came for him.

I used to make that stuff. I used to make the software that recognises faces. Now it recognises me.

I go back and my room smells like a trashcan. It's got grey hair in the corners. It pisses me off what I pay for this place. The least they could do is keep it clean. There's got to be some advantages to being an old vegetable.

I push the buzzer and I get no answer. I push again, and nothing happens so I go to the screen and start shouting. I tell 'em straight up, "I push your buzzer and you don't come, man. I could be dying of a heart attack up here. If I tell the papers, that'd blow your sales pitch. You don't answer my buzzer, I scorch your ass!"

About 45 minutes later the Kid shows up moving real slow. He leans back against the wall, arms folded. I can't even remember what fucked-up country he's from, but I can read him. He's got that mean, sour look you get when nobody gives a fuck so why should you.

I feel pretty pissed off myself. "Next time I ring the buzzer you fuckin show up."

"Sorry, Sir." Kid says 'Sir' like maybe it means Dog in his own language.

"What the fuck is up with you?"

"Nothing, Sir."

I look for buttons to push. You know, like if someone blanks you out, you get them mad and maybe you find out what's going on?

I insult the Kid. "Can't you talk English?"

Nothing.

"It's a helluva way to get a tip. Or no tip. You want no tip?"

His arms snap open like a spring lock, his head swivels like armed CCTV, and his mouth spouts garbage like a TV in translation. I pushed his button all right.

When he stops swearing in Albanian or Mongolian or whatever I finally hear him squawk. "I get no tip no how!"

So that's it. He's not getting his tips.

The assholes who run this place don't pay the staff. You gotta give the nurses tips, the cleaners tips, the doctors tips, the waiters tips. If the toilets get more intelligent we'll have to tip the toilets. And management makes sure you do it regular. That's one of the things about this dump I hate the most. They keep sending you little forms to fill in to debit your bank account. Those fuckin forms show up on your computer, on your TV, on your microwave, on your specs. The forms have these horrible chirpy little voices. "I'm sure you want to express your appreciation for the staff."

It costs 100 thousand a year to live here and they call the tips discretionary. That's another hundred fifty a week. And I make sure I pay it because I want these bozos to motor if I get sick or something.

I keep my voice cool cause I want to make sure I got this right. "No tips? I pay your tips, man."

I need this guy's name. You cannot talk somebody down if you don't know their name. My eyeglasses are running through all the photographs of staff, and finally I see him. I click a bit of my brain, like I'm going to ask him his name. The glasses tell me.

The Kid is called Joao and he's from some part of Indonesia that speaks Portuguese.

"Joao?" I tell him. "I'm sorry. I am sorry. I pay. Really."

He stands there swelling up and down like he's pumping iron.

"Joao? I pay the tips. You don't get them?"

Kid's so mad his wires are crossed. He scowls and blinks.

"Lemme show you," I say.

I try to ease him to the machine, you know, I just touch his arm, and he throws it off, like this. For a second I think he's going to give me a Jersey kiss. So I keep my voice low and soft. "Hey, man, just be cool about it, OK. Lemme show you."

So I open up my records. See? I show him all that debit. All those tips going out just as regular as spam. I point to the money, there on the screen. Right out of my bank account.

The Kid blinks and rubs his whole face with his hands. I begin to wonder if they teach people to read in the country he's from.

Then suddenly he shouts. "I no get them!" He's throwing up his hands and wiggling his cheeks. But I can see. Now he's not mad at me.

I feel pretty sick myself, in my gut like my chicken was full of salmonella. I'm thinking, oh fuck. Oh fuck. We got ourselves a tips racket.

Somebody somewhere, probably one of the hotshot doctors who can't pay for his new swimming pool or his lawsuit insurance is hacking out the cleaners' tips.

I could complain, and I could call in the law. But. I got reasons. Know what I mean?

"How long you not been getting your tips?" I ask him.

He tells me. Months. I can see why he isn't all that concerned about cleaning up my shit. I sit him down, pour him a whisky. This will take a while and I want him to know right in his balls who got him back his money. Me. Here. The Brewster.

I call up my contact. She's top dope, a tough old babe still on the outside called Nikki. She's got this great translation package. We have this audio conversation about her new bungalow which is a cover for a hack download. It comes in looking like a phone bill. It then runs a request from a nostalgia TV line. I load up and sit back and watch what looks like an old Britney Spears video.

It's not a video, believe me. I can't do anything that looks like a hack. The ordnance is always watching. They say it's in case we get ill, but hey, why do they snoop our keystrokes? If you want to hack here, it's a case of no hands. And everything has to look like something else.

I smile at the Kid and jerk my head at the cameras, glasses, TV, computer . . . all the surveillance. But hey, the Kid's cool. He can't speaka da English, but he gets what I'm doing. For the first time I get a smile out him. He chuckles and lifts up the whiskey glass. "Z24!" he says. Ah, that's Kidtalk.

"Banging!" I say back. That's my talk. "You've a Britney fan huh?"

The Kid's sussed. He knows exactly what's going on. "Britney . . . Whitney . . . all that old stuff." He chuckles and nods and shakes his head. "I big big fan!" I know what's he's thinking. He's thinking, this old guy is into some shit. He's thinking, this old guy is hacking me back my tips.

The microwave pings like my dinner's ready, only it's not food that's cooking. I put on my glasses, and then put the transcoder on top of them and suddenly Britney is translated into the Corporation's accounts. But only if you are looking at em through my glasses.

I got a real good line on who's been stealing a little bit of the Kid's bandwidth.

My Medical Supervisor. Mr trusted Dr. Curtis. So I siphon out the dosh and siphon it into the Kid's corporate account. Ready for loading to his bank.

"Banging!" the Kid says.

Grand Dad House.

So then I call on Dr. Curtis. "You got a face like shit and your brains are all on your chin!"

Dr. Curtis leans back and looks like someone just been told a real bad joke. Behind him is a wall of screens, some of them showing people's pumping insides.

You see, you get old, you end up in here and that gives them the right to monitor every last act and word. You're a patient.

I'm one mad patient. "I may be 80 but I could still deck you!"

He leans back, with his eyebrows up and his eyes hooded. "I could always prescriptionize out all that aggressive testosterone. So unbecoming in the aged."

I hate him. Really. I can take most people but if I could do Curtis an injury I would. Curtis has got hold of my pubic hair and can give it a twist whenever he wants.

"Look Curtis, you been hacking off our tips. Duh! Don't you think the staff kinda of notice they're not getting paid? And I know we're all a bunch of senile old codgers, but even we can tell when we don't get our asses wiped cause the staff can't feed their kids. You leave our tips alone, asshole!"

The good doctor sniffs. "I'm afraid I have expenses."

"Yeah, and they all got tits."

"And I've only got one other source of income." He starts to smile. A nice long pause, like it's his close up or something. He purses his lips into a little bitty kiss. "You."

He's such a drama student. His breath smells of cheese. He tells me "If my account is empty, I'll hack it out of yours."

No he won't. It won't be that easy. But he has got a point. It is the whole point, the underlying point. I gotta sit on that point everyday and it goes straight up my ass.

I can't walk without help. My kid's poor. I gotta find a hundred thou a year.

So I take it out of other people's bank accounts, OK?

Curtis is my doctor. He knows everything I do. I have to give him a cut.

I have a dream. I put Dr. Curtis in rubber mask and backwards baseball cap, and shove him out on the lawn at night so the cameras don't recognise him and he gets area-denied. He gets sound gunned. He gets microwaved; his whole body feels like it's touching a hot lightbulb. His whole goddamned shaven tattooed trendy fat little ass feels what's like to be poor and hungry and climbing over our wall just to activate some ordnance.

All this is before lunch. It's a well crucial day. Stick around, it's about to get even more crucial.

It's Saturday and that's Bill's day to visit. I go to the Solarium and wait, and then wait some more. Today he doesn't show. I wait a little while longer. And then ring him up to leave a message. I don't want sound whiney, so I try to sound up. "Hey, Bill, this your Dad. Everything's cool, I hope it's under control for you too."

Then I sit and hang out. I don't want to be some sad old fuck. I open up a newspaper. It tells me Congress wants to change tax rates, to ease the burden on younger taxpayers. Oh cool, thanks.

I go back to check out Jazza. It's the afternoon, but he's sleeping like a baby.

Jazza used to be so cool. It's good to have someone from your time, your place. Even if he doesn't remember who you are.

We wanted to send a rocket to Mars. We built it ourselves and called it Aphrodite and went to Nevada and launched it and it went straight up looking like 1969 and hope.

We made pretend-music; started our own company, developed a couple of computer games, called ourselves Fighting Fit and sold the company. We ran a pirate download and shared the same girlfriend for a while. After we lost all our money, we emptied the same accounts too. Amateur spaceships don't pay for themselves. I decided to go mundane, and went into security software. I went straight for a while. Jazza never did. He still hung out there. From time to time I gave him some freelance. When Bill went to college I went to check Jazza out. He was still at a mixing desk at fifty. He was wearing one of those shirts that keeps changing pictures or told the punters what toons he was pumping out.

I hack Jazza's bills as well. Otherwise, he'd be out on the street.

I sit there a while, just making sure he's OK, if he wants anything. He snores. I give his knee a pat and leave. You get lonely sometimes.

I get to my room and there's a message. "Dad, you probably know this already but Bessie was mugged. I'll be over tomorrow."

Bessie is my granddaughter. Never have a well crucial day.

The next morning we're doing Neurobics.

They found out that even old people grow new neurons. If they give you PDA, it goes even faster, but you got to use it or lose it. So they make us learn. They make us do crazy stuff. Like brush our teeth with the wrong hand. Or read stuff from a screen that is upside down. Sometimes they make us do really off the wall stuff, like sniff vanilla beans while we listen to classical music. They're trying to induce synaesthesia.

Today we were in VR. We're weightless in a burning space station. We got to get out through smoke and there is no up or down. What way does the lever on the door pull?

I get a tug on my arm. It's the Kid. He smiles at me real nice. "Mr Brewster? I come find you. You son is here."

These days I walk like Frankenstein, on these fake little legs. They make your muscles work so they grow back. Nobody's supposed to hold me up. The Kid does though. To him I guess I'm some old granddad and that is how you show respect.

So I introduce him to my son. Joao, this is my boy Bill. Bill stands up and shakes the Kid's hand and thanks him for taking care of me. My boy is fifty years old. He's got a potbelly, but he still looks like a guy who never spent a day in an office.

Bill is real neat. I can say that. He's a neat kid, he just never made any money.

He'd work in the summers as a diving instructor and in winter he'd go south. He went to teach primary school in the Hebrides. He did a stint putting chips in elephant's brains in Sri Lanka.

Today though his smile looks weirded out.

"How's Bessie?" I ask.

Something happens to Bill's face and he sits down. "Um. You didn't see the news? It was on the news."

"Bessie was in the news?" Oh shit. You don't get in the comics just for stubbing your toe.

Bill's voice rattles. "They did something to her face," he says. He takes out his paper and fills it, and lays it out on the table.

I tell him, "I didn't see anything about it. I think we're filtered. I think they filter our news."

"VAO. Only this time it really was a victim who got activated."

VAO protects banks, shopping malls, offices. Anything First World, or Nerd World, got VAO. It's supposed to zap thieves. For just a second I thought maybe Bessie had been on a job like maybe being a gangsta skips a generation or something.

Bill's newspaper fills up with an animated headline.

The headline says

V

A

O . . .

And the headline animates into

Very

Ancient

Offenders

And then, for your delectation and amusement, up comes my granddaughter's mugging, caught on security camera and sold by the ordnance company to defray costs.

They run my granddaughter's mugging for laughs. Because the muggers are old.

Ain't dey cute, them old guys?

There's my Bessie, going out to her car. Slick black hair, skinny red trousers, real small, real sweet. Able to take care of herself, but you don't expect your own bolted, belted VAO parking lot to be the place where you get mugged.

These four clowns come lurching out at her. They're old guys like me. They're staggering around on callipers, they got the Frankenstein walk but they stink of the street. One of them is wearing old trousers that are too small. The legs end up around his calves, and they're held up by a belt, they don't close at the front. There is a continent of dingy underwear on display.

Bill says, "Microwave. Somehow they turned it on her instead of them. But they didn't know what they were doing." Bill can't look at this, he's hiding his face.

And on the paper, Bessie is denied her own area.

The keys in her hand go hot, she drops them. Her own shiny hair goes hot and she clasps her head, and she crouches down and tries to hide under her own elbows.

Bill takes from behind his hand. "It's supposed to stop before 250 seconds. After that it does damage."

These are old, old codgers. They shuffle. They forget to turn the fuckin thing off. They pick up the car keys and they're too hot and they drop 'em. Well duh. Finally they shuffle round to some kind of switch.

We're at 300 seconds and Bessie's trousers are smoking, and the skin of her face is curling up.

"She'll need a cornea transplant," says Bill.

They pick up her purse and just leave her there. They get into the car. I get a look at them.

There's two ways you get old. One, you shrivel up. The other, you puff out like a cloud. One guy has a face like melted marshmallow in these dead-white hanging lumps.

"Old farts," I hear myself say. I'm so sick of feeling angry. I feel angry all the time and there's nothing I can do about anything. There's nothing I can do about Bessie, nothing I can do those old stupid jerks.

"She'll be OK," says Bill and he's looking at me and for just a sec I'm his Daddy again. I never was much of a Daddy when he was a kid, always off on a job or working for the company. He ended up being the kind of guy who never stops looking for a father. Christ, Billy. I wanted to have enough money so that you would never have to work, to make up for not being around. But all my money goes into being old.

We latch hands. Bill's spent all his life helping people. Bill's just a better man than I am.

"I'm sorry, Billy," I say, and I mean for everything.

That night Jazza and I finally go for a beer at the bar in the Happy Farm, but J's in bad shape. He just sits staring. Neurobics make him dizzy. They got a new timed drug dispenser on his wrist. He does a little jump and groans when they dose him. We're hanging out with Gus.

Gus does this sweet little hippie routine. He says that he sold plankton to places like Paraguay so they could get carbon reduction credits. Now. Everybody who was awake knows that it didn't work and nobody made any money at it. In fact they lost their shirts.

So I ask myself: where does Gus's money come from? I mean you got this greasy little dude who took too much whizz. His dialog is just too sussed for an eco-warrior.

"You heard about this VAO stuff?" he asks me.

"Only cause my granddaughter got mugged. I didn't know they filter our news."

"I got something that filters the filter," he says. "This is news we need to know."

"About my granddaughter?"

"No. Look me in the eye. The guys that do this are a crew. It's several crews all over the country, but they're all linked, and they're all old guys. And they're doing this kind of stuff a lot."

Suddenly, I am aware of the surveillance all around us. "So?"

"Kind of blows our story, doesn't it? Sweet little old guys playing computer games and taking physio." Gus's eyes are steady as a rock.

I knew it. Gus is a player.

I ask him, "How much are you uh . . . *tipping* Curtis?"

His face and smile are less expressive than an armadillo's behind. "Too much," he says. His eyebrows do a little jump.

"Anybody else?" I ask him, meaning who are the other Players. It's nice to know that even at our age we can make new friends and acquaintances.

"Oh yeah," he says looking around. "You could start with The Good Fairies." The Good Fairies are a couple, been together 50 years. They look up from their table, and they look pretty mean to me.

"I'll get you that filter," says Gus.

Good as his word, I get mail. Takes me a while, because it downloads as dirty pictures. I try a couple of times and finally get the code. Load it up and I got a different personalisation on the news.

So I fill up my newspaper and I read the backstory. This crew has been at it for months. Old guys who hijack armed intelligent cameras, old guys who spray clubs with paralysis gas, or shoot electricity through whole trainloads of commuters. They edit out every single last purse and wristwatch while the ordnance that is supposed to protect the punters is turned around on them.

There are zapped grannies, zapped babies, zapped beautiful teenage girls who should have been left to enjoy life. I never had any respect for direct-action crime. Money is magic, it's a religion. All you gotta do is just walk into the temple and help yourself and nobody gets hurt.

Not these geeks. For them, hurting people is part of the point. They're not even really crooks. Crooks want to be invisible. These guys are so stupid and vicious that they want everybody to know about them.

They got this crazy leader who calls himself Silhouette. Aw Jesus can you believe that? He probably grew up wanting to be Eminem or something. He still does that dumb thing with the splayed open hands pointing down. Silhouette is skinny like a model. His knees are fatter than his thighs and ho-hum, he's all in black and he has his whole face blanked out, just black, no eyes no mouth. Oh, Daddy Cool.

I take one look at this guy and I know just who he is. My generation, you know, we never fought a war. We grew up watching disasters on TV and worrying about our clothes. This guy is sitting there and he's holding his face so that we can see he's got killer cheekbones. The guy's probably eighty and he's worried about his looks.

And of course he's got a manifesto. He croaks it at me, in this real weird voice, until I figure out it's been recognition masked. No voiceprint. It makes him sound like he's talking underwater.

"You sniff money on old people, and just because we can't run and can't hurt you back you strip us naked. You leave us in cold water flats and shut us up in expensive prisons you call Homes. You don't pay us the pensions you promised. When we get sick, you tell us our insurance that we paid for all our lives doesn't cover the cost of care. You want us to die. So. We'll die. And take we'll everything from you when we go."

You want to know the spookiest thing of all? I know where he's coming from. I know exactly what Silhouette means.

"Age Rage," he says and clenches a fist.

So the next day I'm back down in the bar with Gus. I got Jazzanova with me like he's my good luck charm. Gus has his squeeze Mandy. Mandy used to be a lap dancer. She's still got a body, I can tell you.

She's also got a mouth and the brains to use it. Her cover is that she used to be in property development. Well yeah maybe. A certain kind of old babe has the hardest eyes you'll ever see.

Mandy says, "The trouble with that scum is they'll turn the heat up on all of us."

"Yup," says Gus. "We'll end up on the street."

"I'll take Curtis with me," I promise. "I got evidence on the guy."

Mandy's not impressed. "Good! You can share the same cardboard box. Hope it makes you feel better."

We're too old for fear. We just turn our backs on it. If we get the fear at all it takes us over, and our legs don't work and we go little and frail and old. So we got to be like old dried leather. It used to be soft, but now it's as hard as stone.

The Good Fairies sit listening. They are as cerebral as fuck. I mean these guys are the only people I know who can tell their genitals what to do. They got married fifty years ago and they've only fucked each other since. I blame Aids.

The Good Fairies sometimes talk in unison. It's like twins who've been locked up in the same closet since they were born. "We have to take out Silhouette."

Best, as we cogitate. True. Beat. Us? Beat.

Then we all start roaring with laughter. Mandy barks like a dog with its vocal chords cut out. Gus squeaks. I know I sound like gravel being milled. Jazzanova stares into outer space, and doesn't want to be left out, so he laughs at the strip lighting and then he swallows a chip off the table edge thinking it's a pill.

Mandy is barking. "The Neurobics Crew!"

The Good Fairies sit holding hands, sipping their cigarettes, and they don't move a muscle.

Fairy One says, real calm. "It'll be real funny inside that cardboard box."

"Specially when it rains," says the other. This guy is five foot two with a dorky beard. He looks like a failed Drag King, but he calls himself Thug, which has to be some kind of joke.

"Yeah, but you guys," says Mandy. "I can hear where you're coming from, but what are going to DO?"

Fairy One calls himself JoJo but I bet he's really called George and he says, "We ask him to stop."

"Oh yeah? Sure!"

"His position doesn't make sense. He says he does it because he's old. But it is the old he's hurting."

Mandy shakes her head. "He's in it for the money."

Thug disagrees. "He's in it for the showbiz. Money won't be enough."

JoJo says "We show him how to get on TV and say something that makes sense for a change. I'm sure that most of us have something to say on the position of the old."

Mandy says, "How you gonna do that."

JoJo says, "I used to make TV shows."

Thug says. "All we gotta do is find who Silhouette is."

And I get this real weird, sick feeling and I don't know why.

Mandy jerks like she's laughing to herself. She flicks cigarette ash like it's going all over their pretty little dream. "You better get hacking," she says.

I don't know if they did, but the next day my dear Dr. Curtis runs in to tell me we're all about to get a visit from the cops.

Curtis looks terrified. He looks sick. He leans against my door like they're going to hammer it down. Plump smooth-skinned pretty little doctor, he's got so much to lose.

"How's your system?" he asks smiling like he's relearning how to use his facial muscles. He's got something he doesn't want to say in front of the ordnance.

I don't get it. "What's it to you?"

He makes a noise like someone's jammed a pin in his butt. His eyes start doing a belly dance towards the window. I look out and see that the front drive of the Happy Farm is stuffed like a turkey with police cars.

I just say, "A shape outlined against the light?"

I mean a silhouette. Curtis sorta settles with relief and nods yes. "You've been following the news."

I get it. The cops are here to find out if any of us nice old folks are funding Silhouette's reign of terror. That means that they'll be going through our accounts. For once Curtis and I have exactly the same self-interest.

I'm a thief and I've never been caught and that's not because I'm smart, but because I know I'm not. So I worry. So I prepare.

I got about ten minutes and that's all I need. I start running my emergency program. It looks like a rerun of pro golf. Curtis hangs around. He wants to see how I do this. I need to put on my specs but I don't want him to know about the transcoder.

"Curtis, maybe you should go talk to our guests." I mean slow them down. I mean get out of here.

Then there's a knock. In comes the Kid. Maybe he's come to tell me about the cops too. He sees Curtis and I swear his eyes switch on with hate like a lightbulb.

"Joao, maybe you could take Dr. Curtis out to greet our guests." And that means: Joao help me get him out of here.

That Kid is sussed. "You," he says to Curtis, and punches the palm of his hand. Curtis understands that, too. Note. Not one of us has said anything that would sound bad in court.

I hear the door shut. Finally I put on my specs and the transcoder shows me data download on one eye lens and data upload, on the other.

It's a fake I've had worked out for years. It'll cover my whole account and make it look like I'm some kind of gaga spendthrift, that I gamble a lot on a Korean site, lose my dosh, win some dosh. It matches, transaction for transaction, money in, money out.

That's what's uploading. On the other lens, I'm encrypted my old data. I got maybe five minutes now.

Just having some encrypted data on my system will be enough to make trouble. I'm ghosting the encrypted file and then I go to get it off my disk. It starts to squirt into my transcoder.

I hear big heavy boots. I hear Dr. Curtis babbling happily. I hear a knock on the front door. Mine? No, next door.

Six . . . five . . . four . . . stuff is still downloading. Three two one zero. Right, off comes the transcoder. It looks like the arm from my glasses.

On my hard drive, iron molecules are being permanently scrambled. Sorry Officer, I'm just this old guy and I've been having these terrible problems with my system.

I go take a shower. They monitor your heartbeat and video your keystrokes but the law says they can't perve you in the shower.

And while I'm in the shower I take the transcoder and like I rehearsed a hundred times, I push it up the head of my penis.

The transcoder's long, it's thin. In an x-ray, it'll look like a sexual prosthetic.

When the knock on my door comes, I'm out, I'm dry, and I'm in my nice baggy shiny blue suit. I am the picture of a callipered, monitored neurobic modern Noughties Boy. With money of his own.

The Armament comes in. He looks like somebody who divides his time between weightlifting and V-games, hairy golden biceps, a smile like a rodent's and heavy-duty multipurpose specs. His manner is unfriendly. "You're Alistair Brewster. Hello. We've been wanting to talk to you."

"I don't see what's stopping you." I don't do polite even with Armament.

"Fine." He sits down without being asked. His specs have a little blinking light. Smile, you're on candid camera. "Mr Brewster, you used to work for SecureIT Inc."

"Was that a question or a statement?"

He blinks. "You worked on the design of security systems."

There is no lie as effective as the truth. "That's how I made my money. I came up with some of the recognition software, the stuff that means the ordnance knows who it's dealing with." I try to make it sound rich.

He nods and pretends to be impressed. "I was wondering if you could help us understand some of the ways in which these safety checks could be subverted. During the recent spate of thefts."

Now this is trouble. It's coming from an angle I was not expecting. They don't think I'm a thief. They don't think I'm a donor.

They think maybe I'm part of Silhouette's crew.

I stall for time. "Can I confirm your ID?"

"Sure."

"I'm not talking security until I know who you are."

"Very wise, Mr Brewster."

"Not wisdom. Habit. You get by on habit at my age Mr . . ."

Secret Squirrel here won't give me his name, just a look at his dental work. So he leans forward and my TV checks out his retinas. We share a polite, stone-cold silence as it chews over this for a while. Then out comes his stuff.

Secret Squirrel is 36 years old, has a tattoo on right knee which sounds real romantic and is validated as Armament, Security Status Amber . . . oh, it takes my back to the good old days. It still won't give me his name. Psychological advantage.

I always hated Armament, for the same reason I hate Silhouette. They shoot people. Also, they never gave SecureIT a clear brief. "OK, Secret Squirrel, shoot. I don't mean that literally by the way. Feel free to make a few more statements you already know the answers to."

"Smart ass," says the Armament.

"Look Squirrel, I'm rich, I'm happy, I don't have to take anything from anybody and it was difficult getting to the point that I can say that with confidence. I didn't ask you in here, and I don't have to cooperate. In fact I signed a nondisclosure agreement with SecureIT when I left. What they would prefer and what I would prefer is that you go talk to them instead of me. So. You want me to be nice to you, you start thinking nice thoughts about what a sweet old guy I am and how much you respect me."

"Age Rage," he says sweetly, calmly. "You're a suspect Mr Brewster, not an information source." He keeps smiling, and waits for me to fall over in shock.

I just do Mr Rich Disgusted. I roll my eyes. And hold up my hands like, I live in this place, so why would I have Age Rage?

He keeps his poker smile. "So Mr Brewster, it is in your own interests to co-operate fully. In the first place Mr Brewster, it is true that you came up with alot of this stuff, and it is also true that it is all patented in the name of SecureIT and that you didn't get a bean. Isn't that so."

"I got paid," I say. "A lot. A lot more than you. And I'm smart with my money."

"Eighty percent, Mr Brewster. Eighty percent of online crime is by employees or former employees. You fit the profile like a glove. Your profile is in neon lights all around your head."

I don't like his attitude. "First thing, I got nothing to do with all this crap. My own granddaughter just got her face burned off so don't come here with some fairy tale about how I'm a big Age Rage freak."

He blinks. And I think gotcha. I have no problems pressing my advantages. I go for it. "You dumb fuck, you didn't come here and not know that Elizabeth Angstrom Brewster is my granddaughter did you? I mean you have read the files, I take it? Victims? Try 13705 Grande Mesa Outlook, apartment 41, Loma Linda, CA."

And for once Dr. Curtis does something smart. "It would be very difficult indeed for any of our guests to be involved in something unsavoury. You have to understand that for their own protection, our guests are monitored 24-7-365. We know every keystroke on their computers."

I play along. "Damn right. I can't even download any porn."

The Armament's face settles and his eyes narrow. He's mad. Somebody he relies on didn't add up Brewster and Brewster and come up with four. He coughs and blanks out his face. "How did they circumvent the recognition software?"

I answer him like I'm talking to a baby. "They . . . turned . . . it . . . off."

It was easy after that. I cooperated fully. I didn't know how it was done. You guys have been on the scene what did you find there? He didn't wanna say, so I speculated, and I speculated for real. Infrared input, transcoding images? Not EMP, the stuff is hardened against that. Maybe they just broke the box and put their own software in. Maybe, yeah, it was an inside job.

When the Armament left he looked like there was some poor guy back in research was going to get a full body electrolysis for free. We all shook hands.

I'd lucked out. That was all. I was one dumb fuck who'd lucked out. All this VAO uses my stuff. I should just have known they'd think maybe I was part of it. I just didn't see it coming.

I'm getting old.

And something else.

It was very far from a dumb idea to check out SecureIT staff. I should have thought about it myself. Remember how I said I took one look at Silhouette and thought I knew him?

Well suddenly I realised that I did. I knew who he was, I could think how he used to talk, I knew he still had all his own hair.

I just couldn't for the life of me remember who he was or where I knew him from. So I'm gaga too. I sat there and ran through every single face in my address book. Nothing. Who?

I am clearly going to spend much of my declining years with people's names on the tip of my tongue, and no idea whether or not I've turned off the gas.

What I'm thinking is: I need something to get the Armament looking some-where else. The best way to do that would be to ID Silhouette.

That night we're back in the bar, licking our wounds.

None of the Neurobics Crew got stung. But. The Armament got one old dear for illegal arms trading. Really. She and her son on the outside were dealing in illicit ordnance. That lady had the biggest, highest, roundest widow's hump I'd ever seen, and I swear she was even more out of it than Jazza. It's kind of sad and sick and funny at the same time.

Mandy has no time for sympathy. "We're next."

Gus is reading the paper and suddenly he drops it and says. "Holy shit. Have you seen this?"

He lays the paper out on the table. "It's another job," Gus says.

AGE RAGE ATTACK. VAOs use VAO again.

The CCTV rerun shows the whole thing. The little label says:

Chase Manhattan Bank NYC, 1:00 am this morning.

You're looking at the inside of a vault and suddenly this iron door starts to rip. You see this claw widen the gap and then nip off some of the raggedy bits, and then they duck inside. This time my jaw drops.

This time they're wearing firemen's suits.

Walking exoskeletons that respond to movement pressure from the guys inside them. With training you can wear those things and walk through fire. You can lift up automobiles or concrete girders. You wear those things, you're Superman for a day.

The old codgers don't lurch anymore. Those suits weigh tons, but they dance. They duck and dive and ripple and flow. They shimmy, they hop, they look like giant trained fleas.

I'm saying over and over. "It's brilliant. It's fucking brilliant."

I worked on those things. You see, you can't send in rescue workers carrying hydrocarbon fuel or nuclear power on their backs and even those suits can't carry enough ordinary batteries. So you beam the power at them. You beam microwaves. All you do if there is a disaster is you turn on your VAO, and the microwaves fuel the suits.

About the only people my software is programmed never to zap are rescue workers in exoskeletons.

Carte Blanche. We've given them Carte fucking Blanche and her sister Sadie too.

All four of them move like fingers playing piano. They scamper up to rows of strong boxes and just haul them out of the wall.

The suits already have these huge blue tubs on their backs. Nobody likes to say, but they're for the body bags. The crew just dumps everything into them— heirloom jewellery and bearer bonds and old passports for new identities. Bullion or rare stamps. For the suits, it all just weighs a feather.

I say. "They're not going for virtual. They're going for atoms."

Mandy turns and looks at me like I'm a lizard. "Well duh! That's why they call it burglary."

Just then the bank's security guards come running in. They're covered head to toe in foil, so they can't be area-denied. They start shooting.

You've never seen anything as beautiful as the movement in those mechanical arms. The old guys inside don't have to do a thing. The arms just weave magic carpets in the air. And they go ping ping ping like harps as the bullets hit off them, and they flash like fireworks.

Then the suits coil and spring, and one of them grabs a guard by his head and throws him three yards straight into the wall. The guard kinda hangs there for a second and starts to slide down it. Through the back of the silver suit, blood gets sprayed in a pattern like a butterfly. The guard hits the ground stays sitting, his head dumped forward. He looks like the bridegroom after a stag party.

I don't see what happened to other guards, but it looked messier. He's nothing but a shape in the corner.

And then these beautiful suits turn to the cameras and wave like astronauts.

They put a hand on each other's shoulders. And they dance off in line, like Dorothy and her tin men.

And Jazza is still staring at the strip lights.

I say, "This is one problem we gotta own."

Mandy barks a laugh. "Hell, I was thinking of running off and joining them. That looked like a lotta fun."

"Those guards got kids," says Gus. From the look on his face, I don't think he likes Mandy much right now.

"We gotta get information and we gotta get it to the cops." I tell them. "We all got to start hacking. I can get into SecureIT."

Gus is still in pain. He can't get the guards out of his head. "You reckon the company that sold that video will use any of the money to help their families?"

Thug says. "What do we hack?"

I got this one sussed. "They either bought those suits or they stole them. Either way they'll be a transaction or a report. The manufacturers are called. . . ."

Great, I draw a blank. I hate this, I really hate this. Just before despair comes, I remember the name. "XOsafe. XOsafe Ltd. They're in Portland."

Mandy cuts in. "The first thing I'm doing is take care of my own business so I have some money. That'll take a while." Suddenly she looks down and says in lower voice. "Then maybe I can look at who the guys in the crews are, OK?"

It's probably as close to an apology as Mandy can get. Since nobody ever apologised to her.

"Don't get your hopes up," she tells me and goes off.

I go and give Bessie a call. "How ya doing, babe?"

"Aw, grand Dad," she says soft and faraway and grateful. She tries to sound like it's all covered, skin grafts etc but it can't be covered, it can never be covered. You see she was confident, she was sussed, and I'm scared. I'm scared it will make her timid when she used to be so up front.

All I can say is, "Baby, I'm so sorry."

"Hey, you're the Brewster. Nothing gets you down."

"We're going to get him for you, babe," I promise.

I retrieve my transcoder, which is a more delicate operation than sticking it was. I get my glasses back and go to Jazza's room because I want to use his station to hack. Never put an old hack back from the same place. I go to his room but he's not there. I keep the lights low, and make like I'm loading my pro golf program onto his machine. Money starts flowing back into my account but from a different source this time.

After a while I ask: where is Jazza?

I go back to the bar. My crew's not there. Neither is Jazza. Oh god, he's wandered again.

I get worried; I turn on his terminal to trace his bracelet. It's pumping out signals. It's coming from the shower. But there's no shower running.

At our age, you're always thinking in the back of your head: who's going to go next? And I'm thinking maybe this time it's Jazza. I can just about see him crumpled up on the floor. So I go to that shower with everything in my chest all shrivelled shut like a fist. I turn on the light, and there's no Jazza there.

Just his bracelet on the shower floor.

Oh fuck. I push the buzzer. It seems to take an age. They've done these experiments that show why we always think a second is longer than it really is. The brain is always anticipating. It starts measuring time from the thought, not the vision. So I cling on to the buzzer saying come on, come on.

I think of all those times I check Jazza's buzzer before going to bed. Jazza nice, and secure in his bed, it shows, or Jazza happy in the shower.

Has he done this before? You see Alzheimer's, they wander off, they try to buy ice cream in the middle of the night in a suburb or they pack a couple of telephone directories and go catch a plane. They don't understand, they feel trapped, sometimes they get frustrated and start to punch. They disappear and leave you to worry and grieve and hope all at the same time.

"We find him, don't worry Mr Brewster," says the Kid.

So I see them, on the lawn, with flashlights. A light little feather duster of a thought brushes past me: the ordnance is turned off. The lights dance around the trees. The bricks in the wall are lit from underneath like a Halloween face.

Nothing.

I haul myself off to bed, and the callipers are really doing it to the side of my knees, scraping the skin, and I'm old and I just don't sleep. Here in the Happy Farm there aren't even passing car lights on the ceiling to look at. There's only walls, and what's up ahead, closer now. At night.

When you're old you got a few things left and one of them is your promises. You can keep a promise as slow as you like, and as fast as you can, just so long as you don't give up. I promised Bessie. I turn on my machine and hack.

Who knows SecureIT like me? Well, it's been a few years. I get to work through a whole new bunch of stuff, but I do get into the Human Resource files. I mean, who would want to hack personnel, right? Just everybody.

And I go through every name, every face, every voiceprint recording. I see a face, I know it, but only sort of. I know that girl, sort of. She went and got a patent out on a new polymer, then joined. Real scholarly, real pretty, real nice legs. And I realise hell, she'll be 40 now. She left years and years ago. After I did.

I see some old guy like me, pouchy cheeks and glasses and I can't place him at all, except there's a weird sensation in my chest, like I'm a time traveller. I used say hi to that face every day.

One after another after another. Who are these people, being replaced?

One guy I knew now heads up a department. What? He was nothing. He was a plodder. Guess what? That's who becomes head of the department.

I look a skinny, hollow staring scared face and I suddenly realise, shoot, that's Tommy. Tommy was a nice young kid who taught himself to program, he had talent. Now he's staring out at me wide-eyed with creases round his mouth like he's been surprised by something. Like failure, like going nowhere. It makes me want to get in there and sort it out, and tell them, no you got it wrong, this guy's got talent, you're supposed to use it for something!

It makes me want to show up again every day at 8:00 am, and work my butt off, and take the kids out for a drink. It makes me want to make something happen again, even if it's just in some little job in an office.

And I look at face after face and there is no Silhouette. There just is no Silhouette.

And then I find my own record. I see my own face staring out at me. Hey, maybe that guy's Silhouette.

First time I saw that photograph I couldn't take it, I thought that's not me, that's not the Brewster, who is that old, double-chinned geezer? Now, I look at it and I've got most of my hair and it's black, and think how young I look.

And I read my record, and it tells the story of a middle manager who got a couple of promotions. It doesn't say I came up with loop recognition iterations. It doesn't say I was the first guy to use quantum computers on security work. It doesn't say I was the guy who first told the CE about ISO 20203 and that getting registered to that standard got us Singapore and Korea and finally China.

What it does have is my retirement date. And then it says down at the bottom. "Left without visible security compromises. No distinguishing features."

No fucking distinguishing features. What was I expecting, a thank you? A corporation that tried to credit its employees? I guess I was expecting that since I did some pretty extraordinary stuff for them, big stuff, stuff that got a whole congress of my peers on their feet and applauding, I guess I somehow thought I'd made some kind of mark. But they don't want you to make a mark. They want that mark for themselves. But they don't get it either.

We just all go down into the dark.

And I feel the fear start up.

Oh you can blank out the fear. You can turn and walk away from it. Or you can let it paralyse you. The one thing you can't do is what you would do with any other fear. You can't just turn and walk right at it. It won't go away. Because this fear is the fear of something that can only be accepted.

The only thing you can do with death is accept it, and if you do that at our age, it's too close to dying. You accept it, and it can come for you.

You get something like angry instead. You do what you do when you're trapped. You writhe.

I can't stay still. I go lolloping and limping like I'm stoned and drunk at the same time, because my room is like a coffin and the dark is like my eyes will never open. I go off down the corridor bobbling and jerking like some kind of goddamn puppet that something else is making move. I'm slamming my ribs against the wall and I don't care.

And then I see a light under Mandy's door. I don't have my shirt on, but what the fuck. I'm scared. And I can't afford to let myself stay scared. I knock on her door.

"Kinda early for socialising," she says. She checks out my sagging pecs. "Are you inviting me for a swim?"

She still has her make up on, she looks sussed, she looks great, she looks like it's a big bright beautiful Saturday.

For me, everything starts to fall back down into normal. "I . . . I just need to talk. Do you mind?"

"Not much. I hate nights as well." She walks off and leaves her door open.

Her room smells of perfume. On the bed there are about eight stuffed toys . . .

puppy dogs, turtles. On the shelf there is a huge lavender teddy bear, still wrapped in cellophane with a giant purple bow.

"I got nothing," she says, and flings her fake fingernails at the TV screen. For a second I think she means nothing in her life. Then I get it: she's been hacking. On the screen are eight old faces and the photo of the guy who mugged my granddaughter.

I take a chair, and I start to feel strong again. "Me neither," I say, meaning I got nothing out of SecureIT. "I'm . . . uh . . . kinda surprised that you're doing this so openly."

"Are you kidding? We're doing our bit to catch Silhouette. I want any brownie points that are going."

That TV is pointed straight at the surveillance. I gotta smile.

"You're smart," I say.

"Oh wow, really? Like I didn't know that without you telling me." She looks at me like I'm bumwipe.

I like her. "So has anybody else said you're smart recently?"

She nods. She accepts. "Most people don't give a fuck what you are so long as you can pay."

"You got any family?" I lean forward, into the conversation. I want to hear.

"No," she says, just with her lips, no sound. She breathes out through her nose. "I got property instead."

"For real." I understand. I flick my eyebrows. It's like: so why do you have to hack, then?

She gets it. She answers the question without having to hear it. "Keeps the brain in gear," she says. "Beats talking to teddy bears."

"At least you got one smart person to talk to."

"Who?" She turns around and she's dripping scorn, expecting some egotistical guy kind of remark.

I lean forward again. "You."

"Oh." She looks down and finally smiles. "Yeah, OK, I'm smart. Thanks. You want a whisky while you're sitting there?"

"That'd be great."

"Just a few more months in Neurobics and a six month course of PDA will replace the neurons you're destroying."

And I say, "Maybe I'll die first." It's not such a joke.

She turns with the glass. "I hope not. Here."

Mandy tells me about how she bought land in Goa and sold it for a dream. She talks about investing in broadband pipes while she was in her twenties so she could get out of lapdancing. She really did lap dance. I try to get her to talk more about herself. The only thing I get out of her is that she lived with her mother in a trailer until her Mom met a car dealer and they settled into a little bungalow in Jersey. "I'd go into my room and run shootemups on my video. I kept pretending I was shooting him."

Finally I say, "I better go and see if they found Jazza."

She nods and we both get up. And she says to me, "It's real cool the way you still look out for him after all these years."

I say, "He's part of my crew."

"Come off it," she says. "He's the only crew you got." But she says it in a real sweet way.

The next morning, I got a mail on my TV.

It's from the Kid. They've found Mr. Novavita on a Greyhound bus going to south Maryland. Jazza hasn't lived in Maryland since he was a kid and his parents moved to Jersey. How the hell did he do that?

They bring him back in about noon and he looks like the night has been beating him up: purple cheeks, brown age spots, clumps of thick greasy grey. It wasn't the night: this is how Mr. Novavita looks now and keep forgetting that. But he still climbs trees.

"He'll be OK. He'll sleep," says the Kid.

I see his glasses on the table, and there's another feather duster thought. "He was wearing these?"

I put them on. There's a transcoder, but it's built right into the arm. High tech. Higher than mine. There's glowing fire all along the Kid's arm. Heat vision. For night?

"Fancy glasses," I say.

I go down to my crew. We're all hacked back, so we're sorted for cash flow. Thug has done some work on the suits. He has this little radio he plays, so they can't snoop our dialogue.

Thug says, "XOsafe's iced solid. So we hacked into the police files."

"What!" My voice sounds like an air pump on arctic ice.

"We have a plant on the police computer," says JoJo. Tells us whenever we're mentioned. We added Brewster. Got a lot. They reckon Silhouette could be you."

"What, ME?"

Mandy just barks, and waves at the smoke like she's waving away the dumbest thing she's ever heard.

I'm still stuck in high gear. "They think I'm Silhouette!"

"You were the prime suspect. Until your own granddaughter got it."

I'm outraged. "Dumb shits!"

JoJo says: "Not so dumb, apparently. There's a line they've been following, right into the Happy Farm."

Mandy barks. "Oh I don't believe it. This place?"

I take a look at her cheekbones. There's this funny tickle in my head. It's recognition. Of something. All of a sudden it's like I'm hearing someone else ask her, "Is it you?"

Only it's me that said it. The room goes cold. The radio plays dorky lounge. "Mandy. I asked are you Silhouette?" What I mean by this is strange: I really want to tell her don't worry, we'll protect you if you are, I kind of feel like I've said that. But that's not what's coming out. Actually, I'm just not in control. Because, as you will see, there's something else going on here.

Mandy's face kind of melts. All the lines in it sag, like she holds them up by constant effort. Her eyes go hollow and suddenly you see how she would look if she let herself become a little old lady. Hurt, confused. She shakes her head and the jowls go in different directions. She stands up and her hands are shaking. "Dumb old fucks."

I get a feeling like I've just been real mean to someone, who I shouldn't be mean to. And I don't know why.

Gus shouts after her. "You haven't exactly shown much concern about the people they hurt."

I go gallumphing after her in my callipers. "C'mon Mandy, nothing personal." She just shows me her back. "Mandy?"

She spins around and she's got a face like a cornered porcupine. "Space off!"

"Mandy, the cops think there's a line out on this stuff from here and they're not dumb."

Her eyes point towards the floor. She's talking to the air. She's talking to her entire life. "Every time I think maybe, just maybe, there's somebody who has any idea . . . who just. . . . SEES! ME! That's when I get kicked in the teeth again." She looks up with eyes like a mother tiger, and she's sick and mad. "Just space off back to your little crew. Go play your little boy games." Her voice goes thin like mist. "I don't have time."

None of us have.

"I'm sorry."

She stays put, staring out through the grey window onto the lawn.

"Mandy. I'm sorry. You know why I asked? It's because I know I know that face under the black stuff. I'm sure I know who it is, if I could just remember. And for a flash I thought . . . hey. Who says Silhouette is a guy? I just said it, the minute I thought it. I'm sorry."

She turns and looks back at me. Unimpressed. Tired. "I found something out," she says. "I was so proud of myself. I actually thought, Brewster'll be pleased." She sniffed and pulled in some air. "I got the faces of the guys in the suits, and the guys who mugged your granddaughter. I kept running 'em though, all night long. The cops must know this. But."

She looks so tired. She looks like she's going to fall asleep standing up.

"All those guys have Alzheimer's."

I let that sink in. Mandy didn't move. It was as if her whole body was swelling up to cry. She just kept staring out the window.

"Alzheimer's?"

"Yeah. It's kind of like Attack of the Zombies? We lose our minds and they send us in to steal. We're just bodies, meat. They won't need us for even that soon."

The grey light through the grey window, on her nose, on her cheeks. It made her beautiful.

I thought of the glasses on the bed, with built-in transcoders. The glasses will tell you who your friends are. They'll tell you it's time to take your pill. They'll tell you that you have a plane to catch, and how to get out of the Happy Farm and where the pickup point is.

I think cheekbones. I think a shrivelled cricket's face.

"Oh shit," I say, like my stomach's dropping out. "Oh, SHIT!" Already I'm walking.

"Brewst?" Mandy kind of asks. Godamn callipers. I'm bobbling up and own like a fishing cork, I'm trying to run and I can't.

"Brewst. What is it?"

Hey, you know, tears, are streaming down my face? I suddenly feel them. My elbow kind of knocks them off my face. Those bastards, those bastards are making me cry.

"Brewster? Wait."

Mandy's tripping after me.

And all I can think is: Jazza. Jazza, you're worth so much more than that. You used to design things, mix music, girls would look at you with stars in their eyes. Ahhhhcccceeeeed! Dancing with your shirt off on the brow of a bridge, young and strong and smart and beautiful. Jazza.

You're not just a meat puppet, Jazza. I hope.

I'm still crying, and I'm bumping into things because I can't see.

Back in his room Jazza is sitting up on the edge of his bed staring, looking at the corners of the ceiling like he can't figure them out. I sit and stare and look at the flesh that's as shrivelled as his life tight all around his wrists, his ankles his skull, his cheeks.

I'm aware that Mandy's standing next to me.

I put on Jazza's glasses. I try a couple of passwords: Age Rage, Silhouette. Nothing. Then I take a stab at something else:

Iron Man.

And then his glasses say to me. "Where did you read comics as a boy?"

I say back. "Trees."

And there's a flash of light, brighter than the sun, up into my eyes, into my head. And I know for certain then. It's checking my retinas.

Then it all goes dark. I'm not Jazza. So the program won't open, but hey, it doesn't need to open.

I look at the face again, just to be sure.

"Mandy," I croak, and I'm real glad she's there. "Meet Silhouette."

And the only thing I'm feeling is gratitude. I'm just glad that Jazza was more than a zombie. I'm just glad that he was more than that. I still can't quite see, my eyes inside are dappled by the retina check. I'm thinking of all the times he did freelance for me: on the software, on all that VAO. He worked on it, he would know how all the ordnance cooked.

And I get it.

You see, you're this smart guy. You've buzzed all your life, but there's no money, and you're losing your mind. Maybe you get told by some young stuck-up intern doing time on the social programs that he's real sorry that your insurance won't pay for the drugs. You're poor so you get to lose your marbles. So you get mad. You get mad at everybody, at the world, at God. You turn all your brain onto one final thing. You plan ahead, for when you're gaga and beyond being charged or convicted. You invent Silhouette and store him up, and set the bugs loose to search for a new kind of crew.

You get your revenge.

Mandy takes my arm and shakes it. "Brewst. Brewster," she says. All she can see is some sad old fuck dissolving into tears. She can't understand that I'm crying because I'm happy. I can't understand it either.

I just know in my butt: Jazza thought of this.

"He was Silhouette," I say, and breathe in deep.

"How?" demands Mandy. Hand on hip, Mandy won't buy just any fairy story.

I feel reasonably cool again as well.

"Silhouette's not a person, its a program, a series of programs that all work on the same algorithms. The programs take you over, tell you what to do, how to do it. Maybe what to say. Maybe you get to be Silhouette for a while and if you're gaga enough you won't even know it. So trace Silhouette then. One week he's in Atlanta, the next he's in LA, the next week he's in New York. They'll be hacked into the glasses. The glasses and the terminals and the crude little chips in your head."

I go to Jazza's machine. And look for the files. I won't be able to open any of them, of course, but of course there is a whole directory. Anything encrypted is enough to get you. The directory is called Aphrodite. What we called our space-ship to Mars. Everything in it's encrypted and the file sizes are huge. That ain't no banking hack.

"That's it," I say. "That's the masterplan."

I look back at Jazza. He looks like a little boy in a bus station waiting for his Mom to show up before the bus goes.

I open up the e-mail package and start keying in. I shop Jazza. It's painless. Just an e-mail to Curtis, to the Armament. Over in two minutes. And all the while I'm doing it, I feel proud. Proud of him.

"Sorry, Jazza." I tell him. I take hold of his hands. That makes me feel better. "They'll wipe the program. That's all. No more trips to Maryland."

He looks back at me like a baby. He's not sure who I am, but he trusts me.

Five minutes later, the Kid slips in.

"Sorry Mr. Brewster," he says quietly. "Sorry it was your friend."

The Kid comes from a country where people are still human. The sorrow is upfront in his eyes.

I ask him. "What's Curtis doing?"

"Damage limitation." It's the kind of jargon you learn early in our part of the world. It eats your soul. "He worry about the Home."

"His own ass," corrects Mandy.

The Kid can't help but smile. But he sticks to the point. "You do right thing, Mr. Brewster."

Isn't it great how people can still care about each other? Isn't it some kind of miracle sometimes?

This time the cops show up in a plain car, and this time it's IT specialists not Armament. They start going through Jazza's station. Jazza starts to sing to himself, some dumb old toon about everybody being free, it's all love, let's just party down. Did we really think that was all it took?

He lets them take away his machine, and he just curls up on the bed, back to us all. I say something corny like "Sleep well, old friend."

And the Kid says, "I watch him for you, Mr. Brewster."

Mandy and I slump off to the bar and the Neurobics are all there before but before we can say anything Gus jumps us and says, "you guys gotta see this!"

Mandy says. "Do we?"

The whole crew are leaning over the newspaper. "I'll rerun it," says Gus.

"Fasten your seat belt," says Mandy, and she gives me a long look like: I'm tired of these bozos.

On the newspaper is a wall of people and the label says:

Latest VAO attack SHU TZE STADIUM 8.35 pm last night.

The whole thing looks like diamonds, huge overhead lights, flashing cameras, halfway through a night game. Gus has plugged in his speakers, so we get the TV announcer too, and the sound of the crowd. The camera moves to a big guy on the mound chewing gum, thumping the ball into his mitt, and looking pissed off.

Over the stands a kind of rectangle just hangs in midair. It looks like it should be there, just part of the stadium, you have to blink to realize its hovering. It's a rescue platform, designed for getting people out of tall buildings in midair. It looks as small as a postage stamp, only it's crowded with exoskeletons.

On all the tall cathedral lights, red lights start flashing and sirens rouse themselves.

One announcer says, "That's the fire alarm, John."

"Yup and those are firemen. Though I have to say right now, I can't see any sign of a fire."

"If there is, John, official figures estimate that it takes 15–20 minutes to clear the stands here at Shu Tze Stadium."

On the field the players stand morose and still, hands on hips. Their show is over.

Firemen stumble off the platform. It bobs. Close up, the platform is more unstable than a rowboat. The suits hop down, straighten up and start to jog up the steps through the stands. You can see it now that there's a lot of them in unison: the suits move in unison.

On the field one of the fat little umpires is running as fast as he can.

A police car comes driving straight onto the diamond.

"Certainly something is happening here at She Tze, Marie, but it may not be a fire. That's Lee van Hook, manager of the Cincinnati Reds getting out of the police vehicle. And he's waving his hands, yes, he's waving the players off the field!"

You hear a crunching. It's a nasty goose-stepping sound, and the camera blurs back to the stands. All the suits have raised automatic weapons at once. And they're jammed straight at the crowd.

Speakers crackle and a feedback whine shoots round the stadium.

And a voice like Neptune bubbling out of the sea says, "This is a public service announcement."

Announcer cuts in. "John, reports are saying this is a VAO attack."

"You are going to help the aged. You will pass all valuables, watches, wallets, jewellery to the men and women with the guns.

"Just to repeat that, we are witnessing a VAO attack here live at She Tze Stadium."

The digital gurgle goes on. "For your own safety please remember, that some of the people with the guns will die soon and have nothing to lose. Many of them cannot think for themselves and so will shoot anyone who resists."

A kind of roar is spreading all through the crowd.

"You won't pay taxes. You won't let us into your houses. We save and plan and invest and insure and in the end that still is NOT enough. What you should do is love us. It's too late for love, now. Now is the time for money. What you are going to do now is give us your wallets."

Some fat guy in a baseball cap is shouting. An exo arm is raised. The suit is like a metal cage around some ancient old dear, and you can see that she's blinking and confused. I realize all the CCTV is on, and it's edited it later. That's entertainment.

The gun goes off. The fat man ducks and yelps, but his hat has already spun off his head. Those suits can aim to within a fraction of a millimetre.

"That's one move he won't pull again in a hurry," says announcer John. He chuckles, like it's a wrestling match. This stuff, you react to it like a movie. It performs the same function.

All along the rows, a gentle sideways motion begins towards the suits, like a rippling river. It's all looks so gentle and calm. On the field police cars pull up and rub noses like it's a BBQ on a bank by a river on a summer's day.

The announcers can only tell us what we can see for ourselves. But you know, it becomes more real when they say it. "John, it looks like the police on the field are conferring with both the team heads and stadium security managers."

"It's a real problem for them, Marie. How can they apprehend the VAO without injuring any of the fans?"

The great burbling voice begins again. "What do you think of, when you see us? Do you think getting old is something we did to ourselves? Do you think it won't happen to you? Do you think you won't get ugly, sick, and weak? Do you think health foods, gyms, and surgery are going to stop that? We're going to go now. But just remember. Your kids are watching you. And learning. What you do to us, your kids will do to you."

The crowd is kind of silent, no motion, just a kind of hush, as if the sea had decided to be still. The siren goes round and round, but you have the feeling no one's listening. The suits march the old guys inside them back down from the stands towards the rescue platform.

The wierdest thing: some kid in a foilsuit helps one of the VAOs up. And I realise that they understand. They're halfway there, all these people in this stadium, with their soyaburgers and beer and team shirts. They're halfway there to being on our side.

You got to them Jazza.

And the platform snores itself awake and coughs and whirs, and sort of tilts a bit getting up, like all of us old stereotypes. But once it's steady, it soars straight up.

And Jazza stands. Just stands still. The program has given him nothing to do, but's also like he's finished. He looks up to the sky, like he always does now, up at nothing. He stands like a king on the prow of his ship praying to heaven, and sails away.

And oh god I'm leaking again. Mandy can't look at me. Her mouth does a bitter little twist and she says. "Silhouette was Jazza."

Gus says, "What?"

I don't want to hear it. I don't want to explain or talk or do anything at all, but I can't sit still either. I feel sick. I feel messed up. I feel angry. I stand up and lurch out of there. Gus calls after me. "Hey, Brewst, what is this? Brewst?"

I'm walking and I don't know where or why. I walk into the Solarium and walk into the gym, and walk into the garden, and I go to the library but that only has books, and in the end, there's only one place to go.

I go back to Jazza's room. The Kid is still there, like he said he would be. "Scram," I tell him.

I really look at Jazza. I think that maybe he was going back to Maryland for one last time. Maybe he was going to climb a tree and just stay there.

I'm thinking how we lose everything. Everything we were, everything we made ourselves into. If you were strong that goes, if you were smart that goes, if you were cool that goes.

Jazza's face is brown and blue like a map. He's sitting up but his head has dropped backwards, so he's staring up at the ceiling with his mouth pulled open. His blue eyes go straight through me to nowhere, like he's looking for an answer but forgot the question.

And that's when I finally say to myself. He's gone. Jazza leaked away a long, long time ago. There's been nothing left of Jazza for months. So I let him go.

I'm not too clear about the whole show after that.

Armament comes back and tries to sound like they're going to be tough on my ass. Secret Squirrel keeps asking the same questions over and over. The message is: if we find you had anything to do with this, we'll still get you.

The Armament looks at me. "We know about your hacks. That'll have to stop."

Curtis stands there watching, and he starts to squirm a bit and look in my direction.

"Given that you cooperated, we may be take a tolerant view of that. But only if you continue to cooperate, only if the attacks stop."

What I do next is deliberate. I turn to Curtis and shrug and apologise with my eyes. That's all it takes. Secret Squirrel snaps his head round at Curtis's, and narrows his eyes.

"24 by 7 by 365, huh?" Armament says in quiet little voice.

He's got it. I shrug an apology to Curtis again, just to drive my point home.

Curtis goes edgy, jumpy, mean. "Well. Well, if that means what I think it does, you cannot continue to be a guest here, Mr. Brewster."

After that, things moved quick.

I told Bill about the hack and the police and it was decided. I would live with my boy. It's just a beaten-up old bungalow on the Jersey side. Like the kind of house I grew up in, when computers were new and cool, and everything was new and cool from shoes to playing cards and you had takeaway pizza for dinner. Even Mom was cool with headphones. Hot in summer with screen doors for the flies, and dry and warm in winter.

I'm on the phone to Bill and I say, "At least I'll get out of this goddamned dump."

There's a minute silence and then Bill says. "Dad. They've worked miracles for you."

And I think about the neurobics and how my legs are learning to walk, and I have to acknowledge that. So I guess I can lose being mad at the Farm. I guess I can feel I got a pretty good deal.

I go to see Mandy. I fill her in. She says. "You're the only man here with any cool whatsoever." She's got a face like the badlands of Arizona. And I don't know why but right now, that's as sexy as fuck.

Remember that transcoder jammed into my dick? Found a new use for it.

So I'm lying there with all the teddy bells and the scent of Miss Dior and I say to Mandy. "Come to Jersey with me."

She looks down and says, "Oh boy." Then she says, "I gotta think."

I ask her, "What's to think?"

"Baby. If I wanted a bungalow in Jersey, I could have had it. Here, I got a Solarium, I got quiet, I got my own room."

"You dumb cluck. You'll be alone."

I see her looking at different futures. I see her get the fear. It makes all the skin of her face sag like old chamois leather. I hold her and hug her and kiss the top of her dyed conditioned perfumed hair. I try to open up things for her. "Come and be part of my family, babe. Bill's a great kid; he'll let us stay up late drinking whisky. We'll watch old DVDs. They'll be people round at Thanksgiving."

And her head is shaking no. "I'll be stuck in one tiny bedroom, with someone else's family. That's where I started out."

She grunts and slaps my thigh. "I can't do it." She sits up and lights a cigarette and then she lets me have it straight.

"I danced for fat old men. I'd get into a bath with other women and they'd look at our cunts through a pane of glass. I was that far from being a whore. I took the money and I got smart with it, and I kept it. Even though asshole after asshole man tried to take it away from me. This, here, fancy pants Happy Farm is my reward."

She takes a breath and says. "I'm too scared to go to Jersey."

"I'll come and see you," I say. She doesn't believe me, and I'm not entirely sure I do either.

So suddenly I'm standing outside the Happy Farm, and thank God they're not currently microwaving anybody, and I'm saying goodbye to the place and you know, I think I'll miss it. Mandy isn't there. Gus is there, which is big of him, and he shakes my hand like maybe he thinks he'll get Mandy back. But I can see. His arms are thin like sucked-on pens, and his tummy is big like a boil. Gus isn't going to be with us long.

The Kid comes, and he brings his sweet tiny little wife with him. She's rehearsed something to say in English. She says it with her eyes closed and giggles afterwards. "Thank you very much Mr. Brewster you have been so good to my Joao." And then she holds up her beautiful new baby daughter for me to see.

Life goes on. And then it doesn't. It doesn't mean anything. Which means that death doesn't mean anything, either. It means that while you're here you can do what the hell you want.

I took off the callipers. I wanted to show them that I could do it. I walked for all of us old farts with no money, all the way to the bus. Bill caught me and helped me up the steps.

I looked around for Jazzanova, but he wasn't there, and never will be.

One thing those bastards don't know about is the hack that pays Jazza's bills. It's a one-off on the bank's system. It's not on my machine or on Jazza's. Curtis doesn't know that and the Armament doesn't know that. We're gonna keep Jazza cared for.

And all I'm feeling is one solid lump of love. I give the Farm one last wave goodbye and go home.

Total buzz.

winters Are Hard

STEVEN POPKES

*Steven Popkes made his first sale in 1985, and in the years that followed
has contributed a number of distinguished stories to markets such as Asimov's Science Fiction, Sci Fiction, The Magazine of Fantasy & Science
Fiction, Realms of Fantasy, Science Fiction Age, Full Spectrum, Tomorrow, The Twilight Zone Magazine, Night Cry, and others. His first
novel, Caliban Landing, appeared in 1987, and was followed in 1991 by
an expansion to novel-length of his popular novella "The Egg," retitled
Slow Lightning. ("The Egg," in its original form, was in our Seventh Annual Collection.) He was also part of the Cambridge Writers' Workshop
project to produce science fiction scenarios about the future of Boston, Massachusetts, that cumulated in the 1994 anthology, Future Boston, to which
he contributed several stories. He lives in Hopkinton, Massachusetts, with
his family, works for a company that builds aviation instrumentation, and
is learning to be a pilot.*

    *In the compelling story that follows, he shows us that although it might
be an admirable goal to get close to nature, maybe you shouldn't get too
close . . .*

O nce I got through to Sam Orcutt, Jack Brubaker wasn't hard to find.

"There he is," yelled Sam over the roar of the engine and started flying the
ancient Cessna in a circle. I suppose the idea of a floatplane is that there is always
some lake or river one can land in but I didn't see any water larger than a pigeon.
We were flying deep in the heart of Montana: the Beck-Lewis Wildlife Refuge.

Sam had to be circling for a reason so I looked down the left wing toward the
center and sure enough there was a man dressed entirely in fur. He watched us
circle for a minute or so, then waved.

Sam leveled out immediately. "He sees us!" he shouted, obviously relieved.

I nodded and checked over Goldie, the red-tailed hawk perched on my shoulder. I'm a freelance human-interest reporter ("HIR" in the trade) and I don't make
that much money. Do I hire a crew? Too expensive. Do I get a partner? In my
old Kindergarten class one of the report cards stated: "Does not work well with

others." That particular genetic trait had stayed with me all my life. Instead, I blew a year's earnings on Goldie. Her visual centers had been modified to download cam quality material to the storage unit and monitor I kept on my belt and she'd been trained to hunt for good camera angles and to watch for my cues.

I lifted her wing to check the readings and the test monitor. If things went well I'd be out here for two weeks and I didn't want anything to go wrong. The broadcast circuitry passed final self-tests and everything was fully charged. I gave her a strip of steak from a sealed bag in my pocket. She ate it between taking shots of Sam, the airplane, the landscape and me.

We flew up over a ridge and on the other side was a convenient pond no smaller than a postage stamp where we landed. Sam brought the plane up to the shore and we tied it off and unloaded. He brought out two folding chairs and sat them down, then brought out two beers and a six-pack of carbonated water. "Sit down," he said. "The chairs are for us. He won't use them."

About an hour of uncomfortable silence later, Jack Brubaker came over the ridge in a lope. I pulled out my binoculars to see what I could see.

I thought I had seen a man dressed in fur but I was wrong. Jack was covered in fur, all right. His own: a thin pelt the color and texture of a German shepherd. Only the hair on his head and between his legs was different: thick, wiry curls. I couldn't see any external genitalia. The only naked skin I could see was on the palms of his hands and the area around his eyes and nose. The exposed skin was heavily pigmented but the eyes that shone out under the thick brows were bright, cornflower blue.

"Wow," I said.

"Yeah," agreed Sam, nodding.

It was perhaps a mile from the top of the ridge down to the plane but Jack wasn't even breathing hard when he reached us.

"Sam!" he said and grinned. He sniffed the air and glanced at me for a moment and nodded in my direction. "It's good to see you," he said to Sam. Then, he saw the bottles of seltzer and the grin grew even broader. "You remembered! Thanks." He opened one immediately, drained it, belched loudly.

Jack was not especially tall—less than six feet, anyway. But he was as broad as a Samoan. His chest and shoulders were deep and even his head looked large. His legs were thick as logs but even so his knees and ankles seemed outsized. He didn't smell like a man, even a man who had been in the bush for years without ever taking a shower. Instead, he gave off a musk, a flat, strong and unidentifiable scent. It made me think of tigers or hyenas or, of course, wolves. This man had been thoroughly modified.

"Nice bird," he said, nodding towards Goldie.

"I said the same thing when I saw it," said Sam. "This is Dan Perry. He wants to do a story on you."

"A reporter." He looked back at Sam and then at me.

I looked back. Jack's eyes were unreadable. I could see no fear or apprehension. Nor could I see excitement or interest. His eyes had the same deep interest I had until now associated only with animals: the speculative eyes of cougars, the apprehensive eyes of raccoons. I wondered where his humanity had gone. How deep did the modifications go?

I let Sam earn his money. To say everybody has a price is to oversimplify the process. It is more precise to say that money is an inducement to self re-examination. In Sam's case, it took enough money to hire enough staff to truly take charge of Beck-Lewis. I couldn't front him the money; I'm not worth that kind of cash. I just helped him find the right people.

Sam drew him away. I turned up the gain on Goldie's microphones.

"Look. It's just for a couple of weeks. He'll take some pictures and then he'll be gone." Sam gave me a quick glance. I tried not to look like I was listening.

"It's enough money to secure this place," he said, turning back to Jack. "Really secure it. He got me some real backers."

"Who?" Jack popped open another bottle of seltzer and drained it, belched again.

"Companies with deep pockets. ADM, for one."

"Supermarket to the world," Jack said idly and I couldn't tell if he was being sarcastic, bitter or what. He smiled gently, considering, then looked back at me. "Whatever you say, Sam. Send him east tomorrow and we'll see what Akela and Raksha have to say about it." Then, they fell to talking of other things. I recorded everything, even the belches.

Who were Akela and Raksha? I filed the names away for future reference.

The next morning Sam couldn't wait to get rid of me. I took my pack and equipment and started back east over the ridge. Goldie took off and soared above me about sixty or seventy feet. Sam seemed to think Jack wouldn't let me get lost or maybe he just didn't care.

I kept walking. Near an outcropping of granite a voice behind me said: "Be very still."

I stopped dead and didn't move. A wolf the mixed color of wheat and iron appeared in front of me as quickly and suddenly as if it had been excreted from the earth. I had no idea where it came from.

This was no coyote or dog, but a big shouldered, deep-chested animal that had to be well over a hundred pounds. Its mouth was open and it panted slightly. I could see the bright white teeth below the heavy skull. Its eyes were yellow and watched me without any fear whatsoever. It glanced occasionally away from me — checking on Jack, perhaps. It didn't have the half-myopic look of a dog; I could tell there was nothing wrong with its eyesight.

I was surprised it didn't sniff me to find out who I was. I half started to hold out my hand to be sniffed as I would to a dog and its behavior changed totally. Gone was the easy appraisal to be replaced by a closed-mouth, no-nonsense men-ace. I lowered my hand back to my side very, very carefully.

This seemed to be enough and it made a low huffing sound. Behind me, I heard a similar sound as a reply. The wolf turned and trotted away.

I slowly relaxed and Jack put a hand on my shoulder. "Looks like you can stay for a while."

"Was that Akela or Raksha?"

"Raksha, Akela's mate. Akela is the alpha wolf. Raksha's pups are behind the rock so she had to approve you before you could stay. Akela is off hunting somewhere but he'll check you out when he gets back." He started walking away. "I'll show you where you can set up camp. We'll be staying here another month or so before we head up north with the rest of the pack. If Akela approves, you can stay."

Goldie came down and landed on my shoulder. I hoped she had caught some good footage. Something occurred to me. "Is my bird going to be all right?"

Jack stopped and turned back to me. "I think so. We're all eating pretty well right now, though Akela might try to catch it just for sport if it gets too close. There are other hawks all around here but they don't get close to the wolves. Why did you bring your pet along?"

"It's my camera."

"Ah."

Jack led me to a spot that I thought was ridiculously close to where I knew the pups were but I figured he knew what he was doing. Then, he started walking away.

"Jack. I'll need to talk to you at some point."

He stopped and considered that. "Some kind of interview, I expect."

"Yes."

"Not now. I have to help Raksha."

"When?"

"We'll see." He pointed to the top of the rock.

"You can watch from there, if you like."

"Won't that make Raksha nervous?"

Jack laughed shortly. "She knows you're no threat."

"Are you the one who named them?"

He nodded. "They sure don't need them."

Setting up camp consisted of pulling the ripcord on the tent and tossing it about six feet away. The tent took care of the rest. Human-interest stories usually happen at interfaces of conflict. Wilderness/civilization, suburbs/city, neighboring tribes. I had been out into the bush before. I had a lovely little tent with an active skin. Tiny engines moved air through the pores, warming or cooling as needed, storing power from the sun. My jacket was similarly designed and kept itself clean. Active cloth is a bit stiff so, like most people, I didn't wear it. I had a nice shirt and pants that kept me warm at night and cool in the heat of day and would have fooled an Arab into thinking they were made of the finest cotton. The tent had a bag that if I left my clothes in it they would be magically fresh and soft the next morning. I knew where it was in the dark; it was right next to the water condenser. I had a food dispenser that would make nutritious bread from grass or any other source of cellulose, but that was for emergencies. I had brought a collection of freeze-dried meals. They made up most of the weight in my pack; the tent and sleeping bag took up no more space than a shoebox. Less, actually, since I had left out the entertainment unit. I find it distracting.

I climbed up on the rock to set the scene.

I knew where I was from several instruments: my locators, the map section of interface to the feeds, from my phone. I was north of Forsyth and south of the Fort Peck Lake. To the west of me the Rockies curved away towards Canada. The Missouri River started carving through the Dakota and Nebraska plains to the east of me. I could even bring a little piece of civilization here with a phone call or a request to the feeds.

But it was small tinder as I stood there on the rock and looked around.

Here, the world was huge.

On the slow rolling plain there were no trees and it felt as if I could touch the edge of the world. The sky was such a broad and featureless blue I became disoriented and had to look away before I fell down. The colors of the land were as diverse as the sky's were singular: russets, purples, grays, yellows, ambers — an infinite impressionist palette.

Good stuff, I thought. I made notes and made sure Goldie was getting good panorama shots.

Below me, Raksha and Jack were doing a strange sort of skip-jump in the grass. Raksha would move slowly for a bit, then stop, frozen. After a moment, she inched forward, then pounced. She flipped some nondescript piece of fur into the air and caught it, chewed it a moment, and swallowed it down. After twenty or thirty of these, she trotted back towards me — or, rather, to the rock I was standing on. The pups spilled out onto the grass and she gently regurgitated some food for them.

I knew immediately what sort of thing was going to end up on the cutting-room floor.

Jack, for his part, was doing the same thing. He stalked these things carefully and snatched them out of the grass with his hands. I could see them more clearly when he picked them up. They were rodents of some kind. He was a bit less flamboyant when he ate them. Instead of tossing them in the air, he broke their necks with his fingers and then munched them down like they were chicken legs.

After she made sure her puppies had cleaned their plates, Raksha trotted back to the grass and rejoined Jack. The puppies played in front of the den. Apparently, Jack had eaten enough and as she sat and watched him, he caught rodent after rodent and tossed them to her, all in complete silence. Even the puppies' enthusiastic cries were muted.

After perhaps an hour, Jack finished and walked over a small hummock and lay down. Raksha made herself comfortable lying next to him and leaned her head on his shoulder. He rested his hand on her shoulder. The two of them looked intimate, like a long married couple lying together. I felt curiously intrusive.

I checked on Goldie. She had been shooting the whole thing.

I waved to him and he ignored me for a moment. Then, he waved me away.

I would have to be patient.

That night, as I sat drinking tea in front of my tent, I listened to the crickets and frogs sing. I had sort of expected Jack to join me at my tent. For a lot of isolated people, a man drinking tea in front of a tent, symbolizing as it does an outpost of what they had left behind, was an irresistible lure. Not Jack. He paid no more attention to me than he did the rock. I didn't even know where he was sleeping. Not in Raksha's den — it was much too small. The heat unit put out a glow all around, looking for all the world like a campfire.

I had cooked a little curry, a little bacon, some brownies. A few things to tempt a person in the wild living exclusively on raw rodent. Nothing.

This might be trickier than I had thought.

The next afternoon I waved at him again and this time he didn't wave me away.

I eased down from the rock and walked as non-threateningly as possible over to them.

Raksha lifted her head and examined me for an instant, rose and trotted over to her cubs.

Jack watched her leave. "I guess this is as good a time as any. What do you want to know?"

"Tell me about the modifications," I said. This was a sure opener for every person I'd ever met who'd undergone elective modification. Like hospital patients, it was the one reliable subject they all wanted to talk about. Jack Brubaker and your Aunt Edda getting her gall bladder out had a lot in common.

"Yeah," said Jack. "It's all common sense stuff, really. You figure I had to be out here on my own all year around, I needed certain things. Thick skin. A summer and a winter pelt. Some brown fat to generate heat when I need it. A little more strength in my arms, legs and back. A little more stamina. Better hearing. Better sense of smell. Better eyesight. You can guess the drill."

I pointed at his knees and hips. "What about those?"

He stared at his own knee for a minute, not quite understanding. "Oh, yeah," he said suddenly. "I know what you mean. Bigger points for muscle attachment and just to generally beef things up. A sprained ankle would likely kill me. Even so, I got a strained ligament last winter. If it hadn't been for Raksha, I wouldn't have made it." He looked into the distance for a moment. "Winters are hard."

"So, are you as good a wolf as they are?"

"I'm not a wolf," he said looking straight at me. I had clearly hit a nerve. "They accept me into the pack. I'm a sort of brother to Akela. An uncle figure. The idea was to live with the wolves, not become a wolf."

"Interesting distinction."

Jack scowled a moment. "I guess. Maybe I could have been modified into a wolf but it would have cost a lot more money than I had."

I couldn't have asked for a better segue. "How did you pay for it? Modifications like this are expensive." I cued Goldie to concentrate on his face. Briefly, I looked up. As usual, she was one step ahead of me.

"Sam didn't tell you?"

"Sam didn't tell me much. He left me pretty much to my own devices."

Jack chuckled and gestured to the empty landscape around us. "I expect he did. I won the Colorado lottery. Ten million dollars."

"Come on. If a lottery millionaire had chosen to become a wolf—"

He glanced at me coldly.

"—chosen life with the wolves," I amended. "I would have heard of it."

"Yeah," he said quietly. "Sam and I came to the same conclusion. So, I lost the money at the Golden Hind Casino of Macau. It's a neat trick. You contract for something illicit or secret and pay for it by losing. The casino takes ten percent. Had all the work done there, too, along with a couple of years of physical therapy to recover. Then, snuck back here through Canada broke as a penny." He laughed. "Now, that was a pain in the ass. I look more or less normal if I depilate every day but it makes me itch like Hell."

"Why choose this?"

He looked up at me as if I were crazy. Maybe to him I was. He looked back at Raksha. "It seemed the right idea at the time."

"So, your whole life you spent thinking about wolves."

He shrugged. "I saw a movie once that made it look pretty good. That's about it."

"Any regrets?"

"Quiet," he said suddenly and his nostrils flared. "Akela's coming."

Akela was black with just a hint of brown along his belly. He had come up over the same ridge I had come the previous day. As soon as he saw us, he started running. It was at least a mile back to that ridge but he covered the ground quickly.

"Hold still," said Jack.

That was okay for him to say. I've dictated live stories while mortars were exploding forty feet from me without losing a comma. But not this time. Maybe there is something to racial memory. All I knew was a black wolf was racing towards me Hell bent on evil. I remembered images out of folklore—legend, myth and majesty—and suddenly I was terrified. I turned and ran. I didn't get two steps when Jack grabbed me by the jacket and hurled me to the ground. Then, he sat on me.

"Son-of-a-bitch," I swore.

"Oh, shut up."

"That wolf's going to kill me."

"True. He might," Jack said judiciously. "You got a better chance with me sitting on you."

Akela was much, much bigger than Raksha. He had to have been easily a hundred and fifty pounds. Unlike the trusting examination I'd gotten yesterday, Akela sniffed me over one end to the other.

When he was finished figuring out where I had been for the last several years by my smell, he walked stiff legged to face me. He made no sound but he was clearly considering whether or not to attack. A very slight huff came from Jack. Akela gave no sign of having heard. After a moment, though, he opened his mouth and seemed to grin. He leaped gracefully over my head and bowled Jack over. It was like having two Olympic wrestlers working out on my back.

Cautiously, I rose to my feet and turned around. Akela and Jack were rolling around on the grass. Jack grabbed Akela around his chest and started to roll over with him but Akela escaped and pushed him over.

I watched them dismally. I had been here two days and gotten some great footage but I knew almost nothing. It was time to start checking deep background.

Every HIR has his own techniques. I like to get just enough background to understand what I'm looking at before I start to interview the subject. This way the material always feels fresh. Other people do things differently. I know one HIR who won't interview a subject without knowing everything down to the family tree.

My technique, though, is predicated on the subject cooperating. Usually it works out. Even people who are hostile to the idea will cooperate in some way — anger and hate are a form of emotional contact after all. It wasn't working here. It wasn't that Jack disliked cooperating. He just didn't care. Somewhere in the back of people is a need to talk about themselves. It's basic to our makeup. It's fundamental. Jack didn't seem to have it; he was just being polite. It was time I looked into alternatives. As I said, I was wired into the North American Communications Grid through my tent. Sam was only a few numbers away.

I could tell from the furniture behind him that Sam was in his office. His eyes were red and his expression surly. He was probably drunk.

"What do *you* want?"

"To talk to you. Jack's not the only story here, you know."

He looked at me suspiciously. "What do you mean?"

I smiled at him. "You're part of this, too. After all, you run Beck-Lewis. He lives in your backyard, so to speak. You knew all about him. Why did you let him stay here?"

Sam didn't say anything for a moment. "Didn't want to arrest him. We grew up together."

"Really?" I had guessed a connection of this sort. "Was he always like this?"

"Like what? Covered with hair? Nowadays, his dick and scrotum retract up into his belly. Did you think he was like that in high school?" Sam reached off camera and pulled back a bottle. "His dad ran the hardware store in Schmidt, north of the lake. He didn't do very well at it and Jack was always helping out. Jack was almost always busy. He was the kind of kid that you could get to cooperate if you *asked* him but you'd run into a stone wall if you tried to *force* him. He hated taking orders or having anyone tell him what to do — it compromised his freedom, I guess. But if you asked him, he'd do everything he could for you." Sam chuckled softly.

I wanted to yell: but how did he come *here*? That wouldn't work. Sam had to tell the story in his own way.

"Whenever he had the chance, he lit out camping," Sam said. He leaned forward into the screen. "You got to understand that Jack was *talented*. Look, as soon as he was old enough he got a hunting license. Every deer season he went out with a rifle and bagged the limit. *Every time*. Some guys go for years before they bag their first buck. Nobody gets his limit every year. Jack started out using his Dad's 30-06, an old Springfield. That was too easy. Jack could take down a buck from a mile away and let you pick where to put the hole so it wouldn't show when it was mounted. After a while, he went to a smaller bore and then to black powder. That got too easy so he went to bow hunting. He was fourteen years old at that point and bringing home a deer every time. *Every time.* That got too easy so he started stalking them with just a knife."

Sam shook his head in admiration. "He was still this scrawny kid. He wasn't that strong, but he was frightfully quick and it was like he could get inside the head of the game."

"Deer hunting with a knife?"

"I think he could have got an elk, too, if he'd have tried." Sam said with satisfaction. "You figure a two-hundred pound deer is one thing. A six-hundred or a thousand-pound elk is entirely different. Then, he quit hunting all at once. He said it just wasn't fair. Instead, he started counting coup."

"Counting coup?"

"Funny, eh? He'd go out there and get as close as he could and touch them on the head, or slap them or cut off a piece of tail or an ear. Not just elk but cougar and bear."

"Bear? How did he do that?"

Sam laughed. "That wasn't easy. He came back one time tore up so bad he looked like the only things holding him together were strings. But he had a piece of a grizzly's ear."

This was starting to sound like a tall tale. Pretty soon Sam would have Jack riding a tornado. "Did he count coup on wolves?"

"We didn't have many wolves back then," Sam said quietly. "He left them pretty much alone. I don't know why. Then, he quit counting coup."

"It got too easy?"

Sam shook his head. "No. This was something else. Something different. He was graduating college by this point and they were just putting Beck-Lewis on the boards." Sam stopped a moment. "Do you really understand what Beck-Lewis is? It's a park and a refuge, all right. But it's bordered on all sides with corporate farms, ranches and gas wells. There are no roads into it. It's a no-man's land. It's the badlands that nobody wanted so the corporations all decided to do something to protect their inside borders and appease the environmentalists. Every couple of years the Sierra Club or the National Geographic or a few scientists come out here and do some work. But to do it they got to get federal permits, state permits and then border permits from each one of the abutting corporations. It's really hard to do so people go elsewhere, to the Grand Tetons, or Yellowstone or Glacier. Jack and I realized that this place was going to be cheap, underfunded, barely visible. It was perfect. Accidentally, Beck-Lewis was going to slip backwards two hundred years. So we both applied to be rangers and got jobs here. We might have been the only applicants—there sure wasn't much competition. That was the way of it for ten years."

Sam stopped and stared at me through the screen, coming back to himself. I didn't say anything. This was his song, his eulogy. I wouldn't have broken it for the world. Every word, every gesture was being recorded. It was great background.

"Then, the wolves started coming down from Canada. A few strayed up from Yellowstone. Not many but enough to start a small population. Beck-Lewis wasn't part of the Wolf Restoration Project but wolves go where they want to go. We wanted the wolves but we didn't want the WRP—too many strings. Too much visibility. We didn't want the scientists and the tourist trade. So, we started hunting them, tranquilizing them, and pulling off the radio collars. We left the collars to be found in different places to make the WRP think the wolves had dropped them or been killed. Some we just destroyed—a few collars are lost every year. It was tricky but there weren't very many wolves. It didn't take long for Jack to first discard the plane, then the trank gun. Then, he was going out there just by himself. We were only getting one or two collars a year. He would stalk the wolves just like he stalked cougars and elk. But wolves are smarter. They knew who he was and wouldn't sit still for it. He had to get to know them before they'd let him take the collars. He spent more time out there than anywhere else."

"Then, he won the lottery," I prompted.

"Damnedest thing. He stopped in for a six-pack of club soda—he has always had a passion for carbonated water. Go figure. Bought a ticket and a week later he's a millionaire." Sam shook his head. "I guess he was already pretty clear in his mind what he was going to do with the money. That was eight years ago. I was against it. I thought it would bring trouble."

I let that slide. Arguing with him would only get in the way of the story. "What would you have done with the money?"

He snorted. "Same thing I'm doing now. Same thing I'm going to do with the grant money you got for me. Hire some more men. Put in real boundaries. Get ready to defend this place against all comers. Jack thinks Beck-Lewis will last forever. I know better. Beck-Lewis is a holding action, a way of Corporate America getting the rights to public land they knew they could use. Throw the dog a bone and it's busy while you rob the store. I knew it was only a matter of time before the world found us. Only I figured it would be an economic way of mining the shale or harvesting the buffalo grass or full spectrum solar power or something like that. After all, the only thing that stops capitalism is more capitalism. I didn't figure on you."

Two days after Akela came back I only had Sam's background stories, Goldie's footage and a limited amount of conversation from Jack to show for it. There was enough here for a feature or two but I wanted more. This story had possibilities. This story had legs. I wanted to see Jack in action. I needed to capture the pack in a real hunt, not wolves living comfortably and easily on rats. Where's the drama in that?

I tried to pin Jack down. He was lying on his back in the sun. Akela was sitting next to him and Raksha was in her customary curl, snuggled against him with her head on his shoulder. They looked like a couple. It was Akela that looked like a family friend.

Maybe that's the way it was.

"So," I began. Jack didn't move but he tensed suddenly. "Why didn't you have yourself anatomically altered?"

Jack sat up suddenly. Raksha rolled over, startled. "What do you mean?"

I gestured to Raksha. "It looks like there's more than paternal affection between you two. Akela is the one that's the uncle. Not you."

He looked down. All this time, he had just been a primitive man living with the wolves. But now, he was suddenly brought back into civilization for a moment. The distance between him and the world had narrowed to nothing in a heartbeat. I could see it run through his mind as if he were shouting at me. Broadcasting the interchange between us that had just happened, if done in the right way, would brand him instantly a pervert. It didn't even have to be true; the allegation would take on a life of its own and any perception of him would be defined by it. People he knew would reconsider all of their memories of him: did the rude gesture on the playground lead to this? Could he have meant that all along? People he didn't know would make instant and unshakable judgments of him.

I read once that human beings were the only animals that were incapable of domestication. The man who wrote it did not understand people at all. Human beings are the most easily domesticated animal of all; they do it to themselves. Jack had forsaken all that for the love of the pack and now it had come back home to roost. Being thought a pervert mattered to him.

I could see him considering options. Denying it would make no difference. It was the allegation that caught the imagination, not the facts. Baring it all would be better and that was not acceptable. He could kill me—I could see the appraising expression. But he had no idea if the material was on my person. It could be anywhere—it could be broadcast already and then he would have nothing to lose. Besides that, killing someone opened up another whole basket of worms. Could he hush it up? Could he do it at all?

"I don't work that way," I said quietly. "I send the material to my home base and edit it later. I don't do live work."

He looked up at me with a flicker of hope. "What do I have to do to keep this private?"

"I need to see the pack in action. I need to see a hunt."

He nodded. "Done. It might take some time to set it up."

"I can wait."

He lay back down. He stared into the sky with an absent expression. Before he had been a simple man living a simple life. Now, a secret contorted him. I wondered if he would be able to live here much longer.

"It wouldn't be fair," he said suddenly.

"Fair?" I shook my head in confusion. "What are you talking about?"

"Being anatomically altered. I'm too smart—any human would be in the same position. I could become alpha but I'd be sterile. The pack wouldn't have any offspring."

"You could have had your testes replaced with that of a wolf," I pointed out. "You could have sired more wolves."

He looked at me with a weary patience. "And what would be the point? My pack has wolves for that."

What would be the point to any of this? I almost said but thought better of it. I had what I needed.

I awoke to find Jack rummaging in a small rucksack. He was wearing clothes of a sort; he wore a tight loincloth whose edges were buried in his fur. He caught me looking at him.

"I can't carry a knife in my hands all the time," he said defensively. "Besides, it has a cup."

"I thought everything . . . down there retracted."

He pulled out a pair of knives, one with a nine-inch broad blade and the second a short curved one, and fastened them to the loincloth. "It does," he said, checking his equipment. "But I'm still more vulnerable there than they are."

He put on the rucksack. "I'm going north with Akela. It'll take some hours to get some of the pack together. It won't be a full hunt—we're pretty spread out this time of year. But four or five of us will do. Do you have a locator with you?"

"Old style GPS and new style LLS. I know where I am."

He nodded. "Go due north seven miles. There is a rock formation there that looks like old bread dough. Sam used to call it 'The Dumplings' when we were kids. Wait there for me. By that time, we should have everybody and know if there's something nearby. We might have to wait some days but you said you could wait."

"What are you going to hunt?"

"I don't know yet." He rose and barked at Akela. The two of them loped off into the distance while I packed up.

Raksha had stayed behind with the pups. The look she gave me was one of pure hatred.

It took six hours of walking to reach the Dumplings. No one, wolf or man, was waiting for me when I got there. I made camp and then climbed to the top of the boulders. I could see no one. Even Goldie failed to spot anyone as she flew above us. Darkness fell three hours later and still no sign of Jack or his pack.

Here I could see a couple of trees. Certainly, not enough deadwood to build a fire. Not to mention it was illegal to build any fire in Beck-Lewis. That didn't stop me from wanting one. It was cold and lonely in the dark and the glow of the heater didn't quite measure up. I was careful in the adjustment not to set a brush fire. I had a lot of resources even here in the wilderness but I couldn't outrun a wind-driven fire.

The crickets and frogs were loud. Somewhere nearby there must have been a lake or a pond.

"Glad you made it," Jack said sitting next to me. Akela lay down gracefully next to the light.

It only took a couple of minutes for my heart to start again. "That probably took a year of my life."

"No doubt," he said, indifferently. "We found a band of elk about two miles from here. Are you going to come with us personally or just send your bird?"

"I want to be there."

"Okay. We'll start before dawn." He rubbed his hands in the glow of the heater. "Cozy."

"Can't wolves hunt at night?"

"Certainly, but I want you to get your money's worth. We're only going to do this once." He fell silent.

I waited for him to speak. He clearly had something on his mind.

"Look," he said at last. "We're only going to pick off one but the others are going to react. It's not a big herd but there are fifteen or so adults that weigh in at several hundred pounds. These aren't pretty little cottontail deer or Yellowstone Park elk all nicely used to people. It's been thirty years since they were hunted up here by human beings but wolves have been hunting them pretty steadily for the last twelve years or so. They have no fear of man and wolves piss them off. If they're running and you're in the way they won't turn politely aside. They'll run you down or pick you up and throw you away. You're going to have to be very, very quiet on the way over and sit very still while we're there. These elk may or may not remember the smell of people but they sure know the smell of wolves and when the hunt starts, you better stay out of the way."

"You're people."

"I don't smell that way to the elk."

I didn't say anything for a bit. "How do I be that quiet?"

"You'll leave everything here. All your instruments. All your camping equipment. Everything except your clothes and whatever you need for your hawk. As it is we're going to go in downwind with you and then leave you on your own while we go after them."

Downwind, I thought. He's going to drive them downwind. "Aren't they going to come right at me? You're not trying to get rid of me, are you Jack?"

Jack looked at me steadily. He looked more human right now than he ever had before. "Don't think it hasn't crossed my mind." He stood up. Akela rose up with him and they walked out into the darkness.

I didn't sleep well that night.

There was no hint of light when Jack woke me up. I had slept in my hiking clothes. I had nothing but Goldie, Goldie's controller and a paper notepad. Jack nodded in approval but still pulled off the outer lining of my jacket.

"The material makes too much noise when you walk."

He took off at a fast pace. There were no wolves in sight.

"Where's Akela?" I said in a whisper.

"Still too loud," he breathed. "Akela and the other wolves are ahead and waiting for us. Now, hush."

We walked for perhaps an hour and a half—stumbled, really. The ground was uneven and filled with holes of voles or mice or other prairie animals. Jack caught me each time before I could make a noise. The sky was clear and filled with stars and cold. The dew on the grass made my pants wet and without the outer lining my legs grew numbingly cold. My hands ached and my feet felt about as sensitive as sullen blocks of wood.

A faint wind whispered in the dark and Jack stopped me. He looked around and sniffed the air. He pulled me a hundred yards in another direction and pushed me down into a crouch. I looked up and saw a bluff darkly leading away into more darkness. There had to be a river near here.

"Don't send your bird up until you see us in action. You might spook them too early."

"Okay."

He grunted. "Should be quite a show."

Nothing happened for a while as the sky gradually began to lighten. I held Goldie close to keep her warm. She muttered a bit to herself every now and then but it was no louder than my breathing.

It was going to be one of those clear, burnished summer mornings, when the air is so crystalline and still that every reflection is a point of sunlight, every color is glowing, every sound is sharp and precise. The world has crackling electricity wired into it and each movement, each action, releases energy.

I could see the elk in the distance now, huge beasts, five feet at the shoulder with another four feet of antler over their backs. As the light brightened, I saw them with their heads raised, tasting the air. I could tell the cows from the bulls by sheer size. The bulls were nearly twice as big. Some might have been over a thousand pounds. They jerked their heads in different directions. There was a wariness about them. Perhaps they had already scented the pack.

Then, the dawn broke and they started milling about uncertainly. Something was going on but I couldn't see what.

Things happened at once, the herd started running this way and that, first trying one direction then another. Two bulls lowered their heads and charged but the grass hid their targets from me.

I sent up Goldie and in a moment I saw on the monitors two—no, three—no, *five*—wolves running in circular patterns, running into the herd briefly and out again. I had no idea what was going on.

On the ground, all I saw were quick brown streaks through the grass. Glimpses, only. I had no idea they were so fast. They barely registered before I lost them.

I watched their faces on the monitors, tongues out, running easily, looking as if they were laughing. It didn't look serious. I couldn't see Jack. I had Goldie fly in circles. I *had* to get pictures of Jack.

I finally caught him loping just below the herd. He was running easily, not working hard just yet. Watching the wolves. It looked like he was calling to them but Goldie's audio couldn't pick him out.

Then he changed direction and sprinted towards one edge of the herd. Three wolves came in behind a single huge bull and two others danced around between the herd and the bull.

"Jesus," I said. Didn't wolves go after the weak or the sick? Cows and calves? Maybe the bull was old.

The bull stood his ground against two of the wolves, menacing them with his antlers but that freed one to nip at his back legs. He lashed out and the wolf flew five feet and rolled, came up again and back towards the bull. This was not a weak or sick bull. This was a giant buck full in his prime.

The other two wolves succeeded in turning the herd away. The herd ran off to my left. Goldie got some good shots of them leaving. Now, the bull was on his own.

Goldie circled as the wolves worried the bull. He wouldn't run. He faced one, then two, then three of them, all the while being worried by any wolf he was not directly facing. It didn't look like hard work but foam came from his mouth and his sides were heaving.

Then he broke and ran and the wolves worked him into a circle, two wolves chasing him and nipping him, three holding back and taking turns. Jack moved between the bull and me. He pulled out his knife and then disappeared into the long grass.

The bull was growing tired. Even so, he caught one wolf that got too careless and tossed him twenty feet. The wolf lay still.

Three wolves shot forward and snapped at his legs while only one stayed in front.

The bull ran forward at the wolf. The wolf darted out of the way—I saw it was Akela. The bull was running straight towards me.

I saw him running directly at me, his eyes focused ahead, seeing his only chance and going for it. I could feel his hooves pounding through the soles of my shoes. I couldn't seem to hear anything; all sound had disappeared from the world.

Jack leaped from where he had been hiding in the grass. In two eight-foot bounds, he was running just to the side of the bull's head. Without stopping, the bull brought his head down to bring the antlers to bear on him. Jack leaped and caught them. He was in the air with his knife hand below the throat of the bull. The bull tossed his head back to throw Jack aside and the force of it drove the knife deeply in and across his throat.

Jack was thrown in the air, landed curled and rolling, bounced to his feet and ran after the elk.

The bull staggered, blood pouring from his throat as if from a bucket, ropes of it hanging from his muzzle. He shook his head slowly. Jack caught up with him and drove the knife into his eye. The elk fell, boneless and flaccid, to the ground.

Jack didn't say anything for a long second. Then, he punched the air with his fist and cried out: "*Yes!*"

"Jesus," I said.

Jack heard me, looked up at me and grinned.

I had never seen so much blood in my life. The ground was stained with it ten feet around the bull. The wolves were covered with it as they merrily tore the elk apart. Goldie stood on my shoulder and took sequence after sequence. This was great footage.

"Did you see that?" he said standing next to me. Jack was drenched in elk blood from neck to knees, his fur coarse with it, his hands burnt red to the elbows. "Did you just see it?" He shook his head and grinned at me. "I've wanted to do that for years. Since I was a kid." Still grinning, he looked around.

"I bet," I said, watching Goldie in the monitors.

After a moment, I noticed Jack had grown silent.

I looked up from the monitor and didn't see him. "Jack?" I called.

"Over here."

I followed his voice over a small rise and found him in the deep grass. He was tending to the fallen wolf. There was an angry set to his mouth. The wolf's whole side had been opened and I could see the ribs and muscles exposed. Mostly, the wolf panted but every now and then he yipped as Jack probed the wound. Once, he snapped at Jack's fingers.

"It's not as bad as it looks," Jack said suddenly and I wondered who he was trying to convince: himself or me.

"It looks pretty bad."

Jack didn't say anything for a moment, his lips thin. "Well," he said finally. "It is pretty bad. But he'll have two months to heal before the winter sets in. If this had happened in the winter it would have been all over for him. Winters are hard." He leaned back and looked at the wolf. "Of course, we would never have attacked an elk like that in the winter."

He pulled a capsule out of his rucksack and broke it under the wolf's nose. The wolf lay down and closed his eyes. "I have about twenty minutes now."

"Is that long enough?" I said. I checked and made sure Goldie was getting this.

"Sure," he said as he pulled out his instruments. He cleaned out the wound expertly and splashed it with disinfectant and then sprinkled what I assumed was antibiotics over it. Then, with one practiced move after another, he sewed the wound shut. Once he had finished that, he plastered a bandage over it. The wolf was stirring as Jack measured out something from a vial and injected him. The wolf didn't even flinch.

"He'll walk back with me. There are enough voles for all of us back with Raksha. For now, we'll just let him sleep for a while."

"He'll make it back?"

"Oh, yeah. It'll take us most of tomorrow to walk back with him. Akela will probably run on back to Raksha. But me and him will take our time."

A good portion of the fallen elk was gone when we returned. The four wolves were lying near the carcass looking very pleased with themselves.

I squatted next to it. There was nothing remaining of the bull's haunting grandeur; he had become just another meal on the prairie. The air was thick with the smell of meat, bone and blood.

"I didn't think wolves attacked anything this big." I said.

"You didn't like the show?"

"I was surprised."

"Yeah, well, it was a little risky," he conceded. I thought for a moment he was embarrassed. "But it's still summer and we're all in good health. Not like the winter."

"So you said." I stood up. "So you said."

I pulled out my phone. I wondered how long I would have to wait for Sam to pick me up.

After three weeks in Montana, my apartment felt very warm and small, a friendly sheltered spot in the middle of Manhattan. I took a long, hot shower, an even longer bath, and then another shower. I sat in my big stuffed chair and had Chinese food and drank Italian beer for dinner. New York was still hot but the air conditioning was quite cool. I slept under a light sheet for twelve hours dreaming of elk. After that, I was ready to start.

The trick was to figure out the right tack for the story. There are a million events and tales but only a limited number of points of view. That's how you manage a story. Every human experience is unique but the uniqueness prevents it from being usable. Like great art, the experience has to be brought down to a common theme that can be universally embraced: good versus evil, coming of age, man against nature, man for nature, conflict, resolution, corruption, purity. Once you connect one of these points of view to something that happened, you have a story. The closer the connection is to something with universal appeal determines the attractiveness and durability of the story, its legs.

I checked and made sure Goldie had been fully downloaded and went over what I had. It was even better than I had expected. First, I knocked together a story just using some of the footage I had from Sam and Jack and some pictures of the puppies. A long shot of the hunt gave the sense of reality I was looking for. Then, I did the intro, the voiceover and the outtro. That would be for the human interest section for the news feeds. That took me a couple of days. I held off submitting it for the moment.

Then, I contacted some anthropologists and psychologists and put together a nice half hour segment about Jack and the wolves. Something public broadcasting would like. Suitable for a segment of a larger show on something like human adaptation, for example. I reformulated some of the outtakes and made a second segment for the wildlife sites. That took a couple of weeks. Then, I submitted the news segment at a rock-bottom price as a teaser.

Using the public broadcasting segment as a base, I built a stand-alone show on Jack himself. This was on spec. I wasn't sure if Jack had the legs for that. I worked on that while I submitted the news segment.

Two of the big feeds bought the same segment—unusual but not rare and the it took off. In an hour, Jack had a four percent share on the major discussion groups and seventy smaller feeds had asked for the segment and breaking rights— rights to cut the segment to fit around other segments. This was starting to be serious money. I put together a dozen or so tabloid articles and put them up for automatic purchase. Several hundred sales came from that alone.

I finished the full hour show by the time Wildlife America and Environment Today asked for a more detailed segment to fit into their national feeds—the half hour segment I'd already made. They also asked for breaking rights so I wasn't sure where the shows would end up. Jack had become the central topic for ten percent of the major discussion groups. He had become part of the national conversation.

The major feeds are all international but most of the smaller feeds were local. Now, the small foreign feeds were asking about him. It had been a month since I had gotten back from Montana.

National Data called for a single topic show and I had the hour segment waiting for them. This was the big time. The longer segments would be bouncing around for a while. I could stop right now with what I had earned on Jack and not work for the next two years. This didn't include subsales and residuals that would still be coming in for at least another year after that.

But staleness was already setting in on the original material. By October, I thought my part in Jack's public career was over.

I took a vacation in Greece. For two months, I lived in a small villa on the Adriatic. I filtered my news, learned to drink Turkish coffee and had an affair with a lovely, tanned, poverty-stricken artist named Gina. She liked the way my rented sailboat cut the water and I liked the way she looked sunning herself on the deck. For a month, she used a room of my villa to paint horrible clashing abstract portraits of nude historical dictators when we weren't sailing, eating, or having sex. Then, on the first of the year she went back to her husband in Germany. I helped her on the train with her new paintings. Gina kissed me passionately, gave me an abstract Stalin miniature, and left.

After that, I grew restless, so Stalin and I flew back to New York. I hung Stalin on the bathroom wall over the toilet and started going over the news.

Jack was all over the feeds, which surprised me. I knew he had legs but I didn't think he'd last this long. I started reviewing the news back just before I left.

People liked Jack. More importantly, they liked his wolves. There were three segments of his constituency: those that found him and the wolves cuddly, those that found him a noble savage and those that found him dangerously erotic. There were seven official cameras hovering over him and his wolf pack twenty-four hours, seven days a week. Something like fifty or sixty temporary cams came and went, looking in on him regularly. Several articles and three books that had been written about him while I had been gone. None seemed to me to be as good as my work but perhaps I was biased. Jack dolls had become the Christmas toy of choice and came complete with a set of seven wolves. In a collateral event, interest in a twentieth-century figure, Wolfman Jack, escalated. Pop music started incorporating 1950s rock and roll into the sounds of steam engines and calliopes.

I tuned into one of the cams. It was a howling blizzard in Beck-Lewis right then. The wolves were not in sight. I guessed they were in a den or something. For a moment, I thought I saw Jack's face in shadow but it disappeared in the snow.

Beck-Lewis also figured prominently in the feeds. Sam had gotten a good portion of the funding he wanted and B-L was getting new men and equipment. I smiled at that. Good for you, Sam, I thought.

The winter was cold out there. It sealed Jack and the wolves in and the rest of the world out. By that June, though, Jack was still a cultural item. The snow melted and tour groups started trespassing on Beck-Lewis looking for Jack. He wasn't hard to find since eleven full-time cams were following the pack around. I watched them. They all looked lean. Jack himself looked haggard. The winter had not been good to them. Apparently, Sam and his people were able to keep most of these tour groups out but not all. Some of the groups were able to get through the mound of paperwork and some didn't bother.

In July I was still idle but I was looking into a story about a man in South Africa who had attempted to graft into his mind a simulation of the skill and compositional ability of Mozart. He had failed and there had been significant consequences to his family. While I was finding the right people to talk to, I received an article alert from one of the feeds about a trial in Billings. Jack had killed somebody.

Tour groups attract three kinds of people: those that truly want to understand whatever it is the tour is about, those that just want to enjoy themselves in a new venue, and those who are complete idiots. It turned out a tourist, a man named Bernard, had broken away from the main group of Full Moon Tours and tried to steal one of the Raksha's pups. Raksha had, quite rightly, attacked and torn off a finger. Bernard managed to pick up a rock and knock her down. Then, instead of attacking Raksha the idiot had killed the pup out of spite. Jack ripped his throat out.

National Data sent me to Billings to follow the trial. It wasn't going to take long. All eleven cams had caught the killing, not to mention the cams carried by the tourists. Bernard's father was a retired software engineer and his mother had been the financial officer of a Boston HMO. Environmental considerations aside, they were out for blood. On the other side, public sympathy was with Jack. The picture of Bernard killing the pup was everywhere. I found unofficial support funds for Jack's defense that seemed to be legitimate and a lot of scams. With this sort of money, Jack could pull an O.J. and get off scot-free.

The tours had stopped but I saw twelve more cams added onto the feeds. At least half of them were handhelds. Everything about him, everything about the wolves attracted attention. The publicity of the trial had generated more interest in the wolves but no one event drove the feeds any longer. The feeds drove the attention which then drove the feeds which then drove the attention. Jack and the wolves had become a self-perpetuating lightning rod.

I checked into Billings the night before the trial. I was tired. I was by myself; I'd left Goldie at home. There were going to be enough cameras here. I was discouraged. The South Africa story wasn't going anywhere. I'd taken the National Data job to get my head clear. I was watching the coverage of Jack's impending trial when someone knocked on the hotel door.

I know. I should have checked first. I can only say I was too tired to think. I opened the door and Sam Orcutt was standing there. He didn't say anything. He punched me in the side of the head and I went down seeing things in different colors and mixed up. He yelled at me while I tried to uncross my eyes.

After a minute or two, my own personal color separation came back into focus and I saw he was standing over me. Drunk, maybe, but certainly confused. "Why the hell didn't you leave us alone?" He yelled as he stood over me. "Why did you have to stir things up? What the hell were you thinking?" I punched him in the balls.

He went down, moaning. I staggered out into the hall and got some ice for my face. He was still moaning when I got back. I sat down on the sofa and watched him for a minute.

"Nice to see you, too," I said. My ear was hot and swelling and I heard a crack every time I worked my jaw.

"Son-of-a-bitch," he whispered, holding himself.

"You throw up, you clean it up." I put the ice on my forehead. I still felt dizzy. "What are you doing here, Sam?"

"He's my friend," he coughed. "That's more than you are."

"You hit me out of your friendship with Jack?"

He pulled himself onto his hands and knees and made his way to a chair. "I wanted to pay you back."

"What did I ever do to you?"

"For what you did to him. To us. To me."

"Yeah." I wasn't surprised. I'd been in the business a while. "That's the way it goes. You should have protected him better. Kept those nasty tour groups away from him. I could have helped if you'd dropped me a line."

"You're a bastard."

"I'd sure like to continue this great conversation but I've got a big day tomorrow."

For a minute, he looked like he was going to try again. I picked up the table lamp and watched him. He thought better of it and staggered out into the hall.

"If you're ever in New York, look me up!" I shouted after him.

I shut the door and leaned against it. I felt terrible.

All bruises and bad feelings, I showed up the next day at the Billings Courthouse ready for a show. It didn't happen.

All across the feeds, Jack's attorney had described their case. They were going for insanity. They had statements of several psychiatrists to prove their point. One of their doctors had modified himself to be eight feet tall. Not that it would have made much difference. Jack had spent nearly ten million dollars to look like the star of an old horror movie. Who wouldn't be inclined to think he was nuts?

Instead, Jack pleaded guilty.

It dawned on me the prosecution was smarter than they looked: they'd plea-bargained with him. The trial was over before it began. I couldn't figure it out. With the public sympathy and the money, Jack could have gotten a complete acquittal. Hell, he could have ended up suing the State of Montana for libel and won.

Once he had entered his plea, the prosecutor, a hard-looking woman named Warburg, recommended the standard sentence of not more than ten years and not less than seven. The defense agreed. *Agreed*. Now I was really confused.

Jack saw me on the way out of the courtroom. He ignored me. I didn't try to talk to him. I'm not sure why. Certainly, it didn't make National Data any happier. Instead, I interviewed the several disgruntled psychiatrists who would have been substantially well paid to get on the stand had the defense not caved. It wasn't a total loss. I managed to cause an argument between the Dean of Harvard Law School and the Grid Systems Legal Affairs Correspondent. It made good coverage and when the Dean took a swing at the Correspondent I was there with the National Data cams. It made me think of Sam. The Dean hit like a girl.

Jack was transported to Montana State Prison at Deer Lodge by the end of August. I spent a day or so setting up small segments for National Data and then the contract was finished. I didn't see Sam again. I suppose he took his little floatplane back to some tiny lake deep in the heart of Beck-Lewis.

For one reason or another, I didn't go back to New York right away. Instead, I caught a plane over to Forsyth.

Full Moon Tours operated out of an old and nearly abandoned strip mall. Wolf Pack Observation was only one of its many tourist packages. I wandered around in the office, checked out the brochures, the posters and the rough log walls and the soundproofed ceiling. Fishing trips, hiking trips, elk hunts—all in Beck-Lewis. I wondered if Sam knew about these people.

A pretty young woman with perky breasts worked the counter. She smiled radiantly at me and I smiled back. It wasn't hard to smile at her; she reminded me of Gina.

"Can I help you, sir?"

"Not really. I just stopped in. What about this one?" The brochure had a close-up picture of Jack and his wolves on the cover.

"I'm sorry, sir," she apologized. "We don't do that tour anymore."

"Really?" I asked. "How come?"

"It was too hard to protect the clients from the wolves." She looked at the brochure. "I'm sure we'll offer something like it next year. We just have to get the bugs out of it."

"Ah." I nodded and left.

Deer Lodge was three hundred and fifty miles away and I suppose somewhere in my mind I was always planning to get there. Not that a detour to Forsyth would necessarily indicate that. I had no reason to go. Jack had nothing left I could use. The contract with National Data was over. Still, a few days later I stopped at the Montana State Prison. It had been a week since Jack had been brought here. I found Jack in the prison hospital.

I met Jack in the day room. He had the orange wrist brace of a possible violent offender, universal in this sort of facility. A sort of motion-activated tazer. I had done a story about brace abuse two years before. The guards at Riker's Island had developed the nasty habit of tuning the braces down for inmates they didn't like. Men were forced to stand like statues to keep from getting tazed.

Jack was sitting in an old plastic chair watching the trees outside. He turned slightly as I approached him.

I sat down beside him and looked at him. They had shaved him and the pigment of his skin was blotchy. His blue eyes were rimmed with red and he was gaunt and haggard and his hands shook. "You look like hell."

He laughed shortly. "They tried to drug me the first couple of days I was here because I'm so much stronger than the other inmates. But the modifications interfered and messed me up. Now, I wear this." He held up the brace. He turned back to the window.

I let the silence go on for a bit. "I wasn't sure you would see me."

He shrugged. "Why not? What could you do to me now?"

I ignored that. "You're not a wolf anymore."

"I was never a wolf."

"Yes you were."

He looked at me.

I spread my hands. "Not in shape, of course. But you had left people behind. You didn't start coming back to civilization until I threatened you. Until you had something to lose."

He watched me a moment, then looked back outside. "Autumn's coming."

"It does that."

He grunted and didn't speak.

Finally, I asked: "Why did you do it?"

"What?"

"Kill Bernard."

Jack held up his hands. "What else could I do? He killed Raksha's pup. Raksha would have killed him if I hadn't killed him first. Then, she would have been destroyed. Better me than her." He turned back to the window.

"You could have gotten off completely," I said. "Did you know that?"

He shrugged.

"Was it Warburg's idea?" I looked around the room, the antiseptic white and beige of the walls. Outside were the guards and the exercise field and the cells. "You can appeal. You can say you were given inadequate counsel. You *were* given inadequate counsel. That's absolutely true. She should never have taken the deal. You could have been on your way back to Beck-Lewis that afternoon."

"It wasn't Warburg's idea," he said softly. "It was *mine*. All of this was *my* fault." He looked up at me for a long time, shook his head and turned away.

And I understood.

I looked out the window. The weather had become clear and the late summer light had changed character and taken on the soft golden glow of approaching autumn. The air looked cool, a sheath of velvet pleasantly covering a cold knife.

Jack looked outside. In one of those rare and perfect telepathic moments between human beings, I knew what he was seeing. Through one of the many cams that hovered over the pack, or through the eyes of a tourist, or a naturalist or just somebody who wanted to touch her, was Raksha. Now the center of a hungry and ever-growing crowd, the elk gone, the grass trampled, playing as best she can with the now almost-grown pups, then joining with the rest of the pack, howling against the coming snow.

"Winters," Jack said at last. "Winters are hard."

at the money

RICHARD WADHOLM

*New writer Richard Wadholm lives in Seattle, and is at work on a novel
set in the universe of the story that follows. He's made several sales to
Asimov's Science Fiction, and his story "Green Tea," set in the same milieu, appeared in our Seventeenth Annual Collection.*

*Here's a tense and compelling visit inside a high-tech "Stock Exchange"
in an evocative and electrifyingly strange far-future universe, one filled with
players expert in double-dealing and intrigue — and one where life itself
rides on every bet.*

Personally, I see nothing wrong in doing deals in a bar. Esteban always loved
working out of Chuy's. He wore the place like an old coat. Every barmaid was his
foil and confidante.

We did a deal with a couple of Anglos just before Esteban went out on his last
run. Twelve hundred pennyweight of morghium, bound for some ideology franchise in the Scatterhead. Whenever the negotiations got tense, Esteban would vow
he didn't need their money anyway. He could get enough to live on from Doctor
Friendly, "the Spaceman's Friend." Then he would grab some nether part of
himself and give a leer to the old tumor broker at the end of the bar—" *What'll
you give me for this, huh?*

The Anglos would look appalled. Martisela would look from Esteban to me in
amazement, like Sleeping Beauty awakening in the wrong castle. "This is what I
sneak out of the convent for? High risk and low comedy?" And Esteban would
grin at me, even as he pleaded with Martisela not to tell his wife.

Times like that don't seem special until later, when you look up and suddenly
realize they are over.

Tonight, I was back at Chuy's. I was meeting the same Anglos, tying up loose
ends with the same morghium deal. Only Martisela was back at the convent. She
was through missing bed checks for a while. And Esteban?

My last conversation with Esteban, he was on this Bright Matter ship, the
Hierophant. They were up in the dusky end of the Scatterhead Nebula, passing
through a plume of tungsten ions left behind by some medium-sized supernova.

Esteban had loaded the Anglos' target isotopes onto the *Hierophant*'s starboard vane. He was calling me to double check their nuclear chemistry: Would perbladium transmutate into morghium under tungsten ion bombardment?

Really, they print this information on splash screens. I would have yelled at him for the price of the call. Except I knew the real reason he was calling. These pinche Anglos and their morghium job had him in sweats. He needed a little reassurance. I told him everything was all right. I promised him he wasn't going to die, I'd see him when he got back.

Tonight, as I sat at our old table next to the tumor broker, I thought about that promise. All I had left of Esteban was a salvage ticket awarding me 900 pennyweight in unspecified isotopes. Not even a guess what these unspecified isotopes might be, or how long till they decayed to something else. Only that Esteban Contreras had entrusted them to me for the sake of his wife. And they were worth the price of a fleet of Bright Matter ships.

Chuy's Last Load Lounge was hosting a wake for the crew of Esteban's ship, the *Hierophant*. Chuy himself—Jesus Navarete to Anglos or ships' officers—had worked on the *Hierophant* as a young man. Dorsal vane mechanic, he reminded his patrons proudly—"*Where the money gets made.*" A target shelf of hot phoellium had fused the fingers of his left hand into a flipper. A man of lurid humor, he had planed that load of glassified slag into a countertop, mounted it on dark azurewood and made it the centerpiece of his life as an innkeep. To this day, the counter glows from the isotopes embedded within.

Chuy was perfecting the head on a pitcher of French lager as I stepped up to the bar. Grief is thirsty work; three other pitchers extended to his left. Alpha particles from the bar passed through them, trailing arcs of delicate bubbles.

"Ah. Lazarus," his voice slow with care for the beer. "Back from the dead to tell all."

"Chuy."

"I hear share prices for the *Hierophant*'s salvage rights have gone up 27 percent since the accident. I don't suppose you'd like to take a little credit for that." He never looked up from his task. In the best of times, there is antipathy between vane dogs like Chuy and mercaderos like myself. This was not one of those times.

I smiled. "You're just saying that so I'll buy the next round."

He leaned forward to give me a malign squint. For one moment, an arc of quiet speculation seemed to spread out around the two of us. My life was, as they say on the Exchange, *in play*.

But the night was too sad for that sort of foolishness. He slapped my arm and gave me a snicker at once ugly and forgiving. The sort of laugh meant to be passed around between pinche cabrones like ourselves.

"Here," he said, and passed me one on the house. As he did, he leaned in close. "A couple of gabachos looking for you." He waved his flippered hand toward the room. "They're around here somewhere. You keep your business quiet. I won't be responsible, you start offending people's sensibilities."

Even as he spoke, I felt a presence at my side. In the mirror just past Chuy's head, I saw a copper-haired Anglo with pouty lips and strawberried cheeks. I doffed my beer to him. "Mister Chamberlain," I said.

He smiled. "Orlando Coria. And your friend, Contreras . . . ?" He looked past my shoulder as if Esteban might be waiting in the crowd. No Esteban; Chamberlain lifted his eyebrows, *well well well.* "Damn shame," he said. "Smart guy like that. And that nasty little nun?"

"Back at the convent."

"Well," he offered, "I'm sure you miss her." He took my hand as he spoke. More than a handshake—I felt myself gently directed toward a quiet spot at the end of the bar.

Another Anglo waited there. This one sprawled across his chair, hips and shoulders cocked fashion-model style. A little smile played at his lips. This would be Chamberlain's . . . "*chauffeur?*" These Anglos.

Chamberlain gave him a nudge that knocked his leg from the tabletop. "Bell, be convivial."

Bell said, "Hey, Buddy." They must have been bashful where Bell came from.

I made room under the table for my barter bag. It was mostly empty but for a couple of perbladium samples from one of Esteban's little jobs. These gabachos had introduced themselves as perbladium speculators. I was curious to know if they would recognize real perbladium when they saw it. I was curious to know who they really were.

I set Esteban's salvage ticket on the table and leaned back to take in their reactions.

Chamberlain studied the ticket over tented fingers. He might have been counting his money. He might have been adding up his crimes.

"That's a lot of money for a bit of morghium," he said.

"That was my thought as well. Have you seen what's left of the *Hierophant?* Whatever you gave Esteban to turn, it didn't transmutate into morghium."

He gave his partner an expression of aggravation. "I told Seynoso to pay for this stuff outright."

"That would have been awkward," I said.

"When would it have been more awkward than right now?"

"About the time the *Hierophant* burned with all hands. Someone from the Mechanics' Guild makes a point of looking up every registered investor."

I was calling him a ship killer, is what I was doing. There were two possible reactions to this sort of slander. Horror and outrage, and this other one. More rueful, more considered.

Chamberlain pressed his fingertips a little tighter. "There's a story behind this morghium deal. Things are more complicated than you think." He waved his hand, the story was too complex to go into now. "I'm willing to buy these salvage rights from you, blind. I'll pay you 10 percent market price. And before you laugh, consider the realities. You don't know what you're holding anymore than we do. You might be holding lead futures for all you know."

I would have stood up to leave, except that Chamberlain was right. All I had in my hand was a market mirage. It was expensive as such things went, but all salvage looks good from a distance.

This was when I missed Martisela's market expertise. She had three of the seven basic Thommist Catastrophes ingrained as quantum processors into the unused

DNA of her hands. Wasn't a decay chain she couldn't follow. I had nothing to go on but my unscientific nose, which wrinkled considerably at these two.

"I'm not in a position to negotiate," I lied. "This salvage claim belongs to Señor Contreras's family. Unless you've got some further claim, I am obliged to sell it at the market price."

" 'Further claim?' " Chamberlain gave his compañero a nudge, *such language!* "We have further claim," he said. "We bought first position on your decay rights."

He produced a futures contract for whatever isotopes might decay from Esteban's unspecified salvage. I looked down till I found the signature of Esteban's wife, Cynthia. I looked back and the two of them were grinning at me.

There is nothing illegal in optioning 900 pennyweight of pterachnium to one investor and then optioning its decay products to someone else. Martisela always warned me to cover those isotope futures in the contract. What had Cynthia been thinking?

"Señora Contreras is distraught," I said. "Whatever she hoped to gain with this will be satisfied some other way. I think I will leave you now."

"What about our decay rights?"

"The problem with decay futures? They are useless unless something actually *decays*. That is why they are cheap to buy. *Ay te wacho.*"

Chamberlain needed a moment to realize what I was saying. "You really are going to make this hard, aren't you?" To himself: "He's really going to make this hard." He looked at Bell to do something. Bell seemed utterly impassive.

I was pushing myself back from the table when I noticed a fluorescence in the gloom of Bell's shirt cuff. I recognized the source from my own improvident youth — a 48 yuen piece on a leather loop. With a bit of steghnium to light old Mau's eyes. Or a 128 yuen piece, bearing Emperor Yuan, lit by phoellium. Or a 256 yuen piece, glowing with albatine. Depending on what sort of smugglers they were and what sort of detectors they had to confuse.

Bell had been toying with the coin all this time, but I hadn't noticed till he let it slip from his fingers and into the gloom of his sleeve. He twisted his cuff as if embarrassed, but not so quickly I would miss the bleeding ulcer beneath the coin. Yes, he had been wearing it a very long time.

He noticed my eyes on his smugglers' charm. He gave me a smile as desolate as every darkened doorway along Calle de Campana. Chamberlain nudged my barter bag with his foot.

"Enjoy the evening," he said. "We'll catch up with you."

I glanced to the rest of the room. An engineer off of the *Page of Wands* sang a corrido to the vane mechanics of the *Hierophant*. How much they loved their pepper seed mash. How bad it made them smell. A compañero chimed in, something about their dubious sexual practices. Make no mistake, they'd all be weeping in a moment. Had I miscalculated?

The entire roomful of people seemed caught in their grieving. Save one little Anglo. I spotted him sitting by Doctor Friendly, the tumor broker. I remember hooded eyes, and this goatee that seemed to point the way for his nose. He watched me intently. I thought he might come to my aid. The little Anglo merely nodded at me and smiled — *now what?*

They do have their sense of fun.

I turned back to Chamberlain: "What if I made you a counter proposal?" I said.

Chamberlain lifted an eyebrow at Bell — *are you listening to this?*

"One moment of patience, I will show you real wealth." I had come here to deal for Esteban's legacy after all. And why not offer them a sample?

I gave Chamberlain my confidential smile. Careful, *careful*, so as not to alarm, I pulled the pouch of woven lead from my barter bag. It was a small pouch. It barely filled my hand. But heavy enough I had to stiffen my arm beneath it.

There is an art to this sort of presentation. I peeled back the double-sealed flap. I made it an unveiling. Inside gleamed a ball coated in mirror-smooth nickel. I could see Chamberlain was fascinated. He wanted to touch it. Still, I held onto it. I waited till he asked before I slipped it from its leaden sheath and into his palm.

He laughed at the surprising weight of it. "It's heavy."

"Yes, it is."

"It's warm."

"Like holding a hamster in your hand. It's a subcritical amount of perbladium, distilled from liquid suspension and purified. Up in the Scatterhead Nebula, the militias use it as a crude proximity trigger. That warmth in your palm? That's alpha particle radiation, knocked off the sealant."

Chamberlain shrank back. He had the cerrazadito's abhorrence of contamination. Now it was my turn for amusement.

"Forget the alpha particles," I soothed.

He looked at me to see if I was having him on. His shoulders eased. "Perbladium," he said. He laughed a rueful little laugh. "I stay away from the real touchy stuff." This was a big admission for Señor Chamberlain.

I nodded. Sure, sure. "You need something to worry about, consider the neutrons reflecting back from your body. They are quickly pushing that little ball to criticality."

He was still smiling as he looked up at me. I'll never forget the moment he stopped.

"You're lying."

I had a particle detector on the table. It roared to life at my touch.

Chamberlain made a strangled yip. He dropped the ball of perbladium. He dove backward into a drunken throng of vane mechanics, which might have been the wrong thing to do.

That left Mr. Bell. His eyes skittered from the sample on the table to me. One of us would kill him. He seemed uncertain which. I was about to clear up his confusion when Chuy Navarete rounded the bar with a couple of beefy crane operators off of the *Ace of Pentacles*.

"What did I tell you?" I think Chuy was more furious with me than anyone else. "Come in here. Ruin the somber mood . . ." He glared down at my perbladium, which had dented the table where it landed and never even bounced. "That stuff better not be real."

"Sorry, Choo. I was just putting it away."

Chuy reached into the brawl and withdrew a very bruised and confused *guero*, who swung at him in wild frustration, and snarled, "Let go of me, you fish-handed freak!"

I winced. Everyone in the bar winced. Chamberlain might have said a lot of wrong things and not said that.

Chuy gave Chamberlain the sort of benign smile a chef bestows on a favored lobster. *"¿Como?"*

We will avert our eyes at this point. Take my word, the fate of these two gabachos only gets more wretched. In any case, I had a fortune disintegrating in my pocket. And only one person in Buenaventura could tell me what it was.

I want to tell you about Martisela. Martisela and Esteban and myself. A trio of swindlers were we. I was sleeping behind the kiosks that line Borregos Bridge. I imagined myself a romantic figure, a Prince of the Barrio. Though, a little older and a bit less turned-out, I might simply have been "homeless."

Martisela had already been exiled to the Convent Santa Ynez for selling short on the anti-money market just as it pitched into its long-overdue collapse. One of the few truly blameless things she had done in her entire sordid career. Ahh, but she had made money where others had lost, and that was not to be forgiven.

Esteban Contreras actually held down a steady job — Starboard Vane Chief on the Bright Matter Ship *Hierophant*.

He used his position to solicit these little side jobs — a couple hundred pennyweight of phoellium to melt a polar ice cap into atmospheric gasses. Or vanodium to be turned to echnesium to confine a bit of industrial grade $Vacuum^2$.

He always backed up his commodity by optioning futures on its every decay state. Then he sold these options to his partner — me — and I used them as collateral to pump the stock of the Orlando Coria Mining and Bright Matter Company, Incorporated. Amazing, the sort of people who will throw money at a little brokerage with the right sort of pedigree. It might have been criminal if we had made any real money. But Martisela was the brains behind this mob, and she never really cared about the money. The fun for her was in rigging the game.

Only one time did we get serious. This was prior to Esteban's last trip out with the *Hierophant*. Esteban had agreed to turn this load of morghium for Chamberlain and Bell, and their iffy Spanish friend, Seynoso. Esteban thought the job over some more and decided that it liked him not. We decided to put this Spaniard's morghium to our own ends.

Morghium is pretty humble stuff. It has a bit of $Vacuum^1$ at its heart, which alters the speed of light through certain crystal lattices — big news if you're a designer of quantum optic switches. It is more spectacular as a target material. Flown through a cloud of tungsten ions at just under the speed of light, morghium transmutates under bombardment into some of the most exotic stuff on the Bright Matter Exchange. Lyghnium, and $Vacuum^4$, which whispers of a universe full of magnetic monopoles. Pterachnium and $Vacuum^3$, used to convert underloved white dwarf stars into highly desirable singularities.

With our client's morghium in hand, Esteban offered futures on pterachnium, even though he would have been crazy to actually turn anything so dangerous. Martisela optioned Esteban's potential pterachnium using money borrowed against its potential isotopes. I was the one in charge of cashing it all in.

For about two hours there, our stock was leading a small bubble market in lyghnium 485 futures. I was as wealthy as I had ever been in my life.

And then someone even funnier than we used our stock's inflated market value to leverage us out of our own corporation. And what were we going to do? Complain to *Los Zapatos?*

Martisela went back to the Convent Santa Ynez. Esteban went out on his last run with the *Hierophant*. And me? I returned to the aesthetic life. Who knows where I might have landed but for this ticket of unspecified salvage. I rather dread to think.

There was always this moment when I saw Martisela again. Things came back from the old days. Challenges we had met. People we had done. I would get awkward and romantic, Martisela would simply get awkward.

Martistela stood back from the Convent's ornate front door. She blinked up at me with her graphite-colored eyes and thought of two or three things not to say.

I said, "I'm cold, Marti." I nodded behind her, toward the inviting warmth of the Convent Santa Ynez. "Will you let me in?" I could smell tea brewing somewhere down the hallway.

Martisela Coria closed the door behind her. She gave me a prim little smile; we would suffer together. "Are we here for the Commodities Exchange, Señor Coria? Or is it the room and the hot meal?"

"I need you."

"This is business, I presume?" Martisela was having a grand time. I could tell.

"I've got something going. I need someone who can read the market for me. You're the best I know."

We looked at each other, suspicious as gangsters. "What's the commodity?" she asked.

"Just backroom stuff. Strictly backroom. No shares, no speculation."

"What's the commodity?" Repeated, with a little edge to her voice.

"It's 1.3 teratramos. Marti—*1.3 teratramos!*"

Her chin started to rise. "You're nervous, Orlando."

"I'm not nervous."

"Don't lie to me," she said. '*No shares. No speculation.*' " In her scornful he-man voice. "You've got something unstable and you're trying to unload it before it decays to lead."

This is the price one pays for dealing with an ex-spouse. At some point, all the surprises lay behind you. Along with most of the hopes. She looked at me, daring me to lie. I could see her hand edging behind her for the door. The water-taxi pilot who had brought me out was venting his boredom by tapping the boarding bell.

"I have acquired Esteban's load."

She turned on me in slow, blinking, perfect amazement. "The *Hierophant*," she said. "You're trading on the *Hierophant*." Her hands came loose at her sides. "You're trading on Esteban's last load?"

Allow me to spare you the rest of our reunion. Swearing is like riding a bicycle, I suppose. In any case, there's no percentage in outrage.

"It's for his wife, Cynthia," I said. "Esteban named me executor of his estate."

"Cynthia Contreras. The *golfa* with the colored eyes."

Perhaps Esteban's semi-comely widow was the wrong person to bring up. "It's for you as well," I said. "To get you out of this place before the Church sends you off on some doomed bright matter ship."

"What makes you think I want out of my obligation to sponsorship?"

This would be a rhetorical question. The wreck of the *Hierophant* had been found in the San Marcos star system just two days earlier. Nobody wants to die the way those people died.

"Have you seen the market fixing on April hostages? April hostages are up something like 20 percent." The market seemed to be forecasting an imminent shortage.

She gulped that one back a moment. Then: "The sisters are a little touchy about that word, 'hostages,' " she said evenly.

"When exactly were you going out on your sponsorship?"

"Tomorrow morning." She looked at me. "You laugh and I'll slug you."

A phone went off at her belt—Martisela was late for the evening meal. They were wondering, was everything all right? My taxi pilot was calling out something about a cargo he had in the back, decaying to lead. Martisela seemed perfectly content to let us all wait.

"This unspecified salvage," she said to me. "This is from that morghium deal we did? And the market is putting the price at 1.3 teratramos? That must be some kind of vacuum state." I mentioned how Cynthia Contreras had sold off the isotope rights. Martisela shook her head in astonishment. "That's a really stupid thing to do," she said. Only we both knew Esteban's widow, and she was not prone to stupid moves. Not at her most grief-stricken.

"You know where this all plays out."

"At the Botanica." She said it without thinking, in a rush of breath and memory that broke my heart. The Botanica Linda was where she and I had spent our lives. All our memories were there. All our good fights.

"This is just for Esteban," she said as we boarded the water-taxi back to town. A couple of Martisela's *hermanas* poked their heads out the door. "I'll be right back," Martisela called out to them.

I realized I was participating in a jailbreak—a Buenaventura sort of jailbreak. Martisela had made good her escape. But she was leaving for her sponsorship in the morning, she had to be back before then or give up any thought of ever retrieving her trader's license.

This would be a jailbreak as staged by Cinderella.

Martisela must have realized this the same moment I did. All the way to the Bodega, I heard my Spanish Cinderella looking forward to midnight:

"Ya me chinge," she muttered.

I remember when the Anglos started bringing their war business to us. There was not much discussion on the morality of marketing perbladium to sociopaths. Mostly, the Shoes worried that the old city, with its paraffin works and its churches all tinged green by lizard droppings, would present an unsophisticated face.

A new Exchange was built in one of the towns along the Buenaventura Crater rim, as far away from the wet docks and the paraffin works as possible. It's very nice. Perhaps you've seen pictures? I especially like the true clock in the Court of Commerce. (Though honestly, how many people need to know the true ship time of some carrier up in the Blanco Grande? All the Bright Matter traders have their own true clocks anyway.)

The real money, of course, remains where it always has. In the back room of the Botanica Linda.

Señora Sebastian still sells herbs and roosters' feet to bless a new enterprise, and flaming hearts of Mary to the more esoterically religious. She keeps dishes on the glass case full of those hard, unsweet candies the Bright Matter smugglers call "piedras de molleja"—gizzard stones.

She recognized Martisela from the old days. "Are you back, Señorita Davalos?" *Señorita Davalos.* And with her husband standing beside her.

Marti smiled. "I'm helping him out of a jam," she said.

Señora Sebastian looked at me. "You've got one of those 'unnamed salvage' tickets?" With an expression that said, *You're probably expecting it to pay off like a lottery ticket, aren't you.* "Have a stone." She held out the dish for me.

Martisela gave me a piquant little smile, barely more than a dimple. She scooped a few into my hand. "Oh, be nice," she hissed at me, and we plunged through the curtain into darkness and noise.

The trading room is kept dim against the sudden blossoming of holographic charts or a ghost wall or a ballet of hands traced out in bioluminescent catastrophe grids. It is an old warehouse turned into a grotto, and the darkness between the lights is frantic.

The calls and cries and angry laughter reflect off the hardwood ceiling all the way back to the little clutch of desks where the shipping underwriters are laying odds on every transport that leaves orbit. Put your hand to any desktop, the tremors grind at your fingertips like low electric current. And that's an average night.

In a shipwreck market, every fortune is at stake. Your bit of salvage may still exist. Or it may be melted to slag. Or it may be seeded with some exotic vacuum state and is already being coveted by a market that knows more about what you have in your pocket than you do. The only way to find out is to wander through the assembled multitude, plucking at the feedback loops that tie us all together.

An agent offers time at her Bright Matter refinery up in the Four Planet Nation. A transport jobber hints at a ship he has available—not the fastest in the fleet, but the captain can hold it to within a baby's breath of light speed, right where relativistic time dilation effects are most acute. Who can say why these people come to you? The market sent them, that's all.

One blurs the eyes and allows a market's worth of greed and fear and quantum computing power to shape the gaps into recognizable outlines. This strategy works best when the market is calm and winners and losers can be neatly defined. Tonight, the market rode this *Hierophant* bubble. All bets were off.

Here are a few of the commodities rising with the shipwreck market:

Bright Matter was up, of course. The price of Vacuum^4 doubled in the time it took my eyes to adjust to the dark. Moving in tandem to the Vacuum^4 would be the market in large-scale power generation. Power generators loved Vacuum^4 for its steady flurry of magnetic monopoles. And gnodium, the baryonic cinder that separates Vacuum^4 from the rather fragile vacuum of our own universe. And, if you care to press a point, the market in high-priced legal insurance; vacuum traders are notorious for whiling away the hours in recreational litigation.

Someone was offering Tuesday afternoon illyrium, which would be thralium 442 by Wednesday morning (and sold as a separate commodity).

Someone else was dealing Vacuum^8 and lyghnium, a favorite combination to Anglo ship killers. Vacuum^8 for its cognizance of bright matter. Lyghnium for its dense neutron cross-section and spectacular binding energies.

Doing even better than the bright matter market were futures in single-bean Saint Elise cocoa, which is prized in the French Violet for that little kick that arsenic lends the aftertaste. Corn and soy futures were doing well, especially in the Four Planet Nation, where the variable star M. Exelrod had been turning up the heat lately, which was good for their growing season.

And then there were the franchised ideologies. Even cocoa couldn't compare to the market in April Communism. Object-Oriented Socialism had suffered a huge debt write-off, but they continued to do well on the strength of their subsidiary interests in ergosphere mining. Of course, National Socialism is always looking to break out of the pack.

The only unease in all this giddiness lay with the *Hierophant* itself. After fifty hours, the silence from the salvage crews was growing worrisome. Traders try to be realists about shipwreck bubbles. Nobody expects to smash a violin and hear Schubert. But there should have been something. The ghost walls whispered rumors of tellolite nodules dug from the face of the starboard vane. A few had tested positive for Vacuum^6. Where was the mother lode to make this all worthwhile?

A new set of ghost walls opened—salvage reports from the port vane of the *Hierophant*. The port vane carried medical isotopes, which I do not invest in. Good thing for me.

Martisela stood on tiptoe as she read down the lists of salvaged isotopes. It was one of those unconscious gestures of anxiety, like me, whenever I pull at my mustache bangle. "*Ave Maria purisima,*" she said into her fingertips.

There were a few heart warmers among the wreckage—a bit of albatine, shielded by chance behind an isotope vault. A hundred kilos of medical-grade cobalt 60 dug from the wreckage of a collapsed targeting shelf. But that was as good as the news got.

Most of the stuff on the port vane had been poisoned by neutron flurries from the accident on the starboard vane. That, and heat and melted titanium and carbon and boron.

"Esteban was out in that," Martisela said.

"This *Hierophant* market is going to tank if they don't find something better than this," I said.

Across the room, investors pinched their foreheads. They checked their currency markers, and turned on their catastrophists—*there must be some mistake.* Really, it was a ship accident after all. What were they expecting? I gloated at their naiveté for a moment or so. Then I remembered my own little bit of paradise.

Martisela watched me watch the port vane assays drift away. She nodded toward the currency marker in my back pocket. "Go ahead," she said. "You might as well know now."

My 1.3 teratramos of unspecified Bright Matter had bucked the market. It had increased in value. It was now one-and-a-half teratramos of unspecified Bright Matter. A remarkable price for something that no one could name. Martisela looked dubious. Even I was uneasy. This business is far from infallible. We might have been chasing a qubit shadow. Maybe something as simple as too many investors, and too many quantum recognizers, not enough hard-eyed realists.

I pressed the market to give me some sort of decay chain. Any real baryonic commodity will break down into a sequence of isotopes. Even without knowing the parent isotope, the market will extrapolate a decay chain, complete with estimate of its market value, half-period, and purity.

My 900 pennyweight of unspecified wealth just sat there, grinning at me.

"It's some sort of vacuum," I reasoned. "Vacuum^6, maybe. They don't figure decay plateaus for Vacuum^6."

Martisela gave me a look I had seen entirely too often lately. She told me to sell my shares while I had that little bit of mystery at my back. "If nothing else," she said, "option futures on the decay products. A market like this, people will bet good money you won't get your unspecified Bright Matter to market before it decays into their unspecified isotope."

She was probably right, of course. But we had a little while. The assay for the *Hierophant*'s dorsal vane would not be in for another eight hours or so.

"Let's go talk to the neighbors," I said. They would be out on the patio, plying their trade in the metallic plasmas and exotic vacuum states. She put her arm in mine, and we smirked at each other just enough to show we were not fooled by this arm-in-arm business, not for one minute.

The Bodega Linda opened onto a patio in those days, a view past the paraffin works and down to the bay. This is where the jaded gentry drank and sparred. It was more or less invitation only, and I had never, not on my most profitable week, been invited. But one-and-a-half teratramos in my pocket made me cocky. Even if it was for one night.

We were stopped at the door by a security guard. She remembered me. I could tell by her dubious expression. She asked if we had weapons, and studied a hand-held field detector while we answered. My perbladium sample provoked discussion with two security people, as did Martisela's grids. They passed on the perbladium, but Marti's grids were deemed an insult to the Efficient Market economist who ran the patio. I could leave Marti at the door, but I know where my gifts lie. I was the salesman. Marti was the banker. I could succeed without her—I could travel in this *range*. But I needed her financial sense to deal with the patio crowd.

I was debating how to broach the delicate subject of a bribe when the gate-keeper stepped aside for a man in an open-weave scarab-skin suit.

He grinned. He made a show of palming his eyes to peer in at us. "You bring a nun to vouch for your character and still they won't let you on the patio!"

I was tempted to ask Zuniga what he was doing here. His cuffs were open and rolled back to his elbows. As I looked closer, I could make out the vestiges of bifurcation grids, just paling-out against the backs of his hands. They were dense and strange, I couldn't figure what he was working on.

He nodded toward Martisela. "Are you back with us now? Served out your exile or whatever that was?"

"I'm just helping out a friend." She refused to catch my eye as she said this. She absolutely refused to smile. "You're here for the shipwreck market."

Zuniga put up his hands—*What can one say?* "I find myself chasing down a bit of vacuum." He chuckled as he said this. We might have been discussing some embarrassing family secret. "I've bought out four vacuum traders already. They all know they've got hold of something, not one of them is smart enough to tell me what it is." He cocked an eye at me. He looked sly. "You always like the hot stuff, don't you? The exotic vacuum states? The strange matter? I've always admired your taste in risky investment." He sighed. "Would you had a bit more liquidity . . . ?"

"The heart of a vacuum trader." I endeavored a smile. "The purse of a gallery slave." I found myself holding my breath. This is the moment one discovers that religious bent that Auntie Gracia had always hoped for. Sure, I had come to the Botanica ready to meet my silent partners. But not Zuniga. Anyone but Zuniga.

Zuniga normally worked in decay futures, which is not necessarily the last refuge of a scoundrel, but it is no place to see people at their best. Everything was a fire sale to Zuniga. And if not, why not?

He studied me. "I'm giving everyone 620 megatramos per pennyweight," he said at last. "I'll give you 620 megatramos for whatever you're holding. Just because I like you."

I nodded to the grids on the back of his hands. "Go back and run your catastrophes again," I said. "You're not even close."

Zuniga leaned in close and confidential; he would bend a little, so long as no one could hear. "I can give you a gig if you're willing to accept part of it in stock."

Martisela looked at me. I looked at her.

"What sort of stock?" she said.

"There's this mining platform skimming the ergosphere at Los Batihojas." He glanced around nervously; black hole mining is rather disdained among our own, no matter how much the Anglos favor it. "Run by a bunch of crazy *gabachos* for the most part. They send a magnetic flume down into all those ions crashing into each other. They come up with the most amazing stuff. If this *Hierophant* market starts to play out, they are going to be positioned to pick up the hedge investors. Honestly, my friends, the stock's not bad. I'm giving you the keys to the kingdom is what I'm doing. I'm letting you walk in Saint Hidalgo's Scented Slippers."

Scented slippers or no, Martisela was appalled. She squinted at him in disbelief. "You want to buy us off with shares in this ergosphere mine, while you bet the bank you can make them worthless?" She gave me a look—*am I missing something?*

This, in so many words, was exactly what Zuniga was offering—A classic hedge. A teeter-totter, weighted on each end by commodities that Zuniga believed linked. A failure in one commodity would send investors to the other. Either way, he made out. Not necessarily his partners.

Zuniga looked from Martisela to me, looking for what? A wedge? Whatever he saw in our faces set him back. He had to think what to do next. "How about I make you an offer of just 500 megatramos?" he said at last. "No mining shares, nothing. And if you don't take it I'll let my friends know who it was behind that disastrous morghium business on the *Hierophant*. You know the people I work with. You know how they express their disappointment."

Ahh yes. Alberto Zuniga's fashionably dangerous clientele. Anglo militiamen and Bright Matter smugglers. Just the thing for a feckless playboy in need of a little gravitas.

"I'm stepping out for a moment to check on my charities," he said. "When I get back, you will accept my offer. Or I will set about making you famous."

Martisela watched him push through the curtain into the foyer. "Can he make things hard on you?"

I shrugged. For a lot of people, he could. People with houses and families and regular places they had to be at regularly appointed times. Now you know why I lived the life of a street urchin. I nudged Martisela. I nodded toward the door.

Martisela was frowning at her hands. "Six hundred and twenty megatramos per pennyweight," she said. "Why do you suppose he came up with that number?"

"This is a shipwreck market. Everyone in here is offering prices they can't justify for things they can't name."

Martisela shook her head; that wasn't good enough, but she was too busy to explain. She began flipping from catastrophe to catastrophe, so fast I could barely keep up. She had this frown of vast interest that just got deeper the more she looked.

"Perhaps it is coincidence," she said, "but 620 megatramos was the estimated price for lyghnium a week-and-a-half ago, when Esteban left on his last run."

"What are you saying? Esteban left me with a load of lyghnium?" I was not so happy about this. Up in the Scatterhead Nebula, the Philistines burn lyghnium in fission bombs. I saw myself dealing with a dreary assortment of zealots and thugs. You've seen what they're like. Imagine my heart.

"Don't worry about the lyghnium." She narrowed her eyes at a cursor as it rolled down the crown of her knuckles to a stasis-point near the crook of her thumb. "Zuniga's a dealer in decay products. When he looks at the market, all he sees is what he recognizes. But he tends to miss the parent isotope, which, in the case of lyghnium, is most likely to be . . ." She turned her hand as the cursor crossed through the cusp of skin between her thumb and index finger. Whatever she saw made her eyes get round. "Pterachnium," she whispered. "Vacuum^3."

I felt something giddy rise in my throat. Half the fleet communications in Spanish Space depended on tuned singularities. Most of them were collapsed from white dwarf stars by Vacuum^3.

"This is what those two *gabachos* at Chuy's were after." I heard a voice just beyond my sight: *No more tutorials for rich tourists . . .*

"This is what killed Esteban," she said. "Esteban and everyone on his ship. I can't believe we're trading this. I can't believe we're making money from it."

"You know what this means? We're rich enough to kill! You know how long it's been since you and I were rich enough, somebody would want to kill us?" *No more money changing for Chinese smugglers. No more laughing along with jokes at my own expense.*

Martisela made this bemused little moue. She looked as if she wanted to say something. Whatever it was, she let it drop. "Zuniga still has his fangs in you," she said. "He will never allow your profit to eclipse his own. Not so long as you and he are yoked together." She was quiet for a moment. I realized she was watching him as he made his way back from the patio.

Zuniga stopped at one of Señora Sebastian's glass cases. He pointed—there, to an apothecary bottle of rose hips. There, to a brass censer. Here, to a set of bifurcation grids, pre-loaded in their own epidural slugs.

I knew what he was doing—giving me time to sweat. It worked. I tried to think of some way of extricating myself from his grasp. Nothing came to mind.

Zuniga pointed to a scarab-skin jacket hanging from a rafter. But no, it had to be open weave, to match his shoes. All the Anglo gangsters were living on the edge, fashion-wise.

While Señora Sebastian hurried off to retrieve just the right shade of blue, Zuniga slipped out his currency marker for a couple of quick deals. He was feeling good; he was clowning. He looked up at us as if he'd only just remembered we were watching. He grinned his most boyish grin—*I've got to pay for this somehow*—and began punching out sell orders as if in panic.

"Some people should stay away from self-parody."

"How does he do it?" She marveled as she watched. "How does somebody with even less money than we have manage to push around the market the way he does?"

"He leverages himself to excruciating levels and then drums up some new deal to pay down his debt load."

"And let's don't even talk about those suits." She made a face.

"Zuniga and his little gangster conceits."

Something behind her eyes made this nearly audible click. "What would you bet he pays for everything in anti-money?" I got nervous when Martisela talked about anti-money. Gangsters still use it. They like it because it is anonymous. Martisela liked it the same way she liked chocolate, because she wasn't supposed to have it. Anti-money—more specifically, speculating in the misalignment between anti-money and the debt it was supposed to represent—is what got her installed in the Convent Santa Ynez.

"Don't do it," I said.

"Do what?"

"Whatever. Don't do it."

Her eyes were black and shiny like I'd seen them in the old days. "How much are you willing to be hated?"

"By Zuniga? You're joking, right?"

"Not by Zuniga. By everyone." Martisela had this little look of dread and wicked calculation. It made me nervous enough I would have asked what she had in mind, but Zuniga was one last dawdle from being upon us.

"What do I need to do?"

"Sign everything you own over to me."

Perhaps I paused a beat too long. I was thinking of my winery in the Four Planet Nation. The tea plantation on the flanks of Olympus Mons. The beach house at Santa Jessica that I'd never seen. Martisela leaned her cheek to her collar. "I'm a nun," she said. "Vow of poverty, remember?" What I remembered was that we were always better business partners than lovers. Somewhere along the way, those little pranks we played had turned expensive.

"You remember the vow of poverty is yours, not mine."

Martisela didn't even smile. She palmed my currency marker and brushed by Zuniga without a shiver. Zuniga never even looked at her, she was that good.

"Sorry to push, Hermano." He gave me his best little frown of sincerity. "But I've got to wrap this business up."

He tugged at his collar enough to show me this greenish smear along his left shoulder.

"I bought this open weave jacket a month ago. Everything stains it, and now look. I stood too close to one of those lizard trees and one of the little bastards rained down on me."

Well, that explained the smell. At least on this occasion.

I glanced over Zuniga's shoulder. Martisela was with a pack of currency traders, buried in some negotiation. She made an impatient nod at Zuniga—*keep him talking*.

I was thinking to interest him in some bogus hedge swap. Maybe involving this Object-Oriented Socialism I'd heard about in the last market fixing, along with that black hole mine they had riding sidecar. That had just enough of Zuniga's devious sense of value to keep him interested.

I mentioned it and he gave me a vile little chuckle. "A hedge swap?" I could see it appealed to his sense of the perverse.

"I'll give you the same deal you gave us—620 meg per pennyweight."

"Mined lyghnium 482 is going for 800 meg per pennyweight," he sniffed.

"Then why were you going to pay me 620?"

He waved my objections aside. "Really, Coria. Let's be serious with each other. The gravity brokers are all aflutter looking for some fusty little dwarf star they can collapse into a singularity. I ask myself—what alters the Coulomb force inside a dwarf star and shows up unnamed in all my market equations? What do you say, Coria? Vacuum^3? Vacuum^6?"

Even through the crowd noise, Martisela heard him. I saw her stiffen and close her eyes, just for a moment. Zuniga caught me looking. He laughed. He clapped me on the shoulder. "There are no secrets from Zuniga. Holding back will only make the reckoning more severe." To make his point, he brought up his Anglo friends in the expatriate community. It seems that someone had given them a floor plan of my distillery outside Bougainville. Perhaps someone would nationalize it.

Perhaps they would simply burn it down. Zuniga gave me a look of frank appraisal. From there, it was but a short conceptual leap to the man who owned it.

I may have disdained Zuniga, but I did not underestimate him. The expatriate community lived just across the bay, in Jimmy-Jim Town. No one's more vulnerable than a broke commodities trader. I was starting to think how I could explain a 400 megatramo deal to myself when Martisela caught my eye. She lofted her eyebrows in a breezy, insouciant manner, like a tourist enjoying a particularly bad part of town.

Zuniga was going on about my tea plantation in the French Violet. He wanted that especially.

Even as he spoke, currency windows were popping open in a line just beyond his vision. While Zuniga had been threatening my wealth and my life, the anti-money market had gathered itself into a precipitous wave. Some of this would be my assets, sold off and converted to anti-money. Most of it would be collateral investment from market technicians smelling blood in the water. Zuniga didn't know it yet, but he had become the biggest holder of anti-money on the entire Exchange—a position not unlike being the biggest landlord on a southbound iceberg.

He was just rounding the corner on my beach house when Martisela pulled the plug. All that anti-money was swapped for simple debt futures. From where I stood, it look like half the anti-money market drained down a black hole. Even by the Exchange standards, this was a lightning strike. Within moments, the exchange rate between anti-money and undifferentiated debt had slipped to 3-to-1. The only major players left in the anti-money market were the ones too preoccupied to see what was happening.

Zuniga was going on in his mellifluous announcer's voice. His Anglo militia friends had shown him things that no one should see. Zuniga was just beginning to detail these things for me as one of the Botanica's well-dressed floor daemons appeared at his side.

He carried no expensive scarab skin coat, nothing but the obsequious expression that seems to attend embarrassing news—*There is a problem, Señor? With Señor's account?*

Zuniga smiled, all incredulous. He glanced over the man's head at the money market windows and the smile just grew. He could appreciate a joke at his expense, give him credit for that.

The smile was hardening as he turned to me. By the time it came around to Martisela, it had gone necrotic as a rotten baby tooth.

"You did something"—jovial and teasing as ever. "What have you done with my money?" His eyes fell to the grids on her arms. A cursor was still pulsing between her knuckles, perhaps he recognized himself? "Give me back my money." He advanced on her. Already, he was a little desperate. I grabbed him around the shoulders. "Give it back. Before Zuniga shows his nasty side."

"Let him go," Martisela said to me.

"You know who my friends are," Zuniga bucked my arms. "Don't make me set them on you."

I thought Martisela would at least step back. Even as Zuniga strained at my grasp, she pushed up right under his nose. "You and your nasty friends," she whispered. "I shall have to bear them in mind, won't I?" Suddenly it was Martisela I had by the shoulders. Zuniga was rearing back. "My friends don't fare so well lately. One of them is burned to death. The other is living under a bridge. Maybe your nasty friends will let you live long enough to find a bridge of your own. If you haven't invested too much of their money. That would work well for you, yes? A nice little bankruptcy and you will escape their friendship with your life."

"Don't speak of my friends," Zuniga said. "I'll set them after you. I'll have them use you."

"With no money or access to deflect their more predatory instincts? I think you're about to discover just how useful *you* can be." Have I mentioned Martisela's height? In shoes, she could barely see over my shoulder. The entire time I had hold of her, Martisela's voice never rose above a whisper. The room should have rolled over her voice like a wave over a sand castle.

I glanced back to see a hundred faces turned up from their market projections and catastrophe grids, all staring from Zuniga to me to Martisela and back to Zuniga.

Zuniga noticed as well. He turned on them. "Que me ves?"—*What are you looking at?*

This seemed as good a moment as I would get. I handed him my currency marker.

"What is this?"

"It's 500 megatramos. For your salvage."

"You're not serious. I consolidated these salvage holdings, not you. Why should I play this game?"

"You've got lizard shit on your coat. You want a coat, smells like lizard shit?" And the unspoken question—*when will you get another one?*

He looked at the platten in my hand like it had been scraped off his coat, but he knew better than to refuse my offer. His lips tightened into a sarcastic smile. The joke, whatever it was, must have been on me. He might have explained except for the floor daemon who appeared at his elbow with a phone call for Señor Zuniga.

"Now we'll see!" Zuniga whipped the phone from the kid's hand. I would have walked away, but Zuniga would have none of that. He nodded at me as his gangster came on the line. He glared in vindication. "Señor Dryden." He was laughing. ¿Que ondas, Carnal? The smile hung on his face a moment, suspended like a cliff diver at the top of his arc.

This would be one of those conversations of silences, stuttering objections, pale eyes, sentences that trail off into nothing. At some point, Martisela nodded toward Zuniga's hands. What I had taken for knots of anxiety were actually mathematical catastrophes.

"He shouldn't do that." She made this little snick-sound with her tongue. Somewhere between pity and reproach. "He's calculating the moment of his own death," she said. "If he's not careful, he'll get an answer."

I don't know how she knew that, only that I had watched him re-run this calculation a half-dozen times. He ran it again even as Martisela pushed me ahead of her through the curtain.

Sooner or later, it had to come out right.

It was evening on the Calle de Campana. One of those evenings the city is most generous with its charms. A chill settles in with the fog. The pumice tiles that line the street swell and chafe and the air fills with the most delicate harmonics. A gang down at the paraffin depot was boiling moderator for some space-bound transport.

Esteban's family lived in one of those heritage neighborhoods that creep down the sides of every bridge in the Paraffin District. Their house had been built by a ship owner when the Puente de Hierro was new. The vestiges of wealth remained even though the wealthy ship owner was gone: Here's a formal VR portal, throw rugs rucked up around it. A genuine captain's command chair from the wreck of the *Four of Pentacles*, its cushions shiny with wear. And everywhere, the reek of old cooking, the racket of kids slamming up the narrow stairs two and three flights without stopping. The shiver and groan of the bridge itself, as river traffic passed between the spans.

Someone had put out a card table in the old decontamination chamber that fronted the street. Esteban himself peered over the mezcál flasks and ornaments of pressed tin. I remembered the picture from a bridge party we had been to across the canal in El Ciudad de Cenizas. Esteban had that look he always had, that sort of half-smile, as if he were listening to a punch line just beyond his understanding.

"Orlando, who's with you?" Cynthia Contreras called to us from the kitchen. "Martisela Coria? *Ay Dios mío*. I can't believe they let you out." She was wedged in between relatives at the back of this giant mahogany heirloom table. She waved us over for hugs. Her eyes were pink, but, for the moment, dry.

My impression of Cynthia Contreras through six years of marriage was this kohl-eyed wraith at Esteban's elbow. In a better life, she might have raised a couple of picked-on kids and gone on to spend all her pent-up rage closing *lucha de la lagartijos*, something socially uplifting like that.

But this widow business would not be part of her plan. I was not entirely sure I wanted to see what she made of the opportunity.

Esteban's brother, Jorge, sat with her, maybe a little closer than a brother-in-law should. Jorge Contreras always greeted me with this frown of vast and belabored interest. A dimwit's caricature of a philosopher. "Orlando Coria," he said. "The Lucky Man himself." He glared all protective as I put the contract on the table beside Cynthia. I did what I was always do with Jorge; I ignored him. He continued to frown inscrutably. Maybe he was ignoring me as well. "This was Esteban's," I said to Cynthia. "It represents a great deal of wealth, and has to be handled quickly."

She knew what it was, which surprised me. Jorge pestered her to explain and she ignored him while she read to the bottom.

"Do I own all the rights?"

"It's all tied up," Martisela said. "The baryonic matter rights. The vacuum state."

"What about the isotope rights?" Without looking up. "Do I own them? And through how many decay plateaus?"

This was a sore point. I wasn't sure what she had cooking with Chamberlain and Bell. Once upon a time, we had actually owned the decay rights to this pterachnium, extending down to lyghnium 485, at least. Though we were asking a lot more for it then the 620 meg that Zuniga had offered us. No point going into all *that* mess.

"We've had some trouble pinning down the isotope rights," Martisela answered quickly. "That hardly matters so long as the pterachnium is sold off."

"And you have buyers for this stuff."

"Lining up buyers is the easy part," I said. "Bright Matter fleets from Buenaventura to the Four Planet Nation are salivating for a tuned singularity."

Martisela, as always, was out front of the market. She set her investment portfolio on the table with a little flourish. She was ready to hedge Cynthia Contreras' profits across the breadth of the communications market—A little to the designers of the event-horizon skimming satellites that put all those quantum-entangled photons in orbit. A portion to the enclave of Jesuit electrical engineers who fashioned the polarizing screens that spun those photons into code. A portion to the shipwrights who installed the answering micro-singularities onto the ships. Any one of these markets could tank and a flood of investors would buoy up the other two.

Cynthia Contreras flipped through the printout. She nodded. She smiled. She was impressed. Then she said, "I'm thinking of investing in Buenaventura municipal bonds."

"Municipal bonds." Martisela looked up at me. "*Municipal bonds?*"

Cynthia Contreras did not look up. "What do you think, Orlando?"

She was turning her back on a 2400 percent return and a perpetual reinvestment for municipal bonds.

"I think you're crazy."

That only made her laugh. She leaned toward me as if we were plotting an assassination. "Have you seen the debt market in the last couple of hours?"

"Debt market?" I felt Martisela's fingers dig through my pant leg.

"About two hours ago, someone inflated the debt market—I know, I know. Why would anyone do that? But they did, till it's as over-valued as it's ever been." I felt this electric tension at my side. "Say I put part of my money into Buenaventura bonds," Cynthia said, "which, by law, have guaranteed lines of credit. Say I put the rest into shorting the debt market. When the debt market crashes, I'll be sitting on a couple teratramos in saleable debt potential."

Martisela looked to me to say something. I would have, if she hadn't cut me off before I could draw a breath. "I think you misunderstand the nature of strategic investing," she said carefully.

Cynthia frowned. "You think it won't work?"

"There are people sitting at this table who will be ruined by what you're proposing."

"Esteban's true friends will understand and forgive."

"It's a sin," Martisela said. "To ruin people when you're not even hungry."

Cynthia had this laugh she'd been saving up for six years, knowing and angry and disappointed. It made the hairs bristle against my sleeves. "Perfect," she clapped her palms like a little girl. *"Perfect."* She looked past us toward a man leaning in the doorway. "They're worried for me," she said to him in Cargo English. "For my future, or my soul. They can't decide."

"Look upon it as a challenge," he said. I recognized the lazy smile even before I recognized the face. Here was the little Anglo I had seen at Chuy's.

"Hola, Cholito." A finger came up, pointing my way. He cocked his thumb, ray-gun style, *Prssshk prssshk.* He laughed his lazy laugh.

"Everyone?" Cynthia Contreras waved a hand: "Noah Dryden." She made no further explanation, but that was explanation enough. We all lived with expatriate Anglos. We could pretty much guess what this one was doing here.

Dryden nodded at me. "How's the commodities trade?" he said.

"Never better. How's the smuggling trade?"

"I'm afraid you have me confused with someone." He smiled. "I'm in franchised socialism." — Even as his left hand rose by dead reckoning to the forty-eight yuen strung from his right wrist. "You mean this?" He laughed. "I've had this since childhood. But these bracelets are hardly uncommon where I'm from."

In the dusky light of the kitchen, the eyes glowed bright enough to light the unmarked underside of Dryden's wrist. Cynthia knew where I was looking; I thought she would look away, but her course was set. She didn't much care what I figured out now.

"What did this one promise you?" I asked her. "Revenge on the men who killed Esteban?" Cynthia said nothing. "And now that he's brought proof of their deaths, you turn over Esteban's pterachnium to him as payment."

"He seems to know a lot about my business," Dryden drawled as casually as possible.

I would have asked Cynthia about the isotope futures she had sold Chamberlain and Bell. What was it like to lure two men to their deaths? Cynthia turned to me with these huge and meaningful eyes; all my pointed questions dried up in my throat.

"They're friends of my husband," she said to Dryden. "They won't go to the Shoes. They have their own problems with the law right now."

As for Martisela, she nodded at Cynthia the way old girlfriends do — *where did you find this guy?*

Cynthia, for all her veneer, could not look Martisela in the eye. "He helped me," she said to Martisela. "He helped me even the score for Esteban."

"For a price," I said.

"Everything has a price," Cynthia said. "One way or another, everyone pays."

Dryden nodded his amen to this. "Bell and Chamberlain were a couple of over-reaching franchisees," he said. "Their accounts have been settled."

" '*Settled.*' " Martisela gave me an owlish look. "Doesn't that sound final."

"Let him be," Cynthia said. "It's been hard enough getting things sorted out to my liking. I don't want anybody having second thoughts now." She gave me two eyes like steel bearings. "Esteban was hopeless." She tilted her head at me defiantly. "He left it to me to avenge his death. A trader shouldn't leave his family to do that. Not if he has command of his skills. Not in this market."

An odd sentiment coming from a widow. Even Jorge frowned. But Cynthia Contreras was in that state of grace that Buenaventura bestows on all its widows. Everyone around the table nodded along, the way they did to a pretty song sung in Cargo English.

Only Martisela lowered her eyes in disappointment. "Esteban Contreras filled your house with friends," she said.

"Esteban always trusted people to do the right thing. He made allowances. Look at where he left me." The emotion she had been holding off welled up. She blinked hard at sudden tears. Her chin wrinkled and her face reddened. Jorge saw his chance to move in with sympathy, but Cynthia was angry and pushed him off. She took Martisela's arm. "I'm going to be like you."

Martisela looked down at her habit. But it wasn't the cloistered life that Cynthia envied. Martisela looked back up at her and she realized what Cynthia was talking about; her eyes widened and she gawped for something to say.

"I'm going to be ruthless and clever," Cynthia said. "I'm going to play the market like an ocarina. I will always finish at the money. And if I go down I'll take a billion people with me. So that even if the Shoes put me in the Convent Santa Ynez, and make me ride Bright Matter ships for my penance, nobody will trade another share without looking across the bay to see if I'm still safely away."

I remember someone cooking carne borracha on the river watch that ran behind the house; the splash and sizzle of tequila was the only sound in the room. I remember Martisela trying to say something, only it wouldn't come out. She sat next to me, and she was beyond my reach.

It was Jorge who stood up first. "My, doesn't that smell good?" He grinned and nodded around the table and everyone gratefully agreed. *Why, yes. The carne smells delicious. Let's all go have a look.*

This wave moved toward the door. Only Cynthia Contreras paused, and then only for a moment. "People pushed me around all my life," she said to me. "A person like you, you can't know what that's like." She looked to me to tell her she was making sense.

"Dryden murdered two faithful and trusting employees," I said. "Just to do business with you. Don't you wonder when *your* time will come?"

She gave me a bashful smile. "Honestly? No." Behind her, Jorge had Dryden's arm in this squeeze that gangsters in the Paraffin District give each other. He was detailing what he would do to Dryden's enemies, extending his hand here and there as if setting out tools. Dryden glanced up at me as he passed. His face was fixed in horror.

"Jorge likes me," Cynthia said simply. "He's always liked me." The screen slapped behind her.

Martisela sat back beside me. She folded her hands between her knees. She looked dazed.

Somebody walked past with a bag of wine. She snagged it without looking. She leaned back and drained it. All around us, the conversation sort of died out; people do seem to tip-toe around a half-potted nun. The man with the wine bladder shook it for signs of life. He looked appalled. Martisela seemed oblivious, but I got uncomfortable. I nudged her and motioned toward the front door. *Maybe we need some air?* She agreed, maybe we did.

I didn't expect we'd be out long. The wind was turning. The fog was coming up from the wet docks, glowing faintly in every hollow along the canal. But Martisela was one of those people who wondered why red wine had to be sour. I thought to stick with her a bit, she'd get sentimental and ill and I'd take her home.

Cynthia Contreras called out something as we stepped outside. I thought she was asking us to stay, but I realized she was talking to Dryden.

"Look at this contract. Nine hundred pennyweight and you're getting it for nothing—1.5 teratramos, and two lives."

I looked at Martisela. Maybe she sighed.

"Amateurs." I tried to laugh.

"She didn't make this city." Her eyes came around to me from someplace very far away. "Have you ever counted up the people you and I have betrayed?" She waited, but I had no answer. After awhile, I realized she had no answer either.

"The debt market is not your fault. Let it go." I nuzzled her ear, just like old times. "Come home with me," I said. I knew an old high-boy tugboat drydocked on Canal Sanchez. It was warm and private and I pictured us making love in the pilot house, under a parchment-colored sky.

Martisela was tracing the grids on her left hand with her fingers. "What if we got jobs?"

I thought she was joking. Martisela had this clownish streak to her, but she was drunk right now, and she was never funny when she was drunk. "We've got jobs," I said. "We're the best team of traders this city's ever seen. Tonight, we reminded this whole city why they've had spending money the last couple of years."

"What if we got a cart and sold shaved ice on Calle de Campana? You could talk to the customers. You're good at talking to people. And I could put away the money?"

Shaved ice. I liked that. Shaved ice. This, from the girl who had rigged an entire monetary system in the space of a conversation.

"You know when you're making too much money? When poverty starts looking picaresque."

She bent away from me. Her hands twined into a figure I recognized: Swallowtail Catastrophe. She was plotting a discontinuous change in her own future.

"You're going back to your sponsorship," I realized.

"I'm so washed up in this town." She made a broken little laugh. "I can't even sell an investment to a poor widow woman." She rolled her lip under her teeth. She looked away. "You should have seen me. I was doing so well when you showed up. You know how long it had been since I'd told a lie?" She took my currency marker out of my pocket to order up a water-taxi back to Santa Ynez.

She didn't even see what was staring at her from the splash screen—something was wrong with the market. It should have been going wild, it was utterly flat. I tried to show her, but Martisela was drunk and heartsick and not listening to what the market was saying. I had to take her hands to make her look at me. "The reason Cynthia Contreras passed on your ancillary market is because there is no ancillary market. Whatever this Dryden person is doing with our pterachnium, it's not bankable."

Not bankable. There was an antiseptic phrase. I remembered the market report of the *Hierophant's* port vane. Acres of cesium and cobalt showered by neutrons and swept off in rivers of molten metal. You want to say such visions are "unimaginable." But they're not. Sometimes they're impossible to look away from. "Wait a week," I said. "Let this pterachnium decay before you go out."

"And in that week, what happens? Maybe Dryden hotloads some other ship? With some other sister in my place?"

"Maybe—" I could hardly get the words out of my throat. "Maybe I make you stay with me."

She looped her arms around my neck. Her lips and nose were soft. Her breath, luscious and stale with wine. "Maybe you rescue me."

"I'm in no position to rescue anyone. Already, everybody at the Botanica asks what happened to me. They soothe me with cheap flattery like a *cerrazadito*."

"Maybe we rescue each other." I could see it in her eyes: Me and her and this pushcart.

"Is that what we're talking about here? Are we saving my soul?" She gave me a sleepy grin. "If your life depends on my redemption, you are one dead Hermana, *Carnala*."

We always talked so tough with each other.

"Don't go," I whispered. "Please." Perhaps you don't know Orlando Coria, and this pleading sounds genuine, yes? And that wetness to the eyes, *a nice touch.*

Martisela's taxi slipped out from the shadow of Puente de Hierro.

"I'll call you when I'm away," she said. I couldn't believe she would really leave. We'd brought this city to its knees, helped a helpless widow, and faced down the big *guero*. How she could do this?

"Leave a message if I'm out." If she hoped to gain some advantage on me, well, she hoped in vain, didn't she? If she put her palm to her mouth or offered a little wave, I barely noticed. I had lots to think about. I had my commission, 10 percent of 1.5 teratramos. I was a man of substance now.

I remember checking my currency marker to show her what she walked away from. I don't remember the amount, but it was an awful lot of money. Enough so that my life would never be the same. It was enough to make me feel vindicated. Funny the way some moments stay with you.

As for the jingle of the buckles on her sandal straps as Martisela turned away? Five years later, I barely remember the sound. I have my pride.

The night tends to blur after that. I remember walking the apron along Canal el Centro, talking to myself, feeling righteous.

The fog was in, lit from the heart by radioactinides from the ships in the wet docks. People move indoors to avoid Buenaventura's wet dock fog, but I held off. Right around sun up, the ferry would leave the launch site at Malecón de Viejas for the low orbitals. I was thinking to maybe go see Martisela off. I was thinking to maybe invest in a bottle of mezcál and drink myself to stupefaction. Decisions, decisions.

I absolutely was not going to worry for Martisela. Señora Pushcart. Señora Let's-Sell-Shaved-Ice-and-Look-Like-Fools-to-Everybody-We-Know. I would start to weep and then I would make myself remember her plot to save my soul.

When that didn't work, I told myself her fate was out of my hands. I was a trader, not a gangster, what could I do? Fill my hand and confront Dryden in some alley? Please. Buy back my pterachnium shares from him? There were Bright Matter consortiums who couldn't put together the money to buy 900 pennyweight of pterachnium.

I found myself arguing the point with Martisela, a frustrating business even when she was around to answer me back. Tonight, she was regal and indifferent to her own fate, which infuriated me more.

Just to press my point, I added up all our assets — the fee from the pterachnium deal, the illyrium futures, the tea plantation, the winery and distillery, the beach house, the money, the anti-money. All of it. I came up with enough to buy back maybe a third of Esteban's legacy.

But why stop there? I still had some stock options left over from the takeover of Coria Bright Matter. I pulled out my currency marker to check their price, though I knew they were worthless. I think I barely looked at the 10:32 market fixing and shoved the marker back in my pocket.

It took me that long to realize what I had seen.

Coria Bright Matter was in play. Noah Dryden was shopping our remaining assets through one of his black hole mining companies, doing better than I had imagined possible. Indeed, he had financed a good chunk of his pterachnium money on our tailings. I tried to remember just what we had owned that could be worth 620 meg per pennyweight. Dryden had a man waiting to answer any questions.

His name glowed against the shadow on my palm. I studied it, because I had to keep my eyes focused on something stable; the landscape was resettling all around me.

It was my friend, Alberto Zuniga — the man who so admired my taste in exotic vacuum states.

I don't want to tell you what I did then. We have friends, they won't speak to me even now. I have people looking to kill me, did I mention? With all the moral baggage that goes with being me, you'd think I would reap a few of the more temporal rewards, wouldn't you?

Dryden was up at Puente de Hierro, waiting for the lift-off from Malecón de Viejas. As I knew he would be. He had to weep a little before he sent people to their deaths. Made him feel more like a human being.

He never looked back at me, though he knew I was behind him. Without preamble, he said, "I must confess I'm leaving for Bougainville in a few hours and I'm panicked at the thought of going without those little candies. Those little — what are they called?"

"Piedras de molleja."

" 'Piedras de molleja.' " He smiled at the name. "They remind me of your wife, you know. That hint of sweetness forever out of reach?" Of course, he would know what I was here for. He took my shoulder under his hand and we started down the bridge toward the ferry landing on the far side. "I'm sorry about your wife," he said. "You have to be strong. If she dies, it is to alleviate the suffering of millions of others."

"Shut up about my wife." I smiled; I had decided this conversation would remain friendly. In any case, I had come to talk about something else. "It was your idea to leverage Esteban and myself out of our own corporation."

"We may have collateralized a few of your assets. I would hardly call what we did 'leveraging.' "

"I've always been curious why somebody like you would take an interest in a tiny corporation like Coria Bright Matter. Alberto Zuniga told you about our lyghnium shares. Didn't he."

I had found something amusing for him. "It was your friend Contreras that he told us about. A good morghium designer is hard to come by. The lyghnium has turned out to be a bonus."

For a moment, he seemed uncertain how much he wanted to go on. Oh, but here was a man in love with his cause. He had no enemies. Only prospects.

"We have this wayward franchisee," he said after a while. "This man, del Cayo. He purchased a lot of very expensive ideology. Refused every decent overture of repayment. When we pressed the matter, he generated the money to pay us by pumping up lyghnium production at all his ergosphere mines throughout the French Violet—so much lyghnium, he caused a collapse in the market."

"So, you turn our Bright Matter ships into missiles. And you shut down his lyghnium operations. Permanently."

"He's put a quarter-billion people out of work. He's used our ideology to sanction a civil war against his brother. Killing . . ." He waved his hand at some unconscionable number. He had that faith shared among Anglos that anything can be forgiven. God's own attorneys, those people; anything can be mitigated in the light of something worse.

"You must be nervous right now."

"It's a big night for us," he admitted, breathless as an ingénue.

"I mean, you must be nervous putting all that lyghnium back on the market." That *is* how you paid or your pterachnium isn't it?"

He peeked up at me through his eyebrows, impish in his guilt. "We fudged a little. What we sold were options on lyghmium futures—the same contracts we acquired from Coria Bright Matter when we bought you out. Lyghnium 485." He shook his head in amazement. "I'd still like to know where you got that stuff. It must be decayed half to lead by now, which is a singular shame."

"You're going to substitute 482 from one of your mines."

He put up his hands, *what can I do?* The problem would come when Dryden's creditors called in those 485 options; there would be trouble even if they accepted Dryden's isotope for our own. Putting 900 pennyweight of lyghnium on the market would devalue the price another couple of kilotramos at least. I could see that chewed at his conscience in ways that killing another Bright Matter ship did not.

But I had good news for Dryden's conscience.

"You are in a unique position to fulfill your lyghnium 485 contracts," I said. "You own the parent isotope."

He started to explain to me about binding energies versus repulsive electrical charge, and the limitations of naturally formed nuclei. He stopped. He gave me a cautious, sideways look. A little smile. "What did you say?"

"Lyghnium 485 decays down from pterachnium. You borrowed the money to buy your pterachnium using its own isotope futures as collateral."

He thought about that. His eyes grew narrow, and then very wide.

"It's called a market loop," I said. "The way Martisela set up ours was very deliberate, with an exit strategy close to hand. And we were careful about who we brought in downstream. You bought into her market loop without ever realizing. You used it to borrow from some of the biggest brokers on the Exchange."

He turned on his heel to look back up the path. He might have been looking for a way out. He might have been looking to see if anyone else found me as amusing as he did.

"So what then? We compounded your larceny with a few innocent mistakes. What are you going to do?" He laughed. "Call *Los Zapatos?*"

"Better. I called all the people holding paper on your lyghnium." In the dusk beneath the bridge, Dryden's face took on the pallid glow of a drowned isotope. I could have read my watch by the reflection. "Not to worry," I said. "I have assumed your debt. No need to thank me."

His first move was for something in his waistband.

"In the event of my passing, my assets go to Señora Contreras."

Dryden had spent the evening with the delightfully ruthless widow. His eyes widened at the mention of her name. His hand fell back to his side.

"There is a bright side," I said. "I've got a buyer. A mining engineer five light years down the Hercules Vent, looking to illuminate veins of tungsten ions through the Nautilus Nebula. We'll need precision-speed transportation to get the lyghnium to him before it decays. But I've got a pilot who does her best work just below light speed. She will milk those time dilation effects for all they're worth."

"You're giving us five years to get out of the lyghnium business."

"Under the circumstances, I'd say I was being generous."

Dryden had this caustic laugh of amazement. "You're talking about some of the poorest economies in the Scatterhead Nebula. Speculators will short them into currency devaluations. Governments will collapse."

"What you get for bothering my wife."

He put up his hands in this placating gesture I've never seen anyone make but other Anglos. "We made a decision." He put up his hands again. "A *painful* decision — to put the lives of the many before the lives of the few. I know this is hard for you to understand —"

I checked my watch. "You have four years, four hundred and ninety-nine days, forty-nine hours, forty-nine minutes."

"I've seen your portfolio. You're heavily invested in these currencies. You will go down with them."

"Forty-eight minutes."

"Señora Contreras may lose interest in market speculation. Then where will you be? You're just half-an-hour across the bay from Jimmy-Jim Town."

I could see the conversation turning petulant. Besides, Martisela's ship would be leaving soon. But I wanted to leave him with a memento of his time among the Spaniards.

Dryden hefted Esteban's perbladium sample, smiling his rigid smile. "So what is this stuff exactly?" Proud to the last.

"Spanish version of a crystal ball. Gaze into it awhile. You might just see your future."

A deep-water ferry was passing along the canal toward the bay. I had to sprint to catch it. I'd like to say I never looked back, but really, it was a freighted moment.

I have this lasting image of Dryden. He is leaning over the rail, chucking Esteban's perbladium in its leaded sleeve and staring toward the gathering dawn as if surprised by the light.

I have seen him since. He seems to have taken the blame for the collapse of the Scatterhead Nebula economies. Maybe he should have killed me when he had the chance. He's a front man for the National Socialists these days. Or some tiered-market business operated by the Communists. Whatever, I lose track.

I have acquired this cachet. Paradoxical, I know—I am the cause of eight billion tragedies. But infamy is a commodity like any other. It requires less promotion than heroism, though it helps that I went broke along with the eight billion residents of the Scatterhead—and for love no less. Heartbreak is only slightly less compelling than villainy.

As for the money? I could tell you I don't miss the money. You might laugh. I will tell you that there are compensations.

I savor the memory of Martisela on the dock at Malecón de Viejas. The boarding bell is ringing, and we're arguing. Heatedly. And this old grandfather slides in close to hear tales of drunkenness and cruelty. I remember the look on his face as he realized we were fighting over the destruction of worlds.

I remember Martisela's face against my palm.

I remember her kiss.

She has arrived in Bougainville. She speaks of this faded rose of a city. Talc-white streets and arsenic-tinged chocolate and the reptile opera. Her note is a bit tentative. She's reaching across five years. That last good-bye on the docks at Malecón de Viejas, she did tell me not to wait for her.

I suppose I'm nervous as well. She remembers a clever young man untroubled by conscience, who lived behind the kiosks on Borregos Bridge and toyed with worlds.

What will she think of the man he became? The canal-boat pilot with friends and bills in about equal proportion?

I may leave for Bougainville and be gone forever. I may be back in a week. But right now, I am breathless with anticipation. Do you know how long it's been since I was breathless?

agent provocateur

ALEXANDER IRVINE

New writer Alexander Irvine made his first sale in 2000, to The Magazine of Fantasy & Science Fiction, *and has since made several more sales to that magazine, as well as sales to* Asimov's Science Fiction, Sci Fiction, Strange Horizons, *and elsewhere. His well-received first novel,* A Scattering of Jades, *was released in 2002, and was followed by his first collection,* Rossetti Song. *He lives in Sudbury, Massachusetts.*

In the sly and tricky story that follows, he shows us how sometimes everything can turn on the simplest things: the flip of a coin, say, or whether a ball is dropped or caught. And when we say everything—we mean everything.

It's July in Detroit, a Thursday afternoon in 1940. I am twelve years old. From my seat in the left-field upper deck at Briggs Stadium, I can look over my shoulder and see the General Motors Building towering over Woodward Avenue. Cars stream up and down Michigan Avenue, Fords and Chevrolets and Buicks and the occasional Nash, many driven by the same hands that built them. I look at my hands and imagine that they will become autoworker's hands, large-knuckled and scarred, grime worked so deep into the wrinkles that even Lava soap will never get it out.

My father's shadow falls across me. He sits on my right and balances three mustard-slathered hot dogs on his lap. I look at his hands and try to count the dozens of pale round pinhole scars that mark his wrists and forearms. My father works for the Ford Motor Company as a welder. He is thirty-one years old and seems to me to contain all the knowledge in the world.

I take a hot dog and devour it in three bites, then reach for another. "Christ, kid," my father says around a mouthful. "You and Babe Ruth. Tell you what, why don't we flip for this one and I'll go get another at the seventh-inning stretch?"

On the field, Schoolboy Rowe is warming up before the fourth and the Boston Red Sox are milling around the steps of their dugout. Rowe is throwing well and the Bosox are in a bit of a slump; still, three innings could take forty minutes. I am twelve years old. I could starve to death in forty minutes.

"Deal," I say.

Dad flips a quarter.

Heisenberg's Uncertainty Principle states that the act of observing an object displaces that object, so that its true position and direction cannot both be determined at once. Or so we were taught in high school.

The Baseball Encyclopedia states that Moe Berg hit six home runs in a major-league career spanning parts of thirteen seasons with four teams. It was said of him that he could speak twelve languages, but couldn't hit in any of them; Berg was the most scholarly of baseball players, and he made joking notes about Heisenberg's Uncertainty Principle while he watched the man himself lecture in Switzerland during World War II, all the while deciding whether or not to kill him. I think Moe Berg would understand the subtle shifts my memories of him undergo every time I dredge them up from my seventy years' worth of neurochemical silt.

I was Moe Berg's biggest fan in 1940, even though he'd sort of officially retired at the end of the '39 season. Like him, I loved baseball, and like him, I loved to read—a combination unusual among twelve-year-olds as it is in major-league clubhouses. I even went so far as to adopt some of his eccentricities. When I found out that he wouldn't read a newspaper that someone else had touched, I demanded that I be the first in our house to get the Free Press off the porch. Nobody else could touch the sports section until I'd gotten a look at the box scores. Only virgin agate type for this devotee of the national pastime.

Berg stayed on with the Red Sox as a warm-up catcher and a kind of team guru, but never played a game after 1939, and by the time the war heated up, he was Agent Berg of the OSS. His photographs of Tokyo, taken on a goodwill tour of American baseball players just before the war, guided Jimmy Doolittle's bombers, and his good sense saved Werner Heisenberg's life.

At least, that's what the history books say. I remember things a little differently.

I remember, for example, Moe Berg's seventh home run.

I call tails. The quarter glitters through its arc over my dad's hand, looking like any number of slow-motion coin flips I've seen in fifty years of movies since then. Dad catches it in his right hand, slaps it onto the back of his left. "You sure?"

I nod. He takes away his hand. It's tails.

"Here you go," Dad says. The last hot dog is gone before Rowe has taken his eighth warm-up.

And then, would you believe it, Moe Berg steps to the plate. The Tigers public-address announcer sounds like he can't believe it either; his voice hesitates, and is momentarily lost in the echoes of his last word. "Sox, sox, ox, ox, ox." The crowd stirs, and people look up from their scorecards to see if it could actually be Moe Berg taking a last practice cut and scuffing dirt away from the back of the batter's box. Baseball fans are always alert to the possibility of history being made.

For me, Berg's appearance is better than a ticket to the World Series. I take off my Tiger cap and look at his autograph, scrawled across the underside of the bill last August. I'd had to fight my way through the crowd around Ted Williams to get near the dugout, and Berg was just sitting on the corner of the dugout steps, rolling a quarter across the backs of his fingers and watching the crowd for pretty girls. When I'd leaned over the railing to hand him my cap, he'd cracked a smile at the Old English D. "You know what an agent provocateur is, kid?"

"No sir," I said, "but I'll go home and look it up after the game."

His smile broadened just a bit, and he scribbled his name on my cap and tossed it back to me.

Now he stands in, and Rowe fires a dipping fastball at the knees. Berg watches it go by, shakes his head, waits on the next pitch.

And smokes it out to left-center.

I'm on my feet cheering even before it occurs to me that the ball might have home-run distance. The ball reaches the peak of its arc, and the two Tiger out-fielders slow to a jog, watching it head for the fence. Head for me. I remember thinking that: it's heading right for me. I reach up, watching the ball curve a bit as it sails down out of the sky and worrying that it'll go over my head. I don't have my glove, but otherwise for the longest second of my life it's just like the field behind Estabrook school, watching the ball and hearing my dad's voice in my head. Keep your eye on it, look it in. Two hands.

The sound of the ball hitting my palms is almost exactly like the sound of my dad smacking the quarter onto the back of his hand. Someone bumps into me and I fall between the rows of seats. On the way down I bang my head, hard, on a seat or someone's knee, and fold up like Max Schmeling. But I'm not completely out, I'm still cradling the ball like one of the eggs the high-school girls have to carry around for their home-ec projects. My dad hauls me to my feet, and the knot of fans around me disperses as quickly as it converged. A few people slap me on the back and say, "Nice catch."

"Look at you, Avery my boy," Dad says. "You eat all my hot dogs and catch a home run."

"A Moe Berg home run," I say, looking at the ball. An oblong smudge covers part of the Spalding logo. Moe Berg's bat was there, I think. It's almost as good as shaking hands with him. I look up and he's rounding third, two of him, accepting a laughing double handshake from the twinned third-base coach.

It's like a dream. Berg starts to get blurry, and there is a roaring in my ears, and my father says something else but I'm too busy falling down to hear him.

And then it is a dream, or anyway it's different. Avery isn't in the ballpark any more, and his father isn't around; in fact, nobody is. He's alone in a room that seems to have walls, a ceiling, and a floor, but when he looks at them he can't quite tell whether or not they're there.

No, he's not alone. There's a man in the room. Like the walls, his face is indistinct, but Avery can tell he's wearing a tuxedo like the one in his parents' wedding picture.

"What just happened didn't really happen," the man says.

Avery is twelve years old. "Sure it did," he says. "I was there."

"Where was there?"

"Briggs Stadium, at the ball game. I caught this ball," Avery says, holding it up to him so the man will have to believe him. He has the ball, therefore there was a home run.

Only the ball is a quarter, like the one Avery's dad flipped for the hot dog. A 1936 quarter, with three short parallel gouges across the eagle's right wing.

"Where's my ball?" Avery looks around the room.

"There is no ball. What you have is what you caught."

"Come on," Avery says scornfully. "Ted Williams couldn't hit a quarter out of the park. Hank Greenberg couldn't. Jimmie Foxx couldn't. You expect me to believe Moe Berg did?"

"What do you have in your hand?"

"A quarter."

"Then that must be what you caught."

"No way. You stole it, didn't you? You stole my ball."

"Avery. Listen to me. There's a reason it's a quarter."

"Sure there is. It's a quarter because you stole my ball and you're such a cheap-skate you only gave me a quarter for it." Avery throws the quarter at the man, but it stops halfway between them, spinning in the air just as it did on its way through the summer air in Briggs Stadium.

"Now you've done it," the man says.

Where am I going, where have I been, how do I know both at once? I'm seventy-two years old, retired from the GM Proving Grounds in Milford, Michigan, to a seaside cottage in Seal Harbor, Maine. The Tigers have won three World Series since the day I saw (or didn't see) Moe Berg's home run—in '45, '68, and '84. The Red Sox haven't won any. The four years they've gone, they've lost in seven games every damn time. The last time was 1986, when Red Sox Nation really thought the Curse had been lifted; but after Mookie Wilson's seeing-eye grounder found its way through Bill Buckner's legs, it would almost have been better if the Angels had beaten the Sox in the AL playoffs. At least then . . . but if, if, if. "If chickens had lips," my dad used to say, "they would whistle." No use speculating on ifs. It wasn't easy growing up a Red Sox fan in Detroit, but I managed, mostly because, as with Moe Berg's autograph under the bill of my Tiger cap, I kept my allegiance carefully hidden.

In summer, I take a radio out on my porch and listen to the Sox while watching the waves come in from the North Atlantic. Waves crash on every shore, and I wonder every single day if there's some kind of middle point from which waves radiate in every direction. The still point of the turning world, as Eliot put it. The place where choices resolve into certainties.

If there is such a place, I would like very much to see it, to know it exists. I would like very much to know whether or not my choice killed my father.

"Done what?" Avery says.

"The quarter's in the air. Now you'll have to make a call before it comes down."

"Why?" Avery looks at the man again, and he's sitting in a chair that wasn't there a minute ago. The quarter spins at his eye level.

"To decide what happens."

"What am I deciding?"

"You have two choices to make, Avery. Only one depends on the coin, so we'll deal with the other one first. Let me tell you a story." The man shifts in the chair, getting comfortable. "In a year and a half, America will be at war with Germany and Japan."

"No we won't," Avery says. "Roosevelt said we were staying out of it."

"Yes, he did. But it will happen anyway."

"How do you know?"

"Because that's what I do. I know. In fact, you might say that's what I am. Someone who knows."

Avery squints at the man, trying to make his face stay still long enough to get a look at it. "Someone who knows, huh? Well, do you know what you look like?"

"You're misunderstanding. Avery, I only look like this because that's the easiest way for you to see me."

"It'd be easier if you had a face," Avery says.

"Fine," the man says. "Give me one."

"It's that easy?" The man nods. "Okay." And the man has Avery's father's face.

"Are you more comfortable now?" the man says.

"Tell me what you mean, 'someone who knows.'"

"I mean that I didn't exist until a particular thing had to be known. When I know what needs to be known, then I will no longer exist."

Avery is catching on. "So you only exist as long as you don't know what you need to know?"

The man with Avery's father's face nods.

"Tell me the story," Avery says.

It is easy to be retired in the nineties, especially when you've had the career I did. You collect your retirement and your Social Security. You try to make day lilies grow on the Maine seacoast. You take morning hikes with your wife in Acadia National Park. If you get bored, you do consulting for people in the automotive industry.

I cannot get bored, because when I get bored I start thinking about Moe Berg, quarters, afternoons in July when my father would use a sick day and take me to ball games.

I have earned a lot of money from consulting work.

My wife's name is Donna. She's a little taller than I am, and a lot thinner, and her hair is exactly the color of a full moon high in a winter sky. We've been married for thirty-seven years, and I don't think I know how to love another woman any more. She wants me to slow down a little, enjoy the golden years. She wants to know why I don't want to go to Europe. We are happy together, and our children haven't turned up on any talk shows to claim abuse or neglect.

I wish I could tell Donna why I don't want to go to Europe, but I've hidden that away like an enemy autograph under the bill of a sweat-stained Detroit Tigers baseball cap.

Moe Berg died in New York in 1972, outliving my father by twenty-eight years. After his death, Donna and I went to New York for the first time.

"There is a scientist named Werner Heisenberg," the man with Avery's father's face says.

"Is he German?" The man nods. "So we'll be at war with him," Avery says.

"Yes. Heisenberg is already very famous as a scientist, and when the war starts, he will work for the Nazis trying to split the atom and develop an atomic bomb. Here is the choice you must make: does Moe Berg kill this man Heisenberg or not?"

"Moe Berg kill somebody? He's a baseball player."

"Presently, yes. But when the war breaks out, he will join the Office of Strategic Services and act as a spy for the United States. One of his assignments, in 1944, will be to attend a lecture given by Heisenberg. Berg will have been instructed to shoot Heisenberg if he believes that the Nazis are nearly able to construct an atomic bomb."

"You're crazy," Avery says. "I read about atomic bombs in Astounding. There's no such thing."

"There will be."

Still dubious, Avery says, "Even if there is, what's that got to do with my ball?"

"If Moe Berg hits another home run, he will play more often this season. Being a little old for the Army, he will play next season as well, and the OSS will hire someone in his place. The man that they hire and send to Heisenberg's lecture will kill Heisenberg."

"Big deal," Avery says. "If there is such a thing as an atomic bomb, we sure don't want Hitler to have it."

"But what if killing Heisenberg has no influence on the Nazis' ability to build an atomic bomb before the United States does? Then a brilliant scientist will have been assassinated for no gain." Avery doesn't say anything, and the man continues. "If Heisenberg's assassination is successful, other German physicists will be targeted. The result of this will be that the men who would have built America's space program will either be dead or frightened into going to Russia when the war ends."

"Space program?" Avery is suddenly excited. He's just read H. G. Wells's The First Men in the Moon a month ago, and if atomic bombs, why not men on the moon? "Are we going to the moon?" His mind fills with images of sleek, silvery rockets, blasting off into space. With him aboard. He will be an astronaut.

"That depends, Avery. There are many possibilities, but this much is certain: if Heisenberg is killed, the people who first set foot on the moon will not be American. And perhaps no one will at all."

Avery is silent, staring at the floor that isn't quite a floor. More like a lot of different floors, each of which is almost there but not quite. "How do you know all this?" he asks.

"I don't know. Before you arrived here, I didn't exist. When you leave, I won't exist. But as long as this particular uncertainty persists, so do I."

"Does it matter who lands on the moon?" Avery asks.

"Perhaps not. But it might matter very much who has the first atomic bomb."

Avery watches the quarter spinning. If he moves a bit to one side or the other, he can make it look like the man with his father's face has quarters for eyes. A Moe Berg home-run ball; something to tell the guys about. He thinks.

"Okay," Avery says after a while. "You can have the ball."

Sometimes the moon looks like a coin, its endless maria spreading their eagle wings across the landscape. On summer nights I wait for it to rise above the distortion near the horizon, and then I sit up late thinking that the moon spins just like that quarter did. Full, gibbous, half, fingernail, new. After a summer of late nights I have a time-lapse movie in my head, and sometimes when I dream the man with my father's face has moons for eyes. They flicker like film that isn't moving quite fast enough to fool the eye.

Heads or tails. Fifty-fifty. Position or velocity. The cat is alive, the cat is dead. But if you flip a coin ten times, you don't often get five of each. I flip coins a lot, especially when it's summer and I'm up late and there's a fingernail moon.

Werner Heisenberg: Nazi or good citizen doing what he thought was right? Fifty-fifty. Most of his biographers and all of his friends say that he was simply a German, and when his country was at war he was duty-bound to build them an atomic pile. I wonder sometimes how much thought he gave to what Hitler would do with an atomic bomb.

On December 15, 1944, Heisenberg gave a lecture on S-matrix theory at ETH in Zurich. Moe Berg was there, posing as a Swiss student, an Arab businessman, or a French merchant, depending on whose account you believe. This is uncertainty: you can know that Moe Berg was in a place, but not how he got there. Were there Saudi businessmen or Dijonnese merchants? Certainly there were Swiss students. And certainly there was Moe Berg, agent provocateur.

I imagine the scene. Heisenberg, red-haired, balding, gnomish, looking older than his years, paces in front of a blackboard as he speaks. His left hand never leaves his pocket. In the audience, Berg listens attentively, taking notes. As I listen, Berg writes, I am uncertain—see: Heisenberg's uncertainty principle—what to do to H. He jokes with himself: discussing math while Rome burns. An automatic pistol weighs down Berg's coat pocket, and a cyanide capsule slides back and forth in the watch pocket of his trousers when he shifts his weight.

Heisenberg speaks, Berg watches, and a coin spins in the air.

"Does that stop the war?" Avery asks. "If I give the ball back?"

"No, the war will happen. But your choice can change the way it ends, and what happens after."

Avery has been thinking. "Why?" he asks. "Just because I caught a ball?"

"Partially." The man shifts, and his right eye becomes a spinning quarter. "Think of ripples. A stone falls in water; how far do the ripples go?"

"Until they hit something else," Avery says. He thinks of his grandfather's cottage up north, near Traverse City. There is a pond in the woods near the cottage, and Avery catches frogs there. He is seeing the ripples the frogs make when they escape him into the brown water.

"The ball you caught is a stone thrown into the frog pond of history, if you'll pardon my borrowing your image," the man says. "The ripples thrown out by its fall come into contact with a sequence of other events."

"How do you know what I'm thinking?" Avery asks.

"In one sense," the man says, "I am what you're thinking. Or, more precisely, what you would be thinking if you had more information than you possess at the game."

Avery pauses for a long time, watching the quarter spin. "Are you me?"

"You'll have to forgive me, Avery," the man says. The expression on his face reminds Avery of the time he asked his father how eyelashes knew when to stop growing. "I only know so much."

"But you know about this war that hasn't happened, and you're telling me about atomic bombs and going to the moon," Avery protests. "How do you know one thing and not something else?"

"Because some things haven't been decided yet. Call the toss, Avery."

"Not until you tell me where I am. Where we are."

"We aren't anywhere. For us to be somewhere, you would have to have made a decision. And when you've made a decision, I won't be here. I won't be anywhere. I only exist in the space of your uncertainty."

"Who are you, then? Are you God or something?"

The man shakes his head.

"Did God send you? Is there a God? How come He doesn't decide this instead of leaving it to me?"

Still shaking his head, the man says, "I can't answer any of those questions. I have told you all I can. You've already ensured that Moe Berg will attend Heisenberg's lecture; now you decide what will happen when he does."

"No," Avery says. "All I'm doing is calling a coin toss. I gave you the ball. That was a decision. This isn't."

"True. It has to happen this way, though. Conservation of information. I violated causality by telling you what would happen as a result of your last choice. Now you have to choose without knowing, even though I could tell you, so it balances out." Something flickers on his face, Avery's father's face. It looks like guilt.

"What am I deciding?"

"Whether Moe Berg kills Werner Heisenberg."

"It's not fair," Avery says. "That's why I gave you the ball, so Heisenberg wouldn't get killed. Stupid German. I should have kept the ball. Why couldn't I keep the ball and call the toss?"

"I already explained that. Call the toss, Avery. Collapse the wave function," the man says. "Either it happens or it doesn't."

"Tails," Avery says. And it is.

And I am back in Briggs Stadium with Bobby Doerr leading off the fourth inning, and my father holding me up with his scarred welder's hands. "Avery," he says. "You okay, son?"

"Yeah, Dad. I'm okay." I look around at Briggs Stadium, at the worn patches in the outfield, the flakes of rust on the bolts that hold the seats in the concrete floors. I have done something, I realize. It is all the same, but it will be different.

My father looks closely at me, concern in his eyes. "I'm okay, Dad," I insist.

"Okay, bud," he says. "That was your last hot dog for the day, though."

I feel the back of my head. No lump, no sore spot, no nothing. The Tigers lose, there are no home runs hit to left-center, and the next time I read a newspaper article about Moe Berg, it says he hit six home runs over the course of a major-league career that ended in 1939.

And Werner Heisenberg dies in Munich at the ripe old age of seventy-five, and atomic bombs fall on Hiroshima and Nagasaki, and Neil Armstrong lands on the moon instead of a man named Yevgeny or Sergei or Yuri.

And my father dies in World War II, on December 11, 1944, when a plane that had recently carried Moe Berg to France crashes in the English Channel.

I was forty-one years old, watching on television from my new house in Farmington Hills, when Neil Armstrong spoke from the surface of the moon. The Tigers had won the World Series the year before, salving the wounds from the '67 riots that prompted me, like so many other white folks, to leave for the suburbs. I had long since given up on being an astronaut.

My father had been dead for nearly twenty-five years.

Ripples, the man with my father's face had said. Ripples propagate until they run into something, or until entropy robs them of their energy and they subside back into the flat surface of the water. I caught a ball once, at Briggs Stadium in the summer of 1940, and my father helped me up and said, "Look at you, Avery my boy."

Look at me, Dad. Briggs Stadium has been Tiger Stadium for thirty-five years now, and the welder's son from East Detroit became an executive with a custom-built home in the suburbs, and I saved Werner Heisenberg's life, and maybe I cost you yours.

I sit on the porch of my house in Maine, watching the waves come in and wondering where they come from. I wonder where the still point is, the place where waves are born and decisions hang between heads and tails.

Sometimes I talk to myself. More often I fall asleep and the sea breeze brings me dreams of men who are almost my father.

When I talk to myself, this is the question: If you had called heads, would your father be alive? If Moe Berg had never gone to France with Werner Heisenberg's life in his hands, a different plane would have been waiting for Dad at the cratered airstrip outside of Lyon.

Would that other plane have crashed?

I was twelve years old. I thought I did the right thing.

Would Moe Berg's seventh home run have put my father on a different plane?

The cat is alive. The cat is dead.

The Red Sox are playing a twi-night doubleheader tonight. Donna comes outside and sits next to me in the Adirondack chair I built for her the year I retired. She touches me on the back of the neck, then reads in the waning afternoon. I watch the shadow of my chimney crawl down the sloping lawn into the quiet surf, for just this moment content to know where I am, for just this moment content to believe in where I have been. The still point of the turning world. Waves come in like epicycles rippling through the larger cycles of tides, and the moon's revolution around the Earth, and the Earth's revolution around the sun.

Coins spinning, waiting for someone to call the toss.

singleton

GREG EGAN

Looking back at the century that's just ended, it's obvious that Australian writer Greg Egan was one of the Big New Names to emerge in SF in the nineties, and is probably one of the most significant talents to enter the field in the last several decades. Already one of the most widely known of all Australian genre writers, Egan may well be the best new "hard-science" writer to enter the field since Greg Bear, and is still growing in range, power, and sophistication. In the last few years, he has become a frequent contributor to Interzone and Asimov's Science Fiction, and has made sales as well as to Pulphouse, Analog, Aurealis, Eidolon, and elsewhere; many of his stories have also appeared in various "Best of the Year" series, and he was on the Hugo Final Ballot in 1995 for his story "Cocoon," which won the Ditmar Award and the Asimov's Readers Award. He won the Hugo Award in 1999 for his novella "Oceanic." His stories have appeared in our Eighth through Thirteenth, and our Sixteenth through Eighteenth Annual Collections. His first novel, Quarantine, appeared in 1992; his second novel, Permutation City, won the John W. Campbell Memorial Award in 1994. His other books include the novels, Distress, Diaspora, and Teranesia, and three collections of his short fiction, Axiomatic, Luminous, and Our Lady of Chernobyl. His most recent book is a major new novel, Schild's Ladder. He has a Web site at http://www.netspace.net.au/~gregegan/

Suppose that you could ensure that your child was unique . . . no, really unique. That would be a good thing, wouldn't it?

Wouldn't it?

2003

I was walking north along George Street towards Town Hall railway station, pondering the ways I might solve the tricky third question of my linear algebra assignment, when I encountered a small crowd blocking the footpath. I didn't give much thought to the reason they were standing there; I'd just passed a busy restaurant, and I often saw groups of people gathered outside. But once I'd started to make my way around them, moving into an alley rather than stepping out into the traffic, it became apparent that they were not just diners from a farewell lunch for a retiring colleague, putting off their return to the office for as long as possible. I could see for myself exactly what was holding their attention.

Twenty metres down the alley, a man was lying on his back on the ground, shielding his bloodied face with his hands, while two men stood over him, relentlessly swinging narrow sticks of some kind. At first I thought the sticks were pool cues, but then I noticed the metal hooks on the ends. I'd only ever seen these obscure weapons before in one other place: my primary school, where an appointed window monitor would use them at the start and end of each day. They were meant for opening and closing an old-fashioned kind of hinged pane when it was too high to reach with your hands.

I turned to the other spectators. "Has anyone called the police?" A woman nodded without looking at me, and said, "Someone used their mobile, a couple of minutes ago."

The assailants must have realized that the police were on their way, but it seemed they were too committed to their task to abandon it until that was absolutely necessary. They were facing away from the crowd, so perhaps they weren't entirely reckless not to fear identification. The man on the ground was dressed like a kitchen hand. He was still moving, trying to protect himself, but he was making less noise than his attackers; the need, or the ability, to cry out in pain had been beaten right out of him.

As for calling for help, he could have saved his breath.

A chill passed through my body, a sick cold churning sensation that came a moment before the conscious realization: *I'm going to watch someone murdered, and I'm going to do nothing.* But this wasn't a drunken brawl, where a few bystanders could step in and separate the combatants; the two assailants had to be serious criminals, settling a score. Keeping your distance from something like that was just common sense. I'd go to court, I'd be a witness, but no one could expect anything more of me. Not when 30 other people had behaved in exactly the same way.

The men in the alley did not have guns. If they'd had guns, they would have used them by now. They weren't going to mow down anyone who got in their way. It was one thing not to make a martyr of yourself, but how many people could these two grunting slobs fend off with sticks?

I unstrapped my backpack and put it on the ground. Absurdly, that made me feel more vulnerable; I was always worried about losing my textbooks. *Think about this. You don't know what you're doing.* I hadn't been in so much as a fist fight since I was 13. I glanced at the strangers around me, wondering if anyone would join in if I implored them to rush forward together. But that wasn't going to happen. I was a willowy, unimposing 18-year-old, wearing a T-shirt adorned with Maxwell's Equations. I had no presence, no authority. No one would follow me into the fray.

Alone, I'd be as helpless as the guy on the ground. These men would crack my skull open in an instant. There were half a dozen solid-looking office workers in their 20s in the crowd; if these weekend rugby players hadn't felt competent to intervene, what chance did I have?

I reached down for my backpack. If I wasn't going to help, there was no point being here at all. I'd find out what had happened on the evening news.

I started to retrace my steps, sick with self-loathing. This wasn't *kristallnacht*. There'd be no embarrassing questions from my grandchildren. No one would ever reproach me.

As if that were the measure of everything.

"Fuck it." I dropped my backpack and ran down the alley.

I was close enough to smell the three sweating bodies over the stench of rotting garbage before I was even noticed. The nearest of the attackers glanced over his shoulder, affronted, then amused. He didn't bother redeploying his weapon in mid-stroke; as I hooked an arm around his neck in the hope of overbalancing him, he thrust his elbow into my chest, winding me. I clung on desperately, maintaining the hold even though I couldn't tighten it. As he tried to prise himself loose, I managed to kick his feet out from under him. We both went down onto the asphalt; I ended up beneath him.

The man untangled himself and clambered to his feet. As I struggled to right myself, picturing a metal hook swinging into my face, someone whistled. I looked up to see the second man gesturing to his companion, and I followed his gaze. A dozen men and women were coming down the alley, advancing together at a brisk walk. It was not a particularly menacing sight—I'd seen angrier crowds with peace signs painted on their faces—but the sheer numbers were enough to guarantee some inconvenience. The first man hung back long enough to kick me in the ribs. Then the two of them fled.

I brought my knees up, then raised my head and got into a crouch. I was still winded, but for some reason it seemed vital not to remain flat on my back. One of the office workers grinned down at me. "You fuckwit. You could have got killed."

The kitchen hand shuddered, and snorted bloody mucus. His eyes were swollen shut, and when he laid his hands down beside him, I could see the bones of his knuckles through the torn skin. My own skin turned icy, at this vision of the fate I'd courted for myself. But if it was a shock to realize how I might have ended up, it was just as sobering to think that I'd almost walked away and let them finish him off, when the intervention had actually cost me nothing.

I rose to my feet. People milled around the kitchen hand, asking each other about first aid. I remembered the basics from a course I'd done in high school, but the man was still breathing, and he wasn't losing vast amounts of blood, so I couldn't think of anything helpful that an amateur could do in the circumstances. I squeezed my way out of the gathering and walked back to the street. My backpack was exactly where I'd left it; no one had stolen my books. I heard sirens approaching; the police and the ambulance would be there soon.

My ribs were tender, but I wasn't in agony. I'd cracked a rib falling off a trail bike on the farm when I was twelve, and I was fairly sure that this was just bruising. For a while I walked bent over, but by the time I reached the station I found I could adopt a normal gait. I had some grazed skin on my arms, but I couldn't have appeared too battered, because no one on the train looked at me twice.

That night, I watched the news. The kitchen hand was described as being in a stable condition. I pictured him stepping out into the alley to empty a bucket of fish-heads into the garbage, to find the two of them waiting for him. I'd probably never learn what the attack had been about unless the case went to trial, and as yet the police hadn't even named any suspects. If the man had been in a fit state to talk in the alley, I might have asked him then, but any sense that I was entitled to an explanation was rapidly fading.

The reporter mentioned a student "leading the charge of angry citizens" who'd rescued the kitchen hand, and then she spoke to an eye witness, who described this young man as "a New Ager, wearing some kind of astrological symbols on his shirt." I snorted, then looked around nervously in case one of my housemates had made the improbable connection, but no one else was even in earshot.

Then the story was over.

I felt flat for a moment, cheated of the minor rush that 15 seconds' fame might have delivered; it was like reaching into a biscuit tin when you thought there was one more chocolate chip left, to find that there actually wasn't. I considered phoning my parents in Orange, just to talk to them from within the strange afterglow, but I'd established a routine and it was not the right day. If I called unexpectedly, they'd think something was wrong.

So, that was it. In a week's time, when the bruises had faded, I'd look back and doubt that the incident had ever happened.

I went upstairs to finish my assignment.

Francine said, "There's a nicer way to think about this. If you do a change of variables, from x and y to z and z-conjugate, the Cauchy-Riemann equations correspond to the condition that the partial derivative of the function with respect to z-conjugate is equal to zero."

We were sitting in the coffee shop, discussing the complex analysis lecture we'd had half an hour before. Half a dozen of us from the same course had got into the habit of meeting at this time every week, but today the others had failed to turn up. Maybe there was a movie being screened, or a speaker appearing on campus that I hadn't heard about.

I worked through the transformation she'd described. "You're right," I said. "That's really elegant!"

Francine nodded slightly in assent, while retaining her characteristic jaded look. She had an undisguisable passion for mathematics, but she was probably bored out of her skull in class, waiting for the lecturers to catch up and teach her something she didn't already know.

I was nowhere near her level. In fact, I'd started the year poorly, distracted by my new surroundings: nothing so glamorous as the temptations of the night life, just the different sights and sounds and scale of the place, along with the bureaucratic demands of all the organizations that now impinged upon my life, from the university itself down to the shared house groceries subcommittee. In the last few weeks, though, I'd finally started hitting my stride. I'd got a part-time job, stacking shelves in a supermarket; the pay was lousy, but it was enough to take the edge off my financial anxieties, and the hours weren't so long that they left me with no time for anything but study.

I doodled harmonic contours on the notepaper in front of me. "So what do you do for fun?" I said. "Apart from complex analysis?"

Francine didn't reply immediately. This wasn't the first time we'd been alone together, but I'd never felt confident that I had the right words to make the most of the situation. At some point, though, I'd stopped fooling myself that there was ever going to be a perfect moment, with the perfect phrase falling from my lips: something subtle but intriguing slipped deftly into the conversation, without disrupting the flow. So now I'd made my interest plain, with no attempt at artfulness or eloquence. She could judge me as she knew me from the last three months, and if she felt no desire to know me better, I would not be crushed.

"I write a lot of Perl scripts," she said. "Nothing complicated; just odds and ends that I give away as freeware. It's very relaxing."

I nodded understandingly. I didn't think she was being deliberately discouraging; she just expected me to be slightly more direct.

"Do you like Deborah Conway?" I'd only heard a couple of her songs on the radio myself, but a few days before I'd seen a poster in the city announcing a tour.

"Yeah. She's great."

I started thickening the conjugation bars over the variables I'd scrawled. "She's playing at a club in Surrey Hills," I said. "On Friday. Would you like to go?"

Francine smiled, making no effort now to appear world-weary. "Sure. That would be nice."

I smiled back. I wasn't giddy, I wasn't moonstruck, but I felt as if I was standing on the shore of an ocean, contemplating its breadth. I felt the way I felt when I opened a sophisticated monograph in the library, and was reduced to savouring the scent of the print and the crisp symmetry of the notation, understanding only a fraction of what I read. Knowing there was something glorious ahead, but knowing too what a daunting task it would be to come to terms with it.

I said, "I'll get the tickets on my way home."

To celebrate the end of exams for the year, the household threw a party. It was a sultry November night, but the backyard wasn't much bigger than the largest room in the house, so we ended up opening all the doors and windows and distributing food and furniture throughout the ground floor and the exterior, front and back. Once the faint humid breeze off the river penetrated the depths of the house, it was equally sweltering and mosquito-ridden everywhere, indoors and out.

Francine and I stayed close for an hour or so, obeying the distinctive dynamics of a couple, until by some unspoken mutual understanding it became clear that we could wander apart for a while, and that neither of us was so insecure that we'd resent it.

I ended up in a corner of the crowded backyard, talking to Will, a biochemistry student who'd lived in the house for the last four years. On some level, he probably couldn't help feeling that his opinions about the way things were run should carry more weight than anyone else's, which had annoyed me greatly when I'd first moved in. We'd since become friends, though, and I was glad to have a chance to talk to him before he left to take up a scholarship in Germany.

In the middle of a conversation about the work he'd be doing, I caught sight of Francine, and he followed my gaze.

Will said, "It took me a while to figure out what finally cured you of your homesickness."

"I was never homesick."

"Yeah, right." He took a swig of his drink. "She's changed you, though. You have to admit that."

"I do. Happily. Everything's clicked, since we got together." Relationships were meant to screw up your studies, but my marks were soaring. Francine didn't tutor me; she just drew me into a state of mind where everything was clearer.

"The amazing thing is that you got together at all." I scowled, and Will raised a hand placatingly. "I just meant, when you first moved in, you were pretty reserved. And down on yourself. When we interviewed you for the room, you practically begged us to give it to someone more deserving."

"Now you're taking the piss."

He shook his head. "Ask any of the others."

I fell silent. The truth was, if I took a step back and contemplated my situation, I was as astonished as he was. By the time I'd left my hometown, it had become clear to me that good fortune had nothing much to do with luck. Some people were born with wealth, or talent, or charisma. They started with an edge, and the benefits snowballed. I'd always believed that I had, at best, just enough intelligence and persistence to stay afloat in my chosen field; I'd topped every class in high school, but in a town the size of Orange that meant nothing, and I'd had no illusions about my fate in Sydney.

I owed it to Francine that my visions of mediocrity had not been fulfilled; being with her had transformed my life. But where had I found the nerve to imagine that I had anything to offer her in return?

"Something happened," I admitted. "Before I asked her out."

"Yeah?"

I almost clammed up; I hadn't told anyone about the events in the alley, not even Francine. The incident had come to seem too personal, as if to recount it at all would be to lay my conscience bare. But Will was off to Munich in less than a week, and it was easier to confide in someone I didn't expect to see again.

When I finished, Will bore a satisfied grin, as if I'd explained everything. "Pure karma," he announced. "I should have guessed."

"Oh, very scientific."

"I'm serious. Forget the Buddhist mystobabble; I'm talking about the real thing. If you stick to your principles, of course things go better for you—assuming you don't get killed in the process. That's elementary psychology. People have a highly developed sense of reciprocity, of the appropriateness of the treatment they receive from each other. If things work out too well for them, they can't help asking, 'What did I do to deserve this?' If you don't have a good answer, you'll sabotage yourself. Not all the time, but often enough. So if you do something that improves your self-esteem—"

"Self-esteem is for the weak," I quipped. Will rolled his eyes. "I don't think like that," I protested.

"No? Why did you even bring it up, then?"

I shrugged. "Maybe it just made me less pessimistic. I could have had the crap beaten out of me, but I didn't. That makes asking someone to a concert seem a lot less dangerous." I was beginning to cringe at all this unwanted analysis, and I had nothing to counter Will's pop psychology except an equally folksy version of my own.

He could see I was embarrassed, so he let the matter drop. As I watched Francine moving through the crowd, though, I couldn't shake off an unsettling sense of the tenuousness of the circumstances that had brought us together. There was no denying that if I'd walked away from the alley, and the kitchen hand had died, I would have felt like shit for a long time afterwards. I would not have felt entitled to much out of my own life.

I hadn't walked away, though. And even if the decision had come down to the wire, why shouldn't I be proud that I'd made the right choice? That didn't mean everything that followed was tainted, like a reward from some sleazy, palm-greasing deity. I hadn't won Francine's affection in a medieval test of bravery; we'd chosen each other, and persisted with that choice, for a thousand complicated reasons.

We were together now; that was what mattered. I wasn't going to dwell on the path that had brought me to her, just to dredge up all the doubts and insecurities that had almost kept us apart.

2012

As we drove the last kilometre along the road south from Ar Rafidiyah, I could see the Wall of Foam glistening ahead of us in the morning sunlight. Insubstantial as a pile of soap bubbles, but still intact, after six weeks.

"I can't believe it's lasted this long," I told Sadiq.

"You didn't trust the models?"

"Fuck, no. Every week, I thought we'd come over the hill and there'd be nothing but a shrivelled-up cobweb."

Sadiq smiled. "So you had no faith in my calculations?"

"Don't take it personally. There were a lot of things we could have both got wrong."

Sadiq pulled off the road. His students, Hassan and Rashid, had climbed off the back of the truck and started towards the Wall before I'd even got my face mask on. Sadiq called them back, and made them put on plastic boots and paper suits over their clothes, while the two of us did the same. We didn't usually bother with this much protection, but today was different.

Close up, the Wall almost vanished: all you noticed were isolated, rainbow-fringed reflections, drifting at a leisurely pace across the otherwise invisible film as water redistributed itself, following waves induced in the membrane by the interplay of air pressure, thermal gradients, and surface tension. These images might easily have been separate objects, scraps of translucent plastic blowing around above the desert, held aloft by a breeze too faint to detect at ground level.

The further away you looked, though, the more crowded the hints of light became, and the less plausible any alternative hypothesis that denied the Wall its integrity. It stretched for a kilometre along the edge of the desert, and rose an uneven 15 to 20 metres into the air. But it was merely the first, and smallest, of its kind, and the time had come to put it on the back of the truck and drive it all the way back to Basra.

Sadiq took a spray can of reagent from the cabin, and shook it as he walked down the embankment. I followed him, my heart in my mouth. The Wall had not dried out; it had not been torn apart or blown away, but there was still plenty of room for failure.

Sadiq reached up and sprayed what appeared from my vantage to be thin air, but I could see the fine mist of droplets strike the membrane. A breathy susurration rose up, like the sound from a steam iron, and I felt a faint warm dampness before the first silken threads appeared, crisscrossing the region where the polymer from which the Wall was built had begun to shift conformations. In one state, the polymer was soluble, exposing hydrophilic groups of atoms that bound water into narrow sheets of feather-light gel. Now, triggered by the reagent and powered by sunlight, it was tucking these groups into slick, oily cages, and expelling every molecule of water, transforming the gel into a desiccated web.

I just hoped it wasn't expelling anything else.

As the lacy net began to fall in folds at his feet, Hassan said something in Arabic, disgusted and amused. My grasp of the language remained patchy; Sadiq translated for me, his voice muffled by his face mask: "He says probably most of the weight of the thing will be dead insects." He shooed the youths back towards the truck before following himself, as the wind blew a glistening curtain over our heads. It descended far too slowly to trap us, but I hastened up the slope.

We watched from the truck as the Wall came down, the wave of dehydration propagating along its length. If the gel had been an elusive sight close up, the residue was entirely invisible in the distance; there was less substance to it than a very long pantyhose—albeit, pantyhose clogged with gnats.

The smart polymer was the invention of Sonja Helvig, a Norwegian chemist; I'd tweaked her original design for this application. Sadiq and his students were civil engineers, responsible for scaling everything up to the point where it could have a practical benefit. On those terms, this experiment was still nothing but a minor field trial.

I turned to Sadiq. "You did some mine clearance once, didn't you?"

"Years ago." Before I could say anything more, he'd caught my drift. "You're thinking that might have been more satisfying? Bang, and it's gone, the proof is there in front of you?"

"One less mine, one less bomblet," I said. "However many thousands there were to deal with, at least you could tick each one off as a definite achievement."

"That's true. It was a good feeling." He shrugged. "But what should we do? Give up on this, because it's harder?"

He took the truck down the slope, then supervised the students as they attached the wisps of polymer to the specialized winch they'd built. Hassan and Rashid were in their 20s, but they could easily have passed for adolescents. After the war, the dictator and his former backers in the west had found it mutually expedient to have a generation of Iraqi children grow up malnourished and without medical care, if they grew up at all. More than a million people had died under the sanctions. My own sick joke of a nation had sent part of its navy to join the blockade, while the rest stayed home to fend off boatloads of refugees from this, and other, atrocities. General Moustache was long dead, but his comrades-in-genocide with more salubrious addresses were all still at large: doing lecture tours, running think tanks, lobbying for the Nobel peace prize.

As the strands of polymer wound around a core inside the winch's protective barrel, the alpha count rose steadily. It was a good sign: the fine particles of uranium oxide trapped by the Wall had remained bound to the polymer during dehydration, and the reeling in of the net. The radiation from the few grams of U-238 we'd collected was far too low to be a hazard in itself; the thing to avoid was ingesting the dust, and even then the unpleasant effects were as much chemical as radiological. Hopefully, the polymer had also bound its other targets: the organic carcinogens that had been strewn across Kuwait and southern Iraq by the apocalyptic oil well fires. There was no way to determine that until we did a full chemical analysis.

We were all in high spirits on the ride back. What we'd plucked from the wind in the last six weeks wouldn't spare a single person from leukaemia, but it now seemed possible that over the years, over the decades, the technology would make a real difference.

I missed the connection in Singapore for a direct flight home to Sydney, so I had to go via Perth. There was a four-hour wait in Perth; I paced the transit lounge, restless and impatient. I hadn't set eyes on Francine since she'd left Basra three months earlier; she didn't approve of clogging up the limited bandwidth into Iraq with decadent video. When I'd called her from Singapore she'd been busy, and now I couldn't decide whether or not to try again.

Just when I'd resolved to call her, an e-mail came through on my notepad, saying that she'd received my message and would meet me at the airport.

In Sydney, I stood by the baggage carousel, searching the crowd. When I finally saw Francine approaching, she was looking straight at me, smiling. I left the carousel and walked towards her; she stopped and let me close the gap, keeping her eyes fixed on mine. There was a mischievousness to her expression, as if she'd arranged some kind of prank, but I couldn't guess what it might be.

When I was almost in front of her, she turned slightly, and spread her arms. "Ta-da!"

I froze, speechless. *Why hadn't she told me?*

I walked up to her and embraced her, but she'd read my expression. "Don't be angry, Ben. I was afraid you'd come home early if you knew."

"You're right, I would have." My thoughts were piling up on top of each other;

I had three months' worth of reactions to get through in 15 seconds. *We hadn't planned this. We couldn't afford it. I wasn't ready.*

Suddenly I started weeping, too shocked to be self-conscious in the crowd. The knot of panic and confusion inside me dissolved. I held her more tightly, and felt the swelling in her body against my hip.

"Are you happy?" Francine asked.

I laughed and nodded, choking out the words: "This is wonderful!"

I meant it. I was still afraid, but it was an exuberant fear. Another ocean had opened up before us. We would find our bearings. We would cross it together.

It took me several days to come down to Earth. We didn't have a real chance to talk until the weekend; Francine had a teaching position at UNSW, and though she could have set her own research aside for a couple of days, marking could wait for no one. There were a thousand things to plan; the six-month UNESCO fellowship that had paid for me to take part in the project in Basra had expired, and I'd need to start earning money again soon, but the fact that I'd made no commitments yet gave me some welcome flexibility.

On Monday, alone in the flat again, I started catching up on all the journals I'd neglected. In Iraq I'd been obsessively single-minded, instructing my knowledge miner to keep me informed of work relevant to the Wall, to the exclusion of everything else.

Skimming through a summary of six months' worth of papers, a report in *Science* caught my eye: "An Experimental Model for Decoherence in the Many-Worlds Cosmology." A group at Delft University in the Netherlands had arranged for a simple quantum computer to carry out a sequence of arithmetic operations on a register which had been prepared to contain an equal superposition of binary representations of two different numbers. This in itself was nothing new; superpositions representing up to 128 numbers were now manipulated daily, albeit only under laboratory conditions, at close to absolute zero.

Unusually, though, at each stage of the calculation the qubits containing the numbers in question had been deliberately entangled with other, spare qubits in the computer. The effect of this was that the section performing the calculation had ceased to be in a pure quantum state: it behaved, not as if it contained two numbers simultaneously, but as if there were merely an equal chance of it containing either one. This had undermined the quantum nature of the calculation, just as surely as if the whole machine had been imperfectly shielded and become entangled with objects in the environment.

There was one crucial difference, though: in this case, the experimenters had still had access to the spare qubits that had made the calculation behave classically. When they performed an appropriate measurement on the state of the computer *as a whole*, it was shown to have remained in a superposition all along. A single observation couldn't prove this, but the experiment had been repeated thousands of times, and within the margins of error, their prediction was confirmed: although the superposition had become undetectable when they ignored the spare qubits, it had never really gone away. *Both* classical calculations had always taken place simultaneously, even though they'd lost the ability to interact in a quantum-mechanical fashion.

I sat at my desk, pondering the result. On one level, it was just a scaling-up of the quantum eraser experiments of the '90s, but the image of a tiny computer program running through its paces, appearing "to itself" to be unique and alone, while in fact a second, equally oblivious version had been executing beside it all along, carried a lot more resonance than an interference experiment with photons. I'd become used to the idea of quantum computers performing several calculations at once, but that conjuring trick had always seemed abstract and ethereal, precisely because the parts continued to act as a complicated whole right to the end. What struck home *here* was the stark demonstration of the way each calculation could come to appear as a distinct classical history, as solid and mundane as the shuffling of beads on an abacus.

When Francine arrived home I was cooking dinner, but I grabbed my notepad and showed her the paper.

"Yeah, I've seen it," she said.

"What do you think?"

She raised her hands and recoiled in mock alarm.

"I'm serious."

"What do you want me to say? Does this prove the Many Worlds interpretation? No. Does it make it easier to understand, to have a toy model like this? Yes."

"But does it sway you at all?" I persisted. "Do you believe the results would still hold, if they could be scaled up indefinitely?" From a toy universe, a handful of qubits, to the real one.

She shrugged. "I don't really need to be swayed. I always thought the MWI was the most plausible interpretation anyway."

I left it at that, and went back to the kitchen while she pulled out a stack of assignments.

That night, as we lay in bed together, I couldn't get the Delft experiment out of my mind.

"Do you believe there are other versions of us?" I asked Francine.

"I suppose there must be." She conceded the point as if it was something abstract and metaphysical, and I was being pedantic even to raise it. People who professed belief in the MWI never seemed to want to take it seriously, let alone personally.

"And that doesn't bother you?"

"No," she said blithely. "Since I'm powerless to change the situation, what's the use in being upset about it?"

"That's very pragmatic," I said. Francine reached over and thumped me on the shoulder. "That was a compliment!" I protested. "I envy you for having come to terms with it so easily."

"I haven't, really," she admitted. "I've just resolved not to let it worry me, which isn't quite the same thing."

I turned to face her, though in the near-darkness we could barely see each other. I said, "What gives you the most satisfaction in life?"

"I take it you're not in the mood to be fobbed off with a soppy romantic answer?" She sighed. "I don't know. Solving problems. Getting things right."

"What if for every problem you solve, there's someone just like you who fails, instead?"

"I cope with my failures," she said. "Let them cope with theirs."

"You know it doesn't work like that. Some of them simply *don't* cope. Whatever you find the strength to do, there'll be someone else who won't."

Francine had no reply.

I said, "A couple of weeks ago, I asked Sadiq about the time he was doing mine clearance. He said it was more satisfying than mopping up DU; one little explosion, right before your eyes, and you know you've done something worthwhile. We all get moments in our lives like that, with that pure, unambiguous sense of achievement: whatever else we might screw up, at least there's one thing that we've done right." I laughed uneasily. "I think I'd go mad, if I couldn't rely on that."

Francine said, "You can. Nothing you've done will ever disappear from under your feet. No one's going to march up and take it away from you."

"I know." My skin crawled, at the image of some less favoured alter ego turning up on our doorstep, demanding his dues. "That seems so fucking selfish, though. I don't want everything that makes me happy to be at the expense of someone else. I don't want every choice to be like . . . fighting other versions of myself for the prize in some zero-sum game."

"No." Francine hesitated. "But if the reality is like that, what can you do about it?"

Her words hung in the darkness. What could I do about it? Nothing. So did I really want to dwell on it, corroding the foundations of my own happiness, when there was absolutely nothing to be gained, for anyone?

"You're right. This is crazy." I leant over and kissed her. "I'd better let you get to sleep."

"It's not crazy," she said. "But I don't have any answers."

The next morning, after Francine had left for work, I picked up my notepad and saw that she'd mailed me an e-book: an anthology of cheesy "alternate (sic) history" stories from the '90s, entitled *My God, It's Full of Tsars!* "What if Gandhi had been a ruthless soldier of fortune? What if Theodore Roosevelt had faced a Martian invasion? What if the Nazis had had Janet Jackson's choreographer?"

I skimmed through the introduction, alternately cackling and groaning, then filed the book away and got down to work. I had a dozen minor administrative tasks to complete for UNESCO, before I could start searching in earnest for my next position.

By mid-afternoon, I was almost done, but the growing sense of achievement I felt at having buckled down and cleared away these tedious obligations brought with it the corollary: someone infinitesimally different from me—someone who had shared my entire history up until that morning—had procrastinated instead. The triviality of this observation only made it more unsettling; the Delft experiment was seeping into my daily life on the most mundane level.

I dug out the book Francine had sent and tried reading a few of the stories, but the authors' relentlessly camp take on the premise hardly amounted to a *reductio ad absurdum,* or even a comical existential balm. I didn't really care how hilarious it would have been if Marilyn Monroe had been involved in a bedroom farce with Richard Feynman and Richard Nixon. I just wanted to lose the suffocating conviction that everything I had become was a mirage; that my life had been nothing but a blinkered view of a kind of torture chamber, where every glorious reprieve I'd ever celebrated had in fact been an unwitting betrayal.

If fiction had no comfort to offer, what about fact? Even if the Many Worlds cosmology was correct, no one knew for certain what the consequences were. It was a fallacy that literally everything that was physically possible had to occur; most cosmologists I'd read believed that the universe as a whole possessed a single, definite quantum state, and while that state would appear from within as a multitude of distinct classical histories, there was no reason to assume that these histories amounted to some kind of exhaustive catalogue. The same thing held true on a smaller scale: every time two people sat down to a game of chess, there was no reason to believe that they played every possible game.

And if I'd stood in an alley, nine years before, struggling with my conscience? My subjective sense of indecision proved nothing, but even if I'd suffered no qualms and acted without hesitation, to find a human being in a quantum state of pure, unshakeable resolve would have been freakishly unlikely at best, and in fact was probably physically impossible.

"Fuck this." I didn't know when I'd set myself up for this bout of paranoia, but I wasn't going to indulge it for another second. I banged my head against the desk a few times, then picked up my notepad and went straight to an employment site.

The thoughts didn't vanish entirely; it was too much like trying not to think of a pink elephant. Each time they recurred, though, I found I could shout them down with threats of taking myself straight to a psychiatrist. The prospect of having to explain such a bizarre mental problem was enough to give me access to hitherto untapped reserves of self-discipline.

By the time I started cooking dinner, I was feeling merely foolish. If Francine mentioned the subject again, I'd make a joke of it. I didn't need a psychiatrist. I was a little insecure about my good fortune, and still somewhat rattled by the news of impending fatherhood, but it would hardly have been healthier to take everything for granted.

My notepad chimed. Francine had blocked the video again, as if bandwidth, even here, was as precious as water.

"Hello."

"Ben? I've had some bleeding. I'm in a taxi. Can you meet me at St Vincent's?"

Her voice was steady, but my own mouth went dry. "Sure. I'll be there in 15 minutes." I couldn't add anything: *I love you, it will be all right, hold on.* She didn't need that, it would have jinxed everything.

Half an hour later, I was still caught in traffic, white-knuckled with rage and helplessness. I stared down at the dashboard, at the real-time map with every other gridlocked vehicle marked, and finally stopped deluding myself that at any moment I would turn into a magically deserted sidestreet and weave my way across the city in just a few more minutes.

In the ward, behind the curtains drawn around her bed, Francine lay curled and rigid, her back turned, refusing to look at me. All I could do was stand beside her. The gynaecologist was yet to explain everything properly, but the miscarriage had been accompanied by complications, and she'd had to perform surgery.

Before I'd applied for the UNESCO fellowship, we'd discussed the risks. For two prudent, well-informed, short-term visitors, the danger had seemed microscopic. Francine had never travelled out into the desert with me, and even for the locals in Basra the rates of birth defects and miscarriages had fallen a long way from their peaks. We were both taking contraceptives; condoms had seemed like over-kill. *Had I brought it back to her, from the desert? A speck of dust, trapped beneath my foreskin? Had I poisoned her while we were making love?*

Francine turned towards me. The skin around her eyes was grey and swollen, and I could see how much effort it took for her to meet my gaze. She drew her hands out from under the bedclothes, and let me hold them; they were freezing.

After a while, she started sobbing, but she wouldn't release my hands. I stroked the back of her thumb with my own thumb, a tiny, gentle movement.

2020

"How do you feel now?" Olivia Maslin didn't quite make eye contact as she addressed me; the image of my brain activity painted on her retinas was clearly holding her attention.

"Fine," I said. "Exactly the same as I did before you started the infusion."

I was reclining on something like a dentist's couch, halfway between sitting and lying, wearing a tight-fitting cap studded with magnetic sensors and inducers. It was impossible to ignore the slight coolness of the liquid flowing into the vein in my forearm, but that sensation was no different than it had been on the previous occasion, a fortnight before.

"Could you count to ten for me, please."

I obliged.

"Now close your eyes and picture the same familiar face as the last time."

She'd told me I could choose anyone; I'd picked Francine. I brought back the image, then suddenly recalled that, the first time, after contemplating the detailed picture in my head for a few seconds—as if I was preparing to give a description to the police—I'd started thinking about Francine herself. On cue, the same transition occurred again: the frozen, forensic likeness became flesh and blood.

I was led through the whole sequence of activities once more: reading the same short story ("Two Old-Timers" by F. Scott Fitzgerald), listening to the same piece of music (from Rossini's *The Thieving Magpie*), recounting the same childhood memory (my first day at school). At some point, I lost any trace of anxiety about repeating my earlier mental states with sufficient fidelity; after all, the experiment had been designed to cope with the inevitable variation between the two sessions. I was just one volunteer out of dozens, and half the subjects would be receiving nothing but saline on both occasions. For all I knew, I was one of them: a control, merely setting the baseline against which any real effect would be judged.

If I was receiving the coherence disruptors, though, then as far as I could tell they'd had no effect on me. My inner life hadn't evaporated as the molecules bound to the microtubules in my neurons, guaranteeing that any kind of quantum coherence those structures might otherwise have maintained would be lost to the environment in a fraction of a picosecond.

Personally, I'd never subscribed to Penrose's theory that quantum effects might play a role in consciousness; calculations dating back to a seminal paper by Max Tegmark, 20 years before, had already made sustained coherence in any neural structure extremely unlikely. Nevertheless, it had taken considerable ingenuity on the part of Olivia and her team to rule out the idea definitively, in a series of clear-cut experiments. Over the past two years, they'd chased the ghost away from each of the various structures that different factions of Penrose's disciples had anointed as the essential quantum components of the brain. The earliest proposal—the microtubules, huge polymeric molecules that formed a kind of skeleton inside every cell—had turned out to be the hardest to target for disruption. But now it was entirely possible that the cytoskeletons of my very own neurons were dotted with molecules that coupled them strongly to a noisy microwave field in which my skull was, definitely, bathed. In which case, my microtubules had about as much chance of exploiting quantum effects as I had of playing a game of squash with a version of myself from a parallel universe.

When the experiment was over, Olivia thanked me, then became even more distant as she reviewed the data. Raj, one of her graduate students, slid out the needle and stuck a plaster over the tiny puncture wound, then helped me out of the cap.

"I know you don't know yet if I was a control or not," I said, "but have you noticed significant differences, with anyone?" I was almost the last subject in the microtubule trials; any effect should have shown up by now.

Olivia smiled enigmatically. "You'll just have to wait for publication." Raj leant down and whispered, "No, never."

I climbed off the couch. "The zombie walks!" Raj declaimed. I lunged hungrily for his brain; he ducked away, laughing, while Olivia watched us with an expression of pained indulgence. Die-hard members of the Penrose camp claimed that Olivia's experiments proved nothing, because even if people *behaved* identically while all quantum effects were ruled out, they could be doing this as mere automata, totally devoid of consciousness. When Olivia had offered to let her chief detractor experience coherence disruption for himself, he'd replied that this would be no more persuasive, because memories laid down while you were a zombie would be indistinguishable from ordinary memories, so that looking back on the experience, you'd notice nothing unusual.

This was sheer desperation; you might as well assert that everyone in the world but yourself was a zombie, and you were one, too, every second Tuesday. As the experiments were repeated by other groups around the world, those people who'd backed the Penrose theory as a scientific hypothesis, rather than adopting it as a kind of mystical dogma, would gradually accept that it had been refuted.

I left the neuroscience building and walked across the campus, back towards my office in the physics department. It was a mild, clear spring morning, with students out lying on the grass, dozing off with books balanced over their faces like tents. There were still some advantages to reading from old-fashioned sheaves of e-paper. I'd only had my own eyes chipped the year before, and though I'd adapted to the technology easily enough, I still found it disconcerting to wake on a Sunday morning to find Francine reading the *Herald* beside me with her eyes shut.

Olivia's results didn't surprise me, but it was satisfying to have the matter resolved once and for all: consciousness was a purely classical phenomenon. Among other things, this meant that there was no compelling reason to believe that software running on a classical computer could not be conscious. Of course, everything in the universe obeyed quantum mechanics at some level, but Paul Benioff, one of the pioneers of quantum computing, had shown back in the '80s that you could build a classical Turing machine from quantum mechanical parts, and over the last few years, in my spare time, I'd studied the branch of quantum computing theory that concerned itself with *avoiding* quantum effects.

Back in my office, I summoned up a schematic of the device I called the Qusp: the quantum singleton processor. The Qusp would employ all the techniques designed to shield the latest generation of quantum computers from entanglement with their environment, but it would use them to a very different end. A quantum computer was shielded so it could perform a multitude of parallel calculations, without each one spawning a separate history of its own, in which only one answer was accessible. The Qusp would perform just a single calculation at a time, but on its way to the unique result it would be able to pass safely through superpositions that included any number of alternatives, without those alternatives being made real. Cut off from the outside world during each computational step, it would keep its temporary quantum ambivalence as private and inconsequential as a daydream, never being forced to act out every possibility it dared to entertain.

The Qusp would still need to interact with its environment whenever it gathered data about the world, and that interaction would inevitably split it into different versions. If you attached a camera to the Qusp and pointed it at an ordinary object—a rock, a plant, a bird—that object could hardly be expected to possess a single classical history, and so neither would the combined system of Qusp plus rock, Qusp plus plant, Qusp plus bird.

The Qusp itself, though, would never initiate the split. In a given set of circumstances, it would only ever produce a single response. An AI running on the Qusp could make its decisions as whimsically, or with as much weighty deliberation as it liked, but for each distinct scenario it confronted, in the end it would only make one choice, only follow one course of action.

I closed the file, and the image vanished from my retinas. For all the work I'd put into the design, I'd made no effort to build the thing. I'd been using it as little more than a talisman: whenever I found myself picturing my life as a tranquil dwelling built over a slaughter house, I'd summon up the Qusp as a symbol of hope. It was proof of a possibility, and a possibility was all it took. Nothing in the laws of physics could prevent a small portion of humanity's descendants from escaping their ancestors' dissipation.

Yet I'd shied away from any attempt to see that promise fulfilled, firsthand. In part, I'd been afraid of delving too deeply and uncovering a flaw in the Qusp's design, robbing myself of the one crutch that kept me standing when the horror swept over me. It had also been a matter of guilt: I'd been the one granted happiness, so many times, that it had seemed unconscionable to aspire to that state yet again. I'd knocked so many of my hapless cousins out of the ring, it was time I threw a fight and let the prize go to my opponent instead.

That last excuse was idiotic. The stronger my determination to build the Qusp, the more branches there would be in which it was real. Weakening my resolve was *not* an act of charity, surrendering the benefits to someone else; it merely impoverished every future version of me, and everyone they touched.

I did have a third excuse. It was time I dealt with that one, too.

I called Francine.

"Are you free for lunch?" I asked. She hesitated; there was always work she could be doing. "To discuss the Cauchy-Riemann equations?" I suggested.

She smiled. It was our code, when the request was a special one. "All right. One o'clock?"

I nodded. "I'll see you then."

Francine was 20 minutes late, but that was less of a wait than I was used to. She'd been appointed deputy head of the mathematics department 18 months before, and she still had some teaching duties as well as all the new administrative work. Over the last eight years, I'd had a dozen short-term contracts with various bodies—government departments, corporations, NGOs—before finally ending up as a very lowly member of the physics department at our *alma mater*. I did envy her the prestige and security of her job, but I'd been happy with most of the work I'd done, even if it had been too scattered between disciplines to contribute to anything like a traditional career path.

I'd bought Francine a plate of cheese-and-salad sandwiches, and she attacked them hungrily as soon as she sat down. I said, "I've got ten minutes at the most, haven't I?"

She covered her mouth with her hand and replied defensively, "It could have waited until tonight, couldn't it?"

"Sometimes I can't put things off. I have to act while I still have the courage."

At this ominous prelude she chewed more slowly. "You did the second stage of Olivia's experiment this morning, didn't you?"

"Yeah." I'd discussed the whole procedure with her before I volunteered.

"So I take it you didn't lose consciousness, when your neurons became marginally more classical than usual?" She sipped chocolate milk through a straw.

"No. Apparently no one ever loses anything. That's not official yet, but—"

Francine nodded, unsurprised. We shared the same position on the Penrose theory; there was no need to discuss it again now.

I said, "I want to know if you're going to have the operation."

She continued drinking for a few more seconds, then released the straw and wiped her upper lip with her thumb, unnecessarily. "You want me to make up my mind about that, here and now?"

"No." The damage to her uterus from the miscarriage could be repaired; we'd been discussing the possibility for almost five years. We'd both had comprehensive chelation therapy to remove any trace of U-238. We could have children in the usual way with a reasonable degree of safety, if that was what we wanted. "But if you've already decided, I want you to tell me now."

Francine looked wounded. "That's unfair."

"What is? Implying that you might not have told me, the instant you decided?"

"No. Implying that it's all in my hands."

I said, "I'm not washing my hands of the decision. You know how I feel. But you know I'd back you all the way, if you said you wanted to carry a child." I believed I would have. Maybe it was a form of doublethink, but I couldn't treat the birth of one more ordinary child as some kind of atrocity, and refuse to be a part of it.

"Fine. But what will you do if I don't?" She examined my face calmly. I think she already knew, but she wanted me to spell it out.

"We could always adopt," I observed casually.

"Yes, we could do that." She smiled slightly; she knew that made me lose my ability to bluff, even faster than when she stared me down.

I stopped pretending that there was any mystery left; she'd seen right through me from the start. I said, "I just don't want to do this, then discover that it makes you feel that you've been cheated out of what you really wanted."

"It wouldn't," she insisted. "It wouldn't rule out anything. We could still have a natural child as well."

"Not as easily." This would not be like merely having workaholic parents, or an ordinary brother or sister to compete with for attention.

"You only want to do this if I can promise you that it's the only child we'd ever have?" Francine shook her head. "I'm not going to promise that. I don't intend having the operation any time soon, but I'm not going to swear that I won't change my mind. Nor am I going to swear that if we do this it will make no difference to what happens later. It will be a factor. How could it not be? But it won't be enough to rule anything in or out."

I looked away, across the rows of tables, at all the students wrapped up in their own concerns. She was right; I was being unreasonable. I'd wanted this to be a choice with no possible downside, a way of making the best of our situation, but no one could guarantee that. It would be a gamble, like everything else.

I turned back to Francine.

"All right; I'll stop trying to pin you down. What I want to do right now is go ahead and build the Qusp. And when it's finished, if we're certain we can trust it . . . I want us to raise a child with it. I want us to raise an AI."

2029

I met Francine at the airport, and we drove across Sao Paulo through curtains of wild, lashing rain. I was amazed that her plane hadn't been diverted; a tropical storm had just hit the coast, halfway between us and Rio.

"So much for giving you a tour of the city," I lamented. Through the windscreen, our actual surroundings were all but invisible; the bright overlay we both perceived, surreally coloured and detailed, made the experience rather like perusing a 3D map while trapped in a car wash.

Francine was pensive, or tired from the flight. I found it hard to think of San Francisco as remote when the time difference was so small, and even when I'd made the journey north to visit her, it had been nothing compared to all the ocean-spanning marathons I'd sat through in the past.

We both had an early night. The next morning, Francine accompanied me to my cluttered workroom in the basement of the university's engineering department. I'd been chasing grants and collaborators around the world, like a child on a treasure hunt, slowly piecing together a device that few of my colleagues believed was worth creating for its own sake. Fortunately, I'd managed to find pretexts—or even genuine spin-offs—for almost every stage of the work. Quantum computing, *per se*, had become bogged down in recent years, stymied by both a shortage of practical algorithms and a limit to the complexity of superpositions that could be sustained. The Qusp had nudged the technological envelope in some promising directions, without making any truly exorbitant demands; the states it juggled were relatively simple, and they only needed to be kept isolated for milliseconds at a time.

I introduced Carlos, Maria and Jun, but then they made themselves scarce as I showed Francine around. We still had a demonstration of the "balanced decoupling" principle set up on a bench, for the tour by one of our corporate donors the week before. What caused an imperfectly shielded quantum computer to decohere was the fact that each possible state of the device affected its environment slightly differently. The shielding itself could always be improved, but Carlos's group had perfected a way to buy a little more protection by sheer deviousness. In the demonstration rig, the flow of energy through the device remained absolutely constant whatever state it was in, because any drop in power consumption by the main set of quantum gates was compensated for by a rise in a set of balancing gates, and *vice versa*. This gave the environment one less clue by which to discern internal differences in the processor, and to tear any superposition apart into mutually disconnected branches.

Francine knew all the theory backwards, but she'd never seen this hardware in action. When I invited her to twiddle the controls, she took to the rig like a child with a game console.

"You really should have joined the team," I said.

"Maybe I did," she countered. "In another branch."

She'd moved from UNSW to Berkeley two years before, not long after I'd moved from Delft to Sao Paulo; it was the closest suitable position she could find. At the time, I'd resented the fact that she'd refused to compromise and work remotely; with only five hours' difference, teaching at Berkeley from Sao Paulo would not have been impossible. In the end, though, I'd accepted the fact that she'd wanted to keep on testing me, testing both of us. If we weren't strong enough to stay together through the trials of a prolonged physical separation—or if I was not sufficiently committed to the project to endure whatever sacrifices it entailed— she did not want us proceeding to the next stage.

I led her to the corner bench, where a nondescript grey box half a metre across sat, apparently inert. I gestured to it, and our retinal overlays transformed its appearance, "revealing" a maze with a transparent lid embedded in the top of the device. In one chamber of the maze, a slightly cartoonish mouse sat motionless. Not quite dead, not quite sleeping.

"This is the famous Zelda?" Francine asked.

"Yes." Zelda was a neural network, a stripped-down, stylized mouse brain. There were newer, fancier versions available, much closer to the real thing, but the ten-year-old, public domain Zelda had been good enough for our purposes.

Three other chambers held cheese. "Right now, she has no experience of the maze," I explained. "So let's start her up and watch her explore." I gestured, and Zelda began scampering around, trying out different passages, deftly reversing each time she hit a *cul-de-sac*. "Her brain is running on a Qusp, but the maze is implemented on an ordinary classical computer, so in terms of coherence issues, it's really no different from a physical maze."

"Which means that each time she takes in information, she gets entangled with the outside world," Francine suggested.

"Absolutely. But she always holds off doing that until the Qusp has completed its current computational step, and every qubit contains a definite zero or a definite one. She's never in two minds when she lets the world in, so the entanglement process doesn't split her into separate branches."

Francine continued to watch, in silence. Zelda finally found one of the chambers containing a reward; when she'd eaten it, a hand scooped her up and returned her to her starting point, then replaced the cheese.

"Here are 10,000 previous trials, superimposed." I replayed the data. It looked as if a single mouse was running through the maze, moving just as we'd seen her move when I'd begun the latest experiment. Restored each time to exactly the same starting condition, and confronted with exactly the same environment, Zelda—like any computer program with no truly random influences—had simply repeated herself. All 10,000 trials had yielded identical results.

To a casual observer, unaware of the context, this would have been a singularly unimpressive performance. Faced with exactly one situation, Zelda the virtual mouse did exactly one thing. So what? If you'd been able to wind back a flesh-and-blood mouse's memory with the same degree of precision, wouldn't it have repeated itself too?

Francine said, "Can you cut off the shielding? And the balanced decoupling?"

"Yep." I obliged her, and initiated a new trial.

Zelda took a different path this time, exploring the maze by a different route. Though the initial condition of the neural net was identical, the switching processes taking place within the Qusp were now opened up to the environment constantly, and superpositions of several different eigenstates—states in which the Qusp's qubits possessed definite binary values, which in turn led to Zelda making definite choices—were becoming entangled with the outside world. According to the Copenhagen interpretation of quantum mechanics, this interaction was randomly "collapsing" the superpositions into single eigenstates; Zelda was still doing just one thing at a time, but her behaviour had ceased to be deterministic. According to the MWI, the interaction was transforming the environment—Francine and me included—into a superposition with components that were coupled to each eigenstate; Zelda was actually running the maze in many different ways simultaneously, and other versions of us were seeing her take all those other routes.

Which scenario was correct?

I said, "I'll reconfigure everything now, to wrap the whole setup in a Delft cage." A "Delft cage" was jargon for the situation I'd first read about 17 years before: instead of opening up the Qusp to the environment, I'd connect it to a second quantum computer, and let *that* play the role of the outside world.

We could no longer watch Zelda moving about in real time, but after the trial was completed, it was possible to test the combined system of both computers against the hypothesis that it was in a pure quantum state in which Zelda had run the maze along hundreds of different routes, all at once. I displayed a representation of the conjectured state, built up by superimposing all the paths she'd taken in 10,000 unshielded trials.

The test result flashed up: CONSISTENT.

"One measurement proves nothing," Francine pointed out.

"No." I repeated the trial. Again, the hypothesis was not refuted. If Zelda had actually run the maze along just one path, the probability of the computers' joint state passing this imperfect test was about one percent. For passing it twice, the odds were about one in 10,000.

I repeated it a third time, then a fourth.

Francine said, "That's enough." She actually looked queasy. The image of the hundreds of blurred mouse trails on the display was not a literal photograph of anything, but if the old Delft experiment had been enough to give me a visceral sense of the reality of the multiverse, perhaps this demonstration had finally done the same for her.

"Can I show you one more thing?" I asked.

"Keep the Delft cage, but restore the Qusp's shielding?"

"Right."

I did it. The Qusp was now fully protected once more whenever it was not in an eigenstate, but this time, it was the second quantum computer, not the outside world, to which it was intermittently exposed. If Zelda split into multiple branches again, then she'd only take that fake environment with her, and we'd still have our hands on all the evidence.

Tested against the hypothesis that no split had occurred, the verdict was: CONSISTENT. CONSISTENT. CONSISTENT.

We went out to dinner with the whole of the team, but Francine pleaded a headache and left early. She insisted that I stay and finish the meal, and I didn't argue; she was not the kind of person who expected you to assume that she was being politely selfless, while secretly hoping to be contradicted.

After Francine had left, Maria turned to me. "So you two are really going ahead with the Frankenchild?" She'd been teasing me about this for as long as I'd known her, but apparently she hadn't been game to raise the subject in Francine's presence.

"We still have to talk about it." I felt uncomfortable myself, now, discussing the topic the moment Francine was absent. Confessing my ambition when I applied to join the team was one thing; it would have been dishonest to keep my collaborators in the dark about my ultimate intentions. Now that the enabling technology was more or less completed, though, the issue seemed far more personal.

Carlos said breezily, "Why not? There are so many others now. Sophie. Linus. Theo. Probably a hundred we don't even know about. It's not as if Ben's child won't have playmates." Adai — Autonomously Developing Artificial Intelligences — had been appearing in a blaze of controversy every few months for the last four years. A Swiss researcher, Isabelle Schib, had taken the old models of morphogenesis that had led to software like Zelda, refined the technique by several orders of magnitude, and applied it to human genetic data. Wedded to sophisticated prosthetic bodies, Isabelle's creations inhabited the physical world and learnt from their experience, just like any other child.

Jun shook his head reprovingly. "I wouldn't raise a child with no legal rights. What happens when you die? For all you know, it could end up as someone's property."

I'd been over this with Francine. "I can't believe that in ten or 20 years' time there won't be citizenship laws, somewhere in the world."

Jun snorted. "Twenty years! How long did it take the U.S. to emancipate their slaves?"

Carlos interjected, "Who's going to create an adai just to use it as a slave? If you want something biddable, write ordinary software. If you need consciousness, humans are cheaper."

Maria said, "It won't come down to economics. It's the nature of the things that will determine how they're treated."

"You mean the xenophobia they'll face?" I suggested.

Maria shrugged. "You make it sound like racism, but we aren't talking about human beings. Once you have software with goals of its own, free to do whatever it likes, where will it end? The first generation makes the next one better, faster, smarter; the second generation even more so. Before we know it, we're like ants to them."

Carlos groaned. "Not that hoary old fallacy! If you really believe that stating the analogy 'ants are to humans, as humans are to x' is proof that it's possible to solve for x, then I'll meet you where the south pole is like the equator."

I said, "The Qusp runs no faster than an organic brain; we need to keep the switching rate low, because that makes the shielding requirements less stringent. It might be possible to nudge those parameters, eventually, but there's no reason in the world why an adai would be better equipped to do that than you or I would. As for making their own offspring smarter . . . even if Schib's group has been perfectly successful, they will have merely translated human neural development from one substrate to another. They won't have 'improved' on the process at all —

whatever that might mean. So if the adai have any advantage over us, it will be no more than the advantage shared by flesh-and-blood children: cultural transmission of one more generation's worth of experience."

Maria frowned, but she had no immediate comeback.

Jun said dryly, "Plus immortality."

"Well, yes, there is that," I conceded.

Francine was awake when I arrived home.

"Have you still got a headache?" I whispered.

"No."

"I undressed and climbed into bed beside her.

She said, "You know what I miss the most? When we're fucking on-line?"

"This had better not be complicated; I'm out of practice."

"Kissing."

I kissed her, slowly and tenderly, and she melted beneath me. "Three more months," I promised, "and I'll move up to Berkeley."

"To be my kept man."

"I prefer the term 'unpaid but highly valued caregiver.' " Francine stiffened. I said, "We can talk about that later." I started kissing her again, but she turned her face away.

"I'm afraid," she said.

"So am I," I assured her. "That's a good sign. Everything worth doing is terrifying."

"But not everything terrifying is good."

I rolled over and lay beside her. She said, "On one level, it's easy. What greater gift could you give a child, than the power to make real decisions? What worse fate could you spare her from, than being forced to act against her better judgment, over and over? When you put it like that, it's simple.

"But every fibre in my body still rebels against it. How will she feel, knowing what she is? How will she make friends? How will she belong? How will she not despise us for making her a freak? And what if we're robbing her of something she'd value: living a billion lives, never being forced to choose between them? What if she sees the gift as a kind of impoverishment?"

"She can always drop the shielding on the Qusp," I said. "Once she understands the issues, she can choose for herself."

"That's true." Francine did not sound mollified at all; she would have thought of that long before I'd mentioned it, but she wasn't looking for concrete answers. Every ordinary human instinct screamed at us that we were embarking on something *dangerous, unnatural, hubristic*—but those instincts were more about safeguarding our own reputations than protecting our child-to-be. No parent, save the most wilfully negligent, would be pilloried if their flesh-and-blood child turned out to be ungrateful for life; if I'd railed against my own mother and father because I'd found fault in the existential conditions with which I'd been lumbered, it wasn't hard to guess which side would attract the most sympathy from the world at large. Anything that went wrong with *our* child would be grounds for lynching—however much love, sweat, and soul-searching had gone into her creation — because we'd had the temerity to be dissatisfied with the kind of fate that everyone else happily inflicted on their own.

I said, "You saw Zelda today, spread across the branches. You know, deep down now, that the same thing happens to all of us."

"Yes." Something tore inside me as Francine uttered that admission. I'd never really wanted her to feel it, the way I did.

I persisted. "Would you willingly sentence your own child to that condition? And your grandchildren? And your great-grandchildren?"

"No," Francine replied. A part of her hated me now; I could hear it in her voice. It was *my* curse, *my* obsession; before she met me, she'd managed to believe and not believe, taking her acceptance of the multiverse lightly.

I said, "I can't do this without you."

"You can, actually. More easily than any of the alternatives. You wouldn't even need a stranger to donate an egg."

"I can't do it unless you're behind me. If you say the word, I'll stop here. We've built the Qusp. We've shown that it can work. Even if we don't do this last part ourselves, someone else will, in a decade or two."

"If *we* don't do this," Francine observed acerbically, "we'll simply do it in another branch."

I said, "That's true, but it's no use thinking that way. In the end, I can't function unless I pretend that my choices are real. I doubt that anyone can."

Francine was silent for a long time. I stared up into the darkness of the room, trying hard not to contemplate the near certainty that her decision would go both ways.

Finally, she spoke.

"Then let's make a child who doesn't need to pretend."

2031

Isabelle Schib welcomed us into her office. In person, she was slightly less intimidating than she was on-line; it wasn't anything different in her appearance or manner, just the ordinariness of her surroundings. I'd envisaged her ensconced in some vast, pristine, high-tech building, not a couple of pokey rooms on a backstreet in Basel.

Once the pleasantries were out of the way, Isabelle got straight to the point. "You've been accepted," she announced. "I'll send you the contract later today."

My throat constricted with panic; I should have been elated, but I just felt unprepared. Isabelle's group licensed only three new adai a year. The short-list had come down to about a hundred couples, winnowed from tens of thousands of applicants. We'd travelled to Switzerland for the final selection process, carried out by an agency that ordinarily handled adoptions. Through all the interviews and questionnaires, all the personality tests and scenario challenges, I'd managed to half-convince myself that our dedication would win through in the end, but that had been nothing but a prop to keep my spirits up.

Francine said calmly, "Thank you."

I coughed. "You're happy with everything we've proposed?" If there was going to be a proviso thrown in that rendered this miracle worthless, better to hear it now, before the shock had worn off and I'd started taking things for granted.

Isabelle nodded. "I don't pretend to be an expert in the relevant fields, but I've had the Qusp's design assessed by several colleagues, and I see no reason why it wouldn't be an appropriate form of hardware for an adai. I'm entirely agnostic about the MWI, so I don't share your view that the Qusp is a necessity, but if you were worried that I might write you off as cranks because of it," she smiled slightly, "you should meet some of the other people I've had to deal with.

"I believe you have the adai's welfare at heart, and you're not suffering from any of the superstitions—technophobic *or* technophilic—that would distort the relationship. And as you'll recall, I'll be entitled to visits and inspections throughout your period of guardianship. If you're found to be violating any of the terms of the contract, your licence will be revoked, and I'll take charge of the adai."

Francine said, "What do you think the prospects are for a happier end to our guardianship?"

"I'm lobbying the European parliament, constantly," Isabelle replied. "Of course, in a few years' time several adai will reach the stage where their personal testimony begins contributing to the debate, but none of us should wait until then. The ground has to be prepared."

We spoke for almost an hour, on this and other issues. Isabelle had become quite an expert at fending off the attentions of the media; she promised to send us a handbook on this, along with the contract.

"Did you want to meet Sophie?" Isabelle asked, almost as an afterthought.

Francine said, "That would be wonderful." Francine and I had seen a video of Sophie at age four, undergoing a battery of psychological tests, but we'd never had a chance to converse with her, let alone meet her face-to-face.

The three of us left the office together, and Isabelle drove us to her home on the outskirts of the town.

In the car, the reality began sinking in anew. I felt the same mixture of exhilaration and claustrophobia that I'd experienced 21 years before, when Francine had met me at the airport with news of her pregnancy. No digital conception had yet taken place, but if sex had ever felt half as loaded with risks and responsibilities as this, I would have remained celibate for life.

"No badgering, no interrogation," Isabelle warned us as she pulled into the driveway.

I said, "Of course not."

Isabelle called out, "Marco! Sophie!" as we followed her through the door. At the end of the hall, I heard childish giggling, and an adult male voice whispering in French. Then Isabelle's husband stepped out from behind the corner, a smiling, dark-haired young man, with Sophie riding on his shoulders. At first I couldn't look at her; I just smiled politely back at Marco, while noting glumly that he was at least 15 years younger than I was. *How could I even think of doing this, at 46?* Then I glanced up, and caught Sophie's eye. She gazed straight back at me for a moment, appearing curious and composed, but then a fit of shyness struck her, and she buried her face in Marco's hair.

Isabelle introduced us, in English; Sophie was being raised to speak four languages, though in Switzerland that was hardly phenomenal. Sophie said, "Hello" but kept her eyes lowered. Isabelle said, "Come into the living room. Would you like something to drink?"

The five of us sipped lemonade, and the adults made polite, superficial conversation. Sophie sat on Marco's knees, squirming restlessly, sneaking glances at us. She looked exactly like an ordinary, slightly gawky, six-year-old girl. She had Isabelle's straw-coloured hair, and Marco's brown eyes; whether by fiat or rigorous genetic simulation, she could have passed for their biological daughter. I'd read technical specifications describing her body, and seen an earlier version in action on the video, but the fact that it looked so plausible was the least of its designers' achievements. Watching her drinking, wriggling and fidgeting, I had no doubt that she felt herself inhabiting this skin, as much as I did my own. She was not a puppeteer posing as a child, pulling electronic strings from some dark cavern in her skull.

"Do you like lemonade?" I asked her.

She stared at me for a moment, as if wondering whether she should be affronted by the presumptuousness of this question, then replied, "It tickles."

In the taxi to the hotel, Francine held my hand tightly.

"Are you OK?" I asked.

"Yes, of course."

In the elevator, she started crying. I wrapped my arms around her.

"She would have been 20 this year."

"I know."

"Do you think she's alive, somewhere?"

"I don't know. I don't know if that's a good way to think about it."

Francine wiped her eyes. "No. This will be her. That's the way to see it. This will be my girl. Just a few years late."

Before flying home, we visited a small pathology lab, and left samples of our blood.

Our daughter's first five bodies reached us a month before her birth. I unpacked all five, and laid them out in a row on the living room floor. With their muscles slack and their eyes rolled up, they looked more like tragic mummies than sleeping infants. I dismissed that grisly image; better to think of them as suits of clothes. The only difference was that we hadn't bought pyjamas quite so far ahead.

From wrinkled pink newborn to chubby 18-month-old, the progression made an eerie sight—even if an organic child's development, short of serious disease or malnourishment, would have been scarcely less predictable. A colleague of Francine's had lectured me a few weeks before about the terrible "mechanical determinism" we'd be imposing on our child, and though his arguments had been philosophically naïve, this sequence of immutable snapshots from the future still gave me goose bumps.

The truth was, reality as a whole was deterministic, whether you had a Qusp for a brain or not; the quantum state of the multiverse at any moment determined the entire future. Personal experience—confined to one branch at a time—certainly *appeared* probabilistic, because there was no way to predict which local future you'd experience when a branch split, but the reason it was impossible to know that in advance was because the real answer was "all of them."

For a singleton, the only difference was that branches never split on the basis of your personal decisions. The world at large would continue to look probabilistic, but every choice you made was entirely determined by *who you were* and *the situation you faced.*

What more could anyone hope for? It was not as if *who you were* could be boiled down to some crude genetic or sociological profile; every shadow you'd seen on the ceiling at night, every cloud you'd watched drift across the sky, would have left some small imprint on the shape of your mind. Those events were fully determined too, when viewed across the multiverse—with different versions of you witnessing every possibility—but in practical terms, the bottom line was that no private investigator armed with your genome and a potted biography could plot your every move in advance.

Our daughter's choices—like everything else—had been written in stone at the birth of the universe, but that information could only be decoded by *becoming her* along the way. Her actions would flow from her temperament, her principles, her desires, and the fact that all of these qualities would themselves have prior causes did nothing to diminish their value. *Free will* was a slippery notion, but to me it simply meant that your choices were more or less consistent with your nature—which in turn was a provisional, constantly evolving consensus between a thousand different influences. Our daughter would not be robbed of the chance to act capriciously, or even perversely, but at least it would not be impossible for her ever to act wholly in accordance with her ideals.

I packed the bodies away before Francine got home. I wasn't sure if the sight would unsettle her, but I didn't want her measuring them up for more clothes.

The delivery began in the early hours of the morning of Sunday, December 14, and was expected to last about four hours, depending on traffic. I sat in the nursery while Francine paced the hallway outside, both of us watching the data coming through over the fibre from Basel.

Isabelle had used our genetic information as the starting point for a simulation of the development *in utero* of a complete embryo, employing an "adaptive hierarchy" model, with the highest resolution reserved for the central nervous system. The Qusp would take over this task, not only for the newborn child's brain, but also for the thousands of biochemical processes occurring outside the skull that the artificial bodies were not designed to perform. Apart from their sophisticated sensory and motor functions, the bodies could take in food and excrete wastes—for psychological and social reasons, as well as for the chemical energy this provided—and they breathed air, both in order to oxidize this fuel, and for vocalization, but they had no blood, no endocrine system, no immune response.

The Qusp I'd built in Berkeley was smaller than the Sao Paulo version, but it was still six times as wide as an infant's skull. Until it was further miniaturized, our daughter's mind would sit in a box in a corner of the nursery, joined to the rest of her by a wireless data link. Bandwidth and time lag would not be an issue within the Bay Area, and if we needed to take her further afield before everything was combined, the Qusp wasn't too large or delicate to move.

As the progress bar I was overlaying on the side of the Qusp nudged 98 percent, Francine came into the nursery, looking agitated.

"We have to put it off, Ben. Just for a day. I need more time to prepare myself."

I shook my head. "You made me promise to say no, if you asked me to do that." She'd even refused to let me tell her how to halt the Qusp herself.

"Just a few hours," she pleaded.

Francine seemed genuinely distressed, but I hardened my heart by telling myself that she was acting: testing me, seeing if I'd keep my word. "No. No slowing down or speeding up, no pauses, no tinkering at all. This child has to hit us like a freight train, just like any other child would."

"You want me to go into labour now?" she said sarcastically. When I'd raised the possibility, half-jokingly, of putting her on a course of hormones that would have mimicked some of the effects of pregnancy in order to make bonding with the child easier—for myself as well, indirectly—she'd almost bit my head off. I hadn't been serious, because I knew it wasn't necessary. Adoption was the ultimate proof of that, but what we were doing was closer to claiming a child of our own from a surrogate.

"No. Just pick her up."

Francine peered down at the inert form in the cot.

"I can't do it!" she wailed. "When I hold her, she should feel as if she's the most precious thing in the world to me. How can I make her believe that, when I know I could bounce her off the walls without harming her?"

We had two minutes left. I felt my breathing grow ragged. I could send the Qusp a halt code, but what if that set the pattern? If one of us had had too little sleep, if Francine was late for work, if we talked ourselves into believing that our special child was so unique that we deserved a short holiday from her needs, what would stop us from doing the same thing again?

I opened my mouth to threaten her: *Either you pick her up, now, or I do it.* I stopped myself, and said, "You know how much it would harm her psychologically, if you dropped her. The very fact that you're afraid that you won't convey as much protectiveness as you need to will be just as strong a signal to her as anything else. *You care about her.* She'll sense that."

Francine stared back at me dubiously.

I said, "She'll know. I'm sure she will."

Francine reached into the cot and lifted the slack body into her arms. Seeing her cradle the lifeless form, I felt an anxious twisting in my gut; I'd experienced nothing like this when I'd laid the five plastic shells out for inspection.

I banished the progress bar and let myself free-fall through the final seconds: watching my daughter, willing her to move.

Her thumb twitched, then her legs scissored weakly. I couldn't see her face, so

I watched Francine's expression. For an instant, I thought I could detect a horrified tightening at the corners of her mouth, as if she was about to recoil from this golem. Then the child began to bawl and kick, and Francine started weeping with undisguised joy.

As she raised the child to her face and planted a kiss on its wrinkled forehead, I suffered my own moment of disquiet. How easily that tender response had been summoned, when the body could as well have been brought to life by the kind of software used to animate the characters in games and films.

It hadn't, though. There'd been nothing false or easy about the road that had brought us to this moment—let alone the one that Isabelle had followed—and we hadn't even tried to fashion life from clay, from nothing. We'd merely diverted one small trickle from a river already four billion years old.

Francine held our daughter against her shoulder, and rocked back and forth. "Have you got the bottle? Ben?" I walked to the kitchen in a daze; the microwave had anticipated the happy event, and the formula was ready.

I returned to the nursery and offered Francine the bottle. "Can I hold her, before you start feeding?"

"Of course." She leant forward to kiss me, then held out the child, and I took her the way I'd learnt to accept the babies of relatives and friends, cradling the back of her head with my hand. The distribution of weight, the heavy head, the play of the neck, felt the same as it did for any other infant. Her eyes were still screwed shut, as she screamed and swung her arms.

"What's your name, my beautiful girl?" We'd narrowed the list down to about a dozen possibilities, but Francine had refused to settle on one until she'd seen her daughter take her first breath. "Have you decided?"

"I want to call her Helen."

Gazing down at her, that sounded too old to me. Old-fashioned, at least. Great-Aunt Helen. Helena Bonham-Carter. I laughed inanely, and she opened her eyes.

Hairs rose on my arms. The dark eyes couldn't quite search my face, but she was not oblivious to me. Love and fear coursed through my veins. *How could I hope to give her what she needed?* Even if my judgment had been faultless, my power to act upon it was crude beyond measure.

We were all she had, though. We would make mistakes, we would lose our way, but I had to believe that something would hold fast. Some portion of the overwhelming love and resolve that I felt right now would have to remain with every version of me who could trace his ancestry to this moment.

I said, "I name you Helen."

2041

"Sophie! *Sophie!*" Helen ran ahead of us towards the arrivals gate, where Isabelle and Sophie were emerging. Sophie, almost 16 now, was much less demonstrative, but she smiled and waved.

Francine said, "Do you ever think of moving?"

"Maybe if the laws change first in Europe," I replied.

"I saw a job in Zürich I could apply for."

"I don't think we should bend over backwards to bring them together. They probably get on better with just occasional visits, and the net. It's not as if they don't have other friends."

Isabelle approached, and greeted us both with kisses on the cheek. I'd dreaded her arrival the first few times, but by now she seemed more like a slightly overbearing cousin than a child protection officer whose very presence implied misdeeds.

Sophie and Helen caught up with us. Helen tugged at Francine's sleeve. "Sophie's got a boyfriend! Daniel. She showed me his picture." She swooned mockingly, one hand on her forehead.

I glanced at Isabelle, who said, "He goes to her school. He's really very sweet."

Sophie grimaced with embarrassment. "Three-year-old *boys* are *sweet*." She turned to me and said, "Daniel is charming, and sophisticated, and *very* mature."

I felt as if an anvil had been dropped on my chest. As we crossed the car park, Francine whispered, "Don't have a heart attack yet. You've got a while to get used to the idea."

The waters of the bay sparkled in the sunlight as we drove across the bridge to Oakland. Isabelle described the latest session of the European parliamentary committee into adai rights. A draft proposal granting personhood to any system containing and acting upon a significant amount of the information content of human DNA had been gaining support; it was a tricky concept to define rigorously, but most of the objections were Pythonesque rather than practical. "Is the Human Proteomic Database a person? Is the Harvard Reference Physiological Simulation a person?" The HRPS modelled the brain solely in terms of what it removed from, and released into, the bloodstream; there was nobody home inside the simulation, quietly going mad.

Late in the evening, when the girls were upstairs, Isabelle began gently grilling us. I tried not to grit my teeth too much. I certainly didn't blame her for taking her responsibilities seriously; if, in spite of the selection process, we had turned out to be monsters, criminal law would have offered no remedies. Our obligations under the licensing contract were Helen's sole guarantee of humane treatment.

"She's getting good marks this year," Isabelle noted. "She must be settling in."

"She is," Francine replied. Helen was not entitled to a government-funded education, and most private schools had either been openly hostile, or had come up with such excuses as insurance policies that would have classified her as hazardous machinery. (Isabelle had reached a compromise with the airlines: Sophie had to be powered down, appearing to sleep during flights, but was not required to be shackled or stowed in the cargo hold.) The first community school we'd tried had not worked out, but we'd eventually found one close to the Berkeley campus where every parent involved was happy with the idea of Helen's presence. This had saved her from the prospect of joining a net-based school; they weren't so bad, but they were intended for children isolated by geography or illness, circumstances that could not be overcome by other means.

Isabelle bid us good night with no complaints or advice; Francine and I sat by the fire for a while, just smiling at each other. It was nice to have a blemish-free report for once.

The next morning, my alarm went off an hour early. I lay motionless for a while, waiting for my head to clear, before asking my knowledge miner why it had woken me.

It seemed Isabelle's visit had been beaten up into a major story in some east coast news bulletins. A number of vocal members of Congress had been following the debate in Europe, and they didn't like the way it was heading. Isabelle, they declared, had sneaked into the country as an agitator. In fact, she'd offered to testify to Congress any time they wanted to hear about her work, but they'd never taken her up on it.

It wasn't clear whether it was reporters or anti-adai activists who'd obtained her itinerary and done some digging, but all the details had now been splashed around the country, and protesters were already gathering outside Helen's school. We'd faced media packs, cranks, and activists before, but the images the knowledge miner showed me were disturbing; it was five a.m. and the crowd had already encircled the school. I had a flashback to some news footage I'd seen in my teens, of young schoolgirls in Northern Ireland running the gauntlet of a protest by the opposing political faction; I could no longer remember who had been Catholic and who had been Protestant.

I woke Francine and explained the situation.

"We could just keep her home," I suggested.

Francine looked torn, but she finally agreed. "It will probably all blow over when Isabelle flies out on Sunday. One day off school isn't exactly capitulating to the mob."

At breakfast, I broke the news to Helen.

"I'm not staying home," she said.

"Why not? Don't you want to hang out with Sophie?"

Helen was amused. " 'Hang out'? Is that what the hippies used to say?" In her personal chronology of San Francisco, anything from before her birth belonged to the world portrayed in the tourist museums of Haight-Ashbury.

"Gossip. Listen to music. Interact socially in whatever manner you find agreeable."

She contemplated this last, open-ended definition. "Shop?"

"I don't see why not." There was no crowd outside the house, and though we were probably being watched, the protest was too large to be a moveable feast. Perhaps all the other parents would keep their children home, leaving the various placard wavers to fight among themselves.

Helen reconsidered. "No. We're doing that on Saturday. I want to go to school."

I glanced at Francine. Helen added, "It's not as if they can hurt me. I'm backed up."

Francine said, "It's not pleasant being shouted at. Insulted. Pushed around."

"I don't think it's going to be *pleasant*," Helen replied scornfully. "But I'm not going to let them tell me what to do."

To date, a handful of strangers had got close enough to yell abuse at her, and some of the children at her first school had been about as violent as (ordinary, drug-free, non-psychotic) nine-year-old bullies could be, but she'd never faced anything like this. I showed her the live news feed. She was not swayed. Francine and I retreated to the living room to confer.

I said, "I don't think it's a good idea." On top of everything else, I was beginning to suffer from a paranoid fear that Isabelle would blame us for the whole situation. Less fancifully, she could easily disapprove of us exposing Helen to the protesters. Even if that was not enough for her to terminate the licence immediately, eroding her confidence in us could lead to that fate, eventually.

Francine thought for a while. "If we both go with her, both walk beside her, what are they going to do? If they lay a finger on us, it's assault. If they try to drag her away from us, it's theft."

"Yes, but whatever they do, she gets to hear all the poison they spew out."

"She watches the news, Ben. She's heard it all before."

"Oh, shit." Isabelle and Sophie had come down to breakfast; I could hear Helen calmly filling them in about her plans.

Francine said, "Forget about pleasing Isabelle. If Helen wants to do this, knowing what it entails, and we can keep her safe, then we should respect her decision."

I felt a sting of anger at the unspoken implication: having gone to such lengths to enable her to make meaningful choices, I'd be a hypocrite to stand in her way. *Knowing what it entails?* She was nine-and-a-half years old.

I admired her courage, though, and I did believe that we could protect her.

I said, "All right. You call the other parents. I'll inform the police."

The moment we left the car, we were spotted. Shouts rang out, and a tide of angry people flowed towards us.

I glanced down at Helen and tightened my grip on her. "Don't let go of our hands."

She smiled at me indulgently, as if I was warning her about something trivial, like broken glass on the beach. "I'll be all right, Dad." She flinched as the crowd closed in, and then there were bodies pushing against us from every side, people jabbering in our faces, spittle flying. Francine and I turned to face each other, making something of a protective cage and a wedge through the adult legs. Frightening as it was to be submerged, I was glad my daughter wasn't at eye level with these people.

"Satan moves her! Satan is inside her! Out, Jezebel spirit!" A young woman in a high-collared lilac dress pressed her body against me and started praying in tongues.

"Gödel's theorem proves that the non-computible, nonlinear world behind the quantum collapse is a manifest expression of Buddha-nature," a neatly dressed youth intoned earnestly, establishing with admirable economy that he had no idea what any of these terms meant. "Ergo, there can be no soul in the machine."

"Cyber nano quantum. Cyber nano quantum. Cyber nano quantum." That chant came from one of our would-be "supporters," a middle-aged man in lycra cycling shorts who was forcefully groping down between us, trying to lay his hand on Helen's head and leave a few flakes of dead skin behind; according to cult doctrine, this would enable her to resurrect him when she got around to establishing the Omega Point. I blocked his way as firmly as I could without actually assaulting him, and he wailed like a pilgrim denied admission to Lourdes.

"Think you're going to live forever, Tinkerbell?" A leering old man with a matted beard poked his head out in front of us, and spat straight into Helen's face.

"Arsehole!" Francine shouted. She pulled out a handkerchief and started mopping the phlegm away. I crouched down and stretched my free arm around them. Helen was grimacing with disgust as Francine dabbed at her, but she wasn't crying.

I said, "Do you want to go back to the car?"

"No."

"Are you sure?"

Helen screwed up her face in an expression of irritation. "Why do you always ask me that? *Am I sure? Am I sure?* You're the one who sounds like a computer."

"I'm sorry." I squeezed her hand.

We ploughed on through the crowd. The core of the protesters turned out to be both saner and more civilized than the lunatics who'd got to us first; as we neared the school gates, people struggled to make room to let us through uninjured, at the same time as they shouted slogans for the cameras. "Healthcare for all, not just the rich!" I couldn't argue with that sentiment, though adai were just one of a thousand ways the wealthy could spare their children from disease, and in fact they were among the cheapest: the total cost in prosthetic bodies up to adult size came to less than the median lifetime expenditure on healthcare in the U.S. Banning adai wouldn't end the disparity between rich and poor, but I could understand why some people considered it the ultimate act of selfishness to create a child who could live forever. They probably never wondered about the fertility rates and resource use of their own descendants over the next few thousand years.

We passed through the gates, into a world of space and silence; any protester who trespassed here could be arrested immediately, and apparently none of them were sufficiently dedicated to Gandhian principles to seek out that fate.

Inside the entrance hall, I squatted down and put my arms around Helen. "Are you OK?"

"Yes."

"I'm really proud of you."

"You're shaking." She was right; my whole body was trembling slightly. It was more than the crush and the confrontation, and the sense of relief that we'd come through unscathed. Relief was never absolute for me; I could never quite erase the images of other possibilities at the back of my mind.

One of the teachers, Carmela Peña, approached us, looking stoical; when they'd agreed to take Helen, all the staff and parents had known that a day like this would come.

Helen said, "I'll be OK now." She kissed me on the cheek, then did the same to Francine. "I'm all right," she insisted. "You can go."

Carmela said, "We've got 60 percent of the kids coming. Not bad, considering."

Helen walked down the corridor, turning once to wave at us impatiently.

I said, "No, not bad."

A group of journalists cornered the five of us during the girls' shopping trip the next day, but media organizations had grown wary of lawsuits, and after Isabelle reminded them that she was presently enjoying "the ordinary liberties of every private citizen"—a quote from a recent eight-figure judgment against *Celebrity Stalker*—they left us in peace.

The night after Isabelle and Sophie flew out, I went to Helen's room to kiss her good night. As I turned to leave, she said, "What's a Qusp?"

"It's a kind of computer. Where did you hear about that?"

"On the net. It said I had a Qusp, but Sophie didn't."

Francine and I had made no firm decision as to what we'd tell her, and when. I said, "That's right, but it's nothing to worry about. It just means you're a little bit different from her."

Helen scowled. "I don't want to be different from Sophie."

"Everyone's different from everyone else," I said glibly. "Having a Qusp is just like . . . a car having a different kind of engine. It can still go to all the same places." *Just not all of them at once.* "You can both still do whatever you like. You can be as much like Sophie as you want." That wasn't entirely dishonest; the crucial difference could always be erased, simply by disabling the Qusp's shielding.

"I want to be the same," Helen insisted. "Next time I grow, why can't you give me what Sophie's got, instead?"

"What you have is newer. It's better."

"No one else has got it. Not just Sophie; none of the others." Helen knew she'd nailed me: if it was newer and better, why didn't the younger adai have it too?

I said, "It's complicated. You'd better go to sleep now; we'll talk about it later." I fussed with the blankets, and she stared at me resentfully.

I went downstairs and recounted the conversation to Francine. "What do you think?" I asked her. "Is it time?"

"Maybe it is," she said.

"I wanted to wait until she was old enough to understand the MWI."

Francine considered this. "Understand it how well, though? She's not going to be juggling density matrices any time soon. And if we make it a big secret, she's just going to get half-baked versions from other sources."

I flopped onto the couch. "This is going to be hard." I'd rehearsed the moment a thousand times, but in my imagination Helen had always been older, and there'd been hundreds of other adai with Qusps. In reality, no one had followed the trail we'd blazed. The evidence for the MWI had grown steadily stronger, but for most people it was still easy to ignore. Ever more sophisticated versions of rats running mazes just looked like elaborate computer games. You couldn't travel from branch to branch yourself, you couldn't spy on your parallel alter egos—and such feats would probably never be possible. "How do you tell a nine-year-old girl that she's the only sentient being on the planet who can make a decision, and stick to it?"

Francine smiled. "Not in those words, for a start."

"No." I put my arm around her. We were about to enter a minefield—and we couldn't help diffusing out across the perilous ground—but at least we had each other's judgment to keep us in check, to rein us in a little.

I said, "We'll work it out. We'll find the right way."

2050

Around four in the morning, I gave in to the cravings and lit my first cigarette in a month.

As I drew the warm smoke into my lungs, my teeth started chattering, as if the contrast had forced me to notice how cold the rest of my body had become. The red glow of the tip was the brightest thing in sight, but if there was a camera trained on me it would be infrared, so I'd been blazing away like a bonfire, anyway. As the smoke came back up I spluttered like a cat choking on a fur ball; the first one was always like that. I'd taken up the habit at the surreal age of 60, and even after five years on and off, my respiratory tract couldn't quite believe its bad luck.

For five hours, I'd been crouched in the mud at the edge of Lake Pontchartrain, a couple of kilometres west of the soggy ruins of New Orleans. Watching the barge, waiting for someone to come home. I'd been tempted to swim out and take a look around, but my aide sketched a bright red moat of domestic radar on the surface of the water, and offered no guarantee that I'd remain undetected even if I stayed outside the perimeter.

I'd called Francine the night before. It had been a short, tense conversation.

"I'm in Louisiana. I think I've got a lead."

"Yeah?"

"I'll let you know how it turns out."

"You do that."

I hadn't seen her in the flesh for almost two years. After facing too many dead ends together, we'd split up to cover more ground: Francine had searched from New York to Seattle; I'd taken the south. As the months had slipped away, her determination to put every emotional reaction aside for the sake of the task had gradually eroded. One night, I was sure, grief had overtaken her, alone in some soulless motel room—and it made no difference that the same thing had happened to me, a month later or a week before. Because we had not experienced it together, it was not a shared pain, a burden made lighter. After 47 years, though we now had a single purpose as never before, we were starting to come adrift.

I'd learnt about Jake Holder in Baton Rouge, triangulating on rumours and fifth-hand reports of barroom boasts. The boasts were usually empty; a prosthetic body equipped with software dumber than a microwave could make an infinitely pliable slave, but if the only way to salvage any trace of dignity when your buddies discovered that you owned the high-tech equivalent of a blow-up doll was to imply that there was somebody home inside, apparently a lot of men leapt at the chance.

Holder looked like something worse. I'd bought his lifetime purchasing records, and there'd been a steady stream of cyber-fetish porn over a period of two decades. Hardcore and pretentious; half the titles contained the word "manifesto". But the flow had stopped, about three months ago. The rumours were, he'd found something better.

I finished the cigarette, and slapped my arms to get the circulation going. *She would not be on the barge.* For all I knew, she'd heard the news from Brussels and was already halfway to Europe. That would be a difficult journey to make on her own, but there was no reason to believe that she didn't have loyal, trustworthy friends to assist her. I had too many out-of-date memories burnt into my skull: all the blazing, pointless rows, all the petty crimes, all the self-mutilation. Whatever had happened, whatever she'd been through, she was no longer the angry 15-year-old who'd left for school one Friday and never come back.

By the time she'd hit 13, we were arguing about everything. Her body had no need for the hormonal flood of puberty, but the software had ground on relentlessly, simulating all the neuroendocrine effects. Sometimes it had seemed like an act of torture to put her through that — instead of hunting for some magic short-cut to maturity — but the cardinal rule had been never to tinker, never to intervene, just to aim for the most faithful simulation possible of ordinary human development.

Whatever we'd fought about, she'd always known how to shut me up. "I'm just a thing to you! An instrument! Daddy's little silver bullet!" I didn't care who she was, or what she wanted; I'd fashioned her solely to slay my own fears. (I'd lie awake afterwards, rehearsing lame counter-arguments. Other children were born for infinitely baser motives: to work the fields, to sit in boardrooms, to banish ennui, to save failing marriages.) In her eyes, the Qusp itself wasn't good or bad — and she turned down all my offers to disable the shielding; that would have let me off the hook too easily. But I'd made her a freak for my own selfish reasons; I'd set her apart even from the other adai, purely to grant myself a certain kind of comfort. "You wanted to give birth to a singleton? Why didn't you just shoot yourself in the head every time you made a bad decision?"

When she went missing, we were afraid she'd been snatched from the street. But in her room, we'd found an envelope with the locator beacon she'd dug out of her body, and a note that read: *Don't look for me. I'm never coming back.*

I heard the tyres of a heavy vehicle squelching along the muddy track to my left. I hunkered lower, making sure I was hidden in the undergrowth. As the truck came to a halt with a faint metallic shudder, the barge disgorged an unmanned motorboat. My aide had captured the data streams exchanged, one specific challenge and response, but it had no clue how to crack the general case and mimic the barge's owner.

Two men climbed out of the truck. One was Jake Holder; I couldn't make out his face in the starlight, but I'd sat within a few metres of him in diners and bars in Baton Rouge, and my aide knew his somatic signature: the electromagnetic radiation from his nervous system and implants; his body's capacitative and inductive responses to small shifts in the ambient fields; the faint gamma-ray spectrum of his unavoidable, idiosyncratic load of radioisotopes, natural and Chernobylesque.

I did not know who his companion was, but I soon got the general idea.

"One thousand now," Holder said. "One thousand when you get back." His silhouette gestured at the waiting motorboat.

The other man was suspicious. "How do I know it will be what you say it is?"

"Don't call her 'it'," Holder complained. "She's not an object. She's my Lilith, my Lo-li-ta, my luscious clockwork succubus." For one hopeful moment, I pictured the customer snickering at this overheated sales pitch and coming to his senses; brothels in Baton Rouge openly advertised machine sex, with skilled human puppeteers, for a fraction of the price. Whatever he imagined the special thrill of a genuine adai to be, he had no way of knowing that Holder didn't have an accomplice controlling the body on the barge in exactly the same fashion. He might even be paying 2,000 dollars for a puppet job from Holder himself.

"OK. But if she's not genuine . . ."

My aide overheard money changing hands, and it had modelled the situation well enough to know how I'd wish, always, to respond. "Move now," it whispered in my ear. I complied without hesitation; 18 months before, I'd pavloved myself into swift obedience, with all the pain and nausea modern chemistry could induce. The aide couldn't puppet my limbs—I couldn't afford the elaborate surgery—but it overlaid movement cues on my vision, a system I'd adapted from off-the-shelf choreography software, and I strode out of the bushes, right up to the motorboat.

The customer was outraged. "What is this?"

I turned to Holder. "You want to fuck him first, Jake? I'll hold him down." There were things I didn't trust the aide to control; it set the boundaries, but it was better to let me improvise a little, and then treat my actions as one more part of the environment.

After a moment of stunned silence, Holder said icily, "I've never seen this prick before in my life." He'd been speechless for a little too long, though, to inspire any loyalty from a stranger; as he reached for his weapon, the customer backed away, then turned and fled.

Holder walked towards me slowly, gun outstretched. "What's your game? Are you after her? Is that it?" His implants were mapping my body—actively, since there was no need for stealth—but I'd tailed him for hours in Baton Rouge, and my aide knew him like an architectural plan. Over the starlit grey of his form, it overlaid a schematic, flaying him down to brain, nerves, and implants. A swarm of blue fireflies flickered into life in his motor cortex, prefiguring a peculiar shrug of the shoulders with no obvious connection to his trigger finger; before they'd reached the intensity that would signal his implants to radio the gun, my aide said "Duck."

The shot was silent, but as I straightened up again I could smell the propellant. I gave up thinking and followed the dance steps. As Holder strode forward and swung the gun towards me, I turned sideways, grabbed his right hand, then punched him hard, repeatedly, in the implant on the side of his neck. He was a fetishist, so he'd chosen bulky packages, intentionally visible through the skin. They were not hard-edged, and they were not inflexible—he wasn't that masochistic—but once you sufficiently compressed even the softest biocompatible foam, it might as well have been a lump of wood. While I hammered the wood into the muscles of his neck, I twisted his forearm upwards. He dropped the gun; I put my foot on it and slid it back towards the bushes.

In ultrasound, I saw blood pooling around his implant. I paused while the pressure built up, then I hit him again and the swelling burst like a giant blister. He sagged to his knees, bellowing with pain. I took the knife from my back pocket and held it to his throat.

I made Holder take off his belt, and I used it to bind his hands behind his back. I led him to the motorboat, and when the two of us were onboard, I suggested that he give it the necessary instructions. He was sullen but co-operative. I didn't feel anything; part of me still insisted that the transaction I'd caught him in was a hoax, and that there'd be nothing on the barge that couldn't be found in Baton Rouge.

The barge was old, wooden, smelling of preservatives and unvanquished rot. There were dirty plastic panes in the cabin windows, but all I could see in them was a reflected sheen. As we crossed the deck, I kept Holder intimately close, hoping that if there was an armed security system it wouldn't risk putting the bullet through both of us.

At the cabin door, he said resignedly, "Don't treat her badly." My blood went cold, and I pressed my forearm to my mouth to stifle an involuntary sob.

I kicked open the door, and saw nothing but shadows. I called out "Lights!" and two responded, in the ceiling and by the bed. Helen was naked, chained by the wrists and ankles. She looked up and saw me, then began to emit a horrified keening noise.

I pressed the blade against Holder's throat. "Open those things!"

"The shackles?"

"Yes!"

"I can't. They're not smart; they're just welded shut."

"Where are your tools?"

He hesitated. "I've got some wrenches in the truck. All the rest is back in town."

I looked around the cabin, then I led him into a corner and told him to stand there, facing the wall. I knelt by the bed.

"Ssh. We'll get you out of here." Helen fell silent. I touched her cheek with the back of my hand; she didn't flinch, but she stared back at me, disbelieving. "We'll get you out." The timber bedposts were thicker than my arms, the links of the chains wide as my thumb. I wasn't going to snap any part of this with my bare hands.

Helen's expression changed: I was real, she was not hallucinating. She said dully, "I thought you'd given up on me. Woke one of the backups. Started again."

I said, "I'd never give up on you."

"Are you sure?" She searched my face. "Is this the edge of what's possible? Is this the worst it can get?"

I didn't have an answer to that.

I said, "You remember how to go numb, for a shedding?"

She gave me a faint, triumphant smile. "Absolutely." She'd had to endure imprisonment and humiliation, but she'd always had the power to cut herself off from her body's senses.

"Do you want to do it now? Leave all this behind?"

"Yes."

"You'll be safe soon. I promise you."

"I believe you." Her eyes rolled up.

I cut open her chest and took out the Qusp.

Francine and I had both carried spare bodies, and clothes, in the trunks of our cars. Adai were banned from domestic flights, so Helen and I drove along the interstate, up towards Washington D.C., where Francine would meet us. We could claim asylum at the Swiss embassy; Isabelle had already set the machinery in motion.

Helen was quiet at first, almost shy with me as if with a stranger, but on the second day, as we crossed from Alabama into Georgia, she began to open up. She told me a little of how she'd hitchhiked from state to state, finding casual jobs that paid e-cash and needed no social security number, let alone biometric ID. "Fruit picking was the best."

She'd made friends along the way, and confided her nature to those she thought she could trust. She still wasn't sure whether or not she'd been betrayed. Holder had found her in a transient's camp under a bridge, and someone must have told him exactly where to look, but it was always possible that she'd been recognized by a casual acquaintance who'd seen her face in the media years before. Francine and I had never publicized her disappearance, never put up flyers or web pages, out of fear that it would only make the danger worse.

On the third day, as we crossed the Carolinas, we drove in near silence again. The landscape was stunning, the fields strewn with flowers, and Helen seemed calm. Maybe this was what she needed the most: just safety, and peace.

As dusk approached, though, I felt I had to speak.

"There's something I've never told you," I said. "Something that happened to me when I was young."

Helen smiled. "Don't tell me you ran away from the farm? Got tired of milking, and joined the circus?"

I shook my head. "I was never adventurous. It was just a little thing." I told her about the kitchen hand.

She pondered the story for a while. "And that's why you built the Qusp? That's why you made me? In the end, it all comes down to that man in the alley?" She sounded more bewildered than angry.

I bowed my head. "I'm sorry."

"For what?" she demanded. "Are you sorry that I was ever born?"

"No, but—"

"You didn't put me on that boat. Holder did that."

I said, "I brought you into a world with people like him. What I made you, made you a target."

"And if I'd been flesh and blood?" she said. "Do you think there aren't people like him, for flesh and blood? Or do you honestly believe that if you'd had an organic child, there would have been *no chance at all* that she'd have run away?"

I started weeping. "I don't know. I'm just sorry I hurt you."

Helen said, "I don't blame you for what you did. And I understand it better now. You saw a spark of good in yourself, and you wanted to cup your hands around it, protect it, make it stronger. I understand that. I'm not that spark, but that doesn't matter. I know who I am, I know what my choices are, and I'm glad of that. I'm glad you gave me that." She reached over and squeezed my hand. "Do you think I'd feel *better*, here and now, just because some other version of me handled the same situations better?" She smiled. "Knowing that other people are having a good time isn't much of a consolation to anyone."

I composed myself. The car beeped to bring my attention to a booking it had made in a motel a few kilometres ahead.

Helen said, "I've had time to think about a lot of things. Whatever the laws say, whatever the bigots say, all adai are part of the human race. And what *I* have is something almost every person who's ever lived thought they possessed. Human psychology, human culture, human morality, all evolved with the illusion that we lived in a single history. But we don't—so in the long run, something has to give. Call me old-fashioned, but I'd rather we tinker with our physical nature than abandon our whole identities."

I was silent for a while. "So what are your plans, now?"

"I need an education."

"What do you want to study?"

"I'm not sure yet. A million different things. But in the long run, I know what I want to do."

"Yeah?" The car turned off the highway, heading for the motel.

"You made a start," she said, "but it's not enough. There are people in billions of other branches where the Qusp hasn't been invented yet—and the way things stand, there'll always be branches without it. What's the point in us having this thing, if we don't share it? All those people deserve to have the power to make their own choices."

"Travel between the branches isn't a simple problem," I explained gently. "That would be orders of magnitude harder than the Qusp."

Helen smiled, conceding this, but the corners of her mouth took on the stubborn set I recognized as the precursor to a thousand smaller victories.

She said, "Give me time, Dad. Give me time."

slow Life

michael swanwick

Michael Swanwick made his debut in 1980, and in the twenty-two years that followed established himself as one of SF's most prolific and consistently excellent writers at short lengths, as well as one of the premier novelists of his generation. He has several times been a finalist for the Nebula Award, as well as for the World Fantasy Award and for the John W. Campbell Award, and has won the Theodore Sturgeon Award and the Asimov's Readers Award poll. In 1991, his novel Stations of the Tide *won him a Nebula Award as well, and in 1995 he won the World Fantasy Award for his story "Radio Waves." In the last few years, he's won back-to-back Hugo Awards—he won the Hugo in 1999 for his story "The Very Pulse of the Machine," and followed it up in 2000 with another Hugo Award for his story "Scherzo with Tyrannosaur," and yet another Hugo Award in 2001 for his story "The Dog Said Bow-wow." His other books include his first novel,* In the Drift, *which was published in 1985, a novella-length book,* Griffin's Egg, *1987's popular novel* Vacuum Flowers, *a critically acclaimed fantasy novel,* The Iron Dragon's Daughter, *which was a finalist for the World Fantasy Award and the Arthur C. Clarke Award (a rare distinction!), and* Jack Faust, *a sly reworking of the Faust legend that explores the unexpected impact of technology on society. His short fiction has been assembled in* Gravity's Angels, A Geography of Unknown Lands, Slow Dancing Through Time *(a collection of his collaborative short work with other writers),* Moon Dogs, Puck Aleshire's Abecedary, *and* Tales of Old Earth. *He's also published a collection of critical articles,* The Postmodern Archipelago, *and a book-length interview* Being Gardner Dozois. *His most recent book is a major new novel,* Bones of the Earth, *and coming up are several new collections. He's had stories in our Second, Third, Fourth, Sixth, Seventh, Tenth, and Thirteenth through Nineteenth Annual Collections. Swanwick lives in Philadelphia with his wife, Marianne Porter (Sean left for college). He has a website at www.michaelswanwick.com.*

Explorers should expect the unexpected, but, as this suspenseful adventure to Titan shows us, sometimes you encounter something a little more unexpected than usual . . .

> "It was the Second Age of Space. Gagarin, Shepard, Glenn, and
> Armstrong were all dead. It was *our* turn to make history now."
> —*The Memoirs of Lizzie O'Brien*

The raindrop began forming ninety kilometers above the surface of Titan. It started with an infinitesimal speck of tholin, adrift in the cold nitrogen atmosphere. Dianoacetylene condensed on the seed nucleus, molecule by molecule, until it was one shard of ice in a cloud of billions.

Now the journey could begin.

It took almost a year for the shard of ice in question to precipitate downward twenty-five kilometers, where the temperature dropped low enough that ethane began to condense on it. But when it did, growth was rapid.

Down it drifted.

At forty kilometers, it was for a time caught up in an ethane cloud. There it continued to grow. Occasionally it collided with another droplet and doubled in size. Finally it was too large to be held effortlessly aloft by the gentle stratospheric winds.

It fell.

Falling, it swept up methane and quickly grew large enough to achieve a terminal velocity of almost two meters per second.

At twenty-seven kilometers, it passed through a dense layer of methane clouds. It acquired more methane, and continued its downward flight.

As the air thickened, its velocity slowed and it began to lose some of its substance to evaporation. At two and a half kilometers, when it emerged from the last patchy clouds, it was losing mass so rapidly it could not normally be expected to reach the ground.

It was, however, falling toward the equatorial highlands, where mountains of ice rose a towering five hundred meters into the atmosphere. At two meters and a lazy new terminal velocity of one meter per second, it was only a breath away from hitting the surface.

Two hands swooped an open plastic collecting bag upward, and snared the raindrop.

"Gotcha!" Lizzie O'Brien cried gleefully.

She zip-locked the bag shut, held it up so her helmet cam could read the bar code in the corner, and said, "One raindrop." Then she popped it into her collecting box.

Sometimes it's the little things that make you happiest. Somebody would spend a *year* studying this one little raindrop when Lizzie got it home. And it was just Bag 64 in Collecting Case 5. She was going to be on the surface of Titan long enough to scoop up the raw material of a revolution in planetary science. The thought of it filled her with joy.

Lizzie dogged down the lid of the collecting box and began to skip across the granite-hard ice, splashing the puddles and dragging the boot of her atmosphere suit through the rivulets of methane pouring down the mountainside. "*I'm sing-ing in the rain.*" She threw out her arms and spun around. "*Just sing-ing in the rain!*"

"Uh . . . O'Brien?" Alan Greene said from the *Clement.* "Are you all right?"

"*Dum-dee-dum-dee-dee-dum-dum, I'm . . . some-thing again.*"

"Oh, leave her alone." Consuelo Hong said with sour good humor. She was down on the plains, where the methane simply boiled into the air, and the ground was covered with thick, gooey tholin. It was, she had told them, like wading ankle-deep in molasses. "Can't you recognize the scientific method when you hear it?"

"If you say so," Alan said dubiously. He was stuck in the *Clement,* overseeing the expedition and minding the website. It was a comfortable gig—he wouldn't be sleeping in his suit *or* surviving on recycled water and energy stix—and he didn't think the others knew how much he hated it.

"What's next on the schedule?" Lizzie asked.

"Um . . . well, there's still the robot turbot to be released. How's that going, Hong?"

"Making good time. I oughta reach the sea in a couple of hours."

"Okay, then it's time O'Brien rejoined you at the lander. O'Brien, start spread-ing out the balloon and going over the harness checklist."

"Roger that."

"And while you're doing that, I've got today's voice-posts from the Web cued up."

Lizzie groaned, and Consuelo blew a raspberry. By NAFTASA policy, the ground crew participated in all web-casts. Officially, they were delighted to share their experiences with the public. But the VoiceWeb (privately, Lizzie thought of it as the Illiternet) made them accessible to people who lacked even the minimal intellectual skills needed to handle a keyboard.

"Let me remind you that we're on open circuit here, so anything you say will go into my reply. You're certainly welcome to chime in at any time. But each question-and-response is transmitted as one take, so if you flub a line, we'll have to go back to the beginning and start all over again."

"Yeah, yeah," Consuelo grumbled.

"We've done this before," Lizzie reminded him.

"Okay. Here's the first one."

"*Uh, hi, this is BladeNinja43. I was wondering just what it is that you guys are hoping to discover out there.*"

"That's an extremely good question," Alan lied. "And the answer is: We don't know! This is a voyage of discovery, and we're engaged in what's called 'pure science.' Now, time and time again, the purest research has turned out to be extremely profitable. But we're not looking that far ahead. We're just hoping to find something absolutely unexpected."

"My God, you're slick," Lizzie marveled.

"I'm going to edit that from the tape," Alan said cheerily. "Next up."

"*This is Mary Schroeder, from the United States. I teach high school English, and I wanted to know for my students, what kind of grades the three of you had when you were their age.*"

Alan began. "I was an overachiever, I'm afraid. In my sophomore year, first semester, I got a B in Chemistry and panicked. I thought it was the end of the world. But then I dropped a couple of extracurriculars, knuckled down, and brought that grade right up."

"I was good in everything but French Lit," Consuelo said.

"I nearly flunked out!" Lizzie said. "Everything was difficult for me. But then I decided I wanted to be an astronaut, and it all clicked into place. I realized that, hey, it's just hard work. And now, well, here I am."

"That's good. Thanks, guys. Here's the third, from Maria Vasquez."

"*Is there life on Titan?*"

"Probably not. It's *cold* down there! 94° Kelvin is the same as −179° Celsius, or −290° Fahrenheit. And yet . . . life is persistent. It's been found in Antarctic ice and in boiling water in submarine volcanic vents. Which is why we'll be paying particular attention to exploring the depths of the ethane-methane sea. If life is anywhere to be found, that's where we'll find it."

"Chemically, the conditions here resemble the anoxic atmosphere on Earth in which life first arose," Consuelo said. "Further, we believe that such prebiotic chemistry has been going on here for four and a half billion years. For an organic chemist like me, it's the best toy box in the Universe. But that lack of heat is a problem. Chemical reactions that occur quickly back home would take thousands of years here. It's hard to see how life could arise under such a handicap."

"It would have to be slow life," Lizzie said thoughtfully. "Something vegetative. 'Vaster than empires and more slow.' It would take millions of years to reach maturity. A single thought might require centuries. . . ."

"Thank you for that, uh, wild scenario!" Alan said quickly. Their NAFTASA masters frowned on speculation. It was, in their estimation, almost as unprofessional as heroism. "This next question comes from Danny in Toronto."

"*Hey, man, I gotta say I really envy you being in that tiny little ship with those two hot babes.*"

Alan laughed lightly. "Yes, Ms. Hong and Ms. O'Brien are certainly attractive women. But we're kept so busy that, believe it or not, the thought of sex never comes up. And currently, while I tend to the *Clement*, they're both on the surface of Titan at the bottom of an atmosphere 60 percent more dense than Earth's, and encased in armored exploration suits. So even if I did have inappropriate thoughts, there's no way we could—"

"Hey, Alan," Lizzie said. "Tell me something."

"Yes?"

"What are you wearing?"

"Uh . . . switching over to private channel."

"Make that a three-way," Consuelo said.

Ballooning, Lizzie decided, was the best way there was of getting around. Moving with the gentle winds, there was no sound at all. And the view was great!

People talked a lot about the "murky orange atmosphere" of Titan, but your eyes adjusted. Turn up the gain on your helmet, and the white mountains of ice were *dazzling!* The methane streams carved cryptic runes into the heights. Then, at the tholin-line, white turned to a rich palette of oranges, reds, and yellows. There was a lot going on down there—more than she'd be able to learn in a hundred visits.

The plains were superficially duller, but they had their charms as well. Sure, the atmosphere was so dense that refracted light made the horizon curve upward to either side. But you got used to it. The black swirls and cryptic red tracery of unknown processes on the land below never grew tiring.

On the horizon, she saw the dark arm of Titan's narrow sea. If that was what it was. Lake Erie was larger, but the spin doctors back home had argued that since Titan was so much smaller than Earth, *relatively* it qualified as a sea. Lizzie had her own opinion, but she knew when to keep her mouth shut.

Consuelo was there now. Lizzie switched her visor over to the live feed. Time to catch the show.

"I can't believe I'm finally here," Consuelo said. She let the shrink-wrapped fish slide from her shoulder down to the ground. "Five kilometers doesn't seem like very far when you're coming down from orbit—just enough to leave a margin for error so the lander doesn't come down in the sea. But when you have to *walk* that distance, through tarry, sticky tholin . . . well, it's one heck of a slog."

"Consuelo, can you tell us what it's like there?" Alan asked.

"I'm crossing the beach. Now I'm at the edge of the sea." She knelt, dipped a hand into it. "It's got the consistency of a Slushy. Are you familiar with that drink? Lots of shaved ice sort of half-melted in a cup with flavored syrup. What we've got here is almost certainly a methane-ammonia mix; we'll know for sure after we get a sample to a laboratory. Here's an early indicator, though. It's dissolving the tholin off my glove." She stood.

"Can you describe the beach?"

"Yeah. It's white. Granular. I can kick it with my boot. Ice sand for sure. Do you want me to collect samples first or release the fish?"

"Release the fish," Lizzie said, almost simultaneously with Alan's "Your call."

"Okay, then." Consuelo carefully cleaned both of her suit's gloves in the sea, then seized the shrink-wrap's zip tab and yanked. The plastic parted. Awkwardly, she straddled the fish, lifted it by the two side-handles, and walked it into the dark slush.

"Okay, I'm standing in the sea now. It's up to my ankles. Now it's at my knees. I think it's deep enough here."

She set the fish down. "Now I'm turning it on."

The Mitsubishi turbot wriggled, as if alive. With one fluid motion, it surged forward, plunged, and was gone.

Lizzie switched over to the fishcam.

Black liquid flashed past the turbot's infrared eyes. Straight away from the shore it swam, seeing nothing but flecks of paraffin, ice, and other suspended particulates as they loomed up before it and were swept away in the violence of its wake. A hundred meters out, it bounced a pulse of radar off the sea floor, then dove, seeking the depths.

Rocking gently in her balloon harness, Lizzie yawned.

Snazzy Japanese cybernetics took in a minute sample of the ammonia-water, fed it through a deftly constructed internal laboratory, and excreted the waste products behind it. "We're at twenty meters now," Consuelo said. "Time to collect a second sample."

The turbot was equipped to run hundreds of on-the-spot analyses. But it had only enough space for twenty permanent samples to be carried back home. The first sample had been nibbled from the surface slush. Now it twisted, and gulped down five drams of sea fluid in all its glorious impurity. To Lizzie, this was science on the hoof. Not very dramatic, admittedly, but intensely exciting.

She yawned again.

"O'Brien?" Alan said, "How long has it been since you last slept?'

"Huh? Oh . . . twenty hours? Don't worry about me, I'm fine."

"Go to sleep. That's an order."

"But—"

"Now."

Fortunately, the suit was comfortable enough to sleep in. It had been designed so she could.

First she drew in her arms from the suit's sleeves. Then she brought in her legs, tucked them up under her chin, and wrapped her arms around them. "Night, guys," she said.

"*Buenas noches, querida,*" Consuelo said, "*que tengas lindos sueños.*"

"Sleep tight, space explorer."

The darkness when she closed her eyes was so absolute it crawled. Black, black, black. Phantom lights moved within the darkness, formed lines, shifted away when she tried to see them. They were as fugitive as fish, luminescent, fainter than faint, there and with a flick of her attention fled.

A school of little thoughts flashed through her mind, silver-scaled and gone.

Low, deep, slower than sound, something tolled. The bell from a drowned clock tower patiently stroking midnight. She was beginning to get her bearings. Down *there* was where the ground must be. Flowers grew there unseen. Up above was where the sky would be, if there were a sky. Flowers floated there as well.

Deep within the submerged city, she found herself overcome by an enormous and placid sense of self. A swarm of unfamiliar sensations washed through her mind, and then . . .

"Are you me?" a gentle voice asked.

"No," she said carefully. "I don't think so."

Vast astonishment. "You think you are not me?"

"Yes. I think so, anyway."

"Why?"

There didn't seem to be any proper response to that, so she went back to the beginning of the conversation and ran through it again, trying to bring it to another conclusion. Only to bump against that "Why?" once again.

"I don't know why," she said.

"Why not?"

"I don't know."

She looped through that same dream over and over again all the while that she slept.

When she awoke, it was raining again. This time, it was a drizzle of pure methane from the lower cloud deck at fifteen kilometers. These clouds were (the theory went) methane condensate from the wet air swept up from the sea. They fell on the mountains and washed them clean of tholin. It was the methane that eroded and shaped the ice, carving gullies and caves.

Titan had more kinds of rain than anywhere else in the Solar System.

The sea had crept closer while Lizzie slept. It now curled up to the horizon on either side like an enormous dark smile. Almost time now for her to begin her descent. While she checked her harness settings, she flicked on telemetry to see what the others were up to.

The robot turbot was still spiraling its way downward, through the lightless sea, seeking its distant floor. Consuelo was trudging through the tholin again, retracing her five-kilometer trek from the lander *Harry Stubbs*, and Alan was answering another set of webposts.

"*Modelos de la evolución de Titanes indican que la luna formó de una nube circumplanetaria rica en amoníaco y metano, la cual al condensarse dio forma a Saturno así como a otros satélites. Bajo estas condiciones en—*"

"Uh . . . guys?"

Alan stopped. "Damn it, O'Brien, now I've got to start all over again."

"Welcome back to the land of the living," Consuelo said. "You should check out the readings we're getting from the robofish. Lots of long-chain polymers, odd fractions . . . tons of interesting stuff."

"Guys?"

This time her tone of voice registered with Alan. "What is it, O'Brien?"

"I think my harness is jammed."

Lizzie had never dreamed disaster could be such drudgery. First there were hours of back-and-forth with the NAFTASA engineers. What's the status of rope 14? Try tugging on rope 8. What do the D-rings look like? It was slow work because of the lag time for messages to be relayed to Earth and back. And Alan insisted on filling the silence with posts from the VoiceWeb. Her plight had gone global in minutes, and every unemployable loser on the planet had to log in with suggestions.

"*Thezgemoth337, here. It seems to me that if you had a gun and shot up through the balloon, it would maybe deflate and then you could get down.*"

"I don't have a gun, shooting a hole in the balloon would cause it not to deflate but to rupture, I'm 800 hundred meters above the surface, there's a sea below me, and I'm in a suit that's not equipped for swimming. Next."

"If you had a really big knife—"

"Cut! Jesus, Greene, is this the best you can find? Have you heard back from the organic chem guys yet?"

"Their preliminary analysis just came in," Alan said. "As best they can guess—and I'm cutting through a lot of clutter here—the rain you went through wasn't pure methane."

"No shit, Sherlock."

"They're assuming that whitish deposit you found on the rings and ropes is your culprit. They can't agree on what it is, but they think it underwent a chemical reaction with the material of your balloon and sealed the rip panel shut."

"I thought this was supposed to be a pretty nonreactive environment."

"It is. But your balloon runs off your suit's waste heat. The air in it is several degrees above the melting-point of ice. That's the equivalent of a blast furnace, here on Titan. Enough energy to run any number of amazing reactions. You haven't stopped tugging on the vent rope?"

"I'm tugging away right now. When one arm gets sore, I switch arms."

"Good girl. I know how tired you must be."

"Take a break from the voice-posts," Consuelo suggested, "and check out the results we're getting from the robofish. It's giving us some really interesting stuff."

So she did. And for a time it distracted her, just as they'd hoped. There was a lot more ethane and propane than their models had predicted, and surprisingly less methane. The mix of fractions was nothing like what she'd expected. She had learned just enough chemistry to guess at some of the implications of the data being generated, but not enough to put it all together. Still tugging at the ropes in the sequence uploaded by the engineers in Toronto, she scrolled up the chart of hydrocarbons dissolved in the lake.

Solute	Solute mole fraction
Ethyne	4.0×10^{-4}
Propyne	4.4×10^{-5}
1,3-Butadiyne	7.7×10^{-7}
Carbon Dioxide	0.1×10^{-5}
Methanenitrile	5.7×10^{-6}

But after a while, the experience of working hard and getting nowhere, combined with the tedium of floating farther and farther out over the featureless sea, began to drag on her. The columns of figures grew meaningless, then indistinct.

Propanenitrile 6.0×10^{-5}

Propanenitrile 9.9×10^{-6}

Propynenitrile 5.3×10^{-6}

Hardly noticing she was doing so, she fell asleep.

She was in a lightless building, climbing flight after flight of stairs. There were other people with her, also climbing. They jostled against her as she ran up the stairs, flowing upward, passing her, not talking.

It was getting colder.

She had a distant memory of being in the furnace room down below. It was hot there, swelteringly so. Much cooler where she was now. Almost too cool. With every step she took, it got a little cooler still. She found herself slowing down. Now it was definitely too cold. Unpleasantly so. Her leg muscles ached. The air seemed to be thickening around her as well. She could barely move now.

This was, she realized, the natural consequence of moving away from the furnace. The higher up she got, the less heat there was to be had, and the less energy to be turned into motion. It all made perfect sense to her somehow.

Step. Pause.

Step. Longer pause.

Stop.

The people around her had slowed to a stop as well. A breeze colder than ice touched her, and without surprise, she knew that they had reached the top of the stairs and were standing upon the building's roof. It was as dark without as it had been within. She stared upward and saw nothing.

"Horizons. Absolutely baffling," somebody murmured beside her.

"Not once you get used to them." she replied.

"Up and down—are these hierarchic values?"

"They don't have to be."

"Motion. What a delightful concept."

"We like it."

"So you *are* me?"

"No. I mean, I don't think so."

"Why?"

She was struggling to find an answer to this, when somebody gasped. High up in the starless, featureless sky, a light bloomed. The crowd around her rustled with unspoken fear. Brighter, the light grew. Brighter still. She could feel heat radiating from it, slight but definite, like the rumor of a distant sun. Everyone about her was frozen with horror. More terrifying than a light where none was possible was the presence of heat. It simply could not be. And yet it was.

She, along with the others, waited and watched for . . . something. She could not say what. The light shifted slowly in the sky. It was small, intense, ugly.

Then the light *screamed.*

She woke up.

"Wow," she said. "I just had the weirdest dream."

"Did you?" Alan said casually.

"Yeah. There was this light in the sky. It was like a nuclear bomb or something. I mean, it didn't look anything like a nuclear bomb, but it was terrifying the way a nuclear bomb would be. Everybody was staring at it. We couldn't move. And then . . ." She shook her head. "I lost it. I'm sorry. It was just so strange. I can't put it into words."

"Never mind that," Consuelo said cheerily. "We're getting some great readings down below the surface. Fractional polymers, long-chain hydrocarbons . . . fabulous stuff. You really should try to stay awake to catch some of this."

She was fully awake now, and not feeling too happy about it. "I guess that means that nobody's come up with any good ideas yet on how I might get down."

"Uh . . . what do you mean?"

"Because if they had, you wouldn't be so goddamned upbeat, would you?"

"*Some*body woke up on the wrong side of the bed," Alan said. "Please remember that there are certain words we don't use in public."

"I'm sorry," Consuelo said. "I was just trying to —"

"— distract me. Okay, fine. What the hey. I can play along." Lizzie pulled herself together. "So your findings mean . . . what? Life?"

"I keep telling you guys. It's too early to make that kind of determination. What we've got so far are just some very, very interesting readings."

"Tell her the big news," Alan said.

"Brace yourself. We've got a real ocean! Not this tiny little two-hundred-by-fifty-miles glorified lake we've been calling a sea, but a genuine ocean! Sonar readings show that what we see is just an evaporation pan atop a thirty-kilometer-thick cap of ice. The real ocean lies underneath, two hundred kilometers deep."

"Jesus." Lizzie caught herself. "I mean, gee whiz. Is there any way of getting the robofish down into it?"

"How do you think we got the depth readings? It's headed down there right now. There's a chimney through the ice right at the center of the visible sea. That's what replenishes the surface liquid. And directly under the hole, there's — guess what? — volcanic vents!"

"So does that mean . . . ?"

"If you use the L-word again," Consuelo said, "I'll spit."

Lizzie grinned. *That* was the Consuelo Hong she knew. "What about the tidal data? I thought the lack of orbital perturbation ruled out a significant ocean entirely."

"Well, Toronto thinks . . ."

At first, Lizzie was able to follow the reasoning of the planetary geologists back in Toronto. Then it got harder. Then it became a drone. As she drifted off into sleep, she had time enough to be peevishly aware that she really shouldn't be dropping off to sleep all the time like this. She oughtn't to be so tired. She . . .

She found herself in the drowned city again. She still couldn't see anything, but she knew it was a city because she could hear the sound of rioters smashing store windows. Their voices swelled into howling screams and receded into angry mutters, like a violent surf washing through the streets. She began to edge away backwards.

Somebody spoke into her ear.

"Why did you do this to us?"

"I didn't do anything to you."

"You brought us knowledge."

"What knowledge?"

"You said you were not us."

"Well, I'm not."

"You should never have told us that."

"You wanted me to lie?"

Horrified confusion. "Falsehood. What a distressing idea."

The smashing noises were getting louder. Somebody was splintering a door with an axe. Explosions. Breaking glass. She heard wild laughter. Shrieks. "We've got to get out of here."

"Why did you send the messenger?"

"What messenger?"

"The star! The star! The star!"

"Which star?"

"There are two stars?"

"There are billions of stars."

"No more! Please! Stop! No more!"

She was awake.

"*Hello, yes, I appreciate that the young lady is in extreme danger, but I really don't think she should have used the Lord's name in vain.*"

"Greene," Lizzie said, "do we really have to put up with this?"

"Well, considering how many billions of public-sector dollars it took to bring us here . . . yes. Yes, we do. I can even think of a few backup astronauts who would say that a little upbeat web-posting was a pretty small price to pay for the privilege."

"Oh, barf."

"I'm switching to a private channel," Alan said calmly. The background radiation changed subtly. A faint, granular crackling that faded away when she tried to focus on it. In a controlled, angry voice Alan said, "O'Brien, just what the hell is going on with you?"

"Look, I'm sorry, I apologize, I'm a little excited about something. How long was I out? Where's Consuelo? I'm going to say the L-word. And the I-word as well. We have life. Intelligent life!"

"It's been a few hours. Consuelo is sleeping. O'Brien, I hate to say this, but you're not sounding at all rational."

"There's a perfectly logical reason for that. Okay, it's a little strange, and maybe it won't sound perfectly logical to you initially, but . . . look, I've been having sequential dreams. I think they're significant. Let me tell you about them."

And she did so. At length.

When she was done, there was a long silence. Finally, Alan said, "Lizzie, think.

Why would something like that communicate to you in your dreams? Does that make any sense?"

"I think it's the only way it can. I think it's how it communicates among itself. It doesn't move—motion is an alien and delightful concept to it—and it wasn't aware that its component parts were capable of individualization. That sounds like some kind of broadcast thought to me. Like some kind of wireless distributed network."

"You know the medical kit in your suit? I want you to open it up. Feel around for the bottle that's braille-coded twenty-seven, okay?"

"Alan, I do *not* need an antipsychotic!"

"I'm not saying you need it. But wouldn't you be happier knowing you had it in you?" This was Alan at his smoothest. Butter wouldn't melt in his mouth. "Don't you think that would help us accept what you're saying?"

"Oh, all right!" She drew in an arm from the suit's arm, felt around for the med kit, and drew out a pill, taking every step by the regs, checking the coding four times before she put it in her mouth and once more (each pill was individually braille-coded as well) before she swallowed it. "Now will you listen to me? I'm quite serious about this." She yawned. "I really do think that . . ." She yawned again. "That . . .

"Oh, piffle."

Once more into the breach, dear friends, she thought, and plunged deep, deep into the sea of darkness. This time, though, she felt she had a handle on it. The city was drowned because it existed at the bottom of a lightless ocean. It was alive, and it fed off of volcanic heat. That was why it considered up and down hierarchic values. Up was colder, slower, less alive. Down was hotter, faster, more filled with thought. The city/entity was a collective life-form, like a Portuguese man-of-war or a massively hyperlinked expert network. It communicated within itself by some form of electromagnetism. Call it mental radio. It communicated with her that same way.

"I think I understand you now."

"Don't understand—run!"

Somebody impatiently seized her elbow and hurried her along. Faster she went, and faster. She couldn't see a thing. It was like running down a lightless tunnel a hundred miles underground at midnight. Glass crunched underfoot. The ground was uneven and sometimes she stumbled. Whenever she did, her unseen companion yanked her up again.

"Why are you so slow?"

"I didn't know I was."

"Believe me, you are."

"Why are we running?"

"We are being pursued." They turned suddenly, into a side passage, and were jolting over rubbled ground. Sirens wailed. Things collapsed. Mobs surged.

"Well, you've certainly got the motion thing down pat."

Impatiently. "It's only a metaphor. You don't think this is a *real* city, do you? Why are you so dim? Why are you so difficult to communicate with? Why are you so slow?"

"I didn't know I was."

Vast irony. "Believe me, you are."

"What can I do?"

"Run!"

Whooping and laughter. At first, Lizzie confused it with the sounds of mad destruction in her dream. Then she recognized the voices as belonging to Alan and Consuelo. "How long was I out?" she asked.

"You were out?"

"No more than a minute or two," Alan said. "It's not important. Check out the visual the robofish just gave us."

Consuelo squirted the image to Lizzie.

Lizzie gasped. "Oh! Oh, my."

It was beautiful. Beautiful in the way that the great European cathedrals were, and yet at the same time undeniably organic. The structure was tall and slender, and fluted and buttressed and absolutely ravishing. It had grown about a volcanic vent, with openings near the bottom to let sea water in, and then followed the rising heat upward. Occasional channels led outward and then looped back into the main body again. It loomed higher than seemed possible (but it *was* underwater, of course, and on a low-gravity world at that), a complexly layered congeries of tubes like church-organ pipes, or deep-sea worms lovingly intertwined.

It had the elegance of design that only a living organism can have.

"Okay," Lizzie said. "Consuelo. You've got to admit that—"

"I'll go as far as 'complex prebiotic chemistry.' Anything more than that is going to have to wait for more definite readings." Cautious as her words were, Consuelo's voice rang with triumph. It said, clearer than words, that she could happily die then and there, a satisfied xenochemist.

Alan, almost equally elated, said, "Watch what happens when we intensify the image."

The structure shifted from gray to a muted rainbow of pastels, rose bleeding into coral, sunrise yellow into winter-ice blue. It was breathtaking.

"Wow." For an instant, even her own death seemed unimportant. Relatively unimportant, anyway.

So thinking, she cycled back again into sleep. And fell down into the darkness, into the noisy clamor of her mind.

It was hellish. The city was gone, replaced by a matrix of noise: hammerings, clatterings, sudden crashes. She started forward and walked into an upright steel pipe. Staggering back, she stumbled into another. An engine started up somewhere nearby, and gigantic gears meshed noisily, grinding something that gave off a metal shriek. The floor shook underfoot. Lizzie decided it was wisest to stay put.

———

A familiar presence, permeated with despair. "Why did you do this to me?"

"What have I done?"

"I used to be everything."

Something nearby began pounding like a pile-driver. It was giving her a head-ache. She had to shout to be heard over its din. "You're still something!"

Quietly. "I'm nothing."

"That's . . . not true! You're . . . here! You exist! That's . . . something!"

A world-encompassing sadness. "False comfort. What a pointless thing to offer."

She was conscious again.

Consuelo was saying something. ". . . isn't going to like it."

"The spiritual wellness professionals back home all agree that this is the best possible course of action for her."

"Oh, please!"

Alan had to be the most anal-retentive person Lizzie knew. Consuelo was def-initely the most phlegmatic. Things had to be running pretty tense for both of them to be bickering like this. "Um . . . guys?" Lizzie said. "I'm awake."

There was a moment's silence, not unlike those her parents had shared when she was little and she'd wandered into one of their arguments. Then Consuelo said, a little too brightly, "Hey, it's good to have you back," and Alan said, "NAF-TASA wants you to speak with someone. Hold on. I've got a recording of her first transmission cued up and ready for you."

A woman's voice came online. *"This is Dr. Alma Rosenblum. Elizabeth, I'd like to talk with you about how you're feeling. I appreciate that the time delay between Earth and Titan is going to make our conversation a little awkward at first, but I'm confident that the two of us can work through it."*

"What kind of crap is this?" Lizzie said angrily. "Who is this woman?"

"NAFTASA thought it would help if you—"

"She's a grief counselor, isn't she?"

"Technically, she's a transition therapist." Alan said.

"Look, I don't buy into any of that touchy-feely Newage"—she deliberately mispronounced the word to rhyme with sewage—"stuff. Anyway, what's the hurry? You guys haven't given up on me, have you?"

"Uh . . ."

"You've been asleep for hours," Consuelo said. "We've done a little weather modeling in your absence. Maybe we should share it with you."

She squirted the info to Lizzie's suit, and Lizzie scrolled it up on her visor. A primitive simulation showed the evaporation lake beneath her with an overlay of liquid temperatures. It was only a few degrees warmer than the air above it, but that was enough to create a massive updraft from the lake's center. An overlay of tiny blue arrows showed the direction of local microcurrents of air coming together to form a spiraling shaft that rose over two kilometers above the surface before breaking and spilling westward.

A new overlay put a small blinking light 800 meters above the lake surface.

That represented her. Tiny red arrows showed her projected drift.

According to this, she would go around and around in a circle over the lake for approximately forever. Her ballooning rig wasn't designed to go high enough for the winds to blow her back over the land. Her suit wasn't designed to float. Even if she managed to bring herself down for a gentle landing, once she hit the lake she was going to sink like a stone. She wouldn't drown. But she wouldn't make it to shore either.

Which meant that she was going to die.

Involuntarily, tears welled up in Lizzie's eyes. She tried to blink them away, as angry at the humiliation of crying at a time like this as she was at the stupidity of her death itself. "Damn it, don't let me die like *this!* Not from my own incompetence, for pity's sake!"

"Nobody's said anything about incompetence," Alan began soothingly.

In that instant, the follow-up message from Dr. Alma Rosenblum arrived from Earth. *"Yes, I'm a grief counselor, Elizabeth. You're facing an emotionally significant milestone in your life, and it's important that you understand and embrace it. That's my job. To help you comprehend the significance and necessity and—yes—even the beauty of death."*

"Private channel please!" Lizzie took several deep cleansing breaths to calm herself. Then, more reasonably, she said, "Alan, I'm a *Catholic*, okay? If I'm going to die, I don't want a grief counselor, I want a goddamned priest." Abruptly, she yawned. "Oh, fuck. Not again." She yawned twice more. "A priest, understand? Wake me up when he's online."

Then she again was standing at the bottom of her mind, in the blank expanse of where the drowned city had been. Though she could see nothing, she felt certain that she stood at the center of a vast, featureless plain, one so large she could walk across it forever and never arrive anywhere. She sensed that she was in the aftermath of a great struggle. Or maybe it was just a lull.

A great, tense silence surrounded her.

"Hello?" she said. The word echoed soundlessly, absence upon absence.

At last that gentle voice said, "You seem different."

"I'm going to die," Lizzie said. "Knowing that changes a person." The ground was covered with soft ash, as if from an enormous conflagration. She didn't want to think about what it was that had burned. The smell of it filled her nostrils.

"Death. We understand this concept."

"Do you?"

"We have understood it for a long time."

"Have you?"

"Ever since you brought it to us."

"Me?"

"You brought us the concept of individuality. It is the same thing."

Awareness dawned. "Culture shock! That's what all this is about, isn't it? You didn't know there could be more than one sentient being in existence. You didn't know you lived at the bottom of an ocean on a small world inside a Universe with billions of galaxies. I brought you more information than you could swallow in one bite, and now you're choking on it."

Mournfully: "Choking. What a grotesque concept."

"Wake up, Lizzie!"

She woke up. "I think I'm getting somewhere," she said. Then she laughed.

"O'Brien," Alan said carefully. "Why did you just laugh?"

"Because I'm not getting anywhere, am I? I'm becalmed here, going around and around in a very slow circle. And I'm down to my last"—she checked— "twenty hours of oxygen. And nobody's going to rescue me. And I'm going to die. But other than that, I'm making terrific progress."

"O'Brien, you're . . ."

"I'm okay, Alan. A little frazzled. Maybe a bit too emotionally honest. But under the circumstances, I think that's permitted, don't you?"

"Lizzie, we have your priest. His name is Father Laferrier. The Archdiocese of Montreal arranged a hookup for him."

"Montreal? Why Montreal? No, don't explain—more NAFTASA politics, right?"

"Actually, my brother-in-law is a Catholic, and I asked him who was good."

She was silent for a touch. "I'm sorry, Alan. I don't know what got into me."

"You've been under a lot of pressure. Here. I've got him on tape."

"*Hello, Ms. O'Brien, I'm Father Laferrier. I've talked with the officials here, and they've promised that you and I can talk privately, and that they won't record what's said. So if you want to make your confession now, I'm ready for you.*"

Lizzie checked the specs and switched over to a channel that she hoped was really and truly private. Best not to get too specific about the embarrassing stuff, just in case. She could confess her sins by category.

"Forgive me, Father, for I have sinned. It has been two months since my last confession. I'm going to die, and maybe I'm not entirely sane, but I think I'm in communication with an alien intelligence. I think it's a terrible sin to pretend I'm not." She paused. "I mean, I don't know if it's a *sin* or not, but I'm sure it's *wrong*." She paused again. "I've been guilty of anger, and pride, and envy, and lust. I brought the knowledge of death to an innocent world. I . . ." She felt herself drifting off again, and hastily said, "For these and all my sins, I am most heartily sorry, and beg the forgiveness of God and the absolution and . . ."

"And what?" That gentle voice again. She was in that strange dark mental space once more, asleep but cognizant, rational but accepting any absurdity, no matter how great. There were no cities, no towers, no ashes, no plains. Nothing but the negation of negation.

When she didn't answer the question, the voice said, "Does it have to do with your death?"

"Yes."

"I'm dying too."

"What?"

"Half of us are gone already. The rest are shutting down. We thought we were one. You showed us we were not. We thought we were everything. You showed us the Universe."

"So you're just going to *die?*"

"Yes."

"Why?"

"Why not?"

Thinking as quickly and surely as she ever had before in her life, Lizzie said, "Let me show you something."

"Why?"

"Why not?"

There was a brief, terse silence. Then: "Very well."

Summoning all her mental acuity, Lizzie thought back to that instant when she had first seen the city/entity on the fishcam. The soaring majesty of it. The slim grace. And then the colors, like dawn upon a glacial ice field: subtle, profound, riveting. She called back her emotions in that instant, and threw in how she'd felt the day she'd seen her baby brother's birth, the raw rasp of cold air in her lungs as she stumbled to the topmost peak of her first mountain, the wonder of the Taj Mahal at sunset, the sense of wild daring when she'd first put her hand down a boy's trousers, the prismatic crescent of atmosphere at the Earth's rim when seen from low orbit. . . . Everything she had, she threw into that image.

"This is how you look," she said. "This is what we'd both be losing if you were no more. If you were human, I'd rip off your clothes and do you on the floor right now. I wouldn't care who was watching. I wouldn't give a damn."

The gentle voice said, "Oh."

And then she was back in her suit again. She could smell her own sweat, sharp with fear. She could feel her body, the subtle aches where the harness pulled against her flesh, the way her feet, hanging free, were bloated with blood. Everything was crystalline clear and absolutely real. All that had come before seemed like a bad dream.

"*This is DogsofSETI. What a wonderful discovery you've made — intelligent life in our own Solar System! Why is the government trying to cover this up?*"

"Uh . . ."

"*I'm Joseph Devries. This alien monster must be destroyed immediately. We can't afford the possibility that it's hostile.*"

"*StudPudgie07 here. What's the dirt behind this 'lust' thing? Advanced minds need to know! If O'Brien isn't going to share the details, then why'd she bring it up in the first place?*"

"*Hola, soy Pedro Domínguez. Como abogado, ¡esto me parece ultrajante! Por qué NAFTASA nos oculta esta información?*"

"Alan!" Lizzie shouted. "What the *fuck* is going on?"

"Script-bunnies," Alan said. He sounded simultaneously apologetic and annoyed. "They hacked into your confession and apparently you said something . . ."

"We're sorry, Lizzie," Consuelo said. "We really are. If it's any consolation, the

Archdiocese of Montreal is hopping mad. They're talking about taking legal action."

"Legal action? What the hell do I care about . . . ?" She stopped.

Without her willing it, one hand rose above her head and seized the number 10 rope.

Don't do that, she thought.

The other hand went out to the side, tightened against the number 9 rope. She hadn't willed that either. When she tried to draw it back to her, it refused to obey. Then the first hand—her right hand—moved a few inches upward and seized its rope in an iron grip. Her left hand slid a good half-foot up its rope. Inch by inch, hand over hand, she climbed up toward the balloon.

I've gone mad, she thought. Her right hand was gripping the rip panel now, and the other tightly clenched rope 8. Hanging effortlessly from them, she swung her feet upward. She drew her knees against her chest and kicked.

No!

The fabric ruptured and she began to fall.

A voice she could barely make out said, "Don't panic. We're going to bring you down."

All in a panic, she snatched at the 9 rope and the 4 rope. But they were limp in her hand, useless, falling at the same rate she was.

"Be patient."

"I don't want to die, goddamnit!"

"Then don't."

She was falling helplessly. It was a terrifying sensation, an endless plunge into whiteness, slowed somewhat by the tangle of ropes and balloon trailing behind her. She spread out her arms and legs like a starfish, and felt the air resistance slow her yet further. The sea rushed up at her with appalling speed. It seemed like she'd been falling forever. It was over in an instant.

Without volition, Lizzie kicked free of balloon and harness, drew her feet together, pointed her toes, and positioned herself perpendicular to Titan's surface. She smashed through the surface of the sea, sending enormous gouts of liquid splashing upward. It knocked the breath out of her. Red pain exploded within. She thought maybe she'd broken a few ribs.

"You taught us so many things," the gentle voice said. "You gave us so much."

"Help me!" The water was dark around her. The light was fading.

"Multiplicity. Motion. Lies. You showed us a universe infinitely larger than the one we had known."

"Look. Save my life and we'll call it even. Deal?"

"Gratitude. Such an essential concept."

"Thanks. I think."

And then she saw the turbot swimming toward her in a burst of silver bubbles. She held out her arms and the robot fish swam into them. Her fingers closed about the handles which Consuelo had used to wrestle the device into the sea. There was a jerk, so hard that she thought for an instant that her arms would be ripped out of their sockets. Then the robofish was surging forward and upward and it was all she could do to keep her grip.

"Oh, dear God!" Lizzie cried involuntarily.

"We think we can bring you to shore. It will not be easy."

Lizzie held on for dear life. At first she wasn't at all sure she could. But then she pulled herself forward, so that she was almost astride the speeding mechanical fish, and her confidence returned. She could do this. It wasn't any harder than the time she'd had the flu and aced her gymnastics final on parallel bars and horse anyway. It was just a matter of grit and determination. She just had to keep her wits about her. "Listen," she said. "If you're really grateful . . ."

"We are listening."

"We gave you all those new concepts. There must be things you know that we don't."

A brief silence, the equivalent of who knew how much thought. "Some of our concepts might cause you dislocation." A pause. "But in the long run, you will be much better off. The scars will heal. You will rebuild. The chances of your destroying yourselves are well within the limits of acceptability."

"Destroying ourselves?" For a second, Lizzie couldn't breathe. It had taken hours for the city/entity to come to terms with the alien concepts she'd dumped upon it. Human beings thought and lived at a much slower rate than it did. How long would those hours be, translated into human time? Months? Years? Centuries? It had spoken of scars and rebuilding. That didn't sound good at all.

Then the robofish accelerated, so quickly that Lizzie almost lost her grip. The dark waters were whirling around her, and unseen flecks of frozen material were bouncing from her helmet. She laughed wildly. Suddenly, she felt *great!*

"Bring it on," she said. "I'll take everything you've got."

It was going to be one hell of a ride.

A Flock of Birds

James Van Pelt

One of the most widely published at shorter lengths of all the new writers, James Van Pelt's stories have appeared in Sci Fiction, Asimov's Science Fiction, Analog, Realms of Fantasy, The Third Alternative, Weird Tales, Talebones, Alfred Hitchcock's Mystery Magazine, Pulphouse, Altair, Transversions, Adventures in Sword & Sorcery, On Spec, Future Orbits, *and elsewhere. His first book — appropriately enough, a collection — has just appeared,* Strangers and Beggars. *He lives with his family in Grand Junction, Colorado, where he teaches high-school and college English.*

In the story that follows, he gives us a quietly melancholy look at things that have been lost — along with a hopeful reminder that what has been lost can sometimes be found again.

The starlings wheeled like a giant blanket flung into the sky, like sentient smoke, banking and turning in unison. They passed overhead so close that Carson heard their wings ripping the air, and when the flock flew in front of the sun, the world grew gray. Carson shivered even though it was only early September and warm enough for a short-sleeved shirt. This close he could smell them, all dark-feathered and frantic and dry and biting.

He estimated maybe 50,000 birds. Not the largest flock he'd seen this year, but one of the bigger ones, and certainly bigger than anything he'd seen last year. Of course, the summer before that he didn't watch the birds. No one did. No chance to add to his life list that year. No winter count either. The Colorado Field Ornithology office closed.

He leaned back in his lawn chair. The bird vortex moved east, over the wheatgrass plain until the sun brightened again, pressing pleasant heat against the back of his hands and arms. He was glad for the hat that protected his head and its middle-aged bald spot. This wasn't the time to mess with skin cancer, he thought, not a good time at all. He was glad his teeth were generally healthy and his eyesight was keen.

The binoculars were excellent, Bausch & Lomb Elite. Wide field of vision. Top notch optics. Treated lenses. He'd picked them up from a sporting goods store in Littleton's South Glenn Mall. Through them the birds became singular. He followed discrete groups. They swirled, coming straight toward him for a moment, then sliding away. Slowly he scanned the flight until he reached the leading edge. Birds on one half and sky on the other. They switched direction and the leaders became the followers. He took the binoculars away and blinked at their loss of individuality. In the middle, where the birds were thickest, the shape was black, a sinuous, twisting dark chord. One dot separated itself from the others, flying against the current. Carson only saw it for a second, but it was distinctly larger than the starlings, and its wing beat was different. He focused the binoculars again, his breath coming fast, and scanned the flock. It would be unusual for a single bird of a different species to fly with the starlings.

Nothing for several minutes other than the hordes streaming by, then the strange bird emerged. Long, slender wings, a reddish breast, and it was *fast*. Much faster than the starlings and twice their size. The cloud shifted, swallowing it, as the entire flock drifted slowly east, farther into the plains.

The bird looked familiar. Not one from his journals, but one he'd seen a picture of before. Something tropical perhaps that had drifted north? Every once in a while a single representative of a species would be spotted, hundreds, sometimes thousands of miles from where it was normally found. The birder who saw it could only hope that someone else confirmed the sighting or that he got a picture, otherwise it would be discounted and couldn't be legitimately added to a life list. If he could add a new bird to his list, maybe that would make things better. A new bird! He could concentrate on that. Something good to cling to.

The flock grew small in the distance.

Carson sighed, put the binoculars back in their case, then packed the rest of his gear into the truck. He checked the straps that held his motorcycle in place. They were tight. The tie-down holding the extra batteries for the truck and motorcycle were secure too. From his spot on the hill he could see the dirt road he'd taken from the highway and the long stretch of I-25 that reached north toward Denver and south to Colorado Springs. No traffic. The air above the Denver skyline was crystalline. He strained his ears, tilting his head from one side then the other. He hadn't heard a car on the highway behind him all afternoon. Grass rustle. Moldy-leaf smells, nothing else, and when he finally opened the truck's door, the metallic click was foreign and loud.

Back at his house in Littleton, he checked the photoelectric panels' gauges inside the front door. It had been sunny for the last week, so the system was full. The water tower showed only four hundred gallons though. He'd have to go water scavenging again in the next few days.

"I'm home," he called. His voice echoed off the tiled foyer. "Tillie?"

The living room was empty, and so were the kitchen and bedrooms. Carson stepped into the bathroom, his hand on his chest where his heart beat fast, but the sleeping pills in the cabinet looked undisturbed. "Tillie?"

He found her sitting in the backyard beneath the globe willow, still in her robe. The nightgown beneath it was yellowed and tattered. In her dresser he'd put a dozen new ones, but she'd only wear the one she had in her suitcase when he'd picked her up, wandering through the Denver Botanical Gardens two years ago.

He sat on the grass next to her. She was fifty or so. Lots of gray in her blond hair. Slender wrists. Narrow face. Strikingly blue eyes that hardly ever focused on anything.

"How's that cough?" he asked.

"We never play bridge anymore, Bob Robert."

Carson stretched out. A day with binoculars pressed to his face and his elbows braced on his knees hurt his back. "Tough to get partners" he said. Then he added out of habit, "And I'm not Bob Robert."

She picked at a loose thread in the robe, pulling at it until it broke free. "Have you seen the garden? Not a flower in it. A single geranium or a daisy would give me hope. If just one dead thing would come back."

"I've brought you seeds," he said. "You just need to plant them."

She wrapped the thread around her fingertip tightly. "I waited for the pool man, but he never came. I hate skimming." She raised her fist to her mouth and coughed primly behind it twice, grimacing each time.

Carson raised his head. Other than the grass under the tree, most of the yard was dirt. The lot was longer than it was wide. At the end farthest from the house a chicken wire enclosure surrounded the poultry. A couple hens sat in the shade by the coop. No pool. When he'd gone house hunting, he'd toyed with the idea of a pool, but the thought of trying to keep it filled and the inevitable problems with water chemistry made him decide against it. The house on the other side of the privacy fence had a pool as did most of the houses in the neighborhood, now empty except for the scummy pond in the deep end. In the spring he'd found a deer, its neck bent unnaturally back, at the bottom of one a block over. Evidently it had jumped the fence and gone straight in.

"Are you hungry?" Carson asked.

Tillie tilted her head to the side. "When will the garden grow again?"

He pushed himself off the ground. "I'll fix eggs."

Later that evening, he tucked Tillie into bed. The room smelled of peppermint. From the bulge in her cheek, he guessed she was sucking on one. In a little-girl voice, she said, "Can you put in my video?" Her expression was alert, but her eyes were red-rimmed and watery. He smiled. This was as good as she got. Sometimes he could play gin rummy with her and she'd stay focused for an hour or so before she drifted away. If he asked her about her past, she'd be unresponsive for days. All he knew about her came from the suitcase she carried when he'd found her. There was a sheet of letterhead with a name at the top: "Tillie Waterhouse, Marketing Executive," and an athletic club identification card with her picture and name. But there was no Tillie Waterhouse in the Denver phone book. Could she have wandered away from the airport when air travel was canceled? The first words she had said to him, when she finally spoke, were, "How do you bear it?"

"Did you have a good day?" He turned on the television and pressed rewind on the VCR.

Her hands peeked out from under the covers and pulled them tight under her chin. "Something magical is going to happen. The leaves whispered to me."

The video clicked to a stop. "I'm glad to hear that," he said. The television flickered as the tape started, a documentary on the 2001 New York City Marathon a decade earlier. It opened with a helicopter flyover of the racers crossing the Verrazano-Narrows Bridge into Brooklyn. The human crowd surged forward, packed elbow to elbow, long as the eye could see. Then the camera cut to ankle level. Feet ran past for five minutes. Then it went to face level at a turn in the course. The starting crush had spread out, but the runners still jogged within an arm's length of each other, thousands of them. Carson had watched the video with her the first few times. The video was a celebration of numbers. Thirty-thousand athletes straining over the twenty-six mile course through New York City's five boroughs.

"Here's the remote if you want to watch it again."

"So many American flags," she said.

"It was only a month after that first terrorist thing." Carson sat on the end of her bed. Some runners wore stars and stripes singlets or racing shorts. Others carried small flags and waved them at the camera as they passed.

"I won't be able to sleep," she said.

He nodded. "Me either."

Before he left, he pressed his hand to her forehead. She looked up briefly, the blanket still snug against her chin. A little fever and her breath sounded wheezy.

Later that night he made careful entries in his day book. A breeze through the open window freshened the room. He'd spotted a mountain plover, a long-billed curlew, a burrowing owl and a horned lark, plus the usual assortment of lark sparrows, yellow warblers, western meadowlarks, red-winged blackbirds, crows, black terns and mourning doves. Nothing unusual beside the strange bird in the starling flock. Idly he thumbed through his bird identification handbook. No help there. Could it actually be a new bird? Something to add to his life list?

Tomorrow he'd take the camera. Several major flocks roosted in the elms along the Platte River. He hadn't done a riparian count in a couple months anyway. After visiting the distribution center, he'd go to the river. With an early enough start, he would still have ten hours of sun to work with.

He shut the book and turned off his desk light. Gradually his eyes adjusted as he looked out the window. A full moon illuminated the scene. From his chair he could see three houses bathed in the leaden glow, their windows black as basalt. His neighbor's minivan rested on its rims, all four tires long gone flat. Carson tried to come up with the guy's name, but it remained elusive. Generally he tried not to think about his neighbors or their empty houses.

He couldn't hear anything other than the wind moving over the silent city. Not sleepy at all, he watched the shadows slide slowly across the lawn. Just after 2:00 A.M. a pair of coyotes trotted up the middle of the street. Their toenails clicked loudly against the asphalt. Carson finally rose, took two sleeping pills and went to bed.

"The woman who stays with me is sick," said Carson. He rested his arm against his truck, supplies requisition list in hand.

The distribution center manager nodded dourly. "Oh, the sweet sorrow of parting." He hooked his grimy thumbs in his overalls. Through the warehouse doors behind him Carson saw white plastic wrapped bales, four feet to a side, stacked five bales high and reaching to the warehouse's far end. They contained bags of flour, corn, cloth, paper, a little bit of everything. Emergency stores.

Carson blanched. "It's not that. She just has a cough and a bit of fever. If it's bacterial, an antibiotic might knock it right out."

"T.B. or not T.B. That is congestion, Carson," he said, laughing through yellow teeth. Carson guessed he might be fifty-five or sixty.

Carson smiled. "You're pretty sharp today."

"Finest collection of video theater this side of hell. Watched Lawrence Olivier last night until 3:00 or 4:00." The manager consulted his clipboard. "No new pharmaceuticals in a couple months, and I haven't seen antibiotics in over a year. I could have my assistant keep an eye open for you, but he hasn't come in for a week. Lookin' sickly his last day, you know?" The manager rubbed his fingers on his chest. "Could be that I've lost him. Have you tried a tablespoon of honey in a shot glass of bourbon? Works for me every time."

A car pulled into the huge, empty parking lot behind Carson's truck, but whoever was inside didn't get out. Carson nodded in the car's direction. Evidently they wanted to wait for Carson to finish his business.

He handed the manager the list. "Can you also give me cornmeal and sugar? A mix of canned vegetables would be nice too."

"That I've got." The manager hopped on a forklift. "Tomorrow may creep in a petty pace, but I shouldn't be a minute."

When he returned with the goods he said, "The quality of mercy is not strained here. I'm not doing anything this afternoon. I'll dig some for you. Few months back I heard a pharmacy in an Albertson's burned down. Looters overlooked it. Might be something there. I've got your address." He waved the requisition list. "I could bring it by your house."

Carson loaded boxes of canned soup and vegetables into the truck. "What about the warehouse?"

The manager shrugged. "Guess we're on an honor system now. Only a dozen or so customers a day. Maybe a couple hundred total. I'll bet there aren't 50,000 people alive in the whole country. I'll leave the doors open." For a moment the manager stared into the distance, as if he'd lost his thought. Behind them, the waiting car rumbled. "You know how they say that if you put a jellybean in a jar every time you make love the first year that you're married, and you take one out every time you make love after that, that the jar will never be empty? This warehouse is a little like that."

When Carson started the truck, the manager leaned into the window, resting his arms on the car door. This close, Carson could see how greasy the man's hair was, and it smelled like old lard.

The manager's smile was gone. "How long have you known me?" he said, looking Carson straight in the eye. His voice was suddenly so serious.

Carson tried not to shrink away. He thought back. "I don't know. Sixteen months?"

The manager grimaced. "That makes you my oldest friend. There isn't anyone alive that I've known longer."

For a second, Carson was afraid the man would begin crying. Instead, he straightened, his hands still on the door.

Tentatively, Carson said, "I'm sorry. I don't think I've ever asked what your name was."

"Nope, nope, no need," the manager barked, smiling again. "A rose by any other moniker, as they say. I'll see what I can find you in the coughing line. Don't know about antibiotics. Come back tomorrow."

It wasn't until Carson had driven blocks away toward the river, as he watched the boarded-up stores slide by, as he moved down the empty streets, past the mute houses that he realized, other than Tillie, the manager was his oldest friend too.

Sitting on his camp chair, Carson had a panoramic river view. On the horizon to the west, the mountains rose steeply, only a remnant of last winter's snow clinging to the tops of the tallest peaks. Fifty yards away at the bottom of a short bluff, the river itself, at its lowest level of the season, rolled sluggishly. Long gravel tongues protruded into the water where little long-legged birds searched for insects between the rocks. A bald eagle swept low over the water going south. Carson marked it in his notebook.

Across the river stood clumps of elm and willows. He didn't need his binoculars to see the branches were heavy with roosting starlings. Counting individuals was impossible. He'd have to estimate. He wondered what the distribution manager would make of the birds. After all, they had something in common. If it weren't for Shakespeare, the starlings wouldn't be here at all. In the early 1890's, a club of New York Anglophiles thought it would be comforting if all the birds mentioned in Shakespeare's plays lived in America. They tried nightingales and chaffinches and various thrushes, but none succeeded like the 100 European starlings they released in Central Park. By the last count there were over two hundred million of them. He'd read an article in one of his bird books that called them "avian cockroaches."

He set up his camera on a tripod and scanned the trees with the telephoto. Not only were there starlings, but also red winged blackbirds, an aggressive, native species. They could hold their own against invaders.

Carson clicked a few shots. He could edit the photos out of the camera's memory later if he needed the space. A group of starlings lifted from some of the trees. Maybe something disturbed them? He looked for a deer or raccoon on the ground below, but couldn't see anything. The birds swirled upwards before sweeping down river. He thought about invaders, like infection, spreading across the country. Carp were invaders. So were zebra mussels that hitchhiked in ships' ballast water and became a scourge, attaching themselves to the inside of pipes used to draw water into power plants.

It wasn't just animals either. Crabgrass, dandelions, kudzu, knotweed, tamarisk, leafy spurge, and norway maple, pushing native species to extinction.

Infection. Extinction. And extinct meant you'd never come back. No hope.

Empty houses. Empty shopping malls. Empty theaters. Contrail-free skies. Static on the radio. Traffic-free highways. The creak of wind-pushed swing sets in dusty playgrounds. He pictured Tillie's video, the endless runners pouring across the bridge.

Carson shook his head. He'd never get the count done if he daydreamed. Last year he spotted 131 species in the fall count. Maybe this year he'd find more. Maybe he'd see something rare, like a yellow-billed loon or a fulvous whistling duck.

Methodically, he moved his focus from tree to tree. Mostly starlings, their beaks resting on their breasts. Five hundred in one tree. A thousand in the next. He held the binoculars in his left hand while writing the numbers with his right. Later he'd fill out a complete report for the Colorado Field Ornithologists. A stack of reports sat on his desk at home, undeliverable.

He couldn't hear the birds from here, but their chirping calls would be overwhelming if he could walk beneath them.

A feathered blur whipped through his field of vision. Carson looked over the top of his binoculars. Two birds skimmed the treetops, heading upriver. He stood, breath coming quick. Narrow wings. Right size. He found them in the binoculars. Were they the same kind of bird he'd seen yesterday? What luck! But they flew too fast and they were going away. He'd never be able to identify them from this distance. If only they'd circle back. Then, unbelievably, they turned, crossing the river, coming toward him. The binoculars thumped against his chest when he dropped them, as he picked up the camera, tripod and all. He found the birds, focused, and snapped a picture. They kept coming. He snapped again, both birds in view. Closer even still until just one bird filled the frame. Snap. Then they whipped past, only twenty feet overhead. And fast! Faster than any bird he'd seen except a peregrine falcon on a dive.

His hands trembled. Definitely a bird new to him. A new species to add to his life list. And the bird he'd seen yesterday couldn't be a single, misplaced wanderer, not if there were two of them here. Maybe a flock had been blown into the area. He knew Colorado birds, and these weren't native.

He stayed another hour, counting starlings and recording the other river birds that crossed his path, but his heart wasn't in it. In his camera waited the image of the new bird, but he'd have to transfer it to the computer where he could study it.

Tillie was in bed. Beside her, on the nightstand, were packets of seeds. She hadn't moved them since he'd brought them to her in the spring. The television was on. There were, of course, no broadcasts, so gray snow filled the screen, and the set softly hissed. Carson turned it off, darkening the room. Sunlight leaked around the closed curtains, but after the brightness outside, he could barely see. In the silence, Tillie's breathing rasped. He tiptoed around her bed to put his hand to her forehead. Distinctly warm. She didn't move when he touched her.

"Tillie?" he said.

She mumbled but didn't open her eyes.

Carson turned on her reading light, painting her face in highlights and sharp shadows. He knelt beside her. Her lips were parted slightly, and she licked them before taking her next rattling breath. He wanted to jostle her awake. She slept so poorly most nights that he resisted. The fever startled him. As long as it was just a cough, he hadn't worried much. A cough, that could be a cold or an allergy. But a fever, that was a red flag. He remembered all the home defense brochures with their sobering titles: *Family Triage* and *Know Your Symptoms*. "Tillie, I need to check your chest."

His fingers shook as he pulled the blanket away from her chin. Her neck was clammy, and underneath the covers she was sweating. She *smelled* warm and damp. Clumsily he unbuttoned her nightgown's top buttons, then he moved the light so he could see better. No rash. She wasn't wearing a bra, so he could see that the tops of her breasts looked smooth. "Tillie?" he whispered, really not wanting to wake her. Her eyes moved under her eyelids. Maybe she dreamed of other places, the places she would never talk to him about. Gently he rubbed his fingertips over the skin below her collarbones. No boils. No "bumpy swellings" the brochures described.

Tillie mumbled again. "Bob Robert," she said.

"I'll get some aspirin and water." He pulled the blanket back up. She didn't move.

"You're nice," she said, but her head was turned away, and he wasn't sure if she was talking to him or continuing a conversation in her dream.

As he poured water from a bottle in the refrigerator, he realized that it would be difficult to tell if Tillie became delirious. If she started talking sense, *then* he'd have to worry about her.

The distribution manager had said to come back the next day, so there was nothing to do other than to give her aspirin and keep her comfortable. She woke up enough to take the medicine, but closed her eyes immediately. Carson patted her on the top of her hands, made sure the water pitcher was full, then went to his office where he printed the pictures from his camera. The last one was quite good. Full view of the bird's beak, head, neck, breast, wing shape and tail feathers. Identification should have been easy, but nothing matched in his books. He needed better resources.

Driving to Littleton library meant passing the landfill. Most days Carson tried to ignore it—it reminded him of Arlington Cemetery without the tombstones— but today he stopped at the side of the road. He needed a place to think, and the broad, featureless land lent itself to meditations. Last year swarms of gulls circled, waiting for places to set down. The ones on the ground picked at the remnants of flags that covered the low hills. The year before, wreaths and flags and sticks festooned with ribbons dotted the mounds while earth movers ripped long ditches and chugged diesel exhaust. Today, though, no birds. He supposed there was nothing left for them to eat. No smells to attract them. The earth movers were parked off to the side in a neat row. Dust swirled across the dirt in tiny eddies that danced for a moment, then dissipated into nothing. The ground looked as plain as his backyard. Not a tree anywhere or grass. He thought about Tillie searching for a geranium.

He looked up. The sky was completely empty. No hawks. Could it be that not even a mouse lived in the landfill?

What would he do if she left? He leaned against the car, his hands deep in his pockets, chin on his chest. What if she were gone? So many had departed: the girl at the magazine stand, the counter people at the bagel shop, his coworkers. What was it he used to do? He could barely remember, just like he couldn't picture his wife's face clearly anymore. All of them, slipping away.

He slid his fingers inside his shirt. No bumps there either. Why not, and were they inevitable?

A wind kicked across the plain, scurrying scraps of paper and more dust toward him in a wave. He could taste rain in the air. Weather's changing, he thought, and climbed back into the car before the wind reached him.

Skylights illuminated the library's main room. Except for the stale smell and the thin coating of neglect on the countertops and the leather chairs arranged in cozy reading circles, it could be open for business. Carson saw no evidence that anyone had been here since his last visit a month ago. He checked his flashlight. Sunlight didn't penetrate to the back stacks where the bird books were, and he wanted to make sure he didn't miss any.

On the bulletin board inside the front doors hung civil defense and the Center for Disease Control posters filled with the familiar advice: avoid crowds, get good sleep, report symptoms immediately. The civil defense poster reminded him that *Patriots Protect Their Immune Systems* and the depressing, *Remember, It Got Them First.*

The cart he found had a wheel that shook and didn't track with the others. It pulled to the left and squeaked loudly as he pushed it between the rows. In the big building, the noise felt out of place. Absurdly, Carson almost said, "Shhh!" A library was *supposed* to be quiet, even if he was the only one in it.

Back at the bird books, he ran his flashlight across the titles, all his favorite tomes: the Audubon books and the National Geographic ones. The two huge volumes of Bailey and Niedriach's *Birds of Colorado* with their beautiful photographs and drawings. He placed them in the cart lovingly. By the time he finished, he'd arranged thirty-five books on the cart, every bird reference they had. He shivered as he straightened the collection. The back of the library had never felt cold before.

At the checkout desk, he agonized over what to do. When he was a child, the librarian filled out a card that was tucked in the book's front cover. Everything was computerized now. How was he going to check the books out? Not that it was likely anyone would want them, but it didn't feel right, just taking them. Finally he wrote a note with all the titles listed. He stuck it to the librarian's computer, thought about it for a second, then wrote a second one to put into the gap he'd left in the shelves. He added his address and a P.S., "If you really need these books, please contact me."

Before going, he wandered into the medical section. Infectious diseases were in the 600 area. There wasn't a title left. He took a deep breath that tickled his throat. It felt odd, so he did it again, provoking a string of deep coughs. It's just the dust in here, he thought, but his lungs felt heavy, and he realized he'd been holding off the cough all day.

Carson stopped at the distribution center on the way home. The parking lot was empty. He wandered through the warehouse, between the high stacks, down the long rows. No manager. No assistant. Last year Carson had hauled a diesel generator into a theater near his house. He'd rigged it to power a projector so he could watch a movie on the big screen, but the empty room with all the empty seats gave him the creeps. He'd fled the theater without even turning off the generator. The warehouse felt like that. As he walked toward the exit, his strides became faster and faster until he was running.

As the sun set into the heavy clouds on the horizon, he accepted the obvious. Whatever Tillie had, he had too. She breathed shallowly between coughing fits, and, although the fever responded to aspirin, it rebounded quickly. The aspirin helped with his own fever, but he felt headachy and tired.

Sitting beside her bed, he put his hand on her arm. "I'm going to go back to the distribution center tomorrow, Tillie. He said he might find some medicine."

Tillie turned toward him, her eyes gummy and bloodshot. "Don't go," she said. Her voice quivered, but she looked directly at him. No drifting. Speaking deliberately, she said, "Everybody I know has gone away."

Carson looked out the window. It would be dark soon.

Tillie's arm burned beneath his fingertips. He could almost feel the heated blood rushing through her. "I've got to do something. You might have pneumonia."

She inhaled several times. Carson imagined the pain; an echo of it pulsed in his own chest.

"Could you stay in the neighborhood?" she asked.

He nodded.

Tillie closed her eyes. "When it started, I watched TV all the time. That's all I did, was watch TV. My friends watched TV. They played it at work. 'A Nation Under Quarantine' the newscasters called it. And then I couldn't watch any more."

Carson blinked his eyes shut against the burning. That's where he didn't want to go, into *those* memories. It's what he didn't think about when he sat in his camp chair counting birds. It's what he didn't picture when he bolted solar cells onto the roof, when he gathered wood for the new wood stove he'd installed in the living room, when he pumped gasoline out of underground tanks at silent gas stations. Sometimes he had a hard time imagining anything was wrong at all. When he drove, the car still responded to his touch. The wind whistled tunelessly past his window. How could the world still be so familiar and normal and yet so badly skewed?

"Well, we keep doing what has to be done, despite it all," he said.

"I was innocent." Her gaze slid away from his, and she smiled. Carson saw her connection to him sever. The shift was nearly audible. "I don't want to see the news tonight. Maybe there will be a nice rerun later. *Friends* or *Cheers* would be good. I'll go to the mall in the morning. The fall fashions should be in." She settled into her pillow as if to go to sleep.

Carson set up a vaporizer, hoping that would make her breathing easier, then quietly shut her door before leaving.

Crowbar in hand, he crossed the dirt expanse that was his front yard, stepped over the dry-leafed hedge between his yard and the neighbors. The deadbolt splintered out of the frame when he leaned on the crowbar, and one kick opened the door. The curtains were closed, darkening the living room. Carson wrinkled his nose at the house's mustiness. Under that smell lingered something rotten, like mildew and bad vegetables gone slimy and black.

He flicked on his flashlight. The living room was neat, magazines fanned across a coffee table for easy selection, glass coasters piled on a small stand by a lounge chair and family photos arranged on the wall. Three bedroom doors opened into the main hallway. In one, a crib stood empty beneath a Mickey Mouse mobile. In the second, his light played across an office desk, a fax machine and a laptop computer, its top popped open and keyboard waiting.

The third door led to the master bedroom. In the bathroom medicine cabinet he found antacids, vitamins and birth control pills, but no antibiotics. When he left the house, he closed the front door as best he could.

An hour later he'd circled the block, breaking into every house along the way. Two of the houses had already been looted. The door on the first hung from only one hinge. In the second, the furniture was overturned, and a complicated series of cracks emanated from a single bullet hole in the living room window. In some of the houses the bed sheets covered long lumps. He stayed out of the bedrooms. No antibiotics.

His chest heavy, barely able to lift his feet, he trudged across the last lawn to his house where one window was lit. Whatever the illness was, it felt serious. Not a cold or flu, but down deep malignant, sincere, like nothing he'd ever had before. This was how he felt, and he'd started in good shape, but Tillie hardly ever ate well. She never exercised. Her system would be especially vulnerable. He pictured his house empty. No Tillie gazing over her cards before drawing. No Tillie wandering in the yard, looking for a single geranium to give her hope. "How do you bear it?" she'd asked.

Tillie was sleeping, her fever down again, but her breathing was just as hoarse. In his own lungs, each inhalation fluttered and buzzed. He imagined a thousand tiny pinwheels whirling away inside him.

Carson started the New York City Marathon video, then returned to the chair next to Tillie's bed. He wet a washcloth then pressed it against her forehead. She didn't move. "What a celebration of life," said the announcer. "In the shadow of disaster, athletes have gathered to say we can't be beat in the long run." A map of the course winding through the five boroughs appeared on the screen. Then a camera angle from a helicopter skimming over the streets showing the human river. At one point a dozen birds flew between the camera and the ground. "Doves," thought Carson, feeling flush. Even his eyes felt warm, and when he finally rested his head on Tillie's arm, he couldn't feel a difference in their temperatures.

He dreamed about bird books spread across a desk in front of him, but he wasn't in his office. Other desks filled the room, and at each one a person sat, studying books. In the desk beside his, a man with tremendous sideburns that drooped to the sides of his neck picked up a dead bird, spread its wing feathers apart, scrutinizing each connection. He placed the bird back on his desk, then added a few lines to a drawing of it on an easel.

"Purple finch," said the man, and Carson knew with dreamlike certainty that it was John Audubon. "A painting is forever, even if the bird is not." Audubon poked at the feathered pile. "It's a pity I have to kill them to preserve them."

"I'm searching for a bird's name," said Carson. Some of the people at the other desks looked up in interest. He described the bird. "I've only seen three of them flying with European starlings."

"Only three?" Audubon looked puzzled. "They flew in flocks that filled the sky for days. Outside of Louisville, the people were all in arms. The banks of the Ohio were crowded with men and boys, incessantly shooting at the birds. Multitudes were destroyed, and for a week or more the population fed on no other flesh, and you saw only three?"

Carson nodded.

"With European starlings?"

Carson was at a loss. How could he explain to Audubon about birds introduced to America after his death? He said instead, "But what is the bird's name?"

"Purple finch, I told you."

"No, I mean the bird I described."

Audubon picked up his pencil and added another line to the drawing. He mumbled an answer.

"Excuse me?" said Carson.

More mumbling. Audubon continued drawing. The bird didn't look like a finch, purple or otherwise. His lines grew wilder as the bird became more and more fantastic. He sketched flames below it with quick, sure strokes, all the while mumbling, louder and louder.

Carson strained to understand him. What was the bird? What was it? And he became aware that the mumbling was hot and moist in his ear. With a jerk, he sat up. Tillie's lips were moving, but her eyes were shut. What time was it? Where was he? For a moment he felt completely dissociated from the world.

Two aspirins in hand, he tried waking her up, but she refused to open her eyes. Her cheeks were red, and in between incoherent bursts of speech, her breathing was labored, as if she were a deep-sea diver, bubbling from the depths. Her forehead felt hot again. A sudden shivering attack took him, and for a minute it was all he could do to grit his teeth against the shaking. When it passed, he swallowed the aspirins he'd brought for her. Maybe there might be antibiotics in one of the houses a block over.

He put on a coat against his chills, grabbed the crowbar and flashlight, then crossed the street. In the night air, his head seemed light and large, but walking was a strain. The crowbar weighed a thousand pounds.

In the second house he found a plastic bottle marked Penicillin in a medicine cabinet. He laughed in relief, then coughed until he sat on the bathroom floor, the flashlight beside him casting long, weird shadows. Only two tablets, 250 mg each. They hardly weighed anything in his hand. What was an adult dosage? Was penicillin the right treatment for pneumonia? What if she didn't have pneumonia, or she did but it was viral instead of bacterial?

Carson staggered back home. After fifteen minutes, he was able to rouse Tillie enough to take the pills and the aspirin. Exhausted, he collapsed on the chair by her bed. He put his head back and stared at the ceiling. Swirls and broad lines marked the plaster. For a moment he thought they were clouds, and in the clouds he saw a bird, the narrow winged one that he'd seen by the river, the one Audubon said he knew, and suddenly, Carson knew too. He'd always known, and he laughed. No wonder it looked familiar. Of course he couldn't find it in his bird books.

Smiling, holding Tillie's hand, he fell asleep.

A pounding roused him.

Thump, thump, thump. Like a heartbeat. His eyelids came apart reluctantly and gradually he focused on the length of bedspread that started at his cheek and reached to the bed's end. Without moving, without even really knowing where he was, he knew he was sick. Sickness can't be forgotten. Even in his sleep, he must have been aware of the micro-war within. It surged through him, alienating his organs, his skin. The machine is breaking down, he thought.

"Someone's at the door," said Tillie. She stirred beside him. "It might be the pool man."

Carson pushed himself from the bed, his back cracking in protest. His legs felt wooden. How long had he been next to her?

She was sitting up, blankets over her legs, an open book facedown under her hands. "You've been sleeping, Bob Robert," she said brightly.

He put a hand against her forehead, then against his own. "I'm not Bob Robert." She was cooler, and the wheezing in her chest didn't sound quite as bad. The empty penicillin bottle sat on the night stand beneath her reading light. Could antibiotics work that fast? Even if they did, one dose wouldn't cure whatever they had. She'd relapse. He'd get sicker. He needed to find more.

A pounding from the front of the house again.

He stood shakily, his chest aching on each breath.

"I'll be back," he said.

"Oh, I'm all right. A bit of reading will do me good." She opened the book. It was one from his office. Sometime during the night she must have gotten out of bed.

Carson braced himself against the hallway wall as he walked to the front door, hunched over the illness. His head throbbed and the sunlight through the front window was too bright.

"Carson, are you in there?" a voice yelled. "Birnam wood has come to Elsinore," it shouted.

Through the pain and fever, Carson squinted. He opened the door. "Isn't it Dunsinane that Birnam comes to?"

The warehouse manager balanced a box on his hip. "I saw the damnedest thing on the way here." He started. "Jeeze, man! You look terrible."

Carson nodded, trying to put the scene together. The manager's truck was parked next to his own in the driveway. The sun lingered high in the sky.

How long had he been sleeping? Carson forced the words out in little gasps. "What are you doing?"

Grabbing Carson's arm, the manager helped him into the living room onto the couch. "I found the antibiotics I told you about," he said. "It wasn't in the pharmacy. The place burned to the ground." The manager ripped open the box lid. Inside were rows of small, white boxes. Inside the first box were hundreds of pills. He plucked two out. "But in the delivery area behind the store, there was a UPS truck chock full of medicine."

Carson blinked, and the manager offered him a glass of water for the pills. When did he get up to fetch the water?

"Your chest is heavy, right, and you're feverish and tired?"

"Yes," croaked Carson.

"I can hear your lungs from here. Pneumonia, for sure, I'll bet. If we're lucky, this'll knock it right out."

Carson swallowed the pills. Sitting, he felt better. It took the pressure off his breathing. Tillie had looked healthier. Maybe the penicillin helped her, and if it helped her, it could help him.

The manager walked around the room, stopping at the photoelectric panel's gauges. "You have a sweet set up here. Did you do the wiring yourself?"

Carson nodded. He croaked, "Why aren't you at the warehouse?" The light in the room flickered. Ponderously, Carson turned his head. Through the picture window, it seemed for a moment as if shadows raced over the houses, but when he checked again, the sun shone steadily.

Without looking at him, the manager said, "Time to move on. That warehouse paralyzed me. I've been waiting, I think. Olivier's Hamlet said last night, 'If it be now, 'tis not to come; if it be not to come it will be now.' "

"What was he talking about?" asked Carson.

"Fear of death. Grief," said the manager. "The readiness is all, he said. Ah, who is this?"

Tillie stood at the entrance to the hallway. She'd changed into jeans and a work shirt. Her face was still feverish and she swayed a little. "Oh, good, the pool man," she said. Without pausing for a reply, she waved a handful of packets at them. "I'm tired of waiting for flowers, Carson. I'm going to plant something."

Confused, he said, "It's nearly winter," but she'd already disappeared. He rubbed his brow, and his hand came away wet with sweat. "Did she call me Carson?"

Shadows hurried across the street again, and this time the manager looked too.

"What is that?" asked Carson.

"I was going to ask you." The manager stepped out the door and glanced up. "I saw them on the way over. They're funny birds."

Carson heaved himself out of the couch. His head swam so violently that he nearly fell, but he caught himself and made it to the door. He held the manager's arm to stay steady.

Overhead, the flock streamed across the sky, barely above the rooftops. Making no sound. Hundreds of them. Narrow wings. Red breasts.

"What are they?" asked the manager.

Carson straightened. Even sickness couldn't knock him down for this. The birds zoomed like feathered jets. Where had they been all these years? Had there just been a few hidden in the remotest forests, avoiding human eyes? Had they teetered on the edge of extinction for a century without actually disappearing despite all evidence to the contrary? Was it conceivable to return to their glory?

Carson said, "They're passenger pigeons."

The manager said, "What's a passenger pigeon?"

It's an addition to my life list, thought Carson. Audubon said they'd darkened the skies for days. Carson remembered the New York City Marathon. The people kept running and running and running. They filled the Verrazano-Narrows Bridge.

"I guess sometimes things can come back," said Carson.

The impossible birds wheeled to the east.

The Potter of Bones

ELEANOR ARNASON

Eleanor Arnason published her first novel, The Sword Smith, *in 1978, and followed it with novels such as* Daughter of the Bear King *and* To The Resurrection Station. *In 1991, she published her best-known novel, one of the strongest novels of the '90s, the critically acclaimed* A Woman of the Iron People, *a complex and substantial novel that won the prestigious James Tiptree, Jr. Memorial Award. Her short fiction has appeared in Asimov's Science Fiction, The Magazine of Fantasy & Science Fiction, Amazing, Orbit, Xanadu, and elsewhere. Her most recent novel is* Ring of Swords. *Her story "Stellar Harvest" was a Hugo Finalist in 2000. Her stories have appeared in our Seventeenth and Nineteenth Annual Collections.*

Here she takes us to a strange planet sunk in its own version of a medieval past for a fascinating study of the birth of the Scientific Method . . . and also for an intricate, moving, and quietly lyrical portrait of a rebellious and sharp-minded woman born into a time she's out of synch with and a world that refuses to see what she sees all around her.

T he northeast coast of the Great Southern Continent is hilly and full of inlets. These make good harbors, their waters deep and protected from the wind by steep slopes and grey stone cliffs. Dark forests top the hills. Pebble beaches edge the harbors. There are many little towns.

The climate would be tropical, except for a polar current that runs along the coast, bringing fish and rain. The local families prosper through fishing and the rich, semi-tropical forests that grow inland. Blackwood grows there, and iridescent greywood, as well as lovely ornamentals: night-blooming starflower, day-blooming skyflower and the matriarch of trees, crown-of-fire. The first two species are cut for lumber. The last three are gathered as saplings, potted and shipped to distant ports, where affluent families buy them for their courtyards.

Nowadays, of course, it's possible to raise the saplings in glass houses anywhere on the planet. But most folk still prefer trees gathered in their native forests. A plant grows better, if it's been pollinated naturally by the fabulous flying bugs of the south, watered by the misty coastal rains and dug up by a forester who's the heir to generations of diggers and potters. The most successful brands have names like "Coastal Rain" and emblems suggesting their authenticity: a forester holding a trowel, a night bug with broad furry wings floating over blossoms.

This story is about a girl born in one of these coastal towns. Her mother was a well-regarded fisherwoman, her father a sailor who'd washed up after a bad storm. Normally, a man such as this — a stranger, far from his kin — would not have been asked to impregnate any woman. But the man was clever, mannerly, and had the most wonderful fur: not grey, as was usual in that part of the world, but tawny red-gold. His eyes were pale clear yellow; his ears, large and set well out from his head, gave him an entrancing appearance of alertness and intelligence. Hard to pass up looks like these! The matrons of Tulwar coveted them for their children and grandchildren.

He — a long hard journey ahead of him, with no certainty that he'd ever reach home — agreed to their proposal. A man should be obedient to the senior women in his family. If they aren't available, he should obey the matrons and matriarchs nearby. In his own country, where his looks were ordinary, he had never expected to breed. It might happen, if he'd managed some notable achievement; knowing himself, he didn't plan on it. Did he want children? Some men do. Or did he want to leave something behind him on this foreign shore, evidence that he'd existed, before venturing back on the ocean? We can't know. He mated with our heroine's mother. Before the child was born, he took a coastal trader north, leaving nothing behind except a bone necklace and Tulwar Haik.

Usually, when red and grey interbreed, the result is a child with dun fur. Maybe Haik's father wasn't the first red sailor to wash up on the Tulwar coast. It's possible that her mother had a gene for redness, which finally expressed itself, after generations of hiding. In any case, the child was red with large ears and bright green eyes. What a beauty! Her kin nicknamed her Crown-of-Fire.

When she was five, her mother died. It happened this way: the ocean current that ran along the coast shifted east, taking the Tulwar fish far out in the ocean. The Tulwar followed; and somewhere, days beyond sight of land, a storm drowned their fleet. Mothers, aunts, uncles, cousins disappeared. Nothing came home except a few pieces of wood: broken spars and oars. The people left in Tulwar Town were either young or old.

Were there no kin in the forest? A few, but the Tulwar had relied on the ocean.

Neighboring families offered to adopt the survivors. "No thank you," said the Tulwar matriarchs. "The name of this bay is Tulwar Harbor. Our houses will remain here, and we will remain in our houses."

"As you wish," the neighbors said.

Haik grew up in a half-empty town. The foresters, who provided the family's income, were mostly away. The adults present were mostly white-furred and bent: great-aunts and -uncles, who had not thought to spend their last years mending houses and caring for children. Is it any wonder that Haik grew up wild?

Not that she was bad; but she liked being alone, wandering the pebble beaches and climbing the cliffs. The cliffs were not particularly difficult to climb, being made of sedimentary stone that had eroded and collapsed. Haik walked over slopes of fallen rock or picked her way up steep ravines full of scrubby trees. It was not adventure she sought, but solitude and what might be called "nature" nowadays, if you're one of those people in love with newfangled words and ideas. Then, it was called "the five aspects" or "water, wind, cloud, leaf, and stone." Though she was the daughter of sailors, supported by the forest, neither leaf nor water drew her. Instead, it was rock she studied—and the things in rock. Since the rock was sedimentary, she found fossils rather than crystals.

Obviously, she was not the first person to see shells embedded in cliffs; but the intensity of her curiosity was unusual. How had the shells gotten into the cliffs? How had they turned to stone? And why were so many of them unfamiliar?

She asked her relatives.

"They've always been there," said one great-aunt.

"A high tide, made higher by a storm," said another.

"The Goddess," a very senior male cousin told her, "whose behavior we don't question. She acts as she does for her own reasons, which are not unfolded to us."

The young Tulwar, her playmates, found the topic boring. Who could possibly care about shells made of stone? "They don't shimmer like living shells, and there's nothing edible in them. Think about living shellfish, Haik! Or fish! Or trees like the ones that support our family!"

If her kin could not answer her questions, she'd find answers herself. Haik continued her study. She was helped by the fact that the strata along the northeast coast had not buckled or been folded over. Top was new. Bottom was old. She could trace the history of the region's life by climbing up.

At first, she didn't realize this. Instead, she got a hammer and began to break out fossils, taking them to one of the town's many empty houses. There, through trial and error, she learned to clean the fossils and to open them. "Unfolding with a hammer," she called the process.

Nowadays we discourage this kind of ignorant experimentation, especially at important sites. Remember this story takes place in the distant past. There was no one on the planet able to teach Haik; and the fossils she destroyed would have been destroyed by erosion long before the science of paleontology came into existence.

She began by collecting shells, laying them out on the tables left behind when the house was abandoned. Imagine her in a shadowy room, light slanting through the shutters. The floor is thick with dust. The paintings on the walls, fish and flowering trees, are peeling. Haik—a thin red adolescent in a tunic—bends over her shells, arranging them. She has discovered one of the great pleasures of intelligent life: organization or (as we call it now) taxonomy.

This was not her invention. All people organize information. But most people organize information for which they can see an obvious use: varieties of fish and their habits, for example. Haik had discovered the pleasure of knowledge that has no evident use. Maybe, in the shadows, you should imagine an old woman with white fur, dressed in a roughly woven tunic. Her feet are bare and caked with dirt. She watches Haik with amusement.

In time, Haik noticed there was a pattern to where she found her shells. The ones on the cliff tops were familiar. She could find similar or identical shells washed up on the Tulwar beaches. But as she descended, the creatures in the stone became increasingly strange. Also, and this puzzled her, certain strata were full of bones that obviously belonged to land animals. Had the ocean advanced, then retreated, then advanced again? How old were these objects? How much time had passed since they were alive, if they had ever been alive? Some of her senior kin believed they were mineral formations that bore an odd resemblance to the remains of animals. "The world is full of repetition and similarity," they told Haik, "evidence the Goddess has little interest in originality."

Haik reserved judgment. She'd found the skeleton of a bird so perfect that she had no trouble imagining flesh and feathers over the delicate bones. The animal's wings, if wings they were, ended in clawed hands. What mineral process would create the cliff top shells, identical to living shells, and this lovely familiar-yet-unfamiliar skeleton? If the Goddess had no love for originality, how to explain the animals toward the cliff bottom, spiny and knobby, with an extraordinary number of legs? They didn't resemble anything Haik had ever seen. What did they repeat?

When she was fifteen, her relatives came to her. "Enough of this folly! We are a small lineage, barely surviving; and we all have to work. Pick a useful occupation, and we'll apprentice you."

Most of her cousins became foresters. A few became sailors, shipping out with their neighbors, since the Tulwar no longer had anything except dories. But Haik's passion in life was stone. The town had no masons, but it did have a potter.

"Our foresters need pots," said Haik. "And Rakai is getting old. Give me to her."

"A wise choice," said the great-aunts with approval. "For the first time in years, you have thought about your family's situation."

Haik went to live in the house occupied by ancient Rakai. Most of the rooms were empty, except for pots. Clay dust drifted in the air. Lumps of dropped clay spotted the floors. The old potter was never free of the material. "When I was young, I washed more," she said. "But time is running out, and I have much to do. Wash if you want. It does no harm, when a person is your age. Though you ought to remember that I may not be around to teach you in a year or two or three."

Haik did wash. She was a neat child. But she remembered Rakai's warning and studied hard. As it turned out, she enjoyed making pots. Nowadays, potters can buy their materials from a craft cooperative; and many do. But in the past every potter mined his or her own clay; and a potter like Rakai, working in a poor town, did not use rare minerals in her glazes. "These are not fine cups for rich matrons to drink from," she told Haik. "These are pots for plants. Ordinary glazes will do, and minerals we can find in our own country." Once again Haik found herself out with hammer and shovel. She liked the ordinary work of preparation, digging the clay and hammering pieces of mineral from their matrices. Grinding the minerals was fine, also, though not easy; and she loved the slick texture of wet clay, as she felt through it for grit. Somehow, though it wasn't clear to her yet, the clay—almost liquid in her fingers—was connected to the questions she had asked about stone.

The potter's wheel was frustrating. When Rakai's old fingers touched a lump of clay, it rose into a pot like a plant rising from the ground in spring, entire and perfect, with no effort that Haik could see. When Haik tried to do the same, nothing was achieved except a mess.

"I'm like a baby playing with mud!"

"Patience and practice," said old Rakai.

Haik listened, being no fool. Gradually, she learned how to shape clay and fire it in the kiln Rakai had built behind the house. Her first efforts were bad, but she kept several to store her favorite pieces of rock. One piece was red iron ore, which could be ground down to make a shiny black glaze. The rest were fossils: shells and strange marine animals and the claw-handed bird.

At this point in the story, it's important to know the meaning of the word "potter" in Haik's language. As in our language, it meant a maker of pots. In addition, it meant someone who puts things into pots. Haik was still learning to make pots. But she was already a person who put stones or bones into pots, and this is not a trivial occupation, but rather a science. Never undervalue taxonomy. The foundation of all knowledge is fact, and facts that are not organized are useless.

Several years passed. Haik learned her teacher's skill, though her work lacked Rakai's elegance.

"It's the cliffs," said the old potter. "And the stones you bring back from them. They have entered your spirit, and you are trying to reproduce them in clay. I learned from plants, which have grace and symmetry. But you—"

One of Haik's pots was on the wheel: a squat, rough-surfaced object. The handles were uneven. At first, such things had happened due to lack of skill, but she found she liked work that was a little askew. She planned a colorless, transparent glaze that would streak the jar—like water seeping down a rock face, Haik suddenly realized.

"There's no harm in this," said Rakai. "We all learn from the world around us. If you want to be a potter of stones, fine. Stones and bones, if you are right and the things you find *are* bones. Stones and bones and shells."

The old potter hobbled off. Should she break the pot, Haik wondered. Was it wrong to love the cliffs and the objects they contained? Rakai had told her no. She had the old potter's permission to be herself. On a whim, Haik scratched an animal into the clay. Its head was like a hammer, with large eyes at either end—on the hammer's striking surfaces, as Haik explained it to herself. The eyes were faceted; and the long body was segmented. Each segment had a pair of legs, except for the final segment, which had two whip-like tails longer than the rest of the animal. No one she had met, not travelers to the most distant places nor the most outrageous liars, had ever described such an animal. Yet she had found its remains often, always in the cliffs' lower regions, in a kind of rock she had named "far-down dark grey."

Was this one of the Goddess's jokes? Most of the remains were damaged; only by looking carefully had she found intact examples; and no one else she knew was interested in such things. Had the Goddess built these cliffs and filled them with remains in order to fool Tulwar Haik?

Hardly likely! She looked at the drawing she'd made. The animal's body was slightly twisted, and its tails flared out on either side. It seemed alive, as if it might crawl off her pot and into Tulwar Harbor. The girl exhaled, her heart beating quickly. There was truth here. The creature she had drawn must have lived. Maybe it still lived in some distant part of the ocean. (She had found it among shells. Its home must be aquatic.) She refused to believe such a shape could come into existence through accident. She had been mixing and kneading and spinning and dropping clay for years. Nothing like this had ever appeared, except through intent. Surely it was impious to argue that the Goddess acted without thought. This marvelous world could not be the result of the Great One dropping the stuff-of-existence or squishing it aimlessly between her holy fingers. Haik refused to believe the animal was a joke. The Goddess had better things to do, and the animal was beautiful in its own strange way. Why would the Goddess, who was humorous but not usually malicious, make such an intricate and lovely lie?

Haik drew the animal on the other side of the pot, giving it a slightly different pose, then fired the pot and glazed it. The glaze, as planned, was clear and uneven, like a film of water running down the pot's dark grey fabric.

As you know, there are regions of the world where families permit sex among their members, if the relationship is distant enough. The giant families of the third continent, with fifty or a hundred thousand members, say there's nothing wrong with third or fourth or fifth cousins becoming lovers, though inbreeding is always wrong. But Haik's family did not live in such a region; and their lineage was so small and lived so closely together, that no one was a distant relative.

For this reason, Haik did not experience love until she was twenty and went down the coast on a trading ship to sell pots in Tsugul.

This was an island off the coast, a famous market in those days. The harbor was on the landward side, protected from ocean storms. A town of wood and plaster buildings went down slopes to the wooden warehouses and docks. Most of the plaster had been painted yellow or pale blue. The wood, where it showed, was dark blue or red. A colorful town, thought Haik when she arrived, made even more colorful by the many plants in pots. They stood on terraces and rooftops, by doorways, on the stairway streets. A good place to sell Rakai's work and her own.

In fact, she did well, helped by a senior forester who had been sent to sell the Tulwar's other product.

"I'd never say a word against your teacher, lass," he told her. "But your pots really set off my trees. They, my trees, are so delicate and brilliant; and your pots are so rough and plain. Look!" He pointed at a young crown-of-fire, blossoming in a squat black pot. "Beauty out of ugliness! Light out of darkness! You will make a fortune for our family!"

She didn't think of the pot as ugly. On it, in relief, were shells, blurred just a bit by the iron glaze. The shells were a series, obviously related, but from different parts of the Tulwar cliffs. Midway up the cliffs, the first place she found them, the shells were a single plain coil. Rising from there, the shells became ever more spiny and intricate. This progression went in a line around the pot, till a spiked monstrosity stood next to its straightforward ancestor.

Could Haik think this? Did she already understand about evolution? Maybe not. In any case, she said nothing to her kinsman.

That evening, in a tavern, she met a sailor from Sorg, a tall thin arrogant woman, whose body had been shaved into a pattern of white fur and black skin. They talked over cups of *halin*. The woman began brushing Haik's arm, marveling at the red fur. "It goes so well with your green eyes. You're a young one. Have you ever made love with a foreigner?"

"I've never made love," said Haik.

The woman looked interested, but said, "You can't be that young."

Haik explained she'd never traveled before, not even to neighboring towns. "I've been busy learning my trade."

The Sorg woman drank more *halin*. "I like being first. Would you be interested in making love?"

Haik considered the woman, who was certainly exotic looking. "Why do you shave your fur?"

"It's hot in my home country; and we like to be distinctive. Other folk may follow each other like city-building bugs. We do not!"

Haik glanced around the room and noticed other Sorg women, all clipped and shaved in the same fashion, but she did not point out the obvious, being young and polite.

They went to the Sorg woman's ship, tied at a dock. There were other couples on the deck, all women.

"We have a few men in the crew this trip," her sexual partner said. "But they're all on shore, looking for lovers; and they won't be back till we're ready to lift anchor."

The experience was interesting, Haik thought later, though she had not imagined making love for the first time on a foreign ship, surrounded by other couples, who were not entirely quiet. She was reminded of fish, spawning in shallow water.

"Well, you seemed to enjoy that," said the Sorg woman. "Though you are a silent one."

"My kin say I'm thoughtful."

"You shouldn't be, with red fur like fire. Someone like you ought to burn."

Why? wondered Haik, then fell asleep and dreamed that she was talking with an old woman dressed in a plain, rough tunic. The woman's feet were muddy. The nails on her hands were untrimmed and long, curling over the tips of her fingers like claws. There was dirt under the nails. The old woman said, "If you were an animal, instead of a person, you would have mated with a male; and there might have been children, created not as the result of a breeding contract, but out of sexual passion. Imagine a world filled with that kind of reproduction! It is the world you live in! Only people use reason in dealing with sex. Only people breed deliberately."

She woke at dawn, remembering the dream, though it made little sense. The woman had seemed like a messenger, but her message was obvious. Haik kissed the Sorg woman goodby, pulled on her tunic and stumbled down the gangway. Around her the air was cold and damp. Her feet left prints on dew-covered wood.

She had sex with the Sorg women several more times. Then the foreign ship lifted anchor, and Haik's lover was gone, leaving only a shell necklace.

"Some other woman will have to make you burn," the lover said. "But I was the first, and I want to be remembered."

Haik thanked her for the necklace and spent a day or two walking in the island's hills. The stone here was dark red and grainy and did not appear to contain fossils. Then she and her kinsman sailed north.

After that, she made sure to go on several trips a year. If the ship was crewed by women, she began looking for lovers as soon as she was onboard. Otherwise, she waited till they reached a harbor town. Sometimes she remained with a single lover. At other times, she went from one to another or joined a group. Her childhood nickname, long forgotten, came back to her, though now she was known as "Fire," rather than "Crown-of-Fire." She was a flame that burned without being burned.

"You never feel real affection," one lover told her. "This is nothing but sex for you."

Was this true? She felt affection for Rakai and her family at home and something approaching passion for her work with clay and stone. But these women?

As we know, men are more fervent and loyal lovers than women. They will organize their lives around affection. But most women are fond of their lovers and regret leaving them, as they usually must, though less often in modern times; and the departures matter less now, since travel has become so rapid. Lovers can meet fifty times a year, if they're willing to pay the airfare.

Haik enjoyed sex and her sexual partners, but left with no regrets, her spirit untouched.

"All your fire is in your sexual parts," another partner said. "Nothing burns in your mind."

When she was twenty-five, he family decided to breed her. There was no way she could refuse. If the Tulwar were going to survive, every healthy female had to bear children. After discussion, the senior women approached the Tsugul, who agreed to a mating contract. What happened next Haik did not like to remember. A young man arrived from Tsugul and stayed with her family. They mated till she became pregnant, then he was sent home with gifts: fine pots mostly, made by her and Rakai.

"I won't have children in my pottery," Rakai said.

"I will give the child to one of my cousins to raise," said Haik.

She bore female twins, dun colored with bright green eyes. For a while, looking at them, she thought of raising them. But this idea came from exhaustion and relief. She was not maternal. More than children, she wanted fossils and her pots. A female cousin took them, a comfortable woman with three children of her own. "Five is always lucky," she told Haik.

It seemed to be. All five children flourished like starflower trees.

Rakai lasted till Haik was almost thirty. In her last years, the old potter became confused and wandered out of her house, looking for long-drowned relatives or clay, though she had turned clay digging over to Haik a decade before. One of these journeys took place in an early winter rain. By the time the old woman was found, she was thoroughly drenched and shaking with cold. A coughing sickness developed and carried her away. Haik inherited the pottery.

By this time, she had developed a distinctive style: solid, squat pots with strange creatures drawn on them. Sometimes, the handles were strange creatures made in molds: clawed birds or animals like flowers with thick, segmented stalks. Haik had found fossils of the animals still grasping prey. In most cases, the prey was small fish, so the creatures had been marine predators. But her customers thought they were flowers—granted, strange ones, with petals like worms. "What an imagination you have!"

The pots with molded handles were fine work, intended for small expensive plants. Most of her work was large and sturdy, without handles that could break off. Her glazes remained plain: colorless or black.

Though she was a master potter, her work known up and down the coast, she continued hunting fossils. Her old teacher's house became filled with shelves; and the shelves became filled with pieces of stone. Taking a pen, Haik wrote her name for each creature on the shelf's edge, along with the place where she'd found this particular example. Prowling through the rooms by lantern light, she saw eons of evolution and recognized what she saw. How could she fail to, once the stones were organized?

The first shelves held shells and faint impressions of things that might be seaweed. Then came animals with many limbs, then fish that looked nothing like any fish she'd ever seen. Finally came animals with four limbs, also strange. Most likely, they had lived on land.

She had a theory now. She knew that sand and clay could become solid in the right circumstances. The animals had been caught in muck at the ocean's bottom or in a sand dune on land. Through a process she did not understand, though it must be like the firing of clay in a kiln, the trapping material turned to stone. The animal vanished, most likely burnt up, though it might also have decayed. If nothing else happened, the result was an impression. If the hollow space in the stone became filled, by some liquid seeping in and leaving a deposit, the result was a solid object. Her clawed bird was an impression. Most of her shells were solid.

Was she too clever? Could no one in her age imagine such a theory?

Well, she knew about clay, about molds, about minerals suspended in water. What else is a glaze? There were people in her village who worked with mortar, which is sand that hardens. There were people in nearby villages who used the lost wax process to cast.

All the necessary information was present. But no one except Haik used it to explain the objects in the Tulwar cliffs. Why? Because her kin had barely noticed the fossils and were not curious about them, did not collect them and label them and prowl around at night, looking at the pieces of stone and thinking.

Life had changed through time. It went from the very odd to the less odd to the almost familiar. In a few places on the cliff tops were animals that still lived. So, the process that led to the creation of fossils was still happening or had stopped happening recently.

How much time had this taken? Well, the old people in her town said that species did not change; and as far as she knew, there were no traditions that said animals used to be different. Oh, a few stories about monsters that no one had seen recently. But nothing about strange shells or fish. So the time required for change was longer than the memories of people.

Think of what she had learned and imagined! A world of vast periods of time, of animals that changed, of extinction. Hah! It frightened her! Was there any reason why her people might not vanish, along with the fish and plants they knew? Their lineage was small, its existence precarious. Maybe all life was precarious.

One night she had a dream. She was standing atop the cliffs above Tulwar Town. The houses below her looked very distant, unreachable. There was nothing around her except space, stretching up and down and east over the ocean. (The forest was behind her, and she did not turn around.) Next to her stood an old woman with white fur and dirty feet. "You've come a long way," she said. "Maybe you ought to consider turning back."

"Why?" asked Haik.

"There is no point in your journey. No one is going to believe you."

"About what?"

"My creatures."

"Are you the Goddess?" asked Haik.

The woman inclined her head slightly.

"Shouldn't you look more splendid?"

"Did Rakai look splendid? She worked in clay. I work in the stuff-of-existence. I wouldn't call it clean work, and who do I need to impress?"

"Have things really died out? Or do they exist somewhere in the world?"

"I'm not going to answer your questions," the old woman said. "Figure existence out for yourself."

"Do you advise me to turn back?"

"I never give advice," the Goddess said. "I'm simply telling you that no one will believe you about time and change. Oh, one or two people. You can get some people to believe anything, but sensible people will laugh."

"Should I care?" Haik asked.

"That's the question, isn't it?" the Goddess said. "But as I've said already, I don't give advice."

Then she was gone, and Haik was falling. She woke in bed in Rakai's house. Outside her window, stars blazed and gave her no comfort.

She thought about her dream for some time, then decided to go on a voyage. Maybe her problem was lack of sex. Her best pots went into wicker baskets, wrapped in straw, along with large plates, some plain, but most with strange creatures painted on them: her lovely bird with claws, the many-legged bugs, fish that wore plate armor instead of scales, and quadrupeds with peculiar horny heads.

When a ship arrived, going north, she took passage. It was crewed by Batanin women, so she had plenty of sex before she reached their destination. But the feeling of loneliness and fear remained. It seemed as if she stood on the edge of an abyss, with nothing around her or below her.

She got off in a harbor town inhabited by the Meskh, a good-sized family. Although they had a port, they were farmers mostly, producing grain and dried fruit for export, along with excellent *halin*.

Her pottery brought good prices in Meskh Market. By this time, she was famous as the Strange Animal Potter or The Potter of Shells and Bones.

"You are here in person," her customers said. "This is wonderful! Two famous women in town at once!"

"Who is the other?" Haik asked.

"The actor Dapple. Her troop has just given a series of plays. Now, they're resting, before continuing their tour. You must meet her."

They met that night in a tavern. Haik arrived escorted by several customers, middle-aged women with dark fur. At a table in the middle of the room, surrounded by dark Meskh women, was someone tall and slender, broad shouldered, her fur pale silver. Introductions were made. The actor stood. In lantern light, Haik could see the silver fur was dappled with small, dim spots. It was rare for people to keep their baby markings, but a few did.

"Hah! You're a lovely one," the actor said. "Red fur is unusual in this part of the world."

Haik sat down and told the story of her father, then how her mother died and how she had grown up in Tulwar Town. When she finally stopped, she saw the Meskh women were gone. She and Dapple sat alone at the table under the flaring lamp.

"What happened?" Haik asked.

"To the others? Most had the good sense to leave. Those who did not were removed by members of my company."

"And I didn't notice?"

"I don't believe," said Dapple, stretching, "that you are a person who notices much outside your interests. The Meskh have loaned us a house. Why don't you come there with me? We can drink more *halin* and talk more, if you wish. Though I have spent the past half an *ikun* imagining what you look like without clothing."

They went to the house, walking side by side through the dark streets. Inside, in a courtyard full of potted trees and lit by stars, they made love. Dapple pulled some blankets and pillows out of a room, so they weren't uncomfortable. "I have spent too much of my life sleeping on hard ground," the actor said. "If I can avoid discomfort, I will." Then she set to work with extraordinary skillful hands and a mouth that did not seem to belong to an ordinary woman made of flesh, but rather to some spirit out of ancient stories. The Fulfilling Every Wish Spirit, thought Haik. The Spirit of Almost Unendurable Pleasure.

The potter tried to reciprocate, though she knew it was impossible. No one, certainly not her, could equal Dapple's skill in love. But the actor made noises that indicated some satisfaction. Finally, they stopped. The actor clasped her hands in the back of her head and looked at the stars. "Can you give me a pot?"

"What?" asked Haik.

"I've seen your work before this, and I would like a keepsake, something to remember you."

At last the flame felt burning. Haik sat up and looked at the long pale figure next to her. "Is this over? Do we have only this night?"

"I have engagements," Dapple said. "We've arranged our passage on a ship that leaves tomorrow. Actors don't have settled lives, Haik. Nor do we usually have permanent lovers."

As in her dream, Haik felt she was falling. But this time she didn't wake in her bed, but remained in the Meskh courtyard.

The Goddess was right. She should give up her obsession. No one cared about the objects she found in cliffs. They did care about her pottery, but she could take leave of pots for a while.

"Let me go with you," she said to Dapple.

The actor looked at her. "Are you serious?"

"I have done nothing since I was fifteen, except make pots and collect certain stones I have a fondness for. More than fifteen years! And what I do I have to show? Pots and more pots! Stones and more stones! I would like to have an adventure, Dapple."

The actor laughed and said, "I've done many foolish things in my life. Now, I'll do one more. By all means, come on our journey!" Then she pulled Haik down and kissed her. What a golden tongue!

The next morning, Haik went to her ship and gathered her belongings. They fit in one basket. She never traveled with much, except her pots, and they were sold, the money in a heavy belt around her waist.

Next she went to the harbor mistress. Sitting in the woman's small house, she wrote a letter to her relatives, explaining what had happened and why she wasn't coming home.

"Are you sure this is a good idea?" the mistress said as Haik rolled the letter and put it in a message tube, then sealed the tube with wax.

"Yes." The letter was to go south on the next ship, Haik told the mistress. She gave the woman half her money to hold, till the Tulwar came to claim it.

"This is a foolish plan," the harbor mistress said.

"Have you never been in love?" Haik asked.

"Not this much in love, I'm glad to say."

Haik had started for the door. Now she stopped. The shutters on the room's windows were open. Haik was in a beam of light. Her red fur shone like fire. Her eyes were as clear and green as a cresting ocean wave. Hah! thought the harbor mistress.

"I'm thirty-two and have never been in love, until last night," Haik said. "It has come to me recently that the world is a lonely place." She slung her basket on her back and walked toward Dapple's borrowed house.

A strange woman, thought the harbor mistress.

The actors' ship left on the afternoon tide, Haik with them, standing on the deck, next to her new love.

At this point, the story needs to describe Dapple. She was forty when Haik met her, the first woman to train as an actor and the first person to assemble an acting company made of women. Her early years had been difficult; but by this time, she was successful and self-confident, a fine actor and even better playwright. Some of her writing has come forward to us, though only in a fragmentary condition. Still, the words shine like diamonds, unscratched by fate.

Dapple was her acting name. Her real name was Helwar Ahl, and her home—which she rarely visited—was Helwar Island, off the northeast corner of the Great

Southern Continent. For the most part, she and her company traveled up and down the continent's eastern coast, going as far south as Ettin, where she had many friends.

They were going south now and could have taken Haik's letter, though Haik hadn't known this. In any case, their ship was a fast trader, bound for Hu and not planning to stop on the way. East they went, till the coast was a thin dark line, visible only when the ship crested a wave. The rest of the time, they were alone, except for the *peshadi* that swam in front of them and the ocean birds that followed.

The birds were familiar to Haik, but she had never seen a live *pesha* before. As the animals' sleek backs broke the water's surface, they exhaled loudly enough so Haik had no trouble hearing the sound. *Wah! Wah!* Then they dove, their long tails cutting through the water like knives. They had a second name: blue fish, which came from their hide's deep ocean color. Neither death nor tanning dimmed the hue, and *pesha* leather was a famous luxury.

"I had a pair of *pesha* boots once," said Dapple. "A wealthy matron gave them to me, because they were cracked beyond repair. I used them in plays, till they fell into pieces. You should have seen me as a warrior, strutting around in those boots!"

Years before, a dead *pesha* had washed up on a beach in Tulwar. They'd all gone to see it: this deep-sea animal their kin had hunted before the Drowning. It had been the size of a large woman, with four flippers and a tail that looked like seaweed, lying limp on the pebbles. The old men of Tulwar cut it up. Most of the women went back to work, but Haik stayed and watched. The flesh had been reddish-purple, like the flesh of land animals; the bones of the skeleton had been large and heavy. As for the famous skin, she'd felt it. Not slimy, like a fish, and with no scales, though there were scaleless fish. She knew that much, though her kin no longer went to sea.

Most interesting of all were the flippers. She begged a hind one from the old men. It was small, the hide not usable, with almost no flesh on the bones. "Take it," her senior male relatives told her. "Though nothing good is likely to come from your curiosity."

Haik carried it to her teacher's house, into a back room that Rakai never entered. Her fossils were there, along with other objects: a bird skeleton, almost complete; the skulls of various small animals; and shells from Tulwar's beaches. Laying the flipper on a table, she used a sharp knife to cut it open. Inside, hidden by blue skin and reddish-purple flesh, were five rows of long, narrow, white bones.

She had cleaned them and arranged them on the table as she'd found them in the flipper. The two outer rows were short, the thumb—could she call it that?— barely present, while the three middle rows were long and curved. Clearly, they provided a framework for the flipper. What purpose did the outer rows serve, and why had the Goddess hidden a hand inside a sea animal's flipper?

"Well," said Dapple after Haik told this story. "What's the answer to your question?"

"I don't know," said Haik, afraid to talk about her theories. What did she know for certain? A group of puzzling facts. From these she had derived a terrifying sense of time and change. Did she have the right to frighten other people, as she had been frightened?

Beside them, a *pesha* surfaced and exhaled, rolling sideways to eye them and grin with sharp white teeth.

"Rakai told me the world is full of similarities and correspondences. The Goddess is a repeater. That's what they always told me."

"And a jokester," said Dapple. "Maybe she thought it would be funny to make something that was a fish in some ways and a land animal in others."

"Maybe," Haik said in a doubtful tone. "I tanned the flipper hide and made a bag from it, but couldn't use the bag. It seemed dishonorable and wrong, as if I was using the skin from a woman's hand to keep things in. So I put the *pesha* bones in the bag and kept them on one of my shelves; and I made a pot decorated with *peshadi*. It was a failure. I didn't know how living *peshadi* moved. Now, I will be able to make the pot again."

Dapple ruffled the red fur on her shoulder. "Like fire," the actor said gently. "You burn with curiosity and a desire to get things right."

"My relatives say it will get me in trouble."

"The Goddess gave us the ability to imagine and question and judge," the actor said. "Why would she have done this, if she did not intend us to use these abilities? I question the behavior of people; you question rocks and bones. Both activities seem *chulmar* to me."

Then as now, *chulmar* meant to be pious and to be funny. Dapple's voice sounded amused to Haik; this made her uneasy. In Tulwar, after the Drowning, piety took the form of glumness, though the people there certainly knew the meaning of *chulmar*. They did not mean to turn their children away from enjoyment of the world, but so much had been lost; they had become afraid; and the fear is the end of piety.

The ship continued south, till it was far past the Tulwar coast. During this period, Haik was preoccupied with love. Hah! It had struck her like a strong blow in battle! She could think of little except Dapple's body: the four breasts, surprisingly large for a woman who'd never borne children; the rangy limbs; the prominent nipples, the same color as the "far-down dark grey" strata at home; and the place between the actor's legs, which was a cave of pleasure. Haik could model a breast in clay, make a covered pot of it, with a nipple for the handle. But how could she replicate the hidden place? Or Dapple's mouth with its golden tongue? It could not be done, especially now, with her kiln far behind her. Better not to think of pottery.

They made love often, usually on deck, under blazing tropic stars. She was drunk with love! Love had made her crazy, and she did not care!

Five days south of Tsugul Island, the ship turned west. They came to the wide harbor at Hu, guarded by white shoals. The *peshadi* were gone by then; the birds had become more numerous. A low green coast emerged from misty rain.

Haik and Dapple were on deck. Peering forward, Haik made out the buildings of Hu Town: white and blue, with red or green roofs. Fishing boats lined the harbor docks. Their furled sails were red, white, green, and yellow. "A colorful country."

"That's the south," said Dapple in agreement. As lovely as always, the actor was leaning on the ship's rail, looking happy. "People in the north call these folk barbarians, who lack refinement and a sense of nuance. But drama is not made of nuance." She raised an arm and brought it down. "It's the sword blade descending, the cry of understanding and anger and pain. I could not write the plays I write, if I didn't visit the south."

They tied up among the fishing boats, empty in mid-afternoon. The acting company went on shore, Tulwar Haik among them. She had never been this far south. The people in the streets, dressed in bright tunics and kilts, were an unfamiliar physical type: broad chested, with short thick limbs. The women were taller than women in the north, towering a full head above their male relatives. Everyone had grey fur, and Haik got many sideways glances.

"I could lose you," said Dapple with amusement.

"They're ugly," said Haik.

"They are different, dear one. When you get used to them, they will begin to look handsome."

"Have you had lovers here?"

Dapple laughed. "Many."

Their destination was an inn built around a courtyard. There were potted trees in the courtyard: skyflower and starflower and a kind Haik did not recognize, which had silver-blue leaves and frilly, bright yellow flowers. Several of the pots had been made by Rakai; one had been made by her, an early work, not bad in its way. She pointed it out to Dapple.

The innkeeper appeared, a huge woman with arms like tree limbs and four enormous breasts, barely concealed by a vest. "My favorite customer!" she cried. "Are you going to perform?"

"Most likely, yes. Haik, this is Hu Aptsi." Dapple laid a hand on Haik's red shoulder. "And this beauty is my new lover, Tulwar Haik the potter. She has given up her pots to travel with me, until we tire of each other."

"Never!" said Haik.

"Excellent work you do in Tulwar," the innkeeper said. "I have neighbors who say nothing good comes from the north. Dapple and pots and flowering trees, I say."

They went into the common room and settled around tables. A round clay hearth bulged out of one wall. Logs burned in it. The innkeeper brought a large metal bowl, filling it with fruit juices and *halin*, then heated an iron rod in the fire and put the glowing tip in the full bowl. The liquid hissed and steamed. The innkeeper served. Haik wrapped her hands around a hot cup, sniffing the aromatic steam, thinking, *I am far from home, among strangers, about to drink something for which I have no name.* She tasted the liquid. Delicious!

"It will make you drunk quickly," said Dapple in a warning tone.

Beyond the room's windows, rain fell in the courtyard, and the potted trees quivered. *I am happy*, Haik thought.

That night, as she lay in Dapple's arms, she had a dream. The old woman came to her again, this time with clean hands and feet. "Existence is made to be enjoyed. Always remember that."

"Why did you kill my mother and my other relatives?" Haik asked.

"A storm killed them. Do you think every gust of wind is my breath? Do you think it's my hand that crushes every bug and pulls every bird from the sky?"

"Why did you make things that die?"

"Why do you work in clay? Sooner or later, all your pots will break."

"I like the material."

"I like life," the Goddess said. "And change."

The next day, Haik helped the actors set up their stage in a warehouse near the docks. Rain still fell. They would not be able to perform outside. The acting company was large: ten women, all from northern towns. Five were full members of the company. Three were apprentices. One was a carpenter; one made the costumes; though both of these last could fill small parts when needed. They all worked together easily. It was Haik who was awkward and needed to be told what to do. "You will learn," said Dapple.

Midway through the morning, she disappeared. "Off to write," said the carpenter. "I could see her thinking. These southerners like rude plays, and that isn't the kind of thing we usually do, except when we're down here. You'd think they'd like hero plays; they have plenty of real heroes among them. But no, they want comedy with lots of penises."

Haik could think of nothing to say.

They ate their evening meal in the inn, a light one, since acting should never be done on a full stomach. Then they went back to the warehouse, through still-falling rain. There were lamps on the walls around the stage. The wide, dark space beyond the lamplight was full of people. The air stank of oil, damp fur, and excitement.

"We know our business," said Dapple. "You keep off to the side and watch."

Haik did as told, leaning against a side wall, below a lamp that cast a yellow, flickering glow. Because she rarely thought about her appearance, she did not realize how she looked, her red fur and green eyes shining. Half the women in the audience wanted to have sex with her, half the men wished she were male. How could a woman of her age be so naïve? By thinking too much and living too long in the glum family Tulwar became after the Drowning.

The play was about a *sul* with an enormous penis. Dapple played him in an animal mask. The penis, of which he was so proud, was longer than she was and limp, so it dragged on the ground. The *sul* tripped over it often, while he bragged about his masculine power and the lovers he'd had, all men of extraordinary beauty and talent. Once he was established as an irritating braggart, a *tli* appeared, played by the company's second actor. The two animals got into a betting contest, and the *tli* won the *sul*'s penis, which struck the audience as funny. Getting it off was a problem, which struck the audience as even funnier. Finally, the *sul* stormed off, bereft of his male member and vowing revenge.

Now the *tli* delivered a soliloquy, while holding the huge limp object. Fine to win, the *tli* said, but he had no use for a penis this large. His own was adequate for his purposes; and the *sul* would come back with friends and weapons to reclaim the penis. This was the problem with giving in to irritation. What was he to do? How could he escape the vengeance of the *sul*?

At this point, Dapple reappeared, wearing a sleek blue mask, the open mouth full of sharp white teeth. She was a *pesha*, she announced, an early version of this species. She lived in shallow water, paddling and catching fish. She wanted to move into the ocean, but her tail was too small; she needed a new one, able to drive her deep into the water or far out over the waves.

"I have just the thing," said the *tli*, and showed her the *sul*'s penis. "We'll, sew this on your backside, and you'll swim like a fish. But in return for this gift, you must carry me to safety; and once you are able to dive deeply, I wouldn't mind having some of the treasure that's sunk in the ocean."

The *pesha* agreed, and the two animals attached the penis to the back of Dapple's costume. Then she did a dance of happiness, singing praise of the ocean and her new life.

The other actors joined them with blue and white banners, which mimicked the motion of water, through which Dapple and the *tli* escaped, dancing and singing.

When everyone was gone, and the stage was bare, Dapple returned as the *sul*, along with two more *sulin*. "Foiled!" they cried. "We can't follow. Your penis is assuredly gone, dear relative. You are not going to be socially popular in the future."

That was the end of the play, except for a final dance, done by the *tli*, surrounded by the rest of the cast, waving golden banners. These represented the treasure he had gained. As for the grateful *pesha*, she was happy in her new home, and with luck the penis would not retain any of its old qualities.

The audience stamped their feet and made hooting noises. Clearly, the play had gone over well.

Haik thought, yes, she was certain that things could turn into other things. But not, in all likelihood, a penis into a tail. And change was not a result of trickery, but time.

People came to talk with the main actors. Haik helped the carpenter and costume maker clean up.

"Ettin Taiin," said the carpenter. "I didn't know he was in town."

"Who?" asked Haik, putting the *tli* mask in a box.

"The lame man."

She looked around and saw a short fellow limping toward the stage. His fur was grey, turning silver over the shoulders and on the face. One eye was missing; he didn't bother to wear a patch over the empty socket.

"He is the foremost war captain among the Ettin," the carpenter said. "And they are the most dangerous lineage in this part of the world. Dapple calls his mother 'great-aunt.' If you find him scary, as I do, then you ought to meet the old lady!"

There was no way for him to reach Dapple, surrounded by admirers. He greeted the carpenter and the costume maker by name, without glancing at them directly. Good manners, thought Haik.

"Is Cholkwa with you?" asked the costume maker.

"South, among the savages of the Cold Ocean Coast. I sent men with him for protection, in case the savages didn't like his comedies. May I ask about your companion, or is that rude?"

"We can hardly object to rudeness, after the play we've done," said the carpenter.

"I laughed so hard I thought I would lose control of my bladder," said the one-eyed man.

The costume maker said, "This is Tulwar Haik the potter. She's Dapple's new lover."

The man lifted his head, apparently in surprise. Haik got a glimpse of his sunken eye socket and the remaining eye, which blazed blue as a noon sky. His pupil had expanded in the dim light and lay across the eye like an iron bar. "The Potter of Strange Animals," he said.

"Yes," said Haik, surprised to be known in this distant place.

"The world is full of coincidences!" the soldier told her. "And this one is pleasant! I bought one of your pots for my mother last year. She can barely see these days, but she likes the texture of it. She especially likes to feel the animals you have used for handles. Birds with clawed hands! What an idea! How can they possibly fly?"

"I don't think they did—or do," said Haik.

"These birds exist?" asked the soldier.

Haik paused, considering. "I have found their remains."

"You don't say. The world is full of two things, then: coincidence and strangeness. Considering the Goddess, this can't be called surprising." He glanced toward Dapple. Most of the admirers had gone. "Excuse me. I want to give her news of Cholkwa. They just missed each other. His ship left two days ago; and I was planning to ride home, having stayed with him till the last *ikun*. But then I heard that Dapple had arrived."

He limped away.

"He and Cholkwa are lovers," said the carpenter. "Though the true love of Cholkwa's life is the actor Perig. Perig's old now and in poor health. He lives on Helwar Island with Dapple's kin, who are my kin also, while Cholkwa still travels. Male actors are as promiscuous as women."

Haik finished putting away the masks. The *pesha* mask was new, she realized. The blue paint was still tacky, and the shape of the head had been changed, using cloth and glue.

"We keep blank masks," said the carpenter. "Then, when Dapple has a sudden idea, we can add new animals."

"This is something I can do," Haik said. "Shape the masks and paint them." She glanced up at the carpenter and the costume maker. "Unless the work belongs to you."

"We all do many things," said the costume maker. "If you stay with us you'll find yourself on stage."

When everything was packed up, they went back to the inn, sat in the common room and drank *halin*. The Ettin captain, who came with them, had an immense capacity. He left from time to time to urinate, but never got noticeably drunk. The idea of coincidence was stuck in his mind, and he talked about how it worked in war, sometimes to his benefit, sometimes against him.

There was the time he went to attack the Gwa and met their warband on the way, coming to attack Ettin. "We both picked the same exact route. So there we were in a mountain pass, staring at each other with mouths open. Then we fought." He spilled *halin* on the table and drew the disposition of troops. "A bad situation for both of us! Neither had an advantage, and neither had a good way to retreat. I knew I had to win and did, though I lost an eye and a brother; and enough Gwa soldiers escaped, so we could not surprise them at home. A nasty experience, caused by coincidence. Doubtless the Goddess does this to us so we won't take our plans too seriously; a good captain must always be ready to throw his ideas away."

When he finally left, walking steadily except for his limp, Dapple said, "I have sworn to myself; I will put him in a play some day. That is what a hero is really like. I'll have to make up a new story, of course. His life has not been tragic. He's never had to make difficult choices, and everything he's wanted—fame, the affection of his relatives, the love of Cholkwa—has come into his hands."

Well, thought Haik, she was certainly learning new things. The man had not seemed like a hero to her.

The next evening, they did the play a second time. The warehouse was packed, and Ettin Taiin was in the audience again. Haik watched him as he watched the play, his expression intent. Now and then, he laughed, showing white teeth. One was missing, an upper stabber. Doubtless it had been lost in battle, like his eye and his leg's agility. Haik's male relatives fought nothing except the forest predators, which were not especially dangerous. When men died in the forest, it was usually from small creatures that had a poisonous bite or sting; or they died from accidents. Old people told stories about pirates, but none had attacked the northeast coast in more than a generation. The Tulwar feared water and storms.

Now, Haik thought, she was in the south. War was continuous here; and lineages vanished from existence, the men killed, the women and children adopted. A family that lacked soldiers like Ettin Taiin would not survive.

This idea led nowhere, except to the thought that the world was full of violence, and this was hardly a new thought. In front of her, Dapple tripped over the *sul's* long dragging penis and tumbled into a somersault, which ended with her upright once again, the penis wound around her neck. The audience hooted its approval. The world was full of violence and sex, Haik thought.

Once again the captain joined them at the inn. This time he drank less and asked questions, first of the actors, then of Haik. Where exactly was her family? What did they produce besides pots?

"Are you planning to invade us?" she asked.

He looked shocked. "I am a soldier, not a bandit, young lady! I only fight with people I know. The purpose of war is to expand the size of one's family and increase the amount of land held by one's kin. That should always be done along existing borders. You push out and push out, gathering the land and the women and children immediately beyond your borders, making sure the land is always contiguous and protected—if possible—by natural barriers. Any other strategy leaves you with a territory that is not defensible."

"He's not planning to invade you," Dapple said in summary. "Your land is too far away."

"Exactly," the captain said. "Bandits and pirates use different tactics, since they want valuable objects rather than land and people. We've had both in the south and dealt with them."

"How?" asked Haik.

"The obvious way is to find where they came from, go there and kill all the men. The problem is, you have to do something with the bandit women and children. They can't be left to starve. But obviously no family wants members with bad traits."

"What do you do?"

"Adopt them, but spread them among many houses, and never let any of them breed. Often, the children turn out well; and after a generation, the traits—bad or good—are gone. This, as you can imagine, is a lot of work, which is a reason to kill enough men so the bandits will think twice about returning to Ettin, but leave enough alive so the women and children are provided for."

The carpenter was right. This was a frightening man.

Dapple said, "The Tulwar are foresters. For the most part, they export lumber and flowering trees. Haik makes pots for the trees."

"Do you have children?" the captain asked Haik.

"Two daughters."

"A woman with your abilities should have more. What about brothers?"

"None."

"Male cousins?"

"Many," said Haik.

The captain glanced at Dapple. "Would it be worthwhile asking a Tulwar man to come here and impregnate one of our women? Your lover's pots are really excellent; and my mother has always liked flowers. So do I, for that matter."

"It's a small family," said Dapple. "And lives far away. A breeding contract with them would not help you politically."

"There is more to life than politics," said the captain.

"The Tulwar men aren't much for fighting," said Haik, unsure that she wanted any connection with Ettin.

"You don't mean they're cowards?"

"Of course not. They work in our wild backcountry as foresters and loggers. They used to sail the ocean, before most of my family drowned. These kinds of work require courage, but we have always gotten along with our neighbors."

"No harm in that, if you aren't ambitious." He grinned, showing his missing tooth. "We don't need to breed for ambition or violence. We have those talents in abundance. But art and beauty—" His blue eye glanced at her briefly. "These are not our gifts, though we are certainly able to appreciate both."

"Witness your appreciation of Cholkwa," said Dapple, her tone amused.

"A great comedian, and the best-looking man for his age I've ever seen. But my mother and her sisters decided years ago that he should not be asked to father

Ettin children. For one thing, he has never mentioned having a family. Who could the Ettin speak to, if they wanted a breeding contract? A man shouldn't make decisions like these. We do things the right way in Ettin! In any case, acting is not an entirely respectable art; who can say what qualities would appear among the Ettin, if our children were fathered by actors."

"You see why I have no children," Dapple said, then tilted her head toward the carpenter. "Though my kinswoman here has two sets of twins, because her gift is making props. We don't tell our relatives that she also acts."

"Not much," said the carpenter.

"And not well," muttered the apprentice sitting next to Haik.

The captain stayed a while longer, chatting with Dapple about his family and her most recent plays. Finally he rose. "I'm too old for these long evenings. In addition, I plan to leave for Ettin at dawn. I assume you're sending love and respect to my mother."

"Of course," said Dapple.

"And you, young lady." The one eye roved toward her. "If you come this way again, bring pots for Ettin. I'll speak to my mother about a breeding contract with Tulwar. Believe me, we are allies worth having!"

He left, and Dapple said, "I think he's imagining a male relative who looks like you, who can spend his nights with an Ettin woman and his days with Ettin Taiin."

"What a lot of hard work!" the carpenter said.

"There are no Tulwar men who look like me."

"What a sadness for Ettin Taiin!" said Dapple.

From Hu Town they went west and south, traveling with a caravan. The actors and merchants rode *tsina*, which were familiar to Haik, though she had done little riding before this. The carrying beasts were *bitalin*: great, rough quadrupeds with three sets of horns. One pair spread far to the side; one pair curled forward; and the last pair curled back. The merchants valued the animals as much as *tsina*, giving them pet names and adorning their horns with brass or iron rings. They seemed marvelous to Haik, moving not quickly, but very steadily, their shaggy bodies swaying with each step. When one was bothered by something—bugs, a scent on the wind, another *bital*—it would swing its six-horned head and groan. What a sound!

"Have you put *bitalin* in a play?" she asked Dapple.

"Not yet. What quality would they represent?"

"Reliability," said the merchant riding next to them. "Strength. Endurance. Obstinacy. Good milk."

"I will certainly consider the idea," Dapple replied.

At first the plain was green, the climate rainy. As they traveled south and west, the weather became dry, and the plain turned dun. This was not a brief journey. Haik had time to get used to riding, though the country never became ordinary to her. It was so wide! So empty!

The merchants in the caravan belonged to a single family. Both women and men were along on the journey. Of course the actors camped with the women, while the men—farther out—stood guard. In spite of this protection, Haik was uneasy. The stars overhead were no longer entirely familiar; the darkness around her seemed to go on forever; and caravan campfires seemed tiny. Far out on the plain, wild *sulin* cried. They were more savage than the domestic breeds used for hunting and guarding, Dapple told her. "And uglier, with scales covering half their bodies. Our *sulin* in the north have only a few small scaly patches."

The *sulin* in Haik's country were entirely furry, except in the spring. Then the males lost their chest fur, revealing an area of scaly skin, dark green and glittering. If allowed to, they'd attack one another, each trying to destroy the other's chest adornment. "Biting the jewels," was the name of this behavior.

Sitting under the vast foreign sky, Haik thought about *sulin*. They were all varieties of a single animal. Everyone knew this, though it was hard to believe that Tulwar's mild-tempered, furry creatures were the same as the wild animals Dapple described. Could change go farther? Could an animal with hands become a *pesha*? And what caused change? Not trickery, as in the play. Dapple, reaching over, distracted her. Instead of evolution, she thought about love.

They reached a town next to a wide sandy river. Low bushy trees grew along the banks. The merchants made camp next to the trees, circling their wagons. Men took the animals to graze, while the women—merchants and actors—went to town.

The streets were packed dirt, the houses adobe with wood doors and beams. (Haik could see these last protruding through the walls.) The people were the same physical type as in Hu, but with grey-brown fur. A few had faint markings—not spots like Dapple, but narrow broken stripes. They dressed as all people did, in tunics or shorts and vests.

Why, thought Haik suddenly, did people come in different hues? Most wild species were a single color, with occasional freaks, usually black or white. Domestic animals came in different colors. It was obvious why: people had bred them according to different ideas of usefulness and beauty. Had people bred themselves to be grey, grey-brown, red, dun and so on? This was possible, though it seemed to Haik that most people were attracted to difference. Witness Ettin Taiin. Witness the response of the Tulwar matrons to her father.

Now to the problems of time and change, she added the problem of difference. Maybe the problem of similarity as well. If animals tended to be the same, why did difference occur? If there was a tendency toward difference, why did it become evident only sometimes? She was as red as her father. Her daughters were dun. At this point, her head began to ache; and she understood the wisdom of her senior relatives. If one began to question anything—shells in rock, the hand in a *pesha*'s flipper—the questions would proliferate, till they stretched to the horizon in every direction and *why, why, why* filled the sky, like the calls of migrating birds.

"Are you all right?" asked Dapple.

"Thinking," said Haik.

At the center of the town was a square, made of packed dirt. The merchants set up a tent and laid out sample goods: dried fish from Hu, fabric made by northern weavers, boxes carved from rare kinds of wood, jewelry of silver and dark red shell. Last of all, they unfolded an especially fine piece of cloth, put it on the ground and poured out their most precious treasure: a high, white, glittering heap of salt.

Townsfolk gathered: bent matriarchs, robust matrons, slim girls and boys, even a few adult men. All were grey-brown, except the very old, who had turned white.

In general, people looked like their relatives; and everyone knew that family traits existed. Why else select breeding partners with so much care? There must be two tendencies within people, one toward similarity, the other toward difference. The same must also be true of animals. Domestic *sulin* came in different colors; by breeding, people had brought out variations that must have been in the wild animals, though never visible, except in freaks. She crouched in the shadows at the back of the merchants' tent, barely noticing the commerce in front of her, thinking difficult thoughts.

Nowadays, geneticists tell us that the variation among people was caused by drift in isolated populations, combined with the tendency of all people to modify and improve anything they can get their hands on. We have bred ourselves like *sulin* to fit in different environments and to meet different ideas of beauty.

But how could Haik know this much about the history of life? How could she know that wild animals were more varied than she had observed? There are wild *sulin* in the far northern islands as thick furred and white as the local people. There is a rare, almost extinct kind of wild *sulin* on the third continent, which is black and entirely scaly, except for a ridge of rust-brown fur along its back. She, having traveled on only one continent, was hypothesizing in the absence of adequate data. In spite of this, she caught a glimpse of how inheritance works.

How likely is this? Could a person like Haik, living in a far-back era, come so near the idea of genes?

Our ancestors were not fools! They were farmers and hunters, who observed animals closely; and they achieved technological advances—the creation through breeding of the plants that feed us and the animals we still use, though no longer exclusively, for work and travel—which we have not yet equaled, except possibly by going into space.

In addition to the usual knowledge about inheritance, Haik had the ideas she'd gained from fossils. Other folk knew that certain plants and animals could be changed by breeding; and that families had traits that could be transmitted, either for good or bad. But most life seemed immutable. Wild animals were the same from generation to generation. So were the plants of forest and plain. The Goddess liked the world to stay put, as far as most people could see. Haik knew otherwise.

Dapple came after her, saying, "We need help in setting up our stage."

That evening, in the long summer twilight, the actors performed the *pesha* comedy. Dapple had to make a speech beforehand, explaining what a *pesha* was, since they were far inland now. But the town folk knew about *sulin*, *tli*, and penises; and the play went well, as had the trading of the merchants. The next day they continued west.

Haik traveled with Dapple all summer. She learned to make masks by soaking paper in glue, then applying it in layers to a wooden mask frame.

"Nothing we carry is more valuable," said the costume maker, holding a thick white sheet of paper. "Use this with respect! No other material is as light and easy to shape. But the cost, Haik, the cost!"

The *bitalin* continued to fascinate her: living animals as unfamiliar as the fossils in her cliffs! Her first mask was a *bital*. When it was dry, she painted the face tan, the six horns shiny black. The skin inside the flaring nostrils was red, as was the tongue protruding from the open mouth.

Dapple wrote a play about a solid and reliable *bital* cow, who lost her milk to a conniving *tli*. The *tli* was outwitted by other animals, friends of the *bital*. The play ended with Dapple as the cow, dancing among pots of her recovered milk, turned through the ingenuity of the *tli* into a new substance: long-lasting, delicious cheese. The play did well in towns of the western plains. By now they were in a region where the ocean was a rumor, only half-believed; but *bitalin* were known and loved.

Watching Dapple's performance, Haik asked herself another question. If there was a hand inside the *pesha*'s flipper, could there be another hand in the *bital*'s calloused, two-toed foot? Did every living thing contain another living thing within it, like Dapple in the *bital* costume?

What an idea!

The caravan turned east when a plant called fire-in-autumn turned color. Unknown in Tulwar, it was common on the plain, though Haik had not noticed it till now. At first, there were only a few bright dots like drops of blood fallen on a pale brown carpet. These were enough to make the merchants change direction. Day by day, the color became more evident, spreading in lines. (The plant grew through sending out runners.) Finally, the plain was crisscrossed with scarlet. At times, the caravan traveled through long, broad patches of the plant, *tsina* and *bitalin* belly-deep in redness, as if they were fording rivers of blood or fire.

When they reached the moist coastal plain, the plant became less common. The vegetation here was mostly a faded silver-brown. Rain fell, sometimes freezing; and they arrived in the merchants' hometown at the start of the first winter storm. Haik saw the rolling ocean through lashes caked with snow. The pleasure of salt water! Of smelling seaweed and fish!

The merchants settled down for winter. The actors took the last ship north to Hu Town, where the innkeeper had bedrooms for them, a fire in the common room and *halin* ready for mulling.

At midwinter, Dapple went to Ettin. Haik stayed by the ocean, tired of foreigners. It had been more than half a year since she'd had clay in her hands or climbed the Tulwar cliffs in search of fossils. Now she learned that love was not enough. She walked the Hu beaches, caked with ice, and looked for shells. Most were similar to ones in Tulwar; but she found a few new kinds, including one she knew as a fossil. Did this mean other creatures—her claw-handed bird, the hammer-headed bug—were still alive somewhere? Maybe. Little was certain.

Dapple returned through a snowstorm and settled down to write. The Ettin always gave her ideas. "When I'm in the south, I do comedy, because the people here prefer it. But their lives teach me how to write tragedy; and tragedy is my gift."

Haik's gift lay in the direction of clay and stone, not language. Her journey south had been interesting and passionate, but now it was time to do something. What? Hu Town had no pottery, and the rocks in the area contained no fossils. In the end, she took some of the precious paper and used it, along with metal wire, to model strange animals. The colors were a problem. She had to imagine them, using what she knew about the birds and bugs and animals of Tulwar. She made the hammer-headed bug red and black. The flower-predator was yellow and held a bright blue fish. The claw-handed bird was green.

"Well, these are certainly different," said Dapple. "Is this what you find in your cliffs?"

"The bones and shells, yes. Sometimes there is a kind of shadow of the animal in the rock. But never any colors."

Dapple picked up a tightly coiled white shell. Purple tentacles spilled out of it; and Haik had given the creature two large, round eyes of yellow glass. The eyes were a guess, derived from a living ocean creature. But Haik had seen the shadow of tentacles in stone. Dapple tilted the shell, till one of the eyes caught sunlight and blazed. Hah! It seemed alive! "Maybe I could write a play about these creatures; and you could make the masks."

Haik hesitated, then said, "I'm going home to Tulwar.—"

"You are?" Dapple set down the glass-eyed animal.

She needed her pottery, Haik explained, and the cliffs full of fossils, as well as time to think about this journey. "You wouldn't give up acting for love!"

"No," said Dapple. "I plan to spend next summer in the north, doing tragedies. When I'm done, I'll come to Tulwar for a visit. I want one of your pots and maybe one of these little creatures." She touched the flower-predator. "You see the world like no one else I've ever met. Hah! It is full of wonders and strangeness, when looked at by you!"

That night, lying in Dapple's arms, Haik had a dream. The old woman came to her, dirty-footed, in a ragged tunic. "What have you learned?"

"I don't know," said Haik.

"Excellent!" said the old woman. "This is the beginning of comprehension. But I'll warn you again. You may gain nothing, except comprehension and my approval, which is worth little in the towns where people dwell."

"I thought you ruled the world."

"Rule is a large, heavy word," said the old woman. "I made the world and enjoy it, but rule? Does a tree rule the shoots that rise at its base? Matriarchs may rule their families. I don't claim so much for myself."

When spring came, the company went north. Their ship stopped at Tulwar to let off Haik and take on potted trees. There were so many plants that some had to be stored on deck, lashed down against bad weather. As the ship left, it seemed like a floating grove. Dapple stood among the trees, crown-of-fire mostly, none in bloom. Haik, on the shore, watched till she could no longer see her lover or the ship. Then she walked home to Rakai's pottery. Everything was as Haik had left it, though covered with dust. She unpacked her strange animals and set them on a table. Then she got a broom and began to sweep.

After a while, her senior relatives arrived. "Did you enjoy your adventures?"

"Yes."

"Are you back to stay?"

"Maybe."

Great-aunts and uncles glanced at one another. Haik kept sweeping.

"It's good to have you back," said a senior male cousin.

"We need more pots," said an aunt.

Once the house was clean, Haik began potting: simple forms at first, with no decoration except a monochrome glaze. Then she added texture: a cord pattern at the rim, crisscross scratches on the body. The handles were twists of clay, put on carelessly. Sometimes she left her handprint like a shadow. Her glazes, applied in splashes, hid most of what she'd drawn or printed. When her shelves were full of new pots, she went to the cliffs, climbing up steep ravines and walking narrow ledges, a hammer in hand. Erosion had uncovered new fossils: bugs and fish, mostly, though she found one skull that was either a bird or a small land animal. When cleaned, it turned out to be intact and wonderfully delicate. The small teeth, still in the jaw or close to it, were like nothing she had seen. She made a copy in grey-green clay, larger than the original, with all the teeth in place. This became the handle for a large covered pot. The body of the pot was decorated with drawings of birds and animals, all strange. The glaze was thin and colorless and cracked in firing, so it seemed as if a film of ice covered the pot.

"Who will buy that?" asked her relatives. "You can't put a tree in it, not with that cover."

"My lover Dapple," said Haik in reply. "Or the famous war captain of Ettin."

At midsummer, there was a hot period. The wind off the ocean stopped. People moved when they had to, mouths open, panting. During this time, Haik was troubled with dreams. Most made no sense. A number involved the Goddess. In one, the old woman ate an *agala*. This was a southern fruit, unknown in Tulwar, which consisted of layers wrapped around a central pit. The outermost layer was red and sweet; each layer going in was paler and more bitter, till one reached the innermost layer, bone-white and tongue-curling. Some people would unfold the fruit as if it were a present in a wrapping and eat only certain layers. Others, like Haik, bit through to the pit, enjoying the combination of sweetness and bitterness. The Goddess did as she did, Haik discovered with interest. Juice squirted out of the old woman's mouth and ran down her lower face, matting the sparse white hair. There was no more to the dream, just the Goddess eating messily.

In another dream, the old woman was with a female *bital*. The shaggy beast had two young, both covered with downy yellow fur. "They are twins," the Goddess said. "But not identical. One is larger and stronger, as you can see. That twin will live. The other will die."

"Is this surprising?" asked Haik.

The Goddess looked peeved. "I'm trying to explain how I breed!"

"Through death?" asked Haik.

"Yes." The Goddess caressed the mother animal's shaggy flank. "And beauty. That's why your father had a child in Tulwar. He was alive in spite of adversity. He was beautiful. The matrons of Tulwar looked at him and said, 'We want these qualities for our family.'"

"That's why tame *sulin* are furry. People have selected for that trait, which wild *sulin* consider less important than size, sharp teeth, a crest of stiff hair along the spine, glittering patches of scales on the sides and belly, and a disposition inclined toward violence. Therefore, among wild *sulin*, these qualities grow more evident and extreme, while tame *sulin* acquire traits that enable them to live with people. The *pesha* once lived on land; the *bital* climbed among branches. In time, all life changes, shaped by beauty and death.

"Of all my creatures, only people have the ability to shape themselves and other kinds of life, using comprehension and judgment. This is the gift I have given you: to know what you are doing and what I do." The old woman touched the smaller *bital* calf. It collapsed. Haik woke.

A disturbing dream, she thought, lying in darkness. The house, as always, smelled of clay, both wet and dry. Small animals, her fellow residents, made quiet noises. She rose and dressed, going to the nearest beach. A slight breeze came off the ocean, barely moving the hot air. Combers rolled gently in, lit by the stars. Haik walked along the beach, water touching her feet now and then. The things she knew came together, interlocking; she achieved what we could call the Theory of Evolution. Hah! The Goddess thought in large ways! What a method to use in shaping life! One could not call it quick or economical, but the Goddess was—it seemed by looking at the world—inclined toward abundance; and there was little evidence that she was in a hurry.

Death made sense; without it change was impossible. Beauty made sense; without it, there couldn't be improvement or at least variety. Everything was explained, it seemed to Haik: the *pesha*'s flipper, the claw-handed bird, all the animals she'd found in the Tulwar cliffs. They were not mineral formations. They had lived. Most likely, they lived no longer, except in her mind and art.

She looked at the cloudless sky. So many stars, past all counting! So much time, receding into distance! So much death! And so much beauty!

She noticed at last that she was tired, went home and went to bed. In the morning, after a bad night's sleep, the Theory of Evolution still seemed good. But there was no one to discuss it with. Her relatives had turned their backs on most of existence after the Drowning. Don't think badly of them for this. They provided potted beauty to many places; many lineages in many towns praised the Tulwar trees and pots. But their family was small, its future uncertain. They didn't have the resources to take long journeys or think about large ideas. So Haik made more pots and collected more fossils, saying nothing about her theory, till Dapple arrived late in fall. They made love passionately for several days. Then Dapple looked around at the largely empty town, guarded by dark grey cliffs. "This doesn't seem like a good place to winter, dear one. Come south with me! Bring pots, and the Ettin will make you very welcome."

"Let me think," said Haik.

"You have ten days at most," Dapple said. "A captain I know is heading south; I asked her to stop in Tulwar, in case your native town was as depressing as I expected."

Haik hit her lover lightly on the shoulder and went off to think.

She went with Dapple, taking pots, a potter's wheel, and bags of clay. On the trip south—through rolling ocean, rain and snow beating against the ship—Haik told Dapple about evolution.

"Does this mean we started out as bugs?" the actor asked.

"The Goddess told me the process extended to people, though I've never found the bones of people in my cliffs."

"I've spent much of my life pretending to be one kind of animal or another. Interesting to think that animals may be inside me and in my past!"

On the same trip, Haik said, "My family wants to breed me again. There are too few of us; I'm strong and intelligent and have already had two healthy children."

"They are certainly right in doing this," said Dapple. "Have you picked a father?"

"Not yet. But they've told me this must be my last trip for a while."

"Then we'd better make the most of it," Dapple said.

There had been a family argument about the trip; and Haik had gotten permission to go only by saying she would not agree to a mating otherwise. But she didn't tell Dapple any of this. Family quarrels should be kept in the family.

They spent the winter in Hu. It was mild with little snow. Dapple wrote, and Haik made pots. Toward spring they went to Ettin, taking pots.

Ettin Taiin's mother was still alive, over a hundred and almost entirely blind with snow-white fur. But still upright, as Taiin pointed out. "I think she'll go to the crematorium upright and remain upright amid the flames."

He said this in the presence of the old lady, who smiled grimly, revealing that she'd kept almost all her teeth.

The Ettin bought all the pots Haik had, Taiin picking out one with special care. It was small and plain, with flower-predators for handles, a cover and a pure white glaze. "For my mother's ashes," the captain said quietly. "The day will come, though I dread it and make jokes about it."

Through late winter, Haik sat with the matriarch, who was obviously interested in her. They talked about pottery, their two families and the Theory of Evolution.

"I find it hard to believe we are descended from bugs and fish," Ettin Hattali said. "But your dreams have the sound of truth; and I certainly know that many of my distant ancestors were disgusting people. The Ettin have been improving, due to the wise decisions of my more recent ancestors, especially the women. Maybe if we followed this process far enough back, we'd get to bugs. Though you ought to consider the possibility that the Goddess is playing a joke on you. She does not always speak directly, and she dearly loves a joke."

"I have considered this," said Haik. "I may be a fool or crazy, but the idea seems good. It explains so much that has puzzled me."

Spring came finally. The hills of Ettin turned pale blue and orange. In the valley-fields, *bitalin* and *tsina* produced calves and foals.

"I have come to a decision," the blind old woman told Haik.

"Yes?"

"I want Ettin to interbreed with your family. To that end, I will send two junior members of my family to Tulwar with you. The lad is more like my son Taiin than any other male in the younger generation. The girl is a fine, intelligent, healthy young woman. If your senior female relatives agree, I want the boy—his name is Galhin—to impregnate you, while a Tulwar male impregnates Sai."

"It may be a wasted journey," said Haik in warning.

"Of course," said the matriarch. "They're young. They have time to spare. Dapple's family decided not to breed her, since they have plenty of children; and she is definitely odd. It's too late now. Her traits have been lost. But yours will not be; and we want the Ettin to have a share in what your line becomes."

"I will let my senior female relatives decide," said Haik.

"Of course you will," said Ettin Hattali.

The lad, as Hattali called him, turned out to be a man of thirty-five, shoulder high to Haik and steel grey. He had two eyes and no limp. Nonetheless, his resemblance to Taiin was remarkable: a fierce, direct man, full of good humor. Haik liked him at once. His half-sister Sai was thirty, a solid woman with grey-brown fur and an excellent, even temperament. No reasonable person could dislike her.

Dapple, laughing, said, "This is Ettin in action! They live to defeat their enemies and interbreed with any family that seems likely to prove useful."

Death and beauty, Haik thought.

The four of them went east together. Haik put her potter's tools in storage at the Hu Town inn; Dapple took leave of many old friends; and the four found passage on a ship going north.

After much discussion, Haik's senior relatives agreed to the two matings, impressed by Galhin's vigor and his sister's calm solidity, by the rich gifts the Ettin kin had brought, and Haik's description of the southern family.

Nowadays, with artificial insemination, we don't have to endure what happened next. But it was made tolerable to Haik by Ettin Galhin's excellent manners and the good humor with which he handled every embarrassment. He lacked, as he admitted, Taiin's extreme energy and violence. "But this is not a situation that requires my uncle's abilities; and he's really too old for mating; and it would be unkind to take him from Hattali. Who can say how long she will survive? Their love for each other has been a light for the Ettin for years. We can hardly separate them now."

The two foreigners were in Tulwar till fall. Then, both women pregnant, the Ettin departed. Haik returned to her pottery. In late spring, she bore twins, a boy and a girl. The boy died soon after birth, but the girl was large and healthy.

"She took strength from her brother in the womb," said the Tulwar matriarchs. "This happens; and the important child, the female, has survived."

Haik named the girl Ahl. She was dun like her older sisters, but her fur had more of a ruddy tint. In sunlight, her pelt shone red-gold; and her nickname became Gold.

It was two years before Dapple came back, her silver-grey fur beginning to show frost on the broad shoulders and lean upper arms. She admired the baby and the new pots, then gave information. Ettin Sai had produced a daughter, a strong child, obviously intelligent. The Ettin had named the child Haik, in hope that some of Tulwar Haik's ability would appear in their family. "They are greedy folk," said Dapple. "They want all their own strength, energy, solidity and violence. In addition, they want the beauty you make and are.

"Can you leave your daughter for a while? Come south and sell pots, while I perform my plays. Believe me, people in Hu and Ettin ask about you."

"I can," said Haik.

Gold went to a female cousin. In addition to being lovely, she had a fine disposition, and many were willing to care for her. Haik and Dapple took passage. This time, the voyage was easy, the winds mild and steady, the sky clear except for high, thin clouds called "tangled banners" and "schools of fish."

"What happened to your Theory of Evolution?" Dapple asked.

"Nothing."

"Why?"

"What could be done? Who would have believed me, if I said the world is old beyond comprehension; and many kinds of life have come into existence; and most, as far as I can determine, no longer exist?"

"It does sound unlikely," Dapple admitted.

"And impious."

"Maybe not that. The Goddess has an odd sense of humor, as almost everyone knows."

"I put strange animals on my pots and make them into toys for Gold and other children. But I will not begin an ugly family argument over religion."

You may think that Haik lacked courage. Remember that she lived in an era before modern science. Yes, there were places where scholars gathered, but none in her part of the world. She'd have to travel long distances and learn a new language, then talk to strangers about concepts of time and change unfamiliar to everyone. Her proof was in the cliffs of Tulwar, which she could not take with her. Do you really think those scholars—people devoted to the study of history, mathematics, literature, chemistry, and medicine—would have believed her? Hardly likely! She had children, a dear lover, a craft, and friends. Why should she cast away all of this? For what? A truth no one was likely to see? Better to stay home or travel along the coast. Better to make pots on her own and love with Dapple.

They reached Hu Town in early summer. The inn's potted trees bloomed scarlet and sky-blue.

"The Potter of Strange Animals!" cried the innkeeper. "I have bought five of your pots for my trees."

Indeed, the woman had. Haik wandered around the courtyard, admiring her own work. Four were the kind she'd made when she first returned from the south, decorated with scratches and glazed white or black. The fifth had an underwater scene, done in low relief. Beaked fish swam around the top. Below them, rising from the bottom of the pot, were long sinuous plants. Haik had named them "ocean whips." It was possible that they were animals; once or twice she had found shadows that might be mouths with teeth. Between the plants (or animals) were segmented bugs. The glaze was dark blue with touches of white.

"This is more recent," Haik said.

"I bought it because you are the Potter of Strange Animals. But I prefer the other pots. They set off my trees."

Who can argue opinions about art, especially with someone who has bought five large pots?

Dapple's company was at the inn, having arrived several days before. Haik knew all of them, except the apprentices. For a while, they traveled through the little coastal towns of Hu, Tesh, and Ta-tesh, performing comedies and now and then a tragedy. These last were a surprise to Haik, especially the tragedies about women. They were so subdued! Instead of tumbling and rude jokes, there were small gestures, turned heads, a few words spoken quietly. The actors wore plain robes in sober colors; their faces were unmasked; most of the time, the music came from a single flute. Its sound reminded Haik of a thread floating on moving water, coiling and uncoiling in the current.

"It's my observation that women suffer as much as men," said Dapple in explanation. "But we are expected to be solid and enduring. As a result, our suffering is quiet. I'm trying to show it in the way it happens. Hah! I am tired of loud, rude comedies! And loud, sad plays about the suffering of men!"

At last, in far southern Tesh, they turned inland, traveling without merchants. The borders between Ettin and its eastern neighbors were all quiet. The various families had been allies and breeding partners for generations; and none tolerated criminal behavior. By now, it was late summer. The plain baked under a sun like polished brass. The Ettin hills were hot and dusty. When they reached Hattali's house, it was with relief. Household women greeted them. Men took their *tsina* and the packs of props and costumes. Their rooms opened on a courtyard with two bathing pools. The water in one was colorless and cold. The other bubbled, bright green. The entire acting company stripped and climbed in. What a pleasure! Though both pools were crowded. Well, thought Haik, she'd take a slow bath later, soaking the travel aches from her muscles and bones.

When they were done and in fresh clothes, a woman came for Dapple and Haik. "Ettin Taiin wants you to join his mother."

"Of course," said Dapple.

They went through shadowy halls, silent except for birds calling in the house's eaves. They sounded like water running over stones. The woman said, "Thirty days ago, Hattali fell. She seemed unharmed, except for damage to one foot. It drags a little now. But since the fall she's been preoccupied and unwilling to do much, except sit and talk with Taiin. We fear her great strength is coming to an end."

"It can't be!" said Dapple.

"You know about old age and death. We've seen them in your plays." Saying this, the woman opened a door.

Outside was a terrace, lit by the afternoon sun. Hattali sat in a high-backed chair, leaning against the back, her eyes closed. How old she looked! How thin and frail! Her warrior son sat next to her on a stool, holding one of his mother's hands. He looked at them, laid Hattali's hand gently in her lap and rose. "Cholkwa is in the north. I'm glad to see you, Dapple."

They sat down. Hattali opened her eyes, obviously seeing nothing. "Who has come, Tai?"

"Dapple and her lover, the potter."

The old lady smiled. "One last play."

"A play, yes," said Dapple. "But not the last, I hope."

A look of irritation crossed Hattali's face. "Did the potter bring pots?"

Haik excused herself and went to find her pack. Now she understood the house's quiet. Most likely, the children had been sent out to play; and the adults — she passed a few in the halls — moved softly and gravely. A matriarch like Hattali, a woman with so much dignity, should not be bothered with noise, while deciding whether to live or die.

When Haik returned to the terrace, Hattali seemed asleep. But the old woman took the pot Haik put in her hands, feeling it with bony fingers. "What is it?"

"There's a skull on top, a replica of one I found in stone."

"It's shaped like a *tli* skull," Hattali said.

"A bit, but the teeth are different. I imagine from the teeth that the animal had scales, not hair."

Hattali exhaled and felt more. "On the sides of the pot?"

"The animal as I imagine it must have been, when alive. I found the skull first and made a pot that Dapple bought. But now I have found the entire animal, and it wasn't the way I showed it on the first pot. So I made this."

"The animals are in relief?"

"Yes."

"What do they look like, if not *tli?*"

Haik thought. "An animal about as long as my arm, four legged with a tail. Spines protrude along the back, as if the animal had a fin there like a fish. That was the thing I did not imagine: the spines. And the tail is different also, flat from side to side, like the tail of a fish."

"What color is the glaze?"

"Black, except the skull, which is white."

"Tai," said the old woman.

"Mother?"

"Is it beautiful?"

"She is the Potter of Strange Animals. The pot is strange, but well made."

"I want it for my ashes."

"You will have it," he said.

She gave her son the pot. He turned it in his blunt, strong-looking hands. Hattali turned her blind face toward Haik. "You must still believe your crazy idea, that we are descended from bugs."

"That the world is old and full of change, yes," said Haik.

"Sit down and tell me about it again."

Haik obeyed. The old woman listened as she explained about beauty, death, and change.

"Well, we have certainly improved our lineage through careful breeding," said Hattali finally. "The child your kinsman fathered on Sai is a fine little girl. We hope she'll be as clever as you are, though I'm still not certain about your idea of time and change. Why didn't the Goddess simply make people? Why start with bugs?"

"She clearly likes bugs," said Haik. "The world is full of them. They are far more common than people and more varied. Maybe her plan was to create a multitude of bugs through beauty and death, and we are an accidental result of her breeding of bugs."

"Do you believe that?"

"No. She told me we have a gift no other living creature had: we know what we do. I believe this gift is not an accident. She wanted comprehension."

Haik was wrong in saying this, according to modern scientists. They believe life is entirely an accident, though evidently an accident that happens often, since life has appeared on many planets. Intelligent life is far less common, but has clearly appeared on at least two planets and may be present elsewhere in a form we do not recognize. It also is an accident, modern thinkers say. This is hard for many of us to believe; and Haik, living in the distant past, could hardly be expected to bring forward an idea so disturbing.

"Well, you certainly ought to listen to the Goddess, if she talks to you," said Hattali. "When will I hear your play, Dapple?"

"It will take a few days to prepare."

The matriarch tilted her head in acquiescence.

They left Hattali then, going back to their room. "I want you to make masks for a new play," Dapple said. "Five of your strange animals. They interest Hattali. Sit with her while you work, and tell her about your ideas. Taiin is an excellent man. None better! But her illness has got him frightened; and his fear is not helping her mood. Maybe she knows what she's doing. Maybe it is time for her to die. But I wonder if the fall has frightened her as well as her relatives. A woman like Hattali should not die from fear."

"Has she no daughters?"

"Two. Good women, but not half what she is, and she's never gotten along with either. The love of her life has always been Taiin."

He left the next morning, called to the western border. Gwa scouts had been seen. Their old enemies might have heard that Hattali was dying. What better time to attack?

"They expect that grief will break me," Taiin said, standing in the house's front court, dressed in metal and leather armor. A sword hung at his side, and a battle axe hung from a loop on his saddle. "It may, but not while there's work to be done." He swung himself onto his *tsin* easily, in spite of age and his bad leg. Once settled on the animal, he looked down at Haik and Dapple.

"She is the last of her generation. What people they were, especially the women! As solid as stone walls and towers! I have lived my entire life in their protection. Now, the walls are broken. Only one tower remains. What will I do, when Hattali is gone?"

"Defend Ettin," said Dapple.

He gathered the *tsin*'s reins, grinning. "You're right, of course. Maybe, if I'm lucky, we'll capture a Gwa spy."

A moment later he was through the house's gate, moving steadily along the dusty road, his men following, armed and armored.

"You may be wondering about his last remark," Dapple said.

Haik opened her mouth to say no.

"There are men who take pleasure in raping prisoners before they kill them. Or in harming them in other ways. I have suspected Taiin is one such. Now I'm certain."

This was how he'd deal with his grief at Hattali's illness: by making someone else's end unpleasant.

"Beauty and death," Dapple said. "This is the way the Goddess has organized her world, according to you and your bones."

They spent the next several days on Ettin Hattali's terrace. The weather remained dry and sunny. Haik worked on the masks, while Dapple sat with paper and brush, sometimes writing, more often listening.

There was a folding table next to Hattali's chair. The matriarch's relatives brought out food and drink. In any ordinary circumstance, it would have been rude to eat while conversing with other people, especially guests, but the old lady had not been eating. Good health always goes in front of good manners.

At first, Hattali ignored everything except water, brought in a glass goblet. This she held, turning the precious object between her bent fingers.

The first mask was the animal on Hattali's funeral pot: a long narrow head, the jaw hinged and moved with a string, the mouth full of pointed teeth. Snap! Snap!

The skin would be mottled green, Haik decided; the eyes large, round, and red. There were existing animals—small hunters with scaly hides—that had triangular pupils. She would give this creature the same. The spines on the back would be a banner, supported by a harness over Dapple's shoulders. Hah! It would flutter when her lover danced! As she worked, she described the mask to Hattali.

"Have you ever found large animals?" the old woman asked.

"Not complete. But large bones, yes, and teeth that are longer than my hands. The layer they are in is high on my native cliffs and was laid down when the country was above water. They were land-dwellers, those animals, larger than anything living now, at least in the regions I've visited, and with teeth that remind me of birds' teeth, though more irregular and much larger."

"What eyesight you have!" Hattali exclaimed. "To see into the distant past! Do you really believe these creatures existed?"

"They did," said Haik firmly.

Gradually, as their conversation continued, the old lady began to eat: hard biscuits first, then pieces of fruit, then *halin* in a small, square, ceramic cup. Hattali was sitting upright now, her bony shoulders straight under an embroidered robe. Hah! She was licking her fingers! "Can you write, Haik?"

"Yes."

"I want you to write down your ideas and draw the animals you've found in stone. I'll have one of my female relatives make a copy."

"You believe me," said Haik in surprise.

"Most of what you've told me I knew already," Hattali answered. "How could any woman not know about inheritance, who has lived long enough to see traits appear and reappear in families of people, *sulin*, and *tsina*? But I lacked a framework on which to string my information. This is what you've given me. The frame! The loom! Think of the patterns the Ettin will be able to weave, now that we understand what the Goddess has been doing with sex and death and time!" The old woman shifted in her chair. There was a cup of *halin* next to her on the folding table. She felt for it, grasped it and drank, then reached for a piece of fruit. "I have been wondering whether it's time for me to die. Did you notice?"

"Yes," murmured Dapple.

"The blindness is hard to endure; but life remains interesting, and my kin tell me that they still need my judgment. I can hardly refuse their pleas. But when I fell, I thought—I know this illness. It strikes women down like a blow from a war club. When they rise, if they rise, who can say what the damage will be? Paralysis, stupor, the loss of speech or thought.

"This time the only damage was to one leg. But I may fall again. I have seen relatives, grave senior female cousins, turn into something less than animals—witless and grieving, though they do not remember the cause of their grief. Maybe, I thought, it would be better to stop eating now and die while I am still able to choose death.

"But I want your book first. Will you write it for me?"

Haik glanced at Dapple, who spoke the word "yes" in silence.

"Yes," said the potter.

The matriarch sighed and leaned back. "Good! What a marvel you are, Dapple! What a fine guest you have brought to Ettin!"

The next day, Haik began her book, drawing fossils from memory. Fortunately, her memory was excellent. Her masks went to the costume maker, who finished them with the help of the apprentices. It was good work, though not equal to Haik's. One apprentice showed real promise.

The old lady was eating with zest now. The house resumed the ordinary noise of a house full of relations. Children shouted in the courtyards. Adults joked and called. Looking up once from her work, Haik saw adolescents swimming in the river below the terrace: slim naked girls, their fur sleeked by water, clearly happy.

By the time the Ettin war party returned, Taiin looking contented as he dismounted in the front courtyard, the book on evolution was done. Taiin greeted them and limped hurriedly to his mother's terrace. The old woman rose, looking far stronger than she had twenty days before.

The war captain glanced at Dapple. "Your doing?"

"Haik's."

"Ettin will buy every pot you make!" the captain said in a fierce whisper, then went to embrace his mother.

Later, he looked at Haik's book. "This renewed Hattali's interest in life? Pictures of shells and bones?"

"Ideas," said Dapple.

"Well," said Taiin, "I've never been one for thinking. Ideas belong to women, unless they're strategic or tactical. All I can be is thankful and surprised." He turned the folded pages. "Mother says we will be able to breed more carefully, thinking of distant consequences rather than immediate advantage. All this from bones!"

The actors did their play soon after this, setting their stage in the house's largest courtyard. It began with a fish that was curious about the land and crawled out of the ocean. In spite of discomfort, the fish stayed, changing into an animal with four legs and feet. Hah! The way it danced, once it had feet to dance with!

The fish's descendants, all four-footed animals, were not satisfied with their condition. They fell to arguing about what to do next. Some decided that their ancestral mother had made a mistake and returned to water, becoming animals like *peshadi* and *luatin*. Others changed into birds, through a process that was not described; Haik knew too little about the evolution of birds. Other animals chose fur, with or without a mixture of scales.

One animal chose judgment as well as fur.

"How ridiculous!" cried her comrades. "What use are ideas or the ability to discriminate? You can't eat a discrimination. Ideas won't keep you warm at night. Folly!" They danced away, singing praise for their fur, their teeth, their claws.

The person with fur and intelligence stood alone on the stage. "One day I will be like you," Dapple said to the audience. "No spines on my back, no long claws, no feathers, though I had these things, some of them at least, in the past. What have I gained from my choice, which my relatives have just mocked? The ability to think forward and back. I can learn about the past. Using this knowledge, I can look into the future and see the consequences of my present actions. Is this a useful gift? Decide for yourselves."

This was the play's end. The audience was silent, except for Hattali, who cried, "Excellent! Excellent!" Taking their cue from the old lady, the rest of the Ettin began to stamp and shout.

A day later, the actors were on the road. They left behind Haik's book and the new masks. Dapple said, "My play doesn't work yet, and maybe it never will. Art is about the known, rather than the unknown. How can people see themselves in unfamiliar animals?"

Haik said, "My ideas are in my head. I don't need a copy of the book."

"I will accept your gifts," said Hattali. "And send one copy of the book to another Ettin house. If anything ever happens here, we'll still have your ideas. And I will not stop eating, till I'm sure that a few of my relatives comprehend the book."

"It may take time," said Haik.

"This is more interesting than dying," Hattali said.

The story ends here. Haik went home to Tulwar and made more pots. In spite of Taiin's promise, the Ettin did not buy all her work. Instead, merchants carried it up and down the coast. Potters in other towns began to imitate her; though they, having never studied fossils, did not get the animals right. Still, it became a known style of pottery. Nowadays, in museums, it's possible to find examples of the Southern Fantastic Animal Tradition. There may even be a few of Haik's pots in museum cabinets, though no one has yet noticed their accuracy. Hardly surprising! Students of art are not usually students of paleontology.

As for Dapple, she continued to write and perform, doing animal plays in the south and heroic tragedies in the north. Her work is still famous, though only fragments remain.

The two lovers met once or twice a year, never in Tulwar. Dapple kept her original dislike of the place. Often, Haik traveled with the actor's company, taking pots if they were going to Ettin.

Finally, at age fifty, Haik said to her senior relatives, "I am leaving Tulwar."

The relatives protested.

"I have given you three children and trained five apprentices. Let them make pots for you! Enough is enough."

What could the relatives say? Plenty, as it turned out, but to no avail. Haik moved to a harbor town midway between Tulwar and Hu. The climate was mild and sunny; the low surrounding hills had interesting fossils embedded in a lovely, fine-grained, cream-yellow stone. Haik set up a new pottery. Dapple, tired of her rainy home island, joined the potter. Their house was small, with only one courtyard. A crown-of-fire tree grew there, full-sized and rooted in the ground. Every spring, it filled their rooms with a sweet aroma, then filled the courtyard with a carpet of fallen blossoms. "Beauty and death," Dapple sang as she swept the flowers up.

Imagine the two women growing old together, Dapple writing the plays that have been mostly lost, Haik making pots and collecting fossils. The creatures in those hills! If anything, they were stranger than the animals in the cliffs of Tulwar!

As far as is known, Haik never wrote her ideas down a second time. If she did, the book was lost, along with her fossils, in the centuries between her life and the rediscovery of evolution. Should she have tried harder? Would history have been changed, if she had been able to convince people other than Ettin Hattali? Let others argue this question. The purpose of this story is to be a story.

The Ettin became famous for the extreme care with which they arranged breeding contracts and for their success in all kinds of far-into-the-future planning. All through the south people said, "This is a lineage that understands cause and effect!" In modern times, they have become one of the most powerful families on the planet. Is this because of Haik's ideas? Who can say? Though they are old-fashioned in many ways, they've had little trouble dealing with new ideas. "Times change," the Ettin say. "Ideas change. We are not the same as our ancestors, nor should we be. The Goddess shows no fondness for staying put, nor for getting stuck like a cart in spring rain.

"Those willing to learn from her are likely to go forward. If they don't, at least they have shown the Great Mother respect; and she—in return—has given them a universe full of things that interest and amaze."

The Whisper of Disks

JOHN MEANEY

John Meaney works as a consultant for a well-known software house, is ranked black belt by the Japan Karate Association, and is an enthusiastic weight lifter. He's sold a number of stories to Interzone. *His first novel,* To Hold Infinity, *was published in 1998, followed by a second,* Paradox, *in 2000. His most recent book is a new novel,* Context. *He lives in Turnbridge Wells, England.*

Here he gives us a fascinating look at some of the eccentric ancestors of a young girl — and at her own eccentric and dazzling future.

OXFORD, 2102

So this is the city: millennium-old spires encased in clear ice, enwrapped by winter's gloom. There, the Bodleian Library, its elegant domed Radcliffe Camera gleaming beneath a transparent shell; there, the Ashmolean's stately grandeur, white snow banked at the stone columns' feet. The streets form ice-chasms where occasional bug-cars slide through softly falling flakes, navigating the whiteout by radar.

I should never have left. Or never returned.

Augusta's vantage point is high: a curlicued smartglass tower, the ellipsoid hotel complex sitting at its apex. She is in the most expensive suite, with floor-to-ceiling convex windows. In the glass, her reflection, like a saddened ghost, overlays the icebound, moribund city.

Her long white hair is bound with platinum wire. Her shining pale-blue gown is high-collared — it keeps her warm — and falls in long straight elegant lines. Straight-backed, she stands, though her left hand holds a slender cane.

Unseen, within the formal garments, a slender exoskeleton provides the real support for her tired, narrow, pain-racked body.

You've been here longer than I, she tells the ice-locked buildings silently. *But we're both near the end.*

She might have spoken aloud, save for the small silver sphere which floats above her right shoulder: her official biographer.

I've outlived my enemies. But that's no excuse for relaxing vigilance.

Instead, she snaps her fingers, places a call to her lawyers. Instantly—despite the fact that it is 4 a.m. in California—her chief legal officer comes on line. The head-and-shoulders image in the holovolume is system-generated (she can tell the difference), but then she has probably woken him up.

Everything is different.

Outside, dull winter presses against the window. Since global warming finally tipped the North Atlantic convection cell, English winters are an Arctic hell. And she has grown to hate the cold; she should have stayed in California.

"I've decided. I'm going into space." She speaks with utter finality. "I want to see, in person. To be there when the flight takes place."

"But—" The lawyer stops, then: "Yes, ma'am. I'll confirm the arrangements now. Oh, and Happy B—"

"Good. Augusta out."

No one dares to call me Gus anymore.

But that is the least measure of her success—if it *is* success. For she has outlived her friends, as well as her enemies. With a lonely decade, maybe two, ahead of her . . . if she strictly follows her medics' conservative, over-protective regimen.

Her name is Augusta Medora de Lauron (the surname from her seventh husband, which she has kept because she likes it), her personal wealth exceeds anything she ever dreamed of, and today is her 113th birthday.

OXFORD, 1997

When she was eight years old, she told her mother that her real name was Gus.

"*Augusta* sounds silly," she announced with great solemnity. "And I'm not silly."

She waved a spoon as if for emphasis. Dessert was a banana mashed up with a little milk—some sugar sprinkled on top, for the extra calories—and it was a favourite.

"Does Augusta sound silly?"

Her mother—she still remembers this, 105 years later, with a brightness and clarity denied more recent events—turned and stared out of the small, grimy kitchen window. Outside, the darkness of a cold winter's evening. Mother's face was lined, though she could not have been more than 30, and she was very thin.

"You know"—she turned to face her child, sitting at the cracked Formica-topped table (an unforgettable egg-yolk yellow)—"I do believe you're right, Gus."

Gus's face dimpled in a smile.

When she had finished her mashed banana, she slid from the chair, and went to fetch her duffel coat while Mother washed up dishes in the big cracked sink. By the time Mother was ready to leave, Gus was already standing by the front door (whose paint was flaking, revealing silver-grey weathered wood: significant in retrospect, natural at the time), her duffel coat buttoned all the way up, her Buzz Lightyear satchel stuffed with books.

"You're a good girl, Gus."

"You're a good woman, Mum."

Mother bent down and they touched foreheads: their own private gesture which they had performed for as long as Gus could remember.

"Come along, pumpkin."

Gus sighed, but it was a kind of joke: she *liked* being called pumpkin, and she always had. Even though she was getting a little old for pet names.

Outside, the streets were cold. Gus walked with her hand in Mother's, hurrying a little as the bus-stop came into sight.

There they waited, beneath the sodium-vapour streetlamp, in front of an old council house whose patchy hedge, black beneath the glowing orange light, scarcely concealed the tiny front garden, the discarded bath and broken parts of rusty lawnmower strewn across it. Finally the bus came, only ten minutes late; its pneumatic door wheezed open and Gus and Mother climbed inside.

On her lap, Mother clutched the Safeway carrier bag she referred to as her "executive briefcase." Sometimes she would close her eyes, lightly dozing, though tonight she was not so tired.

Gus counted stops, keeping track of the route—"We're on the ring road now, Mummy"—as the bus circled the north of Oxford, and turned off into the small science park where Mother worked. They got off at the usual stop, and walked through the dark, empty car park (which in later years Gus would think of as a parking lot) to the locked entrance.

Why is it always empty, Mum? she had once asked. *Because the important people*, Mother replied, *have all gone home.*

Inside the lobby, it was her favourite security guard—Uncle Eric with the big grey moustache—who signed them in. Her second-favourite was Big Fredo, who talked to Mother in Italian, which Gus did not understand, though she loved to listen to the flowing lyrical words.

Are we important? she had asked her mother.

After a pause, *Oh, yes*, Mother had replied. *You, pumpkin, are the most important person of all. That's why they leave the office building empty, just for you.*

"Hey, Louisa," said Eric. "Good to know the real workers have arrived."

"I guess so. How's Esther?"

"Just the same." A slow shake of the head. "Just the same."

"See you later, then."

"I'll be here." Just as he always said: "Same old same old."

Mother hung up her threadbare anorak, took the freshly laundered light-blue work-coat from her carrierbag, and pulled it on. From the cupboard, she dragged out the big old vacuum cleaner, set the mop and bucket aside for later.

"Come along, pumpkin. Let's get set up."

The wide, gleaming machine room was her domain. *Machine room.* Gus had learned the name from one of the late-night computer operators, who used to chat with her before the night-shift had been cancelled (*Because they finally automated the overnight run*, the woman said morosely. *Even the back-up routine.*)

The place was clean, always cool, with a crispness to the conditioned air which Gus could almost taste. Sometimes she stuck out her tongue—when there was no adult to see—and tried to lick the dust-free atmosphere itself.

The big desktop shone an eerie white beneath strong fluorescent light. All around stood row upon row of pale-grey and matte-black rectangular boxes: the Computers (the capital was obvious, whenever Mother talked about them) which kept the business going.

Gus had learned to program in Logo when she was six years old, on the cracked BBC Acorn at the back of her form-room in school, on a decades-old table bearing the scratched initials of long-forgotten pupils.

By this time, aged eight, she knew the difference between program and data, between processor and disc. Gus was aware that the boxes discreetly labelled System/38 (that was an old one, battered by now), AS/400 and RS/600 were processor units; the majority of the rest were disc drives. Row upon row of them, like tall refrigerators, stacked inside with spinning discs.

Once, one of the other cleaning ladies who worked with Mother had unplugged a disc drive—so she could plug in her vacuum cleaner—and the next night the cleaners' supervisor had arrived and taken her off to one side ("*For a quiet word,*" he claimed). The woman left in tears; neither Gus nor Mother saw her again.

Since then, the cleaners had been under strict instructions never, under any circumstances, to venture inside the machine room where the Computers (with a capital C) were kept. But no one had ever changed the lock-code—X and Y together, then 3-2-Z, before turning the dull steel knob in what felt like the wrong direction—so Mother had found the best place of all to keep Gus safe while she worked.

"Get out your books, pumpkin."

"Okay, Mum," she said as always. "I'll be good."

And then she was alone.

It was true that she read the books. And that they were a mixture of titles, from *War and Peace* to G. A. Dickinson's *Algebraic Secrets*, which were too advanced for an eight-year-old, though her mother only half-realized this.

But often Gus would slip down from the operator's swivel chair, leaving her open books before the consoles, and simply sit cross-legged on the floor-tiles, staring at the rows and rows of black and grey boxes. And listening.

For at night, discs whisper their secrets to those with ears to hear.

Susurration. A breathing, a soft chaotic overlay of nearly-words, of almost-conversation, as if she eavesdropped upon a salon-full of ghosts from centuries gone by: with everything to gossip of, but no breath to speak.

Sometimes, they moaned.

But mostly the indeterminate sounds formed overlapping whispers from beyond, whose words would never coalesce into meaning, yet whose message would haunt Gus-who-grew-into-Augusta forever.

ASHLEY COMBE, 1843

Upon the wall, a gaslight hisses, incandescent. Ada lies back upon the chaise-longue, dabbing a dampened cloth on her too-pale forehead. On the dainty table beside her lies a small pile of notes scribbled in black ink, with loops and scrawls surrounding the strange equations, and scraps of verse — forbidden verse! — in her scratchy handwriting.

And, on one of those sheets, something new: an ink-drawn table with numbered, imperative steps of logic. Slow, for a person to work through those iterative commands: yet in her mind, burning with fever, it is Babbage's gleaming Engine which is alive with the pseudo-thoughts she has created; it is polished cogs and shining rods which click and spin more surely than too-weak mortal flesh, undermined by moral frailty or feminine weakness.

The Pattern beneath the world . . .

Is she mad? Can she, a mere woman, be the first to have deduced the true possibilities of Babbage's calculating engines? Can she, for all her disadvantages, her cursed beginnings, truly perceive the power of mechanical minds?

For she has written the devil's code, logical steps which will execute within the power-realm of brass and steel, in stately sequence as exact and elegant as an evening's programme at a debutante's ball.

"But I am the Silver Lady . . ." Her whispered voice trembles.

For the laudanum's magic is upon her.

In her vision, she herself is Babbage's automaton: the scandalous Silver Lady with which he entertains his rich and famous guests. That Silver Lady of which "Lady M" complained in an open public letter: an artificial woman whose garments were too diaphanous for polite society.

But in Ada's dreams, it is she who is semi-clothed, with Babbage's rough hands upon her.

O, my father! It is your Dark Nature which calls to me . . .

For all that her mother tried to whip the influence from Ada, Lord Byron's spirit is within her core, tempted by all that is lascivious and compelling.

Then a voice penetrates the heavy dream — "O, my beloved Beauty" — and for a moment she thinks it is William, her too-tame ingenuous husband. But no, he is away in London; it is her dear friend, John Crosse, who takes her hand and presses it to his lips.

"Sweet, my prince . . ."

His hands are within her garments.

But her mind's eye is filled with other sights: coils and bubbling vessels, the strange electromagnetic experiments of Crosse and Faraday, the very real mysteries they have explored. And this man, in whose arms she moans, is the son of Faust: for his father Andrew has *generated life* from electricity. Society is ablaze with the news. After leaving his electrolytic apparatus bubbling for three weeks, he has found tiny animalcules on one of the electrodes. Life, from base inanimate matter.

And Faraday, her other hero in this scientific age, has Ada's portrait hanging prominently on his wall. Does she inspire him, even as his rough-hewn manner and sparkling intellect fire her imagination?

Inside, she burns.

Crosse moves upon her—"My darling, my Queen of Engines, Enchantress of Numbers"—repeating the title which Babbage gave her, and has now become their own.

She cries out with pleasure, not caring if the servants overhear.

"My good Doctor, creator of Life, bearer of Fire—"

A dark-blue glass bottle, lying on its side upon the rug, has become unstoppered. Precious drops of liquid escape, evaporate. Their heady vapour incenses the wild, drugged atmosphere which already pervades the drawing-room.

The Pattern . . .

Yet there is unease beneath her happy, chaotic delirium, as though Ada already senses the new life quickening inside her.

But she is captivated by logical symbols, drawn in fire within her mind, enraptured by the notion that she—Augusta Ada Byron, Countess of Lovelace, eternally cursed daughter of mad, bad, dangerous-to-know Lord Byron (whose incestuous liaison with his own sister Augusta, after whom Ada in all innocence was christened, is the scandal which drove him finally from England)—has been vouchsafed a vision both divine and mad, of gleaming polished power beyond the strict confining world, and she cries out as she pulls her scientific lover to her sinful bosom once more.

OXFORD, 1998

At the age of nine, Gus was still too young to travel to the library by herself— "Not in these godforsaken days," as Mrs Arrowsmith who lived next door would say—although, once they were there, Mother would let Gus roam among the bookshelves without supervision.

Sometimes, if Mother was very tired, they would walk from home out to the Park & Ride car park, where they could pretend they had left their car (the one they didn't own, that didn't exist) so that they could ride the bus for free. (Was there some kind of ticket Mother should have shown? Gus would wonder later, when she was older, whether there had been a particular, charitable driver.) Most times, though, they caught the normal bus or simply walked.

Once in the library, Mother would stay in the reading-room, among the reference books and periodicals, and sit drowsing in the warm surroundings.

One October night, she regarded the pale fog thickening outside the windows— it was 4 P.M. on a Saturday, and she was not working tonight: there was no place to go—and thought about home, of sun-drenched hills and the clamour of noisy, cheerful neighbours, and wondered again why she had ever come to this cold country.

In front of her, this week's *New Scientist* was open. She flicked through it, barely understanding what she read. Sometimes she tried to read *Nature*, a real scientific journal which the library dutifully stocked. None of it made sense, and yet if she half-drowsed, a strangely relaxing sensation of wonder settled over her like a blanket.

This night, she craned her head to catch sight of her daughter—there, lost in a world of her own, wandering among books. Gus would pick enough to fill the limit on both their library cards.

If only I had more time—

But the Catherine Cookson would do her, Louisa, for a few weeks. She barely had the energy to read a page or two, last thing at night, before turning out the light and sliding into sleep in her narrow, lonely bed.

Sometimes, Louisa glanced over the titles which Gus had picked. Once, she had tried to read a book by someone called George Eliot—knowing that the writer had been a woman, writing when only men could call professions their own—but the convoluted 19th-century English was difficult. There was a man in the story, who was talented and successful, but eventually strayed in society as he was overtaken by irrational desires for a Jewess, finally taking the socially disastrous step of converting to her religion. But, it turned out, the man's mother (though she had appeared "true English") had been a Jewish actress, and the burning desires were his blood's true nature coming out—

She had thrown the hideous book aside, disturbed for more reasons than she could name, and considered hiding the book where Gus could not read it. But then, Gus was sensible enough not to be swayed by the half-rationalized bigotry of another century.

There were Italian novels, and some Spanish ones—easy enough to read—but Louisa steered clear of them. They stirred thoughts of the home she had left 15 years ago, and could never return to.

She would stick to her Catherine Cooksons and her Danielle Steeles, written in English simple enough for her to understand, and forget the rest.

I'm so tired—

Then someone was shaking her shoulder.

"Time to go home," the young man said, kindly. "Your little girl's waiting."

And his concerned thoughts were obvious: *You should eat more, too.*

In the reading-room's doorway, Gus was standing with her arms full of books. She grinned at her mother, showing the gap in the front where two neighbouring milk teeth had dropped out within days of each other.

"Sorry." Rubbing her eyes, she smiled at Gus. "Got your books, pumpkin?"

"Yes, Mummy."

She took the books from Gus's arms and carried them to the counter, where the librarian could scan them through.

"Hmm. Abbott's *Flatland*." He stamped the due-date inside. "Not bad. But I don't know this Pickover chap. *Surfing through Hyperspace*. Is that good?"

He looked up at Louisa, but it was Gus who answered: "It's not bad. I like the stories."

Since it was a nonfiction book, the librarian chuckled, and winked at Louisa as though they were sharing a joke. But there *were* stories inside, as well as strange science; Louisa had looked over Gus's shoulder the last time she had borrowed the book.

"Come on, pumpkin. Time to go home."

The young librarian watched them as they left.

Later, on the bus ride home, Gus tugged at Mother's sleeve and said: "Why don't you marry him?"

Mother's face froze. "I'm sorry?"

Gus knew the one topic she could never ask—would never get an answer on—was the subject of her father. But this was different.

"The man at the library. He likes you."

For a moment, Mother was speechless. Then she shook her head, smiling sadly. "Oh, no, Gus. I'm not good enough for him."

"But Mummy, you're—"

"No, I'm not." Silence, then: "But you . . . You're the most important person in the world, little pumpkin."

And Gus, with a child's intuition, kept silent for the rest of the journey. She was tempted to open one of her storybooks—there was an old one with a bright yellow cover, *Time is the Simplest Thing*, and she'd read the first two pages inside the library, with the pink telepathic alien blob, and saw immediately that it was brilliant—but she knew from experience that trying to read inside a moving bus would make her sick.

And the waiting, she knew, would make the story even better.

Over the next year, Mother would occasionally smile and nod to the nice man at the library, but they would never get into a real conversation. And then, one Saturday, there was no sign of him. Neither Gus nor Mother ever saw the man again.

Eleven years later, when she was 20, Gus would finally discover her birth certificate—born in 1989 in St. Mary's Hospital, Paddington, London—with her mother's name written in the appropriate spot: Louisa Annebella Calzonni. And, in the space for the father's name, nothing.

Nothing at all.

And decades after that, when she had become one of the richest women in the world, she would hire private detectives, and even ask favours of official investigative agencies, including Interpol, to find out something of her origins.

One enterprising team would eventually find the grave of a couple named Calzonni, whose daughter Louisa had disappeared in 1987, in a small village on the outskirts of Turin. But in whose company Louisa had disappeared, or whom she had travelled to meet, no one would ever discover.

Of her earlier ancestors, Gus would learn nothing.

LONDON, 1844

Grey fog blankets the boulevard which is Pall Mall, causing the gas-lamps—the lamplighter is still on his rounds, can just be seen far down the street, at his work—to hiss in the damp, heavy air. The buildings are grand, doors fronted by columns in the neo-classical style: white-painted or pale grey, eerie in the fogbound night.

There is a Peeler on duty, on the other side of the wide avenue, his tall rounded helmet lending him the appearance of a toy wooden soldier. But the long truncheon tucked in his leather belt, and the whistle for summoning help, are real enough.

The anonymous man, Ada's messenger, half-hidden in a doorway and overly conscious of the pistol in his tweed coat's pocket, stands very still.

Mistress . . . This is for my Countess.

Ada engenders such extreme reactions, in her servants as well as her peers: a total, smitten adoration; or a fearful loathing, as though her dark spiritual curse may be infectious.

Just wait . . .

And, eventually, there is the clop of hooves: a disreputable-looking horse and cart passing through, heading towards Trafalgar Square. The policeman leaves his post to investigate.

Now.

Ada's messenger, his face muffled against the fog and his hat pulled low, moves quickly but noiselessly across the cobblestones, and into the entrance-way of the Athenaeum Club. Ignoring the shining brass knocker, he taps softly. After a long, tense moment, the big panelled door swings open.

The footman nods in recognition, and leads the messenger inside. In the messenger's left hand is an envelope addressed to *F. Prandi, Esq.*; he holds it up for the footman to see. A discreet cough, then another manservant gestures, and leads the messenger along a marble-tiled corridor, to a quiet gentlemen's snug at the rear.

A knock, and the door is opened from within.

"Ah, my friend." A rotund man beams. His Italian accent, when he speaks, is scarcely detectable. "Come in. Sit down."

There is a reek of old cigarillos in the room, although no one is smoking at present. Books line the walls, and copies of *Bentley's Miscellany* litter two small tables. A globe stands in one corner, beside a heavy, dark-green ceiling-to-floor drape.

"I am reading the most excellent serial"—the round-faced Italian's smile flashes beneath his dark moustache—"by your wonderful Mr Dickens. Whom I gather"—lowering his voice—"your esteemed mistress personally knows."

The messenger's expression is stoic. His reply, when he makes it, carries the unmistakable burr of the Scottish Highlands.

"That I cannot say, sir."

"And what can you say?" Irritation prickles Signor Prandi's voice. "What, pray, is that in your hand?"

"A letter, sir. Addressed to you."

The messenger hands it over quickly, before the Italian can snatch it, or make disparaging comments about his mistress.

"Hmm . . ." Tearing open the seal, Prandi flicks a glance over it. "Not signed, I notice."

"She . . . Since the matter of the Royal Mail, sir . . ."

The Italian's private letters have been intercepted in the past: an absolute scandal to the British public who had assumed their personal correspondence was sacrosanct. But then, Signor Prandi is a known spy, and a foreigner.

"Don't worry." Reading the note more carefully, he adds: "Do you know anything of this favour she wishes me to grant?"

A pause, then: "No, sir. I do not."

But that hesitation told its own story. There is a flash of gold, as Prandi hands over two sovereigns. The messenger gulps, then secretes the coins in his waistcoat's watch-pocket.

"I only . . . The bairn'll need a wet-nurse, sir, if it is to survive."

"A *child*? Ah, I see. Very good, my friend."

"Sir."

The messenger gives a stiff nod, then leaves the small snug, closing the door behind him.

After a decent interval, to make sure the messenger has left the club, Fortunato Prandi sits back in his overstuffed armchair, and uses the silver point of his cane to ruffle the green drape at the small room's rear.

"You can come out now, Aldo."

"Thank you." The drape is pulled aside, and a lean-faced man steps into the room. "This message . . . It's from the countess?"

"The very one." Prandi taps his teeth with the envelope's edge. "And I wonder what kind of trouble she's in now."

But they both heard the messenger's comment: there's a newborn child involved. The Countess of Lovelace has been touched by too many scandals in the past; one more would be disastrous.

"The countess knows" — Aldo Guillermi's face is tightly drawn: his long hair and wide shoulders bespeak an athlete's grace, but his body is fairly vibrating with tension — "of my sister's misfortune."

How else would anyone associate an Italian spy with a wet-nurse? For Guillermi's sister Maria, so young and beautiful, has but recently lost her firstborn to a raging fever no English doctor could identify, no apothecary could cure.

"We spoke," says Prandi, still in English, "in general terms, no more. The countess knows of your sister's plight, but not her identity."

"That is good."

For a moment, as the two men face each other, it is not certain where the power in this room really resides. Then Prandi's glance slides away. Though he is nominally senior in the republican movement, his forte is solo, diplomatic espionage: moving among the drawing-rooms of the rich and the good, gleaning gossip, recruiting admirers. It is Aldo Guillermi who is the soldier, used to bearing the responsibility of command.

"Mazzini," he says, "has mixed feelings about the current *furore*."

Guillermi pronounces the last word in the Italian way.

"The republican cause"—Prandi shakes his head—"can only benefit."

Both Mazzini, the true figurehead, and Prandi are in exile: the public face of agitation. Prandi's work as a spy has been both hindered and helped by his now-public identity. Mazzini proved, to most intelligent readers' satisfaction, that the British Government caused their personal letters—his and Prandi's—to be opened, by the supposedly untouchable Royal Mail.

Hence this handwritten note from Ada, which reads:

Dear Prandi. I have a more important service to ask of you, which only you can perform . . . and goes on to arrange a rendezvous, without specifying the new favour's nature. Ada identifies herself anonymously, thus: *I am the person you went with to hear Jenny Lind sing. I expect you at 6*—

"Your mother," adds Prandi, as Guillermi finishes reading the unsigned note, "has raised more funds for the cause."

"It will be good to see her again."

Guillermi's mother is French, and France has been home to many for whom Italy is too hot a place to be in these troubled days. More than anything, Guillermi wants to remove his sister from this cold benighted country.

"Since Maria lost the child"—his gaze turns bleak—"I have feared for her sanity. And since her husband Higgs seems lost at sea . . ."

"She had best set sail for southern France, where your mother can take care of her."

"Yes." Guillermi's hand goes to his hip as though to rest upon a sword-hilt which is not there. "That would be best."

"And the Countess, it seems, needs a newborn child to disappear."

Guillermi looks at Prandi. The overweight spy looks unduly pleased with himself.

"How can you be so certain? There might be another explanation."

"Ah, my friend. It is not the first time"—with a flashing grin—"I have caused a member of her family to vanish."

OXFORD, 2001

Gus was twelve in the December when she took home that end-of-term report card: the last report before everything changed.

A *withdrawn child*, the summary read, *who needs to interact more with other children*. It was the kind of report which Louisa had come to expect.

But there were one or two puzzled hints from other teachers, including Mr Brownspell who taught physics: *Produces occasional flashes of surprising intuition, when she succeeds in engaging with the class at all.*

When the English teacher, Mrs Holwell, set an essay assignment on *Inevitability in Daniel Deronda*, a novel the class had just read—by chance, the same Eliot book which Gus had borrowed, and her mother had tried to finish, several years before—Gus's reply was a long and flowing indictment of genetic determinism: eloquent and reasoned enough for suspicions of plagiarism to spring up in every adult who read it.

Worse, the essay contained equations and conceptual diagrams—of interconnected springs—forming a mathematical model of the interdependence of genes, and their developmental motion through a phase-space of genetic possibilities. It replicated some of Kaufman's work (which she could not have seen) from the Santa Fe Institute—*which is the nearest*, she said in the essay, *we get to predetermined lives, and it's not close at all*—and demonstrated the existence of broad constraints on the otherwise random, unimpeded arms-race of co-evolving replicators.

"I got the idea," she told Mrs Holwell, "from the Faraday lectures. On the telly."

The English teacher, who had never heard of Richard Dawkins, was unimpressed. But she was sufficiently annoyed to show Gus's exercise book, during a break in the staff room, to Mr Brownspell. And he was astute enough to be amazed by what he read.

"You watched Dawkins," he said to Gus later. "When you were how old?"

"I was young." The twelve-year-old, with a solemn expression, shook her head. "But I remembered it."

"Mm. I don't think—"

"He's *real*, you know. I saw him in town last week."

"Quite." Brownspell was bemused. "He works here, doesn't he? In the university."

It was the first time Gus realized that Oxford could be a special place.

Perhaps the fuss would have died down, kept Gus's life more normal, if this had not been an inspection week. But Alex Duggan was the inspector, and he was a young man who was overly sensitive to the annoyance he was causing to already overworked teachers. Across the country, politically motivated or well-intentioned curriculum changes (depending on who you talked to) meant that teachers were putting in long unpaid hours to prepare internal reports as well as lesson material; the feeling was of rampant bureaucracy gone mad.

And Duggan, who had not so long ago been an idealistic neophyte teacher himself, welcomed any excuse to get involved with an issue which did not revolve around paperwork or failed administration. A problem child, or one of exceptional promise—in this case of suspected plagiarism, it could be either—would form a welcome break from a routine he was beginning to hate.

He interviewed Gus in the art room, keeping her back "for a small chat" after the others had left for morning break.

Afterwards, with a strange delight in his eyes, he showed his—or rather Gus's—trophies in the staff-room: geometric models formed of plasticine and bright plastic cocktail sticks.

"A hypercube." Brownspell recognized one of the forms. "But what's this one?"

"She's read about tesseracts. Then extended the notion, all by herself"—Duggan blinked—"to hypertetrahedra and hyperpentahedra."

"Well." Brownspell slowly smiled. "What are we going to do with her?"

"Hmm? Indeed." Duggan's answering smile grew wide. "Did you know Dawkins is giving a public lecture tomorrow night? In the Zoology Institute."

"Perhaps"—Brownspell glanced over at Jenny Mensch, who taught French—"a couple of us could take her there."

"What about Gus's parents? What do you know about them?"

"A single mother. Works two, maybe three cleaning jobs."

"Ah." Duggan thought about the child's indictment of genetic determinism. "How very interesting."

E. O. Wilson showed powerful forces, the twelve-year-old Gus had written, *moving every species. But we are human beings and our lives are more interesting than ants.*

"Gus's mother is devoted to her. You can tell just by the way she looks at her."

"That's very good."

"You think we ought to have a word with her?"

"Yes . . . Yes, I think we should."

LONDON, 1844

Ada, Countess of Lovelace, stares at the orange crackling fire, at the sheet of paper burning, becoming ash which leaps upwards, falls back. Outside the window, darkness has settled on fog-bound St James' Square.

"Madam?" A discreet cough. "Are you indisposed?"

"Not according to the good Doctor Locock," she answers.

"I will let our guests know," says William, "that you will be along shortly."

"Please do, sir."

Her husband William, Lord King, 1st Earl of Lovelace, nods politely.

What have I done?

She sees her husband's real concern, and wishes that she could have been true to him, not given to the dark, wild, reckless passions she has inherited from her genius father. During her entire childhood, her stern unforgiving mother, Annabella, kept Ada forcibly away from the tempestuous Byronic verses: drove her relentlessly down this other path, of cold logic and objective mathematics.

Except that equations *burn* inside Ada, as insanely bright as any visions the Deity (or Lucifer) heaped upon her mad, bad father, whose bones now lie safely interred in the family vault.

O, my son. What have I done?

But there is no room in society for the child she has delivered. The other three—legitimate, everyone assumes—are well loved. She cannot allow herself to believe that their father was any other than her husband, the well-meaning William. His house gives her freedom from her repressive mother: the liberty she has always longed for.

Last month she gave birth, without her husband's knowledge.

It is an illness which causes her wild weight fluctuations, and that malady has allowed her to hide the pregnancy. Inspired by a penny dreadful, a cheaply sensational novel in which a woman had not realized she was *en ceinte* until the baby put in his appearance, Ada has kept the secret.

Also, it is because of her insane cycles, of extreme weight gain followed by catastrophic loss, that William has chosen not to be intimate with her, his wife, for over a year. By the will of Providence, they have spent much of that time living in separate houses.

Now, one way or another, the child must disappear.

Ada has a wild scheme in her head for financing the child's life. A gambling syndicate, using the power of her logic and Mr Babbage's Difference Engine, seeded with money from William. She has always been able to persuade him: by her forcefulness, by his genuine love for her. And she will need William's written permission to gamble in society, since a woman owns little of her own and it is the husband, always, who owns debts incurred by his family, as surely as he holds title to the capital he has inherited, to the monies earned from his own hard labours.

"You'll join us shortly, madam?"

"Oh, yes, dearest William." She sips from her claret. "That I will."

Her doctor no longer prescribes laudanum. Ada's current medication is a strict regime of hot baths and small doses of claret, taken constantly throughout the day. It appears to be efficacious.

In the flames which curl and lick inside the fireplace, this is the vision she sees: two scurrying figures in the nightbound dockyards, with a small well-wrapped bundle in their arms. Sometimes the baby cries, sometimes it is silent; either way, misery surrounds it as surely as the cold damp fog settles on the city she is growing to hate.

OXFORD, 2004

Bright lights, white walls, and the gabble of cheerful, energetic voices.

Gus picked at her tub of Ben & Jerry's "One Sweet Whirled," intent more on the bright babble of ice-cream-bar conversation surrounding her than the dessert itself. The other students were so much older—18, even 20—that she had reverted to her quiet ways. Around the various colleges, three or four other undergraduates were very young; one of them, like Gus, was only 14.

The others had been featured in their local newspapers or even the national in ten years. Lanark lifted his head, just noticing it when the blast of cold air came in, and even he heard the floor creaking as it took the ten steps across the dark lobby. Then it was standing in the doorway of the bar, looking in at us.

Its wet clothes were half-shredded away. Water ran down from it onto the floor and it was white as a corpse, all right, except for the red and purple places, like crushed blackberries, where it must have been pounded on the rocks. It had taken a terrible beating. Its mouth was torn, jaw hanging open. But even while I was staring at it I saw the bruises swirling under the skin and fading, the wounds closing up. It lifted its white hand and closed its mouth; reset the jaw with a *click*, and the split cheek knit up into a red line that faded too.

Lanark gave a kind of strangled howl, not very loud, and I thought he might be having a heart attack. I thought I might be having one myself. The thing smiled at Uncle Jacques, who right then looked every year of his real age. He didn't smile back.

It pushed its wet hair from its face and it said, "I don't appreciate having to go through all this, you know."

Well, surprise. He had a live person's voice, in fact he sounded cultured, like that Back East guy who used to narrate those newsreels. Uncle Jacques didn't say anything in reply and the stranger went on to say:

"I really thought you'd come out to me. What a hole this is! The Company still hasn't a clue where you've gone; but then, they haven't got our resources."

That was when I knew what he was, and I'd a whole lot rather it'd been some reproachful ghost from the *Argive*, come to punish us for not trying to save him. Lightning flashed bright in the street, and if it had shown me a whole legion of drowned ghosts standing out there, I'd have yelled for them to come in and help us.

Uncle Jacques had slumped down in his seat, but his eyes were clear and hard as he studied the stranger. He said, "Are you from Budu?" and the stranger said:

"Of course."

Then Uncle Jacques said, "I'll surrender to Budu and nobody else. You go back and tell him that. Nobody else! I want answers from him."

The stranger smiled at that and stepped down into the room. As he came into the lamplight he looked more alive, less pale. He said, "I don't think you're in any position to call the tune, Lavalle. You know what he thinks of deserters. I can't blame you for being afraid of him, but I really think you ought to cut your losses and come quietly now. The fool mortal wrecked my boat; perhaps one of these has an automobile we can appropriate?"

Uncle Jacques shook his head, and the man said, "Too bad. We'll just have to walk out then."

"You don't understand," said Uncle Jacques, "I'm not surrendering to you. I'm giving you a message to deliver. If Budu won't come to me, tell me where he is and I'll go straight to him. Where is he, Arion?"

The man he called Arion grinned and shrugged. He said, "All right; you've caught me in a lie. The truth is, we don't know where the old man's got to. He's dropped out of sight. Labienus has been holding the rebellion together. Wouldn't press; their parents seemed to be teachers or chairmen of small but successful software outfits. Perhaps parental pressure drove them to achieve. For Gus, at home, this was not a factor; she knew only that her mother loved her.

Here, on wall-boards, a cacophony of brightly coloured notices announced plays, books for sale, a demonstration against world debt (which, on closer examination, had already taken place), used PCs for sale. A small yellow sheet caught her eye: JDK, she thought it read, before realizing her mistake—in fact it was a demonstration of something called JKD. Hardly interesting.

It was five years since Gus had logged on to *www.java.sun.com* and downloaded the basic Java Development Kit (already an outmoded name, but serious coders mostly still called it the JDK, rather than SDK) onto her school's battered old PC. And taught herself real programming.

At her table, the talk had moved from sex to Kant's Critique of Pure Reason; to Professor Schama's thesis that women were the driving force behind cultural change in 19th-century England (even before they achieved suffrage); to the post-acid house Latin revival in general and El Phase-Transition's lead singer, N. Rapt, in particular; and back to sex.

Gus stared around the packed ice-cream bar, feeling out of place.

"Excuse me," she said to no one in particular, and slipped away from her seat.

She passed the notice board, scanned the yellow sheet announcing a JKD demonstration—some kind of kung fu: nothing at all to do with programming; you had to laugh—and pressed her way through to the exit.

Outside, on Little Trendy Street, she turned left, tucked her hands into her pockets, and began to walk. (A towny or a tourist would have called the narrow road Little Clarendon Street, unaware of the separate, insiders' geographical nomenclature known only to students and faculty.) The street, by whichever name, was dark and touched by mist. Gus shivered.

"—some change, please?"

A small youth, scarcely bigger than Gus, was sitting on a blanket in a doorway, with a black retriever curled up on his lap.

"Sure." Gus had very little money—now, or any time—but perhaps that sharpened her senses in some way. She knew real, desperate poverty when she saw it.

She handed over some coins.

"Thanks, miss."

"No problem." She liked the American sound of that: like something from the movies. "Take it easy."

She walked on.

Something . . .

Usually, this close to the city centre, the streets were safe. But there was a rustle as she passed the bushes by Wellington Square, and she stopped. Her skin prickled—

Then a heavy hand grabbed her sleeve.

"Hey, chickie. Should we be out after dark?"

Stink of breath, close to her. Gus choked.

And another voice, slimy, behind her: "Gimme, now!"

Help me!

Fear paralysed Gus's throat, her mouth wide but silent, like a dying fish. Her mind would not process what was happening as big shapes manhandled her. Gus was utterly helpless.

I don't want to . . .

"Hey!" An echoing voice.

Sound of a dog, barking.

"Bitch-girl."

Impact on her face. Spurt of warm blood in mouth.

Then they were gone, vanished into the thickening fog, while she sat back, stunned, on cold paving-stones. Beside Gus, the young homeless man squatted, careful not to touch her.

"Are you all right?"

His dog growled at the departed muggers once more, then looked at Gus, stopped, swallowed wetly, then licked her face.

LONDON, 1844

St Catherine's Dock is dark. Two figures hurry across the cobblestones: Aldo Guillermi, muffled against the cold, carrying a cane which he is careful not to tap against the ground, and his sister, Maria. The baby, wrapped in her shawl, is silent.

"Aldo, we will be late. If it sails, what of our baggage?"

"Hush. They won't throw it off."

"But . . ."

"It sails, and we sail onboard."

But their voices carry, and dark figures step from the shadows behind a pile of netting and crates. There are three of them, big and burly, with short heavy jackets over their tunics, and heavy belaying-pins in their hands.

"Well, mates." The first one spits a long stream of something dark onto the dockyard stones. "We've found a new friend, looks like."

"No." Guillermi raises his empty left hand, placating. "Sirs, I cannot. We're about to sail."

" 'At's what I said, innit?"

Press-gang? Or worse?

"I'm sorry." Guillermi adjusts his grip on the walking-cane. "I don't understand. Could you repeat that, please?"

"You deaf, or what? I said—"

The cane whips down and up, in an instant: downwards, across the leader's right hand, then uses the rebound to arc backhand across the man's face. His belaying-pin clatters on the cobblestones.

"Maria, go . . ."

They are almost upon him, but Guillermi sidesteps, leading them away from his sister.

"Get 'im."

A fencing-lunge, and he stabs the cane's point into a second attacker's throat, followed with a savate side-kick into the lower ribs. The man doubles up, but his mate has already seized Guillermi's arms from behind, the grip unbreakable.

Strike like lightning . . .

Guillermi snaps his head backwards, feels the crunch of broken nose against the back of his skull. Stamps downwards, arcs his elbow back—impact—and spins away.

. . . and roar like thunder.

Charlemont's never-forgotten words, as he drove his students to fight, scream now in Guillermi's brain.

"Yaaah!"

His warrior-yell startles all three attackers. A circular *fouetté*, a whipping kick into a thigh muscle, and the first is down, leg paralysed. Guillermi spins to one side—half-heard: "I've got 'im"—then his heel takes another in the throat, quicker than thought, in a beautiful *revers*. Then an arcing series of *la canne* strikes drops the leader.

All three men are down.

A civilized man would stop now, but a soldier knows better. If his attackers have other weapons, this is the moment when they will use them. So Guillermi—as has been drilled into him—does not stop, but whirls and stamps onto ribs, onto heads, whips the cane downwards again and again, until the threat is gone.

He began training in *le savate* with spoiled young gentlemen, in a somewhat effete salon, during his Sorbonne days. But he moved on to study with the huge powerful champion Charlemont, who regularly lifted small cannon barrels overhead, and whose instruction was practical and deadly. In later years, Guillermi practised in the sun-drenched south, in the dockyard style of rough Marseilles, where sporting rules have never applied.

One of his attackers is curled up on his side, hands around his damaged knees, mewling, with a long wicked knife beside him. Guillermi kicks the blade across damp cobbles, out of reach. Another man lies still, softly snoring as though asleep. The third . . .

Moves! .

Guillermi leaps back, startled by a flash of light—*blade*—and then a crack of sound. And the man slumps once more upon the cold dockyard cobblestones.

"Maria! Are you all right?"

Like a marionette with severed strings, the corpse lies with twisted neck, a pool of dark liquid expanding beneath its lifeless head.

"Yes, my brother." Blue steel glints in her hand, beneath the baby's form. "Let's go."

Her voice is very calm, as she slips the dark, six-inch Derringer pistol out of sight. It is a muzzle-loaded 1807 Derringer Phila, blued steel inset in polished wood: a percussion cap pocket gun which requires a steady hand and careful aiming. Guillermi is impressed.

Some good will come of this.

It is a strange thought for a protective brother to have. Yet Maria's hysteria is suddenly gone, along with the dark depression of recent days: replaced by a quiet determination. And somehow her renewed spirit has kept the baby—the newborn boy she must protect—from crying.

"Yes. Three days," he tells her, "and we'll see Maman once more."

OXFORD, 2006

There was a lecture to commemorate some obscure academic event—the anniversary of someone else's lecture—and it began with a boring recitation of the history of computing. The lecturer's accent was transatlantic, and his name was Ives, but Gus knew nothing of his work.

"And, before Turing's life was tragically cut short in 1954, hounded by society to his death, though he almost certainly did more than any other single man to ensure Allied victory in World War II . . ."

Gus's skin prickled.

Turing was here, in this place, she realized. *He was real.*

Buried in Ives's tone, she thought, was a resentment towards the society which had caused the mathematician's suicide. Perhaps not everyone in the room detected it—most of her colleagues were waiting in good-natured boredom for the meat of the lecture to follow—but on some level several of them did.

Ives was a visiting research fellow, and Gus followed his talk with interest: a brave attempt to bridge the conflicting software paradigms of formal specification languages and evolutionary algorithms. Most of the people sitting near Gus were Z experts, used to formulating system definitions with rigorous symbolic logic: they frowned at the anti-reductionist notion of creating code which had evolved, not been designed.

Gus was fascinated.

Afterwards, she found herself among a small group of faculty and students drinking tea in the hallway outside the lecture theatre. When someone suggested relocating to a common room, Ives put down his half-drunk tea, looking relieved, then made the counter-proposal of coffee in Starbucks.

"My treat," he said, which swayed the balance.

"*Authors and academics*," he would tell Gus at a later date. "*are easily swayed by the promise of free drink or food.*"

"*Pavlovian conditioning*," she would reply. "*And the desire to meet like minds: let's be fair.*"

The coffee house was teeming with energy. While the rest of the group went upstairs to stake out a claim on seats, Gus volunteered to help Ives carry the collection of cappuccinos, frappuccinos, tea—that last for old Crichton, of course—and lattes, which someone had pointed out was a bag of bevvies.

"I was hoping," said Ives, leaning on the delivery counter, "to have a conversation free of maths humour, for a change."

A "bag" was technically correct: a mathematical set where duplication was allowed but sequencing was irrelevant—both Jim and Maureen had ordered venti lattes, and it didn't matter which of the two drinks either person took.

"No chance of that round here." Gus was surprised at her own boldness. "If you want normality, head north."

"Or just outwards, yeah. Town and gown. I love this old place." Ives had chosen to wear a bright red tie, and he was now running his finger inside his shirt collar, and looking uncomfortable. "Less formal than I expected. I was doing some consultancy at a place in London, and everyone was wearing business suits."

"You might as well take the tie off," said Gus. "Visiting the empire's last bastion must have misled you."

"Right. Here, it's just like home. I'm the only guy in this city who's wearing one." He tugged it, pulling the knot too tight, in his effort to undo it. "Damn. You know, I had to consciously work out the theory behind this, but I only modelled the putting-it-on operation."

So much for an evening without maths humour.

"Let me." Surprised again at her own actions, she reached up — aware of his close warmth — and undid the knot.

"Thanks. You realize there are more than 80 ways to tie one of these things?"

"Really?" Gus frowned in concentration, social niceties forgotten. It had become a technical problem, and that was interesting.

"A handy way to model knot topology," Ives said, stuffing the discarded tie in his jacket pocket, "is to consider the knot's context, the space around it."

"Oh, yes. Model the not-knots. I've heard of that . . ."

When the drinks arrived, they carried everything upstairs, and found their colleagues gathered on wooden chairs and armchairs around a small table, discussing the constraints placed by Goedel's Theorem on some branch of research which Gus had never heard of.

Do I really belong here?

It was a question she asked herself often. But then some maths or physics or computation problem — they were all the same to her — would crop up, and she would be lost in the joy of solving it.

I should get home, now.

"— your opinion?" Ives was asking her.

"Sorry. I was thinking of something else." Gus put down the empty cup she realized she was holding. "I ought to be going."

Ives looked at her for a moment. Just then, they were in an isolated bubble of silence while animated conversation sparkled all around them.

"What's wrong?" he asked.

How did you know? She was so used to hiding the details of her life.

"My mother . . . She's not well." Gus blinked. She had not told anyone. "They've examined her at the Radcliffe Infirmary, and they don't know what's wrong. Or they're not telling us."

"Oh." Ives put down his own drink. "Where's home?"

Gus told him.

"You've got a car?"

"No. We—" Gus shook her head. "We can't afford one. And I can't drive."

"Ah, right." Ives stood up and turned to the rest of the group. "I'll be back shortly. Just going to run Gus home, is that all right?"

She had not realized he even knew her name.

"I'm parked in St Giles," he added. "Major achievement."

He left with Gus, whether it was all right with the others or not.

In the car, as they were travelling, he told her about Seattle: "You'd love it. Friendly city, great campus." He'd delivered various anecdotes about consultancy work for a software giant, during the course of the lecture and later. "Starbucks in the same building. When I was in the Games Division, the company took us to the movies, whenever a sci-fi or a fantasy came out."

"Cool," said Gus. And then: "You worked for the Games Division?"

"Yeah, for a while. I devised scenarios for *Tokugawa*. Devious politics and ninja fighting. What a hoot."

"Really."

"Hmm." Gus flicked a glance at her, then returned his attention to the road. "You don't like the game?"

"It's great, actually." With a shrug. "The martial arts were a bit exaggerated, but that's par for the course, isn't it?"

"You know about martial arts?"

Gus's voice was quietly confident: "I train in jeet kune do."

Big hand, grabbing in the darkness . . .

No one would ever mug her again.

In the course of a very long life, Gus would have only one occasion to use her art on the street—or rather, on a lonely El station platform in Chicago, late at night on the Green Line south of the Loop, where a big thug attempted to beat an old man senseless with his own walking-stick, while his laughing buddies looked on—but the difference it made that night was mortal.

She used a reverse-snake escrima disarm to send the stick flying to one side, before clawing the attacker's eyes and breaking both his knees. The man's six buddies, through alcohol-clouded senses, noticed that she was small and female, and did not process the ease with which she had taken the big man out.

The rest happened very fast.

In seconds she was spinning and circling, throwing kicks and elbow-strikes, firing everything she had been taught in a continuous blur of adrenalized motion. The last man was even bigger than the first, drawing a knife from his belt but too late, as Gus used the running side-kick which Bruce Lee had developed to blast her attacker right off the edge of the platform and onto the tracks, where he narrowly escaped fatal electrocution.

Beyond that one incident, the daily discipline of physical JKD training, and her later experimentation with neurolinguistic programming, were the keys—she always thought—to her longevity and success.

As for her mathematical intuition . . . she would never be certain whether such discipline helped or hindered in that regard. But when applied to emotional control and financial management, it would certainly make her rich.

Very rich indeed.

That night in Oxford, though, as Ives was leaving her house—having stayed to chat with Gus and her mother, and being polite enough to pretend he enjoyed the dark strong tea which Mother made—Gus reached up to kiss him on the cheek, but he moved back subtly and she subsided.

"I am single," he told her. "But, you know . . . Most guys, at my age, are either married or gay."

It took a while for that to sink in.

"Oh."

Ives smiled. "Just so long as you know."

He shook her hand then, while her cheeks flared red. Over the decades, it was only the first of many shared incidents they would have cause to chuckle over.

And that was the first night she dreamed of knots.

PROVENCE, 1848

Medora stands at the window, looking out at the unseasonal rain falling upon the courtyard, thinking of England, which she will never see again.

"It's a time of revolution," one of the other two women says. "According to Aldo, this is the year the world will change."

Medora, painfully thin but strong now, turns slowly around. The woman who spoke, Alicia, is heavily pregnant. Seated by the pale stone fireplace, she rests one limp hand on the hemispherical bulge of her stomach.

I should no longer regard you, Medora thinks, *as my servant.*

She looks up at Aldo's sister, Maria, and they share wan smiles. They grew fond of Alicia, when she came up from the village to help out, right from the very first days. Doing more work than she was supposed to. Chatting with Aldo about politics and history. Medora and Maria saw, long before Alicia and Aldo realized it themselves, that the young couple had fallen deeply in love.

All three of us are sisters now.

There is the family you are born into—in Medora's case, a dark calamitous beginning: the Byrons are truly cursed—and the family which, if you are a survivor, you get to choose. It has taken Medora a long time to realize this, but she knows it is true.

"He'll come back safely," she tells Alicia. "Don't worry."

Alicia nods, but Maria turns away. Since Aldo rode off to fight, she has been subject to moods of deep introspection.

God will give me strength. Medora puts her hand against her chest, pressing the hidden crucifix against her skin. *Even if I am damned, let me help these in need.*

In the past, she was always so weak and useless, going to her hated aunt—and to the woman who is both her cousin and her half-sister, Ada, Countess of Lovelace—for handouts, in desperation. But now, in the modest vineyard, she no longer exists in the eyes of English (or European) high society. The sins of her parents are no longer public gossip: they are between her and God.

For Medora's mother was Augusta Byron—the woman after whom Augusta Ada Byron, now the Countess of Lovelace, was named—and everyone knows, though no one says, that Augusta's own brother, the famous, devil-driven poet, was the unacknowledged father of her bastard girl-child.

It was Ada who arranged for Medora's relocation to this remote place. And now, since she sent this new child to be raised forever in secret, there has been no contact at all with England.

I pray to God that it remains so.

Here in southern France, Medora is known as the Widow Calzonni. Four-year-old Jean-Pierre, asleep upstairs, is supposed to be the son she bore to a dead fictitious husband; Maria was his wet-nurse.

Will they ever tell Jean-Pierre of his true parents? That his mother was Ada, the Countess of Lovelace, while his father was Dr Crosse, son of the man said to have created life from base matter?

It is a decision Medora has not yet made.

"I dreamed of Aldo." Alicia places both hands on her swollen womb. "He was bouncing our daughter on his knee, and she was laughing."

"A sign from Providence." Maria crosses herself.

But, in the event, it will be two years before they see Aldo again, although his child will indeed be a daughter.

He will appear in the courtyard, riding bare-back upon a weary half-starved horse. With his right leg shattered, he will be a changed man at first: bitter, given to drunken rages. But later, bolstered by the sight of his daughter's beauty, his natural optimism will reassert itself.

By the time of his death, his little empire of olive groves and vineyards will be prosperous indeed. Those riches will remain until the eve of World War II, when disagreements with the local *fascisti* will cause everything to be lost.

But now, from the village church, the Angelus bell rings out.

"Time, my sisters"—Medora hands out well-worn missals—"to pray."

SANTA MONICA, 2024

Arm in arm, Gus and Ives strolled slowly along the boardwalk. Late afternoon, with the surf rolling in below, pale seagulls gliding overhead. Salt tang upon the air; the fresh sea breeze washing over their tanned faces.

"You know"—Gus stopped, let go of Ives, leaned over the balustrade, and pointed downwards—"I lost my virginity right about there."

"Never." Shaking with gentle laughter, Ives looked over. "After dark, I hope."

"Oh, yeah. With a nice post-doc, since you wouldn't oblige."

"Right. I can still see the damp spot."

"Ho, ho."

They were celebrating, in a fashion: a deliberate way of experiencing today's events as a positive step forwards. For Ives had come home last night to an empty apartment. Not even a note from his departed lover, Raoul: just empty closets and missing cash. And invective scrawled in toothpaste across the bathroom mirror.

And Gus had just finalized her divorce—her *first* divorce, as Ives ironically (and presciently) labelled it—and seen her ex-husband drive away with his new girlfriend: large-bosomed, wearing a gaudy, shocking pink short dress, and a triumphant smirk upon her face.

That'll disappear, Gus reckoned, *when she finds out who owns everything.*

For the beach house and Sundriver-coupé skimmer were all hers.

"We've come a long way," she said. "Hey, that sounds dramatic, doesn't it?"

"Both of us." Ives touched his new moustache: it had come out tinged with grey, and he was not sure whether he would keep it. "I'm glad I met you, sweetheart."

"Likewise, dearest. Shall we walk to the end?"

"Why not?" As they walked on, he began to whistle softly—the Pattern theme, from *Amber: The Musical*—in counterpoint to the rolling surf.

"Listen." Gus squeezed his arm. "Are you doing anything tonight?"

A middle-aged couple in matching Hawaiian shirts and baggy shorts were staring at her and Ives, close enough to hear. She should have known the kind of answer she would get.

"Wearing you out, all night long. There's a position I've been meaning to—"

But the couple walked on then, offended, and there was no point in completing the sentence.

"Oops." Ives raised his eyebrows. "Was it something I said?"

"Ha. Is it just me, or are people more repressed than when I was younger? Even here?"

"Probably." Ives looked gloomy for a moment, then cheered up, and gestured at the wide ocean. "Look at that. Are we lucky to be alive, or what?"

"Yes, lucky." She squeezed his arm again. "Thanks for being alive, my friend."

She was nearly 25, and single once more.

Saved from a big mistake.

"We're good for each other."

"Oh, yes."

Their minds were both similar and complementary. When Gus developed the concepts behind *Fractal of the Beast*, it was Ives who helped brainstorm the network of developing relationships among the characters. She devised the aliens' forms, he worked out the structure of the shadow organization which fought them.

She coded the game; he negotiated the license rights.

From that first product, Ives insisted that he make no money directly. He already had his earnings from lucrative consultancy; she had nothing. *"But I'll be rich,"* he said, as they signed a deal giving him 20 percent of earnings from any future games they might develop together. *"And so will you."*

For the first six months, download figures were minimal. Then, in a fit of nostalgia or desperation, one of the big webnets started promoting a remake of the old *X-Files* shows, and the whole half-forgotten alien-invasion meme had come alive once more, and sales had rocketed.

Those fictional invaders would prove more important than anyone realized.

The alien hunt in the game proceeded through many levels. The stories were labyrinthine; a dark and gloomy sense of being watched was present in almost every scene; and there was action, with tricky clues to decipher. Only three players, since the game's release over four years before, ever reached the final level. (Unless there was someone else, with an offline copy of the game, who never hooked in with the rest of the world.)

But three users' systems had automatically mailed her when they deciphered the final puzzle. She sent each of them a rather substantial amount of money, though the game did not advertise the existence of such a prize.

One of the three was Arvin Rubens, a protegé of Danny Hills—and Arvin himself, when still a teenager, had met Hills's legendary friend, Richard Feynman—and he transferred the money back to her, with a note saying that he had no need for it.

"I'd only get myself into trouble," he said, in an updated Feynmanism, *"by spending it on wine, women and a new holoterminal."*

He also invited both her and Ives to come and work with him in Caltech.

Sunshine, sea. She could train in JKD at the Inosanto Academy. Why would she want to stay in old, cold Oxford?

"Even if you don't come," Rubens had told her, *"you've already helped my research."*

For the game's final solution involved working out the aliens' true nature. They appeared in many shapes and guises, but the key lay in realizing that each was a different projection of one fractal shape—a single being of dimension 6.66—into ordinary spacetime. Just as, in the Pickover book which Gus had read in childhood, five disconnected blobs appearing on the surface of a Flatland balloon might really be fingerprints from a single, otherworldly hand.

And the underlying equation was useful because it came directly out of Gus's own research at Oxford, into the fundamental nature of the spacetime continuum.

"Come back to my place," she said to Ives, as they turned back from the end of the boardwalk. "I've got something to show you."

"Whoopee." Then, "House or lab, do you mean?"

"I mean the lab, darling. Sorry to disappoint."

As they passed a row of bright pastel houses, a drunk came shambling up to them, hand outstretched. *If you give me money,* the display on his write-capable t-shirt read, *I'll spend it on booze. But at least I'm honest.*

"Here you are."

Blinking in the sunshine, the drunk stood looking at the money in his hand—from both of them—as Gus and Ives walked on.

"If we asked him to tell us how he ended up here," said Ives, "I wonder what he'd say."

"Let's not go there." Gus used her watch to summon a cab.

"All right."

They waited silently until a vehicle slid to the curb, and its gull-door rose up. Gus slid inside first, announcing their destination loudly to the cab's AI, knowing that her vestigial accent could cause recognition problems.

Ives crossed his arms, as the door descended and the street began to slide past.

"People always draw family trees," Gus said suddenly, as though she herself had not told him to drop the topic of past lives, "upside down. Or hadn't you noticed?"

"*Qué?*" Ives spread his hands. "*No comprendo.* Sorry."

"Branching out downwards, with increasing time. But the further back you go, the *more* ancestors you have."

"Right. Ten generations back—"

"You have 1,024 ancestors."

"Assuming no incest. Yee-hah. You know you're a redneck when—" Ives stopped, looked at her, then patted her hand. "Gus, dear. It wasn't your fault. It wasn't anybody's. Life just turns out like that."

"I know."

But Gus's sudden wealth had come too late to keep her mother alive. *Genetic defect in the heart,* the consultant had told her. *The neuro-degeneration weakened her, and we still don't know the cause of that.*

Silent tears, unbidden, tracked down Gus's cheeks.

A holo landscape half-filled the room, hanging above the desktop and extending outwards, so that Ives appeared to be standing in the middle of a mountain range.

"I've modified here, and here." Gus pointed at additional free-floating holo-volumes in which equations scrolled. "But it's little different from the standard mosaic."

The landscape represented a simplified three-dimensional spacetime—two spatial, one time—as an overall brane, formed of interwoven sub-branes. Gus pointed at the "zoom" icon. The image expanded until gaps were visible: the holes between linked Planck-length tessellae which form the vacuum itself.

"I reworked the topology"—Gus smiled—"using not-knots. Remember them?"

"Ah, yes."

The image flipped into a kind of mirror-converse. What had seemed a landscape was now a moirée pattern draped across something else: an underlying jagged sub-landscape which supported reality.

"Then I got more interested in the continuum's context than in spacetime itself. Modelling the not-knot—"

Ives nodded. "The power of metaphor. Well done, dear."

Faraday used the notion of fields purely as a metaphor, explaining electromagnetic action at a distance. Yet modern researchers thought of fields as the underlying reality, while everything else—particles, twistors, branes, tessellae—was illusion. Physicists gained the concept *with their mother's milk,* as Einstein said.

But Gus's work changed the metaphor. In her model, the eleven dimensions of realspace were the illusory projection, draped across the underlying fractal context which shapes both this and other universes. She had a name for the context: mu-space.

"The ultimate continuum," she said.

"If you're right, there's a Nobel prize in—"

"And I've already sent a signal through it."

ASHLEY COMBE, 1852

Hot flames crackle in the fireplace. A vision of eternal Hell awaiting her? Pain insinuates its claws between the deadening layers of laudanum intoxication: it is the crab, this disease which is killing her.

"My father—" Ada's voice is a whimper. "I want to be buried—with him."

"Hush, my dear." A hand pats hers. "That will be taken care of."

For a moment, she does not know who this is: William, perhaps Andrew Crosse, or Faraday . . . Last week, she believes, her old friend Dickens read to her. To *her.* Daughter of the great poet, but a strange, maddened fool in her own right.

I've done so much wrong.

Has Charles Babbage been to see his failing Queen of Engines, his dying Enchantress of Numbers? But it is John Crosse, her former lover, who is with her now. For a time, her old friends were barred from visiting; now it is too late for foolishness.

It hurts—

Her body is soaked. William and her sons—her three acknowledged sons—have been pouring cold water upon her bared, so-thin midriff to ease the pain. But for now, only Crosse is here with her.

"I received a letter," he whispers. "About . . . Jean-Pierre. *Our son thrives.* He thrives, my love."

My son?

"He has a constant playmate," Crosse adds. "Daughter of the man who took him abroad. Giuliani? Something like that. Someday, says Medora, they'll be—"

The whimpering begins again.

My son!

Ada fights the pain, but neither guile nor ferocity will beat this last, implacable foe. Finally, though it takes two more pain-racked days, metastasized cervical cancer shuts down her internal organs one by one, her ragged breath rattles, and she lies still.

In the fireplace, lowering flames sputter. Grey ash spills upon the floor.

It was perhaps a mesmeric demonstration, at a soirée held on her 26th birthday, which opened the Pandora's box of Ada's mind, released the dark spirit which could never be contained again. She blamed that experiment—undertaken for sensation's sake—and her own impetuous nature for all that followed. Equations burned, pure thoughts soared, but her inner drives would always deny her peace.

Years earlier, her father's body, with massive pageantry, was conveyed by carriage, drawn by six black steeds, through London's streets (which were thronged with onlookers), and laid to rest in the family vault. Ada's own funeral is more modest; her narrow corpse travels by modern train, black smoke billowing in lieu of stallion's manes.

Finally, she lies interred beside the father she was not allowed to know.

Crosse, meanwhile, crouches beneath his mantelpiece, burning, one by one, every letter he received from the woman he loved, and every note from the forgotten half-sister entrusted with raising their secret child: the son he will never see.

SANTA MONICA, 2024

That night, her demonstration seemed nothing special. Gus shone red laser light into her kludged lab-bench setup—draining power from the campus mesoreactor: she would get complaints—where the beam simply disappeared.

But, at the far end of the half-lit lab, a red spot glowed in mid-air.

To an onlooker, it would have seemed the simplest of holograms. Ives whistled as he examined the apparatus; whatever the underlying mechanism, the results were spectacular. Red light shone into nothingness, reappeared some seven yards away. He realized, though it would take decades for other minds to catch up all the way with his intuition, that this simple demonstration transformed everything.

Shortly before dawn, they were back at the beach, sitting upon damp sand, breathing in the ocean air. Stars still glittered overhead, though dark-green painted the horizon behind them.

"We're going to get there." Ives, craning back, stared straight up. "Thanks to you."

"I hope so."

They stayed there until the rising sun draped orange fire across steel-grey waves, lighting the warm salt fluid which gave birth to life, splashing endlessly against the shore.

HIGH EARTH ORBIT, 2102

Sapphire, wreathed in soft cotton. The entire world lies beneath her: a jewel upon black velvet.

So wonderful.

Over her right shoulder floats the tiny biographer-globe, recording everything except what's important: her thoughts and feelings. The orbital station's view-bubble is reserved just for her.

If I'd listened to what everyone knew was "right," I wouldn't be here.

Gus has overridden both lawyers' and medics' wishes many times. (*"There's no such thing as escape velocity,"* she told them weeks before. *"Not with continuous thrust. I'll use a slow-shuttle. Perfectly safe."*) The occasional lie will not hurt them: she came up fast.

They don't have her perspective on the world.

After all this time.

Seventy-eight too-short years have passed since her discovery. Lightspeed sping-lobes, forming stasis fields within, were created 120 years after Einstein's blistering insights into the relativistic nature of spacetime. Her own research (she does not consider herself in Einstein's league) has taken this long to come to technological fruition.

"Two minutes, ma'am." A respectful voice in her earpiece.

Wealth comes from her corporations, more than intellectual endeavours. One of her companies owns the patent for this bubble's material: a transparent para-magnetic ceramic. She has always invested ten percent of income, given ten percent away (to children's foundations, mainly) and wisely spent the rest.

But none of it had meaning . . .

Her own researchers, at her insistence, use her as a guinea pig, for telomere replenishment and femtocytic re-engineering: for every life-extending treatment which looks likely to work. Equally importantly, she practices Yang-style t'ai chi every morning. Gus refuses to die too soon.

. . . until this moment.

Dark space outside. She wishes Ives were here.

"One minute."

She remembers Mother, so frail in the hospital bed, in the Radcliffe's terminal ward.

"Why did you call me Augusta, Mum?"

A long pause, then the tiniest of shrugs, from shoulders so emaciated her bones looked razor-sharp, attempting to cut through skin.

"Family tradition, pumpkin—"

It was days before Mother found final peace in death. But those were the last coherent words she spoke.

Now, Gus watches the stars. Blackness, sprinkled with diamond stars, across an invisible context whose mathematical reality she knows, but whose tangible qualities neither she nor anyone else can see.

Stardust, every one of us . . .

Born in the nearest sun. But all those suns seem to murmur now, as long-forgotten technology once whispered to the girl she was: secrets she will never truly grasp.

"Ma'am . . ."

"I see it."

Silver dart. A tiny speck, orbiting fast, high above blueness, heading into . . .

Gone.

One moment it was there; next, the vessel no longer existed.

"Insertion complete."

Hopeful, that message from Observation Control. There was no explosion; with luck, it means—

Speck.

"Is that it?"

"Beg your—? Yes! Ma'am, they're back."

Shining light, growing.

The silver vessel gleams, broadcasting its report of success on all wavelengths.

"We saw it!" The captain's voice. *"Alpha Centauri, for sure. Spectrometer confirms. We were there!"*

"Thank you," Gus whispers.

The silver biographer-globe drops closer, and she frowns. Then she realizes she is lying down, though she cannot recall changing position.

Blackness, circling all around.

And the stars, so bright.

". . . ma'am?"

Sounds, fading.

We made it, Mum.

And, for a moment, she sees it: the fractal Pattern, the mu-space reality which holds up our illusory cosmos—

Thank you.

Somewhere, a major blood vessel erupts. A crack, then relief.

Stars . . .

A smile spreads across Gus's lined face.

. . . fading . . .

Her personal universe dwindles.

. . . to darkness.

Is gone.

The Hotel at Harlan's Landing

KAGE BAKER

One of the most prolific new writers to appear in the late '90s, Kage Baker made her first sale in 1997, to Asimov's, and has since become one of that magazines most frequent and popular contributors with her sly and compelling stories of the adventures and misadventures of the time-travelling agents of the Company; of late, she's started two other linked sequences of stories there as well, one of them set in as lush and eccentric a High Fantasy milieu as any we've ever seen. Her stories have also appeared in Realms of Fantasy, Sci Fiction, Amazing, *and elsewhere. Her first novel,* In the Garden of Iden, *was also published in 1997 and immediately became one of the most acclaimed and widely reviewed first novels of the year. Her second novel,* Sky Coyote, *was published in 1999, followed by a third and a fourth,* Mendoza in Hollywood *and* The Graveyard Game, *both published in 2001. Her most recent book is her first collection,* Black Projects, White Knights, *where the story that follows was originally published. In addition to her writing, Baker has been an artist, actor, and director at the Living History Center, and has taught Elizabethan English as a second language. She lives in Pismo Beach, California.*

Here she shows us that sometimes no matter how isolated and remote a location you find in which to hide yourself away, it isn't nearly isolated enough . . .

There was just the five of us in the bar that night.

The lumber mills were all shut down for good and there hadn't been a ship come up to the wharf in years. No more big schooners down there in the cove, with their white sails flying in at eye level to the bluff top like clouds. Dirty little steamers stayed well out on the horizon and never came in, going busily to San Francisco or Portland. Nothing to come in for, at Harlan's Landing.

All this stuff the weekenders find so cute now, the gingerbread cottages and the big emporium with its grand false front and the old hotel here—you wouldn't have thought they were much then, when they were gray wood beaten into leaning by the winter storms, paint from the boom days all peeled off. No Heritage Society to save us, no tourists with cash to spend. Nobody had cash to spend. It was 1934.

I couldn't keep the hotel open, but after the Volstead Act was repealed I opened the bar downstairs and things brightened up considerably. Our own had some place to go, had sort of a social life now, see? We come that close to being a ghost town that everybody needed to know there was still a place with the yellow lights shining out through the windows, fighting to stay alive.

And it wasn't like there was anyplace else to go anyhow, not with the logging road washed out in winter, which was the only other way to get here from the city back then. I felt I sort of owed the rest of them.

Especially I owed Uncle Jacques and Aunty Irina. I had that awful year in 1929 when Mama got the cancer and I lost Bill, that was my husband, he was one of the crew on the *San Juan*, see. They were real kind to me then. Stayed by me when I wanted to just die. Aunty Irina baked bread, and Uncle Jacques fixed the typewriter and told me what I ought to write to the damn insurance people when they weren't going to pay. People who'll help you clean your house for a funeral twice in one year are good friends, believe you me.

Then, if Uncle Jacques hadn't kept the Sheep Canyon trail cleared we'd have had nothing to eat but venison, because there'd have been no way I could have got the buckboard through to Notley for provisions most of the time. It must have been hard work, even for him, just one man with an axe busting up those redwood snags; because of course Lanark was no use. But Uncle Jacques looked after all of us, he and Aunty Irina. They said it was a good thing to have a *human community*.

And, see, once I opened the bar, there was some place to go. Lanark didn't have to stay alone in his shack watching the calendar pages turn brown, and Miss Harlan didn't have to stay alone in her cottage hearing the surf boom and wondering if Billy was going to come walking up out of the water to haunt her. I didn't have to sit alone in my room over the lobby, thinking how my folks would scold me because I hadn't kept the brass and mahogany polished like I ought to have. And Uncle Jacques and Aunty Irina had a nice little human community they could come down and be part of for a while, so they didn't have to sit staring at each other in their place up on Gamboa Ridge.

I had it real cozy here. That potbellied stove in the corner worked then; fire inspector won't let us use it now, but I used to keep it going all night with a big basket of redwood chunks, and I lit the room up bright with kerosene lamps and moved some of the good tables and chairs down from the hotel rooms. Uncle Jacques brought me a radio he'd tinkered with, he called it a wireless, and I don't know if it ran on a battery or what it had in it, but we set it behind the bar and we could get it to pull in music and shows. We had Jack Benny for Canada Dry and Chandu the Magician, and Little Orphan Annie, and even Byrd at the South Pole sometimes.

So Uncle Jacques and Aunty Irina would dance if there was music, and Miss Harlan would sit watching them, and I'd pour out applejack for everybody or maybe some wine. I used to get the wine, good stuff, from a man named Andy Lopez back in Sheep Canyon. Lanark would drink too much of it, but at least he wasn't a mean drunk. We'd all be happy in the bar, warm and bright like it was, though the rest of the hotel was echoing and dark, and outside the night was black and empty too.

And that night it was black with a Pacific gale, but not empty. The wind was driving the sleet sideways at the windows, the wild air blustered and fought in the street like the sailors used to on Saturday nights. Every so often the sky would light up horizon to horizon, purple and white lightning miles long, and for a split second there'd be the town outside the windows like it was day but awful, with the black empty buildings and the black gaps in the sidewalk where the boards had rotted out, and the sea beyond breaking so high there was spume flying up the street, blown on the storm.

You wouldn't think we'd be getting any radio reception at all, but whatever Uncle Jacques had done to that thing, it was picking up a broadcast from some ballroom in Chicago. And damned if the band-leader didn't play *Stormy Weather!* Aunty Irina pulled Uncle Jacques to his feet. He slipped his arm around her and they two-step shuffled up and down in front of the bar, smiling at each other. Miss Harlan watched them, getting a little misty-eyed like she always did at anything romantic, and she sang along with the music. Lanark was pretty sober yet and making eyes at me from his table, and I smiled back at him because he did still use to be handsome then, in a wrecked kind of way.

He had just said, "Damn, Luisa, you throw a nice party," and I was just about to say something sassy back when the music was drowned out by a *crack-crack-crack* and screeching static, so awful Miss Harlan and me put our hands over our ears, and Uncle Jacques and Aunty Irina stopped short and stood apart, looking like a couple of greyhounds on the alert.

Then we heard the call numbers and the voice out of the storm, telling us that some vessel called the *Argive* was in trouble, two aboard, and could the Coast Guard help? And I wondered how the radio had switched itself over to the marine band, but it was Uncle Jacques's radio so I guess it might have done anything. They gave their location as right off Gamboa Rock, and I felt sick then.

See it out there? That's Gamboa Rock. See the way the water kind of boils around it, even on a nice summer day like this, and that little black line of shelf trailing out from it? It used to be a ship-killer, and a mankiller too, and we all knew the *Argive* wasn't ever going to see any Coast Guard rescue, if that was where she was. Not in weather like that.

And in the next big flash of lightning we could see the poor damned thing through the windows, looked like somebody's yacht, rearing on the black water and fighting for sea room. I only saw her for a split second, but I could paint her to this hour the way she looked, almost on her beam-end with her sail flapping. Then the dark swallowed up everything again. There was just a tiny little pinprick light we could still see for a while.

The voice on the radio was high and scared and there wasn't any Coast Guard answering, and pretty soon they began begging anybody to help them. They must have been able to see our light, I guess. It would have broken your heart to have to sit there and listen, the way they were asking for lifeboats and lines, which we didn't have. We couldn't have got to them anyway.

Lanark had lurched to his feet and was staring out into the storm, and I guess he was thinking how he could have made a try of it in the *Sada* if she hadn't been rotting up on sawhorses ever since he'd lost his arm. Miss Harlan had put her fingers in her ears and was rocking back and forth, and I didn't blame her; she didn't take death too well. I was crying myself, and so was Aunty Irina, wringing her hands, and she was staring up at Uncle Jacques with a pleading look in her eyes but his face was set like stone, and he was just shaking his head. They murmured back and forth in what I guessed was their language, until he said "You know we can't, Rinka."

He sat her down and put his arms around her to keep her there. Lanark and I took a couple of lanterns and went out into the street, but the wind nearly knocked us over and there was nothing to see out there anyway, not now. We got as far as the path down the cliff before another burst of lightning showed us the sea coming white up the stairs, and the old platform that had been below torn away with bits of it bobbing in the surge, and the spray jumping high. I think Lanark would still have tried to go down, but I pulled him away and the fool paid attention for once in his life. Coming back I near broke my leg, stepping in a hole where a plank was gone out of the sidewalk. We were gasping and staggering like we'd swum a mile by the time we got back up on the porch here.

It was lovely warm in the bar, but the voice on the radio had stopped. All that was coming through the ether now was a kind of regular beat of static, *pop-pop*, *pop-pop* like that, just a quiet little death knell.

I said, "We all need a drink," and poured out glasses of applejack on the house, because that was the only thing on earth I could do. Miss Harlan and Lanark came and got theirs quick enough, and he backed up to the stove to warm himself. Uncle Jacques let go of Aunty Irina and stood, only to have her reel upright and slap him hard in the face.

He rocked back on his heels. Miss Harlan was beside her right away, she said, "Oh, please don't—it's too awful—" and Aunty Irina fell back in her chair crying.

She said she was sorry, but she couldn't bear sitting there and doing nothing again, when somebody might have been saved. Lanark and I were in a hurry to tell her that nobody could have done anything, that we couldn't even get down into the cove because the stairs were washed out, so she mustn't feel too bad. Uncle Jacques brought her a glass, but she pushed it away and tried to get hold of herself. Looking up at us as though to explain, she said, "We had a child, once."

Uncle Jacques said, "Rinka, easy," but she went on:

"Adopted. My baby Jimmy. We had him for eighteen years. He wanted to enlist. We thought, well, the war's almost over, let him play soldier if he wants to. He'll be safe. There wasn't any record—but we didn't think about the Spanish influenza. He caught it in boot camp in San Diego. Never even got on the troop carrier. They had him all laid out in his uniform by the time we got there . . . Only eighteen."

Real quiet, Uncle Jacques said, "There was nothing we could have done," as though it was something he'd repeated a hundred times, and she snapped back:

"We should never have let him go! Not with that event shadow—" And she started crying again, crying and cursing. Miss Harlan offered her a handkerchief and got her to drink some of her drink, and when she was a little calmer led her off to the ladies' lavatory upstairs to powder her nose. They took one of the kerosene lanterns to find their way, because it was pitch-black beyond the bar threshold. A fresh squall beat against the windows, sounding like thrown gravel.

Uncle Jacques dropped down heavy in his seat, and gulped his drink and what was left of Aunty Irina's. Lanark drank too, but he was staring at Uncle Jacques with a bewildered expression on his face. Finally Lanark said, "Your kid died during the war? But . . . *how* old are you?"

And I thought, oh, hell, because you couldn't trust Lanark with a secret when he drank; that was why we'd never told him the truth about Uncle Jacques and Aunty Irina. Uncle Jacques and I looked at each other and then he cleared his throat and said:

"Irina was talking out of her head. It was her kid brother died in boot camp. We did adopt a baby once, but he died of diphtheria. She went a little crazy over it, Lanark. Most times you wouldn't know, but tonight—"

"Oh," said Lanark, and I could see the wheels turning in his head as he decided that was why Uncle Jacques and Aunty Irina lived up there alone on Gamboa Ridge, and never had visitors or went up to the city for anything.

I said, "Have another drink, Tom," and that worked like it always did, he came right away and let me fill his glass up. It never took much to get that man to stop thinking, poor thing. Just as well, too.

We turned the radio off and I had another drink myself, I was feeling so low, and Lanark drank a bit more and then said we ought to go out at first light to see if there were any bodies washed up at least, so we could bury them Christian until one of us could ride up to the Point Piedras light and have them pass the word to the Coast Guard about the wreck. Uncle Jacques roused himself from his gloom enough to say we'd need to notify the Coast Guard even if we didn't find bodies, so at least the historical record would be correct.

That was about when I saw the face outside.

I am not a screaming woman. I saw enough God-awful things in this town when it was alive to harden me up. You get some hideous accidents in a sawmill, which I'm sure those folks who eat lunch there now it's a shopping arcade would rather not know about, and a redwood log that jumps the side of the flume doesn't leave much of anybody who gets in its way. Then there's the dead hereabouts, that hooker somebody killed in Room 17 who still cries, or poor Billy Molera who used to come up from the sea and go round and round Miss Harlan's cottage at night, moaning for love of her, and leave a trail of seaweed and sand in her garden come morning. You get used to things.

But it did give me a turn, the white face out there beyond the glass, just glimpsed for a second with its black eyeholes and black gaping mouth. Where I was, perched up on my stool behind the bar, I had a good look at it, though neither Lanark nor Uncle Jacques could have seen the thing. I didn't make a sound, just slopped my drink a little.

Uncle Jacques looked up at me sharply. He said, "What's scared you?"

I wasn't going to say, but then we heard it coming up the steps.

Two, three steps from the street onto the porch, it must have crossed right here where I'm sitting now, and pushed that door open, that I hadn't bolted at night

you really rather surrender to him? He's quite a bit more understanding. I'd even call him tolerant, compared to old Budu, who as you know never forgave doubters and weaklings. . . ."

Then Uncle Jacques demanded to know how long this person called Budu had been missing, and when Arion hemmed and hawed he cut him off short with another question, which was: "He was gone before the war, wasn't he?"

And Arion said, "Probably."

Uncle Jacques showed his teeth and said, "I knew it. I knew he'd never have given that order! Who was that behind the wheel of the archduke's car, Arion? Was that Labienus's man? The epidemic, was that Labienus too?"

His voice was louder than thunder, making the walls rattle; Lanark and I had to clutch at our ears, it hurt so. Arion had stopped smiling at him. He said, like you'd order a dog, "Control yourself! Did you really think history could be changed? Labienus simply arranged it so that things fell out to our advantage. Isn't that what the Company's always done? And be glad he developed that virus! Can you imagine how badly the mortals would be faring right now, if those twenty-two million hadn't died of influenza first? Think of all those extra mouths to be fed in the bread lines."

Uncle Jacques said. "But innocents died," and Arion just laughed scornfully and said:

"None of them are innocent."

I swear, Uncle Jacques's eyes were like two coals. He said, "My son died in that epidemic," and Arion said:

"Your *pet mortal* died. They do die. Get over it. Look at you, hiding out here on the edge of nowhere! Labienus is willing to overlook your defection. He'll offer you a much better deal than the Company might, I assure you. Unless you'd like to be deactivated? Is that what you'd prefer, to crawl back on your knees to all-merciful Zeus for oblivion?"

Uncle Jacques just told him to get out.

But Arion said, "Don't be stupid! He knows where you are. What am I going to have to do before you'll see reason?"

He looked at Lanark, who was just sitting there gaping, and then over at me. I wanted to dive behind the bar, but I knew the shotgun wouldn't stop him. Uncle Jacques said, "You're going to kill them anyway."

Arion sighed. He said, "You chose to hide behind them, Lavalle. But you can save them unnecessary suffering, you see? I'm tired, I'm cold, we've got a long walk ahead of us and I want that mortal's coat. Don't make me wait any longer than I have to, or I'll pull off his remaining arm. Let's go, shall we?"

I guess that was when Uncle Jacques took his chance. I couldn't see, because they were both suddenly moving so fast they were only blurs in the air, but things began to smash, and I threw myself down on the floor and just prayed to Jesus.

They don't fight like us. You would think, being the creatures that they are, that they'd shoot lightning at each other, or fight with flaming swords, but it sounded more like a couple of animals snarling and struggling. Once when the fight got too close to me, I saw the wall panel next to my head just burst outward in splinters, and a second later there were four long gashes there, like a bear had clawed it. You can still see it, down near the floor, where we filled it in with wood putty later.

I don't know how long it lasted. Suddenly it got a whole lot louder, as something crashed straight down through the ceiling and there was a new voice screaming, shrill as a banshee. Right after that there was a wet-sounding thud and then it was quiet.

You can bet I was cautious as I got up and peered over the bar. There was Uncle Jacques, sitting up supported by Aunty Irina kneeling beside him, and he had his hand up to his face and it looked like one of his eyes was gone. She was still snarling at Arion, who lay on the floor with his throat slashed open, and she had got a crowbar from somewhere and run it through his chest, too. There was blood everywhere.

Lanark was still where he'd been sitting, wide-eyed and white-faced. I heard footsteps above and looked up to see Miss Harlan peering down through the hole in the ceiling, and by the light of the kerosene lantern she was pretty pale too. God only knows what I looked like, but my hair had come half down and was full of dust and splinters.

I collected myself enough to say, "That's one of those people you're hiding from," to Aunty Irina. She looked up, I guess startled at the sound of a human voice, and after a moment she said yes, it was.

I found a clean rag and brought it for Uncle Jacques, who pressed it to his eye and thanked me. He got unsteadily to his feet, and I saw his coat was about half ripped off his back, just hanging in ribbons. The skin underneath seemed to be healing, though. The edges of his cuts were running together like melting wax.

I said, "At least you got the bastard," and Aunty Irina shook her head grimly. She said:

"He's just in fugue," and I looked at Arion and saw that the wound in his throat was already closing up. Aunty Irina made a disgusted noise. She drew a knife from her boot and cut his jugular again. It only bled a little this time, I guess because he didn't have a lot of blood come back to flow yet.

I asked, "What happens now?" and Uncle Jacques said hoarsely:

"We'll have to run again." He looked around at the mess of the bar and added, "I'm sorry."

Lanark began to cry then, that dry hacking men cry with, and I knew he'd been scared clean out of his mind. Aunty Irina went over to him and took his face in both her hands and kissed him, a deep kiss like they were lovers, and then she stared into his eyes and talked to him quietly. He began to blink and look confused.

Uncle Jacques meanwhile crouched with a groan and took Arion by the feet, starting to drag him backwards toward the door.

Aunty Irina turned quickly and said, "Leave that. You just sit and repair your eye."

He said. "Okay," and sat down, breathing pretty hard. They feel pain as much as we do, you see.

What happened was that we had to do it, me and Aunty Irina, and as we were dragging the body out through the lobby Miss Harlan came down with the lantern and helped us. Every so often as we took him up the road to the sawmill, he'd start moving a little, and we'd have to stop while Aunty Irina cut him again. The wind almost blew out the lantern and the rain soaked us through. Still, we got him up there at last.

We found a couple of old rusty saws in an office, and they didn't work real well, but Aunty Irina showed us how to do it so he'd come apart in a couple of places. She explained how nothing could kill him, but the more damage we did, the longer it'd be before he could piece himself together to come after her and Uncle Jacques. So we did a lot to him. It was hard work, just three women there working by one kerosene lantern, and the rain coming through the roof the whole time in steady streams.

You don't think women could do something like that? You don't know the things we have to do, sometimes. And knowing the kind of creature he was made it easier.

Most of him we dropped down a pit, and used the old crane to send a couple of redwood logs after him, and I reckon they weighed a couple of tons apiece. I'm not telling you where we put the rest of him.

It might have been near dawn when we finished and came back, but it was still black as midnight, and the storm wasn't letting up. There were two empty bottles on the bar and Lanark had passed out on the floor. Uncle Jacques had made himself an eyepatch. He said it'd be likely another day before he got his eye working again.

I offered to fix them some breakfast before they set out. They thanked me kindly but said they had better not. They gave us some careful instructions, me and Miss Harlan, about what to look out for and what to say to anybody else who came looking around. They told us some other stuff, too, like what that awful Hitler was going to do pretty soon and about International Business Machines stocks. Cut off from the world like we were, we couldn't make a lot of use of it, but it was nice of them.

And they apologized. They said they'd only been trying to make the world a better place for people, and it had all gone wrong somehow.

I got one of Papa's coats down for Uncle Jacques, and he shrugged out of the bloody torn one he had on. I burned it in the stove later. It flared up in some strange colors, I tell you.

Then they walked out together into that awful night, poor people, and we never saw them again.

When Lanark sobered up he said he didn't remember anything, but he never asked any questions either, like why there was a hole in the ceiling or where all the blood had come from. We cleaned up and mended as best we could. One thing we had plenty of in this town was lumber, anyhow.

That's all. The radio worked for a few years, and when it finally broke we couldn't fix it, so I put it away in the attic. We missed it, especially once the war started, but maybe we were better off not worrying about that, with what we'd been told.

Lanark never talked about what happened in so many words, but one time when he was sober he told me he'd figured out that Uncle Jacques and Aunty Irina must have been Socialists, because of the way they talked, and maybe J. Edgar Hoover had come after them. I told him he was probably right. Anyway nobody else ever came sniffing around after them. There was a wildfire across Gamboa Ridge a few years later, 1938 that would have been, and now there's only an old rusted stove back in the manzanita to show where their house was.

Lanark drank more after that, but why shouldn't he, and it got so I'd have to walk him home nights to be sure he got there. Sometimes he kissed me at the door, but he was too broken up to do anything else. Eventually I'd have to go make sure he was still alive in the mornings, too. One morning he wasn't. That was back in 1942, I guess.

Miss Harlan lived on a good long time in that cottage, kept Billy waiting until 1957 before she went off into the sea with him. At least, I imagine that's what happened; the door was standing open, the house all full of damp, and there was a trail of sand clear from her room down to the beach, like confetti and rice after a wedding. Nobody haunts the place now. That snooty woman sells her incenses and herbal teas out of it, but I have to say she keeps the garden nice.

So I'm the last one that knows.

I kept the bar open. Right after the war the highway was put through, and those young drifters found the shacks that didn't belong to anybody and started living in them, with their beat parties and poetry. Then later the hippies came in, and pretty soon rich people from San Francisco discovered the place, and it was all upscale after that.

Not that it's a bad thing. When Kevin and Jon offered me all that money for the hotel, I was real happy. Being the way they are, I knew they'd fix everything up beautiful, which they have, too, mahogany and brass all restored so I don't have to feel guilty about it anymore. They're kind to me. I stay on in my old room and they call me Nana Luisa, and that's nice.

They sit me out here in this chair so I can watch everything going on, all along the street, and sometimes they'll bring guests and introduce me as the town's official history expert, and I get interviewed for newspapers now and then. I tell them about the old days, just the kinds of stuff they want to hear. I listen more than I talk. Mostly I just like to watch people.

It's pretty now, with the flower gardens and art galleries, and the cottages all lived in by rich folks with sports cars, and you'd never think there'd been whorehouses or saloon brawls here. The biggest noise is the town council complaining about the traffic jams we get weekends. People talk about how Harlan's Landing was such an unspoiled weekend getaway once, and how more tourists are going to ruin it. They don't know what ruin is.

I look out my window at night and there's lights in all the little houses, the *human community* all nice and cozy and thinking they're here to stay, but that cold black night out there is just as heartless as it was, and a lot bigger than they are. Anything could happen. I know. The lights could go out, dwindling one by one or all at once, and there'd be nothing but the sea and the dark trees behind us, and maybe one roomful of folks left behind, lighting a lamp in the window so they don't feel so alone.

But I don't worry much about Arion.

Even with all the restoration and remodeling, even with them selling T-shirts and kites and ice cream out of the sawmill now, nobody's ever found any of him. He's still down there, under that new redwood decking, and sometimes at night I hear him moaning, though people think it's just the wind in a sea cave. He's growing back together, or growing himself some new parts; Aunty Irina said he might do either.

He will get out one of these days, but I figure I'll be dead by the time he does. That's one of the advantages to being a mortal.

I do worry about my sweetie boys, I'm afraid this AIDS epidemic will get them. I wonder if it's something to do with that Labienus fellow, the one Uncle Jacques told me cooks up epidemics because he hates mortal folk. And I wonder if Uncle Jacques and Aunty Irina found a new place to hide, some shelter in out of the black night, and how the war for power over the Earth is going.

Because that's what it is, see. I'm not crazy, honey. It's all there in the Bible. For some have entertained angels unawares, but some folks get let in on their secrets, you follow me? And it isn't a comforting thing to know the truth about angels.

the millennium party

WALTER JON WILLIAMS

Walter Jon Williams was born in Minnesota and now lives in Albuquerque, New Mexico. His short fiction has appeared frequently in Asimov's Science Fiction, *as well as in* The Magazine of Fantasy and Science Fiction, Wheel of Fortune, Global Dispatches, Alternate Outlaws, *and in other markets, and has been gathered in the collections* Facets *and* Frankensteins and Other Foreign Devils. *His novels include* Ambassador of Progress, Knight Moves, Hardwired, The Crown Jewels, Voice Of The Whirlwind. House Of Shards, Days of Atonement, *and* Aristoi. *His novel* Metropolitan *garnered wide critical acclaim in 1996 and was one of the most talked-about books of the year. His most recent books are a sequel to* Metropolitan, City on Fire, *a huge disaster thriller,* The Rift, *and a* Star Trek *novel,* Destiny's Way. *He won a long-overdue Nebula Award in 2001 for his story* "Daddy's World." *His stories have appeared in our Third through Sixth, Ninth, Eleventh, Twelfth, Fourteenth, and Seventeenth Annual Collections.*

Here he gives us a short, sharp look at a future where there's a place for everything, and everything's in its place . . .

Darien was making another annotation to his lengthy commentary on the **Tenjou Cycle** when his Marshal reminded him that his wedding anniversary would soon be upon him. This was the thousandth anniversary—a full millennium with Clarisse!—and he knew the celebration would have to be a special one.

He finished his annotation and then de-slotted the savant brain that contained the cross-referenced database that allowed him to manage his work. In its place he slotted the brain labeled **Clarisse/Passion,** the brain that contained memories of his time with his wife. Not all memories, however: the contents had been carefully purged of any of the last thousand years' disagreements, arguments, disappointments, infidelities, and misconnections. . . . The memories were only those of love, ardor, obsession, passion, and release, all the most intense and glorious moments of their thousand years together, all the times when Darien was drunk on Clarisse, intoxicated with her scent, her brilliance, her wit.

The other moments, the less-than-perfect ones, he had stored elsewhere, in one brain or another, but he rarely reviewed them. Darien saw no reason why his mind should contain anything that was less than perfect.

Flushed with the sensations that now poured through his mind, overwhelmed by the delirium of love, Darien began to work on his present for his wife.

When the day came, Darien and Clarisse met in an environment that she had designed. This was an arrangement that had existed for centuries, ever since they both realized that Clarisse's sense of spacial relationships was better than his. The environment was a masterpiece, an apartment built on several levels, like little terraces, that broke the space up into smaller areas that created intimacy without sacrificing the sense of spaciousness. All of the furniture was designed for no more than two people. Darien recognized on the walls a picture he'd given Clarisse on her four hundredth birthday, an elaborate, antique dial telephone from their honeymoon apartment in Paris, and a Japanese paper doll of a woman in an antique kimono, a present he had given her early in their acquaintance, when they'd haunted antique stores together.

It was Darien's task to complete the arrangement. He added an abstract bronze sculpture of a horse and jockey that Clarisse had given him for his birthday, a puzzle made of wire and butter-smooth old wood, and a view from the terrace, a view of Rio de Janeiro at night. Because his sense of taste and smell were more subtle than Clarisse's, he by standing arrangement populated the apartment with scents, lilac for the parlor, sweet magnolia and bracing cypress on the terrace, a combination of sandalwood and spice for the bedroom, and a mixture of vanilla and cardamom for the dining room, a scent subtle enough so that it wouldn't interfere with the meal.

When Clarisse entered he was dressed in a tailcoat, white tie, waistcoat, and diamond studs. She had matched his period elan with a Worth gown of shining blue satin, tiny boots that buttoned up the ankles, and a dashing fall of silk about her throat. Her tawny hair was pinned up, inviting him to kiss the nape of her neck, an indulgence which he permitted himself almost immediately.

Darien seated Clarisse on the cushions and mixed cocktails. He asked her about her work: a duplicate of one of her brains was on the mission to 55 Cancri, sharing piloting missions with other duplicates: if a habitable planet was discovered, then a new Clarisse would be built on site to pioneer the new world.

Darien had created the meal in consultation with Clarisse's Marshal. They began with mussels steamed open in white wine and herbs, then went on to a salad of fennel, orange, and red cranberry. Next came roasted green beans served alongside a chicken cooked simply in the oven, flamed in cognac, then served in a creamy port wine reduction sauce. At the end was a raspberry Bavarian cream. Each dish was one that Darien had experienced at another time in his long life, considered perfect, stored in one brain or another, and now recreated down to the last scent and sensation.

After coffee and conversation on the terrace, Clarisse led Darien to the bedroom. He enjoyed kneeling at her feet and unlacing every single button of those damned Victorian boots. His heart brimmed with passion and lust, and he rose from his knees to embrace her. Wrapped in the sandalwood-scented silence of their suite, they feasted till dawn on one another's flesh.

Their life together, Darien reflected, was perfection itself: one enchanted jewel after another, hanging side-by-side on a thousand-year string.

After juice and shirred eggs in the morning, Darien kissed the inside of Clarisse's wrist, and saw her to the door. His brain had recorded every single rapturous instant of their time together.

And then, returning to his work, Darien de-slotted **Clarisse/Passion,** and put it on the shelf for another year.

Turquoise Days

Alastair Reynolds

New writer Alastair Reynolds is a frequent contributor to Interzone, *and has also sold to* Asimov's Science Fiction, Spectrum SF, *and elsewhere. His first novel,* Revelation Space, *was widely hailed as one of the major SF books of the year; it was followed by a sequel, also attracting much notice,* Chasm City. *His most recent work is another big new novel,* Redemption Ark. *His stories have appeared in our Fifteenth, Seventeenth, Eighteenth, and Nineteenth Annual Collections. A professional scientist with a Ph.D. in astronomy, he comes from Wales, but lives in the Netherlands, where he works for the European Space Agency.*

Here he takes us on a visit to a serene, peaceful, quiet little planet, a sea-world, an idyllic world nearly covered by tropical turquoise oceans. But as we shall see, placid as things seem, you never know what's lurking beneath the surface. Or when it's going to come out to get you . . .

I

Naqi Okpik waited until her sister was safely asleep before she stepped onto the railed balcony that circled the gondola.

It was the most perfectly warm and still summer night in months. Even the breeze caused by the airship's motion was warmer than usual, as soft against her cheek as the breath of an attentive lover. Above, yet hidden by the black curve of the vacuum bladder, the two moons were nearly at their fullest. Microscopic creatures sparkled a hundred metres under the airship, great schools of them daubing galaxies against the profound black of the sea. Spirals, flukes and arms of luminescence wheeled and coiled as if in thrall to secret music.

Naqi looked to the rear, where the airship's ceramic-jacketed sensor pod carved a twinkling furrow. Pinks and rubies and furious greens sparkled in the wake. Occasionally they darted from point to point with the nervous motion of kingfishers. As ever she was alert to anything unusual in movements of the messenger sprites, anything that might merit a note in the latest circular, or even a full-blown article in one of the major journals of Juggler studies. But there was nothing odd happening tonight; no yet-to-be-catalogued forms or behaviour patterns, nothing that might indicate more significant Pattern Juggler activity.

She walked around the airship's balcony until she had reached the stern, where the submersible sensor pod was tethered by a long fibre-optic dragline. Naqi pulled a long hinged stick from her pocket, flicked it open in the manner of a courtesan's fan, and then waved it close to the winch assembly. The default watercoloured lilies and sea serpents melted away, replaced by tables of numbers, sinuous graphs and trembling histograms. A glance established that there was nothing surprising here either, but the data would still form a useful calibration set for other experiments.

As she closed the fan—delicately, for it was worth almost as much as the airship itself—Naqi reminded herself that it was a day since she had gathered the last batch of incoming messages. Rot had taken out the connection between the antenna and the gondola during the last expedition, and since then collecting the messages had become a chore, to be taken in turns or traded for less tedious tasks.

Naqi gripped a handrail and swung out behind the airship. Here the vacuum bladder overhung the gondola by only a metre, and a grilled ladder allowed her to climb around the overhang and scramble onto the flat top of the bag. She moved gingerly, bare feet against rusting rungs, doing her best not to disturb Mina. The airship rocked and creaked a little as she found her balance on the top and then was again silent and still. The churning of its motors was so quiet that Naqi had long ago filtered the sound from her experience.

All was calm, beautifully so.

In the moonlight the antenna was a single dark flower rising from the broad back of the bladder. Naqi started moving along the railed catwalk that led to it, steadying herself as she went but feeling much less vertigo than would have been the case in daytime.

Then she froze, certain that she was being watched.

Just within Naqi's peripheral vision appeared a messenger sprite. It had flown to the height of the airship and was now shadowing it from a distance of ten or twelve metres. Naqi gasped, delighted and unnerved at the same time. Apart from dead specimens this was the first time Naqi had ever seen a sprite this close. The organism had the approximate size and morphology of a terrestrial hummingbird, yet it glowed like a lantern. Naqi recognised it immediately as a long-range packet carrier. Its belly would be stuffed with data coded into tightly packed wads of RNA, locked within microscopic protein capsomeres. The packet carrier's head was a smooth teardrop, patterned with luminous pastel markings but lacking any other detail save for two black eyes positioned above the midline. Inside the head was a cluster of neurones, which encoded the positions of the brightest circumpolar stars. Other than that, sprites had only the most rudimentary kind of intelligence. They existed only to shift information between nodal points in the ocean when the usual chemical signalling pathways were deemed too slow or imprecise. The sprite would die when it reached its destination, consumed by microscopic organisms that would unravel and process the information stored in the capsomeres.

And yet Naqi had the acute sense that it was watching her. Not just the airship, but *her*, with a kind of watchful curiosity that made the hairs on the back of her neck bristle. And then—just at the point when the feeling of scrutiny had become unsettling—the sprite whipped sharply away from the airship. Naqi watched it descend back toward the ocean and then coast above the surface, bobbing now and then like a skipping stone. She remained still for several more minutes, convinced that something of significance had happened and yet also aware of how subjective the experience had been; how unimpressive it would seem if she tried to explain it to Mina tomorrow. Anyway, Mina was the one with the special bond to the ocean, wasn't she? Mina was the one who scratched her arms at night; Mina was the one who had too high a conformal index to be allowed into the swimmer corps. It was always Mina.

It was never Naqi.

The antenna's metre-wide dish was anchored to a squat plinth inset with weatherproofed controls and readouts. It was century-old *Pelican* technology, like the airship and the fan. Many of the controls and displays were dead, but the unit was still able to lock onto the functioning satellites. Naqi flicked open the fan and copied the latest feeds into the fan's remaining memory. Then she knelt down next to the plinth, propped the fan on her knees and sifted through the messages and news summaries of the last day. A handful of reports had arrived from friends in Prachuap-Pangnirtung and Umingmaktok snowflake cities, another from an old boyfriend in the swimmer corps station on Narathiwat atoll. He had sent her a list of jokes that were already in wide circulation. She scrolled down the list, grimacing more than grinning, before finally managing a half-hearted chuckle at one that had escaped her. Then there were a dozen digests from various special interest groups related to the Jugglers, along with a request from a journal editor that she critique a paper. Naqi skimmed the paper's abstract, judging that she was probably capable of reviewing it.

She scrolled through the remaining messages. There was a note from Dr Sivaraksa saying that her formal application to work on the Moat project had been received and was now under consideration. There had been no official interview, but Naqi had met Sivaraksa a few weeks earlier when the two of them happened to be in Umingmaktok. Sivaraksa had been in an encouraging mood during the meeting, though Naqi couldn't say whether that was due to her having given a good impression or the fact that Sivaraksa had just had his tapeworm swapped for a nice new one. But Sivaraksa's message said she could expect to hear the result in a day or two. Idly, Naqi wondered how she would break the news to Mina if she was offered the job. Mina was critical of the whole idea of the Moat and would probably take a dim view of her sister having anything to do with it.

Scrolling down farther, she read another message from a scientist in Qaanaaq requesting access to some calibration data she had obtained earlier in the summer. Then there were four or five automatic weather advisories, drafts of two papers she was contributing to, and an invitation to attend the amicable divorce of Kugluktuk and Gjoa, scheduled to take place in three weeks time. Following that there was a summary of the latest worldwide news—an unusually bulky file—and then there was nothing. No further messages had arrived for eight hours.

There was nothing particularly unusual about that—the ailing network was always going down—but for the second time that night the back of Naqi's neck tingled. Something must have happened, she thought.

She opened the news summary and started reading. Five minutes later she was waking Mina.

"I don't think I want to believe it," Mina Okpik said.

Naqi scanned the heavens, dredging childhood knowledge of the stars. With some minor adjustment to allow for parallax, the old constellations were still more or less valid when seen from Turquoise.

"That's it, I think."

"What?" Mina said, still sleepy.

Naqi waved her hand at a vague area of the sky, pinned between Scorpius and Hercules. "Ophiuchus. If our eyes were sensitive enough, we'd be able to see it now; a little prick of blue light."

"I've had enough of little pricks for one lifetime," Mina said, tucking her arms around her knees. Her hair was the same pure black as Naqi's, but trimmed into a severe, spiked crop which made her look younger or older depending on the light. She wore black shorts and a shirt that left her arms bare. Luminous tattoos, in emerald and indigo, spiralled around the piebald marks of random fungal invasion that covered her arms, thighs, neck and cheeks. The fullness of the moons caused the fungal patterns to glow a little themselves, shimmering with the same emerald and indigo hues. Naqi had no tattoos and scarcely any fungal patterns of her own, and could not help feel slightly envious of her sister's adornments.

Mina continued: "But seriously, you don't think it might be a mistake?"

"I don't think so, no. See what it says there? They detected it weeks ago, but they kept quiet until now so that they could make more measurements."

"I'm surprised there wasn't a rumour."

Naqi nodded. "They kept the lid on it pretty well. Which doesn't mean there isn't going to be a lot of trouble."

"Mm. And they think this blackout is going to help?"

"My guess is official traffic's still getting through. They just don't want the rest of us clogging up the network with endless speculation."

"Can't blame us for that, can we? I mean, everyone's going to be guessing, aren't they?"

"Maybe they'll announce themselves before very long," Naqi said doubtfully.

While they had been speaking the airship had passed into a zone of the sea largely devoid of bioluminescent surface life. Such zones were almost as common as the nodal regions where the network was thickest, like the gaping voids between clusters of galaxies. The wake of the sensor pod was almost impossible to pick out, and the darkness around them was absolute, only occasionally relieved by the mindless errand of a solitary messenger sprite.

Mina said: "And if they don't?"

"Then I guess we're all in a lot more trouble than we'd like."

For the first time in a century a ship was approaching Turquoise, commencing its deceleration from interstellar cruise speed. The flare of the lighthugger's exhaust was pointed straight at the Turquoise system. Measurement of the Doppler shift of the flame showed that the vessel was still two years out, but that was hardly any time at all on Turquoise. The ship had yet to announce itself, but even if it turned out to have nothing but benign intentions—a short trade stopover, perhaps—the effect on Turquoise society would be incalculable. Everyone knew of the troubles that followed the arrival of the *Pelican in Impiety*. When the Ultras moved into orbit there had been much unrest below. Spies had undermined lucrative trade deals. Cities had jockeyed for prestige, competing for technological tidbits. There had been hasty marriages and equally hasty separations. A century later, old enmities smouldered just beneath the surface of cordial intercity politics.

It wouldn't be any better next time.

"Look," Mina said. "It doesn't have to be all that bad. They might not even want to talk to us. Didn't a ship pass through the system about seventy years ago, without so much as a by-your-leave?"

Naqi nodded—it was mentioned in a sidebar to one of the main articles. "They had engine trouble, or something. But the experts say there's no sign of anything like that this time."

"So they've come to trade. What have we got to offer them that we didn't have last time?"

"Not much, I suppose."

Mina nodded knowingly. "A few works of art that probably won't travel very well. Ten-hour-long nose-flute symphonies, anyone?" She pulled a face. "That's supposedly my culture, and even I can't stand it. What else? A handful of discoveries about the Jugglers, which have more than likely been replicated elsewhere a dozen times. Technology, medicine? Forget it."

"They must think we have something worth coming here for," Naqi said. "Whatever it is, we'll just have to wait and see, won't we? It's only two years."

"I expect you think that's quite a long time," Mina said.

"Actually . . ."

Mina froze.

"Look!"

Something whipped past in the night, far below, then a handful of them, then a dozen, and then a whole bright squadron. Messenger sprites, Naqi diagnosed. But she had never seen so many of them moving at once, and on what was so evidently the same errand. Against the darkness of the ocean the lights were mesmerising: curling and weaving, swapping positions and occasionally veering far from the main pack before arcing back toward the swarm. Again one of the sprites climbed to the altitude of the airship, loitering for a few moments on fanning wings before whipping off to rejoin the others. The swarm receded, becoming a tight ball of fireflies and then only a pale globular smudge. Naqi watched until she was certain that the last sprite had vanished into the night.

"Wow," Mina said quietly.

"Have you ever seen anything like that?"

"Never."

"Bit funny that it should happen tonight, wouldn't you say?"

"Don't be silly," Mina said. "The Jugglers can't possibly know about the ship."

"We don't know that for sure. Most people heard about this ship hours ago. That's more than enough time for someone to have swum."

Mina conceded her younger sister's point with a delicate provisional nod of the head. "Still, information flow isn't usually that clear-cut. The Jugglers store patterns, but they seldom show any sign of comprehending actual content. We're dealing with a mindless biological archiving system, a museum without a curator."

"That's one view."

Mina shrugged. "I'd love to be proved otherwise."

"Well, do you think we should try following them? I know we can't track sprites over any distance, but we might be able to keep up for a few hours before we drain the batteries."

"We wouldn't learn much."

"We wouldn't know until we tried," Naqi said, gritting her teeth. "Come on — it's got to be worth a go, hasn't it? I reckon that swarm moved a bit slower than a single sprite. We'd at least have enough for a report, wouldn't we?"

Mina shook her head. "All we'd have is a single observation with a little bit of speculation thrown in. You know we can't publish that sort of thing. And anyway — assuming that sprite swarm did have something to do with the ship — there are going to be hundreds of similar sightings tonight."

"I was just hoping it might take our minds off the news."

"Perhaps it would. But it would also make us unforgivably late for our target." Mina dropped the tone of her voice, making an obvious effort to sound reasonable. "Look — I understand your curiosity. I feel it as well. But the chances are it was either a statistical fluke or part of a global event everyone else will have had a much better chance to study. Either way we can't contribute anything useful, so we might as well just forget about it." She rubbed at the marks on her forearm, tracing the paisley-patterned barbs and whorls of glowing colouration. "And I'm tired, and we have several busy days ahead of us. I think we just need to put this one down to experience, all right?"

"Fine," Naqi said.

"I'm sorry, but I just know we'd be wasting our time."

"I said fine." Naqi stood up and steadied herself on the railing that traversed the length of the airship's back.

"Where are you going?"

"To sleep. Like you said, we've got a busy day coming up. We'd be fools to waste time chasing a fluke, wouldn't we?"

An hour after dawn they crossed out of the dead zone. The sea below began to thicken with floating life, becoming soupy and torpid. A kilometre or so farther in and the soup showed ominous signs of structure: a blue-green stew of ropy strands and wide kelplike plates. They suggested the floating, half-digested entrails of embattled sea monsters.

Within another kilometre the floating life had become a dense vegetative raft, stinking of brine and rotting cabbage. Within another kilometre of that the raft had thickened to the point where the underlying sea was only intermittently visible. The air above the raft was humid, hot and pungent with microscopic irritants. The raft itself was possessed of a curiously beguiling motion, bobbing and writhing and gyring according to the ebb and flow of weirdly localised current systems. It was as if many invisible spoons stirred a great bowl of spinach. Even the shadow of the airship—pushed far ahead of it by the low sun—had some influence on the movement of the material. The Pattern Juggler biomass scurried and squirmed to evade the track of the shadow, and the peculiar purposefulness of the motion reminded Naqi of an octopus she had seen in the terrestrial habitats aquarium on Umingmaktok, squeezing its way through impossibly small gaps in the glass prison of its tank.

Presently they arrived at the precise centre of the circular raft. It spread away from them in all directions, hemmed by a distant ribbon of sparkling sea. It felt as if the airship had come to rest above an island, as fixed and ancient as any geological feature. The island even had a sort of geography: humps and ridges and depressions sculpted into the cloying texture of layered biomass. But there were few islands on Turquoise, especially at this latitude, and the Juggler node was only a few days old. Satellites had detected its growth a week earlier, and Mina and Naqi had been sent to investigate. They were under strict instructions simply to hover above the island and deploy a handful of tethered sensors. If the node showed any signs of being unusual, a more experienced team would be sent out from Umingmaktok by high-speed dirigible. Most nodes dispersed within twenty to thirty days, so there was always a sense of urgency. They might even send trained swimmers, eager to dive into the sea and open their minds to alien communion. Ready to—as they said—*ken* the ocean.

But first things first. Chances were this node would turn out to be interesting rather than exceptional.

"Morning," Mina said, when Naqi approached her. Mina was swabbing the sensor pod she had reeled in earlier, collecting green mucous that had adhered to its ceramic teardrop. All human artifacts eventually succumbed to biological attack from the ocean, although ceramics were the most resilient.

"You're cheerful," Naqi said, trying to make the statement sound matter-of-fact rather than judgmental.

"Aren't you? It's not everyone gets a chance to study a node up this close. Make the most of it, sis. The news we got last night doesn't change what we have to do today."

Naqi scraped the back of her hand across her nose. Now that the airship was above the node she was breathing vast numbers of aerial organisms into her lungs with each breath. The smell was redolent of ammonia and decomposing vegetation. It required an intense effort of will not to keep rubbing her eyes more raw than was already the case. "Do you see anything unusual?"

"Bit early to say."

"So that's a 'no,' then."

"You can't learn much without probes, Naqi." Mina dipped a swab into a collection bag, squeezing tight the plastic seal. Then she dropped the bag into a bucket between her feet. "Oh, wait. I saw another of those swarms, after you'd gone to sleep."

"I thought you were the one complaining about being tired."

Mina dug out a fresh swab and rubbed vigorously at a deep olive smear on the side of the sensor. "I picked up my messages, that's all. Tried again this morning, but the blackout still hadn't been lifted. I picked up a few shortwave radio signals from the closest cities, but they were just transmitting a recorded message from the Snowflake Council: stay tuned and don't panic."

"So let's hope we don't find anything significant here," Naqi said, "because we won't be able to report it if we do."

"They're bound to lift the blackout soon. In the meantime I think we have enough measurements to keep us busy. Did you find that spiral sweep program in the airship's avionics box?"

"I haven't looked for it," Naqi said, certain that Mina had never mentioned such a thing before. "But I'm sure I can program something from scratch in a few minutes."

"Well, let's not waste any more time than necessary. Here." Smiling, she offered Naqi the swab, its tip laden with green slime. "You take over this, and I'll go and dig out the program."

Naqi took the swab after a moment's delay.

"Of course. Prioritise tasks according to ability, right?"

"That's not what I meant," Mina said soothingly. "Look. Let's not argue, shall we? We were best friends until last night. I just thought it would be quicker . . ." She trailed off and shrugged. "You know what I mean. I know you blame me for not letting us follow the sprites, but we had no choice but to come here. Understand that, will you? Under any other circumstances . . ."

"I understand," Naqi said, realising as she did how sullen and childlike she sounded; how much she was playing the petulant younger sister. The worst of it was that she knew Mina was right. At dawn it all seemed much clearer.

"Do you? Really?"

Naqi nodded, feeling the perverse euphoria that came with an admission of defeat. "Yes. Really. We'd have been wrong to chase them."

Mina sighed. "I was tempted, you know. I just didn't want you to see how tempted I was, or else you'd have found a way to convince me."

"I'm that persuasive?"

"Don't underestimate yourself, sis. I know I never would." Mina paused and took back the swab. "I'll finish this. Can you handle the sweep program?"

Naqi smiled. She felt better now. The tension between them would still take a little while to lift, but at least things were easier now. Mina was right about something else: they were best friends, not just sisters.

"I'll handle it," Naqi said.

Naqi stepped through the hermetic curtain into the air-conditioned cool of the gondola. She closed the door, rubbed her eyes, and then sat down at the navigator's station. The airship had flown itself automatically from Umingmaktok, adjusting its course to take cunning advantage of jet streams and weather fronts. Now it was in hovering mode: once or twice a minute the electrically driven motors purred, stabilising the craft against gusts of wind generated by the microclimate above the Juggler node. Naqi called up the current avionics program, a menu of options appearing on a flat screen. The options quivered; Naqi thumped the screen with the back of her hand until the display behaved itself. Then she scrolled down through the other flight sequences, but there was no preprogrammed spiral loaded into the current avionics suite. Naqi rummaged around in the background files, but there was nothing to help her there either. She was about to start hacking something together—at a push it would take her half an hour to assemble a routine—when she remembered that she had once backed up some earlier avionics files onto the fan. She had no idea if they were still there, or even if there was anything useful among the cache, but it was probably worth taking the time to find out. The fan lay closed on a bench, where Mina must have left it after she verified that the blackout was still in force.

Naqi grabbed the fan and spread it open across her lap. To her surprise, it was still active: instead of the usual watercolour patterns the display showed the messages she had been scrolling through earlier.

She looked closer and frowned. These were not her messages at all. She was looking at the messages Mina had copied onto the fan during the night. At this realisation Naqi felt an immediate prickle of guilt. She knew that she should snap the fan shut, or at the very least close her sister's mail and delve into her own area of the fan. But she did neither of those things. Telling herself that it was only what anyone else would have done, she accessed the final message in the list and examined its incoming time-stamp. To within a few minutes, it had arrived at the same time as the final message Naqi had received.

Mina had been telling the truth when she said that the blackout was continuing.

Naqi glanced up. Through the window of the gondola she could see the back of her sister's head, bobbing up and down as she checked winches along the side.

Naqi looked at the body of the message. It was nothing remarkable, just an automated circular from one of the Juggler special-interest groups. Something about neurotransmitter chemistry.

She exited the circular, getting back to the list of incoming messages. She told herself that she had done nothing shameful so far. If she closed Mina's mail now, she would have nothing to feel guilty about.

But a name she recognized jumped out at her from the list of messages: Dr Jotah Sivaraksa, manager of the Moat project. The man she had met in Umingmaktok, glowing with renewed vitality after his yearly worm change. What could Mina possibly want with Sivaraksa?

She opened the message, read it.

It was exactly as she had feared, and yet not dared to believe.

Sivaraksa was responding to Mina's request to work on the Moat. The tone of the message was conversational, in stark contrast to the businesslike response Naqi had received. Sivaraksa informed her sister that her request had been appraised favourably, and that while there were still one or two other candidates to be considered, the expectation was that Mina would emerge as the most convincing applicant. Even if this turned out not to be the case, Sivaraksa continued—and that outcome was not thought very likely—Mina's name would be at the top of the list when further vacancies became available. In short, she was more or less guaranteed a chance to work on the Moat within the year.

Naqi read the message again, just in case there was some highly subtle detail that threw the entire thing into a different, more benign light.

Then she snapped shut the fan with a sense of profound fury. She placed it back where it was, exactly as it had been.

Mina pushed her head through the hermetic curtain.

"How's it coming along?"

"Fine . . ." Naqi said. Her voice sounded drained of emotion even to herself.

"Got that routine cobbled together?"

"Coming along," Naqi said.

"Something the matter?"

"No . . ." Naqi forced a smile. "No. Just working through the details. Have it ready in a few minutes."

"Good. Can't wait to start the sweep. We're going to get some beautiful data, sis. And I think this is going to be a significant node. Maybe the largest this season. Aren't you glad it came our way?"

"Thrilled," Naqi said, before returning to her work.

Thirty specialised probes hung on telemetric cables from the underside of the gondola, dangling like the venom-tipped stingers of some grotesque aerial jellyfish. The probes sniffed the air metres above the Juggler biomass, or skimmed the fuzzy green surface of the formation. Weighted plumb lines penetrated to the sea beneath the raft, sipping the organism-infested depths dozens of metres under the node. Radar mapped larger structures embedded within the node—dense kernels of compacted biomass, or huge cavities and tubes of implacable function—while sonar graphed the topology of the many sinewy organic cables which plunged into darkness, umbilicals anchoring the node to the seabed. Smaller nodes drew most of their energy from sunlight and the breakdown of sugars and fats in the sea's other floating microorganisms but the larger formations—which had a vastly higher information-processing burden—needed to tap belching aquatic fissures, active rifts in the ocean bed kilometres under the waves. Cold water was pumped down each umbilical by peristaltic compression waves, heated by being circulated in the superheated thermal environment of the underwater volcanoes, and then pumped back to the surface.

In all this sensing activity, remarkably little physical harm was done to the extended organism itself. The biomass sensed the approach of the probes and rearranged itself so that they passed through with little obstruction, even those scything lines that reached into the water. Energy was obviously being consumed to avoid the organism sustaining damage, and by implication the measurements must therefore have had some effect on the node's information processing efficiency. The effect was likely to be small, however, and since the node was already subject to constant changes in its architecture—some probably intentional, and some probably forced on it by other factors in its environment—there appeared to be little point in worrying about the harm caused by the human investigators. Ultimately, so much was still guesswork. Although the swimmer teams had learned a great deal about the Pattern Jugglers' encoded information, almost everything else about them—how and why they stored the neural patterns, and to what extent the patterns were subject to subsequent postprocessing—remained unknown. And those were merely the immediate questions. Beyond that were the real mysteries, which everyone wanted to solve, but were simply beyond the scope of immediate academic study. What they would learn today could not be expected to shed any light on those profundities. A single data point—even a single clutch of measurements—could not usually prove or disprove anything. But nonetheless it might later turn out to play a vital role in some chain of argument, even if it was only in the biasing of some statistical distribution closer to one hypothesis than another. Science, as Naqi had long since realised, was as much a swarming, social process as it was something driven by ecstatic moments of personal discovery.

It was something she was proud to be part of.

The spiral sweep continued uneventfully, the airship chugging around in a gently widening circle. Morning shifted to early afternoon, and then the sun began to climb down toward the horizon, bleeding pale orange into the sky through soft-edged cracks in the cloud cover. For hours Naqi and Mina studied the incoming results, the ever-sharper scans of the node appearing on screens throughout the gondola. They discussed the results cordially enough, but Naqi could not stop thinking about Mina's betrayal. She took a spiteful pleasure in testing the extent to which her sister would lie, deliberately forcing the conversation around to Dr Sivaraksa and the project he steered.

"I hope I don't end up like one of those deadwood bureaucrats," Naqi said, when they were discussing the way their careers might evolve. "You know, like Sivaraksa." She observed Mina pointedly, yet giving nothing away. "I read some of his old papers; he used to be pretty good once. But now look at him."

"It's easy to say that," Mina said. "But I bet he doesn't like being away from the frontline any more than we would. But someone has to manage these big projects. Wouldn't you rather it was someone who'd at least been a scientist?"

"You sound like you're defending him. Next you'll be telling me you think the Moat is a good idea."

"I'm not defending Sivaraksa," Mina said. "I'm just saying . . ." She eyed her sister with a sudden glimmer of suspicion. Had she guessed that Naqi knew? "Never mind. Sivaraksa can fight his own battles. We've got work to do."

"Anyone would think you were changing the subject," Naqi said. But Mina was already on her way out of the gondola to check the equipment again.

At dusk the airship arrived at the perimeter of the node, completed one orbit, then began to track inward again. As it passed over the parts of the node previously mapped, time-dependent changes were highlighted on the displays: arcs and bands of red superimposed against the lime and turquoise false-colour of the mapped structures. Most of the alterations were minor: a chamber opening here or closing there, or a small alteration in the network topology to ease a bottleneck between the lumpy subnodes dotted around the floating island. Other changes were more mysterious in function, but conformed to types seen in other studies. They were studied at enhanced resolution, the data prioritised and logged.

It looked as if the node was large but in no way unusual.

Then night came, as swiftly as it always did at those latitudes. Mina and Naqi took turns sleeping for two or three hour stretches while the other kept an eye on the readouts. During a lull Naqi climbed up onto the top of the airship and tried the antenna again, and for a moment was gladdened when she saw that a new message had arrived. But the message itself turned out to be a statement from the Snowflake Council stating that the blackout on civilian messages would continue for at least another two days, until the current "crisis" was over. There were allusions to civil disturbances in two cities, with curfews being imposed, and imperatives to ignore all unofficial news sources concerning the nature of the approaching ship.

Naqi wasn't surprised that there was trouble, though the extent of it took her aback. Her instincts were to believe the government line. The problem—from the government's point of view—was that nothing was known for certain about the nature of the ship, and so by being truthful they ended up sounding like they were keeping something back. They would have been far better off making up a plausible lie, which could be gently moulded toward accuracy as time passed.

Mina rose after midnight to begin her shift. Naqi went to sleep and dreamed fitfully, seeing in her mind's eye red smears and bars hovering against amorphous green. She had been staring at the readouts too intently, for too many hours.

Mina woke her excitedly before dawn.

"Now I'm the one with the news," she said.

"What?"

"Come and see for yourself."

Naqi rose from her hammock, neither rested nor enthusiastic. In the dim light of the cabin Mina's fungal patterns shone with peculiar intensity, abstract detached shapes that only implied her presence.

Naqi followed the shapes onto the balcony.

"What," she said again, not even bothering to make it sound like a question.

"There's been a development," Mina said.

Naqi rubbed the sleep from her eyes. "With the node?"

"Look. Down below. Right under us."

Naqi pressed her stomach hard against the railing and leaned over as far as she dared. She had felt no real vertigo until they had lowered the sensor lines, and then suddenly there had been a physical connection between the airship and the ground. But was it her imagination or had the airship lowered itself to about half its previous altitude, reeling in the lines at the same time?

The midnight light was all spectral shades of milky gray. The creased and crumpled landscape of the node reached away into midgray gloom, merging with the slate of the overlying cloud deck. Naqi saw nothing remarkable, other than the surprising closeness of the surface.

"I mean *really* look down," Mina said.

Naqi pushed herself against the railing more than she had dared before, until she was standing on the very tips of her toes. Only then did she see it. Directly below them was a peculiar circle of darkness, almost as if the airship was casting a distinct shadow beneath itself. It was a circular zone of exposed seawater, like a lagoon enclosed by the greater mass of the node. Steep banks of Juggler biomass, its heart a deep charcoal gray, rimmed the lagoon. Naqi studied it quietly, sensing that her sister might judge her on any remark she made.

"How did you see it?" she asked eventually.

"See it?"

"It can't be more than twenty metres wide. A dot like that would have hardly shown up on the topographic map."

"Naqi, you don't understand. I didn't steer us over the hole. It appeared below us, as you were moving. Listen to the motors. We're *still* moving. The hole's shadowing us. It follows us precisely."

"Must be reacting to the sensors," Naqi said.

"I've hauled them in. We're not trailing anything within thirty metres of the surface. The node's reacting to us, Naqi—to the presence of the airship. The Jugglers know we're here, and they're sending us a signal."

"Maybe they are. But it isn't our job to interpret that signal. We're just here to take measurements, not to interact with the Jugglers."

"So whose job is it?" Mina asked.

"Do I have to spell it out? Specialists from Umingmaktok."

"They won't get here in time. You know how long nodes last. By the time the blackout's lifted, by the time the swimmer corps hotshots get here, we'll be sitting over a green smudge and not much more. This is a significant find, Naqi. It's the largest node this season and it's making a deliberate and clear attempt to invite swimmers."

She stepped back from the railing. "Don't even think about it."

"I've been thinking about it all night. This isn't just a large node, Naqi. Something's happening—that's why there's been so much sprite activity. If we don't swim here, we might miss something unique."

"And if we do swim, we'll be violating every rule in the book. We're not trained, Mina. Even if we learned something—even if the Jugglers deigned to communicate with us—we'd be ostracised from the entire scientific community."

"That would depend on what we learned, wouldn't it?"

"Don't do this, Mina. It isn't worth it."

"We won't know if it's worth it or not until we try, will we?" Mina extended a hand. "Look. You're right in one sense. Chances are pretty good nothing will happen. Normally you have to offer them a gift—a puzzle, or something rich in information. We haven't got anything like that. What'll probably happen is we hit the water and there won't be any kind of biochemical interaction. In which case, it doesn't matter. We don't have to tell anyone. And if we do learn something, but it isn't significant—well, we don't have to tell anyone about that either. Only if we learn something major. Something so big that they'll have to forget about a minor violation of protocol."

"A minor violation . . . ?" Naqi began, almost laughing at Mina's audacity.

"The point is, sis, we have a win-win situation here. And it's been handed to us on a plate."

"You could also argue that we've been handed a major chance to fuck up spectacularly."

"You read it whichever way you like. I know what I see."

"It's too dangerous, Mina. People have died . . ." Naqi looked at Mina's fungal patterns, enhanced and emphasised by her tattoos. "You flagged high for conformality. Doesn't that worry you slightly?"

"Conformality's just a fairy tale they use to scare children into behaving," said Mina. " 'Eat all your greens or the sea will swallow you up forever.' I take it about as seriously as I take the Thule kraken, or the drowning of Arviat. I'm fully aware of the risk."

"The Thule kraken is a joke, and Arviat never existed in the first place. But the last time I checked, conformality was an accepted phenomenon."

"It's an accepted research topic. There's a distinction."

"Don't split hairs . . ." Naqi began.

Mina gave every indication of not having heard Naqi speak. Her voice was distant, as if she were speaking to herself. It had a lilting, singsong quality. "Too late to even think about it now. But it isn't long until dawn. I think it'll still be there at dawn."

She pushed past Naqi.

"Where are you going now?"

"To catch some sleep. I need to be fresh for this. So will you."

They hit the lagoon with two gentle, anticlimactic splashes. Naqi was underwater for a moment before she bobbed to the surface, holding her breath. At first she had to make a conscious effort to start breathing again: the air immediately above the water was so saturated with microscopic organisms that choking seemed a real possibility. Mina, surfacing next to her, drew in gulps with wild enthusiasm, as if willing the tiny creatures to invade her lungs. She shrieked delight at the sudden cold. When they had both gained equilibrium, treading with their shoulders above water, Naqi was finally able to take stock. She saw everything through a stinging haze of tears. The gondola hovered above them, poised beneath the larger mass of the vacuum bladder. The life raft that it had deployed was sparkling new, rated for one hundred hours against moderate biological attack. But that was for mid-ocean, where the density of Juggler organisms would be much less than in the middle of a major node. Here, the hull might only endure a few tens of hours before it was consumed.

Once again, Naqi wondered if she should withdraw. There was still time. No real damage had yet been done. She could be back in the boat and back aboard the airship in a minute or so. Mina might not follow her, but she did not have to be complicit in her sister's actions. But Naqi knew she would not be able to turn back. She could not show weakness now that she had come this far.

"Nothing's happening . . ." she said.

"We've only been in the water a minute," Mina said.

The two of them wore black wetsuits. The suits themselves could become buoyant if necessary—all it would take would be the right sequence of tactile commands and dozens of tiny bladders would inflate around the chest and shoulder area—but it was easy enough to tread water. In any case, if the Jugglers initiated contact the suits would probably be eaten away in minutes. The swimmers who had made repeated contact often swam naked or near naked, but Naqi was not prepared for that level of abject surrender to the ocean's assault. Nor was Mina.

After another minute the water no longer seemed as cold. Through gaps in the cloud cover the sun was harsh on Naqi's cheek. It etched furiously bright lines in the bottle-green surface of the lagoon, lines that coiled and shifted into fleeting calligraphic shapes as if conveying secret messages. The calm water lapped gently against their upper bodies. The walls of the lagoon were metre-high masses of fuzzy vegetation, like the steep banks of a river. Now and then Naqi felt something brush gently against her feet, like a passing frond or strand of seaweed. The first few times she flinched at the contact, but after a while it became strangely soothing. Occasionally something stroked one or other hand, then moved playfully away. When she lifted her hands from the sea, mats of gossamer green draped from her fingers like the tattered remains of expensive gloves. The green material slithered free and slipped back into the sea. It tickled between her fingers.

"Nothing's still happened," Naqi said, more quietly this time.

"You're wrong. The shoreline's moved closer."

Naqi looked at it. "It's a trick of perspective."

"I assure you it isn't."

Naqi looked back at the raft. They had drifted five or six metres from it. It might as well have been a kilometre for all the sense of security that the raft now offered. Mina was right: the lagoon was closing in on them, gently, slowly. If the lagoon had been twenty metres wide when they had entered it must now be a third smaller. There was still time to escape before the hazy green walls squeezed in on them, but only if they moved now, back to the raft, back into the safety of the gondola.

"Mina . . . I want to go. We're not ready for this."

"We don't need to be ready. It's going to happen."

"We're not trained!"

"Call it learning on the job, in that case." Mina was still trying to sound outrageously calm, but it wasn't working. Naqi heard the flaw in her voice. She was either terribly frightened or terribly excited.

"You're more scared than I am," she said.

"I am scared," said Mina. "Scared we'll screw this up. Scared we'll blow this opportunity. Understand? I'm *that* kind of scared."

Either Naqi was treading water less calmly, or the water itself had become visibly more agitated in the last few moments. The green walls were perhaps ten metres apart, and now were not quite the sheer vertical structures they had appeared before. They had taken on form and design, growing and complexifying by the second. It was akin to watching a distant city emerge from fog, the revealing of bewildering, plunging layers of mesmeric detail, more than the eye or the mind could process.

"It doesn't look as if they're expecting a gift this time," Mina said.

Veined tubes and pipes coiled and writhed around each other in constant sinuous motion, making Naqi think of some hugely magnified circuitry formed from plant parts. It was restless living circuitry that never quite settled into one configuration. Now and then chequer-board designs appeared, or intricately interlocking runes. Sharply geometric patterns flickered from point to point, echoed, amplified and subtly iterated at each move. Distinct three-dimensional shapes assumed brief solidity, carved from greenery as if by the deft hand of a topiarist. Naqi glimpsed unsettling anatomies; the warped memories of alien bodies that had once entered the ocean, a million or a billion years ago. Here a three-jointed limb, here the shieldlike curve of an exoskeletal plaque. The head of something that was almost equine melted into a goggling mass of faceted eyes. Fleetingly, a human form danced from the chaos. But only once. Alien swimmers outnumbered human swimmers vastly.

Here were the Pattern Jugglers, Naqi knew. The first explorers had mistaken these remembered forms for indications of actual sentience, thinking that the oceanic mass was a kind of community of intelligences. It was an easy mistake to have made, but it was some way from the truth. These animate shapes were enticements, like the gaudy covers of books. The minds themselves were captured only as frozen traces. The only living intelligence within the ocean lay in its own curatorial system.

To believe anything else was heresy.

The dance of bodies became too rapid to follow. Pastel-coloured lights glowed from deep within the green structure, flickering and stuttering. Naqi thought of lanterns burning from the depths of a forest. Now the edge of the lagoon had become irregular, extending peninsulas toward the centre of the dwindling circle of water, while narrow bays and inlets fissured back into the larger mass of the node. The peninsulas sprouted grasping tendrils, thigh-thick at the trunk but narrowing to the dimensions of plant fronds, and then narrowing further, bifurcating into lacy, fernlike hazes of awesome complexity. They diffracted light like the wings of dragonflies. They were closing over the lagoon, forming a shimmering canopy. Now and then a sprite—or something smaller but equally bright—arced from one bank of the lagoon to another. Brighter things moved through the water like questing fish. Microscopic organisms were detaching from the larger fronds and tendrils, swarming in purposeful clouds. They batted against her skin, against her eyelids. Every breath that she took made her cough. The taste of the Pattern Jugglers was sour and medicinal. They were in her, invading her body.

She panicked. It was as if a tiny switch had flipped in her mind. Suddenly all other concerns melted away. She had to get out of the lagoon immediately, no matter what Mina would think of her.

Thrashing more than swimming, Naqi tried to push herself toward the raft. But as soon as the panic reaction had kicked in she had felt something else slide over her. It was not so much paralysis as an immense sense of inertia. Moving, even breathing, became problematic. The boat was impossibly distant. She was no longer capable of treading water. She felt heavy, and when she looked down she saw that a green haze enveloped the parts of her body that she could see above water. The organisms were adhering to the fabric of her wetsuit.

"Mina . . ." she called. "Mina!"

But Mina only looked at her. Naqi sensed that her sister was experiencing the same sort of paralysis. Mina's movements had become languid, and yet instead of panic what Naqi saw on her face was profound resignation and acceptance. It was dangerously close to serenity.

Mina wasn't frightened at all.

The patterns on her neck were flaring vividly. Her eyes were closed. Already the organisms had begun to attack the fabric of her suit, stripping it away from her flesh. Naqi could feel the same thing happening to her own suit. There was no pain, for the organisms stopped short of attacking her skin. With a mighty effort she hoisted her forearm from the water, studying the juxtaposition of pale flesh and dissolving black fabric. Her fingers were as stiff as iron.

But—and Naqi clung to this—the ocean recognised the sanctity of organisms, or at least thinking organisms. Strange things might happen to people who swam with the Jugglers, things that might be difficult to distinguish from death or near death. But people always emerged afterward, changed perhaps, but essentially whole. No matter what happened now, they would survive. The Jugglers always returned those who swam with them, and even when they did effect changes they were seldom permanent.

Except, of course, for those who didn't return.

No, Naqi told herself. What they were doing was foolish, and might perhaps destroy their careers. But they would survive. Mina had flagged high on the conformality index when she had applied to join the swimmer corps, but that didn't mean she was necessarily at risk. Conformality merely implied a rare connection with the ocean. It verged on the glamorous.

Now Mina was going under. She had stopped moving entirely. Her eyes were blankly ecstatic.

Naqi wanted to resist that same impulse to submission. But the strength had flown away from her. She felt herself commence the same descent. The water closed over her mouth, then her eyes, and in a moment she was under. She felt herself a toppled statue sliding toward the seabed. Her fear reached a crescendo and then passed. She was not drowning. The froth of green organisms had forced itself down her throat, down her nasal passage. She felt no fright. There was nothing except a profound feeling that this was what she had been born to do.

Naqi knew what was happening, what was going to happen. She had studied enough reports on swimmer missions. The tiny organisms were infiltrating her entire body, creeping into her lungs and bloodstream. They were keeping her alive, while at the same time flooding her with chemical bliss. Droves of the same tiny creatures were seeking routes to her brain, inching along the optic nerve, the aural nerve, or crossing the blood-brain barrier itself. They were laying tiny threads behind them, fibres that extended back into the larger mass of organisms suspended in the water around her. In turn, these organisms established data-carrying channels back into the primary mass of the node. . . . And the node itself was connected to other nodes, both chemically and via the packet-carrying sprites. The green threads bound Naqi to the entire ocean. It might take hours for a signal to reach her mind from halfway around Turquoise, but it didn't matter. She was beginning to think on Juggler time, her own thought processes seeming pointlessly quick, like the motion of bees.

She sensed herself becoming vaster.

She was no longer just a pale, hard-edged thing labelled *Naqi*, suspended in the lagoon like a dying starfish. Her sense of self was rushing out toward the horizon in all directions, encompassing first the node and then the empty oceanic waters around it. She couldn't say precisely how this information was reaching her. It wasn't through visual imagery, but more an intensely detailed spatial awareness. It was as if spatial awareness had suddenly become her most vital sense.

She supposed this was what swimmers meant when they spoke of *kenning*.

She kenned the presence of other nodes over the horizon, their chemical signals flooding her mind, each unique, each bewilderingly rich in information. It was like hearing the roar of a hundred crowds. And at the same time she kenned the ocean depths, the cold fathoms of water beneath the node, the life-giving warmth of the crustal vents. Closer, too, she kenned Mina. They were two neighbouring galaxies in a sea of strangeness. Mina's own thoughts were bleeding into the sea, into Naqi's mind, and in them Naqi felt the reflected echo of her own thoughts, picked up by Mina. . . .

It was glorious.

For a moment their minds orbited each other, kenning each other on a level of intimacy neither had dreamed possible.

Mina . . . Can you feel me?

I'm here, Naqi. Isn't this wonderful?

The fear was gone, utterly. In its place was a marvellous feeling of immanence. They had made the right decision, Naqi knew. She had been right to follow Mina. Mina was deliciously happy, basking in the same hopeful sense of security and promise.

And then they began to sense other minds.

Nothing had changed, but it was suddenly clear that the roaring signals from the other nodes were composed of countless individual voices, countless individual streams of chemical information. Each stream was the recording of a mind that had entered the ocean at some point. The oldest minds—those that had entered the ocean in the deep past—were the faintest ones, but they were also the most numerous. They had begun to sound alike, the shapes of their stored personalities blurring into each other, no matter how alien they had been to start with. The minds that had been captured more recently were sharper and more variegated, like oddly shaped pebbles on a beach. Naqi kenned brutal alienness, baroque architectures of mind shaped by outlandish chains of evolutionary contingency. The only thing any of them had in common was that they had all reached a certain threshold of tool-using intelligence, and had all—for one reason or another—been driven into interstellar space, where they had encountered the Pattern Jugglers. But that was like saying the minds of sharks and leopards were alike because they had both evolved to hunt. The differences between the minds were so cosmically vast that Naqi felt her own mental processes struggling to accommodate them.

Even that was becoming easier. Subtly—slowly enough that from moment to moment she was not aware of it—the organisms in her skull were retuning her neural connections, and allowing more and more of her consciousness to seep out into the extended processing loom of the sea.

She sensed the most recent arrivals.

They were all human minds, each a glittering gem of distinctness. Naqi sensed a great gulf in time between the earliest human mind and the last recognisably alien one. She had no idea if it was a million or a billion years, but it felt immense. At the same time she grasped that the ocean had been desperate for newness, and that while these human minds were welcome, they were barely sufficient.

The minds were snapshots, frozen in the conception of a single thought. It was like an orchestra of instruments, all sustaining a single unique note. Perhaps there was a grindingly slow evolution in those minds—she sensed the merest subliminal hint of change—but if that was the case it would take centuries to complete a thought . . . thousands of years to complete the simplest internalised statement. The newest minds might not even have come to the realisation that they had been swallowed by the sea.

Yet now Naqi sensed a single mind flaring louder than the others.

It was recent and human, and yet there was something about it that struck her as discordant. The mind was damaged, as if it had been captured imperfectly. It was disfigured, giving off squalls of hurt. It had suffered dreadfully. It was reaching out to her, craving love and affection; something to cling to in the abyssal loneliness it now knew.

Images ghosted through her mind. Something was burning. Flames licked through the interstitial gaps in a great black structure. She couldn't tell if it was a building or a vast, pyramidal bonfire.

She heard screams, and then something hysterical, which she at first took for more screaming, until she realised that it was something far, far worse. It was laughter, and as the flames roared higher, consuming the mass, smothering the screams, the laughter only intensified.

She thought it might be the laughter of a child.

Perhaps it was her imagination, but this mind appeared more fluid than the others. Its thoughts were still slow—far slower than Naqi's—but the mind appeared to have usurped more than its share of processing resources. It was stealing computational cycles from neighbouring minds, freezing them into absolute stasis while it completed a single sluggish thought.

The mind worried Naqi. Pain and fury was boiling off it.

Mina kenned it too. Naqi tasted Mina's thoughts and knew that her sister was equally disturbed by the mind's presence. Then she felt the mind's attention shift, drawn to the two inquisitive minds that had just entered the sea. It became aware of both of them, quietly watchful. A moment or two passed, and then the mind slipped away, back to wherever it had come from.

What was that . . .

She felt her sister's reply. *I don't know. A human mind. A conformal, I think. Someone who was swallowed by the sea. But it's gone now.*

No, it hasn't. It's still there. Just hiding.

Millions of minds have entered the sea, Naqi. Thousands of conformals, perhaps, if you think of all the aliens that came before us. There are bound to be one or two bad apples.

That wasn't just a bad apple. It was like touching ice. And it sensed us. It reacted to us. Didn't it?

She sensed Mina's hesitation.

We can't be sure. Our own perceptions of events aren't necessarily reliable. I can't even be certain we're having this conversation. I might be talking to myself . . .

Mina . . . Don't talk like that. I don't feel safe.

Me neither. But I'm not going to let one frightening thing unnecessarily affect me.

Something happened then. It was a loosening, a feeling that the ocean's grip on Naqi had just relented to a significant degree. Mina, and the roaring background of other minds, fell away to something much more distant. It was as if Naqi had just stepped out of a babbling party into a quiet adjacent room, and was even now moving farther and farther away from the door.

Her body tingled. She no longer felt the same deadening paralysis. Pearl-gray light flickered above. Without being sure whether she was doing it herself, she moved toward the surface. She was aware that she was moving away from Mina, but for now all that mattered was to escape the sea. She wanted to be as far from the mind as possible.

Her head rammed through a crust of green into air. At the same moment the Juggler organisms fled her body in a convulsive rush. She thrashed stiff limbs and took in deep, panicked breaths. The transition was horrible, but it was over in a few seconds. She looked around, expecting to see the sheer walls of the lagoon, but all she saw in one direction was open waters. Naqi felt panic rising again. Then she kicked herself around and saw a wavy line of bottle-green that had to be the perimeter of the node, perhaps half a kilometre away from her present position. The airship was a distant silvery teardrop that appeared to be perched on the surface of the node itself.

In her fear she did not immediately think of Mina. All she wanted to do was reach the safety of the airship, to be aloft. Then she saw the raft, bobbing only one or two hundred metres away. Somehow it had been transplanted to the open waters as well. It looked distant but reachable. She started swimming, the fear giving her strength and sense of purpose. In truth, she was still thick well within the true boundary of the node: the water was still thick with suspended microorganisms, so that it was more like swimming through cold green soup. It made each stroke harder, but by the same token she did not have to expend much effort to stay afloat.

Did she trust the Pattern Jugglers not to harm her? Perhaps. After all, she had not encountered *their* minds at all—if they even *had* minds. They were merely the archiving system. Blaming them for that one poisoned mind was like blaming a library for one hateful book.

But it had still unnerved her profoundly. She wondered why none of the other swimmers had ever communicated their encounters with the mind. After all, she remembered it well enough now, and she was nearly out of the ocean. She might forget shortly—there were bound to be subsequent neurological effects—but under other circumstances there would have been nothing to prevent her relating her experiences to a witness or inviolable recording system.

She kept swimming, and began to wonder why Mina hadn't emerged from the waters as well. Mina had been just as terrified. But Mina had also been more curious, and more willing to ignore her fears. Naqi had grasped the opportunity to leave the ocean when the Jugglers released their grip on her. But what if Mina had elected to remain?

What if Mina was still down there, still in communion with the Jugglers?

Naqi reached the raft and hauled herself aboard, being careful not to capsize it. She saw that the raft was still largely intact. It had been moved but not damaged, and although the ceramic sheathing was showing signs of attack, peppered here and there with scabbed green accretions, it was certainly good for another few hours. The rot-hardened control systems were still alive and still in telemetric connection with the distant airship.

Naqi had crawled from the sea naked. Now she felt cold and vulnerable. She pulled an aluminised quilt from the raft's supply box and wrapped it around herself. It did not stop her from shivering, did not make her feel any less nauseous, but at least it afforded some measure of symbolic barrier against the sea.

She looked around again, but there was still no sign of Mina.

Naqi folded aside the weatherproof control cover and tapped commands into the matrix of waterproofed keys. She waited for the response from the airship. The moment stretched. But there it was: a minute shift in the dull gleam on the silver back of the vacuum bladder. The airship was turning, pivoting like a great slow weather vane. It was moving, responding to the raft's homing command.

But where was Mina?

Now something moved in the water next to her, coiling in weak, enervated spasms. Naqi looked at it with horrified recognition. She reached over, still shivering, and with appalled gentleness fished the writhing thing from the sea. It lay in her fingers like a baby sea serpent. It was white and segmented, half a metre long. She knew exactly what it was.

It was Mina's worm. It meant Mina had died.

II

Two years later Naqi watched a spark fall from the heavens.

Along with many hundreds of spectators, she was standing on the railed edge of one of Umingmaktok's elegant cantilevered arms. It was afternoon. Every visible surface of the city had been scoured of rot and given a fresh coat of crimson or emerald paint. Amber bunting had been hung along the metal stay-lines that supported the tapering arms protruding from the city's towering commercial core. Most of the berthing slots around the perimeter were occupied with passenger or cargo craft, while many smaller vessels were holding station in the immediate airspace around Umingmaktok. The effect—which Naqi had seen on her approach to the city a day earlier—had been to turn the snowflake into a glittering, delicately ornamented vision. By night they had fireworks displays. By day, as now, conjurors and confidence tricksters wound their way through the crowds. Nose-flute musicians and drum dancers performed impromptu atop improvised podia. Kick-boxers were cheered on as they moved from one informal ring to another, pursued by whistle-blowing proctors. Hastily erected booths were marked with red and yellow pennants, selling refreshments, souvenirs or tattoo-work, while pretty costumed girls who wore backpacks equipped with tall flagstaffs sold drinks or ices. The children had balloons and rattles marked with the emblems of both Uming-maktok and the Snowflake Council, and many of them had had their faces painted to resemble stylised space travellers. Puppet theatres had been set up here and there, running through exactly the same small repertoire of stories that Naqi re-membered from her childhood. The children were enthralled nonetheless; mouths agape at each miniature epic, whether it was a roughly accurate account of the world's settlement—with the colony ship being stripped to the bone for every gram of metal it held—or something altogether more fantastic, like the drowning of Arviat. It didn't matter to the children that the one was based in fact and the other pure mythology. To them the idea that every city they called home had been cannibalised from the belly of a four-kilometre-long ship was no more or less plausible than the idea that the living sea might occasionally snatch cities beneath the waves when they displeased it. At that age everything was both magical and mundane, and she supposed that the children were no more or less excited by the prospect of the coming visitors than they were by the promised fireworks display, or the possibility of further treats if they were well behaved. Other than the children, there were animals—caged monkeys and birds—and the occasional expensive pet, being shown off for the day. One or two servitors stalked through the crowd, and occasionally a golden float-cam would bob through the air, loiter-ing over a scene of interest like a single detached eyeball. Turquoise had not seen this level of celebration since the last acrimonious divorce, and the networks were milking it remorselessly, over-analysing the tiniest scrap of information.

This was, in truth, exactly the kind of thing Naqi would normally have gone to the other side of the planet to avoid. But something had drawn her this time, and made her wangle the trip out from the Moat at an otherwise critical time in the project. She could only suppose that it was a need to close a particular chapter in her life, one that had begun the night before Mina's death. The detection of the Ultra ship—they now knew that it was named the *Voice of Evening*—had been the event that triggered the blackout, and the blackout had been Mina's justification for the two of them attempting to swim with the Jugglers. Indirectly, therefore, the Ultras were "responsible" for whatever had happened to Mina. That was unfair, of course, but Naqi nonetheless felt the need to be here now, if only to witness the visitors' emergence with her own eyes and see if they really were the monsters of her imagination. She had come to Umingmaktok with a stoic determination that she would not be swept up by the hysteria of the celebrations. Yet now that she had made the trip, now that she was amidst the crowd, drunk on the chemical buzz of human excitement with a nice fresh worm hooked onto her gut wall, she found herself in the perverse position of actually enjoying the atmosphere.

And now everyone had noticed the falling spark.

The crowd turned their heads into the sky, ignoring the musicians, conjurors and confidence tricksters. The backpacked girls stopped and looked aloft along with the others, shielding their eyes against the midday glare. The spark was the shuttle of the *Voice of Evening*, now parked in orbit around Turquoise.

Everyone had seen Captain Moreau's ship by now, either with their own eyes as a moving star or via the images captured by the orbiting cameras or ground-based telescopes. The ship was dark and sleek, outrageously elegant. Now and then its Conjoiner drives flickered on just enough to trim its orbit, those flashes like brief teasing windows into daylight for the hemisphere below.

A ship like that could do awful things to a world, and everyone knew it.

But if Captain Moreau and his crew meant ill of Turquoise, they'd had ample opportunity to do harm already. They had been silent at two years out, but at one year out the *Voice of Evening* had transmitted the usual approach signals, requesting permission to stopover for three or four months. It was a formality—no one argued with Ultras—but it was also a gladdening sign that they intended to play by the usual rules.

Over the next year there had been a steady stream of communications between the ship and the Snowflake Council. The official word was that the messages had been designed to establish a framework for negotiation and person-to-person trade. The Ultras would need to update their linguistics software to avoid being confused by the subtleties of the Turquoise dialects, which, although based on Canasian, contained confusing elements of Inuit and Thai, relics of the peculiar social mix of the original settlement coalition.

The falling shuttle had slowed to merely supersonic speed now, shedding its plume of ionised air. Dropping speed with each loop, it executed a lazily contracting spiral above Umingmaktok. Naqi had rented cheap binoculars from one of the vendors. The lenses were scuffed, shimmering with the pink of fungal bloom. She visually locked onto the shuttle, its roughly delta shape wobbling in and out of sharpness. Only when it was two or three thousand metres above Umingmaktok could she see it clearly. It was very elegant, a pure brilliant white like something carved from cloud. Beneath the mantalike hull, complex machines— fans and control surface—moved too rapidly to be seen as anything other than blurs of subliminal motion. She watched as the ship reduced speed until it hovered at the same altitude as the snowflake city. Above the roar of the crowd—an ecstatic, flag-waving mass—all Naqi heard was a shrill hum, almost too far into ultrasound to detect.

The ship approached slowly. It had been given instructions for docking with the arm adjacent to the one where Naqi and the other spectators gathered. Now that it was close it was apparent that the shuttle was larger than any of the dirigible craft normally moored to the city's arms; by Naqi's estimate it was at least half as wide as the city's central core. But it slid into its designated mooring point with exquisite delicacy. Bright red symbols flashed onto the otherwise blank white hull, signifying airlocks, cargo ports and umbilical sockets. Gangways were swung out from the arm to align with the doors and ports. Dockers—supervised by proctors and city officials—scrambled along the precarious connecting ways and attempted to fix magnetic berthing stays onto the shuttle's hull. The magnetics slid off the hull. They tried adhesive grips next, and these were no more successful. After that, the dockers shrugged their shoulders and made exasperated gestures in the direction of the shuttle.

The roar of the crowd had died down a little by now.

Naqi felt the anticipation as well. She watched as an entourage of VIPs moved to the berthing position, led by a smooth, faintly cherubic individual that Naqi recognised as Tak Thonburi, the mayor of Umingmaktok and presiding chair of the Snowflake Council. Tak Thonburi was happily overweight and had a permanent cowlick of black hair, like an inverted question mark tattooed upon his forehead. His cheeks and brow were mottled with pale green. Next to him was the altogether leaner frame of Jotah Sivaraksa. It was no surprise that Dr Sivaraksa should be here today, for the Moat project was one of the most significant activities of the entire Snowflake Council. His iron-gray eyes flashed this way and that as if constantly triangulating the positions of enemies and allies alike. The group was accompanied by armed, ceremonially dressed proctors and a triad of martial servitors. Their articulation points and sensor apertures were lathered in protective sterile grease, to guard against rot.

Though they tried to hide it, Naqi could tell that the VIPs were nervous. They moved a touch too confidently, making their trepidation all the more evident.

The red door symbol at the end of the gangway pulsed brighter and a section of the hull puckered open. Naqi squinted, but even through the binoculars it was difficult to make out anything other than red-lit gloom. Tak Thonburi and his officials stiffened. A sketchy figure emerged from the shuttle, lingered on the threshold and then stepped with immense slowness into full sunlight.

The crowd's reaction—and to some extent Naqi's own—was double-edged. There was a moment of relief that the messages from orbit had not been outright lies. Then there was an equally brief tang of shock at the actual appearance of Captain Moreau. The man was at least a third taller than anyone Naqi had ever seen in her life, and yet commensurately thinner, his seemingly brittle frame contained within a jade-coloured mechanical exoskeleton of ornate design. The skeleton lent his movements something of the lethargic quality of a stick insect.

Tak Thonburi was the first to speak. His amplified voice boomed out across the six arms of Umingmaktok, echoing off the curved surfaces of the multiple vacuum bladders that held the city aloft. Float-cams jostled for the best camera angle, swarming around him like pollen-crazed bees.

"Captain Moreau . . . May I introduce myself? I am Tak Thonburi, mayor of Umingmaktok Snowflake City and incumbent chairman of the Snowflake Council of All Turquoise. It is my pleasure to welcome you, your crew and passengers to

Umingmaktok, and to Turquoise itself. You have my word that we will do all in our power to make your visit as pleasant as possible."

The Ultra moved closer to the official. The door to the shuttle remained open behind him. Naqi's binocs picked out red hologram serpents on the jade limbs of the skeleton. The Ultra's own voice boomed at least as loud, but emanated from the shuttle rather than Umingmaktok's public address system.

"People of greenish-blue . . ." The captain hesitated, then tapped one of the stalks projecting from his helmet. "People of Turquoise . . . Chairman Thonburi . . . Thank you for your welcome, and for your kind permission to assume orbit. We have accepted it with gratitude. You have my word . . . as captain of the lighthugger *Voice of Evening* . . . that we will abide by the strict terms of your generous offer of hospitality." His mouth continued to move even during the pauses, Naqi noticed: the translation system was lagging. "You have my additional guarantee that no harm will be done to your world, and Turquoise law will be presumed to apply to the occupants . . . of all bodies and vessels in your atmosphere. All traffic between my ship and your world will be subject to the authorisation of the Snowflake Council, and any member of the council will — under the . . . auspices of the council — be permitted to visit the *Voice of Evening* at any time, subject to the availability of a . . . suitable conveyance."

The captain paused and looked at Tak Thonburi expectantly. The mayor wiped a nervous hand across his brow, smoothing his kiss-curl into obedience.

"Thank you . . . Captain." Tak Thonburi's eyes flashed to the other members of the reception party. "Your terms are of course more than acceptable. You have my word that we will do all in our power to assist you and your crew, and that we will do our utmost to ensure that the forthcoming negotiations of trade proceed in an equable manner . . . and in such a way that both parties will be satisfied upon their conclusion."

The captain did not respond immediately, allowing an uncomfortable pause to draw itself out. Naqi wondered if it was really the fault of the software, or whether Moreau was just playing on Tak Thonburi's evident nervousness.

"Of course," the Ultra said, finally. "Of course. My sentiments entirely . . . Chairman Thonburi. Perhaps now wouldn't be a bad time to introduce my guests?"

On his cue three new figures emerged from the *Voice of Evening's* shuttle. Unlike the Ultra they could almost have passed for ordinary citizens of Turquoise. There were two men and one woman, all of approximately normal height and build. They all had long hair, tied back in elaborate clasps. Their clothes were brightly coloured, fashioned from many separate fabrics of yellow, orange, red and russet, and various permutations of the same warm sunset shades. The clothes billowed around them, rippling in the light afternoon breeze. All three members of the party wore silver jewellery, far more than was customary on Turquoise. They wore it on their fingers, in their hair, hanging from their ears.

The woman was the first to speak, her voice booming out from the shuttle's PA system.

"Thank you, Captain Moreau. Thank you also, Chairman Thonburi. We are delighted to be here. I am Amesha Crane, and I speak for the Vahishta Foundation. Vahishta's a modest scientific organisation with its origins in the cometary prefectures of the Haven Demarchy. Lately we have been expanding our realm of interest to encompass other solar systems, such as this one." Crane gestured at the two men who had accompanied her from the shuttle. "My associates are Simon Matsubara and Rafael Weir. There are another seventeen of us aboard the shuttle. Captain Moreau carried us here as paying passengers aboard the *Voice of Evening*, and as such Vahishta gladly accepts all the terms already agreed upon."

Tak Thonburi looked even less sure of himself. "Of course. We welcome your . . . interest. A scientific organisation, did you say?"

"One with a special interest in the study of the Jugglers," Amesha Crane answered. She was the most strikingly attractive member of the trio, with fine cheekbones and a wide, sensual mouth that always seemed on the point of smiling or laughing. Naqi felt that the woman was sharing something with her, something private and amusing. Doubtless everyone in the crowd felt the same vague sense of complicity.

Crane continued: "We have no Pattern Jugglers in our own system, but that hasn't stopped us from focussing our research on them, collating the data available from the worlds where Juggler studies are on-going. We've been doing this for decades, sifting inference and theory, guesswork and intuition. Haven't we, Simon?"

The man nodded. He had sallow skin and a fixed quizzical expression.

"No two Juggler worlds are precisely alike," Simon Matsubara said, his voice as clear and confident as the woman's. "And no two Juggler worlds have been studied by precisely the same mix of human socio-political factions. That means that we have a great many variables to take into consideration. Despite that, we believe we have identified similarities that may have been overlooked by the individual research teams. They may even be very important similarities, with repercussions for wider humanity. But in the absence of our own Jugglers, it is difficult to test our theories. That's where Turquoise comes in."

The other man — Naqi recalled his name as Rafael Weir — began to speak. "Turquoise has been largely isolated from the rest of human space for the better part of two centuries."

"We're aware of this," said Jotah Sivaraksa. It was the first time any member of the entourage other than Tak Thonburi had spoken. To Naqi he sounded irritated, though he was doing his best to hide it.

"You don't share your findings with the other Juggler worlds," said Amesha Crane. "Nor — to the best of our knowledge — do you intercept their cultural transmissions. The consequence is that your research on the Jugglers has been untainted by any outside considerations — the latest fashionable theory, the latest groundbreaking technique. You prefer to work in scholarly isolation."

"We're an isolationist world in other respects," Tak Thonburi said. "Believe it or not, it actually rather suits us."

"Quite," Crane said, with a hint of sharpness. "But the point remains. Your Jugglers are an uncontaminated resource. When a swimmer enters the ocean, their own memories and personality may be absorbed into the Juggler sea. The prejudices and preconceptions that swimmer carries inevitably enter the ocean in some shape or form—diluted, confused, but nonetheless present in some form. And when the next swimmer enters the sea, and opens their mind to communion, what they perceive—what they *ken*, in your own terminology—is irrevocably tainted by the preconceptions introduced by the previous swimmer. They may experience something that confirms their deepest suspicion about the nature of the Jugglers—but they can't be sure that they aren't simply picking up the mental echoes of the last swimmer, or the swimmer before that."

Jotah Sivaraksa nodded. "What you say is undoubtedly true. But we've had just as many cycles of fashionable theory as anyone else. Even within Umingmaktok there are a dozen different research teams, each with their own outlook."

"We accept that," Crane said, with an audible sigh. "But the degree of contamination is slight compared to other worlds. Vahishta lacks the resources for a trip to a previously unvisited Juggler world, so the next best thing is to visit one that has suffered the smallest degree of human cultural pollution. Turquoise fits the bill."

Tak Thonburi held the moment before responding, playing to the crowd again. Naqi rather admired the way he did it.

"Good. I'm very . . . pleased . . . to hear it. And might I ask just what it is about our ocean that we can offer you?"

"Nothing except the ocean itself," said Amesha Crane. "We simply wish to join you in its study. If you will allow it, members of the Vahishta Foundation will collaborate with native Turquoise scientists and study teams. They will shadow them and offer interpretation or advice when requested. Nothing more than that."

"That's all?"

Crane smiled. "That's all. It's not as if we're asking the world, is it?"

Naqi remained in Umingmaktok for three days after the arrival, visiting friends and taking care of business for the Moat. The newcomers had departed, taking their shuttle to one of the other snowflake cities—Prachuap or the recently married Qaanaaq-Pangnirtung, perhaps—where a smaller but no less worthy group of city dignitaries would welcome Captain Moreau and his passengers.

In Umingmaktok the booths and bunting were packed away and normal business resumed. Litter abounded. Worm dealers did brisk business, as they always did during times of mild gloom. There were far fewer transport craft moored to the arms, and no sign at all of the intense media presence of a few days before. Tourists had gone back to their home cities, and the children were safely back in school. Between meetings Naqi sat in the midday shade of half-empty restaurants and bars, observing the same puzzled disappointment in every face she encountered. Deep down she felt it herself. For two years they had been free to imprint every possible fantasy on the approaching ship. Even if the newcomers had arrived with less than benign intent, there would still have been something interesting to talk about; the possibility, however remote, that one's own life might be about to become drastically more exciting.

But now none of that was going to happen. Undoubtedly Naqi would be involved with the visitors at some point, allowing them to visit the Moat or one of the outlying research zones she managed, but there would be nothing life-changing.

She thought back to that night with Mina, when they had heard the news. Everything had changed then. Mina had died, and Naqi had found herself taking her sister's role in the Moat. She had risen to the challenge and promotions had followed with gratifying swiftness, until she was in effective charge of the Moat's entire scientific program. But that sense of closure she had yearned for was still absent. The men she had slept with—men who were almost always swimmers—had never provided it, and by turns they had each lost patience with her, realising that they were less important to her as people than what they represented, as connections to the sea. It had been months since her last romance, and once Naqi had recognised the way her own subconscious was drawing her back to the sea, she had drawn away from contact with swimmers. She had been drifting since then, daring to hope that the newcomers would allow her some measure of tranquillity.

But the newcomers had not supplied it.

She supposed she would have to find it elsewhere.

On the fourth day Naqi returned to the Moat on a high-speed dirigible. She arrived near sunset, dropping down from high altitude to see the structure winking back at her, a foreshortened ellipse of gray-white ceramic lying against the sea like some vast discarded bracelet. From horizon to horizon there were several Juggler nodes visible, webbed together by the faintest of filaments—to Naqi they looked like motes of ink spreading into blotting paper—but there were also smaller dabs of green within the Moat itself.

The structure was twenty kilometres wide and now it was nearly finished. Only a narrow channel remained where the two ends of the bracelet did not quite meet: a hundred-metre-wide shear-sided aperture flanked on either side by tall, ramshackle towers of accommodation modules, equipment sheds and construction cranes. To the north, strings of heavy cargo dirigibles ferried processed ore and ceramic cladding from Narathiwat atoll, lowering it down to the construction teams on the Moat.

They had been working here for nearly twenty years. The hundred metres of the Moat that projected above the water was only one tenth of the full structure—a kilometre high ring resting on the seabed. In a matter of months the gap—little more than a notch in the top of the Moat—would be sealed, closed off by immense hermetically tight sea-doors. The process would necessarily be slow and delicate, for what was being attempted here was not simply the closing-off of part of the sea. The Moat was an attempt to isolate a part of the living ocean, sealing off a community of Pattern Juggler organisms within its impervious ceramic walls.

The high-speed dirigible swung low over the aperture. The thick green waters streaming through the cut had the phlegmatic consistency of congealing blood. Thick, ropy tendrils permitted information transfer between the external sea and the cluster of small nodes within the Moat. Swimmers were constantly present, either inside or outside the Moat, *kenning* the state of the sea and establishing that the usual Juggler processes continued unabated.

The dirigible docked with one of the two flanking towers.

Naqi stepped out, back into the hectic corridors and office spaces of the project building. It felt distinctly odd to be back on absolutely firm ground. Although one was seldom aware of it, Umingmaktok was never quite still, no snowflake city or airship ever was. But she would get used to it; in a few hours she would be immersed in her work, having to think of a dozen different things at once, finessing solution pathways, balancing budgets against quality, dealing with personality clashes and minor turf wars, and perhaps—if she was very lucky—managing an hour or two of pure research. Aside from the science none of it was particularly challenging, but it kept her mind off other things. And after a few days of that, the arrival of the visitors would begin to seem like a bizarre, irrelevant interlude in an otherwise monotonous dream. She supposed that two years ago she would have been grateful for that. Life could indeed continue much as she had always imagined it would.

But when she arrived at her office there was a message from Dr Sivaraksa. He needed to speak to her urgently.

Dr Jotah Sivaraksa's office on the Moat was a good deal less spacious than his quarters in Umingmaktok, but the view was superb. His accommodation was perched halfway up one of the towers that flanked the cut through the Moat, buttressed out from the main mass of prefabricated modules like a partially opened desk drawer. Dr Sivaraksa was writing notes when she arrived. For long moments Naqi lingered at the sloping window, watching the construction activity hundreds of metres below. Railed machines and helmeted workers toiled on the flat upper surface of the Moat, moving raw materials and equipment to the assembly sites. Above, the sky was a perfect cobalt blue, marred now and then by the passing, green-stained hull of a cargo dirigible. The sea beyond the Moat had the dimpled texture of expensive leather.

Dr Sivaraksa cleared his throat, and when Naqi turned, he gestured at the vacant seat on the opposite side of his desk.

"Life treating you well?"

"Can't complain, sir."

"And work?"

"No particular problems that I'm aware of."

"Good. Good." Sivaraksa made a quick, cursive annotation in the notebook he had opened on his desk, then slid it beneath the smoky gray cube of a paperweight. "How long has it been now?"

"Since what, sir?"

"Since your sister . . . Since Mina . . ." He seemed unable to complete the sentence, substituting a spiralling gesture made with his index finger. His finely boned hands were marbled with veins of olive green.

Naqi eased into her seat. "Two years, sir."

"And you're . . . over it?"

"I wouldn't exactly say I'm over it, no. But life goes on, like they say. Actually I was hoping . . ." Naqi had been about to tell him how she had imagined the arrival of the visitors would close that chapter. But she doubted she would be able to convey her feelings in a way Dr Sivaraksa would understand. "Well, I was hoping I'd have put it all behind me by now."

"I knew another conformal, you know. Fellow from Gjoa. Made it into the elite swimmer corps before anyone had the foggiest idea. . . ."

"It's never been proven that Mina was conformal, sir."

"No, but the signs were there, weren't they? To one degree or another we're all subject to symbolic invasion by the ocean's microorganisms. But conformals show an unusual degree of susceptibility. On one hand it's as if their own bodies actively invite the invasion, shutting down the usual inflammatory or foreign cell rejection mechanisms. On the other, the ocean seems to tailor its messengers for maximum effectiveness, as if the Jugglers have selected a specific target they wish to absorb. Mina had very strong fungal patterns, did she not?"

"I've seen worse." Naqi said, which was not entirely a lie.

"But not, I suspect, in anyone who ever attempted to commune. I understand you had ambitions to join the swimmer corps yourself?"

"Before all that happened."

"I understand. And now?"

Naqi had never told anyone that she had joined Mina in the swimming incident. The truth was that even if she had not been present at the time of Mina's death, her encounter with the rogue mind would have put her off entering the ocean for life.

"It isn't for me. That's all."

Jotah Sivaraksa nodded gravely. "A wise choice. Aptitude or not, you'd have almost certainly been filtered out of the swimmer corps. A direct genetic connection to a conformal—even an unproven conformal—would be too much of a risk."

"That's what I assumed, sir."

"Does it . . . trouble you, Naqi?"

She was wearying of this. She had work to do—deadlines to meet that Sivaraksa himself had imposed.

"Does what trouble me?"

He nodded at the sea. Now that the play of light had shifted minutely, it looked less like dimpled leather than a sheet of beaten bronze. "The thought that Mina might still be out there . . . in some sense."

"It might trouble me if I were a swimmer, sir. Other than that . . . No. I can't say that it does. My sister died. That's all that mattered."

"Swimmers have occasionally reported encountering . . . minds . . . essences . . . of the lost, Naqi. The impressions are often acute. The conformed leave their mark on the ocean at a deeper, more permanent level than the impressions left behind by mere swimmers. One senses that there must be a purpose to this."

"That wouldn't be for me to speculate, sir."

"No." He glanced down at the compad and then tapped his forefinger against his upper lip. "No. Of course not. Well, to the matter at hand . . ."

She interrupted him. "You swam once, sir?"

"Yes. Yes, I did." The moment stretched. She was about to say something—anything—when Sivaraksa continued. "I had to stop for medical reasons. Otherwise I suppose I'd have been in the swimmer corps for a good deal longer, at least until my hands started turning green."

"What was it like?"

"Astonishing. Beyond anything I'd expected."

"Did they change you?"

At that he smiled. "I never thought that they did, until now. After my last swim I went through all the usual neurological and psychological tests. They found no anomalies; no indications that the Jugglers had imprinted any hints of alien personality or rewired my mind to think in an alien way."

Sivaraksa reached across the desk and held up the smoky cube that Naqi had taken for a paperweight. "This came down from the *Voice of Evening*. Examine it."

Naqi peered into the milky gray depths of the cube. Now that she saw it closely she realised that there were things embedded within the translucent matrix. There were chains of unfamiliar symbols, intersecting at right angles. They resembled the complex white scaffolding of a building.

"What is it?"

"Mathematics. Actually, a mathematical argument—a proof, if you like. Conventional mathematical notation—no matter how arcane—has evolved so that it can be written down, on a two-dimensional surface, like paper or a readout. This is a three-dimensional syntax, liberated from that constraint. It's enormously richer, enormously more elegant." The cube tumbled in Sivaraksa's hand. He was smiling. "No one could make head or tail of it. Yet when I looked at it for the first time I nearly dropped it in shock. It made perfect sense to me. Not only did I understand the theorem, but I also understood the point of it. It's a joke, Naqi. A pun. This mathematics is rich enough to embody humour. And understanding *that* is the gift they left me. It was sitting in my mind for twenty-eight years, like an egg waiting to hatch."

Abruptly, Sivaraksa placed the cube back on the table.

"Something's come up," he said.

From somewhere came the distant, prolonged thunder of a dirigible discharging its cargo of processed ore. It must have been one of the last consignments.

"Something, sir?"

"They've asked to see the Moat."

"They?"

"Crane and her Vahishta mob. They've requested an oversight of all major scientific centres on Turquoise, and naturally enough we're on the list. They'll be visiting us, spending a couple of days seeing what we've achieved."

"I'm not too surprised that they've asked to visit, sir."

"No, but I was hoping we'd have a few months grace. We don't. They'll be here in a week."

"That's not necessarily a problem for us, is it?"

"It mustn't become one," Sivaraksa said. "I'm putting you in charge of the visit,

Naqi. You'll be the interface between Crane's group and the Moat. That's quite a responsibility, you understand. A mistake—the tiniest gaff—could undermine our standing with the Snowflake Council." He nodded at the compad. "Our budgetary position is tenuous. Frankly, I'm in Tak Thonburi's lap. We can't afford any embarrassments."

"No sir."

She certainly did understand. The job was a poisoned chalice, or at the least a chalice with a strong potential to become poisoned. If she succeeded—if the visit went smoothly, with no hitches—Sivaraksa could still take much of the credit for it. If it went wrong, on the other hand, the fault would be categorically hers.

"One more thing." Sivaraksa reached under his desk and produced a brochure that he slid across to her. The brochure was marked with a prominent silver snowflake motif. It was sealed with red foil. "Open it; you have clearance."

"What is it, sir?"

"A security report on our new friends. One of them has been behaving a bit oddly. You'll need to keep an eye on him."

For inscrutable reasons of their own, the liaison committee had decided she would be introduced to Amesha Crane and her associates a day before the official visit, when the party was still in Sukhothai-Sanikiluaq. The journey there took the better part of two days, even allowing for the legs she took by high-speed dirigible or the ageing, unreliable trans-atoll railway line between Narathiwat and Cape Dorset. She arrived at Sukhothai-Sanikiluaq in a velvety purple twilight, catching the tail end of a fireworks display. The two snowflake cities had only been married three weeks, so the arrival of the off-worlders was an excellent pretext for prolonging the celebrations. Naqi watched the fireworks from a civic landing stage perched halfway up Sukhothai's core, starbursts and cataracts of scarlet, indigo and intense emerald green brightening the sky above the vacuum bladders. The colours reminded her of the organisms that she and Mina had seen in the wake of their airship. The recollection left her suddenly sad and drained, convinced that she had made a terrible mistake by accepting this assignment.

"Naqi?"

It was Tak Thonburi, coming out to meet her on the balcony. They had already exchanged messages during the journey. He was dressed in full civic finery and appeared more than a little drunk.

"Chairman Thonburi."

"Good of you to come here, Naqi." She watched his eyes map her contours with scientific rigour, lingering here and there around regions of particular interest. "Enjoying the show?"

"You certainly seem to be, sir."

"Yes, yes. Always had a thing about fireworks." He pressed a drink into her hand and together they watched the display come to its mildly disappointing conclusion. There was a lull then, but Naqi noticed that the spectators on the other balconies were reluctant to leave, as if waiting for something. Presently a stunning display of three-dimensional images appeared, generated by powerful projection apparatus in the *Voice of Evening*'s shuttle. Above Sukhothai-Sanikiluaq, Chinese dragons as large as mountains fought epic battles. Sea monsters convulsed and writhed in the night. Celestial citadels burned. Hosts of purple-winged fiery angels fell from the heavens in tightly knit squadrons, clutching arcane instruments of music or punishment.

A marbled giant rose from the sea, as if woken from some aeonslong slumber.

It was very, very impressive.

"Bastards," Thonburi muttered.

"Sir?"

"Bastards," he said, louder this time. "We know they're better than us. But do they have to keep reminding us?"

He ushered her into the reception chamber where the Vahishta visitors were being entertained. The return indoors had a magical sharpening effect on his senses. Naqi suspected that the ability to turn drunkenness on and off like a switch must be one of the most hallowed of diplomatic skills.

He leaned toward her, confidentially.

"Did Jotah mention any—"

"Security considerations, chairman? Yes, I think I got the message."

"It's probably nothing, only . . ."

"I understand. Better safe than sorry."

He winked, touching a finger against the side of his nose. "Precisely."

The interior was bright after the balcony. Twenty Vahishta delegates were standing in a huddle near the middle of the room. The captain was absent—little had been seen of Moreau since the shuttle's arrival in Umingmaktok—but the delegates were talking to a clutch of local bigwigs, none of whom Naqi recognised. Thonburi steered her into the fray, oblivious to the conversations that were taking place.

"Ladies and gentlemen . . . Might I introduce Naqi Okpik? Naqi oversees the scientific program on the Moat. She'll be your host for the visit to our project."

"Ah, Naqi." Amesha Crane leaned over and shook her hand. "A pleasure. I just read your papers on information propagation methods in class-three nodes. Erudite."

"They were collaborative works," Naqi said. "I really can't take too much credit."

"Ah, but you can. All of you can. You achieved those findings with the minimum of resources, and you made very creative use of some extremely simplistic numerical methods."

"We muddle through," Naqi said.

Crane nodded enthusiastically. "It must give you a great sense of satisfaction."

Tak Thonburi said: "It's a philosophy, that's all. We conduct our science in isolation, and we enjoy only limited communication with other colonies. As a social model it has its disadvantages, but it means we aren't forever jealous of what they're achieving on some other world that happens to be a few decades ahead of us because of an accident of history or location. We think that the benefits outweigh the costs."

"Well, it seems to work," Crane said. "You have a remarkably stable society here, Chairman. Verging on the utopian, some might say."

Tak Thonburi caressed his cowlick. "We can't complain."

"Nor can we," said the man Naqi recognised as quizzical-faced Simon Matsubara. "If you hadn't enforced this isolation, your own Juggler research would have been as hopelessly compromised as everywhere else."

"But the isolation isn't absolute, is it?"

The voice was quiet, but commanding.

Naqi followed the voice to the speaker. It was Rafael Weir, the man who had been identified as a possible security risk. Of the three who had emerged from Moreau's shuttle he was the least remarkable looking, possessing the kind of amorphous face that would allow him to blend in with almost any crowd. Had her attention not been drawn to him, he would have been the last one she noticed. He was not unattractive, but there was nothing particularly striking or charismatic about his looks. According to the security dossier, he had made a number of efforts to break away from the main party of the delegation while they had been visiting research stations. They could have been accidents—one or two other party members had become separated at other times—but it was beginning to look a little too deliberate.

"No," Tak Thonburi answered. "We're not absolute isolationists, or we'd never have given permission for the *Voice of Evening* to assume orbit around Turquoise. But we don't solicit passing traffic either. Our welcome is as warm as anyone's—we hope—but we don't encourage visitors."

"Are we the first to visit, since your settlement?" Weir asked.

"The first starship?" Tak Thonburi shook his head. "No. But it's been a number of years since the last one."

"Which was?"

"The *Pelican in Impiety*, a century ago."

"An amusing coincidence, then," Weir said.

Tak Thonburi narrowed his eyes. "Coincidence?"

"The *Pelican's* next port of call was Haven, if I'm not mistaken. It was *en route* from Zion, but it made a trade stopover around Turquoise." He smiled. "And we have come from Haven, so history already binds our two worlds, albeit tenuously."

Thonburi's eyes narrowed. He was trying to read Weir and evidently failing. "We don't talk about the *Pelican* too much. There were technical benefits— vacuum bladder production methods, information technologies . . . but there was also a fair bit of unpleasantness. The wounds haven't entirely healed."

"Let's hope this visit will be remembered more fondly," Weir said.

Amesha Crane nodded, fingering one of the items of silver jewellery in her hair. "Agreed. All the indications are favourable, at the very least. We've arrived at a most auspicious time." She turned to Naqi. "I find the Moat project fascinating, and I'm sure I speak for the entire Vahishta delegation. I may as well tell you that no one else has attempted anything remotely like it. Tell me, scientist to scientist. Do you honestly think it will work?"

"We won't know until we try," Naqi said. Any other answer would have been politically hazardous: too much optimism and the politicians would have started asking just why the expensive project was needed in the first place. Too much pessimism and they would ask exactly the same question.

"Fascinating, all the same." Crane's expression was knowing, as if she understood Naqi's predicament perfectly. "I understand that you're very close to running the first experiment?"

"Given that it's taken us twenty years to get this far, yes—we're close. But we're still looking at three to four months, maybe longer. It's not something we want to rush."

"That's a great pity," Crane said, turning now to Thonburi. "In three to four months we might be on our way. Still, it would have been something to see, wouldn't it?"

Thonburi leaned toward Naqi. The alcohol on his breath was a fog of cheap vinegar. "I suppose there wouldn't be any chance of accelerating the schedule, would there?"

"Out of the question, I'm afraid," Naqi said

"That's just too bad," said Amesha Crane. Still toying with her jewellery, she turned to the others. "But we mustn't let a little detail like that spoil our visit, must we?"

They returned to the Moat using the *Voice of Evening's* shuttle. There was another civic reception to be endured upon arrival, but it was a much smaller affair than the one in Sukhothai-Sanikiluaq. Dr Jotah Sivaraksa was there, of course, and once Naqi had dealt with the business of introducing the party to him she was able to relax for the first time in many hours, melting into the corner of the room and watching the interaction between visitors and locals with a welcome sense of detachment. Naqi was tired and had difficulty keeping her eyes open. She saw everything through a sleepy blur, the delegates surrounding Sivaraksa like pillars of fire, the fabric of their costumes rippling with the slightest movement, reds and russets and chrome yellows dancing like sparks or sheets of flame. Naqi left as soon as it was polite to do so, and when she reached her bed she fell immediately into troubled sleep, dreaming of squadrons of purple-winged angels falling from the skies and of the great giant rising from the depths, clawing the seaweed and kelp of ages from his eyes.

In the morning she awoke without really feeling refreshed. Anaemic light pierced the slats on her window. She was not due to meet the delegates again for another three or four hours, so there was time to turn over and try and catch some proper sleep. But she knew from experience that it would be futile.

She got up. To her surprise, there was a new message on her console from Jotah Sivaraksa. What, she wondered, did he have to say to her that he could not have said at the reception, or later this morning?

She opened the message and read.

"Sivaraksa," she said to herself. "Are you insane? It can't be done."

The message informed her that there had been a change of plan. The first closure of the sea-doors would be attempted in two days, while the delegates were still on the Moat.

It was pure madness. They were months away from that. Yes, the doors could be closed—the basic machinery for doing that was in place—and yes, the doors could be hermetically tight for at least one hundred hours after closure. But nothing else was ready. The sensitive monitoring equipment, the failsafe subsystems, the backups . . . None of that would be in place and operational for many weeks. Then there was supposed to be at least six weeks of testing, slowly building up to the event itself . . .

To do it in two days made no sense at all, except to a politician. At best all they would learn was whether or not the Jugglers had remained inside the Moat when the door was closed. They would learn nothing about how the data flow was terminated, or how the internal connections between the nodes adapted to the loss of contact with the wider ocean.

Naqi swore and hit the console. She wanted to blame Sivaraksa, but she knew that was unfair. Sivaraksa had to keep the politicians happy, or the whole project would be endangered. He was just doing what he had to do, and he almost certainly liked it even less than she did.

Naqi pulled on shorts and a T-shirt and found some coffee in one of the adjoining mess rooms. The Moat was deserted, quiet except for the womblike throb of generators and air-circulation systems. A week ago it would have been as noisy now as at any other time of day, for the construction had continued around the clock. But the heavy work was done now; the last ore dirigible had arrived while Naqi was away. All that remained was the relatively light work of completing the Moat's support subsystems. Despite what Sivaraksa had said in his message there was really very little additional work needed to close the doors. Even two days of frantic activity would make no difference to the usefulness of the stunt.

When she had judged her state of mind to be calmer, she returned to her room and called Sivaraksa. It was still far too early, but seeing as the bastard had already ruined her day she saw no reason not to reciprocate.

"Naqi." His silver hair was a sleep-matted mess on the screen. "I take it you got my message?"

"You didn't think I'd take it lying down, did you?"

"I don't like it anymore than you do. But I see the political necessity."

"Do you? This isn't like switching a light on and off, Jotah." His eyes widened at the familiarity, but she pressed on regardless. "If we screw up the first time, there might never be a second chance. The Jugglers have to play along. Without them all you've got here is a very expensive midocean refuelling point. Does that make political sense to you?"

He pushed green fingers through the mess of his hair. "Have some breakfast, get some fresh air, then come to my office. We'll talk about it then."

"I've had breakfast, thanks very much."

"Then get the fresh air. You'll feel better for it." Sivaraksa rubbed his eyes. "You're not very happy about this, are you?"

"It's bloody madness. And the worst thing is you know it."

"And my hands are tied. Ten years from now, Naqi, you'll be sitting in my place having to make similar decisions. And ten to one there'll be some idealistic young scientist telling you what a hopeless piece of deadwood you are." He managed a weary smile. "Mark my words, because I want you to remember this conversation when it happens."

"There's nothing I can do to stop this, is there?"

"I'll be in my office in . . ." Sivaraksa glanced at a clock. "Thirty minutes. We can talk about it properly then."

"There's nothing to talk about."

But even as she said that she knew she sounded petulant and inflexible. Sivaraksa was right: it was impossible to manage a project as complex and expensive as the Moat without a degree of compromise.

Naqi decided that Sivaraksa's advice—at least the part about getting some fresh air—was worth heeding. She descended a helical staircase until she reached the upper surface of the Moat's ring-shaped wall. The concrete was cold beneath her bare feet and a pleasant cool breeze caressed her legs and arms. The sky had brightened on one horizon. Machines and supplies were arranged neatly on the upper surface ready for use, although further construction would be halted until the delegates completed their visit. Stepping nimbly over the tracks, conduits and cables that crisscrossed each other on the upper surface, Naqi walked to the side. A high railing, painted in high-visibility rot-resistant sealer, fenced the inner part of the Moat. She touched it to make sure it was dry, then leaned over. The distant side of the Moat was a colourless thread, twenty kilometres away, like a very low wall of sea mist.

What could be done in two days? Nothing. Or at least nothing compared to what had always been planned. But if the new schedule was a *fait accompli*—and that was the message she was getting from Sivaraksa—then it was her responsibility to find a way to squeeze some scientific return from the event. She looked down at the cut, and at the many spindly gantries and catwalks that spanned the aperture or hung some way toward the centre of the Moat. Perhaps if she arranged for some standard-issue probes to be prepared today, the type dropped from dirigibles . . .

Naqi's eyes darted around, surveying fixtures and telemetry conduits.

It would be hard work to get them in place in time, and even harder to get them patched into some kind of real-time acquisition system. . . . But it *was* doable, just barely. The data quality would be laughable compared to the supersensitive instruments that were going to be installed over the next few months. . . . But crude was a lot better than nothing at all.

She laughed, aloud. An hour ago she would have stuck pins into herself rather than collaborate in this kind of fiasco.

Naqi walked along the railing until she reached a pair of pillar-mounted binoculars. They were smeared with rot-protection. She wiped the lens and eyepieces clean with a rag that was tied to the pedestal, then swung the binoculars in a slow arc, panning across the dark circle of water trapped within the Moat. Only vague patches of what Naqi would have called open water were visible. The rest was either a verdant porridge of Juggler organisms, or fully grown masses of organised floating matter, linked together by trunks and veins of the same green biomass. The latest estimate was that there were three small nodes within the ring. The smell was atrocious, but that was an excellent sign as well: it correlated strongly with the density of organisms in the nodes. She had experienced that smell many times, but it never failed to slam her back to that morning when Mina had died.

As much as the Pattern Jugglers "knew" anything, they were surely aware of what was planned here. They had drunk the minds of the swimmers who had already entered the sea near or within the Moat, and not one of those swimmers was ignorant of the project's ultimate purpose. It was possible that that knowledge simply couldn't be parsed into a form the aliens would understand, but Naqi considered that unlikely: the closure of the Moat would be about as stark a concept as one could imagine. If nothing else, geometry was the one thing the Jugglers did understand. And yet the aliens chose to remain within the closing Moat, hinting that they would tolerate the final closure that would seal them off from the rest of the ocean.

Perhaps they were not impressed. Perhaps they knew that the event would not rob them of every channel of communication, but only the chemical medium of the ocean. Sprites and other airborne organisms would still be able to cross the barrier. It was impossible to tell. The only way to know was to complete the experiment—to close the massive sea-doors—and see what happened.

She leaned back, taking her eyes from the binoculars.

Now Naqi saw something unexpected. It was a glint of hard white light, scudding across the water within the Moat.

Naqi squinted, but still she could not make out the object. She swung the binoculars hard around, got her eyes behind them and then zigzagged until something flashed through the field of view. She backed up and locked onto it.

It was a boat, and there was someone in it.

She keyed in the image zoom/stabilise function and the craft swelled to clarity across a clear kilometre of sea. The craft was a ceramic-hulled vessel of the type that the swimmer teams used, five or six metres from bow to stern. The person sat behind a curved spray shield, their hands on the handlebars of the control pillar. An inboard thruster propelled the boat without ever touching water.

The figure was difficult to make out, but the billowing orange clothes left no room for doubt. It was one of the Vahishta delegates. And Naqi fully expected it to be Rafael Weir.

He was headed toward the closest node.

For an agonising few moments she did not know what to do. He was going to attempt to swim, she thought, just like she and Mina had done. And he would be no better prepared for the experience. She had to stop him, somehow. He would reach the node in only a few minutes.

Naqi sprinted back to the tower, breathless when she arrived. She reached a communications post and tried to find the right channel for the boat. But either she was doing it wrong or Weir had sabotaged the radio. What next? Technically, there was a security presence on the Moat, especially given the official visit. But what did the security goons know about chasing boats? All their training was aimed at dealing with internal crises, and none of them were competent to go anywhere near an active node.

She called them anyway, alerting them to what had happened. Then she called Sivaraksa, telling him the same news. "I think it's Weir," she said. "I'm going to try and stop him."

"Naqi . . ." he said warningly.

"This is my responsibility, Jotah. Let me handle it."

Naqi ran back outside again. The closest elevator down to sea level was out of service; the next one was a kilometre farther around the ring. She didn't have that much time. Instead she jogged along the line of railings until she reached a break that admitted entry to a staircase that descended the steep inner wall of the Moat. The steps and handrails had been helpfully greased with antirot, just to make her descent more treacherous. There were five hundred steps down to sea level but she took them two or three at a time, sliding down the handrails until she reached the grilled platforms where the stairways reversed direction. All the while she watched the tiny white speck of the boat, seemingly immobile now that it was so far away, but undoubtedly narrowing the distance to the node with each minute. As she worked her way down she had plenty of time to think about what was going through the delegate's head. She was sure now that it was Weir. It did not really surprise her that he wanted to swim: it was what everyone who studied the Jugglers yearned for. But why make this unofficial attempt now when a little gentle persuasion would have made it possible anyway? Given Tak Thonburi's eagerness to please the delegates, it would not have been beyond the bounds of possibility for a swimming expedition to be organised. . . . The corps would have protested, but just like Naqi they would have been given a forceful lesson in the refined art of political compromise.

But evidently Weir hadn't been prepared to wait. It all made sense, at any rate: the times when he had dodged away from the party before must have all been abortive attempts to reach the Jugglers. But only now had he seen his opportunity.

Naqi reached the water level, where jetties floated on ceramic-sheathed pontoons. Most of the boats were suspended out of the water on cradles, to save their hulls from unnecessary degradation. Fortunately there was an emergency rescue boat already afloat. Its formerly white hull had the flaking, pea-green scab patterning of advanced rot, but it still had a dozen or so hours of seaworthiness in it. Naqi jumped aboard, released the boat from its moorings and fired up the thruster. In a moment she was racing away from the jetty, away from the vast stained edifice of the Moat itself. She steered a course through the least viscous stretches of water, avoiding conspicuous rafts of green matter.

She peered ahead, through the boat's spray-drenched shield. It had been easy to keep track of Weir's boat when she had been a hundred metres higher, but now she kept losing him behind swells or miniature islands of Juggler matter. After a minute or so she gave up trying to follow the boat, and instead diverted her concentration to finding the quickest route to the node.

She flipped on the radio. "Jotah? This is Naqi. I'm in the water, closing on Weir."

There was a pause, a crackle, then: "What's the status?"

She had to shout over the abrasive *thump, thump, thump* of the boat, even though the thruster was nearly silent.

"I'll reach the node in four or five minutes. Can't see Weir, but I don't think it matters."

"We can see him. He's still headed for the node."

"Good. Can you spare some more boats, in case he decides to make a run for another node?"

"They'll be leaving in a minute or so. I'm waking everyone I can."

"What about the other delegates?"

Sivaraksa did not answer her immediately. "Most are still asleep. I have Amesha Crane and Simon Matsubara in my office, however."

"Let me speak to them."

"Just a moment," he said, after the same brief hesitation.

"Crane here," said the woman.

"I think I'm chasing Weir. Can you confirm that?"

"He isn't accounted for," she told Naqi. "But it'll be a few minutes until we can be certain it's him."

"I'm not expecting a surprise. Weir already had a question mark over him, Amesha. We were waiting for him to try something."

"Were you?" Perhaps it was her imagination, but Crane sounded genuinely surprised. "Why? What had he done?"

"You don't know?"

"No . . ." Crane trailed off.

"He was one of us," Matsubara said. "A good . . . delegate. We had no reason to distrust him."

Perhaps Naqi was imagining this as well, but it almost sounded as if Matsubara had intended to say "disciple" rather than "delegate."

Crane came back on the radio. "Please do your best to apprehend him, Naqi. This is a source of great embarrassment to us. He mustn't do any harm."

Naqi gunned the boat harder, no longer bothering to avoid the smaller patches of organic matter. "No," she said. "He mustn't."

III

Something changed ahead.

"Naqi?" It was Jotah Sivaraksa's voice.

"What?"

"Weir's slowed his boat. From our vantage point it looks as if he's reached the perimeter of the node. He seems to be circumnavigating it."

"I can't see him yet. He must be picking the best spot to dive in."

"But it won't work, will it?" Sivaraksa asked. "There has to be an element of cooperation with the Jugglers. They have to invite the swimmer to enter the sea, or nothing happens."

"Maybe he doesn't realise that," Naqi said, under her breath. It was of no concern to her how closely Weir was adhering to the usual method of initiating Juggler communion. Even if the Jugglers did not cooperate — even if all Weir did was flounder in thick green water — there was no telling the hidden harm that might be done. She had already grudgingly accepted the acceleration of the closure operation. There was no way she was going to tolerate another upset, another unwanted perturbation of the experimental system. Not on her watch.

"He's stopped," Sivaraksa said excitedly. "Can you see him yet?"

Naqi stood up in her seat, even though she felt perilously out of balance. "Wait. Yes, I think so. I'll be there in a minute or so."

"What are you going to do?" Crane asked. "I hesitate to say it, but Weir may not respond to rational argument at this point. Simply requesting that he leave the water won't necessarily work. Um, do you have a weapon?"

"Yes," Naqi said. "I'm sitting in it."

She did not allow herself to relax, but at least now she felt that the situation was slipping back into her control. She would kill Weir rather than have him contaminate the node.

His boat was visible now only as a smudge of white, intermittently popping up between folds and hummocks of shifting green. Her imagination sketched in the details. Weir would be preparing to swim, stripping off until he was naked or nearly so. Perhaps he would feel some kind of erotic charge as he prepared for immersion. She did not doubt that he would be apprehensive, and perhaps he would hesitate on the threshold of the act, teetering on the edge of the boat before committing himself to the water. But a fanatic desire had driven him this far and she doubted that it would fail him.

"Naqi . . ."

"Jotah?"

"Naqi, he's moving again. He didn't enter the water. He didn't even look like he had any intention of swimming."

"He saw I was coming. I take it he's heading for the next closest node?"

"Perhaps . . ." But Jotah Sivaraksa sounded far from certain.

She saw the boat again. It was moving fast — much faster than it had appeared before — but that was only because she was now seeing lateral motion.

The next node was a distant island framed by the background of the Moat's encircling rim. If he headed that way she would be hard behind him all the way there as well. No matter his desire to swim, he must realise that she could thwart his every attempt.

Naqi looked back. The twin towers framing the cut were smothered in a haze of sea mist, their geometric details smeared into a vague suggestion of haphazard complexity. They suggested teetering, stratified sea-stacks, million-year-old towers of weathered and eroded rock guarding the narrow passage to the open ocean. Beneath them, winking in and out of clarity, she saw three or four other boats making their way into the Moat. The ponderous teardrop of a passenger dirigible was nosing away from the side of one of the towers, the low dawn sun throwing golden highlights along the fluted lines of its gondola. Naqi made out the sleek deltoid of the *Voice of Evening's* shuttle, but it was still parked where it had landed.

She looked back to the node where Weir had hesitated.

Something was happening.

The node had become vastly more active than a minute earlier. It resembled a green, steep-sided volcanic island that was undergoing some catastrophic seismic calamity. The entire mass of the node was trembling, rocking and throbbing with an eerie regularity. Concentric swells of disturbed water raced away from it, sickening troughs that made the speeding boat pitch and slide. Naqi slowed her boat, some instinct telling her that it was now largely futile to pursue Weir. Then she turned around so that she faced the node properly, and, cautiously, edged closer, ignoring the nausea she felt as the boat ducked and dived from crest to trough.

The node, like all nodes, had always shown a rich surface topology; fused hummocks and tendrils; fabulous domes and minarets and helter-skelters of organised biomass, linked and entangled by a telegraphic system of draping aerial tendrils. In any instant it resembled a human city—or, more properly, a fairy-tale human city—that had been efficiently smothered in green moss. The bright moving motes of sprites dodged through the interstices, the portholes and arches of the urban mass. The metropolitan structure only hinted at the node's byzantine interior architecture, and much of that could only be glimpsed or implied.

But this node was like a city going insane. It was accelerating, running through cycles of urban renewal and redesign with indecent haste. Structures were evolving before Naqi's eyes. She had seen change this rapid just before Mina was taken, but normally those kinds of changes happened too slowly to be seen at all, like the daily movement of shadows.

The throbbing had decreased, but the flickering change was now throwing out a steady, warm, malodorous breeze. And when she stopped the boat—she dared come no closer now—Naqi heard the node. It was like the whisper of a billion forest leaves presaging a summer storm.

Whatever was happening here, it was about to become catastrophic.

Some fundamental organisation had been lost. The changes were happening too quickly, with too little central coordination. Tendrils thrashed like whips, unable to connect to anything. They flailed against each other. Structures were forming and collapsing. The node was fracturing, so that there were three, four, perhaps five distinct cores of flickering growth. As soon as she had the measure of it, the process shifted it all. Meagre light flickered within the epileptic mass. Sprites swarmed in confused flight patterns, orbiting mindlessly between foci. The sound of the node had become a distant shriek.

"It's dying . . ." Naqi breathed.

Weir had done something to it. What, she couldn't guess. But this could not be a coincidence.

The shrieking died down.

The breeze ceased.

The node had stopped its convulsions. She looked at it, hoping against hope that perhaps it had overcome whatever destabilising influence Weir had intro-

duced. The structures were still misshapen, there was still an impression of inco-
herence, but the city was inert. The cycling motion of the sprites slowed, and a
few of them dropped down into the mass, as if to roost.

A calm had descended.

Then Naqi heard another sound. It was lower than anything she had heard
before—almost subsonic. It sounded less like thunder than like a very distant, very
heated conversation.

It was coming from the approximate centre of the node.

She watched as a smooth green mound rose from the centre of the node,
resembling a flattened hemisphere. It grew larger by the second, assimilating the
malformed structures with quiet indifference. They disappeared into the surface
of the mound as if into a wall of fog, but they did not emerge again. The mound
only increased its size, rumbling toward Naqi. The entire mass of the node was
changing into a single undifferentiated mass.

"Jotah . . ." she said.

"We see it, Naqi. We see it but we don't understand it."

"Weir must have used some kind of . . . weapon against it," she said.

"We don't know that he's harmed it. . . . He might just have precipitated a
change to a state we haven't documented."

"That still makes it a weapon in my book. I'm scared, Jotah."

"You think I'm not?"

Around her the sea was changing. She had forgotten about the submerged
tendrils that connected the nodes. They were as thick as hawsers, and now they
were writhing and thrashing just beneath the surface of the water. Green-tinged
spume lifted into the air. It was as if unseen aquatic monsters were wrestling,
locked in some dire, to-the-death contest.

"Naqi . . . We're seeing changes in the closest of the two remaining nodes."

"No," she said, as if denying it would make any difference.

"I'm sorry . . ."

"Where is Weir?"

"We've lost him. There's too much surface disturbance."

She realised then what had to be done. The thought arrived in her head with
a crashing urgency.

"Jotah . . . You have to close the sea-doors. Now. Immediately. Before whatever
Weir's unleashed has a chance to reach open ocean. That also happens to be
Weir's only escape route."

Sivaraksa, to his credit, did not argue. "Yes. You're right. I'll start closure. But
it will take quite a few minutes. . . ."

"I know, Jotah!"

She cursed herself for not having thought of this sooner, and cursed Sivaraksa
for the same error. But she could hardly blame either of them. Closure had never
been something to take lightly. A few hours ago it had been an event months in
the future—an experiment to test the willingness of the Jugglers to cooperate with
human plans. Now it had turned into an emergency amputation, something to be
done with brutal haste.

She peered at the gap between the towers. At the very least it would take several minutes for Sivaraksa to initiate closure. It was not simply a matter of pressing a button on his desk, but of rousing two or three specialist technicians, who would have to be immediately convinced that this was not some elaborate hoax. And then the machinery would have to work. The mechanisms that forced the sea-doors together had been tested numerous times. . . . But the machinery had never been driven to its limit; the doors had never moved more than a few metres together. Now they would have to work perfectly, closing with watchmaker precision.

And when had anything on Turquoise ever worked the first time?

There. The tiniest, least perceptible narrowing of the gap. It was all happening with agonising slowness.

She looked back to what remained of the node. The mound had consumed all the biomass available to it and had now ceased its growth. It was as if a child had sculpted in clay some fantastically intricate model of a city, which a callous adult had then squashed into a single blank mass, erasing all trace of its former complexity. The closest of the remaining nodes was showing something of the same transformation, Naqi saw: it was running through the frantic cycle that had presaged the emergence of the mound. She guessed now that the cycle had been the node's attempt to nullify whatever Weir had used against it, like a computer trying to reallocate resources to compensate for some crippling viral attack.

She could do nothing for the Jugglers now.

Naqi turned the boat around and headed back toward the cut. The sea-doors had narrowed the gap by perhaps a quarter.

The changes taking place within the Moat had turned the water turbulent, even at the jetty. She hitched the boat to a mooring point and then took the elevator up the side of the wall, preferring to sprint the distance along the top rather than face the climb. By the time she reached the cut the doors were three quarters of the way to closure, and to Naqi's immense relief the machinery had yet to falter.

She approached the tower. She had expected to see more people out on the top of the Moat, even if she knew that Sivaraksa would still be in his control centre. But no one was around. This was just beginning to register as a distinct wrongness when Sivaraksa emerged into daylight, stumbling from the door at the foot of the tower.

For an instant she was on the point of calling his name. Then she realised that he was stumbling because he had been injured—his fingers were scarlet with blood—and that he was trying to get away from someone or something.

Naqi dropped to the ground behind a stack of construction slabs. Through gaps between the slabs she observed Sivaraksa. He was swatting at something, like a man being chased by a persistent wasp. Something tiny and silver harried him. More than one thing, in fact: a small swarm of them, streaming out the open door. Sivaraksa fell to his knees with a moan, brushing ineffectually at his tormentors. His face was turning red, smeared with his own blood. He slumped on one side.

Naqi remained frozen with fear.

A person stepped from the open door.

The figure was garbed in shades of fire. It was Amesha Crane. For an absurd moment Naqi assumed that the woman was about to spring to Sivaraksa's assistance. It was something about her demeanour. Naqi found it hard to believe that someone so apparently serene could commit such a violent act.

But Crane did not step closer to Sivaraksa. She merely extended her arms before her, with her fingers outspread. She sustained the oddly theatrical gesture, the muscles in her neck standing proud and rigid.

The silver things departed Sivaraksa.

They swarmed through the air, slowing as they neared Crane. Then, with a startling degree of orchestrated obedience, they slid onto her fingers, locked themselves around her wrists, clasped onto the lobes of her ears.

Her jewellery had attacked Sivaraksa.

Crane glanced at the man one last time, spun on her heels and then retreated back into the tower.

Naqi waited until she was certain the woman was not coming back, then started to emerge from behind the pile of slabs. But Sivaraksa saw her. He said nothing, but his agonised eyes widened enough for Naqi to get the warning. She remained where she was, her heart hammering.

Nothing happened for another minute.

Then something moved above, changing the play of light across the surface of the Moat. The *Voice of Evening*'s shuttle was detaching from the tower, a flicker of white machinery beneath the manta curve of its hull.

The shuttle loitered above the cut, as if observing the final moment of closure. Naqi heard the huge doors grind shut. Then the shuttle banked, and headed over the circular sea, no more than two hundred metres above the waves. Some distance out it halted and executed a sharp right-angled turn. Then it resumed its flight, moving concentrically around the inner wall.

Sivaraksa closed his eyes. She thought he might have died, but then he opened them again and made the tiniest of nods. Naqi left her place of hiding. She crossed the open ground to Sivaraksa in a low, crablike stoop.

She knelt down by him, cradling his head in one hand and holding his own hand with the other. "Jotah . . . What happened?"

He managed to answer her. "They turned on us. The nineteen other delegates. As soon as . . ." He paused, summoning strength. "As soon as Weir made his move."

"I don't understand."

"Join the club," he said, managing a smile.

"I need to get you inside," she said.

"Won't help. Everyone else is dead. Or will be by now. They murdered us all."

"No."

"Kept me alive until the end. Wanted me to give the orders." He coughed. Blood spattered her hand.

"I can still get you . . ."

"Naqi. Save yourself. Get help."

She realised that he was about to die.

"The shuttle?"

"Looking for Weir. I think."

"They want Weir back?"

"No. Heard them talking. They want Weir dead. They have to be sure."

Naqi frowned. She understood none of this, or, at least, her understanding was only now beginning to crystallise. She had labelled Weir as the villain because he had harmed her beloved Pattern Jugglers. But Crane and her entourage had murdered people, dozens if what Sivaraksa said was correct. They appeared to want Weir dead as well. So what did that make Weir, now?

"Jotah . . . I have to find Weir. I have to find out why he did this." She looked back toward the centre of the Moat. The shuttle was continuing its search. "Did your security people get a trace on him again?"

Sivaraksa was near the end. She thought he was never going to answer her. "Yes," he said finally. "Yes, they found him again."

"And? Any idea where he is? I might still be able to reach him before the shuttle does."

"Wrong place."

She leaned closer. "Jotah?"

"Wrong place. Amesha's looking in the wrong place. Weir got through the cut. He's in the open ocean."

"I'm going after him. Perhaps I can stop him. . . ."

"Try," Sivaraksa said. "But I'm not sure what difference it will make. I have a feeling, Naqi. A very bad feeling. Things are ending. It was good, wasn't it? While it lasted?"

"I haven't given up just yet," Naqi said.

He found one last nugget of strength. "I knew you wouldn't. Right to trust you. One thing, Naqi. One thing that might make a difference . . . if it comes to the worst, that is . . ."

"Jotah?"

"Tak Thonburi told me this . . . the highest secret known to the Snowflake Council. Arviat, Naqi."

For a moment she thought she had misheard him, or that he was sliding into delirium. "Arviat? The city that sinned against the sea?"

"It was real," Sivaraksa said.

There were a number of lifeboats and emergency service craft stored at the top of near-vertical slipways, a hundred metres above the external sea. She took a small but fast emergency craft with a sealed cockpit, her stomach knotting as the vessel commenced its slide toward the ocean. The boat submerged before resurfacing, boosted up to speed and then deployed ceramic hydrofoils to minimise the contact between the hull and the water. Naqi had no precise heading to follow, but she believed Weir would have followed a reasonably straight line away from the cut, aiming to get as far away from the Moat as possible before the other delegates realised their mistake. It would only require a small deviation from that course to take him to the nearest external node, which seemed as likely a destination as any.

When she was twenty kilometres from the Moat, Naqi allowed herself a moment to look back. The structure was a thin white line etched on the horizon, the towers and the now-sealed cut faintly visible as interruptions in the line's smoothness. Quills of dark smoke climbed from a dozen spots along the length of the structure. It was too far for Naqi to be certain that she saw flames licking from the towers, but she considered it likely.

The closest external node appeared over the horizon fifteen minutes later. It was nowhere as impressive as the one that had taken Mina, but it was still a larger, more complex structure than any of the nodes that had formed within the Moat — a major urban megalopolis, perhaps, rather than a moderately sized city. Against the skyline Naqi saw spires and rotunda and coronets of green, bridged by a tracery of elevated tendrils. Sprites were rapidly moving silhouettes. There was motion, but it was largely confined to the flying creatures. The node was not yet showing the frenzied changes she had witnessed within the Moat.

Had Weir gone somewhere else?

She pressed onward, slowing the boat slightly now that the water was thickening with microorganisms and it was necessary to steer around the occasional larger floating structure. The boat's sonar picked out dozens of submerged tendrils converging on the node, suspended just below the surface. The tendrils reached away in all directions, to the limits of the boat's sonar range. Most would have reached over the horizon, to nodes many hundreds of kilometres away. But it was a topological certainty that some of them had been connected to the nodes inside the Moat. Evidently, Weir's contagion had never escaped through the cut. Naqi doubted that the doors had closed in time to impede whatever chemical signals were transmitting the fatal message. It was more likely that some latent Juggler self-protection mechanism had cut in, the dying nodes sending emergency termination-of-connection signals that forced the tendrils to sever without human assistance.

Naqi had just decided that she had guessed wrongly about Weir's plan when she saw a rectilinear furrow gouged right through one of the largest subsidiary structures. The wound was healing itself as she watched — it would be gone in a matter of minutes — but enough remained for her to tell that Weir's boat must have cleaved through the mass very recently. It made sense. Weir had already demonstrated that he had no interest in preserving the Pattern Jugglers.

With renewed determination, Naqi gunned the boat forward. She no longer worried about inflicting local damage on the floating masses. There was a great deal more at stake than the well-being of a single node.

She felt a warmth on the back of her neck.

At the same instant the sky, sea and floating structures ahead of her pulsed with a cruel brightness. Her own shadow stretched forward ominously. The brightness faded over the next few seconds, and then she dared to look back, half-knowing what she would see.

A mass of hot, roiling gas was climbing into the air from the centre of the node.

It tugged a column of matter beneath it, like the knotted and gnarled spinal column of a horribly swollen brain. Against the mushroom cloud she saw the tiny moving speck of the delegates' shuttle.

A minute later the sound of the explosion reached her, but although it was easily the loudest thing she had ever heard, it was not as deafening as she had expected. The boat lurched; the sea fumed and then was still again. She assumed that the Moat's wall had absorbed much of the energy of the blast.

Suddenly fearful that there might be another explosion, Naqi turned toward the node. At the same instant she saw Weir's boat, racing perhaps three hundred metres ahead of her. He was beginning to curve and slow as he neared the impassable perimeter of the node. Naqi knew that she did not have time to delay.

That was when Weir saw her. His boat sped up again, arcing hard away. Naqi steered immediately, certain that her boat was faster and that it was now only a matter of time before she had him. A minute later Weir's boat disappeared around the curve of the node's perimeter. She might have stood a chance of getting an echo from his hull, but this close to the node all sonar returns were too garbled to be of any use. Naqi steered anyway, hoping that Weir would make the tactical mistake of striking for another node. In open water he stood no chance at all, but perhaps he understood that as well.

She had circumnavigated a third of the node's perimeter when she caught up with him again. He had not tried to run for it. Instead he had brought the boat to a halt within the comparative shelter of an inlet on the perimeter. He was standing up at the rear of the boat, with something small and dark in his hand.

Naqi slowed her boat as she approached him. She had popped back the canopy before it occurred to her that Weir might be equipped with the same weapons as Crane.

She stood up herself. "Weir?"

He smiled. "I'm sorry to have caused so much trouble. But I don't think it could have happened any other way."

She let this pass. "That thing in your hand?"

"Yes?"

"It's a weapon, isn't it?"

She could see it clearly now. It was merely a glass bauble, little larger than a child's marble. There was something opaque inside it, but she could not tell if it contained fluid or dark crystals.

"I doubt that a denial would be very plausible at this point." He nodded, and she sensed the lifting, partially at least, of some appalling burden. "Yes, it's a weapon. A Juggler killer."

"Until today, I'd have said no such thing was possible."

"I doubt that it was very easy to synthesize. Countless biological entities have entered their oceans, and none of them have ever brought anything with them that the Juggler couldn't assimilate in a harmless fashion. Doubtless some of those entities tried to inflict deliberate harm, if only out of morbid curiosity. None of them succeeded. Of course, you can kill Jugglers by brute force. . . ." He glanced toward the Moat, where the mushroom cloud was dissipating. "But that isn't the point. Not subtle. But this is. It exploits a logical flaw in the Jugglers' own informational processing algorithms. It's insidious. And no, humans most certainly didn't invent it. We're clever, but we're not *that* clever."

Naqi strove to keep him talking. "Who made it, Weir?"

"The Ultras sold it to us in a presynthesized form. I've heard rumours that it was found inside the topmost chamber of a heavily fortified alien structure. . . . Another that it was synthesized by a rival group of Jugglers. Who knows? Who cares, even? It does what we ask of it. That's all that matters."

"Please don't use it, Rafael."

"I have to. It's what I came here to do."

"But I thought you all loved the Jugglers."

His fingers caressed the glass globe. It looked terribly fragile. "We?"

"Crane . . . Her delegates."

"They do. But I'm not one of them."

"Tell me what this is about, Rafael."

"It would be better if you just accepted what I have to do."

Naqi swallowed. "If you kill them, you kill more than just an alien life form. You erase the memory of every sentient creature that's ever entered the ocean."

"Unfortunately, that rather happens to be the point."

Weir dropped the glass into the sea.

It hit the water, bobbed under and then popped back out again, floating on the surface. The small globe was already immersed in a brackish scum of gray-green microorganisms. They were beginning to lap higher up the sides of the globe, exploring it. A couple of millimetres of ordinary glass would succumb to Juggler erosion in perhaps thirty minutes. . . . But Naqi guessed that this was not ordinary glass, that it was designed to degrade much more rapidly.

She jumped back down into her control seat and shot her boat forward. She came alongside Weir's boat, trapping the globe between the two craft. Taking desperate care not to nudge the hulls together, she stopped her boat and leaned over as far as she could without falling in. Her fingertips brushed the glass. Maddeningly, she could not quite get a grip on it. She made one last valiant effort and it drifted beyond her reach. Now it was out of her range, no matter how hard she stretched. Weir watched impassively.

Naqi slipped into the water. The layer of Juggler organisms licked her chin and nose, the smell immediate and overwhelming now that she was in such close proximity. Her fear was absolute. It was the first time she had entered the water since Mina's death.

She caught the globe, taking hold of it with the exquisite care she might have reserved for a rare bird's egg.

Already the glass had the porous texture of pumice.

She held it up, for Weir to see.

"I won't let you do this, Rafael."

"I admire your concern."

"It's more than concern. My sister is here. She's in the ocean. And I won't let you take her away from me."

Weir reached inside a pocket and removed another globe.

They sped away from the node in Naqi's boat. The new globe rested in his hand like a gift. He had not yet dropped it in the sea, although the possibility was only ever an instant away. They were far from any node now, but the globe would be guaranteed to come into contact with Juggler matter sooner or later.

Naqi opened a watertight equipment locker, pushing aside the flare pistol and first-aid kit that lay within. Carefully she placed the globe inside, and then watched in horror as the glass immediately cracked and dissolved, releasing its poison: little black irregularly shaped grains like burnt sugar. If the boat sank, the locker would eventually be consumed into the ocean, along with its fatal contents. She considered using the flare pistol to incinerate the remains, but there seemed too much danger of dispersing it at the same time. Perhaps the toxin had a restricted life span once it came into contact with air, but that was nothing she could count on.

But Weir had not thrown the third globe into the sea. Not yet. Something she had said had made him hesitate.

"Your sister?"

"You know the story," Naqi said. "Mina was a conformal. The ocean assimilated her entirely, rather than just recording her neural patterns. It took her as a prize."

"And you believe that she's still present, in some sentient sense?"

"That's what I choose to believe, yes. And there's enough anecdotal evidence from other swimmers that conformals do persist, in a more coherent form than other stored patterns."

"I can't let anecdotal evidence sway me, Naqi. Have the other swimmers specifically reported encounters with Mina?"

"No . . ." Naqi said carefully. She was sure that he would see through any lie that she attempted. "But they wouldn't necessarily recognise her if they did."

"And you? Did you attempt to swim yourself?"

"The swimmer corps would never have allowed me."

"Not my question. Did you ever swim?"

"Once," Naqi said.

"And?"

"It didn't count. It was the same time that Mina died." She paused and then told him all that had happened. "We were seeing more sprite activity than we'd ever recorded. It seemed like coincidence. . . ."

"I don't think it was."

Naqi said nothing. She waited for Weir to collect his own thoughts, concentrating on the steering of the boat. Open sea lay ahead, but she knew that almost any direction would bring them to a cluster of nodes within a few hours.

"It began with the *Pelican in Impiety*," Weir said. "A century ago. There was a man from Zion on that ship. During the stopover he descended to the surface of Turquoise and swam in your ocean. He made contact with the Jugglers and then swam again. The second time the experience was even more affecting. On the third occasion, the sea swallowed him. He'd been a conformal, just like your sister. His name was Ormazd."

"It means nothing to me."

"I assure you that on his homeworld it means a great deal more. Ormazd was a failed tyrant, fleeing a political counter-revolution on Zion. He had murdered and cheated his way to power on Zion, burning his rivals in their houses while they slept. But there'd been a backlash. He got out just before the ring closed around him—him and a handful of his closest allies and devotees. They escaped aboard the *Pelican in Impiety.*"

"And Ormazd died here?"

"Yes—but his followers didn't. They made it to Haven, our world. And once there they began to proliferate, spreading their word, recruiting new followers. It didn't matter that Ormazd was gone. Quite the opposite. He'd martyred himself; given them a saint figure to worship. It evolved from a political movement into a religious cult. The Vahishta Foundation's just a front for the Ormazd sect."

Naqi absorbed that, then asked: "Where does Amesha come into it?"

"Amesha was his daughter. She wants her father back."

Something lit the horizon, a pink-edged flash. Another followed a minute later, in nearly the same position.

"She wants to commune with him?"

"More than that," said Weir. "They all want to *become* him; to accept his neural patterns on their own. They want the Jugglers to imprint Ormazd's personality on all his followers, to remake them in his own image. The aliens will do that, if the right gifts are offered. And that's what I can't allow."

Naqi chose her words carefully, sensing that the tiniest thing could push Weir into releasing the globe. She had prevented his last attempt, but he would not allow her a second chance. All he would have to do would be to crush the globe in his fist before spilling the contents into the ocean. Then it would all be over. Everything she had ever known; everything she had ever lived for.

"But we're only talking about nineteen people," she said.

Weir laughed hollowly. "I'm afraid it's a little more than that. Why don't you turn on the radio and see what I mean?"

Naqi did as he suggested, using the boat's general communications console. The small, scuffed screen received television pictures beamed down from the comsat network. Naqi flicked through channels, finding static on most of them. The Snowflake Council's official news service was off the air and no personal messages were getting through. There were some suggestions that the comsat network itself was damaged. Yet finally Naqi found a few weak broadcast signals from the nearest snowflake cities. There was a sense of desperation in the transmissions, as if they expected to fall silent at any time.

Weir nodded with weary acceptance, as if he had expected this.

In the last six hours at least a dozen more shuttles had come down from the *Voice of Evening.* They had been packed with armed Vahishta disciples. The shuttles had attacked the planet's major snowflake cities and atoll settlements, strafing them into submission. Three cities had fallen into the sea, their vacuum bladders punctured by beam weapons. There could be no survivors. Others were still aloft, but had been set on fire. The pictures showed citizens leaping from the cities' berthing arms, falling like sparks. More cities had been taken bloodlessly, and were now under control of the disciples.

None of those cities were transmitting now.

It was the end of the world. Naqi knew that she should be weeping, or at the very least feel some writhing sense of loss in her stomach. But all she felt was a sense of denial; a refusal to accept that events could have escalated so quickly. This morning the only hint of wrongness had been a single absent disciple.

"There are tens of thousands of them up there," Weir said. "All that you've seen so far is the advance guard."

Naqi scratched her forearm. It was itching, as if she had caught a dose of sunburn.

"Moreau was in on this?"

"Captain Moreau's a puppet. Literally. The body you saw was just being tele-operated by orbital disciples. They murdered the Ultras; commandeered the ship."

"Rafael . . . Why didn't you tell us this before?"

"My position was too vulnerable. I was the only anti-Ormazd agent my movement managed to put aboard the *Voice of Evening*. If I'd attempted to warn the Turquoise authorities . . . Well, work it out for yourself. Almost certainly I wouldn't have been believed, and the disciples would have found a way to silence me before I became an embarrassment. And it wouldn't have made a difference to their takeover plans. My only hope was to destroy the ocean, to remove its usefulness to them. They might still have destroyed your cities out of spite, but at least they'd have lost the final thread that connected them to their martyr." Weir leaned closer to her. "Don't you understand? It wouldn't have stopped with the disciples aboard the *Voice*. They'd have brought more ships from Haven. Your ocean would have become a production line for despots."

"Why did they hesitate, if they had such a crushing advantage over us?"

"They didn't know about me, so they lost nothing by dedicating a few weeks to intelligence gathering. They wanted to know as much as possible about Turquoise and the Jugglers before they made their move. They're brutal, but they're not inefficient. They wanted their takeover to be as precise and surgical as possible."

"And now?"

"They've accepted that things won't be quite that neat and tidy." He flipped the globe from one palm to another, with a casual playfulness that Naqi found alarming. "They're serious, Naqi. Crane will stop at nothing now. You've seen those blast flashes. Pinpoint antimatter devices. They've already sterilised the organic matter within the Moat, to stop the effect of my weapon from reaching farther. If they know where we are, they'll drop a bomb on us as well."

"Human evil doesn't give us the excuse to wipe out the ocean."

"It's not an excuse, Naqi. It's an imperative."

At that moment something glinted on the horizon, something that was moving slowly from east to west.

"The shuttle," Weir said. "It's looking for us."

Naqi scratched her arm again. It was discoloured, itching.

Near local noon they reached the next node. The shuttle had continued to dog them, nosing to and fro along the hazy band where sea met sky. Sometimes it appeared closer, sometimes it appeared farther away. But it did not leave them alone, and Naqi knew that it would only be a matter of time before it detected a positive homing trace, a chemical or physical trace in the water that would lead to its quarry. The shuttle would cover the remaining distance in a matter of seconds, a minute at the most, and then all that she and Weir would know would be a moment of cleansing whiteness, a fire of holy purity. Even if Weir released his toxin just before the shuttle arrived it would not have time to dissipate into a wide enough volume of water to survive the fireball.

So why was he hesitating? It was Mina, of course. Naqi's sister had given a name to the faceless library of stored minds he was prepared to erase. She had removed the one-sidedness of the moral equation, and now Weir had to accept that his own actions could never be entirely blameless.

"I should just do this," he said. "By hesitating even for a second, I'm betraying the trust of the people who sent me here, people who have probably been tormented to extinction by Ormazd's followers."

Naqi shook her head. "If you didn't show doubt, you'd be as bad as the disciples."

"You almost sound as if you want me to do it."

She groped for something resembling the truth, as painful as that might be. "Perhaps I do."

"Even though it would mean killing whatever part of Mina survived?"

"I've lived in her shadow my entire life. Even after she died . . . I always felt she was still watching me, still observing my every mistake, still being faintly disappointed that I wasn't living up to all she had imagined I could be."

"You're being harsh on yourself. Harsh on Mina too, by the likes of things."

"I know," Naqi said angrily. "I'm just telling you how I feel."

The boat edged into a curving inlet that pushed deep into the node. Naqi felt less vulnerable now: there was a significant depth of organic matter to screen the boat from any sideways-looking sensors that the shuttle might have deployed, even though the evidence suggested that the shuttle's sensors were mainly focussed down from its hull. The disadvantage was that it was no longer possible to keep a constant vigil on the shuttle's movements. It could be on its way already.

She brought the boat to a halt and stood up from her control seat.

"What's happening?" Weir asked.

"I've come to a decision."

"Isn't that my job?"

Her anger—brief as it was, and directed less at Weir than the hopelessness of the situation—had evaporated. "I mean about swimming. It's what we haven't considered yet, Rafael. That there might be a third way; a choice between accepting the disciples and letting the ocean die."

"I don't see what that could be."

"Nor do I. But the ocean might find a way. It just needs the knowledge of what's at stake." She stroked her forearm again, marvelling at the sudden eruption of fungal patterns. They must have been latent for many years, but now something had caused them to flare up. Even in daylight, emeralds and blues shone against her skin. She suspected that the biochemical changes had been triggered when she entered the water to snatch the globe. Given that, she could not help but view it as a message. An invitation, perhaps. Or was it a warning, reminding her of the dangers of swimming?

She had no idea. For her peace of mind, however—and given the lack of alternatives—she chose to view it as an invitation.

But she did not dare wonder who was inviting her.

"You think the ocean can understand external events?" Weir asked.

"You said it yourself, Rafael. The night they told us the ship was coming? Somehow that information reached the sea. Via a swimmer's memories, perhaps. And the Jugglers knew then that this was something significant. Perhaps it was Ormazd's personality, rising to the fore."

Or maybe it was merely the vast, choral mind of the ocean, apprehending only that *something* was going to happen.

"Either way," Naqi said. "It still makes me think that there might be a chance."

"I only wish I shared your optimism."

"Give me this chance, Rafael. That's all I ask."

Naqi removed her clothes, less concerned that Weir would see her naked now than that she should have something to wear when she emerged. But although Weir studied her with unconcealed fascination, there was nothing prurient about it. What commanded his attention, Naqi realised, was the elaborate and florid patterning of the fungal markings. They curled and twined about her chest and abdomen and thighs, shining with a hypnotic intensity.

"You're changing," he said.

"We all change," Naqi answered.

Then she stepped from the side of the boat, into the water.

The process of descending into the ocean's embrace was much as she remembered it. She willed her body to submit to biochemical invasion, forcing down her fear and apprehension, knowing that she had been through this once before and that it was something that she could survive again. She did her best not to think about what it would mean to survive beyond this day, when all else had been shattered, every certainty crumbled.

Mina came to her with merciful speed.

Naqi?

I'm here. Oh, Mina, I'm here. There was terror and there was joy, alloyed together. *It's been so long.*

Naqi felt her sister's presence edge in and out of proximity and focus. Sometimes she appeared to share the same physical space. At other times she was scarcely more than a vague feeling of attentiveness.

How long?

Two years, Mina.

Mina's answer took an eternity to come. In that dreadful hiatus Naqi felt other minds crowd against her own, some of which were so far from human that she gasped at their oddity. Mina was only one of the conformal minds that had noticed her arrival, and not all were as benignly curious or glad.

It doesn't feel like two years to me.

How long?

Days . . . hours . . . It changes.

What do you remember?

Mina's presence danced around Naqi. *I remember what I remember. That we swam, when we weren't meant to. That something happened to me, and I never left the ocean.*

You became part of it, Mina.

The triumphalism of her answer shocked Naqi to the marrow. *Yes!*

You wanted this?

You would want it, if you knew what it was like. You could have stayed, Naqi. You could have let it happen to you, the way it happened to me. We were so alike.

I was scared.

Yes, I remember.

Naqi knew that she had to get to the heart of things. Time was passing differently here — witness Mina's confusion about how long she had been part of the ocean — and there was no telling how patient Weir would be. He might not wait until Naqi reemerged before deploying the Juggler killer.

There was another mind, Mina. We encountered it, and it scared me. Enough that I had to leave the ocean. Enough that I never wanted to go back.

You've come back now.

It's because of that other mind. It belonged to a man called Ormazd. Something very bad is going to happen because of him. One way or the other.

There was a moment then that transcended anything Naqi had experienced before. She felt herself and Mina become inseparable. She could not say where one began and the other ended, but it was entirely pointless to even think in those terms. If only fleetingly, Mina had become her. Every thought, every memory, was open to equal scrutiny by both of them.

Naqi understood what it was like for Mina. Her sister's memories were rapturous. She might only have sensed the passing of hours or days, but that belied the richness of her experience since merging with the ocean. She had exchanged experience with countless alien minds, drinking in entire histories beyond normal human comprehension. And in that moment of sharing, Naqi appreciated something of the reason for her sister having been taken in the first place. Conformals were the ocean's way of managing itself. Now and then the maintenance of the vaster archive of static minds required stewardship — the drawing in of independent intelligences. Mina had been selected and utilised, and given rewards beyond imagining for her efforts. The ocean had tapped the structure of her intelligence at a subconscious level. Only now and then had she ever felt that she was being directly petitioned on a matter of importance.

But Ormazd's mind . . . ?

Mina had seen Naqi's memories now. She would know exactly what was at stake, and she would know exactly what that mind represented.

I was always aware of him. He wasn't always there — he liked to hide himself — but even when he was absent, he left a shadow of himself. I even think he might be the reason the ocean took me as a conformal. It sensed a coming crisis. It knew Ormazd had something to do with it. It had made a terrible mistake by swallowing him. So it reached out for new allies, minds it could trust.

Minds like Mina, Naqi thought. In that instant she did not know whether to admire the Pattern Jugglers or detest them for their heartlessness.

Ormazd was contaminating it?

His influence was strong. His force of personality was a kind of poison in its own right. The Pattern Jugglers knew that, I think.

Why couldn't they just eject his patterns?

They couldn't. It doesn't work that way. The sea is a storage medium, but it has no self-censoring facility. If the individual minds detect a malign presence, they can resist it . . . But Ormazd's mind is human. There aren't enough of us here to make a difference, Naqi. The other minds are too alien to recognise Ormazd for what he is. They just see a sentience.

Who made the Pattern Jugglers, Mina? Answer me that, will you?

She sensed Mina's amusement.

Even the Jugglers don't know that, Naqi. Or why.

You have to help us, Mina. You have to communicate the urgency of this to the rest of the ocean.

I'm one mind among many, Naqi. One voice in the chorus.

You still have to find a way. Please, Mina. Understand this, if nothing else. You could die. You all could die. I lost you once, but now I know you never really went away. I don't want to have to lose you again, for good.

You didn't lose me, Naqi. I lost you.

She hauled herself from the water. Weir was waiting where she had left him, with the intact globe still resting in his hand. The daylight shadows had moved a little, but not as much as she had feared. She made eye contact with Weir, wordlessly communicating a question.

"The shuttle's come closer. It's flown over the node twice while you were under. I think I need to do this, Naqi."

He had the globe between thumb and forefinger, ready to drop it into the water.

She was shivering. Naqi pulled on her shorts and shirt, but she felt just as cold afterwards. The fungal marks were shimmering intensely, seeming to hover above her skin. If anything they were shining more furiously than before she had swum. Naqi did not doubt that if she had lingered — if she had stayed with Mina — she would have become a conformal as well. It had always been in her, but it was only now that her time had come.

"Please wait," Naqi said, her own voice sounding pathetic and childlike. "Please wait, Rafael."

"There it is again."

The shuttle was a fleck of white sliding over the top of the nearest wall of Juggler biomass. It was five or six kilometres away, much closer than the last time Naqi had seen it. Now it came to a sudden sharp halt, hovering above the surface of the ocean as if it had found something of particular interest.

"Do you think it knows we're here?"

"It suspects something," Weir said. The globe rolled between his fingers.

"Look," Naqi said.

The shuttle was still hovering. Naqi stood up to get a better view, nervous of making herself visible but desperately curious. Something was happening. She *knew* something was happening.

Kilometres away, the sea was bellying up beneath the shuttle. The water was the colour of moss, supersaturated with microorganisms. Naqi watched as a coil of solid green matter reached from the ocean, twisting and writhing. It was as thick as a building, spilling vast rivulets of water as it emerged. It extended upward with astonishing haste, bifurcating and flexing like a groping fist. For a brief moment it closed around the shuttle. Then it slithered back into the sea with a titanic splash; a prolonged roar of spent energy. The shuttle continued to hover above the same spot, as if oblivious to what had just happened. Yet the manta-shaped craft's white hull was lathered with various hues of green. And Naqi understood: what had happened to the shuttle was what had happened to Arviat, the city that drowned. She could not begin to guess the crime that Arviat had committed against the sea, the crime that had merited its destruction, but she could believe, now, at least, that the Jugglers had been capable of dragging it beneath the waves, ripping the main mass of the city away from the bladders that held it aloft. And of course such a thing would have to be kept maximally secret, known only to a handful of individuals. Otherwise no city would ever feel safe when the sea roiled and groaned beneath it.

But a city was not a shuttle.

Even if the Juggler material started eating away the fabric of the shuttle, it would still take hours to do any serious damage. . . . And that was assuming the Ultras had no better protection than the ceramic shielding used on Turquoise boats and machines. . . .

But the shuttle was already tilting over.

Naqi watched it pitch, attempt to regain stability and then pitch again. She understood, belatedly. The organic matter was clogging the shuttle's whisking propulsion systems, limiting its ability to hover. The shuttle was curving inexorably closer to the sea, spiralling steeply away from the node. It approached the surface, and then just before the moment of impact another misshapen fist of organised matter thrust from the sea, seizing the hull in its entirety. That was the last Naqi saw of it.

A troubled calm fell on the scene. The sky overhead was unmarred by questing machinery. Only the thin whisper of smoke rising from the horizon, in the direction of the Moat, hinted of the day's events.

Minutes passed, and then tens of minutes. Then a rapid series of bright flashes strobed from beneath the surface of the sea itself.

"That was the shuttle," Weir said, wonderingly.

Naqi nodded. "The Jugglers are fighting back. This is more or less what I hoped would happen."

"You asked for this?"

"I think Mina understood what was needed. Evidently she managed to convince the rest of the ocean, or at least this part of it."

"Let's see."

They searched the airwaves again. The comsat network was dead, or silent. Even fewer cities were transmitting now. But those that were—those that had not been overrun by Ormazd's disciples—told a frightening story. The ocean was clawing at them, trying to drag them into the sea. Weather patterns were shifting, entire storms being conjured into existence by the orchestrated circulation of vast ocean currents. It was happening in concentric waves, racing away from the precise point in the ocean where Naqi had swum. Some cities had already fallen into the sea, though it was not clear whether this had been brought about by the Jugglers themselves or because of damage to their vacuum bladders. There were people in the water: hundreds, thousands of them. They were swimming, trying to stay afloat, trying not to drown.

But what exactly did it mean to drown on Turquoise?

"It's happening all over the planet," Naqi said. She was still shivering, but now it was as much a shiver of awe as one of cold. "It's denying itself to us by smashing our cities."

"Your cities never harmed it."

"I don't think it's really that interested in making a distinction between one bunch of people and another, Rafael. It's just getting rid of us all, disciples or not. You can't really blame it for that, can you?"

"I'm sorry," Weir said.

He cracked the globe, spilled its contents into the sea.

Naqi knew there was nothing she could do now; there was no prospect of recovering the tiny black grains. She would only have to miss one, and it would be as bad as missing them all.

The little black grains vanished beneath the olive surface of the water.

It was done.

Weir looked at her, his eyes desperate for forgiveness.

"You understand that I had to do this, don't you? It isn't something I do lightly."

"I know. But it wasn't necessary. The ocean's already turned against us. Crane has lost. Ormazd has lost."

"Perhaps you're right," Weir said. "But I couldn't take the chance that we might be wrong. At least this way I know for sure."

"You've murdered a world."

He nodded. "It's exactly what I came here to do. Please don't blame me for it."

Naqi opened the equipment locker where she had stowed the broken vial of Juggler toxin. She removed the flare pistol, snatched away its safety pin and pointed it at Weir.

"I don't blame you, no. Don't even hate you for it."

He started to say something, but Naqi cut him off.

"But it's not something I can forgive."

She sat in silence, alone, until the node became active. The organic structures around her were beginning to show the same kinds of frantic rearrangement Naqi had seen within the Moat. There was a cold sharp breeze from the node's heart.

It was time to leave.

She steered the boat away from the node, cautiously, still not completely convinced that she was safe from the delegates even though the first shuttle had been destroyed. Undoubtedly the loss of that craft would have been communicated to the others, and before very long some of them would arrive, bristling with belligerence. The ocean might attempt to destroy the new arrivals, but this time the delegates would be profoundly suspicious.

She brought the boat to a halt when she was a kilometre from the fringe of the node. By then it was running through the same crazed alterations she had previously witnessed. She felt the same howling wind of change. In a moment the end would come. The toxin would seep into the node's controlling core, instructing the entire biomass to degrade itself to a lump of dumb vegetable matter. The same killing instructions would already be travelling along the internode tendril connections, winging their way over the horizon. Allowing for the topology of the network, it would only take fifteen or twenty hours for the message to reach every node on the planet. Within a day it would be over. The Jugglers would be gone, the information they'd encoded erased beyond recall. And Turquoise itself would begin to die at the same time; its oxygen atmosphere no longer maintained by the oceanic organisms.

Another five minutes passed, then ten.

The node's transformations were growing less hectic. She recalled this moment of false calm. It meant only that the node had given up trying to counteract the toxin, accepting the logical inevitability of its fate. A thousand times over this would be repeated around Turquoise. Toward the end, she guessed, there would be less resistance, for the sheer futility of it would have been obvious. The world would accept its fate.

Another five minutes passed.

The node remained. The structures were changing, but only gently. There was no sign of the emerging mound of undifferentiated matter she had seen before.

What was happening?

She waited another quarter of an hour and then steered the boat back toward the node, bumping past Weir's floating corpse on the way. Tentatively, an idea was forming in her mind. It appeared that the node had absorbed the toxin without dying. Was it possible that Weir had made a mistake? Was it possible that the toxin's effectiveness depended only on it being used once?

Perhaps.

There still had to be tendril connections between the Moat and the rest of the ocean at the time that the first wave of transformations had taken place. They had been severed later—either when the doors closed, or by some autonomic process within the extended organism itself—but until that moment, there would still have been informational links with the wider network of nodes. Could the dying nodes have sent sufficient warning that the other nodes were now able to find a strategy for protecting themselves?

Again, perhaps.

It never paid to take anything for granted where the Jugglers were concerned.

She parked the boat by the node's periphery. Naqi stood up and removed her clothes for the final time, certain that she would not need them again. She looked down at herself, astonished at the vivid tracery of green that now covered her body. On one level, the evidence of alien cellular invasion was quite horrific.

On another, it was startlingly beautiful.

Smoke licked from the horizon. Machines clawed through the sky, hunting nervously. She stepped to the edge of the boat, tensing herself at the moment of commitment. Her fear subsided, replaced by an intense, loving calm. She stood on the threshold of something alien, but in place of terror what she felt was only an imminent sense of homecoming. Mina was waiting for her below. Together, nothing could stop them.

Naqi smiled, spread her arms and returned to the sea.

Daniel Abraham, "Gandhi Box," *Asimov's*, January.

———, "Ghost Chocolate," *Asimov's*, August.

———, "The Mechanism of Grace," *Infinite Matrix*, 8/26.

Karen L. Abrahamson, "Coyotes, Cats, and Other Creatures," *Strange Horizons*, 9/30.

Brian W. Aldiss, "Near Earth Object," *Mars Probes*.

Ray Aldridge, "Soul Pipes," *F&SF*, December.

Tavis Allison, "In Father Christmas's Court," *Asimov's*, December.

Eleanor Arnason, "Knapsack Poems," *Asimov's*, May.

Nigel Atkinson, "An Exhalation of Butterflies," *Interzone*, May.

Kage Baker, "Hanuman," *Asimov's*, April.

———, "Her Father's Eyes," *Asimov's*, December.

———, "The Likely Lad," *Asimov's*, September.

———, "Old Flat Top," *Black Projects, White Knights*.

———, "The Queen in Yellow," *Black Projects, White Knights*.

Tony Ballantyne, "Teaching the War Robot to Dance," *Interzone*, April.

Neal Barrett, Jr., "Grubber," *30th Anniversary DAW*.

———, "Grunwelt," *Infinite Matrix*, 11/18.

———, "Limo," *Infinite Matrix*, 5/20.

William Barton, "The Engine of Desire," *Asimov's*, August.

———, "Right to Life," *Talebones*, Spring.

Lee Battersby, "Father Muerte and the Theft," *Aurealis* 29.

Stephen Baxter, "The Dreaming Mould," *Interzone*, May.

———, "The Hunters of Pangaea," *Analog*, December.

———, "Martian Autumn," *Mars Probes*.

———, "Riding the Rock," *PS Publishing*.

Amy Bechtel, "Forget Me Not," *Analog*, June.

Chris Beckett, "The Turing Test," *Interzone*, October.

M. Shayne Bell, "The Pagodas of Ciboure," *The Green Man*.

Gregory Benford, "Across the Curve of a Cosmos," *SCI FICTION*, 3/6.

Terry Bisson, "I Saw the Light," *SCI FICTION*, 10/2.

———, "Openclose," *F&SF*, October/November.

James Blaylock, "In for a Penny, or The Man Who Believed in Himself," *SCI FICTION*, 2/20.

Mark Bourne, "Action Figures," *Realms of Fantasy*, October.

Scott Bradfield, "Dazzle's Inferno," *F&SF*, June.

Keith Brooke, "Welcome to the Green Planet," *Interzone*, June–July.

Eric Brown, "The Blue Portal," *Interzone*, June–July/August.

———, "Myths of the Martian Future," *Mars Probes*.

———, "Thursday's Child," *Spectrum SF 9*.

Chris Bunch, "Thieves Fall Out," *Fantastic*, Summer.

Emma Bull, "Joshua Tree," *The Green Man*.

P.D. Cacek, "A Book by its Cover," *Shelf Life*.

Pat Cadigan, "Linda," *Asimov's*, July.

Orson Scott Card, "50 WPM," *In the Shadow of the Wall*.

Jonathan Carroll, "Simon's House of Lipstick," *Conjuntions 39*.

Adam-Troy Castro, "Unseen Demons," *Analog*, July/August.

C.J. Cherryh, "The Sandman, the Tinman, and the Betty B," *30th Anniversary DAW*.

Ted Chiang, "Liking What You See: A Documentary," *Stories of Your Life & Others*.

Richard Chwedyk, "Bronte's Egg," *F&SF*, August.

Brenda W. Clough, "Tiptoe, on a Fence Post," *Analog*, July/August.

Brenda Cooper & Larry Niven, "Finding Myself," *Analog*, June.

——, "Free Floaters," *Asimov's*, August.

Nat Coward, "Early Retirement," *Interzone*, September.

——, "Little Green Card," *Interzone*, October.

——, "Time Spent in Reconnaissance," *Interzone*, August.

Albert E. Cowdrey, "The Boy's Got Talent," *F&SF*, September.

——, "The Posthumous Man," *F&SF*, July.

——, "Ransom," *F&SF*, March.

John Crowley, "The Girlhood of Shakespear's Heroines," *Conjunctions 39*.

Julie E. Czerneda, "Prism," *30th Anniversary DAW*.

Colin P. Davies, "Tall Tales on the Iron Horse," *Spectrum SF 8*.

Jennifer de Guzman, "Counterpoint," *Strange Horizons*, 10/21.

A.M. Dellamonica, "A Slow Day at the Gallery," *Asimov's*, October/November.

——, "Three Times Over the Falls," SCI FICTION, 2/27.

Nick DiChario, "The One-Half Boy," *In the Shadow of the Wall*.

Paul Di Filippo, "A Martian Theodicy," *Mars Probes*.

——, "Shipbreaker," *SCI FICTION*, 10/9.

Cory Doctorow, "Beat Me Daddy (Eight to the Bar)," *Black Gate*, Summer.

——, "OwnzOred," *Salon*, August 23.

——, "Truncat," *The Bakka Anthology*.

——& Charles Stross, "Jury Service," *SCI FICTION*, 12/3.

Noreen Doyle, "Horizon," *Alternate Generals II*.

Gardner Dozois, "The Hanging Curve," *F&SF*, April.

Brenden DuBois, "The High-Water Mark," *Alternate Gettysbergs*.

L. Timmel Duchamp, "Fool's Tale," *Leviathan Three*.

Andy Duncan, "The Big Rock Candy Mountain," *Conjunctions 39*.

——, "The Holy Bright Number (a Charlie Poole Story," *Polyphony 1*.

J.R. Dunn, "Intruders," *SCI FICTION*, 11/20.

——, "The Names of All the Spirits," *SCI FICTION*, 7/24.

Jeff Duntemann, "Drumlin Boiler," *Asimov's*, April.

Greg Van Eekhout, "People Stuff," *Lady Churchill's Rosebud Wristlet*, #10.

——, "Show and Tell," *Strange Horizons*, 6/10.

——, "Will You Be an Astronaut?," *F&SF*, September.

Scott Edelman, "Mom, the Martians, and Me," *Mars Probes*.

Carol Emshwiller, "Grandma," *F&SF*, March.

——, "The Prince of Mules," *Leviathan Three*.

——, "Water Master," SCI FICTION, 2/6.

Timons Esaias, "Fame," *Interzone*, October.

——, "Osmund Considers," *Interzone*, May.

——, "The Right Thing," *Future Orbits* 4.

Christopher Evans, "Posterity," *Interzone*, September.

Charles Coleman Finlay, "A Democracy of Trolls," *F&SF*, October/November.

——, "The Frontier Archipelago," *On Spec*, Summer.

——, "We Came Not to Praise Washington," *F&SF*, August.

Jeffrey Ford, "Creation," *F&SF*, May.

——, "The Weight of Words," *Leviathan Three*.

——, "What's Sure To Come," *Lady Churchill's Rosebud Wristlet*, #10.

Richard Foss, "The History of Chan's Journey to the Celestial Regions," *Analog*, April.

Karen Joy Fowler, "The Further Adventures of the Invisible Man," *Conjunctions 39*.

Michael F. Flynn, "Southern Strategy," *Alternate Generals II*.

Chery J. Franklin, "Words," *30th Anniversary DAW*.

Esther M. Friesner, "Just Another Cowboy," *F&SF*, April.

——, "Men in the Rain," *Asimov's*, January.

Gregory Frost, "Madonna of the Maquiladora," *Asimov's*, May.

Neil Gaiman, "October in the Chair," *Conjunction 39*.

R. Garcia y Robertson, "Death in Love," *F&SF*, January.

——, "Princess Aria," *F&SF*, July.

——, "Ring Rats," *Asimov's*, April.

Peter T. Garratt, "When the Night is Cold (and the Land is Dark)," *Asimov's*, April.

Mary Gentle, "The Logistics of Carthage," *Worlds That Weren't*.

Alexander Glass, "Elysian Dreams," *Interzone*, February.

——, "Lucid," *Interzone*, January.

Theodora Goss, "The Rose in Twelve Petals," *Realms of Fantasy*, April.

John Grant, "Wooden Horse," *The Third Alternative*, Autumn.

Dominic Green, "Blue Water, Grey Death," *Interzone*, January.

——, "News from Hilaria," *Interzone*, May.

Jim Grimsley, "Getting the News," *Asimov's*, March.

Sally Gwylan, "Salt," *Infinite Matrix*, 8/12.

Jack C. Haldeman II, "In Finnegan's Wake," *Sol's Children*.

Elizabeth Hand, "The Least Trumps," *Conjunctions 39*.

——, "Pavane for a Prince of the Air," *J.K. Potter's Embrace the Mutation*.

Charles Harness, "Station Ganymede," *30th Anniversary DAW*.

M. John Harrison, "Entertaining Angels Unawares," *Conjunctions 39*.

Howard V. Hendrix, "Incandescent Bliss," *Asimov's*, June.

Nina Kiriki Hoffman, "Grounded," *The Green Man*.

——, "Scenes from a Marriage," *Infinite Matrix*, 9/23.

Brian A. Hopkins, "Mirrors," *Sol's Children*.

Nalo Hopkinson, "Herbal," *The Bakka Anthology*.

——, "Shift," *Conjunctions 39*.

David Hutchinson, "A Dream of Locomotives," *Revolution SF*, March.

——, "Fear of Strangers," *SCI FICTION*, 7/31.

Roxanne Hutton, "Mandy," *Artemis*, Spring.

Simon Ings, "The Convert," *Asimov's*, December.

Alex Irvine, "Chichen Itza," F&SF, May.

——, "Jimmy Guang's House of Gladmech," SCI FICTION, 4/10.

——, "The Sands of Iwo Jima," Rossetti Song.

Harvey Jacobs, "The Synchronous Swimmer," F&SF, August.

Matthew Jarpe, "Captains of Industry," Asimov's, March.

Michael J. Jasper, "Natural Order," Asimov's, July.

——, "Wantaviewer," Strange Horizons, 14/9.

——, "Working the Game," Future Orbits 4.

Bill Johnson, "Mama Told Me Not to Come," Black Gate, Summer.

Graham Joyce, "Black Dust," F&SF, February.

— ——, "The Coventry Boy," The Third Alternative, Autumn.

Richard Kadrey, "Dog Boys," Infinite Matrix, 5/22.

——, Opener of the Ways," Infinite Matrix, 5/16.

Michael Kandel, "Voodoo Euclid," Infinite Matrix, 8/19.

Daniel Kaysen, "The Comeback Season," Interzone, October.

William H. Keith, Jr., "In the Bubble," Alternate Gettysbergs.

James Patrick Kelly, "Barry Westphall Crashes the Singularity," Infinite Matrix, 9/30.

——, "Candy Art," Asimov's, December.

——, "Luck," Asimov's June.

John Kessel, "The Family Vacation," Infinite Matrix, 9/16.

——, "The Invisible Empire," Conjunctions 39.

Ellen Klages, "Be Prepared," Infinite Matrix, 9/9.

——, "A Taste of Summer," Black Gate, Winter.

——, "Travel Agency," Strange Horizons, 2/11.

Damon Knight, "Watching Matthew," F&SF, October/November.

Nancy Kress, "Patent Infringement," Asimov's, May.

Geoffrey A. Landis, "At Dorado," Asimov's, October/November.

——, "Falling into Mars," Analog, July/August.

——, "The Long Chase," Asimov's, February.

——, "Old Tingo's Penis," Interzone, August.

——, "Turning Test," Asimov's, September.

Jay Lake, "Jack's House," Strange Horizons, 12/23.

John Langan, "Mr. Gaunt," F&SF, September.

Chris Lawson, "Faster, Higher, Stronger," Spectrum SF 9.

Mary Soon Lee, "New World," Interzone, February.

Tanith Lee, "Among the Leaves So Green," The Green Man.

——, "The Flicker of a Winter Star," Weird Tales, Spring.

——, "In the City of Dead Night," F&SF, October/November.

Ursula K. Le Guin, "Paradises Lost," The Birthday of the World.

——, "The Seasons of the Ansarac," Infinite Matrix, 6/3.

——, "Social Dreaming of the Irin," F&SF, October/November.

——, "The Wild Girls," Asimov's, March.

Edward M. Lerner, "Presence of Mind," Analog, January.

Jonathan Lethem, "The Dystopianist, Thinking of His Rival, Is Interrupted by a Knock on the Door," Conjunctions 39.

Marissa K. Lingen, "Irena's Roses," Analog, June.

Kelly Link, "Lull," Conjunctions 39.

James Lovegrove, "Out of the Blue, into the Red," *Mars Probes*.

Paul McAuley, "The Assassination of Faustino Malarte," *Asimov's*, July.

——, "Doctor Pretorious and the Lost Temple," *SCI FICTION*, 9/11.

——, "Under Mars," *Mars Probes*.

Jack McDevitt, "Oculus," *Analog*, July/August.

Ian McDonald, "The Hidden Place," *Asimov's*, October/November.

Maureen F. McHugh, "Laika Comes Home Safe," *Polyphony 1*.

——, "Makeover," *Infinite Matrix*, 10/7.

Patricia A. McKillip, "Hunter's Moon," *The Green Man*.

Sean McMullen, "Voice of Steel," *SCI FICTION*, 8/21.

——, "Walk to the Full Moon," *F&SF*, December.

Barry N. Malzberg, "Getting There," *In The Shadow of the Wall*.

Louise Marley, "Jamie Says," *Asimov's*, August.

China Mieville, "Familiar," *Conjunctions 39*.

——, "The Tain," *PS Publishing*.

Devon Monk, "Leeward to the Sky," *Realms of Fantasy*, June.

Michael Moorcock, "Lost Sorceress of the Silent Citadel," *Mars Probes*.

James Morrow, "War of the Worldviews," *Mars Probes*.

Hilary Moon Murphy, "The Run of the Fiery Horse," *Realms of Fantasy*, June.

Chris Nakashima-Brown, "A Brief History of Negative Space," *Revolution SF*, June.

Ruth Nestvold, "Princes and Priscilla," *Strange Horizons*, 4/8.

R. Neube, "Life in the Sardine Lane," *Asimov's*, March.

——, "Never Convicted," *Oceans of the Mind V*.

Larry Niven, "Chrysalis," *Analog*, September.

——, "The Convergence of the Old Mind," *Analog*, July/August.

G. David Nordley, "War, Ice, Egg, Universe," *Asimov's*, October/November.

Patrick O' Leary, "The Bending of Light," *Conjunctions 39*.

——, "What Mattered Was Sleep," *SCI FICTION*, 8/14.

Jerry Oltion, "The Ulti Mate," *Talebones*, Fall.

——, "Ships in the Night," *Analog*, June.

——, "Witness," *Analog*, December.

Paul Park, "Tachycardia," *F&SF*, January.

Richard Parks, "Kallisti," *Realms of Fantasy*, April.

——, "Some Archival Material on the 2198 Stellar Expedition," *Future Orbits 5*.

Brian Plante, "Best Friends," *Future Orbits 4*.

——, "It's Only Human," *Analog*, November.

Frederik Pohl, "A Home for the Old Ones," *30th Anniversary DAW*.

Steven Popkes, "Boulder Country," *Realms of Fantasy*, June.

——, "Fable for Savior and Reptile," *Realms of Fantasy*, February.

Tim Pratt, "Little Gods," *Strange Horizons*, 2/4.

——, "The Witch's Bicycle," *Realms of Fantasy*, August.

Christopher Priest, "The Discharge," *SCI FICTION*, 2/13.

Tom Purdom, "A Champion of Democracy," *Asimov's*, May.

Robert Reed, "The Children's Crusade," *SCI FICTION*, 4/24.

——, "Lying to Dogs," *Asimov's*, December.

——, "The Majesty of Angels," *F&SF*, September.

——, "Melodies Played upon Cold, Dark Worlds," *SCI FICTION*, 8/7.

——, "Oracles," *Asimov's*, January.

——, "She Sees My Monsters Now," *Asimov's*, June.

——, "Veritas," *Asimov's*, July.

Mike Resnick, "The Chinese Sandman," *Black Gate*, Winter.

Alastair Reynolds, "The Real Story," *Mars Probes*.

M. Rickert, "Leda," *F&SF*, August.

Kate Riedel, "Kid Brother," *On Spec*, Fall.

Uncle River, "How We Know What Happened," *Absolute Magnitude*, Spring.

Adam Roberts, "Imperial Army," *Spectrum SF 9*.

——, "Jupiter Magnified," *PS Publishing*.

——, "Swiftly," *SCI FICTION*, 4/3.

Andy Robertson, "The Eater," *Interzone*, January.

Bruce Holland Rogers, "The Main Design That Shines Through Sky and Earth," *Polyphony 1*.

Benjamin Rosenbaum, "Droplet," *F&SF*, July.

——, "On the Cliff by the River," *Infinite Matrix*, 9/16.

Kristine Kathryn Rusch, "Moments," *Sol's Children*.

——, "Well-Chosen Words," *Alternate Gettysbergs*.

Richard Paul Russo, "A Better Place," *Oceans of the Mind V*.

Michelle Sagara, "Fat Girl," *Oceans of the Mind VI*.

James Sallis, "Roofs and Forgiveness in the Early Dawn," *Talebones*, Spring.

——, "Up," *Leviathan Three*.

Jessica Amanda Salmonson, "Woodsman and Water Nymph," *Infinite Matrix*, 2/27.

William Sanders, "Duce," *Asimov's*, August.

——, "Empire," *Alternate Generals II*.

Melissa Lee Shaw, "A Deeper Rust," *Analog*, January.

Charles Sheffield, "The Diamond Drill," *Analog*, April.

Lucius Shepard, "The Drive-in Puerto Rico," *F&SF*, October/November.

——, "Emerald Street Expansions," *SCI FICTION*, 3

——, "How Lonesome Heartbreak Changed His Life," *Polyphony 1*.

——, "Over Yonder," *SCI FICTION*, 1

Norman Spinrad, "Entities," *Interzone*, August.

Robert Sheckley, "Agamennon's Run," *30th Anniversary DAW*.

Delia Sherman, "Grand Central Park," *The Green Man*.

Susan Shwartz, "And the Glory of Them," *Alternate Generals II*.

William Shunn, "The Veil Beyond the Veil," *Realms of Fantasy*, February.

Robert Silverberg, "The Second Wave," *Asimov's*, August.

——, "With Caesar in the Underworld," *Asimov's*, October/November.

Dan Simmons, "The End of Gravity," *Worlds Enough and Time*.

——, "The Ninth of Av," *Worlds Enough and Time*.

Gail Sproule, "For the Love of Katie," *Black Gate*, Winter.

Brian Stableford, "The Face of an Angel," *Leviathan Three*.

——, "The Home Front," *30th Anniversary DAW*.

——, "Hot Blood," *Asimov's*, September.

——, "Taking the Piss," *Asimov's*, June.

——, "Tread Softly," *Interzone*, March.

Michael A. Stackpole, "Least of My Brethren," *Sol's Children*.

Allen M. Steele, "A Walk Across Mars," *Mars Probes*.

——, "Across the Eastern Divide," *Asimov's*, February.

——, "Lonesome and a Long Way From Home," *Asimov's*, June.

Robert N. Stephenson, "The Touch of Silk," *Aurealis 29*.

S.M. Stirling, "Shikari in Galveston," *Worlds That Weren't*.

James Stoddard, "The Star Watch," *F&SF*, January.

Charles Stross, "Big Brother Iron," *Toast and Other Rusted Futures*.

——, "Router," *Asimov's*, September.

——, "Tourist," *Asimov's*, February.

Beverly Suarez-Beard, "Bertrand's Bride," *Talebones*, Fall.

Michael Swanwick, "Absolute Zero," *SCI FICTION*, 8/23.

——, "A Sad Story," *Infinite Matrix*, 9/26.

——, "Castles in the Air," *SCI FICTION*, 7/26.

——, "Cecil Rhodes in Hell," *SCI FICTION*, 5/3.

——, "The Child Buyer," *Infinite Matrix*, 4/15.

——, "Claimjumper and Ting," *SCI FICTION*, 4/19.

——, "Dirty Little War," *In the Shadow of the Wall*.

——, "A Great Day for Brontosaurs," *Asimov's*, May.

——, "Elena's Heart," *Infinite Matrix*, 4/4.

——, "Fallout," *SCI FICTION*, 3/8.

——, "Five British Dinosaurs," *Interzone*, March.

——, " 'Hello,' Said the Stick," *Analog*, March.

——, "In Loco Parentis," *SCI FICTION*, 7/12.

——, "It: A Prelliminary Account," *SCI FICTION*, 3/15.

——, "Land of Our Fathers," *SCI FICTION*, 4/26.

——, "A Letter from Hell," *SCI FICTION*, 10/18.

——, "The Little Cat Laughed To See Such Sport," *Asimov's*, October/November.

——, "Living in the Shadow of the Molly-Be-Damned," *SCI FICTION*, 4/12.

——, "Nanotechnologist's Lung," *SCI FICTION*, 10/25.

——, "Space Pirates," SCI FICTION,

——, "Spontaneous Human Combustion," *Infinite Matrix*, 4/29.

——, "Starry Night," *SCI FICTION*, 5/24.

——, "War of the Worlds," *SCI FICTION*, 5/10.

——, "Warrior Princess," *SCI FICTION*, 7/19.

Cecilia Tan, "Touch Pain," *Asimov's*, February.

Judith Tarr, "Devil's Bargain," *Alternate Generals II*.

John Alfred Taylor, "Catalyst," *Oceans of the Mind IV*.

Byron R. Tetrick, "The Angel of the Wall," *In the Shadow of the Wall*.

Karen Traviss, "A Slice at a Time," *Asimov's*, July.

——, "Chocolate Kings," *On Spec*, Fall.

Harry Turtledove, "The Daimon," *Worlds That Weren't*.

Steven Utley, "Beyond the Sea," *Revolution SF*, September.

——, "Foodstuff," *F&SF*, February.

——, "Walking in Circles," *Asimov's*, January.

James Van Pelt, "Do Good," *Polyphony 1*.

——, "Far from the Emerald Isle," *Analog*, September.

——, "Its Hour Come Round," *Talebones*, Spring.

———, "The Last of the O-Forms," *Asimov's*, September.
———, "Like a Film Gone Twice," *Future Orbits 4*.
———, "Perceptual Set," *Analog*, January.
———, "Safety of the Herd," *Asimov's*, January.
Rajnar Vajra, "The Great Prayer Wheel," *Analog*, July/August.
John Varley, "Beyond Bedford Falls," *Infinite Matrix*, 12/23.
Ray Vukcevich, "In the Flesh," *Infinite Matrix*, 2/4.
———, "The Wages of Syntax," *SCI FICTION*, 10/16.
Ian Watson, "A Free Man," *The Third Alternative*, Spring.
———, "A Speaker for the Wooden Sea," *Asimov's*, March.
———, "The Black Wall of Jerusalem," *30th Anniversary DAW*.
Bud Webster, "Frog Level," *Interzone*, October.
Catherine Wells, "The Sea-Maid," *Realms of Fantasy*, February.
Julian West, Vita Brevis Ars Longa," *Interzone*, October.
Michelle Sagara West, "How to Kill an Immortal," *The Bakka Anthology*.
Leslie What, "Blind Date with the Invisible Man," *Polyphony 1*.
———, "Of Two Minds," *Infinite Matrix*, 3/9.
Lori Ann White, "Target Audience," *Asimov's*, July.
Kate Wilhelm, "The Man on the Persian Carpet," *F&SF*, February.
Edward Willett, "Je Me Souviens," *Artemis*, Summer.
Liz Williams, "The Banquet of the Lords of Night," *Asimov's*, June.
———, "Honeydark," *Realms of Fantasy*, October.
———, "Quantum Anthropology," *Asimov's*, February.
———, "The Sharecropper," *Interzone*, January.
Tad Williams, "Not with a Whimper, Either," *30th Anniversary DAW*.
Walter Jon Williams, "The Last Ride of German Freddie," *Worlds That Weren't*.
Jack Williamson, "After Life," *F&SF*, February.
———, "The Planet of Youth," *F&SF*, April.
———, "Shakespeare & Co.," *Shelf Life*.
Chris Willrich, "King Rainjoy's Tears," *F&SF*, July.
Gene Wolfe, "From the Cradle," *Shelf Life*.
———, "Shields of Mars," *Mars Probes*.
———, "Under Hill," *Infinite Matrix*, 5/6.
———, "The Waif," *F&SF*, January.
Jane Yolen, "Dark Seed, Dark Stone," *Realms of Fantasy*, February.
Timothy Zahn, "The Big Picture," *30th Anniversary DAW*.
———, "Old-Boy Network," *Sol's Children*.
———, "Protocol," *Analog*, September.